# The Sinful

## To Slay a God

# Sean Michael Carter

*To everyone who waited for me to finish this story.*
*Thanks for waiting for me…*

Published in 2019 by FeedARead.com Publishing

First Edition

A CIP catalogue record for this title is available from the British
Library.

# Preface

*The* story of the Simal will be told in several volumes. This is volume one: *To Slay a God*. For those still interested in the world of Pangaea after the other volumes telling the particular story of the Simal, there are other numerous short stories and other great tales of adventure that I plan to share and publish, especially in relation to some of the sub characters mentioned throughout the volumes, whose adventures before or after the Simal, are stories that deserve to be told in their own right.

The tale of the Simal is set in the world of Pangaea, a time before the continents had split and the world was still one great mass of land, partially surrounded by numerous archipelagos, as well as isolated small or large islands. Although Pangaea is widely accepted as having existed as a geological entity in the history of our world, the story I tell, the peoples, cultures, kingdoms and so on, that take place upon Pangaea are entirely fictional or inspired by history.

At the centre of the main land mass in my tale, is a place called the Everglow, surrounded by the Great Wall that starts in the Panthalassic Ocean in the west, stretches 6,000 miles across Pangaea to the Tethys Ocean in the east, runs 3,000 miles to the south, and then back west and north again to complete itself for a square mileage of roughly 18,000 miles.

From what we think we know about the geological history of this world, the Tethys Sea more or less separated the two great Mesozoic supercontinents of Laurasia in the north, and Gondwana, in the south. The Panthalassic was the super ocean that surrounded the supercontinent of Pangaea. For creative purposes, I have taken license with geological data and hence in this story these oceans exist around the main supercontinent of Pangaea and the surrounding islands.

In this book, Pangaea is the first of Nine Worlds, or dimensions if you prefer. Pangaea is the physical world, sometimes referred to in the tale as the Outer World, in the same sense as we understand and interpret our own physical world. The other worlds gradually become more ethereal in substance, and gradually less physical. The gods in the story are mostly confined to the more ethereal realms, although some are trying to enter into physical reality to exert their dominance. Humans, after death, or due to higher forms of technology, are also able to cross these realms. I refer to these items in the book as magic items, but as you will see, there are some characters who understand that what appears to others as magic or miracle, is merely due to it not being widely understood that magical events or items are higher forms of technology that more primitive minds cannot comprehend. Although the main substance of this story is set in the world of Pangaea, after death, or using 'magical' portals or items there are occasions when some characters are forced to travel within and experience the other worlds which are realms beyond the physical. However, it is mainly within the Everglow, on Pangaea, that the epic adventure that is this story unfolds.

Within the Everglow are ancient Obelisks, the Arnath, created by an ancient being long ago. The Arnath provide a doorway between the nine different realms, which are: The Outer World; Nefastus; the Labyrinth; Garama Aethoros; the Deadlands; the Dark Paths; Fair Havens; The Barren Waste; The Desolation, also known as the Void. These are collectively called the Nine Worlds, and are in effect different dimensions of Pangaea, not separate physical planets.

There are many types of creature and races that inhabit the Nine Worlds, the human ones, are divided into three main groups: Fell-bloods; Half-bloods and Pure-bloods. The people that make up these different distinctions are not unified groups, and consist

3

of different empires, kingdoms, cultures and civilisations that are often at war with each other.

The Pure-bloods, often referred to as Akkadians, are initially born as babies in their first lifetime, but are unique among the human races in that, after they experience physical death, their lifeforce can be returned from the Deadlands by the Arnath, back to the physical realm of Pangaea. When this happens, the physical age of their new body begins at thirty. They have the same looks, deformities and disabilities or lack of, as they had with their first ever birth. Diseases or injuries gained during their last life, are not present. After what is called the *Awakening*, they regain enough essential memories to remember who they are, but after being in the Deadlands and returning, they have often forgotten things, lost certain knowledge or skills, and have to acquire them again, or wait until their memories fully return. The *Awakening* is often a traumatic experience for many Pure-bloods.

The average life-span for a Pure-blood depends on many factors, but a good age to die would normally be considered seventy to ninety years of age, but the Everglow is a cruel and dangerous place so very few have the good fortune to live a long and natural life. The longest living Akkadian on record, lived for one hundred and ninety-six lifetimes before they met the *Final-death* and were returned no more. This gives you, the reader, an inclination as to just how old, not in physicality, but in their life experiences, some of the characters in this tale are. In contrast, the Fell-bloods and Half-bloods, just like us, only have one life to live in their world, and when they die, it is final.

The historical events concerning empires and kingdoms that have and still populate the Pangaean world of this book, bear little resemblance to actual history, and any similarity is coincidental. Like every author though, I have drawn from human history and the myths and legends of many ancient civilisations, are a rich source of inspiration for anyone wishing to tell epic tales, and therefore, all manner of creatures and species lurk in the primeval jungles, roam the vast plains, swim in the seas, or inhabit the various wild places, kingdoms and empires of Pangaea and the Nine Worlds.

The Simal is set near the end of the Sixth Age of history, a tumultuous time when the powers of gods and men are shifting. The Nine Aeldar who were charged with governance of the world by En-Sof, but were corrupted by their fall from spirit to matter, have been returned to spirit form, and are imprisoned in the Void. The Simal, a powerful object through which they can be summoned to Pangaea, has been discovered by the Kappian Empire, along with the means to use it.

This will be enough by way of introduction to the world of Pangaea, so let us join our characters in their life and death struggles. Let us begin our epic tale, not with our main character, the Priestess Janorra, who has a plan to slay a god, but with a Fell-blood slave, whose limited understanding of the world he lives in is about to change forever.

# Chapter One: *Into the Everglow*

*What a vile and treacherous clan I found the Ikma to be.*
*Temmison Vol VII, Book 1: Davari Tribes and Clans.*

*Temmison, Alberto Hethrin, linguist, explorer and historian, b. 8742 in Kappia. Date of Final-death not known. He lived for 162 lifetimes. In his final-life he was secretary and librarian at the Kappian Library and Professor of History at the Shakawraith University, Kappia city. His most important work was the Fifteen Volume masterpiece based on his travels both within and without the Everglow.*
*Spalding and Marson, Encyclopedia Vol II, Book 1: Famous People of the Everglow.*

*The* large caravan of slaves consisted of roughly twelve hundred captives, chained together in rows of four, and three hundred in length. Many of their number had died during the arduous journey from their Davari homelands in the icy-south, from where they had been pitilessly captured, to where they marched now, within distance of the Great Southern Wall of the Everglow. The slaves were ordered to halt by their ruthless captors, the Ikma, who rode up and down the lines, their horses whinnying and snorting, as the riders cracked their whips in the air and barked their orders. They reined their steeds to a sudden halt when the slave-train had fully come to a still.

The hot desert sun beat down mercilessly on slave and captor alike. The manacles the slaves wore were made of black iron, were thick and heavy, and caused chaffing of their already sunburnt skin. The chains clinked loudly as many of the slaves collapsed through exhaustion onto the hard-baked desert sand. They gasped for breath, and their pleas for water were uttered in vain, for the Ikma paid them no heed. Other slaves, also fatigued, sat down more carefully, glad of the respite, however brief it might be.

Only a very few slaves remained standing, to better see what was happening, and among them was Scarand, a young Davari thrall from the Vanyr clan. He was a man of strength and agility, powerfully built, supple as a snow-panther. On his clean-cut limbs were evidences of scarcely healed wounds. His tangled black mane, soaked with sweat, hung loosely around his head. The tattered rags that clothed him provided little protection from the ferocious sun. The step-son of Thorgrum the Great, a hunter of renown, said to be a beast, before his capture by the Ikma, Scarand had fared little better than other thralls, his only advantage that he had often been taken into the wilds with his father to be trained in the art of hunting.

Born in a land of mountains, ice and snow, it had never occurred to Scarand that the sun could burn so fiercely. He took short, sharp breaths as he scanned the land around him. *The sun bakes the land*, he complained to himself. It was a true wasteland, a barren place where nothing grew. It was the wall, however, that mainly drew his attention. The looming black rampart of the Everglow that it was said stretched the entire width of Pangaea, from the Western Panthalassic Ocean, to the Eastern Tethys Sea, had been revealed by the rise of the morning sun. It stood to the north towering over them, at a distance of about a league. The black gate amidmost the wall and the six towers either side sent a chill down his spine. He felt an abrupt fear, soon replaced by anger, when the massive gate was thrown open with a clang that shook the ground, and from it rode forth a small company of black clad soldiers, no more than a dozen in number. They carried a single fluttering banner, black, with a red tear surrounded by a red shackle as the emblem.

Scarand's wild instinct tempted him to try again to break free from his chains. He knew such an attempt was futile, so he resisted the urge in order to save his failing strength. Ever since he had been taken, his only thought had been to stay alive, so that he might rescue his two sisters. Heart hammering in his chest, *I must stay alive for Marciea and Oliviana,* he said to himself, not for the first time since his capture. They were words he had spoken to himself many times on that dreadful march northwards. He repeated them once more in the quietness of his mind. *For Marciea and Oliviana.*

Scarand looked to his grandfather, Muro, chained in the same row, to his right. The old man knew that Scarand was in fact the illegitimate son of Thaine, and therefore half-brother to Imrand, who was chained to Scarand's left. It was a secret Muro, and Scarand, kept from Imrand.

Scarand remembered the power it was whispered that Muro possessed. He briefly studied the inked patterns on the back of the old man's hands, a matrix of swirling lines. He resented him for doing nothing when the Ikma had arrived, and not for the first time on that dreadful journey, he resisted the urge to throttle the old man with his own chains. It was a temptation that had often visited him since their capture, and it was only a deep-seated fear of the old man and what he might be capable of, that had stayed his hands. *For Marciea and Oliviana.*

Scarand had heard it said that his grandfather had willingly sacrificed his left eye to the runes when he was young, as part of his initiation into the secretive sect of Ruik Priests, after which he disappeared for many years. It was said of him ever since, that his blind eye saw much further than his living one ever had. He had spent his years and days alone in one of the secret rune-caves or in the company of other Ruik in their sacred groves of oak and mistletoe, where their altars reeked of rotting carrion and human flesh. Human sacrifices, those captured from other Davari clans, were offered in such groves. It was said the victims were partially drowned in a sacred pool, and then had their blood drained from the jugular vein. Death was administered by the ritual of garrotting – a technique of crushing the windpipe by twisting a knotted rope around the neck. It was not a ritual Scarand had ever witnessed, but he had heard about it in whispers around many a hearth and campfire, and those selected each year to take offerings of meat and fur to the Ruik, returned with dark tales of the deeds and sights they had witnessed. Most talked about and feared by those who returned, was the forest of the hanged, where numerous victims were hanged so that the Ruik might see other worlds through the eyes of the dead. It was also said of the Ruik Sect that they had whole secret libraries of dark works bound in skin flayed from living human victims, and that in the nameless pits below their sacred mountain they trafficked with powerful dark forces, and traded screaming victims for unholy secrets.

Scarand had never met Muro, until the day when his grandfather had returned to his village, just a few days before the Ikma arrived in numbers, to slaughter, rob, pillage and enslave his people.

"The runes have told me I must go with the Ikma, it is the will of Yig," were the only words Muro had moodily muttered when the village elders had fearfully inquired the reason for his unexpected return. It had been an ill omen for the village. After those words, he had sat and meditated outside the village, and had put up no resistance when the Ikma arrived in large numbers, slaying those who fought, slaughtering the elderly and infirm, and using nets and traps to ensnare those of the Vanyr that could be sold as slaves.

*Why did you not use the runes of ice and fire that are carved into your hands to help us?* Scarand had often thought whenever he looked at the old man, but he never gave voice to the words, for respect and fear for the Ruik had been ingrained in him from as early as he could remember, and that kept his anger and resentment at bay.

Muro had not even resisted when, with a sound like the crack of thunder a dark portal had appeared among the Ikma, and from out of it emerged three terrible figures. One had been a woman, wearing glass armour the colour of the darkest night, made with a skill and workmanship none of the Vanyr had seen before. The breastplate, gorget, spaulders and greaves were made of fine black glass and forged in such a way it mimicked the curve of her perfect feminine form. She wore a necklace, with a small black obelisk – a Neblan, hanging upon a golden chain. Upon the breastplate of her armour had been an intricate design, red in colour of two crossed hammers, at the base of which was wrapped a single golden snake. Fine rings of a mail tunic were visible between the plates and beneath that a thin layer of red cloth so expertly tailored it separated the pieces of armour so that when she moved, the armour made not a sound. Her head had been encased in a helmet forged with an expressionless face that was at the same time beautiful and cruel. Nine horns, each shaped differently, rose from the helm. She had been terrible to behold, so much so, that some of the Vanyr warriors had thought that a goddess had come amongst them, and the more superstitious of them had dared not raise a weapon against her, and surrendered without a fight.

The second figure to appear had been attired the same as the first, except his armour revealed a masculine form with exaggerated muscles. The third, though attired in the same magnificent armour, had clearly been a hunch-back. Not even the armour had been able to hide his disfigurements though it had made them appear deceptively graceful and full of charm. These two had also worn a similar obelisk upon a necklace.

Muro had done nothing during the short battle, nor afterwards when purely for sport, had the three terrors set a pack of wild dogs upon his own illegitimate daughter, Scarand's mother, Marcella. Neither had he resisted them when they took Marciea and Oliviana, and another maiden from the village, back through the portal with them. To be born out of wedlock in Davari culture, meant to be born into the status of a thrall, and considered lesser than those born with honour.

Scarand himself had been ensnared and immobilised by a net, and then thrown into a cage. Like a trapped animal he had crouched there silently watching, full of despair and helplessness, as the events unfolded. He had seen his grandfather just sitting there, meditating, murmuring prayers and chanting rituals whilst their kin were taken or killed around about him. Scarand despised the old man for doing nothing about it. He had also wished that his father, who had been slain by a wild pack of wargs the previous year, had still been alive to help his people during the catastrophe that had befallen them.

Scarand's attention returned to the present as the man next to him, his half-brother, Imrand, the legitimate son of the famous War Chief of their tribe, snarled. When Imrand spoke, his voice was harsh and croaked - the result of a parched mouth.

"I will kill her one day, very slowly. I have sworn it as a blood-vow. I will paint my face in the blue woad - this I have sworn!"

Scarand followed Imrand's angry gaze. His skin crawled as he watched the cruel loremaster dismount from her braying donkey. When a Vanyr warrior painted their face in blue woad, it was more than a decoration, it was a sacred rite meaning that they would rather die than turn back or fail to fulfil their vow. Of all those captured, Imrand and his wife Sarkisi, had suffered the most at the hands of the Ikma, and the loremaster had been their main tormentor.

The loremaster was old but with hair unbound, falling in iron-grey straggle tails to her shoulders. Despite the heat, she wore a multi-coloured robe of various animal skins and furs patched together, fastened at the waist with a belt looped like a mans and hung about with all manner of things: a couple of drawstring purses, the skull of a small animal, the tail bone of a snake. Around her neck she wore a circle of white beads as large as gull eggs. Each bead had mysterious blue runes carved into them that glowed whenever it was dark. She carried a large wooden staff, knotted in a twisted clump at the end. A black raven always perched on her shoulder, unless it was flying on some errand that she had sent it upon.

Scarand recalled how, when chained and shackled on the ship during the voyage up the river his people called the Yarno, the loremaster had enjoyed the job of branding each of the slaves. She had cackled with glee as their soft flesh was seared with scorching iron and their chests forever scarred with a tear surrounded by a shackle, the mark of a slave. The loremaster, who was named Gerdar, had taken a particular dislike towards Sarkisi, perhaps because of the dignified defiance she had shown during the branding. She alone of the women had refused to cry out in pain. Sarkisi, famed among all of the Davari clans for her great beauty, had stared the old hag in the eyes and had not winced, even when she had kept the iron brand pressing against her chest for a lot longer than was necessary.

The Vanyr were a proud people and did not show weakness easily, yet Sarkisi and her husband had paid a heavy price for her pride and defiance. During the times of rare rest, Gerdar had often selected Sarkisi and took her to Bahri, the leader of the Ikma slavers. The hag had then delighted in taunting Imrand with lurid details of how Bahri and his men had used his wife. Not content with that, which was torment enough, she had often delighted in describing the fate that would most likely await Sarkisi once she was within the walls of the Everglow. She had spoken in great detail of the hideous future awaiting such a beauty in the brothels of one of the great cities, provoking Imrand with the knowledge that his beloved wife would be used for the pleasure of men until she died, riddled with disease or that she would be bought as the mere toy of some old, fat and sweaty land owner, who when he grew bored of her, would give her to his other slaves for their use and amusement.

Despite his own suffering, and his torment and fear for the future of his sisters already taken beyond the wall, Scarand had felt great pity as Imrand had roared furiously and fought in vain against his chains, attempting to seize Gerdar, during the times she had tormented him with her taunts, whenever Sarkisi had been taken to Bahri. A Vanyr warrior was never supposed to show weakness, it was against the blade-code they had sworn at the Sacred Ceremony of Knives. But in the quiet darkness of the night, whenever Sarkisi had been taken, Scarand had heard Imrand softly weeping for his beloved wife.

The squawking of Gerdar's raven brought Scarand's mind back to the present. He watched as she whispered something to the bird, still perched on her shoulder. It squawked again, flapped its wings, took off and flew in the direction of the riders who were now covered from view by a cloud of dust. Gerdar and the Ikma watched anxiously as the raven flew to the north, towards the riders. When it drew near to them, the bird dipped into the dust cloud, emerging again a few seconds later.

Dressed in leather armour of various shades of brown, with an assortment of cloaks and robes and rough boots, the shaven headed Ikma all looked similar due to the masks they always wore, dirty brown masks that were as emotionless and merciless in their appearance as the hearts of the wild and vicious men whose faces they covered. As a precaution against the approaching riders, they strung and drew their bows. Those without bows unsheathed swords and sabres, or unstrapped axes or cleavers secured across their backs.

The raven soon returned to Gerdar and squawked in her ear. She understood its meaning, and frowned as a mark of displeasure. She shouted something to Bahri; her voice was shrill and husky. The only words that Scarand could make out clearly were, "*Seesnari,*" and then, "*Sasna.*"

Bahri rode over to Gerdar, and removed his mask. He reached for the water skin that was fastened to his belt between two sabres, the blades of which were notched with use. After taking a draught, he rolled his shoulders to loosen his joints, and bellowed an order for his men to dismount. They did so, and then unstrung their bows and sheathed their weapons.

The Ikma ordered the few slaves still standing to sit. Scarand and Imrand, who were among the last still standing, sat down on the hard ground. To disobey would just mean another pointless whipping. Neither of them had the strength to endure another one of those.

The dust cloud grew bigger as the riders approached. Scarand could hear the sound of their horses nickering and snorting along with the thud of their hooves on the ground. A line of no more than a dozen or so horse riders emerged from the cloud. Slowing down they rode up to Bahri, before reining in their horses to a halt, except the lead rider who rode past him towards the slaves, before drawing the rein with a jerk that set the steed rearing and neighing loudly.

The riders dusted the layers of sand and dirt that had covered them, revealing the black clothing and hauberks beneath. Their trousers were puffed where they tucked into knee length black boots, also soiled by the dust.

Bahri began scratching himself uncomfortably as he bellowed out orders to his men to start setting the tents out and unpacking the wagons and to water the slaves. The lead rider dismounted the horse, a palfrey, with an agile leap from the saddle, as another rider drew up and also dismounted. The two of them walked past the Ikma guarding the slaves without acknowledging them and walked down the first few rows of the captives, stopping only to give them a quick visual inspection. They stopped near to Scarand as Bahri rode his horse up to them and then dismounted, followed by Gerdar who walked over, looking warily at the two Seesnari.

The one who had been the lead rider removed the black hood and scarf that covered her head, revealing the startlingly beautiful face of a woman, wide-eyed under a thick line of kohl. Fetchingly clad in black linen covered by skilfully wrought leather armour and a broad girdle repeatedly wrapped around her slender stomach, and wide silk pantaloons that were tucked into knee length leather boots, she was a fetching sight. Her skin was roasted a deep chestnut from the desert sun, she was tall and lithe and walked with the confidence of nobility. Her long jet-black hair tied back in a knot was immaculately styled. Sheathed across her back, she carried a pair of perfectly matched double-bladed curved scimitars.

Bahri and the others were all close enough that Scarand could hear their conversation which was conducted in the Common Tongue.

"Lady Sasna," Bahri uttered with an accent so strong he struggled to make the words coherent. "We will go west and take these slaves to the gates of Samothrane or Markose if you do not pay double what you did last time."

Sasna's voice was light and sweet, but not without authority and firmness. She answered whilst closely inspecting the slaves.

"Most of these will be dead of thirst before you reach either of those lands. The Parnam Pool has dried up; you will find no water source between here and there. I will pay you what I did last time, less ten-percent."

Bahri curled his nose up furiously and shouted, "You will pay double. The Davari retreat ever southward, far from civilized lands into the wilds. Many have gone deep into the snow, where the winters are hard. The journey is long and troublesome, and difficult for us to find them. You will pay double!"

Sasna inspected the teeth of a female slave, as she declared, "We can no longer send them east along the River Erin. The tolls along the western route of the river grow larger, and my expenses grow and grow. Our own profits are smaller in these troublesome days. I will pay what I did last time, less ten-percent."

Bahri spat on the ground in disgust. "The wargs are a constant plague, their packs grow larger and are ever bolder; I need more guards to protect the slaves. I have lost many Ikma. You will pay double!"

Sasna finished inspecting a female slave. "Spare me your troubles Bahri; I have enough of my own. That is my price or you take them west."

Gerdar whispered something in Bahri's ear. He nodded, and a sly smirk spread across his face. The tone of his voice changed to that of a man offering some assistance. "We hear rumours that the Bruthon King threatens war against the Seesnari, and Ashgiliath will soon be overcome. Pay what we ask or we go west and sell them to those who would also turn on you when war breaks out. You will need these slaves for coin to fund your defence. The Seesnari should take precautions." Bahri nodded victoriously to Gerdar and some of the other Bahri who had gathered around as the haggling continued.

"It's a shame your father did not take precautions, Bahri," Sasna said, "or spill his seed upon your mother's back. This world did not need or want another like you."

Both the Ikma and the Seesnari who had gathered around laughed at her comment, much to Bahri's annoyance. Gerdar frowned and the raven squawked.

Bahri's tone changed again, to one of anger. "We will bring you no more slaves if you do not pay our price, war will come to you, and we will bring you no more!"

Scarand did not care about the tenseness of the situation, it mattered not to whom he was sold, he was familiar with the life of a slave, although the harshness of his own situation had been lessened due to who his father was. He was determined that whoever his new master was, somehow, he would escape, find his sisters and return to his homeland. He raked back his dirty black locks absently, and as he had done every day since capture, he remained alert, hoping that some opportunity for escape might offer itself. If it did not, he would bide his time, and be ready for the hour when it did. *For Marciea and Oliviana.*

Sasna remained calm and firm when she answered Bahri. "Do not listen to the tales spun in Port Marachus or the Windshores. The Bruthon plan no war against us. They look north, as they have forged a new alliance with the Kappian Empire. Their war will be with the Giant Halls or the Baothein, not with us."

Bahri continued to protest, and Scarand noticed that Sasna's tone changed to one who was repeating a pre-prepared script rather than speaking from the heart. "It is not for me to question the High Warden of Ashgiliath and the price he sets for which I must buy, nor is it for you to refuse him that price."

The haggling continued for some time, but was soon out of Scarand's earshot as Sasna and Bahri walked down the line of slaves, still arguing over the price. Scarand became distracted as the Ikma collected water skins from the wagons and began walking up and down the slave rows, pouring water into thirsty mouths from their cracked kidney shaped leather drinking bags. By the time his row had been watered, Bahri and Sasna had returned to a spot near where they had started the negotiations, and it appeared a price had been agreed upon.

10

Sasna sighed, and then spoke. "It is agreed then. I pay the same price as last time for the female virgins, twenty-percent less for the women you have defiled, and the same price, less than ten-percent for the married ones. For the men of fighting age, I will pay you ten-percent more than last time."

Bahri pretended he was not happy, but it was obvious by the smile he tried to repress, that he was pleased with the prices despite his previous displays of anger, and the protestations he still uttered. "*Never trust a Seesnari*," he stated in feigned displeasure and spat on the ground. "Next time I head straight to Samothrane or Markose, but this time I give you these prices."

"Those women you say are virgins had better be so," Sasna said, "or we will not buy untouched from you again and nor will any other respectable slaver, for we will spread word to all the markets in the Everglow, that Bahri of the Ikma is not to be trusted. We lose good money for every one you have despoiled."

"Those females marked as virgin are untouched, at least by us," Bahri alleged. "Gerdar checked them herself."

The loremaster, standing nearby heard her name and walked over.

"You checked the untouched?" Bahri asked her.

"With my own fingers," she answered as she sniffed her fingers, and the raven on her shoulder squawked eagerly.

Sasna threw a disgusted look at Gerdar, and then snatched a ledger offered to her by one of the Ikma and studied it. "Seventy-two are children, in addition to the women. The rest are men of different age and class. You have lost many, according to this. We need more slaves than this Bahri, and not children and the old. We told you that last time." She flicked her fingers in the air and one of the Seesnari men ran over. He caught the ledger as she tossed it to him.

"Branad here will make the arrangements for payment," she said to Bahri.

Bahri and the Seesnari man named Branad, began to discuss the ledger, and walked towards the wagons, deep in discussion.

Sasna walked towards her horse and took a leather pouch from the saddle-bag before mounting the horse. "Follow me Farir," she snapped at the Seesnari man who stood nearest to her. He also mounted his horse. She un-wrapped the leather package, and took out a piece of paper that was worn at the edges. She spurred her horse towards the end row of slaves, and then rode up the line shouting something in the Common Tongue that Scarand could not quite hear until she neared his row.

"Can any read the runes of the Vanyr? Stand if you can," she shouted. "It will go better for you if you can read the runes."

Scarand heard the clink of chains next to him, and turned his head to see his grandfather, Muro, stand up. Sasna also noticed, and rode up to him, dismounting in one graceful movement. She thrust the piece of parchment, upon which were strange letters, and the symbols of runes, in front of Muro.

"You can read these?" she asked him indifferently and with the manner of one who did not expect to be given the answer she desired.

"The runes have sent me here for this purpose, it is the will of Yig," Muro replied.

Sasna, still holding the reins, steadied her horse, which neighed nervously. The man called Farir also dismounted and walked over to where she stood, and took the reins of her horse.

"Sit," Sasna said, and then crouched down next to Muro, and used her riding whip to turn his face as she examined it. Scarand noticed that her eyes were a deep brown, and surrounded by thick lines of kohl dark mascara, that gave her an exotic, mesmerising look. He could smell the strong waft of her perfume mixed with her sweat

11

and the dust on her clothes, and for a moment he gazed at her, spellbound, and his pulse hammered in his temples.

Sasna held the parchment closer to Muro and repeated the question. "You can read this? Do not waste my time old man," she said, her voiced edged with impatience. "Your life depends upon it."

"Bring it closer," Muro urged.

Sasna frowned impatiently, but thrust the piece of parchment closer to him. Muro squinted with his one good eye to get a better view of it. He scanned the parchment up and down, smiled knowingly, and slowly moved the palms of his bound hands over the text, which momentarily glowed. "The runes have sent me here, to read this, it is the will of Yig. What is your interest in this text? It should not be in the hands of such as you."

"Hold your tongue, slave," Farir admonished angrily.

"Quiet Farir," Sasna ordered, and then looking at Muro, asked, "the words, I thought I saw them glow when you moved your hand across them, what did you do?"

Muro stared at her moodily. "The knowledge in this text is beyond you, and is not your concern. Another has paid you to find me, a dwarf perhaps?"

Sasna took the parchment and warily folded it back inside the leather pouch. She stood and stared at Muro for a long time, a look of wonderment on her face, which soon turned to pleasure. "At last," she murmured.

The man next to her, Farir, intervened again. "For near on a year you have sought somebody to read that. Whatever scheme you are wasting your time on, sister, be about the business quickly. We should get back; uncle will want to know how the trade has gone."

Sasna continued to stare at Muro, as though trying to weigh up if he was telling the truth. Eventually, her voice edged with threat, she advised, "It will not go well for you, old man, if you lie. Somebody has offered me a lot of gold for one who can read this text." Noticing the markings on the back of his hands, she traced the spiral designs with the end of her whip, and then turned his hands over with it to look in his palms. She gasped with astonishment when she saw in his right hand, a rune of fire imbedded, and in his left, a rune of ice. She then asked, "I have not seen these markings before, or runes in the hand of a Davari, you are Ruik?"

"I am Vanyr - I am Ruik. The runes have sent me to read that parchment, it is the will of Yig," was his reply, and he raised his hands and moved them in a circle across the air. Scarand was sure he saw a flash of light shoot from one of the runes in one of his hands and hit Sasna in the eyes. She did not appear to notice and nor did Farir, her brother.

An excited and wild gleam shone in the eyes of Sasna. "Unchain this one from the others, but keep him shackled," she ordered one of the Ikma as she pointed at Muro.

"Sasna, what is this folly?" Farir asked her, as he watched the Ikma unchain Muro from the row. "I have been patient this last year whilst you paraded this text before other Davari, but he looks dangerous and you have him unchained from the others?"

"Quiet brother, I will explain when the time is right."

It was then that she noticed Scarand still staring at her. He continued his gaze as she studied the markings on his chest, now partially covered by the brand of a slave, and then the tattoos on his hands, using her riding whip to turn his hands so she could inspect them.

"You are also Vanyr?"

"He is a mere thrall," Imrand said derisively, "illegitimately conceived by the lowest of thralls and raised by a bellowing bull."

12

Scarand ignored him, and nodded at Sasna.

"And this tattoo is the mark of a hunter? Do you excel at it? Are you a good tracker?"

Scarand answered immediately. "I was taught to hunt from birth, part sense, and part instinct. I read the terrain and search for signs of prey passing. I barely eat or sleep, can run for hours, and corner my quarry until I close in for the kill. I have tracked and hunted snow trolls and once, with my father, killed a giant white warg, a matriarch of the Gunarain Wargs, the terrors that hunt in the mists of the Snow-crowned Mountains. I have shot deer and boar in the Winter Forest that has no end."

"How many years have you seen?" she asked him, eyeing him curiously.

"Twenty," he replied.

"Most of the time he is cleaning latrines or sweeping the floors of the huts of better men," Imrand sneered.

Sasna then turned her gaze upon Imrand, who had a similar marking of the Vanyr on his chest and warrior tattoos on his hands. She stepped over the chains and crouched before him, gently tapping the marking on his chest with her riding whip. Imrand's reaction was more instinctive than thought out. Chains clinked noisily as he grabbed the riding whip, stood, and tried to pull Sasna towards him. Her own reactions were lightning fast. She was too quick, letting go of the whip she stood to her full height and kicked Imrand's legs from under him with a swipe of her own. He fell heavily to the ground. She drew her sabres, the tips of which were prodding his neck in a flash. Farir was instantly by her side, also with weapons drawn.

Imrand recovered. Still holding the whip that he had snatched from her, he stood slowly stood to his feet, with the chains clanking around him once more, and the point of Sasna's sabres still pressed to his neck.

Sasna looked him up and down, and Scarand thought she was about to slay him as rage flashed in her eyes. Imrand was a tall man, and despite the hardships the journey had taken on his body, now caked in dirt and clothed in tattered rags, he was muscular and lithe in appearance and movement. His blonde hair was unkempt and covered with filth. His once well-groomed moustache had sprouted into a shaggy beard.

"If you ever touch me again, Davari, I will have the skin flayed from your bones," Sasna threatened. Her frown glittered like poisonous water. She pressed the tip of the swords into his neck, puncturing the skin and causing a trickle of blood to flow. Imrand said nothing, but offered the whip back to her, handle first. She sheathed her swords and took it.

Gerdar and Bahri rushed over to the commotion, the raven on the loremaster's shoulder squawking excitedly.

"Full of trouble this one is," Gerdar howled with rage. "Sell him to the worst fighting pits in the slums, and his whore of a wife to a disease-ridden brothel."

Sasna looked at Gerdar at first with contempt, and then interest. "His wife is here?"

The old woman nodded, dribble frothing down her chin in her rage.

Sasna stepped towards Bahri and then pointed at Scarand and Imrand. "Keep them shackled, but separate them from the rest, and bring me the wife, wherever she is in this mire of misery. I have a special use for them."

Bahri barked some orders and an Ikma with a key rushed over and began unlocking shackles to separate Scarand and Imrand from the rest of the rows of slaves.

"Have these three, and the woman taken to Frema," Sasna ordered Farir. "The old man will be of use to me. The other three will be prepared as a gift for the Baron; I think he will find them pleasing."

13

The chain fell noisily to the ground as Scarand and Imrand were released from the main train of slaves. Still shackled and chained to each other, they were led by the Ikma, at sword point, towards a horse and cart the Ikma were preparing. Scarand considered if it might be worth trying to seize the moment, grab the key from the Ikma, and fight them before unlocking himself, but he quickly concluded it would be a foolish and pointless gesture with no chance of success. *I must stay alive for Marciea and Oliviana,* he said to himself as the three of them were forced onto the back of the cart and chained and locked to the side of it.

Farir rode up to the cart, and threw them some dried dates, and a water bag, which, hindered by the chains, they caught with some difficulty. Munching on the dates and taking turns to quench their thirst, they waited.

A few moments later, one of the Ikma rode up. Across his saddle bow a limp shape hung, a woman, face down, her long and loose hair flowing around the man's stirrup. She wore torn sandals and a tattered dress that barely covered her modesty. He dumped her unceremoniously onto the ground.

The atmosphere changed, Imrand's rage was mixed with joy and relief as he noticed his wife, Sarkisi. Seeing the expression on his face, the Ikma guarding the cart growled a warning. Imrand yanked furiously at his chains to no avail, and was met with a whip which made a loud cracking noise as it lashed across his back.

"Have sense," Scarand urgently said to him. As a hunter, but also a thrall, he had been trained in the ways of patience; as a warrior, Imrand was rash, and often acted before thinking, an attitude which at this moment would serve him no good.

Imrand paid him no heed, he struggled at his chains until his arms were seized and he was forced to be still. Imrand watched like a wild animal as Sarkisi was picked up, put into the cart and chained alongside him.

When she was secure, the Ikma let Imrand go. Sarkisi had fainted from thirst and weariness. Imrand held her tenderly as Scarand poured some water between her parched lips. She moaned presently and stirred vaguely. Her face was bruised and her eyes bloodshot when she opened them, but she instantly recognised Imrand and cried with delight and relief. They kissed and embraced, and did not hold back in their joy, until they remembered their dire situation, and Sarkisi wept as Imrand comforted her.

"Give them encouragement," Sasna shouted to the Seesnari as she remounted her horse and looked at the slaves still chained in the caravan. Several Seesnari rode their horses down the rows of slaves and began speaking to them. Sasna stood near the front row, still close enough to Scarand that he and the others in the cart could also hear what she said.

"You are now the property of Saroth Arnton, the High Warden of Ashgiliath, Conqueror of the Seven Towers of Samothrane, Slayer of Barnoth the Wicked. Your journey has been long and hard but this stage is near to an end. You will be taken into the Everglow, to the city of Ashgiliath, jewel of the clan-kingdom of Seesnari. Your wounds will be tended, your needs met. You will be given food, water, and rest." Her horse neighed, as though sensing it would soon be out of the hot sun.

"In thirty sunrises, you will be sold to Akkadian masters, your fate is then no longer mine to decide. They are not gods, as some will tell you, they are Pure-bloods, but still just men and women, Children of the Arnath, the ancient Obelisks. When a Pure-blood dies, the Obelisks return them to this world with a new body. You will recognise them by the natural mark of an Obelisk each of them has below the left eye."

Scarand had heard of these people, Akkadians, *Children of the Obelisks,* but until then, he had considered them mere myth and legend, and even hearing Sasna's words, he doubted if such a thing could really be true. *People resurrected by Ancient Obelisks?*

"You are Davari Fell-bloods, the descendants of those who betrayed the gods, and as such, the Arnath will not resurrect you. Both within and outside of the Everglow, you have but one life to live. Your Davari legends state that if you die within the walls of the Everglow, your spirits will be doomed to torment at the hands of the gods in the Deadlands. I know not if that is true or false. I am not Akkadian. I am Seesnari, and therefore superior to you, but I too am Fell-blood, and have but one life to live as do you. I do know this, that when my spirit leaves my body, I will go to the Deadlands like you, and will face with courage whatever awaits me there, trusting in the gods of my people. I know little of that future and this day it does not concern me. I will speak only of what I know."

Her horse reared up with a slight flourish.

"It is not unknown for Davari slaves who serve their Akkadian masters well, to be granted their freedom. Many of those who do earn freedom discard the fears they once held and build good lives for themselves and their families within the great cities of the Everglow, some even within the lands of the Kappian Empire itself. Some others return to their Davari homelands, that is their free choice and the reward of the gift of freedom. If one day, you want to be granted that choice, and be given your freedom, then serve your masters well. Be true and faithful to them and hold on to this hope. Do what they demand of you, whatever that may be, no matter how hard or unpleasant the deed, or the indignities you might suffer, for in that fate you currently have no choice. Be not afraid of the future. Face your fate with courage. Do not attempt to escape, for the punishment of such a crime is worse than death itself. You are marked, you will be hunted down. There is no escape for a Davari slave."

Sasna spurred her horse and it reared up with a magnificent flourish and snorted and neighed. She then spoke to Bahri.

"My brother Farir will return tomorrow and will assist you in escorting the remainder of these slaves into Ashgiliath. You and your men have permission from the High Warden to enter our city, stay for only seven days to refresh and entertain yourselves as you see fit. Respect our laws and customs and it will go well for you."

Without waiting for a reply, she spurred her horse once and followed by all but a few of the riders, she headed back towards the direction of the black gate creating a new cloud of dust in her wake.

Scarand turned towards Imrand, who was still holding Sarkisi and whispering comforting words and promises of escape in her ear. He looked at his grandfather, Muro, also in the cart, who had closed his eye and was sullenly chanting. He then looked at the black gate amidmost the wall and the towers either side. Suddenly, he remembered all the tales of the storytellers, the travellers and the minstrels about the horrors and evils beyond that wall. He remembered the warning that Davari mothers would say to their misbehaving children in the hope it would amend their ways: "If you do not behave, one day you will find yourself within the Everglow." He fought back the primal and instinctive fear that tried to engulf him, as the cart lunged forward and began to rumble towards the gate, taking him towards the Everglow.

*For Marciea and Oliviana,* he said to himself.

# Chapter Two: *The Argona Temple*

*You think this universe of the human senses is all there is? Who are you in this vast multiverse? You are but a speck of dust that blows upon the pages of a book written long before you ever came into existence. What mysteries lie beyond the reach of your senses? Did mind emerge from matter, or did the mind of the Nameless Maker imagine and thus create all matter?*
***Segment from the Prophecy of Karthal***

*The* Priestess Janorra moved swiftly and silently through the torch-lit corridors of the Argona Temple; her two female assistants followed obediently. The only noise at such a late hour was the soft patter of their footsteps as their silk slippers hit against the hard-stone floor. Janorra could sense her assistants fear, she saw it in their eyes every time she looked at them. She could also sense him following them, unseen, Azzadan the Assassin, a would-be *Godslayer*. Unlike her assistants, he made no noise, but she knew he was there. Her stomach tightened with revulsion at the thought of the ceremony she would soon be a part of. *It is the last time* she told herself. *If all goes to plan, I will soon be free.* That thought did little to silence her doubts or calm the fears that still gnawed deeply within her. So much could still go wrong. *Ashareth will give me courage*, she told herself, as she took a deep breath.

Slowing her pace, Janorra clasped her hands gently across her stomach and lowered her head as she passed the temple guards positioned just in front of the large ornate doors that led into the Hall of Titans; her assistants followed suite. The two guards, Hammer Knights, as they were known in the outside world, or Knight Militants within the temple, were dressed in ceremonial armour, red in colour and trimmed with gold. Nine ornamental horns sprung from their plumed helms. Their eyes followed the trio as they passed through the open doors. They honoured the procession by slowly banging the double-head of the large, black metallic war-hammer each held, three times on the hard-stone floor. *Thunk! Thunk! Thunk!*

Janorra hardly noticed the familiar sound. Her mind was on the task ahead, but she did notice the familiar, strong odour of the linseed oil and rosin varnish the knights used to keep their armour in perfect condition. The guards were impressive and hard looking men, seasoned warriors, Fifth Circle members of the Hammer Knights. They were warrior priests who had earned the right to guard the most sacred areas of the Argona Temple, an honour only bestowed upon those who had proven themselves through many lifetimes of service to their High Quaester, Mazdek de Lorion of Clarevont, the head of their sacred order.

Their red chest pieces, emblazoned with crossed golden hammers with a snake wrapped around the shafts, glittered in the shimmering light that sprung from burning torches flickering on the bronze sconces lining the walls. The hammers were the symbol of Thuranotos, the chief god of the Aeldar, the snake the symbol of Ahrimakan, his servant. The golden, red-trimmed cloaks hanging from the knights' shoulders fluttered slightly as a gentle breeze found its way up from some depth below, and through the corridor.

As was the custom, neither Janorra nor her assistants acknowledged the guards, who were forbidden, on pain of death, to speak to a Seeress like her, except in exceptional circumstances. Despite this, she always felt their lingering gaze as she passed them by. She had a natural sway of her hips that always drew the attention of men. Knowing full well the thoughts and desires passing through their minds, she would have all the guards made into eunuchs if it were her choice, or make them take vows of chastity during their time of service. After all, it was only for one lifecycle they had the honour to guard the sacred places in the temple. They would have new bodies after their next resurrection, after which they would enter the Sixth Circle and be given a prominent rank in their military order, or a position in the Imperial Honour Guard of the Empress Shaka herself; they might even be promoted to the position of an Inquisitor or even a Guardian of the Ancient Forge, a high honour indeed.

In stature Janorra was tall. A great mass of golden hair, neatly plaited, fell to her hips; around her neck was a great golden necklace from which hung a jewelled Talisman of Summoning, which bore the image of Ahrimakan, the snake-god, one of the nine Aeldar Gods. It was Ahrimakan's sacred day, the first day of the month of Lupoor, and he was the god whom she and her assistants were due to honour through the sacrificial ceremony.

It had been nine years to the day since she had last performed the ceremony and summoned the vile snake-god, and experienced a painful death as the final and high-sacrifice made to him. The memory of his body wrapping itself around her, the flick of his tongue, the bite of his fangs, sent a shiver down her spine. *This time, it will be different*, she told herself. Honouring Ahrimakan, or allowing herself to again be sacrificed to the vile creature, was certainly not what she and the assassin had planned. *Today, a god will be slain. Today, I will take the Simal and escape.*

Janorra wore the white tunic of a priestess with the thick golden mantle of a Seeress, fastened with a brooch. She was voluptuous and lithe, and by every good measure, a great beauty. She had always considered her beauty a curse, as it had led to her many years of imprisonment, torment and suffering in the temple. She shuddered that even once, when he was in man-form, Ahrimakan had requested her. Twenty-seven lifetimes ago, it had been her misfortune to love a man, a man the Empress Shaka once desired on a whim. He was no more, of that she was sure, whilst she had been condemned to be a repeated sacrifice to Ahrimakan, once very nine years, until all her lives had expired. It was only the fact that it was discovered she was a Seeress during her first death, that High Quaester Mazdek and his Council had spared her from her turn in the regular daily sacrifices that took place in honour of the Aeldar. It had been decided she was of more use to them to be trained as a priestess, so she was sent to the secret Mystery Schools and taught and trained in the arts of being a Seeress, rather than wasted as a regular sacrifice, that had spared her this long. This did not stop her being a sacrifice, however, whenever the lot fell to her on the annual holy day when Ahrimakan was honoured. She took her turn, once every nine years, along with eight other priestesses, all who had been chosen by Ahrimakan himself.

As Janorra and her assistants moved through the ancient stone hallways, and approached the Hall of Titans, a feeling of dread came over her, as it always did. The hall was tens of thousands of years old, or perhaps even more. Nobody knew exactly how old it was. Entering it always filled Janorra with a sense of horror, she still dreaded every step when passing through there, despite the countless times she had done so during her twenty-seven lifetimes spent in the temple. This night was no different. She shuddered as she and her assistants passed under the arched entrance into the barrel-vaulted hall. The smallest assistant let out a small whimper of terror at the sight of the gigantic stone statues of the Titans feasting in the hall. Janorra had reacted in a similar way the first time she had seen them, so long ago, when she had first been led through that hall, in the same manner as the two terrified young women.

"Quiet child," she whispered gently and reassuringly. "They are made of stone and cannot harm you." *Unlike the serpentine monstrosity we will soon encounter.*

17

Many myths and legends surrounded the statues of the feasting Titans. Some said that they were once the actual bodies of Titans, now turned to stone, during an age long ago, an age of pre-history, a time long forgotten by anyone living, and now only mentioned in rare and ancient crumbling texts, or copies of such. These texts described how the Aeldar and the Titans, their own sons, the *Firstborn*, had once fought a brutal war among themselves.

At the end of the war, lured by false pretences, it was said the Aeldar tricked the *Firstborn*, inviting them for a feast to cement a peace. Legend stated that those among the Titans who had been foolish enough to accept the invitation, were cruelly betrayed. They were turned to stone by their Aeldar fathers in the midst of their feasting, forever trapping their eternally living spirits within the stone prisons of their former bodies of flesh and blood. To add to their harsh punishment, it was said that the flawless diamonds that now formed their eyes, enabled their trapped spirits to forever look with frustration upon the Outer World, the realm of the living, knowing they could never return. This punishment the Aeldar inflicted upon the Titans, was for their rebellion; it was a cruel retribution for their forging the Arkooms, weapons that could slay the bodies of the Aeldar and trap their spirits in powerful Arzaks.

Janorra believed this story was no mere myth or legend. In the Deadlands, where she had travelled after each of her deaths, she had seen and heard things, read ancient scrolls and seen macabre images drawn by hands that were not human, that depicted the *Stone Feast* as it had become known to legend. Since that discovery, every time she entered the hall, where before she told herself she imagined it, she felt she could sense the rage, anger and hopelessness emanating from the immortal spirits of the Titans who were still trapped within their eternal prisons of stone. She considered it cruel of the Aeldar, to trick their own children at the height of their mirth and frivolity, so that the joyous expressions frozen on their stone faces, forever denied the torment and suffering they experienced within their eternal prisons of stone - but the Aeldar had a reputation for sadistic malice, a reputation she knew from personal experience was well deserved.

It was small wonder the sight of the stone Titans filled her assistants with terror, but Janorra knew the terror they felt then, was nothing compared to that which they would shortly feel, when they would come face to face for the first time with the snake-god, the Aeldar named Ahrimakan. She genuinely felt for her assistants. *I wish I could save them*, she told herself.

As Janorra and her assistants walked past them, the gargantuan, stone statues of the imprisoned Titans seemed to flicker into life amidst the shadows the flame-lit candelabras cast upon them. To her left was Grishna, a grotesque troll-like giant over twenty feet tall, draining the contents from a goblet filled with wine which dripped down a face expressing mirth. Next to him was Drakon, a dragon-like Titan, the son of Drakan the god of fire, one of the elemental gods of the nine Aeldar. Drakon had a look of surprise in his eyes as he bit into the flesh of cooked meat, as though he realised at the very last second, as his body began to turn to stone, the trick the Aeldar had played upon him. The one that always disturbed her the most though, was Arhatak, a repulsive snake-like Titan who had wrapped himself around the feasting table and was in the process of consuming an entire roasted pig. When she was in the hall, his eyes always seemed to follow her wherever she went, even though they never actually moved. She sensed sheer primeval rage emanating from the spirit trapped within the stone figure. It was Arhatak's father, Ahrimakan, they would soon summon and meet this night. Dread and fear, at the thought of the encounter, washed over her like a tide of despair. *Ashareth give me strength. This time, it will be different. Today is the day to slay a god. Today, I will steal the Simal and escape.*

18

Despite her revulsion, Janorra had always been reluctant to carry out the ceremonial spitting at the empty chair in the hall. Legend chronicled that one of the Titan lords had realised what was happening, and had fought and managed to escape the *Stone Feast*, hence the empty stone chair – to represent him as well as the Titans who had refused to attend the feast. It was the duty of every priest and priestess to spit at the empty chair at the end of the table whenever they passed it. More often than not, if nobody was around to watch her, such as on a night like this, she did not carry out the custom. Her assistants would not know the tradition, as she was supposed to teach it to them on this, their first visit, so they would not question her for not carrying it out.

Many pilgrims to the temple often honoured the Titans by placing flowers and incense at the base of their statues. Whenever she could, Janorra had always shown them proper respect, and not solely for the reason it was one of her priestly duties to honour those of the Titans who had been trapped at the feast - she genuinely was afraid of the rage she sensed in them, and to a degree she sympathised at their supposed fate. *The Aeldar Gods can be so cruel.*

This night, there was not time to pause, let alone honour the Titans by reciting the *Ancient Song of Soothing* in the High Vakkan Tongue, the language it was recorded the Titans had spoken, so she passed them by with scarcely a glimpse, and walked quickly past the empty chair without showing disrespect to it. If all went to plan, it would be the last time she would ever pass through the hall, and that thought gave her the courage to ignore custom and press on with what she must do.

Janorra breathed a sigh of relief when she and her assistants eventually left the Hall of Titans and entered the Sanctuary of the Nine. A large domed chamber, it contained nine shrines and altars, the greatest of which was that dedicated to Thuranotos, whose terrifying golden image stood at the front and centre of the sanctuary, dominating the vast space and towering over the statues of the eight other Aeldar Gods, that stood four each side of it. The posture of Thuranotos was rigid, standing, holding a giant double-headed war-hammer with head downwards touching the stone floor. His face was expressionless, at the same time beautiful and cruel. Nine horns, each shaped differently, rose towards the vaulted ceiling as they sprung from a mass of hair on the head. The sight was too much for the small assistant who had previously whimpered. She burst into tears and fell to the ground. The sounds of her cries echoed around the empty sanctuary.

"You must compose yourself," Janorra urged her, in what she hoped was a reassuring manner. "We are the first here. The others will arrive at the death of this hour. Remember your training. Be strong." *Oh Ashareth, I pity them. I felt the same fear and terror when long ago I was first brought into this place.* "You will be in the Deadlands for only a short time, the Seekers will find you and lead you to the Great Obelisk Horshan, here in the heart of the Argona. It is a great honour to be chosen as a sacrifice for Ahrimakan; glory awaits you." *You are most unfortunate they chose you to be the victim of that foul creature.* "You have been chosen for your purity." *You have been chosen because of your beauty and your fear. Ahrimakan feeds on fear; the more you show, the greater his deviant pleasure shall be.*

"Jezareal, come, we must be brave. Father would want us to be brave," the other assistant urged the smaller one who was weeping on the floor.

*They are sisters?*

Although the assistant tried to sound brave when she encouraged her sister, Janorra could hear the trembling in her voice and see the shaking of her hand, as she put it on her sister's shoulder.

*Ashareth, I cannot bear to think on what they will suffer this night.* Janorra was forbidden to speak to them, a rule she had already broken. If they put up any resistance, her duty was

19

to call the Hammer Knights who would, if necessary, drag them to the Summoning Chamber, also known as the *Seat of the Gods*, but this night, of all nights, she did not want the guards near – not yet. *I found my courage and walked there when I was in your position. You must find your strength.*

Janorra looked around her. She sensed the assassin was near, hidden and unseen, but to her relief no guards, nor anyone else had yet entered the sanctuary. It would be no more than an hour before the assembly gathered for the sacrifice, but she had some time.

*What do I care if Ahrimakan's banquet does not taste as full of fear as he desires? If all goes to plan, it will be his last feast. He will rise from Thrainok in the Void no more. The Halls of Hammerfell will not see him again. Maybe I can bring some comfort to them. They look so young.*

"You are sisters?" Janorra asked the slightly taller one, even though she knew the answer to the question.

"We are twins, Lady Seeress. I am older than Jezareal by just a few minutes or so."

"What is your name?" *Why did I ask? It will only make carrying out my duties this night even harder.*

"My name is Sezareal, Lady Seeress. Please, tell us, is it beautiful in the Deadlands? Will we travel from there to the Fair Havens and see Ashareth? Will the Aeldar come and kiss us with their blessing? They say that only Seers like you can see in the worlds beyond the Outer World."

*It is better they do not know the truth.* "The Deadlands is a land of sun. The trees smile at you when you pass them by. The waters are fresh, and as clear as blue crystal. The mountains are more beautiful than those of Trinity Peaks, the forests greener than the freshest limes." *It is often a bleak, barren landscape, broken only by twisted trees and billowing mists. The waters are dark and full of loathsome things. There are mountains full of underground caverns and tunnels, inhabited by terrible creatures that feast on souls they catch. The forests are black, and are places where howling spirits, or far worse things, will hunt you. The way to Fair Havens is lost.*

"It sounds so beautiful," Sezareal said, with a tremor of doubt tainting her voice. "Is it true that each time we die, we get closer to the light of eternal bliss?"

*They won't remember the Deadlands when they resurrect. A comforting lie is kinder than the truth, isn't it?* "One day, we hope to bask in the glory of the Aeldar, who will smile radiantly upon us. On the day of our *Final-death*, beautiful guardians will take our hand and lead us to the Fair Havens. Those of us who have helped to return the Aeldar to this world, where they belong, will enjoy the paradise the Aeldar have prepared for us." *The Aeldar are destroyers, whose aim is the destruction of everything, so that they may take the shattered ruins of creation and twist it into their image and vision. Their followers are blinded and deluded by false promises of unrestrained power.*

"But I have heard that, the only two Aeldar who have thus far been summoned to this world, Ahrimakan, and the other, are terrible to behold?" Sezareal asked, fear turning her face pale.

"Who told you that, child?" *They should not have tormented you with a truth that you will soon discover for yourself.* "This world distorts the beauty of their actual nature, what you will see this night, is but an illusion and distortion of true reality."

Her words seemed to bring some small comfort to the sisters. Sezareal helped her sister off the floor, and used the sleeve of her gown to wipe her tears away. "There, sister," she encouraged. "The Lady Seeress tells us that we have nothing to fear, we must be brave."

*Ashareth forgive me!* Janorra hated lying to the two sisters. The guilt she had previously felt, gnawed at her even more deeply. She studied their features closely and observed that the only noticeable difference between them she could tell, was that which she had

20

previously noticed, that Jezareal was the shorter of the two by a few inches. Both sisters' heads were shaven, as was the custom for first time sacrifices. Their eyes were brown and round. Even in the dim light she could see that their skin was white and pure, no blemishes. They were quite lovely to behold. *Of course, they are, they would not have been selected if they were not. In this place, beauty is a curse.*

Janorra placed a comforting hand on Jezareal's shoulder. "This night will be over soon. Remember what you have been taught at the Theostar, and take comfort in those teachings when you resurrect. It is a great honour you have been given, to be chosen as a sacrifice to Ahrimakan." Once more, the lie wrenched at Janorra's heart.

"We have not yet been taken to the Theostar, Lady Seeress," Sezareal answered meekly.

*What?* "What do you mean?" Janorra asked, feeling perplexed.

"We were born in the Skunfill district of the city. That's where we lived with father, until a few months ago. He kept us locked away, to protect us from any disease."

Janorra was too startled to say anything at first. *Skunfill? An impoverished, disease-ridden district of Kappia city. Since when has the temple recruited sacrifices from there?* It dawned upon Janorra that they had mentioned their father again. *They should never have known their parents.* "Skunfill? You were not taken as milk-babes and raised in the Theostar?"

"No, Lady Seeress," Sezareal replied. "Father only recently converted from the *Old Faith*. He became a worshipper of Ahrimakan and as a skilled mason he joined the Clarevont Guild and found work as a mason in the Cloisters. We moved there, with father, after leaving Skunfill. High Quaester Mazdek noticed us after father met his *Final-death*, not more than three months ago. He selected us for this night. He told us our father wished this for us, and that we will be trained in the Theostar after we resurrect.

*No wonder they are so terrified, they are like me when I was first brought here and selected as a sacrifice. They have not been brainwashed and conditioned like those prepared in the Theostar over many years.*

"If you came from Skunfill, how is that you lived there until the age of resurrection, without succumbing to disease or death? Not many Pure-bloods can survive in that part of the city, yet you have done so without any blemish to your skin?"

The sisters looked at each other, blushed, but did not answer.

*Your father was no mason, or you would not be here, he traded milathran, I see the effects on your unblemished skin and that is why you both look so young.* Pure-bloods who died, before their thirtieth year, for reasons unknown to any, were rarely brought back to life by the Obelisks. It was a reason why Pure-blood children were often carefully protected by their parents, until that age. It was at this age, the Mark of the Arnath, the outline image of a small Obelisk, appeared before the left eye. If a person was a Seer, then after they had died and resurrected, this image was filled in, and that is how Seers were recognised. The Argona Temple however, often sacrificed those who had not reached the age of resurrection and used the Obelisks to return them by dark and sinister arts.

"Before he worked at the Cloisters, did your father travel often? Did he go away from home for long periods?"

"Yes, he was a very skilled mason and much in demand for specialist work all over the Empire."

"How did your father meet the *Final-death*? How many lives had he lived beforehand?"

"We do not know. The Hammer Knights took him and us away one night, and told us he fell from a building, and never resurrected. It was just his time; he must have lived many lives and the last one expired."

21

*He was caught illegally trading milathran and sentenced to the Final-death. Only traders sanctioned by the Milathran Guild can sell it within Kappia city. You too are being punished for his crimes. You will be sacrificed to Ahrimakan every time he is summoned, until all of your lives have expired.*

Janorra suddenly regretted getting involved. She wished she had not asked any questions. It was one thing for those taken from the Theostar to be sacrificed, as that would only happen once every nine years, or even longer if selected by lot. Even though those trained in the Theostar were prepared for it, the sacrificial process was still traumatic. It was quite another thing for those unprepared, and they would be repeatedly sacrificed, sometimes almost immediately after being resurrected again.

"This is your first lifetime?"

"Yes," Sezareal answered.

*Your only hope then, is that you return from the Deadlands, and turn out to be Seers, like I did, although the chances of that are very small.*

"We do not want to be here Lady Seeress, we are afraid," Jezareal whimpered, speaking for the first time. "We want to go home."

*Why did I get involved? I feel for them, but I must go ahead with my mission. I cannot take any chances. I have suffered too much to stay here any longer and there is nothing I can do to help them. Is there?*

Janorra felt a sharp prod in her back that jolted her forward slightly and made her exhale her breath. It was the assassin. He was clearly not happy and wanted to speak with her. She lifted up her right hand, and showed the sisters the ring that adorned her index finger. The ring was gold with a rune-shaped amethyst placed in the centre. "Look at the jewel in this ring," she urged with an authority that caused the girls to immediately look at it. "*Hasoose*," she said gently.

A light flashed from the jewel for a fraction of a second. The girls fell into a trance-like-state, eyes still open, but Janorra knew they would be temporarily unaware of everything happening around them. She took them by the hand and led them to the front of the Sanctuary of the Nine, to the foot of the statue of Ahrimakan which stood immediately to the right of that of Thuranotos. She opened a door at the base and led them into a small, candlelit room, the shrine of Ahrimakan. Closing the door behind her, she led her assistants to two small altars either side of a slightly larger one, situated in front of a small statue of the snake-god. She gently manoeuvred them into a kneeling position.

"What is it?" she asked. "Show yourself, Azzadan."

From out of thin air, a man appeared. Janorra had not been positively impressed by her first impression of Azzadan the Assassin, whom she had met almost a year ago to the day when he had come to the temple, unseen, to seek her out. He had come across as rough, crude, cruel and full of a sinister dark humour. The blackness of his eyes revealed there was very little mercy in his heart, if any at all. The subsequent meetings with him had not changed her opinion. He was handsome enough, in a rough and rugged way, but a streak of cruelty about his features had made her uneasy then, as it did now. Many lifetimes of evil deeds were etched upon his face. He also bore the mark of a Seer. A powerfully built man, Azzadan's black wavy hair hung over his bearded face. He was booted and dressed in black trousers and hauberk. A grey ethereal cloak with a dim silver pattern of a clawed hand stitched upon it, swung across his shoulders, and was clasped together at the front with a clawed brooch. With the hood up, he had been invisible. With it down, he could be seen.

Through his previous communications with her, Janorra knew that Azzadan belonged to the Order of Ithkall, also known as the Guild of the Clawed Hand, or the

Brotherhood of Ishar. It was an ancient Order of assassins and thieves, that had been outlawed long ago, and with good reason. They had been famed and feared in equal measure by rich and poor alike. They worshipped Skipilos, the god of thieves and murder, and that was their trade, which they plied with deadly skill and uncanny precision.

Janorra had gone to the temple libraries and read many tomes and iron-bound books about the Order since first meeting Azzadan. She had discovered that it was said Skipilos had long ago taught Ithkall, the founder of the Order the many skills and talents the members now used in their dark arts. It was written that Skipilos taught them secret arts of crafting and tailoring, so that each member could craft legendary items of great power, such as the ethereal cloak currently worn by Azzadan, that was adorned with strange looking glyphs. Such a cloak enabled the most skilled of them to vanish, even whilst mounted on horse, enabling man and beast to disappear entirely, in the flash of an eye. It was rumoured members of the Order travelled far and wide collecting and gathering the rare fabrics and items needed to make such an item. The books she had read, did not reveal what the ingredients were, for none but the Brotherhood knew and they did not give up their secrets easily or willingly. It was believed that the final ingredient was extremely rare and required travelling outside of the Everglow and risking the *Final-death* to find it.

To become a fully initiated member of the Brotherhood, involved the passing of many tests, and required successfully murdering numerous targets. From their secret locations in the many cities throughout the Kappian Empire, it was quietly whispered that members of the Order slipped unnoticed among the populace to fall like black spiders, silent, deadly, upon their chosen targets. Their preferred weapons were clubs, daggers, or the many throwing stars and blades they carried hidden about their person, the latter often tipped with rare and deadly poisons, each an object of beauty made with precise engineering crafted by the assassins themselves. Each throwing star had its own speciality, with a different weight and thickness that required different handling. These weapons would only give one death though, it was the Arkiths they owned that inspired the most fear.

Some believed the Brotherhood owned several rare Arkiths, blades that were forged in a time long ago, created with foul soul-gems in their hilt, gems called Arzaks, created by methods now forgotten and by means that even the Brotherhood did not know. Death by such a weapon, would forever trap any soul within the harsh gem. To die by an Arkith meant the *Final-death*, even for Pure-blood Akkadians, for once their soul was trapped within the gem, the Obelisks could no longer reach and resurrect the victim. It was a cruel death, and one that even the stoutest Pure-bloods feared. The one hope for those who had the Brotherhood hired against them, was that they only gave death by an Arkith in exceptional circumstances, and for a very high price in coin, which most who hired them for their services, could not afford to pay.

To become a Supreme Master of the Brotherhood required success in only the most dangerous of tasks, and that, was the very reason that Azzadan was with Janorra in the temple, standing before her now. His only mission, was to slay a god, and take her and the Simal to the Baothein - she knew that. As she looked at him, she was again reminded of the seriousness of what they were about to attempt, and her stomach tightened in a knot. A wooden club hung from one side of his belt, but it was the sheathed dagger in the middle that reminded her just what business they were about that night. It was not an Arkith, it was something far worse - an Arkoom. An Arkoom was one of the weapons said to be crafted by the Titans, Elves, Dwarves and Men of old. It was a weapon with a black Arzak crafted into it, a soul-gem so foul and powerful, that if the Arkoom blade it was joined with was used to kill the physical body of a summoned Aeldar, the Arzak could trap the spirit and essence of the god within it. It was the creation of these terrible weapons that led to the Aeldar deciding upon such a cruel punishment for the *Firstborn* Titans, who had shared their knowledges with lesser races.

Sheathed in glass, the ancient jaded-blade shimmered green in colour, and looked very old indeed. On the handle of the dagger, was the Arzak itself. It seemed almost unbelievable to Janorra, just looking at it, that such a dull looking black jewel could imprison even a god. In that moment though, she felt its presence, and it made her nervous, for she could feel dread and impurity oozing and emanating from within it. *What unfortunate creatures and spirits are already trapped inside of it for it to give off such a disturbing presence? It is truly a prison for the gods themselves.*

"Is there a way we can do this and take them with us?" Janorra asked him, as she cast a sympathetic glance at the two sisters, still kneeling trance-like on the silk cushions at the altars. "The blood of the Davari sacrifices will give Ahrimakan physical form, he can be slain then, these two do not need to die, do they?"

Azzadan sat down on one of the stone seats in the small shrine and put his feet up on a nearby table. Despite the immensity and importance of the task at hand that night, it struck Janorra that he seemed calm, relaxed even, without any hint of anxiety or apprehension. He took a green apple from a small fruit bowl on a table next to him and took a bite, as he looked at the two sisters and then pointed at the ring on Janorra's finger.

"It is forbidden to eat those apples," she counselled, feeling alarmed. "Three of them are placed in that bowl. After the sacrifice, my heart, and that of those two, will be placed in the bowl, symbolising our oneness with the Aeldar. If the High Quaester notices before the ceremony one has been tampered with, he might suspect something is wrong."

Azzadan laughed, loudly. "Your newly found devotion to the Aeldar touches me right here," he said sarcastically as he thumped the apple over his heart for effect, after which he took another bite of it, before throwing it carelessly back into the bowl, which rattled loudly.

"Shush, you must be quiet," Janorra insisted in a panicked tone as she turned the apple so the bite marks could not be seen. "The sanctuary might be empty, but it is still unwise to make any noise above that of our whispered words, lest a guard does wander in." She threw him an accusing look. "You are supposed to be a professional and skilled at what you do, yet you raise your voice and eat from a sacred apple?"

Azzadan forcefully snatched her hand and inspected the ring with which she had dazed the two sisters.

"That's a handy trinket, I have seen that you always wear it, but I did not know it did that," he said, inadvertently spitting out some of the apple which he was still chewing. "Why does a priestess need a trinket like this?"

She blushed. "They are given to all priestesses; this one is called *Arnazia*. Some pilgrims who come to the temple believe they will receive a great blessing if they lay with us, especially with a Seeress like myself. We have made vows of chastity, so it protects us in times when we are in private council giving guidance to pilgrims who, well, might wish to impose their will upon us by force." *It did not protect me that one time from Ahrimakan himself when, in the form of a man, he called for me.*

"What else does it do?" he asked suspiciously.

*I do not trust you enough to tell you the true power of such a ring, and what I have taught it with knowledge I learned in the Deadlands and in the sacred libraries of the Mystery Schools.* "It only has one use, to pacify troublesome pilgrims who come to the temple."

"Or to calm such as them?" he asked, looking at the two sisters.

She shook her head, and spoke in a lowered voice. "It is forbidden to use it on our assistants. If they resist going to the sacrifice, the Hammer Knights are to be called and they will be taken there by force. This of all nights I do not wish to pursue that course of action, so I use my ring."

She pulled her hand away from his, and frowned. "Can these two be taken with us, when we escape? Can we just snatch the Simal, and escape with them?" As much as she hated him, Janorra would forsake seeing Ahrimakan slain, if it now meant having the opportunity of saving these two unfortunate sisters. What did it matter if Ahrimakan was left to rot in the Void, or in the Arzak of the Arkoom?

Azzadan smiled cruelly as he swallowed the bit of chewed apple. "Why do you care for them? This is not the first time you have seen such as they sent to this fate, with your own hand as accomplice to the deed."

"These two are different. They have not been trained in the Theostar, and despite what they have been told, they will not be taken there when they resurrect, unless they are Seers. They will repeatedly be given a horrid death until all their lives have expired. I want to take them with us. It will give me some peace to know that I have saved them from such a dark fate."

Azzadan reached under his cloak and took out a green cloth which he unravelled, revealing two, silver circlet headbands, each decorated with purple runes. A small glass phial full of pink liquid was attached to the gem at the centre of each. He placed the headbands on the table.

"Do you remember what I taught you about these?" he asked with an impatient growl.

She nodded. *Unfortunately, she did, but she was hoping beyond hope.*

Azzadan tapped the circlet with a finger. "These are not Juram; try as we might, we could not find any to steal or buy, even for such a task as this. These are Jula!" His tone became aggressive and resentful. "One of them cost the price of a small kingdom, the other, was stolen by a Kirani who only just managed to escape with her life."

She could tell by the tone of his voice, and the scowl on his face that his annoyance was growing.

"What is the plan?" he asked with a fierceness that unnerved her as he stared at her grimly. "Tell me, so that I can have renewed confidence you recall it."

"By Ashareth lower your voice," she pleaded, and swallowed hard before meekly answering. "When Ahrimakan comes to consume me, so that he can take the form of a man, before he wraps himself around me, you will slay him with the Arkoom. I will be holding the Simal. We escape with it, each using one of the Jula."

The snarl on his face turned even more ferocious. "What is the phial and liquid called?" he asked in a condescending manner as he pointed to one of the phials.

"We do not have time for this," she quietly protested as she looked at the door of the shrine, fearful lest somebody might hear them.

"We will make time for this," he snarled as he took his feet off the table and stood menacingly over her. "What are they called?"

*Be quiet, or we will be discovered.* "The gem is the Jula, the phial holds the liquid Elestar that powers it." *Once used the phial often breaks and the circlet becomes a mere collector's piece, next to worthless and of no functional use.*

He slowly nodded his head, the way a teacher might towards a dense student who gave an obvious answer.

"Nobody living has the knowledge to craft Jula anymore, at least nobody known, and no alchemist can brew such a potion as Elestar," he cautioned as he prodded a finger towards the circlets. "It required the greatest skill and talent of Armun of the Tarath Guëan, to shape the runes so that these will take us to where we need to go. The slightest imbalance, will cause results we cannot predict, as these will take us over the seas, rivers and canals of the Underglow itself. We only have one chance to slay Ahrimakan, and escape with the Simal. One chance!"

Azzadan's impatience and aggression intensified. "I take no pleasure in whatever fate befalls them," he said as he glanced at the two sisters, "but nor do I care. I have sworn a blood-oath before the Brotherhood of Ithkall, I have placed a Bethratikus before the Altar of Skipilos, that I will slay the snake-god this night, and bring you and the Simal to the Baothein."

Janorra nodded. "I understand…" She did not get to finish the sentence.

Azzadan wrapped the Jula circlets back in the cloth, and he placed them under his cloak. His hand then unexpectedly lunged forward with lightning speed. Grabbing her by the hair he pulled her head roughly backwards so she was forced to look up at him. She winced in pain as his rough hand twisted her hair in a knot which curled around his knuckles. With his other hand he drew the Arkoom from its sheath, and held the blade just in front of her throat. The blade shimmered more brightly than before. The black jewel on the hilt, the Arzak, began to light up as though it anticipated a feast. If it even scratched her, death would be final. He moved the blade and waved it before her eyes.

Janorra could see haunted and tormented faces within the gem, rising to the surface.

"You dare say I am unprofessional?" he snarled, his voice dark and sinister. He slowly pointed the tip of the blade at her eye.

She felt dizzy with dread. It felt like a filthy evil emerged from the blade, polluting the very air around it. He stared intently into her eyes, but she could not take her eyes off of the Arkoom. The runes shone, they were very intricate and clear. She felt as though her lifeforce was already being sucked into the Arzak.

"There are very few who can read these runes," he said, enjoying her fear. "It is said they are curses from another age, curses the Titans uttered towards the Aeldar, at the time these blades were forged, in smitheries dark and deep."

"Please, let me go," she begged, as he tightened his grip in her hair and pushed her face closer to the blade, the point of which was now next to her eye. She froze, and dared not move, for the slightest motion might cause the tip of the blade to pierce her eye.

"They cannot come with us, is that clear?" he asked.

She wanted to nod, but dare not, for the point of the blade was still too close.

"Yes," she answered softly, her voice trembling. "I understand."

Azzadan let her go and she fell to the floor. Sheathing the Arkoom, he looked at her and advised. "When I slay the snake, be ready to take the Simal. Forget these sisters, their fate is not our concern." With that, he pulled the hood of his cloak over his head, and disappeared.

Janorra sat on the floor trembling for several minutes. There was no sound she could hear outside of the shrine, nor inside of it, except for her own rapid breathing. After she had gathered herself, she stood, and walked over to each of her assistants in turn and whispered, "*Hassostias.*"

The sisters slowly began to awaken from their trance, looking confused and disorientated. Janorra knelt on the cushion at the central altar in between them.

"Pray and meditate quietly," she said calmly to the sisters, "and prepare yourselves for when the High Quaester comes for us. We do not have long."

26

# Chapter Three: *The River Queen*

*The River Erin is the greatest river in the Everglow, in terms of the volume of its flow and the area of its basin. The northernmost source is high in the Kappian Mountains where it flows through the plateau cascading into the Panharin Lake basin, before spiralling south, where it divides, flowing east into the Tethys Sea, and west as far as the famed city of Zinabar.*
*Temmison Vol III, Book 5: Natural Wonders of the Everglow.*

*An* unsettling breeze came from the Wytchwood Forest, on the port side of the *River Queen,* as she slowly moved through the fog, came around the point and entered the anchorage known as Grey Cradle. Sasna emerged from her cabin, and curled her nose up at the stifling air the wind carried. It was night and the crew had lit the night-fire in the great iron brazier amidships. A bandy-legged sailor stoked the fire with an iron, whilst another carefully filled lamps with oil which he ladled from a nearby barrel. They laughed at her reaction of disgust to the breeze.

"The Wytchwood always carries a foul air, stinks, no matter what time of year," the one stoking the fire said to her.

Sasna felt his leering eyes look her up and down, but she ignored him. It was not the first time she had made the journey from Ashgiliath to Berecoth, and she was well acquainted with the River Erin. She walked to the side of the ship and leaned carefully over the rail, and took a few deep breaths despite the foulness of the air. She found the gentle splashing of the oars soothing, the grunts of the unseen slaves powering them less so. A small gust of wind carried not only the stench of the Wytchwood, but that of the oar-slaves, which rose from the lower deck, and wafted across where she was standing. A crewman laughed as she coughed and held her hand over her veiled nose. She then walked towards the quarterdeck where she could just make out the image of the grossly overweight captain standing near the ship's wheel. Her gown slid uneasily over the ladder as she made her way up it. The captain frowned at her as she approached.

"A palla is no dress to be worn on a ship," he barked as he studied her with a disapproving glare.

Sasna knew he was right. The palla she wore was a glamourous silk gown, in her case purple, the colour of royalty as her blood-line could be traced back to ancient kings, and she had been the daughter of the third cousin to the last king to sit upon a throne at Ashgiliath, King Seros IV.

Her attire showed both leg and breast aplenty, and her midriff was only partially covered by a sash worn around it. Custom dictated the clothing had to be worn with a veil covering the lower-part of the face. She wore the same kohl make-up she usually wore, making her eyes stand out prominently. According to Seesnari culture, the palla was worn by single women, supposedly to protect them from the solicitations of men, as a single woman could not be approached by a Seesnari or other male with impure intentions. It was supposed to advertise the female wares, to would be suitors, whilst signalling not available to those with less than honourable intentions. It all seemed a bit ironic to most outsiders, given just how much flesh the palla revealed.

"Baron Daramir will expect me to dine with him this evening. I have to deliver the tribute and slaves personally." *He will expect me to be dressed appropriately.* "He takes great offence if Fell-blood women do not know their place and do not observe expected etiquette," she said as she squatted away a large river fly buzzing around her head.

She looked to the north, where lay the foreboding Wytchwood a few hundred yards off the port bow hidden from sight by the mist. A shiver went down her spine. *It is a cold night.*

The captain continued to frown. "It's not right for a woman to be dressed so on a ship, it will distract the crew. At least cover yourself with a robe."

Sasna stared angrily back at him. *You are an ignorant fool. A Seesnari woman is not allowed to cover herself when she is wearing a palla.* "I have travelled on this ship many times before. But not with you as captain, where is the other one, what was his name?"

"Belus? He died in the Vargo Goss drinking contest. Choked on his own vomit but made it as far as Elcester. It was their ales that finished him, so I was told." The captain's face softened as he laughed to himself. "Mind you, it worked out well for me. I'm done with sailing the Tethys Sea. I signed off at Berecoth and the patrician offered me command of this little beauty." He patted the ship's wheel to emphasise the point. "The life of a river cap'n will suit me just fine now."

*Could it be possible he might have met Vardy? It is a slim chance.* "Did you ever come across a Seesnari by the name of Vardy on your travels?" Sasna had often wondered what might have happened to her oldest brother, who had run away long ago to sail the Tethys Sea. Her mind drifted back to when she was a young girl. She and her siblings had always been fascinated by the stories their nursemaid had told them about the great ocean on the eastern shores of Pangaea. Nurse told them it was filled with great sea-beasts, that it was a place brimming with pirates, and many adventures could be had.

The captain shook his head. "Not that I recall," he answered bluntly.

A brief wave of disappointment brushed over her, but it was soon replaced with an excitement that made her skin tingle. *Soon, I will get to see the Tethys Sea for myself, and can ask for Vardy in places far and near.* The instructions her uncle had given to her and Farir were very clear: '*deliver the tribute gold and the three slaves to Baron Daramir. Pay all due courtesies, arouse no suspicions. State you have business in Berecoth and leave Castle Greytears when politeness allows. Travel with the River Queen to Berecoth. People are waiting for you there, and will escort you to Harwind, and from there you will go directly to the Sea Lords. You are to be my secret envoys to negotiate with them, so that we can again take our slaves by ship along the Erin, all the way to Harwind and even up to Kappia.*' Sasna had jumped at the chance of a new venture. It was so much more exciting than her usual routine of dealing with the Ikma and the likes of Bahri, and then bringing a tribute of gold, and three wretched slaves to Castle Greytears, the ancient seat of Baron Daramir, otherwise known as the *Bloody Baron*. She had made this trip on many occasions, but this time, it was different. In addition to her secret mission to the Sea Lords, she had found a Davari who could read the scrap piece of text she had been given, and that would make her a fast and tidy profit. After spending just enough time to be polite with the Baron, she would take the slave named Muro to the Pike and Pickle Tavern, hand him and the text over to the dwarf who wanted to buy him, and make a tidy profit for very little work. *That dwarf is so foolish. More gold than sense.*

Sasna noticed the captain was still staring at her, somewhat inappropriately. *You are new to the Erin. You need to learn how business is carried out here. I already told you, the Baron is easily offended if etiquette is not followed.* "I will not have you question my attire again," she said, indignantly.

The captain huffed. "From what I hear, 'tis with good reason they call him the *Bloody Baron*, doesn't take much to give him cause for offense nor much reason to satisfy his lust for blood. Besides, we won't be docking this evening, so you can get changed again into something more suited."

Sasna did not attempt to hide either her surprise or her annoyance at the news. "Why won't we be docking, what's happened?"

The captain took a crinkled note out from the pocket of his trousers and handed it to Sasna. "Read it yourself, a raven came with this message from the castle about an hour ago. 'Cos of the fog they've put the iron net across the port mouth."

She looked at the captain contemptuously. "I've entered the port before in fog, this is the first time I've ever heard of them using the net to block it?"

He nodded towards the note. "Read it. Last night pirates raided Berecoth. As a precaution, the Harbour Master at Greytears has ordered nothing is coming in and out of port at night, or whilst there is fog. The net stays up until they can see what comes in and out. Like it or not, we won't be able to dock till morning and then only if the fog has lifted."

Sasna read the crinkled note, and then threw it on the deck in disgust. Her revulsion soon turned to alarm when the news sank in. *Berecoth raided? Since when have pirates ventured that far west along the Erin?* Doubts assailed her. *Perhaps we should return to Ashgiliath immediately? But my uncle will be furious if I return without having spoken to the Sea Lords.*

"No need to be worried little lady," the captain said patronisingly. "The patrician is a shrewd man. He will pay a bribe to the raiders. His ships won't get touched. We'll not be harmed."

There was something in his tone that sounded insincere, and Sasna did not like the disrespectful way he addressed her, but she had more important matters to deal with. She gazed around the upper deck, looking closely at the crew tending to their business about the ship. It was the first time she had left her cabin since they had sailed from Ashgiliath three days before. It dawned upon her, that she did not recognise any of them. She looked up at the rigging. Normally, heavily armed Seranim archers were stationed in the rigging and masts, instead, it was some raggedy looking men, only armed with what looked like poorly made bows. The patrician at Berecoth was a shrewd man, but she knew him well. He would not pay a bribe to stop his ships being attacked. He always protected them, and those who hired them, by paying skilled Seranim mercenaries to make sure they stayed safe from any harm. More doubts assailed her. *Something is definitely not right.*

"The High Warden of Ashgiliath, my uncle, pays for this ship to take me where I wish to go. I will consult with my brother. We may wish to return to Ashgiliath," she said demandingly to the captain. *But if I return having given up on uncle's orders so easily, he will never trust me with anything important again.*

The captain took a deep breath, held it for a second before breathing out noisily. "Don't worry your pretty head. The fog will be lifted by morning, you can be about your business with the Baron. We will learn if it is safe to continue to Berecoth. If not, I'll take you straight back to Ashgiliath." He then smiled, showing a mouth of gold teeth, with some missing.

*I can wait until morning, at least, and then see what news a new day brings,* Sasna thought.

"Best get back to your cabin now, missy," he said obnoxiously. "We are approaching the anchorage. A ship going to anchor is no place for a scantily-dressed woman." The captain hawked up some phlegm in his throat and spat on the deck.

Sasna gritted her teeth in a mixture of frustration and disgust.

"Gnarn!" the captain shouted, "Gnarn, get here you stunted little rat!"

Sasna then noticed a badly disfigured boy curled up by some ropes on the deck behind the captain. The boy was fast asleep, and did not wake, even after the third time the captain called him.

29

"Gnarn! Where are you? You dumb, filthy little toad!" The captain turned around, noticed the boy curled up by the ropes, lunged over and kicked him very hard. The boy woke with a start, a grunt and a wheeze.

"Take the Lady Sasna back to her cabin, and make sure she has all that she needs. Do you understand me boy?"

Gnarn nodded, and flinched as the captain held up a fist. The boy scuttled ahead of Sasna, using both his hands and feet to move along the deck, and signalled for her to follow. She glowered at the captain, who dismissed her annoyance with an indifferent grunt and a dismissive wave of his hand.

Sasna resisted the temptation to remind the captain of his place. That could wait for a more suitable time, besides, the uneasy feeling growing within her was intensifying, and she wanted to speak to Farir.

The captain took the rope of the ship's bell in his hand. He rang the bell several times as he shouted, "Prepare for anchor!"

Sasna left the quarterdeck, following Gnarn down the ladder, and headed towards the cabin where she was staying. The sound of the ringing bell had been muffled by the fog, but nonetheless, had alerted more crew who were emerging from below deck or scuttling about the focsle preparing ropes and chains. She ignored the lustful stares and quiet mutterings of the sailors as she passed them. Entering the cabin without knocking, she left Gnarn outside, and closed the door behind her before she removed her veil. She was not sure what was worse, the rancid smell of the River Erin and the Wytchwood, or the smell of sour wine that hung in the air of the cabin.

The cabin was the captains, but it had been turned over to Sasna's use when they had sailed from Ashgiliath. Although small, it was quite luxurious but very untidy. A table in the middle of the cabin bore a battlefield of carafes, goblets, tin plates and dishes with half-eaten food still on them, and was liberally littered with used ivory handled cutlery. A goblet had fallen over on the creased tablecloth causing a discoloured purple patch where the red wine had stained it.

The cabin was dimly lit by a few wax lamps and a large candlestick in the centre of the table, causing the tablecloth to be stiff with the wax that had trickled down the side of the candelabra. A pile of cushions remained sprawled where Sasna had been previously sleeping. Farir, lying on the hammock, swung his legs over the side and stood up, losing his balance slightly as the ship surged forward with the movement of the oars. He rubbed the side of his head.

"I hate travelling on this cursed river," he moaned grumpily as he poured a glass of red wine from a bottle on a nearby table which also had the remnants of half-eaten food left on it. "Besides, this wine is sour." He took a sip of wine and winced from the taste.

Sasna took a long look at her younger brother. His dishevelled hair had been pulled back and tied in a knot behind his head. He was unshaven, with a lined ascetic face out of which two bloodshot and bleary eyes stared.

"Farir, you make the same complaint every trip. I would rather suffer the river, than face another raiding band of Chatti. It is rumoured they crossed the Erin from the Tarenmoors again and this time they have a Gragor with them. The road from Ashgiliath to Greytears is not safe." *Neither is the river at the moment, with these damned pirates.*

"I thought uncle had sent peace envoys to Malagrim?"

"Do not speak of that in public; besides, peace or not, I would not want to fall into the hands of raiding Chatti, they are a law unto themselves. "

Farir looked his sister up and down and sneered. "Well I don't like this captain. He has a look about him. What happened to the other one, what was his name? Belus or something, now he was a man I could drink with and at least enjoy my time on board this dilapidated raft." He took a deep gulp of wine, winced with disgust, yet refilled the glass and drank some more anyway.

Sasna reached out to take the glass away from him, but Farir raised it above his head out of her reach.

"Farir, I need you sober. I have an uneasy feeling something is not right, we are not docking alongside Greytears but staying at anchor over-night, and longer if this fog does not clear."

Farir drained the glass of its contents and refilled it again. "We've docked in fog before, what's different this time?" He appeared to be more curious than concerned.

"I don't know," Sasna replied, as she took off the palla, and quickly dressed in black leathers and light armour, and wrapped the sash around her waist. Her sabres were sheathed and hung on a hook by the door. She took them down, and strapped them across her shoulders. "This captain shows me no respect. There are no Seranim aboard, I don't recognise any of the crew and pirates have raided Berecoth. I am concerned that we were unaware they are now raiding this far down the Erin."

Farir snorted derisively. "You always see trouble where there is none."

Something did not feel right, Sasna sensed it, and felt annoyed with Farir that he was oblivious to the same sense of foreboding she felt, probably because of the wine.

"Farir, something is not right, I am worried! We must be vigilant, just in case."

Farir placed his empty glass clumsily on the table. He slurred when he said, "Of course something is not right. Do you think I did not notice that you and uncle were in deep discussions I was not allowed to be a part of, and that we left again without our own men to guard us? It might be time you told me what was really going on."

"Brother, I love you, but you spend too much time in wine cups. One loose word from you, would and still can put everything at risk. Leave business matters to me; just be about your wits."

Farir crossed his arms defensively and said petulantly, "Here we go again. Uncle is still angry at me for that Spanian whore incident, isn't he? How was I to know she was a spy? Besides she was caught before she got our ledgers to Marakose. I said sorry, you and uncle should just let it go."

Sasna moved towards him and placed her hand tenderly on his shoulder. "It was my decision not to allow you in on our plans, I will tell you soon enough when the time is right. I promise."

Farir sulkily shrugged her hand from his shoulder, and picked up his glass of wine. "What grand schemes have you and uncle came up with this time? It's bound to lead to trouble of some sort." He staggered and pointed his glass at her. "I bet it's to do with that old text you've been waving about to those Davari, isn't it?"

"That is just a business transaction to earn us gold, nothing more, it has nothing to do with the business we are about," she replied. *I dare not trust him to know about our mission to the Sea Lords. Not until we are safely on our way to Harwind.*

Farir pressed the matter when she did not answer. "It's that text, I knew it. I wondered why you kept waving it about to the Davari, wanting to find somebody who could read it. Every time I asked you why, you gave me no answer."

*The only thing I care about that text is the gold that Gildaora will pay for any Davari that can read it. It's the reason I'm selling that old-man to her. He won't fetch a good price anywhere else and those runes in his hands will scare off other buyers.*

"That old man said he can read it. Well, why not bring him up here, have him tell us what it is and what it says?" Farir asked in between slugging wine.

31

*I questioned him many times at Ashgiliath. He wouldn't answer me.* Sasna looked away from her brother and didn't answer him. *I hate it when he is drunk.*

"Bring him up here, sister, I want to know what this text is! I want to know what you have got us involved in now."

Sasna ignored him and walked over to the side of the cabin, and peered out of the porthole. "Fifty cables," she heard a voice from the bow of the ship shout, and then "forty-five."

There was a pause, and then the captain shouted, "Raise oars!" From below deck the order was repeated and there was a gentle splashing sound as the oars lifted from the water. It went strangely quiet as the drum beating the rhythm for the oars went suddenly silent. The *River Queen* continued to glide along at a very slow pace.

"Forty cables," the voice at the bow of the ship shouted, then "thirty cables." It was not long before the ship came to a virtual halt, and the command to drop anchor was given.

Sasna listened as the chain rattled and the anchor splashed into the water. She turned towards Farir; he was busy filling his glass with yet more wine.

"It's probably some treasure map," he mumbled.

Not for the first time, curiosity mixed with suspicion struck Sasna. She had known the dwarf, Gildaora, for many years, and knew that she searched the libraries and markets for old texts, and often paid far too much for them. She had always thought it was just a strange hobby the dwarf had, combined with far too much gold to spend on it. Over a year ago now, Gildaora had come to her at Ashgiliath and said she would pay three times the usual price in gold, if Sasna could find a Davari slave who could read the piece of text she then handed to her, after which she left.

*It's to do with some lore probably, she studies them. It doesn't look like a treasure map.*

Sasna walked over to the large chest in the centre of the cabin, that held her belongings, and took from it a small lock box. She pressed the secret catches hidden on the box. The lid sprang open and she took a leather pouch from it, and removed the text from the pouch. It was a very old and weathered piece of parchment, frayed at the edges, and the only writing on it was some strange letters, in what appeared to be two languages, neither of which Sasna knew, and some very strange old runes at the bottom of the page. She had looked at parchment before, quite a few times, but had seen nothing special about it so she had paid it little more attention other than to find somebody who could read it for the dwarf. This time, she looked at it more intensely than at any other time. It was hard to see the contents in the dim light, so she walked over to a candle, and being careful not to get it too close to the flame, she held the parchment in its light. To her surprise, other runes and letters appeared on it, and began to glow, and then the parchment set on fire. She dropped it, and tried to stamp out the flames, to no avail.

"It is bewitched," Sasna shouted, as a worried look spread across her face. Taking a jug of water, she threw the contents onto the parchment, but it had no effect. It stayed alight.

"Look, Farir," she said as she bent over and looked more closely. "It is not damaged by the fire, and the water has no effect on the flame." She put her hand teasingly over the flaming text. "The flame is not even hot," she said as she gingerly picked it up. The flame instantly went out. She could barely contain her excitement as she placed the text on the table, as new letters and runes briefly appeared, and then faded. Farir was less impressed.

"Any street magician can temporarily charm a text to glow, and not burn, for the price of a mug of ale. I can understand why it is a novelty but sister, surely you cannot be so naive?"

She picked the text up again, and gently tested the edge. Trying to tear it, she found she could not. She tried again, with more force. It would not tear, no matter how hard she tried.

Farir looked at it curiously. "It is strange, I'll give you that," he slurred, after which he took a swig of wine straight from the bottle. "Where did you get it, in fact?"

"Bring the old man to me, what was his name…Muro," Sasna said.

Farir looked bemused, but put the bottle of wine and glass on the table, shrugged his shoulders and said, "If it will enable me to find out what's going on, then fine, I'll fetch him."

*       *       *

About ten minutes later, Farir opened the door and staggered into the cabin, followed by Muro. The disfigured boy followed them, scuttling in using his hands and feet. His face, scarred and deformed by fire in the distant past, gave what Sasna assumed was an attempt of a smile. Farir went to kick him, but lost his balance and fell on his backside. The boy dodged out the way and sat in the corner whimpering. He grunted something unintelligible, taking deep gasps of breath as he did so and looked over at the table of food and back at Sasna.

"Leave him alone," Sasna ordered Farir as he stumbled to his feet.

"Gnarn has not eaten for three days," the boy said, as he continued to look at her with wide, pleading eyes. "Gnarn took your brother to get the slave!"

"Come here," she softly said to Gnarn, who rushed over to her. "Take a sweetcake with you, when you leave."

Gnarn's eyes shone with delight as he stood to his feet, as upright as it was possible for him to do. Hobbling over to the table next to Farir, he took a sweetcake from a platter, and a half-eaten chicken leg, nodded gratefully and left the cabin, clutching the precious food, and shutting the door behind him.

Sasna took a key from her pocket, and unchained Muro's wrists. "Take a seat," she said to him.

Muro, dressed in a faded blue tunic, trousers and leggings, rubbed his wrinkled and chaffed wrists as he moodily looked at her, and took a seat on a cushioned bench fixed to the bulkhead.

Sasna picked up the text from the desk, scraped an oak chair across the deck of the cabin, cushioned with comfortable looking back and armrests, placed it in front of Muro and sat in it.

Farir took some swigs from the bottle of wine he took from the table, emptying it, and then staggered over to the bureau and took another bottle from it. Sasna could see by his expression that he had already lost attention, and was suddenly indifferent and bored. He popped the cork from the bottle and took a few swigs. *He will be of little help to me.*

"I am tired of your insolence. Tell me what the words mean," she said, turning her attention to Muro and holding the text before him. Why do you believe you have been sent to read them?" *Allowed yourself to be enslaved, even.* Previously, she had put Muro down as a madman at worst, or slightly deranged at least. Now, she was genuinely curious, and wanted an answer.

33

Muro blinked with his one eye and said. "Only Ruik and Reisic are permitted to read such a text."

*The same answer, every time.* Sasna frowned impatiently. "I don't care about your lore or mysteries. You can read this, and that makes you valuable to the dwarf who wishes to buy you from me. Just tell me, is this a treasure map?" *If it is, Gildaora has tried to cheat me.*

Farir nosily stumbled over to her. He stood and looked at Sasna for a few seconds, she could not tell by his expression what he was thinking. A smile slowly started to spread across his face until he burst out laughing, bending over double, spilling his wine and then slapping his leg in sheer merriment. When his laughter subsided, and he straightened up and could speak, he said, as though kicking himself he had not remembered before, "He asked you, on the day we bought him, if a dwarf had given the text to you." He became more serious, but his tone was mocking, "Gildaora gave that to you? That goat-loving, weird little dwarf is involved in all of this? I might have known the goat obsessed freak would be filling your head with some sort of nonsense."

Sasna's eyes blazed passionately. "Nonsense?" she asked scathingly. "Do you think I enjoy being on this stinking ship any more than you do? Is your understanding of me so low that you think my highest ambition is to spend my life selling stinking slaves along this filthy river?" She stood, snatched the bottle of wine from Farir's hand and threw it onto the cabin deck, where it smashed into a myriad of broken shards, spilling the wine onto the wooden planks. She raised her voice to a shout. "You lack ambition, unless it is losing your wits and mind in another bottle, or your member into the crutch of another whore!"

Farir reacted angrily at the insult. "Then why are we not even now lounging on some silk cushioned divan like our cousins? How many schemes of yours to get us wealth of our own have ended in dismal failure? But here we are, in this hovel of a cabin, with you plotting yet another scheme that will probably not end well for us!"

*This text is not the reason we are here, it is an aside, to earn us coin.* "You are such a fool," she shouted angrily.

Farir stumbled back to the table, laughing mockingly, and perched unsteadily on it, and took yet another bottle from the bureau to refill his glass with wine, and emptied it in a few gulps.

Sasna turned back towards Muro. His one eye was staring at her intently.

"You are both fools," he scorned, forebodingly.

Farir scowled at him, the mocking grin gone from his face in an instant. He banged his fist angrily on the table, knocking the bottle off of it. It fell onto the floor and rolled around until it came to a natural rest. He spoke heatedly, in a raised voice "It's one thing for me to have words with my sister, but I'll not tolerate a Davari slave showing her disrespect." He slammed his glass down, breaking the stem and cutting the palm of his hand.

Muro turned his gaze upon Farir, and such was the shadowy intensity with which he stared at him, Farir became unsure of himself, and involuntarily lowered his gaze.

"I will give you one more chance, to tell me what this says," Sasna said sternly to Muro, "or I will forsake the gold the dwarf will pay me for you. She can have you for free, but I will throw this text into the river."

Uncertainty spread across Muro's face.

Farir opened the porthole, "I for one, will be pleased that this latest obsession of yours is over, give it to me," he said.

Sasna held up her hand and offered the text to Farir. She was not serious about letting him throw it out the porthole. *I won't let Gildaora and this slave mock me. If he won't tell me what it is, she will, for I will not let her have it or him, until I discover their true worth.*

34

"No," Muro said, in a tone tainted with uncertainty and anger. "I will tell you what I can." His manner changed, as though warning her. "Do not throw it away."

Sasna withdrew the text, before Farir could take it from her. He sighed with frustration.

Muro's attitude changed once more. "If you want to know, so be it, but the day will come when you wish you had not asked." His voice became menacing and dark. "There are forces at work beyond your knowledge," he warned. "That text has knowledge and secrets worth more than a few mere trinkets or jewels, not even all of the gold in the world would match the worth of the knowledge it contains. It is priceless."

"Priceless, you say?" A greedy smile spread across Sasna's face, whilst Farir instinctively frowned. "It turns out that luck and fortune has smiled on us then, brother, and the dwarf and this slave were trying to hold out on us. It seems we might be able to haggle a better price to sell him to Gildaora, and as for the text, she should tell us how she intends making money from it. I will demand half of whatever she gets for it – this will finally make us rich."

Farir grunted, clearly unimpressed. "I'll believe that when the gold is in my pocket."

"Do not get involved in this business, any more than you already are, Seesnari," Muro advised her with an ominous warning tone. "I will not tell you what it says, but I will tell you what it is. But you will first answer my questions."

A flash of anger rose up in Sasna at his insolence. Before she could reprove him, Muro demanded, "First, tell me where you are taking me."

Sasna thought for a moment as to whether she should scold him, or answer his question, and then decided on the latter, for she also wanted answers. *I will play your game old man, as long as you tell me what this text is and who will value it the most.* "I was planning to sell you to a dwarf named Gildaora. This is…was, her text, but has been in my possession for almost a year. If it is as valuable as you say, then I might consider keeping it for myself, for surely, I am being cheated? I could find a buyer who will give me the true value for both you and this." *Curse that dwarf! She clearly tried to trick me, not telling me the true worth of this text or the Davari who can read it.*

"Give it to me," Muro said, as he reached out and slowly took the text from Sasna. She wanted to snatch it away from him, but did not, or rather could not, and to her own surprise, let him take it from her. *He has bewitched me?*

Muro looked at her and Farir. "Do not get involved in this matter, any further than you are. I see death for you, and him, if you try to frustrate the will of Yig. The runes have sent me to read this text, you cannot contend with the forces at work here." The candles in the cabin flickered and almost went out, but sprang back to life. The temperature suddenly dropped, the sudden coldness and his words sent a chill down Sasna's spine.

Farir hurriedly shut the porthole, but by the look on his face, Sasna knew that even he knew that was not the cause of the sudden chill. Before she could press him on the matter, Muro continued.

"The three Davari kept in the hold with me, what plans do you have for them? Answer me that question, and I will tell you what you need to know."

Sasna hesitated, *it is best he does not know.* However, an overwhelming urge came upon her to tell the truth, and her mind felt suddenly foggy and her eyes glazed. She tried to resist the urge to speak, but could not. "They will be given to the *Bloody Baron* who rules the castle. The pirates at Harwind have stopped us trading slaves with Kappia, for the tariffs they demand at Harwind are too expensive, and they will plunder our cargo if we try to pass them."

"So why bring just three slaves to Castle Greytears?" Muro demanded.

Farir protested, "Sasna, hold your tongue, he has bewitched you."

Sasna wanted to, but again, she could not. "The *Bloody Baron* demands that we give him three slaves every time we buy from the Ikma, and a percentage of the price we paid for our shipment. He considers it a neighbourly tribute and a courtesy."

"Why?"

"It is an agreement he made with my uncle, in return for again allowing our ships to pass and trade, when the pirate threat of Harwind is no more."

"What does he do with the slaves you give to him?"

*I will not tell you.* She tried to resist, clenching her fists and gritting her teeth, but the urge to speak and tell Muro was too strong. "No," she finally blurted out, winning over the urge. "I have answered your questions, now you must answer mine."

Muro raised his hands and moved them in a circle across the air. Sasna was sure she saw a flash of light shoot from one of the runes in one of his hands and hit Farir in the eyes

"He hunts them for sport," Farir said.

"Quiet," Sasna said reprovingly, suddenly coming to her senses. Farir's eyes were glazed over.

"No," Farir replied. "I warned you before, sister, your schemes will one day get us killed. Do you remember that time you thought you had found a map that led to the treasure of some old king? All it led to was a cave empty of anything except the bear that tried to tear us limb from limb. Your schemes will never make us rich; you have failed every time."

Sasna felt incredibly hurt by the remark. "It is different this time Farir, we have something that may be of great value. If the dwarf will not pay us what he is worth, then we should take him and the text to somebody who will."

Muro laughed, it was sinister and mocking. "Ask him anything you wish; he will have little choice but to speak truthfully."

"Stop this, stop it," Sasna demanded, but when she tried to rise from her seat to reach for her sabres, she found she could not.

"What will this Baron do with the three slaves?" Muro asked, directing his gaze and question at Farir. "Answer me that, and I will tell you both what this is." He tantalizingly waved the fragment of text.

Farir took a deep breath. "The Baron delights in certain sports and pleasures, such as hunting human prey. He asks for three of them, a man and wife, and a hunter. He does not enjoy easy hunts, so requests that at least one of the slaves has some skill in reading the land. They never get away though, the Baron enjoys a difficult hunt, but traps are set for them and he always catches his prey - always."

"What does he do when he catches them?" Muro queried.

"The Baron is amused to force the husband to watch as he and then all his men take a turn at the wife. The husband and the hunter will then be killed in whatever gruesome manner Daramir finds most amusing at the time. It would be better for them if they had never been born when Daramir catches them, but he will catch them for they always make the same mistakes and head into the traps he sets."

"That is enough," Sasna shouted at Muro. "Your questions have been answered, whatever you have done to us, stop it, please."

Muro laughed, and raised his hands and moved them in a circle, the opposite way than before. Sasna felt indignant at the mocking tone of his laughter. She could suddenly stand, which she did, and drew her sabres. The glaze had left Farir's eyes, and he also drew his weapons.

"This is a Murien text," Muro said, without any prompting.

Sasna, had been about to lunge at him in an attempt to remove his head, but she checked herself, and stopped Farir, who appeared to be about to attempt the same.

Muro continued. "Murien is a coded language that will only be revealed on this text, when those who know the languages of Rokkan, Sangdalen, and Báith Rahmèra gather to read aloud the words on this page."

"You and Gildaora can read these languages?" Sasna asked.

"I can read Rokkan, as I am Ruik, if the dwarf is Reisic, she can read Sangdalen. I believe she is Reisic, or she would not have known to ask you to seek one such as me. A third will be needed, one who is yet to be revealed, a Pure-blood. One who can read Báith Rahmèra, the language of the dead, and then a fourth also, will need to be revealed, the one who can read the Murien itself. Few there are, with that knowledge, and older than time, they will be. Yig will read the Murien."

"The language of the dead?" Farir asked, somewhat nervously.

Muro held the text up. "This was written by one, who hid the Aeldar Riddles, in a time, so very long ago."

"Whoa!" Farir interjected. Of a sudden, he seemed to sober up at hearing those words and a look of sheer terror spread across his face. "The Aeldar? Sister, you know that history and religion bore me, but even I know that the Aeldar religion has spread like a virus, and was the main cause behind the Kappian Civil War. Their Inquisition is not to be trifled with. If that text is anything to do with them, we should be rid of it as fast as possible before we are caught in possession of it. It is surely only a stroke of good fortune we have not been discovered with it already, considering the manner in which you have openly waved it about for so long."

"Quiet, brother," Sasna snapped reprovingly. It was true, the reputation of the Aeldar Inquisition was terrifying and formidable, but the text, and now Muro, had found themselves in her hands. *Maybe I should consider offering them both to the Empire to buy?*

"So, who would buy it?" she eagerly asked Muro. "The Empire would surely pay a fortune for you and the text?"

She tried to take the Murien off him, but much to her annoyance, he pulled it away.

Muro chuckled, but it was absent of mirth. "Many will seek this, if they hear the word Murien spoken, but those who want it, will not pay the likes of you for it. They will take it, and you and your weakling brother will not be able to stop them. There is only one path you should choose."

"What path?" Sasna asked. "I care not about the myth and legend of the Aeldar, but I do care as to who will pay me what you and that text are truly worth?"

"Myth? Legend?" Muro asked, fixing his eye on her. "The Aeldar Gods, are not merely myth and legend."

Farir laughed uncertainly, stroked his chin thoughtfully, and then let out a long-concerned groan before saying. "Sister, abandon this foolishness now, I implore you. You are out of your depth. We have all heard tales of what the Aeldar Inquisition does to people who cross them or interferes in any of their business." He pointed at the fragment of text that Muro still held. "Hand that thing to the priest or the Inquisitor at Greytears, and be done with it. Let them deal with it as they see fit."

Sasna drew deadly serious, but ignored her brother.

"What path should I choose, to whom should I sell this? If you know, tell me?"

Muro offered her the text. "If it lets you take it, you can choose your own path. If it resists you, then its will is fixed, and only death will meet you on whatever path you choose."

Sasna reached out to the take the text, but when she touched it, her hand felt like it was on fire. She screamed, and pulled back her hand. "What have you done to it? Have you set some spell upon it, or me, so I can no longer touch it?"

Muro took the leather pouch from her and gave an ominous warning. "I protected you from it, lest your folly kills you before you lead me to the dwarf. You will not touch this text again. Take me to the dwarf, ask her what price you will, but do not seek to influence these matters any further. Take whatever gold she offers, and walk away from this matter, whilst you still can. My fate is tied to this, yours is not, unless you choose it to be so – but your fate will be death."

Farir scratched his head, and then walked speedily over to Sasna, and pulled her away. Looking at Muro and the parchment he said, "Take it, we will sell you to the dwarf, for the price my sister previously agreed. You and that goat-freak can both do with it what you will, we want no further part in this."

Sasna watched with dismay as Muro folded the text and slipped it back into the pouch which he slid inside his clothing. "How dare you? You are just a slave!" she yelped, huffily. Something in the look on Muro's face made, her nervous.

"Leave it, sister," Farir urged. "Hand him over to the dwarf, take whatever gold she offers, or let her have him and that text even if she offers none."

As Sasna studied Muro's face, fear crept along her spine. The look on the old Davari's face was sinister, other-worldly. It lasted but a moment, but it had seemed as though a demon had taken control of his features.

"This does not belong to you, and this matter no longer concerns you," he said menacingly. "This is your last warning. Walk away, whilst you still can, or death will come for you. Listen to your brother. Take me to the dwarf, if she offers gold, take it, if she does not, walk away."

Sasna felt her face flush with anger. She wanted to protest further, but did not, as the look that had crossed Muro's face had unnerved her, and by the look on Farir's face, she could tell he felt similar.

Muro pointed to the cabin door, raised his finger to his mouth, and looking at Sasna whispered, "This matter might be beyond your control, even now. The fates are awake, the boy listens, we must commit ourselves to our paths." He looked at Farir. "Open the door, Seesnari, and bring me the boy."

# Chapter Four: *To Slay a God*

*It will be a war of souls, steeped in lore forbidden to men. In their ignorance, they will explore the dark shadows, where evil dwells.*
**Segment from the Prophecy of Karthal.**

*The* hammer banged loudly on the door of the shrine to Ahrimakan. Sezareal and Jezareal began to whimper with fear.

"It is time," Janorra said to them in a low voice. "There is no way for you to escape this fate, nowhere for you to run. The Hammer Knights will use their war-hammers to break your legs if you try." She took each of their hands and squeezed them, trying to offer some small comfort. "It will be all over soon. You must present yourself calmly before High Quaester Mazdek. Think of the Fair Havens!"

The sisters wiped away their tears and tried to steady themselves.

After the ninth and final knock, Janorra stood and looked at the door that led out of the shrine, to the *Seat of the Gods*. "Enter, she said in a loud, clear voice." As the door began to open, she spoke under her breath to the girls. "Whatever horrors you are about to see, remember, it will all be over quickly."

Mazdek, the High Quaester, entered the shrine followed by two Hammer Knights. He wore a scarlet hooded robe, decorated with the hammers of Thuranotos and the snake symbol. "Are you ready, my children," he said in a voice that tried to sound soothing, but was full of hidden malice.

"We are ready," Janorra said as, taking the hands of her two assistants, she stepped forward. The two Hammer Knights positioned themselves behind the two sisters and roughly pushed them forward with their hammers. The girls whimpered, but followed without resistance as Mazdek turned and walked out of the door onto the stairway that led to the *Seat of the Gods*, followed by Janorra and the others.

Then began the deafening throbbing of drums, somewhere deep in darkness and out of sight. *Boom! Boom! Boom!*

Thin men dressed in black-hooded-robes, leaning on staffs, lined the wide stair. Their faces were gaunt white ovals in their hoods. Each of them rang a toneless temple bell and began to chant in a low guttural manner as the party passed, adding to the noise of the drums. Beads of sweat formed on Janorra's brow. *This is it. There is no turning back now. Ashareth give me strength. It is time to slay a god. It is time to steal the Simal and escape.*

It was a tiring and fearful walk up the ninety-nine steps to the entrance area to the *Seat of the Gods*. With each step, Janorra's heart beat almost as loudly as the drums. *Boom! Boom! Boom!* The bells made her head ring. *Clang! Clang! Clang!* She rubbed her forehead with her fingers. The sound of the haunting chanting made her stomach tighten. She felt sick with fear. Summoning her inner-calmness, she fought to push back the terrifying thoughts of what would happen to her if everything went wrong. She took deep and slow breaths. *This time tomorrow, I will be free. Oh Ashareth, give me courage!*

When the sacrificial party reached the top of the stair, the drums, bells and chanting grew to a crescendo. A tall hawk-faced man waited for them at the top. Janorra knew him to be Marnir, the Grand Inquisitor. He held a torch that burned with a steady, unearthly glow which pulsed and simmered, dripping flakes of quivering golden flame onto the black stones about it. She took her two assistants by their hands and squeezed reassuringly, as Marnir turned and led them across the marbled floor towards two arched golden doors elaborately carved with the coloured images of the Aeldar Gods.

At the side of each closed door, two colossal anthrophags made from living black stone stood guard, their dog like heads clothed in decorated headdresses atop slim human bodies, clothed only in pleated loincloths fashioned in striped golden stone.

"What are they?" Jezareal asked hysterically. She fell to her knees in terror, but was forced to her feet again by one of the guards who shoved her roughly.

"Keep moving!" he growled.

When the party reached the doors, Janorra let go of the hands of her assistants and detached the golden Staff of Summoning, which was in the hands of one of the carvings on the door, a carved robed priest, who was bowing to the images of the Aeldar. The staff had looked like it was a part of the carving, but as she picked it up, a dazzling glow emanated from a great red-jewel at the top of the staff, held in place by clasps fashioned in the form of snake and hammers.

Marnir looked at Janorra and her assistants; his face was ashy and corpse-like. "Show your willingness to be given to a god," he said to them, his voice sounding hollow and ghostly, against the din of noise.

Janorra banged on the door with the end of the staff three times, and shouted aloud, "*Epitaphan... Ensensasa... Aquilon! Baquan!*" Epitaphan and Ensensasa were the names of the anthrophag guards. *'Aquilon,'* in the ancient tongue of High Vakkan, meant awake whereas *'baquan'* was the word for open.

The sound of stone grating upon stone rang out as one of the anthrophags slowly began to move its head, looking down at the small party of people below it. Jezareal let out another short, hysterical scream. The second anthrophag moved its head also. Their small yellow eyes glinted emotionless in their dog-like heads as they looked at Janorra and her assistants.

With measured, mechanical and awkward movements and a sickening hoarse noise, Epitaphan and Ensensasa turned to the doors and began to push them, opening them inwards. Their muscled, black stone bodies rippled and quivered as they pushed. With a cloud of dust and a loud grating sound that echoed in the air, the doors swung open.

Jezareal grunted in fear and began to slowly back away, but was pushed forward again by the hammer of the knight behind her. Sezareal took her by the hand. "Don't, sister," she said tenderly. "We will conduct ourselves with dignity. It will soon be over." Jezareal steadied herself and nodded, but tears were streaming down her cheeks, and her hands visibly trembled.

Once again, Janorra felt a wave of compassion for the two sisters, and hated being complicit in what was about to happen to them, but she was stripped of choice. *Forgive me, Ashareth. I did not choose this fate for myself; I have not chosen it for them.* She bit her lip. *This will be the last time,* she told herself. *This will be the last time I will have a part in such a foul deed.*

It was not just the sisters who were frightened. Panic began to rise within Janorra. She fought to contain her own terror. It was not the sights that terrified her, she was used to them. It was the thought of the magnitude of the act she and Azzadan were about to attempt. In an effort to bring her own heart back under control, she tried to think of other things. She thought about the time, when, as a little girl, her father used to sing the *Song of Pargir* to her whenever she was frightened. It felt so many lifetimes ago, but the words of one of the lines came to her. She sang the words softly, under her breath, so nobody but herself would hear. "Seven dolls for seven trolls, a gold coin for a picture. That will solve all our ills, when we are much richer."

Mazdek and Marnir were the first to pass through the doors. Janorra and the two sisters followed next, and after them the two knights, followed by the black-robed figures who had lined the stair. The *Seat of the Gods* contained a large half-amphitheatre that surrounded one half of a black pit, called the Summoning Pit, or the Sacred Deep.

40

Eight Davari, four men and four women, were tied to wooden posts around the front part of the pit of the Sacred Deep, several feet away from the edge of the precipice. A Hammer Knight stood before each of them. Next to each of the posts, in a wooden cage, was a large snake. In the middle of the Davari was an elegant black altar, to which was tied another Davari, who appeared to be sleeping, but as Janorra knew, was in fact already dead. It was this unfortunate who would become the host body for Ahrimakan, after the snake-god had consumed the two assistants, and then Janorra herself.

Thousands of Hammer Knights, priests and priestesses, nobles, dignitaries and invited guests were seated around the amphitheatre. They all watched in silent anticipation as the sacrificial party entered the *Seat of the Gods*. The men in black robes processed towards the amphitheatre and joined the crowd.

Seated on a throne fashioned in the image of golden snakes, in the middle of the amphitheatre, sat the Empress Shakara IX, of House Shakawraith, or Shaka as she preferred to be called. The doors noisily shut behind the procession when the last of them had entered. All except the Empress, stood, and began to shout and chant as the sacrificial party took their positions around the Sacred Deep. The knights began to bang their hammers on the floor as they chanted, "*Araman! Araman! Araman!*" It was an ancient chant that showed respect and worship towards the god about to be summoned, and meant '*great one.*'

Many rumours, myths and legends surrounded the Empress Shaka. It was said that few men could resist her, even though to be lured by her meant certain death. Those who served her, knew terror. Evil worked its way through her palace like maggots chewing through rotting meat. It was believed of her, by many, that behind the image of a woman of matchless beauty lurked a terrifying serpent woman, a creature with a perverse kind of beauty that overtook her body at will. This terrible curse was the result of her once becoming impregnated by Ahrimakan, the snake-god, whose seed assimilated itself into the body of the Empress, forever changing her into half-goddess and half-human. The child of this union was the Titan Erespatagor, a giant, half-snake, half-man that lived deep beneath the Argona Palace. Janorra shuddered, and wished what was said of the Empress, might not be true. She tried to repress the memories the sight of the Empress Shaka and the thought of Erespatagor evoked in her; memories of abject terror and despair.

It was alleged Shaka's desire for men was insatiable, that they pleasured her by day, and by night she consumed them, a process that was repeated if they were Pure-bloods, until she grew tired of them and sent them to their *Final-death*. It was that desire that had been the ruin of Janorra so long ago. Once an aspiring actress in Kappia city, she and her husband, a Half-blood by the name of Thurmon had been summoned to perform the *Echirea Elvenasar* and several other plays before the Empress at a resurrection celebration. Shaka had barely even noticed Janorra, but Thurmon, a handsome man, had caught her eye. It had been the last Janorra had ever seen of him. She had been sent to the Bloody Tower for crimes she had not then known, where she had been mistreated by Prince *Ivanar* Regineo and his guards, and subjected to virtually every indignity and horror imaginable, before being killed in the most gruesome of manner. It had been her *First-death*, and it was only after resurrection that the *Mark of the Obelisk* under her eye was coloured, and the priests discovered she had the gift of a Seeress. It was then she had entered the Theostar, and then the Argona Temple for training, and she had been there ever since, for twenty-seven lifetimes. Her mind briefly flicked over the suffering she had endured in that place. *Not today*, she told herself. *Today, I will not be a sacrifice. It is not I who will die. It is Ahrimakan, one of the Aeldar, who will die. Ashareth, may it be so!*

41

Janorra felt fresh courage, born out of the hope of escape. She looked up at the Empress, and stared at her, despite the distance between them. Shaka was surrounded by her two sons and her daughter, and many court officials. Shaka coldly returned Janorra's stare. As always, Janorra saw no sign of recognition in Shaka's eyes. She had not been important or significant enough for the Empress to remember either her, or the awful fate she had inflicted upon her husband. Janorra smiled to herself. *That will change today. You, Shaka, will forever remember me. You will never again forget me.* The thought, and the lust of her hate, strengthened Janorra's courage. *Azzadan, I hope you are near,* she thought to herself.

Shaka stood to her feet and raised her hands. The drums stopped booming, the bells ceased clanging, and all in the *Seat of the Gods* grew quiet. She wore a long, elegant Kappian gown. The cut of the gown bared part of her left breast, and the colour of the scarlet silk complimented her lengthy, jet black hair. She raised her jewelled hand and stared at Mazdek who stood across from her on the other side of the pit, next to Janorra.

"Let it begin," Shaka ordered. "Summon our beloved."

The crowd roared as Mazdek walked towards the black altar in front of the pit. All of the Davari stared in horror at him. Janorra and her assistants followed - Jezareal still whimpering. Behind the altar, resting in a golden hand with nine fingers and no thumb, sat the Simal, glittering with a myriad of bright and dark colours – colours from this world and those from beyond.

Mazdek picked up the Simal and held it high in both hands. Light from it shot out in many different directions, filling the *Seat of the Gods* with a myriad of colours.

"Through the Simal, and the Riddle of an Aeldar Wife, Ahrimakan's true name will be uttered this night. He will come, once again, into this world to fulfil the next stage of his destiny. We shall all share in the kingdom that will be, when the Aeldar return, and the Seventh Age begins!"

The Hammer Knights in the amphitheatre began to thump their hammers onto the floor, slowly at first, and then speeding up as hysteria took them over so they were thumping them wildly.

Prince *Ivanar* Caspus, the youngest son of Shaka, dressed in only a simple brown robe tied at the waist by a rope, walked down the steps of the amphitheatre, around the edge of the Summoning Pit, approached Marnir and took the torch from him. He then strolled over to where the Davari were tied to a post. His nervous smile did not mask his utterly ruthless nature. The knights undid the locks on the cages of the snakes, and the creatures slithered out of the openings.

From a place unseen, musicians began to play an eerie tune. Prince Caspus began to dance, and each of the snakes reared its head up. The light from the torch glistened on their scales. Their beady eyes glittered and their tongues forked in and out. Caspus continued to dance, scarcely moving his feet or his arms, as he held aloft the torch. The snakes danced with him, weaving and swaying, as though mesmerized by the music and the strange light. They then slithered towards the Davari, who, helplessly tied to the posts, began to scream in terror. Each snake slowly wrapped itself around one of the victims, looping around them with their coils.

Janorra could never watch such a black and diabolic act of cruelty unmoved. Two of the Davari women, looked at each other, and above the din Janorra heard one shriek in the Common Tongue, "Have strength, tonight we dine with our ancestors in our sacred halls."

The other woman had tears running down her eyes. "All is lost, all is lost," she wailed.

42

The Davari soon became silent, as they and the snakes slowly melted together. Soon it was impossible to tell which was which. The knights undid the bindings that still bound the grotesque abominations to the posts. Then, of a sudden, with one jerk and movement they separated, and once more human and snake could be told apart. The Davari and the snakes slumped to the ground as though dead.

The music stopped and a hushed silence fell over all present, as slowly, convulsions racked the bodies, and both the Davari and snakes began to move once more. The Davari did not stand, but slithered along on their bellies, as snakes travel, their heads swaying from side to side, their tongues darting back and forth from their mouths. The serpents arched their necks up, and rearing up to almost their full lengths, they tried to stand as a man or woman would, but they fell to the ground writhing, only to repeat and fail again.

The crowed began to howl, cheer, and then chant. Janorra felt the urge to retch. The ghastly ceremony had never brought her any pleasure. Through black, primordial sorcery, Caspus had transferred the souls of the Davari into the bodies of the snakes, and vice-versa. The victims, Davari and snakes, writhed in agony side by side as they tried to act out their natural instincts in bodies that were alien to them.

Janorra held back her revulsion as she watched, despite it being a sight she had seen many times before. *Never again will I have to witness such a vile act,* she told herself. *Never again!*

Caspus signalled to Marnir, who nodded to the Hammer Knights. They each raised their hammers, and with one swing smashed it down upon the heads of Davari and snake alike, with a sickening crunch, until each was dead. The knights then lay down their hammers, dragged the bodies to a place where grooves were carved in the ground, leading to a chalice placed in a hole. They drew a knife and cut the throats of Davari and beast, allowing the blood to run down the grooves into the chalices. They then picked up the lifeless bodies, raised them high over their heads and threw them into the Sacred Deep, an act that was accompanied by a loud cheer and roar from the crowd. The cups were full, so they removed them, spilling blood over the sides as they did so.

The knights then walked over to Mazdek, who lowered the Simal so that the blood of the Davari and snakes could be tipped over it. The ghastly sphere still shimmered and shined through the running blood. The knights were careful to not look into the Simal, or to touch it.

The Simal shone with an intensity and brilliance far greater than before. A humming noise emerged from it. Mazdek placed it back upon the golden hand behind the altar, and raised his hands. In an instant, everyone in the *Seat of the Gods* became quiet. The only noise was the loud whimpering of Jezareal and her sister, drowned out by the humming of the Simal. He turned towards Janorra, and nodded his head once.

*It is time. This is it! This is it!* Janorra walked to the edge of the precipice of the Sacred Deep. She looked into it, and saw only empty blackness. She raised the Staff of Summoning above her head and slowly swung it in a circle as she began to sing the summoning song in the Ancient Tongue. "Ahrimakan, Ahrimakan, *el tie em re hema,*" which means 'come to me this night.' "*El, Tie ʒi ey louvoir…*" 'Come to be my lover.' "*Ilyiado, el tie bescato ey blousonay…*" 'Sacred one, come to receive my worship' "*Ey louv, esparto manifesto hiy mtwant tie mou jallaley…*" 'My love, spirit, soul, body, I give to you freely.' "*Baquan, baquan, hiy baquan eylefs tie mou…*" 'Open, open, I open myself to you.'

The hidden drums in the deep began to throb again and the black-robed men rang their bells and chanted. Janorra began to sway hypnotically as she slowly circled the staff above her head and repeated the song again, as Marnir and Mazdek also swayed and danced rhythmically, Marnir waving his own staff above his head.

43

The third time she sang the song, a bolt of light shot out from the Simal and hit the Staff of Summoning, from which came a bright light from the tip, filling the whole pit. A spectre in female form appeared briefly from out of the Simal, and spoke words in a tongue unintelligible to any who heard. It then returned to the Simal, and from within, it loudly whispered, "Ahrimakan, Vispin calls you! Your Riddle has been spoken; you have been named! Leave the Void, come to the Outer World!" The voice repeated the words again, and then again.

A gust of roaring wind rose upwards, from deep within the Sacred Deep, causing the flames of the torches in the *Seat of the Gods* to dance eagerly. Janorra's hair and robe also danced wildly in its path.

"He comes," she shouted. "Vispin has spoken the Riddle of Ahrimakan, she has named him, spoken the words that created him at the forging of the worlds."

Janorra steeled herself to continue the ceremony. *"Pushta Efrecar, frone dha'l macoundir mour myseerikin, merou halmorfor byyangondori, merou ilyiado,"* she screamed, meaning – 'Mighty Aeldar, none shall defile your memory, our beautiful guardian, our sacred one.' *"Ilyefso, ilyefso, braetho garni hiy twant tie mou!"* 'Sacrifice, sacrifice, life blood I give to you.' "Ahrimakan, Ahrimakan, *el louv mou merou araman, el ousa ern hema."* 'Ahrimakan, Ahrimakan, we love you our great one, come from the night!' *"Vispin shous mou! Mou harse ziin nostrand. Vispin harc exholed mour raddler. Mour ilyefsos arn brody aren arraile mour toucreh!"* 'Vispin calls you! You have been named. Vispin has spoken your Riddle. Your sacrifices are ready and await your embrace!'

The wind suddenly stopped, Janorra and everybody in the *Seat of the Gods* became quiet. The sound of a deep rumbling and hissing began to rise up from the pit, though it sounded other-worldly.

Jezareal squealed at the sound coming from the pit, turned, and tried to run. The knight behind her, who had slung his hammer over his shoulders, caught her and held her tightly by the arms so she could not move. Sezareal, tried to run over to help her sister, but the knight behind her seized her tightly.

"Stay or I will break your legs child," he said coarsely, as she struggled and he continued to forcibly hold her. The hissing and rumbling coming from the Sacred Deep grew louder.

"Ahrimakan, sacred of the Aeldar, rise and come forth, return to your rightful and ancient seat of power here in the Everglow. Return to us, we implore you!" Janorra shrieked at the top of her voice.

From the Sacred Deep, a low guttural primeval roar followed by furious hissing could be heard. Another gust of wind came rushing up from the pit, and increased in intensity to such a degree that Janorra struggled to stay standing. A blinding light rose from the pit, causing her to shield her eyes with her spare hand. A portal of many colours appeared above the pit, it spun around at a furious rate and then began to slow, until it was finally still. The wind slowly ceased, the light faded, and the portal opened.

Janorra slowly lowered the staff until it touched the floor, and removed her hand from her eyes. A giant spirit, in the form of a hideous snake-man, stepped from out of the portal, and hovered menacingly above the abyss. Terrifying and cruel was the appearance of the creature before Janorra; she had seen it many times, but still she was repulsed by the horror that floated above the pit. Ahrimakan was still in watery form, not completely materialised. The lower part of his body was pure snake, the upper torso human, though scaled, his head that of a horned cobra. The yellow eyes that stared at Janorra shone with pure malice, black evil. His body writhed, as though stretching from a long sleep.

Ahrimakan descended onto the floor of the *Seat of the Gods*, his form shrinking to about the size of ten feet tall. He held his scaled hand in front of his face, studying it as he slowly clenched and unclenched his hand. When he had finished, he stared once more at Janorra who had turned to watch him. He hissed with primal rage as he viciously attempted to seize her by the throat, but his wispy talons gripped the air in vain and passed harmlessly through her body.

*I am protected by the talisman, foul creature. Only when I remove it will I become your sacrifice, but tonight, I shall not take it off.*

Janorra outwardly showed no signs of fear, even though within she wrestled and fought it, so she would not lose control. Long ago, she had mastered the horrible, black dread that enveloped those who came into the presence of this Aeldar that stood before her now. She unemotionally returned the spirit's gaze.

"I honour you lord," she said. *I despise you. Tonight, you will die, vile beast.*

She walked over to the altar, laid the Staff of Summoning upon it, picked up the Simal, and went and stood between Jezareal and Sezareal.

Ahrimakan slithered over towards Jezareal, who was paralysed with sheer terror. As he loomed over her, she urinated where she stood, as his tongue flicked out towards her and lightly stroked her skin. The knight who stood behind her, let go the grip on her arms, cowered and turned his face away from Ahrimakan.

Janorra spoke. "Master, a body has been prepared for you to inhabit. It waits for you upon the altar. You will enjoy the sacrifice more, if you first take physical form." *I will save these sisters if I can.*

Ahrimakan looked at Janorra. His voice was full of malice, and was accompanied by hissing, as his tongue flicked in and out of his mouth between the words. "You dare to *quessstion* me mortal?" he hissed. He spoke in the Ancient Tongue, a language only a very few in the amphitheatre understood. "*Ssshe isss* mine." The coils of his wraith-like body wrapped slowly around Jezareal.

The sound of Jezareal's bones, crunching and breaking, made Janorra feel nauseous. Sezareal shrieked in horror as Ahrimakan's jaws dislocated with a stomach-turning sound, and stretched wide. She covered her eyes, so as not to witness the fate of her sister, and fell to the floor. In a matter of moments, he had half consumed Jezareal's limp body whole, head first, and it did not take him long to finish the rest. He swallowed the last part of the lifeless girl, and his jaws clicked back into place. His form became more physical, more solid.

Inwardly, Janorra gasped with horror. *Ahrimakan is not following protocol. He was supposed to consume the corpse of the ninth Davari.* She knew the ceremony well. She would accompany him as he slithered towards the altar, where the body of the dead Davari was upon it, having been prepared by special rituals. The Simal would use the main Argona Obelisk, in a twist against nature, to bring the spirit of the Davari back to the corpse. His eyes would no doubt suddenly open, as one waking from sleep, and he would scream in horror at the thing hovering over him. Ahrimakan would first consume the spirit of the man, which would enter the mouth of the wraith-like beast with a loud noise as it entered like smoke being inhaled. He would then consume the corpse, which would give his wraith-like body a degree of physical form, a snake-beast in the flesh, and over several hours he would slowly morph into the form of a man. During this period, usually immediately after devouring the body of the last Davari, he would eat the two assistants and then slowly consume Janorra, the main sacrifice, for pure pleasure.

Janorra knew that the body of the Davari that Ahrimakan would inhabit would only last for more than three days or so, maybe even up to five days depending on the physical strength of it, before the corruption became too much and Ahrimakan's spirit would be forced to leave and return again to the Void, by way of the Sacred Deep. Only when all nine of the Aeldar were present would it be possible for them to regain permanent physicality in their own form, or that of an inhabited one. For now, only three Aeldar could be summoned, for only three Aeldar Wives had been discovered and three Aeldar Riddles known. Only two Aeldar had ever been called, though, for Ahrimakan, for reasons never stated, had forbidden the third be summoned until he chose the time.

Ahrimakan was the only one who would be summoned this night, as it was his annual sacred day to be honoured. Just like a parasite, he needed a host body, so he could once more walk in this world, albeit but for a short time. It was the reason he had to remain in the *Seat of the Gods*, and during his stay his every need would be catered for, his every desire and whim indulged.

Janorra knew he would meter out his foul pleasures upon whom he pleased, perhaps even Jezareal and Sezareal after the Obelisk had brought them back, and the poor girls would suffer terribly, as she herself had once done when in the form of a man, he had once called for her. Ahrimakan would then spend his time in twisted and corrupted pleasures with the Empress Shaka.

On that day, Azzadan was supposed to slay Ahrimakan, after he had consumed the second assistant, when he would be fully vulnerable in his true physical form.

"Lift her" Ahrimakan said to the Hammer Knight cringing behind Sezareal. The man, steadied himself, and did as he was instructed.

Out of the corner of her eye, Janorra noticed that Mazdek and Marnir appeared agitated that the ceremony was not going to plan, but they said nothing.

Sezareal uncovered her eyes, and stared at Ahrimakan in horror.

"Give her the *Sssimal*" he hissed at Janorra.

Janorra tried to stutter something, but no words came out, and she could not move. She did not know what to do. *No, this is not how it is supposed to be.* As though entranced, Sezareal reached out, and took the Simal from her. Janorra suddenly felt frozen with fear, and was unable to stop her.

Sezareal stared into the Simal, a look of amazement, then horror, and then insanity spreading across her face.

"I *desssire* you next," Ahrimakan said to Janorra with that awful, slow hissing voice, his tongue flicking in and out between the words, hideously caressing her face, as his coils began to wrap around her body.

"My lord," Mazdek said as he stepped forward, but stopped mid-sentence when Ahrimakan shot him a hateful glare and hissed, "It *isss* her or you." Mazdek bowed his head respectfully, and stepped back.

It had already dawned upon Janorra. *He intends to consume me next; even then he will not have full bodily form.* "Now Azzadan, now," Janorra whispered, hoping he might be near enough to hear her. Nothing. Ahrimakan looked at her curiously. She had no idea if the Arkoom would even work on him, when he was not fully in physical form.

She felt the life being squeezed out of her, as the coils tightened, and the jaws of Ahrimakan began to dislocate, in preparation of consuming her. Darkness glowed in his eyes.

"Azzadan, you still need me, do it!" she shouted at the top of her voice. Nothing.

Ahrimakan, even as his jaws widened, looked at her suspiciously, even with an element of confusion. His coils tightened, and Janorra fought to catch her breath, and she felt her as though at any moment her bones might snap.

"Azzadan, do it, I beg of you!" she shrieked, with the last of her breath, as Ahrimakan's saliva dripped upon her face.

46

Azzadan appeared from out of nowhere. Janorra watched him leap upon Ahrimakan. He plunged the Arkoom deep into his chest. Ahrimakan was taken by complete surprise due to the swiftness of the attack. He looked down at his chest, and saw the hilt of the Arkoom, still gripped by Azzadan, protruding from it.

Janorra felt the coils loosen, and she fell, as Ahrimakan roared and hissed in pain. The Arkoom was ripped out of Azzadan's hand as he was knocked to the floor by the thrashing tail of the wounded fiend. Azzadan lay there momentarily dazed as Ahrimakan rolled on the floor, his body thrashing about wildly, writhing in agony as he tried to remove the Arkoom.

Azzadan stood to his feet and shouted at the top of his voice. "Know the doer of the deed claims the title *Godslayer*!"

Janorra struggled to catch her breath, she got to her feet, panting.

It took a few seconds for the crowd in the amphitheatre to understand what was happening, and when they did, a great commotion broke out. Hammer Knights left the amphitheatre and began to run around the edges of the Sacred Deep, towards the altar, furiously shouting orders. The men in black robes howled in rage, and some waved their staffs, and the orbs on the end began to glow.

Somehow, Azzadan managed to jump on Ahrimakan and remove the Arkoom from his chest. The hilt was covered in green blood that burnt through his glove as he gripped it. He screamed in pain as his hand began to sizzle and bubble. He let go of the Arkoom and was again knocked to the floor as Ahrimakan thrashed about. The Arkoom clattered along the floor and slid over the edge of the precipice into the Sacred Deep.

Ahrimakan rolled about in his death throes, his body teetering on the edge of the Sacred Deep. The essence of his spirit, foul and green, left his ruined body, and with a piercing scream, it was sucked over the side of the Sacred Deep, but Janorra could not tell if it had gone into the gem at the hilt of the Arkoom, which was out of sight, or if it was returning to the Void. One more spasmodic writhe and his body fell over the edge into the inky blackness, plummeting with a hiss that echoed and faded as it fell deeper into the pit, until it could be heard no more.

Azzadan was slightly stunned, so Janorra rushed to his aid, and kicked Marnir, who had pointed his staff at him. Marnir dropped the staff as he fell back, over the edge of the Sacred Deep, and squealed in fear as he clung on to the edge, for his very existence. A bolt of red lightning flashed from the tip of the staff he had pointed at Azzadan, but it went harmlessly into the air. Azzadan was quickly back on his feet and in the fray again. He swung his club and knocked Mazdek senseless as he tried to pick up Marnir's staff. Caspus looked on in horror, dropped the torch he was holding, and turned and fled in terror.

The knight who had been holding Jezareal lunged for Janorra, swinging his hammer wildly at her head. She ducked, and only with a wisp managed to avoid the deadly blow.

A poisoned star flew through the air. Azzadan's aim was deadly, it imbedded itself in the man's forehead. The poison worked almost instantaneously and he was dead before he hit the ground.

The knight who had been holding Sezareal, let her go and launched his hammer towards Janorra. It flipped awkwardly through the air, and caught her slightly on the side of the head. She lost her balance and staggered back, falling to the floor. The knight rushed over and picked up his hammer, and advanced towards Janorra. He swung the hammer over his head to swing down and crush her skull. A pointed throwing star hit him in the forehead. He too, was dead before he hit the ground.

Azzadan rushed over to Janorra. By now he was already wearing one of the Circlets of Jula. He slammed the other upon her head. "Grab the Simal and leave, now," he shouted at her as bolts of red lightning from the staffs of the black-robed men flew all around them, some just narrowly missing. It was fortunate they were still the other side of the Sacred Deep, and their aim was poor. Hammer Knights were still running the edge of the Sacred Deep. Some were nearly in range to throw their hammers. They launched them. The weapons fell short of their targets, but only just. One slid along the floor and hit Janorra on the foot, and she heard the snap of her ankle. She lost her balance and staggered back, falling to the floor. The circlet fell from her head and rolled over to the feet of Sezareal, who still stood there, staring in horror into the Simal.

Azzadan wasted no time. He dragged Janorra along the floor to where the circlet was, placed it roughly on her head, and lifted her to her feet so she was stood directly in front of Sezareal. He turned his attention to the knights, the fastest of whom, now unburdened by the hammers they had thrown, were almost upon them. Azzadan dispatched them with yet more stars. He had once boasted to her that he rarely missed and Janorra was glad there was truth behind the boast.

Janorra knew what was required of her. She attempted to snatch the Simal out of Sezareal's hands, but it was as though the girl had become a statue. She would not let go and it would not budge. It was impossible to retrieve it.

Above the din, Janorra could hear Shaka shouting at the top of her voice, but could not make out what she was saying. From the corner of her eye, she thought she saw the Empress turning into something hideous, but she was not sure.

Azzadan, was clearly in pain as his hand bubbled. It was almost nothing but bone, as the flesh had almost entirely melted away. He looked at Janorra, as she continued to try and wrench the Simal from Sezareal's hands, but her assistant stood there gripping it with a strength that was not human.

"Flee," Azzadan said to Janorra, before saying an incantation. With a loud crack, a portal opened up before him. He fell through it, rather than stepped through it. It closed behind him with an equally loud cracking noise.

The Hammer Knights were almost upon Janorra. "*Baforme, entrendren,*" she yelled. With a loud crack a portal opened before her. As she let go of the Simal, and threw herself into the portal, she felt Sezareal grab hold of her. There was not the time to struggle or pull free; Sezareal was pulled through the portal with her. It closed behind them with a loud crack.

*    *    *

It felt to Janorra that she was spinning through time in slow motion. The sensation lasted for a few seconds, before she and Sezareal were thrown out through a portal into a wooded area. Janorra heard a loud snap as she felt her leg break against a tree. Sezareal landed on her feet, upon a patch of grass about ten feet away. She appeared unhurt, and stood there, still just staring into the Simal.

Janorra looked around, she was in some sort of forest, surrounded by sickly looking trees. Azzadan was nowhere to be seen. The jump through the portal had been successful, she had escaped from the temple, but just as Azzadan had warned, with another person present, the Jula had not taken her to where she was supposed to be. She had no idea where she was.

Janorra tried to stand, but not only was the pain in her leg and ankle too much, one arm and the other leg were tightly glued to a silky thread. Horror spread through her, as it dawned upon her, she was caught in a giant cobweb.

Sezareal continued to stare into the Simal.

"Help me, Sezareal help me please," Janorra said, beginning to panic. "I cannot die here. I must take the Simal to a place of safety."

Sezareal said nothing. Staring into the Simal, she walked off into the forest, and was soon out of sight. Janorra called after her, pleading for help, but to no avail.

Janorra sat there quietly whimpering for a few minutes. She could not stand, and neither could she pull free from the silky strands that bound her. Her attention was soon drawn to a rustling sound in the boughs of the trees nearby. At the same time as she noticed movement out of the corner of her eye, she heard another sound, a gurgling, bubbling noise and then a long venomous hiss. Whatever it was, was now directly above her. She looked up and could only see the branches, but something as yet hidden from her sight, was clearly above her in the foliage. The bubbling hiss drew nearer; the branches creaked as the weight of some creature bore down upon them. She felt a malign intelligence studying her. A look of horror spread on her face as she fearfully stared back at a number of eyes that suddenly appeared, and were glaring at her. She tried to fight off the sickness and fear that quickly enveloped her.

"Sezareal, I am begging you, help me," she implored, shouting in the direction she had gone, with no hope other than absolute desperation.

The stench of death clouded over her. "Sezareal," she called out loudly, one final time.

From out of the foliage emerged the most loathsome shape Janorra had ever beheld this side of the Deadlands. Horrible beyond the horror of even her worst of nightmares, it was only matched by the things she had seen in the temple, including the snake beast that she hoped was now forever slain. A spider it was, but bigger than a horse. A cluster of malign eyes stared unmercifully out of an out-thrust head attached to a huge swollen body that looked like a bloated bag, swaying and sagging between legs which were bent with great knobbed joints high above its head. Hairs like steel spines stuck out from each leg, and at each leg's end was a cruel looking claw. The spider stopped.

Janorra felt nauseous as she realized that behind those unmerciful eyes there was indeed, a cruel intelligence, that was focussed entirely on her. It hissed with delight to see that its prey was helpless. The more she struggled and screamed, the more caught up she became in the sticky threads. The spider moved with horrible speed, snatched her in its claws and with a thrust of its sting, pierced her chest and her heart.

Janorra began to drift from consciousness as she felt the life slowly ebbing away from her. The spider began to wind her from ankle to toe in sticky threads that spewed out of its mouth.

The last sight Janorra saw was the angry malice in the spider's eyes as she was spun about furiously in its claws; the last smell the overwhelming stench from the creature, and the last feeling, intense pain from the mortal wound she had sustained. Janorra died as the last of the threads sealed her body within a sticky tomb.

# Chapter Five: *Danger on the River Erin*

*The saying, 'Never trust a Seesnari,' is reputed to stem from the time of King Baaseiah, who obtained the crown by usurpation. He attempted to wipe out all recorded history and any records of kings before him, though some histories can still be seen carved in ancient monuments around the city of Ashgiliath. Baaseiah was originally an officer of the army under King Nidib II, son of Jerich I. Whilst the army was besieging Girrethan, he slew Nidin his king and mounted the throne. Despite the promise of an amnesty, when they surrendered, he executed the whole House of Nidin. Baaseiah was a warlike ruler, and broke every treaty he ever made, hence emerged the saying, 'Never trust a Seesnari.' He died in his bed after a reign of thirty-four years; his dynasty was extinguished just two years after his death.*
*Temmison Vol III, Book 5: Peoples of the Everglow.*

*Sasna* looked suspiciously at the door to the cabin as Farir quietly approached it. He tiptoed lightly, slightly wobbling, and put his hand on the handle. She thought she heard a faint noise outside, and a quiet but involuntary wheeze.

Muro's face was brooding and dark as he whispered to her, "This Murien is the reason the runes have sent me here. Your business should be trying to survive this night. I sense trickery followed by danger is afoot for you."

Farir had visibly sobered up after hearing Muro's words about the text, and then the sound outside. Sasna motioned with her eyes for him to open the cabin door. Despite the amount of wine, he had consumed, he was suddenly quite alert. He put his finger to his lips, signalling for everyone to be quiet. He turned the handle and opened it with one swift movement. Gnarn, with his ear pressed to the door, fell into the cabin. Farir grabbed him by the scruff of the collar, wrenching him to his feet, and kicked the cabin door shut behind him. "He must have heard everything," he said in alarm as he cuffed Gnarn violently around the side of the head.

Gnarn wheezed and screamed at the same time.

Farir cuffed Gnarn again, and then angrily smacked him roughly around the head several time in succession before throwing him on the floor, pressing the heel of his boot on the lad's neck. "How much did you hear boy, how much?"

"Let him go, Farir," Sasna said with an air of authority that made the reluctant Farir comply.

Gnarn stood to his feet, as far as he was able. He rubbed his neck which was red from the mark made by Farir's boot. He flinched and ran to the corner, where he cowered, and began crying and wheezing.

Sasna sheathed her sabres, went over to him, knelt down, and gently put her hand upon his face and tenderly stroked it. "Nobody here will hurt you Gnarn, if you tell me what you heard."

Gnarn stopped crying, and sluggishly sat up. He slowly raised his eyes and looked with surprise at Sasna. There was a still silence. He had a look of shock on his face. "Nobody has ever touched Gnarn with kindness before," he whispered, as he finally began to catch his breath. "Take Gnarn with you mistress, take Gnarn with you and he will tell you of master's plans to harm you this very night. Master will burn Gnarn or kill him for being caught but Gnarn will tell you what he plans if you take Gnarn."

Sasna gave an involuntary puzzled look towards Farir and Muro, and then turned her attention back on Gnarn, and frowned.

"What plans? Gnarn what do you mean he plans to harm us?"

"Not until you promise you will take Gnarn with you," he answered, quivering with fear and looking nervously around.

Sasna looked at Farir. "We have no choice," she said to him.

Farir drew his sword. "I agree, let's kill the bilge-rat," he snarled.

Gnarn flinched, shrieked and began wheezing again.

"Please mistress, don't let him kill Gnarn. Gnarn will tell you what master has planned if you take Gnarn with you."

Sasna looked at Gnarn and smiled softly, hiding the concern lurking within her heart. "I will take you with me if you promise to tell me everything you know about your master's plans."

"You promise?" Gnarn asked doubtfully, as he looked at her with a desperate plea in his eyes.

"I do," she said, and then glancing over to Muro, added, "but he will badly hurt you, and use magic to force you to tell me the truth if I suspect you are lying. You would not like that, would you Gnarn?"

Gnarn glanced over at Muro, who had a dark and brooding look as he watched the deformed boy. Gnarn shook his head. "Gnarn would not like that."

"I promise you will not be harmed, and can come with me, if you tell me what you know," Sasna said as she removed an attractive ring from one of her fingers. "This is of great value," she lied. "It is worth more than a wagon full of gold, but its value to me is far greater as it belonged to my mother. Return it to me when you consider my promise fulfilled." *Kindness, not cruelty will work with this boy.* The ring was expensive, but certainly not of the value she had just said and it had never belonged to her mother. She had taken a liking to it after seeing it on the finger of a female Davari slave in the last shipment, so had taken it.

Gnarn nodded, snatched the ring and hid it underneath the ragged and torn sackcloth he wore. "Gnarn is sorry mistress," he wheezed with difficulty, in between panting gasps for breath. "Gnarn's master makes him listen in on good people like you. Gnarn learns a lot that way and tells master what he hears."

"And what did you hear?" Sasna asked him gently.

"Gnarn heard nothing mistress," he said as he put a finger in his ear as though cleaning it out. "It is a thick door, Gnarn heard nothing."

Farir unsheathed a knife from his belt and together with the sword in his hand he took a step towards Gnarn whose eyes widened in fear. "His soul is crooked; there is no truth in him. If you won't let me kill him, let me cut out his tongue. That way we are sure he will not repeat anything if he did hear it." He stood menacingly over Gnarn.

"Gnarn will tell you mistress," he squealed in a panic. "Gnarn heard it all, mistress, for twice I listened at your door, once before he was brought here and then again afterwards." He cast a quick glance at Muro and then continued as he watched Farir point the knife at him. "Gnarn heard something about a text. Murien. Gnarn doesn't know what that is. Gnarn heard it is priceless and the old man can read it. Gnarn didn't understand much though and it won't matter, for you will be taken tonight."

"Who will take us?" Farir demanded.

Gnarn sounded like a wounded animal when he spoke. "Promise Gnarn you will take him with you mistress; master will burn Gnarn in the night-fire and feed him to the river fish if he tells you this and you don't take him." Gnarn started to cry.

"Hush boy," Farir said, sheathing his knife and sword. "You'll not be harmed if you tell us what you know."

"You have my ring as a promise, tell us what you know, Gnarn," Sasna said reassuringly, trying to coax him, "or I will hand you over to him." She glanced again at

51

Muro once more, for effect, and Gnarn followed her gaze. Muro stood, raised his palms, and the runes in them began to glow.

Gnarn went cross-eyed with fear for a few seconds. Visibly shaking, he seemed unsure what to do. Sasna took him by the hands and held them comfortingly between her own hands, as a mother would her own child.

"Tell me Gnarn. If you do, I have promised I will take you away from here to a place where nobody will hurt you. What do you mean we will be taken?"

"Master is not who he says he is. He is a very bad man. He does not work for the patrician; he works for somebody far worse."

Sasna felt both startled and confused. "You're not making sense Gnarn, start from the beginning."

"The patrician left Berecoth and came to Harwind, about a month ago. On what business Gnarn does not know. Gnarn was sitting in the Mermaid Tavern. The patrician gambled at Harendale with a ferocious pirate captain, the one they call Redboots. He lost; she took one of his fingers but he couldn't pay the rest of the debt. She was going to nail him to her mast and make him an offering to the sea god Jorgen. To pay the debt, he gave her the *River Queen* and told her that he often carried Seesnari nobility from Ashgiliath to Greytears." He wheezed before continuing. "Master is her man, and all the crew. When the midnight bell tolls and you sleep, master plans to take you and your brother by surprise and deliver you to Redboots so she can hold you for ransom." Gnarn wheezed and let out a whimper. "That is all Gnarn knows. Gnarn swears it."

Sasna chided herself for not acting on her earlier suspicions. *I knew something was not right.* "Is this pirate captain, Redboots, the same one who raided Berecoth?"

"She is. Gnarn does not know the reason but the patrician foolishly offended her once again. She sailed her ship and several others all the way from the Tethys Sea right into Berecoth and cut his throat, and then for good measure hanged him."

*The patrician is dead?*

Gnarn whimpered in fear. "Oh, Gnarn will be in so much trouble if master finds out Gnarn told you this. If your uncle does not pay the ransom, they will make you suffer for it, I heard."

Sasna and Farir looked at each other uneasily. Outside the cabin, the sound of the ship's bell rang out - eleven bells.

"We have less than an hour, we need to think and act fast," Sasna said.

"Let me start by killing him," Farir suggested as he took a step towards Gnarn who squealed, ducked and pulling his hands away from Sasna's grasp covered his head with them for protection.

Gnarn crawled and hid in the corner of the cabin, still covering his head with his hands and cowering.

"No!" Sasna said. "Do not shed his blood. I will keep my promise to him. I need to think." She then asked Farir, "How many weapons do we have?"

"Just our sabres, some daggers and this knife," he replied.

Muro was already on his feet. He stood and walked over to Gnarn, who involuntarily looked at the runes. A light came from them and entered Gnarn's eyes.

"The Davari in the hold, you are to set them free," Muro said.

Farir objected profusely. "They belong to Sasna and I; they are our slaves. What are they to you, old man? You have shown them no concern until now."

Muro's face contorted with hate as he answered Farir. "I care nothing for them, nor for you and your sister. I submit myself to the runes. I surrender to my fate. This night, the Davari are to aid me in my destiny."

Farir snorted derisively. "You forget you still belong to us as well, slave."

Muro held up his hands threateningly, the runes in his palms began to glow. The red one glowed with fire, the white one with ice. "I am Ruik, you would be dead already, and I would be a free man, if I had not submitted myself to the will of the runes," he said menacingly to Farir. "Try me now, if you wish, Seesnari!"

Farir wavered and backed down.

"Enough!" Sasna shouted. She stood and nervously paced to and thro for a few seconds, and then looked at Muro. "If you help Farir and I to escape whatever trap is set for us, you can go your own way," she said. *There is a full crew on board this ship. We need all the help we can get to escape from this.*

"Gnarn, come here, I need you to do something for me," Sasna said gently as she knelt and beckoned him to come to her. Slowly, reluctantly, Gnarn left the corner and moved towards her on all fours. She held him gently by the shoulders. "Those three Davari in the hold, the ones chained alone down there, do you know how to get to them?"

Gnarn nodded.

"Give him the key to the chains, Farir," she said.

Farir hesitated and looked at her questioningly, but then sighed and handed Gnarn the keys.

"Do you know where the key to the armoury is?" Sasna asked Gnarn.

Gnarn nodded again. "The key is in the master's cabin. Gnarn knows all the keys on the ship. Gnarn knows where the armoury key is."

"Good," Sasna said reassuringly. "Did you enjoy that sweetcake I gave you earlier?"

Gnarn nodded.

"Well, if you do what I ask of you, you can come and live with me, and I promise you sweetcakes whenever you want them. Nobody will ever harm you or hold your face to the night-fire again. My ring is the token I will keep my promise; can I trust you to do what I ask?"

Gnarn nodded again.

"Then I want you to go and let those Davari in the hold free. Take them to the armoury and let them arm themselves. Lead them onto the upper deck but tell them, and this is very important Gnarn, tell them when they come onto the upper deck, they are to look to me and follow my lead. Tell them our survival depends on them following my lead. Will you do that for me Gnarn?"

Gnarn nodded once more.

"Act now, fast but calm, Gnarn," Sasna said.

Gnarn scuttled on all fours to the cabin door, opened it, left and slammed it shut behind him.

"I don't trust him," Farir said gloomily. "I hope you know what you are doing sister. What if he betrays us?"

"He will not betray me," Muro said, "the runes have him charmed."

It was obvious to Sasna that Farir did not trust either Muro, or her plans; she could tell that by the way his face had suddenly become ashy, and the questioning expression that spread across his features. The truth was, she had no plan, she was not sure what to do, and only knew she had to try something – anything, to get off of the ship before she was taken.

"Do not give voice to doubt, we have no time to discuss this," she said to Farir, then, "come, let us calmly pretend to enjoy the night air, foul as it is. You will both follow my lead." She took a dagger from a drawer and tucked it beneath the folds of the sash around her waist. Her manner set the tone for how they were to act as she walked towards the cabin door. She adjusted the sabre straps and sheathes over her shoulders.

Opening the cabin door, she stepped out, and walked calmly onto the deck of the *River Queen*, followed by Farir and Muro.

Sasna walked over to the night-fire, where a bare-chested crewman warmed himself. He was the one who had earlier been filling the lamps, a job he had not finished as several lamps still stood around the barrel of oil, and he had not yet replaced the lid. He looked at her suspiciously as she put her hands out as if to warm them.

"What are you doing?" he asked. "Why are you armed?" He looked suspiciously at Muro and Farir

"The night is cold. I wish to warm myself, and should I not be armed if pirates are raiding this river?"

The crewman grunted, turned and headed towards the quarterdeck.

The mist had thickened since Sasna had last been on the deck a short while before. She scanned her surroundings, and could see that the poorly armed bowmen were still in the rigging. She could also see that the captain was still on the quarterdeck. He was pacing up and down and yelling instructions to several crew members who were at the bow of the ship untying ropes and loosening chains, as they adjusted the anchor against the current. He stopped when the crewman reached him and whispered something in his ear. The captain rushed over to the railing, and peered over at her.

Sasna looked at the side of the ship, and wished she and Farir had learnt to swim. The Erin was a treacherous river, with fierce undercurrents and unpredictable eddies, but at that moment she would take Farir and jump overboard, and take her chances, if she could only swim.

"Get back in your cabin and sleep," the captain bellowed aggressively. "And chain that Davari slave up. I'll not have a slave wandering about here at night!"

"My good captain," Sasna replied, trying desperately to think what she should say or do. "Can we not stretch our legs and warm ourselves by the night-fire? We wish to trade words with the slave before we secure him for the night. Then my brother and I will retire. It has been a long day; we will drink wine and will sleep as soon as our heads hit the pillow, but for now I would have fresh air and warm myself."

The captain paused briefly, and then growled, "Very well, just keep out of the way, and don't be long."

From below the deck came muffled sounds of shouting and the clash of steel. The captain looked at his crewman. "Go and see what the commotion is about," he ordered. Before the man had even got down the ladder of the quarterdeck, Imrand burst through the door from the lower deck, brandishing two swords. Bare-footed and bare-chested, he and the swords he held were splattered in blood. Scarand followed behind him and with hardly a pause, fired off three quick arrows into the rigging. The first hit a furled sail, the second and third their targets - the poorly armed men on guard in the rigging. They let out screams as they fell to the deck, landing with a hard thud.

"The fools," Sasna shouted to Farir. "They were supposed to follow my lead."

The crewman on the quarterdeck, reached the bottom of the ladder, and let out a surprised yelp. He then drew a cutlass and charged Farir. Farir drew his sabres and managed to defend the man's blow. The two men began a deadly battle, as the captain began to furiously ring the ship's bell to alert more of the crew.

Imrand ran up to Sasna. He had a wild look in his eyes, "Sarkisi! To me!" he shouted. Sarkisi, brandishing a bow and wearing a quiver full of arrows, was by his side in an instant. She fired off arrows at any crew member she saw. Her mark was deadly. She wore a blue palla, the mark of a married woman, this being a piece of cloth wrapped around the body with one end over the shoulder and draped over the back of the head leaving the face uncovered, with a sash around the middle of the garment. It was a strange site for Sasna to behold seeing her, so attired, dealing out death so swiftly. She was dressed in that manner, having been made ready to be presented to the Baron.

Without warning Imrand took a swipe at Sasna's head with his swords. She barely managed to duck and avoid the double attack, but was able to move agilely on her feet and put the brazier in between herself and him. Imrand stepped towards her, snarling, as she turned to face him drawing her own weapons.

"Imrand, we are in great danger; follow my lead, we need to work together," she pleaded nervously as he snarled at her, his lips writhing back in a bestial grin of hate showing glistening white teeth.

"I'll make my own fortune from here bitch, and send you to whatever filthy gods you profanely serve," he avowed with an almost inhuman snarl slavering from his throat. He then raised one of his swords and lunged, attempting to strike at her again.

Sasna's skin crawled with instinctive fear, but her training mastered it. Without hesitating, she dodged the blow and kicked over the brazier that held the night-fire, spreading burning coals all over the upper deck. The heavy frame of the night-fire rolled into Imrand. Being off-footed, he tripped, stumbled, and fell headlong, throwing out one hand to save himself. One of his swords flew from his hand and clattered away from him and landed at her feet. The brazier continued rolling, spilling burning coals across the deck until it came to the barrel of oil, which it hit. The force was not enough to tip the barrel over, but it did rock it, causing some of the oil to spill over the rim. It immediately caught fire.

Without conscious plan or thought, Sasna hurled one of her sabres at the barrel of oil. The point of the blade embedded in the wood of the barrel, splitting the side so that the entire contents spilled out onto the deck, causing a massive eruption of fire.

By now, many of the crew were coming through hatches and doorways and emerging onto the upper deck. Scarand and Sarkisi were rapidly firing arrows, bringing many of them down as soon as they emerged. Muro was pointing his hands towards the ship's masts and rigging. Fire and ice emerged from the palms of his hand, killing the remaining bowmen who were either instantly frozen to death, falling to the deck as though a lump of ice, or consumed in a bursting ball of flame. The mast, rigging and furled away sails burst into flame. The *River Queen* was quickly turning into a blazing inferno.

Imrand galvanized, rising on one knee and a hand. He leaped over the brazier and burning coals, as his remaining sword slashed at Sasna's head. She managed to fend off one blow, steel against steel, but stumbled as the second slashed her shoulder causing a deep wound. She screamed in pain and dropped her sabre, but grabbing the sword on the deck near her, she held it up to fend off Imrand's next blow.

Farir, having finished his foe, was by her side in an instant, but unsteady on his feet. He barged Imrand so that he was knocked to the deck. He stepped in front of Sasna, and stood protectively in front of her as Imrand got back up. Farir opened his mouth to say something to Imrand but did not get the chance. An arrow, shot by Sarkisi, hit him in the shoulder, the force of which knocked him backwards onto the deck and into the burning oil. He screamed as his clothes caught alight in an instant. He stood, the flames upon him spreading rapidly. In sheer panic, he ran screaming towards the side of the ship and jumped over into the Erin, despite Sasna desperately calling to him.

Imrand took a swipe at Sasna's head. She only barely managed to fend off the attack with the sword she held in her uninjured arm, but the force of the blow knocked it from her grasp and it fell to the deck. The wound in her shoulder gushed blood.

Muro, with a speed that belayed his age, rushed to her side, and raised both of his hands and held them in front of himself towards Imrand. The fire and ice runes began to glow from under the skin of his palms. Sasna could feel the power that came from them. It made her shudder.

A foreboding grimace spread across Muro's face. "These will shatter you or burn you to a crisp. She is needed alive, now leave," he menacingly warned Imrand.

Imrand, who was preparing for a death blow on Sasna, hesitated as Muro stepped forward and stood between her and him. The fire on the ship was spreading and raging all around them, black smoke billowing into the air.

"What is she to you, old man?" Imrand shouted above the roar of the flames.

"She is nothing to me, as you are nothing, but I saved your wretched life for the runes, and for the same reason, I save hers." Muro glanced at Scarand, as the young Davari joined him by his side. Scarand loaded an arrow, and aimed it at Imrand, and then Sarkisi, who pointed a notched arrow at him in return.

"Don't," Scarand growled at Imrand, as they both glared at each other with wild rage in their eyes. "The Seesnari knows where my sisters are. If she dies, Sarkisi is next!"

The runes in the palms of Muro's hand began to glow brighter.

"Vile thrall, traitorous scum," Imrand scowled accusingly. He then pointed his sword at Muro. "I will not forget how you did not come to my aid in my time of need." Looking at Sasna and pointing his sword at her, he warned, "This is not over, slaver. I will have my revenge!" He lowered his sword, turned, and taking Sarkisi by the hand, he ran with her to the side of the ship and they both jumped overboard into the Erin.

More crew members emerged from the lower deck. The captain bellowed orders. "Kill them!" he roared. "Kill them!"

Weakened by the loss of blood, Sasna dropped to her knees, "Farir!" she cried into the mist and smoke in the direction where he had already gone overboard. She hardly noticed Scarand, who stood over her, again firing arrows into the mist, each one hitting a crew member as they emerged from below.

Flames shot from the rune in one of Muro's hands, instantly setting alight both man and ship where it struck, and ice came forth from the other, freezing men to death, and putting out the fire where it touched.

Any sailors who charged the deck, fell before they got close. The last one to charge, was felled in an instant by an arrow through the eye. The crew began to panic as the chaos and fire spread, and they charged no more, choosing instead to jump into the Erin as they saw the ship was lost to the flames.

Thick smoke was still swirling up amongst the mist. Muro walked into the black smoke, stood by the side of the ship, and standing straight he allowed himself to topple over the side saying, "I submit myself to the runes!" He then disappeared from sight.

Scarand slung the bow across his shoulder, picked up one of Sasna's fallen sabres and slid it between his belt and trousers. She did not resist as he took her by the hand and dragged her away from the flames. "Farir, my Farir," she sobbed. Weakened by the blow to the shoulder Scarand had to carry her. He flung her over his shoulder as he climbed up onto the quarterdeck to try and escape the flames. The captain, obscured by a mast and the mist, was still furiously ringing the ship's bell and still shouting for all hands to come to the deck, but no more emerged. He stopped and turned as Scarand laid Sasna on the deck of the ship.

Scarand unslung his bow, and cocked an arrow.

The captain drew a cutlass. "You whore of a bitch!" he shouted to Sasna who lay there bleeding. He then glared at Scarand. "You think you can best me you Davari scum?" he roared. "Put the bow down and face me like a man, blade to blade." He lunged at Scarand.

Scarand let loose the arrow; it hit the captain square in the forehead. He was dead before he hit the deck. "Thralls are not taught to use a sword," he said derisively as he stood over the lifeless body of the captain. Sasna managed to get to her feet and looked at the scene before her. The *River Queen* was almost entirely engulfed in flames.

Sasna could hear screams and splashes in the water, but could not make out what was happening in the chaos as the smoke and mist hid the scene from her. She stumbled over to the side of the ship, confused and disorientated. "Farir!" she shouted. "Farir?" Hearing nothing, bewildered and confused, she ran over to the other side and called from there to her brother.

Scarand stood before her, and drew the sabre from his belt. His face and arms were covered in dirt, sweat and blood. The fierceness in his eye unnerved her; she had not noticed that in him before. He walked towards her as she backed up, until she pressed as far as she could against the rail on the side of the ship. "That's far enough," he said to her.

*So, this is it, this is my end?* Sasna resigned herself to her death. "Just do it," she shouted as she tried to stand to her full height. She looked him defiantly in the eyes, before partly closing her own. "I will join my Farir in the Fair Havens."

Scarand raised the sabre above his head and brought it down in one swift motion. Instinctively she flinched. The sound of steel cutting through rope rang out through the mist, followed by a whoosh of air, the spinning of tackle and a loud splash of water. She opened her eyes fully. Scarand was looking over the side of the *River Queen* at the ship's boat which he had released into the river. The ship had turned so that the current pushed the boat against the stern of the starboard side. "I don't know about you, but I can't swim," he said.

"Neither can I, and these currents can be death," she replied, somewhat surprised she still lived and breathed.

Scarand clambered down the netting on the side of the *River Queen* into the waiting boat. He held his hand up to her, "Come," he urged, "it is your only chance."

Sasna took one last look at the *River Queen*, which was nearly completely engulfed in fire, smoke and mist. With the last of her strength, she swung over the side, and with her good arm she uneasily climbed down the rope ladder as far as she could, and was helped by Scarand into the bottom of the boat where she collapsed in a heap.

"Farewell Farir," she cried, as she drifted into unconsciousness.

# Chapter Six: *The Empress and a Council of Fools*

*That weirdly, dreeing cry, from realms, deep and unmeasurable. I wish I had never stared into the Simal, for afterwards, I was mad for fifteen lifetimes.*
**Confessions of the Priest named Rual.**

*Treachery from an unexpected source broke the Kappian lines, and the once proud palace guards turned and fled. Before chronicling this treachery, it might be well to briefly glance at the state to which the Kappian Empire had fallen into during the time of which I write. Untold wealth had rolled into the capital by conquest. As a result, the rulers replaced simple and hardy living with sumptuous splendour fuelled by untold wealth, but this wealth was not shared out with the people, many of whom starved in the streets whilst lavish banquets were held in the palaces nearby. Degeneracy had sapped the rulers' former strength. Arrogance supplanted their previous simplicity. They treated their own people with contempt, and thus talk of revolt and savage retaliations simmered among the populace who, for the first time in their history, in the year 9142, finally rose up and rebelled.*
**Temmison Vol II, Book 2: History of the Kappian Empire.**

*The* throne hall was long and wide. Bright midday sunbeams fell in glimmering shafts of light from the lofty windows high under the deep eaves. The floor was paved with marble stones of many hues, the centre display of which depicted a large coiled snake. The pillars reaching up from the floor to a high vaulted ceiling were richly carved with runes of gold and half-colours. Elaborate paintings of glorious scenes that told the tale of Kappian antiquity adorned the ceiling itself: the battles fought; the peoples conquered; the cities razed. The images of Titans and the Aeldar Gods were emblazoned on tapestries hanging from the walls, where beneath them marble busts of the Empress Shaka of House Shakawraith, her three children and many of their ancestors, stood proudly on pedestals around the sides of the hall.

Supreme Lord General Karkson, the Commander-in-Chief of the Kappian Legions, momentarily stood in the entrance to the hall and observed the familiar sight before him. He took a deep breath, and then swallowed hard, trying to rid himself of the rising anxiety he felt. His eyes lowered as he saw the Empress Shaka, who sat on a red velvet cushion, placed upon the ruby throne, which was shaped like a snake wrapped around two hammers. It rested upon a dais with nine golden steps carved to represent the circling coils of a serpent. The throne shimmered with gold and jewels which were partly covered by the exquisite furs that draped it.

To the left of Shaka, her three children stood on the dais, on the step below the throne. Each had been granted the ancestral title *Ivanar*, a title that meant *Privileged One*. Anyone given the title was above the law of the Empire, as was the Empress herself according to the recently adapted constitution. As a result of gaining the title *Ivanar*, the princes and princess were feared throughout all regions and provinces of the Empire. Their pointless cruelty and brutality were well known and documented, but was never punished. Karkson had vainly hoped they would not be present for this audience. In fact, it alarmed him that the hall was full of dignitaries.

Prince *Ivanar* Regineo, an ugly looking hunch-backed man, his right foot twisted and lame, was dressed in black and red garb made of silks woven through with intricate designs of fine gold thread. A black circlet with a white pearl at the centre adorned his head. Princess *Ivanar* Aspess, a fine-looking young woman, was dressed in elegant black breeches and a plain white silk shirt tied at the waist by a red sash, attached to which was a cruel looking dagger sheathed in a decorative glass scabbard. Her long black hair glittered due to the many precious coloured jewels and gems that adorned it. She looked out from her position contemptuously at all who stood below her. Next to her, a nervous looking man, Prince *Ivanar* Caspus, her twin, in stark contrast was dressed more plainly in a simple linen gown tied at the waist with a crude rope. His hair and beard were unkempt, in the manner of a desert contemplate. He had the appearance of one who had not washed for several days; his sandaled feet were covered in dust and dirt. Below a tangled mess of hair, from under a bushy brow, shifty eyes nervously darted to and thro, watching the assembled crowd.

To the right of Shaka, two steps below the throne, stood a man who wore a simple black hooded robe, the only decoration of which was the red hammers and snake symbol. His brow was capped with a circlet fashioned in the image of hammers. He leant heavily upon a wooden staff, atop of which was a large cerulean gem that glistened in the light. The man had a pale wise face and heavy-lidded eyes surrounded by dark circles. He was Marnir, the Grand Inquisitor, the Master of Intelligence and one of the most feared men in the Kappian Empire.

Next to him, stood a man wearing a long, jade coloured robe embroidered with red thread, his head adorned also with a hammer circlet. He was Renlak, a balding thin-faced man, Hand and Chamberlain to the Empress. At the bottom of the dais, to the sides, stood several Serveri, dressed in blue togas, the working garb of the Kappian servant class. The togas were elaborate garments that ravelled around their bodies and ended in a spiral shaped headdress. Behind the Serveri were several maids, one of whom was Karkson's own secret daughter, Myrene. As she had often been instructed by her father, she showed no sign or recognition of him when he appeared at the entrance to the throne hall. He made sure their eyes did not meet. Her survival depended on the secrecy of her ancestry being kept. Only Karkson, Myrene herself, and her mother, the wife of a senator, knew that she was Karkson's Pure-blood child, and that she also had a twin brother named Cordius who was a griffin rider at Kara Duram.

Karkson, dressed in full ceremonial armour of white and red, decorated on the chest piece with the image of a golden griffin, began the long and slow walk from the entrance of the hall towards the throne. He led the High Quaester Mazdek by a chain attached to an iron collar around his neck, though the chain was slack as Mazdek walked at his side, not behind. As Karkson had feared, the sight of the High Quaester chained and being led like a common prisoner caused a whisper of protest and complaint to rise up from many of the Hammer Knights present, some of whom sprang at once to their feet and barred the way with their large war-hammers. Karkson knew they would not heed his own command to move out of the way, so to save himself public embarrassment, he whispered quietly to Mazdek.

"Did I not counsel you that your lust for the Simal would bring you to ruin? Command them to move out of our way, or they will be the next to feel the chaos of your folly."

Mazdek answered him, whispering under his breath. "For too long you have counselled against wisdom, general. Choose your words this day with care. Our positions may yet be reversed."

Karkson was taken aback at the threat. *I am not the one the Empress ordered to be brought here on a chain.* "Tell them to move," he said in a barely audible whisper.

There was something in the way that Mazdek confidently smiled, that unnerved Karkson even more, but nonetheless Mazdek gave the order.

"Let us through, my cherished ones," he said confidently to the knights who were barring the way. The knights parted reluctantly as the two men walked forward.

The lords and ladies of the imperial court frowned and muttered among themselves as the two men walked down the long aisle towards the throne. Karkson could sense the uneasiness and tension present in the place. It seemed to him that every footstep he took, loudly echoed around the hall.

"It is an offence and a blasphemy to the Aeldar, to see our High Quaester treated so shamefully," one of the Hammer Knights protested a little too loudly, voicing the concern felt in the hall. The numerous courtiers behind the lords and ladies, dressed in brightly coloured clothes of various styles, mumbled similar feelings among themselves.

"Shame on you general," Karkson heard another one of them mutter.

There was a row of sentries arrayed before the throne, selecting who should be allowed to approach. Karkson reflected that it was not that long since the Praetorian Guard, made up from Pure-blood men he himself had personally selected from the legions, would have been the ones guarding the Empress. They would have shown him respect, but these Hammer Knights merely scowled at him as they moved aside so he and Mazdek could reach the bottom step of the throne.

Shaka coldly watched their every move. Upon her head she wore the magnificent imperial crown, encrusted with nine jewels. The three largest jewels were in the centre: of these three the first was a unique ruby, a peerless masterpiece of the Dwarves' gem making craft; the next, was a green emerald of unrivalled magnificence, said to have been shaped in an ancient age by the Titan Darnicus; the third, in the centre of the crown, was a dazzling blue diamond of such beauty that one could stare at it for hours on end and still marvel in awe. The other six jewels, three either side of the larger ones, were each splendid in their own right. Slightly below the rim of the crown, she wore a thin golden circlet fashioned in the form of a snake. It sat upon her brow, the eyes of which were two red jewels that glittered whenever a shaft of sunlight hit them. On her forearms were snake shaped bracelets. On the finger of her right hand she wore a ring also fashioned in the image of a snake. A large green jewel was set in the middle, cleverly held by clasps made to look like its fangs. Clad in a red silk gown that only barely concealed her nakedness and allowed her comely form to be admired, she watched contemptuously as the two men approached. Karkson and Mazdek stopped when they reached the bottom step of the dais, and both knelt on one knee.

"Rise," Shaka commanded with a disdainful sneer.

Karkson and Mazdek stood to their feet. Mazdek gave a flamboyant bow, that made his chains rattle.

Karkson knew by the dark scowl on her face, which was twisted in rage, that Shaka was in a dangerous and unpredictable mood. Her face had a cruel beauty at the best of times but today she looked terrifying. Her make-up was exotic and perfect in detail, with spiral red patterns on her high angular cheekbones, but that just made her look crueller. He trembled slightly, knowing how impulsive and rash she could be at such times.

Karkson felt a mixture of fear and shame at his current predicament. He was a soldier who enjoyed the honesty of battle. He had never known paralysing fear on the battlefield, but he often felt it when he stood before Shaka. He was skilled in every known battle tactic, but the intrigues, deception and ways of the imperial court had always confused him, and he always felt out of his depth.

The Kappian Empire's history was a portrait of despotism, haunted by terror and shadowed by blood. Its history was a nightmare, from which it was impossible for the citizens to awake. Many had seen the dimming of their own liberties, but they had been powerless to do anything about it. Karkson always regretted that he was unable, or rather unwilling, to stand up to the Empire's exactions. He always opted to keep his head down, his gaze averted. These crimes of omission as well as his complicity in the brutal repression of any rebellion, seemed never to have been cleansed from his conscience. His worst wrongdoing in his own eyes, however, was keeping his head down as Mazdek had grown in power and influence. Of a sudden, he regretted his negligence.

For a long time Karkson had wanted to openly warn Shaka to be cautious about Mazdek. Even when the Praetorian Guard had been replaced with Hammer Knights as the imperial bodyguard, despite desiring to do so, he had stayed silent instead of cautioning her about the folly of allowing Mazdek's Hammer Knights to be her sole personal protectors.

Karkson had tried to play the same game as others did in the imperial court. He had thought that the whispering of a confidant, such as his undisclosed daughter, Myrene, in Shaka's ear might work, or the anonymous passing of a document to her, secretly obtained, would have a large impact. They did not. Karkson lamented that unlike Mazdek, who often gave inspiring public orations to the Senate and Magistracy, great oratory was a skill he lacked. His own speeches were somewhat dull and lacked the flare and critical skills which Mazdek had exercised. Thus, slowly, Mazdek had gained in power and influence, and had outwitted Karkson at every turn in seeking to win influence over the Empress and the imperial court – until now. *I must see that Mazdek's influence is ended this day!*

The day before, Karkson had received an urgent message, sent by raven. He had been summoned to come with all haste to the Kappia Palace. He had set out immediately from Kara Duram, flying by a griffin. On his arrival he had been informed about the events of the last few days, that the Simal had been stolen and Ahrimakan the Aeldar God, lover of Shaka, had been slain. Immediately he had sought a private audience with the Empress, but, just as he had expected, it had not been granted. Renlak had refused to allow him into her private quarters where she had locked herself away, swallowed in grief and wrath at the death of Ahrimakan, and bitterly mourning the theft of the Simal.

At first, it had given Karkson great joy to learn that Mazdek was being blamed for the whole fiasco, for he despised the man and mistrusted him with a deep suspicion. Yet, he had wanted to counsel Shaka not to have him publicly humiliated. He feared it would cause grievous offence to the Hammer Knights.

Soon after arriving and hearing the rumours being spread at the imperial court, Karkson's initial joy had quickly turned into outright alarm. Gossip and rumours always flowed among the lords and ladies of the court, but this time, in just the short time since he had arrived, Karkson had discovered that there was a dangerous mood in Kappia. The entire atmosphere was toxic, against the Empress herself. She, not Mazdek, was being blamed for the theft of the Simal and the death of Ahrimakan. Her fitness and ability to rule were also being questioned. Treasonous statements were being passed about by means of anonymous documents amongst the nobles. Posters against the Empress were often put up by unknown groups in the cities and towns of the Empire, but some of the ones Karkson had seen, suggested they were endorsed by some members of the Senate and Magistracy. *Has nobody told the Empress?*

The graffiti, which was always rampant in the city, was often a good indicator of the public mood. On his way to the palace Karkson had seen less than generous comments about Shaka. She and her children were being portrayed in harsh and mocking caricatures, but, rather than words and images being anonymous, some of them were endorsed by well-known and influential nobles. He sensed a dangerous mood in the city, rebellion was in the air. He felt the same tenseness in the imperial court. Had he been given access to Shaka, he would have tried to persuade her to be cautious in her treatment of Mazdek, but her anger at the loss of the Simal, and the assassination of Ahrimakan, had been as he had expected. She had acted, as Karkson feared she would, rashly and without good judgement and informed counsel. She had impulsively and foolishly ordered the public arrest of the High Quaester.

The news of the loss of the Simal and the assassination of an Aeldar had spread fast and caused panic in Kappia. After all, it had happened at a major religious festival, the first day of Lupoor, so the news was impossible to contain - too many people had witnessed it. On his arrival Karkson had been informed that rioting had earlier broken out in the Skunfill section of the city. Some of the public buildings had been set on fire and an outraged mob had tried to storm the Argona Temple itself. The city guard had arrested and killed several hundred Fell-bloods, and even some Pure-bloods, and had finally brought the city under control.

Karkson opened his mouth to speak, but Mazdek beat him to it.

"My Sarissa," Mazdek said, addressing the Empress and using one of her most ancient and sacred titles. "None could have predicted or foreseen the catastrophe that recently occurred. The scheme was well hidden. Even our greatest Seers and spies, in both the Everglow and the Deadlands, had heard no whisper concerning the abominable outrage inflicted upon us."

Regineo, the hunch-backed prince shuffled on his feet and spoke, his face contorted with barely concealed malice. "It pains us to see you in such circumstances Quaester Mazdek, but the death of Ahrimakan and the loss of the Simal has caused deep unrest in the city, and that is not to even mention the grief and distress it has caused my mother," he croaked. "It is felt you are to blame, and you must pay some price for your negligence."

Whispers of disapproval rose up from the Hammer Knights and the court. Karkson shifted uneasily on his feet as he looked around, unwittingly causing the chains that bound Mazdek to rattle.

"My Sarissa," he said, also using the same ancient title that he knew it pleased the Empress to be addressed by. "This matter is best resolved within the discretion of the Privy Council Chamber. I urge you to dismiss the court that we might discuss these matters in private?"

The face of the Empress twisted with rage. "Silence!" she shouted. She looked at the nearest Hammer Knight, who lowered his gaze as her piercing emerald green eyes met his. "The Hammer Knights are my bodyguard and have sworn loyalty to me. If I order any one of them to crunch the head of this priest with a sacred hammer, they will obey, or they will face my wrath!"

Karkson inwardly winced at the lack of tact and respect his beloved Empress showed towards Mazdek, especially referring to him as though he was merely a common and ordinary priest. Fresh remorse swept over him that he had not more openly warned her and others about the progressively growing influence of Mazdek. *Why did I tame my speeches and hold back on my words when I addressed the Senate and the Magistracy? Why did I allow timidity to restrain my tongue, the very few times of late, when I did gain an audience with my Sarissa?*

Karkson had realised far too late that Mazdek and Marnir had vastly extended the imperial network of spies, informers and confessors. Through such means, they had discovered the secret vices of the most powerful, as well as many ordinary citizens, of Kappia. *Renlak was always loyal to the Empress. What do they have on him, that he does not want revealed? There is no other reason his loyalty would be so corrupted against her.*

It was only as he stood there, openly hearing the murmurings of the Hammer Knights and nobles, that he realised the extent of disdain with which the court held the imperial family. Worst though, they seemed oblivious to it, thinking the murmurings were against Mazdek. He scolded himself. *Why have I been so slow to see the extent of this until now?*

It had only been the day before, that Karkson had discovered that Mazdek had formed a Council of the Learned in Law, legal experts and judges who were richly rewarded solely for their loyalty to him. These men and women had gone through ancient laws and created a system of bonds and fines, designed to penalise the lords and ladies of the court, and even members of the Senate and Magistrate themselves. By such means, many had found themselves caught in Mazdek's web and financially indebted to him, if they even unwittingly broke any of those laws. To oppose Mazdek, meant facing a trumped-up charge and possible financial ruin, not just for the accused, but their family as well. Blackmail. *This is surely the reason some endorse posters and graffiti against the Empress herself. My Sarissa is blind to just how much power and influence Mazdek has obtained. Can she not see how precarious her hold on power is?*

The only consolation Karkson felt, was that due to newly revived ancient laws, no legion had been allowed to camp within seventy miles of the capital, unless they were specifically requested to do so by written decree. Such a decree had to have the full support of both the Senate and Magistracy. This had enabled the unchecked rise of the Hammer Knights, both politically and militarily, but there was one small benefit; due to the legions retreating to Kara Duram, it had saved their most prominent leaders from either financial ruin or becoming indebted to Mazdek. *The legions will remain loyal.*

The withdrawal of the legions from Kappia and its immediate regions, had also led to the rise of the political wing of the Hammer Knights. Many of them had taken political offices within the Senate, Assembly and the Magistrate. The Empress, once so shrewd and vigilant, had trusted Mazdek too much, and had become distracted. She had become totally obsessed with the Aeldar God Ahrimakan. He had chosen her to be his lover whenever he took physical form, and had mated with her, in an act so violent and degrading, it was said that it had once led to the spawning of a new Titan.

Shaka had been so convinced that she was being elevated to become a goddess, 'Queen of the Aeldar,' that she had assumed that Mazdek and the Hammer Knights, who themselves were devoted worshippers of the Aeldar, all understood the sacred role being given to her. The result was that she had believed in their total allegiance towards what she had considered their common goal – her elevation. It had not even occurred to her that Mazdek might not be trusted, and not once had she questioned his loyalty.

Karkson could still hear the whispering and murmurings of discontent behind him. He knew they were directed at Shaka, but she and her children were still in the mistaken belief that it was Mazdek the court murmured against. *Oh, my Sarissa, I have realised this all too late. Forgive me!*

The awe, with which Mazdek was held, was mostly due to it being well known in Kappia that it was one of his ancestors, Galaeroth, who had discovered Tharakoin, deep in the Void, and stared over its edge. Another of his ancestors had found a way through the Maze of Magnarakroth and entered the City of Lost Souls; he also entered the Labyrinth and discovered the lost Simal. The Simal, and the knowledge gained, had been passed on to Mazdek, and he had been the first and only Seer to ever knock on the dreadful doors of Hammerfell where he consulted with Thuranotos himself, who told him of the Aeldar Riddles, also known as the Aeldar Wives. It was Mazdek who discovered where the first Aeldar Wives were to be found, and through them, he discovered the secret knowledge of how to summon three of the Aeldar back to the Outer World.

Mazdek's deeds were well known, because he often boasted publicly how he had located Hammerfell, banged on its doors, and had spoken face to face with Thuranotos himself. In great detail he described the Aeldar, and converted many to the cult he formed around them. Songs had been written about how he had discovered the first three Aeldar Riddles, including Vispin, so that through the power of the Simal, the Aeldar Ahrimakan was able to be summoned to the land of the living. That had been more than thirty years ago, and Ahrimakan had been summoned many times since then, and taken on temporary physical form, as had one other Aeldar, but Ahrimakan had forbidden the third be summoned.

Ahrimakan's goal, was for the other Aeldar Riddles to be discovered, and he had ordered that the Empire must focus all of its efforts and resources on finding them, and especially the Riddle that could summon Thuranotos himself.

Ahrimakan had made sure it was his own symbol of the snake that was proudly adorned along with that of the Hammers of Thuranotos, so that he among the Aeldar became famed and prominent throughout the Empire. He had chosen Shaka to be his lover, and she had become obsessed with him the moment he had first touched her. She had allowed the power and influence of Mazdek to rise mostly unchecked, because she was convinced, he understood her divine destiny, but now her most powerful ally, Ahrimakan, was no more.

On one rare occasion, Karkson had counselled caution in regards to the use of the Simal, but all his words had achieved were to provoke the Empress and Mazdek to wrath. Lately, he had been summoned to give advice less and less. He had been often blocked by Mazdek from entering Privy Council meetings or not informed when they were taking place, and no doubt his absence would have been explained as his own indifference, so of late he had mostly remained in Kara Duram, the fortress and training camp of the legions. It was only due to the events of the previous few days and the arrest of Mazdek that the Empress had finally sent for him to come before the imperial court, but he suspected it was not to listen to his counsel.

Karkson had not been happy when he discovered he had been ordered to lead Mazdek into the imperial court in chains. As far as appearances looked, it would seem to those gathered he was responsible for the order to have Mazdek arrested. Mazdek was the one in chains, but it dawned on Karkson that Mazdek's warning was correct - it was his own position that was far more precarious. Despite her tone towards Mazdek, it was possible that the Empress regretted her rashness, and was looking for somebody else to blame for it, and Karkson knew he would be the perfect scapegoat.

Mazdek did not respond to the insult of being referred to merely as a 'priest,' by the Empress, nor did he rise to the threat she had made. He replied calmly. "My Sarissa, the loyalty of the Hammer Knights to you is without question. You have kept to the way of the Aeldar and have been most diligent in our common cause. Aeldar temples are now spread far and wide. Even in Bruthon lands the heresies of the old ways are being replaced by the light of the Aeldar and the knowledge they bring. The faith prospers under your guidance and we are grateful for this." He turned his head and faced the Hammer Knights and raised his hands. Despite the clinking of the chains, they gave murmurs of approval, but Karkson sensed it was more in support of Mazdek than agreement with his words of praise for the Empress.

Mazdek turned his head back to Shaka and continued. "Ahrimakan himself anointed me as High Quaester. It was in your presence and that of the High Council and the Grand Inquisition, that he spoke those sacred words. I beg you listen to my counsel now, for I have much to say on recent events and have yet to be heard on them."

Karkson could sense the veiled loathing and slyness in the words of Mazdek as he addressed the Empress, but she was oblivious to it. A pained look spread across her face; she squeezed her fist so tightly the knuckles on her hand turned white.

"The Simal is stolen from us, and Ahrimakan, my lover, my sun and stars, is slain," she said as she pointed an accusing finger at Mazdek. "And who is responsible, if not you, priest?"

Karkson was again unsettled by the way Mazdek did not seem phased, but just coolly smiled in the face of such a scathing accusation, his eyes darting shiftily around him to gauge the responses of those within his line of vision. The Hammer Knights were clearly not pleased at hearing their High Quaester so insulted yet again. If, as Karkson suspected, the Empress was looking to shift blame, her anger and wrath was clouding her judgement and objectivity and in that, he knew she was making a fatal mistake.

"Oh, my Sarissa, we do not know for a fact that Ahrimakan was slain," Mazdek declared with a knowing smile.

Karkson gasped with surprise at the statement, as did most of those present in the throne hall, many of whom had themselves witnessed what they had presumed was the death of Ahrimakan. Before Shaka could respond, Mazdek looked accusingly at Karkson. "I have reason to think this betrayal of you, my Sarissa, and the Aeldar, might have been carried out by the friend of the man that now holds the chains I am bound with, and General Karkson failed to act to stop him."

Karkson was speechless. The fear simmering away inside of him evaporated in an instant, as the soldier in him took over. If he had been wearing a sword, he would have been tempted to have drawn it and cut off Mazdek's head despite the consequences, so great was the rage that quickly swelled up within his breast. For the first time, he was almost glad that no member of the legions, himself included, were any longer allowed to carry a weapon in the presence of the Empress since the time the Hammer Knights were made her bodyguard.

"You blame me for this situation?" he asked indignantly.

"I do," Mazdek forcefully replied. "You failed to detect the treachery of one of your own Captain Generals, and now he has plotted with the Baothein Queen to try to bring us to ruin, that is where your blame lies!"

Karkson felt the rage rising up within him increase. The words being uttered by Mazdek were false, and a slander to the honour and code by which Karkson tried to conduct himself. However, it was only a momentary reaction, his fear quickly took over again when Shaka stood to her feet and took slow deliberate steps to reach the bottom of the dais. She walked purposefully up to Mazdek, her face trembling with anticipation as she stared him in the eyes. "Explain," she ordered curtly, as she turned to Marnir, who knew what she expected of him.

Marnir lifted the staff he held over his head and boomed in a deep voice. "Behold, a fragment from the great Jewel of Baramir, Eye of the Morsef. No falsehood or lie may be told in its presence, when one is tested by it. Speak truth only, High Quaester. Diseased, debased, degraded you shall be and all manner of suffering will be yours if you utter dark and false words before the fragment of such a sacred jewel, and the *Final-death* shall be your sentence, if we test you and find you false."

Karkson watched with fearful fascination as Mazdek stared past the Empress at the staff. Everybody in the throne hall knew that the rare and ancient fragment from the Jewel of Baramir set within it was also referred to by some as a Truth Stone. Marnir was correct, if a person was tested by the jewel, no lie or falsehood could be told in its presence without it glowing brightly and shooting a sliver of light at the lips of the one who dared do so, that they may be exposed. The threat of *Final-death*, however, was a penalty of law rather than the result of the power of the jewel itself. Not so, the other consequences.

Mazdek smiled and nodded his head politely towards the Empress. "If you wish me to be tested, the Jewel of Baramir will testify to the truth of my words, as well as bear witness that I alone have a plan to recover that which has been taken. But remember, those who bring an accusation unfounded, into the presence of such a sacred jewel, will have a price to pay themselves, if the jewel finds no guilt in the accused."

Shaka slowly glanced at the fragment from the Jewel of Baramir upon the staff, which Marnir once again held in his right hand, and lent against for support. "There will be no need to test you, High Quaester."

*I will challenge the Eye of Morsef to test him, Karkson wanted to shout!* But his courage failed him, and the opportune moment passed.

Mazdek put a hand to the iron collar around his neck and lightly tugged at it as he looked at the Empress. "This is unnecessary, my Sarissa. It is so undignified and chafes at my neck in a most unpleasant manner. For us to discover the depth of the schemes against your sacred self, I will need to be free from it." He smiled pleasantly, showing yellow, crooked teeth.

"Release him," Shaka ordered without hesitation.

Had this order been given earlier, Karkson would have felt relieved. It had not been wise for the Empress to parade such a powerful and influential man in a way designed for public humiliation. As the situation was, somebody apart from the Empress would have to be blamed for Mazdek's treatment, and Karkson once again felt a sense of dread as he knew who that somebody would be – himself.

Taking a key from a purse attached to his belt, Karkson unlocked the collar around Mazdek's neck. He let it fall to the ground noisily along with the chain that he dropped his hold of. Two Serveri scurried forward and immediately picked them up and removed them from sight. Mazdek rubbed his neck with his hands. He then ran his fingers through his thick long hair and beard, both of which were grey and tangled. Although bent with age, he straightened as best he could.

"Speak and do not delay," Regineo demanded, snarling like a rabid dog.

Mazdek looked at him and smiled. "Prince *Ivanar* Regineo. Before my arrest, I requested one of the throwing stars that was used by one of the conspirators and was informed that you took them? If so, may I request if one of them is about your person that you give it to me, or that one may be fetched, if not? For I will show you a wonder you have never seen before."

Regineo paused, and looked at his mother for guidance.

Shaka gave a quick nod of assent.

Regineo pointed to one of the Serveri, "Fetch one," he ordered, and then as an afterthought added, "handle it with care for it is laced with the deadliest of poisons." The Serveri bowed and rushed off towards an exit a few yards behind the throne.

"Tell me of Ahrimakan," Shaka demanded. "Was he not slain with an Arkoom? Is his spirit not forever trapped within the imbedded Arzak of such an obscene weapon? My grief cannot bear delay if this is so. Tested by the truth stone you will be, if I sense your words are crooked."

Mazdek smiled slyly and spoke measuredly. "With respect, my Sarissa, the order to have me chained and imprisoned so soon after the events of a few nights ago is an understandable mistake to make." He looked at Karkson. "Fools counsel you," he said. Before Karkson could protest that he had given no counsel, nor had he been present, Mazdek continued and once more the opportunity was lost. "Had I been conscious at

66

the time, I would have spoken to you immediately, but it was a harsh blow to my frail head that I received. I was fortunate it did not slay me."

To Karkson's dismay, Mazdek again cast him a quick look as though seeking to shift the blame to him. "Ill-advised you were, during my absence, my Sarissa."

"My Sarissa," Karkson tried to interject, but Shaka shot him a venomous look.

"Silence! The High Quaester will speak!"

Karkson knew that Mazdek understood it was solely the will and decision of the Empress to have him arrested and imprisoned, and that he also knew well enough the intrigues and complex etiquette of the imperial court so that Mazdek would not dare point a finger of blame at her for the decision. With carefully chosen words, and well-timed glances, the suggestion to all present was that he, Karkson, was to blame. He knew it was useless to try to defend himself or protest that he had not even been in the city or made aware of recent events until his arrival in Kappia.

"If only I could have saved you from a time of grief and despair my Sarissa," Mazdek wailed. He coughed and signalled to one of the Serveri.

"Bring me water, my mouth is dry and I have not received any refreshment this day. In fact, make it water mixed with some wine."

After receiving a nod of assent from the Empress, the Serveri poured water and wine from separate decanters on a nearby table into a crystal glass, and passed it to Mazdek. Karkson knew that Mazdek was now clearly in control of the situation and was starting to enjoy the tension felt by all others in the hall.

Mazdek took a few sips from the glass and passed it back to the Serveri. Karkson looked uneasily at the Empress; seventeen lifetimes he had now served her as her Supreme Lord General, Commander-in-Chief of the Kappian Legions, and he knew her well. He could tell she was fighting to contain her rage and impatience and was desperate to discover what Mazdek knew. Perhaps that was why she overlooked his impertinence, but even so, Mazdek was still treading on very dangerous ground. Her unpredictability and rage could get the better of her at any moment and unleash itself without any warning.

Karkson had no desire for the loyalty of the Hammer Knights to be publicly tested, but his own position was becoming extremely dangerous, so his only hope might be if Mazdek overplayed his hand and pushed her patience too far. If so, she would act rashly, but Karkson did not know if the Hammer Knights would obey a command to harm their High Quaester. If they disobeyed the Empress in front of the imperial court, her authority would be greatly diminished, and her position precarious. However, although usually a cautious man, Karkson felt it was a gamble he needed to take – he needed to get the Empress to act rashly towards Mazdek.

Karkson cast a discreet eye around the throne hall. Ever since guarding the Empress had become the responsibility of the Hammer Knights, he was well aware he had few friends and was very much alone, among enemies even, whenever he came to the imperial court. If things turned sour, there was nobody to back him up.

The Hammer Knights seemed less agitated now that Mazdek was not chained. They were the only military order that was not under the direct control of Karkson as Supreme Lord General. Mazdek alone, under the guise of obedience to the Empress, was firmly in control of them. For the last few decades, their numbers had swelled with each passing moon and even members of the Kappia City Guard had joined them. The oath-bound soldiers of the legions would have joined the Order as well, had not he, Karkson, taken steps to forbid their doing so. He had rightly pointed out that whilst the oath-bound served under the imperial banner, their oath was made to the Captain

General of their particular legion, who swore an oath of loyalty to the Empress alone and none other, not even to himself as Supreme Lord General.

The Hammer Knights, however, swore an oath directly to Mazdek, who swore an oath on their behalf to the Aeldar Gods and the Empress. A god had more power than even an Empress, and as Mazdek was the Aeldar representative, he could claim to be acting by an authority even greater than the Empress herself. It was a dangerous technicality that Karkson had once tried to discreetly explain to the Empress, but she had insisted that both Mazdek and the Hammer Knights knew that she was on the same level as the Aeldar, in that she was Ahrimakan's lover and wife, and would one day be crowned as an Aeldar Queen. Shaka, once so vigilant on all matters of state down to the finest detail, had had her head turned and her mind distracted by the wretched snake beast that had been summoned from some deep abyss where once it had been cast and imprisoned. Karkson had never seen Ahrimakan summoned, but he had heard many a tale of the creature, and it revolted and alarmed him in equal measure to think his beloved Empress was under the sway of such a foul monster.

Mazdek spoke. "My Sarissa, when the Nameless One allowed En-Sof to imagine the Nine Worlds, he made this one the greatest and grandest of all. Nine Aeldar were given stewardship over all life, the chief and supreme of whom was Thuranotos, with Ahrimakan as his minion, guide and counsellor. Next was…"

Princess Aspess interrupted him. "We do not have time for one of your sermons, Quaester, get to the point."

The Empress looked at the nearest Hammer Knight. "If he has not told me of the fate of Ahrimakan by the time I am seated on my throne, you are to crush his skull, or you will be fed alive to Erespatagor."

Karkson winced inwardly again. Although he needed Mazdek to make a mistake, he also knew that it would require tact from the Empress in how she dealt with it. He sensed it would not be wise in the current atmosphere for her to have Mazdek harmed. That would test and strain the loyalty of the Hammer Knights too far. She was better having him taken back to a cell so that any punishment could be administered secretly and the consequences carefully managed afterwards. *Tread carefully, my Sarissa*, he said to himself whilst trying to catch her attention with his eyes in an attempt to warn her.

The knight shuffled uneasily on his feet, looking around him for someone to give him direction or support. None looked him in the eye, they looked as uncertain as he did. If he disobeyed his Empress, he indirectly broke his sacred oath to her, and would be punished immediately. If he struck the High Quaester, he equally broke another sacred oath made directly to the Aeldar and the punishments for that were equally harsh.

"My Sarissa," Mazdek protested. "This body does need to be replaced and a visit to the Deadlands will rid me of this old shell and give me a new and more youthful one, but we do not have the luxury that I spend time in the Deadlands, for each passing moment we delay, the Simal may get further away."

"You make a valid point," the Empress said as she paused on the steps, and briefly turned her head. Glancing at the knight, she ordered him. "You will break one of his legs, and then the other, if I am not satisfied with the information I have, by the time I am seated. You will then crush his loins so that the temple whores might get a night's rest."

Turning her head away, she began to slowly and purposefully ascend the dais step by step towards the throne. For the first time Mazdek looked uncomfortable.

*That threat has unsettled the old buzzard*, Karkson thought to himself, but the situation gave him no amusement. He watched and observed as the knight who had been given the order, looked around again at his companions for guidance as what to do. They stared impassively back, giving nothing away, though some gripped the shafts of their two-handed war-hammers even more tightly. Karkson instinctively felt that they would not allow any harm to come to their High Quaester. He looked at those standing around the throne to try to gauge their thoughts. Marnir and Renlak were standing there impassively, also giving nothing away, though Karkson knew their loyalties lay with Mazdek. Regineo, Aspess and Caspus seemed as oblivious and as unaware as their mother of the secret undercurrents flowing through the hall.

*They are so corrupted with the arrogance of power, they do not even see when it is seeping away from them,* Karkson thought.

When Mazdek composed himself and finally spoke, before the Empress had reached the top steps, his words were calm and serene.

"My Sarissa, the unsullied light of the Simal can only summon an Aeldar from Hammerfell when the Aeldar Riddle that is attached to them is known and contained within the Simal." He coughed and cleared his throat.

"Only an Arkoom can slay the body of an Aeldar, and only an Arzak powerful enough can imprison the spirit of such a sacred god. The one used in the assassination attempt was lost in the Sacred Deep." He glanced at Marnir, "A fate our Inquisitor nearly shared, had not one of the knights pulled him from the precipice."

"Get to the point," Regineo snapped.

"My Sarissa, Ahrimakan was not fully physical when the Arkoom was thrust into him. It might be that he is not imprisoned within the Arzak at all, but that his spirit has returned to Hammerfell. Even if he were, by some small chance, trapped within the Arzak, on the day Thuranotos rises, he, the mightiest of the Aeldar, can recall him from it." Mazdek coughed, and then continued. "This makes our quest to find the location of the other Aeldar Wives, even more urgent, but even above that, we must find and return the Simal. No sacrifice should be considered too small, no plan too daring, for this aim must be our top priority. We must sacrifice what we must, and consider the cost a mere offering we give to the Aeldar, who will recompense us fully when they return, and know we made it possible."

Shaka reached the top step of the dais, turned and sat calmly upon the throne. The knight she had ordered looked uneasily at Mazdek, and then nervously at her for guidance.

"Then you are convinced the attempt on Ahrimakan's life failed?" she asked expectantly.

Mazdek nodded his head elatedly. "Those who planned this atrocity are not as versed in the ways of the Aeldar as they think. Ahrimakan might still be returned to us. Either way, all is not lost."

"He can be summoned again?" Shaka breathlessly asked, as she stood to her feet, anticipation and hope spreading across her previously twisted features. "Then you must go to Hammerfell, to discover if he has returned there."

"With respect, my Sarissa, that would take far more time than we have, for the journey is very, very long. Our top priority must be to find the Simal, and when we do, we can attempt to summon him again. That way, we can discover his fate, and make our plans to discover the riddle that can summon Thuranotos. Either way, Ahrimakan will one day be returned to you."

Shaka's mouth twitched for several moments, and then she breathed a huge sigh of relief. "This news is pleasing to me," she exclaimed. The tension in the throne hall seemed to lessen as excited whispers broke out among all present. The knight who had been given the order to break Mazdek's legs visibly relaxed, the anxious strain on his face lifting instantly.

"But without the Simal, we can no longer summon Thuranotos to this world, even if we had his Riddle. You have lost the Simal," Shaka shrieked with fresh venom in her voice. The tension in the room heightened once more. "Tell me why I should delay your next journey to the Deadlands? As long as it takes, should you not visit the Void, travel to Hammerfell and consult with the Aeldar to seek their will? Others can find and return the Simal."

Mazdek slowly shook his head. "We both know what the will of the Aeldar is. To execute it, I am needed here, in the land of the living. You know that of which I speak; the time has now come, for us to execute the plan Ahrimakan revealed to us, my Sarissa."

Her mood switched in an instant, and Shaka suddenly looked visibly uncertain. "It would be a bold move, full of risk," she suggested hesitantly and less angrily.

In all of his years of service to her, Karkson had never seen Shaka look so tentative.

"Perhaps the words that must now be spoken, are for the ears of the Privy Council alone," Mazdek replied measuredly.

"Such a move risks taking the Empire down a dangerous path," Shaka said with an air of distrust, ignoring his request to dismiss the imperial court. "Ahrimakan told us he would let us know when the time for such an action was at hand. Without him to guide us and give us the will and wisdom of Thuranotos, we cannot take such a risk. Now we have lost the Simal, we cannot summon the other two Aeldar whose Riddles are known, or seek their direct counsel on the matter."

"What hope have you to crush the enemies that lurk in the shadows, whispering their vile rebellions, poisoning the minds of the people, whilst they wait for an opportune time to clench their fist and raise it against your royal person?" Mazdek asked. "The will of Ahrimakan has been spoken to us both; I am ready to obey him, but can you find the courage to do so as well, my Sarissa?"

A slight but audible gasp rose up from many in the hall. Mazdek's words were bold and audacious. "Now is surely the time," he urged.

"Explain the reason you allow such discourtesy to leave your lips when addressing the Empress?" Regineo snarled, his face contorting with barely supressed rage.

Mazdek continued in a calm and measured manner, looking only at the Empress.

"I am the greatest Seer of our age," he said, somewhat arrogantly as he became more animated, raised his hands, and slowly turned in a full circle so he could address all in the hall. "I was the one who first revealed to you all that the Aeldar Gods existed. I showed you they could be summoned, a feat I proved to you all. Several moons ago, whilst in physical form, Ahrimakan himself confirmed to me, the time would soon be here, when our loyalty would be tested, and to do the will of Thuranotos would require bold and decisive decisions. The *Prophecy of Karthal* must come to pass, and we are the ones who will make it happen!" He finished his circled turn, lowered his arms, and again looked directly at the Empress. He closed his eyes, lowered his head and said solemnly.

"The destiny of our Empire hangs on a knife-edge. The world itself stands on the edge of chaos, and is falling into deep shadows."

He slowly looked up, opening his eyes, and Karkson could tell they were full of sly deceit. *If he says anything, that I am confident is a lie, I will challenge him to be tested by the Jewel of Baramir. If he speaks true though, it is I who will suffer.*

Mazdek pointed to his chest and tapped it several times for emphasis as his voice reached near frantic proportions. "I only want to see you elevated to where you truly belong, my Sarissa, and for the Aeldar to take their rightful place as they walk once again within the Everglow." He dropped to his knees, pleadingly. "For that to happen, you must surely know the time is now right to implement Ahrimakan's instruction and to see *Karthal's Prophecy* fulfilled."

Karkson felt alarmed that he was unaware as to exactly what Mazdek was proposing. He could tell that both princes, and the princess, also shared a similar confusion as they looked at each other with questioning looks.

At that moment, the Serveri who had been sent to fetch the throwing star that had killed one of the Hammer Knights the evening before, returned, holding the star, which was wrapped in a thick, red cloth.

"Give it to me," Mazdek ordered, holding out his hand and beckoning impatiently as he stood to his feet, "and all will become clear."

The Serveri looked at Regineo who ordered, "Give it to him."

The Serveri handed the cloth to Mazdek, who carefully un-wrapped the star from it, whilst warily still using the cloth to carefully hold it in the palm of his hand.

"I possess a certain gift that few Seers have. Only in the Deadlands can this rare knowledge be learnt. It is not something to be acquired or passed on here in the land of the living, nor can it be taught, for the method used cannot be explained in the words of any language known in this world. I shall speak Báith Rahmèra!"

A hushed gasp arose from the assembled nobles.

Mazdek raised his hand and held the star up high. "I am the only Seer who can discover the secrets and memory this weapon has. To access its secret, I need Manroth, my Seers' Ring," Mazdek said as he looked at Karkson, pointed at him and with a hint of accusation and anger hissed, "he ordered it to be taken from me."

By the way Shaka looked at him, Karkson knew he was on dangerous ground, even though the accusation was false. He adopted an apologetic tone, even though he felt indignant at the unfounded accusation. "These are powerful objects, my Sarissa. The prison guards took it from him as a precaution, an order not given by me. It was only handed to me when, by your imperial order, I arrived to escort him here. I have it with me."

"Then give it to him!" Shaka ordered, impatiently.

Karkson took the ring out of his pocket and slipped it on the finger that Mazdek held out in anticipation. Mazdek gazed at it as though reunited with a lost friend, and then looked at the Empress.

"We know the Seer who betrayed us, my Sarissa. Her name is Janorra, a low-born Pure-blood. She is highly skilled and a great Seeress with many powers that few possess. Her knowledge is vast and her powers strong, she had reached the Ninth Order, but even so, there is much that she still does not know, and that we may count as our good fortune."

"Why would a Seeress who has attained such a high level betray us?" Aspess demanded. "Was she not treated kindly within the confines of the Argona Temple and the secret Mystery Schools? What would lead to such devious and malicious treachery from one who has been taught and given so much?"

Mazdek looked uncomfortable as he shuffled on his feet. "Such matters are best forgotten, my Sarissa," he said, addressing the Empress.

"You know the cause of her betrayal but will not speak of it?" Aspess asked indignantly.

"Speak, and do not hold back, whatever the cause may be," Shaka ordered.

Mazdek closed his eyes, took a deep breath and then opened them. He reluctantly said, "Very well, as you wish. She was known to you, my Sarissa. She was once an actress of rising fame within our Empire. Her stage name was *Elfonia Elfie Ancient-clan*.

71

She wrote the famous play *The Legend of the Last Elf*, and won much acclaim throughout the land performing many of the mythic elf-legends of the forgotten cities."

"I remember that play," Shaka said. "What happened to her? It has been many lifetimes since that play has been performed here."

Karkson was surprised Shaka had forgotten, and he could tell, by the way he raised his eyebrows, that Mazdek was also surprised she did not recall the incident.

After a pause, Mazdek asked, "You have forgotten what happened, my Sarissa? No matter. It is not important."

"I remember," Regineo said. "She was summoned along with her troupe of actors to perform here in Kappia at the Royal Amphitheatre, in your presence, mother. She performed the play *The Lost Child of the Lake*, as well as *The Legend of the Last Elf*.

"She won much acclaim and praise from all who saw the plays, even from you, my Sarissa," Mazdek exclaimed.

Regineo's face twisted with hate. "It was the time when the Royal Privy Council had ordered the Senate to pass the *Edict of Varscal*, to make it illegal for Pure-bloods to marry or be in marriage to Fell-bloods or Half-bloods."

Karkson also remembered that time, although he had only been a Praetorian Guard with low rank. The incident had disturbed him greatly. He had always remembered the treatment of the unfortunate actress Janorra who, after performing, had been summoned along with the rest of the cast to the very hall they stood in, to be complimented for their performance. Unwittingly, she had caused great offence to the Empress.

At the time, Varscal, a scholar of some note, had called for action against the genetically undesirable. His teachings had gained much renown in Kappia, where he had taught that it was absurd to selectively breed horses and sheep, and improve the stock of pigs and fowls, whilst Pure-blood Akkadians were allowed to marry and mate in the most heedless of manner with Fell-bloods and Half-bloods. He had stated that the children of such marriage polluted the purity of the ancient Akkadian bloodlines, and that is why even the Obelisks considered any not of Pure-blood unfit to resurrect. He had taught that Half-bloods, were mostly moral delinquents, and had been the cause of much of the strife and chaos in the world. He had declared that the Fell-bloods, those with not even one parent of pure Akkadian blood, were mostly the poor, the drunkards, the gluttons and the lazy, and had crippled the Empire financially due to their inability to produce wealth. The fact that many Fell-bloods and even Half-bloods at the time were some of the wealthiest merchants had gone mostly ignored. His edict resulted in them being taxed heavily, some even had their wealth taken from them and given to more deserving families of Pure-bloods. It had become fashionable at the time for the noble families, to gather around them the finest specimens of Pure-blood humanity and to make sure they guarded the bloodlines.

Even though the Senate had not made any decision on the edict proposed by Varscal, nor had the Assembly yet voted on the matter, everyone knew it was a foregone conclusion that all marriages to any but Pure-bloods would be dissolved, as the court of public opinion among the nobility in Kappia had decided that it would be so, mostly because Shaka herself was in favour of it. When summoned before the Empress to be commended for her performance, the poor actress Janorra, unaware of this, introduced her co-lead, as also being her husband. He was a Half-blood. It had caused grievous offence to many nobles and the royal family, and Shaka had considered it a direct insult, even though the unfortunate woman had no idea about the teachings of Varscal, as it was an idea and proposal that was only floating around the noble and political upper-classes of Kappian society. Her fate was sealed when, under fierce and angry questioning, the Empress had discovered the woman was carrying a Half-blood child.

Regineo's face curled with contempt. "She was married to some Half-blood fool, whose name I forget. Had we not acted and punished her, she would have been another one polluting our society and bloodlines with their Half-breed spawn." He spat in disgust. The spit landed on the floor below the dais and was quickly cleaned up by one of the Serveri, using the sleeve of his robe.

"This was the cause of her offence, that she was punished for this?" Aspess asked incredulously. "How pathetic she would betray us, over an illegal marriage to a Half-blood who she could only know for one lifetime."

Karkson felt a wave of guilt flood through him. He had been one of the guards who, under orders, had thrown Janorra into prison, and then later was commanded to drag the terrified woman to Regineo's chambers, where he dreaded to think what atrocities she had endured.

"That alone was not the cause," Mazdek exclaimed, and then hesitated before continuing. "My Sarissa, you took offence that she brought a Half-blood into the royal presence, that is true, yet her husband was a man of exceptional beauty."

Karkson knew that Mazdek dare not finish the sentence, though the insinuation was there. Karkson remembered that the Empress had desired the Half-blood. He had been summoned to her bedchamber and had never been seen again. The fact they could never see the irony of such situations, and the hypocrisy the imperial family showed, was always a source of bewilderment to him.

Aspess understood the insinuation, and took deep offence, but not at Mazdek. "She should have felt privileged the Empress honoured her in this way. It is disgraceful she felt more for a lowly Half-blood than she did her Empress," she declared in disbelief.

"I do not recall these events, it is too many lifetimes ago," Shaka pronounced with a cruel impatience. "But that does not explain how she became a Seeress or why she would betray her own kind and most of all me, her Empress? It sounds like she was a person of most vile character."

Mazdek looked clearly uncomfortable. He took a deep breath. "She had not experienced her *First-death*, she was young, it was her first lifetime, she was a *Firstling*. When it was discovered she was a Seeress, we had an obligation to train her in the Theostar and the Mystery Schools. I felt the punishment she had already received, had satisfied the imperial wrath and justice."

"What was her just punishment?" Shaka asked.

Karkson remembered that what had happened to Janorra had been anything but just. Shaka's then body was old and withered and she had taken exception to Janorra's beauty. He remembered the punishment, and looked at Mazdek and wondered if he dared to remined Shaka of it.

"You gifted her to Prince Regineo," Mazdek announced.

Karkson felt shame at the memory. Regineo had been deeply attracted to the beautiful actress Janorra. He and his closest friends had defiled and disfigured her in the most unpleasant of ways, and as a result she lost the child in her womb. When they grew bored of entertaining themselves with her, they sent her to the dungeons, where she was executed and sent to the Deadlands in the cruellest of manners.

Turning to Regineo, the Empress appeared unconcerned. "I am sure she was treated well by my son, despite her crimes, and given a merciful *First-death*."

"She was executed humanely," Regineo said dishonestly, "and taught not to repeat such a mistake in her future lifetimes."

Once again Karkson felt sick at the hypocrisy. The way the imperial family could commit their foul deeds openly, and then lie in front of the imperial court, without blushing with shame, was a mark of just how degenerate they had all become. However, he also knew there was a method behind it: they knew that knowledge of their deeds created terror and fear in those who were hearing about them, especially as the title they held of *Ivanar*, meant none of them would ever be held to account by law. As much as he treasured the Empire and was oath-bound to the Empress, and even admired, perhaps even loved her for her strength and exquisiteness, he had little respect for all of the intrigue and corruption, and none at all for the many injustices carried out. For all its unrivalled achievements and surpassing splendour, there was an infinitely darker side to the Kappian Empire. Nowhere were the stakes higher, the passions fiercer or the politicking more dangerous and murderous than they were at the very top, in the imperial court. It was a dangerous place to be, even at the best of times, as the poor Janorra had found out.

Karkson recollected how he had felt sickened at the time by the manner in which Janorra had been unjustly treated, but he had never showed it in any expression on his face, nor spoke it with any word, and never even hinted at his true feelings. Even showing sympathy for the plight of somebody the imperial family had turned upon, was considered an act of treason itself. He had stayed silent at the time, and felt the lesser man for it. *I did not realise she had become a Seer, though. I always assumed that upon resurrecting she had been expelled from the city. I understand why she has done what she has done.* Had his own immediate predicament not been so precarious, Karkson might have taken some time to find satisfaction that, in her own way, and after so long, Janorra had found a way to strike back at the imperial family.

Regineo's face flushed red with anger. "She clearly resented our mercy towards her, mother. She now justifies her wickedness and treachery towards the Empire and our royal-selves, because she was sentenced for her own wrongdoings in the past?"

A darkness grew over Shaka's face; her expression became cruel and hard. "When we capture her, we shall not show any mercy. She will suffer for the rest of her lifetimes, until the *Final-death* takes her. Even in the Deadlands the day will come when the Aeldar will punish her for what she has done. What greater crime is there than that of stealing the Simal and plotting to slay my beloved Ahrimakan? She is an abomination." Shaka grimaced as though in pain, and then glared murderously at Mazdek, and with a voice full of indignation, ordered him, "Tell me, why did you allow one of such vulgar virtue to become a Seeress within our very own sacred Argona Temple?"

Mazdek stuttered tentatively before he replied. "It was her *First-death*. On her first resurrection, the Mark of a Seer was upon her. After her first *Awakening*, memory came back to her very quickly. She spoke of many things she had seen in the Deadlands. She had an exceptional gift to *Awaken* quickly, and had such extraordinary clarity and memory of what she had seen and heard, so..." Mazdek hesitated. "It was decided she should train as a Seeress."

"Only you have the authority to allow one to train as such," Regineo said. "Loyalty to the Empire must be uttermost in the hearts of those entrusted with such sacred positions. How did she deceive you and hide such disloyalty in her heart for so long, Quaester?"

"After each *Awakening*, when memory returned, she spoke of nothing but love and loyalty towards you, my Sarissa. She said she understood how she had embarrassed you by marrying a Half-blood."

"Her words were false?" Aspess asked resentfully.

74

"Of course, they were. She was an actress, and clearly Mazdek could not see through her deceit," Regineo exclaimed with an air of contempt and disgust.

Mazdek looked solemn. "I now fear she must have met somebody, or something in the Deadlands who told her to practice deceit on her return to the living. Always, she swore loyalty to you, and never had she given the slightest reason to doubt her sincerity…until now."

"Should then, the Eye of Morsef be used to test the sincerity of all Seers from now on?" Aspess asked.

Mazdek looked at Marnir and the staff he held. "When the Eye of Morsef opens in the Jewel of Baramir, and looks upon one, it considerably shortens the number of lifetimes even of innocent Pure-bloods, and those of the accuser, be the accusation true or false. Such a test should be used only in the gravest of circumstances."

"These circumstances are not grave enough?" Aspess asked incredulously.

"With hindsight, yes, princess," Mazdek replied, "but not once, on any occasion, did we ever have reason to doubt her devotion. On appearances, she was a loyal and ardent servant to the Aeldar, and never once complained, nor ever uttered a word against the imperial family. We had no good reason to test her."

When Marnir spoke, his voice was grim, and he spoke in defence of Mazdek. "When the Eye of Morsef looks upon this world, it might demand truth to be spoken, by any present, so careful selection is made of those who shall be assembled. It takes a special council time, to prepare for a test, and they must be willing to have the number of their lifetimes shortened." Marnir looked at Shaka. "The High Quaester is correct, such tests, using such power, should only ever be carried out when there is good reason for it to be so."

Mazdek seized on the glimmer of reprieve, and looked at Shaka. "I never had any reason to suspect the Seeress Janorra had ever spoken falsely, my Sarissa. Had I even once, been given reason to doubt her words, I would not have hesitated to have had her tested."

"You were deceived fool," Regineo yelled with barely concealed rage. "The great Quaester deceived all this time by a common whore of an actress."

Karkson noticed the respectful demeanour of Mazdek was starting to lift. He observed by the twitch of Mazdek's mouth, that wrath instead of uneasiness was taking its place. He noticed something he had not seen in him before. A dark and ancient rage twisted his features for the mere flicker of a second, before he regained his composure. Mazdek responded serenely, but cautiously.

"The fault is entirely mine," Mazdek replied. "You are right my royal prince for I was deceived by her, yet she could not have made such an audacious plan by herself. This is why we need to unlock the memory of this Assassin's Star. I can discover her co-conspirators." He looked at Shaka. "Let me make amends, my Sarissa?"

"Then enough words and be about it," Shaka ordered scathingly. "My Aspess carries an Arkith, and old is the Arzak crafted into its hilt. With it she will send you to your *Final-death* if what you present does not offer solution to this crisis. Your existence in this world hangs in the balance, High Quaester."

Mazdek nodded. "I think you will not be disappointed, my Sarissa."

His words were reassuring, but the general noticed that Mazdek himself once more looked angry. He clearly did not take kindly to being threatened with the *Final-death* in front of the imperial court.

Foolishly, Karkson noted, the Empress was seeking to remind everybody of her authority. Karkson glanced sideways, and could tell by the way they scowled and gripped their weapons that the Hammer Knights present, did not appreciate the threat against their High Quaester. They looked uneasy and uncertain. Karkson quickly weighed up the odds, and in that moment, made a decision. *It might be a rash and foolish move on her part, but it might be the only chance to save the Empire from Mazdek. I have to time it perfectly – I must urge the Empress to order his Final-death, in secret, later, today. I think the Hammer Knights will do nothing immediately, as they will be leaderless for a while. That will give me time to recall the legions to Kappia and prevent a civil war among the Kappian faction. Even if war comes, the legions will back the Empress, and we will prevail.*

Mazdek held the star, resting on the cloth, in the palm of his hand. He held up his right hand upon which he wore *Manroth*, and then looked at all around him. "My Sarissa, a lesser skilled Seer would take many hours, days, months, or even years to sift through all of the memories contained within this object, before they found that which is of importance for our situation. I have the skill to find what we need in a very short time, but I require full concentration, and no sound must be made." He slowly turned in a slow, full circle as he again looked at all around himself, and then at Shaka. "Despite the marvel I will display, with your permission, my Sarissa, none shall speak until I am done. If I find a memory and it is disturbed during the process, it may become distorted, and even I may not be able to get it back in a pure form. All present must quietly watch and listen until the memory is told."

"Understood," the Empress said. "None shall speak."

Mazdek stared intensely at the star. He cautiously lowered it and placed it upon the ground. *"Mazouk, mazouk, hashayesay,"* he whispered. Everyone gasped, even Karkson himself, as the star rose slowly into mid-air of its own accord. *"Hashayesay mortol enkarno."* The star slowly began to rotate mid-air, as if being turned by an unseen hand. It stopped when a light connected it to the ring on Mazdek's finger. Images began to form in the air around it, until they took almost solid form.

Everybody in the throne room stayed silent, clearly in awe at the unusual spectacle as they watched the forms talk and move. A ruggedly handsome man hammered at metal upon a forge. Sparks flew and with each blow the metal began to take the form of a star. A robed man, dark against the orange glow of the forge, watched him and then spoke. His voice was noble and calm.

"Your skill grows, my young apprentice. Shaping the metal is the easiest part. It requires greater skill to tip it with dragon steel and coat it with toxins that will be deadly to the touch of human skin, but I think you are ready, young Azzadan, for me to teach you this new skill."

"It is knowledge I crave, Master Ithkall," the man named Azzadan replied, after which the image faded away.

"Ithkall met the *Final-death* long ago, his order was banished and the last of them hunted down and destroyed," Regineo objected. "You cannot be suggesting they had a part in what happened?"

"Quiet!" Mazdek shouted crossly. "There is more to see. You will disturb the memories and they will be lost."

Regineo glared indignantly at Mazdek, but after his mother frowned at him, he stayed silent.

*"Hashayesay mortol enkarno,"* Mazdek said again. The star rotated once more, stopping when light from the ring connected to it once again. More images began to emerge. A musty scholar's laboratory filled with shelves of dusty tomes, scrolls and phials filled or half-filled with varying liquids of differing colour appeared. Azzadan, wearing black leathered armour, stood and laughed at a man cowering in the corner. "You have it," the man said with a quavering voice. "You know the location of the Arkoom. I am just

a Half-blood, if you slay me, I have no resurrection. I have given you what you want, I beg you for mercy."

Azzadan, now a decade older than in the first image, unmercifully laughed at the man's pleas. In one hand Azzadan held a scroll, neatly rolled up. With his other, he pulled the star from beneath his cloak. "I need to practice my aim old man," he said laughingly, as he threw the star, hitting the man in the neck. In an instant, the man's neck and face swelled up and turned a sickly green. Death followed quickly afterwards. The image began to fade as Azzadan, grinning callously, walked over to the dead man and retrieved the star. The image disappeared.

Once more the star turned, but in a different direction, until it again connected with light that came from Mazdek's ring, *Manroth*. A woman entered a small room. Looking out into the corridor beyond, she checked nobody was around and shut the door behind her. Azzadan appeared, from ethereal form. He spoke. "All is in place. The day of your vengeance is near, Janorra. The Baothein have promised you safe sanctuary, if the Simal is brought to them."

In the image, the woman Janorra stared at Azzadan for a brief moment. When she spoke, her voice was uncertain. "On the first day of Lupoor, be ready. I will take the Simal, you will slay Ahrimakan, that monstrosity she loves."

Karkson noticed the Empress was barely containing her rage as she fidgeted on the throne, but she stayed silent, her gaze fixed to the star as it turned once more, again in a different direction, and again until the light connected to it. More images appeared. Azzadan was sat at a long silver table, surrounded by robed men and women, and one, a woman of immeasurable beauty. She was dressed in white and wearing a crown that shone so radiantly it awed the eye even in the vision. "I secretly enter the Argona Temple in Kappia tomorrow," Azzadan said to the woman. "The Seeress is nervous, but I am confident she will follow through on the plan."

The woman spoke, her voice gentle and melodic. "My greatest Seeress, has met her in the Deadlands, and much they have discussed. The woman Janorra has knowledge which will aid us in the downfall of the evil germ who rules in Kappia." She turned her head and addressed the others around the table. "We have still to secure the alliance of the Lord of the Northern city of Aleskian, Captain General Borach. Much aid he can give us in causing the House of Shakawraith to fall. We will convince him to side with us in our war against the Kappians. He will swear blood-oaths to me."

The light from the ring on Mazdek's finger went out, and the star fell to the floor with a clatter. Many people in the throne room gasped and began to murmur at the images they had seen and the words that had been spoken.

Karkson wanted to speak, to assure the Empress of the unquestioning loyalty of his friend, Lord Borach towards her, but he could not find the right words quickly enough. Shaka screamed with a primeval roar that sent a shiver down the spine of even the stoutest heart. She stood from the throne and fell to her knees and screamed, "Treachery! Treachery! Long have I suspected that mongrel in Aleskian of treachery and here is the proof." She turned towards Karkson and pointed at him accusingly. "You defended him at every turn, swore he never spoke of ill plans against me!"

Karkson felt a tremor of fear rush through him, but he somehow found his voice. "I will gladly face the test, by the Jewel of Baramir, if any dare to call me liar," he answered, in disbelief at all he was hearing. "I swear, my Sarissa, not once have any utterances of betrayal ever passed the lips of Lord Borach in my presence. The images do not show that the Baothein actually made approaches to him, if they had, he would have reported it immediately. He is loyal to you, I swear."

The Empress, whimpering with rage, took some deep breaths, but did not calm. "Your judgement is ill if you could not see the treachery lurking behind his false smiles and treacherous words."

"The images, they are not proof that he betrayed you, my Sarissa." Karkson pleaded. He noticed Mazdek smiling smugly next to him.

"Have myself, and Lord Borach tested by the Eye of Morsef, my Sarissa," Karkson said. "I swear to you, he is loyal!"

"Get out! Everybody out! All except my Privy Council leave the imperial court!" Shaka bellowed.

The nobles did not wait to be told twice. It did not take long for the throne hall to empty. They made swift exit, followed by the Hammer Knights. The Serveri were the last to leave, along with the maids. Karkson briefly caught the eye of his daughter, Myrene. She gave him a brief look of alarm and concern, but departed in silence.

*      *      *

Mazdek was grinning inwardly when he accompanied the Empress Shaka into the Council Chamber. Marnir, Renlak, the Imperial Treasurer, a man named Staris and the Imperial Secretary named Bothir, and Shaka's three children, were seated around the large conference table waiting for them. Two guards stood by the door.

When he and Shaka were seated, inwardly Mazdek smiled even more smugly when Shaka turned to him and said, "We discovered much from the Assassin's Star. We know who helped the Seeress, and the loyalty of those who lead my legions has been brought into question. We need to move decisively to undo this treachery."

"A matter I have for some time warned you about," Mazdek answered. "It is now surely the time to remove these corrupt nobles from their military office and have the legions disbanded and subjugated under the careful watch of the Hammer Knights. Not only do we have proof the Baothein have corrupted Lord Borach, they are in league with the Order of Ithkall, a morally diseased band of thieves we believed long ago vanquished and removed from within our Empire."

Shaka turned her head and looked at Renlak, who, with just a glance from her knew the information she required. "Ithkall and his Order are now known only to memory. They were destroyed during the great purge. It is not possible their Order still exists."

"Renlak is genuine in his belief, but wrong, my Sarissa," Mazdek interjected. "The Baothein must have found exiled members of this Order and hired them. The one in the image, Azzadan, is the same one who tried to slay Ahrimakan. I saw him with my own eyes before I was knocked unconscious. This plot runs very deep. Of most concern, is Lord Borach, who from now on should be known as the *Betrayer*. Such a powerful Lord siding with the Baothein is dangerous, very dangerous for us!"

"Who is the Seeress who met with this Janorra in the Deadlands, the one the false Queen of Baothein referred to?" Aspess asked.

Mazdek coughed uncomfortably. "Long has she been a bane to us in the Deadlands. It is even rumoured she is of ancient Elven descent, though it goes back many generations, but such a suggestion is surely a lie. Her name is Ashara. She is a Seeress of no small power and trickery. Long have we hunted her in the Deadlands with little success. Only now, through the memories of the star, have I discovered she has been the link between the Baothein and the traitor Janorra in the Deadlands."

Renlak advised, "Should we not immediately send ravens and messengers to the furthest reaches of the Empire, even to Bruthon lands, to search for this Janorra? Great reward should be offered for her capture and the return of the Simal!"

Aspess suggested sombrely, "Surely she will be safe in Baothein lands with the Simal by now? We have not the strength to assail them. The Simal is lost to us."

Regineo looked at his mother angrily. "In addition to seeking the recapture of the Seeress, we must punish Aleskian and the traitor Borach. He must be immediately arrested."

"Borach sits in Aleskian surrounded by those loyal to him," Aspess said. "If they are sided with the Baothein, they would not allow his arrest; we need to be craftier in our approach to unseat him from Aleskian."

Mazdek again coughed to clear his throat. "My Sarissa, when the assassin and the Seeress attacked Ahrimakan and took the Simal, to leave the Chamber of Summoning, they opened up Jula portals to escape. These are well known to the princes and princess who liberally use up the rare and expensive phials it takes to open these portals, in the pursuit of their hunting Davari for sport. Prince Caspus is a particular expert in them."

"It is Juram we mostly use," Aspess said, correcting him.

Caspus fumbled nervously at the rope about his waist, but said nothing.

"Jula or Juram. I would respectfully council you stop using them for royal entertainments, and now put those few we might acquire, to wiser use," Mazdek urged.

Aspess openly snarled her displeasure at Mazdek, as did Regineo. "You overstep the mark," she warned, as she fingered the Arkith sheathed in her belt.

*You are a fool. They are too rare and precious to be wasted on hunting Davari for sport.* Mazdek ignored her and continued. "My counsel is that we do not send out ravens and messengers informing the Empire that the Simal is lost. The land and sky are perilous in these times and many would not make it. Those that did would bear news only of our vulnerability. We know the trouble the news of the loss of the Simal has caused here in Kappia. This trouble will spread if the news reaches the rest of the Empire. Faith in the Aeldar is still relatively new, and it might be shaken beyond repair unless we act wisely. The rebellious factions in Bruthon might be given new courage to rise up."

Aspess spoke to her mother. "Many people, witnessed the calamity that has overtaken us. It has been openly discussed here today. We cannot stop all ravens from leaving the city, bearing this ill news. Traders and trade caravans leaving the city, will also have such tasty chatter on the tips of their tongues, ready to wag them towards any listening ear. If we cannot prevent the news from spreading, we must control and change that which is spread."

Mazdek sneered slyly at Aspess. "You are your mother's daughter. Wisdom drips from your tongue. We must make a declaration at the rise of the morning sun tomorrow, that the Seeress has been caught, and the Simal returned to us."

Aspess nodded in agreement. "It will not be that hard for the royal jewellers to make something that resembles the Simal. We can parade it through the city along with some wretch that resembles this woman, Janorra. We can silence the wretch and send her to a public *Final-death*. We then announce the matter is dealt with, and new measures have been taken to ensure such a calamity never befalls us again."

Regineo scoffed. "What good is any of this if we do not have the real Simal? It is still lost to us and safe in Baothein lands by now." He looked at his mother. "Your sister, the false Queen of the Baothein, will boast she has it. If she publicly shows it and the Seeress, any lies we tell will be exposed."

Shaka looked at Renlak. "What would you suggest?"

Renlak took a deep breath. "Our treaty with the Bruthon is fragile. Their lands still simmer with rebellion. The Bruthon King has failed to regain control of the rebel provinces north of the Erin, led by the House of Anthain."

"What do you counsel?" Shaka asked him impatiently. "Not what Karkson would," Renlak said. "I spoke to him before entering here. He suggests we return several legions to the capital and the major cities, to keep the peace. His advice is that we limit the role of the Hammer Knights to the Argona Temple and send the rest to their sacred mountain, to meditate and reflect on how they have failed you so badly. He suggests that there, they can choose a new High Quaester."

"What would he have us do with Mazdek?" Shaka asked.

Renlak lowered his eyes apologetically when he looked at Mazdek. "Karkson is a fool, High Quaester," he said. "He wanted to urge the *Final-death* be given to you."

Mazdek supressed the simmering rage the words evoked within him, which was easier to do, due to the fact that Shaka had accepted his advice to not allow Karkson to be present in the meeting until decisions had been reached. "Karkson offers no solutions," he snapped.

Shaka again looked at Mazdek, "That might be, but I asked Renlak to discuss this with the general." She turned to Renlak. "What did Karkson suggest about how the Simal might be returned?"

Renlak looked warily at Mazdek. "I present Karkson's view, not my own," he said. Then addressing the room, he continued. "Karkson would immediately send out every Griffin Rider to hunt for her. He proposed if she lacks more Jula, she might still be travelling in the wilderness or crossing the disputed zone, for the journey to Baothein lands is far on foot, and even by horse. The general hopes she might still be found." Renlak looked nervously at Shaka. "Karkson suggested that if she has already made it to Baothein lands, we should negotiate peace with them, using their ancestral lands in the disputed areas as leverage, and insisting they return the Simal and the Seeress as part of any treaty."

"A foolish notion," Mazdek interjected. "The Baothein would have planned how to quickly get the Simal into their territory, after they took so much trouble to help the Seeress steal it."

"I agree," Renlak quickly said.

"Does the advice Karkson offers, not sound like the words a friend of the Baothein, and Lord Borach, would speak?" Mazdek asked. "General Karkson wants us to search in the wrong place, hand over lands to our enemy, and have the *Aeldar Faith* destroyed by disbanding those most loyal to them and to you, my Sarissa?" Mazdek held his hand out in a gesture that implored Shaka. "My Sarissa, the general is deceiving you, hence my request for him to be denied access to this meeting. He is displaying his ignorance and knows nothing. His traitorous tongue should be forever silenced."

"Explain your reasons for thinking this!" Shaka ordered Mazdek.

Mazdek smirked knowingly. "Karkson is trying to mislead you, my Sarissa. The Simal is not in Baothein lands, but somewhere in the Tarenmoors, or possibly even in Bruthon realms."

Regineo's eyes widened. "Why do you think this?" he demanded.

The expressions of Shaka and all the others in the room showed they were just as surprised by the revelation.

Mazdek looked conceitedly at Marnir. "Tell them," he ordered.

Marnir bowed his head respectfully. "Some of us Seers have the ability to use our rings to slow down time. It is something we can only do very occasionally for it drains us of energy and life, and the ring, of its power for a time. The effect lasts for only a few seconds. I had the wit to do this when the traitors were making their escape, as I clung on to the precipice. At such times I myself cannot move or act with speed, but I can observe. The assassin teleported west, no doubt to Baothein lands; the Seeress with her assistant, unintentionally went south-west with the Simal. A Jula Portal is only meant for one to pass through it. Two going through, interrupted the process and the course that had been planned."

Mazdek grew excited. "Not by her own will, she went south-westerly into the Tarenmoors or maybe as far as Bruthon lands, not into Baothein ones."

"I saw the Jula Portal open at the other end in a vast forest. It is possible she may be in a place called the Wytchwood," Marnir said. "I informed the High Quaester of this when I visited him in his cell earlier this morning, before you summoned him."

Regineo's eyes widened even more. "If those who are disloyal to us in those lands get the Simal, they may sell it to the Baothein, or worse, use it for their own ends. We should offer reward, gold, titles, lands and whatever it takes for it to be returned back to us."

A baffled expression crossed Aspess' face as she spoke. "The two wretches intended for sacrifice; they were a part of the scheme?"

Marnir shook his head. "No, I do not think so my princess. The one who was killed at the ceremony has resurrected; we have interrogated her; she tells no lie when she protests that she and her sister knew nothing of these plans. To make sure, she will be tested by the Eye of Morsef."

Mazdek sounded triumphant when he spoke. "The Seeress had no intention of taking the assistant with her, for she was supposed to have already been sacrificed at the moment they planned to use the Jula."

"Chance ruined her plan of escape," Renlak said.

"Not chance," Mazdek declared. "Have confidence that Ahrimakan changing the way the ceremony was conducted, has worked for the greater good. The Seeress Janorra has gone to a place not of her choosing, and this is to our advantage, for she is far from the safety of Baothein lands as she planned."

Caspus spoke for the first time. His voice was weak and timid, his manner stuttering. He looked to his mother for reassurance. "Mother, if I go to the Chamber of S...s... summoning, I believe I can accurately trace her path and calculate the possibilities where sh...sh... she might have ended up. If sh...sh... she is in this Wytchwood I can confirm it."

*Idiot! Why have you not already done this?* Mazdek looked at Caspus, who still fidgeted nervously, and swallowing his annoyance, respectfully suggested, "It is possible, but the traces fade with time. You must act soon my prince."

"Then no more delay. You should have thought for yourself and done this at once. Be about it now!" Shaka barked furiously to Caspus who stood, bowed, and nervously ran off to do his mother's bidding.

"Once we find her location, I will seek to find and purchase a Juram, and seek her out myself. Aspess and Caspus shall accompany me," Regineo uttered.

Mazdek slowly shook his head. "My prince, your intentions are noble, but you cannot do this. It is a matter beyond your ability."

Regineo's face distorted with animosity. "You dare to insult me, priest?" he roared.

Shaka frowned disdainfully at her son. "The Quaester is right," she said after a short moment. "You would know this had you paid more attention to the study of such things and attended the temple more frequently to hear the *Lore of the Aeldar* recited."

Regineo was visibly hurt by the remark and stared sulkily at his mother but gave no reply.

Mazdek attempted to smile humbly, but struggled to hide the contempt written on his face as he addressed Regineo. "My prince, for you to attempt to return the Simal through a Jula or even a Juram portal, would result in a catastrophic eruption that would most likely entrap you in realms beyond the reach of any Obelisk. Not even I have the knowledge to carry the Simal in such a manner. It remains a mystery to me how Janorra discovered a way to safely do it. The Jula was altered in some way. I suspect the involvement of one of the Tarath Guëan, perhaps a renegade, for only one of their kind might possess such knowledge."

"We can find that out soon enough," Regineo said, "but then, to get the Simal and capture the Seeress, I will go with a company of Hammer Knights and find them," he declared. "I will physically escort the Simal back myself,"

"Close your jabbering lips," Shaka said, venting out her frustration. "You cannot carry the Simal, you are not trained to do so."

Mazdek stared at Regineo. *You are a fool in the ways of the Aeldar.* "The Empress is right," Mazdek said, feigning humility. "There are few who can cast it away once they have stared into its depths or held it in their hands, my prince. The Simal might turn you insane, perhaps irreversibly so." *I would prefer your insanity over your idiocy.*

"Then there is no use offering any reward for its return?" Aspess asked.

Mazdek shook his head. "If we offered reward, many would seek the Simal, and some might find it, but their lust would be seduced by it. They would keep it hidden, like a crow who steals a diamond for no other reason than to look at it and marvel. The Simal would hold them in its power and take their mind. The Seeress has been trained over many lifetimes to resist its power, or she could not have been a part of the summoning ceremony. Any who find her, and take the Simal from her, will not be tempted by any reward to give it up."

Aspess spoke again. "Then that is another reason why we must prevent people looking for it, by making claim we have retrieved it. Anyone who searches for it, and discovers it, might hide away with it in deep places, where they will live with the induced madness. They might never be discovered."

"You are so wise, princess," Mazdek replied sycophantly.

"Then you must take a company of Hammer Knights and retrieve the Simal?" Regineo asked Mazdek.

"That would not be possible," Mazdek said, and he looked at Renlak suggesting he give the reasons why.

Renlak blinked and then said, "The peace we have with Bruthon is fragile. We could not send a significant force into their territories, without being noticed. It would lead to the civil war being ignited once again."

All present knew that in the Empire it was the role of the Senate to make internal laws, as well as to decide diplomatic and foreign policies. The role of the Assembly was to refine the laws and policies, and then vote on them. The task of the Magistracy was to make sure the laws of the Empire were enforced. The role of any military force was to protect the Empire and only wage any offensive wars if the Empress and Senate agreed for such a war to take place, and even then, only if the Assembly had voted and written the specific aims of the war on a numbered vellum parchment called *A War Scroll.*

"It would be seen as an aggressive act," Renlak said, "and with such tension in Kappia at this time, to enter their lands without a *War Scroll*, would cause too many problems in the Senate. The risk of another war with the Bruthon is neither possible, or sensible."

"In addition, we are almost bankrupt," Staris said.

"War with Bruthon is not the only risk, my Sarissa," Renlak added. "Neglected and drained of troops, most of their lords and barons are cooped up in their castles whilst marauding bands of Chatti, Gragor and Barbarians pillage and loot at will in their lands, fighting over the scraps that remain outside. In their eastern realms, Horse Lords raid, to add to their troubles. We would be hindered every step of the way. It would take months or years of fighting before we could even begin to look for the Simal, and by then, it will be safely within Baothein lands."

Mazdek shook his head and sighed. "I agree with the Hand. It would not be possible for us to send a force to the Wytchwood, if that is where the Simal is. The River Erin is plagued with pirates, we could not travel that way, without paying tolls to the Sea Lords that we cannot afford. The Tarenmoors are wild, broken lands, ruined and desolate in places. Many foul things live there. The Fell-bloods who dwell there are savage and uncivilized, their tribes and kings are untrustworthy and warlike. Many of the Obelisks there are lost. It would not be wise or safe to travel through those lands, either alone or by force, either with the Simal if we were to recover it, or without. The rebel provinces of the Anthain are also blocked to us."

"In essence, my Sarissa," Renlak said, either by land or water, we have no means of reaching the Wytchwood with any significant force, and without risk of war."

"You both present many problems, but offer few solutions," Shaka stated to both men, and then asked everyone. "Does anybody actually have any plan at all as to how we might recover the Simal?" The frustration in her voice was clear.

Regineo answered immediately. "We dispatch a battalion of Griffin Riders, and somebody trained to carry the Simal. They must fly high and swiftly, acting as far as possible, in secret. They can search for Janorra, and the Simal."

*Fool!* Mazdek inwardly scoffed. He tempered his anger when he spoke. "The Simal cannot be carried on any beast. A griffin would go wild and unstable, they would become uncontrollable." *You would know this if you attended temple and listened to my sermons on the topic!"*

"Then we use griffins just to locate her, and the Simal. A small force can then bring her and it back by force, on foot," Regineo suggested.

*Your advice is pitiable, Mazdek wanted to reply condescendingly.* He tempered his response. "Even some of our legions' finest generals counsel against the use of griffins, too many times they have turned even on their own in the heat of battle." He raised a finger expressively. "All of our options present perilous choices, with little chance of success." He looked knowingly at the Empress. "You asked if there was a plan to recover the Simal? Yes, all choices, except one, are taken from us. You know that of which I speak!"

"Would you care to tell us what that is?" Regineo inquired, not bothering to hide either his annoyance or contempt.

Mazdek looked at the Empress and bent over in a pleading manner. "My Sarissa, we must be the agents in fulfilling the *Prophecy of Karthal.* Ahrimakan whispered these same words to you, and is this not the time to see them fulfilled?"

"He did," Shaka answered thoughtfully, "but that path is fraught with risk."

"But Ahrimakan instructed us to do it, surely this is the time for such an action?" Mazdek urged. "For many long nights I have deliberated over this issue. I am convinced now is the time for us to act with courage and determination. It is time for us to bend our wills, and force the fulfilment of the prophecy. It will solve many of our ills, and what time, if not now, would be better, my Sarissa?"

"Would you care to enlighten us as to what this prophecy is?" Regineo petulantly asked.

"Tell them," Shaka ordered, looking directly at Mazdek.

Mazdek cleared his throat. "It is a lengthy text, but the part that concerns us is this: *the betrayal by a powerful man, will lead to the death of an Aeldar, his spirit imprisoned in a different place. Yet all is not lost. All threats shall be dealt with, by one decisive action. Those who are considered enemies, shall become allies, and return that which was taken. The land shall be cleansed of the impure. All filthy bloodlines shall vanish. The Everglow will teeter and shake. The Aeldar who was slain, shall rise when Thuranotos returns."*

"You think this has been partly fulfilled by recent events?" Aspess asked.

"Yes, Lord Borach is the *Betrayer*." Mazdek said, and pointed an accusing finger at the door to the room. "Karkson, who waits outside, knew of his plans."

"The general protests his innocence, should he not be tested before the Eye of Morsef, to see if his tongue spews forth lies?" Aspess inquired.

Mazdek responded immediately. "It would take too long to prepare for the test, and time is a luxury we do not have."

"I have heard enough," Shaka said quietly but firmly. "I grow tired of this endless chattering!" She stared at Mazdek coldly. "We must rid ourselves of the Baothein threat, once and for all. The Empire must be cleansed of all who do not worship the Aeldar and would wish our plans to come afoul. We do not have the numbers in our armies to do it ourselves. The Erin is blocked for trade, we are near to bankruptcy. We are stripped of many choices, only one path seems right for us to take." She had not taken her eyes off of Mazdek as she spoke. "Only in such a desperate time as now, will I consider such a bold plan. Speak of it and let all present hear and reflect!"

"It is the only solution I see to this dilemma," Mazdek stated. He stared accusingly at the door where Karkson waited outside, and then as Shaka. "Do not seek his counsel on this. He will try to dissuade you from the only wise course available to us, and I am convinced he is working with Borach *the Betrayer* to hand Aleskian over to the Baothein."

"What is this plan?" Regineo asked? the frustration showing on his face, "and why is this prophecy so important?"

Mazdek stared in turn, at each person in the room. "Ahrimakan told us of the Prophet of Karthal, who died long ago, during an age now forgotten by all, except the Aeldar. He lived in the Kingdom of Karthal, by which we name him, for nobody knows his original name. He discovered and ascended the Forbidden Mountain, and entered the Tent of Meeting, for he found it abandoned. His life was spent there in meditation and visions, until the last few years, when he returned to Karthal and taught the people day and night about all he had seen and heard in that sacred place."

Mazdek paused, and pointed a finger in the air for emphasis when he continued. "Karthal's final words on his deathbed were strange and cryptic, but the meaning was clear. He spoke of a time that would come, when an empress would become a goddess, and ascend to the Aeldar. Who else could this prophecy refer too, but our Sarissa? She was soon to be anointed as an Aeldar Queen, and still will be."

Mazdek noticed the smug look on Shaka's face, and he smiled inwardly, for flattery always stoked her ego. He continued his speech. "Karthal wrote that before the empress he referred to was elevated to her rightful position, a time of great calamity would come, when all would seem lost. It was then, that the only solution, would be an alliance with those considered most foul." He paused for dramatic effect. "In addition to this, Ahrimakan recently told us, he desires that the Golden Horn of Aleskian must be brought here, to Kappia itself, for the Aeldar desire such a relic in the Argona Temple."

There was a gasp of astonishment from all present, all except Shaka who nodded with slow agreement and a lustful sneer.

"Ahrimakan also instructed us to make an alliance with our foulest enemy, for the old order must be shaken, to make way for the new. He said we would know when the time was right to make such a pact."

"You want us to ally with the Baothein?" Regineo asked, looking confused.

"He means the Bantu," Aspess answered softly, under her breath.

"Preposterous," Regineo instinctively yelled, amidst protests and outcries from all but the Empress, Marnir and Mazdek. "Why would you suggest such a thing?" He looked at Mazdek with astonishment, and then at his mother with the same expression etched on his face. "And why would you even consider such a thing, mother?"

Shaka momentarily looked pensive before she replied. It occurred to Mazdek that he had never seen her looking so uncertain and indecisive as she looked at that brief moment, before her arrogance again dominated her facial expressions. "Ahrimakan himself, ordered me to make an alliance with the Bantu. It is the one thing, I have hesitated to obey him in, but we have already started talks with them. Mazdek has already met with Goth Surien, a Lord of the Bantu."

"What? This is madness," Regineo protested.

"Is it?" Mazdek asked him. "Races of old, chiselled the sides of the mountains straight, this side of the wall, on the other, they carved a deep and waterless ravine. Nobody knows why the work was not finished, but the Baothein lands are protected by those mountains and the gorge. Where the land is flat, Aleskian was built to guard the northern gateway in and out of the Everglow. The Bantu cannot climb the wall, as it is deadly to them, empowered by charms ancient and strong, so at Aleskian they pound it even to this day with the great Braka. To what effect?" He looked at Shaka. "It might be time for General Karkson to join us," he suggested.

"Bring in the general, Shaka ordered one of the guards.

*        *        *

Karkson sat on a cushioned seat outside of the door to the Council Chamber where the Privy Council were meeting. The door was made of a thick wood, so even if it had not been for the guards present outside, with his ear pressed to the door, he would still have heard nothing. It not only wounded his pride that he alone, also a member of the Privy Council, had been excluded, it caused him great concern for he knew that whatever counsel Mazdek was giving, was likely to go unopposed.

The door opened, and one of the guards from inside the room, waved a finger at the general bidding him to enter. Karkson stood, and entered the room. The door shut behind him, and as he walked slowly towards the table where Shaka and the others were seated, he felt like he was a condemned man.

"May I?" he asked Shaka, as he pointed to a chair. She nodded her assent, and he took his seat.

Mazdek spoke instantly when Karkson was seated. "Tell us general! There are cracks in the Great Northern Wall, are there not? The ancient charms start to fail us!"

Karkson sensed that Mazdek was setting a trap for him. He would need to be careful with his words. "I am assured the cracks that have appeared are merely cosmetic. The Bantu can never break through the wall," he replied cautiously.

"Oh, but they already have, general," Mazdek announced confidently.

"What? That's impossible," Karkson protested. "If they had breached it, I would know. If they managed to enter the Everglow, they could not pass Aleskian or the network of outer ring-forts. The legions at Aleskian would drive them back."

Mazdek laughed mockingly and pointed at Karkson. "This is the man we trust with the defence of our realm, my Sarissa?"

Karkson clenched his fists in frustration and anger.

"If the wall has been breached, then why have we not been told?" Regineo demanded. He looked at his mother. "Were you aware of this?"

"Yes," she responded solemnly. "Ahrimakan informed me of it."

Mazdek pointed to the floor with his finger. "The foundations of the wall run deep, down to the very foundations of the world, even into other realms, such as the Labyrinth and beyond. Braka has not broken through in this realm, but in another. In the Labyrinth, a hole has appeared. The cracks in the wall, in the Outer World, are the result of this."

Everybody except Mazdek, Marnir and Shaka gasped in horror. Mazdek continued in a self-assured manner, as one who was more knowledgeable than all others present. "The Bantu have yet to discover this, but they will. The breech is in a place where we cannot adequately defend it. It will get larger every time Braka strikes the wall."

"What can be done about it?" Regineo asked, his voice almost panic stricken.

"We have already acted upon it," Mazdek said, and he smiled slyly before continuing. "Goth Surien, exists in both the Outer World, and the Deadlands. We left many messages for him across that realm, informing him that we wished to talk. Myself and many of our bravest Seers met with him. It was an angry and hostile meeting, and full of threats at first, but under a flag of truce, we learnt much from each other, and discovered much of the cause of both our discontent, is from a shared enemy." Mazdek took a deep breath before he continued. "I discovered the Bantu hatred is focused on the Baothein, for long and ancient is their dispute. Yet their section of the Great Northern Wall is impenetrable, for the ravine prevents Braka from hammering it, and the tops of the mountains carved straight are riddled with Baothein watchtowers and forts, though most are now abandoned. In most places those mountains could not be scaled or crossed, as the winds are too strong and the cold too fierce, and the gully, who knows what lurks in the swamps and forests that have grown in it since the time it was carved? Even the Bantu are no match for the beasts prowling down there. This is why Goth Surien has them attack the wall at Aleskian. Goth Surien's grudge is not with us, though. He attacks us only as a means to get to the Baothein." Mazdek stared in turn at each in the hall for effect, excluding Karkson, who felt horrified at what he was hearing.

"This need not be our war." Mazdek continued. "Goth Surien wishes only to clear a path to Baothein lands so his Bantu forces can destroy his ancient enemy. If we gave his forces access through Aleskian, Goth Surien's armies would ally with us and head west into Baothein lands. Their enemy is also ours. The Bantu would scorch Baothein lands, besiege their cities, reclaim what was stolen from them long ago, and then they would retreat back to their own lands and leave us in peace."

Karkson strongly objected, finding a courage which was bolstered by the insanity of the plan Mazdek was suggesting. "The Bantu are wild and savage, they are not to be trusted, let alone this fey wraith!"

Mazdek did not hesitate with his response. "It is true that a dark wind follows every step of Goth Surien, the wraithlike tyrant who has been given command of the Bantu hordes. He is unlike us; he lives in both the world of the living and the dead at the same time, but should we fear him for that? So vast is his army north of the wall, so terrible his armament, that were he to enter the Everglow as our enemy, it would be a war like no other we have experienced. But…" Mazdek again paused for effect and looked every person briefly in the eye. "Until recently, we have never had the chance to ask him why he wishes to make war with us and the reason he wants entry into the Everglow?"

"Do you need to ask a wolf why it hunts deer?" Karkson asked. "It is their nature."

Mazdek ignored him and looked at Renlak. "You have studied Temmison, the Histories, Volume Seven, have you not?"

"I have studied all the works of Temmison, every volume, during each of my lifetimes," Renlak replied and grinned boastfully.

"Can you tell us what that volume is about, and would you give us a brief description."

Renlak blushed. "My memory is not fresh, as it has been many a year in this lifetime since I have read in full all the volumes..."

"Then I shall do so, if you cannot," Mazdek interrupted arrogantly.

Renlak's blush turned a deeper shade of red and he blurted out a response: "But, I remember enough of that particular volume." He cleared his throat before continuing at a slightly more measured pace. "Temmison is the only Akkadian known to have travelled widely beyond the Great Northern Wall of the Everglow, risking *Final-death* to discover what was beyond there."

Regineo yawned for effect, and with a bored tone said, "We know this!"

Renlak continued, this time in a hurried manner. "Temmison reported on his return that the land itself devours the people, that it is uninhabitable and wild. The fauna is as savage and hungry as the beasts that roam it. He tells how he found the Great Northern Forests. He searched for the Cave Dwarves of the Drearth Mountains and the Dark Elves of the Silverlode Valley. He discovered their ruins and evidence of their once great civilisations, but no trace of a living elf did he ever find, so some say."

"Is there a point to this history lesson?" Regineo demanded. "Besides, we are not all ignorant of our history, did not Edegal call Temmison a liar?"

"He did, my prince, and there is a point to this lesson. For it isn't what Temmison didn't find that is important, it is what he did find that is."

"Then get to the point and tell us," Regineo demanded irritably.

Mazdek interrupted and took over from Renlak. "We have never stopped to ask why the Lord of Morkroth sent his servant Goth Surien to wage war on us and seek entrance to the Everglow. We have always assumed it was due to their savage nature and hatred of our kind, and that alone was the reason, but we were wrong." He looked around proudly.

"How so?" Regineo asked, looking perplexed.

Mazdek smiled smugly. "His ancient dispute is with the Baothein, because, before the Bantu civilisation had risen to the power it is today, Temmison stole something from those lands, and carried it away to Baothein."

"What did he take?" Regineo asked.

"You tell them," Mazdek said haughtily to Renlak.

Renlak again cleared his throat before speaking. "Some of you may recall, before our Empire's Civil War, many lifetimes ago, before the White Queen had laid false claim to ancient titles, I was ambassador to her court. In the copies of *The Histories* that we have in Kappia, what Temmison discovered about the dispute between the Bantu and Baothein is not recorded, but in the originals kept in the Baothein library, it is. I had access to the library. I saw what was written in the original text." Renlak blinked several times and licked his lips. "Temmison discovered the tomb of Morkroth. Such was the corpse he had never seen anything like it before. He knew not how to describe it, apart from it was a large being with six wings and many eyes all over its body. He had the Davari who were with him, bring back the mummified remains as a curiosity, along with many other treasures and artefacts, to Baothein lands. Even to this day, the body of Morkroth is there, sealed deep in a hidden place, somewhere deep in the Ibarack Mountains."

"It is that which the Bantu seek," Mazdek declared.

"Why would the Lord of Morkroth desire a spent body?" Aspess asked. "Can't he just resurrect, or steal a new one?"

Mazdek tapped his chest with an air of self-importance. "It is a fair question, princess, and I know the answer. Goth Surien told us that Morkroth, is now shadow only, and he is very old. Unlike the Aeldar he cannot fashion a new body nor can one be made for him. To walk fully in this world again, and to remember all, he must reclaim that which was stolen from his tomb. When his shadow woke from a dark sleep, he discovered his body stolen, and by means we do not know, he found out that it was Temmison of the Baothein who stole it. That is the grievance he has with them. The only reason he attacks us, is we guard the weakest part of the wall, the only part he might possibly breech. His grievance is against the Baothein; his only desire is to reclaim the body that was stolen."

"You are saying the Bantu horde only attack us to forge a path to the Baothein, and we fight a war with them that is unnecessary?" Aspess asked.

Mazdek eagerly answered her. "Aleskian was built to defend the wall. It has drained our treasury, at great cost; our navy has suffered and been reduced to a level where we can no longer even protect the Erin from pirate scum, and pay heavy tariffs with what little trade we do with Harwind. We pay the Sea Lords huge tolls to travel our own seas. We have lost most of our lucrative trade and slave routes, and for what?"

"We have bankrupted ourselves to protect our own enemy, the Baothein," Aspess said, answering the question.

Mazdek nodded exultantly. "An alliance with the Bantu is the solution to the threats we face. We can harness their savagery and use it for our own purposes. If we allow the Bantu to enter the Everglow, they will destroy the Baothein for us. The Bantu can reclaim the body of Morkroth, after which they will return to their abodes in the North. If we surrender Aleskian to them, with the money we save, we can finally deal with the arrogance of the Sea Lords who have troubled and insulted us so deeply. With such new-found wealth, we can conquer and tame the entire Everglow."

"I have never heard such an insane suggestion," Karkson bellowed indignantly. "You would ally with a savage enemy on the basis of some disputed history book and the words of a deceitful half-wraith? Who knows what nature this Goth Surien is who serves the unknown Lord of Morkroth? Both are lying spirits for all we know!"

Mazdek's retort was scathing and sharp. "Is it not you, who polluted your own legions? Did you not allow Dwarves and Davari to join, to form the auxiliaries and mercenary legions, and even join those of the Pure-bloods?"

"We could not have defended the wall or fought outside of it, had we not used them," Karkson replied. "We have limited Neblans!"

Any semblance of calmness was gone. Mazdek exploded with rage. "Long ago, when you still had influence, you persuaded the Council to revoke the *Edict of Varscal*, and that has exhausted our treasury. Now, after twenty-five years of service, the Fell-blood auxiliaries are granted citizenship and farms. We support, for the rest of their miserable lives, those who don't even believe in the idea of Kappia like we Pure-bloods do. They despise the civilisation we have given to them, and many of them plot against us in secret rooms, or openly in taverns and inns. Fell-bloods have little interest in defending Kappia, for most have never even seen our great city; yet, it bleeds us dry to defend them on the lands they now pollute with more of their offspring?"

Mazdek took a breath, and looked pleadingly at each member of the Privy Council in turn. "Is it not time, the war-mongering of Karkson and that despicable *Betrayer* in Aleskian, is put to an end?" He raised his hands in exasperation. "Can you not see, that it is time we cleanse our lands from all Fell-bloods, and purify the Empire again? The Bantu will do this for us, for such a small price!"

"It is time your prattling is brought to an end," Karkson said, his anger fuelling his new-found courage. He instinctively felt for the hilt of his sword, which was not there.

"Quiet, general," Shaka said reprovingly.

"My Sarissa, I…"

The Empress looked at Regineo, and before Karkson could finish his sentence, said, "If the general speaks one more word, you are to cut out his tongue."

"With pleasure mother," Regineo snarled, as he drew a knife, rose from his seat and stood behind Karkson.

Karkson felt his courage evaporate, yet again. He hated himself that he could not find the same courage he had on the battlefield, here in this war of words. This was a battle he did not know how to fight.

Mazdek looked at him contemptuously, and then at the Empress and the other members of the Privy Council. "The lands we control outside of the Kappia Plateau, have little defensive value to our own existence, and cost us more to defend than they give back in coin. Is this not true, Staris?" he asked the Imperial Treasurer.

Staris, a small bald man, partially unrolled a parchment he carried and used a polished magnifying glass to glance at it before speaking. "I have all the figures here, if you want them, my Sarissa," he answered, looking at the Empress.

"Just give the overview," she said impatiently, rubbing her forehead with two fingers.

Staris continued. "The Privy Council are already aware of this, but just to remind us all. Aleskian is a huge drain on the imperial purse, it is too remote to generate much trade and it consumes most of the grain and produce grown in the lands around it. Our borders along the disputed lands are heavily guarded and fortified, and then there is the financial cost of the legions guarding the Aleskian Gate; it is a situation we can no longer afford - we are almost bankrupt!" He looked around expecting questions, but as none came, he continued: "We are not strong enough to make an assault on Baothein fortifications – we are at a stalemate at the disputed lands, some of which the Baothein are now colonising. The border of the Tarenmoors is only lightly guarded, for we do not expect any threat to come from there soon, so we only maintain several forts and castles in the region, but they cost a lot to maintain in materials, goods and repairs, and some are dilapidated to the point of neglect." Again, he looked around for questions, but none came, so he quickly unrolled more of the parchment. "We spend more coin guarding the trade routes to the Kappia Plateau, than we get back as a return. Protecting the towns and cities they pass through, has drained the treasury. I repeat, we are in an impecunious situation!" His uninterrupted pause was brief. "The farming produces harvested off of the Plateau, and the manufacturing items made, are nothing we cannot grow, produce and make on the Plateau itself. The Kappia Plateau is supporting the lands off of it, they are not supporting us. Trade is simply not worth it anymore. We have spent more in keeping strong, well-armed forces to deal with the many Fell-blood bandits that roam outside of the towns and cities robbing the trade caravans, than we have got from the trade itself."

"Get to the point!" Regineo demanded.

"I think I just have, my prince," Staris said respectfully. "The situation we are currently in, is unsustainable. We spend our coin guarding that which brings no profit, and this is the reason we cannot afford a strong imperial navy to deal with the many water born threats we face." He paused and looked solemnly around, and to reinforce and drive the point home, he stated, "The treasury, is virtually empty!"

Mazdek waited for the words to sink in, before he asked Staris: "Your proposed solution?"

"We would be able to make vast profit, if once again, we focused on freeing up trade along the River Erin, and fight the Sea Lords on the Tethys Sea," Staris replied. "Our lack of a navy is the reason that the Sea Lords have dared challenge and extorted us. It will not be long before they entirely block our sea trade, even that of the milathran from the islands around Grona. Soon, our treaties with them along those routes will expire, and they have no reason to renew them: even if they desired to do so, we cannot afford, any longer, to pay for their protection. We need a solution, or the Kappian Empire, is doomed!"

Before any could respond, Mazdek declared. "Karkson has allowed this to happen. Whilst we drain our wealth defending the Aleskian Gate, and empty our resources funding legions to defend Aleskian's needs, our Empire crumbles. Aleskian only defends the Baothein, our enemy. We fight an unnecessary war with the Bantu, which we do not need to fight. Where is the sense in any of this?"

If it were not for the distress of having his tongue cut out, a threat he knew the Empress would carry out, Karkson would have protested, but even then, what would he say? It was his instinct that the Bantu were not to be trusted, and letting them into the Everglow was an insane decision. Aleskian held them back, but to keep Aleskian meant protecting the surrounding provinces and lands that provided the city with what it needed to survive. He could see the military necessity for this, but, as a soldier, and not a man who had to balance monetary books, he simply did not know how to respond. To the best of his knowledge it was true, there was no longer any money to pay the wages of the legions, or fund them. Aleskian was a financial burden the Empire could no longer afford, but the plan Mazdek had was still madness.

Mazdek pressed home the point he was aiming at. "We would become rich if we built up our naval power and took control of the Erin again. Capturing Harwind is the key, for it controls access to the River Erin from the Tethys Sea. If we take Harwind and fortify it, we control the Erin. We then economically strangle Anthain lands, and the Bruthon would not dare to whisper against us for we would have the means to sack and pillage their ports along the Erin if they dared. With a strong navy based at Harwind, we can begin to seize control of the trade routes along the Tethys Sea. The Sea Lords would be forced to co-operate with us."

"If we disband the legions, the Kappia Plateau is still easily and cheaply defended," Staris said. "The devotion of the Hammer Knights means they require very little in terms of pay. With the money we save not paying the legions, we can become a naval power!"

Karkson was not sure if Mazdek was mad or a fool, or both. The Sea Lords commanded the Eastern Tethys Sea. They slew any of the great sea beasts that came into the sea territories under their control, and thus demanded a toll payment from any of the nations, including the Empire, that used any sea routes for trade or fishing. The Sea Lords had great treasury ships anchored outside of each major harbour of every city along the eastern shores of the Everglow, and any ship or even fishing boats entering or leaving harbour had to pay them a toll. The smaller harbours had no treasury ships outside, but even in the small towns and villages they either had an official harbour office, or spies and unofficial toll-masters who kept a tally of what vessels entered and left, and took payment from them. To suggest taking on the powerful Sea Lords, would mean a war that, in Karkson's mind, was one the Empire could not win even if it built up a formidable navy, which would take time and coin, neither of which the Empire had. The plan was madness, wasn't it?

"The Sea Lords are not to be lightly crossed," Staris said. "Any ship or vessel, no matter who owns it that is found trying to avoid the tolls or tariffs, are either sunk or seized. The captain and crew are publicly crucified to the main mast in the Bay of Suffering, or made to pay a terrible salt-price. If they are Pure-bloods, they resurrect at Toseucia, or if east from there, on the Island of Grona, inside the prison."

"If I may," Renlak said. "We still pay the tolls and tariffs for our prison ships to travel to Grona, as we have a milathran mine on a nearby island and they bring back the cargo for us, but the Sea Lords are always increasing the toll and our profits grow ever smaller from that."

"It is an intolerable situation that we have to pay tolls even in our own territorial waters," Aspess said angrily.

"And one for which we have an answer if we only have the courage and will to act upon it," Mazdek interjected. "What I propose, is that we order the legions guarding Aleskian, to go to Kara Duram. The Kappia Plateau is self-sustaining in food and many resources. It is virtually impenetrable and easily defended."

Karkson felt like a small boy when he raised his hand for permission to speak.

"General, you may speak," Shaka said.

"The Plateau needs griffins to defend it, as well as the legions," Karkson countered. *Economically, I see the argument, but militarily, this whole plan is madness and fraught with many risks.* "I believe this plan is not wise, my Sarissa."

"But we only have a few griffins left, unknown diseases have depleted their numbers," Mazdek declared factually.

"Griffins are too unreliable," Regineo added. "Once they lose their rider in a battle, they frequently turn on friend or foe alike. Modern weapons such as strategically placed ballistae and scorpions are more reliable for our air defence, and they are cheaper to maintain than griffins, which also consume a large amount of meat."

Karkson wanted to argue with facts, but he could not: it was true, griffins, though fierce in combat, were notoriously unreliable. Often, in past battles, he himself had witnessed them turn on their own men. He was one of those who had often questioned if they were more trouble than they were worth.

Mazdek had the attention of all listening. "Disband the legions; we do not need them. The Hammer Knights are sufficient to guard the plateau! We allow the Pure-blood legionnaires of disbanded legions to take the farms and homes of Fell-bloods. We can spend the coin we save on slowly and secretly building up our naval power, to deal with the pirate threat first, and then, when we are able, we will take on the Sea Lords themselves."

*The Sea Lords and the pirate threat are one and the same,* Karkson thought, but he dared not voice it.

Mazdek was jubilant, he had the captivated attention of all. "Once we have secured the wealth of the Erin and the trade on the Tethys Sea, we can build up the army again for such a time as we want to conquer and expand." He took a few excited breaths. "I suggest we must issue a call to all Pure-bloods in the Empire, to return to the plateau. We must then enforce the Edict of Varscal again, and have a purposeful Pure-blood breeding programme. All half and Fell-bloods on the plateau will be enslaved, or if a drain on our resources, destroyed. Their properties will be confiscated and given to those more deserving. Those outside the plateau, the Bantu will eradicate them."

"What about Aleskian?" Regineo asked. "Lord Borach *the Betrayer*, will never surrender his ancestral home."

"If he plans to hand Aleskian to the Baothein, let him," Aspess said. "They will then have the cost and responsibility to protect themselves from the Bantu threat."

"There is a better way," Mazdek said. "We cannot allow the Baothein to seize Aleskian, with all of its defences intact. If we abandon it, and allow the Bantu to raze it, the Baothein would have no choice but to wait in their own lands to face the Bantu, or to strike out and attempt to secure the gate to prevent more Bantu hordes from pouring through. Whatever they choose, they will bear the brunt of the cost in coin and manpower. Either choice will drain their wealth and resources."

"What about the *Betrayer*?" Renlak asked. "The Third Legion is mostly Pure-blood and they have served him over many lifetimes, the treachery probably runs deep in them as well. They will not just allow him to be arrested and taken, and though the other legions will withdraw to Kara Duram, they will obey whatever Borach orders them to do."

"We will use cunning, the Hammer Knights, and a well-timed imperial order sent to Aleskian. In this manner, Borach can easily enough be dealt with," Mazdek answered.

"This is all very well, but what about the Simal?" Regineo asked. "How will any of this help us recover the Simal?"

Mazdek again smiled triumphantly. "The Bantu have those they call the Wild Hunt, or the Sacred Band. They will not be affected by the allure of the Simal. They have skin-changers that can turn into flying beasts. They fly high and fast, and if given Janorra's scent, they will be able to track her from vast distances. In a city of a hundred thousand she could not hide from them, nor in a deep cave in the wilds. Nobody can hide from the Wild Hunt, once they have the scent of their prey. They can speedily travel vast distances on a ship that travels on the waters of the Underglow, which they enter through something they call the Rumbling Bridge, a bridge that belongs in a realm not even known to us. They then use moleworms to burrow up into the Everglow itself, to catch their prey by surprise. The Wild Hunt will not rest or give up until they find her, wherever she might be."

"What is to stop the Bantu taking the Simal for themselves?" Aspess asked edgily.

Mazdek took another breath. "Only a Pure-blood Akkadian trained to do so, can summon an Aeldar. The Simal is of no use to them, it is nothing but a pretty bauble; it will serve their purpose for it to be returned to us."

"How so?" Regineo asked, the anger on his face finally being replaced with curiosity.

"Morkroth seeks an alliance with the Aeldar, for he was once allied to them when they walked the world. He wishes to remember better days. Goth Surien will return the Simal to us as a part of any treaty and alliance, of this I am sure. In return we will offer to help them locate the body of Morkroth once the Baothein are destroyed. As a part of this deal, we will demand that the White Queen is handed over to us, so that she will be brought here to Kappia, for her fate to be decided by our Sarissa."

"Do you agree with this plan, mother?" Regineo asked.

"Ahrimakan desired for me to ally with the Bantu forces," Shaka said thoughtfully. "Such an alliance is fraught with risk, but to continue on the path we are on, will surely ruin the Empire and its demise is all but certain." She looked thoughtfully at Mazdek. "Will you negotiate the terms?"

He nodded. "Much discussion has previously taken place between Goth Surien, myself and our envoys. He has invited me to Thar Markoom to see his army, and inspect the Wild Hunt."

"I would like to go with you," Aspess offered.

"Never," Shaka declared. "I will not have my daughter go into the heart of darkness."

"Goth Surien desires this alliance, my Sarissa. Princess Aspess will be quite safe," Mazdek said. "We can both don a Neblan. I have a number of Juram I have kept for such a time as this. We can use them as a means of travel. Princess Aspess will be quite safe."

"You kept Juram hidden from us?" Regineo asked indignantly.

"Only for such a time as this, my prince," Mazdek answered with a respectful bow of his head.

Karkson was horrified at what he was hearing, but he still dared not speak without invitation, for Regineo still hovered behind him. *My best chance is to leave this meeting alive. I must warn Borach, I must warn the legions about the madness being planned and plotted here.*

He felt only slight relief when Regineo asked the question that he wanted to ask. "Why have we not been told before about the ability of the Bantu to open an unworldly bridge that will enable them to sail upon the Underglow? How do we know they will not use it to come to Kappia itself?"

Mazdek looked at the Empress when he answered the question. "My Sarissa, it is the wall that prevents them from entering the Everglow. Only if the wall is breached or the gate opened, can they use that bridge to enter the Underglow. They only have one ship with this ability. It can only carry a few hundred or so of them. It poses no danger to the capital or anywhere else with a good defence, as they cannot transport an army by this means. They will use it only to hunt the Seeress Janorra."

Mazdek held out his hands in an imploring gesture. "All of our problems can be solved with one swift decision, my Sarissa," he implored pleadingly. "With this plan, Kappia will always be safe, our enemies will be destroyed, the Simal returned to us, and in time we will once again regain control of the Erin and the Tethys Sea. It is a bold and audacious plan, but one that we must execute without delay before the opportunity passes. We need a decision now, my Sarissa."

Shaka had become unusually calm, almost serene. Karkson could tell by her appearance that Mazdek had won her over with his madness. She was poised and graceful when, after a long silence, she finally spoke. "This morning, I had lost all hope. I thought my lover was forever slain, my destiny out of reach, but now I know differently. High Quaester Mazdek has shown us the way, and bitterly do I regret ever taking General Karkson's advice, in preference over his." She looked at Karkson, and at that moment he feared his fate was sealed, and that no words would dissuade her otherwise. *There is nothing I can do or say here to change the course of events. I must leave this meeting alive. Borach and the legions must be warned. Together, we can resist this folly.* He closed his eyes as she continued.

"The prophetic utterances of Karthal are clear to me. The race that is most foul to my people, are the ones we must turn to for an alliance, before I am anointed as an Aeldar Wife, a goddess, who will take my rightful place by Ahrimakan's side when he is returned to us." She smiled contentedly. "The Golden Horn of Aleskian must sound its beauty here in Kappia."

Karkson opened his eyes and looked around him. Mazdek had won over all of the Privy Council. Each one of them was looking expectantly at Shaka, for her next words. She paused and looked at each one of them, except Karkson.

"Until now, I had not seen how the hand of the Aeldar is surely guiding all of these events. My grief when I thought I had forever lost Ahrimakan, and my destiny, was too much to bear, it clouded my mind. The High Quaester has opened my eyes. We would be fools not to accept the plan he is proposing to us, so it is my will and my word that we implement it immediately."

Karkson could not help the involuntary groan that issued from his lips.

Shaka looked at him, long and hard. "You have my permission to speak freely," she said. Regineo took his seat again.

"This is madness, my Sarissa," Karkson quietly groaned as his chin slumped onto his chest. *I must warn the others.*

93

"Do you fear the Kappia Plateau itself, might be vulnerable then, general?" she asked him. "Are you not confident the Steps of Narzoum are safe?"

Renlak answered her. "It is impenetrable," he stated. "No army could scale the high cliffs of the plateau without being seen and any would be easily repelled. The Needle Pass is virtually impenetrable. You will recall, my Sarissa, that Treasurer Saris, with your consent, gave permission for the coin to be borrowed from the Hamash Bank to strengthen the pass. If we disband the legions, a single battalion of Hammer Knights could hold it against an army unnumbered. It is said even the blind and the lame could defend the pass, that is how secure it is."

"When this business is complete, you must borrow more money from the Hamash Bank, with which we will build up our navy," Shaka said to Staris, who bowed his head gracefully in acknowledgement.

Karkson breathed heavily as he looked up. He knew by the look the Empress gave him, that there was no more discussion to be had. He understood that no words he could speak would change the course of events now being set in progress. He bitterly regretted his past and present cowardice in the imperial court, a fearfulness born of not being able to play the game of words as well as others like Mazdek. The Empire was setting itself on a course of utter madness, and despite the outrage he felt, he knew there was nothing he could do or say to stop the events about to unfold, and even if there was, he did not know how to give voice to combat such insanity. He did what he had mostly done in such situations, he stayed silent. He had once counselled Shaka that the unity of the Empire was fragile and warned her that using the Simal to summon Ahrimakan and the two other Aeldar whose riddles were known, was foolhardy. He had warned then, that to force the worship of Thuranotos and the Aeldar on the people would split the Kappian Empire, and lead to a costly civil war. She had not listened, and he had not persisted or pressed the matter, but he had been proven right. The Baothein had broken away from Kappia and restored their ancient royal lineage as a result. The Bruthon, always a hotbed simmering with rebellion, had also rebelled and taken up arms. At the start of the war, Karkson had failed to militarily overcome and defeat the border defences of either of the rebel factions and had been forced to adopt a more defensive war over an aggressive push into rebel lands.

*I should have argued my case more vehemently at the time.* Karkson had failed the Empress, he knew it. He had failed her in not realising the folly that would be pursued, as a result of him not putting across his side more forcefully over the many years and lifetimes when he did have her ear. In that moment, he was not only anxious for himself, he feared that the decision that had just been made would cause the collapse of the entire Kappian Empire. It would affect his own Pure-blood children, including Myrene. The Bantu were not to be trusted. They would be unrestrained in the slaughter and destruction they would bring. It was a small consolation to him that he had instructed Myrene, secretly and well, over many lifetimes, and taught her all he had discovered. He had warned her many times to not associate herself with his name, but to keep her mother's marital name. He had used the same tactic for his son, using his power, influence and wealth to unobtrusively put him in a position where he could move through the ranks of the legions, whilst using his mother's marital names and not his. The only regret he had was that his son had not yet risen to the position he had aspired of him; it was a disappointment that he was merely the captain of a griffin scout patrol. Secretly he had educated both of his illegitimate children, in regard to his suspicions about the true nature of the Aeldar; he had warned them of the growing influence of the Hammer Knights, but it was all now too late. *I must warn Borach and others about the madness that has been decided here this day.*

Mazdek slowly pointed a finger accusingly at the general and stared at him for more than a moment for effect, before sneeringly saying. "He failed to defeat the Baothein and the Bruthon during the war that fractured our glorious Empire. The peace he made with the rebellious Bruthon favours them more than it does us, and now he has drained the imperial treasury with an army protecting provinces and lands with no financial or strategic value." He looked at Shaka. "May we have permission to immediately disband the legions, my Sarissa? The Hammer Knights will take their place at a fraction of the cost, for they serve out of loyalty, not for mere pay."

"Let it be done," Shaka replied, "but general, what must we do with you?"

"He could not even see the disloyalty of the betrayer Borach, the one he calls friend," Regineo sneered contemptuously. "We have no need of such an incompetent man."

"His council, is defective and should never be heeded again," Mazdek said, spitting the words out with venom and hate. "He must not be allowed to leave here alive, for he will warn others and leak our plans before they can be executed. I say we give him the *Final-death*, here and now."

It finally dawned upon Karkson. *I was never going to leave this meeting alive.* His strength gave out, through despair, more than fear. He felt frozen to the spot. Sweat dripped down his forehead, and he fought to control his breathing and stop his hands from trembling.

"General, do you have nothing more to say?" Shaka asked beratingly.

Karkson knew it was pointless, and too late, but he cried, "The High Quaester is a heel-biter."

The Empress raised an eyebrow, as did the rest of the Privy Council. They gasped that the general had issued such a grievous insult about the High Quaester, in effect calling him a traitor, but Karkson no longer cared and finally, with the few moments of life he had left, he was determined to speak his mind.

"My Sarissa, I would beg you not to do this, but I see your mind is made up and will not be changed. Any alliance with the Bantu cannot last. I cannot prove it with eloquent words, but I know that Lord Borach has not betrayed you. I would have seen it in his eyes and detected it in his voice, and can say to you, that man is loyal." He looked at Mazdek, whose face was red with rage. "Unlike this heel-biter, who seeks to deceive you for purposes not to your benefit. I challenge him to be tested by the Jewel of Baramir. Let the Eye of Morsef look at him, and discover his true intentions."

"It is too late for that, general," Shaka said. She then looked at Aspess, and said almost respectfully. "It is time our cherished general rests from his labours. Retire him."

Aspess bowed her head knowingly. Leisurely, she stood from her chair. All that remained for him was to face his *Final-death* with some dignity, so he rose to his feet and stood to attention, bowed his head and saluted the Empress.

"My Sarissa, I have always been and remain loyal to you. The Jewel of Baramir would show that no lie has come from my lips. When all others have turned or gone from you, my voice will return to you from the grave. Listen to it then, if not now. Mazdek is a heel-biter, a traitor of the worst kind. My voice alone remains true to you in this council of fools," he said. "I regret I was never gifted with more eloquence in which to expose the deceit that surrounds you, and the danger you are in, for the Empire is about to be brought to ash and ruin. I hope your eyes will be opened, before it is too late for you."

Aspess stalked him, like a wolf approaching a lamb, as she unsheathed the Arkith, a weapon that could send those of Pure-blood to their *Final-death*.

95

Karkson turned to face her. He looked at the blade in her hand, it was long and leaf shaped, clearly of ancient Elven design, created by that lost and forgotten race. A purple soul-gem adorned the hilt, and dread struck him as he realized that within there, he would spend eternity with whatever unfortunate souls were trapped within. Terror gripped him, but he knew that begging for mercy would not help, nor would it change his fate. He had finally spoken his mind, but it was too late. In an arena of battle where he was not skilled, he had lost to Mazdek.

"It is alleged," Aspess said with quiet ferocity, "that if an Arkoom but scratches you, and you die near it, death is final, so powerful is the Arzak it carries. But this is an Arkith, for the Arzak to claim you, it must kill you…"

Even had he wanted too, Karkson had no time to react as Aspess struck with great speed. Karkson shuddered as the Arkith plunged into his chest, penetrating his armour like butter. The purple gem on the hilt of the dagger, the Arzak, glowed as he felt his spirit and essence being sucked into it. She let go of the pommel and watched his fate with glee. He heard the screams of misery from the souls already trapped within the Arzak. His spirit was ripped from his body, which he could already see was lying in a pool of blood on the floor. The last thing he ever saw, heard and felt in the land of the living, was Aspess stroking his forehead gently as she callously said: "Rest in peace from your labours general, many deaths you have had, but from this one is no return." The soul of Karkson, was then sucked into the Arzak, where it would forever remain.

# Chapter Seven: *Scarand's Honour*

*There is an unconquerable ferocity about the men of the ice-lands, yet, I was never afraid when amongst them. They are violent and severe towards those who are their enemy, and revel in wholesale butchery in the heat of a battlefield, but they prefer mercy over cruelty towards the helpless. Their savagery is restrained by a moral code, of which I hope to learn more. They possess a primordial chivalry, and an innate reverence towards womanhood that I find wholly fascinating.*

*Temmison Vol VII, Book 6: The Davari Tribes and Clans – The Vanyr.*

*The* mist from the day before had dispersed, dark rain clouds that threatened to drop their load drifted overhead. Scarand put some more wood on the small fire he had lit next to a cut of rock, which he had built there so the flames could not easily be seen by anyone or anything prowling through the woods. He blew on it to coax the flame. Smoke and sparks flew excitedly into the air as the wood cackled and the flame sprang to new life. Every fibre in him still tingled with outrage from his experience in captivity. Being a thrall, he was no stranger to slavery, but among his own kind, he had experienced a degree of freedom and had not been kept in cages and chains. The Ikma had been cruel and brutal, and his anger seethed towards them. In Ashgiliath, his Seesnari captors had been stern, but had not mistreated him or the other Davari, as long as they kept to the rules, which were enforced. Even so, whilst at Ashgiliath and also whilst on board the *River Queen* for the journey down the River Erin, he had felt the resentment of a caged wild beast, and had been infuriated by the chains that had bound him.

He sat on the log and observed Sasna as she slept. His eyes smouldered with an intensity that the eyes of men bred to civilisation lacked. Her thick kohl make-up had smeared across her face. The outline of her splendid limbs was moulded by her soaked leather clothing. Her chest rose and fell as she breathed. Even in a bedraggled state, she looked exotic and captivating, but he could not help feeling bitter towards her for the part she had played in his enslavement. Despite his youth, he was a man who frequently fought huge melancholies, often interspersed with equally huge bouts of mirth when the situation warranted it. As he scrutinised Sasna, he felt no melancholy or mirth. He was troubled by the question, *what do I do with her when she wakes up?* Despite the fact she had briefly considered him her slave, and she his owner, his own sense of honour had not allowed him to leave her defenceless, at night, in a forest where any manner of creature might come along and bring her harm. It was not just this sense of honour, but a more practical fact as well that had kept him there. He needed information from her if he was to find his sisters. These lands were strange to him and he had no map and little knowledge of them. *For Marciea and Oliviana.*

Scarand wondered if Marciea and Oliviana were still alive, and if so, what they might be doing at that very moment. He feared for them, and vowed anew that he would not stop, until he either found them, or if they were dead, discovered their fate and took revenge upon those he blamed. Not for the first time, he again studied his surroundings. The sombre and primeval forest was not inviting. Above him, lofty green arches were formed by intertwining branches. Giant trees hemmed in the small glade they were in. Apart from a trail to the south made by animals, which probably came to drink at the river, clumps of undergrowth limited his vision, so he had to stay alert, listening, lest some beast try to sneak up upon them. The slightest snap of a twig or branch might indicate movement nearby, or, at any moment there might come the distant cries of men searching for survivors from the wreckage of the *River Queen*.

Sasna shivered, and let out a small cry, as though some nightmare tormented her sleep. Scarand again turned his gaze upon her. She twitched her slender shoulders. Against the background of the somber, primeval forest, she looked out of place. His previous attempts to wake her had proven futile, as she had been in a deep unconscious sleep. He was pleased that she was now showing signs of stirring. She was now sleeping uneasily; she moaned and let out another sharp cry. Blood and puss were seeping through the make-shift bandage he had put around her shoulder.

Scarand was a skilled hunter, and knew much about the animals and vegetation of his own homelands. Here, however, he was among trees and plants that were unfamiliar to him, and he knew not what manner of beasts might live in such a place. At the slave pens of Ashgiliath, a plump Davari free-woman named Frema, a cook who had served the slaves food, had taught him some local forestry and herb lore, and the different types of plants he would find in the Everglow, particularly in the Bruthon lands. Frema had told him that learning new skills, added to his value when he was to be given to his new master at Greytears; she had said such skills might save him from the fighting pits if he could prove more useful outside of them. Although he still could not recognise nor name every herb and plant in the area, for they were different from those of his homeland, when he had searched the immediate surroundings of the glade, he had found some wild potatoes and mashed them into a paste. He knew that placing it beneath the bandage would act as a poultice and soothe Sasna's wound to help prevent infection and swelling. The rest of the potatoes he had cooked upon a flat stone placed over a part of the camp fire he had made.

Sasna woke with a start. Disorientated for a few seconds, she rubbed her eyes and looked around her, but did not notice him straight away. She immediately winced with the pain from her shoulder.

Scarand pointed to her wound. "I need to change that for you, it's been on for a few hours now."

In an instant she transformed into sudden panic when she noticed him sitting there, staring at her. With a stifled cry she tried to get up but fell back down, and then swiftly moved into a half crouching position as though about to lunge at him or run.

Scarand laughed grimly. "If I was going to harm you, you would be dead already." He stood and walked over to her, whilst she watched him warily, not taking her suspicious eyes off of him for a single moment. He crouched and looked at her shoulder, and gently lifted the bandage, peeling it off slightly. She gasped in pain.

"It will heal in time," he said as he watched her bite her lips to quench the discomfort. He then offered her some of the cooked potatoes he took from the stone. "Eat quickly; I will change the dressing for you, and when you have told me what I need to know, I will leave."

Sasna looked around her, confused. She blinked and shook her head, and then sat back down; she began to shiver due to the cold and wet.

"The Baron will have search parties out looking for survivors, especially me and Farir; you must take me to Greytears," she said as she took the potato and moved it from hand to hand, blowing on it to cool it down before taking a bite.

"Wait here," Scarand said, looking at her with narrow eyes. He then made his way to the nearby river bank. The reeds were thick and taller than a man's head, but he waded into the place where the reeds were thinner and the water rose about his thighs, so he could see both up and down the river for a mile each way. He strained his eyes out across the dark and restless water. Up river, on the distant horizon, where the sun was rising, he could still see wisps of smoke rising into the air from the wreckage of the *River Queen*. Down river, he could see no sign of any life, either on the river or along the banks.

He scowled across at the other shore, and wandered if it might have been better to have landed on that side. In the darkness of the night before, as he had paddled downstream, the boat had been caught in a powerful current and drawn near to the southern bank where it hit a submerged rock and had sprung a rapid leak, causing it to sink. He had lost the bow in the accident, but managed to retain the sabre. It was fortunate the water was shallow. In his homeland, the waters were too cold to swim in, so he had never learned how. Even in the shallows of the Erin, it had been with great difficulty he had made his way to the shore, somehow pulling the unconscious Sasna with him as he struggled against the current with endurance and vigour that lesser men would have lacked.

He rinsed out the bloodied cloth in the river until it was as clean as he could get it, and then wrung it as dry as he could. Once again, straining his eyes he looked across the restless water. This time, he thought he saw something moving on the water – a long, low, black shape that submerged beneath the surface. He felt a cold chill go down his spine, and quickly scrambled out of the water, before making his way back to Sasna. He had half expected her to have attempted to run away, and if she had, he would have caught her again easily enough, but she was waiting for him where he had left her as he emerged from the reeds.

She glanced anxiously at him, as she tried to warm herself by the fire. "Have you searched for Farir? The current may have brought him to the shore."

Scarand shook his head as he walked over to her. She instinctively pushed herself back against a rock.

"He is not my concern, you are. I want you to tell me who took my sisters Marciea and Oliviana. Three terrors, dressed in black armour adorned with a symbol of two hammers and a snake wrapped around the shafts, emerged from some portal, and after tormenting my people, they took them. Who were they and where did they take them?" He put some more wood on the fire, giving it fresh life. "Warm yourself woman," he said, "I plan you no harm."

Sasna shivered, and watching him warily, huddled closer to the fire. Her clothing, torn and wet, offered little protection from the wind that blew and whistled through the trees. She looked at the sabre tucked into the belt of his tunic.

"What are your intentions?" she asked suspiciously.

Scarand felt a fierceness rise within him when she did not answer his question, but asked her own. He bent above his captive, hungrily dwelling on each detail of her full red lips, her dark eyes surrounded by long –lashed lids. Part of her bosom was bare, and heaved with each breath she took as her wide clear eyes met his, reflecting the fear she felt as she watched him eyeing her. His voice was harsh with conflicting emotions.

"It will hurt, but keep washing the wound or it will become infected," he suggested as he held out the damp cloth to her." She took the cloth and carefully dabbed the wound. He picked up the remainder of the poultice he had earlier wrapped in a leaf and gave it to her along with a dry piece of tunic he tore from his own raiment.

"This poultice will help, wash the wound quickly and then I will dress it. Now, tell me, who took Marciea and Oliviana?"

"If I tell you what you seek, you will kill me," she said, her voice tense with distrust.

Scarand grunted and his face grew sombre. "The ways of men may vary in different lands, but we Vanyr keep to our word. I'll not harm you if you tell me what I seek." *I'll not harm you even if you don't, but neither will I help you any further if you do not offer me the information I seek.* He still felt a naked elemental anger towards her, for her part in his captivity, but he meant to keep his word. Each memory, every humiliation at being captured and chained, stung him as harshly as the slaver's whips ever had done. He was born and bred in a savage land where the daily struggle for survival was fierce. He was familiar with death, either seeing it, or dealing it out, and bloodshed and violence were no strangers to him for the Vanyr often had savage wars among themselves, wars in which thralls were often called upon to fight. Thralls were not allowed to be trained in the use of swords or other weapons, only bow and arrow, and were used as archers, as were many of the free women.

Despite his fierceness, Scarand still had his own code of honour, and even despite the part Sasna had played in his misfortunes, killing or harming an unarmed and helpless woman was not something he wished or desired to do. *It is cursed work to kill a helpless woman*, he said to himself. There was also something else, and this bothered him the most - he was fascinated by the Seesnari woman. Her beauty was intoxicating even in her bedraggled state, and when she looked at him with her strange dark eyes, he had to silence his primitive imagination lest wild passions consume him, and he lost control. He shook his head to clear his mind.

Sasna looked up at the dark sky; a distant rumble of thunder sounded in the distance and a crack of lightning briefly lit up the sky. Light rain began to fall. "Which direction did the sun rise in? We are south side of the river?"

He nodded and pointed to the east, where the sun, not yet risen above the canopy of trees, also had its light still partially hidden by dark clouds. Her gaze followed the direction his finger pointed towards, and then she looked around the small glade they were in. "Baron Daramir will have seen the flames of the *River Queen*. There will be mounted troops, foot-soldiers, archers and trackers scouting for survivors. How far did we go down river before coming ashore?"

Scarand glanced at the river. "About a mile, the current was strong."

"Then it will not be long before his men find us," she said. "The forest on the southside of the river only runs for a mile or two at the most. We will find the road that leads from Ashgiliath to Castle Greytears, if we head south."

Her words were obviously a comfort to her, but disturbing to him. *I was hoping many miles of forest separated me from civilised roads.* He looked around at the trees, and listened for any sound that might indicate the distant sound of men, but all he heard was the wind whistling in the boughs and another distant crack of thunder, and the occasional chirp of a bird.

Scarand felt a growing impatience with Sasna. He had not been able to wake her the night before, as she was unconscious due to the wound. Now she was awake, she was not answering his question. He did not doubt that it would be true, search parties would be looking for survivors. Already, he had wasted much time in getting ahead of them, and now he was concerned to learn just how close they were to a road built by men. On top of that, he felt exhausted, as he had kept alert all night. He was used to living in an icy, dangerous wilderness; his ears had remained vigilant whilst his eyes had rested, but his sleep had been light and not refreshing. He had no intention of leaving the Everglow until he found out about the fate of Marciea and Oliviana, and at that moment Sasna was the best hope of giving him at least some information. He had questioned Frema back at the slave pens, but she always fell silent when he had asked her about the black terrors, and had refused to discuss the matter.

Scarand tore off another piece of his tunic, took the poultice from Sasna and unwrapped it from the leaf as she blew on the wound to dry it. She continued to look at him uncertainly as he applied the poultice to her shoulder, wrapped the wound with the cloth, and then tied another piece of fabric to keep it in place. When her eyes moved towards the sabre, he warned, "Don't try it." He had no intention of harming her if he could help it, but if she tried to take the sword, he would have little choice but to stop her. Although no trained swordsman, he knew how to swing or stab with one. She looked at him defiantly, but made no move towards the weapon.

"Tell me everything you know about the three black terrors that appeared," he said impatiently. "One of them dragged his right foot and spoke with a broken voice. The other, when she took her helmet off, was wearing jewels in her hair, whilst the third was a nervous looking man. The symbol on their armour was hammers wrapped around by a snake."

"You will not end my life if I tell you what I know?" An angry frown darkened her face as she continued to gently dab the now bandaged wound on her shoulder, as though doing so might ease her obvious discomfort.

"I won't," he said impassively, "unless you refuse to tell me what you know." He tried to make it sound like a threat, but he sensed she could tell it was not. "Now speak." He took a stick from the fire and pushed it around the ashes, causing sparks and smoke to rise up as the flame fought against the rain and refreshed itself.

"If you insist, but you will not like what you hear," Sasna said. "Those you call the terrors, did they have a necklace upon them, in this shape?" She drew a shape in the air with her fingers.

"Yes, over their armour, I noticed such a thing around their necks," Scarand answered sombrely.

"Then they are Akkadians. Pure-bloods risk the *Final-death* if they travel outside of the Everglow, as the Obelisks cannot reach their spirits if they die; they become lost and cannot return to this world. But if they have a necklace of the Obelisks, a Neblan they call them, even if they die, their spirit can survive inside the artefact until they return to the Everglow, where a proper Obelisk can resurrect them." She sighed. "I only know about the three you mention, by tawdry songs sang in taverns to mock them, or a whispered rumour or story here and there, but I think the hunch-back is a prince of Kappia, son to the Empress Shaka who reigns there. His name is Regineo, his mind and soul are more broken and twisted than his body. I will not tell you all of the grisly tales of his rumoured deeds. He is bestial; men and women are no more to him than a writhing maggot is to a fisherman about to put it on a hook. If he takes a fancy to a woman, he will take her so that he can carry out the fantasies of his disordered brain."

Scarand silenced the groan of sick fury that rose up within him, at the thought of Marciea and Oliviana being in the hands of such a man. He then remembered the gentle caresses of their soft, white hands, when they had tended his wounds after a hunt. He could see their delicate skin, white as ivory. To take his mind of his torment, he knocked the potatoes off of the flat stone with a stick. They lay smoking and cooling in the grass as Sasna continued.

"The other two who appeared with him are his siblings; they are twins, brother and sister. The sister, Aspess, is as dangerous as Regineo, but not as cruel. Minstrels sing tawdry ballads of her desires in taverns across the Everglow. They say she prefers the company of female companions, as she is oath-sworn not to lie with a man. It is held that in her chambers, whose marble floors are littered with rare furs, and with walls lavish with golden frieze-work, she chooses the most attractive Davari maids whose slender limbs are weighted with gem-crusted armlets and anklets, and induces them into a drugged slumber, where they sleep on velvet couches around the royal bed with its golden dais and silk canopy, until she wakes them for her pleasure. Caspus is the name of the other. In deep dungeons he performs experiments with people, especially Davari, tampering blasphemously with the naked elements of life itself, for what purpose nobody knows."

An icy chill crept down Scarand's spine, and he could no longer supress the yell, so frightful and inhuman, that rose in his throat and then burst from his lips. He glared fearsomely at Sasna, and she recoiled at his wrath. "Continue," he said, when he had regained his composure.

She tensed, and sounded cautious as she said, "We Seesnari used to sell our slaves at Berecoth where the Kappian Empire would buy most of them. The trade stopped when the Empire had a civil war and split into three factions; they could not stop the Sea Lords from taking over their seas and rivers. We now sell most of the slaves in the West."

Scarand took a deep breath. "Frema gave me some knowledge of the Empire everybody fears. The three factions, Kappian, Baothein and Bruthon. It is Bruthon lands we are now in?"

"Yes," Sasna replied. "The Houses of Kappia and Baothein are still at war, but the Bruthon made peace with the Empress Shaka about ten years ago. Our trade began again, we paid a toll at Harwind, but it has recently stopped as new pirate scum began to make their way from Harwind, raiding along the Erin. We were forced to stop selling slaves to the Empire, as we have no means to transport them to Kappia."

Scarand gritted his teeth. "Why is this relevant to me?"

"Because we now have to send our slaves to Zinibar where they are sold. The Kappian Empire cannot buy them there for they would have to transport them across dangerous wilderness and enemy lands. But, the children of the Empress, have been tainted by a life of ease and luxury, it has given them a thrill for danger. They still have a deal with the Ikma, that on occasion they join them on their raids. They take back slaves with them, through portals by which they can travel vast distances in a moment."

"Where would they have taken my sisters?"

"More than likely to Kappia city. It is there I think you will find them, but you must give up hope, for you are marked as a slave, and they are now slaves in the heart of the Kappian Empire."

Scarand frowned. *Whatever the danger, I will try and find them.*

"Those portals they used; are they magic?"

Sasna laughed. "Magic is a word the uneducated use to explain knowledge which they cannot understand. The portals are opened using an artefact. There is nothing magic about them."

"How many people can travel through these portals?"

"I know little of such matters, but have heard there are three types of portal: Jula, through which only an individual can travel, Juram which can take up to two dozen people, and Jurashe, through which it is said an entire army can travel, but few there are that have the skill to open and use these, and I think the last Jurashe vanished from the world a long time ago."

"If I find somebody with such an artefact, and the knowledge of how to use them, could I use it to take me to where Marciea and Oliviana are?" he asked hopefully.

"I doubt you will ever find one," she answered. "It is said that nobody now has the knowledge to craft the artefacts or brew the liquid they need to work; those that still exist are very rare, and they are so fragile they often break even after a single use. If any are discovered, say in an ancient cache, they sell for a king's fortune at auctions. The princes and princess pay highly for any that are found, and few buyers can match their offers, even if they dared openly bid against them."

Whatever hope Scarand had, was quickly evaporating, and he felt a deep melancholy envelope him, but he still asked, "But it is possible?"

"Yes," Sasna answered as she continued watching him warily. She hesitated, and then added, "The Ikma once told me that the three royal siblings play a game and roll a dice for each of the Davari women they take, and you should hope, or pray to whatever gods you serve, that it was Aspess who won the roll for your sisters, as that is the lesser of ill-fates that could have befallen them."

A very faint hope remained within Scarand, but it was mixed with despair, as he considered the magnitude of the task before him. *I must keep hope alive, for the sake of Marciea and Oliviana. At least I now know who has taken them, and where my search should begin.*

"Will you show me where Kappia is?" he asked Sasna.

Her response was measured. "If you help me get to Castle Greytears, I will draw you a map, but that will be of no use to you unless you become a free man."

"I am free man right now," he growled.

She nodded, took a deep breath and sighed reflectively. "You are in strange lands you do not know, and are branded as a slave. If you help me, I vow to help you. I will arrange for the brand of a free man to be put upon you, and give you the papers to prove your freedom. Without my help you have no way of rescuing those you seek."

He looked at her, but said nothing.

"There is a brand you need, on your neck," she said, to show you have been freed. You will also need papers to get into any free-town, or any city of the Empire, or else you will be treated as an escaped slave. You will never find those you seek within the Everglow, without the brand and having the papers to prove you are a free man. I will give you what you need, in return for your help."

Scarand gazed at her, trying to gauge her sincerity. From his time in the slave pens, he was already familiar with the phrase *never trust a Seesnari*. He took a stick and stabbed a couple of the potatoes on the grass, and offered her the stick. "Eat some more; you will need your strength."

Sasna took the stick, blew on the potatoes, and when they were cool enough, she began to eat, chewing slowly, and not taking her eyes off of him. "We need each other, for a time," she said, after she had swallowed her mouthful.

Scarand grunted, picked up a potato for himself, shuffled it between his hands whilst blowing on it, and when it was cool enough, he bit into it. The taste was sweet and a tad sour, but it gave him fresh energy.

They both finished their scant meal in silence, after which Sasna threw the stick aside and complained, "You are a hunter. Could you not have found us some meat?"

He muttered a curse under his breath. With no bow or arrow to hunt with, it would have taken too long to set a trap or a snare. It occurred to him that she was not familiar with the wild. The rain continued to fall, getting heavier, and the trees they were under offered little shelter from the chill wind. "Which way is Kappia?" he asked.

Sasna shivered, and held out her hands towards the fire to try and draw warmth from it, and put her head between her knees. "It is far away to the north, situated on a large plateau surrounded by unclimbable cliffs. One way to get to it is by a heavily guarded passage called the Steps of Narzoum, which are impossible to pass undetected. A ship or boat along the Erin is the only other way to get there. Kappia starts at the port and descends up the sides of the plateau. With the infestation of pirate scum now reaching as far as Berecoth, I have recently learnt the Erin is now not even safe in these parts. I am on a mission to negotiate safe passages for Seesnari ships."

"I can take care of myself," Scarand said, as he stood. He looked north towards the Erin, once again regretting that even with his raw stamina and strength, he lacked the ability to swim across it. If he could swim, currents or not, he would have made the attempt. The fire started to flicker out, he finished it by kicking some dirt over it. "I fare you well, Seesnari," he said purposefully as he began towards the trail.

"You need me," Sasna called after him, a hint of desperation in her voice. "For the sake of your sisters, see the sense in this."

Scarand turned and looked at her. She pleaded with him. "Take me to Greytears, and then help me to find Farir." She then said resolutely, "If you do, I swear I will not only set you free, I will give you all of the gold you will need to buy back your sisters' freedom."

"I plan to rescue them, not buy them," he answered. The saying again rattled in his head; *never trust a Seesnari.* "Your words here mean nothing. If I take you to that castle, I would be clapped in irons again, and have no means to make you fulfil any promise you might make here. I will take my own chances."

He then pointed to the rough path in the wall of green forest, either side of which the undergrowth was dense. "Any scouts looking for survivors will the more easily find you if you head to the road, but I do not know if the trails will reach that far. If the trackers out looking know their trade, they will find you soon enough if you wait here."

"You can't just leave me here!" Sasna said in alarm. "All manner of beasts prowls the wild places outside of any settlements, and there are creatures that emerge from the river to consume the unsuspecting, who might wait unaware near the banks."

Scarand felt in a quandary, differing emotions raged inside his heart. Every wild instinct of his told him that he was better off making his own way, whilst a more logical part of him, knew that if she did keep her word to him that would be a more sensible path. His own sense of honour, yet again, also urged him from just walking off and leaving her. *Not all predators hunt and feed only at night.*

"Please, I beg you," she said, looking vulnerable. "At least take me as far as the road, and from there make your decision. I do not feel I have the strength left to make it on my own, and I have no blade to clear a path if the way is blocked by the foliage." She shuddered, and looked around at the thick wall of trees. "When you were gone, I was sure I saw a movement in the trees."

It dawned upon Scarand why she had not tried to run when he was washing out the cloth. *She is weak through the injury, and more afraid of what is out there, than she is of me.* He again scanned the thick green wall of trees for any movement, but nothing met his eyes. He tried to listen for any sound or noise beyond the natural, and looked to the reeds, hoping that what he had glimpsed on the river might just be born of imagination. The only sound was of birds chirping amongst the trees, the rain as it pattered around them and the wind as it blew and whistled through the branches and leaves.

The dilemma he felt was almost unbearable. He turned his attention back to Sasna, she looked so helpless. The land was wild and he could see the fear in her eyes when she looked up and observed her surroundings, and worse, he saw fear in her eyes when she looked at him, even though his actions had already surely proven to her that he had no intentions of harming her. He cursed silently under his breath. Despite whom she was and the part she had played in his enslavement, it was just not who he was to abandon her in the wild looking landscape they were in, and besides, although he knew little of civilised ways, the offer of searching for his sisters, whilst not also being an escaped slave, if she kept her word, made sense to him.

*For Marciea and Oliviana.* "Do you swear, that if I give assistance to you now, you will give me the things that prove my freedom?"

"I swear it," she solemnly replied.

*I want to believe you. I will take you as far as the road, and make my decision there.*

He reached his hand out to her. Reluctantly, Sasna used her good arm to take it. He firmly but gently pulled her to her feet. She then pulled her hand away from his, and stood on her own. The sky had grown darker and the light rain was turning into a heavy downpour when they set out into the forest wilderness. The sky flickered with lightning, followed by rumbling thunder.

"We should move fast," he said, leading the way southward towards the trail through the dense undergrowth. His eyes and ears were keenly alert as they made their way through the forest, especially his ears, as no gaze could penetrate the leafy tangle for more than a few feet in either direction. He used the sabre to continue to make the passage easier to traverse, as he cut away more foliage.

It was not long before Sasna started lagging behind, due to being weakened through the wound. She rejected the shoulder he offered her to lean on, so Scarand let her go in front, so he could keep an eye on her progress, and push her forward when she slowed.

They walked in silence; the stillness of the forest trail was primeval, and the only sounds were the song of the birds, the crash of thunder and the pitter-patter of heavy rain, accompanied by the snap of a stick or branch whenever Sasna stumbled, which was becoming more often. They made their way through the path, and were soon on other natural and animal trails. Each time a choice was offered, Scarand chose the trail that looked easier to travel. In places where their route became blocked, he cleared a path with the sabre through the thick undergrowth, until once again they had come across more trails. Apart from where he had to cut a path, he was careful on the trails to make sure there was little trace of his passing, but Sasna was leaving a trail even an untrained eye would be able to follow. He consoled himself that once he had escorted her, and left her by the road, he would be able to find another place to make his escape, and once again leave little or no sign of his passing.

Scarand helped steady Sasna on a few occasions. She was stumbling more and more. It was clear she was getting weaker. The blood had drained from her face, which was pale and sickly looking, and she was panting heavily. She stopped and leant against a tree, taking in some deep breaths. He turned to face her, as she stumbled. Just in time he managed to catch her and keep her on her feet, but she then steadied herself and continued. It was obvious that every step was becoming more of a struggle than the last. Again, leaning again against a tree, she took some more deep breaths. This time, she did not refuse his arm when he offered it to her for support as they set out again. She leant heavily on him.

"You puzzle me Davari," she said as she hung her head with tiredness, and looked up at him with half-closed eyes.

"You should save your breath," he answered impatiently.

"It helps me to talk, it takes my mind off of the pain, and I need to rest but a few moments," she said, slurring the words slightly as she pushed him away, adjusted the bandage, and then fainted and slumped to the floor.

Scarand cursed under his breath. The grey skies had opened fully, and a great downpour of rain fell; the canopy of the forest offered little protection as the rain cascaded down the leaves. Fierce lightning streaked across the sky followed by loud peals of thunder. He looked around, the forest to his left was not so thick. About a hundred yards or so he could see some sort of collapsed structure, overgrown with vines and covered in broken trees and lichen.

Picking Sasna up in his arms, he made his way towards it. Carrying her made his movements a lot slower. Even though it was not far, it was not long before he felt fatigued himself. It was with difficulty he walked along the wet leafy path to a large ruin, mostly reclaimed by the forest. He found a small, derelict tower, partially surrounded by two collapsed walls; it was probably once part of some sort of keep. He made his way through it into a ruined hall, partially collapsed. It provided temporary shelter from the rain that was now pouring down heavily, and from the lightning still streaking across the sky.

Scarand lay Sasna down, with her back towards a wall, under what little shelter the ruin provided. He briefly considered abandoning her to the forest. *I have delayed long enough. For Marciea and Oliviana.* As the thoughts crossed his mind, she awoke.

She had a delirious look in her eyes, and her words were slurred and sluggish when she spoke. "I feel a sickly chill and fear if I pass into sleep again, I may not wake. Find me pirken," she said.

*Pirken? I need to look for a purple flower. It is common in wooded areas. I remember Frema telling me of it.* Scarand rushed into the woods, and quickly found one. He picked it, stalk and all, and returned to Sasna. She was out cold, her breath fast and rapid. *She is dying.* He tried to remember what Frema had taught him about pirken. *'Be careful with it, it is as dangerous as it is good for a cure. If it does not cure you, it will kill you,'* she had said. *'Once picked the whole flower becomes poisonous if it remains exposed to air, and not consumed quickly. Crush the petals in your fingers, eat the petals, then the leaves, and then the stalk. In that order.'*

He shook Sasna awake, patting the side of her face to bring her round. "You must eat this," he said, as he crushed the petals between his fingers. They gave out a sweet and pungent fragrance.

"I think I am dying, Davari," she answered weakly, as he put the crushed petals in her mouth. She ate it, chewing slowly, and swallowed with difficulty. Purple froth oozed through her lips. She closed her eyes.

"Stay awake," he urged, as he crushed the leaves and gave it to her. She ate, and spluttered at the foul taste. He then broke the stalk into several pieces, which he also gave to her. After eating the stalk, her chin fell onto her chest, and no effort of his could wake her. The blue veins under her skin bulged and traced a map of her inner workings. She let out a heavy breath of air and became still. For a moment Scarand thought she had died, but she soon started breathing again, lightly and slowly.

Scarand felt a growing impatience at the delay. He again considered abandoning her to the forest, and cursed himself when he could not find it within himself to do so. He sat there and looked more closely at his surroundings. Some of the stone blocks looked like they would once have been part of a great castle. Where once a mighty curtain wall stood, only scattered blocks of stone remained, blocks so large that it must have taken a hundred men to place them. Some had sunk so deep into the wet mud and bog that only a corner showed. Others lay about like they were the abandoned toy of a giant. They were cracked and crumbling, spotted with lichen and covered in creeping vines.

Scarand managed to find some dry stick in the ruin, and rubbing two sticks together, he made a small fire which he fed with as much dry wood as he could find. He then sat and waited in the ruin, by Sasna's side, and watched, checking for signs of breathing, when it seemed like she was not moving, and using leaves to wipe away the purple froth as it oozed out of her mouth. The blue veins bulging under her skin soon settled, and colour slowly returned to her cheeks. He changed the dressing and applied the last of the poultice.

It was an hour before Sasna awoke. She coughed and spluttered. Scarand picked a large leaf full of rain water. He dribbled the contents onto her lips, and she dank from it thirstily. He poured the remainder of the contents of the leaf until her thirst was satisfied.

"That day on the desert sands, on the Plains of Ashgiliath, you told me you once hunted a giant white warg," she said, as she wearily looked at him.

He was taken aback by the unexpected comment. *You don't hunt a white warg, it hunts you. It kills you, or you kill it.*

"Have you not even wondered why you and the other two slaves, out of all the others, were not taken to Zinibar to be sold, but were being brought to Castle Greytears?" she asked him, as her head flopped sideward, like one drunk.

It had occurred to him, but lacking opportunity to gain answers, he had put the concern aside. Frema had refused to answer any questions on the matter. *'Learn what I teach you about the land and its herbs and flowers. It might save your life,'* was all she ever said when quizzed.

"The Baron is also a hunter, but his prey is men," Sasna said, after which she winced.

*She is delirious with the pain, or from the effects of the pirken.*

"We pay him a regular tribute in gold, and when we buy slaves from the Ikma, he demands a tribute of three. He demands we send a husband and wife, and another. Somebody like yourself, who knows a bit about hunting, and will give them a good chase." Clammy sweat beaded her flesh.

Scarand felt anger rise within him. He silently muttered a silent and savage curse, as he again remembered the saying; *never trust a Seesnari.* He regretted staying to help her.

Sasna smiled cold-bloodedly, and her words were slow and feverish. "No Davari has ever escaped the Baron; his men and dogs always catch their prey," she said.

*You were sending me to be hunted like a wild pig?* Scarand fingered the hilt of the sabre, as once more conflicting emotions flickered about inside of him. He resisted the urge to strike her down where she sat. He had given her his word not to harm her, and nothing she would now say would change that. He released the hilt of the weapon.

*I will leave you here. There are bound to be creatures that will pick up your scent. You will know the fear of being prey.* He cast a look around him at the dense leafy walls to the south, beyond the ruin, his ears ever alert to any sound of danger.

"But I am glad it did not turn out that way," she said, the heartless smile fading from her face, "for you are an honourable man. That is why I promise you with an oath, if you get me to Castle Greytears, and deliver me safely into the hands of the Baron, and help me find my brother, I swear to you I will do everything in my power to help you find those lost to you. When the way is clear, I will go to Kappia and buy your sisters myself, for you, and set them free."

The rage inside of him submerged. *I cannot tell if she is mine enemy, or my hope.*

"I too was once a captive and a slave," she said.

He raised his eyebrows in surprise.

"I was just a young girl when the civil war within the Kappia Empire started, over some rare artefact they had discovered, called the Simal." She coughed, and adjusted the bandage. "War and chaos broke out everywhere, even outside of the Empire. The Nine Kingdoms did not go unscathed. One of them, Spartak, has always been a seething cauldron of violence. It is a cursed place, a land in which no man's holdings were ever safe. Chieftains and princelings led marauding bands, despoiling everything in their paths in pursuit of their bloody feuds. Every other man called himself a king, but only one held any real claim to lordship, King Gharian of the Southern Steppes."

"You can tell me this another time. We need to get moving," Scarand said impatiently. He could tell by the way she kept adjusting the bandage on her shoulder, and rubbing the wound, that it was still causing some discomfort.

"The wound was disturbed when I changed the dressing. The poultice takes a while to work, but the pain should soon subside, and then we must make haste," he said.

She nodded. "I need but a few moments, I am already feeling a bit stronger. The pirken, it might have saved my life." She took a deep breath. "Gharian united the warring factions at the start of the civil war and attacked the Kingdom of Cabeiri. Knowing they would be next in the path of Spartak if Cabeiri fell, the kingdoms of Luciana and Merva allied with them to fight Spartak. The kingdoms of Phoausanos and Samothrane that bordered them, did not send their chariots and come to their aid. It suited them for their neighbours to be locked in a war, as it gave them opportunity to become allied and strike at my people. They attacked us Seesnari, agreeing to share out the spoils of war and the land, my land, among themselves."

She wiped away a tear that rolled down her eye, and Scarand could tell the reminiscing was not easy for her.

"Many of my people were slain, or taken captive. I was just a young girl when Farir and I were captured with my mother and taken as political prisoners to the capital of Samothrane." She gently rubbed her shoulder, taking deep and slow breaths, and continued. "My mother's family had a summer house in the Golden Hills of Valain, the westernmost province of Seesnari. We were taken before we even knew war was declared. My father was a general in the king's army. The armies of the Phoausanos and Samothrane had looted and pillaged the western provinces of Seesnari, but he held them back at a strategic position called *Dead Man's Pass*. He would not surrender and give up the advantage point, so they threatened my mother with the Golden Barrel unless he surrendered the pass."

Sasna broke off. She wiped her face, and Scarand was not sure if she was wiping off a raindrop or a tear. She took another deep breath and looking up at him she asked, "You don't know what that is, do you?"

He shook his head and a vague memory stirred in his brain as he admitted, "No, I do not, but my father once told me that the cruel ways of so-called civilised kingdoms, far exceed the barbarism for which my own people are known." He looked at her attentively. The natural scepticism of an educated man was not his, but his own people told their own mythology through oral stories, and he was curious about the world, so wanted her to continue.

"It is a cruel punishment the Samothrane reserve usually for their own noble women, wives and mistresses of their king mostly, who are unfaithful to him. They cut the arms and legs off the victim, seal and tend the wounds to make sure they stay alive, put them in a golden barrel with just the head on show and parade them through each city of Samothrane, accompanied by jesters and clowns who mock the victim. The barrel is escorted by musicians who dance, blow horns and play the tambourine whilst throwing sweetcakes to the crowd."

Scarand's eyes widened. *They did this to your mother?*

"My father would not surrender the path, even when his wife was threatened with this fate. Farir and I were young, but were given the task of caring for her. We were forced to stand on the wagon that paraded her through the streets of Samothrane. She begged for death, even from us her own children, but we could not do it as we had neither the means nor the will. She died within the year, which was a mercy."

"How did you escape?" he asked her.

"We didn't. Peace came eventually, except for areas along the border where the usual skirmishing between bands of raiders or individuals takes place. My father was killed in the war, so my uncle ransomed us." She curled her nose up, as though she was disgusted at the memory. "It is the only reason I am a slaver. He made me and Farir responsible for the debt for our ransom. He makes us serve him, to pay it back. It is the only reason I am in this foul trade," she said. "But he has entrusted me with a diplomatic mission, and if I succeed in that, and some personal business, the debt can be all but paid and I can choose my own path in this life."

Sasna looked at the ground, pulled her legs up to her chest and began to play with a blade of grass. Tears filled her eyes. It was the first time Scarand was certain he was seeing genuine emotional weakness in her, and it disturbed him greatly though he could not explain why. She again looked so vulnerable sitting shivering in her damp and torn clothes, her hair tangled and wet from the wind and dripping from the rain that had broken from the clouds and was still falling around them, some of it making its way through the ruin in which they sheltered. His heart beat faster and he desired to be near her, to protect her. He felt uncomfortable with his own feelings, he wanted to hate her, to feel bitter and angry, but he did not feel that way about her. As he looked at her, so defenceless, something stirred deep within his own heart, a sudden and unexpected desire to protect her from all the evils of the world. The only previous time he had felt powerful emotions towards a woman not of his family, was when he had once been in the presence of a Davari noblewoman who ruled in Jorthek, a great town where his father had once taken him to sell furs at the market there. He had been captivated by her elegance and noble bearing, and his heart had stirred within him. He shook his head to clear it. *She is bewitching me?*

Sasna plucked the blade of grass and rubbed it with her fingers. She stared at him. Colour was starting to come back into her cheeks, her eyes were becoming clearer and wider open, her voice stronger. "These ruins are old, very old," she said, looking around her. "I often wonder what the people were like whom once lived in places such as this. What made them laugh or cry? What struggles and terrors did they face, were they good or bad people? What calamity led to them abandoning what would once have been a safe home?"

Scarand pointed at a corner stone opposite him. "There is an inscription on it, it is weathered, but it is clearly writing."

Sasna looked at the words on the stone, squinting at the faded inscription. "That is the old Cinoan language, my father taught me this," she said.

"What does it say?" Scarand asked curiously.

"It is hard to read, for they are faint, but I believe it says "I am King Emerides, greatest King of all Kings. My works and name shall stand for all time and will never be forgotten."

"He was a famous king?" Scarand asked. Despite the misery of the weather and the obvious discomfort of her wound, Sasna smiled more widely than before, the pirken had clearly had a good effect.

"I am no scholar of merit like some, and know more of the history of my own people than that of others. But I have read the works and histories of Temmison, and never came across the name of this king. It appears this stone is the only thing that remembers him." She looked around her, at the broken ruins. "What powerful but unrecorded race, once dwelt in this annihilated place. The faeces of foxes sit, where Emerides once did abide."

Scarand could not help but laugh out loud, and Sasna joined in, the wound in her shoulder did not appear to bother her so much. When their laughter faded, he looked at her, yet felt like he was seeing her for the first time. He noticed the small dimple in her cheek, the laughter lines on her eyes. He again felt a wave of affection for her that involuntarily swooped over him. He quickly looked away, lest she might sense what he felt as he looked at her.

Her voice was calm when she finally spoke. "We Seesnari are a proud people, this is not easy for me but..." She trailed off. Scarand sensed what she was about to say was difficult for her.

"Thank you, Davari, you have saved my life," she said.

She held her hand up to him. "I think the pirken and poultice are working, the pain is going away, and I feel suddenly stronger and refreshed."

He took her hand and gently pulled her to her feet.

They set out again and walked in silence until they again found the natural trails in the forest, and for a good half an hour, they made good progress towards the road. Scarand pondered much on the grisly tale she had told him, but his mind was not so consumed that he did not stay alert, ever watching and listening for any signs of danger, and then he found some.

He urgently put his finger to his mouth, ordering silence. He then pointed to some tracks in the forest, tracks that were not made by any natural beast. Sasna's eyes widened in terror, and he could tell she recognised their source. The tracks had come from the south, and then headed west. Whoever had made them wore no footwear. They were not the tracks of men, even though of similar size, apart from one set, far larger than the rest. Sasna looked at him, her face curled with concern as she whispered.

"Those tracks are Chatti, they travel with a Gragor, or a giant as some call them. They are raiding these parts. She stared at him, and then continued. "If these tracks do not make you fearful, they should."

Scarand felt his scalp prickle. He scanned the forest for any sign of life or movement, after which he crouched down to more closely examine the tracks. They were about a day old. Alone he could move through the forest and leave little or no trace of his passing, but with Sasna, that would still not be possible. If those who had made the tracks returned, or if more travelled that way, they would surely discover her tracks, which would be all but impossible to conceal.

"We should find the road quickly," he said. "There could be more, heading this way, or they might return."

Scarand chose a different trail from that which the trackers were upon. It was an hour or so before they finally made it to the road, and by that time the rain had stopped as had the thunder. Scarand looked to the south, to the marshes beyond the road, and then to the south-east, where smoke from pillaged villages was rising into the air. Sasna followed his gaze.

"It looks like the Chatti have raided a village. You must take me to Castle Greytears; the road will not be safe come nightfall," she said. "It is the wisest choice before you!"

Before Scarand could answer, in the distance, they heard the sound of blowing horns, braying dogs, the sound of hoof beats and the shouts of men coming along the road, just over a ridge ahead.

"Choice is stripped from you," Sasna said, "do not consider running, the dogs will follow your scent and you will not escape."

Scarand hesitated, and drew the sabre. "Then I die here!"

"Don't be a fool," Sasna urged. "Even a trained swordsman could not fight so many. If not for yourself, surrender to my plan for Marciea and Oliviana."

Scarand fought against his natural urges, which were to run and seek escape, or to die fighting where he stood. It went against every grain of his instincts when he handed the sabre over to Sasna, hilt first."

"Then I hope you are a Seesnari I can trust," he said resignedly. *For Marciea and Oliviana.*

# Chapter Eight: *The Deadlands*

*It may seem strange to those not of Akkadian Pure-blood, that this is my first published works on the Deadlands, but information is so hard to come by on this subject. I so wish I myself was a Seer, as they are so rare, and those few you do meet, are seldom willing to share about what they have seen in that dreadful place. However, I have managed to tempt one with enough coin, to share his experiences with me, and thus I finally put pen to paper, with at least a measure of authority on the subject.*

*Temmison Vol XIV, Book 1: The Deadlands.*

*Janorra* hovered above her own body, watching in horror as the spider continued to wrap her flesh in gossamer thread. As her spirit body began to slowly form in essence, the physical world of the Everglow began to fade, and slowly the world of the Deadlands formed, until she left her body entirely and became a spirit.

Her silver armour glistened in the fading twilight. She drew the sword named *Fury* and swished it in the air, but as always it could connect with nothing physical in the Outer World, it was only of use in the Deadlands. In the physical world, it was as though the spider sensed her ghostly presence. It dropped her physical body and fled into the trees from whence it came. The world of the Everglow soon disappeared entirely, as her spirit was sucked away from the physical world, until she was fully back in the Deadlands.

*I do not know this part of the Deadlands, it is unfamiliar to me,* she thought, as she surveyed her surroundings. She was on a hill, below which laid a marsh foul and stinking. Her nostrils recoiled at the pungent aromas all around her, wafting up the slopes pushed by the slight breeze. Black clouds in the ever-grey sky of the Deadlands loomed above her. In the distance she heard a ferocious howling. *Netherhounds.* They were down wind of her and would pick up her scent soon enough, and then hunt her down.

*Is there no end to my misfortune?* She wailed to herself. She could take one, maybe two with *Fury*, but she knew not how many netherhounds there might be, and they often hunted in packs of varying sizes. She looked around for a marker, or a path made by a Seer who might have passed that way before, but she could see none. There was no silver tower close by, or in the distance. *This is not good. I need to find the closest Obelisk.* She looked around, and felt disorientated, and did not know which direction to take. If she could find a door or a gateway to the Dark Paths, she could speak to Horin and ask for his assistance and help, but it was almost impossible to find a gate or door to the path unless you knew where one was, and this area was new and strange to her. The chances of stumbling by chance onto a gate or door were very slight, you could easily pass by one just a few feet or even inches away, and not see it. She knew the location of three gates and one door, but not knowing where she was, she guessed they were far away from her, and she had no way of knowing how to get to them.

A change in the sound of the hounds, from howling to excited chatters told her they had picked up her scent. They were closer than she had first thought. She took deep breaths to calm herself. She was no established warrior in the Everglow, the land of the living, but here in the Underglow, the land of the dead, she had proven herself many times. Horin had taught her how to defend herself. It would not be the first time she had fought netherhounds, but she could not risk a second-death here in the Deadlands. If her spirit body was killed, the netherhounds could not see or touch her spirit essence, but she would drift aimlessly until drawn in by an unknown Obelisk, or, even worse, a

Telamone, a soul-eater, could find her, or a servant of the Aeldar who would surely return her to a fate worse than death.

Out of all the horrors in the Deadlands, Telamones were what Seers feared the most, and a reason when possible they only ever entered the Deadlands in large numbers or in areas they knew they had secured, and where they had previously constructed defences or hiding places against such terrible foes. But here, she was in the wild, and alone. Her best chance of survival was to try flight before fight. She sheathed *Fury* in the scabbard that hung across her back.

Attuning to the sound of the hounds yammering, she determined as best she could which direction they were coming from, and without further hesitation, turned and fled in the opposite one, running speedily, but at a rate where she would not exhaust herself too quickly. If the netherhounds caught up with her, which chances were they surely would, regardless how fast she ran, she had to make sure she conserved enough energy and stamina for the fight that would surely follow.

In the grey light under the dark sky, she set off. She slanted to the right to avoid stumbling down the steep slope of the hill, and raced down the stony slope to the vast fen below. Apart from the sound of her panting breath and the yammering of the hounds in the distance, there was black silence.

Janorra reached the marsh in short time. The reek of it filled her nostrils even more than before. Heavy and foul in the air, which had suddenly become still, it caused her to momentarily choke and gasp for air. Stumbling, she fell with a splash into the filthy mire. Regaining her feet, the sound of the hounds had stopped. *They no longer yammer; they have followed my scent and picked up my trail.*

Realising they were close, she set off with fresh vigour, taking deep breaths of the pungent air. Picking up the sound of running water, she headed towards it. Soon she came across the bed of one of one of the many small rivers that trickled down from the surrounding hills to feed the stagnant pools and mires. Running into it, her feet splashed along in the stony stream. Fortunately, it was shallow and did not hinder her speed. She rushed along in the stream until she heard the yammering of the hounds once more. As she had hoped, the stream had covered her scent, but it would not be long before they picked it up again. She paused but for a few moments to catch her breath, and then set off once more, away from the sound of the hounds, which soon began to yammer, telling each other, one of them had picked up her scent again. She picked up her speed, more so when they again became silent as they continued their hunt. The stream soon became less shallow and earthier, before disappearing into a hole in the ground. Noticing a gully to her left, she clambered down the side which was about as tall as a man's height. At its base there were wide flat shelves, made of naturally formed metamorphic grey stone slate. Water ran in a channel on the other side fed by a small waterfall where the stream had again sprung from the ground. She set off but slipped on the wet stone and fell heavily, only avoiding injury by stretching out her hands just in time. As she stood to her feet, she became momentarily disorientated. Above her, on top of the steep grassy mounds that surrounded the gully, she heard the sound of nearby panting. The hounds were upon her.

Janorra drew *Fury*, and braced, readying herself for the beasts that would pounce out of the dull light. She counted the breaths of three, more than she had ever fought before. From the ledge above two of the hounds flung themselves upon her, a mass of black leather hide, horns, claws and gnashing saliva dripping teeth. Far bigger than a bear in the world of the living, the first one knocked her to the ground causing her to fall several feet backwards, which was fortunate in a way as the teeth of the second missed her face by a mere inch. The third pounced, but she had seen it. Thrusting *Fury* forward, the hound made a piercing, whimpering screech as its jaws were skewered. It fell next to her, lifeless.

In the Deadlands, the land of the dead, such a creature as a netherhound would not return to any form of existence. She pulled *Fury* from the jaws of the dead beast, just in time to strike the first hound which had found its feet and launched itself at her once more. Performing a pirouette, she swung *Fury*. Steel met flesh; the hound fell to the stony ground with a thud and a clatter followed by a splash - the thud the sound of its body hitting the ground, the clatter the sound of its parted head as it bounced upon the ground before landing in the water causing the splash. The last hound lunged and clawed at her face but her reactions were quicker, she parted its front legs from it before thrusting *Fury* into its chest. The hound died with an unnerving howl of rage and pain.

Exhausted, Janorra fell to her knees. Her head slumped to her breast as she gasped to catch her breath. After a few moments she stood to her feet and walked over to the stream, where she washed the black blood off of *Fury*. It would be no good to her if the sword stuck to her sheath, next time she needed it. She did not clean the splatters of blood off of her face or armour, instead, she smeared more upon herself. Long ago, Horin had taught her that the scent of slain hounds would soon mask her own, helping her get to a silver tower, whilst possibly being unnoticed by more of them. Netherhounds rarely hunted and attacked each other. Here, in the Deadlands, even the slightest advantage might help her survive and make it to a silver tower where an Obelisk would return her to the Everglow, the land of the living.

Feeling thirst, Janorra longed to take a sip of the water around her, but it was foul-smelling. It would only cause her sickness, which would slow her down. Looking around her, again she could see no sign or clue as to which direction to head off in, so she continued in the same direction as before. She followed the stream for three chill hours until she came to the end of the watercourse, where the water joined a brown bog. The banks became moss grown mounds, not so steep as before. She clambered up the nearest bank and walked through dry reeds that rattled against the armour on her legs. On either side ahead, fens and mires now lay, stretching into the distance until lost in sight in the dim half-light. Mists curled and smoked from gurgling pools, the reek of which hung in the now still and stagnant air. She avoided the pools that gurgled - revolting things often lived in them.

On she went, walking for hours she could not count, around an endless network of pools, soft mires, and half-strangled water courses. It was a dreary and wearisome journey. The only green she saw was the scum of livid weed on the dark greasy surfaces of the sullen waters. Dead grasses and rotting weeds loomed out of the half-light. Her armour, bright at first, became caked in the grime and dirt of the bog. She felt no remorse for this. It helped her move unseen and covered her scent even more.

Occasionally she would hear the sound of some distant creatures; a distant bellow, answered by another, a hiss, a roar, a scream or a yowl. Whenever she heard such a noise, she stopped, crouched down low, and pressed an ear to the earth until she could hear it no more before continuing.

The fen grew wetter, opening into wide stagnant meres, among which it became harder to find firmer ground she could walk upon without sinking into the mud. The air here seemed blacker, and more difficult to breathe. It was not long before she felt a very dark presence, a spirit of great power.

Janorra stopped. She felt she was being watched by powerful unseen eyes, but she sensed whatever it was, was curious about her, perhaps even a little fearful, so she spoke into the air.

"Whatever dark spirit you are, let me pass and do not hinder me, for it will not end well for you. I have power you will not want unleashed against you."

In response, a dark wind blew around her, causing her hair to dance on its breeze. She felt the unseen spirit moving around her, circling her, but it kept is distance. The air filled with the sound of unintelligible whispers. The spirit was trying to talk to her, but the words made no sense. It was a dark tongue, beyond her knowing.

*This is no ordinary wraith or spectre, it is something else, the like of which I have not met before.* Then, an image faintly appeared. It was a hag with pendulous teats and greenish warty like skin. Her black lips snarled with malice, but in contrast, her crusty yellow puss filled eyes were desperate and filled with tears. The hag whispered unintelligible words in another dark tongue.

As from another realm, a wrinkled hand appeared, and a long finger pointed at the image of the hag. "Help her," the dark spirit said.

Janorra drew *Fury* from its scabbard and held it up defensively before her face. "Look at this sword, if you know its legend, then you will know not to follow me, or I will speak words that will reveal your essence and this sword shall end your miserable existence. Keep away from me. That is my only warning to you."

Another form appeared, just as the first hag faded away. Its appearance was also faint and watery. It was a female figure, hideously deformed, trapped inside a sphere wreathed in blue flames. The creature whispered and held out a hand as if seeking help, before it howled in pain and disappeared.

"Help her," the dark spirit said again.

A third apparition appeared. It was a face, grey and wrinkled, aged beyond counting: this hag had seen thousands of years, and the cruelty and misery of each of them had formed the hateful expression on her features. Her eye sockets were coated with filthy slime, and the redness of her lips was caked and crusted as though she had carelessly drunk blood again and again. Her matted, filthy grey hair hung down to her shoulders. A drift of putrescent stink wafted from her mouth as she spoke, causing Janorra to cover her nose with the palm of her hand. Once again, the whispered words were unintelligible. The apparition only appeared for the briefest of moments before it vanished.

"Help her," the dark spirit said for a third time. Janorra could sense cruelty and evil in the hags she had seen in the vision, and a deep anger, but also a great pain. It made her wince and cry out with a whimper when she felt their pain.

Janorra felt the presence of the dark spirit depart, and the darkness seemed to lift considerably. A vague memory woke in her, and she recalled reading something of its kind before, but could not quite remember what it was she had once read. *What could it be?*

As she continued to make her way through the bog, Janorra felt relief that she could no longer sense the spirit, it did not follow. More than ever, she wished that by sheer chance she could find a gate to the Dark Paths. *Horin would know what that spirit was. He would advise me, and point me in the direction of an Obelisk where it would be safe to resurrect at.*

The presence of the spirit had unnerved her, but also, the images it showed her had stirred pity in her. She was unsure why she should feel pity for such wretched creatures, but she could not reason the feeling away.

It was not long before Janorra sensed two other presences, but these were different. One was bitter and enraged; the other was calm and wise. She sensed them very faintly at first, but as she continued in the same direction, the feeling became stronger with each step, until she saw two sets of thick roots from two trees. The roots came down from the sky and touched the land, before burying beneath the surface. The roots were slowly moving, it was as though they were a feature of the landscape, their presence and essence a part of where she was. She considered turning back, away from whatever it was she sensed, for one of the set of roots creaked and moaned in great pain. But, a faint howl in the distance in the direction of where she had come, made her think otherwise, so she continued, taking weary step after weary step as she stepped over the roots and continued in the direction she was headed.

Exhaustion soon overwhelmed Janorra, but she dared not rest for longer than a few minutes at a time, the frequency of which became more necessary the wetter the fen became. *I must get out of this cursed place as fast as I can. Should I turn back and find another way, or should I go on?*

She stood and listened, but all was silent, except for the odd croak coming from a bed of weeds, or the buzzing of a fen fly. Again, she decided turning back was not an option, her strength would not allow her to traverse the way back from whence she had come, and she did not want to chance meeting the strange spirit again. She had sensed it was powerful, very powerful, and though she had yet to meet a foe in the Deadlands that *Fury* could not wound or kill, a battle with such a spirit was not a battle she desired. The images the spirit had shown troubled her. Even though she had sensed malice and evil coming from them, there was a part of her that felt compassion for them, but she knew not why nor what help she could offer. It then dawned upon her. *Could it be Aeldar Wives the spirit showed me? Am I getting near to Aeldar Riddles? If so, why are they revealing themselves to me. If they want me to find them, why? Has the Simal led me to them?* She cast the thoughts from her mind, as she continued taking step after weary step. Her first priority had to be to find a silver tower, and an Obelisk to resurrect at.

Janorra wandered for many more hours. Hope evaporated within her, as fast as her failing strength. Despair soon set in. *I will never find a way out of this bog.*

She caught her foot in some old root or tussock and fell heavily on her hands, which sank deep into sticky ooze. She rested her face on the surface of the foul ground and closed her eyes but a moment, before jolting awake and struggling to her feet. *I cannot stop here or I will never get up again, I must press on.*

As she walked on, step after tired step, she continued to flounder, stepping or falling noisily into mud or a small pool. Her strength was near its final end, her will ready to surrender, when finally, she stepped upon firmer ground, where she felt the air moving, and the stench of the bog being blown back onto itself. Continuing with her last few ounces of strength, she finally reached grass. It was brown, but beneath it was firm ground. She sat, resting her body, but still not wanting to close her eyes in sleep. To keep herself awake, and give some cheer, she softly sang.

'*O misty eyes, which sorrow oft sees.*
*I close them now, to give them some ease.*
*My child so fine, is lost from my sight.*
*The world is dark, the stars do not shine.*
*O misty eyes, you close now in peace.*'

Sleep overtook her, against her will.

*      *      *

On waking several hours later, Janorra scorned herself that it was not the best choice of song to sing to try and stay awake, but exhaustion had weakened her mind as well as her body, and sleep had taken her against her will. Unlike sleep in the physical world, sleep in the Deadlands was never accompanied by dreams. It was just a blank of memory. Regardless of her regret, she felt a new vigour and strength. A light, refreshing breeze blew upon her. Standing, she looked at the sky, it did not seem as dark and foreboding as before. There was no sun in the Deadlands, but the sky shimmered with a faint light and blue.

Janorra walked upon the grass which grew greener with each step until she came to a stream where the water was fresh and clean and led to a small pond, from which she quenched her thirst. The scent of the hounds upon her had long since vanished with the stench of the bog, she was slimed and fouled all over and the stench an offence to her own nostrils. Fully clad in her armour, she lay in the stream and allowed the cool water to wash the stench and filth away. When her armour was clean, she removed it, then her chainmail and then her undergarment. She washed her body all over until free from dirt and mire. Donning her attire again, she set out in the same direction, filled with hope and expectation. She knew she was getting closer to a silver tower, to an Obelisk, and if so, it would not be long before she heard it calling to her.

It took less than an hour of walking before she heard it, a whisper on the wind, "*Come.*"

It was only a short distance until she found an ancient highway, lined by columns that were now only crumbled and broken ruins. *If there are Seers in whatever land of the Everglow this part of the Deadlands shadow, it is long since they have travelled this way, or they are unskilled and know not what to do,* she thought to herself. In the Deadlands that mirrored the Kappia Plateau, strong defences, citadels, roads and many safe places had been constructed for the Seers, and much of the wilds conquered. It was only when they ventured further into strange places in the Deadlands that the Empire's Seers often faced real dangers, and often they were not alone on such occasions.

Looking both directions the highway ran in, she spotted a small and distant spire. "*Come,*" the voice whispered.

Janorra took a deep breath, her former hope and expectation faded as it dawned upon her, she knew not in what place the Obelisk would resurrect her. But she could not stay in the Deadlands, it was too dangerous here in places unknown to her. An Obelisk had found her and she had found it. Sooner or later, it would resurrect her back to the Everglow, the land of the living, unless she moved away from it, and that was something she did not have the strength to do. Choice was taken from her, as the thought of going back the way she had come, or chancing herself in another direction, did not seem worth the risk, especially as finding any other Obelisk would involve the same risks of resurrecting in a hostile or fatal situation. *Ashareth guide me.*

More than one Seer she knew who had travelled away from known ways in the Deadlands, had resurrected at one of the Lost Obelisks located deep in underground lakes of the Everglow, where they had drowned and found themselves quickly back in the Deadlands again. Some had resurrected at an Obelisk buried deep in rock or lava, and death had been just as swift. *I must head towards this silver tower, and take my chances with this Obelisk.*

It was never far from Janorra's thoughts, that the Simal and *Arnazia*, her ring, were both lost in the Everglow, and her chances of finding them were better, the quicker she returned. Setting her face towards the distant tower, she headed towards it until after an hour or so she stood at its base, looking up at the thousands of glimmering runes and symbols of multiple colours that adorned its shining silver surface from top to bottom.

"I do not know these symbols," she said out loud to the tower. Although that was true, she did know that when the runes and symbols of a silver tower and the Obelisk within it were multi-coloured, it was often a sign that the Obelisk the other side, in the

Everglow, was slightly mad and insane, but to quite what degree it was impossible to tell.

"I am a stranger here, please help me," she shouted as she walked around the base of the tower. "You have to open the door for me."

Her voice echoed in the silence and went unanswered. Having no other choice, she walked over to a patch of lush grass nearby, that appeared wet with a morning due, not that the Deadlands had day or night. She sat crossed legged on the lush grass and waited, closing her eyes, but listening intently for any sound that might reveal some unfriendly creature creeping up on her. Back on the Kappia Plateau, all of the Obelisks were surrounded with strong defences that kept out the things not supposed to come near. Many of them were even surrounded with small towns or cities of the dead, constructed over centuries by the Seers. She had helped to build such places. But this place was neglected, no Seer with any skill or knowledge had come here in a long time.

When, after an hour or so, a finger prodded Janorra in the back, she sprung instantly to her feet, and turned with *Fury* drawn ready to face her antagonist. A man made of pure back marble with an expressionless face stood before her. She breathed a sigh of relief, and sheathed *Fury*.

"What is your name, Obelisk, and what land of the living do you open into?"

A smile appeared on the face of the Obelisk, which turned into an expression of absolute delight. It hummed a tune in a deep musical tone.

"Tum de tum. Tum de dah Tum. Tum de tum. Tum de de dah Tum."

"Oh great," Janorra said out loud to herself. "It is definitely one of the mad or eccentric ones."

The Obelisk formed a serious expression on its face. "Evil comes for you, comes it does on tireless feet and in the form of a golden and red beast of the air. Escape will be hard for you; evil waits for you through the door. Tum de de dah tum. Tum de tum. Tum de de dah tum."

Janorra knew better than to try to get an Obelisk such as this to speak in anything less than confusing riddles, but it had said enough to cause her concern. She had met many Obelisks in her time, some that were clear and rational in speech and would answer all questions, others that were rude or angry, but this one was clearly mad, for it had clearly not received the proper attention of any Seer for a very long time. Even with such attention, many Obelisks did not like sharing their knowledge with the Seers anymore. If on rare occasions they were in the mood to do so, they would often speak in unfathomable riddles, allegory, or construct sentences that made little sense.

Many Seers believed that the Obelisks, if they were ancient machines, were slowly breaking down. If they were living beings, then they were dying and going mad due to their great age and knowledge. Whichever was the case, the process of deterioration was accelerated if an Obelisk was neglected, and no skilful Seer attended to it. Even when neglected, the deterioration process lasted tens of thousands of years.

Janorra had once read that the Obelisks were older than the Ancient Ones themselves, and that even the Aeldar were considered young in comparison to them, although some scholars argued they were created during the Aeldar Age. It was said the Obelisks were placed in the Everglow by En-Sof himself. Whatever the truth of their origin, many priests and even Seers often ignored or paid little attention to anything most of them actually said, as much of it appeared to be mere babble and nonsense, and their words had too often proved unreliable on many an occasion.

Even so, Janorra always tried to reason with any Obelisk she met for the first time, and this day she had more reason to do so, than any time before. "Please Obelisk, tell me your name and where I am, for I am afraid of what might await me beyond that door to the Outer World? Your words bring no comfort to me."

Janorra knew that at if an Obelisk told you its name, it gave you the power to ask any knowledge you wished of it and it would answer you.

"Tum de de dah tum. Tum de tum. Tum de de dah tum. Tonight! The first three die: soon to flow; a river of blood. They hunt you young Elfie."

The Obelisk mimicked the frightened voice of a child. "Mother! Mother! Mother! It's dark down here. Mother! I'm frightened. Show me the way."

Janorra recognised the voice, it was her own, a haunting memory from her childhood, many lifetimes ago, when she had become lost in a cave she had ventured into whilst traveling in the acting troupe her parents had raised her in. The troupe had stopped for the night and parked their horse drawn caravans by the side of a small wood. She had been sent to gather wood for the fire, and had fallen into a shallow cave as she did so. Her mother had never come, but her father had heard her screams and rescued her.

Janorra had not recalled that memory in a long time. The once warm recollection, was now just a reminder of a time when life was more simple and pleasant. Now, as she thought of her father holding her in his arms, wiping away her tears and gently saying, "My silly young Elfie," the memory did not bring warmth, only a deep longing to be safe and secure.

"Please do not call me by that name," she said to the Obelisk. "I am now Janorra, not Elfie." Only two men had ever called her Elfie, and that so long ago: her father, then, later that same life, her husband, the man so cruelly taken from her.

The Obelisk looked at her and laughed innocently, and then its voice immediately changed to that of a screaming, hysterical woman. "Johnny! Johnny! Where's my little Johnny? The monster killed my little Johnny-boy!"

The Obelisk grew silent, thoughtful even, and looked sad. It sighed, closed its eyes and smiled again, returning to its normal musical voice.

"Tum de de dah tum. Tum de tum. Tum de de dah tum."

Of a sudden, the Obelisk grew serious and looked at Janorra with what appeared to be genuine concern. "Great evil hunts you, young Elfie. Terrible deeds done to you, if they catch you, much suffering will be yours. Run, Janorra! Run!"

Fear arose within her. The Obelisk was clearly mad, but twice it had given her a similar warning, that whatever was beyond the door that led back to the Everglow, was not good.

"Then please, let me go. Show me the way to another Obelisk. Let me find a safer place to enter the Everglow, please?"

"Too late," the Obelisk said; and then, in a panicked voice, loud, urgent and shrill, it shrieked, "run, Janorra! Run!"

The Obelisk thrust the palm of his hand on Janorra's forehead and drew her to him. It suddenly became calm. "Otan is my name." It narrowed its eyes and drew close to her; their eyes were almost touching. It then said in an urgent, but calm voice. "When you resurrect - run, Janorra! Run!" The Deadlands faded, as Otan returned Janorra back to the land of the living, back to the Outer World of the Everglow.

# Chapter Nine: *Thar Markoom*

*I heard it from good authority that the Bantu do exist, but in all of my time north beyond the great wall, outside of the Everglow, I never came across one, living or dead. It is said they war with the Dark Elves, assailing their last refuges deep in the Northern Winter Forests. Perhaps it is there I should go to discover if both races are real, or just the stuff of mere legend and myth? However, I have discovered a crypt located in an abandoned citadel that I find of most interest. I plan to excavate this tomb before travelling any further to the north.*
*Temmison Vol XV, Book 3: The Northern Badlands.*

*The* Bantu called it Thar Markoom; the Keep of Dagen Forosoth, was the Akkadian name for it. It was a dark and bleak place, but one of the most impressive fortifications either Mazdek or Aspess had ever seen. The citadel was a grandiose complex of buildings, some of which grew into the Black Mountain itself.

Aspess wore no jewels in her hair, a style that she only favoured when in the mood for it. She carried her high-crowned helm under her arm. On her head she wore the hammer and snake circlet on which the Juram was held along with the phial of Elestar. Her body was clothed with a hauberk made with rings forged of steel, black as jet. Above the mail she wore a sur-coat of black, embroidered with the hammer and snake symbol.

Mazdek was dressed more simply, in a black silk robe that covered a hair shirt, with a satchel slung over his shoulder. "Look!" He said to Aspess, as he slowly waved his hand, gesturing at all that was around them. "What an ally against the Baothein we now have." He followed her gaze at their surroundings, and especially at the sight that could be seen over the battlements. Spread out across the vale, reaching out to the Black Hills surrounding the keep and the Black Mountain itself, the campfires of the Bantu host that were lit and burning in the night could not be counted.

"Don't keep 'im waiting," one of their Bantu escorts said to Mazdek in the Common Tongue. "The soft-'ole must wait 'ere."

"What?" Aspess asked Mazdek indignantly. "I was under the impression that I was going to meet Goth Surien as well?"

Both of the Bantu were taller than Mazdek and Aspess, and it was the smaller of the two who answered her. "Maybe later, but soft-'oles ain't allowed beyond 'ere. Now shut ya giggle-mug and wait 'ere with Moggels."

"I refuse to wait here," Aspess responded, her face twitching with fury.

"My apologies, princess, but we agreed we must abide by their etiquette," Mazdek responded.

Aspess' face curled with anger. "We agreed that the reason for my being here, was to report back to my mother what I had seen and heard. If I do not meet Goth Surien, then any talk of an alliance fails right here, right now. On that, you have my solemn vow!"

Mazdek turned to the two Bantu, and said firmly, "Princess Aspess will accompany me. If that is not an option, then we will return immediately to Kappia, and you can explain to Goth Surien the reason we have not met with him."

The two Bantu looked at each other hesitantly, murmured quietly to each other, and then the larger one, Moggels, said to the smaller, "Let 'er go up there Bagballs, Grixen ain't 'ere so it ain't our noggins on the chop."

119

The smaller one, Bagballs, then barked at Mazdek, "Alright, shut ya gas-pipes and don't get all poked-up about it; it was the nose-bagger Grixen who told us that was 'ow it was to be. I don't care either way. Come!"

Mazdek and Aspess followed behind the two Bantu. They passed through a propylon entrance, a square canopied porch with several columns on each side, upon which were carved images of the most grotesque of figures. This opened up into a large courtyard, covered in large painted marble tiles, depicting many battle scenes. Passing through this, they crossed a balcony with the most stupendous views across the Black Plain, and once again Mazdek marvelled to himself that his genius alone had secured a treaty, and more so, an alliance with the leaders of such an army.

"Up there, follow 'im, we'll twiddle our nose pickers and wait 'ere for you," Bagballs said, pointing to a sallow-skinned halfling, holding a lit lantern as it waited at the front of a blackened arch.

Mazdek and Aspess followed the halfling through the arch. The winding stone stairs they climbed, spiralled and ran up through the keep, into the very mountain itself. The steps were old and tired, worn down by countless feet over many centuries. Eventually they came to another arch, through which they could see a large ledge of rock that was way up in the clouds and high enough to be dusted with a layer of snow. The halfling who had led them there, gasped for breath. Stooped with the effects of years of labour, half-starved, and hollow-eyed, it looked warily at several skeletons encased in iron-cages that swayed with the wind, hanging at the end of creaking chains hung on great iron hooks protruding from wooden rafters emerging from the rock face. A few skulls jutted from the end of pikes, some white with age, others fresh but marred, with flesh torn off by carrion. The halfling pointed to a star-shaped pattern and then withdrew into the shadow of the stairway, and hid from sight.

Mazdek fingered the small black Neblan that hung around his neck by means of a silver chain. He and Aspess walked out onto the ledge and stood just within the star shaped pattern. A figure emerged before them, as from an unseen realm. Intangible at first it started to take form.

"Greetings," Mazdek said. "After our encounters in the Deadlands, it is good we finally meet here on this day, to seal our alliance."

Goth Surien flung back his hood. He had a tarnished kingly crown; and yet upon no head visible was it set. Red and yellow fire shone between it, and the mantled shoulders upon which hung a frayed scarlet robe, were but a purple flame. He seemed to glide, more than walk, as he approached Mazdek and Aspess.

Other-worldly whispers could be heard as from a mouth unseen, Goth Surien spoke, his voice bottomless and ghostly, but very much present also in this one.

"I gave instructions you were to ascend to this place alone," he said to Mazdek as he looked at Aspess with disdain.

"And I insisted I would not wait below with your filthy gutter-rats," she retorted back.

Goth Surien studied her for more than a moment, and then asked, "I sense no fear in you, even in this place; are the hosts of Thar Markoom now trusted by she who rules in Kappia?"

"My mother trusted Ahrimakan, and he trusted High Quaester Mazdek. If I fear you who the Aeldar said to trust, would I not be called faithless?"

Goth Surien did not smile, he studied Aspess more intently before answering. "The old order is being washed away. The fresh dawn of a new age is soon to begin. Those who unseated the ancient powers, will be humbled and brought to judgement. The new world will be forged by our vision of how things ought to be. Allied, we will work towards this."

"We shall indeed," Aspess said with a wry smile.

"Then we are agreed?" Mazdek asked.

"The Lord of Morkroth has agreed. The Wild Hunt will find the Seeress for you, and the Shrimakan, that which your own kind call the Simal." Goth Surien's breathless words were chilling and raw. "They will be returned to you, and your promises you will keep, lest much lamentation befall you. As a sign of good will, Aleskian will be given to us!"

Mazdek could not help but lower his gaze as Goth Surien watched him. His fiery yellow eyes glowed with malice and burned with hatred so fierce it took Mazdek's breath away. In the Deadlands, Mazdek had met far more cunning and ferocious opponents, but here, in the Everglow, he did not yet wield the same sort of power, and in this place, he did not want to contend against the Lord of Morkroth's servant. "The Empress has agreed to the plan," he gasped.

"Then we too, will do what we have assured you of," Goth Surien replied, as he continued to fix his gaze upon him. "My servant, Grixen, will return with you to Kappia and speak for the Lord of Morkroth, for he has been fully instructed on my master's will on such matters."

Mazdek nodded agreement.

When Goth Surien next spoke, it was without words, and only Mazdek could hear him. *'Princess Aspess is more magnificent than I would ever have imagined. I sense what she is, that which possesses her, and what she can become. The darkness that lurks within her soul would feed Lord Morkroth. She is a bride the Lord of Shadows himself would desire, for only darkness so pure, will not fear darkness so deep.'*

*'She does not yet fully understand what, or who she is,'* Mazdek replied, also without words. *'The prophecy is vague and even she has not fully grasped the importance of it. If you try to pluck her before she is ripe, sour the fruit will turn out to be.'*

*'Then you must instruct as well as deceive her. We will wait, until the time of harvest,'* Goth Surien hissed, *'For only then can she be considered suitable. If the forces of Vangalen are roused from their slumber, Lord Morkroth will need a means to control or defeat them. She is a potential weapon, but we cannot force such a power to our will, without ruining, breaking, or turning it into another force of chaos. She must come willingly but subdued, broken not mended, aware but still unknowing, taught but lacking the knowledge that is of most importance. You, must prepare her to be supple, able to be twisted to our will when that within her awakes. You, too, have bowed the knee to the Lord of Morkroth, one of the Nine Lost Seraphim. His shadow requires his body; when they are reunited, a worthy womb he seeks to plant within it an heir.'*

*'I will remain loyal to my oath, and will turn Aspess over to you at the opportune time,'* Mazdek replied diplomatically, again without words, as this time he returned Goth Surien's fierce stare. He shut his mind so Goth Surien could no longer hear him. *I have different plans for Aspess, and it is not for her to become a bride of the Lord of Morkroth. A true son honours his father, and not all true sons are born from a mother's womb. False though I may be, I have convinced Thuranotos and the Lord of Morkroth of my trustworthiness, and will continue to do so, until I can rule over them, and all living things.*

Mazdek paused a moment, smiled, and then said, "As we agreed, Princess Aspess and I would see the Wild Hunt and inspect them before my return to Kappia. The Empress will expect this of us." He then again said telepathically. *'The princess must be convinced they will truly assist us with our current quandaries. She would have been most offended if she had not been granted an audience with you. She and her mother are volatile, such an offence almost risked our entire alliance.'*

121

Goth Surien's face twisted sinisterly, and he answered telepathically. *'This is a sacred place. It has offended the spirits, who do not wish to allow her flesh to leave here; they desire to feast upon it, but I am stopping them. Only the descendants of those who defeat the Maradrath, in the Deadlands, as yours have done, are granted the privilege of climbing the revered Steps of Thar Markoom for an audience. There will be a price she must pay for her insolence.'*

Mazdek nodded. *'As you wish, but not until she has served her purpose.'*

When Goth Surien next spoke, it was with audible voice. "Inspect my Wild Hunt, and see that they are most capable of returning the rebellious Seeress and the Shrimakan to you."

Mazdek smiled. "On behalf of my Sarissa, the Empress Shaka, together we will defeat all our foes and see our mutual goals attained."

"It shall be so," Goth Surien said, before he faded away into blackness and another realm, followed by ghostly whispers.

The halfling emerged from the stairway he had cowered in, still holding the lantern in his hands. Fear was in his eyes and he trembled as he wearily beckoned for Mazdek and Aspess to follow. They followed him down the spiral stairs, where the Bantu were waiting for them at the bottom. The smaller of the Bantu brutally kicked the halfling who squealed and scampered away back into the shadows. He and the other then led Mazdek and Aspess back the same way they had come, until they finally emerged again into the small open courtyard, where the two Bantu began arguing among themselves.

"Where's Grixen? 'E was supposed to meet these two orf-chumps once they 'ad seen 'im upstairs. It's my time to pour some grog down me gas-pipes," Bagballs complained.

Moggels shrugged his shoulders. "Now listen 'ere Bagballs, don't get all poked up at me, 'ow the 'eck do I know why that skulkamink ain't 'ere. I don't umble-cum-stumble the ways of 'is posh kind."

Mazdek ignored the two Bantu as they continued arguing between themselves.

"I would have been grievously offended had I not been granted an audience!" Aspess said indignantly to him.

"As would have been your right, my princess," Mazdek replied. "Their ways are strange to us, as our ways will be to them. But look!" Once again, he pointed to the sight of the vast army in the vale. "Look again at the army that will unite with us in our cause. Is this not a marvel to gaze upon?"

Mazdek watched Aspess. He observed her every movement, every twitch of her face, each glance of her eye. *You shall not be wed to the Lord of Morkroth. When the time is right, when the Empire is fully under my control, I shall rid the Everglow of your mother, and you will be mine to control. Together, we shall conquer every corner of the Everglow and beyond, and when you are no longer of use to me...* He felt no love for her, his desire was born of hatred, revenge and a lust for power. Hatred, because he wanted nothing more than to break and humble her for the many times, she had humiliated him. Revenge, on her and her entire family, would be one of the first fruits of power he would enjoy when he finally became the Kappian Emperor. With her broken and obedient at his side, he would show her fully what she was, and then harness and control her power for his own purposes, for it was the lust for power that gripped and mastered his heart.

"It is a magnificently terrifying army," she said, looking awestruck. "Even though Lord Borach has proven himself traitor, to stand against such a host for so long, is a worthy feat."

Mazdek detected a hint of admiration in her voice.

"It is the power imbedded in the Great Wall itself, a power older and greater than Borach *the Betrayer* that has stopped them from entering the Everglow. All he has done is hide behind the walls of Aleskian, or venture forth into these lands on riskless raids and then claim to be a hero. When the wall crumbles, all your mother's enemies shall be vanquished."

Aspess scowled, and said with a hint of uncertainty, "I look at this host, and a part of me wishes not to see them enter the Everglow. The wall has protected us for so long." She fiddled with the Neblan hanging around her neck. "If my mother had not heard the instructions direct from Ahrimakan, I would question the wisdom of such a plan, and even dare to call it folly."

"The person who writes a speech for fools is always sure of a large audience," Mazdek replied dryly, "but folly is our foe. Wisdom is the product of knowledge; the Aeldar guide us all to our destiny and true and lasting greatness." He put a comforting hand on her shoulder. "Think, my princess," he said in a reassuring voice. "Borach *the Betrayer* is the last obstacle that frustrates the will of your mother, our Sarissa, in seeing her sister defeated. This host will soon be at the gates of the Baothein, crushing their defences, burning their cities and devastating their lands. We will again have the Simal, and will summon the Aeldar once again. The Bantu will retreat from the Everglow when the Baothein are destroyed, for then the Lord of Morkroth will have what he desires, and we shall rebuild the wall, and conquer all foes that remain." *In the Deadlands, with the aid of the Aeldar, I will also destroy the Lord of Morkroth and his vile servant Goth Surien, and then the Bantu host will be mine to control. I will be Lord and Master of all I survey!*

Aspess looked at Mazdek's hand still resting upon her shoulder. "Unless you wish to go through the remainder of this lifetime with only one hand, remove it," she said icily.

*I will break you ever so slowly*, Mazdek thought as he slowly took his hand off her shoulder, and pointed. "Look at our allies!" He said.

As the two of them watched the distant host, the two Bantu stopped arguing. Bagballs said to Mazdek, "If you wanna goggle at the Wild 'unt, follow us then, I ain't gonna wait 'ere all night."

*      *      *

Aspess felt both disgusted and excited by the Bantu brutes they followed through the citadel. Despite her many lifetimes and long years, she had never seen a living one. She had heard and read numerous descriptions of them, even seen their decapitated heads when brought before her, mounted as trophies, but she had never seen a living one until that day. She was both fascinated and disgusted by them in equal measure.

Aspess and Mazdek had used a Juram Portal to enter Dagen Forosoth, for a pre-arranged meeting. The two Bantu had waited for them. For as long as anybody could remember, the Bantu and the Kappian Empire had been at war, and Aspess felt the thrill of being in the heart of an ancient enemy keep. Dagen Forosoth was a potentially dangerous and deadly place for both of them to be, if Goth Surien broke his word. If either of them died, or were killed, no Obelisk could reach them, *Final-death* would be certain unless the Neblans were returned to the Everglow, and, although virtually indestructible when empty, they became very fragile indeed when holding a soul. Once again, she touched it with her fingers; *this is my only safety net from the Final-death, if this parley turns sour.* She felt fear, but the type that thrilled her and sent a tingle through her body. Since the meeting of the Privy Council, Mazdek had been very persuasive with his rhetoric, on convincing her mother that she, Aspess, should accompany him to the Bantu fortress to see the army for herself, and she had been willing and keen for the experience. Despite that, she could not shake off the feeling of uneasiness about the alliance.

123

*Ahrimakan wills it. He and my mother know what they are doing*, she thought to herself. She studied the two Bantu they were following. *These beasts are primal and savage, but I do not fear them. They should fear me, what it has been prophesied that I will one day become – my destiny…"*

"They are both fascinating and filthy in equal degrees, are they not?" Mazdek asked her, interrupting her thoughts.

Aspess laughed. "Their stench is not pleasant to me. Do they not have bathing and cleansing rituals like us?"

"They do not, princess. But these types have no titles, so are the least important among their kind. The Wild Hunt, who we will soon meet, are those who have earned high honours in battle!"

∗      ∗      ∗

Mazdek was quietly impressed with the courage that Aspess was showing. *Not many women would have found the courage to willingly take the risk and come here.* Initially, he had entertained some doubts himself. It was only the fact that he knew, without a doubt, that Goth Surien had more to gain by assuring their safety at Dagen Forosoth, than he did by betraying or harming them, that Mazdek had agreed to both he and Aspess visiting. He knew that only she could convince her mother to accept his plan and alliance, and to do that, she had to accompany him into a major stronghold of the Bantu to see for herself that a treaty and an alliance was possible. He wanted her to witness the size and might of the Bantu horde.

They followed the two Bantu as they crossed the courtyard. As they walked, the one called Bagballs spoke in his native language to his companion, unawares that Mazdek understood their tongue.

"I bet the sight of the dark-one wiped the smile off 'er gigglemug, and 'is," he said, and let out a rough laugh, as he turned and poked Mazdek with a cudgel. Mazdek did not react outwardly, but seethed inside. *Many humiliations I have endured on the road I have walked, but he that is patient, will have his reward.*

Moggels spoke. "I bet 'e almost pooped through his gas-pipe when he first saw 'im. He's a right mutton-shunter this one, but the soft-'ole, she's enjoying it all."

The Bantu laughed as they reached the end of the courtyard, turned and signalled for Mazdek and Aspess to follow, and then headed up some winding steps.

"Keep up mutton-shunter," Bagballs said to Mazdek in the Common Tongue.

The Bantu continued talking to each other in low whispers with the odd burst of raucous laughter as they walked up the stairway. Mazdek and Aspess followed in silence.

When they reached the top of the stair, and were stood upon an enclosed landing in a tower, Bagballs asked Moggels, "What about 'er?"

He briefly turned his head and looked lustfully at Aspess. "They gonna let the boys maffick with 'er during 'er visit here? I wouldn't mind shunting 'er soft-'ole with me cosh."

Moggels spat with disgust. "It'll be easier to make a Gragor laugh than get a go at the soft-'ole." He looked angrily towards Mazdek. "This one is a nose-bagger to Goth Surien, so we 'ave orders not to touch 'em. Only an orf-chump would lay an 'and on 'er, she's protected."

"Shame, I'd like to test what the boys on the front line say and see for me-self if these 'uman women really can't take a coshing. I 'eard it makes 'em bleed to death."

"The boys on the front-line only had Fell-bloods, those sent as mercenaries with their men. This one's special, a Pure-blood."

Both of the Bantu laughed. Mazdek said nothing, but he smiled to himself with grim amusement. Irony always entertained him. These two Bantu would poop through their own gas-pipes if they knew the true nature of Aspess, that which lurked deep in her soul, biding its time until it could reveal itself. When that time came, Mazdek was confident he would have gained the allies and the power he needed to subdue Aspess, and then as a sponge absorbed water, he would drain her of that power and he would become invincible in this world and the next. Then, he could dispose of her as and when he wished.

*   *   *

Mazdek and Aspess followed the two Bantu, as they left the tower and walked onto the battlements of the keep, before crossing a wooden bridge held up by wire cables. The bridge swung in the strong wind and creaked and swayed underfoot like a living thing. Even the Bantu had to hold on to the rope rails to steady themselves as they crossed. When Aspess looked over the side, she could see nothing but blackness below. Once safely across, they entered another keep through a covered stone walkway. The echoes of their footsteps mingled with the noise of the wind that howled through it. The door at the end of the walkway was black wood, studded with iron, and barred on the inside. The smaller of the Bantu hammered on the door with his cudgel. After a moment the door was opened from within by a small, pale-faced halfling, who flinched and cowered as the Bantu and their guests walked past it. The halfling shut the door behind them, as the two Bantu escorted Aspess and Mazdek to the bottom of a wooden stairway.

"Up there," Moggels said as he pushed Mazdek with a cudgel. "Me and Bagballs ain't gonna bap-milk you anymore. We got grog to guzzle down our gas-pipes."

Unaccompanied by the two Bantu, Aspess and Mazdek climbed the twisting steps to a corridor formed of black stone walls and floor, at the end of which was a door, half ajar. They traversed the corridor, pushing open the door when they reached it. Aspess entered the large chamber followed by Mazdek. The hall was wooden floored, the walls of stone, and decorated with numerous mounted heads of all manner and types of creatures, large and small. In between the mounted trophies, were carved woodworks, many aged torn tapestries and wall hangings. The stench in the room almost made Aspess retch as it hit her nostrils. She covered her nose with a handkerchief she took from her pocket.

A dozen or so Bantu were seated on stools around a brazier on which meat was spit-roasting. The Bantu glared angrily at them as they entered. As Aspess walked slowly towards the centre of the room, the scent of roasting flesh momentarily overcame the fouler smells, and was so good that her mouth began to water, but another, more foul scent that accompanied it soon overwhelmed it and put her off. She kept her eyes warily on the Bantu. They whispered and murmured among themselves, looking suspiciously at the two guests who stood there. The Bantu continued to tear lumps of meat from the animal roasting in the fire, dipping the chunks in a bowl that contained a sticky black sauce. All of the Bantu in the hall were far larger than the two who had escorted them to the chamber, apart from one who stood and approached them as they entered. He was the smallest Bantu they had yet seen. Garbed in mottled robes of blue and grey, he bowed his head respectfully. To Aspess' surprise, he spoke High Akkadian.

"I am Ambassador Grixen the Literate, servant to my Master Goth Surien."

"You were supposed to meet us when we arrived," Mazdek said dryly.

"My apologies, I was somewhat delayed on other business, but I trust your audience with Goth Surien went well?"

"We have an agreement," Mazdek replied, and then said indignantly. "I know something of your culture. I expected one more educated than you to host us? Why are you, a mere Literate One, not yet a Scribe, entrusted to meet with myself and the princess?"

Aspess noted his tone clearly indicated he was offended, and she felt smug that it was his turn to feel slighted by their hosts.

If Grixen felt affronted by the remark, he did not show it. His tone was polite and well-spoken. He bowed his head apologetically. "I am more than capable of dealing with this matter. I am soon to be promoted to the honoured title of Scribe. The matter of the Shrimakan is a most important and pressing concern to the Lord of Morkroth, who I assure you wishes to assist in its return to you. Unfortunately, our few Scribes have urgent commitments elsewhere."

"Such as?" Mazdek asked suspiciously.

"To the east, The *Fallen* dream of rebuilding Vangalen; not so long ago, we learnt that the corpse of Velentine, Queen of the Dark Undead was stolen from its ancient tomb. She will seek to wake her husband, Lord Voran, that ancient Seraphim whose light is now so dark. It was news of this, which, among other things, persuaded the Lord of Morkroth an alliance with you was most necessary."

"I was not aware of this news," Mazdek answered, "but I suspect the Order of Ithkall might have played a hand in it, for we are now aware they are not extinct, as was once thought."

"That is interesting," Grixen replied. "We suspected others, but when time allows, this is a matter I would very much like to discuss with you. If they do have a hand in it, they must be hunted down before they can meddle further in affairs, they know so little about."

Aspess remembered that long ago, there was once rumours that the Order of Ithkall gathered like rats in a sewer beneath the city of Kappia itself, in secret hideaways and places well hidden. Her mother, had spent vast resources through spy networks trying to find them, and their Obelisk, both in the Everglow and in the Deadlands, but to no avail, so they had dismissed them as just that – rumours. "It was not long ago, we thought they had vanished from the world, and were just a bad memory, but it appears their legend is known to you?"

Grixen nodded. "Recently I have read a lot of Temmison, for his works exist even in our own vast libraries, and I have sought to inform myself on matters past and present concerning the Everglow, in anticipation of my serving my master as ambassador to your imperial court."

"Then perhaps your Wild Hunt might be able to assist us in finding these sewer rats," she said, briefly removing the handkerchief and then replacing it.

"Perhaps," Grixen answered thoughtfully, "but seeking the Shrimakan is the most pressing and immediate concern they have. We will not have them chasing rumours until we have more solid evidence on who it was that disturbed ancient Vangalen."

"That will be pleasing for my mother to hear," Aspess replied, "recapturing the Simal is our highest priority."

"As regaining the stolen body of the Lord of Morkroth is ours," Grixen said, as he attempted a smile, but only managed a crude sneer. "If only we had more resources to devote to it. To the north of us, well, all mixture of enemies lurks in those realms. Once we have recovered Lord Morkroth's body, we will have to leave the Everglow to deal with the troubles we still face there."

The remarks confirmed to Aspess intelligence she had already heard in the Privy Council. Spies had long reported that the Bantu were engaged in another war at the far northern end of Pangaea and had pushed back the tribes and clans of the men and races that lived there. The Bantu had explored the area widely and it was said that they had discovered ancient Elven cities abandoned thousands of years before. Many of their Scribes of note were in those cities discovering their secrets, and that was where it was said that the Bantu had discovered the Shargoroth and Norvaskun, which the Elves once sailed on the waterways of the Underglow. She felt reassured though, that Grixen had confirmed that defeating the Baothein and reclaiming his mummified corpse was a priority for the Lord of Morkroth, despite the troubles they faced in the North. The new alliance would never have reached this far, if they did not have mutual needs each could assist the other with.

"The Simal is of little interest to your kind?" she asked bluntly, seeking to get to press the issue that concerned her the most.

"It is impossible for the Bantu to summon the Aeldar," he replied, "so apart from being a trinket of interest, we would have little use for it. Mazdek has agreed, that after the Simal has been returned to him, he will lead Goth Surien to the gates of Hammerfell itself; there, in the Void, he will seek, on behalf of the Lord of Morkroth, an alliance with the Aeldar face to face." Grixen attempted another smile, which again turned into more of a sneer. "It is in both of our interests, to work together, to ensure the Aeldar can be permanently summoned to the Outer World."

Mazdek beamed with delight at Grixen's words. "It is pleasing to me, to hear your words confirm the agreement I have made with Goth Surien. It is also pleasing to me, and soothing to my ears, that your tongue and words are not as crude as those of your companions."

Grixen snorted. "Indeed not, for I was bred for the purpose of study and am educated in finer things than they. Even I find their conversation, let me say, a little, coarse, at times."

Aspess also allowed herself a rare smile, but she was not interested with small niceties. "What is that awful smell?" she asked as she once more briefly removed the handkerchief, curled her nose in disgust and quickly covered it again.

Grixen grinned. "They eat wild boar meat dipped in Blackweed, a sauce made from the blood of the boar and mixed with a weed that grows in the hills around these parts."

"It stinks," she said as she curled her nose once more.

"Blackweed gives my kind great stamina on a hunt. The smell is strong, and the weed itself is poisonous to the touch and taste of the more delicate human nature. Many a Davari scout spying for your legions, has accidentally brushed against it, and met a slow and painful death. It is a reason why our warriors and hunters sometimes lace their weapons and arrows with it. It is highly flammable, and when fired from a bow, an arrow laced with it will catch light and is hard to extinguish. Something to do with the speed it flies through the air."

Grixen paused a moment, as though enjoying the thought. "Although not of much use if fired when it is raining, as then it will not catch light to begin with." He grunted. "Now let me introduce you to the Wild Hunt, they are all fluent in the Common Tongue," he said, after which he himself switched to it.

"Master Gaishak, you will come please. It is the will of Goth Surien." He gestured with his hand to the largest of the Bantu sitting to his right.

"This is Gaishak *the Corpse-Eater*; he is the Hunt Master, and the Captain of Norvaskun." The Bantu arrogantly got out of the chair and sullenly walked over to where Mazdek and Aspess stood.

There was a light like hot fire behind Gaishak's eyes, that fascinated Aspess; she beamed with delight and whispered under her breath, "Magnificent," as she circled him, looking him up and down. He was a particularly impressive specimen. Two heads and a shoulder above the tallest men in height, he snarled at Aspess, his lips curling back to reveal fanged teeth that almost touched the ring hanging from his flat nose. He wore black leather armour which bore the emblem of two yellow eyes upon a black hole. In his hand he held a long, thick shafted spear with an evil looking point with a cruel barb. A bow and quiver of arrows were strung across his back, a sword and dagger sheathed on each side of his belted waist. His bare, muscular arms were scarred and covered in multiple bronze bands with strange wording and designs upon them. Even the slightest movement of his arms caused the muscles to ripple, showing every indication he was a creature of sheer brute strength. Bits of bone were the only decoration in his long, thick black hair, from which protruded pointed ears from which hung heavy looped earrings.

As she finished circling him, she met Gaishak's gaze unflinchingly. A low guttural rumbling issued from his throat. She sensed his primitive nature, dark and deceitful, cruel beyond measure. She smiled, as she knew, that hidden beneath the surface of her own physical beauty, was a nature just as primitive, just as dark, far more deceitful and intelligent, and yet as cruel as his. She impressed herself at how unflinching she was in the presence of such a fearsome creature, in the middle of its own stronghold.

She briefly looked at Grixen and asked, "So it is true then what I have heard, Bantu only have one name, until they earn a title?" She then turned her gaze again upon Gaishak and asked, "And you have the title *Corpse-eater*?"

Grixen answered her. "That is true, the warrior class recognize each other by their scent, but only warriors who do a deed of worth are given a title after their name. The title is given to them by others based on, well, let us just say the behaviour or characteristic that most describes them during, or after a battle or great deed."

"He is magnificently disgusting," Aspess said.

"Gaishak *the Corpse-eater* is a great hunter, well proven and tested many times, with too many other lesser titles to announce, lest we be here all day, and most self-given I may add. He will lead the hunt for your escaped Seeress.

"The sight of it delights and disgusts me," she said as she purred with delight on touching Gaishak's arm. He did not draw back, but another guttural growl grew in his throat as he bared his fangs.

Grixen pointed to another Bantu who was seated. "That one is Barikoff *the Corpse-defiler*. Hmm, I think it best not to explain what he does to dead enemies to earn that title."

He pointed to another, "And that one is Marigoof *the Mad*." Marigoof stood up, and much to Aspess' delighted disgust, a severed, shrunken Bantu head was strapped on to his shoulder.

Marigoof turned to the decapitated head and chuckled, "If Marigoof gets a snogging and mafficks with the soft-'ole, I'll gis u a turn at the snog."

Grixen whispered apologetically to Mazdek and Aspess. "Marigoof has still not quite got over the death of his brother, so he preserved his shrunken head and carries it with him wherever he goes. Once again, please forgive their crudeness. Those with titles are free to speak as they wish, with no consequences, for it is considered they have earned the right to express themselves."

"How did his brother die?" Aspess asked.

Grixen was clearly embarrassed as he answered. "Marigoof's mother killed him; let us just say that even in Bantu culture trying to forcibly '*maffick*' with one's own mother is not acceptable."

It took Aspess a second for the statement to sink in, and as it did, she smiled to herself in sheer amusement. "What a vile, disgusting breed," she said with glee.

Grixen coughed to hide his embarrassment and continued to point to each of the Bantu in turn. "That is Nordof *the Hairless*, Scopold *the Torturer*, Pakarin *the Pig-rapist*."

"*Pig-rapist?*" Aspess asked, and involuntarily burst out laughing.

Pakarin stood up and indignantly said. "In battle, a thousand warriors or more I 'ave butchered, but do they call me Pakarin *the Slayer?* No. I have coshed a thousand Bantu females and spread my swimming boys far and wide to breed little bap-suckers, but do they call me Pakarin *the Lively-cosh?* No. But I cosh one pig and they call me *Pig-rapist!*"

The other Bantu began to shout and insult him.

"It was more than one," a few of them jeered.

"No, it was just one, I tell ya, now shut your gas-pipes or I'll be calling you for a reckoning," Pakarin shouted back.

"Sit down, *Pig-cosher*," some of them said. Pakarin sat down muttering indignantly.

"Quiet, please," Grixen said, and when they had quietened down a little, he continued to point out the different Bantu. "That is Garkin *the Foul*, Hargoth *the Relentless*, Dotherekin *the Diseased*, Moregin *the Lucky-shot*, Jififig *the Heart-eater* and finally Froglin *the Biter*." Aspess noticed with grim amusement that even for a Bantu, Froglin was particularly ugly and nasty looking; half of his jaw and head had been replaced with metal, and his teeth were iron spikes.

"These are just the leaders of the Wild Hunt, which numbers roughly a hundred and twenty or more," Grixen said to Aspess and Mazdek, and then turning to the Bantu, said, "Come, our guests wish to inspect you, for you will soon begin the hunt."

The Bantu all stood and walked over and stood behind Gaishak. Only slightly smaller than him, they were no less impressive and each with distinctive and recognisable looks. They were each armed in the same way, a bow and quiver of arrows slung across their backs, a sheathed dagger and sword or axe attached to each of their belts, and the heavy spears on the weapon racks no doubt theirs. Their armour was brown leather and hide, with the same emblem as Gaishak's.

*Effective armour, but built for speed*, Aspess observed.

Dotherekin *the Diseased*, a fat Bantu whose features were vastly disfigured and covered in puss bubbles sniffed the air, and spoke in his own tongue. "She smells sweet. I wanna sink my gnasher's into 'er warm flesh."

Pakarin *the Pig Rapist* said, "I wanna stick me cosh into 'er gigglemug make 'er choke on it."

"Those baps look tasty, I'll bet Froglin would like to chew on them," Scopold said. He had an eye missing.

Froglin laughed hysterically and ground his teeth together. All the Bantu, apart from Grixen and Gaishak laughed.

Aspess had not understood what they had said, but guessed by the tone of it, that it was not polite.

Grixen smiled politely at Aspess, and apologetically at Mazdek and then said to the Bantu, "She is the guest of Goth Surien. If any one of you seeks to harm her, it will be him you answer too, and be aware, that our guest Mazdek, understands our tongue."

"Ya posh gas-piping bap-sucker," Dotherekin said to Grixen, "we're only gattering and snorting. She'll not be 'armed."

"They only jest, it is their way," Grixen said in High Akkadian to Mazdek, who nodded solemnly.

Grixen continued. "Once the Great Wall is compromised, and the Aleskian Gate is open, a tunnel will be burrowed to the Underglow, and the Wild Hunt will sail on the seas and then the canals of it with Norvaskun, and using the Shargoroth, they will locate the Seeress you seek. Janorra is her name, I have been informed?"

129

"Yes," Aspess said, feeling a surge of rage flush through her at the mention of the Seeress.

"A moleworm will travel with them. It can burrow up through the earth. A necromancer of no small accomplishment, with the name Methruille, and title of the *Disloyal*, will also accompany them."

"I have heard of him," Mazdek said, and then asked, "was he not once one of the Tarath Guëan?"

"That was a long time ago," Grixen replied, "and of no consequence now." He paused and then continued. "You were informed we needed something with her scent on it?"

Mazdek unbuckled his satchel, reached into it and took out a white gown. "I took it from her chambers, it was in her laundry, so has not been washed since last worn." He handed it to Grixen who sniffed it.

"Good, good. The Wild Hunt will capture Janorra and the Shrimakan, and return them both to you in Kappia. Meanwhile, you will see to the other terms of our treaty, as the Wild Hunt cannot enter the Everglow until the wall is breeched and the power of it broken. Do you have arrangements in place for that?"

"Arrangements are in place," Aspess answered, and Mazdek nodded.

Grixen bowed his head respectfully and addressing Mazdek asked, "I shall be Goth Surien's Ambassador, speaking for him in the imperial high court of the Argona palace; I understand the Empress has agreed to this?"

"It is agreed," Mazdek answered.

Aspess felt amused. *I look forward to see the faces of those at court when a Bantu walks in.*

Grixen nodded. "Now, you wish to see the skin-changer, he is not far from here, a beast-master is supervising the change. After that, you may leave, and I shall accompany you. Garâtons will be used to exchange messages between myself and Thar Markoom, but your griffins are trained to kill them on sight. That is why the griffins you wish to keep must be kept confined, or those that might be used against our messengers, must be killed."

"The griffins have been more trouble than they are worth," Mazdek replied with disgust. "They are volatile, unpredictable, and I will be glad to be rid of them. Their time is finished."

"I agree," Aspess said. Part of her disdain for griffins, was that neither she or any of her family had ever been able to tame one to ride it, and try as they might, they had each lost a number of lives in their many attempts, being rejected by the griffins in favour of riders from lesser families. "The Baothein have none left, their High Nests died out long ago. The Grey Council have a nest, but they cannot breed them so it is said they have very few. The High Nest at Kara Duram became diseased, and only one or two of the beasts have survived. The nest at Kappia was destroyed, for they were vicious and killed those of us with noble blood who tried to tame them."

"So Aleskian is the last nest of worth?" Grixen asked, even though it was phrased more as an observation then a question.

"It will be disposed of," Mazdek said, but then added. "Do not think though, Grixen the Literate, that the skies above the Kappian Plateau will be unprotected should you decide to change the terms of our treaty."

Grixen raised an eyebrow. "How so?"

"The stretch of the Empire once reached much further than it does now. We absorbed much knowledge, and kept hold of that which was of use. We have fast-breeding wyverns, bred for such a time as this, caged and kept in locations on the plateau, that can be released into our skies any time we wish to control your messenger garâtons, should they become a nuisance, or too populace for our liking."

Aspess felt glad and assured that Mazdek had issued the subtle warning.

"That is noted," Grixen said, and then smiled. "Please, follow me."

Mazdek and Aspess followed Grixen and left the chamber by a different door, whilst the rest of the Bantu took their seats again, to continue tearing off lumps of meat from the roasted carcass and dipping it in the Blackweed as they made more jokes about Aspess and the things they would like to do with her.

Mazdek and Grixen continued talking as they went down more winding steps and left the keep by a different exit, and crossed three wooden bridges, each one narrower than before, but these ones were protected from the elements with wooden walls and a roof. They then entered and passed through several halls, keeps, and numerous corridors. The conversation consisted mainly of niceties, and a history of Dagen Forosoth, the murals, frescoes, statues and trophies they passed as well as the style of architecture, all of which bored Aspess, so she paid scant attention.

Eventually, she grew so bored, so asked, "Are you sure the Wild Hunt will find this traitorous Seeress, and return her and the Simal to us in Kappia? They are impressive physically, but appear to have grotesque interests that might distract them."

"Of course, they will," Grixen replied. "They never fail to find their prey. The hunt is relentless and swift in their pursuit. Success or death is the black-oath they will swear to their lord, before they set out. They may retreat at times if they suffer a temporary set-back, but they will never give up. You see, the Wild Hunt, when sailing on Norvaskun will have…limitations that we do not have when sailing our own waters this side of the Great Wall."

It did not go unnoticed by Aspess that Grixen stopped mid-sentence.

"Which are?" she asked.

Grixen grinned sheepishly.

"Tell her," Mazdek said, "it is time she knew."

Grixen cleared his throat. "Very well then. The Underglow, upon which Norvaskun and the Wild Hunt will row, according to legend, is notoriously difficult and dangerous to navigate. The compass, the Shargoroth, communicates with a flying beast above ground, if that is where the prey is. When the flying beast locates the prey, a way to the surface is needed to tunnel to the surface. But lava, earth or rock is between the surface, often at different layers, so a moleworm is needed, and can only burrow through earth, not rock or lava, nor could it ever burrow under the Great Wall. That is why the Aleskian Gate has to be opened before Norvaskun can enter the Everglow. Even when it does reach there, it will take time for a suitable place where Norvaskun can emerge."

"Then find that place, and if needed, hunt her on foot," Aspess replied curtly.

"That is not the problem," Grixen said. "The creature we use above ground is called a Barclugoth, a shape-shifter."

Aspess shrugged her shoulders impatiently.

"Your griffins, they can smell the scent of a Barclugoth, from vast distances away. They will most likely kill it, before the Seeress is found."

"So, send those things you call garâtons with it, to protect it."

"Garâtons mostly fly in vast swarms, and, their nature often gets the better of them. They too, would slay the Barclugoth."

Aspess was growing more impatient and shot Grixen a frowning questioning look. "So, what's the solution?"

He cleared his throat again before continuing. "The Barclugoth must fly alone, but to be sure it can cross the territory of your Empire safely, your griffin riders must be

131

slain. The Barclugoth and a griffin are evenly matched, but it would only take one rogue griffin rider, and the Barclugoth could be badly wounded, or worse, slain itself and then Norvaskun has no eyes above ground. If Speed is of the essence in reclaiming the Simal, all griffin riders must also be slain, to ensure the safe passage of the Barclugoth."

The frown on her face deepened, but with such a sharp intellect, Aspess saw the necessity of such a radical act, although it disturbed her profoundly.

"We have wyverns that can protect the Kappia Plateau," Mazdek said to her. "They do not have the strength to fly long distances, so are not much use off it, but will still be a force in the air to defend our main cities, should we need it in the future. We can keep some breeding stock of griffins caged at Kappia, to repopulate their numbers, once we have the Simal."

"My family has no personal fondness for griffins, but their tactical use has been an advantage. We have agreed to confine or slay the griffins, but the skill of the riders and the knowledge they have, we might not want to lose. My mother might need some convincing over this," Aspess replied uncertainly.

"Leave that with me, my princess," Mazdek answered. He then said to Grixen, "We pay a heavy price to employ your Wild Hunt. I hope they are worth it."

"The Wild Hunt always catch their prey," Grixen replied. "Time is just the false illusion of security for those the Wild Hunt seeks. There is nowhere for their prey to hide, once they are on the scent. As time is crucial, for this hunt, Norvaskun will be full to capacity. The chiefs of every hunt party have been assigned. You just met them; they are the best of the best at what they do." He looked at Aspess quizzically. "Perhaps when this is over, you might be taken to see the Underglow? I read that parts of it, can be quite stunning to behold, at least the tales of old tell us, when Norvaskun once rowed under the Everglow."

"You are well read," Mazdek remarked.

"We have acquired works from across the Nine Worlds," Grixen replied.

"Now, a little-known fact about the Wild Hunt is this: they cannot be stopped in this world, all the time their real bodies are upon Norvaskun, in the Underglow."

"Their bodies are an illusion?"

"A projection of matter, formed by the power of the Shargoroth. We have mastered its use except for one small matter."

"Which is?"

"When they appear above ground in illusory form, it drains a lot of power from the Shargoroth. We do not know how to recharge it; it has to regain its charge over time."

"Then why do they not risk their physical bodies?" Mazdek asked.

"Oh, they will, when necessity dictates it. But the Shargoroth also powers Norvaskun, which also uses a lot of power. The Wild Hunt will not risk losing Norvaskun, for they are bound to it."

"So, they will not return to a hunt immediately, after a setback?"

"Like all hunters, they must be patient at times," Grixen said, "but eventually, they always catch their prey."

Aspess smiled smugly. "So, to kill the Wild Hunt, one must enter the Underglow?" she asked, although she already knew the answer.

"You learn fast," Grixen replied, accompanied by a knowing nod. "Our peoples have much in common, but also much to learn from each other, when it comes to understanding the true nature of reality."

Aspess felt a sudden lust for knowledge. "Do you have Mystery Schools, like we do, that teach such knowledge?"

"Of course," Grixen answered, "although our understanding of the Nine Worlds differs to your own."

Aspess sneered. "Then we do indeed have similarities. In Kappa, if you listen to a discussion between eleven priests, you will hear twelve opinions." She then peered curiously at Grixen. "Do you, like us, believe the Outer World is superior among all of the nine realms?"

"It is the reason why, all that is spirit, wishes to return here," Grixen answered, "although we understand the origins and history of the other realms differently. Our convictions are different to those of Kappia."

Mazdek interjected, and arrogantly proclaimed. "A world where consciousness comes before matter, was the only realm where En-Sof and the Nameless one could truly rule. Making matter was their error; they lost much of their power, either on purpose, more likely by mistake."

"A contest desired, or a catastrophe caused by error," Grixen said gleefully.

Mazdek nodded. "All spirit falls into vegetation and matter at some point, that is the nature of the fall. It is also the cause of all suffering and confusion. The Aeldar cannot defeat En-Sof in the realms that are spirit, only those that are matter. They wish to destroy spirit, so that only matter can remain. This is the teaching of the Aeldar. That which is considered as spirit must perish, and then the Aeldar will rule supreme."

"That is the reason why the Lord of Morkroth, so desires his body back from the wretched Baothein," Grixen said, a serious look on his face.

"The Aeldar enjoyed the supremacies of the pleasures of matter," Aspess retorted reflectively. "So, all must fall into the world of matter, that, I remember you saying in your sermons, Mazdek."

"I did," he answered. "Only the world of matter is of true importance, for all other worlds will fade into insignificance, but only if we support the Aeldar and win this war."

Aspess then said to Grixen. "In the Deadlands I am a Seeress, and have seen much. But I have only ever seen this world, and that one. Do beings of higher power choose to descend rather than ascend, or are they forced to do so? Do your kind have a theory?"

"Come now," Mazdek said defensively, before Grixen could answer. "Are my skills of oratory and my rhetoric so poor you do not remember the many sermons of mine that you have sat through?"

"Perhaps they are," Aspess replied cuttingly, "you are more often than not, mostly concerned with rules, rituals and regulations, than preferring to speak deep truths."

"Then for that, I am truly sorry," Mazdek said dejectedly. "But you must have heard me say on many an occasion, that the mind of matter thinks in terms of layers, but the mind of the spirit, thinks in terms of perceptions of matter. Understanding the true nature of reality, does not consist of advancing through layers of matter, but of ever greater and growing perceptions of the spirit. Those who understand this, see it, and when they see it, they can, without fear, abolish that which is spirit so that they can rule matter. You have so much learning, but still, you perceive so little?"

Aspess felt insulted, a surge of sudden rage flooded through her. "Do not forget who I am, and be too loose with your tongue," she said scathingly to Mazdek.

He bowed his headed and meekly replied, "That was never my intention, my princess. I think the worlds you can see with your own eyes, this one and the Deadlands, combined with the promises of Ahrimakan, are until now, mostly what you have concerned yourself with." He smiled apologetically. "Maybe you are ready, when the time is agreeable, to visit the Labyrinth and see the wonders there are to behold in that place."

133

"And when the Wild Hunt have succeeded in their chase, I will request that Goth Surien orders them to show you the Underglow, Grixen said.

Aspess felt somewhat pacified, but she continued to look venomously at Mazdek, a number of thoughts rushing through her mind as she thought about the mission and what they were all seeking to achieve. *My mother trusts you, but doubt, and sometimes uncertainty, concerning the wisdom of this plan, visit me often. If it were not for Ahrimakan backing it, I would never have agreed.* She decided, as before, to crush such doubts as one would an annoying fly. Turning her attention to Grixen, she asked him, "The Wild Hunt, they do know that we want the Seeress alive? She must suffer for the calamity she has brought upon my mother and all of Kappia."

Grixen smiled placidly. "They may seem coarse and undisciplined, but they will do everything that is asked of them. I understand your Empress will reward them with Davari women to satisfy their more salacious needs and desires once the hunt is finished?"

"They can have as many Davari women as they wish, if they succeed in their mission," Mazdek answered grimly.

Grixen nodded his approval. "I find most carnal appetites all rather distasteful myself, but I am bred that way. My desire is knowledge so do tell me, if I may be so bold to ask a question." He looked at Mazdek quizzically. "Is there, to your knowledge, a way that one such as I might accompany my Master Goth Surien to the Void, and see the gates of Hammerfell for myself?"

"Not that I know of," Mazdek replied. "Once the Simal has been returned, and the Baothein threat destroyed, I will study the matter."

Grixen's eyes shone with desire. "Have you both seen the three Aeldar already summoned from the Void to this world, with your own eyes, including the snake-god Ahrimakan?"

"Many times," Mazdek replied sombrely. "Though only two have been summoned. Ahrimakan forbade the regular summoning of the second Aeldar, unless it was his festival day. The other Aeldar, the third, we were forbidden to summon him at all. Ahrimakan alone spoke… speaks on behalf of Thuranotos. We trust his counsel, and that is why we are here."

Aspess noted that Grixen literally shook with excitement and could barely contain himself. "This alliance truly is exciting. Those of the pure Akkadian blood still benefit from being returned from the dead, but…" he hesitated a moment. "I hear that the Obelisks are dying and going mad, and that only Seers trained in the Mystery Schools of the Aeldar can slow down their deterioration, but only the Aeldar can truly heal them and return them to their healthy state. Is this true?"

"It is true," Mazdek answered. *You know so little, fool.*

Grixen rubbed his chin thoughtfully and stopped after they had crossed the third bridge. "At first, we Bantu thought it was mere legend that the Riddles can summon the Aeldar from the Void, but then, some years ago our sages said they felt the presence of an Aeldar in the world, and then, that of another. This is all so interesting, very interesting." Grixen was clearly deep in thought as he stared at Mazdek, and then added. "There is a lot of talk among the Scribes and Literate ones of my kind that we Bantu may be granted a similar gift by the Aeldar, our own Obelisks and a return to the land of the living after death if we seek the Riddles and aid their cause. Do you know if this is also true?"

"That is not for me to say. All I know is that the Aeldar wish to meet with Goth Surien, as much as he desires to meet with them. Ahrimakan wished an alliance with the

Lord of Morkroth. He suggested this treaty would be of mutual benefit between the Bantu and the Kappian Empire, as did other Aeldar I spoke to in the Void."

Aspess grew impatient, the conversation began to bore her. "Can we keep moving and walk faster? This wind gets everywhere and I am cold."

Grixen smiled. "Of course, we can. I am excited about this new friendship between our races. It opens up so many possibilities for us all."

Grixen set off again and quickened the pace, and descended winding steps until they came to a large courtyard surrounded on three sides by several caves that had been carved into the mountain itself upon which the keep was built. The fresh stench that hit them was almost unbearable, more so than that of the Bantu and Blackweed. Mazdek covered his nose with a hand, and Aspess hers with her handkerchief.

"This smell is even worse than the Blackweed," she said.

"It is not pleasant, I know," Grixen replied. "We call this place *The Stable*. Here the change is encouraged. Come, I will show you."

They followed Grixen into the third cave. A small halfling with a lantern met them and led the way. They walked at first along a black passage, and then up many worn steps that wound upwards like a turret stair until they emerged from the stony darkness and looked about. They were on a wide flat rock without rail or parapet, lit by the first rays of the early morning sunrise. At the far end a darkened figure stood over a writhing, black lump about the size of a large horse. The darkened figure shuffled over to them. It was a very old and hunched Bantu. The Bantu tapped a small axe tucked into a rope belt.

"The changeling is not to be disturbed, or old splitter 'ere will be relieving ya shoulders of their swollen noggins," he said rudely to Grixen.

"Hugluk, we will not disturb him, our guests just want to look."

The Bantu looked at Mazdek and Aspess questionably, and then scowled with disgust. "A quick gaze with the peepers, then be on ya stride out of 'ere." Hugluk shuffled off towards the writhing black lump. They all followed silently.

It was hard for Aspess to make out exactly what it was she was looking at, as they watched the black lump writhing. It was a slimy black sack made of skin. Some creature within it was moving very slowly, making a sucking and squelching noise as it did so.

"It takes three days to make the change," Grixen said.

"Three days?" Aspess asked, surprised. "That is slow. It has not mastered the technique then."

Grixen looked at her. The astonishment that showed on his face did not last long. "You know of such things? So, what they say about the Empress is true? She is a changeling herself?"

"We are not here to discuss my mother," Aspess answered belligerently.

She noticed that Mazdek gave Grixen a silencing look.

"Apologies, princess," Grixen said, slightly bowing his head deferentially. "My question was too intrusive, but was only born out of sheer curiosity and fascination for the magnificence I have heard emanates from the Empress Shaka."

Aspess felt an indifference towards both the apology and the flattery.

Grixen continued. "Some are under the impression that all changelings can change at will and in an instant, but it requires considerable skill and ample patience, for these ones can take many forms, but it takes time. They have to be fed the right foods, liquids and herbs and a beast-master such as Hugluk, has to massage them and help them take the right shape by pushing the joints into place. It requires copious skill and knowledge from both, and mutual cooperation. Master and changeling have to both learn the secret and technique behind each desired change."

"It is highly unusual for changelings to be able to take different types of form," Mazdek said.

"That is why it takes them time. Most of our changelings can only become garâtons, and we have plenty of natural born garâtons buzzing about the skies, like flies, so we do not require changelings to become one, except to practice the skill of morphing. Now, only the most skilled, like Morfus here, can become a Barclugoth, the glorious flying beast we need for this hunt, although he can take nine different forms in all. He is very old and has mastered each one, though some take longer than others to form. Hugluk was with him at birth and is an expert at helping him take any one of his nine forms."

Hugluk was busy massaging the black lump and muttered some curses under his breath, ignoring Grixen, who continued to speak. "The process is not always a success and a changeling may emerge deformed and have to repeat the process, which is quite painful for them, but you can usually tell after the first day if it is going wrong." Grixen turned his head towards Hugluk. "I am right that the change this time is successful?"

Hugluk glared angrily at Grixen. "Of course, it is. I'm not an orf-chump, 'e'll be 'atched and ready for flight soon. Now off with you. Your peepers 'ad the stare. I still 'ave slog to do."

Mazdek and Aspess followed Grixen as they made their way out from the stable, led by the halfling.

"Hugluk did not seem to hold you with much respect," Aspess said, watching for Grixen's reaction.

Grixen did not appear to be bothered by it. "His is arrogance born of rare skill and knowledge, jealously guarded. Bantu born with changeling blood in them are very rare, and those who are changeling masters like Hugluk are even rarer. His position in Bantu society is very high. A beast-master of his level is above my own station as a mere Literate so his words are acceptable to me. Hugluk is yet to choose an apprentice."

Grixen paused for a moment in his stride and Aspess sensed regret in him. "I had once hoped it would be me," he said before continuing down the stone path.

"You would rather work in this filth than be a literate or scribe?" Aspess asked, genuinely surprised.

"This is a warrior culture, those of us who read and write words and discuss matters of importance with other civilisations and races are despised by most of our own kind, especially the females. Only those rare few scribes who reach the top of the scribe-tree are allowed to mate."

Aspess laughed, derisively and involuntarily, and made no attempt to hide it.

Grixen did not respond but merely said. "Enough of such things, you will now meet one of our War Chiefs before we conclude our business."

The five of them came out onto a different courtyard. Entering through a wooden door, they went into a passage lit by torches burning in iron sconces. Grixen picked up one of the torches. For twenty minutes or so they wove through dark underground passages and corridors until they came to more winding steps which they ascended. On reaching the top, they emerged out onto a large battlement, so wide, a dozen men could walk along it abreast. The sun had risen fully and the light of it was in their eyes. Dark clouds briefly covered it every now and then for a few brief moments.

The battlement was a high wall of ancient stone broken only by the occasional lofty stone tower. A dozen or so Bantu stood beneath a banner of a yellow shield and a clenched fist on a scorched field. The banner flapped noisily in the wind. Grixen walked over to one of the Bantu and stood next to him, signalling for Mazdek and Aspess to follow. The Bantu was fierce and angry looking, as he stared at them, looking them up and down briefly.

136

"Warlord Garuk the Conqueror, the King-eater," Grixen quietly said to Aspess and Mazdek as he pointed with his eyes towards Garuk, who was dressed in dented and dirty heavy black armour that bore the same emblem as the banner. A long two-handed sword, adorned with black runes that shimmered and seemed to move, was sheathed across his back. In the pommel was an Arzak, coloured midnight blue. Mazdek had heard of the sword, it was one of legend and whose name, *Ungweethon*, translated as *Dark-Soul-Biter*. Aspess had believed, until then, the sword was an Arkith, but looking at the different coloured Arzak, she desired the weapon and wondered *is it Arkoom?*

Several heavily armoured Bantu shield-masters, stood around Garuk, and watched Aspess and Mazdek doubtfully.

"Is it almost ready?" Grixen asked Garuk, who merely grunted and pointed at the plain below the battlement.

The plain was filled with a vast host of Bantu, a multitude on multitude of warriors. Company upon company were camped around fires and tents. Huge siege towers and engines were packed, ready to move along the lanes carved out in the muddy earth. Trenches with spikes guarded the camps. Many of the Bantu were looking at the distant Great Wall of the Everglow, about three miles in distance across the plain. The Great Gate of Aleskian was to the south of them, wrought of steel and iron and guarded by towers and bastions of indomitable stone.

"Braka," Garuk said as he smiled fiercely and pointed to a battering ram of immense size positioned to the east of the gate, before the Great Wall.

"The ground-shaker," Grixen said, almost in awe.

Mazdek and Aspess looked in amazement at Braka, they had both heard of it, but the sight even from that distance was greater than the telling. It was a siege-ram about two hundred feet in length, held by mighty chains upon a gigantic wood and steel frame. The gruesome head, wrought of silver steel was shaped in the likeness of a clenched, clawed fist. Some giant cyclops and many Bantu surrounded it, operating the ropes, chains and winches that drew Braka back on the chains ready to be released.

Grixen smiled with pleasure at the sight. "Thirty-days it takes to prepare Braka to strike. Dark spells and fell magic lay upon it to defeat the spells of the Great Wall of the Everglow. Long was Braka forged in the foundry of the Labyrinth to be used as a hammer against our foe."

"We will open the gates for you soon, and have promised to deliver Lord Borach to you. Why do you need to strike the wall again?" Aspess asked.

"Garuk has sworn a black-oath to defeat his foe Borach in battle, and cannot die with honour until he fulfils it. He wishes to demonstrate Braka to you, to show you his power and prowess. He believes that even without this treaty he would soon break through the Great Wall," Grixen said ominously.

Above the Great Wall far in the distance, the griffin banners of Aleskian flew and fluttered in the wind, as numerously as they did among the white turrets of the city of Aleskian itself. Labour of old had built the ancient city. Up, up and up the great white turrets rose into the sky. The Great Citadel, a bastion of stone covered in white marble climbed the five levels on which the city was built. Great houses and winding roads could be seen, despite the distance. Between the Great Wall and the city, a network of several castles stood out strong and clear.

A brazen horn sounded from the plain below. "It is ready to be released," Grixen said softly to Aspess, before walking over to Garuk and whispering something in his ear.

"Rakrash!" Garuk roared. "Rakrash! Let the thumping begin! Let the Great Wall crumble!"

137

One of the Bantu standing nearby, blew a horn, the deep sound of which rolled around the battlement and down into the plain beneath. Several horns on the plain below responded, sounding one after the other. Tens of thousands of drums began to rumble; a multitude of horns accompanied the roar of the vast host below. "Var, var, var," they shouted and screamed as swords clashed against shield. The noise was deafening. In the distance, from the city of Aleskian, even above the din of the Bantu host, a roar of defiance was heard, and trumpets blew, declaring the legions were ready for whatever the Bantu host had prepared for them. Then, a horn blew, the sound of which was so eerie yet mystifyingly intoxicating to the senses, it made Aspess shiver, and the Bantu hold their hands to their ears and cry out in rage.

"The Golden Horn of Aleskian," Aspess said under her breath. She closed her eyes and drank in the sound until it finished with an echo around the plain.

Beneath the Great Wall, a massive brutish cyclops swung a large sledgehammer and struck the heavy iron pin holding Braka in place. The pin fell to the ground with a great clanking sound. Ropes and chains creaked as the ram Braka swung against the Great Wall. The ground literally shook as it hit, as though an earthquake had suddenly taken hold. It felt as though the very earth was being shaken beneath their feet. The sound of a loud thud and crack filled the very plain. Despite the ground shaking and rumbling, the Great Wall still stood. From the walls of Aleskian another roar of defiance went up, trumpets blew, and great stones of fire flew through the air, hurled by great catapults positioned around the city and the outer castles. Burning oil from murder-holes built into the walls, was poured directly onto the ram, and fiery arrows rained down upon those not protected by the ram's covering. The stones bounced off the housing of Braka, and no fire would catch. As the stones hit the ground around it, and arrows found their marks, some of the cyclops and Bantu were crushed or pierced, and a few fled in terror and fear as the burning missiles rained down. The bodies of those who died were soon dragged away and others took their place, taking more care to find cover beneath the casing of Braka.

Aspess turned and looked at Mazdek. Suddenly, she felt no joy or awe, and sensed it was visible in her face, and none sounded in her voice when she spoke with a lowered voice. "I do not feel the delight I felt moments ago, and once more I feel doubt. When I was told I would see Braka released against the wall, I expected joy would be my response at such a sight. But as the defences of Borach *the Betrayer* are weakened, I realise it is also our defences they strike at." She studied Mazdek who looked at her sympathetically as she continued. "They hate us. The doom of the city seems certain to them, but it brings me concern about the course we are set upon. How can the Hammer Knights defend against this horde if they betray us, especially when the legions are disbanded?"

Mazdek smiled, and then answered reassuringly. "It must be this way, princess. These are dark times; the Empire is but a shadow of what it once was. The legions can no longer be trusted to defend us, nor can we afford their greedy demands. Soon, they will depart Aleskian, and will disband at Kara Duram. The Hammer Knights will be far superior defenders of the Empire, loyal to a fault, and require no pay above immediate expenses."

"My brother, Prince Regineo, said it would be better to arrest Borach *the Betrayer*, and have him stand trial in Kappia, and be put to *Final-death* for all to see. Why must he die at the hands of the Bantu?"

Mazdek sighed. "I have explained this. Garuk must be given the chance to defeat Borach in open battle, a black-oath is something the Bantu take very seriously. It was a small concession for us to make; they insisted it be a part of any deal and alliance. The blade he carries will give Borach the *Final-death*. It will save us any unforeseen embarrassments at a trial."

Aspess noticed that Grixen had joined them, and was listening in on their conversation.

"Princess Aspess," he said sincerely. "The Lord of Morkroth wishes only to see the Baothein defeated, and to claim the body they stole from him long ago. We have troubles in the North, and beyond this foray into the Everglow, we have no strategic interests or plans within it. Our forces will retreat back to Thar Markoom, once we have achieved our goals; as will the Wild Hunt as soon as they have recaptured and returned the Simal and the Seeress to you. Our alliance benefits us all."

Mazdek smiled. "The return of the Simal and the vanquishing of the Baothein is all that matters, princess," he said maliciously.

"Perhaps," Grixen said hopefully, "when shadow again meets flesh, an alliance sealed by marriage might enable the trust between our peoples to bring be brought closer together? I am sure there is some bride of worth who might find the Lord of Morkroth as being a worthy and suitable husband?"

Aspess understood the hint, and suddenly, her momentary weakness and doubt about the whole plan was replaced by a rising fury; she felt far from pleased at the hint. "My home and destiny are within the Everglow, in reach of the Obelisks. I suggest the Lord of Morkroth finds an inhabitant of these foul lands to wed."

"Perhaps a discussion for another day," Grixen said.

Aspess looked murderously at him, and then at Mazdek. "No, there is no discussion at all. I would not marry the master of these filthy beasts. Do not overstep your mark and make plans for my future, either of you. That is for my mother, and I to decide. If this alliance is to work, dismiss all thoughts along those lines. Is that clear?"

Aspess noticed anger flash across Grixen's eyes, and an involuntary snarl cross his lips, but then, as though by an act of his will, both were gone, and no trace of discontent revealed itself when he spoke. "Forgive me, I meant no offence. But…" he reached into his pocket and took out a ring. Upon the ring was set a black stone polished to such a high sheen that it resembled a pool of oil. It even seemed to be rippling, as though currents were drifting through its centre. "I almost forgot. Please accept this small token, a gift of good will from the Lord of Morkroth. It symbolises nothing, and is merely a gift of beauty made by our finest jewellers, for the Princess of Kappia."

Aspess looked at the ring, and stared at the stone. For a moment she seemed to be hypnotized by its beauty, her attention so transfixed by it that she did not resist as Grixen slipped it upon her finger.

"Thank you," she said almost drunkenly, before coming to her senses and looking around her, as though she had been unaware of the last few seconds. *What just happened? I have no memory of the last few moments?*

*       *       *

Mazdek smiled and had to contain himself so that he did not shout with triumph. His plan, devised over many long centuries, was finally coming together, piece by piece. He looked at Aspess. *Your arrogance will be broken soon, now that we have taken the first step to harness that vileness which lurks within you. You will quickly learn what it will mean to fear me. Every insult you and your family have cast my way will soon be repaid in full.* "It is a beautiful gift," he said to her.

"What gift?" she asked.

139

"The gift of our sworn allegiance towards our common goals," Grixen answered as he bowed his head respectfully.

"It is a marvellous day," Mazdek declared. The fact that Aspess had accepted the gift of the Lord of Morkroth so easily, gave him immense joy. *After she has served my purpose, perhaps I might consider giving her as a gift to the Lord of Morkroth, she will be of no use to him once I have taken from her the power that we both, desire. After that, I care not what sort of fate might befall her in this dark and dreadful land. Imagine his rage when he realises, she is stripped of that power and is then of no use to him? What punishments would he inflict upon her to quell his rage?* Turning his attention to the horde of Bantu in the plain below, he marvelled that such a chaotic army would soon be ravishing the lands of the Everglow, whilst he, held the only place that could be defended, the Kappia Plateau. If all went to plan, Aleskian would soon be burnt to ashes, and the Empress would surely be the one blamed for such a disaster. As Aspess watched the horde below, Mazdek and Grixen gave each other a knowing look, and smiled.

"War is coming," he whispered under his breath.

"It is indeed," Grixen responded with glee.

# Chapter Ten: *Imrand and the Wytches*

*I heard many strange rumours and tales about the Wytchwood. I so wanted to enter it, but no amount of coin I offered, could tempt my guides to lead me under the green foliage. I stood at the edge with them, and hesitated for a long while. Finally, I decided to go in by myself, but a strange noise coming from something unseen within the forest, about a hundred yards away, and the feeling of being watched, made me decide otherwise. I am still not sure whether I should regret or be grateful for my hesitation. However, all I can write about that place is from hearsay only, not direct experience. Legend states that Wytches dwell there. I use the spelling on purpose, as according to Akkadian folk-lore a Wytch is a different type of fiend as compared to a human witch. It is said a ruined citadel of sorts is hidden deep within the forest, along with other ancient structures, now mostly ruins reclaimed by nature; I could not confirm this, but I can tell you that the Wytchwood itself is an amazing sight to behold even just looking at it from the outside.*

**Temmison Vol III, Book 5: Natural Wonders of the Everglow.**

*The* stillness of the forest trail was so primeval that the very tread of their bare feet was a startling disturbance. At least it seemed so to the ears of Imrand and Sarkisi, as they moved along a trail with great caution. He was glad that, after having lost his sword in the Erin, due to saving Sarkisi, the bodies of one of the crew had washed up on the shore in the morning, and he had retrieved a dagger and a sword from it. He loosened the sword in the scabbard, and held onto its hilt.

"There, behind us," Sarkisi whispered in panic as she drew the dagger. Imrand spun around, just in time to see something flicker in the corner of his vision. He glimpsed a light, just before it disappeared from sight for the tenth time that hour. He had previously attempted to pursue whatever it was, but to no avail, so this time he did not take the trouble. He feared neither man nor beast, nor anything that could feel the bite of steel, but he felt uneasy, and with his sharpened primal instincts, dreaded that whatever it was that was following them, might not be slain with a sword, or by any means that he or Sarkisi possessed.

"This is a cursed place," he muttered.

It was not long before, ahead of them, broken columns glimmered among the tall trees. The irregular lines of crumbling walls rambled off into the shadows, remnants of some prehistoric kingdom, lost and forgotten even before the first men had set foot within the Wytchwood.

Under their feet the ground soon changed to broad paving stones that were cracked and bowed by roots growing beneath. "Maybe we should head back to the river, follow it east or west, there is a dense evil in this forest I do not like," Sarkisi said fearfully.

Imrand looked at his wife, and of a sudden felt overwhelmed with love and pity for her. She had suffered so much, and he had failed to protect her. He had felt the river was not safe, armed search parties might be looking for survivors and escaped slaves. It was better to head into the forest. He gently took her hand, and led her on, deeper into the darkness under the woodland canopy. All the while an animal-like uneasiness possessed him, a sense of lurking peril that he could not shake. The flickering light had not been a creation of their imaginations, it was real, and it was following them.

Among the trees, in the distance, reared a broken dome-like structure, built of gigantic blocks of a peculiar iron-like green stone the like of which neither he or Sarkisi had seen before. It seemed incredible that human hands could have shaped and placed them; it was as though it was the work of the giants of the old myths he had been told

141

about as a boy around his grandfather's campfire. The path, though broken, when they re-joined it led to the broken dome structure. To their left and right, the forest was so dense and so thick they had no choice but to go back, or continue. For a moment, he considered going back. He paused and frowned, something was again flickering in the corner of his vision; it looked like red, blue and green flames rippling through the trees, but when he turned his head to look at it, it was gone. He shook his head and turned his attention back to the structure, edging closer and steadying his breathing. Again, he thought he saw lights, somewhere in his peripheral vision behind them, on the way they had come, but when he turned to look at them, once more they were gone.

"Curse this place," he said under his breath, deciding again there was no other option but to continue forward.

Imrand and Sarkisi reached the domed structure. It was made of ton-heavy blocks, some of which had been smashed and splintered like glass, with sharp shards lying all around. Imrand was no mason, but he knew that only something unnatural could have such an effect on stone as thick as that. He climbed over the debris and peered in, beckoning for Sarkisi to follow. What he saw brought a grunt from him. Within the ruined dome surrounded by stone-dust and bits of broken masonry, lay a giant upon a silver block. He was clad in tarnished silver mail and armour. His black hair, which fell in a square mane to his massive shoulders, was confined about his temples by a narrow-stained silver band. The skin on the face of the giant was shrunken and withered, outlining the shape of the skull beneath. The eyes, long gone, had been replaced by two black stones that rested in the empty sockets. On armoured breast he held a strange dagger with a jewelled pommel, purple-bound hilt, and a long, narrow serrated blade, covered with purple runes, and made with great skill. It bore no signs of age.

The giant was dead; had been for many long centuries. Instead of gazing in awe at the preserved body of a giant, Imrand only lusted for the weapon; it was the only thought that consumed him. Never had the yearning to possess a thing as much as that taken a hold of him before, and when he looked upon it, he desired it above all else. Though just a dagger to the giant, it would serve as a broadsword to a man of his size, perhaps a little unwieldy, but it could disembowel any man with an upward stroke and remove a head or a limb with ease if swung with the skill of a seasoned warrior such as himself.

"Don't, it is not good to disturb the dead," Sarkisi warned as Imrand reached out to take the weapon. No sooner had he touched it a flash of light filled the whole dome. Bolts of red, green and blue lightning erupted from the light with a loud boom and cackling sound.

Imrand pulled Sarkisi to his side, and pointed the newly acquired weapon at the three apparitions that appeared before him. The first, a woman clad in red transparent silks, floated in the air. Golden hair floated slowly around her as though she were drifting in water. The second was similar in appearance but with green silks and white hair with streaks of black and the third also the same, apart from the colour of her silks being blue and her hair dark with white flecks. None of them were unpleasant to look at. His first thought was that they were ghosts or some sort of wraiths, but then it occurred to him the wood was not named for nothing. "Witches," he said under his breath.

"Wytches, not witches," a male voice, coming from a source unknown, whispered.

The first Wytch spoke, her face twisting with sudden rage, her voice menacing and ghostly, as from another world.

"Who is it that defiles the Tomb of Bothgar and steals his prize?"

142

The second Wytch spoke, slowly, deliberately, her voice shrill and accusing. "Who are you thief?"

The third Wytch added angrily. "We don't like thieves!"

"No, we don't," they all hissed in unison.

The hairs on the back of Imrand's neck prickled. It was more instinctive than thought out, as he lunged at the red Wytche's apparition with the weapon. She disappeared like a puff of smoke before he could strike her, only to reappear elsewhere, behind him. He swung around and lunged again, but once more he was not fast enough and the Wytch disappeared before re-appearing in front of him.

"Careful with that," the red Wytch hissed indignantly.

"Yes, careful," the green one chimed in crossly.

He lunged at the blue one, who disappeared and then reappeared elsewhere, laughing sarcastically and saying, "Wits and swords are as straws against the wisdom of the darkness."

"Put it down, thief," red said.

Green followed. "You cannot hurt us!"

Blue grinned. "Such a weak and puny man is no challenge to us."

"Then why do you avoid the attack if you cannot be harmed?" Sarkisi said to the apparitions, whose faces grew dark and furious as they eyed her and began to move in circles, around she and Imrand.

"Why do you disturb the tomb, thief?" the red Wytch asked again.

The other two demanded:

"Tell us!"

"Answer!"

Imrand was about to curse the apparitions and lunge at them again when Sarkisi spoke. "We are Davari, and are far from home. We were taken as slaves from our homeland. Our story is tragic and long, chance not purpose has led us here, for the ship transporting us to our fate was burned and wrecked. Forgive us for disturbing this sacred place, the blade shall be put back and my husband and I shall leave."

Imrand watched as the Wytches' apparitions continued to circle, looking at and talking to each other with a sudden excitement.

The red one asked, "Could it be?"

The green one replied, "If she is wife to him, a prophecy fulfilled it could be."

Blue said, "On burning boat Davari would come. It was written slaves they will be, the children of great warriors!"

"They bear the mark of slaves," the red one said.

The green one sniffed at the air and then confirmed, "Davari they are. It is a stench so foul I remember it from long ago."

The blue one, looking at Imrand and Sarkisi, asked, "Yes, my sisters, but who are they? Has the *Prophecy of Rithguar* finally come to pass?"

Sarkisi spoke again, answering the question as the three Wytches' apparitions circled them. "I am Sarkisi, daughter of Chief Rakri of Clan Ashausi of the Vanyr. This is my husband Imrand, son of Thaine, Chief of Clan Masisa, also of the Vanyr. Forgive us for disturbing this tomb, we meant no dishonour or sacrilege." She turned to Imrand and urged him, "Put the dagger back and we will leave."

Imrand glanced at Sarkisi, and then continued watching the Wytches. "If I put this back, they will kill us or worse. They could not harm us in the wood, and this thing summoned them in this form." He looked contemptuously at the Wytches and challenged them. "You cannot harm us whilst I wield it, I am right, aren't I?"

The Wytches all laughed, shrieking, mockingly, one after the other, and then spoke in the same order as the times before.

Red: "If your tale is true, we do not want to harm you."

Green: "If true, the *Prophecy of Rithguar* is finally fulfilled. It is we who need your help."

Blue: "We will reward you greatly, if *Rithguar's Prophecy* you fulfil."

The three of them continued to circle Imrand and Sarkisi.

"To hell with you," Imrand murmured, but before he could continue cursing them, they disappeared in a flash of light accompanied by loud cracks of coloured lightning. The three Wytches stood before him, no longer as watery apparitions but in bodily form. The red Wytch, wore a tight fitting long red dress that revealed her ample cleavage. She spoke, but her voice was different than before, it was now soothing and calm.

"Neferu is my name. Come with us, my brave warrior, spoken of in the *Prophecy of Rithguar.*" She held out one hand to Imrand, and the other to Sarkisi, who both instinctively recoiled backwards.

The green Wytch, dressed in the same styled long dress but coloured blue, had less cleavage and smaller bust. Her voice was now tranquil and gentle, she said, "I am Lefaria, Bothgar brought us the last page of Rithguar's text. Allies we shall be, if fulfil the prophesy you and your pretty wife do!"

"I am Morna," said the blue Wytch eagerly and then urged expectantly. "Long we have waited. *The Prophecy of Rithguar* said Davari will arrive when the Simal is in our reach. You must come with us!"

"The hell I will," Imrand said as he lunged at Morna with the blade, but she was quicker and gestured with her hand. Imrand and Sarkisi froze in place, unable to move.

Neferu spoke to Morna in panicked tones, "Don't use magic here sister. She will know it, and discover we are awake and near this tomb."

"She will find us," Lefaria added as she fearfully looked up at the sky.

"Bring them to our home, quickly," Morna insisted, at which the other Wytches nodded enthusiastically in agreement.

Each in turn, the Wytches began to scream – quick, piercing, and furious. They screamed in a way that neither Imrand nor Sarkisi had ever heard anyone scream before. Their appearance changed so they looked like demons, and then old hags.

The sound somehow released them; Imrand dropped to his knees; he involuntarily dropped the weapon and clapped his hand over his ears to protect them, as did Sarkisi. He tried to say something as he stood to his feet, to ask them to stop, but as they were formed his words became a strangled cough and he staggered backwards, as thick roots appeared from the wood, snaking through the dome and wrapping around his throat. The red, green and blue lights flashed again but this time they blazed inside his head from where the three Wytches shrieked and screamed at him. The ground beneath him began to open up; he tried to balance himself, reaching out with flailing hands. He howled as he was dragged into the ground as though he were a new-born babe. He clutched at the roots but everywhere around him was erupting, spitting out roots and vines and lashing them around his body. The tendrils tightened web-like over his face. His stomach lurched horrible as he was dragged through the portal that opened beneath him. Then his thoughts grew dim and dark, as consciousness slowly slipped away. The last thing he saw was Sarkisi, covered in the same roots and vines being dragged through the portal with him.

"My love," he shouted as he reached out a hand to her. They clasped hands, before darkness took them.

144

# Chapter Eleven: *The Hedge Knights*

*With their glittering hosts greatly increased by mercenaries, the Bruthon host initially crushed all foes south of the River Erin. As a result of their expansion, they became haughty and intolerant. They taxed their conquered subjects exorbitantly, and conscripted them for their wars of territorial expansion. It was the Kappian Civil War that led to their downfall. Whilst engaged in fierce battles in the North, those in the South, once formerly subjugated, rose up in rebellion. At the battle of the Bossmarch, Bruthon arrogance was tested by the Horse Lords from Rhonbea and the Southern Marches, who united, and rode to battle in numbers that could not be counted. The Bruthon were defeated, and their power broken. Such was the massacre, the Bruthon Lords no longer had the forces to guard their own frontiers. They retreated to their fortresses of old, and surrendered on all other fronts. Facing other foes beyond the great Southern Wall, with only a few exceptions, the Horse Lords did not press the advantage, and like a tide that recedes, so did they.*
*Despite surrendering to Kappia, and the retreat of most of the Horse Lords, the Bruthon's troubles were not over, for that is when the Chatti Raiders first appeared.*
*Bochart Vol II, Book 1: An Account of the Kappian Civil War.*

*It* did not take long for the soldiers and trackers to come into view. The trackers, on foot, were being pulled by large hounds slobbering and barking as they followed a scent. Plainly garbed in wool and boiled leather and armed with bow and dagger, the trackers were a dozen or so in number. Some forty men-at-arms followed on foot, wearing helmets and suits of mail, armed with spears, swords, axes and crossbows, and behind them came a hundred or so mounted knights and soldiers, trotting behind with much clinking of chain and rattle of plate.

At the head of these was a knight, dressed in armour far superior to the others. Silvered steel and gold inlay brightened his armour, and his war helm was crested in a riot of silken plumes, feathers and cunningly wrought fish and birds. Behind him one of the men-at-arms carried a banner that flapped in the wind, upon which was adorned a red castle surrounded by a green hedge and lazuli flowers, set against a yellow background.

"They are Hedge Knights. They must be in service to Baron Daramir," Sasna whispered to Scarand.

Scarand looked at the approaching men, and asked, "Will be they be friend or foe?"

"It will be hard to tell," Sasna said, and then hesitated before continuing. "I have not seen them at the castle before, but these are troubled times so the Baron may have asked for their assistance."

"I know little of knights, only from brief tales of folklore Frema taught me, but they will be honourable men, will they not?" Scarand asked.

"In these lands, such naiveite will get you killed," Sasna replied matter-of-factly. "When they make their oaths to the Hedge Guild, they have to choose three virtues out of nine. The three they choose become their primary ones that guide all of their actions. It makes them fanatical in certain pursuits and dangerous to be around, so say absolutely nothing." She looked seriously at Scarand, and then warned, "A slave is not permitted to address such men, unless they speak to you first. It will immediately cost you your life, if you talk freely in the presence of Hedge Knights. Do you understand?"

Scarand scowled, but nodded.

The trackers did not pause as they approached, but rushed by, pulled by the barking hounds. The foot soldiers followed the trackers, only turning their heads to look at the curious sight of Sasna and the Davari, as they passed them at a fast pace.

Sasna stepped out into the path of the knights. "Well met, my lords, I am lady Sasna of Ashgiliath and this is my slave. I need your assistance," she said as loudly as she could as the knights on the horses approached.

The lead knight held up a hand as he and those mounted behind him stopped. The faces of three gargoyles poked their snouts out from their breastplates through a circle of lapis lazuli flowers, on top of which was the castle and hedge emblem. She knew that the expressions on the gargoyle faces were a symbol of the virtues these knights were sworn to embrace, but she could not remember what these three were.

The knight in the silver armour walked his horse forward a few paces, his long green cloak twisting in the wind blowing off the marshes. He lifted his visor to reveal a thin, cruel looking face. His voice was elegant, haughty and impatient.

"Out of our way peasant, or be ridden down," he snarled.

Sasna realized, although they had passed and were still moving into the distance, he might not have heard her former greeting above the still considerable sound of the hounds and the stamp of the soldiers' iron shod feet on the ground. She repeated her greeting, as loud as she could. "Well met, my lords, I am Lady Sasna of Ashgiliath and this is my slave. I need your assistance. Please inform me, what virtues do you most aspire to?"

The knight's tone was scornful. "I fear I see no lady, and if I did, I do not know her. She is hardly dressed for court or as one who should address me." A couple of the mounted men-at-arms behind laughed in a sycophant manner at his words.

"She looks more like a scullery maid or a vagabond than a lady," another knight sneered contemptuously.

"If only we had time for some sport with her," another said.

"I am known at Castle Greytears. I am a friend and ally of Baron Daramir," Sasna declared as respectfully as she could.

"Baris, you know the going and comings at the castle as well as any there, take a closer look at this filthy wretch," the silver clad knight said.

It occurred to Sasna just how dirty and unkempt she must have appeared.

One of the mounted soldiers, a man-at-arms who had not laughed, was sat upon a big, thick limbed horse, a dappled grey. He trotted towards Sasna and Scarand. He was a Half-blood man of wide shoulders and huge girth, old, scar-faced and grey bearded. He carried a long and heavy spear and was bearing a sword; his armour was plainer than the knights, and dented and well used. He dismounted with an agility that surprised Sasna. He lent his long spear against the side of his horse, and walked up to her, studying her face. He then turned to the lead knight and said, "My Lord Darin, it is indeed Lady Sasna of Ashgiliath."

Sasna swayed slightly, but stood upright. She felt more than a little humiliated at having to stand before these men dressed like a roadside vagabond. She was pleased that Scarand was taking her advice, and staring at the ground, not directly at the knight or his men-at-arms.

"For Marciea and Oliviana," she heard him whisper under his breath.

"My Lord Darin, we have not met before? I was travelling to Castle Greytears, when disaster found the vessel we were boarded upon. No doubt the flames and smoke would have been seen from the castle watchtowers?"

"They were indeed, as were those of the villages and farms destroyed by Chatti raiders a few days ago, so we have no interest in a burnt boat," Darin answered with an air of indifference. "What business did you have travelling up the Erin? My brother's men are acquainted with you. Do you frequent the taverns where they find their beer and wenches?"

*Arrogant fool.* Sasna bit her lip, but did not rise to the unnecessary insult.

"I am no tavern wench, sir. I once traded slaves from Ashgiliath to Berecoth, on behalf of my uncle, Saroth Arnton, the High Warden of Ashgiliath. We now we sell them at Zinibar, due to the routes to Harwind and Kappia being blocked by the pirate scum that now infest the River Erin."

The knight asked, "Then what business did you have at Greytears?"

Sasna answered as politely as she could. "We still give the Baron a tribute of three slaves from each shipment, and a gift of gold, so that we might maintain an alliance for a time more favourable when trade along the Erin can recommence."

"It is true, Lord Darin," Baris said. "I would suggest we give lady Sasna the assistance she requests."

Darin frowned, and curled his nose up in disgust as he looked at Sasna.

Sasna smiled outwardly, but not inwardly. "My uncle, will surely be grateful for any kindness shown to me. Surely Lord Daramir must have made talk about these matters to you, and perhaps made mention of my name?"

Darin's impatience visibly grew. "My brother has more important things to discuss with me than a common slave trader from that dreadful place Ashgiliath. Your name is not known to me." He turned to his men. "Is this why they say *never trust a Seesnari*? They are such liars, calling themselves ladies when they parade about like debauched scullery maids giving themselves titles and importance above their station." His men laughed, all except Baris. Turning back to stare at her, Darin did not even have the courtesy to look at her as he stared into the distance. "I have more urgent business than to trade words with a vagabond Seesnari. We are tracking the Chatti warband, who pillaged villages and farms in the fields of Fornose. You are fortunate you did not run into them."

Sasna bit her lips in frustration at the discourtesy she was being treated with. *If you meet them, I hope they separate that arrogant head from your neck.* Swallowing her pride, she said dutifully, "We have seen tracks, my lord, in the wood this side of the river, but no sign of those who made them, for they were a day or so old."

Darin sighed impatiently. "As I thought, this pursuit is a waste of time. I told the Baron they would have fled as a rat before a wolf, by the time we mount a pursuit." He drew his visor down, and spurred his horse to a trot.

"My Lord Darin," Sasna pleaded loudly as he passed by. "I am in dire need of assistance. I was wounded in the fire on the ship and fear I do not have the strength to make it to the castle. Are your sworn virtues such that they allow you to refuse assistance to an ally of your brother in need of your assistance?" *I feel my life and strength are fading fast, but I will not beg or ask you again, you conceited fool.*

Darin halted his horse, and lifted up his visor again. He stared at Sasna. It was obvious to her he was clearly irritated at the delay and working out what to do.

"Please my lord, she looks like she will not make it without our help," Baris urged.

Darin signalled to him. "Then you assist her to the castle. Do not bother to return to me, for we are on a fool's errand. Inform my brother we will inspect any Chatti tracks, but will then turn our attention to searching for any more survivors from the ship's wreckage. A hunt for escaped slaves might make this folly worth the time." Darin drew down his visor, spurred his horse and followed by all but Baris galloped off in the direction of the trackers and foot soldiers.

Baris grimaced as he looked at the crude bandage on Sasna's shoulder, which still had blood and ooze seeping from it. He went to his horse and took a small glass bottle from a pouch in his saddlebag, and some fresh bandages. "May I, my lady?" He was gruff of speech, but spoke politely as he reached out to her shoulder.

"If it will help," she said.

Baris undid the bandage. He grimaced at the sight of the wound. "This is bad," he said, and then sniffed the poultice. "Wild spuds?"

"My slave was given some basic training in such matters," Sasna replied.

"It may have saved your life," Baris replied. "Did you find pirken in the woodland?" Sasna nodded,

"Well, this is pirken extract," he said as he held up the small bottle. "It will sting, but I need to pour this on it. It will stop any infection from getting worse."

Sasna was beyond caring, as the pain was still very bad. Without ceremony Baris pulled the cork from the bottle and poured it over her shoulder. It stung and burnt with almost unbearable pain, but she bit her lips and closed her eyes. He un-wrapped the clean bandage he held and wound it tightly against the wound. He returned to his saddlebag and took what looked like a small jar and handing it to Sasna he said, "Pirken paste. It is safe, unlike eating the flower. Chew on it. Keep a bit of it under the tongue. It will ease the pain and stop you passing out. I should be able to get you to the castle alive, but the wound is bad, you will still need the help of a proper physician."

"Thank you, Baris," Sasna said, and then asked, "Since when has the Baron had Hedge Knights in his service?"

"As you have already heard, Darin is the Baron's brother. After an absence of an entire lifetime, he returned from the Hinterwaste only a day or so ago. Rumour has it he is equal in cruelty to the Baron."

"May I enquire what the primary virtues of his company are?" Sasna asked.

"Courage, loyalty, and hospitality," Baris answered as he looked resentfully at the Hedge Knights now disappearing into the distance. "I have not met many of them during my long years, but the ones I have, I can speak with experience that they are hypocrites the lot of them. Darin and his company are no different. They interpret their virtues as they see fit, and often at the cost of the virtues they are not sworn to uphold. They care little for Fell-bloods like us, and consider that their oaths and virtues only apply when dealing with Pure-bloods like themselves." He spat as he continued looking at the Hedge Knights who were now almost out of view.

Sasna then asked him, "Do you recall what their charge is, with the three virtues they are sworn to uphold?"

Baris picked up his spear from the side of his horse. "Let me think, I did look it up when they arrived," he said thoughtfully. "Hospitality is something along the lines '*to help the friendless but be ruthless towards the stranger if words they speak are false, deal not harshly with the humble and lowly but strike those who come haughtily to your abode.*' I think that's close enough." He paused momentarily and then continued, "Loyalty is: '*though my friend strikes me I shall do him no scathe, yet will I abide by the enactments of lawful authority and will not see them forsake the ways that are right to me.*' Courage is, '*I will bear with courage the decrees of my heart and seek to fearlessly do what is just in my own eyes.*' The charges are something along those lines."

"I read their *Book of Logic* once, when I was a young girl," Sasna said. "It struck me then that it was strange vows and oaths they took when they embraced their three primary virtues. I have never met a Hedge Knight until just now, but like you, I think I will have little respect for them?"

148

Baris growled, "Their vows can be interpreted by themselves in any way they choose. They delude themselves that they act with honour bound oaths when in truth they are the most despicable among men. Tread carefully around them if your business at Greytears brings you into their presence again, especially Lord Darin. Already I have decided he is the most despicable type of man, but I would hope my words go no further than your ears, my lady."

Sasna smiled. "They will not."

"What do you want me to do with him?" Baris asked as he looked at Scarand. "He will only slow us down and I wish to get you to the castle for treatment as fast as I can. I will make it fast and painless." He lowered his spear and pointed it in the direction of Scarand.

"I am not yet a defenceless old sow, old man," Scarand said as with a speed that caught him by surprise, he snatched the spear from Baris and turned it on him.

"Darn it if I'll not be getting slow in my old age," Baris growled as he drew his sword.

"Scarand, trust me, please," Sasna said as she held out her hand for him to hand over the spear. He looked at her, and she saw doubt and anger in his eyes. Of a sudden, she felt compassion for him and wondered if he already regretted not taking his chance to escape, now it dawned upon him he had so soon been taken back into her power. As a slave again, his life could be taken on a whim and his fate decided by those he did not truly know. *I would slay us both if I were him*, she said to herself.

She then turned to Baris. "He saved my life by treating my wound, and treated me with honour and kindness when I was helpless. Please, I would not see him harmed."

She looked at Scarand and urged him, "For the sake of Marciea and Oliviana, hand me the spear." She could see conflict raging inside of him. "Trust me," she said.

After a moment, with an angry growl Scarand reluctantly handed her the spear. She handed it back to Baris, who sheathed his sword and then took it.

"Hands out front," Baris ordered him. Resting his spear against his horse again, he took a rope from a saddlebag and bound Scarand's hands with it whilst tying the other end of the rope to the pummel on his saddle.

Baris looked sullenly at Sasna. "If he had pulled that trick in front of Darin and his men, he would be dead already. But I am not them. As you wish, I'll not harm him my lady, but if he tries anything like that again, I'll not be caught off guard a second time and will have his head."

Baris took a blanket roll off the back of the saddle, unwrapped it and gave it to Sasna. She wrapped herself in it and was immediately grateful for the warmth the blanket offered and the small protection from the elements. Remounting, Baris helped her onto his horse where she sat behind him, adjusting the blanket. He picked up his spear and they set off, Scarand being pulled along behind the horse, stumbling at first on his feet as he tried to keep up, then matching the pace lest he lose his footing.

It was not too long before they came upon a cobbled road and crossed a small stone bridge that passed over a stream, and then headed along a stone road shaded by trees and surrounded by undergrowth. Every time she felt faint, Sasna took a small bit of the pirken paste from the jar. It revived and refreshed her, giving her new vigour and strength.

They briefly crossed some marshes which were overlaid with raised wooden roads upon stilts that straddled them. After the marshes, were fields. They mostly looked barren but nonetheless workers still toiled upon them, tilling the ground and removing rocks and other obstacles. An hour or so past the fields, darkling against a sallow sky, two black mounds, sheer hills, appeared, standing before them black-boned and bare.

Upon the hills, stood what was known as *The Thorns of Greytears*, two towers strong and tall that guarded the Western Pass, a valley that led between the two hills. Sasna recalled that it was said the towers had been originally built in days long past, in a time even before the Cinoans had ruled the land, which of itself was a time now mostly forgotten with only a little of that period recorded by history. The Thorns, which had once fallen into disrepair and decay, now stood strong again, repaired when the Kappian Empire had spread into the South and then the West conquering the clan-kingdoms that had once dwelt there.

For the Seesnari, the Kappian Civil War had been a blessing in disguise, for had it not been for it, Seesnari would have surely have been the next clan-kingdom to be conquered and occupied by the Empire. The Empire's civil war had saved them. Twenty-seven clan-kingdoms had once existed where the Bruthon now ruled; only the nine to the west had survived the imperial expansion. But times were once more changing; it was widely said that the Bruthon King now looked westward again, where he enviously eyed the remaining clan-kingdoms, and harboured ambitious plans to conquer them; it was only a lack of resources and manpower that had stayed his hand.

Although it had made travel more dangerous, especially by road, Sasna was glad that the Chatti were raiding Bruthon lands. Kappia desired to conquer the Baothein, the Bruthon had ambitions towards her own lands. But the ever-existing threat from the Horse Lords to the south-east of the Bruthon King, and now the Chatti raiders, meant that for now the Seesnari were safe; they could easily fend off the ever-present threat of the other eight clan-kingdoms, as long as the Bruthon did not attack.

Despite feeling reassurance that she was now safe from the dangers of the last days or so, the sight of the Thorns, filled with men and arms, was always a reminder to her that any war between Seesnari and the Bruthon, would be one where her people would be fighting for their own survival, not to gain ground. *Without new allies, the threat remains. I must fulfil my mission to the Sea Lords. The Bruthon must continue to be troubled by many enemies, so that my people will remain safe.*

The security provided by the Thorns was the reason Baron Daramir had neglected the western watchtowers that bordered Seesnari lands, it being too much cost for very little gain. The land between those watchtowers and the Thorns was mostly bleak and barren, although a few villages, towns and farmsteads existed there, and the land to the south the Chatti had raided, had little commercial or agricultural value for the Baron. The Baron had abandoned such towns and villages to their fate, as no Pure-blood Kappians dwelt in such places. Most towns and farmsteads had already been destroyed by the Chatti raiding bands that had plagued the area of recent. It was only now that the raiders were coming within sight of the Thorns, that the Baron was acting. Sasna was shrewd enough to know that the Baron's plan was clever. It would weaken him to defend a vast territory of little value in resources, but strengthen him to defend only that which was necessary.

As they made their way through the valley that ran between the Thorns, Sasna studied the defences. Crossbowman guarded the walls that ran along the top of the valley. Drawbridges, lowered or raised by ropes and chains, crossed the valley so that guardsman could cross from one side to the other, tower to tower or wall to wall, with relative ease. To try to pass between the Thorns, would be a costly endeavour for any army. To try to take them, meant scaling the huge ramparts of stone on top of the hills where they stood. Several other towers were built along the top of the valley.

*They are formidable defences*, Sasna thought as they passed through the first few gates unchallenged. As they headed further into the valley, a grisly sight met them. Hanging by their necks on ropes from the ramparts, the dead bodies of men, women and children swayed in the wind. Their bodies still bore the marks of violence, their skin and tattered clothes stained dark brown with dried blood. Others were nailed to the wooden trestles beneath the ramparts. Most of those nailed to the trestles were still in death, others moved and only their faint moans revealed to Sasna that these poor wretches were still alive and their slow movements not merely the effect from the wind. She shuddered as the smell of decay carried on the breeze.

"Who are they?" she asked.

Baris halted his steed and followed her gaze. "Those who refused to give up the *Old Faith*. Since the peace was made with the Empress, this hammer and snake cult has spread like a virus throughout Bruthon lands."

"You have not embraced it then?"

"At the moment we're not forced to, but we are not allowed to worship the old gods, nor keep their festivals or mark the rites of passage."

Baris looked away and spat on the ground in disgust. "Those bloody fools hanging up there insisted on decorating their houses with moon dolls during the recent solstice, but they didn't deserve that fate."

Sasna turned to check on Scarand, for Baris had ridden at a pace that meant he had needed to run just to keep up. He was caching his breath, and staggering slightly. Baris also turned to look at him, and yanked the rope roughly. Scarand lost his footing and went down hard on one knee. The exhausted look on his face as he glared at Baris turned to fury. For half a heartbeat, Sasna feared that Scarand would attack Baris, which would mean certain death whether he did or did not succeed, for the crossbowmen were vigilant and staring down at the small party in the valley. Baris pulled the rope, and Scarand got back to his feet.

Sasna felt Baris then abruptly spur his horse, "Come on Ranby," he said as the horse picked up its pace again. It took them a full half an hour to reach the end of the valley, from where Castle Greytears could be seen. It was large and ominous. Beyond the battlements a large black keep rose up, its top hidden by low dark clouds. As though a warning or an omen, thunder rumbled in the distance, and Sasna felt a chill run down her spine. For reasons she could not fathom, she suddenly felt uneasy, and felt the sense of a foreboding premonition.

Baris slowed the horse's pace. It took more than an hour to traverse all the roads that led through the town of Greyport situated just outside of the castle. They journeyed along cobbled streets and went past inns, houses and shops of various kinds. Perhaps it was the late hour, but the place seemed quiet to Sasna. A gloom hung over the very air, so thick that she felt she could taste it. She had never enjoyed travelling to Greytears, for she always sensed the same gloom, yet this time it seemed more foreboding than before. Hardly anyone was upon the street, and those who were, quickly rushed into the nearest building as they passed by, some dragging children with them, or they looked down at the ground as Sasna and her two companions passed by.

Finally, they reached the drawbridge that stretched over the moat surrounding the castle. The guards questioned Baris, but let them pass and traverse the drawbridge. Sasna looked around her, it had been a while since she had entered Greytears through this way. Atop the largest and furthest rampart that led to Castle Greytears, was a single gate of solid iron, and upon its battlements, guards paced and watched with anticipation the horse and riders as they approached. Baris took a horn hanging from his saddle and blew it. It was answered from deep within the keep by another horn.

Sasna turned again and stared at Scarand being led behind the horse. "Well, we are here," she said sympathetically to him. "Castle Greytears, one of the great ancient castles of the Bruthon Family, the seat of the third Baron Daramir Bruthon, cousin to the First Lord of Bruthon who is brother to King Lagaelias the Third."

It was clear to her that Scarand had never seen such sights before. It did not please her that he was so obviously in a state of despair. She had never really considered before what the Davari slaves might feel. She knew it was always wise to make the pretence she cared what they felt and feared, as it helped her manage them. But she had never before spent as much time with one as she had with Scarand. It disturbed her greatly to realize that she felt gratitude for his kindness, his help. His obvious anguish at that moment made her feel uneasy. As the chains clanked and the great iron portcullis in front of them lifted, she again wondered if he felt regret that he had not taken his one chance at freedom. She had manipulated him into doing what she wanted, and now he would probably never be free despite the promises she had made to him. A sensation and emotion passed over her she had not felt for many a year, since that time when she and her mother had been prisoners of the Samothrane. She felt guilt. It only lasted as briefly as the pity had, just the most fleeting of moments, but it had been there, and it was real, and it was not nice. She concluded her thoughts and feelings must be the effects of the pirken paste and medicine Baris had given her, so perhaps such thoughts and feelings would be gone when the effects wore off. Reprimanding herself for allowing a momentary lapse into emotional stupidity, she snapped herself out of it and decided not to look at the Davari anymore. She would help him if she could, and hoped that the Baron would allow her to take him to help her search for Farir, but beyond that, she had no responsibility for his fate and she told herself she would be sensible to remember that.

The guards on the battlements watched as the rider with his companions passed beneath the portcullis and entered Castle Greytears. Once inside the castle, they again journeyed upon cobbled stones and went past more inns, houses and shops of various kinds, and a few smaller keeps and guard towers. Again, perhaps it was the late hour, but Sasna sensed the same gloom as in the town. Once more, hardly anyone was upon the street, apart from a few guard patrols. The few civilians who were still about, just like those in the town, quickly rushed into the nearest building as they passed by, or did not look as they hurried along.

Baris and Sasna dismounted the horse near the door of the main keep. Whatever medicine Baris had given her, it had worked. The pain in her shoulder was just a dull throb and she felt awake and alert. Baris must have sensed this, he smiled knowingly.

"Its powerful stuff, my lady," he said. As Baris untied Scarand, Sasna noticed a man, dressed in black and red watching them sombrely from a balcony very high above, his cloak whipping about him in the wind. She felt troubled as she recognised Baron Daramir. The way he looked at her was unsettling. He turned and disappeared from her view. Deep down, Sasna knew that something was wrong; she could sense the Baron was not happy, and when in such a mood, he could be extremely dangerous and unpredictable. It was for good reason they called him the *Bloody Baron. There's no turning back now*, Sasna said to herself, but once again, she felt a sinister sensation and shuddered as she looked at the keep of Castle Greytears.

152

# Chapter Twelve: *Treachery*

*Wandering northward, the Kappians destroyed the ancient Highkarnian Kingdom of Hykros, whose peoples soon adopted many of the ways of their superior conquerors. King Arius had finally welded an empire from the savage clans. He, who was born in a mud-walled, wattle-roofed hut, now sat on a golden throne in the city he built upon the hill of his enemies' woe. He named the city, Aleskian. Arius was, however, not content. He ever remained ferocious, elemental, interested in only war and plunder and the naked primal principles of life. He turned a jealous eye towards what is now known as the Kappian Plateau, and once again, he prepared to conquer all who stood before him, and vowed to break the power of the Eastern kings.*

**Temmison Vol II, Book 2: History of the Kappian Empire.**

*As* he had most mornings the last few days, Borach sat at his desk and waited. He caressed the scroll he held in his hand. He knew that today would be the day when final confirmation of the orders received from Kappia would arrive. His thoughts were interrupted by the stamp of sentries outside his study. Jumping up from his chair, he belted his sword around his waist and waited by his desk. The curtain covering the entrance was pulled back, and a grubby looking dwarf entered. The several guards waited outside.

Borach knew Galin well. The Fourth Commander was in control of the stores of the Third Legion, and responsible for all messages. The dwarf's jerkin was caked with filth and stank from the sweat of his journey. His neatly braided beard was thick with dirt. The dwarf tucked his thumbs into his belt; his grimy fingernails fidgeting with the colourful wool weave of his trousers.

"It's official," he said with frustration. "On top of that, Prince Regineo is several miles or so from the city, camped with an army of Hammer Knights." Galin shifted uncomfortably on his feet. "He told me himself, you should expect him on the morrow. He expects you to obey the imperial order without complaint or the slightest deviance."

Before Borach could reply, another dwarf entered, followed by a man who wore the gold sash of an imperial courier over his griffin rider's attire, which was red dyed boiled leather, thick thigh length heavy boots and a hooded black cloak. Borach placed the scroll he had been holding on the desk, and took the new letter offered by the bowing courier.

The second dwarf said to the courier, "Go and rest in the officers' mess, you know the way?"

The courier nodded.

"Good, eat and drink. If there is a reply, I will bring it to you.

"Thank you Commander Marki," the courier said before saluting, and leaving the study.

Borach did not notice the courier leave. He opened the wax seal and unfolded the vellum parchment. He read carefully, studying the usual platitudes and form that started all imperial letters. As was his habit, he committed every name and phrase to memory, and checked all of the official seals and signatures before reading the meat of the letter that confirmed the orders. He shook his head angrily as he digested its contents.

"What is it?" the dwarf Marki asked him.

Borach looked at his old friend, and handed him the letter. Marki took it, skipped the formalities and went straight to the meat of the orders. He read them, and then re-read them again to make sure he had understood the contents. "Karkson has more hair than wit, and more faults than hairs, if he has willingly signed these orders," he growled before he could stop himself.

"Are the legions prepared to leave?" Borach asked Galin.

"They have been preparing for three days. On your word, they will abandon the ring keeps, and the watch forts; a vanguard of Hammer Knights has already arrived to secure them. A handful from each legion will remain, the rest will march out of Aleskian when the sun rises." He growled. "We, the Third, will be practically the only legion left at Aleskian, tasked with teaching the Hammer Knights all they need to know about the city, but even our numbers will be depleted. When the legions leave tomorrow, the majority of our griffin riders will fly to Kara Duram, and our own Seers, cavalry and archers will march with the other legions when the sun rises." He clenched his fist and gritted his teeth; his next words came out uneasily. "I am loyal to a fault, to you and to the Empress, but this is downright lunacy."

Borach closed his eyes in thought. The truth was, he agreed the orders given made no sense, but they were sent directly from Kappia. He placed the letter on the desk, and picked up the scroll he had been formerly holding. Opening his eyes, he looked expectantly at Marki. "Maybe there is a contradiction in the orders, anything that will allow me to delay, and go to Kara Duram and speak directly with Karkson when he returns from Kappia?"

Marki sighed. "Ravens and griffin riders have confirmed the orders to the generals of each legion. I checked them myself, each and every one. Tomorrow, they must march to Kara Duram, where they will be disbanded." He shook his head, the beads in his beard cracking together and slapping against the iron breastplate on his chest. "It doesn't make sense," he protested. "Galin is right, this is insanity! Why is the defence of Aleskian and the ring keeps being given over to the Hammer Knights?" He angrily banged his fist on the desk. "What is going on Bor?"

Borach wished he knew. For more than three thousand years, his family had been given the sacred task of ruling Aleskian, commanding the northern legions, and guarding the Great Northern Wall from any threats. His father had overseen the building of the ring keeps, a network of seven keeps outside of the city of Aleskian that helped secure the area from the early peril of bandits and marauders, from within the Everglow, in the days when the Empire was plagued by numerous invaders. His grandfather, had repaired and manned the ancient watch forts - the mile keeps along the Great Northern Wall that, in a time before even the Bantu threat had first appeared, were used to secure the Everglow from any foes that might emerge from the Northern Wilds. Before even any of that, his distant ancestors had marched with King Arius.

Marki eyed the scroll that Borach had earlier been caressing with his thumb. "May I, Bor?" he asked.

Borach gestured for his friend to take it. Marki snatched it up, unrolled it, read it, and threw it on the desk in disgust. "That just seals a deal of rotten-meat," he roared.

"What does?" Galin asked.

"In three days, we have to march with the few men we will have left, onto the Aleskian Plain, wait, and formerly hand over the authority of the city and the defence of the wall to Prince Regineo and the Hammer Knights! That is just poking a warg with a stick." Marki paused, and then addressing Borach, asked, "What will you do Bor? You have devoted all of your lifetimes to this city and to guarding the wall."

Borach sighed wearily, and then said, "I would have faithfully discharged my duty, and before my *Final-death*, I would have handed over the responsibility to my own son." He smiled wryly. "The truth is, I am tired from war and conflict. The legions are to be disbanded, so I must stand down as well. I will retire to my estate at Estalda, and will

154

hope to live out the rest of my lives in peace, with Yianna and our children. Maybe this is for the best."

"It's that darn hammer and snake religion, and that upstart Mazdek upturning everything," Galin snarled. "Ruining the old order that once stabilised the Empire. Only chaos will come from this, mark my word!"

Borach smiled. "You two have served with me faithfully, for as many years as I can remember. Maybe it is time you set out to search for your fathers, and see if they ever did discover Frabrim; if you uncovered their fate, maybe your kin would open the doors of the Iron Mountain for you if you chose to return again?"

"They would not open the doors for anything less than our taking a Sangdalen back to them," Galin said, "and few of them there are."

"You would be welcome to live out your days with me and my kin at Estalda," Borach offered sincerely.

"Time enough to consider our future in the days ahead, but first we have to drink a foul medicine and obey these orders," Marki said grumpily. He continued protesting. "There's treachery behind these orders Bor, I feel it in my blood, something's not right."

*I know something is not right, but what can I do?* Borach crumpled the letter in his hand as he rubbed his chin thoughtfully and then looked at Marki. "We are soldiers Marki. These orders have been sent from Kappia, and have been signed with the imperial seal of the Empress Shaka herself, and all of her Privy Council, including Karkson." He heaved a sigh again. "We have no choice but to obey them, no matter how it makes us feel."

"I bet it has something to do with the rumours that the sacred artefact these hammer nuts all go on about was stolen," Galin said. "What was it called again?"

"The Simal," Marki answered him. "We also heard that one of their Aeldar was slain, although if you ask me, I think the whole thing about raising some beast from an abyss is all made up by that madman Mazdek, but if it is true, then no wonder the Empire has turned to madness."

"You will need to guard your tongue in the days ahead," Borach warned. "Whatever your personal misgivings or thoughts on the hammer and snake cult, it has now arrived at Aleskian, and their Inquisition does not tolerate dissent."

"Then maybe you are right Bor," Marki replied gloomily, "perhaps it is time to look for fortune and favour elsewhere. That cult has already brought enough death and destruction to the Empire!"

Borach fumbled about on his desk, and selecting another scroll unrolled it. Reading it briefly, he said, "Official news is that the slaying of an Aeldar is false; the Simal was briefly stolen by a renegade priestess, but she was quickly recaptured and will face retribution. The Simal has been returned to the Argona Temple." He threw the scroll back onto the table. "These are strange times," he muttered to himself, and then looking at the two Dwarves said, "you have your orders, be about them."

Galin and Marki left the room, grumbling and protesting as they did so. When he was alone, Borach sat back down at his desk and thought about the orders and the two Dwarves' comments. They were right, and their words had only confirmed what he himself had concluded. The orders from Kappia were complete and utter madness. The hammer and snake cult were finally taking hold of the last great stronghold of the Kappian Empire; short of outright rebellion, something he had no intention of doing, he had no choice but to obey. He felt perplexed, and un-crumpling the main orders he read them again, hoping he had missed or overlooked something obvious. He re-read the contents, checked every signature and seal. It was official; these were orders from

Kappia sealed by the Empress Shaka herself and the entire Privy Council, including General Karkson. To disobey the order would be an act of treason, although to obey it felt like an act of madness and treachery in itself.

"What is going on?" he whispered to himself as he read the letter yet again. Walking over to a glass weapon's cabinet, he removed *Havwitha,* the only Arkith the Third Legion possessed. It was not a sword he would ever wield willingly, but feared that a time may soon come, when he might have no choice but to put it to use. *What will I do when the hammer and snake cult enforce their will at my own estate of Estalda, will I have peace there or be forced to bend the knee to their gods?*

His troubled thoughts were disturbed when he heard the door to the left of his office open. His wife, Yianna entered. She smiled, and it warmed his heart as it always did. She walked across the room and stood in front of the tall wood-framed mirror near the window, and checked her outfit.

"The orders have been confirmed," he said with a worried look on his face. He opened a drawer, and took a necklace from it, before standing and walking over to her. "It's official, from the Empress herself."

He was pleased to note that Yianna was dressed for riding. She wore black tunic and trousers embroidered with gold, thigh length leather boots and a light black cloak that had the emblem of the Third Legion, a golden griffin stitched on the back. Fastening the cloak around her neck were the emerald brooch and pins that he had gifted to her several lifetimes ago.

He gently handed her the necklace, and held back her long black hair for her as she put it on. Her slender fingers skilfully hooked the clasp behind her neck, and then she turned to face him.

He put a finger over her lips, to gently stop her from speaking.

"You must make haste and ride to Estalda with the children; wait there until I join you. Be wary who you trust," he said.

"I will always obey you my husband, but surely we can send the children to Estalda? Yonnicia will look after them well. My place is by your side," she said as she gently brushed his finger aside and put her head on his chest. "Why would the legions and their families be ordered to Kara Duram? It feels like Aleskian is being evacuated." It was forbidden for the legionnaires to have Pure-blood wives, but many had taken Fell-bloods, and had children with them. The fact that they too, were being ordered out of Aleskian, did indeed make it feel like an evacuation.

"The city has been given to the Hammer Knights," was all he said in reply. He stroked her hair and held her tightly. The thought of being separated from Yianna again, even if for a short time, tormented him. She had accompanied him before on expeditions and various campaigns of the past, but that was before they had been blessed with the gift of children. Sixteen lifetimes they had been married, and she had not conceived during her first lifetime. But, recently, several years ago Yianna had unexpectedly become one of the very few and rare Pure-bloods to become pregnant after their first lifetime. She had given birth to twins, two healthy Pure-bloods, a girl and a boy, who they named Yana and Biran.

"Let me stay with you," she asked gently, as she looked pleadingly into his eyes.

"Not this time, my love. I do not know what is afoot. Something is not right I can feel it, but choices are stripped from me. To defy the order would be an act of treason. I will join you at Estalda soon," he replied as he tenderly stroked her hair.

Borach could tell that something else was on her mind, and he knew her well enough to know what it was without asking, but he asked anyway.

"What is it? Speak openly," he softly said to her.

156

"The religion of hammer and snake has spread everywhere like a poison. It spreads madness and confusion as it does so. Mark my words husband, the end of the Empire as we know it has begun. Never again will the griffin banner fly over Aleskian. I cannot tolerate the thought of those Hammer Knights flying their banners over the city which has been our home for so long."

*I feel the same way, but short of disobeying an imperial order, what other choice is there?* He smiled at her. "It is not the path I would have chosen for us, but the truth is, I am tired of war. I see this as a new start. We can spend the rest of our lives in peace; we need never be apart again after I fulfil my final duties."

She looked up at him worryingly.

"I can tell you have something to add to that," he said, with a half-smile.

"The cult of hammer and snake will allow no peace," she said, and then hesitated before adding. "My words are of no use, for you will not heed them. If I thought for one moment you would, I would beg you to come with me and the children, now, today! I sense betrayal in the air."

*I wish with all of my heart that I could.* "I have to officially hand the city over to Prince Regineo."

"I beg you, feign an illness, for my sake and that of our children. Let Marki hand the city over. Heed my warning, but if you will not, as I suspect, then please, let me stay with you?"

He kissed her passionately on the face, before saying, "I am loyal to the Empress and the Empire, as my father was before me; the Empress will return that loyalty by allowing me to retire in peace. I will join with you soon enough." He softly wiped the tears away from her eyes with his fingers. *I hope your suspicions do not come to pass. I am not naive; I know full well the nature of those I serve.* "All will be well, but the fact that Prince Regineo is coming here, is reason enough for you to leave." *I could never sit and endure what he has forced upon others. I would not have you touched by him. I would cut off his head with Havwitha and throw him over the wall myself if he laid a finger upon you."*

Borach knew that Yianna understood what he meant; she closed her eyes briefly. The royal family all had the title *Ivanar*, which meant they were above any law in the Empire - they were the law. It was a power they often abused, especially when amongst the most powerful families. Regineo's grandfather, Maopold III, was remembered for his insane capriciousness and cruelty. He was a man remembered with loathing and utter terror. Regineo was building a reputation to match.

Shaka had followed in her father's footsteps, and Aspess and Caspus had also acted with impunity and committed many loathsome acts; but none, matched Prince Regineo in following in his grandfather's footsteps. Regineo's actions were as extravagant as his desires were outrageous. His liaisons with daughters of the nobility and married women were just the start. Often, at a feast, he would order the wife of some noble into an adjacent room, emerging later on to discuss and score the woman's sexual skill. Her husband had little choice but to smile and endure the public humiliation. It was said that slaves in his charge fared the worst. He would disguise himself in the fur of a predatory beast and hide in a 'den' before flinging himself at the intimate parts of male and female victims, who were bound to wooden stakes, completely at his mercy, of which he had none. It had been more than two lifetimes ago since Regineo had last entered Aleskian, and Borach had made sure that Yianna and the other wives of prominent nobles in the city had been safely in his mountain estate of Estalda long before he had arrived.

"I will leave immediately, and I will pray to the old gods, or any that will listen, that we might be together again soon," Yianna said.

Borach smiled and took his wife by the hands. "I love you more than life itself," he whispered tenderly. "I do not fully understand the reason for the madness behind these orders, but I do know that our days in Aleskian are finished." *I fear the worst, but must play the last moves out.* "As long as you and the children are safe, I am content."

He twiddled the rare and expensive milathran chain that held the locket hanging from her neck. It was a gift he had given her, so many lifetimes ago. He carefully moved his fingers down the chain to the locket, held it, and flicked the catch so it sprung open. He studied the tiny painting of them together, placed within it. He remembered the words he had said to her on the day he had given it to her as a gift, and he repeated them. "Never forget my face, never forget us," he said.

A tear rolled down her cheek, and she answered him with the same words she had said on that same day so long ago. "How do you think I could ever forget us, or your face?" She tenderly closed the locket and stroked his cheek. "Do not tarry once your business here is finished," she pleaded.

"I will join you in Estalda soon enough," he replied, as he pulled his wife into his lap; they lovingly embraced and kissed passionately.

# Chapter Thirteen: *The Bloody Baron*

*It was said that a long time ago, many a Wytch and monster hunter visited Greytears with plans of entering the Wytchwood and ridding it of its cursed ones. The Baron's treatment of them, soon lessened their numbers, but even then, we heard tales that some entered and never returned. Many mysteries and great evil surrounds that place, it is few who would dare to venture under those cursed boughs.*
**Temmison Vol III, Book 5: Natural Wonders of the Everglow.**

*Baris* tied his horse to a hitching rail, lent his spear against the wall of the keep and led Sasna and Scarand through large iron framed wooden doors, which were opened from the inside by burly sentries. Once they had passed through the doors and stood in the vast porch, the doors were slammed shut behind them.

"The Baron wishes to speak with you," the steward who greeted them said.

Baris became agitated. "I can give you the message Lord Darin has for the Baron. I need to attend to my horse," he protested.

"Not before you exchange words with the Baron," the steward replied haughtily, before turning abruptly. "Follow me!"

*Something still doesn't feel right*, Sasna thought, as they followed the steward and entered the great hall. The sense of foreboding she felt increased with every step. She had been in the hall many times before. The familiar trophies, the heads of a variety of beasts hung from the walls. She noticed a newly mounted trophy, a Gragor's head. Its eyes seemed to follow her as she made her way down the hall. The great fireplace at the far end of the hall was unlit; the long table that stretched the length of it was empty. It was clear no meal or feast was planned for that day. They left the hall and ascended the large spiral staircase that had an exit at every floor. They passed the first floor where the office she conducted trade and business with the Baron's steward was located. They passed the second floor, where the guest rooms were situated. She was also familiar with it having often stayed in a room on that level. They passed that floor, and then the third, fourth, fifth and sixth before they came to the seventh, where she knew Baron Daramir's private chambers were located. The steward led them along the corridor and into a large study.

The steward was the first to enter the room, followed by Sasna, Scarand and then Baris. A man-at-arms was waiting. He looked at Baris and shrugged his shoulders in frustration and resignation as they entered.

"He's in a foul mood, tread with care," the man said to him.

"Thanks for the warning," Baris replied, in a grim whisper.

"Follow," the steward said as he hastened ahead to the far end of the study, where a fire was burning in the hearth, the logs crackling and spitting. He invited Sasna to sit in a chair in front of a great wooden desk, upon which was a feathered quill, some ink in a pot, several ledgers and parchments. Two chairs were the opposite side of the desk. The steward went and knocked on a door in the corner of the room, and waited patiently.

Baris looked at Sasna; instinctively she perceived a look of genuine concern on his face. "Be careful, my lady," he whispered. "The Baron has invited us all in here, unattired for the occasion. That means he is impatient about a matter, and that never bodes well."

Sasna wrapped the blanket just that little tighter around herself. She looked at Scarand, and quietly said, "For the sake of Marciea and Oliviana, do not look him in the eye. It will be instant death for you."

To take her mind off of her concerns, Sasna looked around her. It occurred to her that the slave Scarand may never have seen a study before. He was looking around in bafflement at the many books that lined the shelves that rose from the ground high up into the wooden vaulted ceiling. The floor, carpeted in red inset with flowing traceries of many colours, was littered with more books and scrolls piled in high stacks. It certainly was an impressive personal library Daramir had. A latch in the door to the left clicked and the door opened.

The steward stood aside and bowed his head as Baron Daramir entered the library with a broad grin on his face, but the smile was false and did not touch his eyes. A male scribe, dressed in grey, followed him. Daramir took the seat opposite Sasna, and the scribe the one next to him. He lent on the desk with his elbows, and stared into her eyes. His smile disappeared in an instant.

"Bring him in," he shouted. A fat repellent figure, dangling a bunch of keys entered through the same open door, accompanied by a burly guard who was pushing ahead of him a hooded figure bound by ropes. Sasna knew the fat man; he was the Baron's chief eunuch, Malkili, of whom grisly tales were whispered – a man with whom a monstrous lust for torture took the place of all human passions. Several other guards followed.

The guard pulled the hood off of the captive's head, to reveal a man whose nose was missing as was one eye; the deep scarring showed they were old wounds. He blinked like an owl with his one good eye, and winced from the light shining from candles in the chandelier hanging from the ceiling. His face was badly beaten and bruised. Sasna was both disappointed and horrified. For a moment she hoped it might have been Farir, it was not, but her sense of horror was due to the fact she did recognise the man. He was Marlo, the man through whom she and her uncle had arranged passage, by ship, from Berecoth to Harwind, from where she would then take another ship to meet the Sea Lord Erik Vansoth.

"These pirates sing prettier than any songbird or parrot," a woman's voice said from the corner of the library.

Sasna had not noticed Daramir's sister, Lady Bavira, enter. Sasna stood out of respect. "Lord Daramir, Lady Bavira, I bring you greetings," she said, but was ignored by the both of them.

"The mere threat of flaying and impalement makes his kind willing to speak and give up their little secrets, and their own comrades, when faced with such a fate," Daramir said. The guard yanked the rope violently, causing Marlo to stumble to the floor. Malkili giggled demonically.

"You promised he would soon be mine to entertain myself with," Bavira said, her eyes darting across the pirate lustily and cruelly. She was not an attractive woman; her hair was balding at the front and heavy jowls spread across her otherwise thin face. Her once white garment was grubby and stained with dirt. "Meanwhile, he can do some hard labour for the priest. If he does not work hard for the priest by day, nor entertain me by night, he will pay the price at the next feast. Malkili's apprentice desires to learn and practice new techniques; we should let him do so, and hope this time he does not end him prematurely with his botched manner."

Malkili smiled, and giggled even more demonically, sending a shiver down Sasna's spine.

"Very well sister," Daramir said. He issued an order to a guard.

"Take him to the dungeon. Give him food and water; if the priest wants to use him for manual labour, let him."

The guard nodded and promptly forced the man to his feet before removing him from the library, followed by Malkili. Daramir watched as the man was taken away, and then he turned to Sasna. The harsh look in his eyes unnerved her.

"Lady Sasna, when the raven brought the message that you were bringing us the usual tribute of gold and three Davari slaves, it did not say you intended to try to drown them in the Erin beforehand." He gestured impatiently with his hand towards the chair. "Sit woman, sit," he said.

Sasna sat down again; her shoulder caused her to grimace, as the effect of the medication was starting to wear off. The blood was beginning to seep through the bandage Baris had put on her, and the blanket with which she covered herself.

"That does not look like a pleasant wound," Bavira said with barely hidden glee. "You have had quite the night."

"Indeed," Sasna said, masking the pain she felt, and the fear. *If Marlo has talked, this will not go well.*

"Were there signs of any other survivors?" she asked, hoping she might receive news of Farir, and avoid the questions she knew were soon to come.

Daramir sighed deeply. "Not all of our trackers have returned. We have watchers in the marshes, we scout the riverbanks this side of the river. Only you two, and a few others, have been fortunate, it seems."

Sasna had to restrain herself. Her grief that Farir had not been found reasserted itself. "I fear for my poor brother, but hope still lives. He has always been a strong swimmer." *Yet he was wounded. I cling to the hope that it might still be possible he made it to the shore of the Wytchwood.* "I would request a change of clothes and two horses, one for myself and the other for my slave so that we may go and search for him?"

"Do you know what may have caused this ship's fire?" Daramir asked, ignoring her request.

"No," Sasna lied. "I was sleeping and woke to the sound of shouting. The ship was aflame and covered in smoke. It did cross my mind that maybe pirates had attacked but I could not be sure. I searched, but could not find Farir, so my slave helped me into a boat and got me to the southern shore." She looked at Scarand and smiled gently. She had made sure she spoke in the Common Tongue so that he would know the version of events she had given to Lord Daramir.

Daramir looked contemptuously at Scarand, who, wisely, stared at the floor as instructed, but Sasna could sense the rage and primal instinct the Davari was clearly holding back, and she saw it in his eyes.

"He looks a fierce one," Bavira said of Scarand, "like he needs to be broken and taught his place."

Sasna defended Scarand: "Any anger upon his countenance, is due to the suffering I have endured; it is not disrespect to you, Lady Bavira, or to you Lord Daramir. When we landed on the shore, my slave lit a fire to keep me warm, and guarded me throughout the night. He made a poultice and bandaged my wound. It saved my life. We set out for the castle hoping to meet your men and were not disappointed." *If Baron Daramir has already decided to torment and slay Scarand, there is nothing I can do for him.* She tried to distract Daramir. "Are you sure there are no other survivors this side of the river?" she asked again.

"It is tiresome to repeat myself," Daramir said moodily after which he gave a big yawn. "There is no report of any other survivors this side of the river. We have not checked the Wychtwood, and neither shall we, though some bodies or survivors may end up there as the currents of the Erin may throw people, dead or alive, upon its cursed banks. What remains of that ship is already grounded close to the northern riverbank."

Sasna knew that if she could remove herself and Scarand from Daramir's presence, whatever had troubled and angered him, might not be taken out on them. However, it all depended on what information had been distracted from Marlo. She rubbed her shoulder. "If my slave and I might be excused, my injury throbs. I would see a medic if you would be so kind. The wound is open and needs stitching."

Ignoring her, Daramir drummed his fingers on the desk, and turned his attention to Baris who appeared restless and agitated as he stood waiting. "Look at that," Daramir said as he smiled nastily. "This fool of a half-breed has a message he feels is urgent to give, but he knows better than to interrupt me." He sighed deeply, "Very well, what is it?"

Baris bowed his head respectfully. "Your grace, Lord Darin wishes me to inform you he is inspecting tracks that led from a burned village. At the same time, he will search for any more survivors from the wreckage."

Daramir snarled with rage. "I heard my brother did not leave the taverns until after the warband had already finished their raiding and were leaving my lands, is this true? Lie to me, and I will mount your head on my wall," he threatened.

"Lord Darin set out at a time that seemed right to him," Baris said apologetically and with a tone laced with as much diplomacy as a man like him could muster.

The news did not please Daramir, who frowned at Sasna. "These Chatti and Gragor originate from a land of volcano and ash. They now regularly raid my lands, and I cannot even rely on my own brother to chase them off until he has finished his cavorting and whoring," he said as he continued drumming his fingers on the desk. "On top of this, pirates have sacked and looted Berecoth and killed the patrician there. Had you heard this news?"

*If Marlo told them of my mission, all is lost.* Her cover story would not hold up to any interrogation. She tried not to let the rising panic within her, reveal itself in her voice. She swallowed hard before speaking. "I had heard about the Chatti raiding parties, my uncle has increased our own border security, and the captain of the ship I was on informed me that pirates had raided Berecoth."

"If they had not raided it, did you have business in Berecoth once you had delivered us our tribute?" Lady Bavira asked with a sly look on her face.

"Only on a business matter. The dwarf, Gildaora, wished to purchase a slave from me."

"Are you certain you were not headed to Berecoth to betray us?" Bavira hissed scathingly. "We heard you wanted passage from there to Harwind?"

Sasna panicked as thoughts raced through her mind. *Marlo has told them, they know. But, he and Senzas only knew I wanted an audience with the Sea Lords, not the nature of the discussion.* She thought a half-lie might suffice. "The pirate situation is costing us all money. It was one of the matters I intended to discuss with you, to see whether you had news if the Bruthon King or the Empire had revealed any strategy to deal with the continuing threat and blockade to trade on the Erin. My uncle was going to test the Sea Lords, and see if a regular tribute to them might enable trade to flow once again." Her mouth felt dry; she began to sweat. "As I said, we would not have acted without fully consulting you first, Baron, it was a matter I was going to raise with you, to see if you might agree such a discussion with the Sea Lords might be of mutual benefit to us both?"

"Is that so?" Daramir asked as he cocked an eyebrow.

"She lies," Bavira whispered accusingly in her brother's ear, loud enough for Sasna to hear.

Daramir stroked his chin thoughtfully. "The head of the pirate captain, the one they call Redboots, who raided Berecoth, would look good mounted in my hall, don't you think?"

Sasna slowly nodded in agreement, glad of the change of topic.

"I would like to hang her pretty red boots right next to her head," Bavira said with glee.

Daramir grunted, delighted by the thought. "The prisoner informed me that only three ships and their crews remain in Berecoth, and that Redboots has left there for now. I would like nothing more than to set out for Berecoth immediately, and slay the remaining pirate scum, but Berecoth is a free port. If I enter it with armed men, no matter the circumstances, it will unsettle many of the other free people in Anthain lands. It would be seen as an act of war." He drummed his fingers on the table and continued to stare harshly at Sasna. She looked away briefly, and attempted a half smile when she looked him in the eye again.

Bavira stared her down. "The Empress does nothing to protect the ports, and the Bruthon King idles away his time with wine and women whilst his kingdom false to ruin around him," she said angrily.

Daramir spoke through gritted teeth. "My sister is right, neither the city of Bruthon nor Kappia has the ships to remove this menace from my river, so they do nothing and the flow of slaves and all trade stops. I discovered the patrician at Berecoth had made a deal and was doing business with the pirate scum. I am forced to tolerate having such a port right next to my own borders, and now you seek to sneak past my castle into Berecoth on some errand you claim is in my interest as well as that of you Seesnari?" He stopped drumming his fingers, and clenched both fists tightly as he leant forward towards Sasna. "Do not expect me to believe such a lie," he hissed.

"*Never trust a Seesnari*," Bavira screamed, almost hysterically.

Sasna felt paralysed with fear. Thoughts raced through her mind. They knew the truth, but if she admitted to it, she feared for her future. She would persist in telling the Baron and his sister the half-truth. "I was ordered to discuss the matter with you, so that any proposal made to the Sea Lords, had your full support," she said meekly.

The Baron looked at his steward. "Tell my squire to prepare my horse and armour. I will wear the heavy Arurien-set. Rouse as many men as can be spared, I will join my brother in searching the shores of the Erin once my business with Lady Sasna is concluded."

The steward bowed his head, "Yes, your grace," he said, and promptly left.

Daramir looked at Baris. "You shall ride out to my brother and inform him I will join him shortly. He will wait for me along the road."

"Yes, my lord," Baris said, and then quickly saluted, bowed and hastily left the library.

"That does look like a nasty wound beneath that blanket," Daramir said to Sasna as he pointed to the blood soaking through it. "We must get the physician to see to it soon. How did you get it? Perhaps you caught it on some splintered wood as you fled the ship?"

"Yes," Sasna said, sensing a trap, but not knowing how to answer. "I can't really remember; it all happened so fast, but I did catch it on something."

Bavira walked slowly around the desk and stood behind Sasna. She slowly lifted the blanket, and the bandage, and looked at the wound, before roughly prodding it with her finger. Sasna gasped with the pain.

"This looks like a deep sabre cut to me," Bavira said as she put her bloodied fingers into her mouth and tasted the blood.

"He did this?" Daramir asked, as he shot a hateful look at Scarand.

"No, he saved my life, he did not harm me," Sasna answered.

"Then how did you get this wound," Bavira asked as she sat on the desk and looked at Sasna. "We know what the cut of a sword looks like on human flesh."

"I don't know," Sasna replied, lying. I may have cut it when I fell into the boat or was fleeing from the flames. I do not recall how I received it."

"She lies yet again," Bavira said as she walked around the desk and stood next to her brother. She shook him playfully by the shoulders and put her head next to his as she smiled wildly at Sasna. "She lies," she repeated, and giggled menacingly. Her yellow and blackened teeth chattered up and down.

"You know what they say, brother; *never trust a Seesnari*, so don't trust this one." The mirth in Bavira's voice did not reach her eyes, as both she and Daramir stared ominously at Sasna.

"She does lie," he said. He turned and looked at the scribe, who was furiously scribbling onto the parchment with the quill. "Are you getting this all down?"

"Yes, your grace," the scribe replied.

Sasna felt untameable fear rise up within her. *I need to get out of here, fast.* "Thank you for the assistance I received to bring me here," she said as she fretfully stood to her feet. "I would like to search for Farir without delay. Pirken and the medicine your man Baris gave me, have strengthened me, and though my wound still troubles me, I feel well enough to leave. If I may have a little assistance from your physician, to stitch it, I would be thankful, and then I shall be on my way. I will owe you a great debt of gratitude." The pirken and medicine had helped Sasna a lot, but the effects were wearing off. Pain and dizziness were returning and she felt exhausted, but wanted to leave.

"No, I would not hear of it," Daramir said with an over-exaggerated sense of concern. "Your uncle would never forgive me if I allowed you to go wandering off in this state. Besides, I have forbidden that any enter the Wytchwood, and if your brother lives, then surely he will be there."

"We cannot allow it," Bavira said, "For great evil haunts that place and must not be stirred from its slumber."

Daramir smiled disingenuously. "Indeed, you must rest here until your uncle sends an escort to return you safely back to Ashgiliath or another ship arrives that is headed towards there."

Sasna could sense the insincerity in both Daramir and Bavira. *I must flee, in haste.* She felt she had no choice but to still try and bluff her way out. "Your offer is received with gratitude, but I will leave and must insist on it, even if I must walk, but as you wish I will not enter the Wytchwood," she said as she bowed her head.

"Insist?" Bavira asked indignantly.

The Baron narrowed his eyes. "Even Seesnari from high-society cannot insist anything from Pure-blood Akkadians like us, especially when so much mystery still surrounds your plans to get to Harwind and from there to the Sea Lords."

"Where are your manners?" Bavira chimed in.

*It must be this wound and my grief for Farir. I am not thinking clearly.* "Apologies, my lady, I meant no offence. My concern for my brother overwhelms me, you can understand that? I only wish to be on my way and either find him or have time to grieve for my loss. I can assure you that I had no intention of making any trip to speak with the Sea Lords, without hearing and receiving your own counsel on the matter, and gaining your

164

consent." She looked at Scarand, who stood in chains with his head lowered. "The tribute slaves we had planned to give to you have perished," she lied, switching to the High-Akkadian speech so Scarand would not understand what she was saying. "This Davari slave is newly owned by me, but already on the road here he has proven his loyalty. It saddens me to part with him, but you can keep him. I will send you more, for the trouble this matter has caused you."

Scarand looked up at her, rage glowering in his eyes, as though he instinctively sensed betrayal.

"Perhaps, unless he is to be questioned by Malkili, and his body broken in the doing, I will keep him," Bavira said as she circled Scarand, looking him up and down, admiring his form and looks. "I have always found Davari to be of such an unpleasant and devious disposition, but they do make good sport when we hunt or bed them." She sniffed at him and curled her nose in disgust. "He needs a bath though; the stench of the Erin is upon him."

Sasna felt a twinge of regret that Scarand's fate was now beyond her control, but the feeling did not last long, as her own situation was the most pressing concern.

Bavira glared at her ominously, and then walked over to Daramir. "I grow tired of this charade brother," she said. "Show her."

The smile that slowly spread across Daramir's face sent a chill down Sasna's spine, as much as the words that slipped through his cruel mouth. "It is entertaining to watch her squirm, though, is it not, sister? She has the audacity to come here, ask for our help, and tries to hide her mischief-making from us."

Bavira did not smile. "I grow bored of toying with her." She continued to look harshly at Sasna. "You will not be leaving here," she said spitefully and then spat out the words, "Lady Sasna!"

"If you insist that I must stay here, I gladly accept your hospitality," Sasna said with a polite smile that hid the panic that nearly consumed her. *I need to buy time, plan my escape. It is clear I am to be kept here against my will.* "If that is how it is to be, may I please have a bath and change of clothes and have this wound seen too? I am in much need of rest and sleep. I would be very grateful." She took an exhausted breath. "May I please retire now, Lord Daramir?" she asked weakly.

"Yes, you may," he replied. "We have a skilled physician in the castle; he will tend to your shoulder, who knows what harm this savage has done with his filthy poultices. I should have him flogged for having the insolence to touch you, even if it was to assist."

"There is no need," Sasna said, as she inwardly sighed, albeit with only momentary relief, that she might soon leave the Baron's presence. "He was my slave and is now yours. I would request that he is not harmed, though he is yours to do with as you wish."

Bavira laughed, "She is rather sweet, but the lies that have poured from her mouth still go uncorrected," she said condescendingly. "You will have such fun with her, brother."

*If you lay a finger on me, my uncle will view it as an act of war,* Sasna thought, her panic rising to near uncontrollable levels. She felt her hands begin to tremble, so gripped them together tightly in an attempt to still them.

"When does the Inquisitor return?" Daramir asked, looking at the scribe.

"It may not be for a few weeks; they have found more Seers of the *Old Faith* hiding in the sewers of Bruthon. His apprentice is but a few days' ride from here though; would you have me send for him?"

165

"No, no. He accidentally killed the last one we let him practice on, his methods are still crude. He requires much further training, and we still have much more information to extract from this lying Seesnari!"

"Then use Malkili, brother. He will extract a confession from her!"

"No; if the Seesnari are conspiring with the Sea Lords, we will need the backing of Kappia. Only a confession extracted by the Inquisitor, using a fragment from the Eye of Morsef, will carry authority with the imperial court." He stroked his chin thoughtfully before looking at the scribe, and said, "This matter cannot wait. Send message to the Bruthon King, and the Inquisitor, that we have a prisoner that needs immediate interrogation before the Eye of Morsef. Inform them it is a matter of the uttermost importance."

"If you lay a finger on me, my uncle will consider it an act of war!" Sasna blurted out.

"If you have nothing to hide, you have nothing to fear!" Bavira squealed. "The Eye of Morsef only brings intense suffering to those who speak falsely in its presence. Those who speak truth, suffer less, though it will age you somewhat even if innocent."

Daramir smiled insincerely. "My sister is right. The Inquisitor is highly skilled. Only those who lie, suffer greatly before a fragment of the Eye of Morsef." He sneered. "You need not be alarmed, if our concerns are ill-founded. If they are proven true, well, your uncle will never learn of the fate we have planned for you."

The sweat poured off of Sasna's forehead, and as tightly as she gripped them, she could not prevent the trembling of her hands.

Daramir focused his attention on Scarand, and then looked at the guard who stood next to him. "I am done with him. Take him to the dungeon; allow the priest to use him for labour."

"Are we to allow Malkili to at least question him?" Bavira asked.

"No; we will soon learn all we need to learn from Lady Sasna. Let that annoying priest know he can put the Davari to work, for now. He constantly complains in my ear that he needs help since we killed his last assistant; it may stop his whining for a day or two."

With a nod, the guard led Scarand out of the library.

Despite a previous and genuine desire to save Scarand, Sasna knew his fate was out of her hands. Her focus had to be entirely on rescuing herself from her own dilemma. She felt sick to her stomach; her own situation was precarious, and her own well-being far more important to her than that of a slave. She felt the blood drain from her face as Bavira and Daramir stared impassively at her.

"I will happily answer any questions when the Inquisitor returns," she lied, hearing the quaking in her own voice. "May I rest now?" she asked hopefully, and gave another polite smile, although she felt her lips quiver and tremble as the words rushed out.

"Another question," Daramir said, to her dismay. "The message that you sent mentioned you had a fresh Davari woman for me. I am distraught she has been lost to the flames or the river, was she really as beautiful as you say?" He licked his lips for dramatic effect.

"She was beautiful, Lord Daramir, the bride of the son of a Davari Chief. It is with regret she was not successfully delivered to you." *I'm glad she has been saved from a fate at your hands, repulsive toad.* Sasna forced a nervous smile.

"Come then, follow me," he said as he stood and walked towards the door that led to his personal chambers, opened it and then entered.

"You can rest in here. I have a new goose-feathered mattress. The comfort of my personal chambers will be yours."

Sasna stood, and tailed by a guard, she suspiciously followed Daramir into the chamber next to the library. The scribe and Bavira followed them in, closing the door behind them; she heard it lock behind her. Sasna had an overwhelming sense of unease, a deep instinct that something bad was about to happen, but she was completely helpless to do anything. Unarmed, outnumbered, and wounded, she felt more vulnerable than at any other time in her entire life.

She studied her surroundings like a trapped animal, looking in vain for anything that might help her escape, either right then, or at the earliest opportunity. The chamber was a large square-room lavishly furnished with a large bed in the centre and various wardrobes and large chests-of-drawers aligning the walls, which were adorned with an assortment of paintings and tapestries. It had an exquisitely carpeted floor that covered the entire room except for a far corner of it where the stone was bare. The sight confounded any hope of escape, for, crouched in that corner, far to the left was a naked woman. The hapless woman tried to push herself further into the corner when she saw Daramir look at her. Arms around her knees, she pulled them tight to herself. She was covered in dried blood, and had marks and bruises all over her body. Around her neck was a thick iron collar connected by a heavy chain attached to a massive pin in the wall.

Sasna recognised the broken woman. It was the last Davari female-slave who had been given to Daramir a few months before. She had been the captured wife of a Davari Thegn. The poor woman flinched as Daramir walked up to her.

"Please, no more, show mercy my lord," she begged in the Common Tongue.

Taking a key out of his pocket, Daramir stood over the woman and frowned. She flinched and huddled into a ball and began pleading and begging again.

"I can't take anymore, please, my lord, show me mercy." She wailed and sobbed as Daramir unlocked the collar from her neck and took her by the hand. He dragged her across the floor to an open window. Grabbing her by the hair with one hand and the crotch with the other, in one swift movement he threw her out of the window. Her screams were ended with the sound of a sickening crunch and the thud of her body hitting the cobblestones below.

"Her suffering is over, am I not merciful?" Daramir asked sarcastically, as he turned and shrugged. "I get bored of these Davari women so quickly, although she and her husband managed to evade me for two days when I hunted them for sport, and since then she has kept me entertained long enough until she could be replaced."

He sighed in an exaggerated manner, and looked at his sister. "The one Sasna promised me, is lost to the river or flame. How am I to entertain myself, sister, until the Inquisitor returns?"

Bavira had a sly look as she eyed Sasna up and down. "If she has failed to deliver a fresh Davari to you, then, is it not her moral obligation to replace her?" She gave Sasna a wicked smile. "It will amuse you, brother, at least until the Inquisitor returns and we discover whether she and her filthy clan are as treacherous as we suspect."

Sasna looked at them both with horror. *You would not dare?* She had heard rumour that Daramir was a cruel master, but, until she had seen the poor broken woman in the corner, she had no idea his cruelty extended to that degree. It repulsed her to witness and think on how he had treated the poor-wretch whose demise she had just seen. Again, she tried to buy herself time. "I will willingly answer before the Eye of Morsef, but, if I am shown to be found true, if you mistreat me now, it will have serious repercussions with relations between the Bruthon and Seesnari."

"How naïve," Bavira scoffed. "We will learn the truth from you when the Inquisitor returns, but, even if you are telling the truth, you will never return to Ashgiliath."

A sickening realisation stirred within Sasna. *They will discover the lie if I am here when the Inquisitor returns, but, even if I was not conspiring with the Sea Lords, they are still planning to not let me go.*

"Athwin!" Daramir shouted out loud. A maid opened a door at the far end of the room and entered, quickly followed by seven men who swiftly surrounded Sasna. Two of the men had spears in their hands with broad bright heads. The other five had great bows slung across their backs, almost of their own height, and great quivers full of long green feathered arrows. All had swords by their sides, and were clad in green and browns of various hues, as if better to walk unseen in the wilds.

"These are my fellow huntsmen, who join me for my sport. If your brother is alive, but not trapped in the cursed Wytchwood, my hunters will find him."

Sasna had already backed as far into the wall as she could go.

"Seize her!" Daramir ordered calmly and cruelly.

The men quite quickly and easily overpowered Sasna, dragging her over to the corner of the room where the Davari girl had been chained; she struggled with what little strength remained, whilst the maid, ripped the blanket from her, shook it and examined it. Finding nothing, she used scissors to shear off Sasna's garments, and searched them. Finally, she roughly pulled off the boots Sasna wore and inspected them.

"Nothing, my lord," she said, as Sasna tried to cover her nakedness with her arms and hands. One of the huntsmen pushed her to the floor. Sasna screamed in fear, as the guards forced her arms aside.

Daramir approached her and put the iron collar around her neck, and snapped it shut. He put the key in his pocket.

"This is an outrage," Sasna said, fighting to get her breath. "Why are you doing this? You cannot do this to me. The law forbids it. My uncle will hear of it and will not forgive, he will complain to the Bruthon King. You cannot do this to me I am protected by the law!" Sasna already knew the futility of her protest.

"Ah, your uncle," Daramir said. "He will grieve for you, of that there is no doubt. We will assure him that our physician did everything in his power to keep you alive, but the infection on your wound spread and the fever it caused was incurable."

Sasna grasped at a last straw. "Do you think you can forever keep such a secret when you do this in the company of your own men? These vile pigs will soon have a loose tongue after a night in their cups, and news of my mistreatment will one day reach the ears of my uncle!"

The way Daramir laughed was sinister. He pointed to each man in turn as he said, "Oh, you mean these men who have sworn a greater loyalty to me than even to King Lagaelias Bruthon the Third? These, my hunters and guards, Half-bloods whose living is paid for by me? The very men whose homes, wives, and everything they own have been given to them by me? These men whose children live within the walls of this castle? Whose families reside in the villages and towns on lands I own?"

He laughed. "My guards are loyal, and these men have hunted with me since they were mere boys." He pointed at the huntsmen. "Ask them if they will risk everything to speak of this, even with a wine-addled tongue?"

Sasna could tell by the looks on the men's faces that whatever events happened that day, none would ever breathe a word of it. She said nothing as her hopes sank beneath a wave of despair.

Daramir pointed at the maid. "What about you Athwin? What will you say happened to the Lady Sasna, who was last seen publicly riding on the back of Baris' horse and brought safely and immediately to the physician for her wound to be tended?"

The girl shook her head. "'Tis very sad my lord, was a real tragedy. The Lady Sasna was brought here with a wound already sustained in the shipwreck. A fever took 'old, she became very sick. We all grieved her demise when she died soon after arriving 'ere, despite being treated by the castle's best physician."

"You see," Daramir said to Sasna as he leant over and peered into her face, so she could smell the foulness of his breath. "Nobody here cares about the fate of a Seesnari whore."

Her fear momentarily gave way to rage. Anger flashed within Sasna. "I am no whore," she said defiantly. The anger dissipated as quickly as it had arisen, and the fear returned.

Daramir turned and looked at his men, smiled, and then returning his stare towards her, Sasna's skin crawled as she felt his lingering gaze studying her nakedness. When he spoke, his voice was cold and hard, devoid of mercy and compassion. "Oh, but you will be, if that is what fate I decide for you. They all start out defiant. Perhaps you will secretly remain here as my new toy until such a time as I grow bored of you, even after the Inquisitor has broken you and we have discovered your plans to betray us to the Sea Lords."

Sasna felt sick with distress, and involuntarily wretched, but nothing came out.

The Baron smiled, as though imagining some delight. "Before the Inquisitor has finished with you, you will beg to be sent back to me, and when you are with me, you will beg to be sent back to him, in the vain hope either one of us might show you even a faint glimmer of mercy."

"Isn't it ironic," Bavira said with glee, "that even if just for a time, she will discover what it feels like to be one of those Davari wretches she so often gives to you, brother." She lent in close to Sasna. "You will know what it feels like to suffer how they suffered, and trust me Lady Sasna, suffer they did."

"Why would you do this? I have done you no wrong, I promise you Baron."

"I really don't know how you tainted-bloods can tolerate only one life, and that being so short," Bavira said. "It makes everything you achieve seem so futile and pointless. What did you hope to gain from your plan?"

The chain clinked and rattled as Sasna sat up and pushed herself up against the wall, her arms around her knees which were pulled tight to herself. "I am innocent," she lied. "I swear, I was going to discuss the plans with you."

"Oh? We already know you are not innocent, Lady Sasna," Bavira said so sweetly and sickly.

The Baron laughed mockingly. "A Baron is the law in his own castle. My judgement alone is what matters. I always assume the accused are guilty unless they have proof they are not." He curled his nose up in disgust and spat out the next words contemptuously. "In your case, I have proof already, but due to the spread of this hammer and snake cult, which is spreading across all realms, I am required to obey an imperial edict. We Bruthon believe that only a confession given through torture is reliable, but, to wage war against your people, Kappia will require a confession at the hands of an Inquisitor, in the presence of the Eye." He knelt on one knee and leaned even more closely towards Sasna. His breath smelt of wine and eggs. "The Inquisitor will return soon enough, he will find out all, until then, do not think your stay here will be free from unpleasantness."

Sasna knew that the Inquisitors were carefully selected mages, specifically chosen after years of training and indoctrination in that foul temple of theirs in Kappia. Each possessed a staff with a piece of a very rare fragment that they called the Eye of Morsef. It was impossible to tell a lie in front of a fragment of it when you were tested, for deception was revealed in its presence when an incantation was said, and the deceiver suffered terribly. She did not know what it consisted of, but the test was said to be fierce and agonising for the guilty one.

"He will soon discover I have nothing to hide," Sasna said defensively, her lip tremoring. *I must hold to the lie for as long as I can.*

The Baron smiled cruelly. He stood to his full height, and stared viciously at her in the manner of a beast stalking prey. When he spoke, the cynicism in his voice was plain. "He will discover, that in your stupidity, until recently you did not know the value or worth of the text you waved about for so long; but, the depths of your uncle's plotting and planning, and the secret mission he entrusted you with to conspire with the Sea Lords against the Bruthon, all of that will be revealed."

Sasna sobbed in despair, she knew full well what they were talking about, but she was too terrified to admit anything to them. *How do they know about the text?*

"Did you really think one in your position, and that drunken brother of yours could get away with such a deception?" the Baron asked. "You are merely a trader in slaves, yet involved yourself in matters beyond you."

Sasna felt chilled to the bone with fear. "Just tell me what you think it is you know," she said meekly. She was taking short, deep breaths. Never had she known such a mixture of emotions as she was feeling right then. Rage, terror, humiliation, confusion all oscillated within her as one came to the surface for the briefest of moments to be quickly overshadowed by another. She huddled even tighter to the corner, hoping it would somehow swallow her up and she could be gone from that dreadful place. *How do they know about the text?* she again asked herself.

The Baron crossed his arms. "It is a serious crime to seek to hide a Murien text from the Empire! Surely you were aware of this?"

Sasna would continue to deny the conspiracy with the Sea Lords, but regarding the text, she saw little point trying to deny it; besides, she had not known what it was until the night of the ship's fire. Somehow, they had discovered this, but how?"

"I did not plan to keep it from the Empire," Sasna blurted out, almost involuntarily.

"No, even worse, rather than hand it over as the law demands, you planned to extort the Empress and sell it to her!" Bavira said shrilly.

The Baron and his sister exchanged a glance with one another, and then fixed their gazes back on Sasna. "Where is the text?" he asked her.

"If you tell us, and we find it, and can verify what it is, we will send a message to Kappia that we have found a Murien, and leave you out of it," Bavira said.

Sasna saw no point in lying about the text; it would serve her no purpose.

"I was given the text by the dwarf, Gildaora. She told me she would pay handsomely for any slave who could read it. I did not know what it was, I swear." She took a deep breath. "I assumed her interest was merely academic as she has many eccentricities like that. I was due to meet her here in Greytears, in the Pike and Perch tavern."

"We know that," Bavira said, "but where is the text now?"

"One by the name of Muro has it," Sasna answered.

"Where is the text?" Bavira asked again. "That Davari you travelled with has been searched, it was not with him and we can see it is not about your person, where is it?"

The desperation in her voice was obvious even to herself. "I am speaking the truth. It is currently in the possession of a slave by the name of Muro. I do not know what happened to him after the ship's fire."

Daramir looked at one of his seven huntsmen. "We have searched every tavern for miles. There is no sign of the dwarf anywhere, nor any reported sightings of her."

170

It occurred to Sasna, that the immediate priority of Daramir and his sister, was in finding the text. No surprises there, if they discovered it, no small reward would be theirs. "It could be Gildaora saw the ship burn and returned to Berecoth or the Wytchwood," Sasna said, trying to sound co-operative.

Bavira's nose curled up in distrust. "We have forbidden any to enter that cursed place, lest they wake up the evil that lurks within. Gruck, gryllus and lunggrims roam there as well as diseased roretrolds. Are you telling us she defies that order and goes into that place at will?"

"That, you would have to ask her," Sasna answered.

"The text could have been destroyed in the fire," Bavira said to her brother.

Again, Sasna felt there was no benefit to her for trying to deny her knowledge about the text; the only thing she would not reveal, was the planned conspiracy between Ashgiliath and the Sea Lords against the Bruthon.

"It is with the Ruik named Muro. It is on his living person, or upon his corpse. Neither fire nor water can destroy such a text, and I have seen proof of this. He told me it cannot be ruined by any means known to man. If you want the text, let me search for it with you, and look also for my brother Farir. I will search the banks of the Wytchwood to see if Farir or Muro have washed up there."

"It would be foolish to enter the forest, my lord," one of the huntsmen said to Daramir.

Bavira laughed mockingly at the huntsman, which Sasna thought hypocritical considering her statement moments before. "Is a grown man still terrified of jinxies and fumbleskins?"

The huntsman cast his eyes to the ground at the rebuke, as Bavira looked at her brother. "Perhaps we should reconsider our position. Maybe it is the time to re-enter it?

The Baron looked coldly at his sister. "You know that what is in there is no children's' fable sister," he replied.

Bavira closed her eyes momentarily in frustration. "Think brother, think. That which once haunted it must be long dead if that dwarf can enter it. Many a lifetime has passed since we last heard those evil screams and that doleful wailing in the dark hours of night drifting over the Erin. Too long have we waited, now there is good reason to enter it again. Find your courage, brother?"

"Silence, sister," Daramir barked sinisterly. "Long has that brooding evil shadowed our souls and none more than I wish to know if the crone is finally gone from this world, and I need no longer honour the oath I swore to her; but if the darkness in their still sleeps, foolish are those who would wake it, and if I enter or send any in there, you know the price I must pay."

Sasna did not know what oath Daramir had made, or with what, but she seized upon his words. "Release me, and my slave, for he is skilled in tracking. If we go in there voluntarily, you have not sent us, and your oath still stands. If I find the text, I will send it to you, I swear." *To hell with the Murien, I am done with it. I will look for Farir, and then be done with Castle Greytears unless it is to see the end of the dynasty of Baron Daramir.*

"We will look for the text everywhere else, but not in the Wytchwood," Daramir declared.

Bavira cast a sideward glance at Sasna and asked, "What will you do with her?"

Daramir crouched down, leant over and put his face next to Sasnas. "She has told us all she knows about the text, of that I am sure, but she has lied about her proposed business with the Sea lords. I sense Seesnari treachery. I sense it in my very bones. The Inquisitor will get that information from her."

"After that?" Bavira asked.

171

Daramir sneered. "Long have I secretly desired her and now, I have the chance to take what I want with no consequence. I will keep her here, for myself, as a pet, until I am bored; for now, her death will be announced that she died of injury and fever. If we find her brother, we will make similar sport of him."

Sasna felt another sudden and uncontrollable surge of rage, at the threat towards Farir; she spat in Daramir's face, but instantly regretted it once the impulse was satisfied.

The Baron slowly stood, wiped the spit off his face with his finger, put it in his mouth and tasted it. He turned and looked at his men, smiled, and then turned back to Sasna, his gaze again lingering over her helpless nakedness. "Most of them start out defiant, and display occasional flares of spirit. Breaking you to be compliant to my every desire will be amusing to me," he said callously. "It is a shame I have this business I must attend to, but I will start your breaking in the moment I return, of that you can be sure."

"Do you see how hopeless your situation is?" Bavira asked gleefully.

Sasna did not answer; she tucked her head in between her knees.

Daramir stood and addressed his men. "Make sure you search and question every survivor from the wreck you find; search every corpse washed up for any text or parchment. Leave no stone unturned."

"What about the thing?" one of the huntsmen asked. "Shall we kill it?"

"I almost forgot about it," Daramir replied. "Guard, fetch it in."

A guard entered the room, and following him, to Sasna's surprise, was Gnarn.

Daramir walked over to Gnarn and crouched down to look him in the eyes. Gnarn looked nervously down at the floor.

"He may yet still have his uses," Daramir said, to himself, and then to his men. "He has been a good boy and told us of her lies and the Murien text. I suspect he himself is well practiced in the art of sneaking and deception. One who is so clever and hears much, yet can act so stupid, may be of use to me."

He took Gnarn's chin in his hand. "That's right boy, isn't it? I see through you, you are not totally stupid at all but quite clever, after all, you managed to survive that wreck, and you made your way here."

Gnarn avoided Daramir's eyes when he answered him. "Gnarn is whatever you say, master. To serve you in any form will be Gnarn's honour. Gnarn only knows to do that which you tell him, no more and no less." He stared fidgetingly at the floor.

Daramir laughed. "Good boy. Stay here with her. Seesnari are full of tricks. If she moves, you raise the alarm, do you hear?"

Gnarn nodded and ran over to the corner where he sat hunched near to Sasna, just out of her reach. "Gnarn will scream for the guards if she moves, master."

Daramir ordered Athwin to fetch the physician. "See that he stitches and tends this wound immediately. I do not want her dying; she must be alive and well for when I return." The girl scuttled off to carry out the command.

Daramir addressed the scribe, who had been standing still for some time. "Make sure none but the physician and the guards enter, and the Lady Bavira if she wishes." The scribe bowed his head respectfully, and followed Daramir and the others as they filed out of the room. The last guard slammed the door shut behind them and locked it.

Sasna, still huddling to hide her nakedness, looked nervously at Gnarn, who was looking at the floor and wheezing. "I underestimated you," she said to him.

Gnarn smiled. "So, did he, so did he," he said triumphantly as he held up the key to the collar around Sasna's neck.

Sasna's eyes widened with shock and disbelief. "Gnarn?"

172

"Sneaking and peeking are not Gnarn's only skills," he said with pride as he quickly looked at her, then turned away just as quickly, embarrassed by her nakedness. He half stood and hobbled over to the door and put his ear to it.

"Gnarn is sorry he told him about the text. He hurt Gnarn so hard we had to tell him some things. Gnarn has low tolerance to pain," he said with a wheeze. He hobbled back over to Sasna, and held the key up, looking for approval, but once again taking great care to not look at her nakedness.

She reached out her hand to snatch the key but Gnarn quickly pulled it away. "No, no, no. Not yet, the physician will come and will attend you, you must wait and have patience." He put the key inside his sack-cloth, and went over to where the blanket that had been torn from her lay among her ripped and cut-up clothing. He picked it up and brought it to her, and half-tucking his head into his shoulder so he could not see her body, offered her the blanket. "Take it, take it," he said.

Sasna took the blanket and wrapped it around herself as best she could with the weight of the chain and the pain in her shoulder hindering her.

"Thank you Gnarn, but you must give me the key. I must get out of here; you heard what he said he will do to me?"

"No! No! No! Not yet. Not until mistress has let the physician heal her. Gnarn cannot bear to see mistress hurt. Rest, mistress is tired, tis better to leave when mistress is healed and rested. Gnarn will help mistress when she is stronger, before the bad master returns."

"How do I know I can trust you?" Sasna asked Gnarn suspiciously.

Gnarn looked hurt and wounded by the remark. "Mistress doesn't trust Gnarn?" he asked slowly with a wheeze.

"Why should I when you won't give me the key? Give me the key Gnarn, and then I will trust you. Mistress will trust you if you give me the key."

Gnarn found the courage to look Sasna briefly in the eyes as he said. "Look at Gnarn's face." He pointed to his scarred, burned and deformed face and then pulled up the roughhewn top he wore and spun around to show her the deep scars from multiple whip marks on his back. "Gnarn is tired of serving brutal masters, a life like that will not end well for Gnarn. All despise and hurt Gnarn, but mistress gave him sweetcake and touched his face. Nobody ever touched Gnarn before like mistress did - she touched him like a mother." He lowered his clothing, and turned to face her. "Gnarn knows the touch of a mother for he has seen it when he sneaked and peeked in candle-lit windows in the night. Gnarn wants to call you mother? Tis better?"

"You can," Sasna said to him gently, "if you give me the key."

He ran over and tried each door, they were locked. He scuttled over to the window, and looked out of it. "It's a long way down, and they are clearing up blood and bones down there. There is no way out, only the door. Sleep first, let the physician heal you, then Gnarn gives you the key, he promises. Now sleep, mother."

Sasna did feel exhausted, and her wound was troubling her a lot. "I'm glad you survived Gnarn, but did you see any other survivors, my brother Farir, did you see him?"

"Gnarn did not. Gnarn jumped from the burning ship and swam to the bank of the river. The forest frightened Gnarn so I came here to steal food and to sneak and peak and was caught by guards. Sleep now, mother, Gnarn will wake you when the physician arrives. When you are stronger, Gnarn will give you the key. Gnarn will find a way to get out of here. We need more keys for more doors. There are guards everywhere; Gnarn will plan how to steal their keys."

Sasna lay down on her side, bending her knees to her chest, and cradling her head on her uninjured arm, she answered, "You need to help mother to get out of here, Gnarn, it has to be before the Baron returns or he will hurt mother and make me scream." Exhaustion finally caught up with Sasna. She pulled the blanket tighter around her and fell into a deep and uneasy sleep.

# Chapter Fourteen: *The Third Legion*

*Aleskian will fall, your precious Golden Horn brought to Kappia. The terror your towers inspire, and the pride of your heart have deceived you. You who occupy the heights of the three hills, though you build your nests high as the eagle, from there you will be brought down. You will become an object of horror. All who pass you by will be appalled and will scoff and ask, "Where now is your pride?"*

**A Prophecy of the Prophet Thesius.**

*It* was dawn when the Third Legion set out for Fort Watch. They passed through the first massive timber gate of Aleskian, in the shadow of the thick trusses that supported an arched vault overhead, the sound of their booted feet echoing in unison with each step. The walls were lined with fluted pillars of marble decorated with forest-green emerald designs. Between the pillars were large carved statues depicting a variety of creatures, all skilfully captured with great detail by the sculptor's chisel. Passing under the portcullis of the second gate, known as the Griffin Gate, they marched proudly out from between the two forty-foot-high golden griffin statues that stood proudly either side of it, and made their way down the hill on the wide paved path. The beautiful sounds of the Golden Horn of Aleskian, of which legend said it was made from the severed tusk of a *Firstborn* Titan, floated melodiously across the city and the plain, as it always did when the Lord of Aleskian left or entered the city. It then fell suddenly silent.

Borach sat on his horse to the right of the second century of his cohort, at the centre of the legion's line; next to him was the cohort's cornicen. Each century stood four men across and twenty men deep. It was not long before they were about three miles away from Aleskian, and only one mile away from Fort Watch, the first of the many defensive mile forts that were part of the Great Northern Wall, and the closest to the Great Northern Gate, also called the Aleskian Gate. Both behind and before them, lay the open expanse of the Aleskian Plain that now stood between them and the great city of Aleskian, and the fort they marched towards.

Marki, riding his dapple coloured pony, came alongside Borach. "I'll hold that horn blower to account, he is supposed to play until you reach the fort. On a day such as this, tradition is important," he barked angrily.

Borach did not turn his head to look back towards to the city. "I fear it is the last time I shall ever hear the alluring tones of the Golden Horn," he answered miserably. "Not only that, I miss the screech of griffins overhead as we march out for the last time."

They both looked in vain at the empty sky.

"Perhaps Meron and other riders might yet arrive on the back of one," Borach said.

"I was never a fan of griffins Bor, but I sure miss their presence now they are not here," Marki agreed wistfully. "Most will already be at Kara Duram by now, the riders that remained were given the orders, so, where are they? I can only guess the sickness has spread to the other griffins but surely Meron would have informed us?" With an air of desperation, he then added. "It does not feel right; Regineo and these Hammer Knight are given the city, that's bad enough, but why have we been sent to Fort Watch for you to be relieved of your command? And, with our legion's numbers depleted. It's insane, it makes no sense! There is treachery in the air."

Borach reacted angrily. "What would you suggest? Disobeying an imperial order?" He shared the concerns of his closest friend and advisor, but the orders he had been given were clear and exact, and bore the correct imperial stamps and insignias. To disobey them, would be treasonous and an act of war against Kappia.

"That is exactly what I suggest," Marki grumbled. "There is foul intrigue in the air; we both know it."

Borach turned his head and looked back at Aleskian, the city of his ancestors, built over the ruins of an older city, upon the three hills of The Mannermen. The sight caused him great dismay. Already, the legions' banners, and that of his house, had been lowered and over the walls and turrets of Aleskian, the hammer and snake banners flew.

Marki followed Borach's gaze. "That didn't take them long," he growled.

"Stop complaining, and let us be about this business," Borach snapped back. "As soon as Prince Regineo and his contingent join us, we will give him a tour of Fort Watch and the wall and our business here is done." He let out a deep and pensive sigh. "Maybe it is for the best, I am tired from war and conflict. Aleskian is now our past, not our future." He felt a twinge of regret for his anger, as he looked at the glumness on his oldest friend's face. He stretched across and patted him warmly on the shoulder, and spoke more softly. "It won't be all bad. Yianna has gone ahead of us to Estalda, where there will be wine and song aplenty waiting for us. We can rest from our many labours and hardships, feast, drink and make merry any day we choose, and when we grow bored of days of ease, we will find some new adventure to satisfy our souls…perhaps I will put a Neblan around my neck and journey with you to find your father?"

"Humph," Marki growled, "Yianna would never allow that." He raised his hand to halt the legion. They promptly came to a disciplined still at the spot marked where they were to wait for Prince Regineo to join them before proceeding to the fort.

Marki raised himself from his saddle and looked all around. "Meanwhile, we sit here as dumb as a squeaking mouse sticking its head in a cheese trap." He then pointed towards the Great Northern Wall and the Aleskian Gate. The hammer and snake banners now also flew over them, and along each fort and the area it covered, the ancient banners of Aleskian, the House of Borach the Barathfey, and the banner of the specific legion that had been guarding them was lowered. "I wonder what our Bantu friends will make of that?" Marki asked, as on the battlements of Fort Watch, to the left of the gate, the banner of the Sixth Legion, whose turn at the guard it had been, a red griffin on a white background, was taken down, and on the battlements of Fort Resilient, to the right of the gate, the banner of the Twelfth Legion was the last to come down. In their place, the hammer and snake emblem of the Hammer Knights was raised. Just a few men from each of the other legions had been left to hand over their responsibilities to the Hammer Knights. The main contingents of the legions had already left for Kara Duram where they were to be disbanded.

"I weep for the House of Barathfey, and for Borach, Lord of the great city of Aleskian," Marki wailed, as the new banners unfolded and fluttered in the breeze.

Borach felt the same way; it was a sight he had never expected to see. But he was a soldier, and no matter for how many lives and generations the rank of Captain General had been passed on down through his family line, when the orders came to relinquish his command, what choice did he have but to obey?

Before Borach could articulate or give voice to his solemn thoughts, ahead of them, a loud bell repeatedly sounded. Then, the clanging noise of massive bolts being unlocked could be heard. Borach, Marki and the rest of the depleted Third Legion looked on in initial confusion, which soon turned to horror. In the distance, the heavy Aleskian Gate rumbled as heavy chains slowly began to raise the mammoth bars that locked it.

"They're opening the gate! They're opening the bloody gate!" Marki shouted in alarm. "I knew it, we are betrayed!"

Borach watched helplessly as the Aleskian Gate rumbled and slowly swung open. The counter-weight system used to open it could be heard grinding and thumping even from that distance.

"I might have guessed, in fact I did, that foul High Quaester and his hammer knuckled whoresons had betrayed us," Marki howled, as he watched with horror the scene unfolding before them.

Borach and only a thousand men of the Third Legion had marched out of the city of Aleskian towards the gate. It was only a sixth of their total number. By imperial order, the rest had been commanded to go with their families and the other legions to Kara Duram, on the high Kappian Plateau; Borach had inwardly wept as the legions had left Aleskian, accompanied by pack wagons and their many possessions. The only men of the Third who had remained in the city, were a few who were sick in the hospital, and some of the griffin riders, who remained in the High Nest tending the griffins that were injured or unable to fly at that time, and those charged with flying out with Borach whilst he formerly handed the responsibility of guarding the wall to Regineo and the Hammer Knights. *I held on to the faintest glimmer of hope, but it is true, we are betrayed by Kappia!*

In all of Borach's lifetimes, the sight of every horror, now paled in comparison to the sight unfolding before his eyes. The Hammer Knights, newly charged with guarding Aleskian, were opening the gate that protected the Everglow from the threats beyond the wall. The men with him began to cry out in alarm and panic as a wave of fear rippled through them. Each one of them were hardened veterans of many a campaign, but never had they been in a situation such as this.

"Hold your nerve you snivelling wine curs and stop squealing like a gaggle of frightened geese," Marki bellowed at them.

Because of the safety of the wall, and the impenetrable charms and glamour that protected it, most of the Third Legion had never encountered the Bantu foe in direct hand to hand combat. Throughout the centuries, many Fell-blood mercenaries had been sent beyond the wall, but only rarely Pure-bloods, and then wearing a Neblan so in the event of death their souls could be safely brought back into the Everglow for resurrection. Now, for the first time in known history, their foe was entering the Everglow itself and coming to them. Despair filled them as the first of the Bantu horde began to pour through the gate, even before it was fully open.

Borach looked behind him. The portcullis of the Griffin Gate that led out of the first ring of the city of Aleskian, had already been lowered and the gate shut. The legion would never make it back anyhow, it was too far behind them, and the fact that along the battlements of the city, and on the high towers, the banners of the Hammer Knights were the ones that now fluttered in the wind, was proof enough that way was also barred to them. They were trapped in the open. Whatever decision he made, it had to be quick and decisive as some of the men in the cohorts were beginning to break rank and run as they watched more and more screeching and howling Bantu pouring onto the plain through the gate which was about a quarter of the way open.

The standard-bearer of the third, a man called Poppaeus, noticing the fear and confusion in the ranks, waved the legions standard, a golden griffin on a red staff, and shouted, "Stay with the standard! Do not lose your honour and standard this day! Unless you want the enemy to take your standard stay put." The man, dressed in a wild warg pelt, with an ornamental head of a griffin fixed to the top of the warg's furry head, was the guardian of the Third Legion's morale. Whilst the griffin standard remained upright, the honour of the Third lived. Poppaeus, a much-decorated centurion had served the required five lifetimes in the Third Legion. He was now in his last few months of service, after which he would have retired anyway, be given rich farmland on the Kappia Plateau, and be allowed to marry a Pure-blood wife and raise a family.

The bannerman stood next to Poppaeus, and waved the legion's banner, a golden griffin on a red background, in the air. "You will not find me failing in my duty this day to Lord Borach and Aleskian. To the standard and banner where your honour lays!" he roared.

The gallantry of the standard-bearer and bannerman had the desired effect and Borach was glad for their intervention. He had promoted them both to their honoured positions and time and again it had proven to be a wise choice. Those who had broken ranks, stopped in their tracks, and quickly re-joined them.

Marki pointed to the battlements of Fort Watch and snarled. "Look, that gallant few of the Sixth that remained are making a stand. Bor, look!"

Borach scanned the battlements of Fort Watch and the barbican over the main gate. The few men of the Sixth who had been tasked with handing over their watch to the Hammer Knights, were in fierce combat with them. Nonetheless, the gate continued opening, but then suddenly stopped when it was halfway open. The Bantu horde still poured through the gate, but their progress was slowed as it was lowered again to only a quarter of the way open and then stopped.

It was obvious to Borach the few men of the Sixth were trying to close the gate, and no doubt a battle was taking place within the gatehouse itself. He bitterly regretted being such a fool, and marching willingly into such an obvious trap, but the orders he had received had been very clear. They had come from the Empress Shaka herself, bearing her seal and that of General Karkson, and the seals of every member of the Privy Council. It had also been confirmed by Prince Regineo himself, who had briefly visited the city the evening before, and instructed Borach to march with the remainder of his men onto the Aleskian Plain and await him.

Borach would have faced the *Final-death* to disobey such direct orders, but nonetheless he was mystified. It made no sense to him why the Empress would give such an order, or why she would ally with the Bantu horde and allow them into the Everglow except – *madness, she has gone insane? Or, she has been deposed?* The blowing of Bantu horns and the throbbing of drums returned his attention to the present. *Time enough to ponder this on another day, if we survive this one.* "We will have to figure out the reason for this betrayal another time," he said to his trusted old friend.

"Aye, if we don't do something, and fast, there will be no other time. Our only hope is that the Hammer Knights have forgotten our men still guarding the High Nest. If they can release the remaining griffins, sick and maimed as some of them are, we might have hope," Marki replied. The griffins were the fierce flying beasts that, along with their riders, for thousands of years, had helped protect Aleskian from the Bantu horde. They were powerful and majestic creatures but incredibly cruel, often toying and tormenting their prey as they fed, consuming them piece by piece or dragging them to great heights and dropping them to the ground. They had the body, tail, and back legs of a lion and the head and wings of an eagle and sharp talons were their front feet. They were fierce and deadly in battle, a flurry of beak and claw that rendered armour and tore through flesh and bone as a knife through butter. The Bantu were terrified of them.

Despite Marki's optimism, the truth was, the griffins would be of little help at that time. A mysterious sickness had recently rendered many of them lame. It was unusual for such beasts to be prone to injury or sickness, but now the timing and extent of the recent outbreak, seemed no coincidence. Foul forces were at work.

"Shield wall, three lines!" Borach shouted, as he drew *Havwitha*. He could feel the questioning looks of the men but they were too disciplined to say anything. It seemed madness to try to stand against the ferocious Bantu horde pouring through the partially opened gate, but Borach knew they had little other choice, other than to run, and that would expose their flank. *If we can survive the first wave, we might then make a push and close the gate, or make an orderly retreat to the ruined Dune Fort.*

The men of the Third wedged their shields into the sand to make a wall. Two rows formed behind, ready to reinforce and replace the front line at the shields should they fall. All readied their slings and javelins, and prepared their spears and swords. Marki, who preferred the use of a two-handed long shafted double headed axe he called *Old Trusty*, swung it around his head in practice. The legion's standard and banner were planted in the ground. There, they would make their stand against the horde that was pouring down upon them.

"Hooray for the men of the Sixth!" Marki shouted.

Borach knew he was right. The Bantu, were still pouring through the gate, but not in so many numbers as they would if it were fully open. A bottleneck was being created at the entrance. Although impeded, a lot of the horde had already made it through the gate and were spreading to the left and right as well as charging forward.

"They're gonna surround us Bor," Marki said with concern as he saw the Bantu horde preparing for a scissor manoeuvre.

"Square formation! Three lines!" Borach shouted. It did not take the well drilled Third Legion long to form the square. As before, the front line wedged their shields in the sand to form a wall, the second and third lines stood behind them.

"Bor, defeat is not an option, you cannot die here today. If I die, I'm gone from this world but when you resurrect, you will be in the hands of these Bantu or whoever it is who has betrayed you. You have to get away Bor, and tell the tale of this duplicity. Head to the Dune Fort with the legion. I and a few others will make a stand and hold these brutes back."

Borach knew his friend was right, death on the field of battle that day would mean being resurrected into the hands of whoever had betrayed them. He looked around at the legion; there were a few Fell-blood scouts, but the rest were all Pure-blood Akkadians, just as he was. In addition to some scouts, the only exceptions were his dwarf friends Marki and Galin, who were cousins.

"Enough of such talk," he answered. "If my fate is to be decided here, on the plain where my forefathers once fought, then so be it. Together we will make our stand!"

Borach looked at his men. Beads of nervous sweat formed on the foreheads of some, but all had a steely and determined look on their face. He admired their courage. Many of those in the Third Legion had already served three lifetimes or more, and had faithfully guarded Aleskian and the Empire from the threat beyond the wall. They stood tall and proud in their red armour upon which the symbol of the golden griffin stood proudly on their chests. Each of them between the ages of thirty and forty-five had sworn sacred oaths to the legion. Many of them had half or Fell-blood wives, and therefore Half-blood children and families. They did not have any Pure-blood wives or children, as the law forbade legionnaires from marriage and children during their service to the legion. Many of them had Fell-blood families that as long as they did not flaunt openly, were tolerated. Only Borach as a nobleman, was allowed a Pure-blood family. It was a small relief to Borach that at least the families of his men were safely on their way to Kara Duram, and his own beloved Yianna and his children were on their way to the safety of his mountain estate of Estalda.

Marki sensed what he was thinking. "Yianna and the children are safe?"

Borach nodded. "I hope so." He looked around again, considering the options available to him. A seasoned soldier, he knew too well what was at stake if he and his men were to fall, but they had little choice but to stay disciplined and fight. Their only chance was to push to the gate and help the Sixth to close it, and then make an orderly retreat. To their left, about a mile away was an old Dune Fort. Although mostly a ruin, Borach knew of secret passages beneath it, known only to him as the Lord of Aleskian, and a select few others including Marki. He and his men could use the tunnels to re-enter Aleskian, and if necessary, to leave the city undetected whilst they figured out what was going on. *We have to close that gate though; we cannot leave it open.*

Borach, Marki, his three other commanders and several of his bodyguards were the only ones on horseback. They could easily make it to the fort at a gallop, but abandoning his men was something he would not even consider, nor would he leave the gate open. He also knew that if the legion lost their nerve and tried to run, they would perish. The charging Bantu horde would catch up and butcher them all before they reached the safety of the Dune Fort. *Whatever I choose, order and discipline must be maintained, or we are all doomed.*

"If we can hold off this first wave Marki, we might get a breather, make it to the gate, shut it and then foot it to the Dune Fort, in orderly retreat."

"Aye, that's what I was thinking," Marki said. "And I think the key is to kill that big bugger there!" Marki pointed his axe towards a Bantu, much larger than the others who passed through the gate, which, was now only partially open so they could only do so in pairs.

Surrounded by banners, several giants and heavily armed Bantu, Borach recognised his old foe, Garuk *the Black-blade*. It made his face twist with rage to see him pass through the gate and step upon the Plain of Aleskian, inside the Everglow. This was a day of shame for Borach. For many centuries he and his father and his forefathers before him had held the Great Northern Wall and never before had a Bantu stepped foot within the Everglow, unless as a prisoner. To see his foe arrogantly stride through the gate unopposed, was a sight he never thought he would see. It sent a cold chill down his spine and he let out an involuntary moan.

It was not long before the Third Legion was surrounded by Bantu on all sides, but the gate was neither opening or closing so the numbers of them now coming through were limited. They stopped a few hundred yards away, just out of the range of the slings. All went quiet as Garuk walked to the front line of the horde. There were so many of them trying to cram through the now small opening in the gate that they were crushing each other and pushing the front line of their ranks involuntarily forward, creating a bottleneck that prevented more from entering. The disorder of the Bantu horde, gave the Third Legion their only advantage.

"Men, we've got to kill him, and shut the gate," Borach ordered with a fierce snarl.

"No pressure then," Marki replied wistfully.

Ahead of them Garuk lifted up his sword and shouted. One of the Bantu next to him blew a horn, the deep sound of which rolled around the plain. Several other horns responded, sounding one after the other. From the north, beyond the Great Wall, tens of thousands of drums began to rumble, and a multitude of other horns accompanied the roar of the vast Bantu host, many who were still gathered outside of the gate, as yet unable to come in because of their disorderly pressing forward.

"Garuk! Garuk! Garuk!" The Bantu horde shouted as they waved a variety of weapons in the air. They were a savage looking army, armed with toothed swords, axes even bigger than a man, hammers with handles like small trees and heads like anvils. They were weapons designed to terrify. Others held bows or spears.

180

Borach had seen this sight many times before, for wearing a Neblan he had often led mercenary armies beyond the wall into the land of his enemy. Always, each and every time, his friend Marki had fought beside him. Their last foray had been when Borach had led a foreign legion of Davari he had trained himself. He had led them beyond the wall to try to destroy Braka, and they had all but succeeded, but an ill-timed rain borne of dark forces had quenched the fires they had set upon it, and they were forced to retreat, back through the Aleskian Gate into the Everglow.

But now, on this day, Borach's foe was within the Everglow itself. Whenever the Bantu battle roar had cried out before, from beyond the wall, it had always been answered with defiance by the roar and trumpets of the legions guarding the city, the great wall, gate and forts, and the sound of the Great Horn of Aleskian. He looked back at Aleskian where his banners no longer fluttered in the wind among the battlements or high towers, and to his dismay there was no roar or trumpets sounding nor was any help coming from the city. Now that the horde was within the Everglow, the trumpets were woefully silent, as was the horn.

"The vile bastards!" Marki said, following Borach's gaze and looking at the banner of the Hammer Knights, that were raised and fluttering in the wind. "Mazdek is behind this, Karkson warned us not to trust that babbling swag bellied priest."

Borach refused to consider in that moment the implications or reasons behind the betrayal, for he had more immediate and pressing concerns. One of the Bantu began to run towards the line of the Third, screaming with battle frenzy. It was brought down with a javelin that pierced its belly. Falling to its knees, it pulled the javelin out and defiantly hurled it back at the legion's ranks, before it collapsed in its own death throes.

Borach understood the message Garuk had sent; the Bantu with him were those of the Bashri-Bazerk and were not afraid to die. Their whole energy and lives were devoted to training and combat. They were the elite of the elite.

"If we can hold against the Bazerks, the rest might lose their nerve," Marki said, raising his voice above the din so Borach could hear him.

A giant, carrying a large boulder ran to the front line and hurled the rock at the legion. It hurtled high through the air and fell with a loud thud. It fell short, but such was the force with which it had been thrown it rolled into the lines crushing several men to death, and maiming or scattering some others. The breaches in the lines were closed in seconds by those behind.

Led by the Bazerks, the Bantu host charged. The legion's slingshots and javelins took down many of them before they hit the shield wall, but the Bantu pressed on and were soon in vicious hand to hand combat with the front lines of the legion. There were more breaches in a couple of places where the large hammers of the Bantu crushed shields and smashed their way through the line, but the second line did its work fast and efficiently, spitting the Bantu with sword or spear. Skulls were cleaved, armours rendered, and blood was spilt on both sides. The fast blades of the legion pierced the throats, stomachs and faces of the Bantu. The Bantu weapons had deadly effect when they found a target, but the legion's casualties were less in numbers, due to the skill and fighting prowess of the Third. The legion contested every inch of ground and the Bantu paid dearly.

A giant hurled a massive spear, it pierced Poppaeus through the chest. Even with his last dying breaths he tried to hold the standard up high, but as his life left him and the standard tilted, another legionnaire, his son, Popparus, took it and held it high before it could fall to the ground.

More breaches were made, but they were closed in moments, and the enraged Bantu host began to die in large numbers against the disciplined ranks of the proud and formidable Third Legion, still formed in square formation. More and more Bantu charged, only to perish at the immovable lines of the Third, but it was not without cost, as the Bantu onslaught was relentless. When one died, five others replaced it, or so it seemed to Borach.

Borach paid no attention to the carnage around him but stayed focussed on giving orders when needed. Marki, always by his side pushed back any of the Bantu that made it past the shield walls, those tasked with bringing down the head of the legion, Borach, or those attempting to slay the standard bearer. With a flurry of axe strikes and kicks, the furious dwarf slew many foes, and defended Borach and the standard, with the fierceness of his kind. More of the Bantu broke through the breaches in the wall heading towards Borach in an attempt to slay the famous Lord of Aleskian. They failed in their attempt. Marki and the bodyguard of seven protected him well, and the bodies of the Bantu piled up high around them.

The tenacity of the legion, and their ability to inflict casualties, astonished even the relentless Bashri-Bazerks, but the effect of row after row of their numbers being cut down as they hurled themselves against the legion, affected those not of that elite order, and they began to turn and flee.

When the last of the Bashri-Bazerks fell, orders were issued to the Bantu host through the blasting horns, and they began to back away from the shield wall and regroup, but their attempt to retreat made them easier targets for the slings. The legion remained disciplined and did not charge or follow, tempting as it was. There was silence for a few moments, and the men of the legion welcomed the short reprieve. They closed ranks, took the chance to drink some water, and waited to see what their foe would do next. They did not wait long. The air filled with a lethal glinting rain that darkened the sky.

"Protect!" Borach shouted. Those of the legion, due to fatigue or injury who did not raise their shields in time dropped to their knees, pierced by dozens of black feathered shafts. Cries rang out from the injured and dying. The rain of arrows continued, but clattered against the shields that protected the legion beneath them. The raised shields of his bodyguard protected Borach and themselves, but were not enough to protect the horses, armoured though they were. Each of their noble horses fell to the ground, whinnying in terror and pain as the deadly storm rained down upon them, dealing death and destruction.

"Forward!" Borach shouted, now leading on foot. He knew that the advantage was with the Bantu who could keep sending in fresh warriors if the battle of the gatehouse was lost by the Sixth, and that his own men would not have the strength to continue fighting at the same pace all day. He had to press every little advantage no matter how small and seek to make it to the gate, as his enemy was still bottlenecked there. The only chance of surviving the onslaught was for the gate to be closed.

The Bantu Commanders, who were bellowing orders and blasting horns, regained some discipline and order over the blood-frenzied horde, but as the legion advanced, they cut down those in front of them, and without the presence of the Bashri-Bazerks, the morale of the Bantu slowly began to dissolve.

The legion kept its square formation as it steadily moved forward towards the Aleskian Gate, trampling the bodies of the dead beneath their heeled boots, raising their shields whenever another rain of deadly arrows descended, planting their shields and holding ground whenever the Bantu host charged. Using this tactic, step by step, yard by yard they began to make steady progress towards the gate. Rocks, poorly aimed and thrown by the giants, killed more of the Bantu than they did the men of the legion, who did not waiver or falter as they fought inch by inch towards their goal. Such was the press of Bantu still trying to get through the gate, that it still worked to the legion's advantage. Many of the Bantu were crushed to death by their own surging ranks, but their commanders were slowly regaining order, and the horde was starting to obey.

"Ill-disciplined morons!" Marki shouted as his axe split the head of another Bantu who had made it through the lines and charged at Borach.

"Look," Borach said, as he pointed to Fort Watch. "The banner of the Sixth again flies over the fort."

"And the Twelfth have retaken Fort Resilient!" Marki added, as the banners of the Hammer Knights were toppled, and in their place flew the proud emblems of the respective legion.

A thundering cheer came up from the Third, even as they fought and pressed forward with increased resolve.

The Sixth and Twelfth Legions had a proud history of guarding Aleskian, and it was clear to Borach they could not just watch as their ancient enemy poured through the gate, whilst they, despite their orders, did nothing. They had rebelled and taken up arms against the Hammer Knights.

Behind him, on the battlements of Aleskian itself, it was playing out in a similar fashion. The very few men of the Third, who had been forced to remain in the city, were fighting the Hammer Knights and seeking to retake the battlements. But, the banners of the Hammer Knights there were not toppling.

It took the Third Legion several hours of intense fighting to reach the gate, by which time the men of the Sixth had pushed the Hammer Knights back from the battlements, and had taken much of the barbican from them. Some Hammer Knights were ramming the upper doors to gain entrance to the doors of the mechanism room where a small group from the Sixth had locked themselves inside. It required at least two dozen men to open or close the ancient gate, so it was clear to Borach that however many men were inside, it was not enough to fully close it.

The surge of the Bantu had forced Garuk to move to the west of the gate where he was reforming his forces. All of the giants that had made it within the Everglow, had fallen to the legions well aimed javelins. Countless number of the Bantu had died to the disciplined ranks of the legion, but their own casualties had been high. Only about six hundred or so of the Third Legion, out of the thousand who had marched onto the plain, remained alive, and most of them bore some injury or strain from the battle.

The Third planted its shield at the line of the gate, and still in square formation held its ground there with ease, for the Bantu were still only able to come through in pairs and were easily dealt with. Garuk and his remaining forces, still on the plain, began to retreat towards Aleskian, where to Borach's dismay, an army of Hammer Knights were filing through the Griffin gate and onto the plain. The banner of prince Regineo flew among them.

Borach turned his focus back to the immediate threat. He scanned the battlements of the Great Northern Wall. The Twelfth Legion, had made their way from Fort Resilient along the lower inner battlements, and joined the Sixth. The Hammer Knights were giving ground, but their retreat was orderly and with their fierce hammers they smashed the heads of any from the legions who tried to hound their retreat.

The door to the inner gatehouse was barred from within, and Borach pounded on it with the hilt of Havwitha, shouting, "If friends are within, open for the Lord of Aleskian. If foes, surrender, or we will knock it down and death will be dealt!"

The cry worked. The door was unbarred, unlocked and opened. The men of the Sixth who had been guarding it took up the cry. "For the Lord of Aleskian!"

Borach and Marki rushed into the gatehouse. From above fighting could also be heard.

"There are some Hammer Knights blocking our way to the mechanism room, or the gate would already be closed and locked," one of the men of the Sixth declared.

Borach led the charge up the stairs. The door at the top was broken down with a stone bench, that cracked and broke with the impact. The several Hammer Knights who guarded the room were dispatched after fierce fighting and the loss of two more good legionnaires. A newly positioned statue of one of the Aeldar Gods was used to batter down the next inner door. Within the room several more knights were trying to batter down the door to the mechanism room. Trapped, it was another fierce fight to kill them. Two of Borach's bodyguards died in the fight with the knights, whose heavy hammers dealt deadly blows.

Marki examined the thick, goat-haired under garment that had been exposed through the rent armour and clothes of one of the knights.

"No wonder they are such ill-natured pumpions if this is what they wear under all that," he said as he kicked the bodies of one of them.

The door to the mechanism room was opened when ordered by Borach. Enough of them entered to operate the heavy levers to shut the gate, after which the mechanism to shut the portcullis was also operated by the same men. The counter weights deep below could be heard to move and their heavy chains clanked. Borach breathed a sigh of relief as from outside, the sound of the gate and portcullis shutting with heavy thuds could be heard. The counter weights continued to move and the sound of the Aleskian Gate closing was met with a cheer, as were the screams and roars of the Bantu it crushed as it did so. More cheers went up from both inside and outside the gatehouse as the gate finally shut and the locking mechanism slid into place.

Borach and Marki wasted little time in celebration. They ran out onto the high battlements to survey the scene. The Bantu outside the gate were fleeing. The wall was too high for even the largest siege ladders or towers to mount, and with the gate again closed, the charms and magic that protected it were in place. The men of the Sixth and Twelfth still on the battlements fired the great scorpions and catapults at the fleeing Bantu. The surviving Hammer Knights, had retreated along the battlements to the west of Fort Watch.

Within the gate, on the Aleskian Plain, the remainder of the Bantu were regrouping around Garuk who was now trapped inside. He was issuing and barking orders and retreating deeper into the plain. Regineo and the Hammer Knights were marching at full pace towards Garuk, but all who watched were not naive enough to think he intended to engage them.

Upon the battlements of Aleskian Borach could see the great catapults and scorpions being loaded and readied to fire, but they were not released upon the Bantu horde that remained in the plain. The banners of the Hammer Knights were once again raised, meaning the few men of the Third still within the city, had not succeeded in retaking it.

Marki pointed at the catapults and scorpions far in the distance. "Those bloody things will cut us down before we get near Aleskian. We must make haste for the Dune Fort, and only that mob is blocking the way," he said as he looked at Garuk and the Bantu, gathering rank around their commander. "We have got to kill him and get to the Dune Fort, before Regineo reaches him and they join forces."

Two captains, one from the Sixth and the other the Twelfth, made their way through the crowd with their men following, and stood before Borach. They saluted him, and he returned the gesture. Borach knew and recognised them both. "Galek, I do not know what madness is afoot, but I thank you for your help this day."

"Whatever is afoot, seeing the Bantu inside the Everglow, was more than my men and I could bear," Galek replied. "Imperial orders or not, we could not watch the Third be cut down like rats in a trap."

"Aye," Mustan, the other captain agreed. "If you can tell us what is going on, it would help me and the lads see some sense as to what has occurred this day."

"We have all obeyed imperial orders, sent from the Empress herself, and we were cruelly betrayed. Beyond that, it is as much a mystery for me as it is for you," Borach replied honestly.

"We were shocked when General Longshins said the Sixth and the Twelfth had been ordered to Kara Duram, and only a few of us were to remain," Mustan said.

Galek then complained, "We were commanded to obey every order issued by the commander of the Hammer Knights, who were sent here to relieve us from our watch and learn how to open and close the gate."

Galek looked solemn. "The Hammer Knights spread rumours you had betrayed the Empress and allied with the false Queen of Baothein to hand the city to them; I doubted when I first heard it, tell me there is no truth to it?"

Borach stared him in the eye. "I have been nothing but loyal to the Empress and our people. I do not understand what madness and deception has led to the events of this day. We must figure out the why or where of this another time."

Galek hesitated for a moment. Borach knew him as a loyal man who along with every other legionnaire had not only sworn oaths to the Empress, but also to him as the Lord of Aleskian. "Well, I cannot ask the Empress for her thoughts on this as I've never met her and nor do I think I will, but long have I served and trusted you. If you say you remained loyal, I accept it. You have my sword this day and if needs be tomorrow. I shall answer why, with solemn oaths if I am brought to task for my decisions today."

"Aye, me too," Mustan chimed in.

Then you are all men of the Third, for now," Marki roared.

Both captains then shouted. "For Borach! For Borach!" The other men of the Sixth and Twelfth joined in, as did the men of the Third. "For Borach! For Borach!"

*        *        *

"If I had known you were so incapable of dealing with so few men of the Third, I would have brought more Hammer Knights to Aleskian to help you," Regineo sneered sarcastically at Garuk. About two hundred or so Hammer Knights had marched with him from Aleskian, and now joined their forces with Garuk.

Garuk growled viciously in response. "Shut ya gigglemug orf-chump, or prince or not, I'll give you a flanning. I'm poked up enough that your mutton-shunters did not open the gate fully or I'd already 'ave the egg yolk."

Regineo bit his lip, and felt a surge of fury. It was true, whatever had happened at the gatehouse, it had turned the tide of battle, or Borach and his men would all be lying dead on the Plains of Aleskian by now.

"Gentleman, please," Grixen the Bantu Ambassador said. "We are on the same side, there is no need to trade insults."

"Let's finish this," Regineo said, ignoring Garuk's insult. He spurred his horse, and ordered a full-paced march ahead.

Marki began barking orders to the men to leave the wall and the gatehouse, to restock their used javelins or broken spears from the gatehouse armoury, and to form rank. It did not take long for the newly merged legion to form as one, in front of the gate, in line formation. They were now about eight hundred in number.

"What about the gate?" Mustan asked. "We cannot just abandon it!"

"Know when a battle is lost, but not a war," Marki shouted in response. "We have short supplies, and will be trapped like a honking gosling in a den of foxes if we stay here and fight. I say to the Dune Fort!"

"Marki is right, Mustan," Borach said. "For reasons unknown, the Empire itself has turned upon us this day, and I intend to discover the where and why." Before Mustan could reply, Borach shouted, "Forward!" In response the legion, as one, started to march at full-pace towards the old Dune Fort.

Borach kept a close eye on Garuk and the still sizeable horde of Bantu gathered around him, now reinforced by Regineo and two hundred Hammer Knights, all of whom were also marching at full-pace, and seeing the legion's direction, adjusting to cut them off accordingly.

The legion marched three abreast, ready to turn and face the enemy at any point. Trampling the bodies of the dead beneath their heeled boots, they paid them no heed. The only time they slowed was to pick up their own wounded, whilst dispatching those of the Bantu horde. It soon became clear they would not reach the Dune Fort before their foes, so Borach ordered the legion to head straight towards Regineo and his army, who also adjusted their course, so that it was not long before both armies were face to face, halting a hundred or so yards from each other. The Bantu had all discarded their bows.

"The Bantu are out of arrows, and Regineo has no archers. Finally, a bit of good fortune," Marki said.

Borach felt only a slight relief. They would not have to raise their shields whenever another rain of arrows descended, and the legion had some fresh javelins and missiles for their slings – but it was only a slight advantage.

The two sides watched each other warily, each waiting for the other to make the first manoeuvre.

Borach, who understood the Bantu tongue, listened as Garuk shouted to his warriors that they were to slaughter any among their own ranks who sought to retreat. This was a fight to the death!

He and Garuk had never met on the field of battle before, but both had sworn blood oaths that if they were to meet, they would seek each other out in the mayhem, and their personal battle would be to the death. If Garuk died, it would be only once, he would not return to the land of the living. If Borach died by Garuk's sword, it would also be the *Final-death*, for the foul blade Garuk carried, was an Arkith. The Obelisks would not be able to resurrect Borach, perhaps a mercy, for if they did, he might have many more lifetimes whilst a prisoner, at the mercy of cruel enemies. But he did not wish to die the *Final-death*, not yet, until he understood what had led to the events of the day.

Borach had to silence the many thoughts racing through his mind. His concern was not for himself, but his wife and children somewhere beyond the wall. He had built many secret places for them to hide undetected in the city if ever the need required it, but he breathed a sigh of relief they had already left Aleskian. Time enough for those thoughts later, for now, another battle had to be won.

**186**

*Let us be done with this.* "Advance!" Borach ordered. As one, the legion moved. Step by step, yard by yard they began to make their way towards the remaining Bantu and the Hammer Knights. The horde stood still, and unusually were silent. As the legion approached, Regineo, surrounded by several Hammer Knights rode out from the ranks. One of them was carrying a white flag, which he waved.

Borach held up his hand and ordered his men to halt. The disciplined legion came to a standstill almost instantly.

"They want to talk?" Marki asked, exasperated. "Well there's bloody well nothing those villainous turds can say that I want to hear," he said loud enough for the men of the Third Legion to hear. They roared in approval.

"I recognise the one with the flag, that's General Shinther," Borach said as Regineo and the group with him approached.

Marki squinted his eyes and shook his head in surprise. "Aye, it looks like it is. What the frying frig is he doing here? Was he not until recently Captain General of the Fourteenth Legion, and now he dressed as a blasted Hammer Knight?"

Regineo and his men stopped halfway between the two forces, and waited.

"Don't go, it's a trap," Marki said. "Let's charge them, and take the surprise!"

"No," Borach answered him, and then addressing one of the other commanders said, "Commander Torach, I need you to stay with the legion, if it is a trap you must lead them out of this. Marki, with me."

"Just try stopping me," the dwarf muttered.

Borach and Marki walked towards Prince Regineo and the knights, stopping when they were in ear shot of them. Not knowing how else to respond, Borach slammed his clenched and bloodied fist against his dented armour as a mark of respect to Regineo. "My prince," he said. "None of this makes sense. These are our sworn enemies, yet you ride among them like they are allies and kin?"

"Why do I owe any explanation to Borach *the Betrayer*?" Regineo asked, spitting the words out.

Shinther lifted the visor of his helmet, and spat on the ground.

"Look closely at the catapults Borach *the Betrayer*," he said scathingly, as he pointed behind himself without ever taking his eyes off Borach.

Borach strained to see the catapults clearly, they were too far away.

"Your wife and children are strapped into them. If I lower this white flag, they will be fired. Your family will be hurled over the wall to their *Final-death*. Order your men to lay down your weapons and surrender, immediately.

*It's not possible. Yianna and the children left the city yesterday, didn't they?*

"He lies," Marki said.

Regineo scowled. "Show him," he said contemptuously.

Shinther took a broken milathran chain from his pocket and threw it at the feet of Borach. "Is this not the property of your wife?" he asked.

Borach knelt down and picked the chain up from the sand. It looked like Yianna's chain but where was the locket? She had sworn never to remove it. The chain looked like it had been snatched and broken by force. He gently sniffed it, and felt he could smell a faint scent of Yianna's favourite perfume.

*It could be a trap. If they have the chain, they would have the locket, wouldn't they?* He looked up at the catapults. *Yianna and the children will be safe at Estalda now, won't they? Am I willing to take that chance?*

He looked around at the men of the legion, at his faithful friend Marki, who always stood by his side. *I love Marki, I love the men of the Third Legion, but I would not risk Yianna for any one of them. My life for hers, their life for hers.*

187

"Order the men to lay down their weapons," Borach said to Marki, as he stood, never taking his eyes from the locket.

"Bor, it's a trick," Marki said. "There are other milathran chains, it is well-known by any who knew her she always wears one. They do not have her locket!"

"Do it!" Borach ordered.

Marki grimaced and bit his tongue, turned, and reluctantly bellowed the order for the legion to lay down its weapons. The men hesitated, and Marki bellowed out the order again. Slowly, reluctantly, they obeyed, their weapons dropping one by one onto the floor of the plain with a clatter and thud.

Garuk, accompanied by a smaller, more refined looking Bantu, arrogantly strutted his way towards where Regineo and General Shinther sat upon their horses. "Lord Garuk was promised, if the opportunity arose, single combat with this craven; he would see the promise fulfilled," the smaller Bantu said.

Regineo looked at Borach with disgust. "Ambassador Grixen is correct. Will you seek to regain at least a degree of your honour, and meet Garuk in single combat, or is your traitorous heart to faint to fight him?"

Marki, who had not dropped his axe, took a step forward and swung it in the air. "I'll fight the yellow toothed pignut," he snarled.

Borach wrapped the chain around his wrist, and secured it. His sword already drawn, he stood next to his dearest friend and laid a hand on his wrist. "Go back to the ranks with Torach, whatever happens, the men must surrender. For the sake of Yianna." He then addressed Regineo.

"My prince, my men were only obeying my orders and showing what they thought was loyalty to the city, to your mother the Empress, and to the Empire. If you give me your word they will not be punished, I submit myself to your will, be that what it may."

"What good is the word of an *Ivanar*?" Marki asked, infuriated.

"Quiet," Borach ordered him.

Marki, exasperated, whispered to Borach, "He is a known promise-breaker, and here he is, in league with the Bantu. Bor, don't trust him."

Borach looked up at the catapults holding his family. "Be that as it may, I have given you an order to return to the ranks," he barked, and then, pleading with his stubborn friend, added, "please Marki, for the sake of Yianna and my children."

Marki barely stopped a scream of frustration. Reluctantly, he re-joined the ranks of the legion.

Looking at Garuk, and then at Regineo, Borach said, "I am confused as to what has led to the events of this day. You call me *Betrayer*, my wife and children's' lives are threatened, and I find myself here in this plain having fought this battle against an ancient foe we have long kept outside of the wall, one you now stand among as friends? Am I not owed an explanation at the least?"

Regineo waved away the quibble. "Fight Garuk. If you win, you will, at the least, keep your honour as a soldier and shall be given the chance to answer for your crimes at the Bloody Tower in Kappia. Lose to him, then a warrior's shame will be upon you, and that soul-gem will forever take your spirit."

"My prince, promise me that whatever happens, you will spare my family, and I will fight him at your order, and after I severe his head from his body, I will surrender myself to you, but one request I have."

"You are in no position to make a request, *Betrayer*," Shinther quipped.

"Were we not friends once, and now you insult me, and show me no proof?"

Shinther sneered with disgust. "I am no friend to traitors."

Borach addressed Regineo again. "My loyalty has always been to the Empress, to my Sarissa. You will discover this to be true. I will swear it and publicly face the test, in front of the sacred Jewel of Baramir. All of Kappia will then know that I am loyal and my actions this day were only born out of what I believed was loyalty to my Sarissa and the Empire."

"We will see," Regineo said, as he spurred his horse and along with Shinther and the other knights, re-joined the ranks of his soldiers so that only Garuk and Borach stood in the gap between the two armies.

Garuk strode forward to face Borach in combat. He was a head taller than Borach, and much broader. Blood was spattered across the golden emblem of his armour. Garuk snarled, showing a mouthful of yellowed fangs dripping with saliva. "They call me Warlord Garuk *the Conqueror, the King-eater, the Black-blade*," he said fiercely. "Today a new title will be bestowed upon me, Garuk *the Slayer of Borach the Betrayer*, and that soft-'ole you call wife, will warm my bed and cosh this night, for I will demand it as a spoil for my victory over you."

Borach did not reply. He was too experienced in combat to be goaded into a rash move. He watched as Garuk drew the infamous two-handed sword from across his back, the blade that had earned him the name *Black-blade*. The black runes on the blade shimmered and moved as if in anticipation of a feast of blood, and the jet-black jewel in the pommel glowed in hungry anticipation of a new soul to join those already within its foul prison.

Borach lifted his own sword, *Havwitha*, and waited for Garuk to make the first move, as they started to circle each other, whilst both armies looked on in silent anticipation. Long had Borach and Garuk taunted each other across the wall, and now, after centuries of such conflict, they stood face to face and there could only be one victor. It was fame or shame for them, and only one of them would survive a battle that would be to the death.

Garuk made the first move, and lunged with a speed that belied his size. He aimed a swipe at Borach's neck but it was easily slammed aside. Borach turned in a circle as Garuk moved around him. Steel clashed on steel, and Garuk drew the first blood as he suddenly pirouetted into a crouch and struck at Borach's leg. Borach managed to parry the main force of it, but he was left with a gash across his right leg where the sword had pierced his armour as though it were butter. The pain was immediate, agony flooded into his leg and for a moment he thought he would pass out. He felt that the Arkith itself was screaming at him, demanding he surrender his soul to its dark embrace.

"I have killed you, so easily and quickly," Garuk mocked as he circled Borach once more. Striking again, he cut through Borach's helmet with a blow that would have cloven him in two had he not once more parried it to limit the effect of the landed blow. Borach's head began to immediately ache, abominably. He felt a qualm of nausea, and blood began to clot thickly among his black locks. The pain blossomed at an incredible rate. His head was lolling drunkenly on his shoulders. He knew what it meant; he was dead unless he could get the anti-dote to counter the poison laced upon the Bantu's blade. All men of the legions at Aleskian had carried it; he did not have time to take it from the pouch on his belt, for to attempt to do so would be instant death as Garuk would seize the advantage.

"Die," Garuk grunted as he savagely chopped at him.

Borach managed to fend off the blows, though he barely got his sword up in time. Despite his savagery, Garuk was no unthinking brute who led with his rage, and he was much faster than Borach had anticipated. Borach, feeling more weakened from the

189

poison with every second that passed, realised that Garuk was winning. A fierce cry rose from Garuk's lips - he also sensed the victory.

The Bantu horde, until then silent, raised a raucous shout, and some began to blow horns. As if in response, beyond the Aleskian Gate, more drums and Bantu horns began to blow filling the air with a mighty crescendo.

Borach began to stagger, and then he dropped to his knees as his leg gave out. Behind him, even above the din of the Bantu, he heard Marki shriek with a wail of despair. He lifted his left arm to fend off the next blow. His armour seemed to explode from the force of the blow and the dark charms of the runes. The shattered pieces fell away from his half-severed and broken arm.

"Die," Garuk bellowed again as his metalled boot kicked Borach in the temple so hard his head rang.

Falling flat on his back, *Havwitha* fell away from him. Borach looked up; there was only sky above him. He rolled onto his side and tried to find his feet, but pain shuddered through him and the world throbbed, as the Arkith again screamed out to him. He fell again on his back.

Garuk drew up above him. "Borach *the Betrayer*, you are mine," he bellowed down. "Look in my eyes as I slay you!" He grabbed Borach by the beard, and pulled him to his knees.

Borach fumbled for his sword. It was out of reach. He felt for the dirk he kept in a scabbard, and found its hilt. Garuk loomed overhead, he seemed immense in size. Letting go of Borach's beard, with both hands gripping the hilt, he raised his sword above his head, but instead of landing the killing blow he began to show off to the Bantu who were roaring with pleasure. He flailed and whirled his sword above his head faster and faster, in order to make the final blow as stylish as he could.

With the last ounce of his strength, Borach lunged to his feet and thrust the dagger deep into Garuk's right eye. He tried to shout "you die," but only a croak came from his mouth.

Garuk involuntarily let go of his sword which was flung harmlessly by the motion to the side. He gave a hideous scream and tried to wrench away from the agony, pulling at the hilt of the dirk protruding from his burst eye. A shower of black blood and brain splattered over Borach's face. Garuk died a second later, falling like a heavy sack with a loud thump to the ground. The Bantu host fell silent, as Marki and the men of the Third Legion cheered. The world disappeared, as Borach lost consciousness, a second or so later.

# Chapter Fifteen: *Castle Greytears*

*I have a tale, children of Pangaea, of how nine seeds gave life to worlds those Titans held in trust.*
**Poetry of the Vanyr.**

*"The tentacles of the Inquisition and Aeldar Priests are everywhere. Their order will soon help finance wars, loan money, collect taxes, build castles, run cities, ports and fleets of ships, raise armies, resolve trade disputes to their advantage and carry out political assassinations. I am warning you, listen to me. The only crime I am guilty of is telling the truth. The allegations against me are obscene, false and mendacious, and have been proposed by liars and corruptors. Never, after speaking of virtue by day, did I shake my hips in nocturnal folly and exertion in the brothels of Mendosa and never did I have intimate relations with a donkey. I was put in a dungeon under lock and key. My so-called confession corroborating these accusations was obtained by torture. I was starved, deprived of sleep, shackled, racked, burnt on the feet and hauled up in the strappado until I could bear no more. I only told my black-clad interrogators exactly what they wanted to hear, to make them stop."*
**The last words of the heretic Athswain before his tongue was cut out and he was strapped to a wagon, and then taken to a field where he was burned alive on a sacred Aeldar Pyre.**

$\mathcal{A}$ dull throbbing, as well as the sound of keys jangling in a lock roused Scarand. Every time blood pulsed through his head it brought a fresh wave of pain. He cracked his eyes open and winced from the light shining from a lantern thrust through the cell door that had just been opened. When he tried to sit up, he realized that his hands were tied behind his back. *At least the chains have been replaced with rope,* he thought.

A guard entered the cell, followed by a short, fat man dressed in a brown robe tied at the waist with a crude rope, from which a bunch of keys jangled on a large metal hoop attached to a short chain. The top of the man's head was shaven in the tonsure style. "Untie him, I have much to do and little time to do it all," he said impatiently to the guard.

The guard, an elderly man with a spiteful face and a hooked nose put the lantern on the floor and cut the rope that bound Scarand's hands and feet.

"Why did you beat him?" the man asked the guard.

"It wasn't me your reverence," the guard answered sarcastically, "I wasn't on duty last night. It's just the boys having some fun before they locked him up."

Scarand sat up as the guard shouted at him. "Get up you lazy Davari scum. The priest has work for you."

Scarand stood gingerly to his feet. His limbs were stiff, his head ached.

"Move," the guard said as he shoved Scarand violently towards the exit of the cell. Born of an instinct honed in the wild and savage lands of his birth, Scarand had to control himself not to turn and attack the guard. Overpowering the man and killing him would be easy enough, but escaping from the castle just yet, was another matter. *I must stay alive. For Marciea and Oliviana.*

"That's quite enough of that Ole Benkin, I can control him," the priest said as he looked Scarand up and down and sniffed the air. "If you're going to work with me today, we will get you bathed and a change of clothes. I can't be dealing with the smell of an unwashed Davari all day. You stink of the Erin and it is quite beyond my ability to endure."

The priest left the room, and the guard pushed Scarand out of the cell after him. "Follow him," he barked, as he picked up the lantern."

*For Marciea and Oliviana.*

The guard then unlocked another prisoner from another cell, and he was dragged out to join them. Scarand recognised the man, it was the pirate, Marlo.

The priest wagged his finger at them. "Both of your lives have been spared, for now, so you can do some work for me." He fumbled for a short strange looking stick which he took from beneath his robe and waved threateningly at them. "Work hard today, and cause me no trouble, or I'll have Ole Benkin hold you down and I will use this stinger on you and its very painful you know? I'll then send for Malkili and he will make you sorry if you cause me any trouble, is that clear?"

Scarand and Marlo both nodded.

"Good then, cause me no trouble, and I will also try and put in a good word on your behalf to the Baron. Is that understood?"

Both men nodded again.

"Good, I am Janus, the Aeldar priest of the castle. Now, you are Marlo?"

The man mumbled he was. Scarand took a long look at Marlo. His missing nose and eyes were old wounds, but his body showed signs of more recent acts of brutality and torture. He was clearly a broken man, and stood their shaking as the guard unshackled him.

"Don't send for Malkili, I'll be good," he said pleadingly to Janus.

Janus ignored him, and asked Scarand, "And what is your name?"

"I am Scarand."

"Hmm, I don't like either of those names but they will do for now. Follow me."

Janus led them along several stone passages that were wet with damp. The guard followed closely behind. The lantern only gave enough radiance to barely light the passageways a few steps ahead of them at a time. They walked along many stone passageways, full of cells either empty, or containing rotting corpses or bleached skeletons. Eventually they came to stairs guarded at the top by iron gates.

As they waited for the gates to be unlocked by the sentries, Janus said to Scarand casually, "You should feel lucky you weren't locked in the deeper dungeons, like Marlo here was, until I got him released for work purposes. It's a terrible place down there. Malkili and his apprentice are free to do whatever they like with the prisoners down there, and not all of their prisoners are human. Trust me, it's a terrible place."

When the gates were opened, they passed through, and Scarand heard the gates slamming and locking behind them. He made sure to observe everything as they walked through the castle; he would need to know both where he was, and where to go, when the time came to attempt escape.

Janus led them through corridors with long patterned carpets on the floor, and pictures of men fighting on horseback adorning the walls, before passing through several large rooms with tall glass windows hung with plain drapery. There were chairs with grey velvet and black iron legs, and grim paintings on the walls and large tapestries.

As they made their way, they met the occasional servant carrying linen, a tray or a bucket of soapy water. They passed guards patrolling in twos, or standing outside of rooms with big fancy doors. Eventually, they walked up some winding stairs and entered a room through an arched wooden door. The guard accompanying them stayed outside.

The room was very untidy. It had an unmade bed, a wooden desk with books scattered across it and dirty plates and dishes littered randomly around, some of which still contained rotting food. In the corner was a wooden bath tub, filled with grimy water.

"I have to do everything myself," Janus said, as he sighed and looked around at the room. "I have never known a keep of this size not to give a priest like me his own slaves and servants. I only have use of you two because of the state of the temple, and now the resurrection due to take place today. It's most barbaric and uncivilized. Three days I have had to use the same bathing water, and I hate cold water."

Janus handed Marlo and Scarand a bar of soap each, a towel and clean but tattered looking tunics. "Now, bathe in turn and change out of those foul-smelling rags you wear. When you are done, I will take you to the kitchen for bread and water, and then I expect a good day's work from you. You might not be in a state to work for a long time, if the Inquisitor gets a hold of you, but work hard for me and I will tell him there's no need to bother you two."

*I don't plan on being here long enough to meet the Inquisitor,* Scarand thought to himself.

Although Janus spoke in the Common Tongue, his accent was thick and Scarand was only just able to understand him. The priest pulled a stool from under the desk, and sat on it, whilst Marlo bathed first. Scarand watched as Janus picked up a quill, dipped it in ink and began scribbling notes on pieces of papyrus paper. He paid no attention as Marlo got out the bath, dried himself and dressed, after which Scarand stripped, and with some unease and disgust, got into the grimy bath water. He washed from head to toe as quickly as he could, before getting out, drying himself and putting on the tattered tunic, which, to his relief was at least clean. As unpleasant as the bath water had been, it slightly revived and refreshed him, and eased some of the aches and pains he felt all over his body.

Janus looked up at the two men. "Do you read? No, of course you don't, I am silly to ask. I will return to these letters later. Come now, with me." He put down the quill and rushed impatiently towards the door.

"Come," he said. "I have so much to do and so little time to do it all."

Scarand and Marlo followed Janus out of the room, along a passage, and down some stone steps. The guard followed again. It was a long way, through the castle, but eventually they came to the kitchens. When they arrived, there was a half-opened door behind which was a large kitchen, from which wafted the smell of freshly baked bread that caused Scarand's mouth to water. Janus, still complaining about how busy he was, pushed the door open with his foot and entered, followed by the three men.

The kitchen was full of utensils, pots and pans hung from hooks on the wall and from wires hanging across the ceiling. Helpers were scurrying around carrying heavy sacks of vegetables, hot trays full of cakes or large pots, each trying not to bump into each other. People chopped things on tables, whipped food or were washing pans in a sink as cooks yelled orders. The smell of the food was so good it immediately made Scarand aware of the hunger he felt. A plain looking maid stood at a long table rolling some dough, she looked up and smiled as Janus entered and approached her, whilst the guard, Ole Benkin, went and sat on a chair in the corner and began chatting to a plump female cook who was stirring a large pot hanging over a fireplace.

"Morning your reverence," the maid said cheerfully to Janus.

He scowled at her. "Rosie, you were supposed to change my bath-water and clean up my room, it's uncivilised for me to have to live in such conditions; I have so much work to do there is not enough hours in the day."

"I 'ave me own chores to do," Rosie said defensively. "If master didn't keep killing them few Davari slaves we get sent none of us would 'ave to do menial work like that. Do you know 'ow many rooms I have to clean today as well as do my chores 'ere in the kitchen?"

Janus looked at Scarand and shrugged in frustration, wringing his hands in the air. "See what I have to put up with?" he yelped.

Rosie paid no courtesy to him. Continuing to roll the dough she aired her further complaint. "That's you and me both, your reverence. I'm a servant but I ain't any mongrel-blood. My father was a 'alf-blood Akkadian from the Blue Lake, nice cottage we owned, right by the lake itself." She shook her head and sighed. "My sister works the kitchens in one of the Rose Forts just over the Kappian border, and she 'as twenty Davari slaves working under 'er. Twenty! I'm thinking of giving me notice and go join 'er there."

"I'm just asking that somebody cleans my room," Janus wailed.

Rosie shook her head. "When I'm not preparing master's meals, tidying and cleaning 'is rooms, the cooks 'ere are bellowing at me to do chores for them as well, and then I am supposed to clean and tidy for you as well? It's all getting too much."

She looked over at Ole Benkin the guard, who was still chatting to the plump cook, "And look at the quality of the men 'ere in this place, you turn your back on them for one minute and they are trying to bed somebody else."

"None of those things are my problem," Janus said with a frustrated sigh. "If I ask you to do something, you must do it."

Rosie stopped rolling the dough, blew some flour from the tip of her nose and looked at him. "I told Brindy to do it last evening, but she's all loved up with one of the guards and I ain't seen 'er yet this morning." Her face softened. "I'll make sure somebody does it today, I give you my word your reverence."

Janus looked like he was about to explode with anger. Instead, he took his frustration out on a loaf of bread. He ripped it in half, and taking a knife crudely spread some butter on one half and then on the other. Taking a pot of jam from a shelf, he scooped the jam out and spread some on both halves, and greedily ate them.

Rosie grew agitated. "That blueberry jam belongs to the Baron, 'e likes it for breakfast. If we run out, I'll not be taking the blame for it. I'll tell 'im it was you that scoffed it."

Janus ignored her. Pouring water from a jug into a cup, he washed his food down, only half-chewed. He then tore at the bread and handed a chunk to Scarand and then to Marlo, as well as a cup of water each. Both men took them and ate and drank eagerly.

Rosie looked at Marlo and quipped, "I see Malkili 'as been 'aving some fun." She then looked Scarand up and down, as she continued rolling the dough.

"My, this one is 'ansome; I bet Lady Bavira will make use of 'im afore the master does 'im away for sport or in a fit of temper."

"Quiet, Rosie," Janus rebuked. "I am not interested in such filth!"

Scarand looked at the keys jangling from Janus' belt. He fought the sudden urge to launch himself knocking the priest senseless, and taking the keys and then tackling the guard, Ole Benkin, who was inappropriately touching the cook as she continued to stir the pot; she was only making half-hearted giggling attempts to push his groping hands away. *I must be smarter than my wrath. For Marciea and Oliviana. The kitchen is far too busy for me to get away without an alarm being raised.*

Janus dodged an irritated helper who nearly bumped into him; he spoke to Rosie, whilst greedily chewing another mouthful of bread and jam.

"I will be giving a sermon from the *Book of Aeldar* this evening at six-o'clock. I expect you to be there. I am tired of preaching to an empty sanctuary."

"I can't be there at that time," Rosie protested. "The Baron will be wanting 'is dinner at usual time and..."

Janus interrupted her before she could finish the sentence. "The Baron has ridden out on some business or other, looking for villains or survivors – or both; I doubt he'll be back for dinner."

"Don't matter none," Rosie said. "I always get 'is food ready whether 'e is 'ere or not. That way if 'e turns up unexpected, it's ready for 'im and I stay out of trouble. Besides Lady Bavira still needs feeding and I usually help Sissy prepare 'er Ladyship's broth, as old Sissy always overcooks the carrots and Lady Bavira likes 'em crunchy. Last time 'er ladyship threw the bowl at poor ole Sissy 'cos she overcooked the veg in the broth."

Rosie put down the rolling-pin she was rolling the dough with, dusted the flour off her hands and wiped the remaining dough on her apron and walked over to a cupboard. Opening it, she took out two pies. Walking over to Janus, she showed the pies to him. "Look at these, your reverence," she said as she grinned cheekily. "I made these yesterday. Take them to share as lunch for you and your 'elpers, to take with; and help yourself to a jug of milk, the farmer brought some up from 'is dairy last night - it's all fresh."

Janus put the last morsel of bread into his mouth, drank some water and went to take the pies, but Rosie mischievously put them behind her back. The priest sighed deeply.

"And what do you want for them?" he asked suspiciously, still chewing the bread.

Rosie looked around, to make sure none but those within immediate earshot could hear. "I 'ear that the Obelisk been chattering away all night; at least that's what Ole Jimson the guard is telling everyone. He says that old thing keeps talking about a red and golden-beast of the air, and tireless feet 'unting some Seeress. Ole Jimson said 'e never 'eard the thing babbles on in like manner afore. Whole keep is talking about it this morning."

Janus answered impatiently, spraying bits of half-chewed bread as he spoke. "The Obelisks rarely speak sense, I have yet to get to know the habits of this one well, but I do know enough not to pay much attention to anything it says."

Rosie ignored him and continued.

"No Pure-blood from keep or town has died or we would 'ave heard about it, and if the Baron or one of his men got killed last night a raven would 'ave been sent, and whole keep would be gossiping about it." She leaned in closer, looked around again, and whispered. "Folk are saying an Akkadian might have died on that wreck? Now, who do you think it could possibly be?"

Janus shook his head wearily and swallowed the bread with a gulp. "How am I supposed to know that? Even if it is somebody who died on the wreck, that is no concern of yours. You lot and the guards need to stop this incessant gossiping and speculation."

"'Ere, don't be like that or I'll be putting these pies back," Rosie said indignantly as she frowned, and looked displeasingly at Marlo and then Scarand.

"The guards said the ugly one was caught by the Baron's spies near Berecoth, and the Davari, was washed up with Lady Sasna. Maybe he knows a thing or two about the wreck?"

The mention of Sasna caught Scarand's attention.

"Lady Sasna? She is at the castle?" Janus asked, surprised.

"Was," Rosie replied. "Rumour is she died of a wound overnight, or at the least is very sick with it and won't last the day. Baron's own physician was sent to 'elp 'er, but he ain't no good, at least not as good as the ones at the Rose Forts."

*Sasna is dead or dying?* The news surprised and saddened Scarand.

195

"Why am I always the last to hear anything," Janus moaned as he looked disapprovingly at Scarand. "You didn't tell me you and Lady Sasna were on that wreck? Was a Pure-blood on board as well?"

*I only met you a short while ago, fool, and you haven't stopped moaning and complaining.* "I don't know, I was locked in the hold for most of the journey." *Even if I did know, and got a chance to speak, I would not be telling you.*

"Oh, never mind, I'll find out soon enough who is resurrecting," Janus sighed.

Rosie smiled cheekily. "Tell you what, when Brindy gets 'ere I'll make sure she does your room all spotless like. And, I've got Ranien Steak for the Baron's dinner tonight. I might 'ave some spare for your dinner as well, if you do me a favour."

Janus' eyes widened. "Ranien Steak?" he asked after which he licked his lips. "And what favour do you want, Rosie?"

"Let me come to the resurrection and watch, I ain't never seen one before – Brindy 'asn't either, she wants to come as well - we can 'elp you out."

"It's not really appropriate."

"Please, your reverence?" Rosie whined. "Look at these two? Who knows where they washed up from? They won't know what to do. Brindy and I can take turns fetching things for you."

"Such as?"

"Wine and food, or maybe a blanket if you get cold. You'll be sitting alone, or with these two, waiting for the resurrection and then the *Awakening*. Since master smashed in the head of the last Davari slave you ain't got anybody to help you if not me and Brindy, and these two won't be much good at fetching. What do you say?"

Janus paused for a moment, and scratched his chin thoughtfully. "Ranien steak, you say? From the fields of Phouasanos?"

Rosie nodded and smiled. "The best cuts from a wild auroch-calf, that I'll cook with spices from Merva. The master hired me on the merits of that dish alone."

"Very well," Janus answered after a further moment's pause. "The chamber's already heating up, but it won't be more than a few hours. My guess is the resurrection will happen soon after lunch-time." He looked over at the guard, who was now eating some bread and cheese and still chatting away to the cook. "I'll send, him, whatever his name is, to fetch you?"

Rosie clapped her hands together in glee. "Thank you, your reverence, thank you."

"You must follow my instructions to the letter, it is a very sacred occasion and we do not know who it is resurrecting nor why they are here; they might be a very important person, do you understand?"

Rosie, smiled and squealed with sheer delight, nodded and put the pies on the table. Opening a drawer, she took out some brown paper which she used to wrap them. Walking over to a cupboard, she got a large clay jar full of milk, and taking it down handed the pies and jar to Scarand.

"Don't be dropping these now, 'is reverence likes 'is milk and pies and won't be any too 'appy if a clumsy Davari drops 'em in the dirt."

Scarand took the pies and the milk, and silently followed Janus out of the kitchen. Marlo and Ole Benkin also followed.

Janus moaned and mumbled under his breath, mostly to himself, as they walked down the stone passageway and along several corridors.

"Say what you like about Davari slaves but at least they do what you tell them. That maid's a Half-blood; it makes her protected by law. As such they always go on about their legal rights, contracts and so on. If I took a stick to her, I would end up before the judge, having to answer for breaking the law myself. They won't do anything for the

196

likes of me unless I give them something in return. It's a disgrace I tell you, an absolute disgrace." He continued walking but turned to face Scarand. "I was sent here to convert them to the glorious way of the Aeldar and all I get is grief and hardship. I shall be writing a strongly worded letter to my prelate; of that you can be sure." He stabbed his finger in the air for effect. "A strongly worded letter!"

The four of them reached the end of the last corridor. The wooden door at the end had two iron hinges and upon the wood was carved two hammers and a snake. Scarand recognised the symbol.

"The black terrors," he said quietly under his breath.

"What?" Janus asked. "Oh, never mind, I have no time to be hearing the ramblings of a Davari." He unlocked and opened the door and led them into a large temple with a high vaulted domed ceiling. The sanctuary was full of pews facing an altar. He continued to complain as he shut the door behind them, and locked it. Ole Benkin walked over to one of the pews, laid down on it, made himself comfortable and closed his eyes.

"Useless, utterly useless," Janus mumbled as he looked at the guard. "He's supposed to keep an eye on you two!"

Scarand looked around him in confused amazement. He had never seen such a grand place, even though the sanctuary was far from complete. Scaffolding was erected on the far wall, to the right of the large main doors, but no workers could be seen. At the front a large altar made of polished black marble was positioned beneath a great ebony-pulpit upon which were carved images that Scarand did not know. Above the pulpit was a large metallic sculpture of hammers and a snake, hanging from two chains attached to the ceiling. Some of the plinths at the front of the sanctuary were empty; others had large bronze idols sitting on them, creatures of terrifying appearance. The floor was made of blue marble, inlaid with gold intricate designs, but it was covered in a layer of thin dust due to the work being carried out. Every wall in the sanctuary was covered in black ebony wood, upon which were tapestries, or, painted in a variety of colours, carved images of god-like figures, and terrible beasts and epic battles, along with the hammers and snake symbol which were everywhere. Some of the carvings were finished, others were works under progress. Branches of lit candles were on stands littered around the hall, or on shelves on the walls. The candles, as well as flickering torches in sconces on the wall and chandeliers high up in the ceiling, were its only source of light.

"I even had to get up early and light these candles myself," Janus muttered. "I begged my prelate not to send me to this backwater, but apparently, taking cake from the priory at night when the scullery was closed is behaviour unbecoming a priest." He lifted his hands in exasperation. "I was hungry and the cake had fresh cream. How was I to know it was for the prelate's birthday gathering? It's not worth this punishment I can tell you."

Janus then walked over to one of the pews and sat down upon it, inviting Scarand and Marlo to join him, which they did. He took the pies and milk off Scarand, and placed them in a drawer at the bottom of the pew he was sat upon. "I'll make sure you two get some bread for lunch, I have some left over from a few days before. I think a slice of pie might be too delicate a taste for a Davari and a pirate, and I don't want to see it go to waste."

He looked at Scarand, "And I can't be having you go sick on me, we have a lot of work to do. You don't talk much, do you? You're not dumb, are you? Oh, please don't tell me they have sent me an idiot." He spoke very slowly. "Do…you…understand… me?"

197

"I do," Scarand answered, resisting the urge to grab the priest by the throat.

"Janus then looked at Marlo, who was looking badly bruised and weakened, the result of his recent mistreatment.

"I know you spent time with Malkili, it was only because I need work done here that you were allowed up to the upper dungeon. You are fortunate they didn't cut out your tongue. They enjoy that. Now, you will behave?"

"Yes," Marlo muttered darkly.

"Where is the Lady Sasna, I must speak with her?" Scarand asked, before Janus could utter any more nonsense.

"Sasna? Why would she want to speak with you?" he asked in reply as he looked at Scarand quizzically. "She is Seesnari. There's a saying in these parts; *never trust a Seesnari.* Liars and deceivers the lot of them, they would sell their own mothers if it suits their cause. I know her well, so I speak with authority that she finds Davari distasteful, and would not want to speak with you, especially if she is near to death's door. Or, perhaps she is dead and the rumours are true?" He paused, and then blurted out. "Oh my, you must be delirious. Maybe the guards damaged you when they beat you?" He shook his head sadly. "I ask them time and again not to beat the slaves. I need them strong to do work for me, but do the guards ever listen? No, nobody ever listens to poor Janus," he said pitifully, and then slapping his hands on his knees he stood.

"I will enquire of Lady Sasna's well-being later, but first I have duties to attend." He peered at the two men. It looked like the blood drained from his face. He hesitated before he spoke, and when he did, it was with a slight nervous stutter. "Now listen to me, and pay heed. Baron Daramir is a cruel man with a mercurial disposition, that's why they call him the *Bloody Baron.* I am a Pure-blood Akkadian and protected by laws, well, mostly, as are those Half-bloods like the maids. Even so, we know not to anger him or question any of his business affairs. He comes from a powerful family, and even for me it is not wise to not meddle in the affairs of such people, nor ask too many questions." He looked around at the sanctuary, and wagged his finger at the men. "He rarely comes to this place, but he might today, if he returns in time to meet whoever it is resurrecting. If he does, remember that the Baron hates all people impartially, but particularly slaves, and especially Davari. You are an offence to him simply for being alive. He will take his anger and violence out upon the likes of you, with or without offence. Do not look him in the eye, and whatever you do, for pity's sake do not speak to him, unless spoken too. Is that understood?"

Janus' words stirred in Scarand a deep sense of dread, but also a boiling anger. *I will endure what I must, to stay alive, for Marciea and Oliviana.*

Both men nodded.

"Good. It sickens me, but I can do nothing." Janus noticed them both looking around the splendid but unfinished sanctuary, so he also looked around and gestured with his hands at it, and said somewhat excitedly. "Impressive, isn't it? Just wait until it's finished, it will be one of the marvels of all Bruthon lands. I am only overseeing the building project mind, and get to do all the hard work. I won't get to be the priest here when it's all finished, oh no, some favourite of my prelate will get that privilege and I will be sent who knows where?" He sighed pitifully.

The sanctuary was impressive, but Scarand was in no mood to admire the beauty and workmanship. He was looking for any means of escape. *The windows, the scaffolding. It might be possible.*

"I have given the workmen, the masons and artists several days off, in honour of the festival of Lupoor which is given in honour of the great Ahrimakan, one of our Aeldar Gods. These people, the Bruthon, mostly do not worship them yet, but it is my task to convert them. By letting them honour the festivals, it, well, kind of gives them an incentive to want to embrace the *Aeldar Faith* and all the benefits it has. You two, can help me today, by cleaning!"

He pointed to a corner. "Now, see those brooms over there, pick them up, and start sweeping the floor. The dust these masons cause gets everywhere and they refuse to clean up after themselves. Put the dust in those sacks over there. That is the first job I have for you two today."

Scarand had never used that type of broom before, but he followed Marlo's action, picked one up and used the same sweeping motion as him. He winced in pain from his bruises, but carried on regardless.

Janus walked over to him and watched. "No, no, no," he said, clearly frustrated. He snatched the broom off of Scarand. "Long sweeps," he said as he pushed the broom in a long and slow manner along the floor. "Long sweeps... you try!" He handed the broom back.

Scarand began sweeping in the manner Janus had shown him.

"Good, good, much better," Janus said enthusiastically. "I have some chores to do in the *Chamber of the Obelisk* and will be gone a good hour or more, it will take you that long to sweep this place, then you will need to dust everywhere and sweep again." He looked at the guard who was fast asleep and snoring in the pew, and walked over and shook him awake. The guard opened his eyes, sat up and irritably mumbled something.

"Keep an eye on these two," Janus said. "I will keep the doors locked so they don't go wandering off." He looked at Scarand and Marlo. "Guards are everywhere, and if they find you wandering, it will not go well for you. If you try anything, you will be sent straight to the lower-dungeons, and you don't want that, do you?"

"No," Marlo muttered, panic in his voice.

Scarand nodded, and continued sweeping in long, slow strokes, as Janus scurried over to the far end of the sanctuary before disappearing through a door to the left of the main altar, which he locked behind himself.

Scarand watched the guard, who sat there yawning, before laying down and going back to sleep. He then continued sweeping whilst carefully looking around at his surroundings. The scaffolding was built about a third of the way up the large walls, far below the large arched windows that were near the top, ending where the wall joined to the large vaulted ceiling. *There is no way to reach those windows, yet, not without some sort of ladder. If they complete the scaffolding it may reach up to them but how long will these workers be off for this festival?*

The sanctuary had three exits, the locked door to the side that they had entered by, the one through which the priest had disappeared, and two large double-doors, elaborately carved with the hammer and snake symbol, at the opposite end to the altar, which were clearly the main entrance to the temple. A smaller door was set within them that was probably used for daily purposes. He was trapped, the only way out, would be to forcibly take the keys from the priest when he returned, but as yet, he had no idea what the layout of the castle was. Despite the urge for immediate escape, he restrained his impulses. *I must bide my time, be patient. For Marciea and Oliviana.*

# Chapter Sixteen: *Escape from Aleskian*

*Balian was admired for his chivalry, but he found the Hammer Knights dangerous; he feared them because they were men not attached to the things of this world. After the Battle of Chronicles, he ordered all Hammer Knights captured alive, to be given the Final-death, all except one, Matthias their High-General. For him, he chose special humiliation.*
***Temmison Vol II, Book 5: The Wars and Conquests of the Kappian Empire.***


*Marki's* cheer and that of the Third Legion turned to loud wails as they watched Borach collapse and fall heavily to the dusty ground. He looked up at the battlements where Borach's family had been bound and trussed in the buckets of the catapults. He had no intention of putting them at risk, and for their sake, he was about to throw *Old Trusty* down in frustration, and surrender his and the legion's fate to Prince Regineo. He glanced at the distant battlements upon which were the catapults. The buckets were empty and the arms of the catapults were raised. To his dismay and despair, they had been fired. Shinther had lowered the flag.

"By Balagrim, they fired them." he wailed in misery. He hesitated but a moment, and then shouted to the legion. "They killed Yianna and the bairns! To arms men, to arms!" The legionnaires picked up their weapons and shields.

The Bantu horde, looking at the fallen body of Garuk, started to become unruly and restless, so Marki readied *Old Trusty*.

"They sliced Garuk the *Black-blade*," he heard one of them scream, causing the others to murmur even more.

"That rumble 'ad loaded dice," another shouted accusingly, as the Bantu ranks began to surge forward.

"Blacklegs, the whole stinking lot of 'em," another shouted.

General Shinther's horse began to snort; it became restless and reared up. Shinther hauled back the reins to steady it.

"Stand down," he roared at the nearest group of Bantu.

One of them snarled at him and growled, "I'll be no nose-bagger to 'uman scum." The Bantu lunged forward, and gutted Shinther's horse with a toothed sword. The poor beast whinnied and screamed in terror as its intestines spilled onto the ground. It fell, dismounting Shinther. Before he could even regain a footing, the Bantu were upon him cutting him in pieces.

"Stop, no," the Bantu Ambassador, Grixen, shouted. "In the name of your master, Goth Surien, I order you to stop!"

Prince Regineo shouted an order to the Hammer Knights, "Protect me, protect your prince!" They surged around Regineo, and fighting broke out between the Bantu and the Hammer Knights.

Marki glanced at Borach lying senseless on the ground, and then at the Bantu horde; those not engaged in a fight with the Hammer Knights, were already charging the legion. With a soldier's instinct, he made an immediate decision and barked an order.

"Form a phalanx! At them," he roared, as the Bantu charged. The legion broke into a run, keeping pace with each other, a strong phalanx of a hundred in a row, and several rows deep, hurling javelins and slinging stones on the run. Many Bantu fell. The men continued the charge, their shields locked, and their spears jutting like the horns of a charging bull. The main force smashed into the ranks of the Bantu, whilst a small group surrounded Borach and protected him with a circular shield wall from the chaos, lest his body be trampled or pierced through by a vengeful stroke.

"He's alive, but barely," Galin shouted as he picked up *Havwitha,* the legion's Arkith.

Shouts and curses accompanied the clatter of the Bantu weapons on the legion's shields. The spears thrust forward piercing Bantu armour and flesh. When the spears were broken or stuck in a foe, swords were drawn and used with equally deadly effect. Some of the Bantu, by sheer brute force and the ferocity of their attack and strength of numbers, managed to force several wedges in between the front rank of the legion. The shield wall soon broke, and the battle became more chaotic, and a series of mini-battles in the bigger one.

Marki found himself cut off from the main ranks, he and just several other legionnaires. As if guided by a single hand, the legionnaires with him jabbed forth their sword as one, and several Bantu fell. Marki swung *Old Trusty* at the Bantu straight in front of him and caught him in the left side of his chest. The beast crashed to the floor with a grunt as a shower of blood spurted up from the wound.

Another Bantu swung his hammer at Marki; he ducked, but could not avoid the steel clod foot that smashed into his face. He lost his balance and crashed to the floor, his plumed helmet moving out of place to block his vision, plunging the fight into sheer blackness. He desperately wrenched at the leather chin strap, tearing it loose in time to see one of the legionnaires move himself between him and the Bantu. The man dropped to his knees his head crushed by the hammer blow of the Bantu.

Marki did not hesitate, still lying on the ground he swung *Old Trusty* cutting off both the feet of the Bantu at the ankles. The beast fell to the floor screaming in rage and agony. Another legionnaire finished him off with a sword thrust to the neck. The helmet crest of a legionnaire appeared over Marki, he grabbed the proffered hand and allowed himself to be dragged to his feet. He spat out a mouthful of blood and tested his teeth with a probing finger. He winced as several wobbled at his prodding.

The battle was short and brutal. The Hammer Knights were overwhelmed and killed by the Bantu; the legion, the most effective killing machine and army that Marki knew of, soon slaughtered most of the Bantu. The few that remained fought to the death, until the last one fell to the dusty ground screaming out its fury at defeat. The only survivor from their side, was the ambassador named Grixen, who was spurring his horse and riding at full flight back towards Aleskian. Even Prince Regineo lay dead on the ground, his decapitated head stared back at Marki who, in rage at the senseless killing of Yianna and Borach's children, kicked it like a ball. High into the air it flew, and landed, bouncing several times with sickening thuds.

The Third Legion had also suffered heavy losses, time enough to count exactly how many later, but Marki's quick scan of the battlefield estimated that about fifty had been lost in the exchange. Roughly seven hundred and fifty remained. There was no time to stand and ponder, or wait for more enemies to arrive. The Hammer Knights had retaken the Aleskian Gate, and the sounds of the heavy mechanisms moving boomed across the plain. The gate was being opened, again, and the first of a new wave of Bantu were already beginning to enter the Everglow. "To the Dune Fort," he bellowed, as he grabbed at the reins of a passing horse, until recently ridden by a Hammer Knight.

"Torach, press ahead and open the entrance." Marki handed the reins of the horse to Torach, who mounted and galloped off towards the fort. Marki grabbed the reins of another horse and mounted it.

Picking up their wounded comrades, leaving the dead, the legion reformed and headed towards the Dune Fort at a swift jogging pace. This time they kept their formation loosely and imperfectly, but still ready to fight any foe that might confront them, but the way to the fort was clear.

Marki rode over to a group of legionnaires who were carrying Borach. "Is he dead?" he asked them desperately, as he looked at his friends now purple coloured face.

One of them, running alongside the carriers, answered. "He lives. I have given him Easewood, and he now breathes, but that was a dark and mischievous blade that cut him; there is a malignancy and curse about the wounds, which of themselves are grievous. He needs the aid of a skilled healer if he is to survive, of which I am, but we cannot stop to render that which he needs, lest we be overcome by more foes."

"Make haste to the Dune Fort, we can tend to him there," Marki ordered.

"I found this on the battlefield," the man said, as he cautiously handed Marki a foul blade.

Marki recognised it; it was *Ungweethon,* the blade of Garuk. "I will not touch it," Marki wailed.

Galin, who had also found a horse, caught up. He had sheathed *Havwitha*, and said to the man, "I will take charge of it, for now. It is too foul a blade to fall into the wrong hands."

In the manner one might hand over a deadly toxin, the surgeon passed *Ungweethon* to Galin."

"You need to get that blade far away from Lord Borach; if these wounds kill him when it is near, that gem will suck his soul into it and he dies the *Final-death*," the surgeon shouted breathlessly as they continued at pace towards the Dune Fort.

"What should I do with it?" Galin asked Marki. "If we cannot leave it behind, nor take it with us, what should be done?"

Marki thought for a moment. "The only choice we have, is to send it to the Tarath Guëan, the Grey-Council. One of them came to us, a decade or so ago, what was his name?" Marki scratched his head thoughtfully for a moment and then declared. "Armun, Master Armun he called himself. I do not know what he and Lord Borach discussed, but he might come to our aid or they might send another of their own to assist us at this time of need."

Galin acknowledged with a nod. "I agree we should send it to them, but I do not think they will send any of their number to help us." He turned to one of the legion's Fell-blood scouts. He asked the man a question. "Alwith, do you know the way to High Blackbarrow?"

The man wavered a moment, then said, "I studied the old maps, as all scouts do, but I have never been there, none of us have. It is in the Forbidden Lands." He paused thoughtfully for a moment, and then added, "But I am sure I can find the way. For Lord Borach, I will find the way!"

Galin handed the man *Ungweethon.* He took the sword warily, holding it by the pommel as though it were a poisonous snake that might rise up at any second.

"It is a dangerous journey. The Tarath Guëan might kill you if they believe you have entered their domain with no good reason, but I believe taking them this blade will be reason enough for them to spare you."

A worried look crossed Alwith's face, but was then replaced by a determined scowl. "I accept the risk involved."

"Good," Galin growled. "When we leave Aleskian, you are to take this foul blade with all haste, to the Grey Council who dwell at High Blackbarrow; ask for Master Armun. Tell him, and them, it has inflicted Lord Borach with a mortal wound, which may still kill him yet. They might know what to do with it and send us assistance."

Alwith the legionnaire nodded, and carefully sheathed *Ungweethon* in his own scabbard. "Would it not be better to take Lord Borach directly to them?"

"Fool," Marki growled. "Since the civil war ended, Pure-bloods are not allowed to approach or enter High Blackbarrow; the treaty states the punishment of *Final-death* will meet those who try. The Tarath Guëan will kill Lord Borach if we try to take him there."

*       *       *

The legion made fast progress to the fort. Its walls were crumbled and cracked and there were no gates on the long-abandoned entrance. Torach had raced ahead on horse and had opened the secret tunnel that led under the city, and outside it, to the small military supply camp called Ash Gonath. The entrance to the tunnel was concealed behind some bush and bracken, which Torach had already hacked away. Torches, oil and flints to light them were ready in barrels just inside the entrance, and he had already lit some and was handing them out to the men as well as bellowing at any legionnaire hesitant to enter.

"We are just leaving the dead to resurrect here?" one of them asked as he passed the entrance.

"We have little choice at the moment," Torach replied as he shoved the man through the entrance. "We cannot lay siege to the city."

There was no time for delay, the entrance was only wide enough for them to enter two at a time. The same runes that had opened it would be used to close it, and it would take some time for all the men to enter.

Alwith was the next to enter. Torach gave him some brief instructions how to exit the tunnel by the door at Ash Gonath. Shedding his armour to un-hinder himself, taking a torch to light the way, he sped down it with all haste, attempting to put as much distance between Borach and *Ungweethon* as possible.

Marki jumped off his horse and gave the reins to a soldier with orders to lead the animal through the tunnel. He then shouted after Alwith. "Flee Alwith, flee with as much haste as your strength allows. To the Tarath Guëan at High Blackbarrow!" He watched Alwith go, and when he had disappeared from sight, and even the light of the torch was swallowed by the darkness of the tunnel, he turned his attention to the other immediate issues at hand. He had traversed the secret tunnel many times during his one hundred and seven years with the Third Legion, but each time had just been for a training exercise or to inspect it. This was the first time he had to use it to escape. Nobody could remember when it was built or by whom, and Borach had jealously guarded its secret revealing it to only his most trusted friends and commanders.

Borach's was brought into the tunnel, and the surgeon and his medics began to work on him furiously. Marki winced when he heard him say to those assisting him, "I need to amputate the arm, but will try to save the legs. He has wounds on them both and Fangwoe is in his blood."

The surgeon looked at some men and ordered, "Give me your phials of Easewood, now," at which the men promptly obeyed.

There was nothing Marki could do for Borach, and he did not want to hinder the progress of the surgeon, so he ran up to Torach, grabbed a torch and ordered Galin, and several men to follow him.

"I'm going to see if by any whisker of a hope there might be some trace of Yianna and the bairns back at the house, and we were tricked," he said to Torach. "And I'll not leave *Old Nanna* behind. Once you make Ash Gonath, if I have not caught up, don't wait for me, take whatever supplies you can and head south. I'll catch up with you if I am still alive. Make sure you close this entrance when the last of the men are safely inside."

Torach nodded.

Marki pushed past some legionnaires and entered the tunnel, followed by those he had ordered to follow. Inside the tunnel it was wide enough for the men to walk several abreast. He and his companions raced past the other soldiers, bellowing orders to clear the way, which they did. The tunnel was dark, damp, musty and quite humid within. By the time he and the others had raced about a mile into it, they had all built up a sweat and their breathing had become more laboured. He stopped when he came to what looked like common graffiti on a wall.

"Here it is," he said as he pushed several slabs of stone on the tunnel wall, until one of them moved. He drew it out, and behind it was a wooden lever which he pulled. A door within the wall opened with a loud grating sound. He passed through it and beckoned for the others to quickly follow. Once they were all inside, he pulled out another brick from the wall, and pulled another lever that had been hidden behind it. The door shut, and Marki replaced the brick.

"Remember lads, this is also the way out if this all goes wrong," he said, "but whatever you do, close it behind you when you re-enter the tunnel, or our way of escape will be discovered."

Borach's mansion was in Shreenan's Holdfast, a massive square fortress that nestled in the heart of the Griffin Keep behind walls twelve feet thick and surrounded by a moat filled with iron spikes. It was a castle within a castle. Marki and the men were inside a large wine cellar in the holdfast. Numerous racks and shelves contained bottles of wine of all shapes and sizes, some of which were dusty and had not been touched for a long time. Barrels of ale, brandy and vats of whisky were littered about. As Marki swung the torch in a semi-circle in front of him, he briefly remembered the many times over the long years he and Borach had come down here during some feast to select a rare vintage or to choose a barrel of fine brandy for the servants to carry to the feasting hall.

This was not the time for any nostalgia or sentimental reflection, however, so he quickly made his way through the maze of racks and barrels until he found the stairs that led out of the cellar to the kitchen in Borach's mansion. He opened the door carefully, peering inside. He cried out when he saw that all of the staff were lying dead on the floor in pools of their own blood. He ran into the kitchen and shook his head as he looked at a particularly plump woman whose throat had been cut from ear to ear.

"Oh *Nanna*," he said with grief as he looked upon his favourite Davari cook. She had been with Borach's family ever since she had been brought to Aleskian as a young slave girl some sixty years ago. Marki remembered the first time he had met her in the very same kitchen. Her name was Yinki and she had not then acquired the nickname *Nanna*. It had been some Aeldar feast and Seers from Kappia had come as special guests. Borach had asked Marki to go to the cellar and choose some bottles of the rarest and finest vintages from the vineyards of the Crumbian Valley for the guests, as they had finished the ones already out. This was Borach's code to say to him, '*These guests don't know their wines so give them something decent, not the cheapest, but certainly not the rarest or best.*' It had been on such a trip to the cellar, he had passed through the kitchen, when he had seen *Nanna* for the first time. She had been seven years old. It was the first time she had seen a dwarf, and on noticing the young girl's fear, he had pulled a funny face and pretended to trip over which had made her back away a bit but nervously laugh. He then did a handstand, not a good idea with all the ale he had consumed that evening, and he had crashed into a table and fell on the floor, before vaulting backwards onto his legs, losing balance and knocking over another small table with a dish of rare treats on it.

The head cook at that time, a fierce old Davari woman, had chased him out of the kitchen with a rolling pin cursing the drunken dwarf for his rowdy behaviour. Pulling silly faces at Yinki who he later nicknamed *Nanna* had become his thing, and it had not been long before she was no longer afraid of him during future encounters in the house. When she had grown into an adult, they had become good friends. He had often spent many an hour off duty, just sitting in the kitchen talking to *Nanna* about anything and everything, whilst being treated to the delicious treats she often prepared for him, and the rare ales she collected from the brewery which she knew were his favourites.

"Somebody's going to pay for this, I swear it by Balagrim's beard," he said with half choked tears as he walked past her corpse, regretting that there was not time to stop and give her a decent burial. "Forgive me *Nanna*, I've not the time to bury you lass," he said as he took a kitchen towel, stooped over her and placed it respectfully over her body. "I swear, somebody will pay. I will write this deed in my *Book of Grudges*," he vowed through gritted teeth.

The house was well lit so Marki placed the torch he carried into a sconce on the wall, and then he and the men made their way out of the kitchen and up the winding stone stairs that led to the different levels of the house. They made their way straight to the great hall, which had stairs that led to the upper storey of the main house. As they entered the hall, Marki's skin crawled. All of the marble busts of Borach's family and ancestors, as well as all of the previous Lords of Aleskian before him that lined it, were smashed or knocked off of their pedestals. He saw the familiar mural on the far wall. It depicted Borach, with Marki beside him, standing at the gates of Felucia in Baothein lands, with several of the legions behind them. It had been a hard-won battle and the most famous victory during the Empire's brutal civil war. The city, which until it had fallen, had been hailed by the Baothein as the '*Defender of the West*.' It was still under Kappian control to this day, and the strategic capture of the Great Obelisk Morthan, had helped end the war, as the Baothein had retreated back to the Stallis Mountain range. The mural had been defaced with faeces and the word, *Betrayers!* was written crudely across it.

"What in Balagrim's name went on here?" Marki asked.

Galin gasped, and furiously said, "It's sacrilege."

All of them had been a part of that most famous of battles. To make things worse, the gilded griffin seat where Borach and generations of his family before him had ruled Aleskian in the name of the Empress had been smashed and overturned.

Marki and the others crept stealthily down the length of the hall to the stairs that led to the upper levels of the holdfast where Borach's personal apartments were, and they climbed them swiftly but carefully, listening out for signs of the intruders who had caused the death and carnage. As they entered the main corridor of the upper level, they did not see the two crossbowmen standing behind a patterned paper screen guarding the main living room. They fired the loaded bolts as soon as Marki and the others entered the corridor. Two of the legionnaires were hit. One of them fell to the floor instantly dead, the bolt hitting him in the neck. The other staggered backwards snapping the shaft of the bolt in his clumsy and panicked attempt to pull it free before he fell to the ground.

With a great burst of speed, Marki ran the length of the corridor shouting, "The Iron life, the Iron life!" the ancient battle cry of the Iron Mountains. He made short work of the first crossbowman when he reached him, kicking down the paper screen and slaying him as he was still trying to reload. He crashed the end of *Old Trusty* into the face of the other, causing him to drop his crossbow and fall to the floor in a shower of blood that poured from his nose. He grabbed the man, who looked up at the fierce dwarf, with defiance. The man, a Pure-blood, was not a guard from the holdfast, or Marki would have recognised him. He was also not dressed in the uniform of the Sixth Legion, but he did wear their emblem, crudely stitched to his raiment. The Sixth were the only legion to use crossbows. All the other legions used either big yew longbows, double curved horn and sinew bows, or the great heartwood bows, each of which had their different uses and required a different skill set, which all of the highly trained archers of the legions had acquired.

"Are you a man of the Sixth?" Marki asked him.

"It is none of your business, dwarf. Slay me, I have many ailments in this body and will be glad to be rid of it. I will resurrect soon enough, with all of the dead from your legion."

"You won't resurrect if I slay you with this," Galin warned, as he unsheathed *Havwitha*. The midnight blue Arzak began to glow, and the runes shimmered in anticipation. "This is an Arkith!"

"A *soul-eater*!" the man said, his defiance turning to terror. "Give me your word you'll not slay me with that; I will answer your questions, I swear it," he whimpered.

"You have my word," Marki said, as Galin pressed the tip of the sword to the man's neck. "Now talk, who are you and what was your business here?"

"I am a sell-sword, come up from Kappia with my company."

*A Mercenary, that figures.* "Who pays your coin?" Marki asked.

"The High Quaester, Mazdek."

*I knew it.* "Why did you come to this house?"

"Lord Borach's wife and children, they were intercepted leaving the city, but managed to escape and return here. We were sent to capture them. They were taken away. Me and about twelve others were ordered to stay here and guard the house, lest any others return, like you."

"The kitchen staff, it was you who killed them?" Marki asked, his anger rising.

"Not me, some of the boys had a bit of fun here in the house, that was all. I had nothing to do with killing anyone here."

"You gave him your word not to kill him with this blade," Galin said, as he pointed to the two legionnaires, one of whom lay dead, and the other slowly dying, as a result of the crossbow bolts. "I did not give him mine."

Marki shook his head. "Put the blade away, any Arkith is a foul thing and should not be wielded unless choice is stripped from us." Galin reluctantly sheathed the blade, as, with a swipe of *Old Trusty*, Marki removed the man's head in one blow. The head clattered down the corridor and the corpse collapsed in a spurt of blood. "I gave him the mercy of a resurrection," he snarled. He spat on the two corpses as he opened the door to the main bedroom.

Helped by others, the wounded soldier was dragged into the main living room, the broken shaft of the crossbow bolt still protruding from his chest. Blood seeped from the wound and flowed down the breastplate of his armour.

Marki took a crock of water from a nearby table and poured some for the soldier into a glass. He put the glass to the man's lips; he drank gladly.

"I am sorry I failed you, legionnaire," he said. "You are going to resurrect in the Obelisk of this city, to what fate, I know not, for it is in the hands of our enemies."

The man reached out his hand, Marki took it and squeezed it.

"We are brothers-in-arms," the man whispered faintly, after which the light went from his eyes and his body slumped in death.

One of the men who had carried the mortally wounded comrade into the main room, spoke with fear, panic in his voice.

"This is a cruel death and a worse fate awaits him. The Aleskian Gate is opened again, the Bantu horde is flooding through it and will surely overrun the city. It is a cruel fate to resurrect in their midst!"

Another legionnaire said, "We are trapped; he will resurrect at Obelisk Matrath, here in Aleskian, tomorrow, and be in the hands of our enemies, be they Bantu or Hammer Knight. What endless tortures await him now? How many deaths will he endure only to rise at the same Obelisk to face the same horrors time and time again?"

Yet another soldier in the room spoke. "The prophecies were right; the gift has now become our curse. Blessed are they who do not share our Pure-blood and only face one death."

"Quiet!" Marki said with such force that all the men in the room took note. "We will not forget the betrayal of this day, yet I still do not know how or why it has come about. We need to make our way to the Rookery and the High Nest, but not before we search this house, lest there be any I know, suffering at the hands of mercenary scum. To hell with creeping about, we've not the time." "Galin, take Monso and Rovebin and search this floor. The rest, follow me."

Marki's rage was so great, he did not care who heard him as he charged through the house. In fact, he wanted to come across anyone who might oppose him so he could use *Old Trusty* to vent his fury. He shouted and swore nastily as he ran from room to room in the house. As well as Borach's family home, it had also been his home for nigh on a century, ever since he had had left the barracks and moved into one of the guest rooms, which he had never left.

"Yianna! Yianna!" he shouted, and then the names of some of the servants whose bodies he had not seen in the kitchen. "Avrilain! Mosil! Hildari!" No answer. He continued shouting out the names as he rushed from room to room, frantically searching and looking, but not finding those he was looking for.

"They're not here Marki," Galin said when they eventually both came to the main hallway again. "Twice we've been through here. Nobody is here, but I found this, in Borach's quarters – the door was open." He held out a note. Marki snatched it off of him.

"It's the writing of Yianna, I recognise the style from the notes she used to send me, when she would rebuke me for keeping Borach up for whole nights of drinking," he said as he read aloud the words on the vellum paper.

*'My husband, I do not have much time. Hammer Knights attacked us as we left the city. Our bodyguard were mostly slain, but a few of them managed to bring us back here, but mercenaries are ransacking the mansion. We have locked ourselves in our quarters. We are trapped, and hope to remain hidden until we can try to make it to the tunnel and flee to Ash Gonath. Your love, Yianna.'*

Marki crumpled the note and threw it to the floor in frustration. A tiny glimmer of hope rose within him. "She was trying to get to one of the secret escape tunnels," he said.

"I checked the one in the west wing," Galin said glumly. "There were no tracks in the dust, nobody has used it recently. We're on a fool's errand here and wasting valuable time; we saw them in the catapults."

*He's right, but I refuse to give up hope, yet. It could be possible the people in the catapults were not Yianna and the bairns.* "There is another entrance to the tunnel, let us check there before we give up hope." He ran into the dining room, up the stairs into Borach's office, whilst

207

Galin and the others followed. The door had been smashed down, and there were signs of a struggle in the room; furniture was knocked over, but there were no bodies.

From the corner of his eye, on the floor, partially hidden and only just poking out from under the edge of a chest-of-drawers, Marki noticed something glitter. He bent down, and fished it out with his finger. He immediately recognised it – it was Yianna's locket. It must have fell under there, pulled loose from the chain in a struggle in a struggle. *Oh no.* He picked it up and put it in his pocket. *If she was hindered here, it might be possible she and the children still made it.* It only took him a moment to find the hidden lever cleverly camouflaged on the wall. He pulled it. With a grating noise, a door opened next to the fireplace. Taking a candle from a nearby table, he lit it with a match, and took a step into the passage that had been revealed. The dust on the floor of the passage was undisturbed. He swore and muttered angrily under his breath and threw the candle into the passage in a rage. It went out as it clattered and rolled along the floor.

*It is Yianna's locket, that was her chain Shinther had.* "They were so close, but they didn't make it," he muttered. "They were so near to escaping, but they didn't make it."

Galin did not look him in the eye but said with uncharacteristic softness in his voice, "We have other business to attend too, we should leave."

Marki knew it was time to face facts. Yianna and the children had not escaped and managed to get to Estalda. They had been caught right there, in that room, and had been taken and hurtled over the wall, by the catapults, to their *Final-death.* There would be time for him to mourn them later. The soldier in him took over. "One more thing I need," he said as he left the office, and followed by the others went to his own quarters. On the table next to his bed, lay his personal *Book of Grudges.* "It has been many a year since I have made an entry into this, but these pages will soon be pretty full again," he snarled as he snatched the book and put it in a knapsack which he strapped over his shoulders. "To the Rookery, we need to get word out," he said.

It took Marki and the others about ten minutes to make their way from the house to the Rookery, which was on top of a large tower that was a part of the main keep. To get to it they had to pass the Chapel of Rest. As they ran past, Marki stopped, opened the door and peeked inside. The seven Seers of the Third Legion had all taken their lives the night before, ordered by Kappia on some mission into the Deadlands. Their bodies were all lain out on the stone slabs, dressed in black robes and golden meshed masks. It was nothing unusual for Seers to be sent on missions into the Deadlands, especially whilst garrisoned in Aleskian. The only time they usually travelled with the legion was if it left the city. The Seers, although oath-bound legionnaires, were loyal to the *Aeldar Faith.* He wondered what orders they had been given, and hoped they would be able to assist the men who had just died in battle.

Marki closed the door, and caught up with the others. They were exhausted by the time they reached the tower that led to the Rookery. The tower was dark and looked deserted. The winding stairs echoed with their bootsteps as they ran up them, and, littered on the stairway, they soon came across the dead bodies of some men of the Third, Hammer Knights and also some mercenaries.

"The blood on the stones is dry, this battle took place earlier in the day," Galin observed as he bent and wiped some blood with his finger, which he then smelled.

"You have your telescope?" he asked Galin, who fumbled in his knapsack and handed over the requested item.

It clicked several times as Marki opened it fully and peered through the nearest glassless window. He gazed across the city, over the plain to the distant gate. The Aleskian Gate was now fully open again, and he could see more of the Bantu horde flooding onto the plain. Even worse, the Griffin Gate had also been opened, and some Bantu were already passing through it into Aleskian itself.

"Balagrim's curses," he muttered in horror, as he set his ear to the wind to listen to the sounds coming from the city, beyond the wall of the mansion and keep. Instead of the music and song that usually faintly spilled from some distant tavern, there were sounds of screaming and panic. In the distance he could hear the noise of the Bantu horde roaring and shouting, and the clamour of battle. He could see that those who had spilled from the gate onto the plain were clearly confused that the Third Legion had disappeared from sight. Marki felt relieved that there was no way they could discover or open the tunnel, whose secret was known only to a few.

The Hammer Knights had clearly been betrayed themselves by the Bantu, and he could see some fighting taking place in the city between them and the Bantu. *Who opened the Griffin Gate then?* It was a question that bothered him, but there was no time to ponder any of the mysteries of the day; he had to get word out of the betrayal, tell of the treachery and deceit behind the events that had taken place that day.

"We must hasten," he said; he closed the telescope and handed it back to Galin, and they all climbed the rest of the stairs and left the tower through an upper door and made haste along the parapet to the Rookery. He looked down at the bridge which guarded the keep. It was strewn with the bodies of the guards. A small battle had taken place, and it looked like the keep's guard had been taken by surprise. They certainly had not expected an attack or they would have lifted the bridge.

"Stang? Stang!" Marki shouted as he entered the Rookery, which, like the rest of the holdfast, was abandoned. The loremaster was nowhere to be found. In Stang's study, his ointments and potions were stacked neatly on shelves fixed between large bookcases filled with scrolls and leather-bound books. Marki noticed the familiar phials of the antidote, Easewood, which counteracted the poison that was often coated onto the Bantu blades of those with high rank. The legion, as was standard practice, had all been issued with a phial of it before leaving for the gate. There were only a few of the precious phials left.

"Grab them," Marki said to Galin. The antidote, named Easewood, was the extract of a tiny plant that grew only in a marsh along the eastern part of the River Erin. *Such a small thing to hold the power of life and death.* The leaves had to be aged and washed and then soaked in a sugar water, before a drop of the very rare and expensive milathran was added. The process was slow and difficult, the ingredients expensive and hard to get hold of, so much so that only traders with an imperial license could deal in milathran which was the hardest ingredient to acquire of all, as the only resources of it that were known, were in the harsh Chatti lands far to the west or on an island near the dreaded Isle of Grona. Only the most skilled loremasters trained in alchemy could successfully produce Easewood which made them very valued members of any legion. It was fortunate for the legions that the deadliest poison laced on a Bantu blade, which the legions called Fangwoe, was also just as difficult to produce, so it was mostly only their high ranks like Garuk who dipped their blades in it. The poison would make the muscles in the throat of a man close ever tighter than any fist, shutting off his windpipe. A victim's face turned purple as they died.

Easewood did not always prevent death, which was inevitable once Fangwoe was in a victim's body, but it could prolong it for long periods. Depending on the nature of the wound, when Easewood was applied, a good surgeon could prolong death if a wounded person was in dangerous territory without a safe Obelisk for them to resurrect at. Some surgeons had kept poisoned victims alive for months, applying just the right amount of Easewood when needed. Marki hoped to Balagrim that the surgeon and his assistants,

209

who even now would still be working on and monitoring Borach, would ply their craft as skilfully as they had ever done.

Galin grabbed a large satchel lying on a table, and used a small step-ladder to reach the shelves. He took all of the bottles of Easewood, and placed them in the satchel, and took several other potions, tins and boxes as well, before swinging the satchel over his shoulder and descending the ladder. Whilst his cousin was doing that, Marki absent-mindedly thumbed through the pages of a scholar's book lying randomly on a table, and came upon a page with the detailed drawing of an Obelisk upon it. Not even knowing why, he tore the page from the book, folded it and put it in the small pouch hanging from his belt.

The door to the Rookery, which adjoined the loremaster's study, was stuck fast, so Marki had to put his shoulder to it to open it. He remembered that Stang had often complained that the door got stuck and he could never get a carpenter to come and fix it. The ravens squawked and cawed furiously as Marki fell into the room followed by his companions. "Everyone, write as many messages as you can and send it with a bird."

"What do we write?" one of the legionnaires asked.

"Oh, I don't know, why not wish them a happy Luppoor?" he answered sarcastically, and then, "what do you think man? Write that - *Lord Borach and the Third Legion were betrayed at Aleskian by the Hammer Knights, and handed over to Bantu foes, but we escaped and fled.*"

Marki looked around at the hundreds of cages and birds, and found the cages of the ones trained to take messages to Kara Duram. He and his comrades wasted no time. They scribbled several messages down on the paper using the feathered quills on a large desk. They took ravens out of the cages marked Kara Duram, folded the notes neatly, put them in the small pouches, and attached them to the bird's feet. Walking out onto the battlement, they let the first one go. Somebody, from a place unseen, must have spotted them for they heard distant shouting. The raven took flight, and got about two hundred yards before an arrow took it down. They released the remainder of the birds they were holding, but did not have the time to check if they made it or not, as they heard shouts of, "They're in the Rookery." An arrow, shot from an unseen assailant, thudded into the wooden door frame near Marki's head.

"That'll have to do boys, to the High Nest."

Bounding back along the parapet to the tower, and then down the stairs, they made their way back to another parapet, and headed to the tower that led to the High Nest. They quickly ascended the stairs, ran along the battlement, and reached the door of the High Nest, also known as the Griffin's Roost. As he ran up the thirty-nine steps of the nest, in between panting for breath, Marki hoped that maybe some of the ravens might have made it through. The message sent was short, but he hoped it would make some of the generals at Kara Duram ask some questions at the very least, when news of what had happened at Aleskian started to filter through.

As he climbed, Marki remembered past ascents, especially the first time when he had climbed those very stairs with Borach and Meron so long ago. The griffins had been an awe-inspiring sight for him to see, for the very first time, and he had never quite lost his awe or fear of them, nor his mistrust.

When he reached the top, the view was just as intoxicating as ever, but much more disturbing. Marki could see that the Great Plain of Aleskian was now almost completely filled with Bantu, so vast was their number. He could also see that the fighting taking place in the city streets, was not going the way of the Hammer Knights - they were losing badly. He wanted to gloat, to shout and cheer the fact the those who had betrayed them, had been turned on by the very ones they had allowed through the gate, but he had neither time nor will for it, and at that moment he was not sure if it was the Bantu or the knights that he despised the most. So much of his life had been spent in the service to this city and guarding it from the Bantu, it made him sick to see his loathed enemy, now rampaging through its streets, but the knights were the ones who had let them in. *This just doesn't make any sense.*

In the distance, he saw that some of the great towers of Aleskian were now fully ablaze. *Enough sightseeing. We must find out what has happened to the griffins and their riders, and why they did not help us in the battle? I know each and every one of those riders by name, they would never betray us.*

Marki started to fear the worse when they found the door to the entrance of the High Nest open, and banging in the wind. As they approached, the fact that inside, instead of the click and cawing or even the screeching of the occasional griffin, there was nothing but silence, was telling. His fears were confirmed when he entered. Hanging from the rafters by ropes, swinging in the breeze that came through the open door and from the exposed take off area, the twenty griffin riders of the Third Legion who had remained behind to tend their sick griffins, had all been hanged. There was no sign of resistance, so whoever had executed them, had been trusted and had taken them by surprise. The cages of the griffins were all quiet, the occupants within slain.

Marki heard whimpering in the corner. It was Meron, the legion's Griffin Master. "No! No!" he wailed softly and pitifully as he stared at the dead griffins in the cages.

"What happened here?" Marki asked him.

Meron, a Pure-blood, stood to his feet. He was a man of short stature and balding head. "I went to the apothecary to get some more medicine for my babies," he said as he looked woefully at the griffins, "for even those supposed to fly out today had gone down with a strange illness. A rumour spread through the city that the Aleskian Gate had been opened, and what was left of the legions were attacked. Prince Regineo entered the city with a large contingent of knights and mercenaries. When he left the city with about two hundred of them, the mercenaries and knights began ransacking Aleskian. By the time I had returned here, my babies were all dead." He sobbed. "I should have been here with my babies," he cried, as he fell to his knees next to a cage.

Marki looked inside the cage. A large male griffin lay dead on the floor; it had several large spears protruding from its body. The head was crushed, its tongue lolled lifelessly from its beak. He knew the name and title of the beast, Yarrion the Great. He had been a famed and formidable male griffin that was father to most of the other males, but not the breeding females. The once magnificent beast, had the body, tail, and back legs of a lion; the head and wings of an eagle; and an eagle's talons as its front feet. Its body was red in colour, the feathers on its breast a bright golden hue, as was its head, though its neck was surrounded by orange feathers it wore like a band around it.

Tears rolled down Meron's face at the sight, and he wailed, a long, desperate, painful cry. Marki felt a tear well up in his own. He ran from cage to cage, looking inside. Most of them were empty for most of the healthy griffins had been flown to Kara Duram, but those left behind, about twenty in number, were all dead. In each cage a griffin was slain in similar fashion to Yarrion.

Marki felt for Meron. He had bred those griffins for thousands of years, over many lifetimes. He had carefully guarded the bloodline and managed it down the long centuries. But they had all suffered loss that day, and Marki thought now was not the time to mourn. "Come, friend," he said to Meron. In fact, he and Meron disliked each other intently, and often had bitter arguments, but now was not the time for any pettiness, so Marki put a comforting hand on Meron's shoulder. "Find your strength,

211

we must get back to the legion. All we have found here is more signs of treachery and betrayal."

A voice behind them spoke. "Commander Thaos of the Hammer Knights, was ordered by Shinther to commit this deed."

Due to their haste and grief, Marki and the others were taken by surprise as a dozen or so legionnaires from the Sixth Legion, entered the High Nest, some with bows, the double curved horn and sinew ones favoured for short distant firing. The bows were aimed at Marki and his men. Instinctively, Marki drew and raised *Old Trusty*, readying it in an instant as his comrades drew their swords.

"Stand down, stand down," a large man said as he entered the High Nest. Marki recognised the large and powerful frame of Captain Stamis of the Sixth Legion. He and Stamis had never gotten on, after some tavern brawl many years ago when Stamis had accused Marki of cheating at the card game, Harendale. In most matters Marki was as honest as the day was old, but he did sometimes indulge in a bit of sleight of hand if he wanted to win a particular bet, and Stamis' accusation did have some merit that day, but Marki still fought him in a fist fight when called out over it. He had knocked the man out. Meron and Stamis however, were both cousins and good friends, and that had been the beginning of his feud with them both. Stamis took his helm off, stroked his red beard and looked at Meron. "Come with me, cousin," he said, and then, looking at Marki added, "Put that axe on the floor shorty. I will take you to Commander Thaos."

"I'd rather fricking stick this axe up your hole than be putting it on the floor you red bearded old krunge," Marki said with a snarl that showed his recently chipped and broken teeth.

Stamis looked at one of the bowmen and said, "I swear by Aspess' teats that if this stinking dwarf utters one more word, I'll have your balls for breakfast if you don't skewer him with that arrow right where he stands."

"So be it," Marki said as he tensed up to charge, ready to utter his war cry and lunge at the men. He knew it was certain and instant death, for those bows could fire an arrow that would pierce his armour as though it were butter and each of the bowmen were poised, ready to release. But he had his story ready to tell the Dwarven Shield-Maidens, so they would allow him into the Feasting Halls of Balagrim. He was ready to die, right there, right then.

Galin drew *Havwitha*, "You'll die an unpleasant *Final-death* Stamis the moment after an arrow is released," he snarled.

*'Havwitha,'* Stamis said nervously as he involuntarily took a step back on seeing the Arkith; the bowmen also looked nervously at it, and one of them changed his target to Galin. The bowmen all tensed, pulled back the strings on their bows and nervously readied their aim.

Stang, the loremaster, who Marki had not noticed standing behind the bowmen, stepped forward. "Hold your peace," he said urgently, and then to all present, "all just hold your peace." He put a hand on the notched arrow of the nearest bowmen, and forcefully lowered it towards the ground. "There may be personal grievances some here have with each other, but they do not warrant these actions; we are not sworn enemies."

"That depends," Meron said, as he looked at Stamis. "Cousins we are, but I consider you a friend, nay, a brother. Swear to me you had nothing to do with the slaying of my babies, Stam. I beg of you?"

A puzzled frown quickly spread across Stamis' face, and then he noticed the dead griffins. He looked troubled as he took in the sight.

"Well, answer him, muffin head!" Marki said incredulously.

"Stamis had nothing to do with this," Stang said, answering for him.

The bitter tone on Stamis' voice was evident for all to hear. "I am disappointed you think so little of me cousin," he said to Meron, "but I put your rash words down to your grief and shock on discovering this deed. If an oath it takes, I swear to you, I had no knowledge of this deed until a few moments ago."

"The fault lies at the hand of Regineo, nobody else," Stang said. "Commander Thaos acted on the prince's instructions."

"How do you know this? Marki enquired.

"I was present when the order was given to slay these magnificent beasts, but I was detained attending to Regineo's medical needs. His hump had blistered and was oozing puss. I was commanded to attend to him last night, at his camp; he gave the order that the moment he entered the city on this day, Thaos was to take a contingent of Hammer Knights to slay the remaining griffins and their riders." Sadness swept across the face of Stang. "I had no way of sending any warning or message, for I was watched and kept under guard, until only an hour ago when the city erupted into chaos."

"I fear that Stang speaks true," Stamis said gravely.

"Why is there fighting in the city?" Marki impatiently asked him.

"You know, it is against the law for a prince of the realm to enter Aleskian with more than just a bodyguard in attendance, when the Lord of Aleskian is present; even an *Ivanar* will not break such a code. Regineo waited until Lord Borach had left the city by the Griffin Gate; I was tasked with then allowing him into Aleskian and attending him." Stamis sighed wearily. "He had a foul Bantu Ambassador with him, one they call Grixen. When the Battle of the Plain had begun, and lost by the Bantu, Grixen advised that Regineo only take a small force onto the plain lest the Bantu force thought they were being tricked and surrounded." He paused, and laughed disbelievingly. "When Regineo was slain, and the gate opened, the mercenary captains feared they would be slaughtered. They ordered the city to be sacked, after which they would leave. Thaos tried to stop them, and ordered his knights to attack the mercenaries. And now, the Bantu are also within the city and chaos has descended as every side attacks the other on sight."

"So, what are you doing here, at the High Nest?" Galin asked.

"One of my bowmen saw you at the Rookery, and then your flight here."

"You shot the ravens down?" Marki asked angrily.

"No," Stamis answered, "like you, we wanted to send message to Kara Duram.

"So why do you want to take us to Thaos?" Galin questioned.

Stamis looked uncomfortable when he answered. "I don't know the full ins and outs of it, only the part I was ordered to play. Lord Borach is charged with treason. It was said he conspired to hand Aleskian over to the Baothein Queen." He fidgeted on his feet uneasily. "We were told an alliance had been made with the Bantu, and that those of us left in the city, or at the forts, were to obey General Shinther without question." He sighed wearily. "Each legion was given specific orders, and none of us know what the others were ordered. We didn't know the Hammer Knights planned to open the Aleskian Gate."

Marki felt the rage bubble inside of him. Not only at the accusation that Borach was a traitor, but at the betrayal they were themselves victims of. He himself had doubted the nature of the orders the Third had received, as had Borach himself, but they could not question their legitimacy and that was the brilliance of the conspiracy. Like rats in a trap, they had walked right into it. *But why was the trap set in the first place?* Never, had he heard Borach, or any commander or captain of the Third Legion ever utter a single word against the Empress or the ruling powers in Kappia. They were nothing but loyal servants, and had always obeyed flawlessly and, until recently, without question any order they had been given. It was perhaps that sense of loyalty and commitment that helped him to understand the next words Stamis himself spoke.

"I am a servant of the Empire, as are all the men of the Sixth. We just did our duty, what we were told. Now, surrender and hand yourself over to me without resistance. Regineo and Shinther are dead; until they resurrect, Thaos is in charge. I will take you to him! It will do none of you any good to die here today."

"Balagrim's whiskers," Marki said exasperated. The Bantu are inside the Everglow, within this very city and are now slaying all they come across. You yourself have said you have seen this?"

A look of uncertainty swept over Stamis' face. It was clear to Marki that he was struggling with conflicting thoughts. As a loyal oath bound legionnaire, Stamis was duty bound to follow orders, but these orders were insane.

"I have my orders," Stamis stuttered.

"Then get some common-sense man. How many lifetimes do you need to earn an ounce of wit?" Marki asked with a growl. "Take another look at what is going on!"

Stamis took a few steps back, towards a window, not taking his eyes off Marki except when he briefly glanced at the city. His posture visibly deflated at the sight. He lowered his own sword.

Marki seized upon the opportunity. "Stamis, by Balagrim, whatever has gone on here today it is fuelled by madness. We are heading to Ash Gonath, where we can get supplies and try and figure out what is going on. Come with us, or at the least, let us go without a pointless fight."

Stamis still hesitated and looked at each of his own men around him. They all gave each other brief, anxious, puzzled and concerned looks, and some of them lowered their bows.

Meron interjected. "Stam, please, Marki is right. Battle madness is upon the Bantu. I will go with him to Ash Gonath, for as far as I know, the words spoken about Lord Borach are false; as Griffin Master of the High Nest, I have been in close counsel with him often, and not once has he ever spoken treasonously." With tears in his eyes, he pointed at the dead griffins in the cages and their riders swinging from the rafters. "Look cousin, look at what this Thaos has done!"

"Like us, Thaos was under orders from Prince Regineo; he acted for Kappia!" Stamis muttered uncertainly.

"Remember our first lifetime, when me and you played in here as boys, whilst my father tended the first Yarrion?" Meron asked passionately. He pleaded with Stamis. "Look! Weep, and question; I will go with the Third to Ash Gonath, and hope to hear news from Kara Duram to make sense of this. Come with us, or at the least, don't hinder us from leaving this doomed city."

Stamis looked around him, and grief spread across his face at the sight; from the High Nest, they could all see flames licking into the air. Aleskian was ablaze. He lowered his head and dropped to his knees in despair. His men looked at each other and the last of them lowered their bows.

Marki lowered *Old Trusty*, sheathed it across his back and walked over to Stamis, as did Meron. Even kneeling, Stamis was the same height as Marki. "For now, let us forget old squabbles, you and I," Marki said to him.

"You will never get outside the city; the gate to the Kappia Road is heavily guarded by Hammer Knights, if the Bantu have not already slain them," Stamis mumbled.

"We have another way out of the city," Marki replied glumly as Stamis took Meron's hand and was pulled to his feet. "This city is doomed. It is time we left."

214

# Chapter Seventeen: *Sasna & Gnarn*

*It is said that when Castle Greytears was built, each block of stone was baptised in sacrificial blood. It is a cursed place, and whilst it stands, it is a place where those who dwell within its walls, will only know suffering and see more bloodshed. I tell you, any who might conquer it, earn favour with the gods and men, and destroy it until not a stone remains upon a stone, so even a ruin no longer exists.*
**Segment from The Prophecy of Karthal.**

*The* door creaked as Sasna pressed her ear against it, listening intently. "Somebody's coming," she said to Gnarn when she heard keys unlocking a door and mumbled voices. Her breath quickened with anxious anticipation. "Get ready," she said, as she sat on the bare stone floor, replacing the iron collar around her neck but making sure it did not snap shut. Pain lanced through her shoulder as she adjusted the catch. The evening before, the physician had cured any infection, and stitched the wound, but it would still take a while to knit up and heal properly. Gnarn had unlocked the collar for her so she could sleep more comfortably.

Gnarn revolted Sasna; not only did he stink, he made her skin crawl, and every movement of his appeared to her as a grotesque twist of nature. But he was an essential ally in her desperate situation. They both readied themselves when they heard footsteps in the corridor outside and the voices of the physician and guard. Behind their backs, they concealed the cruel looking daggers they had found the night before when searching the Baron's room. The sound of keys jangling in the lock caused a bead of sweat to form on Sasna's forehead, time felt like it slowed. The lock sluggishly clicked; the door opened.

"Lady Sasna, I have come to bathe and balm the stitching, and change the dressing," the physician said as he entered the room. His tunic was a bright red, embroidered with a green symbol of two hands. He carried some bandages and ointments in small phials. He had been kind and sympathetic the evening before. Not only had he stitched and skilfully attended her wound and provided her with medicine that relieved the pain that allowed the swelling to go down, he had provided her with a plain gown that offered her some modesty, and he had treated her with respect. She was not looking forward to what had to be done; but he was still the Baron's man, and therefore one of her captors. He had politely ignored her pleas for help and therefore, despite his kind-heartedness, that made him complicit in her predicament. If it was his life or hers, she chose to take his. Besides, he was a Pure-blood so would resurrect, unlike the poor Fell-blood guard.

The guard, was the same one who had accompanied the physician the evening before; he was dressed in the same iron helmet and boiled leather armour. He had the keys to the room, her only method of escape. The key Gnarn had stolen only unlocked her chains.

How is your wound, Lady Sasna?" the physician asked as he entered the room. His medicinal satchel was slung over his shoulder, in his hands he carried a bowl of steaming water and some cloths. The guard followed him.

"It still troubles me, but less so," Sasna replied.

The physician placed the bowl of water and cloths on the ground, and leant close to Sasna so he could inspect the wound. "The infection was caught in time, or it could have been a lot worse. It is not good to let the water of the Erin into an open wound, or to wash it with that water un-boiled like you say your slave did, but, although crude and elementary, the other treatment he gave you slowed and counteracted it. You probably owe him your life."

Sasna gave no warning when she thrust the sharp point of the dagger into the physician's neck. She felt it grate upon the neck-bone and pushed it still harder, up to the hilt. Blood ran hot over her fingers, over her wrist, beneath the sleeves of her gown. The physician stared at her with horror.

Gnarn wasted no time either. The neck of the guard was the only part of him unprotected. He jumped onto the hapless man's back and stabbed at his neck furiously and repeatedly.

"I'm sorry," Sasna said to the physician as the blood gurgled from his open wound and the life flowed from him. "You will rise again, but I have only one life to live." She felt guiltier at the guard being killed, whom the physician had referred to the night before as Ole Jimsom by name. He had seemed amiable enough, and even seemed sympathetic towards Sasna when he had given her food and drink. Ole Jimson died with a look of horror on his face and fear in his eyes, as he clutched his neck, trying to hold back the blood that sprayed or oozed from the many puncture wounds Gnarn had inflicted with the deadly blade.

Sasna did not waste any time reflecting on the deed. *It was necessary*, she told herself. Even before Ole Jimson had breathed his last, she was removing his armour and underclothing, and donning it herself. It was a bad fit, and she would not pass any close inspection, but it might allow her to move about the castle unnoticed from a distance if she did not draw any attention to herself. She used the gown she had removed to wipe the blood from the armour, and then buckled the sword belt and sheath around her waist. Taking the keys off the dead twitching guard, she looked at Gnarn, took a deep breath and asked, "Ready?"

Gnarn nodded nervously.

There was no point trying to conceal the bodies, there was too much blood and it would take too long to clean it up. They left the room swiftly, closing and locking the door behind them, and made their way down the corridor until they came to another door. It only took a few attempts at trying different keys before she found the right one that unlocked the door to the spiral stairs leading down to the landings below. She closed and locked the door behind her. They wasted no time making their way down the stairs, and felt relieved when they did not have to waste time with the other doors to the landings below which were unlocked.

Sasna became disorientated, perhaps because of the nausea she felt resulting from the fear she fought every step of the way, and that was the reason that instead of finding herself as expected, in the feasting hall, she opened a door to a large cloistered hallway made of plain stone that led left and right and surrounded an open-air garden. The sound of distant voices and laughter, made her decide not to trace her steps back, so she continued through the door she had opened, closing it behind her and Gnarn, and then pressing her ear to the door to ensure the guards were not coming her way. They were not, the voices and laughter faded.

Sasna took some deep breaths of the fresh air, to quell the rising fear she felt within. She and Gnarn crept into the hallway and moved stealthily along it, crouching when they approached the first cloistered arch. Peering over the edge, she saw a square shaped grassed garden, surrounded on all four sides by the cloisters. There were a few coloured flowerbeds, bushes and marble benches placed neatly in ordered rows.

Looking at the sun in the eastern sky, despite it being a dark and grey day, she knew it was around mid-day. She had hoped that the physician would have come early in the morning, but he had not. She felt glad that as least she was able to get her bearings from the sun's position.

"Stay close and quiet Gnarn," she said, and then took a deep breath and climbed over the edge of the wall and dropped into the garden, where she crawled quickly over to a bush and scrambled beneath it. She winced as the action sent a wave of pain through her shoulder. A stitch had come undone, and she felt it begin to bleed. Gnarn quickly followed.

Sasna ignored the pain and studied her surroundings. Behind her, at the edges of the garden were the cloisters, and beyond that the main wall of the keep from where they had just come from. The cloisters to the left and the right each had a tiled roof, which joined onto an outer wall, on top of which a parapet ran parallel. Small, round, stone towers were situated at each end of the parapets. She figured the walls of those parapets would lead out of the keep and into the streets, but she would have to climb them, both ascending and descending, which would be a problem without a rope, and the aching wound in her shoulder. She judged the height from the parapet would be too far to jump from into the street, and to commit to a risky climb down a wall at mid-day into an open street, even if they found a rope, posed far too much of a risk anyway, somebody might see them and raise the alarm. She had to find another way. *It might be possible to find a way to the street from the towers. I just hope these keys unlock the doors if they are locked.*

Moments before she was about to run over to the eastern cloister, to try the door and if successful climb the stairs to the tower, a door opened from the upper level and two guards strode leisurely onto the parapet. Sasna froze, she and Gnarn could easily be seen if the guards looked in their direction, and attempting to move to a more concealed spot, would almost certainly attract their attention. She held her breath and watched as they chatted to each other. They stopped briefly in the middle to look over the parapet onto the street, but to her relief they did not check the garden. They continued on until they reached the tower at the other end of the parapet and entered it through the door.

When the guards had disappeared, Sasna let out her breath, and took in deep fresh lungfuls of air. She and Gnarn then sprinted across the courtyard, and climbed over the small wall into the northern cloister. The flagged floor stretched away under her feet, and a line of doors with grilles in them, ran to the right and left in front of her. Turning to the left, she and Gnarn moved noiselessly along the line of rooms, glancing briefly into one as they passed, but to their relief, they were empty of people. In one, she caught the glimmer of naked white bones. No doubt some poor wretch had been locked in their long ago for the amusement of the Baron, and left to perish and rot until only the bones remained.

They reached the door to the first tower. It was locked. She wasted precious time trying each of the keys, with no success, so they continued moving quietly along the cloister until they came to another arched hallway that had not been visible from her earlier vantage point. Ahead, she saw the dim outline of a stairway sloping upwards, and downwards. She bit her lip nervously, and hoped it was a stair that would lead down into the streets. Looking around warily for any sign of guards, she headed towards it, and then ran swiftly down the stair, closely followed by Gnarn who scuttled behind on all fours at quite a speed. She felt glad that somehow, he manged to keep his wheezing at a low level so it was only a slight murmur. She felt something like a panic pursue her down the stair, and breathed a heavy sigh of relief when she reached the bottom. She fumbled at the keys to unlock the door, it was the third key that turned in the lock and, much to her relief, it unlocked the door. Opening it, she craned her neck to peer through the open crack, hoping to see the outside street, but to her dismay she looked into a bare stone corridor, dimly lit.

Pausing only to ascertain there were no guards, she then sprinted down the vaulted corridor which ended at another door. The fourth key unlocked and opened it, leading to a stair that went upwards. *This is a never-ending maze!* she thought, fighting back a rush of panic; she had been certain it would lead to an open street. Again, she listened intently, but apart from Gnarn's soft wheezing, she could hear no sound. She did not know in what part of the keep she was now in, and having lost her sense of direction, she did not know which way might lead to the city streets. She trembled as she took Gnarn by the hand, and drew him along the corridor. They halted beside an alcove masked with satin tapestry, and stepped into the niche behind it when they heard the door at the other end of the corridor unlock and then open. They heard it shut, lock, and then the sound of two guards walking, their voices getting ever louder as they drew near.

She squeezed Gnarn's hand, and felt him return the gesture, as his wheezing grew louder with fear. Her eyes revealed their fear to him, as she put her finger to her lips as a gesture for him to quieten his breathing. Gnarn took a deep breath, and held it.

"So, you seeing Rosie this evening then Ole Tomso?" one of the guards asked the other nonchalantly. His voice was loud enough that Sasna knew they were passing the tapestry.

"No, tonight I'm off to the tavern," the other guard replied. "It's my only night off and with the entire stir about this place I think it will be awhile since I get another, so I am in for a good drinking bout."

Their voices faded, and eventually, Sasna heard keys turn in the lock of the door at the end of the corridor. One of the guards swore, and she heard the sound of the door open. "Shouldn't this one be locked?" the guard asked the other, his voice feinter due to the distance.

"It's probably that fat old priest or some dipsy maid, they often forget to lock up when they pass through," the other replied. The door shut, and the sound of it being locked led to Gnarn letting out his breath, his chest heaving up and down as he drew in deep breaths with heavy wheezing.

"Good boy," Sasna said to him, "Good boy Gnarn."

He smiled up at her, and when he had regained his breath, they continued. Without hesitation they glided down the passage, and with reckless disregard, Sasna fumbled at the keys until she found the right one to unlock the next door. In similar manner, they passed through several other corridors. The dank black walls of each one was lit up by the torches in sconces along the wall, and seemed to dance with silhouettes; the fear of sudden death or capture lurked in every doorway and shadow. The tension was palpable as they crept along the deep passages, hiding in niches or behind tapestries and statues and anything that would conceal them if they heard the sounds of the guards.

Eventually, dripping with sweat, they entered a short tunnel, which had a guard sleeping on a chair at the end of it, behind the first of two doors. The first was set with iron bars, the second, was a thick iron door which she hoped would surely lead to the street outside. Sasna had to make a choice, to go on, or to go back and find another way out of the keep. She stepped into the tunnel, and crept a few paces along it. There was nowhere to hide if the guard woke up, she would be spotted instantly, the alarm would be raised and the place would soon be flooded with guards. She looked to see if Gnarn was following her. He was.

Sasna glided to the guard's side and knelt down beside him. He was snoring softly. She reached through the bars, took his head in her hands and with one swift movement

218

tried to snap his neck. Perhaps due to weakness caused by the injury to her shoulder, or lack of skill, death was not instant. The guard yelped in pain and woke with a start. He fell off the chair. With their arms reaching through the bars, in one swift movement she and Gnarn pulled him towards the door and Gnarn put the knife to his neck.

Sasna forced the guard to look at her. She smiled as reassuringly as she could; she resisted the urge to take her own knife and cut his throat. His eyes rolled in their sockets as he focussed on the knife held to his neck, and then on her face, realising his predicament as one who awakens from a dream. She stroked his cheek with a hand as she slid it to his chin, and then to his belt as she began to unfasten the keys from it.

"My brave guard," she said. "I need you to be brave and quiet, and I will spare your life." She skilfully unloosed the keys and dangled them quietly before his face. "Which key?"

He studied the keys for a moment, and then pointed to a slightly rusted medium sized key. Gnarn kept the knife pressed firmly against his neck, whilst Sasna unlocked and opened the iron barred door.

"Gnarn can't leave him alive mother, it is dangerous," he said. The guard tried to say something, but could only gurgle as Gnarn repeatedly stabbed him in the neck until he was still and quiet in death.

"Gnarn, did you need to do that?" she whispered, stepping away from the pool of blood spreading quickly across the stone floor.

"Yes mother, Gnarn did," he wheezed.

They unlocked and opened the second, iron bound door. It did not lead to the street, it led downwards. Light gleamed at the bottom of the winding stairs. Somewhere in a room below distant voices and laughter could be heard. She could make out the distinct high-pitched voice of the eunuch, Malkili.

Sasna swallowed hard, trying to suppress the fear she felt as she and Gnarn crept down the stairs. The voices and occasional burst of laughter were louder as they neared the bottom of them. She peered around the bottom of the stairway wall into a long corridor which was well lit. There were three doors, one set of heavy double doors at the end and two at the side facing each other. Along the sides of one of the walls was a long, oblong shaped observation window, designed so that whoever was inside the room on the right could see who was coming and going. This time, she was certain the double door would lead to the outside street, or one of the castle's many gardens.

Gnarn slumped onto the bottom stair, slapping his hands on the floor as he pushed himself forcefully against the wall as though he wished he could disappear into it. It would be much better if they could sneak through their way past the guards rather than fight. It would only take for one of them to raise an alarm, and far too many guards for them to handle would quickly be upon them, and aware of their attempt to escape.

Sasna heard Malkili say something, and was joined in his squealing laughter by others.

Sasna spoke in a barely audible whisper. "The fat eunuch, he is in the room to the right, I am sure that beyond the heavy double doors are the public gardens, or a street; we must be very quiet Gnarn," she said in a barely audible whisper. He nodded.

She made her way quietly down the corridor until she reached the observation window, which, to her great relief, did not have somebody looking out of it. She did not look behind her as she heard the shuffling noise of Gnarn catching up with her. She motioned for him to stop and placed her ear on the door on the right, that led into the observation room. The voices and laughter were coming from within that room. She heard three distinct voices, and curled up her nose in disgust and fear as she caught snippets of their lewd conversation.

"That Seesnari whore is gonna suffer at the hands of the Baron and his sister, they have some real degenerate ways between them," one of them said laughingly.

"Wouldn't mind a go at her myself, I seen her once last time she was here, not a bad looker that one," another replied and then asked, "What about you Malkili, what will your plans for her be if they let you entertain her down in your dungeon?"

There was a loud grunt followed by a heavily breathed out snort. "I'll make her squeal like a pig if the Baron lets me use my tools on her," Malkili said.

Sasna fought the urge to wretch with dread. The observation window was about three feet from the ground. She lay on her stomach and began to leopard crawl towards the double door at the end of the corridor. When she was clear of the window, she stood up, and noticed Gnarn had not followed her, he was waiting near the door to the observation room. Creeping towards the doorway, she placed the keys quietly into the lock and turned it. The lock snapped open with a crack that seemed to echo like thunder. The laughter in the room stopped.

"Did you hear something?" one of the guards asked.

Sasna froze in her tracks. She heard the unmistakable sound of chairs scraping along the ground and knew the men were getting up to investigate the noise. She quickly but carefully turned the handle of the door and began to open it, hoping she might squeeze through before she was seen. The door creaked on its hinges, a noise that seemed to her far louder than it was in reality. The door of the observation room opened, and the two guards and Malkili entered the passageway and saw her immediately.

"It's the Seesnari!" one of the guards shouted. They were the last words he ever spoke as Gnarn was upon him stabbing furiously. Sana wasted no time; she drew her sword and ran towards the other guard. Her sword had pierced through him before he could draw his own sword. Malkili was unarmed. He raised his hands in the air as Sasna pulled the sword from the guard and put the tip of it to Malkili's throat.

"I'm unarmed!" he squealed.

"Then before you make a threat against a Seesnari, you should always arm yourself," she said before plunging the sword through his neck, killing him instantly. She cleaned the sword, wiped the blood from her armour, and then wasted no time going through the door, which did lead into one of the public gardens. She and Gnarn sped along the paths with great haste, passing bushes shaped by the craft of topiary, various flower beds and trees until they came at last to a public street.

Next to the park exit, there was a small house. An unattended washing line in a small courtyard provided Sasna with an opportunity to change. She opened the gate and wasting no time, took some clothes, and secluded behind a stone outhouse, changed from the guard's armour, thinking it would be a lot easier to talk her way out of a situation if she was not caught posing as a guard. She donned the linen smallclothes and a shift, and put over that a dress of blue silk. She quickly put on a pair of hose for her legs, boots from the outhouse that laced up to her knees, and heavy leather gloves. She then put on a hooded cloak of blue dyed rabbit fur, and drew the hood over her head and tightened the lace to conceal her face.

Sasna put the sword belt on so that it was concealed beneath the cloak. She thumbed the hilt of the sword, and the dagger she had slipped into the belt, and for an instant, she considered what to do with Gnarn. At any moment, the bodies of the dead guards might be discovered, and the whole city alerted to their escape. She could now blend in, but not if Gnarn was with her. He was covered in blood, and the way he scuttled about on all fours, along with his deformities, made him easily recognisable and drew attention. He stood, bent over; looking up at her he smiled in the manner a

220

besotted pet might an owner. *He is a liability. He cannot stay with me if I am to have any chance of escape.*

"What shall we do now, mother?" Gnarn asked her, looking at her trustingly

She slowly squeezed the hilt of the sword. *It will be merciful to end for him the misery that is his existence.* In one swift movement, she would be able to draw the weapon and give Gnarn a merciful and quick end; she figured she could hide his body in the outhouse.

"Mother?" Gnarn asked, a look of confusion spreading across his features as she stared at him.

She fingered the hilt of the sword, and considered the best stroke to make the least messy way of bringing him to his end, so her change of clothes would not reveal the mess from the deed. She pointed to a beautiful yellow flower growing in a flowerbed in the courtyard.

"Gnarn, pick that for mother, will you? Mother finds comfort from beautiful flowers."

Gnarn smiled, turned and shuffled over to the flower. Sasna followed him, her fingers still gripping the hilt of the sword, the sweat of anticipation dripping from her forehead. Try as she might though, she could not go through with such a dark feat. She felt a moment of compassion and empathy for him, despite the danger she was in. She removed her hand from the hilt of the weapon and dismissed the thought of the deed, just as Gnarn picked the flower and handed it to her.

"Good boy," she whispered as she took the flower and placed it a pocket on her clothing.

"Gnarn, do you think you will be able to make your own way out of the city, and meet mother on the other side of the Erin?"

"Gnarn wants to stay with mother," he answered.

"It is not safe," she replied. "We must each make our own way out of the city, the best way we can. Do you understand?"

Gnarn nodded. "Yes, mother," he said.

"Good boy. You cannot stop to steal anything, lest you are seen. Your best chance will be to wait until dark; you can find an outhouse like this to hide in until then, not this one though. If the owner returns, they might notice the missing clothes and search around."

"Gnarn can find a place to hide. Gnarn can wait until dark and swim the river. Gnarn is a good swimmer even though the currents are strong," he said. "Gnarn will find mother, soon."

Sasna stroked his face. "May good fate be with you, Gnarn." With those words, checking nobody was watching, leaving him behind she left the garden, walked down the road and entered the busy streets of the town of Greytears, confident she would never see Gnarn again. She would be long gone by night, when he made his move, by which time she was sure the bodies of the physician and guard would already have been found and the city on high alert. If he was caught, which was likely, as it was hard for such a grotesque to blend in, she would hopefully already be far away from the castle. Even if he did make it out alive, the Erin was a dangerous place to swim across. If he did survive the currents, he might fall prey to any one of the foul creatures that lurked in such a river. It gave her no pleasure that he probably would not survive, but she could not dwell on his fate, all she wanted to do was to survive herself, and try to find her brother. A small part of her, however, hoped that Gnarn would make it.

Sasna knew from her past visits to the town and the castle, roughly where she was. From the high point of the hill on which the castle and town were built, she looked back. Castle Greytears was a great sprawl, a massive stone labyrinth of walls, towers, courtyards and tunnels spreading out in all directions. Beyond these, was the town which she had made it into. To the north, down the hill and beyond the town, she could see the port which joined the river, and beyond that the Cradle where the *River Queen* had been burnt. The river curved around the town, and not far from where she was, stood the Erin Bridge that spanned the river, a bridge large enough for a ship to sail beneath it with ease. On the Erin Bridge, she could see various wagons, carts, riders and people heading into the town or out of it. She figured it might be easy to hide in a supply wagon heading out of the city. The guards didn't appear to be stopping and searching any people or carts leaving, but they were searching everyone and everything entering the town, as the Baron had ordered.

Large gatehouses guarded each end of the bridge. Beyond that, far in the distance, she could see the Wychtwood, which started far to the west on the northern side of the bridge. A dark cloud seemed to hang over it, and the sight of it made her skin crawl, but she had no choice. *That is where I must search for Farir.*

Sasna tried to memorise as many points as she could, especially of the parts of the town she was not familiar with, in case she needed to change direction quickly; she moved at a pace fast enough not to tarry, but not so fast it would draw attention to herself. As she made her way through the streets, which unlike her arrival when they were relatively empty, were now bustling with people, due to it being daytime. She headed towards the bridge. A dark thought occurred to her. *Perhaps Farir himself might try to enter Greytears, and not knowing the events that had unfolded, he would make himself known to the Baron to seek aid.* She did not have time to consider the dreadful implications for him if that happened, and she prayed that if he were alive, he would stay far away from the castle.

The streets were busy, but not crowded, so she wasted no time in making her way to the Erin Bridge. When she arrived at the entrance to the massive gatehouse, she moved swiftly to the wagon at the front of the queue, and without hesitation got up into it and sat next to the driver. He looked at her and was about to protest, when she held her stomach with both hands and winced with feigned pain.

"Please sir, I am newly with child and must travel to my village to see my physician. My husband awaits me the other side of the bridge but I fear the walk is too much for me."

"Do you have coin to pay for it?" the man asked abruptly.

"My husband does. He is a generous man and will reward your kindness, if you transport me across the bridge."

"He better," the man sniped.

For reassurance, Sasna gripped the hilt of the dagger sheathed on her belt, and said to him, "You will get your reward, my hero," complimenting him by using a common phrase in those parts used to give thanks to a man who gave assistance to a woman in distress.

The man grunted, flicked the reins of his horse and the wagon lurched forward towards the gate. Despite the urgency of the situation, Sasna's mind turned to the songs and stories she used to enjoy as a child. The heroes in those stories often rescued maidens from monsters or evil men and their castles, but life was not a song or a story, and in her life, she had met very few heroes.

*There are no real heroes,* she said to herself, and then she turned her head to look back at the castle, and she remembered the Davari, Scarand, and the help he had given her. She bit her lip, and regretted the fate he would face there, a fate that would be made worse as the Baron would no doubt take his rage out on the poor wretch when he learned of the events of the day and her escape. Guilt was not often a sentiment she felt, let alone towards a slave, but in that moment, she felt it, even though rationally she knew it had been beyond her power to help him escape as well. She felt cowardly for leaving him behind, after he had helped her when she was in dire need, but she wanted to be away from Greytears as fast as possible and trying to help him would surely have led to her recapture and doom.

Fear, of a sudden, gripped Sasna's heart like a vice as the castle bells began to loudly clang, sounding the alarm. *The bodies have been found and my escape discovered.* Her heart began to pound so hard, she thought it might at any moment burst through her chest. Some of the guards in the gatehouse looked up at the castle and began to murmur among themselves. A sergeant-at-arms leaned out of a window in one of the towers by the gate, and barked orders for the gate to be closed, and that no more traffic was to be allowed onto the bridge until they found out the reason for the alarm at the castle.

The wagon was approaching the gate but a guard stood in front of it and blocked it. "I need to get my fish to the villages before they start to rot!" the wagon driver protested loudly to the guard, who shrugged his shoulders.

"We can't allow any more traffic on the bridge until we find out what mischief is happening at the castle," he barked moodily as the driver flicked the reins and drew the horse and wagon to a halt, murmuring and complaining bitterly as he did so.

Sasna realised nothing was going to get onto the bridge. *Janus, I must find Janus and beg him to help me.*

She thanked the driver, made some excuse about returning back to her lodgings to rest until the bridge re-opened, got down from the wagon and began to make her way from the gate back into the city. With her hand on her dagger hilt she watched as guards started to appear and block off the town's roads.

"Clear the streets!" a guard shouted to all of the people upon it, and then he looked at her and shouted gruffly, "Off the streets woman, now, back to your home." Her situation could be no more desperate than it was. She rushed over to a man and a woman who were going inside a house and tried to join them.

"What are you doing?" the woman objected. "Go to your own home."

Sasna did not argue or try to push past but turned around and continued back the way she had come. She tried to merge herself with the throngs that were making their way to their homes, as more guards poured onto the streets ordering for them to be cleared. She darted down an alley to avoid some guards who blocked the end of the street she was walking along. The throng of people was beginning to thin out; if she did not hurry, she would be found wandering the streets alone, and would surely be caught. She had no doubt that a house to house search would also soon start. Panic set in. *Janus is my only hope; I will throw myself at his mercy.*

The end of the ally she was in led back to the public gardens outside the keep. Guards were running through the gardens, most making their way to the keep or to the streets. "Conduct a thorough search of the gardens as well," she heard one of them shout.

Terror filled Sasna's heart and mind. She would surely be found. She managed to dodge the guards by hiding in shrubbery and then behind a tree as they ran past, but then she stepped out, and Baris stood in her way. He looked sympathetically at her. "Wait a few minutes, then go down this path and turn left," he said. "If the temple is unlocked, hide in there. If not, wait unseen in the gardens until nightfall. I will return for you and assist you."

"Thank you," Sasna said, as she hid in the bushes again.

She heard Baris bellowing out orders. "Clear the gardens, she's not here. Search the streets!"

Sasna heard guards running past and waited until their footsteps and shouts were distant. Leaving her hiding place, she ran down the path and turned left. Seeing the large double doors of the temple sanctuary at one end of the garden, she made her way towards it. Approaching the temple by a little-used path that ran between close set ornamental trees whose intertwining branches formed a vault overhead, she finally reached the huge mahogany doors. Behind her, she heard guards still shouting and moving about the gardens. There was no time to consider who or what might be behind the doors. She tried the smaller inner door, it opened, and without hesitation she stepped inside and slammed it shut behind her. She stopped and froze in horror, at the sight that met her eyes.

# Chapter Eighteen: *Into the Tarenmoors*

*Nobody really knows the origin of the Obelisks. There are so many myths and legends about them it really is hard to separate any facts from fiction. We do know that there are no records for any Fell-bloods or Half-bloods ever being resurrected by one. Only those born of Akkadian Pure-blood are resurrected. This fact, in my opinion, makes Choaser's thesis that they were originally made by the gods as a gift to our Akkadian ancestors, pretty compelling, and he makes an excellent case for this.*
**Temmison Vol IX, Book 5: The Obelisks.**

*Over* long leagues of gloomy forest, across broad rivers and hills, the warg had relentlessly pursued Alwith, and when it had finally cornered him, he instinctively drew *Ungweethon*, and stood face to face with the shockingly fearsome creature. Drool dripped from the fangs of the beast, landing on the ground in small pools. Its eyes were red and burnt with savagery. A terrible wound, now healed, showed part of its rib cage. Each of its claws appeared to Alwith like daggers. The warg stared at the blade for a long time, as though mesmerized by it, and then, without explanation, it snarled, turned and then trotted across the open space and melted back into the forest without a backward glance.

Alwith shook his head, unable to understand it, but glad of the fact that, for whatever reason, the warg had departed. His limbs were stiff, his wounds, sustained by travelling with rash haste through the rugged and hostile terrain, ached. He expanded his chest and drank in deep breaths of air. He rubbed his bloodshot eyes with the back of his wrist. He had not slept for days, and now the exhaustion was catching up with him. He blinked and took stock of his surroundings. Below him the green wilderness waved and billowed away in a solid mass. In the distance, he saw it for the first time, High Blackbarrow, upon which the Greytower, the abode of the Tarath Guëan, the Grey Council, stood. The sight filled him with dread, but, drinking in more breaths of air and finding his courage, Alwith set out again, with a determination to reach it before nightfall.

*        *        *

Borach's first sensation of returning consciousness was a throbbing pain in his head and cramp all over his body. He struggled to breathe. His throat was dry and his nose was almost completely blocked with clots of blood. He tried to speak, but was unable to move. Through barely open eyes and a daze of vision, he could see the four commanders of the Third Legion, the Dwarves Marki and Galin, and the man Torach. With them, was the griffin-keeper, Meron. Marki held up a lamp as they studied maps laid out on a table within the command pavilion which Borach was so familiar with, for it was his own.

"In the Tarenmoors there are no borders between clans in the northern-parts, none that you'd recognise. It is a mongrel region, full of hill tribes and primitive savages," Marki said gruffly, and then continued. "One chieftain or king says to another, 'this land this side of the forest is mine.' The other chieftain or king agrees, or if he does not, they fight over it. The one who gets the axe or sword in his head loses."

"Then it is perfect for what we plan," Torach said as he breathed a sigh of relief, scratched the lid of his good eye and adjusted the patch over his missing one. "Our scouts say the path to Kara Duram is blocked with Hammer Knights. Estalda is nothing but a smoking ruin. We have no choice; we must go south!"

Borach tried to speak, but he could not. *Look for Yianna! Search for Yianna and my children!*

Galin was more cautious as he spoke. "Advancing without secured supplies is always risky. These maps are old and we have no idea who owns what land now. Our scouts will search far and wide, seeking what they can discover." He then took some snuff out of a silver box, applied a pinch to each nostril, and snorted the contents into his nose with a loud sniff.

Meron contributed. "I heard tavern talk once, some drunken traveller bragging he had been to the central kingdoms. He said they are warlike, but more civilised and organised than the tribes that inhabit the northern Tarenmoors. He made talk of a kingdom called Thurogen. Their capital is an ancient fortress named Thurog Tor. The Thurogenites are ruled by a despot, King Falamore. The traveller said they have a Seeress, and an Obelisk there."

"There is an Obelisk marked on the map, the only one. The others are unknown, lost or dead," Marki said as he prodded the map with a stubby finger. "I say we take a chance and head for there."

"What sort of reception do you think a Tarenmoor king will give to a Kappian legion?" Torach asked. "Depleted as we are, he will still think we are invading, and before we even reach there, we have to pass the northern tribes."

Marki scratched his bearded chin, thoughtfully. "We should send a messenger ahead to Thurog Tor, when we draw near. If they are as warlike as we think, we can offer the legion as a mercenary force, in return for supplies and the use of their Obelisk."

*We are not mercenaries,* Borach wanted to say, but the words would not come. *Go to Estalda, Search for Yianna! Even if it is a ruin, she will hide there and watch for my arrival!*

"It disgusts me to think our proud legion has been reduced to this," Torach moaned, "but Borach is not long for this world. If we do not find a safe Obelisk soon, who knows where he could resurrect at? It could be an Obelisk, lost and drowned deep in a cavernous underground lake or even in boiled lava."

"We have other men sick from their wounds as well, the physician is hardly getting any sleep tending them and trying to keep them all alive," Meron added.

"Then we have no other option," Marki declared. "Every other route is closed to us. I say we head south, and parley with this Tarenmoor king. If he is usurped or dead when we arrive, we will offer our swords to whoever rules."

The other three grunted their agreement.

*Go to Estalda, look for Yianna!*

"We should avoid conflict with the northern tribes, if we can, until we have secured a safe Obelisk," Torach added. "We do not want to risk men in unnecessary battles."

Meron nodded in agreement. "I agree. Avoid the tribes if we can. We did not get many supplies here at Ash Gonath, they will soon run out, so we will have to hunt and forage the land. I say if we follow the Mansosi River south, it will offer another potential food supply, and at least we will have water."

"What about the griffin?" Galin asked. "We will struggle to feed it; it is untrained and too young to be flown. I say we set it free to take its own chances in the world, or we give it a merciful death, and use it for meat."

On their arrival at Ash Gonath, they had found a caged griffin. News of what had happened at Aleskian had already reached there, the Fell-blood guards had fled and abandoned the creature. Just the month before, Meron had rejected it for the breeding programme, because it was smaller than the others, had lost some feathers, and it had a slightly crooked beak. It had been bought as a pet by the men of the keep at Ash Gonath.

"No!" Meron said, reacting with instant fury. "It is the last of the bloodline of Yarrion the Great. If any of you tries to bring harm to the creature, you will have me to tend with."

"Is that a threat?" Galin asked with raised voice, his eyes furrowing with annoyance. "We will barely be able to feed the men let alone a growing griffin!"

"I agree with Galin," Torach pronounced. "The march to Thurog Tor will be one for survival, we cannot chance taking a caged griffin with us."

Meron protested loudly, and the four began to squabble, each offering ardent and vociferous opinions.

*Damn the griffin. Go to Estalda and look for Yianna*, Borach wanted to shout, but not a muscle in his body would move.

*Damn you Marki, damn you Meron! Damn the griffin!* Borach thought. *Damn all of you. Go to Estalda, search again for my Yianna and my children.*

The conversation of the commanders faded, as once more Borach slipped into unconsciousness.

*      *      *

"Quiet!" Marki shouted, as he thumped his fist on the table. It had the desired effect, the three of them went quiet and looked at him. He was the senior commander, in the absence of Borach. Where there was difference of opinion, the decision would ultimately be his.

Meron and Galin both stepped towards him, about to argue for their cause, but he put his finger to his lips. "Quiet, I said, let me think."

Marki was well aware that to end the breeding bloodline of Yarrion the Great, by killing or releasing the griffin, would also receive a mixed reaction among the men. Some would support killing it, resenting the fact that their bellies might have to grumble with hunger whilst a griffin was fed. Others would despise harming the beast. Marki considered the options – the men had to come first. *Better to kill the beast, it will just be a burden and slow us down where we are going.*

"You will lose me, Marki." Meron warned. "I'll defend it to my death if you order it harmed. If you release it, I'll stay with it. I've never disobeyed an order in all my years of service over many lifetimes, but I'll turn on you all if this is the way of it!"

Marki knew, by the countenance on Meron's face, that he was deadly serious. It would be a perilous enough journey, and a struggle to keep the morale of the men up. Their best chance of survival, was to stay together. *If I lose a commander before we have even set out, the legion will surely start to crumble. One by one, they will drift away.*

"Damn it Meron!" Marki roared. "It was the runt of the litter, but keep the featherless chicken if it means that much to you!"

Meron breathed a big sigh of relief. "Thank you Marki, thank you."

Galin snorted with displeasure at the decision. "The thing is half-starved as it is, I'll wager it will die of hunger before the end of the week," he said.

"Then I'll feed it a dwarf!" Meron retorted back.

Galin angrily snapped shut the lid of his silver snuff box and tucked it into a pouch attached to his sword belt.

"Galin, enough," Marki said firmly. "I've made my decision. If we four continue to squabble and lose order, we will never keep the legion together through the perils we now face."

Fort Fearless stood on the southernmost edges of the borders of the Kappian Empire, where it met the Mansosi River, beyond which was the Tarenmoors. Once a mighty fortress, it was now little more than a dilapidated wooden stockade, built amidst a larger pile of stone ruins, sitting on the bank of the river.

The Fell-blood old man stood with the two Fell-blood scouts on the decrepit parapet. He pointed to the ill-repaired and rickety looking bridge that spanned the river, and then to the great chunks of collapsed stone lying in the riverbed, around which the river flowed. "When I was a young lad, the stone bridge was a magnificent structure. Damaged in the Baothein raid, years ago, there was no money to repair it after the war, so it collapsed. The wooden bridge you see, no longer gets used, so there is little point in me trying to maintain it."

The first scout, Maynryn, was a fresh-faced man of about twenty-five years of age. "Why did everyone else leave?" he asked the old guard.

"During the war, the Baothein reduced this fortress to rubble, as they did so many others. Those of us who survived the raid, tried to rebuild afterwards, but when the Empire stopped paying our wages, one by one everybody just drifted away."

"So why did you stay?" the second scout asked. He was a man in his mid-forties, and had a heavily scarred and weathered face.

"My wife was not well, and could not travel, so I stayed with her. When she died, I had nowhere else to go." He pointed to a vegetable patch not far away. "It's a meagre existence, but I get by. The soil here is good to grow some food. I get fish from the river, snare rabbits and even the occasional roebuck."

"Have you ever been over the other side, into the Tarenmoors?" Maynryn asked him."

"Oh, when I was a lad, we often sneaked over, but never went too far, and never at night, it was far too dangerous back then." He looked southwards, towards the Tarenmoors, and looked sad as he reminisced. "For hundreds of years, guards patrolled the log runways of the once mighty stone parapets, day and night, and the bridge itself was heavily guarded. Nobody entered or left the Tarenmoors by this route." He sighed deeply. "By the time I was born, this place was already a shadow of what it once was. Even then it was in decline and falling to ruin. The Baothein raid just finished the job."

"Do you ever see signs of any life over there now, across the river?" Maynryn asked.

The man stared reflectively at the wilderness across the river. "It is a howling wilderness, much of it. I suspect that for hundreds of miles the land runs bare and uninhabited. I see the occasional half-starved looking warg, or the odd deer now and then, but that is all."

The old man laughed, as he fondly recalled another memory. "When I was a boy, we used to climb the battlements and would watch the great migratory herds of deer and wildebeest crossing the Mansosi. They stretched as far as the eye could see, and were always followed by great packs of wargs. It was quite a sight you know." He looked wistful and pointed to the river. "All manner of river beast waited for them to cross. Crocodiles, water-snakes as long and thick as the trunk of a tree. We kept well away from the riverbanks during the migration." He sighed. "It truly was a magnificent sight to behold, but once the herds stopped migrating, the beasts stopped coming."

"Do you know what happened to them, why they stopped coming?" the weathered scout asked.

The old man shook his head. "Not really, there were rumours and tales, some of which I'll tell you if you wish to stop for a bite to eat."

"We don't have time for stories, old man," the weathered scout said, "although we won't turn down a meal, so if that is the price, we must pay for it, so be it."

"When the legion passes through here, you should come with us. An enemy worse and crueller than the Baothein is coming this way," Maynryn said.

The old man blinked his milky eyes. "It was the greatest day of my life when I knelt the knee, and swore fealty to Lady Macraith, in the great hall that once stood over there." He pointed to a crumbled ruin. "She was a Fell-blood woman of extravagant loveliness, exquisite to behold. I swore to her that day, I would never stop guarding this place for her, that I would never leave my post, till my dying breath. It is a vow I intend to keep."

"The enemy that comes is fierce, and unyielding," Maynryn said.

"And they'll find old Ben, just as fierce and unyielding. I made a vow to the lady whose elegance blessed this place in times past, and I'll not break it." He smiled, showing yellowed, worn down teeth. "My sword has a bit of rust on it, but it will still give a nasty nick here and there. I ran out of oils to keep it pristine many years ago, and my armour has seen better days, now brandishing a few dents and a fair bit of corrosion." He wagged his finger at Maynryn. "But mark my words young man, if any enemy comes through here, they'll find old Ben armed and ready, fulfilling his vow."

Pointing to a ramshackle hut, he said, "Now, when you have done looking, I have some piping hot stew bubbling away. Come and eat with me, you are the first visitors I have had in twenty-years. I would be interested to hear news of the outside world."

Old Ben walked away, climbed down the ladder from the parapet to the ground, and headed towards his hut.

The two scouts looked across the river, and observed the barren landscape.

"Go and report to Commander Marki that we found a possible crossing place," Maynryn said to his colleague. "I will head south, see what else I find and look for locations for the legion to camp. But first, I wouldn't mind a bellyful of that hot stew, and to hear a tale or two of his."

"He's a foolish old man, and can keep his tales to himself," scar-face muttered, "but a bowl of that stew, would be welcome, even if he has to bore us with the folly that is his life."

*      *      *

In the Kappian mind, civilisation ended at Fort Fearless. To them it was the last outpost of a civilised world. The legion had cautiously crossed the ill-repaired and rickety bridge that spanned the Mansosi River, and entered the northern Tarenmoors, watched by Old Ben who waved goodbye until they were out of sight.

Heading south, following the river deeper into the Tarenmoors, the legion remained on high alert. Two hundred or so men, mainly those who had joined from the Sixth, Ninth and Twelfth Legions, had deserted during the last few weeks. They were mostly those with families now at Kara Duram, which was where they were probably headed. The tramp of the remaining six hundred plus feet of the legion, the hooves of the few horses they had and the wheels of the carts being pulled by horses or oxen had brought up a swathe of dust that swirled in the light wind and settled on the armour of the legionnaires. Such a force could not move through the difficult terrain without getting attention from any inhabitants.

Scouts had been sent out looking for signs of potential trouble gathering, but it was only after the third week, that they came across any sign of human habitation. Every settlement they discovered, had been abandoned. The huts of whoever once dwelled there, were left intact, apart from where the weather had damaged them, and nobody had made repairs. Some of their possession remained behind, and were neatly stowed, showing they had not been left in a hurry or been plundered. There were no decaying corpses or skeletons left lying around. For some reason, the inhabitants had simply packed up most of their belongings and left.

A broad red moon was shining overhead when Borach gained consciousness again. His head still ached, but felt clearer than before. The cramp had gone from his body, and he could slightly move one of his arms, although he groaned when he realised that below the elbow of the other, it had been amputated. He felt warm and damp compresses on his forehead. The blood was cleared from his nostrils and his breathing was easier. When he tried to move his legs, he could do so, but with difficulty and great pain. The bumping motion he felt, made him soon realise he was on a makeshift stretcher, being dragged along by a horse, following a cart its reins were tied too.

He rubbed his weary eyes and looked around him. The men of the legion looked tired and gaunt; clearly, they had been marching for many days. Ahead of him, a dray, almost empty of provisions, was being pulled by some half-starved oxen, led by reins a legionnaire held.

As if on cue, the horse pulling Borach's stretcher whinnied pitifully in complaint, as it struggled to pull him over a small rise. The few other horses in sight were showing their ribs under a coat of dark dust. To his side, he heard a man mutter a complaint that the water from the river was sour and they were always hungry. Borach turned his head and saw a legionnaire marching beside him.

"My wife, Yianna, my children. What news of them?" he asked the man.

The legionnaire did not answer, instead he started shouting excitedly, "He's awake! Lord Borach is awake!"

"Quiet," another legionnaire barked at him. "Keep the noise down. We don't know what your squawking might attract out of this dark night." The legionnaire was right; all sorts of creatures hunted and prowled the Tarenmoors at night, they were not safe until the camp was set up and guards were patrolling the perimeter, and they would not set up camp until they arrived at a suitable place ahead that the scouts would have already located. The man ran over and looked at Borach and said to the other legionnaire, "Give him water, I'll go and find the surgeon and inform him he is awake."

Just a few minutes later, they must have arrived at the place the scouts had found. Well-practiced, and rigid in discipline, it did not take long for the legion to respond to the orders that filtered through, to set up camp, and have a perimeter guard posted. The legionnaire who had gone to find the surgeon, returned, unattached the stretcher-horse from the back of the cart, and took the reins.

As Borach lay on his stretcher which was dragged bumpily through the camp, it seemed to him as though he were in a dream, as he watched the men of the legion setting up camp-fires to prepare the evening meal, or tending their swords and weapons and oiling their armour with linseed. Some were preparing rough bivouacs to sleep in. Each had a job to do and it would not take long before the camp was set and heavily guarded and protected from the perils of the night.

Borach was led past a cart that carried the caged griffin. The creature was slumped in the cage and looked sickly and weak. It had lost many feathers. Usually, they were noble and ferocious beasts, either flying or strutting on all fours. If being transported in a cage, it was always in a gilded one carried on a richly decorated and elaborate wagon

230

designed for that very purpose. Specially made armour for the griffin would be proudly hanging on the sides, along with a flying saddle for a rider and passenger. The beast in the rusted cage Borach saw, made a mockery of the majesty of such creatures, not that he blamed the beast itself for the miserable condition it was in. It was suffering, and had his thoughts not been dominated by concern for the fate of Yianna and his children, he might have pitied the poor creature.

Borach felt a small degree of comfort at the sight of his own command tent. It was a domed structure made up of light cloth dyed in red and golden stripes, held up with wooden poles that, when on the march, were used to hang supplies from and were carried by the men of the legion. The legion's griffin banner flew proudly above it, and the standard was planted outside.

When the legionnaire led the horse past the tent, Borach asked him, "Where are you taking me?"

"To the surgeon's tent," the man answered.

"The heck you are," he said, as he tested his legs. There was some feeling in them. He undid the buckle and pulled off the leather strap that held him in the stretcher, and with difficulty uneasily stood to his feet, swaying and swaggering.

The legionnaire stopped the horse and moved as if to help him.

"Tend to your own business," Borach ordered as he moodily waved the man away, and staggered his way towards the command tent. He shielded his eyes from the glow of the bronze lamps as he entered the tent. His four commanders were around a table, looking over a map, pointing at it or stabbing fingers upon it as they each made suggestions.

"Yianna, where is Yianna and the children?" Borach asked as, his legs almost giving out, he staggered over to a chair and collapsed into it.

The four commanders turned, and gasped with surprise. Marki was the first to rush to his friend's side.

"Bor, I…" whatever it was Marki wanted to say, he could not. Tears ran from his eyes and he sobbed.

"Lord Borach, you are supposed to be with the surgeon. He has said that when we stop…" Torach broke off mid-sentence, perhaps due to the ferocity with which Borach demanded. "My wife? My children? Did you go to Estalda to fetch them?"

"Estalda, why would we go there?" Marki asked, raising his eyebrows questioningly. "The scouts said it was naught but a smoking ruin."

"That is where Yianna and the children are. I sent them there."

"But Bor, on the plain, Shinther had Yianna's chain. He showed it to you."

"That could have been anyone's chain," Borach said, as he looked at the chain, still wrapped around his wrist. "There was no locket. They would not show me the chain and not the locket!"

"You were willing to surrender us over to our enemies, when you were not even certain it was her chain?" Meron asked suspiciously. The look of hurt that spread across his face, and the expression he wore, was such that Borach had never seen in his old friend and comrade until then.

Borach's anger resided. "I could not take the risk," he said, almost meekly. "I could not take the risk." His meekness did not last long, it disappeared in an instant as he remembered the rest of the events of that day on the Aleskian Plain, and then the later discussion when the commanders had been discussing entering the Tarenmoors.

"You were ordered to surrender, why are we even here? Why did you not obey my order to surrender?"

"We did Bor, we did," Marki said, as tears still welled up in his eyes. "I would gladly give up my life for Yianna and the bairns, even if it was but a small chance it was them that was in those catapults." He wiped away the tears that flowed down his face and onto his beard. "When Garuk fell, the other Bantu went wild and slew Prince Regineo, as well as General Shinther and his Hammer Knights; they then turned on us. The catapults were fired, and it was only then we fought, when the Bantu charged us."

"Then you personally should have checked Estalda," Borach barked. "There was a good chance they made it to Estalda."

Marki answered with an apologetic undertone. "You are not listening Bor, Hammer Knights burned down Estalda. Nobody was there. Our scouts checked." He then took something out of his pocket, and showed it to Borach. It was Yianna's locket. His voice tremored with emotion. "They never made it Bor, Shinther was right, it was Yianna and the bairns in the catapults. They were hurled to their *Final-death*." He sighed, and his head sank to his chest in despair.

Borach took the locket from Marki, and stared at it. He clutched it tightly in the grip of his hand. He had never felt such a terrible pain as he did in that moment, to realize his beloved Yianna and his children were forever gone from the world, forever dead. Within him opened up a grief so fierce, so deep, he could not even give voice or cry to it. He opened his mouth to roar, but nothing came out. He willed the tears of rage and grief to come, but they would not. And then, his grief froze hard inside of him, and was replaced with something else – with intense rage. It was a rage the like of which he had never felt before - it embedded itself as a force and power within him, and it craved only one thing - vengeance.

"If even the gods try to stop me from having vengeance on those behind this foul duplicity, they will tremble when the darkness now inside, rises from within me," he swore.

Marki wept, and the other commanders hung their heads.

The legion's surgeon rushed into the tent, quickly followed by two physicians, carrying a bowl of water, some cloths, satchels and rolled up belts full of medical tools.

"Lord Borach, you were supposed to be carried straight to my tent. I have to operate on you, straight away," the surgeon said as he used a fresh, warm damp cloth to wipe the sweat of Borach's forehead. "How did you manage to walk on these legs? You were supposed to remain laying down."

Borach tried to raise himself from the chair; the medics forced him back down. It was only at that moment that he looked down, and realized his legs were heavily bandaged and again, he could no longer feel them, but he could smell them. It was a putrid, rotting smell, coming from the blood and puss that oozed from the bandages. *The gods mock me ever so cruelly this day, but I will have my vengeance.*

"We could not operate whilst you were sleeping under the influence of Easewood, the shock would have killed you," the surgeon said apologetically.

"We are trying to keep you alive, and get you to a safe Obelisk," Marki said, and then let out some heavy sobs.

"There was not only poison on the Bantu blade, it is a cursed weapon, we need to operate on you quickly," the surgeon said regretfully. He took out a phial from a pouch hanging from his belt. "This is the last of the Easewood, we feared if we gave it to you whilst unconscious, it might kill you. You must drink it, and we must amputate your legs, immediately. The last of the Easewood might slow the spread of the rest of the poison in your body, long enough for us to get to the Obelisk in Thurog Tor."

"Then get on with it," Borach said through gritted teeth. *Whatever it takes, I will stay alive to have my vengeance, and when that is complete, I will find a way to join Yianna in the Final-death.*

Marki respectfully knelt down beside him, and taking his hands within his own, he said, "Bor, if I could have done anything to save Yianna and your bairns, I would have considered the cost of my own life a small price to give in exchange for their safety." He wiped tears from his eyes with his sleeve.

Borach knew that the dwarf meant every word. Marki was fearless and rough, often uncouth, but he was also loyal to a fault and had loved Borach's family as his own.

"I know my friend, I know," Borach said. "Get me to that Obelisk, Marki, for I need a new body. Do whatever it takes. I will not rest until those responsible for our calamities suffer, and their entire bloodline is wiped from this world. I will violate and desecrate their living and their dead. I will empty their tombs and vaults, and those of their ancestors, and throw their bones and treasures in the Skunfill sewer. All record of them shall be removed from this world."

Marki's voice was low, but he spoke in a determined manner, "And by Balagrim, I shall be by your side as you do it."

The surgeon took some herbs from a pouch. "Eat," he said, "the effects are almost immediate. It will dull the pain, and help keep you alive afterwards."

Borach let the surgeon push the herbs into his mouth. He did not chew, just swallowed.

"Do it," he ordered the surgeon. Borach knew there was no fast and painless way to perform an amputation, despite whatever herbs he might be given. He gladly bit down on the piece of wood placed in his mouth. A neat amputation took time and required a flap of skin to be cut to cover the stump. The surgeon's assistants, the physicians, took out a burner from a bag, lit it, washed sharpened knives and a saw in water and then heated them over the burner.

Borach's face felt flushed and was beaded with sweat; he bit down hard on the wood as the medics made the first cut in his right leg after the blades were sufficiently heated. He screwed his face up tight, determined not to make a sound, although he knew worse was to come.

"Don't look," the surgeon said in a murmur as Borach attempted to watch what they were doing.

He was happy to oblige and stared at the roof of the tent when one of the assistants handed the saw to the surgeon. The two assistants pinned him down as the surgeon lifted the flap of skin, and as quickly as he could begin, he started to saw away at the right leg. The pain was unbearable, and despite vowing to himself not to make a noise, Borach grunted and struggled but the surgeon's assistants pinned him tightly to the ground. It was a mercy that he felt himself slowly but un-peacefully drifting once again into the sleep of unconsciousness. There was one word in his mind as he drifted away - *vengeance.*

# Chapter Nineteen: *The Awakening*

*Contrary to the stereotypical view that pirates are an anarchic rabble, they are actually high self-governed and disciplined. Each crew member swears a salt-oath on the Book of Jorgen, and vows allegiance to the captain, agreeing to follow the ship's rules (articles) before departure. Articles vary from pirate ship to pirate ship, but the main provisions are similar and deal with the division of booty. Below is the code of piratical conduct from Captain Barson's fleet, circa 9712.*
*Abbie Marson: True Accounts and Great Swashbuckling Tales.*


*Janorra* took some deep breaths. All of the screaming and crying had hurt her throat and she urgently needed some water. The first memory that returned was an old song. *Seven dolls for seven trolls, a gold coin for a picture. That will solve all our ills, when we are much richer.* Other, more recent memories, had soon began to flood into her mind.

The *Awakening* had been more traumatic than at any other time she had previously experienced it, and it had been much shorter. Numerous memories from all her past lives, both good and bad, minor and major, and the emotions that accompanied each of them had re-entered her in the short space of an hour, when it should have taken days or weeks; sometimes it was months or years before memories from lifetimes before the last one returned. A lot of it depended upon the skill of whoever helped manage the process after a resurrection. Confusion, panic, fear, joy, hope, love, hate and every extreme range of emotion good and bad she had ever experienced in her twenty-eight previous lifetimes flooded through her entire being during the course of that hour, and she had screamed in horror for the next two hours as she remembered some of the things she had seen and experienced.

The *Awakening* was a dangerous time for any Pure-blood. Temporary insanity could occur if it happened too quickly. It was rarely a permanent insanity, but it could last for days, weeks or sometimes even months. Most Seers, however, had the capacity to *Awaken* very quickly with little or no side effects. Janorra coughed, wretched and groaned as the memories began to orientate themselves in a time-line that she could relate too, and fear gripped her as realisation flooded back concerning the most recent events. Her freshest memories, of both the Deadlands and the life before that, slowly clicked into place. She remembered the escape from the Argona Temple, the death by a spider, but could not yet remember where that had been. As the frightening horror of her situation dawned, the uncertainty of where she was caused her heart to beat quickly. She took some deep breaths to still her mind and calm her heart. *Ashareth, show me the way in this life, guide me to the Fair Haven in the next,* she silently prayed.

A clarity that only a Seer of her calibre could experience in such a short span of time helped her make sense of her environment. She lifted her legs over the side of the marble resurrection cradle she was lying in, got out of it and stood up.

The Obelisk, probably tired itself after resurrecting her, appeared asleep, but a fat, overweight Aeldar priest was staring at her with eyes wide with shock.

"How long has my *Awakening* taken?" she asked him.

"Less than an hour," he replied. "I've never seen anything like it, never seen anybody go through it so quickly. It's incredible. You must be a Seer?" He looked at the mark of the Obelisk beneath her eye, and must have realised for the first time it was not an outline only. He prostrated himself, and pressed his forehead to the stone floor. "You are," he said. "Forgive me, I am so unobservant and had not noticed your mark until now. I am unskilled in helping a Seer resurrect; the *Awakening* happened so rapidly and I could not slow it."

She stared at him for a moment whilst she pondered his response, and then felt immediate relief; she had not wasted valuable time in a slow *Awakening*, and he clearly did not know who she was, but the relief soon gave way to a sense of urgency.

"You may rise," she said. With some difficulty due to his weight, the priest rose to his feet.

"Where am I?" she asked him, and then noticed that others were in the chamber and were also staring at her: a fierce looking Davari slave, a maid, a guard and a man with his nose cut off and a missing eye. She suddenly became aware of her nakedness, but had more important matters to contend with than to feel embarrassed by it. The maid ran forward and with a look of awe on her face, curtsied and handed her a plain white gown. Janorra effortlessly slipped it over her body.

The priest still looked shocked. "You are in Castle Greytears, I am Janus, the temple priest. Why has a Seer come here? You must have perished on that ship that was wrecked on the Erin?"

Janorra momentarily closed her eyes and tried to recall if she could place Castle Greytears on a map. As a Seer, her memory was trained to recall many facts, and vast was her knowledge, but due to freshly *Awakening* she could not yet recall where it was. She remembered that the Erin was a long river that stretched in many directions and had numerous habitations and ports along its length, but she could not yet remember or locate the castle in her mind.

"Am I still inside the Empire's borders?" she asked, fearing the answer. The fact an Aeldar priest was there, was proof to her she had not entirely escaped the possible clutches of the Empire, but it might be that she was in a far-off outpost. The Empire and the Aeldar sect believed it was their destiny to civilize and rule the world in the name of the gods they worshipped, and their reach had already stretched to many far-off places, even beyond the borders of the Empire.

"That depends who you are talking to," Janus said apprehensively. "Technically you are not within the borders of the Empire, although some would dispute that; these are Bruthon lands, and though they are now a separated state after the war, the Empire still makes a claim on them."

Another memory returned to Janorra: *Bruthon; these are lands that declared independence from the Empire during the civil war.* "What about the lord or lady of this castle, where does he or she stand on the matter?"

"Baron Daramir? He is loyal to the Bruthon King, who maintains we are now an independent state! But, Kappia still challenges the king's claim; we have peace with Kappia, but it is fragile."

*Then ravens might already have been sent from Kappia with news of the theft of the Simal and the slaying of Ahrimakan. They might be making speed here, now, even as we talk; I cannot chance any delay!* She decided to lie. "I am on business from Kappia, of what nature does not concern your king or the baron of this castle. I will need a horse and some provisions, and will be immediately on my way."

Janus shook his head. "Perhaps you should lie down again; you are clearly traumatised and have not regained all of your memories if you cannot remember the wreckage." He took her by the hand and led her to a seat, which she gladly took as she still felt unsteady on her feet. "It would be irresponsible for me to let you go until you at least remembered what caused your death." He turned to the Davari and asked, "Scarand, do you remember seeing this woman on the ship?"

Another memory returned to Janorra in a flash. *The Wytchwood, I died in the Wytchwood.* She still could not remember exactly where Castle Greytears was, but even though she was no expert in the politics of Bruthon lands, she did remember hearing the name of the particularly cruel baron of the castle and his often reckless and lawless ways, for he had committed some unspeakably cruel acts during the civil war. She held her breath and looked at the Davari named Scarand. He looked at her, curiously, perhaps with a degree of awe and wonder. She assumed by the chaffing on his wrists and ankles, and the bruises on his face, that he was a fairly new slave, and therefore had not yet fully accepted the conditions of his captivity. "Yes, he does remember me," she lied, looking at him, pleading with her eyes for him to support the lie. If he did not, she could claim confusion due to her *Awakening.* Her mind was still unclear, her memories incoherent, and she could not think of a good reason to explain her presence or death in a place where she vaguely remembered reading that people usually did not travel into. Offering absence of memory as an excuse would be a ruse that she might only be able to hold for a short time; the priest's assumption she was on the ship would assist her.

When Scarand spoke, his tone was calm, despite the wildness glaring in his eyes. With cool assurance he said, "I was chained in the hold for most of the journey, and until I set eyes on her just now, had forgotten I had briefly seen her when we boarded. Yes, she was on the *River Queen* when we left Ashgiliath in Seesnari lands six days ago."

His accent was rough and unpolished, but Janorra breathed a short sigh of relief. Not only had this unknown slave given her an excuse for resurrecting at the castle, he had, perhaps astutely, offered her more information to support her lie. Another memory returned to her; she could remember where Ashgiliath was, but still could not quite place where, exactly, along the Erin Castle Greytears was located.

"Ah, you must be the Seer that Inquisitor Feagan requested, he is away on business. We did not expect you for another month or so, though. Why did you come by way of Ashgiliath?"

"My memory has not quite fully returned," Janorra answered, "but I do remember that I am not the Seer that Inquisitor Feagan requested. My business is of a matter that must remain undisclosed. How far away from Kappia am I, as the messenger bird flies?"

"Are you expecting a message to come for you from Kappia?" Janus enquired.

"I need to send one," Janorra answered, lying yet again.

"Well now let me see. Twenty-eight to thirty days if a pigeon, though they often fall prey to larger birds so we send or get very few messages that way. Ravens take about forty days to get here; they are stronger and more cunning and can avoid larger birds such as eagles and hawks more easily, so it will be a while before they receive any message. Is it important?"

Janorra felt relieved the castle would have received no message from Kappia yet. She briefly felt terror in her heart, as she asked the next question, and waited for the answer. "When will the Inquisitor return?"

The Inquisitor would demand to know the nature of her business; her lies would not hold up to him. If she was put to the test, in the presence of a fragment from the Eye of Morsef that all Inquisitors carried, she would fail it and be exposed.

"He is away in the Bruthon capital hunting heretics of the *Old Faith.*" Janus curled his face up in disgust and was about to spit contemptuously, but appearing to remember his surroundings, swallowed it. "Many in these parts still adhere to the teachings of En-Sof, and Feagan hunts them, though I suspect when he hears news of the events happening here, he will return promptly. Whatever your business, you will not be allowed to leave until you have spoken to Inquisitor Feagan. The castle will be on

236

shutdown now – nobody will be allowed to leave. I will send a message to him asking for his immediate return."

The news did not cause the terror inside Janorra to reside. The castle was on shutdown, and she had to act quickly before Feagan returned. She knew she could not tarry at the castle; it was too dangerous; she would have to continue to insist that she left immediately, but if it was on shutdown, it was unlikely she would be allowed. The only other option was to find a way to escape. She needed to somehow reclaim *Arnazia*, her lost ring, as well as the Simal. Another memory returned. *Oh, by Ashareth, Sezareal has the Simal.*

"Come with me, we have some food and water waiting for you in the sanctuary," Janus said to her, and then turned and clapped his hands impatiently at the maid. "Go on Rosie, enough of your gawking. I've let you watch the resurrection and the *Awakening*, so go and get the food, I'm feeling a bit peckish myself after all this work."

"Yes, your reverence," Rosie said as she crossed the chamber, taking another look at Janorra before bounding up the stairs.

Janorra stood, and felt a bit steadier on her feet. Janus walked towards the exit, trailed by the man with no-nose.

"Help her up the stairs," Janus ordered Scarand, "slowly, she has been through a lot and is not to be rushed."

Scarand took her by the arm, and as the other two started up the stairs, he walked Janorra slowly to them.

"You lied," he whispered. "You were not on the *River Queen.*"

She looked him in the eye; "I have good reasons not to tarry here, and by looking at your injuries, I would assume captivity is a new experience for you and one you would not want to become permanent?"

He nodded. "I do not wish to remain here, but there is a woman, goes by the name of Sasna. If I can, I would help her escape this place as well."

"Of what interest is this woman to you? A relative, a friend or a lover?"

A look of confusion crossed his face, as though he was not sure how to answer.

"If she is not close to you, and you wish to leave with me, by any means possible, then we have the same interest," she said in reply.

Scarand looked back at the Obelisk, which still appeared to be resting. "That thing, it has eyes and it speaks," he said. "I had heard of this, that Akkadians were resurrected by some living pillar, but until this day, I had doubted the truth of it."

She did not have the time to talk to him about the mysteries of the Obelisks, or what it meant to be a Pure-blood Akkadian. He had lied for her, and that gave her hope. He looked stern and courageous, and she had decided it was worth the risk in being honest with him. It was clear he was a new slave to the Everglow, and she had gambled that he still entertained thoughts of escape, and much to her relief, it was clear that he did. "There are greater wonders you will see, if you help me get out of here. By any means, I must escape this place as quickly as I can," she whispered.

His eyes blazed as he looked at her, and then he smiled grimly. "We have the same goal," he said softly, "but my honour will not allow me to leave the woman named Sasna behind. She is in deep trouble if she remains here. There is some sort of trouble in the castle, some guards were murdered. It is a situation we might be able to use."

She felt a surge of frustration. *Fool of a Davari, the fate of the world is at stake and you want to help a woman? If you hinder my escape, I will leave you behind!*

"What is your name?" he asked her.

Before she could answer, the large Obelisk in the middle of the chamber opened its eyes. "Her name is Janorra," it said, its voice deep and booming. It stood there, and she looked at it. On this side of the Deadlands, it was like every other Obelisk - tall and black with wide, yellow, blinking eyes. It spoke, again, with an urgency. "Tum de dum. Run Seeress, run! The Wild Hunt comes for you. A terrible beast of the air with red and golden wings searches for you. Beasts also live within these castle walls. Run, Seeress, run!"

Janus scuttled partially back down the stairs and peered at the Obelisk. "Oh, pay it no heed," he said to Janorra as he turned back and beckoned for her to follow him and go up the stairs. "It's been muttering silly phrases like that all day. Last time the Baron died and resurrected, I had to put up with all manner of nonsense from it. Pay it no heed!"

"Yes, they can be like that," Janorra replied as, assisted by Scarand, she walked across the chamber and followed the others up the winding stairs. The words of the Obelisk troubled her. *The Wild Hunt? I have heard of them, but cannot yet recall who or what they are? What beast searches for me? Kappia must have sent griffins to hunt me down!*

They reached the top of the stairway and walked out into the sanctuary, where she was met by a grisly sight and a cacophony of noise. Six dead bodies, wrapped in white linen coverings lay on top of the altar, with only their heads uncovered. Blood was seeping through the linen, a sign the bodies had met a grisly end and not that long ago. Outside of the temple sanctuary, distant bells and alarms were frantically ringing.

"Oh, excuse them," Janus said as he shut and locked the door of the chamber behind them. "There's been murder in the castle, foul deeds, the bodies were wrapped and brought here immediately as Aeldar law dictates. A dangerous prisoner has escaped, Sasna is her name."

"Sasna did this deed?" Scarand blurted out, clearly surprised. "Why didn't you tell me this was her doing?"

"Why? Of what business is it of yours?" Janus asked indignantly. He then said rebukingly to Scarand, "Now mind your own, us Pure-bloods are talking and I'll not have you interrupting."

Janorra noticed Scarand clench his fists and glower angrily at Janus, but the priest was staring at her and muttering. "These Davari slaves always poke their noses into other people's business and that's what angers the baron!" He sighed and still looking at Janorra said, "My apologies for the presence of the Davari when you resurrected. I was supposed to have two maids helping me here, but one of them was hysterical as that one," he pointed to one of the corpses, "Ole Jimson, was her man." He then pointed to some fresh blood on the floor and groaned, "What a mess. This floor is new!" Barking an order at Scarand he said, "Go get the mop and clean that mess up?"

As Scarand fetched a mop and began cleaning up, Janus looked at the guard, who was staring angrily at Scarand.

"He was with the Seesnari bitch when she arrived at the castle, you should let me lock him back up," he said heatedly, and then staring at the man with no nose, he added, "and that piece of pirate scum!" The guard frowned at Janus. "What sort of place allows villains to roam freely? The security at this castle has become a joke since your fat arse arrived and you demanded prisoners from the cells help you." He snorted derisively and looked condescendingly at Janus.

Janus sighed angrily at the guard and answered furiously. "Ole Benkin, I am in charge of them, not you! You go and make yourself useful! Go and tell Lady Bavira, that our guest has resurrected. She might not trouble herself to come down here with all of the fuss at the moment but it's better we let her make that choice, she is Baron Daramir's sister, after all."

Ole Benkin the guard walked sullenly off, in no particular rush.

Janus sat on the front pew and pointed at Rosie, "You are friends with Ole Benkin, warn him I'll report him to the Baron for disrespect! Now, where is the food girl?" He then signalled for Janorra to sit next to him. "My apologies; the guards here are so disrespectful to me." He wiped his face with his hands as though the gesture might remove his irritation. "I know exhaustion will soon hit you. I will have a room prepared for you so you can rest. But, before that, we must wait in case Lady Bavira wishes to speak with you."

Rosie the maid fetched food and water from a basket near the altar.

Janorra took a few deep breaths to calm her racing heart and to quiet the thoughts drumming through her mind. She rubbed her forehead, feeling her own fatigue, and slowly, she summoned her inner calmness. Fighting to push back the terrifying thoughts of what would happen to her if she was discovered a liar, or could not escape from the castle, she silently prayed: *Ashareth, show me the way, guide me in this world, and in the next, to the Fair Haven.* Peace and hope returned, and even if only momentarily, it was a welcome respite. She still did not remember exactly where the castle was, but she was glad she had discovered it was far enough from Kappia that it would take time for ravens or pigeons to arrive with a message of recent events. It was important that she did not panic, or arouse more suspicion than her arrival already had. It was untimely her arrival coincided with an escape attempt from another prisoner. The castle guard would be on high alert. She was sure it would not be long before she remembered from her past study of maps exactly where the castle was. She did know though, that she had to leave, as soon as possible, before Inquisitor Feagan returned. Even if by some small chance he was delayed, the Empire would soon be on her trail, in one form or another, of that she had no doubt, and as the Aeldar sect clearly had a foothold here, it would not remain safe for her for very long. Besides, the Obelisk had already warned her she was being hunted. *Otan, I now remember, that is the Obelisk's name.*

Time was of the essence, but she needed refreshment as fatigue and extreme exhaustion usually followed shortly after a resurrection. It was not unusual for a newly resurrected person to sleep for many hours after the experience. She could already feel the tiredness and exhaustion skulking up on her, but the seriousness of her situation and the alertness she felt, was keeping it at bay, for now. She was glad when Rosie handed her bread with cheese, and gave her water. She ate and drank hungrily, paying little attention to good manners.

"Who is this Sasna, whom you say is the culprit for these murders?" she asked in between taking another bite from the bread.

Janus, who was greedily eating, spoke with his mouth-full, spitting out pieces of bread. "It is most strange. She is a Seesnari noble. I don't know why she was being held or why she might be acting so insanely in killing guards. I'm not entirely sure yet. I'm always the last to be told anything around here." He laughed sardonically, "But you know what they say; *never trust a Seesnari!*" He attempted to smile at her. "You haven't told me your name, or how you died on the *River Queen*; do you remember yet? Was it by fire, smoke inhalation or drowning? I drowned once, several lifetimes ago – horrible death."

"My name is Alydia, and I died by smoke inhalation," Janorra lied. Wanting to take the initiative and garner information, she asked, "What region of Bruthon is this? Tell me everything you know, where the safe Obelisks are and which other lands border these regions?"

"Well, this region is called Bragen, on the border of Seesnari which is to the west. To the north-west are the Branded Lands and the Wytchwood, and in the north-east Anthain and Stargen, the lands of the free cities and free peoples. South of here there are mainly marshes, there are probably a few Obelisks in there but they are lost to memory and outside of the few habitations, so the marsh is a wild and dangerous place to travel. To the south-east are the lands of the Horse Lords of Rhonbea and the Southern Marches; they allow few to trespass there. To the east are the lands and estates of other Bruthon barons, all the Obelisks there are known and safe. There are several in and around the capital Bruthon, which is several days ride from here."

"Was this province loyal to the Bruthon King during the civil war?"

Janus vigorously nodded his head. "Yes, Baron Daramir declared for the Bruthon King. Many other barons though, declared war and independence, as they wanted to keep the ways of the *Old Faith*. King Lagaelias crushed and utterly destroyed most of them, but it bankrupted him, and if Kappia's legions had not been caught in a life and death struggle with the Baothein, they would surely have conquered Bruthon." He shook his head. "The war cost all parts of the Empire dearly, it has never really recovered, and that includes here. The peace in Bruthon lands, is now a very fragile one. But, Lagaelias is allowing the spread of the *Aeldar Faith* and that will bring stability, in time. We are at peace with Kappia, and that is good."

Fear, unbidden and unwelcome, once again crept into Janorra's heart when she heard that she was in a province at peace with the Empress, but she kept her composure. She looked around at the unfinished temple interior, and asked Janus, "How long have you been here?"

"About two years. Inquisitor Feagan has only been here about six months. The *Old Faith* was dying out here long before we arrived, but they are still strong in the Bruthon capital, and he passionately wants to wipe them out. He requested to be posted here." Janus looked at her incredulously. "Can you believe that? Who in their right mind would want to come to this barbaric place?" He then blushed with embarrassment. "Sorry, me and my tact. I do not like it here, the only help I get is from criminals and slaves the baron allows me to use, and even they are often rude to me."

Janorra shuddered as some more memories returned to her, many more in the matter of a few seconds, causing her to gasp for breath and her head to spin so that she nearly fainted. *I know where I am. The Jula has brought me far to the South. I am a long way from the safety of Baothein lands.* She also remembered something she had once been told in the Deadlands about the Wytchwood, something she had not shared with her peers or Mazdek after she had resurrected that particular time. That might explain the strange and sinister presence she had felt in the Deadlands. *A strange spirit once told me that he had reasons to believe Aeldar Riddles were hiding in the Wytchwood. The Simal brought itself here to find the Aeldar Riddles.* She suddenly remembered it all. *That was secretive information I was to share with the Baothein, when I handed the Simal over to them, to further ensure my safety and sanctuary.* She was suddenly filled with a new sense of horror. *Arnazia is with my last body in the Wytchwood. That is where the Simal and Sezareal will be as well. I have to go there and reclaim them.* She looked again at her surroundings, a temple sanctuary of worship to the Aeldar. She then looked at her attire, the robe she wore. With a renewed sense of urgency that pushed back her growing fatigue, she said to Janus. "I need a pair of strong boots, travelling attire, a sword and dagger and if possible, a bow. Please provide me with these, some supplies and a horse."

Janus chuckled politely. "The castle is in shutdown. Nobody will be allowed to leave until the murderer is caught."

"You can arrange a special pass, surely?" She tried to sound as sincere as possible when she told the next lie. "I am on special business from Kappia, I remember it clearly now. If you or anybody here in this castle, causes that business to be delayed, the Empress herself will hear of it and they will be answerable to her!"

240

Janus answered apologetically. "And, if I let you leave, I would be directly answerable to the Baron, and his wrath would be more of an immediate danger to me than that of the Empress, may the Aeldar bless her name and fortune."

Before she could protest, a shrill female voice behind her asked, "So, who is this?"

Janorra spun around, to see a spiteful looking woman staring at her, along with three guards, including the one who had left the sanctuary to fetch Lady Bavira.

"Ah, Lady Bavira," Janus said to the woman, and then turned to Janorra. "Our guest is a Seeress by the name of Alydia. She tells me she is on business from Kappia but died during the wrecking of the *River Queen*."

Suspicion crossed Bavira's face. "What were you doing on the *River Queen*? What business would a Seeress from Kappia have with Ashgiliath from where it set out, and to where would you be headed?"

When Janorra stood and spoke it was with a confidence that hid and masked the fear she felt. More memories came back. *I once spent an entire lifetime serving at the Temple of Lies in the Argona complex. I remember my training, and can use deceit when it serves the greater purpose.* "I had business with the Seesnari authorities. The High Quaester, Mazdek de Lorion of Clarevont of the Argona Temple in Kappia, sent me there to convince them to allow us to start building Aeldar Temples in Seesnari lands."

Bavira looked at her strangely for a long moment, as though thinking how to put together pieces of a puzzle; she then then asked suspiciously. "Does Kappia now feel that we Bruthon are really that naive and simple?"

"I do not understand your meaning," Janorra replied.

Bavira's face twisted with a hatred so intense, it made Janorra shudder. "We recently discovered that the wicked and deceitful Sasna, a Seesnari of most vile character, had been sent to conspire with the Sea Lords, and we now discover a Seeress from Kappia travelled on the same ship with her?"

Out of the corner of her eye, Janorra noticed Scarand begin to slowly move to a position behind the guards.

"I only met her briefly, as I stayed confined to my cabin in meditation," Janorra replied. She tried to think of an excuse as to why she might be travelling along the Erin. "I was hoping to get to a safe port town, where I might hire safe passage by land or river back to Kappia. I know nothing about any conspiracy with the Sea Lords."

"If you were sent on an errand to Ashgiliath, where are your Pure-blood bodyguards?" Bavira asked. "Surely they would also be resurrecting around about this time? The Obelisk is very silent about it, if so."

"They must have survived the wreckage, and be out searching for me," Janorra quickly answered, and then turning to Janus asked, "May I rest now? Exhaustion is overcoming me." That was the truth, she felt utterly exhausted, but resting was not a part of her plan, not that she really had one at that moment.

Janus suddenly stood up, took a step back, and pointed an accusing finger at Janorra. "The Obelisk, he said you were hunted by a beast with red and golden wings, what else could that be but a griffin?" He looked questioningly at Bavira. "Maybe Kappia itself is aware of her plot to sow discord between them and us, and now hunts her down? Why else would a griffin hunt her?"

Janorra felt panicked, and could not think what to say or do, so blurted out, "Stranger coincidences have happened. Neither I nor Kappia have any knowledge of any Seesnari plot with the Sea Lords, if there is one. My mission is as I said, but, if you want to listen to the words of an insane Obelisk about me being hunted, then go ahead, but also take heed of every other insanity it ever speaks about anybody else who it resurrects!"

The intensity in Bavira's stare did not lessen, nor the harshness in her voice. "Feagan will get the truth out of you, by way of the Eye of Morsef, but it might be you tell the truth about your mission, so until then, I will not act hastily in my dealings with a Seeress who claims to be on a mission from Kappia. That is, if you do one thing that I request of you?"

"Which is?" Janorra asked.

"If you are trusted by Kappia to leave the temple, then you are of a high order. Do you do have the power of Báith Rahmèra, and speak the tongue of the Deadlands? If so, has the memory of how to perform the ritual returned yet?"

The memory had returned. So ingrained were many of the rituals and powers a Seeress had, they were often some of the first memories to come back. Janorra knew exactly what was being asked of her, and not knowing what else to do, thought a demonstration of her power might temporarily win the trust of Bavira.

"I remember the Báith Rahmèra. What do you require of me?"

"I want to know what happened, how the Seesnari escaped. If you do this for me, I would be most…appreciative."

Janus shook his head. "I cannot allow this, perhaps in Kappia such things occur but this is not the sort of thing that should happen in my sanctuary."

"Stop your cantankerous complaining priest," Bavira said fiercely to Janus, as she walked over to Janorra and eyed her up and down, and then spoke again to Janus without taking her eyes off of Janorra. "I have heard you boast often of the power of the Aeldar, especially that wielded by those initiated into the higher orders of your faith, such as Seers, but never have I seen a proper demonstration of it. If she can do this, I want to see proof of it, and in so doing learn if anyone in the castle aided the Seesnari in her escape."

Janus looked incredulously at Janorra. "Only a very few Seers have the ability of Báith Rahmèra, and they are in the highest order of the faith and are sworn and dedicated to service only at the Argona Temple. Why would one of such a high order be sent on a mission to Ashgiliath?"

"Perhaps to convince them with a demonstration of Aeldar power," Janorra quickly replied as she looked at Janus. "If a priest such as you were sent, what sort of demonstration beyond your incessant complaining could you show them?"

Bavira stared suspiciously at Janorra, and warily asked her. "Is this true? Are not those who might have the power of Báith Rahmèra sworn to service only at the Argona Temple?"

"The translation of the text that dictates this, is open to interpretation," Janorra replied. "We are sent from the temple, when our skills are needed elsewhere, in service to the temple, not at it. We can leave when the High Quaestar himself grants us a special task and permission. His letter of permission, stamped with his seal, is on my former body."

"The conversion of the untrustworthy Seesnari takes one of your skill?" Bavira asked.

Janorra replied as confidently as she could. "The High Quaester, desires to have the Deadlands in these areas fully mapped out. He has sent me as I have the skills to do such a deed, the mission to Ashgiliath was added to my tasks, but was only of minor importance. I am of the Ninth Order. I have the ability to perform the Báith Rahmèra, and memory of the ritual has already returned. If I demonstrate this to you, perhaps you will stop with these futile accusations about Kappia being involved in some plot against the Bruthon?"

242

"But, with respect, she still does not have the authority," Janus protested, and pleaded with Bavira. "My lady, only the High Quaester or an Inquisitor has the authority to authorise the use of such a disturbing ritual."

"Fetch the *Book of Aeldar Volume III* and turn to the ninth chapter, and read the forty-second verse," Janorra ordered Janus.

Reluctantly, he went to the altar, fumbled through the pages of one of the Aeldar books upon it, and when he found what he was looking for, he read the verse silently, mouthing the words with his lips.

She glanced at him. "Does it not say a Seer or Seeress of the Ninth Order can also authorise the use of the ritual?"

"It does," he answered reluctantly.

Looking back at Bavira, Janorra added, "The High Quaester was most insistent that after I had spoken with the Seesnari authorities, I informed you of my true mission here, and that I obey all reasonable instructions of the Baron, and his sister. Before finding passage back to Kappia, I planned to stop here and request an audience with Baron Daramir."

Bavira still watched her suspiciously, so Janorra urged, "Only the spirit of a half or Fell-blood can be recalled through the Báith Rahmèra, and only then if it has not wandered too far away from the Obelisk. Time is of the essence. If this is to be done, it must be done now."

"Then do it," Bavira said, with quiet ferocity and determination. "The guard was a Fell-blood, all of them are. I want to know what he saw. He might have information that can assist us in finding the Seesnari."

Janus walked over to the corpses still lying on the altar, and Janorra followed. "It is one of these ones, these were the first two corpses brought here," he said, uncovering the first. It was dressed in the garb of a physician, and bore the mark of the Obelisk under the eye.

"I cannot use a Pure-blood, it is impossible, it must be the Fell-blood," she replied.

Janus uncovered the second one. It was the guard. "That's him, that is Ole Jimson."

Rosie let out a squeal of terror, and Ole Benkin mumbled to another guard, "What are they going to do to Ole Jimson's corpse?"

Without warning, another wave of exhaustion swept over Janorra. Under any other circumstance, she would refuse to even attempt to perform such a ritual. It would be difficult without her ring. Even if she had it, it would take a lot of energy out of her. However, this close to an Obelisk, she could use its power, but the Obelisk would not like it, but there were other advantages to her. As well as performing the ritual, it would powerfully energise her physically. *The power of the Obelisk charges the very air all around us. Perhaps this will also remove the effects of my resurrection and Awakening. I am so tired; I can use its power to refresh me.*

"Go ahead," Bavira said taking a few steps back.

"You must kneel here, at the altar, in honour of the Aeldar," Janorra said to Janus, pointing to the cushioned tier at the foot of the altar. "The rest of you, take one of those cushions at the foot of a pew, if you require it, and kneel where you are."

Rosie and the guards hesitated, and looked at each other uncertainly.

"Do it!" Bavira ordered, "everyone, obey now!" she shrilled, before taking a cushion and kneeling.

Scarand shot Janorra a short glance, and she gestured with her eyes for him to do the same. One by one, the others in the sanctuary, followed suit and knelt, except Janorra.

"Confirm his name," she said to Rosie, who mumbled nervously,

"His name was Ole Jimson ma'am."

Without hesitation, Janorra walked over to a kneeling guard and asked for his knife. The guard looked to Bavira, who nodded permission. Janorra took the knife, walked over to the dead body and cut the linen away from it, and put the knife next to it.

Janorra grimaced, for she knew the act would both insult and cause pain to the Obelisk. *Forgive me for what I am about to do, Otan.* "Otan! Otan! *Baragar, akma al a sineiedious,*" she said, using Báith Rahmèra, the tongue of the dead. The sanctuary went dark as the many branches of candles instantly blew out, before strangely lighting themselves again, giving off an eerie unnatural blue light. Deep below, in the Chamber of Resurrection, Otan the Obelisk, wailed and then roared out in booming anger, drowning out the distant clang of the bells still ringing outside of the sanctuary. The sanctuary shook with the sound of his wrath and pain. Janorra did not like treating Otan in such a manner after the help he had given her, but she had little choice. The door of the resurrection chamber blew open, smashing the lock and handle. A light rush of wind blew through the sanctuary, causing the candles to flicker but not go out. The wind died away, and there was silence, except for the whimpering of Rosie and the frightened moans of the guards. Janorra felt the vital energy and power of Otan surging through her body. Any exhaustion she felt, disappeared in an instant, but she knew it would not last long. *Forgive me for this, Otan.*

"Ole Jimson *hasoa en gaharty*," Janorra said, as she waved her hands over the body. Energy in the form of light left her palms, and entered the corpse. Slowly, the body of Ole Jimson began to move. Bones clicked and snapped as it sat up and then awkwardly stepped off the altar. Rosie screamed in terror and covered her face.

"T'is against nature!" Ole Benkin said, aghast.

The movements of Ole Jimson's corpse, were clumsy and spasmodic. Its face was twisted with pain and horror as the eyes opened and looked at Janorra, its voice filled with despair and agony, and when it spoke, it was in the language of Báith Rahmèra, a tongue only Janorra out of those living, could understand.

"Why, why did you bring me back? I know only pain," it wailed.

Rosie covered her face with her hands. "T'is not right," she shrieked in between hysterical sobs.

*Forgive me for this sacrilege. I am so sorry Ole Jimson.* "You will answer my questions," Janorra said to the corpse, also using the Báith Rahmèra speech.

The dead man looked at her, "Send me back. Send me back. The pain of this body I cannot bear, even the dark horror would not torment me so much."

"Tell me how you died, who killed you and what happened? Answer my questions and I will release you back to the dark sleep." The dead man looked at her and wailed, a long, pitiful, painful moan.

"Tell me, or I will leave you in this state, to forever walk the land of the living as tormented flesh, until your bones bleach and crumble."

The dead man wailed again, but seemed to understand what she wanted. "I will tell you, then release me! The agony of this body is too much to bear."

"Who killed you, was it the Seesnari woman?"

"The deformed boy, he thrust the dagger into me. Release me! I beg of you for all the mercy of the gods, release me!"

"Did anybody else assist the Seesnari?"

"Just the boy, just the boy."

Janorra thought for a brief moment. "The portal that sucked you into the Deadlands, was it arched and blue on the outside with black smoke in the middle?"

"It was," the dead man said.

"Forgive me for this, answer this last question, and I will release you," Janorra said to the corpse. She grimaced, "Do you know what happened to the Seesnari, the one they called Sasna?"

The corpse turned, and looked towards the door, and pointed at something. "Seesnari!" it said.

"*Carsa mak el nanrna,*" Janorra said. Air nosily left the lungs and mouth of the corpse, as it clattered lifeless to the floor. The candles went out as a wind blew through the sanctuary and when they relit themselves, their natural light returned. Otan, in the chamber below, began to wail and cry. Janorra turned her head to look at what Ole Jimson had pointed at. A woman stood there, at the entrance to the sanctuary, looking at the scene with horror. She was dressed in blue silk and a hooded cloak of blue dyed rabbit fur.

Everyone stood up, turned, and stared towards the woman.

"You!" Bavira shrilled at the woman and pointed at her. "It is the Seesnari, it is Sasna! Seize her!" she ordered the guards. "Seize her!"

After initially looking startled, the first guard to react was Ole Benkin. He drew his sword and rushed at the woman.

"Sasna!" Scarand shouted. Instinctively, with the speed of a mountain lion, he was on his feet and charged Ole Benkin and rammed into him, knocking him to the floor. Ole Benkin lost grip of his sword, which clattered across the floor and fell at Janorra's feet. Without hesitating she picked it up.

Ole Benkin quickly got back to his feet. "What are you doing you Davari scum?" he shouted at Scarand, then drew a dirk and lunged at him, which he easily and gracefully dodged.

After a moment of initial confusion, Janorra knew. *This might be my only chance to escape, I have to take it.* With a skilful leap and hop, she plunged the sword into the next guard to his feet, killing him almost instantly.

The last guard drew his weapon, yelling at the top of his voice for Janorra to drop the sword, and when she did not, he set about her with a series of lunges and cuts, shouting at the top of his voice to Ole Benkin to call for help.

Ole Benkin immediately began to run towards a large bell in the sanctuary shouting for help as he did so. He was stopped by Marlo who was on his feet, ran at him and tackled him to the ground. Scarand was also upon him in an instant, and smashed Ole Benkin's head repeatedly into the side of a pew until he breathed his last.

Janorra easily parried the attacks of her assailant, but in an instant, she felt the energy she had taken from Otan, evaporate and leave her. The guard did not have a lot of skill, but enough that it was a battle she did not have the time for, and now not even the strength. There was no way she could match him in her weakened state, as exhaustion was again seeping through every bone and muscle of her body. Noticing this, the guard stepped up the attack, swinging his blade high and then low, aiming for head and then knees.

"You are cursed Pure-blood!" he said through teeth gritted with fury. "When you return from the Deadlands, you have no idea what the Baron and his sister will do to you for your deeds this day. Do you believe you can tolerate the pain?" He struck at her head, but missed.

"I'll make you all pay for killing Ole Jarsin 'ere in the sanctuary, and for that dark magic you put on Ole Jimson," he said tauntingly, as she weakly parried his cut and thrusts.

Janorra slipped on the freshly spilt blood from one of the corpses, and fell to the ground. In an instant, the guard pinned her to it with the sword point at her throat. He never saw what hit him as Scarand struck. He smashed him to the ground with a hammer blow from one of the bronze idols he had taken from a plinth. The guard was more than likely dead by the time he hit the marble floor.

Janorra stared up at Scarand. She was panting after the conflict, trembling in every limb. "Help me!" she gasped breathlessly, as she looked at him. He stood like the image of a conquering primordial, his legs braced apart, his head thrust forward. One hand reached out. She took it and he pulled her to her feet.

Bavira was screaming in hysterical fury, Rosie in sheer terror. Bavira's scream was cut short as Sasna pierced her through with a sword.

"If only you had one death to die bitch," she said. Bavira stared at Sasna, and with her last breaths said, "My brother will see Ashgiliath burn to the ground for this!" The light flickered from her eyes. Sasna kicked the corpse from the sword, and it fell clumsily to the floor with a thud.

Rosie held her head in her hands and continued crying and shrieking.

Sasna went to slay her, but Rosie stood to her feet and fled from the sanctuary. "Let her go," Janorra said as Marlo began to pursue her.

Scarand's voice was desperate with strident urgency. "I don't know a way out of here," he said, as he dropped the idol to the floor. It landed with a loud crash.

"I do, I remember now," Janorra said as she bound over to Janus who was unsteadily regaining his feet. She kicked him in the face with the heel of her foot and he fell to the floor.

"I think I lost a tooth," he mumbled through smashed and bloody lips, before noticing the blood spattered upon Janorra, the dead guards, and Lady Bavira, sprawled lifeless on the floor. He wailed in despair.

Outside, alerted by Rosie's screams, the clattering of armed men running and shouting could be heard, their yells getting louder as they neared the sanctuary.

Janorra snatched the keys hanging from Janus' rope belt and threw them to Scarand and shouted at him and Marlo. "Lock the door, bar and bolt it. It won't buy us much time but it might be enough."

Scarand, aided by Marlo wasted no time. They bound over to the main doors and barred them, before quickly shutting and sliding across the bolts on the smaller inset door. They were just in time. As they slid the last bolt across the inset door, it immediately began to rattle as the guards tried to break it down from the outside. Scarand then locked the door for good measure before grabbing a bow, a quiver of arrows and a sword from a guard. He strapped the sword belt to his waist and slung the bow and arrows over his shoulder.

Janorra grabbed Janus' arm and pinned it behind his back as she spun it around whilst holding the sword to his neck. He screamed in pain, "You'll break it," he whimpered.

"Where is your priest-hole that leads to the outside?"

"It's under the altar," Janus wailed as she twisted his arm even further.

Except for the Argona Temple, Janorra had suddenly remembered that every Aeldar temple, contained a secret exit that served as an escape, usually under the altar, in case those of the faith needed to make a quick getaway. It also served as a secret entrance, in case clandestine access was required. Some could be opened by means known to her, others, might take more time, depending on when and how they were constructed and in what land. This one, might prove to be a problem, as it would be engineered specifically for Bruthon lands.

"*Hemasay, ankragor am oosh shekanahri,*" Janorra said as she raised her sword hand. The sanctuary shook slightly and several stands of candles clattered loudly to the floor as a force left her hand, rippled down the sword and out of the tip of the blade. She looked all around her; blue hazy lines dazzled and filled the sanctuary and then disappeared as quickly as they came. The altar lit up, but did not move. Otan the Obelisk, was still letting her use its power, despite the pain and anger she had caused it in performing a dark ritual, raising a dead Fell-blood.

"Thank you, Otan," she whispered.

Deep below in the Chamber of Resurrection, Otan boomed and roared, "Run Janorra, run!"

The temple door shook and rattled. The guards had found something to batter the smaller inset door, some sort of ram, probably a stone bench from the gardens.

Janorra knew she had to act fast. She let go of Janus, and spoke to him as she dropped the sword and pulled the boots and breeches off of one of the fallen guards.

"The High Quaester himself will reward you well if you help me leave this place. I am on an important mission of the uttermost secrecy that can bear no delay. You must help me. Open the exit." She hoped the lie would work, as she pulled the leather hauberk and the shirt off of the same guard. Taking her robe off, she quickly dressed in the dead man's bloodied clothes and hauberk, and then pulled the boots on.

"Look at what you've done!" Janus howled.

"Will you help me?" she asked him, as she took a belt and buckled it around her waist before picking up and sheathing the sword.

Janus was sobbing and wailing in despair, beating his chest with his fists. "You killed the Lady Bavira!" he screamed as Sasna. "Her fury when she resurrects, and that of the Baron, will know no end. Why did you do this?"

"She deserves it. You have no idea what they were planning to do to me," Sasna protested loudly.

The door shook and shuddered, as the ram crashed against it.

Janus panicked and flustered, pulling the hair of his tonsure and then beating his fists against his chest. "You don't know what is down there," he wailed.

Janorra ran over to the altar, and was soon joined by Scarand, Marlo and Sasna. She placed both hands upon it. "*Hemasay, ankragor am esh shekanahri,*" she said desperately, not knowing what else to do. Blue hazy lines dazzled and flowed over the altar, and then disappeared as quickly as they came, but again the altar did not move.

The door shook and shuddered again, as it was hit with even more force causing it to bend and groan with the impact and a hinge to fly off.

"Janus, help me, please," Janorra begged him, as she tried to push the altar, and then slide it. When that didn't work, she looked and felt for a catch and randomly used her fingers and pressed the altar at different parts. "Unlock it for me!"

Scarand was upon Janus in a moment. He grabbed him by the throat with both hands and dragged him over to the altar. "Show her what she needs to know," he said.

Janus shrieked as he looked at the maddened glare in the Davari's blue eyes. "Let go," he spluttered as he tried to prize Scarand's hands away from his throat. "I'll show you, then be gone from this place, and be dammed," he said.

Scarand let go of him.

Janus looked at the altar, and then with a finger, he pressed in specific sequence, several different body parts from some of the carved images.

"It is unlocked, but I am too afraid to remember the incantation," he said as he looked up at Janorra. "The Baron will punish me for this. He has no logic or reason when his fury is let loose."

The door shook and shuddered again, as it was hit with even more impact causing it to bend and groan with the impact and causing another hinge to fly off.

247

Janorra did not know the incantation specific to this altar, but she knew that all altars, when unlocked, should respond to the tongue of Báith Rahmèra. It was a fact she had learnt in the Mystery Schools, but had never put into practice, and now her very existence and fate rested upon it.

*"Hemasay, ankragor am esh shekanahri."* Blue hazy lines dazzled and flowed over the altar again, but once more disappeared as quickly as they came, but to her great relief, the altar effortlessly moved of its own accord, sliding towards the pulpit causing some of the bodies to roll off of it and fall into the newly appeared opening in the ground. At that moment, the inset door groaned and bent at the impact of the battering it was receiving. With a snapping of bolts and hinges, and a rending of wood, the door splintered and burst inwards. Rosie, accompanied by a dozen or so guards, rushed in.

"Murderers," she screamed and pointed at those by the altar. "They are all murderers."

*"Hemasay, ankragor am merkown shekanahri,"* Janorra shouted, as she pointed towards the scaffolding to the right of the door. Blue hazy lines dazzled and flowed over the scaffolding, which lurched, and with a loud crash fell upon the guards who shouted and screamed in panic.

Janus, the priest, rolled into the opening made by the altar, shouting, *"Mafius en toosa,"* the High Akkadian words for 'close and lock.'

"He's trying to shut it," Janorra screamed. "Get inside!" The altar began to slide back to close. She, Scarand, Marlo and Sasna all acted instinctively, and leaped through the opening, and only got safely inside mere moments before the altar shut over their heads, locking with several loud clicking sounds.

# Chapter Twenty: *The Order of Ithkall*

*The famous General Attira of Carapoth, called his more famous than him sword, the Sword of En-Sof, because he boasted that it fell from heaven as a gift for him to slay his enemies. I doubt that is true, for the sword was made at an enchanted blacksmith's forge in the Carovna province. Temmison refers to it when he wrote about the history of that particular region. In order to know about magic swords, we first need to know how a sword is made. Techniques for heat-treating a sword are complex and vary slightly with different smiths, and there are a number of different enchanting methods. However much the methods may vary, to create a magic sword, the process always contains the following four steps.*

*1. Soaking. The metal is brought up to a high temperature – over $700\,^oC$ – and tongs are used to hold it in the heat for up to several hours. Each alloy requires a special temperature.*

*2. Quenching. The metal is cooled very quickly to achieve extreme hardness, usually by quenching it is water, or in most cases, oil. The rate at which the metal is cooled off is very important, as even the difference between ice water and room temperature can make a difference and determine how the crystals will be structured and what precipitates might form. Oils are the most common quenching medium for blades, as they have a very good rate of heat dissipation.*

*3. Tempering. If not carried out correctly, quenching can over-harden the blade and make it brittle, so it is necessary to keep raising the temperature again to around $200\,^oC$. This process is usually carried out repeatedly and eases some of the internal stresses to make the blade softer and less prone to shattering.*

*4. Enchanting. Powers can be added to a sword by enchanting it. The right materials need to be used, in conjunction with the right enchantment. It is a very complicated and extremely difficult process fraught with risk, therefore only the most skilled and trained enchanters should ever make the attempt. Most gain their skills by learning to enchant normal cutlery before they ever even attempt to enchant a weapon. The use of any magic, especially enchantments, can have unforeseen consequences, so again, I cannot stress strongly enough, that nobody should attempt this process without the proper training.*
*Lankray: The Art of Smithing and Enchanting Vol I.*

*Port* Kappia stood strangely quiet in the noonday heat that had followed the fierce dawn storm. The white water cascaded down from the Kappia Plateau high above, and on its descent hit a series of rocky outcrops, giving the effect of many waterfalls rather than just one. Peaceful from a distance, but loud and deafening up close, a mist rose up from the spray of the water as it cascaded into Lake Panharin, then casually flowed on its way as if nothing had occurred.

The capital city of Kappia, to the west of the waterfall, had an upper part, on the top of the plateau itself, and a central section built on massive ramparts which connected it to the lower section, on the shores of the lake. The central and lower sections were heavily guarded by strategically placed forts and watchtowers.

Azzadan paid little attention to the familiar view as he entered the harbour of Kappia situated at the base of the plateau. He threaded his way between the great war-galleys and merchant ships at anchor. He rowed straight towards a jetty a mile or so to the left of the waterfall, where hundreds of small boats similar in make and appearance to the one he was in were tied. The guards on the harbour watchtower paid no attention to him as he made his boat fast to an iron ring set in the wood of the quayside. He made no effort to appear to be in a rush as he spread out his net to dry in the boat, in the pretence of being one of the many fishermen, before picking up a basket of fish, strapping it to his shoulder, and then climbing a ladder onto the top of the jetty, and then another to the top of the stone pier.

Somebody dressed in a fisherman's mantle and carrying a wicker basket of freshly caught fish roused no suspicion. He seemed but an ordinary fisherman returning after a trip afloat, one of the many hundreds who rowed out of the harbour onto the lake every day, and back again. If one had observed him more closely, however, they would have seen the murderous look in his eye, the way his features were twisted in anger, and the manner in which he held a hand on the hilt of a club partly hidden inside his mantle. Nobody cast Azzadan more than a casual glance as he sold his catch to a nearby vendor, a man from his own Order.

"He is waiting for you," the vendor whispered.

Azzadan did not haggle over the offered price, but merely nodded and put the coin in a purse before hastily striding off the pier.

Azzadan noticed a strange restlessness that ran through the people of the capital's port. People whispered to each other, in tones so soft that only those who spoke to each other in such a way could hear them. His whetted primitive instincts sensed there was unrest here. It was no surprise to him, the theft of the Simal and the escape of a Seeress from the temple in such a dramatic manner, and the news about Aleskian, were enough to disturb all who heard about such shocking events.

Azzadan had taken a boat earlier that morning from a house his Order owned on the south-western side of Lake Panharin, ready with nets and fresh fish so he could enter Kappia without arousing suspicion. The house-master had informed him of rumours that the great city of Aleskian had been burned to the ground, the Aleskian Gate had been breached and that Bantu hordes were now pouring into the Everglow, pillaging and destroying everything in their path. He had also heard rumour that the Simal had been recaptured, and would soon be visibly paraded through Kappia along with the Seeress, who would meet a grisly and public *Final-death*. It was that news which bothered him the most – if she and the Simal had been recaptured, then he had already failed in a vital part of his mission. His instincts told him to doubt what he had heard.

Amongst the throng of people Azzadan passed in Kappia, he alone suspected that all may not be as it seemed, and that that the return of the Simal and the captured Seeress, could be just a ruse to assuage the anger of the masses. The house-master had told him it was said the Seeress had made it as far as the vast Golden Vineyards of Sathia, over the border, and was captured trying to sneak past one of the Rose Forts. The house-master, who would not be privy to the business or mission Azzadan had been on, had said that the news was, the would-be assassin who had been with her, had also been captured, and had failed in the task of attempting to kill Ahrimakan. Azzadan wondered, *if that part is not true, about me being captured and Ahrimakan not being slain, what else is false?*

Azzadan had already began his search for Janorra, and the Simal, after she had failed to show up at the rendezvous area, but after he had set out, a coded message had been sent to him by raven. He was commanded to return to the secret base of the Order of Ithkall. The message had not been welcomed by him, but he had no other choice than to obey, for he had sworn utter obedience through sacred vows, as all had to do upon entry into the secretive Order.

He walked swiftly along the waterfront streets with their broad steps that led down to the water. The waft of beer and wine, mixed with tobacco and sweat, floated in the

250

air as he passed the taverns, where sailors and marines drank and played dice and cards, as women danced to music that drifted through the air mingled with raucous laughter and song. He entered the long shadowy streets of the lower part of the city, where people strode along the pavements upon which shops and stalls displayed their wares. The people who traversed the streets were commoners, the odd noble man or women, slaves, tradesmen and harlots. Shoeless children sold wares or begged passers-by for coin. Only a few of the people were Akkadians, some were Half-bloods but most were Fell-bloods. The crowds of people became fewer as he progressed into the more secluded area of the lower-city.

He made his way towards an unobtrusive cottage that stood by itself far from the others, just below the sheer cliff face, and mostly hidden by a copse of trees. The cottage could only be reached by entering through a stone archway, that held warning signs of death to trespassers, and then walking on a walled cobbled path that passed through the trees. When he reached the door of the cottage, he looked around, merely as a precaution, to make sure nobody had followed or was watching, before knocking with a special knock only used by his Order. A hooded man opened the door and bid him come in. The cottage was barely furnished, and the windows were boarded up so none could see in. A fat woman led him silently through the scarcely furnished place and into a walled back garden that consisted of a hedge maze, concealed underneath an overhang in the cliff, so that those walking through the maze could not be observed from above. She said nothing as she closed the door quietly behind him.

The casual visitor or purposeful trespasser to the garden, would not know this was a Davian Maze, which meant that when entered, unless you knew the secret latches and levers, and where and when to press or pull them, no matter which direction you took, you would always end up at the beginning of where you started, by the back door. Even for those who knew the path, it often seemed as though the maze changed shape in order to keep an unwanted wanderer from finding a way through it should they stumble upon a latch or lever by mistake.

Azzadan negotiated the maze with no difficulty, pressing a latch here or pulling a lever there, whilst paying little heed to the sentries he passed, who either posed openly as gardeners, or, still sensed by him, those who remained concealed from sight by their ethereal cloaks. He finally arrived at a small stone wall built flat to the side of the cliff at the back of the overhang, behind which were the secret and sacred halls of his Order, nicknamed by some as the *Rat Warren*.

Azzadan heard a deep rumbling. A huge slab of rock, red and yellow in the torchlight, rose up from the floor with a resounding crash. Within the rock was a doorway, which he passed through. He entered a small cavern, and was met by a hooded man holding a torch. They said nothing to each other. The man pushed a small stone in the wall. The deep rumbling of the door shutting behind him meant there was no turning back now, until his business here was concluded. Azzadan followed the man and they descended a circular stone stairway.

The two of them walked through gloomy halls decorated with faded tapestries, and then passed through cavernous underground courtyards and over bridges which spanned deep chasms below. High walls pressed close on either side as they entered a tunnel with a vaulted ceiling. Azzadan's fingers brushed against rough, unfinished stone to his left and right. The shadows of Azzadan and the man with the torch writhed against the sides of the walls, tall as giants. *Where there is a way in, there is a way out*, he always told himself when he entered the main part of the *Rat Warren*, though in truth he knew that both the way in and out were guarded by unseen and secret sentinels, and the reality was the only way to enter or leave was with permission. He had particular reason

251

to feel concern on this occasion. He was returning without the Simal, or the Seeress. He had failed in his mission, and the consequences could be severe. To accentuate his concern, from somewhere far below him, he heard the screams and echoes of a man and a woman in terrible pain, their pleas for mercy going unanswered.

The heavy bronze door at the end of the tunnel was not locked. The man with the torch opened it, and signalled for Azzadan to enter, but did not follow. The door closed behind Azzadan. He looked around the massive square chamber made of black stone. Torches smouldered in niches in the wall. His booted feet made no sound as he crossed the black marble floor. At the far end an oak door stood partly open, and gliding through this with his hand on the hilt of his club, he came out into a great, dim, shadowy place. The black walls swept upwards toward a lofty ceiling he could not see. Black arched doorways opened into the great circular hall, known as the Hall of Circles, which was lit by bronze lamps that gave an eerie orange glow. On all sides, dim galleries hung like black stone ledges. In the midst of the great hall, stood a black stone alter, massive, sombre, without carving or decoration, and upon it stood the statue of the god Skipilos, the god of thieves, trickery, and murder. Holding a lyre with one good hand whilst playing it with a clawed hand, Skipilos had a mischievous grin on his face and his eyes were cast in such a way that it looked as though he watched the world with mockery.

Azzadan knew this place well. It was here in the secret halls of the *Order of The Clawed Hand*, the halls of *The Dark Brotherhood of the Order of Ithkall*, that he had sworn vows to Skipilos many lifetimes ago. In return for being trained in the secrets of the Order, he had vowed to serve, until he had paid what was called *The Debt*, a vast amount of money that was required in order to buy back his freedom should he wish to do so. It was also the place where a sacred blood-vow was made each time a member of the Order accepted a mission from the brotherhood.

Azzadan, like all his fellows, was a ruthless assassin and thief, trained to follow the brotherhood code. He had sworn never to purposely kill an innocent, unless the success of the assignment required it. He had vowed to obey his superiors in all things, sworn never to betray the brotherhood or expose its secrets. The final vow was never to desert the responsibility of a blood-vow.' This was a vow an assassin of the brotherhood made each time they were given a *Corpse*, their term for an assassination target, or a *Prize*, the term for something they had to steal, or a *Payoff*, if they had to kidnap somebody or something. They shed a drop of their own blood onto an image or icon of the spirit Bethratikus, the servant of Skipilos, and vowed to forfeit their lives even to *Final-death* in the effort to fulfil their sworn mission.

It was in this that Azzadan had failed. In that very hall, he had sworn a blood-vow, more than a year earlier. He had been given the only Arkoom his Order owned, for the purpose of entering the Argona Temple, to slay Ahrimakan, and rescue the Seeress after she had stolen the Simal. She had been told, and believed, that Azzadan had been commissioned to deliver her to the Baothein. Unbeknown to her, she had been a *Payoff*. He had been ordered, by whatever means, to return her and the *Prize*, the Simal, to his own Order. It was the most important mission the Order had ever issued, and it had been entrusted to him. Yet, here he was, returning without the *Prize* or the *Payoff*, even though he had assassinated the target Ahrimakan.

Had Azzadan been successful, not only would the honoured title of *Godslayer* be bestowed upon him, riches upon riches would have been given to him, and he could pay *The Debt*, and become a Master of the Brew and a member of the Council of Fellows, within his Order. Ishar, the son of Ithkall, was now the leader of the Order, but Azzadan had little respect for him as Ishar interpreted the rules of the sacred vows in a manner Azzadan considered disrespectful. On being promoted within the Order, he had intended to gain influence to limit Ishar's harmful influence. But he had failed. *The Debt* would not be repaid, and he had been summoned to give account for his failure, in front of his Order and the leader, Ishar.

Silently, as if from nowhere, hundreds of robed figures appeared in the galleries. At the far end of the hall, a broad black marble stairway with no railing, reached up into the gloom. Ishar descended the stairway, accompanied each side by a band of figures wearing black robes and bestial masks. They walked purposefully towards Azzadan. Azzadan recognised what Ishar held in his hand, and the knowledge of what it meant twisted his insides with emotions he fought to contain. It was the small Bethratikus on which he, Azzadan, had made his blood-vow to return the Simal and the Seeress to this very hall.

Ishar placed the Bethratikus on the base of the stone, at the feet of Skipilos, and removed his hood. He was a bald-headed, authoritative looking man. Along with many members of the Order who were initiated as assassins, Ishar was a Pure-blood, and also a Seer – both of which were requirements to become a higher member of the Order.

Ishar stared impassively at Azzadan and slowly asked, "Brother, where is the *Payoff*, the Seeress Janorra? Where is the *Prize*, the Simal, brother? You made the sacred vow to bring both of them to me." He grimaced. "Where are they?"

Azzadan watched as the robed figures wearing the bestial masks surrounded him, each of them taking a sacred dagger from a scabbard and raising it with two hands above their heads. One of them, he knew not who, held an Arkith, and was ready to give him the *Final-death*, should Ishar order it.

Azzadan's heart began to race but he slowed it by taking some deep breaths. A bead of sweat ran down his forehead, onto his cheek and trickled over his beard, before dropping to the floor with a splash. He did not relish the thought of his soul forever being trapped within such a soul-gem with whatever other hellish things might dwell within. Many of his own victims might be trapped within there, for it might be one of the very Arkiths he had previously used on a mission to slay those who had been made a *Corpse* by the Order. If so, he would be forced to spend eternity with his victims' hate, spite and bitterness aimed towards him.

"Master Ishar, my mission met with a small complication," he replied. "I was seeking to retrieve the *Prize* and the *Payoff*, when I was recalled here. I have not failed my mission; success has just been briefly delayed."

Murmurs of disapproval from those in the galleries rose as one. Ishar raised his hand to silence them.

"You were entrusted with the most sacred mission this Order has ever entrusted to anyone. Neither the *Prize* nor the *Payoff* is with you. You have failed to honour this Bethratikus, upon which you made your sacred vow!" Ishar's face warped with perverse displeasure.

Azzadan held his nerve, despite knowing his life was at stake, and at any moment it might be ordered he be given the *Final-death* by whomever held the Arkith. When he answered, despite the rage and anguish in his heart towards Ishar's accusation, he spoke tranquilly.

"Master Ishar, I have not dishonoured my vow, nor have I failed to honour the Bethratikus. If I had not been recalled, I would be searching for the Seeress and the Simal, at this very moment." His next words did not come out so tranquilly. "The fact you and the Council of Fellows have chosen to recall me here, instead of allowing me to complete my mission, has wasted valuable time. Allow me to continue my mission; my vow will still be fulfilled and I will honour the Bethratikus at the feet of Skipilos when I stand here with both the *Payoff* and the *Prize*.

Ishar studied him intensely, but said nothing, so Azzadan interjected, "I successfully terminated the *Corpse*. Ahrimakan is slain. Give me time to finish the rest of my mission."

"You did indeed slay Ahrimakan, so the revered title of *Godslayer* will be given to you," Ishar answered. "But I now doubt whether or not you are worthy to be considered as a Master of the Brew and a member of the Council of Fellows. As for this Bethratikus, it will now be given to another, one more suited to hunt the *Payoff* and retrieve the *Prize*."

A murmur of surprise rose from the galleries.

On hearing the words, Azzadan felt a surge of rage towards Ishar, but did not allow it to show when he spoke. "Master Ishar, never have I failed to honour a Bethratikus or fulfil a sacred vow, you must give me the chance to redeem myself."

"I must give you nothing" Ishar snapped back. "Be thankful, that even though it goes against the advice of the Council of Fellows, I spare you from the *Final-death* this day. You have delayed my plans considerably with your failure to secure the *Payoff* and the *Prize*." He took a deep breath, and when he spoke next, his tone was more measured. "I will have words with you in private."

Ishar nodded to the robed men wearing the masks; they sheathed their daggers, and the Arkith.

"Come," Ishar then said to Azzadan, before turning around and heading towards the stairway he had come from, "and leave the Bethratikus."

Azzadan seethed with frustration and brimmed with humiliation as he walked away from the statue of Skipilos. Leaving the Bethratikus behind, meant that the Order considered he had failed in his mission and that it had been taken from him and would be given to another. He had been dishonoured in front of other members of the Order, but he had no choice but to follow Ishar up the stairway. During many lifetimes in the Order, he had been up the stairway numerous times, but this time it seemed an age before they reached the top. On top of the stairs, was a huge altar, upon which were all of the active missions of the Order, each symbolised by a Bethratikus, that had been placed there by those who had accepted the mission. On the completion of the mission, they ascended the stairway, reclaimed the Bethratikus, descended and placed it at the feet of Skipilos and then claimed their reward and any titles.

Ishar paid no attention to the altar, but proceeded along a labyrinthine maze of black corridors that confused even Azzadan's sense of direction as he followed. It was the first time he had been that way, and he felt peril in the black shadows around him and unless his eyes deceived him, he thought he saw faint signs of movement that ceased at a quietly muttered command from Ishar.

Ishar at last led him into a chamber lit by a curious nine-branched candelabrum in which black candles burned. The chamber was square and well furnished. The black marble walls were covered with canvassed paintings and tapestries, and some trophy heads of beasts and creatures the like of which Azzadan had never seen before also adorned them. A woman stretched herself on a cushion littered silken couch. She stirred with feline suppleness as the two men entered. Voluptuously figured, her hair was long and elaborately styled, among which was a large blue jewel. Apart from a jewel encrusted girdle about her supple waist, and blue velvet slippers, she was quite naked. She intertwined her sleek fingers behind her head, and regarded Azzadan from under long drooping eyelashes.

Rising lithely, the woman came and circled Azzadan, running a long-painted finger nail around his neck as she did so. Her sharp nail drew blood. She licked it off her finger, and studied him carefully until with some elation, she said, "So, the great and mighty Azzadan has failed to honour the Bethratikus upon which he swore his oath." She laughed cruelly, and then walked over to a glass case, within which were three Arkiths, each with a different coloured Arzak. The case had many empty spaces for more such weapons.

Ishar looked angrily at Azzadan. "Give the Arkoom to her, that she might return it to its rightful place until such a time as it is needed again."

Sweat dripped from Azzadan's brow. "I do not have it, it was not possible for me to retrieve it, after I had slain Ahrimakan." He noticed that Ishar's face twisted with momentary rage, before returning to his normal, calm demeanour. External calmness was something Ishar nearly always showed, despite whatever dark emotions might be boiling under the surface. The fact that he had already unwittingly revealed his emotions a number of times since their meeting on this day, even if momentarily, was a sign to Azzadan just how precarious his own situation still was.

"Do you know, what was required of us, to find and obtain such a rare item?" Ishar asked him, with an acidity in his tone.

Azzadan felt insulted by the question. *I was by your side when we stole it.* He swallowed, took a breath, and when he answered, he did so respectfully. "I was one of those who helped to steal it. I remember well the price some of our Order paid to obtain it, Master Ishar."

"Yet you failed to look after it, and return it here, after slaying Ahrimakan with it," Ishar snarled. "If the Empire now finds the Simal before we do, they will not be so easily fooled next time by our sneaking whilst concealed in ethereal cloaks." He sighed. "It is only a matter of time before Mazdek discovers the whereabouts of the remaining Aeldar Riddles. When he does so, Thuranotos can be summoned. They now possess my Arkoom, in which the spirit of Ahrimakan was imprisoned after his body was slain with it. Possessing the Arkoom, Thuranotos will have the power to summon the spirit of Ahrimakan back to this world in another body prepared for him."

"I am aware of that, Master Ishar. Let me correct this situation. I will find the Seeress and the Simal, and return them here. Then I will discover where the Arkoom is kept. I will take it, and return it. I will not fail to honour the Bethratikus if you let me pick it up again, and return it to the altar."

Ishar said nothing as he walked over to the case, stood next to the woman, and studied the Arkiths. "During the time of my father, this case was once filled with Arkiths. Now, we have only five left, three of which you see here."

"How goes the search for the missing ones?" Azzadan asked as he walked over to where Ishar and the woman stood.

Ishar watched him thoughtfully before replying. "They are scattered. We know the whereabouts of two, and there are those of our Order tasked with searching the location of the others."

Azzadan had heard rumour that Princess Aspess often carried an Arkith once owned by the Order, and that a Sea Lord possessed another. "When do you plan to retrieve the two whose locations are known?" he asked.

Ishar answered, "The one owned by Aspess, will not go anywhere soon, I will let her keep it for now, but there is another, owned by a Sea Lord who does not keep it well hidden. In fact, he shows it off as a trophy whenever he is high in his cups."

"I have heard the Sea Lords own several Arkiths; it would be good to get our own one back, and relieve them of all of the others as well," Azzadan said.

Ishar looked at the Arkiths in the case, and then slanting his head towards Azzadan, asked, "I assume news of the fate of Aleskian has reached your ears?"

Azzadan nodded. "I heard rumours that a Bantu horde destroyed it and have entered the Everglow."

Ishar paused thoughtfully. "Peace is a fragile and temporary thing. The three Houses of the Empire will always find a reason to be at war with each other, but one will never completely destroy the other. The war that is coming now, will be unlike any the Everglow has seen, since times and days now ancient and long past." He paused again, and then whispered quietly, as though to himself, "The destruction of Aleskian has changed everything."

Azzadan wished he could tell what Ishar was thinking, but was sure he would find out soon enough, and he felt it had something to do with why he had been recalled and not allowed to honour his Bethratikus.

Ishar continued. "Cities can be built, burned down, and built again. The great cities of the Empire are nothing compared to what will be built when Skipilos returns, but the Aeldar must perish before he can walk again in these sacred halls."

"Let me do my part in seeing that happen. I will honour my Bethratikus, it is still possible for me to fulfil my mission," Azzadan offered.

Ishar sighed. "These are difficult days for our Order. Our Obelisk, here in our sacred halls, remains hidden and concealed within the Deadlands from the Empire's Seers, but as our numbers grow fewer, it is harder to keep it hidden. If it is discovered, we must leave this place. Already we search for a new home."

Ishar stared at the case that contained the Arkiths. "We have lost possession of most of them, and now the only Arkoom we possessed. In such a time should we not seek new allies?"

*New allies? Surely, he cannot mean the Bantu?* Azzadan frowned. "What is your plan, Master?"

"The Bantu are brutish, wild and unpredictable, but our spies report the Empire is allied with them. Whatever happened at Aleskian, was a mere blip in a far wider plan. A dark warlock by the name of Goth Surien has restored order to the horde, and they again work with Kappia with the common goal of eradicating the Baothein."

Azzadan, was rarely taken by surprise, but the words Ishar had spoken made his eyes widen at the hearing of it. *The Empire allied with the Bantu? Then they allowed Aleskian to be destroyed. It does not make sense.* He stayed silent as Ishar continued.

"It is said my brother, Mazdek, is behind such a scheme. If it were not for his vile betrayal that led to our former halls being discovered and desecrated, I might have considered seeking to offer him the services of our Order, but he is now as dedicated to the Aeldar, as we are to Skipilos, and they are sworn enemies. There is now no common ground between my brother and I, nor the Empire he serves, so I look elsewhere for an alliance."

Azzadan remained silent.

There was a mad exaltation in Ishar's eyes when he next spoke. "Skipilos will reward me by elevating me to become like him, one of the gods. I will take my place in the highest firmaments, if I destroy the Aeldar and help him win the war of all wars, that has now begun." Ishar leered. "You learnt much from my father. He always told me you were a good apprentice and disciple, our best thief and assassin."

"I am honoured to be spoken of in such a manner, by one whose memory I treasure," Azzadan replied.

"That is why I am so disappointed at your failure to secure the Simal and the Seeress," Ishar quipped back, "and that mission shall now be given to another, for I have a new task for you, and that is why, despite the will of Council of Fellows, I spared you the *Final-death,* for it is a mission only you can fulfil."

Azzadan guessed what the new task was, but at that moment, he was more concerned with finding out who would now be commissioned to find the Simal and Janorra. "Who will pick up my existing Bethratikus?" he asked.

It was the woman who answered. "I have advised Master Ishar to entrust it to the one called Skidegeat. He has now been assigned to find them."

"Skidegeat? That devious cat?" Azzadan protested, momentarily losing his outwardly respectful demeanour. "No doubt his disciple, Zasorra, Sasorra or whatever her name is, who stole Murim's cloak will also be a part of this?" It was a sore point for Azzadan. Skidegeat had a disciple, Zasorra, who had once stolen an ethereal cloak from a member of the Order who had died the *Final-death.* She did not belong to the Order, and therefore was not entitled to it, and had never been punished for taking it. Azzadan had insisted to Ishar that the cloak should have been returned, but Ishar had not acted.

"Ishar, this is my mission, I am sworn to it."

"But you failed in it," the woman purred, "and are now more useful elsewhere."

*Who is this opinionated bitch?* Azzadan seethed to himself.

"I have another task for you, Azzadan," Ishar said firmly. "It will not be sworn on a Bethratikus, for I do not wish the Council of Fellows to know of it, just yet, but when you succeed, your *Debt* will be considered fulfilled. As for your desire to become a Master of the Brew, if you succeed, I might, after all, decide to bestow this honour upon you despite your more recent failure."

"But you promised me this upon the slaying of Ahrimakan!"

Ishar snapped, "But you have failed in your other tasks!"

Azzadan felt anger rise up within him. It would be sacrilege for him to swear another blood-vow on a Bethratikus whilst the current one remained unfulfilled. He was glad that at least Ishar had spared him that indignity, but only returning a Bethratikus to Skipilos each time a mission was completed, could pay off a part of the *Debt.* To have the *Debt* considered paid without returning a Bethratikus, was sacrilege. Worse, Ishar was going back on his promise to recommend Azzadan to the Council of Fellows, to be allowed into their inner-circled by becoming a Master of the Brew, for the slaying of Ahrimakan. "Ishar, you must let me complete my mission, or," he swallowed at the thought of the humiliation but said, "or allow me to work with Skidegeat. I must be allowed to honour the Bethratikus, or I dishonour Skipilos and he will be offended with me on the day of his return." *I will also take back the cloak Zasorra stole and punish her for her part in Murim's death.*

Ishar snorted derisively. "I have always known you do not truly care for the honour of Skipilos. You only serve your own pride and ego. It is the worldly riches being in this Order brings you, and the titles and privileges you think you can earn, that motivate you, is it not?"

It was true, Azzadan cared little for the honour of a god he had never seen or met, but the thought of the dishonour that was being brought upon him in the Order, offended him deeply, for honouring a Bethratikus was one of the very few principles and the only moral code he really had left, and without that, he did now know who he was or what to be guided by. He also felt that the chance of becoming an honoured master, was slipping from him.

"Ishar, you cannot ask this from me. I will be forever dishonoured in the eyes of the Order if you force this path for me!"

"Would you prefer the *Final-death?*" the woman hissed as she slowly scratched his neck with her nail and again drew fresh blood.

257

Azzadan did not react, he knew to do so, would mean the *Final-death*, for Ishar had picked up one of the Arkiths. Despite his own speed and skill, Azzadan knew physical combat with Ishar would be hard, as they were evenly matched. Even if he won, and then dispatched the woman, escape from the halls would be all but impossible. If he did escape, killing Ishar would mean becoming a sworn enemy of the brotherhood, and they would surely hunt him down.

The woman walked over to the couch, licking the blood from her fingers, as she watched him.

Ishar stared at him coldly. "The pieces of a great game are all being moved into position. We must adjust and play the game with wisdom and skill, or we shall lose. The mission I have for you, must be kept secret from the Council of Fellows, hence the reason it will not be sworn publicly on a Bethratikus, but only privately before me. Know that it is still of vital importance to us all."

Azzadan swallowed his pride and anger. "What do you require of me?" *I already know what it is you will ask, but not why.*

"Circumstances necessitate you to return to Grona!"

Azzadan lowered his head to his chest and closed his eyes. He was the only man who had ever escaped from the Grona prison. He knew a way in, and a way out. The very name of the place filled even the stoutest hearts with dread. The prison was on the island of Grona, which was on the eastern part of the Tethys Sea. The worst prisoners of the Empire were sent there, it was a particularly harsh punishment, considered worse than the *Final-death*. It had its own Obelisk, so even death was not an escape from the prison for a Pure-blood Akkadian. There were no guards in the prison itself, the prisoners were left alone inside to live and create whatever system they chose. The worst, most twisted scum lived, died and resurrected within there. It was a perpetual living hell from which even death was not an escape. Except for that which he knew, there was no known entrance or exit to the prison. The island was guarded by a particularly vicious monstrosity named Kakath and the way in and out which Azzadan knew, required passing the creature, for the way in and out was in its lair. Getting to the prison itself would be a challenge. Even the Empire's prison ships that took prisoners to Grona did not land on the island of Grona. Only Fell-bloods crewed the ships and they ritually killed the sentenced prisoners when a mile off shore so they would automatically resurrect at the Obelisk inside the prison. The ships of the Empire that guarded the island were crewed by Fell-bloods, very few Pure-bloods would risk going near Grona lest they died and then found themselves forever entombed within there.

Opening his eyes and raising his head, Azzadan said, "That area is circled by a dozen war galleys that protect the milathran mines on the nearby islands around Grona. Only Empire ships go there. If you intend to get me in by becoming a prisoner on one of them, I will resurrect inside with no equipment. I killed a lot of people inside Grona before I escaped. Resurrecting inside of there would put me into the hands of many enemies." He inhaled and exhaled heavily. "Whatever your plans are, they will not remain hidden from Kappia if you try to sneak me in and out on an Empire ship." He then added with uncertainty, "It will be hard for you to find any other captain who will take a ship to Grona."

"I have already found one," Ishar replied.

"Then the Sea Lords will discover what you are doing," Azzadan remarked.

"They already know," Ishar responded as he stared at him dispassionately, "for you will be working with them." He still gripped the Arkith. "It is your choice. Receive the *Final-death*, or accept this new mission. Succeed, and your *Debt* will be paid. I might allow you to stay in these halls with your desired honours, or you will leave these halls, still with the revered title of *Godslayer*. The wealth of your share of the riches you have acquired during your service to the Order, will await you in the Guild Bank at Rothrostan."

It pained Azzadan that abandoning his quest to return the Simal and Janorra to the halls meant a violation of the sacred blood-vow he had made on the Bethratikus, and that it would be the first time he had ever failed to honour one. He fought hard to contain the rage he felt. *Curse that wretched Seeress, it is due to her incompetence in using the Jula that I am so dishonoured. I will have my revenge on her!*

"I accept," he said reluctantly, after a long silence.

"Good," Ishar replied, "Lagrinda here, will provide you with specific instructions for your mission when you resurrect."

"What do you mean when I resurrect?" Azzadan asked suspiciously.

Ishar sneered darkly. "Consider it a mark of my immense displeasure for your recent failings. Do not underestimate my anger that you lost the Arkoom, and failed to return the *Prize* and *Payoff* to me. Or, if you like, look at it as a blessing that you can start this new mission with a newly resurrected body free from any ailments or troublesome ageing."

After Ishar had finished speaking, the woman jumped onto the couch and reared up like a serpent about to strike. Her lips drew back, revealing white fangs. Azzadan realised what she was. *A vampire.*

"Let me feed on him master, let me feed on him, let me drink his immortality that I may be refreshed and forever young to please you," she hissed.

"Feast, my sweet Lagrinda," Ishar said with an evil grin.

Azzadan fought with his own instincts. Despite knowing the futility of it, his first instinctive reaction was to take out a poisoned star and attempt to throw it at the woman, but fast as he was, he was suddenly frozen by bonds and powers he could not see, dark forces being wielded by the mind of either Ishar, or the vampire. He was powerless to do anything as the woman sprang from the couch and slowly approached, fangs still protruded, all the while hissing. There was a black coldness in her eyes he had not seen before, that unnerved even him, the most fearless of men, and one who had experienced all manner of deaths before, but never death by a vampire.

The woman rose on tiptoe, and put her arms slowly around his thick muscular neck. "I am so thirsty," she hissed, "so thirsty. Enjoy the *Stinging Kiss*."

Her head thrown back, eyes closed and lips parted, she slowly pressed her mouth against his powerful neck. He felt a sharp pang at the base of his throat as the teeth pierced his skin and sunk deep into the flesh. Azzadan felt the life draining from him as she drank, and drank, only pausing to purr and groan with pleasure before drinking again. The last memory he had of that life, was when he dropped the poisoned star he had been about to throw, and heard it clatter on the floor, as his spirit was sucked into the Deadlands.

# Chapter Twenty-One: *Escape from Castle Greytears*

*Temmison wrote that Castle Greytears was built by Eurorian Dwarves and Titans long ago. How can anybody take the writings of this fraud seriously? I agree it is an ancient structure, one of six that now reside in lands ruled by the Bruthon, but I would date it to a late period of the Dark Age, or even later. There is evidence that much of the structure of these castles has changed over time, especially that of Greytears. I must admit there are some elements that still appear of Dwarven design, but that could be due to Dwarven architects being employed to make renovations at various points of Greytear's history. Temmison simply has no evidence the original design and build was Dwarven, and to claim that even a fabled race of Titans (that I have argued elsewhere never even existed) also helped to design and build the original structure is such an outlandish claim, that I strongly propose all of his academic work on Castle Greytears is dismissed without further consideration. His books on the topic should be removed from this library, and his scholarly credentials revoked by this esteemed council of scholars to whom I write and make this appeal.*

**A fragment of text found in the Kappian Library - Source believed to be Edegal.**

*To the Kappian Council,*

*I found a page of Sangdalen when excavating in tunnels beneath Castle Greytears, as you know, and was reliably informed that a roguish dwarf had once hidden others in more tunnels to the east of the Wytchwood. I intend to search there once we find an entrance to them. Meanwhile, the Sangdalen text I found beneath Greytears had been translated to me by a Dwarven scholar who preferred coin over tradition. He said the text was proof that Castle Greytears was indeed built by Eurorian Dwarves with the aid of Titans. I submitted this text to you, the Council of the Kappian Library, for you to study for yourselves, and you now inform me it has gone missing? I am outraged at your carelessness. I am convinced there are more of these texts buried below Greytears, but a strange wailing issuing up from the deeper tunnels to which we could not find an access, spooked the workers and they refuse to go back. This makes the loss of the Sangdalen I did send to you, even more of an outrage, for I doubt we can return to find more. I am horrified at your negligence and will write in the strongest terms to the Emperor himself, requesting that this matter is fully investigated and the culprit found. I suspect Edegal is somehow involved in this. If he wishes to bring me before a court of law for the defamation of his character or libel for stating my suspicions about him, let him do so! I will gladly face that scoundrel even if I have to do so in front of the Imperial Kappian Court of Law!*

**An unsigned note found in the Kappian Library – Source believed to be Temmison.**

*As* the altar slid shut over the top of them, Janorra, Scarand, Sasna, Marlo and Janus all fell and tumbled down a small flight of stairs, into a small chamber lit by glowing red stones set within a bricked wall. Janorra and Scarand were the first ones on their feet, kicking aside the dead bodies that had also tumbled down the stairs. Pointing the tip of her sword at Janus' throat, she scathingly said, "You tried to trick us."

Janus shuddered and his face went ashen. "Can you blame me?" he replied in a whimpering tone. "I was looking forward to Ranien Steak for my dinner tonight; now look at the chaos you have caused. You have no idea what is down here, do you?"

Scarand was looking above them where the altar was firmly shut. "Can they get in?" he asked.

"No," Janorra replied. "Aeldar Tunnels are not easily opened by those not trained to do so. Even if you know the catches and sequence, only an initiated priest or Seer can speak words that will open them."

Janorra pressed the tip of her sword so hard against Janus' neck, it drew blood. "Any more trickery, I will send you to the Deadlands."

"Do it, just do it," Janus pleaded, "it will fare better for me if I am killed, the Baron cannot accuse me of aiding you then."

"Maybe we should heed his voice, and do away with him," Marlo growled.

Janorra sheathed her sword and looked at Marlo. "We need him. Aeldar Tunnels are often full of traps and tricks to enable the initiated to escape even the most cunning foe who try to pursue or lead them unwillingly through such a place."

"The builders never had time to complete all of the traps," Janus said, "there were unforeseen problems. You have no idea what is down here."

"Where does it lead?" Janorra demanded, looking at the tunnel that led from the chamber, "and what do you mean, what is down here?"

"Why should I help you or tell you anything?" Janus moaned. "Kill me so I can resurrect. I will face the test of the Jewel of Baramir and prove I had nothing to do with any of this! I will not help you." He looked warily at Marlo. "What was your name, err, Marlo, that's it, it is Marlo. Give me a quick death, or defend me against these two whilst I can open the altar again. If you help me, I will speak well of you to the Baron."

Janorra observed Marlo in detail for the first time. He had the vicious look about him of a man who had committed many dark deeds, but he also appeared broken and traumatised. She gripped the hilt of her sword more tightly, ready to draw it if needed. She wanted Janus to answer her questions, and was not going to let Marlo harm him, yet.

"I will chop your hands and feet off and leave you to die slowly in here," Marlo said to Janus, "now answer her questions."

Janus flinched as Marlo moved aggressively towards him. "Okay, okay," he shrilled. Reluctantly, he mumbled, "This is not a normal Aeldar tunnel, for one thing it is not secret. He cannot open it, but the Baron knows it is here."

"How did he find out?" Janorra asked. "It takes many skilled masons from the Clarevont Guild to build a temple and carve out the tunnel underneath, but they are sworn to secrecy."

"Two teams were digging the tunnel. The first, started right above us and were never detected when the altar was put in place, and the magic charms spoken over it. The second, started from the other end, near the banks of the River Erin. The two teams had almost finished and met in the middle, when a cave-in happened, that revealed ancient tunnels and foul dungeons in deep and dark places, possibly of Dwarven origin. You cannot get to the exit, without going through them."

"That shouldn't have been a problem the masons could not overcome?"

"The masons could not stay and finish the work. They came across some sort of beast living down in the ancient tunnels. The Davari slaves refused to carry on working, even though some were brutally put to death as an example to the others." Janus shuddered and cast a frightened look down the tunnel. "The casualties the beast inflicted on the tunnel teams were many. Some survivors fled into the temple, popping out of the altar just as the Baron and his sister were inspecting the temple. He might not be able to open the tunnel without my help, but he and his sister know it is here, and they know it leads to the Erin."

Janus paused for breath and then said. "I was planning to hide out here, only long enough until all the trouble you had caused up top had been dealt with. It would be madness if we tried to get to the Erin, that thing is still down here, somewhere. You must go back and throw yourself at the mercy of the Baron."

261

"He has no mercy," Sasna said anxiously. "I would rather face death down here then fall back into his hands."

"Then death you will face, for the beast that lurks down here, seemed impervious to every attempt to harm it when the teams tried to defend themselves," Janus whimpered.

Janorra took a deep breath. *Ashareth, guide and help me.* She considered her options. Another death was not an option for her. It would mean resurrecting back at the castle and into the hands of the Baron. No doubt a strong and alert guard would be waiting in the temple above, so turning back was not possible. It would be impossible for the Baron to open the altar, but when the Inquisitor returned, he would be able to do so, which meant they could not wait where they were, even if they had the food and water supplies to do so, which they did not. There was no other choice but to press on. The memory of an ancient invocation suddenly returned to her. *Thank you Ashareth, thank you.* She breathed a sigh of relief. *The Theos Murphor incantation, might tame or pacify the creature, depending on the nature of the beast.* It was a risky option, but trying to pacify it, might be better than attempting to slay it should they come across the beast. She looked down the tunnel, and then at the closed altar above them. *I would rather face any beast than a vengeful man.* "Does the Baron know where the exit of the other tunnel is?"

Janus shook his head. "Aeldar law prevented me and the Inquisitor from discussing it with him when he asked. He was quite angry, and guessed it would be somewhere along the riverbank, but he did not overly press the matter when we told him nothing, for the Inquisitor himself can be quite intimidating, and he acts with the authority of the Bruthon King and the whole of Kappia."

"Along with you and the Inquisitor, was it only the Baron and his sister who knew of the existence of this tunnel?"

Janus nodded, "Until now."

"Then we have no choice," Sasna interjected. "The alarms will cause the Baron to return to the castle, and soon. When he hears what has happened, he will send men to watch the riverbank. Beast or not, we must make haste and attempt to reach the other end."

"Sasna is right," Scarand said. "I would rather face this beast, than wait like a helpless rat in a trap waiting in terror for its fate."

Marlo eagerly agreed. "A year ago, me and some of the boys came to test the depths of the channels in the river. We came ashore looking for some female company to kidnap and take back with us to Berecoth. Some of the lads were captured, I got away. As far as I know, one of the boats we left behind is still lying hidden in the reeds."

Janorra felt immediate disgust towards Marlo, but if what he said was true, he would be of use, so she acknowledged his word with a nod of her head. The words of Otan, went through her mind. *Run, Janorra, run!'*

"Then let us not tarry here," she said, as she pushed Janus into the tunnel. "Lead the way, or I'll make Marlo cut off your hands and we will use you as bait and dinner for whatever the beast thing is!"

*       *       *

They had moved at a rapid pace through the tunnels, in the light of the glowing red stones imbedded in the walls, for nearly an hour, when they finally came to the place where the cave-in had happened. The tunnel ahead was blocked with debris, and there were several large holes in the floor just before where it was blocked, with debris leading into tunnels below that spanned out in several directions. They paused for breath, and to catch their bearings. The physician had done a good job in healing and stitching

Sasna's wound, but such had been the physical exertions involved in seeking to escape, some of the stitching had come undone. *I cannot keep up this pace for long, but I have no choice*, she thought, as fear rose within her. *The Baron's revenge will be brutal for what I have done and what happened to his sister.*

Sasna leant back against the wall, taking in deep draughts of the musky air. *I can't go on much longer.*

"You caused quite a commotion in the castle, but it may turn out in our favour," Janorra said to her. "The guards will most likely wait for instructions directly from the Baron before they act decisively."

Sasna looked into the eyes of the Seeress; they were deep pools of blue, and showed much sadness, but there was also a determination showing in them.

"You look pale and sickly, you are not well," Janorra said emphatically to her, but then added, "I do not have time to tarry if you fall behind. We may have to split-up. I will leave you behind if you cannot keep up."

*Bitch!* "I am near to exhaustion and in much pain" Sasna answered. She undid the jerkin; blood was seeping through the undergarment. She had no doubt that, even though not willingly, the Seeress meant it when she said she would leave her behind. *After all, it is what I would do if I were in her situation.*

"I will stay with her, if that is necessary," Scarand said, "but I am also willing to carry her. We will keep-up."

Sasna stared at him, feeling bewildered, for Scarand himself looked exhausted and the worse for wear. *Even now, in the midst of such danger, he offers to help me? I do not understand what drives this slave!*

Janorra reached out a hand towards Sasna's shoulder. "May I?"

Sasna nodded, and said, "Go ahead." *If you don't do something, I can't go on.*

Janorra carefully moved aside the jerkin, and gently lifted the garment to inspect the wound. A throbbing pain shot through her shoulder when Janorra touched it; Sasna winced in pain and let out an involuntary cry.

"Trust me," Janorra said. "My memories are returning fast, for Ashareth answers me when I call." She stood to her feet and shouted. "Otan, I know you hear me. Lend me your power again. I know it hurts you, but I am in need. Otan, please help me!"

"Shush! shush!" Janus said in a panicked manner. "You have no idea what is down there. It will hear you!"

Sasna watched as a warm glowing light suddenly appeared around Janorra.

"Thank you Otan," Janorra said, as she knelt down and touched Sasna's shoulder again. Placing a hand on the wound, Janorra said, "*Moousa.*"

Instead of pain, Sasna felt a warm healing glow coming from Janorra's hand into her shoulder, and she felt colour coming back to her face. After a moment or two, the pain had entirely ceased. "That is incredible," she said in awe, "what did you do?"

"The Obelisk is near enough that he can still hear me, and he let me use his power to heal. The effect won't last long, but it might be enough." Janorra held out a hand to Sasna, and she took it and was helped to her feet.

"Preserve your strength whilst you can; soon, I will be too far from the Obelisk to be able to use its power," Janorra said as she used the sword to prize one of the red stones from the tunnel wall. She held it in her hand, and it acted as a torch shining a red light wherever she pointed it. "Rest here for a few moments," she said to them all, "except you, Janus. You are coming with me to see if there is another way to get into the exit tunnel." She jabbed him lightly with the sword. "Do not try any more of your trickery."

Muttering and complaining, Janus followed Janorra as she climbed and slid down the debris into the dark tunnels below.

Sasna slid into the sitting position, and Scarand joined her, whilst Marlo studied the stones in the wall, no doubt to see if they had any value, which Sasna knew they did not as Rocha stones such as these were commonly found in underground caves and were often used as lights in dark places.

"In the Baron's library, I thought you had betrayed me," Scarand said to her, with a fierce intensity.

*I had no choice.* "I told you, I would help you if you brought me to Greytears. I had not expected such hostility from the Baron, but I promised I would not leave without you, that's why I came and found you." The lie did not bother her. *You are no longer my concern. If the physician had arrived even just a few minutes earlier, I might already be long gone from this accursed castle.* "Please, let me rest and save my breath, we do not yet know what we might still face in this dreadful place, or how far we still have to go."

*       *       *

Janorra and Janus had explored the lower tunnels for an hour. She was almost suffocated by the mad pounding of her heart, when she finally returned to the pile of debris beneath the Aeldar tunnel from where they had entered the lower ones. Her companions had heard the commotion, for they were peering from above at her, as she stood panting to get her breath. The sound of the beast had caused Janus to panic to such a degree, that his chins had literally wobbled with fear as he ran screaming down a random tunnel, into the darkness, in the opposite direction. Janorra had managed to quell her own fear enough, to retrace her steps and make it back to the junction beneath the debris, where she had left the others. *There is more safety in numbers, if the Theos Murphor incantation does not tame this beast, we will have to try to slay it.*

The others climbed and scrambled down the debris into the tunnel.

"What happened?" Scarand demanded. "We heard noises."

"No time to explain, run!" she said, pointing back to the way she had just come from, "anyway but that way!"

*Ashareth, help me. Let chance or fortune show me the way.* Not knowing the way to go, Janorra randomly picked a tunnel, and with sword in one hand and the light-stone in the other, she set off down it followed by the others. The sound of their panted breaths as they ran, and the pounding noise of their footsteps, was only broken by a distant, awful, hysterical scream coming from Janus, followed by a hideous, primal roar, that echoed through the tunnels. Then there was silence. *The priest did not make it!*

With panting haste, they quickened their pace. It must have been a trick of the red light from the stone, that in the shadows of every opening and tunnel they passed, Janorra felt she saw flickers of movement or the shadow of some beast, but fortunately for them, it was just that, tricks of the light. The noise behind them, however, was not of her imagination. There was no doubt that whatever had chased Janus down and caught him, was now pursuing them, for they heard the distant drum of what sounded like hoofbeats clipping on stone.

They ran with all of the speed they could muster. Other than the distant echoing hoofbeats, there was no sound save their heavy breathing and the rap of their feet, which seemed to grow to an echoing noise, like the slapping of great hands against the cold stone floor. Behind them, the echoes of the creature's galloping footsteps grew louder by the second. The dank black walls lit up by the glowing stone, seemed to dance with silhouettes; the fear of sudden death or capture lurking in every doorway and shadow. The tension was palpable as they ran along the deep passages of the lost tunnels beneath Castle Greytears.

*Asbareth help me, I beg of you, help and guide me for I am in dire need,* Janorra prayed, as they came to a junction and she chose tunnels to run down based on nothing more than instinct. Eventually, dripping with sweat, they came to another pile of debris. It was the opposite side of the cave-in area, and led to the exit tunnel. They had found the second part of the Aeldar tunnel. *"Thank you Asbareth, thank you,"* Janorra cried with relief.

The companions scrambled up the debris, and ran with all of their might down the tunnel, until they came to the end, which was blocked by a black, stone door with strange symbols on it. "This is an Aeldar door, the exit," Janorra said, breathing with relief. "I will need time to discover the incantation to open it." She studied the symbols. *There are many different types of Aeldar door, each with their own incantation to open them, it will only be one word, yet I cannot yet remember them all. Damn that priest, he would know the one to open it. Why did I not think to ask him?*

"It is time we do not have," Scarand breathed.

At the other end of the tunnel, echoing through it, the sound of laughter could be heard. It was unmistakably almost human mirth in its amusement, but Janorra knew that whatever made the sound was far from human. The noise staggered her reason.

"It thinks we are trapped," Marlo blubbered as he began to claw frantically at the door, ripping his nails out in the process.

"We are, if she cannot open the door," Sasna cried out.

Janorra ignored them and continued studying the inscriptions. *I need to concentrate. Asbareth, help me to remember!*

The laughter stopped, and was replaced by an inhuman screech of sheer rage. The creature sniffed the air. The sound of its loud breathing and snorting could be heard, along with the echo of its hooves clipping against the stone floor as it slowly moved down the tunnel towards them.

*"Myrash; Benthos; Heiorthian!"* Nothing happened. Janorra felt a rising sense of panic, and breathed slowly to calm herself. *They are the only three I can remember. Think, think.*

Marlo flattened himself against the back of the wall and screamed in terror, as the sound of the creature drew near.

Holding a sword in front of him, Scarand, with a grim and resolute stare, began to walk towards whatever was coming down the tunnel. Sasna followed him and caught up, and walked by his side, also holding her sword. "They say *never trust a Seesnari,"* she said, "but no matter who or what you are, never corner or trap one either." They grinned grimly at each other in solemn amusement.

Janorra could not think of any more incantations, time was up – she had to face the beast.

"Stop," she said to Scarand and Sasna, as she ran to their side. "Whatever this thing is, fighting it might not be the only way – so let that be our last resort." She put her hands on the blade of their swords, and lowered them.

Taking a few steps in front of them, she waited for the beast to appear, and did not have to wait long. She stared in horror, as slowly, the shape of the beast took form and it emerged into the red glow of the light-stone. Standing several feet in front of her, it stared at her with unblinking, soulless eyes. It was the first time Janorra had seen a Minotaur in the flesh, but she knew what it was from images she had seen in the *Book of Bestiary.* Spiralled horns sprang from the creature's massive, bovine head, which was hung low between grossly oversized shoulders. It had a crumpled, heavily lined face and a thin-lipped, down-turned mouth. The right side of the face was a pink mass of scar tissue, the result of some past terrible wound. The beast stepped forward and reared up horrifically in the flickering light.

Janorra let out a breath she hadn't realised she had been holding, and she felt a sudden qualm of nausea at the stench coming from the beast's breath as it lowered its head and studied her curiously for a moment. She prepared to softly sing the *Theos Murphor Incantation* - a Song of the Ancients she had been taught long ago in the Argona Temple. *At least I remember this. Thank you Ashareth that I remember this!*

# Chapter Twenty-Two: *The Empress Shaka*

*Death stalks through the royal palace, no, rather it slithers. Even so, I stole a jewel-encrusted case from under the pillow of a noblewoman whilst she slept. I have made my fortune; I am done with this trade, but I often grow bored. Could all of the gold in Kappia tempt me to go back again inside that palace of evil? I ask you, are such riches worth more than my life? I answer my own question - that depends on how much the riches are worth, and how much I value my life. But my immortal soul, are all the treasures of Kappia worth more than my immortal soul? Is the answer no? Temptation calls!*
**Lorna Grayson: *The Tales and Exploits of Sinnibar the Rogue*.**

*The* Empress Shaka looked out from the Terrace of the Sun, which was situated on her summer palace high in the Argona Mountains. The Celestial Palace, as it was called, was her favourite place in all of Kappia. She wore a carefully tailored scarlet silk dress, with slits in it that showed her arms and thighs, whilst the rest clung to her shapely body. She drew a white, fur-skin shawl around her shoulders as a cool and gentle fresh breeze wafted across the patio.

The fragrance of roses filled the air, and she sniffed the scent appreciatively. Red roses, replaced without fail every morning, filled the golden vases placed neatly around the edges of the terrace. The floor was white marble covered tastefully with the occasional patterned mosaic. The walls were covered by exquisite velvet tapestries, which along with the red silk canopy that covered the terrace, rippled with the soft breeze.

A large contingent of servants and staff, most with their tongues cut out so they could not disturb the peace of the Empress in this place she favoured as a retreat from the busyness of Kappia, waited in cleverly carved niches in the three marble walls that surrounded the terrace. They watched and remained alert, ready to serve and respond to her every whim. One of the main tasks of the terrace staff was to quickly remove any rose petal that fell to the floor so it would not be a distraction before it was whisked away. No rose petal sat on the floor too long before it was silently, quickly and discreetly moved by the staff whose clothes, skin and hair were all dyed red or white, depending on their assigned tasks, to complement the colour of the surroundings.

It was a clear day, Shaka could see far across the Kappia Plateau. Far below the terrace and to the south, the magnificent buildings of the city of Kappia, jewel of the Empire, bristled with life. The largest and grandest building in the city, the Argona Temple, stood tall and proud in the centre, its ancient spires and steeples rising proudly into the blue sky. Next to it, the Argona Palace, also known as the Imperial Palace, Shaka's home, a grand building with its many terraces and gardens, stood as the next most prominent architectural feature. Outside of the main city wall, within its own walls along with a keep, stood the tall and crooked Bloody Tower, where the Empire's prisoners were kept, within the tower itself, or underground in the subterranean and dark dungeons that spread deep below the complex. Shaka grinned with amusement at the thought that even at that very moment, her enemies and those who had offended her, suffered within the walls of that feared place.

To the south of the city, deep below the plateau, the water of Lake Panharin glistened in the sunlight. Trading ships and war galleys coming to and thro went about their business as they joined or left the two mighty rivers that Panharin fed, the Erin and Lucoth. The Erin went deep into the south, out of sight into Bruthon lands, before splitting west and east; west, as it snaked as far as the lands of the Samothrane and beyond to the great city of Zinibar, and east where it led to the infamous port of Harwind before it fed out into the great Tethys Sea itself. The Lucoth went only a little way to the south-east before stretching east where it broke up into several smaller rivers before they also reached, far out of sight, into the Great Tethys Sea. Any amusement Shaka felt soon left her, when she remembered how the Sea Lords still controlled or blocked so much of the Empire's trade.

On a small island just before the mouth of the Rivers Erin and Lucoth, stood the Vargo, the stone colossuses of the nine Aeldar, built during a time now forgotten. They were placed in a circle from which eight of them looked out, with Thuranotos, whose statue was far larger, placed in the middle, with four sides to his face so that he looked in every direction. Shaka looked at the statue of Ahrimakan, and her heart pined. *I miss you, my love.*

The Kappia Plateau varied from about one hundred and fifty to two hundred miles in width, and about three hundred miles in length. Heavily fortified, it was effectively impregnable, as the sheer cliff faces were virtually unscalable, certainly for any army. Armies could not reach and assail the plateau by either of the two passes that led to it, without passing the many fortifications. Navies could not attack it from the few waterways near it, and even unfriendly flying beasts could not fly onto it without facing the massive bolts from countless ballista that would send them plummeting from the skies, or, until more recently, the fierce griffins and their riders that had been strategically placed at locations on the plateau. As her eyes scanned the plateau, a doubt nagged at Shaka. *Am I right to disband the legions? Is the day of the griffin riders really now past, as Ahrimakan and Mazdek have said?* She dismissed the thoughts as quickly as they came. *I trust your ancient wisdom, Ahrimakan.*

The plateau was not a uniform surface, but presented a variety of forms, from the lofty peaks of some the mountains upon it, to the fertile valleys and expansive fruitful plains that fed the vast populace that lived upon it in settlements, towns and great cities. Averaging about four thousand feet in height above the Panharin and above sea level, it was a virtual fortress in and of itself. Since the time when King Arius had first conquered and then fortified it, no invading army in living memory or recorded history had ever successfully invaded the plateau. The only way by foot to gain entrance upon it was through the narrow Steps of Goldroth to the west, or the hidden Stairway of Narzoum in the north. Through these passages, an army could only pass three abreast and that under the presence of the many forts and watchtowers that overlooked them, making the passes easily defendable and virtually impossible for an opposing force to successfully ascend to the plateau through those means. The only other way onto the plateau, apart from flying beasts, was by the lake, where the port of Kappia was stationed on a long strip of land to the west of the waterfall that poured abundantly over the cliff upon which the main part of Kappia city was built.

Kappia was built high above the lake, near to the western banks of the river that spewed over the edge of the cliffs by the waterfall that fed the lake. On the western side of the city, were a series of canals. The only way from the port on the lake, to the main part of the city and its canals, was by a complicated series of zig-zagging locks if by ship or boat, that enabled ships from the now mostly abandoned shipyards to be lowered to the lake below, or even raised from it. If on foot, the wide zig-zagged steps were the way, which was a momentous physical task for even the fittest of people. Ramps allowed those traveling by horse, horse-drawn-carriage or rickshaws, to ascend or descend from the port to the city or vice-versa. The steps and ramps were not only carved from the rock face of the cliff, they went deep into it at places, tunnelling inside, and were heavily fortified and could also be easily defended. The ramps and steps were only broken at various levels where the city had spilled over into many other habitations and buildings, built upon layered great stone or wooden platforms held up by huge stilts. Some of the lower platforms stretched out over a part of the lake itself

Shaka sat down on a velvet red chair, next to a red stained, beautiful, ornate marble table. Taking a small phial from underneath the table, she carefully pulled the stopper, poured a drop of the contents into a glass which she then filled with wine, before putting the stopper back into the phial and hiding it again under the table. She then picked up a small bell and rang it. A servant, dressed and painted entirely in white, responded immediately to the sweet chimes of the bell, running and flinging himself prostrate before her.

"I am ready for them," she said to him.

The servant lifted himself to his hands and knees, and shuffled backwards a few yards before he stood, bowed, and ran towards a door at the back of the terrace. A few moments later, a servant who still had her tongue, announced, "My Sarissa, I present Grand Inquisitor Marnir, and the Hand of the Empress, Renlak."

Marnir, carrying an elegant box, and Renlak holding a scroll, entered, approached the table and both bowed deeply before Shaka.

"And who is this you have brought?" she asked, as she looked at the handsome young man bound and gagged between two of the Hammer Knights, who was dragged in behind Marnir and Renlak.

"The young man you requested, my Sarissa," Renlak replied. "If you are no longer in the mood for company, I will have him thrown from the terrace as food for the dogs."

The man struggled in vain at his bonds and tried to say something through his gag, but his voice was muffled and his eyes rolled with terror.

"No need," Shaka said, "I am in the mood for company this day. And what is this you hold, Grand Inquisitor?" she asked as she looked at the box that Marnir held.

"A gift for you, my Sarissa," he answered as he slowly blinked his heavy eyelids.

"May I suggest business first," Renlak said as he offered Shaka the scroll. "This contains news from Aleskian, a detailed report you may study at your leisure."

Shaka shuddered. The news from Aleskian was never good of late, and the people in Kappia were deeply troubled and restless when news of its fall had reached the capital.

"Has the traitor Borach been apprehended yet?" she asked him.

Renlak trembled slightly, hesitated a moment before he spoke, and then blurted out. "The traitor Borach has fled into the Tarenmoors with about six hundred men from the Third Legion." He then quickly added. "There are no known safe Obelisks there. If the tribes do not kill them, the pursuing Bantu will. Their fate will not be good, nor should they trouble us anymore."

Shaka closed her eyes, attempting to curb the fury she felt at the news. She looked coldly at Renlak. He continued nervously, before she could say anything.

"We had expected the men of the Third Legion to die in the battle and resurrect as our prisoners, and for Lord Borach to die the *Final-death*. We had not anticipated his victory either on the plains, or in a duel to the death with the Bantu Commander."

"What about his family?"

Renlak blinked and then said, "Once it was understood that all was not going to plan, and General Shinther had met an unfortunate death, the Hammer Knight Captain who took charge, had the wit and presence to give the impression they had been sent to their *Final-death*, but he removed them from the catapults, and had them taken from the city to a secure location at Kara Duram."

"It is just as well," Shaka said. "We will keep them for possible bargaining tools. If Lord Borach resurfaces and causes us trouble, we might need them."

Renlak nodded his head in agreement. "Goth Surien has fully restored order to the Bantu horde. The four hundred men of the Third who died in the battle, as well as the Hammer Knights and any Pure-blood civilians, have all safely resurrected, and were handed over to us by Goth Surien himself. They and the rest of the Third, and the dead from any other legion, have been ordered to Kara Duram where they are being re-educated. It is believed many of them might join the Hammer Knights, as the gracious offer High Quaester Mazdek has made, is a tempting one."

Shaka could tell there was something else Renlak was not telling her. "Tell me what else!" She ordered.

"We have heard no news of Prince Regineo, since he resurrected at Aleskian. He left the city in a rage, accompanied by his personal bodyguard."

"What?" she shouted, banging her fist on the table so that the glassware shook. "He was instructed to return to Kappia, immediately."

"He left in a carriage, rather than using a Jula portal. Perhaps he has found some amusement to occupy himself with, on the return journey," Renlak nervously suggested. "Maybe he is taking his anger out on a few peasants?"

Shaka frowned, but Renlak's suggestion made sense. Regineo had chosen not to use a portal and had opted for a carriage, which he was not particularly fond of. He would want to vent his frustration out somehow, so it was more than likely he was distracted by some grim amusement to assuage his anger. Perhaps some whore he had taken a fancy towards, or the daughters of a peasant family he could torment.

"Let me know the moment news is heard of him."

"Yes, my Sarissa."

"Are the rumours about Aleskian confirmed?"

Renlak winced, and spoke hesitantly. "My Sarissa. Before Goth Surien restored order to the Bantu horde, Aleskian was completely sacked and razed to the ground." He coughed uncertainly, and then continued. "It is now no more than rubble and ash, a smoking ruin, but better that than handed over to the Baothein by Borach *the Betrayer*?"

The news struck Shaka like a thunderbolt from the heavens. She felt the blood draining from her face, and felt faint. She had heard unconfirmed reports the city had been sacked, but not that it had been utterly destroyed.

Renlak continued before she could make any remarks. "Goth Surien has had the Bantu leaders responsible flayed alive. He has promised us reparations, that without any cost to the Empire, the gold will be given to us to rebuild the city from scratch once the Baothein have been dealt with and the Bantu have retreated from the Everglow. The city can be renamed, rebuilt afresh, or left as a ruin and we use the gold elsewhere. The news, after reflection, is not as bad as when first heard."

After a moment of consideration, Shaka calmed slightly. It was true; the city of Aleskian had long been a bane, a thorn in the side of the Empire, and had a history of rebellious lords the last of which had been Lord Borach himself. It was the only city who named its own successor, with all titles being passed down the ancestral lines, with no input or influence from Kappia. In addition, since the civil war, when the milathran trade route had been blocked, defending and supporting Aleskian and the regions to the south, had become a massive drain on the Empire's resources that it could no longer afford. Withdrawing from the city and the Aleskian regions, had often seemed a tempting idea, but one that until recent events, had been delayed and put off time and time again. *Perhaps this might work for our good, but there is still so much to play for.*

"Do we still have assurances the Bantu will leave the Everglow, now that we no longer control the Aleskian Gate?" she asked, feeling momentary doubt at the sheer risk the plan Mazdek had put into operation involved.

"They will cleanse the Everglow of our enemies, and as an assurance they will leave afterwards, many of the sons and daughters of their tribal lords and clans, including the beloved son and daughter of Goth Surien, have been sent to Karaos Duan as hostages. They have also, as a guarantee, sent a vast fortune in treasure to us. It is even now, on its way here to Kappia. It is a treasure the like of which has never been seen before in the Everglow, so priceless is its worth. We get to keep it, but must return their hostages once the Baothein are destroyed and the last of their horde has left the Everglow."

Shaka felt a slight sense of relief. If the Bantu did not keep to their agreement, the treasure horde handed over, would buy a mercenary army so large, she could drive them out of the Everglow by force. If correctly valued, and used wisely, the treasure would save the Empire from the financial ruin it faced.

As she was thinking, Marnir placed the elegant box he had been holding on the table.

"What is this?" she asked as she looked at the strange black box placed before her.

Marnir smiled. "Within it is a gift from the Lord of Morkroth, as an apology for the unforeseen events at Aleskian. The jewels within are said to be worth more than even the most exquisite of those the Dwarves mined in what they call their *Age of Flourish* before they locked themselves away." He pushed the box towards her.

Shaka studied its curious design. Along the rim of the lid nine skulls were carved among intertwining snakes passing through the eye sockets and mouths. She was about to press at the skulls.

"Don't," Marnir warned. "To press them in the wrong order will bring death, for poisoned pins in the shape of a snake's fangs will emerge. The correct order must be used. There is a secret catch, allow me," he said as he pressed the skulls in a certain order, that led to a catch springing up from the lid.

"You give me a poisoned box?" she angrily asked him.

"No, it is purely a safeguard to protect what is within," Marnir replied. "Ambassador Grixen, the Bantu envoy, has taught us its secrets. The box guards the treasures within, that it contains." He pressed the catch and opened the box. Inside were a number of jewels of such exquisite beauty, she quickly forgot her anger as she gazed upon their alluring loveliness.

"Their craftsmanship is incredible," she gasped, as she carefully took one from the box and studied it.

Marnir smiled. "Ambassador Grixen will be present at the feast tonight, he has another, rarer and far more expensive gift he wishes to present to you. It is an exquisite gift to you, and will surely become most treasured and precious among all of your possessions."

"It is a rare gift of exquisite beauty, a gift that can only be put on and taken off in a certain manner, one which you and your staff shall be taught," Renlak said tentatively with a trace of nervousness so slight, Shaka did not think it important, as she felt he was still getting over breaking the bad news he had given to her.

"I'm not sure I want to meet one of those Bantu beasts, even if he is as cultured as you say," she fumed as she turned up her nose in disgust at the thought of meeting the Bantu Ambassador. She had seen their severed heads or dead bodies before, but never in all of her one hundred and thirty-six lifetimes, had she ever seen a living Bantu let alone met one. Now she was obligated to dine with one and actually talk to it.

She looked impatiently at Marnir and Renlak.

"I instructed that General Longshins should replace Karkson, and oversee the disbanding and re-education of the legions. Has this been done?"

Renlak looked nervously at Marnir, who replied, "It has, my Sarissa. But doubt has often been cast over Longshins as a suitable successor. He will be sworn in tomorrow, so it is not too late to accept the Privy Council's recommendation and appoint General Shinther to oversee this delicate situation."

"I have not changed my mind," Shaka snapped impatiently. "Leave me now. I will read and study the detail of the scroll later."

Looking at the two Hammer Knights, and then at the bound and gagged young man, she ordered, "You may leave him, but remove that gag and those ropes that bind him, and then you will also leave."

The two knights did as she ordered, and after removing the man's bonds and gag, quietly left along with Renlak and Marnir, who secured the jewels back into the box, closed it and took it with him.

Shaka paid them no attention as they left; she was more interested in the man, and ravenously looked him up and down. She slowly licked her lips. "Come now, don't be afraid," she purred softly and almost kindly to him. "Come and sit with me, for I am in the mood for lighter and far more pleasant conversation than my officials can provide."

The man, still cowering on the floor, looked nervously at her. She smiled gently at him. *I enjoy their fear.* "Come, sit with me."

He cautiously rose to his feet, walked slowly and doubtfully over to her, and at her bidding sat on the chair next to her. She used a finger to delicately push the crystal goblet full of wine she had earlier poured, towards him, and then poured some for herself.

"Not many of my subjects can say they have had wine poured for them by the Empress herself," she stated playfully, as she took a sip of the wine that she had poured for herself. "You do not need to be afraid of me. I come here to my summer palace to relax and any guests I invite, are only here to help ease me from the pressures of ruling such a vast Empire. Now, drink."

The man picked the goblet up cautiously, and took a sip. His eyes glazed over, ever so slightly.

"Are most of the citizens of Kappia as afraid of me as you are?" she asked him before taking another sip of her own wine.

The man stuttered slightly with fear when he answered her. "They…they say you can change…that… that you can take on the form of a snake…"

Shaka threw her head back and laughed innocently. "Snakes come in two general types; loathsomely sluggish or scarily speedy. The sluggish ones usually crush their prey to death; the fast ones have a bite that poisons. What type do they say I am?"

The man did not answer.

"Oh come, do not believe such tales. I am just a woman of flesh and blood. The only difference between you and I is that I am a Pure-blood Akkadian and have led many lives, you are a Half-blood are you not?"

"I am, your majesty," the man stuttered.

"Please, no formality here today. I told you this is my place to relax and be free from all but the most necessary burdens of state. Call me Shaka."

The man's eyes widened with surprise at her suggestion. "If you wish…your maj…if you wish."

She spoke softly and gently. "Now, drink up, and tell me, what is your name?"

The man drank some more of the wine. His eyes glazed over even more.

"Marden, I am Marden. I am an actor who comes from the town of Greenwood on the eastern side of the plateau. I am here with my troupe to perform at the feast tonight. We plan to perform the play, *The Delinquent Centaur*."

"That is a dark play; until the hero turns the tide," Shaka remarked, as she ran her finger around the rim of the goblet she held. "But it has an important moral lesson, don't you think?"

"Indeed, it does your maj…it does."

"Do you think they exist, somewhere out there?" Shaka asked him, as she stared out at the plateau and beyond.

"Centaurs?" he asked cautiously.

"Of course, Centaurs, do you think they exist, or if not now, did they ever exist?"

Marden looked momentarily perplexed. "I have never really thought about it to be honest. Folk say that a lot of things exist beyond the plateau, but I have never left it. I have read Temmison, every volume and every book, but I am not sure if they are works of fiction or history. At my college we often discussed the merits and authenticity of his works. Edegal certainly hated him. It is said they were once close friends, but fell out over a woman, and after that Edegal vowed to discredit him and his works at every opportunity."

"Temmison was a loathsome, boring little man," Shaka said with contempt. "My grandmother knew him, a long-time ago. When I was new-born, just a little girl, she told me about him. She said he would come to the palace and talk endlessly how he had discovered lost cities, or been the first to enter unexplored jungles, or travelled on savage pirate galleons. He had a particular admiration for some of the Davari clans. Can you imagine that? How can anyone admire such a wretched race?" She laughed derisively, and topped up both of their goblets with wine.

"That's better Marden of the Greenwood town," she said as he drank more freely. "You seem more at ease now. Do you think I am still going to turn into some sort of snake thing?" She gave him a mischievous smile. He smiled back at her, somewhat uncertainly, but he visibly relaxed a little more.

Maren smiled tentatively. "You are not what I expected; I was terrified when they told me I was being brought to meet you, especially when they bound me with ropes. I feared the worst. I did not expect this."

*Fear is more delicious, when the prey is first lured to a false sense of security.* "You should not believe everything they whisper about me in the taverns," she said, eyeing him slyly over the rim of her cup. "Talk to me as though I was one of your college friends, or a member of your troupe. Today, Marden, I do not want to be treated like an Empress, only like a woman."

Marden smiled uncertainly, and then slightly finding his confidence, he nervously replied, "Then I am sure I can find you some food to cook, and then there are some dishes you can wash?"

Shaka was surprised by the audacious jest. She laughed outwardly. "So, I entertain a man with humour in him?" *I have some food, of that you can be sure, but dishes I need not.* She slowly licked her lips. "Now please, do I need to tell you again to call me Shaka?" She lifted her glass and took a sip.

"My humour is often in poor taste, so my friends tell me," he said cautiously as he took another mouthful of wine and relaxed slightly. "What do you think then, Shaka? About Centaurs I mean, do you think they exist?" He then leant forward a little, and then drank some more of the wine, and then drained the final contents of his cup.

Shaka watched him as his eyes glazed over. In a moment, his fear and nervousness seemed to completely leave him, and when he next looked at her, she could see pure lust in his eyes. *The potion is working.*

Shaka poured him another glass of wine and then stared thoughtfully across the plateau before answering. "There are many races that are stragglers from a previous

273

epoch trapped or hiding in this world, some of them rare survivors. Whether the Centaurs are of that kind or not, I do not know. The story of *The Delinquent Centaur* is told on a frieze in the Kappia Museum, you should see it if you have not already, before you go back to your nice home in the Greenwood."

"I will," he replied, as he drained the contents of his goblet in one go. He now had no shame as his eyes slowly looked up and down her body, admiring her voluptuous curves.

"Take a look down there," she said as she pointed to Kappia City and to the palace.
His gaze followed where she pointed.

"In my palace there is a room where there are strange wooden statues of kings who ruled this world before any human king. The priests who tend them say you cannot understand the history of our world until you understand about the three dynasties. You have heard of this?"

Marden shook his head.

"No, of course you have not. It is knowledge taught in the secret Mystery Schools that exist behind large walls; look there is one down there, the ziggurat next to that big market."

Marden had to strain his eyes, to make out the building in the distant. "It is said that people sometimes sneak behind those walls at night, and always, in the morning, their broken bodies are found in the streets outside as a message to all to keep out," he said.

"The knowledge in those places is closely guarded," Shaka replied, almost absently.

"Would you be allowed inside a Mystery School, Shaka?" Marden asked curiously.

"Of course, I spent an entire lifetime studying in one, before I became the Empress. They taught me that true reality is pure light and that the fall of the gods of the First Age and dynasty, and that of all this we see, was a fall from spirit into matter. After that fall, the gods were no longer able to squeeze into the tightening net of physical necessity that covered the world. The power of the creative gods, became limited and they could only exercise it in times of crisis when the people called to them. It was then, that the Aeldar took over in this realm, and brought it under their rule, for they found a way to control matter whilst preserving their powers."

"The Aeldar Days," Marden said with a tone of awe.

"Good, you know your history, you should as an actor," Shaka responded with a smile, "although we here in Kappia refer to it as the Age of the Aeldar, an age we seek to restore."

Marden became excited. "I love history. Now it is said that matter has become so dense, the Aeldar cannot become physical unless through magic and the Simal, and only then if one of their Aeldar wives reveals the riddle of their name."

"I do not like that word magic," Shaka said with disdain. "Only the ignorant use such a term. Any sufficiently advanced knowledge and the use of items that harness unseen powers, are indistinguishable from magic to the untrained eye."

"You are very wise," Marden said, as he unashamedly continued to stare at her body.

Shaka smiled. "The two great turning points in all history are caused by two types of thought. The first, when a great teacher or person thinks of something that nobody has ever thought of before, the second when those thoughts are written in words or captured in art. Magic is just a way of using higher knowledge to manipulate matter, nothing more."

"What would you call it then?" Marden asked, but by the tone of his voice, she could tell he was not interested in the answer. He was again brazenly looking only at her body. The potion had taken full effect.

274

"Higher Knowledge, as magic is just a way of transforming matter through thought and words, using what we know to shape the world around us. It only appears as magic or miracles to the ignorant who do not understand it."

Marden paused, hesitated, but then pressed on with his next question, this time looking her in the eyes. "It is rumoured, in my home the Greenwood, that in the Argona Temple, one of the Aeldar has been called back to this world many times. Is this really true or an exaggeration of what goes on there?"

"Two of them have been summoned, not just one," she answered.

He gasped in awe.

*I grow bored.* "Come, I wish to show you something." Shaka stood, and walked towards a door in the wall at the back of the terrace. Marden followed.

They entered a large windowless room which was furnished only with a large, red, four poster bed, covered with red sheets and pillows and surrounded by red net curtains. Torches set in ornate gold brackets lit the walls of the room.

"Shut the door," Shaka said, at which Marden quickly complied.

He stared around wide-eyed. "This room is incredible," he said.

Shaka pointed to some of the hieroglyphics painted on the wall. "This room is tens of thousands of years old, and so are these images. Look, the Aeldar fell to this world in chariots of fire surrounded by clouds. They fought with the other gods, those of the old dynasties; flashes of lightning came from their chariots and the Aeldar prevailed to become the only ones of their dynasty to remain, but they were unable to reclaim all of the Nine Worlds so they remained here. Each chariot has a wheel which, when it touches the ground, has a second wheel turning crosswise inside of it."

She pointed to other images. "Look, they could move in any direction they wanted. North to south, east to west, as well as up and down. Their chariots were magnificent, made for the gods themselves."

Marden pointed to an image. "But the Obelisks were already here?" he asked excitedly. He then pointed to some large words written in an ancient and strangely scripted language over the headboard of the bed. "What does that say?"

Shaka licked her lips and answered slowly. "It says, everyone wants to be a beast, until it is time to do what beasts by nature, have to do."

"I would love to write a play about this day when I met you, you are so fascinating, as is the history here. Would I be allowed to do so?"

"Would it be a horror story, or one of romance and passion?" she asked him.

"Romance and passion, for you are different to what I expected," he answered.

She looked at him hungrily, and did not reply. Taking him by the hand she led him over to the bed, and looked at him with a mixture of desire and ravenous predatory hunger. "I grow bored of talking of such things. The world over time has become darker, a place of paradox where it is painful to be human, unless our desires are met."

Shaka cast the shawl off of her and threw it onto the ground, and then took a pin from her gown; in one movement it slid effortlessly from her body onto the floor. She stood their naked before Marden.

"Undress," she told him.

Marden did so without hesitation.

Shaka pushed him onto the bed. Within moments she was on top of him, and he was thrusting inside of her. Their love making was loud, furious and passionate.

Both Marden and Shaka were in the throes of passion when she began to turn, to change. It was a slow change. Her face became a bestial serpentine travesty, glowing with exaltation and pleasure, her head, the hood of a serpent. Her legs and torso turned to a scaly horror and coiled around him, yet still she rode him for her pleasure. His eyes glazed widely; the look of lust replaced with that of terror. His outstretched arms were pinned to the bed by the overwhelming strength of her now scaly arms. Poison dripped from the fangs that protruded from her mouth and burnt the skin off his face. He screamed, but still she continued to take her pleasure from him, her head darting to and thro with great speed as she bit him many times. By the time she had finished her pleasure, he had already died a screaming, agonising death, his body a swollen mess bloated with poison and his legs crushed and broken by her powerful coils. She rolled off him flat onto her belly. She was fully in snake form. Her jaw began to crack and dislocate itself, and when wide enough, she started to consume what remained of his shattered and ruined corpse, head first. With such subtlety and deceit, and with the help of a Maia potion, had she seduced and then consumed many an unfortunate victim, before that day when she had invited Marden from the Greenwood, an actor who was to perform in the play *The Delinquent Centaur*, to the Terrace of the Sun at her Celestial Palace.

# Chapter Twenty-Three: *The Theos Murphor*

*How do you like your steak served? Clip its horns and hooves, wipe its arse and roast it. That's how! But what if it's a Minotaur? Then we'll need a bigger oven.*
**A Dwarven Proverb.**

*Stop leaning on the creator, and realise his needs are as great as our own. His woes are more profound than ours, his sense of failure so deep that it mocks our own. He is far from fulfilling his own vision. How can his sorrow not be immeasurably more than our own?*
**The Teachings of Karthal.**

*The* creature hesitated for a brief moment, and looked at Janorra. Cold sweat gathered thick on her body as icy doubts assailed her. *If this doesn't work, the consequences of resurrecting inside the castle again, are terrible to behold.*

A murderous glare formed in its eyes. It sniffed the air, and then strove forward with a thunderous bellow, consumed with a bloodlust at the sight and smell of human prey. It roared at her, its fangs dripping saliva. She could see traces of Janus the priest's flesh and robes, still stuck between its razor-sharp teeth. Her voice was sweet and musical, as she began to sing the *Theos Murphor* incantation in the language of Báith Rahmèra.

> *"The guardian strides through the halls of Bell,*
> *Across his path grim shadows fell,*
> *Awake he did at the sound of foes,*
> *But the smell of the Pure-blood, that he knows."*

The beast tilted its head, puzzled and confused, but clearly listening to the enchanting song. Janorra slowly and cautiously moved toward it as she continued to sing.

> *"The beast he knew this song of old,*
> *Into his ears the words unfold,*
> *Alert he sees I am no foe,*
> *For the sweet smell of a Pure-blood, that he knows."*

The creature leant down and put its nose an inch or so from Janorra's face, and sniffed. Something deep within it stirred; below the level of consciousness, it recognized something in the words she was singing. She fought her fear, and continued singing with the saliva dripping jaws of the beast only inches from her face. She reached out and stroked its muzzle. It snorted.

> *The night is cold in the South tonight,*
> *A full moon bids the clouds farewell,*
> *The beast he cries his mournful woe,*
> *Peace to the Pure-bloods who dwell within the Everglow.*

> *Keep your peace and let me pass,*
> *I know your pain, your grief your rage,*

277

*For long has it troubled you of great age,*
*Let me pass for pure is my blood, peace to you who is not my foe.*

*This tongue of old, you know its tune,*
*An echo from our ancestors who dwelt in peace,*
*This song they sang, before the world was full of woe,*
*And now, today, be not my foe.*

The creature stood up to its full height, and fixed its stare upon Scarand, Sasna and then Marlo, who shook with fear. Janorra moved and stood in front of them. "They are with me, you shall not harm them either," she said gently, but with authority.

The creature hesitated for a brief moment, looked at her, and then at the others, before it sniffed the air once again, turned around, and began to slowly make its way back down the passage.

"That was incredible," Scarand gasped in awe, when it was out of sight.

"How many times have you used that trick?" Sasna asked.

"Including that time? Once," Janorra answered her, panting with relief and nervously wiping away the sweat that dripped down her own face. "We are still not safe; the charm does not last long and might not work a second time. If it returns, we will have to fight it. Come!" She ran up to the Aeldar door and studied the symbols on it again, looking at each one and trying to remember their meaning. And then it came. She shuddered and staggered as more memories returned, and tried to supress the overwhelming emotions that accompanied some of them. She let out an involuntary cry.

"Are you alright?" Scarand queried, as he looked at her with concern.

She nodded. "More memories are returning; I am finding it difficult to process them all. Usually, after the *Awakening*, Pure-bloods are allowed as much rest as they need, to meditate and fully recover."

Despite a host of grim memories that had accompanied the last memory rush, Janorra continued to study the symbols. She was not certain, but she felt she might now know the word required to open the door. She waved her hand across it. "*Maroosh*," she whispered, and to her relief, the door slid open with a grating sound.

Her three companions let out short exulted cries. Fresh air wafted through the door and the sound of flowing water could be heard in the near distance. They heard the bellow of the beast in the background – the incantation had worn off more quickly than she had anticipated, but they were through the door before it reappeared. "*Maransh*," she said, and the door closed behind them, becoming as one with the small rock face so nobody would even guess there was a door there. Aeldar doors were not made to be seen when shut. Even their own makers could rarely find them if their location was forgotten, and when their secrets were lost, nobody could open them. Janorra closed her eyes and breathed a huge sigh of relief. *Thank you, Ashareth.*

The moon was high in the night sky when they emerged into the open air near to the river. Lightning split the skies, etching Castle Greytears against the silver-grey firmament. Seven heartbeats later the thunder boomed like a distant drum. Janorra poised like a statue in between the thunder crashes, listening intently for any sounds that might reveal a nearby foe.

"The river is just ahead," Marlo puffed nervously, as he began to run towards the reeds at the bank of the river. The others followed him.

When they made it to the reeds there was no sound, save for the buzzing of flies and the croak of bullfrogs. But in the castle, a mile away behind them, the blare of trumpets and the ringing of bells could be heard.

"The Baron has returned," Sasna squealed, looking around terrified. "He will discover the foul deeds we have committed and the banks of the river, both sides, will soon be swarming with his men. They already have search parties out looking for survivors of the wreck."

Janorra knew Sasna was right; it would not be long before the banks of both sides of the river would be filled with more search parties, not looking for survivors, but hunting them, so she did not even consider hiding somewhere near the castle until the search passed on. Their only chance of escape still lay in speed.

"Follow Marlo to the boat," she said, trying to suppress her own sense of panic.

The companions splashed through the reeds and shallows of the river, following Marlo as he searched for the boat. Janorra scanned the shallows, very aware that gigantic river snakes or crocodiles could be lurking just beneath the surface. She almost screamed with relief when Marlo found the boat about a quarter of a mile from where they had exited the Aeldar door. By the time they had unmoored the small flat-bottomed boat and began to push it out of the shallows, they could see that across the Erin bridge, silhouetted against the moonlight, scores of armoured knights were rapidly crossing, their lances and plumed helmets making stark shapes against the lightning lit sky. The unmistakable sound of baying hunting dogs filled the silence in between the crashes of thunder.

"Hedge Knights," Sasna whispered.

The companions quickly clambered into the boat. Marlo and Janorra took a paddle each and made haste to the middle of the river, where a strange current took hold of it and began to take them westward. The storm appeared to reach them and spread over them at incredible speed, the sound of the wind drowning out nearly all other noise.

"This is an ill-wind," Scarand said quietly as he scanned the darkened sky.

"Or a fortunate one, if chance or favour has sent it to obscure our passage," Janorra replied as she also scanned the sky.

"That may be, but this is an ill-current and is taking us under the bridge," Marlo said in alarm. "We would be safest if we reached Berecoth but this current takes us away from it."

A strong current had taken hold of the boat, and try as they might to paddle against it, their heroic efforts were futile. The current carried them towards the Erin Bridge where knights and men-at-arms were still crossing in large numbers.

The black clouds of the storm writhed and billowed, swelled and expanded. Janorra had never seen a storm like it before. It rolled and billowed with the fierce wind in its belly and seemed to carry them in its will. The voice of the wind mingled with the thunder, and the rain began to pour down soaking the companions in the boat. They were completely at the mercy of the storm and the great River Erin, caught in its white-capped waves and fierce current.

"I've never known the river act like this before, the current should take us east to Berecoth but it's taking us west under the bridge and towards the Wytchwood," Marlo shouted above the howl of the wind and rain. He then pointed to the water, his face ashen and craven, "Look," he shouted fearfully, "for a moment I thought I saw creatures in the water, moving under the boat."

When the others looked over the side, they saw nothing but the rapid movement of the water.

The sky was torn and convulsed in the lightning flashes as they were swept helplessly along in the current accompanied by the thunder and wind. In the midst of that cacophony of noise, the sound of baying dogs could still be heard. Janorra's flesh crawled as she caught sight of the hunting dogs and their owners on the banks of the river not far from where the boat was passing. *If the current turns and takes us ashore, all is lost.*

To Janorra, it felt like the companions in the boat were naked, afloat in the open where they were bound to be seen; only the dim light was in their favour, but when the lightning flared, it lit up the sky and the entire surroundings. Fortune or fate was with her, as the hunting party, struggling against the elements, passed on without noticing the small boat passing by on the current not a hundred yards from the bank where they searched.

The rain beat down upon the occupants of the boat mercilessly, only ceasing as they passed under the Great Erin Bridge. There was a sensation of unreality as they passed under the bridge, the echoing sound of the water against the stone walls of the structure and the sudden stillness of wind contrasting against the roaring elements sweeping the rest of the river. The current lessened under the bridge, and then took fresh hold once they were past it, and they let the river take them at its own pace, for it was futile to try to paddle against the current. The silhouettes and blackened images of the knights and soldiers still passing the high bridge or fanning out along both sides of the banks of the river were highlighted with every flash of lightning. The occupants of the boat sat still so as not to allow any movement except that of the boat, lest attention be drawn to them.

Sasna sat huddled at the bow, softly sobbing with her head covered in an attempt to keep out the driving wind and rain. Marlo lay flat, but looked poised to jump overboard, as though preferring to take his chances with the river should the boat be drawn towards the banks and the search parties. Scarand sat, looking sullen and grim, gripping his sword whilst Janorra silently prayed to Ashareth for favourable currents to move them past the danger.

As they passed the port of Greytears to the south, a blaze of lightning lit the sky and outlined against its glare they saw the masts of the very few ships safely moored within. So, passed the night, and with the rise of the morning sun, the storm had dissipated and the current ceased to carry them against their will.

"The currents can be strange on the Erin," Marlo said, "but rarely more so than last night. Apart from some strange eddies they mostly flow towards Berecoth and beyond there into the Tethys Sea far to the east."

"Then we must count it good fortune," Janorra said, "for my business is within the Wytchwood." *Good fortune or answered prayers.*

"As is mine," declared Sasna. "My brother Farir could be lost in there."

"Mine should be in Berecoth," Marlo said pensively, "but I'll not be arguing we paddle back east, for chance and luck may not favour us again in such a manner as it did last night."

As Marlo paddled them westward down the river, Janorra tried to sleep, to conserve what little strength she had remaining, but slumber would not come, as more memories seeped and surged into her tormented mind.

On the northern and southern banks of the Erin, for most of the day they saw long green slopes only broken by the occasional rock or tree, but no sign of the enemy that pursued them. But above them, high above in the sky, some beast only just visible to the naked eye appeared and flew on mighty wings in a circle above them. The sight of the beast sent a deep-seated fear into Janorra's heart as she remembered Otan's words. "Tum de dum. Run Seeress, run! The Wild Hunt comes for you. A terrible beast of the air with red and golden wings searches for you. Run, Seeress, run."

All in the boat looked up at the beast and trembled, but Janorra most of all.

280

"What is it?" she demanded of her fellow companions. "Is this a regular sight in these lands and along this river?"

Sasna shook her head uncertainly. "I have never seen such a thing in the skies before, I know it is not a griffin, so I fear to even ask what it might be."

As their voyage continued, aided by Marlo paddling against the current which was now soft and slow, they came to the Branded Land on the north side of the river, the area between the Wytchwood and Stargen. The Branded Land appeared hostile, vast and desolate and there was no sign of living and moving things. The land to the south of the river was green and lined with trees and the banks of the river filled with forests of reeds, where many small birds flitted about, whistling and piping.

"I'll not be going further down this river," Marlo said. "A few more leagues to the west, is the Cradle, and who knows who may be anchored there who would recognise me as an envoy of the Sea Lords. Beyond that the Wytchwood, and I will not paddle past such a cursed place in a vessel as powerless against the currents as this. I'll take my chances going to the south bank and from there west to Ashgiliath where I can by chance find work on a ship sailing waters with lesser fear."

Sasna protested. "You must help me find my brother Farir, and then escort me to Berecoth and then to Harwind. I must conclude my business with Erik Vansoth the Sea Lord. Even if this Redboots plans to take me hostage, as one called Gnarn told me she desired, I must bear the risk and reason with her to let me on my way."

Marlo shook his head. "Redboots did not know of your desire to visit Erik Vansoth, for I kept it from her so I alone could keep the coin you paid. I did not know her plans for you, or shamed I would be to now look you in the eye, and I would now confess my fault had I known she planned to take you hostage."

"Whatever the risk, once I find Farir, I must go to Berecoth and seek passage to Harwind and from there to Lord Vansoth. You must assist me!" Sasna insisted.

Marlo scratched the scar on his face. "I can think of no safe route back to Berecoth so my corsair days are done, for now. Search for a man in Berecoth by the name of Senzas, he was my partner. He knows of the arrangement I had made with you. He might grant you safe passage to where you seek."

"Then will you at least go to Ashgiliath, and inform my uncle of all the tragedy that has befallen me, and tell him that Baron Daramir is aware of our plans and shamefully mistreated me? Inform him I am seeking Farir and when he is found, I will continue with the mission he entrusted me with."

Marlo hesitated for a moment.

"You will be richly rewarded, tell my uncle I promised you a thousand gold coins to deliver this news," Sasna urged.

Marlo's eyes widened. "For that, I would deliver a message to Jorgen himself," he replied, "but they say *never trust a Seesnari*."

"He will pay," Sasna snapped.

Janorra suspected Marlo would never see a single one of the gold coins, but she had no concern for such a trivial matter. "As your last task, take us to the north bank," she ordered him. "That is my direction of travel." In her weakened state, she did not want to be powerless against the currents lest she find herself drifting east back towards Greytears and unable to do anything about it. "Each can make their own choice which bank they wish to depart from. But take caution, and remember that many there are that hunt us, not to mention that dreaded terror that now tracks us from the sky."

Marlo paddled the boat into the shallows of the north bank, where there were gravel-shoals so care with steering was needed.

"I thank you for your help, and fare you well, Marlo," Janorra said to the pirate as she jumped from the boat and waded towards the shore. Sasna and Scarand followed her.

Sasna once again urged Marlo to go with all haste with the news for her uncle, and then the companions bade farewell to him, after which he paddled the craft back into the Erin, waving a final farewell as he made his way to the south bank.

Not far from the bank where they landed ashore, the signs that men and dogs had recently passed, heading west, were a sign a search party had already passed that way. The remaining companions decided to trek north to avoid them, but also because in that direction the trail was firmer than the marshy land leading west.

There was little speech and no laughter, each of the company of three was busy with their own thoughts and more than once did they cast their eye to the sky where the silent winged beast followed. Everyone in the tired and battered group shared the fear to some extent.

Janorra and her two companions continued in a northerly direction until the land became firmer and they turned west. The ground was rough so they made their way slowly and cautiously, as they did not want to injure themselves nor come to the point of total exhaustion. They made their way around the south-western slope of a hill. The land before them sloped away westward but it was wild and pathless; bushes and small trees grew in dense patches with wide barren spaces in between. The grass was scanty, and the further westwards they headed towards the Wychtwood, the coarser and greyer it became. It was a cheerless, gloomy land. They spoke little as they trudged along. Janorra was tired and heavy hearted. She feared that despite the many dangers she had already faced, the ever-present beast in the air was a sign that more might soon appear at any moment. She was too tired and despondent to speak or answer any question, even when Scarand questioned her if the beast might be related to Otan's dire warning to her.

Inwardly, Janorra hoped that the appearance of the beast was just a coincidence, and that it was merely a wild predator, even though that would present a challenge in its own right if it decided to attack. Without her ring her powers were greatly diminished and she was no longer near enough to the Obelisk to draw from its power. More than once it crossed her mind to abandon her quest, and seek some quiet and discreet corner of the Everglow where she might live out the rest of her lives in obscurity. The truth was though, she knew that the Empire would never stop hunting for her, and as such she would never know peace. For that reason, she felt she must continue. Finding the Simal was her main objective, but relocating her ring must be her first priority. She felt insecure without it, and even though finding it again would not remove her fear, it would give her more confidence knowing she had the use of its many and varied powers, as that would greatly aid her in her quest to find the Simal, and somehow take it to the Baothein.

When the dark hours approached, Janorra dreaded them, as did her two companions. They kept watch in pairs by night always two of them awake, expecting at any time the flying beast to descend. But they heard nothing, only the sound of the wind blowing through the patched grass and dead trees. Yet when the dawn finally came, still, the beast was there high in the sky circling them, only this time two other smaller shapes were with it, though the larger beast soon chased them off.

Scarand used his bow and arrows to shoot a brace of wild conies, which they cooked over a fire, saving some of the meat for later. They stopped and drank from streams they passed and made their way ever closer to the Wytchwood, always followed by the beast in the air.

"No one lives in this land. Villages and towns once dwelt here but they were driven away from the darkness in that wood, and here we are headed towards it. A shadow lies on this land," Sasna said gloomily.

"You are not being forced to follow," was all Janorra answered in reply. She was not accustomed to being so discourteous and terse to others, but her own heart was too heavy, her own thoughts too dark and sombre, to take on the complaints of another.

"What other choice do I have?" Sasna asked, despairingly. "I must search for my brother Farir, despite my fear of that place."

The hills now began to shut them in. The travellers came into a long valley; narrow, deeply cloven, dark and silent. It was a small relief to them that some trees hung over the cliffs and their old and twisted roots protruded from the mud at places, providing some cover at which times they stopped to rest. They grew ever wearier but only stopped when necessary, constantly fearing that at any moment the Baron and his men might appear on the horizon or the beast in the air would descend and attack. They had to advance slowly, for the country was pathless and encumbered by tumbled rocks and fallen trees.

"There was once a great battle in this valley, between the armies of Bruthon and the Clans of the Tarenmoors," Sasna said. "But that was so long ago that even the rocks have forgotten it and none speak of it anymore."

"Where did you learn such a tale if men no longer speak of it and if the land itself has forgotten?" Scarand asked.

"The scrolls and books do not forget such things," she said in reply. "Many things I have read and more than I can tell or remember. The histories of these lands are written in books kept in the great libraries of Ashgiliath, and much did I read about them when I was young and still curious about the history of the world."

"What good is knowledge that one soon forgets?" Scarand inquired.

"You never know what you will remember, and when," she replied.

"Do you know of the lands to the north of here?"

I have not walked them, nor do I wish too. To the north of here is the Dale of Yarron where it is said the dead walk, and past them are the Blue Mountains, where monsters and fiends are said to dwell. The only safe way to pass those mountains is to go through them, by way of the Crystal Caves which one can easily get lost in without a knowledgeable guide to lead the way. Beyond them are the Tarenmoors, a harsh and dangerous place if ever there was, one full of wild and savage clans and packs of roaming wargs." She paused for a moment, and then added, "Only a fool would travel north from here."

Scarand and Sasna then both looked into the sky at the ever-present beast and they shuddered.

"If the truth be told, I would rather risk all of those dangers than be beneath that thing which tracks us from the sky, for a purpose we do not know," Sasna said. "Better a possible future danger, then a certain present one."

Janorra briefly stopped and looked tentatively around her. New thoughts came to her mind, and inadvertently she gave voice to them. "It is merely marking our position. Whatever it is that hunts us moves along the ground or by other means; that is why I am anxious to press on." She heard Sasna mutter under her breath, but could not make out what she said.

Janorra only allowed very brief halts during the days march. At such times Scarand stopped, watched and listened for sounds of pursuit but there was none that he could see or hear apart from the beast in the sky, which again was occasionally joined by two flying birds which, each time, it chased off. It was plain the companions could go no further when night came, even if their strength had allowed. They rested by a stream and lit a fire upon which they cooked a large bird Scarand had shot from a dead tree. They reasoned that whatever or whoever it was that was hunting them, the darkness of the night would not hide their presence from them so they might as well enjoy the warmth of a fire for as long as it took to cook the meat.

When daylight eventually came, they set off. To their initial delight the beast in the sky had disappeared, although the two smaller creatures were following them. It was not long before the large beast reappeared again, chased off the birds and was once more on their trail. In the early afternoon they came to a place where the trail they followed plunged into a deep cutting with steep moist walls of red stone. Even if they spoke in whispers their voices echoed so they passed through it in silence. All at once, as if passing through a gate, their path emerged out of the end of the tunnel into the open. There, at the bottom of a short incline lay a long flat mile or so, and beyond that the edge of the Wychtwood.

They eagerly quickened their pace, and were only half way across the flat when the beast in the sky began its descent. Like a great shadow it descended as a falling cloud, hitting the ground ahead of them with a loud thud that made it tremble and shake and the ground crack. It was a winged creature with a red body and golden wings. Quills and feathers that looked like sharp needles covered its entire bulk. It stood on two hind legs that were thicker than a man's body. Its front legs were more like gnarled arms, the end of which were vicious talons that could easily tear a man in two. The head of the creature was like that of a demon of old. Pure hatred shone from every sharp feature. It beat its great wings and screamed with high-pitched ferocity at the companions.

The three companions were filled with madness and terror at the sight of the creature ahead of them, blocking their way to the Wytchwood. Despair filled their hearts, for each cried out in misery.

Instinctively Janorra turned and looked back the way they had come as she heard a loud, muffled rumbling sound, coming from somewhere beyond a ridge a few hundred feet away. It sounded like it came from below the ground. Along the ridge, it appeared as though something large was gliding beneath the surface, causing the ground to move like a wave. It changed direction and headed towards them as though drawn by the screeching noise the flying beast made. A twisting burrow-mound of mud cut through the ridge. From the earth, without warning, burst a gigantic moleworm spraying such a large amount of mud and grass into the air, the sky was momentarily darkened. The heavier clumps landed on the ground with a loud thud, missing the companions, who were only showered with lighter bits of dirt and grass. The creature's body was adorned with bones and skulls of assorted types everywhere. Its great teeth within the cavern circle of its mouth spread like an enormous flower. The decaying odour from it dominated the air. As it closed its mouth, its glistening, barbed body subtracted and withdrew back into the cavernous hole it had made, and in its place a fierce looking man-like figure emerged from the hole in the ground, onto the side of the hill, and was soon joined by others.

Sasna began to scream hysterically at the sight whilst Scarand stood open-mouthed, watching the spectacle with wide-eyed horror, before muttering some unintelligible curse. Janorra knew what these creatures were. She had read about them in books, Otan had warned her she was pursued by them, but, until then, she had never truly believed it was the Wild Hunt who chased her. As was often their way, she had thought that the Obelisk Otan had either been uttering a form of nonsense, or had been speaking cryptically. *He was right about the flying beast. He was right about the Wild Hunt!* A myriad of thoughts flashed through her mind in an instant. *How can they enter the Everglow? The great city in the north, Aleskian, is the ever-watchful guardian preventing such an occurrence. For the Bantu to be within the Everglow, means Aleskian has fallen, but how can that be?*

The largest Bantu scanned his surroundings, and quickly noticed Janorra and her two companions watching him. It snarled and then blew a horn which made a loud, distinctive, bellowing sound. Scores more Bantu soon began to pour from the hole, onto the side of the hill. Taller than men, they stood like threatening statues, creatures from a more primitive and savage age. Janorra felt sheer terror in her heart. *They should not be here. The Bantu could never penetrate the Everglow unless the Great Northern Wall was breeched and the city of Aleskian has fallen. This cannot be possible?* Prophecies from the *Books of Aeldar* had said that all of the time the great city of Aleskian stood, the Bantu would never walk within the Everglow. But here they were. She had never seen a living one before, only dead mummified ones in the Kappian Museum, but she had read many descriptions of them. She did not have time to consider or wonder why or even how they were on her trail, especially those known as the Wild Hunt. They were there, and although she briefly entertained the notion that by some chance of misfortune, it might be one of her two companions she now travelled with they were hunting, Otan had said they were hunting her. In front of her and her companions, the flying beast stood before them, screeching. Behind them, with a terrible cry and the blowing of horns the Bantu began to charge down the hill towards them. Janorra heard Scarand involuntarily cry out, a furious, angered roar, as he drew his bow and notched an arrow, looking between the beast and the Bantu trying to calculate which posed the most immediate threat.

Sasna had found her courage and had drawn her sword, but she looked ashen with fear.

Janorra looked at Scarand and Sasna and said, "You Fell-bloods are most fortunate you only have one death to die. Die well today. Do not let them take you alive!" The words of Otan came back to her. *Run Janorra, run!* Drawing her sword, her terror changed to desperation and then to rage. She screamed in fury, and charged towards the great flying beast that blocked her way to the Wychtwood, and her only possible chance of escape.

# Chapter Twenty-Four: *The Tarath Guëan*

*They know very little of cultured ways, and tend to shun the large cities on the southern plains. They are content to hunt, to love, and generally live uncomplicated lives. If they come across an abandoned wooden fort, they will make it their home for a while, but they fiercely resist living in places built of stone. I tried to teach them the basics of farming, but they refused to learn and showed no interest, so I abandoned my fruitless efforts. I even attempted to teach them how to build fences so they could keep their livestock in pens, but this seemed to offend them greatly, as they believed any animal should be free to wander where it wishes. The pens and fences I made from the woven reed I collected from the riverbank at the bottom of a long slope were never used.*

*Temmison Volume IV, Book 3: The Tribes of the Tarenmoors.*

*In* front of Alwith rose the sheer rocky cliff face of High Blackbarrow, upon which Greytower stood. The place was surrounded by a howling wilderness, filled with the burial mounds of the kings, queens and heroes of old. A narrow ladder-like stair of hand-holds had been niched into the rock. Alwith climbed until he reached the top. The nearest outposts of the Kappian Empire were now hundreds of miles away. *Why do the council choose to live in a place as desolate as this?* he wondered.

When he reached the summit, he walked over and stood in front of the aged tower; the stones were stained with dirt and time, though not a one was broken or crumbling. The sun, hanging high above the wilderness, beamed onto a heavy iron-bound oaken door half-way up the front of the tower, but there was no stairway to reach it that Alwith could see. As he stood there, a doorway previously hidden, opened at the base of the tower.

"Come," he thought he heard a voice whisper on the wind that blew from within the tower, stirring Alwith's tangled mane.

Suspiciously, he approached the door. His knees trembled and his hands shook. The Tarath Guëan, rarely bothered themselves with the affairs of men, but when they did, it was because it benefited their agenda, whatever that was. It was said of them, they were an ancient cult who monopolized certain knowledge and power, which they refused to share with others, believing that such knowledge and power was dangerous for an untrained person to use without being corrupted by it. Of a sudden it puzzled Alwith as to why Commander Marki would seek their help on an issue such as this. Never, in all of Alwith's knowledge, had anyone ever been to the tower. *At least it is located where it is marked on the old maps.* He consoled himself, as he steeled his courage and peered into the soft gloom of the doorway. He panted to catch his breath and, drenched in sweat, he futilely tried to dry his sweaty brow with his equally sweaty hand. He passed through the doorway slowly, cautiously, *Ungweethon* at the ready.

The inside of the tower, was not what he expected. Torches in sconces on the wall mysteriously flickered into life, and the door shut behind him. With lightning like abruptness, Alwith recoiled and spat out a curse, as he leaped into a position of defence. He could not see who or what had closed the door. He looked at his surroundings and observed that he stood in a man-made cavern, dim, shadowy, on the walls of which were haunting images of hideous, half-bestial gods. A dim glow emanated from a small blue stone that he could see through the eye-sockets of what looked like a dragon skull, which stood on a marble podium, around which sat twelve figures. The appearance of the figures startled Alwith. The hands with which he held *Ungweethon*, began to shake.

"That weapon should not be handled by mere mortal men," an unsympathetic voice said, and then ordered, "sheath it, now!"

Alwith looked around in alarm, he was not a man easily abashed, but he felt disconcerted. At first, he could not see where the voice came from. It had not come from any of the figures sat around the table. They did not move, nor did they turn their heads towards him. From out of the shadows, the image of a man appeared. He was seated in a large carved ebony chair, in a sitting position with his legs crossed. Wearing a long, grey robe etched with either the grime or dirt of recent travel, or lack of washing, the starred pattern of which had long since faded, could only just be made out. Along with the rimmed pointed hat he wore, it was obvious to Alwith that he was one of the Tarath Guëan, the Grey-Council. He had one white milky eye, his right one, the other was black, and his stare was intense and harsh. The left side of his face was scarred as from an old burn. His white hair flowed across his shoulders, down his back and was equal in length to his long-flowing beard neatly knotted, styled and speckled with what looked like tiny gold flecks and gems. He held an ebony staff in his right hand, his long fingers impatiently strumming the shaft. On the end of the staff was a white orb streaked with black lightning that shifted and move across the surface. The clasps that held the orb in place were fashioned in the shape of griffin talons. The man was smoking a long briar pipe and blowing smoke rings into the air. He quickly extinguished the pipe in the manner of one with more important matters to deal with.

"Master Armun?" Alwith asked expectantly, somewhat nervously.

The response was bad-tempered. "No, I am Amrus, and shared the same mother's womb as Armun, so we look alike, not that you would have seen either of us before. He has long been among the *Banished*, and *Bane* is now added to his title, though *Nuisance* would be more fitting. He is no longer welcome among the Tarath Guëan. His council we seek no more, his gifts we will not use." Amrus stood to his impressively full height and fixed his powerful gaze upon the blade *Ungweethon*. "Give it to me," he commanded moodily, as he slipped the briar pipe beneath his robe and held out his hand.

Alwith hesitated a moment, but remembering the reason he was there, he handed *Ungweethon* over to Amrus, hilt first.

The mage stared at the blade as he took it, and then into the black jewel on the pommel. "The folly of the Empire still abounds. That is why we no longer offer council on their politics. Why do you bring such a foul blade here to High Blackbarrow?"

"It has inflicted Lord Borach, with a wound that had not killed him when I left but may have done so since. I was sent here to seek your help and advice."

"We have seen the troubles that have beset Aleskian. A beggar in the streets had the mark of *Arvivan*, through her eyes, we saw the city burn. It is now a place of rubble, ash and ruin." He winced with disgust. "The people of Aleskian were forsaken by the rulers of the Empire. The freedom won for Kappia, by the sweat and blood of the legions, has been handed over by treachery to butchers and slavers, but worse is still to come." He stared at Alwith, and the look penetrated his soul. "Your commanders were correct to send us this blade, it does not belong in the realms of mortal men. Your race cannot be trusted with such a weapon. Now, be gone with you!"

"I have come to seek your counsel, as well as to give you *Ungweethon*. It was only by good fortune that I arrived safely. I was pursued for much of the way, by a ferocious looking warg," Alwith said.

"He was not hunting you; he was guarding *Ungweethon* that it might be brought safely to us by your hands. Through his eyes, we watched you on your journey," Amrus replied impatiently. The mage thrust the sword in the empty sheath he wore attached to his thick belt. "Now, be gone with you!"

287

Alwith steeled his nerve. "Not until you have given me the counsel I seek, for I have brought you *Ungweethon*, and in return I demand…" He coughed when Amrus glowered angrily at him. "I request, that you hear me and offer advice."

Amrus strutted over to the skull, and thrust his staff through one of the eye-sockets so it made a blue orb within the skull light up. "Then come," he ordered.

Alwith joined him, warily looking at the twelve figures, which he soon realised were gaunt corpses clothed in hooded robes torn and tattered with age.

"Who were they?" he asked Amrus.

"The last Dragon-King of Darakmorothron, and his oath-sworn knights, but we do not have time for such a tale to be told now," the mage grumbled as he looked down at the runes on the sword *Ungweethon* which shone through the sheath, in the eerie light of the orb. As though they were ghosts, a number of other mages similarly attired to Amrus suddenly appeared as though emerging from fog, and surrounded the skull.

Amrus withdrew his staff and said, "Look into the blue orb within the skull, and tell me what you see and what you hear?"

Cautiously, Alwith peered into the skull and looked at the blue orb. He jumped back with a startled curse, as an image appeared and a voice spoke to him.

"What did you see, what did you hear?" Amrus demanded.

"I saw what looked like a man, but it was not a man. He had wings on his back that were as tattered as the robes that adorn these corpses."

"What did he say? Tell me!" Amrus commanded impatiently.

"He said, *they are coming back*!" Alwith shivered. "I heard him say his name!"

"What was his name?" Amrus loudly demanded.

"He said his name was Migdal," Alwith answered nervously.

Amrus and all of the other mages began to loudly mutter to one another. "More are waking up," one mage yowled.

"Armun was a fool to involve himself and us in this matter, double the fool for losing the Simal," another complained.

"Methruille has used his power in the Everglow, Armun had to leave our midst to bring balance," another retorted defensively. "He should not have been made *Banished*."

Some of them strutted back and forth, men lost in their own thoughts, anxiously talking and arguing among themselves.

Amrus raised his hands requesting silence. When he did not get it, he banged the foot of his staff angrily on the ground. A spark of lightning left the orb and hit the ceiling of the cavern, causing some debris and small rocks to fall to the floor. Alwith watched Amrus with alarm, the mage was clearly agitated, as were the others.

"Comrades, for some time we have known the fools in Kappia have been waking up the Aeldar," he said. "We know the Simal is now abroad, lost to us but not to itself. It is waking the other Aeldar Wives. Poor watchman we have been, to trust a task of such magnitude to Armun alone. It was clearly beyond him. Methruille has learnt much, since he left the Tarath Guën. Imbalance, he has brought, and Armun has not corrected it."

Some of the mages muttered in agreement.

Amrus' face twisted angrily as he continued. "I warned Armun that the Simal has a will of its own, that he should be vigilant, especially in any dealing with the foul Order of Ithkall."

"We do not yet know how Armun lost the Simal," a mage suggested sympathetically.

"We would if he responded to our summons," another remarked.

"The Simal is evil. Its use will only bring more war and suffering to an already grief inflicted world," another lamented.

"I do not understand about such matters, and nor do I care," Alwith said, and then finding his courage asked, "will you assist Lord Borach? Aleskian has fallen, he has fled, but was wounded by the blade *Ungweethon* when he fought with a Bantu named Garuk, the one who wielded it. None of us knows if Borach will die the *Final-death* even if this blade is far from him when his spirit leaves his mortal body."

"It is not for a puny mortal like you to question the Tarath Guëan," a mage answered him angrily.

"Yet the question remains," Amrus said, "and will be answered. This blade cannot steal Borach's soul, the distance between them is now too great, but it has blackened it, and few there are that can now cure the evil that will surely grow inside of him."

"Can you come, and help him?" Alwith pleaded.

One of the mages looked at Amrus and said, "The power of High Blackbarrow will fail, if more of us leave at this time. Methruille will gain much more power, if we bring further imbalance. Already, we can no longer see through our Omphalos Stone as far as we once could. If another of us leaves, we cannot hold back the chaos that will come. The concerns of the Empire nor those who fight for or against it, are ours."

"Then we must watch, and see what we can see, and trust Armun to make right the mischief he has caused, for he has already interfered with the plans of the Aeldar, and the Empire is now their servant and tool to wield as they wish," another mage said. The others, except Amrus, who was deep in thought, muttered in agreement.

"Comrades, we must retire to our studies, to ponder and reflect on what must be done," Amrus said. The others quietly agreed, and as though disappearing into a fog, vanished from out of sight so it was only Alwith and Amrus who remained.

"What about Lord Borach?" Alwith asked impatiently. "You say he is not in danger of the *Final-death*, but what can cure the evil you say this blade has inflicted within him?"

"Follow," Amrus said, as he turned and headed towards a door that he opened. Alwith followed him up a winding stairway and into a stone room filled with all manner of items you might expect in a sorcerer's study: books, scrolls, phials and jars of various sizes full of all manner of liquids, or various items ranging from those pleasant to the eye to the more grotesque. Climbing a rolling ladder, he searched for a book among the upper shelves, and finding what he wanted, climbed back down with it in his hands. Blowing the dust from it, he opened it and mumbled to himself as he flicked through the pages, and finding what he wanted, read and muttered the words to himself.

"As I thought," he murmured. "There is a place in the Deadlands, called the Garden of Masaraso. Few there are that know the way. Consuming the petals from a flower that grows there, consumes all memories of former lives. If one takes Borach there, and gives him a petal to eat, memory will be lost but the curse will be removed. But remind him, *memory is loves final gift*."

"Then I must be away at once, to give this answer for when he awakes."

Amrus looked at Alwith sternly.

"We have griffins that live upon the roof of this tower. I will teach you to ride one, it will eventually return you to Lord Borach, but I want something in return."

"Name your terms," Alwith replied.

"I want you to become *Arvivan*, so we can see through your eyes with the Omphalos stone."

Alwith shook his head resignedly. "I am probably a fool for saying yes to something the Tarath Guëan ask, when I do not know what it is, but on the condition that it will help cure Lord Borach, I will agree to it."

With a speed that belied his age, Amrus, in one move, thrust his staff knocking Alwith on the head with the base. "Good," he heard the mage say, as he drifted into unconsciousness.

\*          \*          \*

As Marki had expected, the Tarenmoors was a howling wilderness. For hundreds of miles the land ran bare and uninhabited. Plundering Ash Gonath had been a fortuitist move for the Third Legion, but their march had been hampered by the speed of the supply train. The heavy carts pulled by oxen had often become stuck on rough ground, and the oxen could only walk about two to three miles an hour. The supplies were now nearly exhausted, so the men had started butchering some of the oxen and abandoning or using for firewood the carts already empty of supplies. Other food sources had been scarce and hard to come by. Hunting and foraging parties were sent out daily, but often returned with little to show for their efforts, apart from one day when they encountered a small herd of deer, some of which they killed before the rest scattered and fled. As well as the fresh meat they provided, the legion had kept the skins as a possible source of trade. Their main source of food had been from the Mansosi River, which had provided fish, eels and some giant crested reptiles that lived in the reed beds, as well as an endless supply of water. Despite it snaking and bending often, closely following the river had been a wise move.

The men of the Third were exhausted, dirty, hungry and discontent. Morale was at its lowest, and more of the men were openly talking of deserting, and taking their chances on their own. Stamis had been one of the main spreaders of discontent, but Marki had hesitated to discipline him unless it became absolutely necessary, as the legion's unity was very fragile, and Stamis and his small group of men were not from the Third. It was for these reasons alone, that Marki had not personally set out to find Thurog Tor, believing he best served Borach by remaining, in an attempt to keep the legion intact. Instead, he had sent out scouts looking for cities or major settlements. The scouts carried sealed letters stating that the presence of a Kappian Legion in the Tarenmoors was entirely peaceful, and that they were in urgent need to use an Obelisk.

The legion was now deep into the Tarenmoors. The tramp of the six-hundred plus feet of the men, the hooves of the few horses they had and the wheels of the carts being pulled by oxen had brought up a swathe of dust that swirled in the light wind and settled on the armour of the legionnaires. Such a force could not move through the difficult terrain without getting attention from any inhabitants. For this reason, other scouts had been sent out to look for signs of potential trouble ahead, but every settlement they had come across, they reported had been abandoned. The huts were left intact apart from where the weather had damaged them and nobody had made repairs. Some possessions had been neatly stowed showing they had not been plundered. There were no decaying corpses or skeletons left lying around. For some reason, the inhabitants had simply packed up most of their belongings and left.

Warriors from the first inhabited settlement they had come across, had attacked them, but the legion had defeated them without any losses to their own. They had killed the warriors, but spared the settlement and moved on. The following week, one of the scouts had come across another inhabited settlement, and the news he carried brought fresh hope.

The settlement was nothing more than a few hundred or so round mud huts with straw roofs. Half-dug into the hillside, they were basic dwellings with round glassless windows and furs or leathers covering the entrances. A rotten wooden palisade surrounded the village from which hung the grinning skulls of men, but there were no towers or ramparts from which the wall could be defended. About fifteen hundred warriors had drawn up outside the palisade. They wore skin loincloths and their bodies were crudely painted with crimson blood and mud, and some wore feathers in their hair. They carried flint axes and crude leather shields painted with animal faces. A few warriors, the most wild and barbaric looking of all, wore human teeth woven into their tangled locks. Their teeth were borne in a grimace; they screamed and yelped war cries.

On the wild hillside meadows around the settlement, sheep and cattle wandered unattended. There were dilapidated pens made from fences formed from the woven reed taken from the riverbank at the bottom of a long slope, but they were not in use, apart from the occasional pig who wandered at will in or out of them, oblivious to the five hundred plus men of the Third Legion poised at the top of the opposite hill overlooking the scene. The other one hundred had been left with the supply train and the griffin a few miles behind. Marki's pony twitched her ears and tail as the flies pestered her, but was otherwise happily taking the chance to munch on some grass.

"There," Maynryn said as he pointed to a crude totem pole in the middle of the village.

Marki squinted, and looked at the pole. "By Balagrim you might be right," he said. "The drawings are basic, but they definitely look like a griffin and an Obelisk."

"It will be another slaughter if we have to fight them, I'd rather we avoid it if we can," Galin said as he took some snuff from a pouch and sniffed it.

Marki agreed. "Aye, I've not the stomach to kill more of these savages, nor to wipe out a settlement, unless we have no other choice. We'll try and talk, reason with them, and see what meaning they put, if any, to their drawings on that pole." He watched as a crimson feathered chief, accompanied by some of his warriors, ran towards them, waving flint axes threateningly. They stopped halfway down the slope that led from their settlement, yelping and gesturing rudely towards Marki.

Marki dismounted from his pony, took the jug of whisky Galin offered to him, and walked towards the chief. Galin and Maynryn joined him at his side.

Marki glanced up at the sun; he guessed it was an hour before sunset. Maynryn had found the settlement the night before, and when the legion broke camp and marched that morning, they had seen a group of the savages following them. They wanted to avoid battle as far as possible, as they did not want to lose any men on needless encounters, as that would further sink morale. The tales and rumours of Obelisks lost under rivers or entombed in dark cavernous places with no chance of escape had put a fear in even the strongest of hearts. It would be all but impossible to search for them, so it simply was not worth risking battle until they had secured a safe Obelisk for the dead to resurrect at.

The Lost Obelisks of the Tarenmoors, were the main reason the Empire, throughout its history, had not sought to enslave and conquer the peoples who dwelt there. Even the greatest Seers feared going into the Deadland realms of the Tarenmoors, as it was a wild and dangerous place even for them. Many who had ventured there long ago in times past had been lost, never to return again, so the Empire had long ago given up attempting to explore it.

The reports that a tribe had been discovered, living in a settlement with a totem pole depicting a griffin and an Obelisk upon it, had temporarily lifted morale significantly. The legion's commanders had unanimously decided that trying to talk and reason with the savages was the best option. They reasoned that it might just be possible that this tribe might know the location of an Obelisk in the area, one that was not lost in an impossible location. Although the tribe probably would not know of their use, for they were all Fell-bloods, it just might be possible they had discovered one, or perhaps more, Obelisks. That was the hope that had driven the legion towards the settlement, for Borach was still dying, but so far, the skill of the surgeon and medics and the amputation of his legs, and part of one arm, had slowed the poison from the Bantu blade enough so that he was stable, for now. But the last of the Easewood had been used. They needed to find an Obelisk, and soon. If Lord Borach died, and resurrected at a lost Obelisk from which he could neither be found, or escape, the commanders feared that would break moral beyond repair. They were concerned it would be the event that would fragment and splinter the legion, and regardless of oaths made, those that remained would also desert.

The chieftain screamed and waved his axe as Marki, Galin and Maynryn walked down the slope into the small valley, and then up the opposite slope towards him. He felt the chief's screaming was more for show than an intention to attack, but Marki was cautious. He crouched, put the jug of whisky on the ground, and took a few paces back down the slope, and gestured with his hand for the chief to take it. The chief watched him suspiciously, then lowered his axe and walked forward with his warriors.

When the chief was next to the jar of whisky, Marki pulled off his helmet so they could better see his face, tucked it under his arm and said in the Common Tongue, "We do not want to fight. You are the chief?"

"I chieftain," the man answered. He then poked his own chest for effect. "I am Ognok. We see Karno?"

His Common Tongue was broken, hard to comprehend, guttural and slurred with a brash accent, but good enough for Marki to recognise. The only word he did not understand was the word *Karno*. Though he paid very little attention to the gods, for a moment he felt grateful that if the myths were true, long ago the gods had taught all men and all races the Common Tongue and it was instinctive in them all. It would save a lot of time in seeking constructive dialogue with the tribe.

"I am Marki," he said as he pointed to himself and then asked, "what or who is Karno?"

The chieftain waved the axe in the air again, but Marki resisted the urge to grab the hilt of *Old Trusty*.

"Karno griffin god you bring, we want see him," Ognok said.

Marki suddenly understood what Ognok was asking for, no doubt his men had seen the griffin in the cage. The poor beast was in a dire condition and nearly dead, but this primitive chief clearly thought it was a god. Marki seized on the initiative. "Yes, yes, we will show you Karno." *You could keep the bedraggled thing or even eat it if it was up to me, but Meron is still insistent we keep it alive.* "We come in peace and mean you no harm. We wish only to talk."

Ognok smiled. "Then you welcome. Karno welcome. You bring him here?"

Marki nodded. "We can do that, I suppose."

Ognok then conferred with his warriors before speaking. "If you not want fight leave weapon on ground, come to home of Ognok."

Marki looked at Galin, who raised his eyebrows, his expression conveying his doubts. Marki shared them, but handed Maynryn his helmet. He then took *Old Trusty* out with measured movements, and with one hand raised in peace, he slowly handed it to Maynryn, and Galin did the same with his helmet and weapon.

"I'll not leave my axe on the hillside for these varmints to steal," Marki muttered to Maynryn. "Return it to my belongings, and then ride with all haste to the supply train and have that darn griffin brought here – if it's still alive."

Maynryn nodded and rushed off immediately.

292

Marki looked at Galin, who was looking doubtful. Marki clenched his fists and muttered, "We are never unarmed when we can still use these, cousin, if it comes to it."

Galin smiled, "Aye cousin."

Galin and Marki joined Ognok, who had picked up the jug of whisky, and then walked with him to the village. "Maidens preserve us," Marki protested under his breath as they headed towards the dilapidated entrance to the settlement, "I can smell the stink of his home from here."

In the village, families were coming out of the houses and leaving the palisade. Women and children with dirt stained faces and clothes, were sheltering behind their menfolk. The warriors had stopped yelping, the women began loudly ululating.

"Is welcome for servants of Karno," Ognok said looking pleased as the high pitch of the women reached a crescendo and then suddenly stopped.

"Gift!" Marki said, as he pointed to the jug of whisky. Ognok looked at the jug, sniffed it, examining it closely, clearly not sure what it was or what to do with it.

Marki pointed to the cork, which made Ognok jump back and wave his axe, but Marki motioned with his hands for the chief to pull the cork, which he did. It made a popping sound as he pulled it out with his mouth, which made him jump again uneasily, before he settled down again. He sniffed the contents, and curled his nose up in disgust.

"Fool of a degenerate, that's a waste of a good and rare whisky," Marki muttered under his breath in alarm as Ognok poured the contents onto the ground, then examined the empty jar.

Ognok blew into the jar; it made a high-pitched sound. The sound made him smile with delight, and he repeated blowing into it several more times. "I like gift," he said as he smiled broadly. "You give more. We talk."

"We've several jars of the stuff left," Galin said to Marki. "I brought them with me from the supply train in case we needed them to trade. I'll go fetch them if you want, but I don't want to give good whisky to the fool if he is going to water the ground with it," he complained, as they reached the broken gate of the village.

Marki sighed deeply, and watched as Ognok passed around the empty jar to the warriors around him, who were each as fascinated as their chief by the sound the jug made when they blew into it.

"We have little choice," Marki said, after which Galin hurried off to fetch the last jugs of whisky.

Marki waited for Galin to return, and watched bemused as Ognok and his men continued to pass around the jug, dancing as they played poorly sounding tunes on it, and laughing hysterically as they did so. A few minutes later, Galin returned, accompanied by several unarmed legionnaires who carried the remaining jugs of whisky.

Marki took one of the jars, popped the cork, made sure Ognok and his men were watching and took a few swigs. "Yummy," he said as he rubbed his stomach and offered the jug to Ognok. "Try it. Drink."

Ognok took the jug, sniffed the contents and was about to tip it on the floor again until Marki bellowed, "Drink it man! For the love of life, drink it!" He gestured that Ognok try to drink it.

Ognok cautiously took a sip, swallowed, and curled his face up in disgust.

"Give it a moment," Marki said, as he watched the chief, whose expression slowly changed into a broad smile as the effect of the whisky slowly took hold.

"That hit the mark, didn't it?" Marki said with a broad smile as Ognok then took several big swigs and swallowed, before passing the jug on to his other warriors who drank eagerly, passing it among themselves.

293

"Steady now, this is Merian whisky, the strong and expensive stuff," Marki warned as the legionnaires handed the remaining jugs to the warriors.

"Come, just you," Ognok said as he pointed to Marki, then turned and headed towards the village, followed by his warriors who popped the corks off the jugs, and continued drinking the whisky.

Marki looked around him, then at Galin and the legionnaires.

"Savages and whisky are a poor mix," Galin warned.

Marki clenched a fist and pummelled it into the palm of his other hand. "Bah, I'll give them a chance. I can crack the skulls of a few drunken savages with my fists if I have too. Have the men set up defences, just in case, and camp here for the night. If I'm not back by morning, it will not be due to my own will."

Galin understood and nodded as Marki followed the chief and his men.

The gate of the palisade was crudely made, and not even on hinges. It was already open, but Marki observed that it had to be lifted in and out of place. Ever the soldier, he carefully observed everything lest he might need to escape from the village. *If they close that behind me, this place could prove tricky to escape.* However, he sensed curiosity, not anger or hostility from the people who watched as he passed them by, and then followed him into the village whispering excitedly among themselves, as some women again started to ululate.

The village itself was not very impressive. Dogs greeted him with a chorus of snarls and growls and wild barking, but he paid them no mind. Wood smoke drifted from between the mud huts as women, clad in furs and leathers and surrounded by unwashed wild looking children, cooked meats over open fires. They watched curiously as Marki followed the chief and the warriors, who were laughing and making a lot of noise as they continued drinking the whisky.

Marki followed Ognok and entered the main hut in the village. Inside the floor was bare, apart from a few blankets and meagre possessions. They all sat cross-legged on the ground.

"You look like bearded child, very small. Why are you short, size of child, and men who follow you bigger?" Ognok asked.

Marki did not show the annoyance he felt. On any other occasion, such a remark might have warranted a cuff around the side of the head, but he realised Ognok was being curious, not rude.

"I am a dwarf, born into a noble race from far away. We are a different race from that of men, and a better one if you ask me."

Ognok and his men conferred in their own tongue before the chief answered. "We have heard of Dwarves, but you are first we see with our eyes."

Marki feigned a smile, hiding his annoyance. *If you have heard of my kind, why the bloody heck did you ask me?*

"Why you come my village. Karno commands?" Ognok asked as he took another chug from the jug.

"I come here as a friend, in need of help." Marki held up the palms of his hands peacefully, and then signalled he wanted to take something from the pouch attached to his belt. The chief and his warriors were alarmed and unsure, so Marki made certain his movements were slow and deliberate as he rummaged through the pouch, and then took the wrinkled and folded page he had torn from the scholar's book whilst escaping from Aleskian. Ognok and his warriors watched curiously as he unfolded it. He pointed to the detailed drawing of the Obelisk upon it. "You have a similar drawing on your totem pole, but have you ever seen one of these for real?" he asked as he showed them the drawing.

Ognok and his men took the page, passed it among themselves, looked at it, understood, and conferred among themselves in their own tongue, before the chief answered, "Talain. Thurog Tor."

*I know there is one at Thurog Tor you bumbling fool, but is there one closer?*" Marki tried not to frown his displeasure. "Have you seen any others, closer than this Thurog Tor?"

Ognok pointed to the torn page. "Talain. Dark soon. Not good time to walk when dark." He prodded his chest to make the point. "Tomorrow, I take you to Talain," he said.

"There is an Obelisk at a place you call Talain?"

"Tomorrow, I show you," Ognok replied. "You will understand."

Marki saw little point in trying to persuade Ognok to take him there immediately, so he took a jug of whisky from a warrior, lifted it up and drank heavily from it, deciding to try and discover more information. He decided to question Ognok on why the settlements they had previously come across had all been abandoned.

"Chief, can you tell me why all of the other settlements we have come across are abandoned?"

"I tell you. But first you answer me. Why you in Tarenmoors? Where you come from?"

"Now that is a long story," Marki replied as he handed the jug of whisky to the warrior next to him, "and I am in no mood to talk about it, but we are not here to fight, that I can tell you,"

"You want women? We have too many. I have spare women; some are fat and eat too much. You give more whisky, I give you our fat women," Ognok said as he drank the last few sips from the jug he held, and then blew into the bottle, laughing at the sound it made.

Marki rolled his eyes in exasperation. "We don't want women and these jugs are the last of the whisky; we just want to find an Obelisk, or if there isn't one, to pass through your lands without fighting."

Ognok looked surprised. "Our women are good at make man happy – they give you good time." He stood and suggestively moved his hips and his hands as though he were taking an imaginary woman, much to the amusement of his men. "Also, they cook good food. You beat them if they get too greedy. Why you not want women? You prefer a cow, sheep or pig for boom?" The chief made more suggestive moves with his hips and hands as he looked at Marki quizzically. The rest of the tribesmen laughed and Ognok sat down overly pleased with himself at his joke.

"What? No, no!" *For goodness sake you degenerate.* "We will take some of those animals for meat though."

"Ognok smiled, "Ah, of course – *for meat*," he said as his men roared with laughter, slapping Marki on the back.

Marki closed his eyes, and swallowed his anger, paused and then said, "Now, tell me why the other tribes have abandoned their homes?"

"Because of dragon skull and *Raven Queen*," Ognok replied.

"Dragon? I once heard tavern talk there were wyverns in the Tarenmoors, but surely dragons have been extinct for hundreds of years?"

Ognok laughed. "Dragon kind are no more - all dead. It is skull of dragon. All other tribes worship dragon skull as their god. They follow *Raven Queen* for great war to the south."

Marki thought about it for a few moments, accepted the jar of whisky passed to him, drank deeply, and passed it to the warrior on his right as he put the pieces of information together. *Some queen has united the tribes using a dragon skull as some kind of god to influence them. The sound of a war to the south is good, if we can offer our services to the side which has an Obelisk.*

"Why have you not joined them?"

"We Beereni tribe, we worship Talain and Karno. We last of Beereni, all rest dead now. We are last of our kind. Talain protects us." Ognok was now slurring his words as he snatched the jug of whisky from another tribesman and drank some more.

*So Talain is a person, an object or a thing, not a place,* Marki thought as he continued to attempt to put the pieces of information together.

"Is Talain a wyvern or a griffin?" Marki asked.

"No, Talain is woman – she only one who can use Obelisk at Thurog Tor. She dies, then lives again. Tomorrow, I show you Talain," Ognok answered.

*Talain is a Pure-blood?* Marki stayed for another hour or so, gleaning as much information as he could, which got harder the drunker the tribesmen became, especially when Ognok began to chant some songs in his own tongue. When all of the whisky was gone and neither the chief or warriors were able to hold a sensible conversation, and were either burbling nonsensically or asleep, Marki decided to withdraw in the hope that in the morning he would be taken to Talain. It was full night when he left the hut and made his way through the sleeping village and past the snarling dogs. With some difficulty he opened the broken and unguarded gate, and made his way out of the village to rejoin the legion, who had already erected defences and a guard along the perimeter of their camp.

*      *      *

The next morning Marki was woken early in his tent by the morning bugle call. He had slept fully clothed, so quickly donned his armour. Picking up *Old Trusty* from where Maynryn had placed it the night before, he gripped it, and was glad to feel its cold embrace as he ran a finger across the iron surface of the axe head. It was not often he and his old friend were separated.

The smell of breakfast wafted between the mud-stained tents as he emerged from his own pavilion, and made his way through the camp. The hillside wind howled over the long grass, and caused the walls of the numerous tents to flap, making a sound similar to a flock of birds taking off. The legionnaires who had just come off of guard duty, were already waiting with spoon and dish in hand at their company kitchen for whatever scanty meal breakfast might consist of. Marki made his way past the waiting line as they shifted forward a few paces, and he watched as the cooks serving, shrugged at the complaints of some of the men about the poor fare they were again being served. Marki walked over to a bench that was sagging under the strain of a soot-stained pot of gruel, made up of mostly water, reptile meat, fish and a few scarce wild root vegetables.

"You've been on enough campaigns to know the game lads," he said to the men next in the queue, whilst thinking, *but this is no ordinary campaign – this is different.* He sniffed the contents of the pot, and instinctively curled his nose up at the smell, before moving off before any of them could pester him for news of his visit to the village. He walked briefly around a part of the camp, stopping occasionally to hang around with groups of men, emerging from their tents, and gathering around the few centurions of the companies to receive orders to carry out after their breakfast. All of them looked tired and gloomy, some visibly miserable and sad, whilst others looked angry.

Marki felt the discontent in the air, though none voiced it when he was present. An experienced veteran, he knew there was the constant griping that legionnaires were always prone to, but this was different – he sensed raw anger and genuine dissent. It was

296

of little surprise. These Pure-blood men had lost their homes, some their families, and were now exiled from the Empire and in a very precarious and dangerous situation. They were oath-bound to Borach and the Third Legion. Their loyalty had been tested to the uttermost and proven beyond a shadow of doubt many times in the past, but there was always a time when even the most loyal of men could break, and he sensed that unless they found an Obelisk soon, for some, that time was not far off.

Marki regretted that their journey into the Tarenmoors had left them with so few choices, but as he reflected on the decisions he and the other commanders had made, he could not see how they could have done anything differently to improve their current lot. It was not the hardship that bothered these men; he knew that it was a combination of things: exile; the loss of home and loved ones along with the concern at having no safe Obelisk to resurrect at, that was testing them to their limit. For these Pure-blood soldiers, death was no release from life, and the thought for many of them that if they died in that region, they could repeatedly resurrect at an Obelisk under water, entombed, or just as worse, and that they would resurrect into suffering until their *Final-death*, had been a concern that had rapidly eaten away at morale, which was the lowest Marki had ever seen it. *Our situation is dire. Even if we had a Seer with us, they might be lost before we find a safe Obelisk*, Marki reflected.

It was perhaps the understanding of their current predicament, and the knowledge that they were safer together, that was the only glue holding the legion together. The oaths they had made had been in the context of service to the Empire, from which they were now exiled.

Marki noticed Stamis sitting around a campfire with the bowmen who had been with him at the High Nest. He walked over to them. Stamis and the men were muttering darkly to themselves, but fell silent as he approached them.

"The chief of the village is going to show us something today, it is connected to an Obelisk," he said to Stamis. "I want you to come and see it with me." Marki figured that allowing Stamis to witness some good news, or evidence of an Obelisk, might dampen his discontent. *I Hope that whatever it is Ognok shows us today, is of some worth and merit, or it might be the last straw for some of these men.*

Stamis, visibly perked up at the news, as did the others.

"Make yourself ready and join me at the perimeter," Marki said as he turned and walked away from the campfire. He could already hear the news being told to others, and by the tone of the animated chatter, it was being met with great excitement and fervour. News would spread quickly around the camp. He could not yet smile though; his own thoughts were riddled with concern. *Ognok, don't let me down. The whole future and existence of what remains of this legion might depend on whatever it is you show me today.*

Marki made his way towards Borach's tent and entered it. His appearance silenced the chattering inside. Braziers lit the inside of the pavilion with a ruddy glow, the coloured fabric dancing with the shadows of the commanders, legates and tribunes who made up the war-council, who were gathered within. They all stared at him expectantly as he entered.

Borach, both legs ending in blood-stained swaddled stumps just above the knee, was lying asleep on a stretcher. He stirred, his eyes slowly flickering open. There was a moment of vagueness before he sat bolt upright and stared at Marki. He winced. Every movement was clearly causing him pain.

Marki recounted to Borach and all in the pavilion about his meeting with Ognok, and that the chief had agreed to show them something, or someone, connected to an Obelisk.

Borach drifted off into unconsciousness before Marki could finish the entire tale, so was left alone with the surgeon to tend to him, whilst Marki continued talking to the others in the tent.

"Is the griffin still alive? The chief wants to see it."

Meron answered him. "I had an ox butchered last night, and fed most of it to him. He has revived somewhat."

"What?" Galin asked, reacting furiously. "I am in charge of stores, and also the oxen. You cannot be butchering one of the beasts without my permission!"

Torach was also not that amused. "Our men have to eat disgusting fish gruel, whilst you give that mangy beast fresh ox to eat?"

"That beast is a griffin bred from the finest stock," Meron protested.

"It was the runt of the litter, and would have been put down if not purchased as a pet for the amusement of the men of Ash Gonath, who had sense enough to leave the wretched creature behind," Galin roared.

"Enough!" Marki bellowed. He took some breaths, and spoke softly through gritted teeth when he continued. "The men are fraught enough, without them hearing us lot in an uproar over some meat." Secretly, he agreed with Galin that feeding the sickly griffin was a waste of resources, and Meron had no right to slaughter an ox without permission, but Meron had been increasingly spending time with Stamis, and had grown sullen and uncooperative during the last few days. *I have to keep the war-council united.* "The beast might yet prove useful," he said, trying to calm the situation, as he walked over to the map table. *If it doesn't, I'll wring the mangy beast's throat myself and then knock some sense into Meron if he takes issue with it.*

The legates and tribunes quickly spread a map across the table so the commanders could look at it. They joined Marki and concentrated on where he pointed his finger. "Now, we will see what Ognok shows us today, and will need to mark it on the map. Unless what he shows us is anything other than an Obelisk, the legion will march tomorrow, but we will have to stop following the river, and from here head south-west towards Thurog Tor. Have any more scouts returned?"

"Not yet," Torach said, "but unless some mishap has prevented them, the ones sent to Thurog Tor should return any time soon."

Let's hope they bring good news, and that our offer to serve as mercenaries in return for the use of their Obelisk is acceptable to them," Marki said. He glanced briefly at Borach, who was out cold. His face was grey, and Marki could tell death was not far away from him. Despair suddenly gripped Marki, but he shook it off. *If the king at Thurog Tor refuses our offer, and whatever Ognok shows us today is not an Obelisk, then we are doomed, but I'll not give into despair without first knowing what today will unveil.*

Before anybody could say anything else, they could hear some sort of disturbance within the camp. A few moments later a guard rushed into the pavilion. "The entire village is tramping up the hill, demanding to see the griffin," he panted as he caught his breath.

Marki and the commanders left the command tent and made their way to the perimeter of the camp. They could hear an excited babble, as saw many people from the tribe trying to push past the guards, who were trying to restrain them and threatening lethal force.

Marki quickly spotted Ognok. *Good, I thought I would have to wake him and he would have a hangover after the whisky.* "Don't use lethal force!" he shouted to the guards as he rushed over to the chief.

"Ognok, tell your people to move back, we cannot let them inside our camp, at least not whilst they are acting like an unruly rabble."

"We want to see Karno, then we show you Talain," Ognok insisted. Some of the guards had drawn their swords, whilst others were tackling to the ground some of the people who had broken through the perimeter.

"We will bring him out, but order your people back from the perimeter of the camp," Marki said to Ognok, having to raise his voice over the chaos and tumult growing around them. To his relief, the chief understood, and in his own strange tongue shrilled an order, which his people obeyed. They drew back. Those who had made it into the perimeter, were shoved forcefully outside, but were unharmed.

"Well let's not disappoint them then. Bring that overgrown turkey out so they can look at it, and be quick about it," Marki bellowed at Meron, who in turn headed into the camp barking orders at some men who followed him.

"Karno! Karno! Karno!" The tribesmen chanted excitedly as the women loudly ululated. It was not long before Meron returned, followed by the men who were pushing and pulling the ox driven cart on which the griffin was caged, to speed its progress. As the cart was taken out of the camp and onto the top of the hill, the excited tribe gathered around the cage to get a closer look at the griffin.

The ox meat it had eaten had clearly revived the griffin somewhat, for it started to become agitated and screeched loudly as it lunged at the bars of the cage, crashing into them and snapping at them with its beak. A dozen or so legionnaires surrounded the cage to stop the villagers from getting too near. Some of them threw scraps of meat into the cage, much to the annoyance of Meron who shouted at them to stop. A sickly griffin overfed, could easily die, unable to digest too much food.

Ognok managed to push past the guards and put his hand inside the cage to stroke the griffin. Fortunately, he was behind it and only touched its back leg. Marki managed to grab him and forcefully push him away from the cage just as the griffin turned its head in rage and snapped at Ognok, just missing his arm. "You frothy-headed simpleton, it'll rip your arm off," he said in exasperation as the chief beamed with delight that he had touched the griffin, which was becoming so infuriated and enraged at the crowd bustling outside its cage, the cage was in danger of breaking as the beast crashed and thrashed against the bars, snapping wildly in the air with its beak. The creature was also injuring itself in the process.

Meron ordered for it to be taken into the camp which was duly done as more legionnaires arrived and cleared a way through the crowd for the cart to pass. He and the other trained handlers were attempting to calm the griffin down as it still thrashed wildly about in its cage, clawing and snapping at the bars in blind fury. They covered the cage in a black silk curtain so it would not get too hot, as well as attempting to get it to stop focusing on the stimulus it had seen and heard outside of the cage. The experienced handlers used calming whistles and grunts to help soothe the sickly young beast. A softly played drum, sent out a soothing rhythmic beat. Slowly, the rage in the beast began to quieten as it left the tumult behind and entered the comparative serenity of the camp.

Some of the tribespeople collected the loose feathers that had fallen from the creature, and shouted "Karno," as they kissed and stroked the griffin's feathers.

Ognok was delirious with joy. "Ognok see Karno, your god. Now you see Talain, mine," he said as his people began to disperse and head back down the hillside, the women ululating with joy or chattering loudly, and the men dancing and singing and blowing into the empty whisky jars from the night before.

"Follow," Ognok said, as he and a few warriors began to trot towards a wooded copse far to the west of the camp.

Marki turned and noticed Galin and Stamis. "You two, follow me," he said. The two men, along with Torach and some legionnaires previously selected for the expedition, joined them with various items of equipment that it was anticipated might be needed. They caught up with Ognok and his men, and together they ran at a steady pace for about an hour until they reached the wooded copse, and entered it.

The copse was dark, and they made their way silently through it. Ognok and his men, who led the way, did not appear to be on the lookout for any danger, so Marki also relaxed a little. He reasoned that these men lived and hunted this land, so if they were calm, he would be calm, but he remained alert. It was not long before they emerged from the wood and before them was a rocky outcrop no larger than a small hill. The sun had risen and, unlike the cold and damp they had previously encountered on most days of their journey, it was scorching hot, so even though it was only a short walk up an incline, they had all broken a sweat by the time they reached a partially hidden cave that descended into the side of a rock face.

The mouth of the cave was half-concealed behind a lichen covered rock. It was merely a cleft in the rock barely wide enough for a dwarf, let alone a man, to pass through. It opened to face the east, so the entrance area, which widened once through the cleft, was lit quite well by the morning sun. Within the rock, the passage descended some forty feet, and when the sun could no longer provide enough light, the way was lit by a legionnaire with a torch.

Marki could hear the sound of running water somewhere deep below as they descended, but soon they reached the end of the passage which opened into a great cavern, filled with the stench of rotting corpses, so that all had to cover their noses with cloth unwrapped from their belts until they adjusted to the smell.

"Talain. Thurog Tor." The chief said as he pointed at four rotting corpses, covered in shrouds, lying on the dusty floor of the cave, and then up at the large charcoal drawing of an Obelisk on the ceiling of the cave.

"Jumping degenerates," Marki said exasperated. "This is the Obelisk?"

"Thurog Tor," Ognok said as he pointed at the drawing, and then said "Talain," as he pointed to the corpses.

"So, I was right, Talain is a person," Marki muttered under his breath, not expecting a response from Ognok.

Marki took the torch off the legionnaire and cautiously walked over to the four corpses. The first one was no more than a pile of bleached bones, wrapped in a torn, thin sheet that looked as though the slightest breeze would blow it away at any moment. The other corpses were three bodies, clearly female, which all appeared to be the same shape and size, though the parts the shrouds did not cover showed they were all at various stages of decay, some more than others.

Marki carefully lifted the shroud off of the second corpse, which he estimated was only about a year old. He thought he could make out a very faint, partial mark of an Obelisk under the right eye, and a strange spiral display carved into the face, but the face was also badly damaged with bite marks made with some very sharp teeth, so it was hard to be sure. The hair was neatly tied back with the feathers of a sparrow-hawk tied into it. The corpse was clothed in plain, boiled leather raiment, a very basic form of light armour. The leather was torn and damaged at the front, which Marki suspected was claw marks, the result of some very sharp ones. He curled his nose in disgust, but inspected the armour and undid the fastenings at the side. Under the layer of leather there was a thin layer of dull metal, and beneath that a backing of linen to make it more comfortable to wear.

"Whoever made this light armour is no artist, but they have some skill in their craft, as it looks good enough to move fast and offer some protection, but not much," he said out loud as the others gathered around.

"Talain make armour," Ognok said.

"Does she now?" Marki asked as he moved over to the third corpse. A section of cloth covering the face and neck of it had come loose, revealing a portion of sunken, lined skin with the same spiral design carved into the face. The face was dry and mummified, not yet fully decomposed, and older than the other corpse, but clearly recognisable as the same woman. This time, however, the mark of the Obelisk was clear, and it was filled in.

"Jumping Jittlejacks she is a Seer," Marki said, barely able to contain his delight. He respectfully removed the shroud. The hair and the raiment were also the same as the other corpses. The damage to the leather armour this time, was the result of multiple blunt instruments, probably crude axes.

He turned to look at Ognok. "Did you or your folk kill her?" he asked, "and if so, where?"

He was not troubled if Ognok and his people had killed her, his only thought was that if she had died in the vicinity, the multiple corpses were evidence that she had safely resurrected at an Obelisk, and returned.

Ognok shook his head. "No. Is Varsi tribe kill Talain. Very bad people. Varsi now with *Raven Queen*."

Marki was satisfied he was telling the truth, but he wanted more information. "Where was she killed, near here?"

Ognok nodded. "Varsi raid us before they leave to join *Raven Queen*. Talain fought with us, she our protector," he said, and then pointed to the corpse clothed in the leather that had been slashed by claws. "Warg kill her that time. We chase it off before it ate her," he said proudly.

"This is either triplets or it is the same woman," Marki said expectantly as he lifted the shroud off of the head of the last corpse. The spiral scars carved into the face were the same, as was the hair. The corpse wore the similar leather raiment. He held his breath as he leant over and examined the face more closely. "This is the same woman," he said triumphantly, resisting the urge to literally jump with joy and hug everybody in sight. It was the freshest corpse, perhaps only a month old. He held the torch over it to see more clearly but keeping it far enough away so that the heat or any dripping embers would not damage it. Under the eye, again, he could clearly make out the sign of an Obelisk, and the woman definitely bore the mark of a Seer.

"It is the same woman, a Pure-blood," he said with delight. "This corpse is only a month or so dead. There has to be a safe Obelisk near here and these bodies prove it."

The commanders and legionnaires let out cheers of absolute delight. Some cried with relief, as they hugged and patted each other. The relief that they were more than likely in the vicinity of a safe Obelisk, in a single moment lifted their darkest thoughts and secret fears that each had carried but not voiced, concerning the horrors any one of them could suffer were they to face the misfortune of death in the vicinity of an unsafe resurrection.

Marki, had held the same fears, not for himself or Galin as it would not affect them as Dwarves, but he loved the men of the legion, and had often stayed awake during the night hours sweating about the possible fate that might befall any one of them, or his believed friend Borach, were they not to find a safe Obelisk. He tried to not let the others see the tears of joy that escaped from his eyes, and he quickly wiped them whilst complaining the dust in the cave being disturbed by the celebrations was the cause.

301

Ognok and his warriors looked on in bemused bafflement. "You very happy to see our god, Talain," he said as he pointed at the corpses.

"Well, technically she is not a goddess, just a Pure-blood woman, but I'm not going to be an open box of pernicious gloating scholars about it," Marki said as he hugged the chief who looked even more baffled, but then grinned with joy as he pointed at the corpses.

"We love Karno, your god. You love Talain, our god," Ognok said.

Marki quickly regained his composure, and his quick mind began to calculate all the facts at hand. "Where is Talain? Do you know where she resurrected at, where the Obelisk is?"

Ognok understood the question and pointed to the drawing of the Obelisk on the roof of the cave. "This at Thurog Tor." He then pointed at the corpses. "Talain lives at Thurog Tor, but she come here often. She is our protector."

Marki looked at the drawing of the Obelisk on the ceiling.

"Talain tell me, in land of dead, she sees all. She walks in dead place with sight and vision," Ognok said enthusiastically.

The commanders and legionnaires were all elated, but it was Torach who was the first to express the doubt that also hit their minds simultaneously, as the grins on their faces slowly disappeared. "How do we know where her loyalties lay?" he asked. "A Pure-blood living in the Tarenmoors, still might have allegiances elsewhere, and she might not be the only one at Thurog Tor."

Marki rubbed his hands through his hair anxiously as the same thought had struck him. He stroked the chin hairs of his beard thoughtfully before replying. "Look at the marks on her face, no Pure-blood of the like I have ever met or known has them, not even Bruthon ones. Kappia has no business in these parts that we know of, and why would a Seeress be interested in a bunch of savages like these?" He paced up and down anxiously for a few seconds before continuing. "This Talain has a story to tell, but my gut tells me she is not working for any faction of the Empire, so there is only one thing for it," he said with grim determination. "We need to speak with her, as well as continue with our plan to do whatever it takes to make peace with whoever rules at Thurog Tor, for if Borach dies, that is where he will resurrect."

"That'll still be a mighty risky business," Galin said, "but I agree. We have to roll the dice on this one. There's no guarantee how long the surgeon can keep Bor breathing, so he will end up there soon enough."

"Then come, we've no more time to waste," Marki said as he turned around and headed back towards the entrance of the cave. "If the scouts have not returned with news, I'll head to Thurog Tor myself to negotiate with whoever rules there. The legion can wait here, for if we enter their borders in force it might be seen as a hostile act. We don't want to start a war with them."

Turning to Ognok, he asked. "Chief, will you take me to Thurog Tor?"

Ognok nodded enthusiastically and prodded his own chest proudly. "Talain my friend, my god," he said with a big toothy smile. "But first, you meet Effgard the *Wargheart*. You only see King Falamore, after speaking with Effgard."

"If that's the way it is, so be it then," Marki said.

# Chapter Twenty-Five: *Captain Redboots*

*Captain Spragge sailed into the harbour of Harwind with a king and four barons hanging by the neck from his yardarms. His deeds have never been equalled in all of the annals of buccaneering.*
*Abbie Marson: True Accounts and Great Swashbuckling Tales.*

*Azzadan* instinctively kept rubbing his throat. There was no trace of the vampire's bite left, his body was new and it was not possible for an Akkadian to be permanently infected by such a creature, but his pride was deeply wounded. Such a death made him feel humiliated, and the fact that Ishar had allowed it, infuriated him. He remembered the feeling of helplessness as the vampire had sucked the life out of him, but rather than feeling fear, he had felt murderous rage. He swore revenge on the vile creature if ever he was given the chance. *Lagrinda, I will not forget that name!* For the first time, he was even beginning to question the vows he had made to his Order. *If Ishar treats me with such contempt, and forces me to dishonour the Bethratikus, how can the Order support him as leader?*

Azzadan had resurrected at the Obelisk in the Hall of the Dark Brotherhood. The Great Obelisk Ithkarn, was hidden by very powerful enchantments so that not even the Seers of the Empire could find it within the Deadlands. Azzadan, himself a Seer, as were many in his Order, had stayed close to Ithkarn during his stay in the Deadlands and due to this, his time there had passed without event. Immediately after he had resurrected and *Awakened*, he had been given the Orange Brew that kept him bound to the Order, and then he had been given a fresh mission, one that he did not particularly like.

Azzadan deeply resented Ishar for taking the Bethratikus from him before it had been honoured, and for humiliating him so publicly in front of the Order. *If Ishar had given me more time, I would have completed my task and found the Seeress Janorra and the Simal.* It was the first time that he had failed to fulfil every part of a blood-vow. Raw emotions conflicted within him. He was still oath-sworn to obey Ishar, but he felt betrayed by him, and was angry that the principals upon which the Order were founded had been violated. He also wondered about Ishar's new friend, and his new mission. *Since when has the Order of Ithkall conspired with blood-suckers?*

It was dusk as he traced his way back through the same streets of the Kappia port as he had the day before, clutching a carefully wrapped linen package tied with string. It contained two letters, one for his cargo after she had been woken up, and the other for the infamous pirate captain he was due to meet. He tucked the package safely away under his cloak, and set out for the docks.

Stopping at an old apothecary shop, Azzadan entered. The bell in the doorway rang as he stepped across the threshold and walked up to the counter. The shop smelt of herbs and various scents. It was filled with assorted jars of salve, tassels of herbs, urns full of powders and phials of liquid. Animal parts hung from hooks attached to beams in the ceiling and a vast assortment of boxes filled shelves and spaces on the floor with almost everything you would expect to find in such a place. The partially bald, elderly man behind the counter, wiped his hands on his leather apron, and gave a toothless smile as Azzadan approached.

"I want something that will deter vampires," Azzadan barked rudely.

"Vampires?" The old man laughed, and was about to make a remark, but the look on Azzadan's face made him think twice. He turned and moved a ladder along a rail, and climbed to the top shelf from which he took a thick and heavy book, and after descending, brought it to the counter where he placed it down with a heavy thud. Brushing the dust off, he said, "I don't get much call for vampire powder these days." He put his glasses on, before opening the book and reading the contents section. "Ah, page five hundred and fifty-nine." Licking his fingers, he flicked the pages of the book until he found the page he was looking for.

"You know, a lot of people think garlic-based potions fend off a vampire, but that's not what it says here," the old man said as he peered at Azzadan from over the rim of his glasses. "Vampire powder is made from the dried blood, ground teeth, dust and powdered bones of a dead one. Vangalen fell such a long, long-time ago, such items are now extremely rare, as well as illegal and very expensive. I don't keep illegal items in stock young fella. I can't help you."

Azzadan took a gold sovereign Kappian coin from his purse and flicked it onto the counter. It spun around the counter in several ever-decreasing circles and rattled in front of the old man before coming to a still. "I'm not the harbour or city watch old man. I know you have vampire powder, as my Order have sold body parts to you in the past."

The old man's eyes widened, at first in fear, and then delight as he picked up the coin, studied it and slipped it inside the pocket of his apron. "Let me see what I have out back," he said before disappearing into a back room.

Azzadan heard the muffled sound of cupboards opening, and floorboards being removed. The old man returned a short while later with several brown paper bags, the powdered contents of which he put into a wooden bowl. Taking a phial from a shelf, he popped the cork and poured a yellow liquid onto the powder, and mashed it all into a pulp with a wooden masher. He then added more liquid, stirred it up, and poured the contents into a phial which he sealed with a cork. He handed the phial to Azzadan and then tapped the page of the book from which he had gotten the recipe. "It says here, that if you drink it, it will last for one lifetime only. A vampire will find the taste of even one drop of your blood so disgusting, it will not drink from you, and it will lose its power and strength for a while if it does. One drop of your blood will make them become as weak as any normal man or woman. I can make more, for the same price?"

Azzadan popped the cork. He took out one of his throwing stars, and tipped drops of the liquid onto the tips of it before he drained the remainder of the contents of the phial in one. The taste was disgusting and his face twisted and curled with revulsion. "This better work old man, or I will be back," he growled, as he threw the empty phial back onto the counter and left the shop.

Azzadan continued to make his way through the streets to the waterfront, and then along to the docks where he found the merchant ship *Galliver*, waiting for him. The captain of the ship was prowling the foredeck scanning the dockside for any sign of his passenger, but did not seem pleased when Azzadan walked up the gangway. The captain rushed over to him when he was on board and dragged him aside. He spoke in a quiet whisper.

"That cargo Ishar ordered me to load; I took a look, it's a sarcophagus and has the seal and insignia of Vangalen on it."

"You have your orders, as I have mine," Azzadan replied.

"Don't tell me we are to actually have one of them on board Azzie," the captain said. "The men won't like it."

"You know better than to question orders, Scithil. Lie to the men; tell them it's probably just hiding contraband. Now get me to Harwind as fast as you can and you will be rid of that thing soon enough." He rubbed his throat again in memory of his own recent encounter with a vampire and then took off the fisherman's mantle he wore and threw it in the sea. It felt much better to be dressed in his usual manner; he stroked his ethereal cloak, that had been hidden underneath the mantle.

It seemed to the crew loading the sarcophagus, a bad omen, when out of nowhere a strong gale blew up, which tore off the sacking covering it. Some of the men gasped in horror when they saw what it was, they were loading.

"Get it on board swiftly," Scithil said in a panic. "If we are discovered in possession of such a thing, we will all pay the price!"

The men hurried to get the sarcophagus on board, but it seemed another bad omen when they were lashed by a sudden and unexpected squall of freezing rain as they were winching it aboard the *Galliver*. The sarcophagus swung so wildly on the ropes that, had it not been made of iron, it would certainly have smashed to bits by hitting the main mast several times before it was lowered clumsily to the deck.

Azzadan stared at the sarcophagus. The countenance of the occupant was carved in hardwood on the lacquered lid, and with such vividness, it appeared as though created of a forgotten art. Archaic hieroglyphic, scrawled across every part of the sarcophagus, made his flesh tremble with a chill when he studied them more closely.

"Get it below quickly," Scithil barked, "before the city watch or harbour master start poking their noses around."

Battling against the wind and rain, the men seemed eager to get it out of sight as quickly as they could. The crew murmured in fear as they loaded the sarcophagus into the hull. It unsettled them even more when they closed the hatches, as the rain and wind ceased as suddenly as they had started.

When the sun had reappeared, Azzadan noticed a particularly attractive young harlot walking along the dockside looking for trade. She looked at him, and smiled seductively, and without invitation walked up the gangplank.

"Where's this ship going?"

"None of your business," he growled.

The harlot licked her lips suggestively. "It can be mighty lonely on the River Erin, don't you think?" When Azzadan didn't answer, she turned around and began heading back down the gangplank, swaying her hips.

"Wait," he shouted, as an idea suddenly occurred to him. She turned her head and looked at him.

"Will you entertain me on the way to Harwind for this?" He took a bronze Kappian coin from his purse and flicked it in the air towards her. The harlot caught it, and her eyes widened in astonishment as she studied it.

"For that, I'll do the whole damn crew to Harwind and back," she answered as she walked back up the gangway.

Azzadan grabbed her arm, and said, "It will only be my needs you will take care of." The solution was perfect. The harlot could entertain him on the way to Harwind, and after she had served that purpose, she could be used to feed the vampire in the hold after he woke it up.

Looking at Captain Scithil, he said, "Sail as soon as you are ready, and have your cabin boy bring jugs of wine to my cabin and lots of food. I don't want to be disturbed until I get to Harwind, and for goodness sake, whatever you and your men do, don't open that coffin or disturb that thing in the hold."

"Don't worry about that Azzie, I've no intention of that happening," Scithil replied nervously.

Azzadan smiled lustily and patted the harlot's bottom. "You're going to have to work hard to make me think I have gotten value for this," he said as he took the coin from her and dropped it between her cleavage.

She giggled, wriggled her chest so the coin slipped out of sight, and said, "Don't you worry about that sir, as long as you can keep it up, I'll keep it happy."

*      *      *

During the passage across Lake Panharin and then down the Erin, the harlot, whose name was Smindy, was as good as her word. No pleasure did she refuse Azzadan, and no complaint did she make when he became rough and even violent during the throes of passion. She submitted to whatever he demanded of her. He decided he liked this wench, not only was she compliant when it mattered, she had a sharp wit that amused him and made the long journey to Harwind less dull. When he drank the ample supplies of wine that were brought to him by the cabin boy, she matched him glass for glass. They often spoke long into the night, and he talked with her about many matters, some of which he should not, but as he planned to feed her to the vampire anyway, he reasoned to himself that her tongue would be silenced soon enough.

Gladly Smindy massaged his body, fetched and boiled sea water for them to bathe in, and took care of his every need. On the fourth day of the voyage, he had grown so fond of her, he considered changing his mind concerning what he had planned for her. *Maybe I won't feed her to that abomination in the hold.*

Smindy was a Fell-blood, long-legged and lean, only of modest bust, but Azzadan liked the firmness of them. Her skin was tanned by the sun and wind chafed. Her black hair was cut short and framed a pretty face of no more than twenty-five years or so. She moved as though she was used to a deck beneath her feet. "This isn't the first time you have been a sea bitch, is it?" he asked after a particularly wild love making session as she lay in his arms, her cheeks flushed red.

"I was born on the Arran coast, my pa sailed the Tethys Sea and hunted the great white basilisks that swim there," she replied.

"A basilisk hunter? Did you ever go to sea with him on such a hunt?"

"No, he never let me go on a hunt, but my sisters and I would often be on board at other times when he did business on his boat which was not so dangerous."

"How did you end up a whore in Kappia? I heard basilisk hunters and their crew can become rich men if they find one with a blue tusk."

Smindy laughed. "He never had such luck, but he scraped a living by selling their bone and meat."

"What happened to him?"

He went out to sea a few summers ago; forty of them set sail, none of them ever came back. He was a gambling man and had debts, so my ma, my sisters and brothers and I were all sold off to pay them. I ended up here in Port Kappia."

"Who owns you?"

"Nobody now, I was bought by a fat merchant to be his plaything, but when his wife found out she threw me from the lodgings he had paid for me. Ever since then I have wandered the docks and lived off my wits and my tits."

*I like her even more.* She gave no resistance as Azzadan fondled her breasts, and then took her for the seventh time that day. After that session, Smindy suggested they get some fresh air. Azzadan put on some boots, wrapped a cloak around him, took the linen package for safekeeping and made his way to the upper deck with Smindy. It was dusk and the upper deck was lightly manned.

"How far from Harwind?" he asked the sailor at the wheel of the ship.

"Dunno sir, I just steer it when on watch. You'll have to ask the navigator." The navigator informed him they were about five days away from Harwind. Azzadan

306

ordered the cabin boy to fetch him cups and a jug of wine, which he promptly did. Azzadan and Smindy then sat on barrels tied to the railings of the ship and drank the wine, and laughed, and talked about nothing in particular or of great importance. Below decks, the sound of raucous drunken singing could also be heard.

Azzadan and Smindy finished the wine, and sat in silence, watching the water of the Erin turn to green, to grey and then black as the sun set. It was at that moment, as he watched her staring at the glorious setting sun that he decided he would not give her to the vampire, he would let her leave when they arrived at Harwind. He would find some beggar on the street instead. It was rare he felt any notion of kindness or empathy towards another, but he also decided he would let her keep the coin. In matters where he had spoken too much about his work, he would swear her to silence.

That night, they slept under the stars, and were only woken in the early misty morning by the pounding of drums sounding out a battle beat. The crew of the *Galliver* were quickly woken and called to battle stations.

"What is it?" Azzadan asked Scithil, who emerged from below decks.

One of the crew pointed to something and shouted in panic, "It's a rammer!"

A small glowing light, swaying to and thro, was growing larger in the mist. It was another ship, heading straight towards them.

"Hard to Port," Scithil screamed, as three of the sailors swung the heavy steering wheel.

It was too late. From out of the mist, the ram of a large war galley appeared, cutting through the choppy waters of the Erin where the river stopped heading south and instead split to the east and west and into several smaller channels. Atop the main mast of the galley was a flag of black, upon which was the emblem of a pair of red boots. The galley rammed into the side of the *Galliver* with such force, that everyone, including Azzadan, was knocked off their feet. He rolled over a few times but leapt back to his feet, checking that the package with the two letters he had closely guarded throughout the voyage were still safely tucked away. To his relief, they were.

The galley tore into the side of the ship smashing it to pieces as though it were matchsticks. The only thing that stopped the *Galliver* from sinking was the clever design of the galley's ram that caused the *Galliver* to rest upon it, with the bow of the galley only slightly pressed down into the water. Before the crew of the *Galliver* could get to their feet and respond a hundred or so pirates had vaulted over the gunwale and landed on the deck of the *Galliver* with sabres drawn. A couple of crew members from the *Galliver* tried to resist when they eventually scrambled to their feet, but they were cut to shreds in seconds. Seeing the futility of the situation, Captain Scithil of the *Galliver* ordered his crew to surrender immediately.

A woman of incredible beauty, only spoilt by a scar that ran down the left side of her face, jumped from the galley onto the *Galliver*. She was tall, full-bosomed and large-limbed, with slender yet muscular shoulders. Her whole figure reflected an unusual strength, without detracting from the femininity of her appearance. She was very much a woman in spite of her bearing and her garments. On her head, she wore a red tricorn hat adorned with a single red plumed feather, that sat on top of her long red hair, which was neatly tied and plaited with golden pins. Around her neck, she wore a golden necklace, hanging from which were numerous human finger bones. On her voluptuous body, she wore a tight, red velvet jacket clasped with a decorated golden belt. Her skirt was uneven, asymmetrical - reaching down to her calf on the left side and, on the right, revealing a hint of flesh not covered by the thigh length soft red leather boots she wore beneath the skirt. In her right hand she carried a cutlass the pommel of which was a silver skull with two rubies for eyes; in the left a dagger, with a matching pommel. The bright red rubies sparkled in the dim light. She waved the cutlass in the air and shouted in a fierce and authoritative voice, "Who be the captain here?"

Nervously, Scithil stepped forward. "I am," he said warily.

The woman pirouetted and with her cutlass cut him in half in one powerful stroke; the two parts of his ruined body fell to the deck in grisly disarray, spattering those nearest with his blood.

"Who be the captain here?" she asked a crew member of the *Galliver*. He looked around him, hoping somebody would give him the answer. The woman struck his head with her cutlass; the steel went crunching through hair and skull, splitting it in two. Blood splattered over her clothing.

"Now you know why I prefer to wear red," she said with a dark smile, revealing white perfect teeth, and one golden one. She wrenched her cutlass free; the man staggered for half a heartbeat, then fell and was dead before he hit the deck, his body twitching out the death throes.

"Are they stupid?" she asked as she turned to her own crewmen who laughed raucously. She approached another crewman of the *Galliver*.

"I'll ask once more, who be the captain here?"

The man hesitated and looked around for help or advice, but none came. As she raised her cutlass he quickly blurted out, uncertainly, "You are?"

The crewman looked at the woman nervously, unsure if it was the right answer or not.

"Finally, they get it," she said as she patted the man on the shoulder with the flat side of her cutlass and then wiped the blood off of it onto his shirt.

"Now help my men get everything of value from this old tub onto my ship, and if you do it without complaint or causing trouble, I'll let you sign the articles or you can leave at the port of Harwind." She clapped her hands, and without argument her own crew and that of the *Galliver* got busy.

The woman noticed Azzadan staring coldly at her. She had the wickedest smile he had ever seen on a woman. She boldly approached him and pressed the tip of her cutlass against his neck. He did not flinch.

"I am Captain Redboots, your master Ishar has recruited me to take you to Grona."

Azzadan had already realised this was the captain he was supposed to meet. "We were supposed to meet at Harwind, you were instructed to find me when we docked," he said angrily.

Redboots laughed mightily. "Oh, were we now? I got bored with the wait. I've spent so long at sea and on water, I've grown a man's appetites." She stepped close and put a hand to the front of his breeches and gave him a squeeze through the cloth. She looked at Smindy, who was standing next to Azzadan and gave her a broad smile.

"He's not gone hard as a mast for me Smindy, has he been this limp for you?"

"No, my captain, he's used his mast a lot and the wood did not soften," Smindy answered as she gave Azzadan a cheeky wink.

"Smindy?" Azzadan turned and looked at her with astonishment before it dawned on him, he had been played. He smiled, amused at the clever subtlety with which Smindy had played her part. "That story about your father was a lie?"

"No, it was all true, except that when that fat merchant purchased me at the debtors' block, Captain Redboots here was watching. When he led me away, she slit his belly open so his guts fell on the floor and she recruited me to her crew. With the gold I've earned I bought the freedom of all my family and they now live in a cottage with no debt to anybody, and now I freely choose to follow the captain."

"But if I hadn't asked you on board?"

"There are many merchant ships that go to Harwind. I'd have paid my way, by warming a captain's bunk or greasing his palm with gold."

She turned to Redboots. "Captain, I'm glad you received the message I sent by raven that the *Galliver* was preparing to sail, and chose to meet us, although I would have enjoyed the rest of the trip if you had waited at Harwind. For a man with many secrets, this one does a lot of pillow talk."

Smindy smiled at Azzadan.

"Answer me one thing my sweet," Redboots said sullenly to Smindy. "Was he cruel to you? If he was, I'll cut it off and he can spend the rest of this lifetime without it."

In one swift movement, Redboots sheathed her cutlass but pressed the dirk against the front of Azzadan's breeches, which she unlaced with her free hand. "My crew is loyal to me because I am loyal to them," she said as she pressed the edge of the dirk against the base of his manhood.

Sweat began to drip from Azzadan's forehead, he was fearless of death, but knew full well what she meant, and had no doubt that she would not hesitate to do it. He did not fancy spending the rest of this life minus an important part of himself, and he could not spare the time to suicide and resurrect in order to get a new body. When he had become violent towards Smindy during their love-making, he felt relieved that because he had liked her, it had not been extreme.

Smindy looked at him and smiled cheekily, and then at Captain Redboots. "He was rough, but I liked it. Let him keep his mast even though I know the end he probably had planned for me at Harwind, if I had been a mere common harlot. I still kind of like him."

Redboots sheathed the dirk.

Azzadan smiled, mostly with relief, as he laced up his breeches. "I hadn't quite made up my mind at first my sweet," he said to Smindy, "but, even if you had been a common harlot, last night I had decided to spare you anyway."

"Then it's good to know romance is not dead in the world," Smindy said as she gave him another mischievous smile.

Azzadan finished lacing up his breeches and looked at Redboots.

"I have something for you," he said as he reached slowly under his cloak and took out the package. Untying the string and unwrapping the covering, he took one of the letters, and checking it was the right one, gave it to her and said, "There was no need to kill Captain Scithil; he was useful to my Order and Ishar will not be pleased."

Redboots waved a dismissive hand. "Not as useful as I will soon be. Every port along the Erin is filled with dock dregs like him willing to sell their principles for coin, but Ishar chose me for this task, so I am a thousand times more useful or he would have hired them. Besides, he answered my question wrong, and for that he had to die."

Redboots opened the letter and read it as Azzadan watched her carefully. He was far from happy that she had killed Scithil.

"I'm surprised you can read," he said sarcastically, trying to soothe some of the anger he felt. "I assume Ishar used big letters and short words to help you understand the nature and terms of this contract, which doesn't include killing Scithil?"

She did not take her eyes off the letter, nor did she rise to the insult. "Dead men can tell no tales," she said emotionlessly. Whilst still reading the letter she then added. "Beat me at Harendale, cards or dice, and I will let you cut off one of my fingers to soothe your anger. Lose, and I get one of yours." She looked up from the letter, and rattled the necklace adorned with finger bones.

"Harendale is as much a game of chance as skill, so only a cheat would issue such a challenge," Azzadan replied.

Redboots finished reading the letter, folded it and slipped it inside her jacket and then held up her left hand. The little finger was missing. "Even cheats can be beaten by a better cheat," she said with a huge smile.

It did not take long before the *Galliver* had been plundered of anything of worth, which along with the sarcophagus was taken aboard the *Cruel Maid*, the aptly named ship of Captain Redboots. Its lean red hull was over a hundred-foot-long, a single tall mast with a folded red sail stood in the centre of a deck long enough for over a hundred men and the fifty oars that sprouted from out of each side. At the prow was the great iron ram in the shape of an arrowhead.

The crew of the *Galliver* turned pale as they stepped aboard the *Cruel Maid*, as tied to the main mast, bound in chains and manacles, was a man. The runes carved into his skin were covered in dried scabs and blood. His lips were sown up with wire. He writhed weakly against his bonds.

"Who is that?" Azzadan asked.

"An offering to Jorgen, the god of sea and river," Reboots answered. "He will die soon. We'll choose one of the crew of the *Galliver* to replace him. Let me know if among them there's anyone you don't like."

Azzadan stared at her and said nothing.

Redboots winked and then walked to the prow of the ship, barking orders to her crew. "Save enough of them for an offering to Jorgen, three for the *Red Tide*, one more for the *Cruel Maid*. You know what to do with the rest boys," she said.

The crew of the *Cruel Maid* possessed not a tender feeling among them as bets of who could despatch the greatest number were made. The slaughter of the remaining crew of the *Galliver* was swift and merciless; all entreaties for mercy were made in vain. The bodies were thrown over the side into the Erin, the shrieks and expiring groans of the few victims still tenderly holding onto life despite their grisly wounds went ignored.

"That was unnecessary, they could have been spared, or signed the articles," Azzadan said gruffly.

"I told you, dead men can tell no tales," was Redboots brazen reply, "and I lied to them about the articles. My crew is full."

The crew strained at the oars as they pulled the *Cruel Maid* off the *Galliver*, which sank almost immediately beneath the surface of the Erin in a froth of bubbles.

"That bitch in Kappia and that old fool in Bruthon who calls himself a king, have sent their best galleys in large numbers after me and my fleet, all their ships now lay at the bottom of the Erin or the Tethys Sea, just like that old tub," Redboots said to Azzadan, and then laughed. "We let some merchant ships go to Harwind, but they pay a heavy tariff to dock there."

"Where is your fleet?" he inquired.

"Most are blockading the Erin from Berecoth, three are waiting in Harwind and will sail to Grona with us."

Redboots led Azzadan and Smindy into her cabin at the rear of the vessel. She flung open the ornately carved double doors. The cabin was elaborately furnished, and ran the width of the ship. A large red and golden rug covered the deck, and upon it were chairs, a desk and divans all nailed and secured to the deck so they couldn't move. The centre piece of the cabin was a table that had the serpent sea god Jorgen elaborately carved along its side. Two benches with red velvet padding were fixed either side. Chests overflowing with gold and jewels were placed in one corner. A large cot bed covered with a red silk blanket was at the back of the room, and next to that sat a bath tub made of pure gold just below the glazed windows, which were clearly strong enough to survive the impact of ramming.

"There is enough wealth here for you to live like a queen, why haven't you retired?" Azzadan asked her as he noticed the impressive wealth displayed.

Redboots removed her jacket and hung it on a stand. She walked over and stood before a golden framed mirror attached to the port bulkhead and removed her tricorn hat. She spun it onto the bed and took out the pins from her hair. The plaits undid themselves as she shook her red hair which spread in all its glory. "I would get bored of retirement. Unlike you Pure-bloods, I only have one life to live and this is how I choose to spend it."

At that moment, Azzadan had never desired any woman as much in his life as he did when he looked upon Reboots. He still felt angry about Scithil's unnecessary death, and knew that the slaughter she had inflicted upon the crew was for no other reason than to satisfy her own hellish propensity for shedding blood, but he was suddenly willing to put it aside. *Scithil was no innocent, and I've taken the lives of better men for lesser reasons than hers*, he reasoned with himself as his anger vaporised to be replaced by lust and yearning for the woman standing before him. He watched her every move as she walked over to a dresser and took some Harendale dice and cards from a drawer, and went and sat at the table and invited him to join her. As he sat down opposite her, she held up her hand with the missing finger, and then tugged her ring finger with the thumb and index finger of her other hand which was bedecked with jewelled rings.

"I don't ever plan to get married, so if I lose, you get this."

"Why would I want your finger?" Azzadan asked as he looked into her emerald green eyes.

"In payment for your friend. I see it angered you and I do not want a Brotherhood Assassin bearing me a grudge," she said with a cruel smile.

"Scithil was no friend, I liked him, but he was scum. I've killed men more decent than him for lesser reasons than you had," he said as he watched her bosom heave and move like a wave on the sea as she breathed in and out.

"Besides, there's other things I might want and will hold no grudge if given them."

Redboots laughed. "That's not on offer. No man can win or buy that, I only give it freely to whomever I choose. I'll have one of my men carve the bone of my finger into an exact figurine of me and paint the boots red with my blood. You can choose a golden chain from my treasures and use it to hang it from your neck. Think of the story you can tell of the day you beat Captain Redboots at Harendale and won her finger, now what'll it be, dice or cards?"

She rolled the five dice on the table, they landed each with the image of emperors on top, an unbeatable roll.

"Cards, I think," he said. "Now who gets to cut the finger off if I win. Me or you?"

"I'll do it myself," she answered.

He looked into her emerald green eyes, and felt drawn into them. They were as deep as the sea and sparkled with raw carefree courage. He had heard about the infamous Captain Redboots, most people who had ever visited a dock or tavern had, but he decided that the stories that followed her name did not even start to boast of the magnificence of the woman herself. He had never in all of his lifetimes met a woman of her like before and he knew he was never likely to again. He wanted her more than he had ever wanted anything in the world. Even just having her finger to hang around his neck to remind him of her, would be enough if he could not have all of her, and it would be his greatest and most valued possession. He wanted to win it, whatever the price.

"Which finger do you want if you win?" he asked Redboots as Smindy sat next to him on the bench and stroked his cheek with her finger.

"Usually, my captain would want one of your own fingers," Smindy answered him. "But, today, if she wins, Captain Redboots will take a Jorgen's favour."

"What the frig is that?" he asked.

Smindy answered him. "It will involve the breaking of none of your oaths, nor the killing or harming of any you love or value. But when a Jorgen's favour is called, on your honour you must do what is asked of you."

"I accept," he said as he picked up the pack of cards, but I'll be handling these for now." He opened the pack and inspected them. They appeared to be a normal pack of Harendale cards so he put them face down on the table.

"What game?" he asked Redboots.

She smiled widely, her golden tooth glinting in the lamplight. "Split the pack. Highest card wins. One shuffles the other chooses first pick."

Azzadan was surprised by Redboots choice of game, and also the one rule. It wouldn't be possible for her to cheat that way. He picked up the pack of cards. "I'll shuffle, you will choose first," he said. She watched him closely as he slowly shuffled the cards, not taking her eyes off of them for even the briefest of moments. He split the pack into two halves, and placed both halves on the table face down.

"I'll even let you go first," she said slyly, "and take two of my fingers if I lose."

Azzadan nodded agreement and grinned.

*It's my choice. It's not possible for her to cheat,* he said to himself as he turned over the top card from the left pack. He let out a yell of delight as he saw it was the golden empress card. Only one other card in the deck could beat it. He did not take his eyes off the other half of the pack as Redboot's fingers slowly picked up the top card. She turned it over.

"Damn it! Damn it to the Deadlands and back," Azzadan shouted as he thumped the table in frustration. She had turned over the golden emperor card, the only one that could beat his; she threw her head back and laughed wildly. He turned over the rest of the cards to check she had not somehow switched the pack; they were still the same normal cards and all appeared to be present.

"You cheated. How did you do that?" he asked, feeling exasperated. He hadn't seen any sleight of hand and she had not touched the cards until turning the top one over.

"I'm just lucky," she said with a devious smile as she got up from the bench and walked over to the bed. Smindy joined her.

"I'm not buying the luck thing, you did something," he said. "If luck was the reason for your win, one day it will run out."

"Then if I lose all my fingers on one hand, I'll cut the hand off and have a hook. I've always fancied one of them," she said as her body shook, and she roared again with laughter, the sound of which filled the entire cabin.

"How many times have you played this game with your finger as the prize?" he asked.

She replied with a look of amusement on her face. "That was the tenth time, and I've only lost once." She held up the hand with a missing finger. "Curse the luck or the cheating hand of a drunken dwarf," she said with a mischievous grin, and then, "I wanted you to win."

"Not as much as I did," he replied ruefully.

She wiggled a digit at him. "Think of the boast in a drinking hall if I showed this as a missing digit and said this one is now worn by Azzadan the *Godslayer* of the Dark Brotherhood of Ithkall."

Azzadan had not read the contents of Ishar's letter that he had handed to her. It was obvious it would mention taking him to Grona after Harwind. What pleased him and

312

made him feel warm, was that the title *Godslayer* was now being used in official correspondence that mentioned him.

"You can still give me your finger," he said seriously, "and make that boast."

"You didn't win it, *Godslayer*," she said as she undid her sword belt and let it fall to the deck. The clank was muffled by the soft rug. She then reached behind her back with both hands and undid some laces. The red dress glided off her body and fell to the floor. She stood there naked as the day she was born, except for the pair of red boots she still wore. Smindy let her own dress slip off of her as they held hands and climbed onto the bed.

"Join us," Redboots said friskily as she held out a hand of invitation to him.

Azzadan looked behind him. Outside of the cabin, the crew of the *Cruel Maid* were going about their business. A hundred men were heaving at the oars to a rhythmic beat of a drum, and the crew could look inside at will, but she clearly did not care. Sailors were walking past dragging ropes or equipment, a turn of their head showing all that would take place.

"Shouldn't we close the cabin doors?" he inquired.

Redboots smiled and licked her teeth, focussing on the golden one, before answering. "And block out the sound of life? Leave them open. I want to hear my crew and they want to hear me. You are a *Godslayer*, don't be Azzadan the *Shy*," she said, and then slowly began to kiss Smindy.

As he walked towards the bed, removing items of clothing on the way, Azzadan looked lustfully at Redboots and Smindy and said, "By Skipilos. I think in this moment I love you both more than life itself."

# Chapter Twenty-Six: *The Foul Guest*

*For one hundred and sixty-years Half-bloods were forbidden to perform and entertain in the sacred imperial palaces, and absent they were in the once and great legendary theatres of Kappia. So dire did the entertainment become during this period, and so detrimental was this edict to the arts, that the Empress Shaka rescinded it in the year 4,132. A history of stage and song in Kappia should be written about these years, for like the Centaurs of legend, surely her existence and reign are delinquent? Who would dare to perform such a play? I would.*
**Sophisticated graffiti found on the walls of the Kappian Theatre, a day after the famous Half-blood actor Marden entered Kappia City to perform his renowned play - The Delinquent Centaur.**

*Our Dear Brochus,*
*Marden mysteriously disappeared this morning, and has not been seen or heard from since. This is most unusual behaviour and we are concerned for his welfare. Could you return and help us search for him? We need to rehearse for tonight's play.*
**A note sent by the acting troupe to Brochus, the brother and manager of the famous Half-blood actor Marden, received whilst dining at a tavern.**

*Shaka* stood on the steps and looked across the banquet room, known as the Feasting Hall. The hall was bedecked in the colours and crest of the royal court - red hammers wrapped by a golden snake on a black background. The mood of the guests at the supper was festive despite the presence of the Bantu Ambassador, whom the Empress knew would be the talk of all in the room. The celebratory mood was abetted by a roaring fire and the ample wine that flowed from fountains, from where it was being liberally poured into large crystal glasses and then served to the guests by the Serveri, assisted by hundreds of scantily-clad female slaves. She could sense in the atmosphere, a palpable sense of relief and excitement that the Simal had been found, and the escaped Seeress recaptured. She smiled to herself: *Ruling those who easily believe lies more effortlessly told is amusing. Such fools forfeit the right to be trusted with the truth.*

As she stood there, inwardly mocking the guests as they were feasting, drinking and talking, she congratulated herself at how she had managed to quell the trouble that could have so easily ensued had she not acted decisively. In addition to the lie the people had accepted, the anticipation in Kappia resulting from the announcement of thirty days of gladiatorial games and chariot races had also lightened the mood in the city. Already, several famous gladiatorial schools on the Kappia Plateau had announced their intention to provide hundreds of fighters. As news of the games reached the more distant lands, soon other schools from the vast reaches of the Empire would send news they would also provide men, women and beasts to fight in the show. *These games will be a spectacular distraction from the current troubles.*

Fighting pits had been a part of the Empire for as long as it had existed, but Shaka's father had first introduced gladiatorial games on a large scale in massive, purpose-built arenas. Such games had since become a regular occurrence. Her father had taught her that they were a useful political and social distraction to take away the focus of the masses from the more unpleasant, but often necessary aspects, of imperial policy. The games were free to attend, for all citizens, and after the contests, at the close of each day, bread, wine and gifts were generously given to the people as they left the arena.

The heralds blew their trumpets, returning her mind to the banquet she was attending. The entire room fell quiet and every head turned and bowed as Shaka walked down the large and lavish central staircase, into the hall. She was escorted by her son Prince Caspus, and announced by one of the Serveri. It felt wonderful to sense all eyes upon her as she confidently, arrogantly, descended the staircase. Her hair was styled with front bangs and a raised bun, where a golden flower at the top stole the limelight, and lavish ornaments, a clasp, as well as pins gave the look a very smooth and elegant touch. A golden shannongrove gorget adorned her neck. She wore a brilliant yellow gown with purple silk trim, set with glittering rubies and diamonds, and a series of gold-thread tassels that hung at the hem and swept the floor as she moved down the stairs and then onto the floor of the hall. Her décolletage was cut low, the bodice lifted, and the waist cinched. The skirt had daring slits up to the thigh on each side. It was perfectly tailored to reveal every trace of her perfect body, the age of which was kept at bay by use of the rare and expensive powder, milathran.

Regineo, who was waiting at the bottom of the stairs, looked at his mother disapprovingly as she stood still, accepting the eager clapping and cheering of the crowd. He whispered to her, "You look beautiful mother, but perhaps you are too fond of the effects of milathran. It is easier to die and resurrect to combat the process of ageing."

Shaka returned the disapproving look of her firstborn son. He was dressed in an elegant doublet fit for the occasion, but neither that nor the embroidered cloak he wore could hide his disfigurements, and despite the white powder and make-up that covered his face, his natural physical ugliness could not be covered. It had always puzzled her how unlucky and cursed were those Pure-bloods such as her son who were born with such imperfections. No amount of resurrections would ever correct them. Each time, when they resurrected, the same disfigurements were always there. She thought herself fortunate and blessed that she had been born with such elegance and beauty, and with no natural physical imperfections. Ageing was her only physical frustration, but milathran kept that at bay until the moment of death. It was too much of an inconvenience to keep dying, and the waste of a life just to get a new and younger body, when the precious milathran removed the ageing process just as effectively. She decided not to answer her son, at least on that issue. "Why has it taken you so long to return to Kappia, after the events at Aleskian?" she demanded of him.

"I am here now," he said bad-temperedly. "I will sit and sup with the Bantu Ambassador, as you command, but I no longer trust them and I will not easily forget what they did at Aleskian!"

"You will hold your tongue and do as I say," she said scolding him. "The path we have embarked upon, will not be without its challenges, but it is the will of Ahrimakan, and of I, your Empress and mother!"

Regineo lowered his eyes, but Shaka was not unaware of the scowl that he then gave, as Caspus, still holding her arm, led her towards her place at the head of the table. As firstborn, it should have been Regineo's role, but his grotesque limp and inability to walk upright, was a source of embarrassment to Shaka so she always gave the role to Caspus at any major or state function. Limping, Regineo followed them. She offered him a word of comfort. "The Golden Horn of Aleskian is now in Kappia, the *Prophecy of Karthal* is being fulfilled."

Regineo snorted dismissively.

Shaka smiled and nodded graciously and politely at all of the lords, ladies and nobility of her court as she passed them. Her smile hid the contempt she felt for them all. They were so easily manipulated and deceived, and this thought elevated her sense of superiority over them. The loss of the Simal, and the shock that an Aeldar had been slain, had been matters that could have caused huge eruptions of social unrest and

315

secret rebellions. She felt grateful to Mazdek whose subtle plans had avoided such troubles, and for the select few Hammer Knights who alone knew the truth that both the recaptured Simal and the Seeress, were false. Their sworn loyalty would ensure the truth never emerged.

Not only had Mazdek's plan deceived the court and all of Kappia, it would in a short time return the actual Simal and the renegade Seeress into the heart of the temple. Shaka had revelled and delighted at the thought of the tortures and punishments she would ensure the wretch named Janorra would experience. Death would not even be a release for her. Other Seers would accompany her into the Deadlands to ensure that each time she died, she would resurrect back at Kappia, so that the retributions could begin again, until all of her lifetimes were expired. She would be punished with a brutal and cruel severity, and Shaka's only regret was that it would not last until the coming of the New Aeldar Age, the Age of the Aeldar, and the end of all time. Even so, that which she could do, she would, and the thought of such revenge, sent a chill of delight running down her back and a tinge of pleasure in her groin area.

Mazdek's plan had been of such genius, it had solved so many problems in one stroke. It had removed an ancient ruling family in the city of Aleskian whose loyalty she had long suspected. It had long been rumoured that Lord Borach, whose own father had once been one of her father's greatest allies and advisors, had become a troublesome *Betrayer*, but now he was of no significance having fled into some obscure exile, from which he would soon be hunted down by pursuing Bantu. The Imperial Treasury had long struggled to cope with the expensive drain of guarding the Aleskian Gate, and supporting the city of Aleskian and the region it controlled. It was an expense she had to endure, no more. The cost of funding the legions, and the expense of their griffin battalions, had also further crippled the struggling economy. Now, at Kara Duram, the legions were being disbanded. The Hammer Knights, who would become the Empire's army and defend the Kappia Plateau, beyond their immediate needs being met, required very little pay, as their service was one of dedication to a higher cause. The Kappian army would soon entirely consist of these holy warriors, who were so militant in their faith, they wanted little other rewards apart from those which the holy books of the Aeldar promised them. The Kappia Plateau was safe under their protection. The money that was saved, meant that she could divert the resources to building a navy to take back control of the once prosperous trade on the Erin, and even to stretch out to the Tethys Sea and challenge the power of the Sea Lords. The thought of the Sea Lords soured her mood slightly. Only lately, had they allowed ships from Kappia to travel on the River Erin, but only as far as Harwind, and no further, and even then, expensive tariffs and tolls were demanded by them for this slight reprieve. She looked forward to crushing the Seal Lords, and regaining the trade routes along the mighty river.

Shaka inwardly congratulated herself. *The drums of war never cease, but mine will soon beat the loudest! The Everglow lies in turmoil. The people need a strong and decisive ruler. That ruler is me!* Her only regret, was that she had not taken such bold and audacious steps before. In addition to all of the benefits Mazdek's plan had provided her, the Bantu horde would soon be ravaging the lands of the Baothein and would surely topple the High-Seat of her rebellious sister, who the people had named the White Queen. The hatred Shaka had for her sister surpassed all other hatreds she had, for the false queen had been the cause for almost a third of the Empire splitting away from the rule of Kappia during the time of the civil war, and that, to Shaka, was unforgivable. It seemed perfectly reasonable to Shaka that if her sister and the Baothein would not accept her rule, then they deserved complete and total annihilation. Yes, Mazdek's plan was bold and

316

audacious, but also sheer genius. The Bantu would destroy the Baothein, and when they had what they wanted and had retreated back to their own lands, her Hammer Knights would march from the Kappia Plateau, and conquer the whole Everglow. *From out of the ashes of chaos, I shall rebuild an Empire larger and stronger that none can resist. I will soon rule the entirety of the Everglow!*

As she approached the table, she noticed Grixen, the Bantu Ambassador watching her. She tried to hide the disgust the sight of the creature evoked in her, for despite his reputedly impeccable manners, he had a sly and foul look about him. *He is now an important ally. When the terms of our treaty are fulfilled, I need never lay eyes on such a creature again.* She smiled politely as she approached.

The seating for the feast was formal. Shaka sat in the prime seat reserved for her, the Empress and the host of the feast. As priests, their temple duties meant that Marnir and Mazdek rarely attended feasts, but on this occasion, she noticed that they were in attendance, and were seated at either end of the top table, a show of false humility, for she knew in truth that they revelled in being seated prominently on most other occasions.

Ambassador Grixen, was seated directly to Shaka's left, and her children in order of age, to her right. Aspess, dressed in a narrow girdle crusted with jewels, her dark eyes shaded by long dusky lashes, had an expressionless look on her face as her mother approached. Other prominent visiting guests of honour were seated in near proximity to Shaka, including Renlak, her Hand, who was to the left of Grixen. After that all of the nobility were carefully seated in positions that indicated their rank and status in society, the most important being on the main table, with the more important being closer to her. The lesser important, were on other tables, with the least significant nobles being the furthest away. The whole seating plan was all designed to enforce everybody to accept the social status and position assigned to them through the complex intricacies of life at the imperial court. Even the main table, and the secondary, third and other tables were laid out with exact precision as dictated by the famous *Book of Carvings* that described in specific detail where everyone and everything for such an occasion should be. The *Book of Carvings* listed the rules and customs that should be followed by those preparing, by those serving, and the guests who would be consuming the dishes: it included everything from the hand washing ceremonies to the exact placement of everything on the table, and the order in which any cutlery or implements should be used.

Everybody continued to stand quietly as Shaka settled into her seat, and only sat down when she nodded to the Master of Ceremony, a Serveri, who loudly banged a large brass symbol with a gong. The deep sound of the symbol echoed throughout the hall. The people sat and then resumed their conversations. After a pause, Shaka turned her head slightly, and looked at Grixen. It repulsed her that he was seated next to her as a guest of honour, for he was most displeasing to the eye. He wore a fine silk black robe with a golden design, but despite the brutal ugliness of his face, there was a savageness about him that did at least evoke her curiosity. Another, albeit small saving grace, was the pleasant revelation to her that he did not have a foul smell: he smelt of rare and exotic perfumes and scents that she was not familiar with, but that gave a pleasingly wild and sensuous aroma.

"I hope your stay in Kappia is proving to be pleasant so far, Ambassador Grixen," she said with a polite nod, acknowledging him.

Grixen gave a warm smile that bared his sharpened fangs. "It is proving to be most educational your grace," he replied, "though I find the wine here rather weak and vapid. My palate has not adjusted to your food, which is tawdry; but both are sufficient as basic sustenance. The dishes tonight do not look much better and the wine smells pungent."

Shaka raised her eyebrow in surprise at the statement. The table was full of the finest fare to be found anywhere in the Empire. She suppressed the flash of rage that surged through her, and took a breath before she answered. "The wine is from the southern slopes of Vintagnia, it is the finest Flararian. I am surprised it is not to your liking?"

"Maybe he would prefer warg piss," Regineo, who was listening in, suggested a bit too loudly.

Shaka silenced her son with a stern look. She then looked at the feast laid out on the table: it contained boar from the Forest of Tethian, which stretched from beneath the eastern most bottom of the Kappia Plateau all the way to the imperial port of Tethia Kappos at the edge of the Tethys Sea; wild venison from the Plains of Occua; rare Ranien steak from the aurochs that roamed the Fields of Phouasanos; numerous other meats, fruits and delicacies, each carefully prepared by the most skilful chefs in the Empire littered the tables that filled the Great Hall of Feasting. "Do you prefer your meat raw?" she asked Grixen, trying not to sound too indignant or rude.

"I prefer it still living," he said, with a foul grin, "and I do like my warg piss warm," he added, as he raised his glass to Regineo and bared his fangs in an attempted smile, that failed to mask the bitter sarcasm behind his words.

Shaka reflected briefly on the ambassador's words, considering if he meant insult, or if it was just the Bantu way, before replying dryly, "Then that, in regards to meat, we have in common. The trouble is, living meat makes so much noise, and tonight I am in the mood for a quieter dish." She laughed politely, as one would, having just told a joke.

As Shaka stared him in the eyes, Grixen returned the smile, and baring his fangs, raised his glass and said, "To quieter fare."

She sensed the surprise her answer effected on the ambassador, and she enjoyed his mild bafflement. Shaka accepted a freshly filled glass of wine, already taste tested and offered to her by a Serveri. She sipped slowly on the wine before adding, "Although, I cannot say I have ever tried the contents of a warg's bladder." Her tone turned slightly sarcastic and acidic when she added, "We have such creatures in our zoo and fighting pits, unless you jest, we can have some brought for you if that is your preferred taste?"

"I assure you, I jest," Grixen replied.

Shaka's first impressions of Grixen were not favourable. She had been told by her aides that his manners were impeccable, but she found his conversation insolent. *If this was any other guest, I would have their tongue removed, have a chef cook and prepare it, and force the offender to eat it in front of me.* Had he also not been an ambassador for the Bantu, she would have, at the very least, considered having him removed from next to her for more agreeable company, but tonight was about diplomacy. Too much was at stake to be risked, on taking umbrage at petty offences, whether they were meant or not. *Nonetheless, I will test him, but not push too far.*

Instead of reacting as she desired, Shaka raised her glass, took another sip of wine and then said politely, "To quieter fare, ambassador." She then drained her glass of wine as elegantly as she could with speed, and placed it on a lace coaster to her right, indicating that the Master of Ceremony could serve the first dish. He loudly banged the symbol. The clutter of conversation across the hall was disturbed as a host of Serveri and slaves began to serve food from the platters, onto the plates of the waiting guests.

Shaka was served her first dish, which was food especially prepared for her and not served from the table in front of her. Her taste tester, a thin Serveri with a crooked nose, took a random sample, sniffed it, ate a piece, and then nodded signalling the plate of food could be served to her, which a slave hastily but carefully did. It was a dish of thinly sliced spiced meats. Shaka picked up a golden knife and fork, and after cutting a small piece off the corner of a piece of meat, she delicately ate it. After she had swallowed it, she dabbed her mouth with a fine laced napkin and pushed the plate aside.

"Are you not eating mother?" Regineo asked her.

"I ate earlier," she replied.

Looking at the ambassador, who to her surprise, was eating with apparently flawless manners, she said to him. "Tell me, ambassador. Have we not allowed an army of your finest warriors to enter the Everglow, with the purpose of razing the cities of the Baothein, pillaging their lands, reducing their kingdom to ash and rubble, and for the White Queen to be delivered to me bound in chains?"

Grixen chewed his food and swallowed. When he answered, much to Shaka's disgust bits of food were stuck to his fangs.

"You have, and we shall all benefit from the alliance."

"Then how is it, that one of your top commanders, could not even defeat Lord Borach and his reduced legion in battle? I am most disappointed he escaped."

Grixen paused for a moment, and then said. "Lovely it is, when the chaos of war reaps its mischief upon the battlefield, and one looks out from the comfort of their castle window, to gaze with contempt upon the great efforts of others."

Shaka felt genuinely surprised by his answer, if not a little offended. "You have read the *Wisdom of Rael*?" she asked him.

"It is not as refined as some of our Bantu literature, but yes, I am familiar with his work."

*I detest the arrogance of this Bantu.* "Rael also wrote, *'to have begun is half the job: be bold and be sensible, and finish what you have set out to do,'* did he not?" She noticed the corner of Grixen's lip rise in a momentary, involuntary snarl, as though angered. *I will press him more, test his resolve.* "Then will you not answer me directly, without evasiveness, as to how Lord Borach slew your commander, defeated your warriors in battle and then escaped?"

The question clearly irritated Grixen, and he could not hide it in his tone of voice. "And will you not answer me, as to why you are so weakened as an empress, that you could not merely order one of your lords arrested without causing another rebellion in your lands?" He then added, somewhat sarcastically, "Your grace."

*If he was not the ambassador, I would have his head for that*, Shaka thought, as she bit her lip to suppress her rising rage at his arrogance. *It was one of your demands that Borach faced battle with your kind.*

Regineo vociferously slammed his glass of wine onto the table, and stared with hostility at Grixen, who bared his fangs.

Renlak, sensing the rising tension, leant over and asked Grixen. "Ambassador, how long will it take for Braka to be moved into position at the Baothein borders, and for the other, more sensitive matter to be resolved?"

Grixen regained his composure. "The Wild Hunt are taking care of business as we speak."

"That is a matter not to be discussed outside of discreet council," Shaka reminded both Grixen and Renlak.

Grixen acknowledged with a nod, and swallowed the mouthful of food he was chewing. "Braka will be in place in a matter of months. Meanwhile, our forces will also build other, but lesser siege engines, whilst we scout and raid Baothein lands. Man-flesh is not the preferred meat of our warriors, but we will send warbands far and wide to imprison captives, and then breed them for a constant supply of fresh young meat."

"We were under the impression this would not be a long war?" Shaka brusquely asked. "But you plan to breed Fell-blood meat and wait for it to be born?"

"Our warriors eat the unborn," Grixen replied. "It will be a supplement to their diet, a delicacy and reward for fighting well. Their main source of food will be brought by our own supply wagons." He stuck his fork into a piece of meat, and continued eating, and only spoke after he had chewed and swallowed. "Mazdek informed us that any Fell-bloods we come across in the Aleskian or Baothein regions, even if they claim allegiance to you, we can consider as ours to do with as we wish, but Pure-bloods we are to return to you unharmed."

"That is correct," Renlak said. "The Fell-bloods breed like rats and defile our ancient bloodlines, and like all vermin, must be destroyed to restore purity to the Everglow. We will keep some as slaves for the more menial tasks, but their numbers will be controlled."

Grixen smiled, as though a thought in his mind caused him amusement. He then grew serious when he said, "We have already sent a large expedition into the place you call the Tarenmoors in search of the one you call Borach *the Betrayer*."

Shaka raised an eyebrow in pleasant surprise, and answered in more measured tones. "In recent times, we have not had cause to trouble ourselves with the Tarenmoors. Those savages have not trespassed or harassed imperial lands since the reign of my father. It would be pleasing though, if after you found *the Betrayer*, your forces were to also cleanse that place of Fell-bloods, for cockroaches always spill out of their crevices at some time or another."

Grixen sneered derisively. "It will not take many of our warriors to wipe out untrained savages. But tell me, were your own legions so afraid of the *Final-death*, or resurrecting at unsafe Obelisks, that they were truly fearful to explore and scout the Tarenmoors themselves?"

Shaka took a moment to compose her thoughts and emotions, and to not give voice to her initial, impulsive angered response at Grixen's further provocation. Her words were curt, but again measured when she replied.

"I seem to recall, that wearing Neblans and leading armies of Davari slaves, in the past we ventured into your lands and caused you heavy losses, did we not?"

Grixen grinned. "Indeed, that's when some of our warriors first experienced the taste of man-flesh."

"The Tarenmoors had nothing we required or needed for us to throw resources at them," Renlak interjected, again trying to calm the rising tension.

"But your legions are now disbanded?"

"They are being replaced by a far superior and loyal force," Shaka answered curtly, as she cut another small piece of meat, and slowly ate it, more to suppress her anger than to satisfy any hunger. "Disbanding an army takes time."

Regineo, who had been eating silently but sullenly listening to the conversation scowled angrily at Grixen. "We have never lightly thrown the lives of our legions away on fool's errands. It takes too long to replenish those of Pure-blood; we have only sacrificed those who are disloyal. These are not your concerns. It is now the main task of your boors to cleanse the Baothein lands, and the renegade Aleskian regions, is it not?"

"It is," Grixen replied, in a more conciliatory tone. "Kappia and Thar Markoom have a lot of mutual interests. There is a border, far to the west of Thar Markoom, where Chatti and Gragor pass beyond the Northern Wall, and transgress and invade Bantu lands. They sneak and raid, and steal the rocks from which milathran is made, and then hide behind the wall. Would it not also be in both our interests to allow us

320

Bantu to see these races destroyed? If so, you might then trade with Goth Surien alone, for the milathran you value so much?"

"After Aleskian, our trust in your forces has been gravely tested," Regineo grumbled.

"And we have been assured by Goth Surien himself, that those responsible, have been brutally punished, and such an occurrence will not be repeated," Renlak said as diplomatically as he could.

Shaka took a sip of wine, and dried her lips with a napkin before she spoke. "Milathran has many uses, all of them of value to us. It used to be shipped through Baothein lands, as well as many other exotic luxuries, but we now have other ways to obtain what we need." She coughed, and tried to make her gestures and words seem polite, but Grixen had severely tested her patience. "I am quite bored of all of this talk of business, ambassador. The terms of our alliance are clearly outlined. Could I suggest we now enjoy the festivities this night offers?"

Grixen smiled. Much to Shaka's disgust, with a leathery tongue he licked off the remnants of some lingering food still stuck to his fangs before he answered her. "We will soon celebrate great victories, and I shall delight in seeing your raw emotions express themselves, of that I am confident."

Shaka looked at the Bantu inquisitively - he seemed overly pleased with himself after their unfavourable exchanges.

After a short silence, Grixen spoke with a confident tone. "We Bantu are worshippers of the Dark Mist; it shall descend upon the Baothein and all that is light there will go out. Some of our generals have already earned a much sought-after title of *Extinguisher of Light*. It is our rarest of titles, and is only given to exemplary warriors, after the complete and utter destruction and genocide of a civilisation opposed to us." He seemed to be revelling in violent thoughts. "Commander Garuk was feared, but he is like a mere mouse to a lion, compared to the generals, the *Extinguishers of Light*, who are already marching from the north, where we have all but won all wars fought there."

Shaka felt a qualm of uneasiness with the manner in which Grixen had spoken about the generals marching from the north.

As though sensing her unease, Renlak said to her, "The alliance states that only enough Bantu to defeat the Baothein will pass through the Aleskian Gate. I have the situation monitored. The generals are merely coming to lead the forces allowed into the Everglow."

She nodded. *I will question you and Mazdek in more detail on this, at the first opportunity.*

Shaka had heard of the Dark Mist; it was said to be the essence of the mysterious god of the Bantu, but she knew little in detail about it. She did not want to appear ignorant in front of Grixen, so decided to make inquiries later from scholars at the imperial court. For now, she said nothing. Instead, she fought to not allow the disgust and dislike she felt for Grixen to openly show in its full force. For the first time, a small part of her grew uneasy that she had allowed such a foul race to enter the Everglow, but when she remembered the benefits of how Mazdek's plan had saved the Empire's economy, she tried to quash any new doubts that arose. The same doubts were momentarily cast aside, when the thought of the Bantu horde finally vanquishing and forever destroying the Baothein and their false queen, fed her own pride and ego, and therefore pushed any troubling thoughts even further away. The image of her sister, the White Queen, being humiliated and subdued, quickly quietened every one of her misgivings, but only for a short while. One niggling thought occurred to her, not for the first time, but from that moment it grew, and kept coming back. *What if the Bantu never willingly leave the Everglow? We have invited death into our home.* She dismissed the troubling thoughts, for now. *Ahrimakan assured me this was the will of the Aeldar. I trust him.*

The banquet had seven courses, but fortunately Shaka could choose when each one finished, and therefore, the moment when the entertainment between each course would begin. She placed her knife and fork across each other on the plate, and then pushed it away, the sign that she had finished that course. The Master of Ceremony banged the gong, the signal for all the guests to follow suit with the Empress. The guests each placed their own knives and forks onto the plate in the same fashion, and pushed their plates away, even if they had not finished the dish. They smiled even if they resented leaving, unfinished, a dish they were particularly enjoying. They all knew it was considered a serious offence towards the Empress if any of them continued eating after the gong to end that particular course had sounded.

Secretly, Shaka hoped the vile Bantu Ambassador might not be aware of this etiquette, and though unlike other guests he would not be punished if he continued eating, she would enjoy making a big public display informing him regarding his lack of manners. To her slight dismay, Grixen had obviously been briefed in the etiquette required at a banquet, and he placed his knife and fork on the plate in the correct manner and pushed it away.

Serveri and the female slaves cleared all of the dishes and cutlery from the tables in less than a minute, and a small bowl of warm water, soap and a towel were brought to each guest to wash their hands. Shaka touched the soap, dipped her fingers in the water and allowed a Serveri to dry them for her.

After she had performed the ceremonial hand washing and the items were removed, the gong sounded again and a troupe of acrobats and dancers appeared on the main floor in the middle of all of the tables. They performed routines of fast dancing, pirouetting and various acrobatic stunts all accompanied by loud and fast music. This lasted for several minutes and when this had finished, silence for a few seconds came back to the hall, to be quickly broken by a round of applause and then the chattering of renewed conversation.

A second course was served, a mixture of meat and fish, savoury and sour dishes. Shaka had no interest in pursuing any further conversation with Grixen, for she found him most unpleasant in every regard. She decided to only respond when politeness required it, or if he directly addressed her. In order not to have to engage with him if he should start a conversation, she signalled to one of the Serveri and ordered him: "Inform Ambassador Grixen, in detail, on the history of each of our culinary customs at our banquets. He might find the topic of great interest."

The Serveri knelt at Grixen's side, and in a quiet monotone manner, explained to him in great detail how creating such a feast as great as he was experiencing took a large team of dedicated kitchen and serving staff. He told him that the process involved ninety-eight cooks, one hundred and fifty scullions, spit-turners and other assorted staff to serve and feed the more than two-thousand guests. He explained that one Serveri and two female slaves served five guests between them on the next lower tables, and that one Serveri and two female slaves served ten guests between them on tables lower than that, and so on. He made sure to point out that the guests at the top table all had their own dedicated Serveri and two female slaves each.

Shaka, although not hungry, made sure that she very slowly nibbled at the delicacies of the dish before her, because the Serveri was boring to the extreme, and she hoped Grixen might express some impatience and verbalise his boredom. It would have made no difference to anything, apart from to give her a tad amount of pleasure that she had tormented him a little. To her dismay and displeasure, Grixen listened to the Serveri

322

with apparent great interest, and even asked numerous questions and requested to be provided with a copy of the *Book of Carvings* that he might better study such an interesting topic.

When Shaka grew bored, she finished the course, and watched the next round of entertainment after which the next course was then served. Again, she slowly ate, more for show, whilst the Serveri continued to explain to Grixen that every process of the feast was carried out with deliberate care and attention. He was laboriously informed that in order for each chef and carver to perform their duties successfully, they had to absorb a very extensive body of specialised knowledge. Each prepared joint, bird, fish or baked meat pie, had to be cooked and then carved and served in its own particular way, and described on the menu with their own very distinctive carving terms. Each dish had to be served with the appropriate accompaniment, syrup, sprinkling or sauce. The Serveri monotonously listed information, written down in the famous *Book of Carvings*, and liberally quoted from it, only becoming silent during the entertainment, after which he continued his next discourse to Grixen.

In this way, Shaka managed to get through each dish by having minimal light talk with the ambassador, dismissing the entertainment quickly on the pretence that as Grixen found the topic of the *Book of Carvings* a matter of such interest, she did not wish to spoil his evening. At times she interjected into the conversation, instructing the Serveri to elaborate and go into further fine detail about some aspect of the feast. Grixen just listened, nodded his head politely, and smiled, and asked more questions. To her displeasure, he visibly showed no sign of boredom, so for her own sanity, in between the next few courses Shaka allowed the entertainment to run its course. Actors performed plays. Minstrels sang songs, poets eloquently orated their poems, and story tellers told tales from one of the volumes of *Temmison's 'Fairy Stories* and *Legends of the Everglow.'*

Before the final dish came out, which would be a sweet one, the Master of Ceremony announced that due to the mysterious absence of Marsden the famed actor, the play *The Delinquent Centaur* had been cancelled. The crowd groaned with disappointment, but gave a little cheer when he announced that the court jester, Gozan, who with his team of misfits appeared at the entrance to the hall, would perform instead.

The surprise announcement pleased Shaka. Gozan knew better than to taunt her or Regineo, or any member of her family. He had learnt his lesson well the first time he thought he could get away with a jest at their expense as he had in the days of her father. Shaka knew that Gozan had not forgotten how, after a jest at her father's expense, a pair of iron shoes had been heated in the fire and he had been made to dance in them until he was nearly dead, and after that he had suffered even more un-pleasantries in the Bloody Tower as a result. It was a mistake he had never repeated. All other guests on such occasions apart from the immediate royal family were fair game however.

Shaka, made a point of holding her wine glass in her left hand. It was her agreed sign to Gozan that, whenever he performed at a banquet, she wanted him to taunt and mock any special guest seated on her left, who in this case, was Ambassador Grixen. He had infuriated her throughout the evening, and deserved to be taunted by Gozan. It satisfied her to know she would enjoy Grixen's negative reaction, if he showed one.

Gozan made a dramatic entrance into the hall, running in and tumbling head over heels several times until he stood and bowed elegantly before Shaka and the head table. It was made to look like he had stumbled and fallen, but it was all part of quite an amazing acrobatic feat that landed him exactly where he had wanted to stand. He was dressed head to toe in bright colours, and bells attached to his costume jingled with every movement. Two other jesters, elaborately dressed, one in red attire and the other in green, both without headgear entered the hall and joined him in a similar manner.

"My Sarissa. You look as beautiful and lovely as ever this evening," Gozan said as he elegantly bowed once more. A roar of approval and agreement rose up from the hall. Shaka smiled and acknowledged the compliment with a nod of her head.

"Prince Regineo, Prince Caspus and Princess Aspess, all adorned with grace and style as usual," Gozan said after which he bowed again. Once more a murmur of approval and agreement rippled throughout the hall as the royal siblings each nodded and acknowledged the compliment without smiling.

When Gozan stood tall after the bow, a sad and exaggerated look had formed across his face. "But there is a situation of great concern that troubles even me and my fools, isn't their lads?" he asked as he turned to each of the jesters, who over exaggeratedly nodded their heads in agreement.

"Great concern," one said.

"A terrible situation," the other replied.

Shaka smiled to herself, she knew this routine of Gozan's as he had used different versions of it before after certain noble ladies in the court had given birth. It was sure to insult the ambassador, who having been given instructions on court etiquette, would have been informed it was just a part of polite entertainment if he was mocked, and no offence was intended.

Gozan looked at Grixen. "Are you aware, Mr Ambassador, that your wife has followed you into the Everglow and sits outside this very hall at this moment, holding a Bantu baby?" Gozan asked him.

Grixen momentarily seemed unaware of how he was expected to respond. To Shaka's delight, he seemed confused and took the bait.

"I have no wife, nor do I have children, for those of my class are eunuchs among my kind," he replied matter-of-factly.

"In that case," Gozan said. "When Ambassador Grixen found a Bantu shopkeeper screwing his wife, they both got something they hadn't bargained for."

"Boom!" shouted the red jester as the crowd in the hall erupted into laughter and Gozan did a tumbling act to land back on his feet.

Shaka smiled even more widely within herself. The worst thing anybody could do was to rise to the taunting of a jester and give them more verbal ammunition. It was better to sit there and take it, and smile as the taunts came in. Grixen, although briefed, was clearly not accustomed to the humour and style of court jesters.

"I hear the Bantu play a game where they throw small golden balls to an opponent, and the winner is the one who catches the most," Gozan said, "but that Ambassador Grixen is terrible at it."

"Sounds fun," the red jester replied. "Does the winner get to keep the balls?"

"Yes, and the loser loses his."

"Boom!" Shouted the red jester.

The crowd roared and clapped with laughter.

"What's the difference between Ambassador Grixen and a horny dwarf?" Gozan asked as he spun around with open arms to the crowd inviting an answer.

"Grixen is a massive vassal with a passive tassel, whilst a horny dwarf is a rigid midget with a frigid digit," the green jester answered.

"Boom!" shouted the red jester as Gozan did the tumbling routine again.

"Apparently," the green jester said, "Ambassador Grixen would make a fine tax collector as he is said to be stubborn and won't take no for an answer."

Gozan retorted, "Although he is rather flexible when it comes to genitalia removal."

"Boom!" shouted the red jester as Gozan tumbled and the crowd roared.

Shaka looked at Grixen, but to her dismay he was sitting there just smiling at the jesters. It was not an amused smile; there was something sinister about it that unnerved even her. It was the smile of somebody who had the air that they felt they would get the last laugh.

"Back to his wife and her lover's baby though, she told us that the Bantu females do not stop breastfeeding, even when the baby's sharp teeth appear, which is after a day or so," Gozan said.

"Do Bantu babies have the terrible twos like human babies?" the green jester asked.

"No, but that's what they called his wife's breasts after she had breastfed her baby," Gozan replied.

Boom!" shouted the red jester as Gozan tumbled and the crowd roared.

Shaka looked at Grixen, who still had the sinister smile on his face. It was not lost to her, that it might be better to not test the point of contact for the new alliance too much on their first meeting, so she stood to her feet.

"Thank you Gozan, but that is enough for now. The ambassador is our guest and may not be used to our humour and customs, so we have laughed at his expense enough this evening."

Gozan and the other two jesters bowed deeply, then turned, ran and tumbled out of the hall to the cheers and applause of the guests.

Taking her seat, Shaka turned and said insincerely to Grixen, "Forgive him ambassador. It is a custom of ours to so tease a guest, but if one is not accustomed to it, then it may not be to their tastes."

Grixen looked back at Shaka, and with a serious look of concern asked. "Who is the Bantu female with the baby outside of the hall? I am not married and I cannot have children. If she claims such it is a lie, and she and the baby must be flayed alive immediately and fed to a kennel of dogs."

Shaka returned his stare and felt a little perplexed. "There is no female or baby, ambassador, it was a joke."

Grixen bared his fangs and grinned. "As was that, your grace," he said.

Shaka smiled politely at him, although inwardly she did not share the joke, for behind the grins and smile she could sense that he was not happy at being mocked.

Grixen's tone of voice and accent suddenly became rough and wild. "We have a saying among my kind, that he who uses his giggle-box to laugh at the discomfort of his guests, is short-sighted, but when the guest becomes the host, he shall never cease to be entertained."

Before Shaka could respond, he continued in the more refined manner in which he had previously spoken all evening. "If etiquette allows, I would like to speak some words and present a gift from Goth Surien to your grace," he said, as he turned to the Master of Ceremony looking for permission.

"If my Sarissa allows, it will be acceptable," the man said.

Shaka nodded agreement. "Such formalities should normally be carried out when the imperial court is in session and not at a banquet, but seeing as you were content for our jesters to have a little fun at your expense, I think we should allow it before the final dish is served."

Grixen stood and looked across the crowded banquet room. The Master of Ceremony banged the symbol and the hall went quiet.

"Your grace," Grixen said as he acknowledged Shaka with a half-bow. "Imperial princes and princess, lords, ladies and distinguished guests. I greet you in the name of my lord and master, Goth Surien, the Samporak to the Lord of Morkroth." A few muffled whispers could be heard rippling around the hall.

"Long has there been mistrust between our peoples. Our enemy, like yours, is the Baothein, and the false White Queen, whose reign insults not only Goth Surien and the Lord of Morkroth, but your own esteemed Empress Shaka!"

The lord and ladies nodded and murmured in agreement. Some of the guests clapped uncertainly. The rest, not sure how to respond, joined in and also clapped, although not very enthusiastically.

"The only reason for our wishing to break through the Great Northern Wall and enter the Everglow, is because of the historic crime the Baothein committed against the Lord of Morkroth. Their foulest deed was the theft of his body from one of our most sacred burial sites."

A deathly quiet filled the hall, the only sound was Grixen's voice. "The White Queen has used her magic and devious ways to cause my kind pain and distress. Death and disease north of the wall are the products of her filthy spells and vile enchantments. Long has her evil been directed towards my kith and kindred. In defence, we had no choice but to try to reach her and our only path to her was through your city of Aleskian. Now that she has shown the true vileness of her nature to your own Empress, betrayed and made war against her, we the Bantu, and the Kappian Empire, have now united. Allied together, we will rid Pangaea of this abominable wretch for all time."

The guests remained quiet.

Grixen held a hand to his chest. "It is with great reassurance and relief, that now peace and an alliance have been reached between your wise Empress and my people - co-operating together, we can rid the world of this evil, false, so-called White Queen!"

He paused for effect. "When that aim is accomplished, we, the Bantu, shall retreat back to the safety of our own lands beyond the wall. Never again will we wish to make war with Kappia, nor seek entrance into the Everglow."

Grixen stared at the crowd and raised his voice. "You, and we, shall have eternal peace, on the day the Baothein and the false queen are destroyed!"

At the end of the table, Mazdek began to clap, very enthusiastically, to encourage the guests and show he supported the alliance. The guests waited, until Shaka, and then her children clapped, and then every person present joined in with cautious rigour and eagerness, before eventually breaking into thunderous applause accompanied by loud cheers and jubilation.

When the clapping died down, Grixen nodded to a Serveri who pulled a curtain aside. Three Bantu emerged, all of similar size to Grixen and dressed as smartly and eloquently as he, although they were clearly female in form. They carried a golden box with a red coloured glass lid. Placing it on the table before Shaka, one of the female Bantu carefully opened the lid.

With curiosity, Shaka peered into the box. Inside, was an arm bracelet and necklace joined by a magnificent gilded chain. Both the bracelet and necklace were made of gold and silver exquisitely crafted with detailed and intricate design; it was clearly workmanship of the highest quality. It was studded with a myriad of dazzling jewels and gems so rare, beautiful and precious, that even Shaka had not seen the like. Even the jewels she had be presented with earlier in the day by Marnir, could not compare to what she looked at in the box. She quickly forgot her anger as she gazed upon the alluring beauty of the long bracelet, necklace, and the chain that joined them together.

It took all three of the female Bantu to pick the jewellery up, and they held it in the air. The piece dazzled under the light of the great lamps that lit the hall. Everyone gasped as they saw the grandeur and beauty of the workmanship.

"The craftsmanship is incredible," Shaka said. "The bracelet will cover most of my arm and require several attendants to put it on."

"It only requires three," Grixen said.

"Mother, it is so splendid," Aspess gasped, looking at it with awe.

"It looks like two separate pieces, but this jewellery is in fact all one piece," Grixen said. "It is unique, and is called the Maidenarz, for such a magnificent piece must have a name. There is a sequence of clasps and catches to open and close it."

Without prompting, the three female Bantu capably opened silver clasps and catches, which were woven through with milathran. "It can only be put on and taken off in a certain manner, one which we shall teach your maids," one of the female Bantu said, her voice adenoidal, yet surprisingly, pleasantly modulated.

The second female Bantu spoke, her voice similar to the first. "In anticipation of a worthy recipient of this gift being found, the most skilled craftsmen of the Deeplands worked day and night for a year to craft the Maidenarz. The gold was mined far to the north, in the ancient, now ruined, Elven Kingdom of Sansia; the jewels and gems were carefully taken from the crowns of some of their vanquished kings and queens of old. The silver came from the famed Silverlode Valley."

The guests gasped at the mention of Sansia, a kingdom many believed had been the substance of myth or legend."

Regineo snorted derisively. "Elves?"

Grixen answered him. "They have long been extinct, and after their demise, their once great civilisation fell to abandonment and ruin. We found their ancient cities, mostly crumbled to dust. Our most gifted miners re-opened the legendary mines they left behind."

Regineo took a swig of wine and laughed mockingly.

Caspus stuttered when he spoke. "Dddd…did you, ffff…find any of their writings?"

Grixen chortled. "We found their great libraries, but many of their works were ravaged by time and crumbled at the touch. We did retrieve some, though, dear prince." He then added, "When this war with the Baothein is over, wearing Neblans, those from Kappia who wish to come with us on our explorations, will be most welcome."

Caspus beamed excitedly.

Turning to Shaka, Grixen said, "Riches shall flow between our races in trade. This priceless and unique possession, is but the first of the gifts we shall give as a token of the friendship of the Lord of Morkroth."

"Great Empress Shaka, you are most worthy of such a gift," the third female Bantu said. "May we have the honour of adorning your beauty with it?"

Shaka looked at the Maidenarz. She was used to wearing the finest jewellery and items of loveliness, but even she had not seen anything that matched its beauty or workmanship. It was more an arm piece than a bracelet, for it started at the wrist and went all the way up to the shoulder, where a gilded chain then joined it to the elegant necklace.

"You may," she answered.

The three female Bantu put the arm bracelet on Shaka's left arm and fastened it up with clasps the like of which she had never seen before, and then did the same to the neck piece. When it was fitted, Shaka stood, and showed it off to the guests who all cheered or murmured with appreciation and wonder.

The Maidenarz felt strangely light and warm. In fact, it did not really feel like she was wearing anything. It felt a part of her, like it was her own arm and neck. So perfect was the fit, and so faultless the workmanship that when she bent her arm it silently adjusted itself to her slightest movement.

"Thank you, ambassador," she said after which she took her seat. "We shall find a gift suiting to the Lord of Morkroth, in return."

The final sweet dish was served, after which the Master of Ceremony closed the proceedings. Shaka, accompanied by Caspus, stood and made her way to the stairs to leave the hall. All of the guest stood and bowed. When she had left the hall, she heard the clang of the symbol again. Although the banquet was officially finished, if the rest of the guests wished to remain and eat and drink more, and enjoy the festivities, they were allowed to do so. Even she, the Empress could go back and mingle unofficially without ceremony if she wished, which she rarely if ever did.

As Shaka made her way to her private apartments, several maids joined her. The nearer she got she felt the Maidenarz begin to slowly tighten. It became uncomfortable, and then painful. She gurgled, and struggled to breathe. "Fetch those female Bantu, I want this thing off," she said to one of her maids, "but do it quietly. Do not cause a scene."

The maid rushed off to obey.

"Open the door," Shaka barked at another maid as she approached the door to her apartment. The maid rushed ahead and opened the door, which, as was usual, was guarded by two Hammer Knights.

Once Shaka, Caspus and the other maids were inside and the door shut, Caspus asked, "Www…what is it, mmm…mother?" Along with the maids, he stared at her with grave concern.

"I don't know. It's this thing. It is hurting me. Something is not right, and it's getting tighter," she said with a sense of growing alarm as she clawed at the Maidenarz. "Get it off me," she panted, struggling to breathe.

In vain, Caspus and the maids fumbled at the clasps, trying to undo them and take it off her. The maids began to cry in fear as Shaka choked.

The third maid entered the apartment, accompanied by the three female Bantu and the two Hammer Knights who had been guarding the door.

"Get this off me!" Shaka angrily ordered the Bantu females.

The Bantu said nothing.

Caspus did not have time to react as, with one blow of his deadly hammer, one of the Hammer Knights, cracked his skull open like it was a frail egg. He was dead before he hit the floor.

Shaka stared at his limp body, feeling total shock, and unable to speak as the Maidenarz was now so tight she could hardly breathe. She could feel her face turning purple. So great was the passion of her anger, that she felt the snake-beast inside of her. She surrendered to it, choosing to change aspect and allow the beast infesting her heart to manifest. In snake form, she could easily overpower these two men, and the female Bantu. None of them would be unable to cause her any serious injury when she changed aspect. But, try as she might, she could not change. When the knights bound and gagged her, and bundled her into a large sack, she was so weak and helpless in her human female form that she could do nothing to resist their overpowering strength and force. When she was in the sack, she felt utterly helpless. The Maidenarz was now so tight, she could not breathe at all. *My power to change, what has happened to my power?* she thought softly to herself, as she began to slip from consciousness.

Continuing to claw in vain at the Maidenarz, the last words Shaka heard before she lost consciousness, were spoken by one of the Hammer Knights to the maids, who were whimpering in terror.

"As long as you cooperate and cause no trouble, you will not be harmed. You are of use to Mazdek."

328

# Chapter Twenty-Seven: *The Courage of Dwarves*

*Dwarven males are aggressive, smelly little things. The females are more docile, unless severely provoked. The males are powerfully built, with hands heavily calloused. Males pride themselves in having elegantly braided beards, the work of untold hours of preening. Contrary to the rumours and myths that abound around the subject, the females are not similar to the males in appearance; in fact, most of the females I saw, I would not class as beautiful, but quite pretty.*

*The Dwarves speak Segdelin among themselves, but use the Common Tongue when conversing with humans. They also have a secret language, Sangdalan, known only to a very few of them. It is believed this language was taught to them by their god, Old Balagrim, long ago. Orally, it is was once used in worship rituals, but not so any more as the Dwarves rarely participate in any form of actual devotion, hence it is a surprise to visitors to their lands that they keep their shrines, statues and temples, all dedicated to Balagrim or the Nine Shield-Maidens, in pristine condition.*

*In written form, Sangdalan is now mostly found on very rare archaic nonsensical texts, which strangely can still sell for a high price and are highly sought after by collectors. As a result of some of these factors, Sangdalan has fallen out of common use and is in danger of becoming a forgotten language. Some of the educated, such as the priestly classes, (their role is solely that of storyteller and requires no ritualist duties), and the scholars still learn Sangdalan, but less so now, as it has mostly become an irrelevant language that provokes only minor scholarly interest. The Reisic, however, a banned sect, still pride themselves in learning Sangdalan to an expert level. Strangely, despite its decline, it is still forbidden on pain of death for a dwarf versed in Sangdalan to use this language in front of other races such as humans, although an odd exception to this law is allowed if a dwarf converses with a rather dangerous and appalling Davari priestly sect called the Ruik, who, I might add, are despised and greatly feared by most Davari clans. The Ruik speak Rokkan.*

*Some scholars believe that Sangdalan is merely the echo of a far more sacred and ancient language now only remembered by the Reisic, as is Rokkan by the Ruik, and that when both languages and tongues are spoken or written together, along with a strange tongue called Báith Rahmera, they form another language called Murien. Now, that is worthy of note, for Murien texts are literally priceless. Well, not quite, everything has a value and price, so let me just say that if you discover a Murien text and find the right buyer, you will become very wealthy indeed. I do digress, so a final word on Sangdalan. It is now forbidden for Sangdalan to be written down by the Dwarves. I suspect it is so that some of them can control the value of the ancient texts and the prices they are sold for. For all we know, the scheming Dwarves could have vast amounts of these texts stored away, and release them only when their greed desires more wealth. This is perhaps the reason that books, letters, texts or even the slightest fragment of a text written in Sangdalan are now so very rare, and that explains their exceptionally high value.*

*Only one complete letter and one book written in Sangdalan are known to exist in the Kappian Library, and a few fragments of texts, but no scholar there can translate them. I was told that some dwarven lords, if they thought there was even a slight chance of victory, would gladly go to war against the Kappian Empire just to get them back.*

**Temmison Vol VIII, Book 1: The Dwarves of the Iron Mountains.**

*F*rom the Wytchwood Gildaora watched the beast land and the moleworm burst through the side of the hill, forming the hole from which the Bantu appeared. She recognised Sasna, who, despite screaming in horror, drew a sword and stood her ground. Next to her, a Davari notched an arrow to a bow and fired it at the beast to no effect. The arrow bounded harmlessly off its thick and calloused hide. The blonde woman with Sasna, also drew a sword and valiantly charged the beast, which was the only thing standing between her and the Wytchwood, the direction it appeared they were heading.

"Time to move me Gaffren," Gildaora said as she frantically dug her heels into the side of the large goat she was riding. Gaffren, his horns curled at the side of his head, snorted, bleated, then shook his head and refused to move. "Come me Gaffren, this is not the time for one of your moods," she said with raised voice and urgency as she not so gently dug her heels in once more and tapped him hard with her staff on one of his horns. Gaffren bleated his displeasure, and reluctantly galloped forward toward the beast, all the while continuing to noisily sound his annoyance.

As Gildaora neared the flying beast, she could see in Gaffren's eyes, which rolled backwards in alarm, that his irritation had turned into panic. He was old, short-sighted, and slightly deaf, so had not seen or heard what he was charging towards until they were near.

"I know me Gaffren, it puts fear in me old bones as well, hold your courage my dear," she said as she patted his head to comfort him. She raised the knotted staff she held and the blue orb at the end of it began to glow. "Oh my, I hope this works me Gaffren. This is a creature of the old world and I've not met it's like before."

The beast must have sensed Gildaora's approach for it suddenly turned, and faced her and Gaffren. It let out a loud shrill and croaking cry that hurt her ears. Gaffren skidded to a halt still bleating in terror, and nearly threw her, as he tried to buck her off. It took all her skill as a rider to remain in the saddle. She understood Gaffren's terror. Her own skin crawled. She instinctively sensed the blackness of the beast's mind and felt the primordial rage that drove it. Dread filled her heart and mind. She shuddered, having never felt so afraid before.

Gildaora held her nerve, and brought Gaffren under control. Closing her eyes, she pointed the staff at the beast. A blue beam shone from it, and connected with the creature's head, causing it momentary disorientation. She spoke telepathically to it, soul to soul, using words not understood by any human tongue, communication that travelled along the beam coming from her staff. The conversation began at a deeper level, beyond the physical, as she reached out and touched the black ambiance of the obscene creature.

"What foul eyrie were you bred upon? I command you to answer me," she roared without words.

Confused, the creature roared back at her in disordered fury, then answered her in the same manner, soul to soul. "Thar Markoom," it involuntarily screamed at her.

"What are you?" she demanded.

"I am Barclugoth!"

"Why are you pursuing these people?"

The creature roared, and then screamed, "We want the Seeress. There is nowhere for her to hide, where we will not find her."

Gildaora then used a very old loremasters' trick she had learnt from her grandmother. Letting go of the rein she held in one hand, she opened her eyes, put her hand on Gaffren's head, and channelled into the dread she could sense in him. Gaffren's terror flowed through her arm and body, into the shaft, through the orb and into the beam. The blue orb on her staff, and the beam, shone more brightly than before as Gaffren's fear shot along the beam and entered the beast.

The trick worked. Although against its ferocious nature, the beast had a rush of uncontrollable terror. Gildaora screamed and ululated at it to compound the unfamiliar feeling of fear the beast felt. Much to her relief, she could sense the panic within Barclugoth, an emotion she intuitively sensed the creature had never felt before.

330

"Be gone from here foul beast for your peril is at my hands," she screamed, soul to soul. The vast wings of the creature outspread and it beat them as it took a panicked jump backwards, its claws scratching at the ground.

Gildaora noticed that the blonde woman was still charging. The woman screamed, "For Ashareth!"

The creature turned its neck to see the woman, sword in hand, rapidly approaching it from behind.

Gildaora dug her heels into Gaffren to continue the charge at it from the front. For the first time in its existence, the great beast felt fear. It beat its hideous wings and leaped screaming into the air away from the peril it sensed.

Gildaora spurred Gaffren into a full gallop and rode with haste towards the blonde woman and did not stop as she passed her by but shouted, "Run, me dear, run for the wood with all haste and wait for me there. The fear in the beast will not last long and soon those others will be upon you."

Gildaora soon caught up with the Davari who had charged with the blonde woman, he had fired several more arrows that each bounced harmlessly off the beasts hide as it took off, but now he had turned, planted his sword in the earth, and stood his ground facing the Bantu, who were charging at full pace.

Sasna stood next to the Davari, also standing her ground.

"Run for the forest and wait at its edge," Gildaora yelled to them. The Davari hesitated, the fury of battle was clearly upon him.

"Run me dears, run," Gildaora shouted to them.

Taking one last look at the Bantu, the Davari fired a defiant shot at them which did not reach its mark, before he took his sword, took Sasna by the arm, turned and together they fled toward the Wytchwood.

It did not take Gildaora long to wheel Gaffren around and catch up with them. She looked around her, the Bantu were extremely fast runners, and were quickly approaching their position. It would not be long before they were in range to throw their spears and fire their bows. It was obvious Sasna was slowing the Davari down, for he was almost pushing her along to increase her speed. Gildaora leant over from the saddle and grabbed Sasna by the scruff of her garments, and with a strength that belied her size yanked her up onto Gaffren. Sasna was all too glad of the assistance and with help managed to scramble behind her onto the back of the goat.

Gildaora spurred Gaffren to gallop at full speed towards the forest. "Run me Gaffren, run!" The goat bleated and hoofed its way towards the Wytchwood as fast as it was able. It was not long before they were caught up with the blonde woman, and the Davari, himself a fast runner, was close behind them.

"Don't stop, follow me," Gildaora panted as Gaffren galloped past the blonde woman. "Do not delay, those things are making fast speed across the ground, my dear."

Gildaora felt a sense of relief as the green shade of the leafy Wytchwood embraced her once again; she slowed Gaffren down so he would not trip over the many roots that criss-crossed the forest floor. She nervously wiped her brow. "Well Gaffer, my dear, that will be a story to tell the Maidens and grumpy Old Balagrim."

The blonde woman and the Davari, soon caught up with her and Sasna. They were panting breathlessly, and stopped for a brief respite. The forest was dark, deep, and scented with pine trees so straight they shot up into the sky. They looked around in uncertain awe.

"There'll be time to admire the view later. For now, run!" Gildaora said. She spurred Gaffer on again, at a more careful pace, and calling to her new companions added, "Try to keep up, we are not safe yet."

Gaffer skilfully jumped the many obstacles. Once they had crossed the buffer of pine trees at the edge of the Wytchwood, they entered the forest proper. There were gnarled oaks, beech and birch and a variety of other trees. Fungi, taller than Gildaora grew randomly. The forest was so thick with trees, fungi and foliage that the way ahead soon became blocked and unpassable, but that was not a problem for her.

"*Mathayain,*" Gildaora said to the forest. The boughs from the trees swung back, making a narrow avenue, allowing them to pass.

"What kind of forest is this?" the Davari asked as he looked around uncertainly as the boughs moved, making a path for them. He muttered a curse, but still followed Gildaora into the avenue made by the trees.

Gildaora did not answer him; there was plenty of time for talk later, if they made it safely to her home. The sheer size of the trunks of the largest trees usually took travellers by surprise; even ten grown men with outstretched arms could not have spanned their girth. The canopy of foliage that rose to about two hundred paces above the forest floor drowned out the sun and would have plunged the place into darkness, but as though on cue, thousands of tiny fireflies of different hues took to the air and provided a spectacular display of light. The visitors did not have time to stop and admire the sheer extravagant beauty of their surroundings.

Gildaora sniffed the air and drew comfort from the familiar smell of wood and foliage. She slowed and trotted Gaffren to a pace, for she could tell he was tired. It also gave an opportunity for the two on foot to be able to catch up, for their progress had slowed, due to the many hindrances of root and brushwood on the ground.

Gildaora snatched a glance over her shoulder. To her surprise, the first of the Bantu had reached the wood and were in relentless, silent pursuit. She had lived by her wits for as long as she could remember and had evaded all manner of creatures before, but she had never seen anything like these or the manner in which they had arrived, and the speed with which they moved even over such irregular terrain as the forest floor. A lifetime of wandering and living much of that time in the wilds had sharpened her senses to an almost unnatural degree. A barely perceptible rushing of air alerted her to an arrow that she just managed to avoid by pulling Gaffren to the right. The black shafted arrow narrowly missed her and sailed past, thudding into a nearby oak tree.

"They travel through the forest as easily as we do my dear, or even easier," she said to Gaffren. She raised her staff, the blue orb shone once more as she allowed her spirit to join with that of the forest and listen to it. She sensed the trees did not like the presence of the creatures that had entered their domain and pursued her. Their very presence was as a wound in the forest's soul. This pleased her as she knew the forest would help expel such unwholesome creatures. She heard the cracking and creaking of wood; the forest was moving behind her blocking the path which she had taken. The pursuers would have to find another way and that would take them time.

Behind Gildaora and her companions, a dire horn blast that sounded like the long lowing cry of a wounded beast rang through the air. The sound was answered by another identical note. Animals began to bolt at the sound; a deer exploded from the forest and scrambled past them; squirrels ran from the ground into the trees. Birds took to flight.

Gaffer bucked in panic, but Gildaora managed to bring him under control. She looked behind her. The forest had moved and formed an impenetrable wall of trunk, branch, brush and thicket that the creatures that pursued would not be able to get through. The two on foot stopped, panting as they again tried to catch their breath.

"We are safe for now me dears," Gildaora said to them. "But we best not linger. The forest will stop them finding our path for now, but it could soon tire and they might find a way. My home is far. Do not trade words as I need to listen to the forest to tell me where those things are, for their horns may soon fall silent."

Instinctively, Gildaora pulled the arrow from out of the tree in which it was imbedded, and attached it by a strap inside Gaffren's saddlebag. She rode the exhausted Gaffren slowly along paths that traced deep into the wood, stopping only occasionally to listen to the forest. The horn blasts faded until they could no longer be heard.

Gaffren trotted clumsily through the glades and paths the forest opened up for them, with little care for concealment or quietness. Soon they reached natural trails and travelled paths. The companions travelled for much of the day, though their pace was slow as those on foot suffered from exhaustion, as did Gaffren. Sasna slept, and Gildaora sensed it was not through choice.

By dusk, they were deep into the forest. Gildaora led them to Martha, her name for the Wisdom Tree which was her home. It was a giant gnarled oak in the middle of a large green glade. The tree was surrounded by carved wooden arches with Elven inscriptions on them. The architecture was elegant and the beams smooth, and seemed at one with the forest. At the base of the trunk of the tree, roots fanned out across the earth. As she approached, she pointed her staff and whispered, "*Markalring.*" The roots of the tree responded to her word; groaning and cracking as they moved, framing an opening in the ground. There were steps leading down underground into the loamy soil. The Davari hesitated before entering.

"This is dark magic," he muttered suspiciously.

"No, it's not, me dear, it is Elven magic, long forgotten."

"But you're a dwarf! Magic is forbidden for your kind!" the Davari stated in disbelief.

"Yes, I am, and yes, it is, me dear," she said with a big smile. "Gildaora is my name though most call me Gilly." She dismounted from Gaffren. "Now, won't you come into my home, me dears, you are most welcome."

*     *     *

Methruille the Necromancer stood at the edge of the Wytchwood, and watched Gaishak and his brutes emerge from it. He wore a yellow hat, robe and a hooded cloak, all adorned with the image of black stars. The hat was a capotain, a tall-crowned, narrow-brimmed, slightly conical hat with a flat top. The robe was tight from the shoulders to the midriff, after which it increasingly flared out into a conical shape. Attached to a purple buckled belt around his waist, were various phials filled with different coloured liquids.

Gaishak spoke with an angry, low guttural rumbling. "Mutter some flutteries with your gas-pipes, the wood 'as an evil eye and wouldn't grease our way."

Methruille, a man long acquainted with the Bantu ways and slang, understood what Gaishak meant: '*Speak magic words, the wood used its own enchantments to bar our way.*'

When Methruille answered, his mood was sombre and his tone dark. "I know this wood of old, I will find a way to subdue it." He paused though, feeling genuinely perplexed. *This is a mystery to me. How can a dwarf use ancient Elven magic?* He spoke out loud to himself, more than to Gaishak, when he quietly said, "But I have never seen a dwarf use magic before, let alone magic of the Elven kind."

Gaishak bared his fangs and replied, "The stumpy plucked our barbstick from a trunker. Use your flutteries to beat the trunkers, and Froglin will use 'is sniffer to find 'er."

The news pleased Methruille. *The dwarf retrieved a Bantu arrow from a tree? Then she is unfamiliar with our hunting methods.*

Methruille waited until Marigoof and Pakarin joined him and Gaishak.

"We will return to Norvaskun," Methruille ordered, "as soon as Morfus returns. I have never seen a Barclugoth react in such a way."

Marigoof turned to the decapitated head on his shoulder, nodded as though agreeing with it, and said moodily to Methruille, "I've been on many a 'unt with Morfus. Never peeped 'im do that. The stumpy used some flutteries on 'im, got 'im all spooked."

Pakarin snarled with rage. He took a white gown from a bag he carried over his shoulder, sniffed it, and then held the garment in the air. He then took a horn slung over his other shoulder, put it to his mouth and blew it. He waited a moment and then sniffed the air before saying. "Morfus is returning, and I'll bet 'e feels mutton shunted for what the stumpy did to 'im. I'll wager 'e is all poked up about it." He scowled, sniffed the white gown again and said, "The soft-'ole Janorra smells good. I'm gammy in me noggin 'ow she blagged a stumpy and some 'alf-wit mollies to 'elp 'er though. Don't they know what we'll do to 'em for 'elping our prey?"

Marigoof answered. "Our reppie ain't established 'ere yet. We got some graft to do, make 'em know they can't mess with the Wild 'unt."

Froglin arrived, and overhearing the conversation, said, "I sniffed 'em, the 'alf-wits. One was Davari, the other soft-'ole, not sniffed 'er kind before."

"She is Seesnari," Methruille seethed, "I know her race from times of old. Capture her alive, if you can." *Her kind cheated me before; I blame the Seesnari for my expulsion from the Tarath Güean. Never trust a Seesnari!*

"Make sure you pass her scent on to Morfus." *When we have captured the Seeress and the Simal, I will have my revenge on all Seesnari!*

"What about the Davari scum?" Gaishak asked.

"The Davari is of no consequence. Kill him, slowly, if it entertains you, but keep the dwarf alive if you can. I wish to question her."

*      *      *

Gilly smiled as Sasna, now awake, and still seated behind her on Gaffer, who looked around at her surroundings in wide-eyed awe, before looking behind to check they were not being pursued.

"Welcome back Miss Sasna, me poor dear. You needed that sleep."

Sasna rubbed her eyes, and then winced in pain, and held her shoulder.

"I'll tend to that soon enough, Miss Sasna, me dear," Gilly said reassuringly. *Oh my, Miss Sasna does not look well.*

Gilly led Gaffren by the reigns down the steps. The other two with them, the Davari and the blonde woman followed. *Hmm, she is a Pure-blood, and a Seer,* Gilly thought, as she observed the blond woman and the Seers' Mark of the Obelisk under her eye. *Why has she come to the Wytchwood?*

Once each of the party had entered the hole, Gilly issued a command and the roots cracked and creaked again, as they closed behind them, sealing them within the tree.

"Thank you, Martha," Gilly said out loud to the tree.

"Am I safe in here?" the blonde woman asked.

Gilly noticed the fear and anxiety on the woman's face. "I think so, me dear. Those beasties should not find us. Martha is concealed by ancient glamour." Her point was confirmed as they passed a hanging mosaic of gossamer runes so dazzlingly beautiful, her three companions gasped in admiration.

334

"Martha?" the woman asked.

"My name for this Wisdom Tree, me dear," Gilly responded.

After descending the steps, they all passed through a slender archway decorated with rich intarsia of platinum and gold, and then stepped out beneath a domed vault of root and thorn, raw in nature in contrast to the entrance they had just passed through. It did not take Gilly long to remove Gaffren's saddle and the saddlebags, which she placed over a wooden horse.

"How's that feel, my dear?" she asked, as she patted him and gave him a big hug and stroked him. "You did so well today my Gaffren." She then opened the saddlebag and took the Bantu arrow she had retrieved from the tree.

"Off to bed with you now, Gaffren, my dear," she said warmly. "I'll come and brush you, and tickle your chin, but later. Old Gilly has some guests to host for now." She affectionately patted and stroked him again. Gaffren then wandered off down a tunnelled path that led to a straw filled pen, where he began drinking water from a trough and eating from a pile of leaves as he bleated contentedly, his former terror blissfully forgotten.

"Now, I know Miss Sasna, but I think some introductions are needed between the rest of us," Gilly said to the Davari and the blonde woman.

The chamber they were in was very old and over the years much of it had silvered and petrified and gave off a luminous glow. The blonde woman stared at it, and Gilly sensed it was with an intellectual curiosity.

"Who are you?" the blonde woman demanded, when she turned her attention to Gilly.

Again, noticing the Mark of the Obelisk under her eye, and that it was coloured, Gilly already knew that the woman was a Pure-blood Seeress. "I already told you. I am Gildaora, but you can call me Gilly, me dear," she answered.

"What is this place?" the Davari asked as he stared around in awe.

Gilly briefly studied him before answering. He was young and handsome; she sensed a noble aura around him, as well as a primal wildness.

"It used to be an Elven Archive me dear, but they abandoned it long ago. I discovered it, so now it's my home whenever I visit the forest."

"Elves?" the Davari asked incredulously. "I believed them to be myth and legend only, but of late I have discovered I have been wrong about many things in this world, and little of its races and creatures do I truly know."

"They lived in these parts once, me dear, in a time now forgotten by Men and Dwarves alike."

"Where are they now?" the Davari inquired.

"Nobody really knows, me dear. I think Elves paid little attention to the affairs of other races. Their last written entry in the archive states that they planned to head north out of the Everglow, seeking sanctuary. That was written long ago. Who knows where they ended up at, or what fate met them there? I don't think anybody has seen an elf for thousands of years now."

"*The Legend of the Last Elf,*" the blonde, Pure-blood woman said quietly.

"Oh, you know that play me dear?" Gilly asked.

The woman did not reply. A deep look of sadness slowly spread across her exhausted face.

"It is a sad tale indeed," Gilly said respectfully. It maybe Elves are extinct, though some Everglow scholars wrote that Elves still live in the northernmost part of Winter Forest, just where it meets the shores of the Tethys Sea. Others say the last of their kind was an elf-maiden named Tamreaile, and that she was the last survivor, and died trying to return to the Everglow, having failed to find sanctuary in the North. If I remember rightly, I think that play was about her?" She looked at the blonde woman who gave no answer.

"Might I know your name, me dear?" Gilly asked her.

"Janorra. My name is Janorra."

She stared at the Davari. "And your name?"

"I am Scarand, a Davari of the Vanyr tribe."

Gilly smiled at them. "Welcome, all of you. I kind of expected you. My Bena birds were watching you. They told me about the wretched flying thing tracking you."

"Have they seen anything of Farir, my brother. I have not seen him since he fell overboard when the *River Queen* was set ablaze."

"Do forgive me, how remiss of me. Yes, Farir is here. He is quite safe, though still a little shaken by events. He is the reason I had my birds out looking for you."

"He is here?" Sasna put her hand over her mouth and stifled a relieved cry. She then let out a loud squeal that was a mixture of relief and delight.

"You must take me to him, please," she said when she had composed herself.

"Then follow me," Gilly said as she made her way from the chamber into another passageway filled with roots, and then into another large chamber, constructed from a single enormous leaf curled around itself in a spiral to create a long tunnel shaped room, which was crammed with shelves laden down with an untold number of books. "We all have much to discuss me dears, but you all look like you are in need of some rest and some good dwarf cooking."

Scarand became more wide-eyed with every step he took. "This is the second library I have now seen," he said, and then asked, "do you know why the Elves left?"

*He asks a lot of questions, but that's good, it shows intelligence*, Gilly said to herself.

"Not exactly, but I have my thoughts, and I think it was very sudden, me dear. They left so much behind, so I guess they left in a rush, taking only what they could carry. What they left behind, was all undisturbed, for age upon age, until I found it. Come now, my delicious stew is cooking and will soon be ready."

They passed through another room filled with towering columns of roots that spiralled overhead twisting into hundreds of wooden statues. Gilly felt she should comment on it. "This room is the archive itself, it tells their history, at least up until the time the Elves left. It is said Elves could sing their stories and the trees would tell it with their roots." She pointed at some of the statues. "Look, there is an elf fishing on the Erin, and some beast from the water pulls him under, but there in the next scene he manages to slay it."

"The images, they change!" Scarand gasped in wide-eyed awe, as the roots creaked and cracked and slowly swirled into new shapes revealing different images that any artist would be proud of.

"Martha senses what we need or want to see and shows us accordingly, me dear. She is very clever. The Elves left some magic in her that still has energy to this day and she can still tell the story of the forest, though she won't tell me why the Elves left. I think it still upsets her." Gilly pointed at one of the images. "Look, an elf-maiden has died, see how the others mourn. Martha often shows me this one, as though the forest itself still mourns this particular elf's passing even after all of this time. I think I know who she was, and why she died, but I shall not speak of it for now, me dears."

Gilly noticed that Janorra was staring at her suspiciously, but also that she looked so weary and exhausted.

Janorra spoke: "If I may eat, to refresh myself, I would be grateful, but I cannot tarry here long. I can't let those things find me."

336

"This is a safe place for you to rest, me dear," Gilly said. "If Martha was alarmed by those beasties, she would show it to me in the archive. I think you are safe here, for a while."

A tear ran down Janorra's face, leaving a clean streak through the dirt of travel. "I am not safe anywhere," she said softly.

Sasna frantically took Gilly by the sleeve. "Take me to Farir, please."

Gilly thought for a moment, and then smiled. "Of course," she said as she made her way out of the archive followed by the others. "I was about to set out to meet you when news reached Berecoth that the ship you were on had met a foul end, so I came here to the Wytchwood. My Bena birds rescued your brother from the Erin the night the ship burnt, and brought him safely here."

"Is he well? He was wounded how is his health?"

"I have tended to his wound with the dew and flower nectar that can only be found in a sacred circular grove in the forest. It is fully healed and he is quite well."

Sasna sighed with relief. Tears of gratitude and joy welled up in her eyes. Gilly noticed the dried blood on the garment of her shoulder.

"You are wounded as well?"

Sasna cast a furtive glance at Janorra. "She healed me, temporarily, but the excesses of our journey have reopened the wound. It is quite itchy and throbs with pain."

"The same dew and nectar that healed Farir will work on that. I also have a honey-brewed ointment that will vanish any scar and rid you of the irritation me dear," Gilly said. "Now, come, me dear, I have something to show you and then I will take you to Farir. My birds also managed to find and rescue a scary looking rune-keeper. He said his name is Muro."

"My grandfather is here?" Scarand blurted out in surprise.

"Muro is your grandfather? Now I wasn't expecting that," Gilly said looking and feeling quite surprised. "It seems I am not the only one with news and stories to share. You will be eager to be reunited no doubt."

"I care nothing for him," Scarand scowled. "He abandoned his kin and kind to follow the corruption of malign gods. He was willing to trade the last shred of his soul for forbidden knowledge, and sacrifice innocent blood to bloodthirsty deities; I care not if I ever see him again."

Gilly stopped for a moment. *There is a dark aura around Muro, but he has been sent to assist me in reading the text.* "All I ask is that in my home you be civil to all, me dear, including him. Set aside all rivalry whilst you dwell under this roof."

"Are you sure it is safe for me to rest here awhile?" Janorra asked, as they walked on though the network of wooded passageways.

"I am quite convinced of it, me dear," Gilly said compassionately and then added, "at least I hope so." She paused for a moment. "Incursions by the foolhardy or trespassers that mean harm are often dealt with harshly by the forest. Many outsiders have lost their lives here, their blood nourishing the forest roots, whilst others the forest lets wander about without interference. The forest has already helped you, even beyond its own borders before you entered it, so, I know it favours you."

"In what way has the forest helped?" Janorra asked suspiciously.

"The sylphs and water nymphs manipulated the weather and currents to bring you safely along the Erin. And then, when you entered the forest, the sprites manipulated wood and brush to allow our passing and block those who pursued."

"Elementals," Janorra said somewhat subdued.

"Yes, air, earth and water elementals. The veil between their realm and ours is thin in this place. Lesser creatures and those with a pure aura are tolerated, but most, especially the foul of heart, are not left alone for long to roam undisturbed in the green and peaceful glades of the Wytchwood." *I fear the forest will not let that fellow Muro wander alone. He has a disturbing look about him, but he is Ruik, and I need him. Perhaps that is why the forest has allowed him sanctuary, for now.*

Gilly scratched her chin. She felt troubled as well as puzzled and intrigued. "I have never seen the like of those creatures pursuing you Sasna, and the manner in which they appeared, though I have read about them and think they are called Bantu? Nor have I ever seen such a fearsome and unholy beast as that which travels with them."

Sasna cast a brief sideways glance at Janorra. "I do not think they were pursuing me." She took a deep breath and then sighed. "But the Baron also pursues us," she added disparagingly, "and I do know it is I, he wishes to capture the most."

Gilly nodded in acknowledgement. "My birds told me the Baron and his men were less than an hour behind you. It seems that whatever events have happened of late, he has found courage or anger enough to come at least this near the Wytchwood, though I think both rashness of rage and courage would still not allow him to foolishly enter here, for he did so once before and has forever regretted the price he paid. The forest does not favour him at all."

"Then I hope he meets those things that appeared and learns another lesson," Sasna said quietly and vindictively.

"Hmm, why does the Baron hunt you?"

"It is a long tale; I will tell it after I have seen Farir."

Gilly looked sympathetically at Janorra. "Why do you think these strange beasts might be after you, me dear?"

Janorra lowered her head, and did not answer, at first.

"Me dear, the more I know, the more assistance I might be able to offer you," Gilly said gently.

Janorra wiped the sweat off of her brow, with a hand that shook with fear. Her voice trembled as she spoke. "I thank you for helping me Gilly, and I accept the chance to rest a little and take refreshment, but I must leave soon. I have lost objects of great value in this forest which I must retrieve. Do you think the forest will allow me to go about my business in peace?"

Gilly felt a flood of compassion as she looked at the woman; she could both feel and see her terror, but she also felt intrigued as to what it was that she may have lost. *There will be time to find out when she has rested.* "You are quite safe for the moment, me dear, perhaps we can discuss your lost possessions when you are fully refreshed, and then we can see what we can do about retrieving them."

"I do not have time to wait here for long," Janorra said, "you must let me leave when I wish."

Gilly noticed that she gripped the hilt of her sword in her fingers.

"You are not my prisoner, me dear, you can leave anytime you want, just say the word and I will lead you to the exit." She smiled reassuringly. "No journey of any merit, can be attempted without occasions of rest. I offer you bowls of stew and a night of peace, so even if just for a short time, your wayfaring is not simply hardship and danger unabated. I only offer you my hospitality."

Janorra let go of the hilt of her sword.

"I also offer you advice, me dears. If you wish or need to wander this forest, it is not the sort of place to be wandering alone, and aimlessly, without the friends of the forest to help you, especially with those beasties now out there."

"I could do with some food," Scarand said, "but I also want to know more about those things that showed up."

338

"Indeed. You will all feel better after a bowl of stew and a nice sleep, me dears," Gilly said. "It's me grandmother's own recipe, might her soul rest in peace. I made it with the mushrooms, vegetables and fruit that grow wildly in the Wytchwood, but let us first try to find the reason why these beasts are hunting you."

Gilly walked over to a desk where a large tablet of wood lay upon it. She pointed to it. Much Elven knowledge is contained within this tree, here me dears, look, an Oculareadus, a living book!"

Janorra and the others joined her and looked at the tablet; strange words and symbols appeared, carved into the wooden pages, and then changed.

Gilly smiled. "Martha shows me what she wishes me to read. If you understand the Elven script there is much to be learnt here."

"Elvish is a lost language, you claim to understand it?" Janorra asked, the amazement mixed with disbelief evident in her tone.

Gilly nodded. "Some of it, me dear. Sometimes I wake up, and it is as though I have learnt a new word or phrase whilst I was sleeping. I think that maybe Martha is teaching it to me, but I am a mere novice in the language, not a master."

Janorra looked at the text inscribed in the wood. "This is priceless knowledge. There are those would pay you a fortune to learn a forgotten tongue and script. I have never met any scholar who can read Ancient Elvish."

Gilly smiled more widely. "As I say, I am just a novice, me dear."

"I don't like this place, it brings me fear and you are delving in matters best left alone," Sasna said to Gilly. She had a look of confusion and concern upon her face. "Take me to Farir, I wish to be gone from here after I have rested, for I must be about my business in Berecoth, or if the way is unpassable, I must find another way. I will not return to Ashgiliath until my quest is completed."

"It is best you all know what and why you are hunted, before you choose your paths and leave," Gilly said to Sasna, and then, a sudden thought occurring to her she cast a kind look at Janorra and added, "are you sure these Bantu hunt you, me dear?"

Janorra answered her dispassionately, and Gilly was well aware she avoided the question. "It is most strange for a dwarf to be delving in Elven matters, let alone that you are able to communicate with Martha, the tree, and with some other life-forms. Somehow, you sent terror into that flying beast, to make it go away. Isn't that why it fled?"

Gilly nodded. "Yes, I used an old loremaster's trick to shoo the wee beastie away. To be honest, I am surprised it worked on it. I am not sure it would do so a second time though, and the beast will return."

"It is most strange to find a dwarf versed in animal-lore," Janorra said suspiciously.

*My interest in the lore of nature led to banishment from my own people.* "It is an area of lore I have long been interested in, me dear. I made a choice to not allow the scholars and priests of my own kind to dissuade me from thinking as I saw fit, and nor would I allow them to stop me from pursuing the knowledge that interests me most."

"You scared away that dumb creature?" Scarand asked incredulously, looking bewildered as he sized Gilly up and down.

"I confused it for now, me dear. It was not dim-witted, but intelligent. It has a cleverness born of its own basic nature. I was able to use that. But I could not get through to those other brutes, the Bantu. I sensed nothing from them except hate, anger and lies and..." She hesitated but a moment, and then said, "Cruelty. I sensed a very deep cruelty in them. I have not met their kind before and I have read just a little about them, but I sensed they would be immune to the trick I played to shoo away the beastie." She took the Bantu arrow from her rucksack. The feathers and wood of the

339

arrow were jet black, as was the cruel looking tip on the end which was split into four barbed, hook like needles. She held it over the living book.

"If I show it objects, sometimes the Oculareadus will explain them to me, if it has come across them before."

Words appeared on the pages of the book, and Gilly read them silently to herself whilst the others looked on and waited. Her horror grew with each word she read. After a few minutes, she looked up and stared intensely at Janorra. *They ARE hunting her! You must run from them, me dear, run from them, as fast and far as you can.* "We must talk and discuss these matters, after we have rested," was all she said for now.

Janorra nodded her head once, knowingly.

"Yes," Sasna said impatiently. "Now, please take me to Farir." She paused briefly, and then blurted out, "Does the slave named Muro, still have the Murien? I still expect payment, as we agreed, but much more for the trouble that thing has brought to me."

*So, Sasna has discovered what it is.* It did not go unnoticed by Gilly that Janorra let out a small gasp and her eyes opened wide at the mention of a Murien text.

"I'll take you to them now, me dear," Gilly said, looking at Sasna cautiously. "It is best we discuss all matters of a business nature when we are rested, we have all had quite a day already. Come now, I have a stew prepared. It will be ready. Follow me please, me dears."

As Gilly began walking towards the exit, one that led to the living quarters, the roots in the vaulted ceiling and upon the walls creaked and groaned and changed shape. The wooden image they showed was of Janorra, but she was dead, and her broken and lifeless body was being wrapped into a cocoon by an enormous spider. It was Gilly's turn to gasp with surprise, and she looked at Janorra again.

"Oh, my poor dear, it seems you had the misfortune to encounter Uilisomor?"

Janorra stood motionless looking up at the image with a mix of horror and terror on her face.

"The Wytchwood is a place of magic and wonder, but it can also be one of great danger," Gilly said. "It was said to have once been a part of the *Blessed Realms*, now it is in the midst of a falling world. Beauty and corruption exist here in equal measure."

Janorra spoke with tremoring voice. "Be that as it may, I must go back to that place. A ring of great value and power, that belongs to me, remains on that discarded body. I need help to get it back, and not only that have I lost, but something of far greater value."

Gilly smiled, but it was outward only. Events were unfolding that troubled her deeply. "It seems you have quite a story to tell, if you are willing to voice it once you have rested me dear. Elven Archives can only show events that have already passed, not those still to come." She opened the door that led to the living quarters. "Come now, me dears, eat first, sleep, and then we can all talk and try to figure out what is going on."

# Chapter Twenty-Eight: *Effgard the Wargheart*

*When the mad King Varys stood on top of the tower, his people gathered below to hear him. "Watch, marvel and behold," he shouted. "If the earth does not cushion and embrace me, one of the gods will step in and save me, for they will not allow one as great as I to meet such an ignoble end." He then jumped from the top of the tower. This testimony was taken from an eyewitness account of the death of the mad King Varys II.*

*Temmison Vol IV, Book 2: History of the Kings and Queens of the Tarenmoors.*

*When* the ground was flat and clear of obstacles, or consisted of vast fertile meadows, Marki rode his pony at a fast gallop. When the ground became uneven, or was littered with hindrances such as small rocks or puddles of water, he slowed down to a canter, and rode at an ambling pace so as not to cause injury to the animal. Ognok had no trouble keeping up with Marki whatever pace he rode at, at times hardly even losing his breath.

During the few times they rested, Marki learnt from Ognok that before the current war, the wild tribes of the Tarenmoors, were mostly friendly to strangers who posed no threat to them. They were happy to trade wolfhounds, pelts, furs and even on occasion their women for weapons or any items they could not make for themselves. It was the civilised kingdoms and provinces, he said, that were often inhospitable to strangers, as the darkness of suspicion lurked in the heart of every king, prince and lord of a realm.

It was a surprise for Marki to learn that traders from Seesnari and from all the Nine Kingdoms made frequent trips to the Tarenmoors. He also discovered that outside of the many so-called civilised kingdoms and provinces, many of the tribes were nomadic, and only a few had made permanent settlements. Most of all, he discovered that when in a large battle, the tribes would fight as individuals. Each man would pick out a target in the front ranks of the enemy, challenge them with war cries from across the battlefield, charge, and attack the specific single enemy they had challenged.

Marki had suspected that was how it would be, and this was the reason he felt confident that the much smaller but impeccably drilled legion working as a unit, would be able to wear down much larger numbers they faced, killing hordes of any enemy who attacked them, with very little losses themselves. When the Kappian legions had faced similar foes before, they marched forward in a three-line formation, with their shields in front. When the enemy stood in front of a legionnaire they had challenged to combat, the legionnaire did not fight him, but would thrust his sword into the side of the unexpecting foe to the left. In this way, they often mowed down armies far larger, as a man with a sickle cuts down wheat. It had been considered a dishonourable method of fighting by tribal people, but it was their bodies heaped up in piles after a battle with the legions taking very few casualties in comparison.

Ognok also informed Marki, that Effgard was more than likely to be staying at a small town, Theinstead Homestead, just within the borders of the Kingdom of Thurogen, where he resided. He had gone to his town of birth to pay homage to his ancestors and ask for their blessing and protection during the battles that would soon be fought. It was there that Ognok was taking him.

Marki and Ognok travelled for three more days, after which they reached the outskirts of civilised areas, where the wild landscape soon began to turn into large areas of patchwork fields, each marked with boundaries of small walls built of roughly cut white stone. Although a few of the men, women and children working the fields glanced more than once, or stood and stared curiously as Marki rode by with Ognok running at his side, they did not seem concerned at the presence of a dwarf and a wildling traversing the paths between the field boundaries.

Marki felt hungry. The rations he had taken with him had not lasted long, and apart from a small muntjac they had caught, they had not had time to hunt any more animals for meat. He was glad when they came to the first recognisable town, Theinstead Homestead, fortified with a wall and guard towers. Ognok and Marki spoke with the guards, merely stating they wished to speak with Effgard to conduct business. The guards mumbled and complained about *'Dwarves and Barbarians,'* and then one of them finally agreed to let them into the town, after which he led Marki and Ognok to an elegant inn named The Golden Sheaf, where, if Effgard was not already currently carousing and drinking, the guard told Marki he could wait until summoned when Effgard was ready for him.

As Marki, Ognok and the guard approached the inn, the sound of music and revelry floated through the air. Posted on the noticeboard outside of the tavern was the following notice:

RULES OF THE INN

NO THIEVES, ROGUES, TINKERS or BARBARIANS –
NO SKULKING LOAFERS -
NO FLEA-BITTEN or LICE INFESTED VAGRANTS –
NO 'SLAPPING or PINCHING' the WENCHES' BACKSIDES –
NO BANGING of the TANKARDS on the TABLES –
NO DEFECATING or URINATING WITHIN the BAR AREA. WE HAVE DUG a HOLE
    In the COURTYARD at the BACK of the INN FOR THAT -
DO NOT EMPTY HOT ASH FROM YOUR PIPE ONTO the FLOOR – IT BURNS the
HANDS and KNEES of SOME CUSTOMERS LEAVING the PREMISES -
MEN – No SHOES or SHIRT = No SERVICE! -
WOMEN – No SHOES or SHIRT ACCOMPANIED by a WILLINGNESS to DANCE
    = FREE ALE! -
IF YOU FIGHT – YOU MOP up YOUR OWN DAMN BLOOD –
IF you're DEAD due to FIGHTING or OVER-INDULGENCE this INN WILL NOT
    PAY for YOUR GRAVE or BURIAL -
DEAD BODIES MUST be COLLECTED by the FAMILIES or FRIENDS of the DECEASED
    BEFORE CLOSING TIME or the CARCASS WILL be DISCARDED at
    BEGGARS END for the STRAY DOGS to EAT…

MEN if YOU are:

| | | | |
|---|---|---|---|
| 1. | HIDING FROM YOUR WIFE | … | 1 Brass Penny |
| 2. | JUST MISSED HIM | … | 2 Brass Pennies |
| 3. | HE JUST HAD ONE DRINK AND LEFT | … | 3 Brass Pennies |
| 4. | HASN'T BEEN IN ALL DAY | … | 4 Brass Pennies |
| 5. | NEVER HEARD OF HIM | … | 5 Brass Pennies |
| 6. | NEVER SEEN HIM WITH NO LADY | … | 1 Silver Shilling |

IF YOU OBEY THESE RULES you will EXPERIENCE a WARM and FRIENDLY WELCOME at the GOLDEN SHEAF INN…

"You'd better wait outside," Marki suggested to Ognok after reading the notice, after which the guard opened the door and led Marki inside. The inn was crowded and noisy. The guests, locals and visitors, were engaged in activities you would expect to find in most inns. Merchants argued with farmers over the price of crops, goods and credit interest. Harlots were trying to tempt those who had money to spend whilst discouraging those who had none. Marki strutted past some drunken nitwits who pinched the backsides of the girls carrying trays full of beer and food to customers. Several town guards were singing a song celebrating their courage, whilst banging their tankards on the table and boasting in graphic and considerable details about what they would do to any enemy army if they ever entered their lands. "So much for rules," Marki muttered to the guard, who snorted derisively.

"Wait at the bar," the guard ordered Marki, who begrudgingly obliged.

Apart from some whispering and curious glances, initially, none paid any undue attention to Marki as he walked up to the bar and perched himself on a stool, apart from the surly looking innkeeper who on noticing him, muttered something to himself. Under different circumstances, Marki would have picked a group of revellers, making himself welcome by buying those around the table a drink before joining them. As these were new lands and the customs unknown, he thought it better to keep his own company, for now, so he took a seat at the bar and sat watching the clientele. He noticed that one of the town guards had stopped his singing and was staring at him. Marki's normal response would have been a rude gesture followed by a threatening stare, but he did not have time for trouble, and wished to avoid it if he could, so he gritted his teeth and sat and observed a group the guard who had led him to the inn approached. The group consisted of six men who were seated at a table in front of a dirty looking red curtain that hid an alcove from view. The guard, whispered some words to these men, and then disappeared behind the curtain, which had the faded image of a golden heart gripped in a hand upon it. The men stared moodily at Marki.

Marki's concentration was broken when the innkeeper growled, "I need to add no Dwarves to my sign."

"Enforce the rules you already have before adding more," Marki growled back. "Now, give me ale and food, enough for myself, and have a wench take some to a wildling who waits outside for me."

Before the innkeeper could respond, Marki took out a silver coin and flicked it onto the bar. It rolled in a circle and then rattled before settling. Whatever it was the innkeeper was about to say, he stayed silent, and his demeanour changed as he picked up the coin, bit it to test it, and then whistled as he studied the coin.

"Keep the change," Marki said.

"This is a Kappian coin," the innkeeper said, his surliness gone in an instant and his voice tinged with amazement. "I recognise the image of their Empress."

"The Empress Shaka," Marki growled, and that silver is purer than any you will find your regular patrons carrying in this den of fleas," he said.

"It has been a long time since a Kappian coin has been passed into my hands," the innkeeper remarked as he slipped the coin into the moneybag slung around his ample waist. "But I still recognise them alright."

The innkeeper poured a large tankard of mead from an even larger jug and pushed it towards Marki, who drank it without ceremony. The drink was a high-alcohol fermentation of water and honey, which tasted quite sweet and not much to Marki's liking. Nonetheless he downed the drink in several gulps and slammed the empty tankard on the table. "Again," he demanded, "keep filling it till I tell you to stop or that coin buys me and my wildling no more."

"You've paid for more than you could eat or drink in a whole month," the innkeeper replied honestly, but then seemed to regret the slip of tongue. A glint of greed crossed his eyes. "Do you have any more of those coins?"

Although the copper and brass coins the other customers used to pay for their drink and food were different in design to the ones Marki carried, the innkeeper did not refuse them when Marki flicked several onto the bar. "For these, I require the loose tongue of an innkeeper such as yourself," he said, as he grabbed the innkeeper's hand before he could pick them up.

The innkeeper nodded, and after Marki had let go of his hand, he picked up the coins, bit another one of them to test it and looked at the intricate design on one side, and the portrait of the Empress Shaka on the other. He weighed them up with the size of local ones, and smiled as they also disappeared into the moneybag slung around his waist, after which he filled the tankard again.

The innkeeper leant on the bar, and spoke in a lowered tone to Marki.

"Your kind has never been around here in great numbers, but we used to see the odd one now and again, until you Dwarves locked yourselves up in those Iron Mountains of yours. You are the first one I've seen for ten years or more now," he said, and then asked, "what brings you here?" He pushed the frothy tankard of ale towards Marki, who said nothing but took a few gulps, wiping the froth from his beard with the sleeve of his tunic after which he let out a loud and unbashful belch.

"I'm paying for food and drink, for a loose tongue and answered questions, not to feed a curious ear," Marki gruffly answered.

"Oh, I know better than to ask strangers their business," the innkeeper said. "In my line of work, it is best to listen more than talk, but I am surprised to see a dwarf in my inn, let alone one who carries imperial coin yet travels with a wildling companion. There's trouble brewing with that lot, mark my words. If it were not for Effgard the *Wargheart*, this would be a land gripped in fear, due to the shadow of war that looms over us and what it is that is coming."

"And what would be coming?" Marki asked nonchalantly, trying not to sound too interested.

The innkeeper smiled, and leant on his elbows as he leaned in closer towards Marki. "You are new to these parts then? Else you would know that a great and glorious bloodshed, a purging, is coming, after which it is said the gods will return." He looked to his left and right to see who was listening. Confident nobody could overhear, he continued. "War is here, it is a war of siblings, for Falamore, Sharwin and Effgard all share the same father but different mothers. When their father was killed in battle, Sharwin and Falamore fought for the throne, with neither winning so peace was made and the kingdom split. An uneasy peace settled for many a year until recent times."

"Peace is only ever temporary, until ambition has finished resting," Marki curtly replied.

The innkeeper nodded. "Ancient relics are being used to prove who has the favour of the gods. A foul and evil spirit entered Queen Sharwin, they now call her the *Raven Queen*. This spirit led her to the Chatti, who allowed her to use a very rare relic, one that united most of the barbarian wildlings and got them to join forces with her to attack King Falamore. She allied with the Gragor and Chatti. They have a common cause. She has some of their number in her midst."

The news both surprised and concerned Marki. *Gragor and Chatti are in the Tarenmoors?* The Gragor were a race of giants, and the Chatti a race of fierce sub-humans. The Kappian legions had never met either in battle before, but their reputation as warriors was formidable.

The innkeeper continued. "The *Wargheart* is considering breaking the alliance either with his sister Sharwin, or their brother Falamore. We are awaiting his decision – he is waiting for a sign from the gods before he decides whom to side with." The innkeeper stared at Marki and then nodded toward the curtain. "If you are here to seek mercenary work, you will find that aplenty at this time, but Effgard's choice will be the key to this war, so seek favour and employment from him if you wish your axe to join a cause."

344

Marki glanced towards the curtain, and at the six men in front of it who were still warily watching him. The guard who had accompanied Marki exited the curtain, looked at him, whispered something to the men around the table, and then marched over to the singing guards. "I'll be back for a few after my watch," he said to them, before he left the inn.

"Not many folks apart from those to gain from it are pleased when the drum beats of war are sounding," Marki said as he turned back and watched the innkeeper wipe the top of the bar with his apron, "and only a rock-headed fool would wish axes and swords wielded by the pious to be let loose upon their land."

The innkeeper continued wiping the top of the bar. "These farmlands and the rural towns are mostly unguarded except for a few lowly paid guards. We are the bread basket for Falamore's kingdom, but he can barely guard the five keeps that are his, so we are left to our own devices." He lowered his voice to even more of a whisper, and glanced nervously at the curtain. "Effgard has come here, to his home town, to decide what to do. His army waits on the Plains of Thurogen. He has to choose to join Sharwin or Falamore. The people here will back whoever he chooses, for we have little other choice, but most of us hope he chooses Falamore. He is fat and useless as kings go, but he does not bother us too much and lets us get on with living. The storm is coming, we just hope it passes us by and Effgard emerges victorious, whomever he backs."

The innkeeper looked at the town guards who had begun another round of their songs, all except the one who had stopped and was still staring at Marki. The innkeeper continued speaking. "Before he can meet Sharwin in battle, Falamore has to deal with some rebel barons who have taken this time of strife as an opportunity to declare allegiance to another king. The fools think Sharwin will let them be and that Falamore has too many troubles and not enough warriors to attack them."

The innkeeper flicked his fingers at a serving girl who walked by, and pointed a finger at a plate of food on it. "Give that to this dwarf, and take some food and mead outside to a wilding who waits," he said. The girl took a plate of food off the tray and placed it in front of Marki without ceremony, before rushing off to serve another customer, and then heading for the door with the remaining food and ale on the tray. *At least they haven't denied Ognok food and drink,* Marki thought to himself.

The food consisted of selected meats, bread, cheese, pickles and a chunk of bread. Marki drained the mead from his tankard, and then tore into the bread and meat, eating hungrily. The innkeeper wrinkled his bulging forehead and wiped the empty tankard on his striped apron, filled it with mead again, and pushed it towards Marki. "This one would be on the house, had you not already paid enough for it," he said, and then grinning he asked, "I'm guessing you are a mercenary, come from Kappian lands to fight in this war, a deserter perhaps? As that is no ordinary armour you wear. Battered though it is, it is imperial, am I right?"

Marki took a gulp of the mead, swallowed the mouthful of food he was chewing and then growled, "Blithering fish lips. For somebody who says they listen more than they talk, you ask a lot of questions."

The innkeeper took from his moneybag one of the coins Marki had given to him, and studied it. "It has been since before living memory, that an Akkadian has visited these parts, if ever one has. Some years ago, some Fell-blood mercenaries came through, returning from a civil war they had fought in. We had all but forgotten an empire existed in the north, and rare was any news we ever heard of events that far away. They liberally spent similar coin to these you carried, that is how I recognise them. They wore armour they had looted from the dead."

"What happened to them?" Marki asked. He had employed many mercenaries himself, and wondered if any might have settled locally that he could visit to garner information from them.

"They drank themselves into a stupor for a few days whilst boasting of their deeds, sobered up and then moved on." The innkeeper sighed. "Such coins as those they spent still circulate sometimes. They are worth a lot around here. You are right, the quality of the copper, brass, silver or gold used to make them are far better than that used in local ones, and only somebody who does not know their worth would offer the equivalent coin."

"Aye, I'm a mercenary, of sorts," Marki said, thinking it best not to divulge too much information or give too much away about his business, until he had spoken to Effgard, but he needed to keep the innkeeper talking so he could find out what he could.

"That's good. Sell swords are welcome in these parts during these troublesome days, as long as they join whatever side Effgard will choose," the innkeeper said.

"So, where is he?" Marki asked, impatiently glancing back at the curtain and the six men. "Behind there?"

The innkeeper glanced warily at the curtain, and gave a toothy but uncertain smile. "He has his own private entrance to this inn, for although I own the building and the business, this land itself is his. I don't know if he is in or not," he said in a manner that made Marki stop chewing his food and look at him warily.

"Then I'll not be wasting any more of my time here," Marki said as he drained the last of his ale, and crammed the last of the meat, bread and cheese into his mouth. He swallowed after hardly chewing, and stood and turned and addressed all those in the room, banging his empty tankard on the top of the bar to get attention. The people fell silent and the music stopped.

"I desire to speak to Effgard, wherever he is," Marki bellowed as he glanced at the curtain. "If any can send word to him, tell him I am waiting, but if he lingers too long, I will go directly to King Falamore and deal with him!"

A few people gasped at the audacity of the dwarf.

"There are patrols and watchtowers you will need to pass. You need permission to travel unhindered to Thurog Tor. The *Wargheart* will either give you permission, or he will kill you," one of the patrons loudly said.

"Too much mead, too much mead," the innkeeper said apologetically to the patrons, and then hastily waved to the musicians. "Play, play some music," he said.

Marki sat back on the stool as the music, song and chatter resumed. "I've not had too much mead. You are talking to a *Vargo Goss Ale Drinking Champion*," he said indignantly.

"Be that as it may, you will get yourself killed," the innkeeper whispered to him urgently, and then with a warning tone added, "you cannot leave this town until Effgard has spoken to you, and that will be at a time of his choosing. I can give you a bed for the night if you need it, but to leave now without Effgard's permission, would mean your certain death. Like it or not, you'll have to wait for him."

Marki looked impatiently around. *I don't have time for this. Bor might be dead already, or if not, soon will be.* The six men in front of the curtain were murmuring among themselves and casting suspicious looks Marki's way. He looked at the mens' armour and swords, and figured, if he had to fight his way out, *Old Trusty* would penetrate their armour easily enough and their swords, as he observed, were in worn out sheaths, so might not be that well maintained. The guards were drunk, and soon began paying little attention as the music began again and the chatter in the inn resumed, but the one who had not stopped looking at Marki, had stood to his feet, and was staggering uneasily towards him. He stopped, and took a jug of ale from a passing maid, and stood there drinking it as she took the coins to pay for it from his purse.

*He won't be a problem to deal with,* Marki thought, but he suddenly regretted his rashness and impatience. *I cannot make an enemy of him they call Wargheart before I have even had the chance to speak with him. I could fight my way out from this rabble, but then what? If Effgard chooses to side with Falamore and I have slain his men, the Obelisk is shut to us. What choice do I have but to wait?*

"Do you know how Effgard got the title *Wargheart?*" The innkeeper asked, as he refilled Marki's tankard with more mead, in an attempt to calm his patience, and ordered a serving girl to put more meat, bread and cheese on his plate.

Marki figured that even if he had had known, the innkeeper would still tell the story so he said nothing, and took a swig at the mead, realising he had but little choice to wait – for now.

"When he was but a young man, Effgard was given a legendary sword that he exchanged for a pure-bred horse. He said he was busy creating his own legend, so he did not need anybody else's sword, to borrow from their legend."

Marki continued drinking, the froth from the mead covering the hair on his upper lip. He looked at the innkeeper, showing just enough interest to keep him wanting to tell the story.

"And did he forge his own legend?" he asked.

The innkeeper's eyes shone with excitement.

"Oh yes, oh yes indeed. In the battle of the Weirmarsh, Effgard's father fell. His army was defeated and routed. You see, Effgard's warriors ride their horses to a battle, but not into one. They fight on foot, whereas the enemy king had cavalry, and they sent wyverns to kill all the horses at the rear of Effgard's army. There was no escape for any of them, surrounded and outnumbered, everyone in his army died, except Effgard."

Marki whistled, and said, "That's some heavy losses."

"Effgard stood fighting alone until the corpses piled up high around him. So, impressed with his skill and courage, the enemy king offered to spare him if he laid down his sword. Death was certain if not, so Effgard agreed to the terms."

"It's only sensible to know when enough is enough," Marki said as he took another gulp of mead. "So, what happened then?"

"Well, he was imprisoned with a minstrel, a troubadour from Aquantain who had offended some noble with a bawdy song. This minstrel soon became devoted to Effgard. With his help, Effgard composed a ballad to the daughter of the king, Princess Blondel, for she often walked with her companions in the street below the cell Effgard was kept in, and he loved her from the moment he first glimpsed her."

"Harrumph, lusted after her more like," Marki cynically suggested.

"Well she is… was once a great beauty. Anyway, one day Blondel heard Effgard's melodious voice drifting through the iron bars of the cell, for he is a fine singer. So fine and romantic were the words he sang to her, she fell in love with him the moment she set eyes upon him. He was secretly taken to her chamber each night, and she was soon with child. When her father the king heard about it, he was furious to be so insulted after he had shown Effgard mercy."

"I should think," Marki said as he tore into another chunk of meat and swigged more mead.

"But King Feydas could not have Effgard murdered. Falamore had seized his own father's throne at Thurog Tor, and Sharwin had seized the lands to the west. Each were offering King Feydas a huge ransom, outbidding each other, for the return of Effgard their brother, for such was his fame as a warrior, it would boost their standing to have him take up their cause."

"King Feydas' kingdom was in great need, and some of his own barons were murmuring against him. His people would not be pleased if Feydas wasted an opportunity for much needed gold. But, in making the daughter of King Feydas pregnant, Effgard had deeply offended and insulted him, humiliated him even. The king regretted his former mercy, and wanted him dead, so he staged an incident, so that his death could be announced as a tragic accident."

Marki shook his head with disgust, "That is the trouble with kings and queens, they do not know the honesty of looking a man in the eyes and taking his life in fair and equal combat. So, what did Feydas do?"

The innkeeper eagerly continued. "The king kept captured wargs in his private zoo, which was next to the prison. One of them was called Nakan, the son of a famous warg king named Nakah, who once terrorised the Tarenmoors until he was captured by the Tarath Guëan and forced into their service."

"I am surprised the Tarath Guëan are known in these parts?"

"They have rarely been here, but it is said they are great movers of deeds, so when they have come, it was noted. One travelled through a year or so ago, though on what business, the likes of me do not know, and nor would I dare to ask. Anyway, Nakan was starved for a few days and then, under the pretence of escaping, was to be released when Effgard was exercising in the prison yard. Blondel had heard of the plot beforehand so she gave Effgard keys to his cell and the prison, and urged him to flee, but he refused. Instead he asked her for forty silk handkerchiefs, which she gave him. He wrapped his forearm in them for protection, and when Nakan jumped over the wall into the yard, Effgard thrust his arm down the warg's throat, reached into its chest and ripped out its heart. He then used the keys to leave the prison, strode to the Great Hall, and threw the still beating heart onto the table in front of the astonished king and his guests who were at supper. Effgard then sprinkled the still pulsating heart with some salt, put some mustard on it, and then ate it with great relish. He is *Wargheart* by deed and name."

Marki finished his drink, and took a last bite of food from his plate. "That's a story worthy of the Shield-Maidens," he said respectfully, "but most stories grow with the telling."

The guards' song, judging by the growing intensity and volume of obscene words, was reaching its grand finale. As Marki slammed his empty tankard onto the bar, he felt a tap on the shoulder, and turned to see the guard who had had been staring at him standing behind him. He was a balding man whose face was disfigured by a scar that ran across his right eyebrow, the bridge of his nose and across his left cheek. Several of his teeth were missing, and grey stubble covered the lower part of his gaunt face. He had an angry look about him.

"It's against the rules to bang your tankard in this place," the guard slurred, staggering slightly due to the influence of drink.

"Don't be causing any trouble, Bergil," the innkeeper said to the guard, who dismissed his concerns with a wave of his hand.

"I'm talking to *Stumpy the Dwarf* here, not to you," the guard garbled.

"My business is with Effgard, not a stewed-prune like you," Marki growled at the guard. He then got off the bar stool, wiped the froth from his beard and said to the innkeeper, "I'll take that room, and wait to speak to the *Wargheart!*" *I need to keep out of trouble. If drunken guards will bother me, I'll wait in a room.*

348

"That's not for you to choose, Stumpy," the guard said as he poked Marki hard in the chest with a finger.

Marki felt the blood begin to boil within him. *Your head would already be parted from your shoulders, if my business with this Effgard was not so urgent.*

The other guards, noticing the commotion, finished their song, stood to their feet and staggered over to join their comrade. They were all the worse for wear with drink.

"Is this dwarf bothering you, Bergil?" one of them asked, his voice just as slurred.

"This dwarf is trying to mind his own business," Marki answered him, and then looking at the innkeeper demanded. "Show me the room you offered. I wish to be away from these curs."

"*Stumpy the Dwarf* is scared," Bergil said in a mocking tone as he prodded Marki again.

"A man of wax like you would have his courage melt in the midday sun, if this was between just me and you," Marki replied threateningly with a growl, as the innkeeper ran from behind the bar with a speed that belied his size.

"Follow me, to your room," he urged Marki.

Marki turned to follow him, but Bergil grabbed him by the hair and swung him around. Marki's reaction was more instinctive than thought out. The punch he landed knocked Bergil backwards several feet, spraying his few remaining teeth along with blood onto the floor of the tavern, whilst he was still mid-air. The other guards tried to seize Marki, and several of them drew weapons. Marki sprang towards them, his veins on fire with madness. He had no time for conscious consecutive thought. Resisting the urge to draw *Old Trusty* and deal fatal blows, he used his fists to punch with powerful effect. Pivoting on his heel, the force of his blows meant only one was needed to fell each guard. He dodged, spun around, and rolled to avoid the clumsy swings they made at him with their swords. In less time than it would take him to drain a mug of mead, all of the guards were soon lying unconscious or incapacitated and groaning incoherently on the tavern floor.

"Anyone else want to interfere in my business?" Marki asked threateningly with a growl as he scanned the room, holding up his fists. The fury within him was overcoming his sense, in that he partly hoped some of them would take up the offer. He looked at the six men before the curtain, who were still watching him. They had not moved, but had put hands on their weapons.

"Are you going to give me trouble, or hold your peace?" he challenged them. They looked at each other uncertainly.

The other guests in the tavern, who had paused to watch the fight, returned to their own drinking or business.

Marki snarled at nobody in particular. "If any whoreson mangy dog of a fool puts another hand on me, or bothers me needlessly, I'll cut his gnash gab head off, you see if I don't." He then turned to the innkeeper and angrily shouted, "And I'll not be clearing their blood off the floor! Make them do it when they sober up!"

"Enough!" A voice boomed authoritatively across the room. A large man drew aside the curtain and was standing in the alcove it had hidden. "Calm your tongue, dwarf, or by the gods I will also bear the title *Dwarfheart* by the end of this day, as I rip yours from your chest and have it for supper."

Marki clenched his fists. It took him a moment or two, before it dawned upon him the significance of the man's words. He realized who it was standing in the alcove – Effgard. Nonetheless, his emotions conflicted within him. Marki wanted to accept the challenge and fight him. It took all of his restraint to remember his reason for being there. *If I didn't need to speak with you, it would be your heart I would feed to the town's stray dogs.*

Reluctantly, Marki lowered his fists. "If you are Effgard, I would exchange words with you. It would do you well to hear me out. If that is not to your liking, then let me leave in peace, or by Balagrim, only one of us will be alive before the innkeeper can serve another ale."

The man laughed; it was a deep, hearty guffaw. "Effgard, I am," he said as he raised his arms. His sleeveless cloak of dyed warg skin parted with the movement to reveal a vest of bronze mail and tautly muscled arms tattooed with red ink. Heavy gold bracelets hung on his wrists and gold rings adorned each of his remaining seven fingers. The parts of his skin that were visible were a mass of long healed scars. He had a bearing of one that was fearless, and expected to be obeyed without question. The clay binding of beard braids clinked together as he took a seat at a chair beside a table in the alcove.

"Come, dwarf, speak to me," he boomed, "and pray to your angry god, Balagrim, the words you speak are of interest to me or your corpse will be pushing up the daisies by morning, or feeding the dogs."

*Damn the circumstance Bor, if it was not for your predicament and that of the legion, I would fight this bedwarmer's' son until only one of us were left breathing.*

The six men, all standing, watched as Marki strode past them. He looked fiercely at them, daring them to make a move but they did nothing, apart from to slide the curtain across behind him when he and Effgard were alone in the alcove. He was in no mood for small talk, so when Effgard beckoned for him to take a seat, he sat moodily down, glowering at Effgard who glowered back. The only noise was the sound beyond the curtain of some women who were laughing at the guards and making stinging comments about them being defeated in a fight by a single dwarf. Marki paid no heed, and then the groans of the guards and the mocking laughter they endured, was drowned out by lively music that began to play.

"Speak then," Effgard said. "Why is a dwarf in my tavern causing trouble?"

"I was here minding my own business, seeking an audience with you when those fopdoodles picked a fight," Marki growled, "and by Balagrim it felt good to crunch some bones with the boys," he added, as he clenched and shook his fists. "Bouncer and Bedtime, I call them." He then broke into an old rowdy dwarf song:

*"If you see my boys a swinging, you'd better step aside*
*Both are made of iron; they'll bounce you on your hide*
*They'll knock you into sleep, oh your women, they will weep*
*If you see my boys a swinging, they have a lot of skill*
*If the left one doesn't get you, the right one certainly will."*

Effgard stared at him intensely for a while, and Marki returned the stare. After a few moments, Effgard roared with laughter, a deep-throated boom gusty as a mountain wind. "I like you dwarf," he said, after which he bellowed to one of the men beyond the curtain to have a maid bring more mead. Within moments, a maid brought a tray full of frothing meads and ales.

"Keep them coming wench," he ordered her, and then taking one, he said to Marki, "Drink!"

Marki took a tankard, and copying Effgard, he downed it in one, letting out a loud burp afterwards. Both man and dwarf laughed, and each took another full tankard that they drank more slowly.

"State your name and your business dwarf," Effgard said.

"Then hold tongue, and I will tell you my tale," Marki replied. He had never been very good at lying the few times he had tried it in his life, and there were few times he

350

saw the need to do so. He could think of no good reason why the truth would not stand as good as any made-up tale, so he told Effgard the truth, and left nothing out. Recounting the fall of Aleskian, the danger Borach was in, the need for a safe Obelisk for him to resurrect at, and the willingness of the legion to sell their swords for the use of one, he told it all and held nothing back. He even told about their griffin, Ognok's remarks about it, and that the wildlings had called it Karno. He also spoke about the Bantu horde that had entered the Everglow, and no doubt would soon be in the Tarenmoors.

Effgard listened quietly, and intently, as deep into the evening Marki spoke. He only interrupted him when he wanted something clarified or repeated. When Marki had finished his tale, he looked at Effgard and said, "Now, have that maid fetch me a pot to piss in, as this mead has to come out some time, and then order more for all this jabbering of my tongue has given me a thirst that scorches more than sucking at a volcanoes teat."

Effgard flicked his fingers and the maid, waiting nearby, fetched a large bowl into which Marki, with a sigh of relief, relieved himself. He then drank thirstily from one of the tankards of fresh mead she had placed on the table.

"You'll not get any more out of me, for there's nothing more to tell. You know the full truth of it, why we have come to these barren pig swills of a land," he said as he stared Effgard defiantly in the eyes.

"We planned to offer our swords in service to your brother, for we need his Obelisk, or if this Sharwin has one, we'll serve her just as well. But Ognok told me of one called Talain, a Pure-blood at Thurog Tor he says can see in the land of the dead?"

Effgard snarled mockingly. "Talain is thoughtless with her gift, for she dies a lot, often as a result of some foolish endeavour. Only recently she wandered out into the wilderness and stumbled into a stingwing nest, and was stung to death. But it is true. The Obelisk at Thurog Tor always brings her back; yet, she learns nothing, for she does not curb her rash endeavours and never stays alive for more than a few months at a time, a year at most. She says she enjoys dying as she learns a lot from what she sees in the Deadlands."

"Then that settles it from my side, for I need an Obelisk, and she is a Seer. But, unless you plan to join your brother, King Falamore, I think my plans will not be to your liking. Unless your sister has an Obelisk, we can use, choice is stripped from me."

Marki liked Effgard, but he realised he might have to kill him and escape the tavern, unless Effgard also planned to join his brother. He readied himself, alert for any eventuality.

A fierce countenance grew on Effgard's face. When he spoke, it was as though he was choosing his words with as much care as if they had been razors.

"I have already chosen my side," he said. "I fight for King Falamore, for I do not like the thought of Chatti and Gragor stalking these lands; it was they who sent the foul spirit that now possesses my sister, and they that allowed her to use the skull of a dragon to recruit the barbarians. I sought a sign to confirm my choice, and your griffin, Karno, is the answer I have looked for. Karno will rally and strengthen our cause."

Marki chuckled. "Well, if you and your men want to worship some skinny griffin that was the sickly runt of a litter, I'll not mock you for it, but neither will I hide my surprise or feign the same deference," he replied.

"I care not if this griffin is or is not a god," Effgard said tautly, "but to my warriors and the people of this land, he will be seen as such and that will serve my cause, and in that it is a sign."

351

Marki nodded in agreement. "Do you think our offer will be acceptable to your brother - our swords in return for the use of his Obelisk?"

Effgard nodded an assent, and Marki let out an immediate sigh of relief.

"I have heard honesty in your words, I will speak truth to you," Effgard said. "Do you think a legion from Kappia, could enter the Tarenmoors and we would not be aware of it?" he asked.

Marki shrugged his shoulders. "The first sign of human life we saw was Ognok and his tribe."

Effgard laughed, but there was no amusement in it. "Our borders to the east are settled, but those to the south and the west, face incessant raids from the barbarians who have joined Sharwin. The hills swarm with them; they are a mindless horde full of murder and rapine." He took a swig of mead, and stared vacantly into the air before looking Marki over again. "Half of my army is less than three days march from here. Ognok sent word to us, the moment one of his tribe spotted your legion. I sent word for him to befriend you. I sent scouts, so that I might have eyes watching your movements. I did not know your intent, if you came as an invader from the North. But with many of the Obelisks in the Tarenmoors lost, it would have been a folly for Pure-bloods to invade, and that with only a tired looking depleted legion. That is why I could not work out your reason for coming here, or what advantage it would have for you. Your words have explained your reasons, and I am content with the truth of it." Effgard smiled and held out his hand. "I offer you a hand of friendship. In the days long ago before they locked themselves away, I had Dwarves fight alongside me. Most have been stubborn, but strong of heart, they are loose and loud with their words, but speak the truth as they see it. There is none I can say I have regretted meeting."

Marki guffawed as he shook Effgard's hand and said, "Then it is Balagrim's luck you have not met the worst of my kind and there be plenty of them, for we have good and bad ones like all other folk."

Effgard's face took on a serious tone. "War was sport when I was younger, now it is an inconvenience. I do not wish for it, or seek it any longer, but nor shall I shrink from it when it comes knocking at my door. I see no lie in your eye, and have accepted your tale, that your legion offers service in return for our assistance. But, your words about the Bantu horde bring me a greater concern than even the trouble brewing with my sister, Sharwin."

Marki nodded in agreement, but let him continue without interruption.

"Whilst we are dealing with the threats to the south and west, I now learn that a new one, just as ferocious, may appear from the North." Effgard sighed deeply, swilling the last remnants of some mead around the bottom of the tankard before drinking it. "The Tarenmoors have always been left to themselves; any intruders that came here with evil intent have never lasted long. The Kappians, until your arrival, due to most of the Obelisks being lost or undiscovered, have never seen it worthwhile to bother with us. But now, you warn of this new Bantu threat? This news troubles me deeply."

"It should," Marki said forcefully.

Effgard nodded. "The Kappian Empire, your legions, have failed in their attempt to stop this horde coming into the Everglow. Now, no more legions are between us and this new threat?"

Marki felt himself blushing. He felt embarrassed that Aleskian had fallen, even though it was due to events beyond his control. He did not like being reminded of the Kappian legions' failure, however it had come about, but Effgard was right to be concerned. Marki wanted to particularly defend the honour of the Third, and then that of the other legions, but for a long moment he said nothing, instead, biting his tongue, until the silence became almost unbearable. He then spoke.

"The only hope is, that the Bantu have a long hatred for the Baothein. Baothein defences are strong, but such might be the numberless horde that now enters the Everglow, who can tell how long before they conquer the Baothein? Especially with the war-machine they call Braka *the Groundshaker*. We have no doubt we were pursued, but did they stop when we entered the Tarenmoors? Will they wait until they have conquered the Baothein, or will they have the numbers to arrive on your doorstep sooner than that? The Kappia Plateau is virtually impenetrable, even if they break any alliances they might make, the Bantu will not bother with that, yet. But I fear they will burn the rest of Kappian lands to the ground. Outside of the Plateau, Kappian defences will be abandoned or will fall. When that happens, there will be no buffer between them and your lands. It is in the Bantu nature to destroy and they will send armies here, of that I have no doubt, it is just a matter of time. No lands are safe anymore." He sighed deeply. "I have many questions, and very few answers, for I do not understand what mischief went on to see my friend and lord, so betrayed. But I offer our swords, and with the use of the Obelisk, we will make our stand and fight with you, for we have nowhere else to go. Whatever enemies we have to face, we can face together."

"Maybe Dwarves were wise, for perhaps your kind has foreseen what you call Rogrok, the end of days," Effgard said. "But we have nowhere to lock ourselves away, except in our fortified cities, but that means abandoning our fields and our food supplies." His face twisted in frustration. "Now is not a wise time for the kingdoms of the Tarenmoors to be war making among themselves, but my sister Sharwin is troublesome. Her offence with our brother, Falamore, is strong; she was firstborn and has the blood right to the throne, so no reason or logic will divert her from her course of destroying him. She has patiently bided her time to strike. War is inevitable with her, but the timing could not be worse."

"She cannot be reasoned with?" Marki asked.

"No more than a starving warg with a bone could be reasoned with to give it up," Effgard replied. "So, we must have this war done with quickly to prepare for the enemy that will now come from the North."

"I agree," Marki said, "but you look acquainted enough with the ways of war to know that by its nature it can be unpredictable and turn up surprises not anticipated. Your northern border is poorly defended, it must be strengthened even as you turn to face the enemies to the south and the west, for that war may not be over as quickly as you would desire."

"I have made the right decision about you," Effgard said as he held out his hand again. "It gladdens me you offer swords to ally with us in this war. You and your legion will fight alongside me, and face whatever enemies we must."

Marki breathed another, deep sigh of relief, and grabbed Effgard's forearm enthusiastically, and Effgard did the same to Marki. They shook rigorously.

"I will take you to Thurog Tor and speak with my brother. I am confident he will agree your men can use the Obelisk, and if he has any sense, he will, for we will be heavily outnumbered on all sides in this war. If your Lord Borach dies, he will be treated well when he resurrects at Thurog Tor. I will send a messenger along with Ognok to speak to your legion, and instruct them where to camp. You will write words on parchment, so they know it is an order from you."

"What if, by any chance, Falamore does not agree?"

"He will agree or he is a fool, for many are his enemies and few are his friends. He will not be wanting to anger me when I have now sided with him against our own sister.

"Good," Marki said, "then it is settled." He then leant towards Effgard.

"Now you tell me, that story of the warg-heart, is it a crock of shite or did that really happen?"

Effgard frowned. "It's all true apart from one thing, but you know how stories grow in the telling."

"Which one thing would that be?" Marki inquired.

Effgard smiled wryly. "I didn't season it with salt or mustard. I prefer a pulsating warg-heart to be eaten unflavoured."

Marki looked at Effgard, banged his fist on the table, and they both roared with laughter.

# Chapter Twenty-Nine: *A Dark Dungeon*

*Nine of the Aeldar there are, summoned they shall be, even those whose bodies were slain by ancient deceit and trickery. When Thuranotos appears, the souls of the eight will rise from the cunning prisons that were their demise. The wrath of his hammers will shake the worlds. In fury shall he summon Skipilos and his minions, and have his revenge. Thus, the war of the gods begins. The tendrils of chaos that creep from the accursed wastes of Vangalen, that taint the land and sow dissent, shall rise again, but will be vanquished. The Dark Lords of the North shall flee before Thuranotos. The ancient thrones shall groan, in the North, in the South, in the West, in the East, rivers of blood shall flow. The world will cry for mercy. When En-Sof appears, he will open the sky. The Nameless One will come forth, weakened he will be, and death shall be his. In this way Thuranotos alone will rule.*
**The Book of Aeldar Prophecies.**


*There* was no window in the small dungeon, no bed, not even a slop bucket. The straw on the floor stank of Shaka's own urine. Once the thick wooden door studded with iron had slammed shut, the dark had been absolute, and she had seen no more. With her groping hands, she touched the cold stone wall for the hundredth time, feeling and pushing, hoping to find some weakness that might lead to her escape, until the chain around her leg drew taut, having reached its limit.

There was no weakness in the wall she could find. The Maidenarz felt suffocating. Primal passions deep within her struggled against its power, her very nature wanted to change, she willed it, wanted it, but, by some power, the Maidenarz would not allow it. *If I could change aspect, would I have the strength to break free from this prison of stone or even then would I still be trapped?*

The dungeon was very deep underground beneath the Bloody Tower in Kappia. The light of the sun or moon could not penetrate her cell, and it was too dark to mark the days on the walls. Shaka had no idea how long she had been kept there. The water and food she had been left with had long gone, her throat was dry with thirst and her lips cracked. She rubbed her fingers over the skin of her face, it felt old and wrinkled. It had been some time since she had applied any milathran to it, and her age had taken affect. It did not matter, she sensed whether through age or other means, her next death was not far away and she would be resurrected again, with a new gift of youth. But to what sort of life would she be resurrected?

The recurring thought and fear that tormented her, was - *What fate does Mazdek have planned for me?*

When Shaka slept, she dreamed: dark, foreboding nightmares so terrible that when she awoke from them, she feared to close her eyes again and resisted sleep until it took her against her will. When awake, there was nothing to do but think. She thought of the many people she had sent to these very same dungeons below the Bloody Tower, never giving them a second thought once they were out of her sight. She thought of the Seeress Janorra, and wondered whether this might even be the very same cell that she had once been imprisoned in long ago. The venom of hatred coursed through her soul as she thought of the wrong inflicted upon her by that woman. Her actions had allowed Mazdek to seize advantage over her. *I will have my revenge on Janorra, she will suffer, as will Mazdek and all who have betrayed me and given allegiance to him.*

In between her dark thoughts of plotted revenge, when she imagined the sufferings she would inflict on her enemies, Shaka often thought of her children, and feared what Mazdek may have done to them. The thought of Aspess in the hands of Mazdek, brought her much torment, for he knew her secret and what she could become, and long had he suggested using her to forge alliances through marriage. Regineo would suffer the most, for many times he had slighted Mazdek and humiliated him before the imperial court. Mazdek had born the insults in silence, but what revenge might he exact now Regineo was in his power? Caspus had suffered a quick but brutal death in her room. He would have resurrected by now, would Mazdek seek to extract by force the dark secrets her son had discovered by his mysterious arcane arts? The thought occurred to her that perhaps they might all be in a cell similar to her own, in the same dungeon. She had called out their names into the darkness, but only silence was the response. It was not knowing their fate that was her biggest torment. *What will you do to my beloved children, Mazdek?*

Whenever her thoughts turned to Mazdek, "Fool," she cried into the darkness as she cursed herself for her carelessness. She could now see clearly how he had wormed his way into her confidence, gained her trust, and lured her into replacing all her guards with the Hammer Knights, men who, when it had been put to the test, had given their loyalty to him. She cursed his name in the darkness for his deeds, but most of all she cursed him for turning her against her loyal generals. It was a painful realisation for her to awaken to the truth that General Karkson had been a true and wise counsellor to her, a loyal confidant. *Curse you Mazdek! What twisted words and crooked council you whispered into my ear to turn me against my loyal General Karkson.*

Doubt had also arisen in her mind as to the alleged betrayal of the Captain General of Aleskian, Borach. *Was Lord Borach really disloyal to me, did he conspire with the Baothein against me or was that all a part of Mazdek's warped lies and perverted schemes?*

She asked herself that question repeatedly, never quite coming up with a conclusion or clear answer. *Did Mazdek carefully, patiently and slyly divert my trust from those truly loyal to me, or was everyone plotting against me?*

Whatever the truth behind it, she could not yet figure it out, but Mazdek's plotting and lies had been the instrument of her ruin, and she had been too distracted to see what was happening right in front of her own eyes. She fell into another tormented sleep, disturbed by dark dreams.

*      *      *

It had felt so long since she had heard anything but the sound of her own voice and wailing, that when Shaka finally heard the distant clinking of keys and the sound of footsteps, she felt she imagined them and it seemed unreal. The next clanking sound of keys in a lock and the grating of the bolts as they were undone, followed by the sound of booted footsteps on stone, were unmistakable, as were the unintelligible voices that she heard talking outside of her cell. The sound of keys jangling in the lock of the door to her cell and bolts being slid, sent a wave of fear and nausea through her. *What fate now awaits me?*

The thick heavy wooden door creaked open, and the sudden light from the torches the men outside held was painful to her eyes. A grimy gaoler was the first to enter. His hand trembled and he nervously thrust a jug of water at her and offered some stale looking bread he took from a filthy pouch around his belted waist. Her lips were parched and cracked, her hunger intense, but Shaka did not take either the food or water, despite feeling powerful urges to grab both to eat ravenously and drink greedily. *What poisons and potions are in that water? Death and resurrection would be welcome, but I will not allow my mind to be drugged if I am to be interrogated.*

356

Shaka stared at the gaoler, and even she could feel the intense hatred and anger burning in her eyes. He dropped the jug, which smashed on the floor spilling the contents, then dropped the bread and ran from the cell in fear pushing past the men outside the door. "I want no part in this," he screamed as he threw his keys at their feet and fled down the hall. The incident gave Shaka a slight feeling of hope. *I am still the Empress, and my subjects still fear me, and so they should, for I shall have my revenge on all who assist Mazdek in his dire plans.*

The Grand Inquisitor Marnir, and then Renlak her Hand, accompanied by a second gaoler who stooped to pick up the keys, entered the cell, stepping over the shattered pieces of the jug and the spilt contents. A third person, whose face was covered in a hood, waited outside. For reasons unknown to her, this figure struck terror into her heart.

Renlak curled his nose up at the stench of the cell. "You should take some refreshment, my Sarissa," he said coldly, as he stooped and dabbed the bread in the water on the floor, and offered it to her. He then said to the second gaoler, "Fetch more water, fresh, and have your cowardly associate flogged and then thrust into a cell like this, not to be fed or watered until he dies. I will deal with him when he resurrects."

"Yes, my lord," the man replied nervously, and rushed off to fetch another jug of water.

Shaka felt uncontrollable hate rise within her as she stared at her betrayers. She resisted the urge to take the soggy bread, and when she spoke, her words were tainted with bitterness. "Hours turn to days in here, or so it seems. Blood, betrayal and broken promises have been my food and water in the dark. I do not need this pitiful fare you offer me."

Renlak dropped the bread onto the floor, and ground it into the grime with his boot. "As you wish," he said.

*How brave you are now, but I know your cowardly heart*, Shaka thought to herself as she noted the look of contempt on his face.

The second gaoler returned with a jug of water and a wooden cup. His hands shook as he poured some water into the cup and offered it to Shaka, turning his head away from her so as not to look into her eyes.

"It is not poisoned or drugged," Renlak said on noticing Shaka's reluctance to drink. He then took the cup from the gaoler, sipped from it, and then offered it to Shaka. She took the cup, and resisting the urge to gulp it down eagerly, instead took several slow sips. *I will not lose more of my dignity in front of these men.*

The water was cool and refreshing, and at that moment tasted better than anything Shaka had ever tasted before. The gaoler put the jug on the ground near her, and she noticed that his hands still shook and trembled with fear. *I still have power and some influence over these wretches,* she thought to herself.

"Leave us," Renlak ordered the gaoler, who eagerly complied and left in a hurry.

"What is the news of my children?" she asked Renlak, her voice croaky and broken.

Renlak chuckled as though an amusing thought or memory suddenly passed through his mind. "The Princess Aspess is amazingly resolute. We knew it would take a different kind of persuasion for her to agree, but she has now decided to support Mazdek's plan and proposal."

"What plan, what proposal?" Shaka asked, trying to mask the desperation in her voice.

"Regineo needed more physical tactics, but it did not take long before he agreed to it. It took Caspus hardly any time at all to be persuaded it was the right course of action for the Empire," Renlak said with a smug smile. "One look at the tools Grixen uses, and he was compliant."

"What are you talking about, what have you forced them to agree to?" *You will suffer most of all Renlak, if the suffering of my children has brought you any pleasure. I will roast you alive slowly, flay the skin from your bones and then invent worse ways for you to suffer each time you resurrect.*

"I will allow Marnir to explain," Renlak said as Marnir stepped forward.

Marnir, a man of few words who usually got straight to the point, said, "High Quaester Mazdek does not wish to usurp the throne from you, instead, you will agree to the marriage proposal he offers you, and will become his Munte bride."

A surge of rage and anger rose up within Shaka. "Never," she hissed. "I will never agree to such a marriage!"

In the Empire there were two types of marriage Pure-blood Kappians could undertake, Munte and Freide. Munte was formal, permanent, and involved the transfer of all of the woman's property, titles, power and wealth being passed over to her husband. The marriage contract continued beyond one lifetime until either husband or wife met the *Final-death*. A Munte marriage was permanent and gave all power to the husband, and for it to be legally recognised, it needed the signed agreement and public support of any heirs or relations that might be affected by it. If they did not give their public support, the marriage would not be legally recognised. In contrast, a Freide marriage was only for one lifetime, and did not require the transfer of wealth or titles, nor did it need the signed and public agreement of the heirs or relations. The concept of Freide was that the woman had been lent rather than given, and her relations could not oppose the loan of the woman if she had agreed to it of her own free will and in peace, as it did not affect them as the contract expired after the lifetime in which it was made. With a Munte marriage, the husband had the power to choose who his legal heirs might be, even if they were not blood related. It gave the man complete power, and if Shaka agreed to the Munte marriage, Mazdek would not be seen as usurper to the throne, but as the legal and legitimate Kappian Emperor.

Although exactly who the father of her children was had been questioned, Shaka's previous and only marriage, during which the birth of her children during her first lifetime had taken place, had been Freide, and after death and then resurrection the man had been quietly disposed of with the *Final-death*. The Munte marriage she was being offered with Mazdek would be binding for all their remaining lifetimes. She had no illusions that if she agreed to the Munte marriage, once he had secured his position as Emperor in the hearts and minds of the people, Mazdek would banish her and her children, which would be his legal right to do, or worse, they would all be quietly disposed of with the *Final-death*. After all, that was how her own father had come to the throne, by forcing her mother into a Munte marriage, after a military conquest in a brutal civil war upon the Kappia plateau, many long centuries ago. The war was remembered as the War of Despair and had handed the Empire over to House Shakawraith, and Shaka would not easily just give it away to another.

"I will never agree to this," she hissed again.

"Oh, I think our guest might be able to persuade you," Marnir said with a sinister tone accompanied by a menacing look.

The hooded figure stepped into the cell, and removed his hood. It was Grixen. He bared his fangs in a gleeful leering smile, and licked them with his leathery tongue. He stepped forward and seized her arm in his fist. Shaka tried to pull away, but his grip was too firm.

358

"Do you like the Maidenarz, a gift from the Lord of Morkroth?" he asked with a sneer, as he forced her arm outwards and shone the torch, he held, over it. The pure gold and the gems on the Maidenarz dazzled in the torchlight and made a mockery of the rags she wore that barely covered her nakedness, rags that not long before had been the beautiful gown she had worn the night of the feast.

If Shaka could change form, she would gladly agree to the marriage to Mazdek, but only so she could consume him on their very wedding bed and take back her throne. But, the Maidenarz was firmly fixed, and no attempt of hers had enabled her to remove it. The foul thing was fixed with spells and charms beyond her means to break and all the time she wore it, she could not change aspect. She only had her physical strength as a woman to help her, her wit and her wile. She would gladly cut her own arm off to be rid of it had she the means to do so, but she even suspected that so strong were the charms on the Maidenarz it might prevent her from doing so. Besides, she would also have to remove her head. She looked at the Maidenarz again and regretted that she had been tricked so easily.

"I have learnt, never to accept a gift from the Lord of Morkroth," she said with a faint and sarcastic smile, full of menace and regret. She pulled her arm free from Grixen's grasp and added, "but the Lord of Morkroth will one day regret that he ever gave me such a gift."

Grixen's laughter was mocking and belittling. "I very much doubt that, for a Maidenarz exists in two worlds, and will follow you even into the Deadlands and then again when you resurrect in the Everglow," he said, "and when you are wed to High Quaester Mazdek, your name and power will soon fade to memory and eventually be forgotten. You have no allies or friends left, *Empress*!" The way he spat out the word *Empress* was scathing and mocking.

"You mock me?" Shaka snarled, as the anger within her surged up again, overtaking her fear. She hit him, hard. It was a slap, backhanded, but she put all of her strength into it, all her fear, all her rage, all her pain.

Grixen staggered back, blood trickled from his lip. In a manner that contradicted the bestial fury on his face, he calmly took a handkerchief out of his pocket and dabbed his lip, and then with his leathery tongue licked his fangs clean. When he spoke, his voice was quiet, but threatening. "I will enjoy persuading you to agree to this Munte marriage, more than I did persuading your children."

Shaka's face flushed red with anger, and she went to strike Grixen again. He stepped back. Marnir's reactions were even faster; he raised his staff and shouted, "*Mossana! Harka mankora deshoconjur.*"

Shaka began choking violently. She felt invisible hands gripping her throat and squeezing the life out of her. Falling to her knees, she tried to wrench the unseen hands away, but could only grasp the air.

"That's enough," Renlak said.

"*Hassostias,*" Marnir said calmly.

Shaka felt the hands release her. She gasped for air as she rubbed her throat.

Marnir spoke quietly but calmly. "A new power has arisen; the old lineage is to be broken. You will submit to this Munte marriage of your own free will, or you will be persuaded by other means."

"You all forget one thing," she retorted back. "I am the *Mother of a Titan*; I am promised to the Aeldar Ahrimakan. When Thuranotos returns, he will release his spirit from the Arzak to again take physical form. My beloved will not tolerate the treatment I have suffered at the hands of my betrayers. You are a devotee of the Aeldar, do you not fear his displeasure? It was promised to me, that I will be an Aeldar Queen for all eternity!"

Grixen laughed; it was a cruel, mocking laugh, but Marnir silenced him with a glance.

Marnir sounded almost compassionate when he answered her. "You were useful to Ahrimakan, for a time, but you failed him. It will be you he blames for having lost the Simal, and for his humiliating death at the hands of an assassin. When we recover the Simal, and when the glorious day comes when Thuranotos is summoned and uses his power to release Ahrimakan from the Arzak, alive or dead you will be presented to the Aeldar in case they wish to express their displeasure at your failing them. They will understand why we deemed it better that you were replaced. After all, you imprisoned and humiliated the High Quaester, of whom it is written in the *Fifth Book of the Aeldar* that any that raise a hand against one in such a position, must be brought down and punished accordingly, regardless of their station."

"Spare me your sermons you babbling fool," Shaka said furiously as she raised her hand to strike Marnir, but then thought better of it as he raised his staff.

"I have been loyal to the Aeldar," she protested. "My devotion and service to them cannot be questioned."

"That is why I have persuaded the High Quaester to let you prove your devotion in a new way. Become his Munte bride, help him secure his reign, and though smaller the part you will play, you will aid the cause we strive for in returning the Aeldar to the Everglow. On the day of their return, they may overlook your past failings and transgressions, if you show your loyalty to them by submitting to your new role with humility and acceptance." He offered a sickly, false and pretentious smile. "You have twenty-four hours to decide. If you still refuse, Ambassador Grixen here, will attempt to persuade you."

Grixen gave her a mocking, cruel smile.

"Twenty-four hours," Marnir repeated, as he, Renlak and Grixen turned and left the cell. The door crashed shut behind them, the keys jangled as they turned in the lock and the bolts were slid firmly across. Shaka blinked as the light vanished. She was prevented from rushing to the door to try and wrench it open by the chain around her leg that rattled and clanked, as it drew taut whenever she tried to get to the door.

*I will never agree to this marriage*, she said defiantly to herself. *They speak lies, my beloved Ahrimakan will not allow the injustices done to me to go unavenged.* But hope and anger left her as she stared into the darkness, and fear returned – she felt so alone. She lowered her head to her chest, curled up on the straw, and for the first time in many lifetimes, the Empress Shaka cried.

# Chapter Thirty: *The Wisdom Tree*

*Temmison wrote that the Elvish races have a magical power in that you forget they exist, just a few days after meeting them. He claims this is why they can stay hidden in the Northern Winter Forest. He claims their existence is known by those who met them, wrote about it, but afterwards forgot all about it, but still had their written account. He boldly asserts that he is one of those who actually met an elf, and the female elf demonstrated her skill as an artisan, archer and healer to him. He said she told him that the Light Elves worshipped the gods of the Upper Worlds, and the Dark Elves those of the Lower ones, and those that left Pangaea for the islands to the north, became High Elves. He claims that he wrote all his knowledge down before he forgot he had met her. Therefore, his claim is based solely upon the fact he said that the reading of his own account at a later date was proof enough to him that he had met an elf. Temmison, I call you a liar sir, yes sir, a liar! Give me proof the Elves exist, or I will conclude your claim to write about them with personal knowledge, is based on nothing more than a lie and a greedy desire to sell more of your books.*

**A fragment of text found in the Kappian Library - Source believed to be Edegal.**

*The museum at Kappia will certainly be willing to pay vast sums for my notes, and I have colluded with them, so that in the event of my Final-death, they will be able to tell apart the authentic and genuine from the many fakes and forgeries. However, I will handsomely reward anyone who finds the thief who stole from me my notes on the Dwarves in relation to the language of Sangdalen. I am just glad that my final draft on this volume was almost complete before the notes were maliciously taken from me. It is a relief to me that I had kept it locked away in a different location to the notes. I suspect Edegal is behind the theft, he has always been envious of my success and wide acclaim whilst his own written works have been given little merit.*

**A Note Found in the Kappian Library - Source Temmison.**

*Janorra* woke from an exhaust driven, but surprisingly peaceful sleep, considering the trauma she had been through of late. She had slept fully clothed and was still wearing her sword, and it gave her immediate comfort when she felt the hilt of it. Opening her eyes and yawning, she heard the sound of voices coming from across the corridor, from the living room where she had eaten the delicious stew Gilly had cooked the evening before.

During the meal, Janorra had eaten in silence. She had watched as Sasna and Farir had been joyously reunited, both sharing tales of their own events of the last few days. After that, everybody else had then mostly eaten in silence, except for Gilly and the man named Muro. They had sat in a corner and spoke in quiet, muffled tones. Janorra had noticed that as the two were speaking, Sasna had watched them suspiciously, but had said nothing. After that, Janorra, driven by exhaustion, had taken up the offer for a bed for the night.

Whatever was being discussed in the dining room now was causing some dissent for voices were raised and angry, but the conversation was muffled. Janorra pushed herself into a sitting position and then with graceful elegance swung her still booted feet down to the floor. The door of the room she had slept in only made a thin, quiet squeak as she opened it. Padding slowly and silently along the rooted corridor to the door of the dining room, she pressed her ear to the wood. She could not fully hear the animated but muffled conversation coming from within, so she pushed the door open slightly, and peaked through the crack in the door.

Unlike the other rooms, the dining room was made of stone, with a chimney that snaked up through the tree, and was the reason why Gilly could light a fire on a stove or in a small fireplace, within the small kitchen area which was a part of it. The dwarf stood by some cooking pots stirring the contents, occasionally adding some spices. Her blonde hair was tied back in a ponytail, and Janorra thought that for a dwarf she was quite pretty, in a strange sort of way. Her wide blue eyes sparkled against the warm glaze of the fire, and she seemed to have a joy and wisdom about her, but she was frowning as she listened to Farir and Sasna in heated debate with one another. Muro and Scarand sat in silence, listening solemnly to the argument between brother and sister.

"I say we go immediately back to Ashgiliath," Farir shouted, and then added in a more measured tone, "you cannot trust that pirate scum to deliver the news of the ill fortune that has befallen us, and he will suspect uncle won't pay him what you promised. Uncle needs to know the Baron is aware of his plans. Besides, from what you have said, if Bantu have appeared, and the Baron hunts you for revenge, the road to Berecoth is too dangerous to travel."

"Oh, be quiet," Sasna shouted back at him. "I will not go back to Ashgiliath without fulfilling to the letter the instructions uncle gave me. You go back if you must; I will take the Davari as a guard and companion if you are too craven!"

"Tell her dwarf, that it is too dangerous," Farir passionately implored Gilly.

"There must be a safe way to travel to Berecoth," Sasna implored her with equal passion. "I have important business that can delay no longer." She and Farir then turned again on each other, arguing to such a degree Janorra could not make out what either of them were saying.

"Be quiet, me dears!" Gilly shouted with exasperation as several times she banged the spoon on the side of the cooking pot. "You are both giving me quite the headache, and Gilly does not like headaches."

When Sasna and Farir were both quiet and looking sulkily at Gilly, she continued. "It is not my business to tell you what to do, but there is a safer way to Berecoth should you choose that path."

Sasna's eyes lit up with excitement, and she cast Farir an *I told you so* look.

"There are ancient Dwarven tunnels beneath the Branded Land. You would have to leave the Wytchwood and cover a mile or so of open ground before you came to the entrance, which is hidden in an old ruin. If you know the path through them, you can emerge on a hill about three miles to the north of Berecoth"

"If we know the path!" Farir emphasised sarcastically. "Meaning if we don't then we could get lost in them?"

"Yes, me dear," Gilly admitted. "It's a real maze down there, and was difficult even for me as a dwarf to explore. I've wandered far from the main tunnels; it is not a place you would want to get lost in. I could draw a map for you, of the way you would need, but if you wandered by intent or mistake from the route, you will easily get lost and might never find a way out."

"Then it is settled, I will leave for Berecoth," Sasna declared, "and you, Gilly, will guide me through the tunnels."

"Well, me dear, I am in a twaddle. I have spoken to some forest creatures this morning and was told those beasties have not tried to enter again, they have disappeared the way they came, back down that hole. Their appearance though, means trouble is brewing. What I saw yesterday, fills me with a dread of the world the like of which I never had before. I wonder if I should find out what is happening, but I am not sure if I want too." She looked emphatically at the door Janorra was hidden behind. Janorra pulled back.

362

"It is Janorra they seek. But why? Is it possible she is the one who could read the third part of the Murien I found? I do wonder?"

*I can read it, and I am curious, but I have enough trouble in finding the Simal, without getting involved in reading a text to solve the curiosity of a dwarf, even though such an opportunity may never come my way again. A Murien is so very rare, could it be connected to the Simal arriving here?*

Gilly paused for thought, and Janorra could tell the dwarf was feeling the dilemma of the situation.

"This is way beyond me. After speaking with Muro, and reading that text with him last night, it is not just a rare Murien, but something much more. I wish I had never found it, nor got involved with all of this."

Janorra again chanced peering through the crack in the door.

Sasna looked at Muro and then back at Gilly. "Seesnari is in deep trouble unless I fulfil my mission, I must be about that business now. I have wasted enough time on that text, and now abandon that path, at least Farir and I agree on that. It is folly for me to be involved any further with the Murien. It took me near on a year to find a Davari who could read it for you, and it is now causing nothing but trouble." She paused. "You still owe me Gilly, a lot. Pay me for the Davari, more than we agreed. But, as part payment, I will also consider you escorting me to Berecoth through those tunnels as part of what you owe me."

Gilly closed her eyes. "I feel current business in the Wytchwood requires my attention, more than you know, me dear."

Sasna was forceful when she replied. "I implore you! The Bruthon prepare for war against my people, the fate of the Seesnari may depend upon the success of my mission."

"Well, maybe I could spare a day or two, me dear," Gilly said, clearly considering the proposal. "The Wychtwood is more than able to look after itself without my help, for a day or so, and I need time to think."

Janorra decided it was time to enter the room. Pushing the door open fully wide, she stepped inside.

Gilly, who had returned to stirring the pot, turned her head towards Janorra, smiled and said, "Good morning me dear, come in, do come in. Did you sleep well? You look refreshed."

Janorra did not answer, she did feel refreshed, but was in no mood for small talk. She gladly took the pot of stew dished up for her by Gilly, who then dished more up and handed a bowl to each of the other occupants of the room. The stew was different than the delicious one she had eaten the night before, but smelt just as tasty. It was a creamy white, thick with leeks, carrots, mushrooms and other vegetables Janorra did not know, but she was glad for it. After blowing on it to cool it, she spooned it up gratefully. It was the sort of stew that invigorated the body.

They ate in uncomfortable silence, until, perhaps sensing the mood Gilly suddenly said, "I shall play for you all whilst we eat." She walked over to where a small lute was hanging on a wall. Taking the instrument, she plucked the strings and began to sing. Her voice was soft, delicate, beautiful, and it seemed as though the tree itself responded to her song, as the leaves outside whispered and the boughs squeaked.

> *"A gold-bright sun, shone in the sky*
> *It was the day, we said goodbye*
> *My love he came, my love he left*
> *To war he went, and I to bed.*

*A gold-bright sun, shone in the sky*
*the day they told me, my love had died.*
*The drums they rolled, the trumpets blast*
*the clash of steel, and he breathed his last.*

*A gold-bright sun, shone in the sky*
*when his body home, they brought to lie.*
*My tears they flowed, my heart did burst,*
*my love was gone, my last and first.*

*A gold-bright sun, shines in the sky,*
*It is today, that I shall die*
*my tears are dry, my heart is free*
*I go to my love, he comes to me."*

Janorra felt the music and words in her breast. They were charged with sounds that made her feel so suddenly aware of herself. She felt her own body and its needs, and was glad that she had taken the time to rest. She listened with intense stillness as Gilly sang again, this time she sang a song about blissful meadows and softly flowing streams.

When they had all finished their meal, Gilly finished her song and put the lute away. She then collected the bowls and spoons, emptying the leftovers into a bucket and placing the bowls into a sink filled with water, where she rinsed them clean. After that she poured water and put a selection of more vegetables into another pot, added some spices and herbs, put it over the fire where the other pot had been and began to stir it with a large ladle. "It seems we will all have a busy day, I will make soup to take on whatever journeys we must go on," she said.

Janorra considered her options. Whatever she chose, she could not linger any longer in the Wisdom Tree. *I must warn these people about what they are now involved in. They will either assist me, or must let me go about my business, alone.* "Gilly, I heard your discussion with Sasna," she said. "As urgent as her business may be, mine is more so. You must assist me in reclaiming the items I have lost in the forest." Janorra ignored the angry look Sasna cast her way.

Janorra noticed that Muro was staring intently at her, and it made her feel uncomfortable.

Gilly smiled knowingly. "Oh, you won't need me to accompany you on that journey, me dear, the forest friends have already helped you. This shows they favour you and I am confident this means they will surely help you again."

Janorra looked suspiciously at the dwarf. "Where was their help when that spider slew me and cocooned what is now the corpse of my last body? I have a ring, an object I need, still on that corpse. I must reclaim that and another item I have lost, an item an associate now carries. She cannot transport it safely, as she is not trained to do so, and I fear for the fate of both her and the item."

"Hmm, most creatures in the forest, me dear, avoid the area where old Uilisomor lives. They usually won't bother her or interfere in her affairs. She rids the forest of maggots, stingwing flies and other fouler things that would otherwise be a constant pest if not for her. She is left alone where she dwells, and is given much respect."

"These forest friends you speak of will not help me recover my items?"

"Oh, they might, as long as you do not intend harming old Uilisomor. But, tell me, me dear. What is the other item you have lost – it must surely be connected to the sudden appearance of these Bantu beasties that have appeared? Martha, the dear tree we rest within, was very clear that it is you they hunt, I saw it in the archive whilst you slept." Gilly scratched her head. "This is so confusing. Will you not tell where you are from and why these items are so important to you?"

Janorra was still aware that Muro still fixed his gaze upon her.

If she was to secure Gilly's help, Janorra felt she should not be too evasive. Besides, the nagging thought that the appearance of a Murien, might somehow be connected to the Simal bringing her here, was growing. She needed answers herself, so had to offer some in return.

*I do not want to endanger these folks any more than I already have.* "The less you know, the better it is for you. Help me find my items, and I can be on my way out of this forest."

"It would help if those who assist you knew what they were looking for, me dear," Gilly answered.

Janorra felt flustered. "You don't understand what you are getting involved in. You have been thrown into events whose beginnings predate the world itself. Even I, only dimly glimpse the hidden powers at work, but with or without hope, I must continue. Beyond the assistance already given, and helping me retrieve my lost items, you need not involve yourselves beyond that."

"If that is true, me dear, which I do not doubt, then you owe it to us to inform us of any peril we are in," Gilly said.

Muro spoke. "The runes showed me in my dreams that very soon, the third one needed to read the Murien will be revealed. Answer me directly, can you read the language of the dead, Báith Rahmèra?"

It felt as though an icy chill filled the room. Sasna pointed challengingly at Janorra, "There was some diabolical ritual she carried out at Castle Greytears. She spoke a strange, haunting language. Do you dare to deny it?"

Janorra felt in a quandary. It was true, she could read Báith Rahmèra, but she feared such a text as a Murien, and what it might reveal. However, she could not deny she spoke Báith Rahmèra, both Sasna and Scarand had witnessed her speak it.

"It is your destiny, along with that of mine and the dwarf, to read the text," Muro said, as Janorra considered her options. "The fates have brought us together for this very purpose. It is the will of Yig."

Janorra closed her eyes and bit her lip, and then finally admitted, "Yes, I can read Báith Rahmèra."

Muro sat there expressionless as he still stared at Janorra. "But, will you?" he asked.

"I fear events might be connected," Janorra replied, "but you would not want to involve yourself any further with the business I am in, were you to know about it. You would do better to walk away, and live without knowing the burden I now carry."

"Well, we are already involved, to some degree, me dear, so perhaps you will tell us your tale, and then we can choose what we do with any knowledge you furnish us with, me dear." Gilly smiled kindly and with sincerity.

*What choice do I have but to tell them?* "I have lost *Arnazia*, my Seers' Ring. I am an Aeldar Seeress, from Kappia. The object I have lost is an artefact that I must find, lest it fall into the wrong hands." Janorra noticed that the word Kappia drew Scarand's attention and interest, as well as Gillys, but the latter continued talking to her.

"Now what would an Aeldar Seeress be doing in these parts? I can't help but think, what with Muro showing up, your appearance is also connected to this text. I do wonder? You might be able to answer some questions, me dear."

"As can you," Janorra replied, as she looked quizzically at Gilly, at Muro and then back at Gilly again. "My knowledge and memories have almost fully returned, and I am well learned in matters relating to Murien texts. You say you can read it? Then you must be a Reisic Dwarf and he a Ruik Priest? Only the Ruik can read Rokkan, and only the Reisic Sangdalen, and the knowledge of Báith Rahmèra is a closely guarded secret of the Mystery Schools, taught to only a very few. Together we can read this text, aloud, and then the Murien words will be revealed, an ancient tongue I do not know. A fourth will be needed, who can read and understand Murien."

"My interest in the text was scholarly only, me dears," Gilly said. "I did not know it might be the cause of all this trouble. But, me dear, I now fear that text is no mere rare Murien. It is something more, much more. I never really expected a Ruik would actually show up, let alone shortly afterwards a Pure-blood who speaks Báith Rahmèra. What else can this mean, except the text wants to be read?"

"Half-truths do not sit well on the lips of your kind," Janorra replied. "There is more to your interest in such a text than a mere academic one."

Gilly blushed. "Very well, me dear. I will tell you the truth of my part in this, if you tell me that of yours," she said, "for I dread that I might now be involved in something far bigger than I intended when I sought a Davari who might read this text with me."

Janorra glanced at Sasna, Farir and then at Scarand before saying to Gilly. "Some conversations are best held, when only those who need to know are present."

Gilly sighed, "You are quite right, me dear." She then looked in turn at Scarand, Farir and then Sasna. "Would you mind leaving, me dears?"

Sasna's face winced with suspicion. "Do I not at the least deserve to know the reason why you have had me search this last year, to find for you one who could read that text?" She pointed at Muro. "He is still my slave, until you pay me, he does not belong to you!"

Farir groaned with frustration, and with more than a hint of desperation in his voice moaned, "Sasna, let us just be done with this business now, it has caused us nothing but trouble."

Still holding a ladle, Gilly left the cooking pot, took a pouch out of her pocket and handed it over to Sasna, who opened it, her eyes widening in wonder at the contents. She showed the contents of the pouch to Farir. His dejected look changed in an instant to one of wonder. He whistled in the air, clearly impressed at what he was looking at – a bag full of a variety of sparkling jewels and rare gold coins.

"Where did you get so many jewels?" Sasna asked as she took a glittering diamond from the pouch and examined it, and then a large red ruby.

"That is my business, me dear," Gilly responded. "They are of the finest quality, and worth more than I promised you in payment, and add to that my promise to now escort you safely to the entrance to the tunnels that lead to Berecoth."

Gilly returned to the cooking pot to commence stirring, and looking at Sasna, said. "Now, me dear, I will shortly escort you safely to the tunnels, and provide you with a map to navigate them, but this business I have with Janorra and Muro, need not be your concern, any further." She looked at Farir for support.

"Agreed, the payment is more than ample reward for my sister's efforts in finding you Muro," Farir declared as he stood up, and pulling Sasna to her feet by the arm said to her, "our involvement in this particular matter is done. If you seem intent on going to Berecoth and then on to the Sea Lords, against my better judgement, I will go with you." He then cast a disapproving look Scarand's way. "Come, slave, you can finally prove yourself useful and carry any supplies we take."

Scarand stared at Farir, and Gilly noticed a beast like ferocity in his gaze.

"You promised to help me find Marciea and Oliviana, in return for the assistance I gave you to get to the castle," Scarand said icily to Sasna. "I demand my freedom."

"How dare you speak to us like that," Farir protested.

Sasna pulled away from Farir's grasp, walked over to Scarand and handed him a letter and said, "I have appreciated your help. I have no seal or official papers on me, but I have written and signed a letter stating, that for services given, I grant you your freedom. Show it at the city hall in Ashgiliath if you can get there, they will arrange the alteration of your branding and give you the correct papers to show you are now a free man. If they give you trouble or delay the process, wait for my return, when I will push it through with all speed." She took another piece of parchment from her pocket and handed it to him. On unfolding it, Janorra saw that she had given him a map.

"It is crude and basic," Sasna said, "and shows none of the terrain features, for I am no cartographer, but on waking this morning, I drew you this map. It might help you find your way to Ashgiliath, where you can obtain a more detailed map, and can plan your journey with care. If they still breathe air, this map shows the location of the city where your sister and your betrothed are likely to be found." She looked at Janorra. "This woman is from Kappia, where your sisters are probably held. It might be that your path is now connected to hers, for a time." She then offered Scarand the diamond she was still holding. "Once you have your papers showing you are free, sell this to Hagrand the Jeweller whose shop is in Trader Street in Ashgiliath. Accept no less than gold sesna coin worth one thousand. That will not only cover the cost of the purchase of the women you seek, it will equip you and fund your journey. If your quest is successful, it will give you the power to choose your own path to follow when you have found them."

"Sister, that is too generous, he is just a slave," Farir protested.

"He saved my life," Sasna replied cuttingly to him, "and for that, I am grateful and consider his service complete, and my debt to him paid."

Sasna looked at Scarand. "I can aid you no further at this time, but want to know, do you also consider my debt to you settled? I have gifted you your freedom, and given you wealth to assist you in your quest."

Scarand took the diamond, and looking at it, said, "I do not thank you for giving back to me the freedom that was always mine, until taken from me, but for this map and this jewel, I do. I consider your promise fulfilled."

Sasna touched Scarand's forearm warmly, causing Farir to blurt out, "Sister, what madness has overcome you? He is a slave!"

Sasna ignored him, and whispered softly to Scarand, "I have been shown little kindness and trust in this world. You, have shown me both, and it confuses me, for you are Davari. I have learnt that when we are trusted, we ourselves become more trustworthy. My promise to you is true. You are free."

Janorra thought she saw an awkward moment of affection between the two of them, and Sasna quickly withdrew her hand as though it was in a fireplace.

Scarand acknowledged with a nod. "It seems that people think that we Davari only like war and violence. I cannot speak for all of my kind, but I only love that which such methods need often defend. If we meet again, I have no grudge to bear you."

"Then fare you well, Davari," Sasna said, and then added, "the saying *never trust a Seesnari*, does not always hold truth."

For a moment, Janorra was certain she saw emotion and sadness in Scarand's eyes as Sasna left the room with her brother. *He's a fool if he feels emotion for that one, she would never return such a love,* she thought to herself. *Her revulsion for slaves runs too deep.*

Gilly turned to Scarand, her tone was soft and gentle when she spoke. "You need to leave as well, me dear, this business we discuss, is not for you."

Scarand frowned, and looking at the map asked, "Will I be allowed to wander through the forest and make my way in peace to Ashgiliath?"

Janorra answered him, before Gilly could. "You still have the brand of a slave, even if you are free. If you try to travel any lands alone, even to Ashgiliath, without the escort of a free person, you will be lynched if caught, and that letter will not save you; and that map will be but a poor guide. Your best path would have been for you to travel with the Seesnari, your hope being that one day they returned with you to Ashgiliath. You need the help of a free person, so there is another path for you to choose…"

Scarand looked at her quizzically.

"You have proven yourself to be strong and brave. Assist me in retrieving the items I have lost, for I need to find a way to Baothein lands and my best chance is to find a ship at Ashgiliath to take me. I will escort you there, in return for any assistance you offer to me."

"Then his path is now with us, and he will need to know the danger of it," Muro said ferociously, speaking for the first time. "If we must be jabbering, then let us be about the business of the text. The runes have sent me for this purpose alone, and no other cause now concerns me. Let us each speak, and learn of each other's part in this matter."

"Very well, Scarand, you may stay, me dear," Gilly said. Looking at the others, she began her account. "I shall tell the first tale, and speak of my part in this." She put the ladle down, and sat on a stool. "I was Reisic, a worshipper of the Giant Bothgar as was my mother, grandmother and theirs before them. The Way of the Reisic, has been passed down to very few, and I am one who knows the mysteries of it and can speak and read the sacred Sangdalen texts, but only together with a Ruik and a speaker of Báith Rahmèra can we read a Murien, for the secret language to be revealed." She breathed, and swallowed hard. It occurred to Janorra that painful memories were returning to Gilly. "Most Dwarves worship the legendary giant they call Old Balagrim, but Reisic follow the teaching of Bothgar, whose mother was Yag, and for that our way and tradition is banned by the Dwarven Balagrim priests, for we practice lore and magic, and that is forbidden by them."

Janorra knew the story of *The Terrible Ones,* Yag, Yig and Yog, or *The Three Wise Sisters,* as some called them. She was tempted to tell it, but remained quiet as Gilly wiped away the tears that rolled down her face. When she had composed herself, she continued. "My mother died when I was a young girl, so I was raised by my grandmother. When it was discovered we were Reisic, we were banished from the Iron Mountains, and told we could only return on two conditions. The first, we were to renounce the way of the Reisic. The second condition, in our wanderings we were to search for one of the lost Sangdalen texts, and return it to the Iron Library in our mountain homeland. We are not the only ones who can read Sangdalen, the priestly cast can, though they will not touch a Murien, for such texts are banned among my kind for the language of Báith Rahmèra is feared by them. Those were the conditions by which we could return." She wiped away another tear that rolled down her cheek. "Without success, I have searched far and wide for a lost Sangdalen and this Murien was the nearest I came. I have left behind and renounced the way of the Reisic, for I have now learnt Elven mysteries, and seen that the way of the Reisic is limiting and too dark for my liking." She sighed deeply. "I have knowledge aplenty, but now, I yearn for the company of my own kind, and wish to return home, but without a Sangdalen, I cannot."

"You may have renounced the way of the Reisic, but the way has not renounced you," Muro grumbled. "The Murien came into your possession, for a reason, now continue your tale, without the self-pity."

Gilly nodded, and continued, speaking with a hint of resignation that showed she had accepted her fate. "My grandmother died on our journey from the Iron Mountains to the Everglow, the telling of which must wait for another time. I entered the Everglow by way of Ashgiliath, and there I bought me Gaffren. We crossed the Erin and wandered east from there. We came upon bandits who chased us, but when we fled into the Wytchwood to escape them, they did not follow. Hence, it was by chance I came to the Wytchwood. Many days I was lost, roaming the forest, unable to find my way out of it, for the very forest paths seemed to shift and change before and behind me. By chance, or by design of the forest, I came upon this tree and entered it, and made it my home. I named her Martha." She smiled fondly at her surroundings. "I felt a deep connection to her, and through Martha, I learned to speak to the forest, and to hear it. I have now spent many years studying the lore of this place, and explored the lands around and about. That is how I found the ancient dwarf tunnels that I will lead Sasna through, in which I searched deep and long, looking for a Sangdalen, so that I might return home. Instead, I found much treasure, the like of which I just gave to Sasna, but I never found a Sangdalen text. But I did find something worth much more, and recognised it for what it was – a Murien." She sighed. "I was hoping it might give me a clue where to find an uncontaminated Sangdalen text, or I might swap it for one, but those at the markets of Ashgiliath told me it was probably a fake. Knowing Sasna likes gold and fine jewels, on the promise of such, I asked her to search for a Davari who could read the text, for without such, a Murien was useless to me."

Gilly looked at each companion, in turn and admitted, "I had quite forgotten about it, until Sasna sent me message she had found a Davari who claimed he could read it." Her face turned ashen. "I am now quite worried, me dears, for I fear my finding that text, is leading to a chain of events beyond my control, beyond the control of any of us." She took a few deep breaths, and addressing Janorra, continued. "Your appearance, and the fact you can read Báith Rahmèra, has come as quite a shock to me."

Gilly looked over at Muro. "What now sends terror through me, delights him. I am afraid that what is coming upon the world is darkness and chaos, and I now believe my kind were right to lock themselves away from the events of this time and age, for whatever this text says, it cannot bode well for the world." She stared at Janorra and said firmly but compassionately. "It is all connected. Your appearance, me dear, cannot be an accident."

Janorra felt her own face turn ashen, and she shook with fear and gagged with nausea. *I had no idea, when I stole the Simal, that this was the path I would find myself on. My role was only to take it, and hand it over to the Whitebeards of the Baothein.*

"I am afraid to read it," she confessed, with a trembling voice, "for I fear I know what it will reveal." *I did not realise what jeopardy I would put myself and the world in, but now, I am starting to see I did not bring the Simal here – it used me and brought itself. I must seek to amend the situation, for nowhere outside of Baothein lands is safe for me now, and they might not let me enter without the Simal.*

Gilly spoke with deep solemnity. "I have read the Sangdalen on the Murien, but Muro refused to read it until the third person was revealed. I fear that time is now. Together, we must read it, and tell each us what we know, me dears, for we have come this far and the rest of the text must be read – by you two!"

Janorra closed her eyes for a few moments, thoughts racing rapidly through her mind. *Only the Baothein can protect me but I cannot go to them absent of the Simal, for they will not give me the sanctuary I seek if I do not have it when I go to them. I fear the text will tell me where to go, and it may be a place I fear to tread."*

She decided, the best choice she could make right then, was to tell those present what she had done, and her part in stealing the Simal. *It is all connected, after all?*

369

With great emotion, Janorra gave a full account of how she and Azzadan had stolen the Simal, how Ahrimakan was possibly slain, and the events that led to that very moment of her recounting the tale. "The Simal is here in the Wytchwood, in the hands of the young Sezareal, but madness has taken a hold of her, for she gazed into it. She may have unwittingly taken it to those whom the Simal seeks. I now suspect I know who it was seeking, and has found them. I fear our reading of the Murien text will confirm that which I fear most, and what I must do."

She looked at Gilly and felt only desperation, "Now you know why my mission is so urgent – the fate of the world as we know it depends upon the success of it. I do not understand how the Bantu have entered the Everglow, or their part in this, only that their presence in the Everglow is only possible if the great guardian city of Aleskian has fallen. It cannot be by mere chance they appear at this time as well. They hunt me thinking I still have the Simal, of that I have no doubt. I can think of no other explanation for their appearance." Looking at Muro, she asked, "But what is it that he seeks and what motive is his for being sent to read the Murien?"

A dark and moody expression was on Muro's face, as he sat there with his eyes closed, rocking to and thro as though meditating.

"Can we trust him?" Janorra asked, momentarily forgetting he could hear her.

Muro opened his eyes; they were dark and filled with an angry foreboding when he looked at Janorra. It sent a shiver down her spine when he cast them upon her with a fixed gaze.

"At the castle, speaking Báith Rahmèra, Sasna told me last night you raised a dead man?" he then glanced at Scarand. "You can confirm this?"

"Ask her, I trust her to speak the truth, and if she chooses silence, then decipher that as you will," Scarand answered moodily. "I care for nothing except finding my sisters."

"You are not the only one with such power," Muro said to Janorra.

"The power used was not mine, the knowledge of how to do it was. The Obelisk Otan let me use his power," she answered.

Muro nodded his head slowly, in acknowledgement. "We Ruik, know that some Seers possess a knowledge that can only be acquired by the dead, and we envy you for it. You can learn it for yourself in the Deadlands, then rise again, to use that knowledge in the land of the living. That, we Ruik cannot do, but we too can see into the Deadlands, and speak to the dead, but we use the tongue of Rokkan."

Janorra noticed that Gilly was visibly shocked by the revelation about the dead.

Muro grunted a laugh to himself and then continued. "We have forests of hanging trees, and can use the men and women we hang upon them, to see into the Deadlands through their eyes, to use their spiritual bodies for a short spell of time, or to raise their physical ones for a few minutes to force them to speak to us. It takes much blood sacrifice, prior to us being able to perform this rite on the hanged. I am one of the few with this gift."

"*The Terrible Ones*, are your goddess'," Janorra whispered, recalling what she had read long ago about the Ruik.

"We Ruik call them *The Three Wise Sisters*, Yag, Yig and Yog." Muro smiled sadistically. "Yag gave birth to the giant, Bothgar, in a time now forgotten. Yig, spoke to the Giant Rithguar, and gave him a prophecy, the knowledge of which she soon forgot. Bothgar slew Rithguar, but even in death, Rithguar did not let go of the sacred pages that he had written down. Bothgar managed to tear from him only the last page. It was he, Yag's son, who stole the last page of the Rithguar, our sacred text. Yag wanted to show Bothgar mercy, Yig wanted to slay him. They had a dreadful fight, until Yog intervened." Muro grinned demonically. "Yog was sent to find Bothgar and return the last page of the *Prophecy of Rithguar.*"

"But Rithguar gave the prophecy to the Seraphim Migdal," Janorra said, finishing for him, "and Yog never returned."

"Yig has spoken to me through the written runes, gifted me with the power of eighteen runes, and promised me much more, if I find Yog, and with her help return the last page of the prophecy to the Ruik." Muro held up his hands, and the runes in them changed colours. "I have the power to cast fire and ice, to heal, to blunt and change steel, to thwart evil intentions, quench flames and calm stormy waters. I can confuse witches and speak to hanged men, bend people to my will and even seduce women." He stood, and seemed to grow in stature and became terrible for Janorra to behold as he took a step towards her, reaching out his hand. A light shone from the rune in his hand, and of a sudden she was overcome with an insatiable desire for Muro to take her. She tried to fight it, but the sensation was too strong. The lust and desire left her, when Muro lowered his hand, smiled cruelly, and sat down again, becoming of normal appearance which was frightening of its own. Janorra felt humiliated by the experience, and resented him for subjecting her to it.

"The runes showed me that Yog has long been here, in this forest, waiting for this time," Muro said. "My tradition states she lives in a palace of ice and rock."

Gilly nearly fell off her stool in surprise. "Here, in this forest? Well, me dear, the climate is too hot for a palace of ice to exist here. It would melt."

Muro ignored her; his focus was solely upon Janorra. "The text revealed, is a language older than time. It will show me where Yog dwells. I believe she is the fourth one, who will read the Murien. I must speak to her. Willingly or unwillingly, you will read it, and there we will go, and both find that which we seek." He turned and looked at Gilly. "You will lead us through the forest, for your assistance might be required," he ordered.

"I promised to lead Sasna through the tunnels to Berecoth, me dear," she stammered.

Muro replied, "That foolish Seesnari woman has been but a puppet in the hands of powers far greater than she knows. Her part in this is done. I have released her to whatever folly she next engages in. Your part is not yet completed, for the nature of a Murien is to reveal more, at a time of its own choosing, and your part may not be complete."

"Me dear, I do not lightly abandon a promise," Gilly replied, composing herself. "I have offered to show her a safe passage to Berecoth, and that I shall do."

Muro raised his hands, and moved one in a circle.

"That silly trick won't work on me, me dear," Gilly said scolding him. "My Bena birds will guide Janorra to reclaim her items. I will help Sasna, and then I shall return and join you all, and go where the Murien guides us, for although fear and regret now dance on my soul, I will play my part in this to the end."

"Then take her to this safe passage, if you must," Muro barked, "but return swiftly." He looked again at Janorra. "Yog will know where Migdal dwells, he has what I seek. Now, the last part must be done. We must read the text!"

A thousand thoughts raced through Janorra's mind; her darkest fears were confirmed. *He mentions Migdal? Then my fears are right, the Simal has come here to find the Aeldar Wives. But I did not know that this Yog he speaks of also dwells here? It must have been her I sensed in the Deadlands, but she was not the only foul presence.* Without thought, and more as a reaction, Janorra blurted out, "Then let us read this cursed text, and learn the path we must now tread." *I have no choice — I can see no other way.*

371

"I put it in there," Gilly said, as she pointed to a drawer, "but I do not wish to touch or gaze upon it again, although I know I must."

Muro stood, walked over and opened the drawer, but he paused a moment, looking with concern at the contents of the draw. Instead of taking out the Murien text, he removed the Bantu arrow, sniffed it and examined it. "Where did you get this?" he asked, angrily. His initial reaction soon changed, and a look of grave concern spread across his features, as he then said, "It was foolish of you to carry this into your home."

"One of the Bantu fired it at us," Scarand answered for Gilly. He stood, and caught the arrow as Muro threw it to him.

"You are a hunter, a bowman, what do you make of it?" Muro asked sourly.

Scarand examined the arrow Gilly had retrieved from the tree. Janorra watched as he carefully turned it, holding it by the shaft and black feathers. He also sniffed it, and turned his nose up at the smell. "I've never seen the like before. We need to be careful with this," he said, "the tip is covered with a foul poison, and a dark magic. I can smell it and sense it, just the holding of it causes me unease."

"Then put it away again me dear," Gilly said.

"No, it must leave this place. It must be broken, and buried, lest those who own it find a way into your very home," Muro sternly said, as he looked around in a way one might who expected an intruder at any moment. "My people have a saying that, *evil things call out to their evil masters.*" He cast a look of disgust at Scarand. "This fool should have warned you of this, but he did not, and he cannot be trusted with the task of disposing of it. It must leave this forest, immediately! Take it, dwarf, and bury it near the tunnels when the time is right."

Gilly put her face in her hands and shook her head. "Oh dear, me dears, oh dear," she said. Scarand wrapped the arrow in a cloth and handed her the arrow, and scowled at Muro, who took the Murien text out of the drawer and handed it to Janorra.

"We have no more time to waste," Muro said. "We are not the only ones who seek what we seek. We must read it!"

All the people in the room gathered around the table as Janorra took the text from Muro, undid the ribbon that bound it, opened it and spread it out upon the table. It lay flat, without curling back up into a roll. Gilly covered her eyes as Janorra studied it. There were words upon it in Rokkan and Sangdalen, and the runes at the bottom. "You must both speak, in turn, exactly the words you see. First you, Muro, then you Gilly, and then I shall read my part, and the runes will reveal the Murien.

Muro looked at the Murien, and said the words in Rokkan, "*Mihioath forendaki Yog hakmak? Ti ensonderi komalias om taradris muka, to okkeaus drek or krakes salk dreek? Mihioath forendaki Yog hakmak?*" Which, when translated means, 'Where does Yog dwell? In forest green or forest deep, in ocean depths or caves that weep? Where does Yog dwell?

Gilly spoke the words of the Sangdalen, the words of which were sweet to the ear and meant, 'Where does Silverberry dwell? In mountains high or deep, in town or keep, we seek, where Silverberry does dwell?'

Janorra spoke the words written in Báith Rahmèra, and as she began to speak, the Wisdom Tree itself creaked and seemed to groan in horror that such words were being spoken within its very trunk. The candles flickered as though in a mighty wind, and went out, and then reignited of themselves when she had finished. The meaning of the words Janorra spoke are thus: "In what realm does the thirdborn now dwell, where in the Nine Worlds is the third sister of *The Terrible Ones?*"

The runes on the page moved, and more words were revealed upon the Murien, but written in a tongue that was neither Rokkan, Sangdalen or Báith Rahmèra. The style of writing that appeared, the stroke of the letters and shape of the words, made all who

372

looked upon them tremble and feel sick at the sight of them, for they were not from this world. Gilly covered her eyes with her hands.

Other familiar words took form on the page. "Musho," Muro said, as a word in Rokkan appeared. "You must keep reading," he impatiently urged Gilly.

Briefly uncovering her eyes, and with a stammer in her voice, Gilly read aloud the Sangdalen word that had appeared, "*Maranth*," she said.

A word in Báith Rahmèra appeared on the text, and Janorra uttered it. "Frearso."

Replacing what was formerly written on there, a crude glowing map appeared upon the parchment, of a location somewhere in the Wytchwood.

"Do you know this place?" Janorra asked Gilly, who, peeking through her hands, looked at the parchment.

"That is in the forbidden part of the forest, where the second Wisdom Tree, Mithilos, dwells. The forest has always warned me not to go there."

"The map of the location only appeared when we spoke the words," Janorra said as she then turned her attention to another word, in Báith Rahmèra, that had appeared. She studiously looked at it. "This is a very rare word," she whispered, and then she spoke it, very quietly. "Frorako." Previously hidden letters appeared on the page and began to glow brightly.

Muro's demeanour changed, the solemn moodiness left him as he gasped with delight, looking at the parchment with wide-eyed awe. "Is this Murien? What does it say?" he asked excitedly.

"I fear these are indeed Murien words," Janorra said. "It is a tongue rarely spoken in the Everglow. Few have uttered such words since the Age of the Titans. None of us can interpret these words, and know their meaning."

"Look!" Muro said, pointing at the text.

Everybody in the room gasped as two hands made of a pure azure and white light, slowly formed in the text and then reached out, touching Janorra on the forehead. A mixture of emotions swept across her face in a single moment: terror; calm; excitement; peace, and then sheer ecstatic delight. The azure and white light filled her eyes and shone from her mouth as well. "I feel everything," she said in an angelic voice not of this world, as she saw visions of time and eternity. "I see what is, what was and all possibilities of what could be." A pure light filled her, as she spoke in a spectral voice. "Everything must come to ash and dust: the sun; moon, day and night. All except time itself will be vanquished. Every particle of existence will change, from one form to another and all will end as ash and dust before the new comes."

"Make it stop," Gilly said as she pointed at Janorra. "Make it stop!" She grabbed her head in her hands and winced as though in great pain, as did the others.

"Everything comes to ash and dust!" Janorra shouted, after which the spell of the text was broken. In an instance, the light left her, the hands withdrew back and Janorra stood there looking at the others in the room. They did not appear to be in pain anymore.

Gilly was the first to speak. "What just happened?" she asked nervously.

Janorra was tremoring when she spoke. "We must go to where the map showed us, to the forbidden part of the forest. The fourth one who must read this, dwells there. She must read the text. She will show us where we need to go."

"Yog," Muro said, with devilish delight. He gasped with ecstasy. "She dwells in a palace of ice and rock. We must leave, go to her, now," he said.

Janorra continued. "I saw the Wild Hunt, Norvaskun is their ship, which the Elves once used to sail upon the roof of the Labyrinth along the ancient waterways. As we speak, the Wild Hunt use this stolen vessel to row upon the waters of the Underglow.

373

They are searching, looking for places where their moleworms, who swim with them, can burrow through to the surface, near to us. They are seeking a way to find me, to enter the Wytchwood, but cannot for now." She pointed to the arrow Gilly carried. "Some of them remain above ground. They are tracking that arrow on foot."

"Then we must burn it," Scarand said.

Janorra shook her head. "It has a dark charm on it, it will still lead them here, after it is destroyed." She turned and looked at Gilly. "Gilly, you must take it with all swiftness outside of the Wytchwood, lead them away from here, but the Bantu will come for you. Discard it before you get to the tunnels. You must then make all haste and get inside them, for their moleworms cannot burrow through stone. Some of them might pursue you on foot, and swift they are."

"How do you know all of this, you were shown?" Scarand asked.

"Yes. I also saw the paths we must tread, but not the outcome," Janorra replied. "If the arrow stays with us, they will enter the Wytchwood. If it is taken outside, they will still find a way, but it will take them longer."

"What else did you see?" Gilly asked.

"I saw that the ancient city of Aleskian, guardian of the Great Northern Wall has been destroyed. The Bantu slaughtered the Obelisk there, and great was its suffering. So great was the fire and the destruction of the city and the Obelisk, a cloud of ash blacked out the sun and the moon. The place that was once Aleskian is still covered in darkness, as the dust of that once great city blows away in the wind." She gritted her teeth, trying to find the courage to say the next words. "That is why the Bantu can now enter the Everglow. I am indeed the prey they hunt." She felt a chill on the back of her neck, and looked worryingly at those in the room. "We do not have time to linger. The Bantu were able to enter the outskirts of the Wytchwood, but the power of the forest has kept them from entering further. The forest grows weaker, as dark magic now works against it, and it will not be able to stop them indefinitely from re-entering. The longer that arrows stays within it, the faster the forest will weaken. They are coming!"

Muro took the Murien, rolled it up and tied it with the ribbon, before putting it into the leather pouch and then inside a pocket on his clothing. "We have read the Murien text, that is why the runes have sent me," he said pragmatically, and then with a force and authority that invited no debate, looking at Janorra he declared, "I will follow you, Janorra, you will take me to Yog. I shall do as you command, until we reach there. Your fear is strong, but you have been sent. We are allies, who, for now, must walk upon the same path."

"I too shall come," Scarand said, "for it seems, I also, have but little choice than to follow the same path. For now."

Gilly went the corner of the room, where, leant against the wall was a large Elven bow and a quiver full of arrows. She took the bow and arrows and gave them to Scarand. "It's too big for me to use, me dear," she said, "and I doubt the original owner will come back for them, so I fetched the bow and arrows from the armoury last night. I think those arrows fired from that bow, will be quite formidable, even against the foes we face. They are yours."

Scarand looked stunned as he took the bow and the arrows and admired the exquisite carvings and workmanship. "This is a rare and useful gift. I don't know what to say, apart from thank you," he said.

Gilly smiled in a way that said she knew it was the right thing to do. Janorra looked at her and urged, "We must tarry here no longer. I now have friends and allies in a place I did not expect to find them, hope refreshes me. Lead me to the friends you say will lead me through the forest to reclaim *Arnazia*. Take the Bantu arrow, discard it outside

374

of the Wytchwood and lead Sasna and her brother to Berecoth, for I saw that a terrible war is coming, and they have a role to play in the events to come."

Gilly nodded. "Very well, me dear. I think the Spriggan are the ones to help us if we are to go into the forbidden part of the forest, where this Yog dwells. I will send them word, through forest ways."

Janorra nodded. "You must then join us, as soon as you can. We need you to speak to the forest on our account, and to guide us through it. It might also be, you are given warning if the Bantu find a way in."

Gilly nodded again. "I will bottle the soup, so that we can each take some with us. It will give us strength, me dears, when we feel weak. Take anything else you might need, but be in haste. We must leave soon. It is good I had the sense earlier to bake a cake. Without it, my Bena birds might get stubborn and refuse to help you."

# Chapter Thirty-One: *King Falamore*

*When Cyrion the Targon held a knife at her throat, Queen Valaryas taunted him. "You are weak man, the last of a weak bloodline soon to be forgotten. You lack the courage, so put down the knife, I shall forgive you, and we will speak of this no more, for no deed of any from the House of Targon shall ever be remembered." Those were the last words she ever spoke.*
*Temmison Vol IV, Book 2: History of the Kings and Queens of the Tarenmoors.*

*Never in my life, have I met a man with as much flatulence as King Falamore of Thurog Tor.*
*An anecdote from the keynote speaker at a dinner given for merchants in Berecoth.*

*The* crowd parted as Marki, Effgard and his men headed up the slope towards the summit, where the long hall of King Falamore the First stood, in the fortified hill city of Thurog Tor. The ride had been fast and hard, and all felt the signs of exhaustion, but Marki most of all, for his journey had been relentless since leaving Aleskian.

Two wooden columns flanked the arched doorway, their tops carved in the likeness of two wargs. An embroidered banner hung between them, sodden with rain and tattered with age, depicting a youthful warrior cutting off the head of a vicious looking warg. Two men guarded the heavy oak doors. The men were crudely armoured. Each had planted a large spear in the ground, atop which fluttered the same banner. They parted and opened the doors so that Effgard and Marki could enter. Effgard's men waited outside.

The Hall of Falamore was long and narrow, with an arcaded upper level. Smoke from lamps swinging in the rafters and the fire-pit in the centre of the hall created light smog in the air. Round shields, both wooden and metal, with a variety of shapes and colours on them hung from the barrier of the arcade alongside trophy heads of various animals such as stags, bears, wolves and wargs, which stared down into the hall. Lavish yet aged embroidery covered the ground floor walls. On one of the embroideries, Marki noticed that a woman, who was surrounded by ravens, stood in an ornate doorway, elaborately carved in a style he knew not the origins of; the doorposts on the embroidery were topped by wyverns; their wings were outstretched and from their heads sprouted long, flickering tongues. In the scene there was a naked giant, who was leaning from an adjacent tower, and caressing the woman on the cheek. A naked man, in the lower border of the embroidery, was lewdly gesturing up the woman's skirt.

"My sister, and her rumoured trysts with giants," Effgard said with mirth, when he noticed Marki looking at it. "Truth is, one of them would break her in two, but it amuses my brother to see her insulted in such a way."

Marki stared at the embroidery and tittered as he and Effgard passed it and then approached Falamore who was seated upon a large wooden throne atop a stepped dais, beneath which a woman was chained. Two guards, and two other men stood in front of Falamore.

"Yizain, the king's steward," Effgard said, pointing to a wiry middle-aged man with a thick black beard and a lazy eye, "and Hozain, his twin brother, the general of the army," he said, pointing to the other.

The resemblance in the brothers was remarkable. Marki could only tell them apart due to the fact that Yizain had a lazy right eye, whereas Hozain had a lazy left one.

Falamore smiled a crooked smile as Marki and Effgard came to a still beneath the dais. Dressed in the most incredible finery, he wore a long ermine cloak, the finery of which was only ruined, in that it was stained with the remnants of food and wine. Heavy gold earrings hung from his ears, and the crown he wore on top of his long red hair was ringed with the fangs of wargs. The grotesquely obese king was greedily gnawing on a haunch of meat. Grease and saliva dribbled down his long, red beard, which was flecked with grey. His appetite was so fierce and he indulged with such intenseness that the veins in his forehead swelled, and he dripped with perspiration, as he tore into the food. When he had chewed most of the meat from the bone, Falamore threw it to the floor. "Eat, my dogs!" he roared.

From under the long table that ran the length along one side of the hall, some pitiful, half-starved men dressed in tattered rags, scuttled out from underneath it. They had no feet, or hands, and their eyes had been removed. They moved awkwardly, scuttling about on their knees and the stubs of their arms, searching frantically for the bone until one of them found it. The others, on hearing him scuttle back to the table, followed and fought with him, to try to seize the bone from him. Falamore laughed hysterically at the sight.

"Seventeen kings and lords fight for the scraps beneath the table of Great King Falamore the Conqueror, who one day, will be the only King of the Tarenmoors," Yizain declared.

Falamore yanked the chain of the scantily-clad woman, no more than sixteen years of age, who was chained to the dais, near his feet. He spoke aggressively to her.

"Did you ever see such a sight in the hall of your mother? A dwarf has come to pay his respects and offer the service of a Kappian legion, to me! Did you ever see such a sight in your mother's hall?"

The young woman did not reply, but cast her sad eyes to the floor as Falamore laughed gustily and reached for a jewelled goblet, full of wine, being held on a tray by a serving wench. He drank lustily, red wine spilling over his fur-lined silk tunic, before soaking into his robes.

The two guards, both holding spears and shields, readied themselves and watched suspiciously as Marki reached the dais. They stood easy when Falamore mumbled something to them. He clapped his hands, and two young boys, no older than fifteen years each, appeared from behind the throne with a woman, who Marki assumed was their mother.

"Queen Blondel and the two sons she bore to Falamore," Effgard whispered, and noticing Marki's surprised expression added, "it's a long story. Over a cup sometime I will tell you how she ended up married to my brother."

The boys held onto Blondel's dress and huddled into her as they looked at Marki with suspicion and fear. Marki studied them both, and although they bore more the likeness of Yizain or Hozain than Falamore, he immediately dismissed the boys as unimportant; he could tell they had been raised in comfort and had no idea of war or loss. Both overweight and dressed well, they were clearly pampered princes not yet weaned from their mother's side. Their uncle, King Effgard, when earlier telling Marki of them had even referred to them as 'soft and spoiled little milklings.'

The angry gleam in their mother's eyes however, told Marki all he needed to know about Falamore's queen. She had known loss and hard times, and according to Effgard, life had made her bitter, and her character was far different from when she was an innocent and carefree youth; she could be a dangerous and treacherous woman.

*So much for young love that has outgrown itself,* Marki thought, remembering the tale of Effgard and Blondel's love in their youth.

Blondel's mass of greying hair was unkempt, her lips curled in a snarl of derision as she intensely watched Marki. She was a head taller than any woman Marki had ever laid eyes upon, and her frame was broad. Her beauty was withered with age, and had a cruel taint to it, one born of much bitterness.

Falamore leant his head towards one of the boys, and pointed a fat ringed-finger at Marki.

"A dwarf! They used to be a common sight here, before you were born, but in these dark days we don't see many of their kind anymore. In fact, it is the first one I have set eyes upon for many a year."

The boys looked Marki up and down, and then again buried their heads in their mother's dress for comfort to shield themselves from the unusual sight of a dwarf.

Falamore continued, this time addressing Marki directly.

"Many of my people believed your race was extinct or locked deep in your mountains far beyond the Everglow. It is said that the only dwarves who wonder above ground are those who are outlaws or banished from their own kind, so which are you dwarf, criminal, banished, or both?"

Marki took a deep breath, to rid himself of the urge to barge past the guards and throttle the fat old king. He would not be baited especially as he desperately needed the help of this man, vile as he was. During the journey to Thurog Tor, Marki had discovered from Effgard that a decade ago, Falamore had been the aggressor in breaking a truce that had been made with their sister, Sharwin. He had also broken other truces by invading some of the smaller kingdoms in the East. Marki felt sympathy for the pitiful men begging for scraps, after all, they had all once been kings or great lords, whose realms had been destroyed by Falamore's army.

Marki had also learnt from Effgard, that the war with Sharwin had gone badly for Falamore in more recent years, and that he was still at war with two other kings. He no longer had enough warriors left to strike a decisive blow, and now, having lost confidence in him, some of his barons had broken away from him and declared themselves kings in their own right.

To make matters worse, Sharwin, his sister, known as the *Raven Queen of the Summer Sun*, had been loaned a relic by the Chatti. She had used it to unite many of the barbarian tribes. A great host was now gathering, and would soon sweep like a swarm into the land of Thurogen. Falamore was sure to be defeated. The news had cheered Marki, for it meant that a legion of Pure-bloods who could resurrect at the Obelisk if killed in battle, gave Falamore much needed swords. Marki was confident they could come to a mutual agreement.

Effgard, had been open in the fact that the main reason he had sided with his brother over his sister, was due to an ancient feud he had with the Chatti and Gragor, both of whom were races he hated with a passion. He despised the thought of them having any influence over the future of Thurogen. He had decided he could never have peace with them.

Despite Effgard now siding with Falamore, and the legion soon to join their ranks, the situation for Falamore was still desperate. Marki had been informed that Falamore's kingdom had suffered heavy losses, militarily and financially. His coffers had been all but emptied in the war. Due to the battlefield losses of many of his native-born army, Falamore had been forced to hire expensive Seranim archers and Shemite slingers, to help him defend the few cities he held onto. The gold was nearly gone, and when it had, with it would go the last of the mercenaries. A company of Normagne Knights and their Footmen, having not been paid that month, had already abandoned Falamore and gone over to Sharwin's side. It had all been good news for Marki to hear. The unfavourable circumstances Falamore found himself in meant he would be desperate for the legion's assistance.

378

"Nice embroidery," Marki said, trying to break the ice, as he glanced back at the embroidery on the wall he had passed.

"They are tapestries," Queen Blondel said indignantly.

"No, they are not," Marki replied knowingly. "A tapestry is woven whereas embroidery is sewn onto a plain linen background, and cheaper to make." His mother, a weaver and seamstress, had been one of those who had woven the famous dwarf tapestry of the *Battle of Iron Conachlan* that covered the entire length of the Iron Hall, where the dwarf king of the Iron Mountains sat upon a throne made entirely of the purest gold, softened only by a large silk cushion, that his mother had also made. She would have been impressed he had taken a stand over such a matter. Queen Blondel, however, was not. Her face twisted with rage and indignation.

"Will you allow this distorted imp to come into my home and insult me?" she hissed at the king.

"Be quiet woman!" Falamore ordered. "I have business to discuss with the dwarf and it won't be interrupted by your prattling. Off with you, the boys have seen the dwarf. Now there must be something more constructive you can do with your time than whittle away at my sanity!"

Blondel stared at Marki with an intense hatred evident in her eyes, which did not disappear as she then looked at her husband. With a hiss of contempt, she turned and haughtily left the hall by the same way she had entered, followed by the two princes who were still clutching her dress.

*I have made an enemy already,* Marki thought as he watched her go. *But tapestry is tapestry and embroidery are embroidery!"*

"I received Effgard's raven, dwarf, and the message intrigues me," Falamore said, speaking with a mouth full of food. "I have discussed the matter with my counsel, and considered it. I will allow your legion the use of my Obelisk, in return for their assistance in the troubles that assail my kingdom. But first, I want to hear from your own mouth, the telling of why a Kappian legion is in the Tarenmoors." After speaking, he took a jug of ale and quaffed from it, with no care or thought to the froth and contents spilling onto his beard and raiment.

"Good!" Marki said in a loud clear voice. "But if we are going to talk, how about you let me take a chair? My bones ache, and I hunger and thirst for some of that meat and ale you are guzzling down your gullet."

The old king paused for a moment and looked at the dwarf with an expression somewhere between blank and amused, as though he was considering whether he had just been insulted or not. He then burst out laughing and slapped the bottom of the serving wench next to him.

"I like the bluntness of Dwarves! Gerda, fetch wine and ale, and plenty of it, and bring more meat, the dwarf needs food and I'm still hungry!"

Gerda rushed off to obey her king's bidding. Falamore attempted to get up from his seat with some difficulty, falling back into it several times before he managed to lurch to his feet with the help of his two guards. He walked past the chained woman and down the two steps of the wooden dais and then over to the long table. He approached a chair at the head of the table, and fell heavily into it, crashing onto the stack of cushions upon it. The chair strained under his weight. He signalled impatiently for Marki and Effgard to join him, as well as Hozain and Yizain. They all took a seat near to Falamore.

Gerda quickly arrived carrying a large tray, and was followed by another wench. It occurred to Marki that they must keep a plentiful supply of meat, wine and ale nearby. Both of the wenches bowed, as best as they could, lade as they each were with a large tray. They each set the tray on their ample hips, and began transferring plates of meat, bowls of fruit and nuts, jugs of ale and skins of wine, as well as goblets onto the table.

"Keep the ale and wine flowing and these goblets full. I'll be drinking till I sleep or vomit," Falamore said as he burped loudly, grabbed a haunch of meat and without ceremony bit into it.

Gerda and the other wench poured wine into the goblets.

"Drink dwarf! Eat!" Falamore bellowed, food spitting from his mouth. He pushed a plain metal goblet filled with wine and a plate of meat towards Marki. "Tell me your tale!"

Marki took the goblet of wine and gulped it down in one go before holding it out for the wench to refill it from the large jug she was holding. He let out a loud burp and Falamore laughed, wiping the grease dripping down his mouth on his ermine sleeve.

The wine was not a good vintage, but it was strong. From what he had seen of the Tarenmoors so far, it occurred to Marki they didn't enjoy a climate favourable for wine making. Though the many different kingdoms had once traded with each other, war had no doubt put a stop to that, and he suspected that even in more peaceful times a good wine would still be rare and cost a lot of coin. Besides, Marki preferred good strong ale or mead over wine any day, but he hadn't been offered that, so he would drink the wine with this king until the ale was offered to him, which he hoped would be soon.

They all listened as Marki spoke of the fall of Aleskian, the woes that had befallen them since, and the Bantu threat that would, at some point, more than likely head south into the Tarenmoors. He finished the account by saying, "We will fight for you, in return for the use of your Obelisk. My friend, Borach, will be dead soon if not already, and the closer the legion comes to Thurog Tor, the more likely it is he will resurrect here anyway."

Marki then took a large bite from a haunch of meat, and not caring about his manners seeing as the king had none, asked without any formality, "Do we have an agreement?" He finished the wine in his glass, and then, perhaps due to feeling the effects of it and giving up any further pretence of manners, pointed to a jug of ale and said, "What I didn't tell you is that I am also a *Vargo Goss Ale Champion*, prior to my going to Aleskian, so why not push a jug of that ale over here, heh?"

Falamore did not seem perturbed by the request. He slapped Gerda hard on the buttocks. "Give the dwarf ale if that's what he wants," he roared.

Gerda took a large jug of ale and gave it to Marki. He drank from it greedily, the froth brimming around his beard.

Falamore, waving another haunch of meat in between chewing it, spoke. "If it is only the use of the Obelisk, and not payment in gold you require, then we may find agreement, but there are other matters to discuss first." He smiled falsely, showing yellow crooked teeth, after which he swigged more wine, tossed the goblet aside so it fell clattering onto the floor, and wiped the back of his hand across his mouth. Gerda picked up the goblet, refilled it with wine and handed it back to him.

"The Obelisk is deep down in the tombs of the ancient kings and queens, in a vault that has not been disturbed for centuries, except by Talain, who uses it often."

*That news is good!* Marki said to himself with a sigh of relief. "Talain, she is the Seeress Ognok mentioned?"

"Who is Ognok?" Falamore asked nonchalantly.

"The barbarian I told you about in my tale," Marki answered impatiently. "The one who led me to Effgard."

Falamore snorted. "Ah yes, I care not about barbarians, but I do like Talain. She is reckless, dying as she pleases, only to pop up alive again a day or so later, or sometimes

380

even weeks later. She then sits and eats with me, and babbles about what she has seen. I am curious about it all, even if such talk sometimes puts apprehension into my otherwise stout bones." Waving the haunch of meat, he then added, "If your lord is already in lands that Talain has died in, he will probably resurrect here, that is almost certain."

Marki felt relief at the news, and the further confirmation about Talain. He felt it travel to his face, and for the first time since leaving Aleskian, he relaxed slightly, and was almost overcome with emotion. *Borach is safe!* He fought the tears that tried to leave his eyes. "Dust allergy," he said defensively, as he wiped away one that did escape. "There must be dust in this hall, it always makes my eyes water," he lied. *The news is all good. Borach and the men of the legion will be safe if they die, and will be well served in the Deadlands by a good Seeress!*

Falamore stared hard and suspiciously at Marki, all mirth gone when he spoke again, almost accusingly. "You have no siege weapons dwarf, and it would take many weeks or months for you to build them, and even then, you would be hard pressed to breech the walls of Thurog Tor. Entertain no other thought than that of allying with me if you hope to use my Obelisk for your legion."

Marki returned his stare. "Then it is just as well, an alliance is my only intention," he said sincerely. "We wish no more, than to use your Obelisk in return for putting our swords, and my axe, to your service. It is an honest exchange!"

Falamore appeared to relax a little, nodded, and then grinned, chewing meat as he did so.

Hozain spoke. "The legion will camp with my army on the Plains of Thurogen. Unless resurrecting, your men can enter within the city walls in groups of no more than fifty at a time. They must be unarmed. They can use the taverns or amenities the city offers. The only exception to not bearing arms, is if they enter to have their swords and weapons sharpened or repaired at one of the forges, but then they can only come in a group of no more than ten at a time, but can bring as many weapons as need attention, including those of their colleagues."

Marki was not concerned about these restrictions, so he nodded. "Agreed," he said, "as long as our own blacksmiths can make use of your forges. They will need to craft new armours and weapons, to replace those left behind or lost on a battlefield. We cannot send resurrected legionnaires naked into battle."

"That is acceptable," Hozain said.

Marki knew his next statement might not be so readily received. "In battle, the legion will fight in its own way, and for this reason will not be under orders from any except our own. In fact, my suggestion is, if you want us to win decisive victories to turn the tide in this war, when he is resurrected and fully *Awakened*, you should give Lord Borach overall command of the entire army during any battle itself."

The look on Hozain's face showed Marki he had just made another enemy, but he was making an important point. The Third Legion had its own style of fighting, and although Falamore's army might be a little more sophisticated than other barbarians, Marki remembered the warriors from the barbarian wooden palisade on a small hill that had attacked the legion. The warriors had fought bravely, but stupidly, showing not the slightest understanding of any sort of tactics.

Sharwin had her own warriors, and some Chatti and Gragor, who all had fierce reputations, but most of the vast army she had amassed consisted of barbarians. It was a reason Marki was confident that the men of the legion would prevail in any battles to come. If they did not, they would die, resurrect, and fight again. It was therefore also important, where possible, that the weapons and armour of any legionnaire killed were retrieved, as even working around the clock it would take the legion's blacksmiths considerable time to forge new ones.

"I am in charge of my warriors during any battle," Hozain declared, "as well as your men."

"The men of the Third Legion are not your warriors, and you will not command them in battle," Marki responded fiercely.

Falamore lifted his hand when Hozain started to protest, and silenced him. "It is a long time since we have ever given much thought to the Kappian Empire, but memories last long, any tales of your legions that are still told, even if rarely and then only by strangers visiting, speak of the ferocity and success you have had in your campaigns."

Hozain's face was glowering red with rage; he stared at Marki, but said nothing.

"However," Falamore said, "there is a saying in the Tarenmoors. Use a chef to cook your meals, a whore to warm your bed, and a wife to suckle your children. Meaning, each has different skills, so let them do what they do best." He smiled confidently. "Effgard has his style of fighting so will command his own men. Hozain will command my army. You command your legion, and fight in the manner you see fit."

*Small wonder this blubber-laden oaf has lost so many battles*, Marki thought, but decided not to give voice to his annoyance. The suggestion was not perfect. Three men in command, each doing their own thing during a battle, was not a good idea, but Marki felt he would prefer that over the legion being commanded by either Effgard or Hozain, for despite their reputations, he had not seen if they themselves understood actual battle tactics and if so, to what degree.

"So, be it!" he declared, "but what about coin? You have none, so I ask none from you, but when my men run out of the coin they carry, they will need it! If there is plunder, we will need a share of it!"

"You can keep ten percent of all you plunder," Falamore said.

"Fifty" Marki countered.

"Twenty," Falamore said.

"Forty and we have a deal," Marki offered.

"Thirty, but for that, there is one thing you have, that you must give to me," Falamore said.

*Blithering flea-bite of a man, what else?* "Go on," Marki said, biting his tongue.

"Give me your griffin!" Falamore declared.

*I'll be glad to be rid of the mangy beast*, Marki thought, and almost said it but checked himself. Meron would not be pleased if the griffin was given away. When Marki had left the legion, despite the hope of soon acquiring the use of an Obelisk, morale had been very low, and it would not take much for it to completely disappear like the morning dew. The legion had shown fierce loyalty to Borach, but even oath-bound men had their breaking points, and Marki knew some of the men of the legion, had been near to reaching theirs for some time. Tensions had been high when he had departed for Thurog Tor. Many of the legionnaires had realised that they might not ever see their families or homes again, and fear at the devastation and mercilessness the Bantu would show had been on every mind, yet a raw pragmatism had still prevailed. The legion had been well trained. They knew that together, they were stronger, and it was a saying in Aleskian that '*every wrong will be made right on the final day when all evil acts are brought to account*,' and that led to the decree that stated, '*but we will stand together to strive for victory over injustice, to right them now, before that day, and if we cannot right them now we will wait for tomorrow or for the more opportune time.*' A shortened version of this formed the legion's motto,

382

'*Where there is unity, there is victory!*' Marki knew that giving the griffin away, would cause trouble. *Meron will feel I have wronged him*, he thought.

"I cannot give away the griffin," Marki said, regretfully. "I'll let you name him Karno or whatever you want to call it: I'll parade it through the city; bring it to the battlefield, but he must stay with us."

Falamore tightly gripped his jewelled goblet, and looked like he was about to hurtle it across the room in rage, until the serving wench refilled it with wine. "Then we have no deal!" he roared. "Be gone from my hall. March with your legion wherever you will, but do not enter my lands. If your master resurrects here with no deal made, I will consider him an enemy!"

The sudden change of mind surprised Marki, and caught him off guard. Under different circumstances, he would gladly have stormed out, but, as distasteful as it was, he had to stay and work something out with this wretched king.

"Stop blustering brother," Effgard said angrily, before Marki could offer a response. "Like it or not, you need the dwarf's help, and he needs yours. Reason, not stubbornness, must rule these negotiations."

Marki was grateful for the intervention.

"I'll not budge on this, I want the griffin," Falamore declared.

Marki could tell by the look on his face and the tone in his voice, he meant it. "Why is it so important to you?" he asked the king.

"I have no care for gods of any kind," Falamore replied, "but my people do! The people of Thurogen have similar beliefs to the barbarian wildlings."

*You are all barbarian wildlings to me*, Marki thought.

Yizain broke in, speaking for the second time. "The people believe in a prophecy that their god Karno will come to them in the form of a griffin. The prophecy states that Karno will give them victory when the hour is darkest. Effgard mentioned the griffin in his message; news of Karno has spread throughout the city and beyond. It has given the people hope! They want Karno, he will be well cared for and worshipped."

Marki felt the dilemma of the situation, but realised he had little choice. For a cruel and greedy man with too much power and no self-restraint, Falamore was remarkably perceptive. He knew he had more leverage in this bargaining.

"Give me the griffin, and our deal is sealed. Refuse, then you must leave," Falamore said with finality.

"Have it then," Marki abruptly barked. *Meron will just have to understand.*

Falamore, his rage gone in an instant, smiled widely, and laughed so hard, his chins wobbled. "I am pleased," he said, "now we will talk of war!"

"Indeed," Effgard broke in. "This Bantu threat may well come in time, but the enemies on our doorstep are the ones we must deal with first."

Falamore grinned. "Thurog Tor is a city as old as the hill it stands upon. It was built by those whose remains now lie near the Obelisk. Once, long ago, it was the capital of the Tarenmoors. After we win the battles ahead, I aim to restore it to that glorified position and become the ruler of all of the Tarenmoors! You, dwarf, and your legion, will help me conquer!"

For the next hour, they spoke of tactics, whilst Yizain wrote down what had been agreed upon, in a document. Hozain informed them that it would be a good six weeks before Sharwin's army would enter the Plains of Thurogen, due to the fact that in order to protect her flanks, she had laid siege to the capital city of the Kingdom of Bellarare; although far to the south-west of Thurog Tor, it bordered Thurogen. It was the only kingdom still allied to Falamore, but not being in a position to make much difference to their plight Falamore had turned away their envoys and refused their pleas for

383

assistance. The capital city was starving, the walls almost breeched, it was just a matter of time before it fell, but it was time that Falamore now had to use quickly and to his advantage whilst the bulk of Sharwin's forces had Bellarare under siege.

There were other enemies to deal with as well. Some savages had come from the forests to the south, strange looking beings, and had built a wooden palisade on a small hill just inside the southern border of Thurogen. It was believed they were there to try to lure Falamore's army away from the Plains of Thurogen, or would attack when Sharwin's army eventually entered the plains. The legion, accompanied by Effgard and some of his men, would deal with that threat, whilst the main army remained in the plains, where the future of Thurogen would be decided. The legion would then head west and take the castles of several small provinces that had broken away from Thurogen and declared their allegiance to one who was called *King Marsin the Pureheart*.

Although it was doubtful these rebel provinces allied to King Marsin posed much of a threat, if they did choose to attack and flank when the battle of the plains started, it could be disastrous.

"Cripple their warriors, or kill them," Falamore said, "I care not which, but I want King Marsin, the rebel barons, their wives and children brought before me alive! We will deal with them, then with Sharwin. After that, we look east. I am at peace with the Shemite and Seranim kingdoms that stretch far to the east and the Normagne to the south, for great forests and mountain ranges separate them from my land of Thurogen, but my ambitions will not be separated by forests and mountains." He spat on the floor in disgust, and then said. "I am the only true king in the Tarenmoors! When the last kings within my reach who oppose my rule, or do not recognise my authority over them, place their crowns at my feet, then I will be content. I want them grovelling and eating scraps from under my table. Only when I am unopposed in the Tarenmoors will I be a happy man!"

Marki had not eaten or drank whilst they had discussed tactics, but he then downed his ale in a few gulps and sighed appreciatively as the serving girl topped his tankard back up. He had no desire to enter a regional war, but once again, he and the legion had little choice. "War is war! So be it!" he declared.

Falamore nodded with delight, his chins wobbling again as he did so, but Marki's next words took the smile away. "We will kill any man who offers a fight or carries a weapon, but we will not slaughter innocents, nor will we enslave their women and children for your pleasure," he said, as he looked at the young woman chained to the dais. He pitied the sufferer whose every feature displayed her misery.

"Sharwin's daughter," Effgard said to Marki, as he too looked towards the dais, and then pointed to the man who had earlier snatched the bone thrown to the floor, "and Sharwin's husband."

The revelation surprised Marki.

Falamore growled. He also glanced at the chained girl, and then at the man still gnawing at the bone. "Then Effgard's men will do for me what you have neither the stomach nor the courage to do! As for these two wretches you look at with dwarfish pity in your eye, my sister married that rogue, some pauper who now shows his true nature, grovelling like a starving dog under my table." He used a haunch of meat to point at the man. "He and the girl were out hunting with hawks and hounds, and only a few guards were with them. A raiding party went by stealth into Sharwin's lands, and set an ambush, and what a prize they caught. I brought them here as hostage to stay Sharwin's hand, or make her pay good gold, but she is stubborn and refuses. She is still intent on making war, regardless what threats we make about the girl."

Marki did understand. The Kappians often lay ambushes for the powerful and wealthy, thrust them into prison, tortured and humiliated them and when they had reduced them to the point of death, or even death and resurrection if they were Pure-bloods, they then offered them for ransom. Borach had found such tactics distasteful, and did not use them, except in time of war and even then, the prisoners were treated justly. It was a reason Marki had been able to serve him all these many long years, for although he understood why hostages were taken and used, he did not like the tactic of mistreating them.

"It is not the dwarven way, nor that of my legion," he said to Falamore. "I am not here to judge the rights or wrongs of this war, we will fight for you, but we will not wound our consciences in the doing of deeds that would stain them."

"Do as you will," Falamore said, "but do not stop others doing as they will."

Falamore sat back, took another goblet of wine handed to him by Gerda, and swirled the contents around, his expression unreadable. He glanced over at the chained girl, and loudly said, "Your legion can have her, do with her what they will." He raised an eyebrow as he asked, "Even Pure-blood Kappian men have needs, do they not?"

The girl overheard, and looked nervously towards Marki.

Falamore continued to swirl the wine around in the goblet as he drummed the fingers of his other hand on the table, waiting for an answer.

Marki looked past the king at the poor unfortunate young woman chained at the dais, and frowned. He then sniffed the air, as he could smell a pungent smell. The source of it, he noticed with a mixture of pity and revulsion, was one of the men from underneath the table who had crept up to him; the half-starved wretch, who was caked in filth and dirt, blindly held out his stubs, begging for food.

Falamore, also noticing the man, waved the haunch of meat he was holding in the air and then pointed it at him. "He was once my oldest enemy, once a king, look at him now, the wretch," he sneered, after which he threw the meat to the man, who seized it with his stubs and began hungrily gnawing at it.

"Your stench offends me," Falamore then roared at the man. He threw a goblet of wine at him; it hit him in the back, covering him and the floor with its spilled scarlet contents. A maid picked up the goblet, returned it and refilled it as the former king scuttled silently away.

"My aim gets better each time," Falamore said jubilantly, "and I would kick him, if I could reach, or had the energy to leave my chair."

Marki looked at Falamore and did not attempt to disguise his disgust as his frown deepened and turned to annoyance. *Degenerate oaf!* Ignoring the sight of the miserable wretch, which revolted him, he turned to Effgard and asked, "Is your sister a woman who honours her word?"

Falamore grunted, and took another haunch of meat and tore into it.

Effgard looked at Falamore, and then answered Marki. "Unlike our brother, she is," he said.

"Careful brother," Falamore said menacingly, with bits of food spitting from his mouth.

"I'll take the girl," Marki said, "but she will not be harmed or touched by any of my men." He took a swig of ale, and continued. "It might be that on the seeing of her daughter, Sharwin might be reasoned with, if we offer her in exchange for peace. When our armies meet on the Plains of Thurogen, the sight of a disciplined legion fighting for you, and the promise of her daughter being given unharmed, might sway her, as might the news of the enemy that may still come from the North."

385

"You do not know my sister," Effgard said. "I doubt she will turn away from this war. The blood-feuds in these parts are strong. This war can only end in the death or capture of kings or queens. Sharwin will leave no claimant to what she believes is her throne alive. We grow weaker, while she grows stronger. It will not be long before she completely surrounds and chokes all of our lands. She will raid the farmlands, and we have not the men to stop her. It is the reason we have challenged her to a decisive battle in the Plains of Thurogen. As yet, she has not taken the bait but sent her forces elsewhere."

"If we lose, we will all perish to her sword," Falamore said. "If we win the battle, it might be at a high price in more of our own men lost, but we will be able to plunder the cities of our enemies and replenish my treasury. A temporary truce would ruin us, the gold to pay the mercenaries would run out."

"It might be, she would make an agreement to permanent peace," Marki said, "for our arrival here, is no small thing. Even if she won the battle on the plains, she could never take Thurog Tor with a Kappian legion of Pure-bloods stationed here defending it, for we would chip away at her forces and make constant raids on her supplies."

"I will never make peace with Sharwin," Falamore roared.

Effgard turned to his brother and said, "I agree, there can be no peace, but Maraya serves no purpose other than that of an ornament here. The dwarf might be able to use her to our advantage."

Falamore sat there in silence for a long while, chewing and swallowing his food before he repeated, more quietly, "I want no peace with Sharwin."

"Sire, I would like more time to build our defences where they are weak or crumbling," Hozain said. "We can break any agreement we make, when we are again in a position of strength. A temporary peace, might give us an advantage."

Yizain followed with, "I would like to get the trade routes open to replenish the treasury. Peace, for now, could work to our advantage, sire."

"I know my sister, she will not give peace, for she does not trust me and on that she is right," Falamore said. "But, Maraya may have strategic value. I told the dwarf he could have her. Lie, cheat, bargain for even a small advantage, but we attack Sharwin when she comes upon the Plains of Thurogen!"

"What about Sharwin's husband?" Marki asked.

"He is just a shell of the man he once was," Falamore said with amusement. "She knows the wretch begs for food under my table, so she would kill him for the shame he has brought upon her. It amuses me to keep him here, and further humiliate her."

"Just the girl then, her name is Maraya?" Marki asked.

"Yes," Effgard answered. "Tell Sharwin, I would have peace with her, but not whilst she is allied with the Chatti and Gragor."

"You mentioned a relic the Chatti had loaned to your sister, what is it?" Marki then asked him.

"A dragon skull," Effgard answered.

"A dragon skull?" Marki failed to hide the incredulous tone in his voice.

"You doubt such a thing exists?" Effgard inquired.

"I've never given it much thought, until I heard about it at the inn," Marki admitted. "Long ago I read in some bestiary that dragons once existed. If your enemies have the skull of one, I guess that proves it, but I will embrace doubt until I see it."

"The Chatti use it for some ancient ritual. Whatever the ritual is, they use it to sway people to their cause. It is how they tainted the mind of our sister," Effgard replied with a hint of disgust, "along with the foul raven spirit that has entered her."

"Stealing it would swing the barbarians to our side then, would it not?" Marki asked.

Before the conversation could continue, the doors of the great hall opened and a ferocious looking girl of about thirty years of age entered, accompanied by a young boy carrying a small lyre. The boy sprinted the length of the hall, into the arms of Effgard.

"Father, I have missed you," the boy said eagerly.

"I've missed you too son," Effgard replied as he proudly embraced his son.

Marki looked at the boy, whose appearance was ruddy, with bright eyes and good-looking. The boy noticed him, and left his father's embrace. He bowed gracefully and with respect to Falamore, and then said, "So it is true, a dwarf has come to your great hall uncle, and look at his armour, it is Kappian!"

Falamore grinned proudly.

"My name is Davgard, I am pleased to meet you sir," the boy said to Marki, who smiled and winked in response.

"Would you like me to play the lyre and sing, sire?" Davgard asked Falamore.

The king looked at the young boy, and answered gruffly, but affectionately. "I am in no mood for music or song, there is business to discuss, be gone with you now, you have seen the dwarf!"

Effgard ruffled his son's curly hair affectionately and said, "Your uncle is right, we have business to discuss. Are you still training with the Shemites?"

"Yes father, I am becoming quite skilful with the sling, and when my arm is strong enough, you must teach me to wield the axe."

"Return to your training then, I shall send for you if we wish you to sing for us later," Effgard replied.

The boy smiled, turned to Marki and said, "It really was nice to meet you sir. Another time, I would love to hear tales of your adventures, for I hear Dwarves are brave and a proud and noble race."

"I like your boy, he's smart," Marki said, as the boy bowed again to Falamore and then sprinted down the hall. By the time he had gone through the doors, the woman who was strutting slowly but confidently down the hall had reached the table.

She bowed to Falamore, "Sire, you sent for me," she said.

Marki recognised the woman from the decaying bodies in the caves, and to his delight, noticed the mark of a Pure-blood Seer upon her.

"The Seeress Talain," Marki said, in between a mouthful of wine and meat.

Talain stared at him.

"You look feral," he blurted out, as his thoughts accidentally turned to words.

"She enjoys the wilds more than the comforts of my city, and can travel back from death. What would you expect such a one as she, to look like?" Falamore asked proudly. "I tried to get her to wear gowns, drench herself in perfume and gild her nails, but she prefers to be like this, so I let her do as she wishes."

Talain's eyes remained fixed on Marki. They were harsh, but she stared at him with fascinated amusement. Her cinnamon locks, plaited with the feathers of a sparrow hawk and tied neatly back made her appearance even wilder as did her worn boiled leather raiment. A spear, seven feet in length and made of black oak, tipped in gleaming iron, was slung across her back, and two daggers were sheathed in scabbards attached to a belt around her waist. The most striking thing about her was the ritual scarring that covered her face: deep, circular grooves that spiralled down from her forehead and surrounded her eyes, adding to her ferocious appearance.

"You do that to your face every time you resurrect lass?" Marki asked mordantly.

Talain ignored the question. Her voice was laced with wild power when she spoke. "It is true then, a dwarf has come to the hall of King Falamore, a Kappian legion offers service, and Karno is coming to us." She looked Marki up and down, and then approaching him she stopped and stared at his groin before staring him in the eyes. "Are you small in all departments dwarf?" she asked mischievously.

Marki took a swig of ale and looked at his groin, then at Talain. "I'll match it against a Gragors any day of the week," he answered.

Talain's expression softened as she, Falamore and Effgard raucously laughed together at the same time. She then sat at the table and helped herself to wine and took an apple from a large bowl of fruit brought by another serving maid.

"So, dwarf, are you learning about the complexities of the Tarenmoors? No doubt you have heard that although Queen Sharwin once sat upon her throne like a queen bee, gorging on the jelly of royal pride fed to her by buzzing flatterers, she now moves against my own king and sire?"

Falamore shoved some meat in his mouth, spraying the contents as he chewed and spoke in between swallowing the food. "The dwarf and his Kappian legion will fight for us, in return for the use of the Obelisk, and you guiding their dead to it."

"I will gladly do it, if it is my sire's wish," Talain said. "Even though, Ognok and his tribe, worship me as a goddess, but the dwarf has brought a griffin god for them to worship as well." She smiled impishly. "We goddesses do not like competition."

Falamore grunted with amusement.

Yizain finally finished the last document, and passed it and the quill to Falamore, who signed it without even reading it.

Marki scanned the document carefully, and then he signed it. "It is as we agreed," he said. "Now, I wouldn't mind some shut eye, for it is late and I am driven to exhaustion. When the sun rises, I wish to inspect the Obelisk, and then return to the legion."

"If they have marched with haste, they would have made good ground, for the route to the Plains of Thurogen is straight. I will be surprised if they do not arrive by tomorrow. Hozain will take you to them," Effgard said.

# Chapter Thirty-Two: *The Humiliated Empress*

*It is my solemn belief, that deviant people are naturally liars - therefore torture is the regrettable but only means to get them to reveal the darkest secrets of their heart, to confess their crimes, or to submit to the righteous and just rule of law. Only through such means can those of us with the responsibility to rule, have a reliable and perpetual record of the truth, for a Jewel of Baramir may not always be readily available. A notary must be present whenever such methods are adopted to record the pure and honest confessions the purity of pain provides. An Inquisitor shall also be present to bear solemn testimony that any confession, or agreement to the will of the sovereign, was willingly given by the deviant being questioned. The role of an Inquisitor is merely that of a moral auditor, it would not be becoming of them to soil their souls by laying their own hands upon any deviant whose soul is being purified by such means. Another, more uncouth type, shall do the actual deed of extracting a pure confession.*
**Maopold III: The Art of Just Rule Vol I.**

*Dawn* arrived, dripping pale fingers of light through the iron bars of the cell in the Bloody Tower where Shaka had been taken, and still the torture continued. She slipped in and out of consciousness as the Bantu, Grixen, worked her torn flesh with hot irons and cruel pincers. The pain was like nothing she had ever endured, but her cruel captor managed to keep her from the quiet mercy of death until a moment of his choosing. As Grixen worked, he muttered dark rhymes and utterings in a tongue she did not understand. In between the rhymes, the grunts and moans he made clearly revealed he was not only enjoying his work, he revelled in it with sadistic delight.

Every now and then, Grixen would stare into Shaka's eyes. At such moments, she felt she was trapped in a nightmare. His eyes seemed to her as deep pools of malice. His lips curled back in a feral grin, revealing teeth that were short and sharp apart from two long and crooked fangs. When he stared at her, she knew fear the like of which she had never known before, but still, somewhere deep within, a small spark of defiance remained within her.

Shaka looked down at her ruined body. "I will have my revenge," she vowed. "My spirit will rise from the wreckage of this body."

"It will," Grixen said with cruel glee. "And then we shall start over again, unless you agree to the Munte marriage." He looked at the notary, who was seated at a table, behind which Marnir, the Grand Inquisitor, stood.

"Make sure you record her defiance," Grixen said to the notary, who nodded compliance and recorded her words, writing them down using an ink quill upon a parchment.

Shaka looked at the Maidenarz, the cursed item that stopped her changing aspect, and hated it with a ferocity that almost sent her insane. That was the last memory she had of that life, as her spirit departed her body for the Deadlands.

\*   \*   \*

The *Awakening* a few days later, was particularly traumatic for Shaka, especially when the memory of recent events came flooding back. The first thing she noticed, was that the Maidenarz was still on her new body. It had indeed followed her between worlds and not even death and resurrection had set her free from it. It was customary on the death of a royal that a hundred Seers were executed to lead them in the Deadlands, and to resurrect them, but for the first time since she had become Empress, she had been given no such courtesy, though she did not doubt that some would have kept an eye on her at the orders of Mazdek, to make sure she did not drift as a sightless wraith away from the Obelisk it was pre-planned she would resurrect at.

There were many Obelisks in Kappia, she had been resurrected secretly in the *Tower of the Obelisk*, situated in a secure location near the prison. The name of the Obelisk was Doomskar. When life had returned to her, it had whispered dark omens to her that she could not yet recall. Shortly after resurrecting, she was taken almost immediately by the Hammer Knights, by way of a curtained horse drawn carriage, in secret, again to the Bloody Tower, which stood on a rocky outcrop overlooking the Pangarin Lake.

As she was dragged unceremoniously, not into the dungeons below, but this time into a cell within the tower itself, the stench and the screams of the victims, weakened her resolve as she remembered what and who was waiting for her. It was not the sight of Marnir or the notary, but that of Grixen, who with them was waiting in the same cell for her arrival, that sent fear into her. He wore the now familiar feral grin, as she was thrown to the floor.

"Shall we begin," he said, taking a cruel looking implement from the rack of tools upon the wall. That was the moment the Empress Shaka finally broke.

*I cannot take anymore. Ahrimakan, if only I could speak to you and ask you to visit vengeance upon my foul betrayers.* The small spark of defiance that had remained within her, evaporated. Rising to her knees, she begged Marnir to not allow her to be harmed anymore. Dignity no longer mattered. She would face any humiliation; agree to anything, as long as Grixen was not allowed to touch her and inflict more torment upon her.

"I agree to it," Shaka gasped in between tears.

"You agree to the Munte marriage?" Marnir asked her, seeking clarity.

"Yes, yes! I will enter into a Munte marriage with Mazdek, just don't allow that beast to touch me," she pleaded, looking at Grixen who appeared to be disappointed his pleasure was to be forsaken.

Marnir nodded, and the notary recorded the words. A contract agreeing to a Munte marriage to Mazdek was then put before her, which she signed. Marnir rolled it up, tied it with a ribbon, and put it inside his robe.

"Bring her," he ordered two Hammer Knights as he stepped from the cell. In such a broken manner, Shaka was led by a crude leather lead tied roughly around her neck, naked apart from the cursed Maidenarz, by two Hammer Knights who pulled her along as though she were a common slave. Marnir led them through the tower and into the dark underground tunnels below the dungeon, and then through secret passageways that ran under the city, until they emerged into a cloistered area of the Argona Temple, a part she had never visited before.

Shaka was led into a stone corridor, lined by a gauntlet of Hammer Knights who methodically banged the heads of their hammers on the floor, and stared coldly and dispassionately at her, as she was led past them. They spoke no word, not a one of them, the sound of their hammers a clanging condemnation, not salutation. At the end of the corridor she was led into a large room, heavily guarded, within which was only a glimmering Spiral Portal. Marnir opened the portal, and she was led into dark, secret and forbidden parts of the temple, until she was taken into a room, where Mazdek and Renlak were waiting for her.

The room was small but ornate, with faded murals on the graceful panelled walls, deep rugs on the granite floor, and with the lofty ceiling adorned with intricate carvings of gods and beasts. From behind a black marble, gold inlaid writing table, Mazdek stared at her. His garments were of rich fabric, elaborately made. Shaka recognised them at once; they were the robes her own father had once worn, as were the rings on Mazdek's fingers and the golden chains around his neck. The small spark of defiance that had evaporated, was suddenly reignited by the sight of such insolence. It was very deep within her, and very dim, but she felt it flicker, even if but for an instant.

Mazdek shifted his focus from her, and scanned his eyes across the yellowed pages of a book open on the desk in front of him. He snorted with derision, and read aloud from the book:

*"Maopold III, liked to sit enthroned for hours, doing nothing much more than wearing his crown, holding his spectre and wearing other symbols of his regality, whilst 'speaking to no man.' Even when his closest advisors, or members of the Senate entered his presence, they were expected to bow low, scrape the knee, lower their eyes, and silently wait in that position for many an hour until he decided to speak to them. If, when he asked their business, they brought some urgent matter of state before him, he would treat them with contempt, shouting that he would not even dismiss a scullion from his kitchens at their request. None dared protest at such behaviour, for he often had fits of rage, shouting aloud from the throne that the laws of the Kappian Empire were 'in his mouth and breast,' and his divine destiny was 'to rule without having to answer to anyone.' His reign was tainted with terror."*

With the sound of a heavy thud, Mazdek slammed the book shut, causing some dust to rise in the air. "The decline of this once great Empire, began during the long and arduous reign of your father," he said to Shaka. "You, have done little to reverse its fortunes," he added, accusingly. He then rested his chin on the cups of his hands and fixed his smouldering black eyes upon her.

Shaka perceived a dark deceptiveness, a fierce intensity and determination in his eyes she had never observed before, and wondered whether it was because he had previously hidden such an attitude, or, consumed by her power and luxuries, she had grown lapse and had merely not noticed it. She concluded that like most cowards, the courage Mazdek now exhibited was due only to the fact he was in a position of absolute power over her.

"Do you offer no defence against this accusation I bring against you and the foul dynasty that has been inflicted upon us for far too many centuries?" he asked.

*Better shun the bait, then to struggle in the snare*, Shaka thought, knowing that no answer she could give, would satisfy the man she stood before.

Marnir handed Mazdek the rolled parchment, which he untied, opened, read and then handed over to Renlak, who rolled it on a table, and took from a drawer a candle, some wax, and the imperial seal.

The three men stared at her, as the two Hammer Knights fixed their gaze ahead. Shaka's body stiffened with rage, when she saw her three betrayers observing her nakedness. But it was not lust in their eyes, she saw something far, far worse – contempt and mockery. Humiliation joined the rage, and both soon gave way to a new fear. It was as though Mazdek could read the contending emotions and thoughts bubbling away inside of her, for when he finished shiftily eyeing her body, he just remained seated, staring at her with his black, emotionless eyes, until she could no longer meet his gaze, and lowered her head. It was only then that he spoke.

"I am pleased that your stay in the tower, has led to you agreeing to my marriage proposal," he said. He then stood from his chair and slowly circled her, studying every aspect of her body, before casually taking his seat again, fixing his gaze upon her once more.

Again, she sensed it was not lust that was driving him. It was the same contempt and mockery as before. She could see it in the expression on his face, and hear it in every tone and reflection in his voice.

"Will you be a good bride to me?" he asked, without attempting to hide the sarcasm.

"Yes," she said in a dull whisper that masked the anger and humiliation still simmering within her, only kept at bay by the fear she had of the pain he could again order to be inflicted upon her at the hands of Grixen.

"Louder," Mazdek growled in a manner as though he was reproaching a petulant child.

"Yes, I have agreed to the marriage," Shaka said as tears rolled involuntarily from her eyes and down her cheeks. The emotional nakedness she felt at that moment was far worse than her physical humiliation.

Mazdek grinned. "The imperial seal is on the table, stamp it, to seal your signature, that the heralds may proclaim the joyous news throughout the city and ravens will be sent to the ends of my Empire."

"Either one of you is capable of stamping it for me," Shaka said, feeling a moment of defiance, as the spark of it flew to the surface."

"You will do it," Mazdek said menacingly, "for if you are ever brought to trial and testing in front of the Jewel of Baramir, you will bear true witness that it was not only signed by your own hand, but you also stamped and sealed it!"

"Do I not get to read it first?" she asked indignantly.

"No need," Marnir answered. "You have signed it, now you must put your seal upon it."

Renlak cleared his throat. "It declares your love for Mazdek. It states how he has guided you with wisdom throughout the recent calamities, and that you believe he is better suited to rule the great Kappian Empire. It records that you willingly submit to him as your husband through a Munte marriage, so by law, you and all other citizens will hail him as the new Emperor."

Throughout her imprisonment Shaka had known this moment was inevitable. Even as she had signed the parchment and agreed to the Munte marriage, she had known what it meant, but hearing the verbal confirmation, that by cunning and manipulation, Mazdek was now usurping her throne, made her feel like vomiting.

"My children's' signatures are not upon it, nor their seals," she said, trying one last throw of the dice.

"Oh, they will be," Mazdek said confidently. "They too are guests in the tower. They have already agreed to sign and seal it, once they see your signature and seal upon it. If they go back on their word, well, Grixen can be quite persuasive, as you yourself have discovered."

Rage twisted inside of Shaka, on hearing the threat to her children, but she fought the urge to scream and shout at Mazdek. *If only I could change aspect, I would devour them all.* She cast a regretful glance at the Morkroth jewellery that made her so helpless, and bemoaned that she had ever set eyes upon such a wicked object, let alone be tricked into allowing it to be willingly put upon her. In the same instant she also regretted how lapse she had become. It had been Mazdek who, over many lifetimes, had whispered in her ear a course of action that had led to the Second Kappian Civil War, a war so costly and damaging, that it had broken the Empire into three factions, and left it deeply in debt to the Hamash Bank. She had supported the war in order that worship of the Aeldar Gods would be enforced, at a faster pace than some of her other advisors had deemed wise.

It was also Mazdek who had turned her against her own generals, whispering of plots and plans so she had mistrusted them the more each day. He was the one who had slowly replaced her Imperial Guard with the wretched Hammer Knights. She rebuked herself for her own stupidity in testing their loyalty, and for her arrogance in believing that nobody would ever dare to challenge her rule and authority as Empress. These were mistakes for which she was now paying a very humiliating, heavy and dangerous price.

It was as though Mazdek read her thoughts, for he sneered at her, and tapped the cover of the book he had previously read aloud to her, the title of which was *The Wicked Reign and Rule of Emperor Maopold III*. It was a book that had long ago been written by a banished member of the Senate, and was a book her father had banned. On pain of *Final-death*, he had only allowed favourable accounts of his rule and reign to be written by authors, and then read by the citizens of Kappia.

"Come now, don't be so upset," Mazdek said insincerely. "I want to have a peaceful marriage. And, after all, did not your father, Maopold, come to the throne, by forcing your very own mother into a Munte marriage?"

Shaka knew the history well. Her father, a Kappian General, had returned from a successful war in the far west of the Everglow, but on his return to the Kappian Plateau, during his victory parade, his men turned on the citizens of Kappia and he seized the city. Giving the then Emperor and Empress the *Final-death*, publicly, he made their daughter, Shaka's mother, the new Empress, and in order to make legal his usurpation of the throne, he forced her into a Munte marriage shortly afterwards. The events led to the *First Kappian Civil War*, a brutal affair that was remembered as the *War of Despair*.

"It is double the pleasure, to usurp the child of one who himself was a usurper," Mazdek said, followed by a smug grin.

Shaka remained silent. All her many lifetimes had not been without hard taught lessons, and ones that she now remembered. Anger would not win her back her throne; she would have to be more cunning and shrewd than the foul wretch before her. *My patience will achieve more than my wrath, for now.*

"Do you have nothing to say?" Mazdek asked her.

Shaka closed her eyes, and swallowed the rage and humiliation she felt. She could not again face being at the merciless whim of Grixen. The very thought made her feel nauseous, and that fear itself led to a further sense of humiliation that also furthered and fuelled her rage, for she was both disgusted and ashamed with herself that she had not been able to endure more at his hands. He could never have done that to her, if it had not been for the cursed Maidenarz. Again, she fought and resisted the rage and fear inside of her. *My patience will achieve more than my wrath.*

Never, in all her lifetimes, had it been harder to say the next words that came from her mouth. She opened her eyes and said, "If you promise not to harm my children, I will submit privately to you, and publicly to the marriage. Princess Aspess and I can go and spend our lives with the Sisters of the Grey Mountain; you can send my sons to the Brothers of Mercy. We will all spend our remaining lifetimes in study and reflection, and private devotion to the Aeldar."

Mazdek said nothing, but eyed her curiously.

She continued. "When you have need of my public support, which at times you will, I can return for a brief time to the Celestial Palace, and appear in public to show my support for you." Shaka knew that to have any hope of reversing what Mazdek was doing, and to regain her power, she would have to plan very carefully, and tread cautiously. Rashness was in her nature, but to show it or be led by it, would be her undoing. To understand all that was at play, she would have to carefully, and with great patience and timing, work away at Mazdek's own weaknesses, and undo the power base he had built, so that she could strike and bring him down when the time was right. His greatest weakness was her own, arrogance and ego. But he had exercised patience, whilst she had been rash. She could see it now, and knew that for the survival of herself and her children, that was something on which she must work.

393

Mazdek pulled open a drawer, and took from it a weapon that Shaka recognised. It was the Arkith Aspess had until recently owned, the one with which she had slain General Karkson. Mazdek fumbled the hilt with his fingers, and then looked at the Arzak, the soul-gem, before turning to look at Renlak and asking him, "Wasn't your father present, when Shaka plunged this very same blade into the heart of her own father, Maopold, giving him the *Final-death* so she could take the throne?"

"He was," Renlak answered. "Although the official account is that he died peacefully in his sleep."

"And do you recall the words she is reputed to have said as his spirit was sucked into the eternal prison of this gem?"

Renlak cleared his throat. "She said, if an injury is to be done to a man, or a woman, it should be so severe or final, that his vengeance might never be feared."

Mazdek looked at Shaka. "Did you enjoy plunging this into your father's heart?"

She offered no response.

"I have often heard you say a true Empress never lacks legitimate reason to break a promise, and I have seen you break many of those, even to those most loyal to you. Why should I trust you?"

Shaka shut her eyes again. When she opened them, it was not calmness or peace that directed her voice and actions, but a cold, calculating malice that pushed down her fears and humiliation, and masqueraded itself as compliance. *I must make him believe he has cowed me into submission.* Her voice was composed when she spoke.

"May I have a robe? I am soon to become your Munte bride, can you not at least allow me to keep some small level of dignity?" She also tugged at the leash attached to the collar around her neck. "And this, is not necessary," she said.

Mazdek signalled with his head to one of the Hammer Knights, who undid the leash and collar. Renlak then opened a nearby chest from which he took a robe and a clasp, and passed it to her. She wrapped it around herself, and fixed the clasp so her modesty was restored.

"Thank you," Shaka said, masking the scathing animosity she felt, for she felt no gratitude in the slightest to these betrayers.

Mazdek was still gazing into the Arzak of the Arkith. "I sometimes wonder, how your father reacted, when General Karkson joined him in this eternal swirl of misery. Was not Karkson once his squire?"

"He was," Shaka answered, trying to appear unruffled.

"Power has no relationship with morals," Mazdek said, as he turned his attention away from the Arkith, and looked with glee and pleasure at the signed document, soon to be legalised with the imperial seal. Shaka knew the real game was on, and the cost of losing it, would be high. She was under no illusion, that once her children had also signed and sealed the marriage document, and the Munte marriage ceremony was publicly performed, for a while they may be sent to the Grey Mountain, sometimes perhaps even recalled to Kappia for show, but, sooner or later, their usefulness would be at an end, and that very Arkith would be plunged into her own heart, and that of her children, and she and they would join her father, General Karkson, and the many others who dwelt within the Arzak, in eternal misery.

Mazdek had bound her with complex strands of intrigue and guile. Shaka knew that every word she spoke from that moment on, every action, had to convince him she had accepted her fate. *I must convince him I have accepted defeat. I must fight for more time, for now, my weapons will be words.* She remembered something General Karkson had once said, about battle. *'The wise man seizes an opportunity at once, whilst the fool dithers with long delays.'* She was in a different type of battle, but a battle nonetheless. She knew, that the opportunity to strike, was not now, but when it did come, she would not have the luxury of delay. *For now, I must choose every word carefully, seizing every opportunity to buy more time, time I will use to plot a return to power, or delay an inevitable Final-death.* With this in mind, Shaka felt it wise to remind Mazdek of a few facts he would need to consider.

"I do have one question," she said, trying to sound poised and calm, despite the conflicting emotions raging inside of her.

Mazdek raised his eyebrows, curiously.

"I am the mother of a Titan. I am pledged to wed Ahrimakan. He has said I will become an Aeldar Wife, a Keeper of a Riddle, a Queen of the Aeldar. Do you not fear his wrath on the day Thuranotos returns and releases him from the Arkoom? I ruled with the blessing of Ahrimakan."

Mazdek smiled cruelly, and his answer both surprised and confused her. "There are powers even greater than the Aeldar, in the worlds soon to be revealed. There is evil in the Void, both timeless and nameless, whose origin mere humans cannot begin to understand, whose purpose has yet to be revealed."

*That is blasphemy*, Shaka thought. She closed her eyes briefly, lest Mazdek guess her thought, and see her shock and disgust. For the first time, she questioned his loyalty to the Aeldar. When she opened them, she observed that even Marnir was looking at Mazdek with a puzzled frown upon his face.

"The Aeldar have no interest in those who sit upon the thrones of men," Mazdek said. "As long as those who do so, aid their own cause, which is their return to the Everglow, they are indulged." He sneered derisively. "When Ahrimakan took the form of a man and lay with you, promised you would one day be an Aeldar Wife wed to him, did it never occur to you why he did not make it so and tell you the riddle of his true name?"

It had occurred to Shaka, often, but she had always trusted the promise Ahrimakan had made, that one day it would be so, so she had never pressed the issue, for his response to being questioned was always a furious and swift brutality against her person, and she had continually feared angering him.

Mazdek looked smug when he next spoke. "I am best suited to assist them now, for the power of the Empire was sifting away under your incompetence. The enemies of the Aeldar have multiplied, but under my reign, they will be crushed. You will be insignificant on the day of their return; they can do with you as they wish. I will be confident if they judge between us, that it is I who will get the reward I deserve."

Shaka seethed within. Fear, anger and hate surged like conflicting tides within her, one superseding the other in an instant, and then back again. She feared, that if Mazdek still considered her defiant, she would be sent back to Grixen, but against her will, her feelings rose to the surface. She was angry, because, she thought, *Ahrimakan loves me, how dare you question that love?* She hated, because, throughout all of her lifetimes, apart from at the hands of her own father, she had never been mistreated by another human until after she had allowed the Morkroth jewellery to be put upon her. It was for that reason, that in that instant, the small spark of defiance within her, flared to the surface, overcoming her resolve to be cunning and patient. She could not control the rage that suddenly burst within her like a volcano.

"You are a rat, not a lion of ancient royal bloodlines like me and my kin," she shouted at Mazdek. She reached out, in an attempt to grab the Arkith from his grasp. His reactions were slow, but fortunately for him, those of the two Hammer Knights were not. One of them seized her, and held her in an iron grip. The other, with both hands holding the hilt, raised his hammer above her head, looking to Mazdek for instruction on what to do next.

It took Mazdek a moment to compose himself. He looked at the Arkith, which he had nearly dropped, and then at Shaka. For the briefest of moments, she saw the intent of madness in his eyes. He stood, gripped the hilt of the Arkith tightly, raised it above his head, and hurled himself recklessly across the desk, attempting to plunge it into her heart.

Marnir stopped him. Grasping his hand and pulling him back, he said with all urgency, "We still need her. We cannot sustain another civil war upon the plateau, not in these times."

Shaka watched, as reason and logic slowly returned to Mazdek. He lowered the Arkith, and took his seat again. After a few moments, the same contemptuous look returned to his face, but Shaka knew she had to seize the initiative. She knew, in that moment, that she could no longer pretend complete compliance. She had meant it, at first, for Grixen had broken her, but now, she had to play a different hand, and gamble, for the sands had shifted yet again.

She looked at the Hammer Knight whose hands were still firmly grasped around her, and then at the one whose hammer was still raised above her head, and said to them as regally and authoritatively as she could, "Do not forget, I am still your Empress! You are oath-bound to me, as much as to the High Quaester." She noticed a slither of uncertainty in both of their expressions, so before Mazdek could address them she said, "I am the lover of Ahrimakan, one of the Aeldar Gods you worship. I am the mother of a Titan, pledged to be an Aeldar Wife and Queen. Lower your weapon!"

There was no containing the delight Shaka felt within her, when she felt, ever so slightly, the tight grip of the knight holding her loosen and become softer, more uncertain, and the fact that the other knight slowly lowered his hammer.

"We still need her," Marnir urged Mazdek.

Mazdek momentarily closed his eyes, composing himself. For a moment Shaka observed that his face was angry, unpredictable, but then it took on a false serenity.

Shaka's quick mind analysed the situation.

*They will not give me the Final-death, here and now, they still need me* - she felt relief.

*But they could return me to Grixen* - she felt fear.

*In rashness, I have reacted* - she felt anger and regret with herself, in allowing her rashness and emotions to override her short-lived resolve of patient action.

"Release me," she ordered the knight, who looked for Mazdek's permission, which he gave with a nod, before doing so. The other knight completely lowered his hammer, resting the head of it on the floor.

After a pause, Mazdek said, in a manner that could not hide the offense he had taken, "It was treachery that exalted your bloodline, not a right to rule."

He opened the book he had earlier quoted from, and flicked through some pages, until he found what he was looking for. Losing his composure again, his finger trembled with pent up rage as he stabbed at the words on the page of the book and read them out loud:

*"Maopold treated the citizens of the Kappian Empire with unreasonable severity, cruelly oppressed high and low, unjustly disinherited many, and caused the death of thousands by starvation and war, especially in the provinces. He was tyrannical, ambitious, rapacious, arrogant, a greedy and ravening wolf destitute of any virtue."*

He looked up from the pages of the book, with an expression showing he wanted an answer, though he had posed no question.

Shaka knew her pretence of full compliance was up, it was a place she could no longer retreat to, for her guard had truly slipped and so quickly after her resolve.

Neither could she again show open defiance. The fear of the threat of Grixen reigned in her anger. She needed to adopt a middle ground.

Again, her quick mind analysed the situation before she spoke. "It may take time for me to surrender to my new role, as your soon to be Munte bride, but for the sake of my children, if you swear to me that neither I, nor they, will be harmed, then with sacred oaths and promises, loyal wife I swear to be." *You have already reminded me, that as the true Empress, I should never lack a legitimate reason to break a promise, especially one made under such duress.*

"Would you be willing to undergo trial by the Jewel of Baramir, to test how true or false such an oath would be?"

Shaka thought quickly. "Such a trial would need to be public. If I failed the test, your reign and the Munte marriage would be invalid, as my vows would show they were involuntary."

"So, you do speak with falseness in your heart and a lie upon your tongue?" Mazdek accused her scathingly.

"I speak with seeing the situation for what it is. You have won the throne and I cannot thwart your aims." *I will win it back!* "Lay no further hand of harm upon me, and none on my children, and that will secure my compliance in public. If, in the privacy of my own heart I still lament the fate now befallen me, can I not be allowed that, as it will bear no relevance to the power or authority of your rule. You need this Munte marriage, or you will never be accepted as a legitimate Emperor."

Mazdek snarled, but Shaka continued. "None of your ancestors' deeds are recorded in the *Annals of the Akkadian Empire*. It will deeply hurt the pride of the noble families to be ruled by a man of such low birth, when others, either by bloodlines or the deeds of their own ancestors, feel and believe they have a greater claim to the imperial throne than you."

Mazdek clenched his fist, clearly angered at the truth. "Galaeroth, my ancestor, found the Simal!"

"That deed is not recorded in the *Annals of the Akkadian Empire*. We only have your word for it. Admired you are for the tales you tell, but you were not born with royal blood, so tales, stories and your own boasting does not give you a legitimate claim for the throne, and others will think this and whisper it in their gatherings." Shaka then asked him, "Is it not better I hurt you with the truth rather than comfort you with a lie?"

"A Munte marriage will overcome these matters," Renlak offered. "To overcome the reluctance of the nobility to your claim to the throne, she must remain alive to legitimize it."

"But we cannot trust her," Mazdek said, looking her derisively up and down.

Shaka's next move was purposeful, though risky. She spat at Mazdek in the face, and then said, "That is the last act of defiance you will ever see from me, I swear to it."

Such was the rage she saw rise up in Mazdek, that he was almost breathless when he wiped away the spittle and drool that had run down his chin. He went to say something, but she spoke first.

"You asked me if I enjoyed plunging that Arkith into my father's heart and watching the Arzak draw his spirit within?" Her face twisted with hate. "The answer is yes," she declared. "You pointed out the flaws in my father, I can point out more. The only thing that stood between him and the suffering he inflicted upon his subjects were the limits of his own conscience, and not once did I ever see him reach that boundary. Did he spare even me his own daughter, when he inflicted his lust upon me whilst I was still virgin and pure? No, I hated him for all of his deeds, but for that most of all, and it brought me immense pleasure to plunge that into him and imprison his spirit for all eternity." *I will not tell you though, that from that profane union, Regineo was born.*

Mazdek laughed bitterly, and when he spoke, he spat out the words venomously. "You judged your father, yet you followed his path. The measure of any person is what they do with power. What did you do with it apart from to satisfy your own decadence and your own unrestrained cruelty?" He tapped the pages of the book with a finger. "You were no better than him, and the written history of your rule will record your own many foul deeds."

"Then answer me this honestly," Shaka retorted immediately. "Do you pretend or think you will be any better, as the new Emperor? Was it not your idea to unleash the Bantu upon Aleskian and the provinces? Have you given thought to the suffering your advice has already inflicted upon the people of the Empire?"

Mazdek banged his fist on the table, and then seemed to curb his own flash of anger. He took some deep breaths, before laughing bitterly and then answering her. "Dominating others is merely a show of strength. True power is mastering and controlling yourself, is it not? I will do what needs to be done, to reach my objectives."

"But will you limit your power, and revoke the ancient title of *Ivanar*, and in thus doing bring yourself under petty human laws?" she asked. "Or, will you embrace such a title and rule with absolute control as I did?" She spotted the other tomes scattered on his desk, and noticing a tome of a *Book of Aeldar Proverbs*, she quoted from it. "*Power itself is not evil, it is neutral. Patience is power. Patience is not an absence of action, it is timing. Wait on the right time to act, and all power will be yours.*" She then noticed a *Book of Aeldar Prophecies* on the desk, and also quoted from that. "*For the powerful, crimes are those which other people commit. If you cannot abuse power, you have too little of it, but absolute power without compassion is the worst of all things.*" She then made her closing case, that would see if her new tactic would play to her advantage, or not. Pointing to the *Book of Aeldar Prophecies*, she again quoted from it. "*It is written, that it is better to obey a noble lion, than a lord of rats. The Aeldar shall restore the noble line of the gods and all rats shall flee and scatter. The noble of creation shall rule whilst En-Sof and his rats flee. In their fury and shame, they will seek to hide in deep and forgotten places, but the fury of the Aeldar will seek them out and justice shall prevail. Not in this or any other realm shall En-Sof hide when the Aeldar regain their ancient power.*" She looked at Mazdek, and said, "We both wish and seek this, do we not? On this purpose, we can be allied and work together? You as Emperor, I as your Munte bride." *I will secretly oppose you, every chance I get.*

Mazdek smiled cruelly. "Very good, your knowledge of our sacred texts is commendable," he said, but his smile disappeared quickly, as she continued.

"In the eyes of the nobles, you are a rat, not a lion of ancient royal bloodlines like me and my kin. This Munte marriage will change all of that for you. My reign may not have left the world a better place than I found it, but I swore that the light of the Aeldar would shine through the Kappian Empire to the ends of Pangaea, so that when they are all summoned, I would be rewarded by becoming as they are. I still serve the same end, but now I will serve it by being loyal wife to you."

Shaka got down on her knees, even though every fibre of her being resented the act, as submitting to Mazdek even in pretence, made her feel nauseous. She felt humiliated by every lie she told, but she was determined to play whatever part she must to regain her power and throne. *The end must be my goal. If this is the price I must pay, to win back my throne and plot my revenge, then I will pay it!*

"Power will destroy you, my husband to be, unless you treat it with respect, something I did not do and now regret. It is the ultimate aphrodisiac is it not? Your lust for it means you have already lost yourself to it. But this day, I swear to you my loyalty, and will submit to you in every way a Munte bride is required to do so." She lowered her head to the floor, and taking one of his sandaled feet from under the desk, kissed it. "I swear my allegiance to you, husband to be. I will be your loyal and faithful Munte. *"I do this for the sake of myself, my children, and to get back my throne.*

When she stood to her feet again, the look on the faces of the three men was one of slight shock, and surprised pleasure, but then Marnir frowned, cocked an eyebrow curiously and said, "You will have a procession from the tower, and then you will enter the city square of Kappia. The marriage will be a simple, public ceremony, performed by myself. You will then consent and submit to the first act of consummation. It will be public."

Shaka involuntarily curled her nose up in disgust. Even when his body was young, Mazdek had no attractive features, his face was thin and bird-like and few women had ever found his looks pleasant to the eye let alone now he was old, but the thought of his timeworn and withered body touching her was not the cause of the disgust she felt.

"Public consummation? Can I at least not be spared the indignity of that?"

Mazdek glared threateningly at her. "You will keep to the assurances you have given here without fault, or I have no use for you. After the document is stamped and sealed, in return, you will be sent back to a cell in the tower, but one with more comfort. Falter once and you will be sent back to the same cell, or dungeon, to be entertained by Grixen, until such a time I choose to dispose of you and your brood."

The thought of returning to the dark dungeon under the tower, where she had first been imprisoned, or the cell where Grixen had inflicted much suffering upon her, was persuasion enough to make her comply, for now. She would stay the course, swallow her rage and endure the public humiliation that she could see no way to avoid.

"If you keep that beast away from me, and do no further harm to my person, or any harm to my children, I consent to all of the terms," she said begrudgingly, but as sincerely as she could falsely muster under the circumstances.

"Even public consummation?" Renlak asked. "Public consummation will leave no question in the minds of the people, that the Munte is legitimate. You must agree, comply and show willingness and desire for your husband."

"Where will I be allowed to dwell after the ceremony?" she asked.

Mazdek smiled impatiently, and answered, "If the ceremony has been completed to my satisfaction, you will be allowed back to the Celestial Palace, where you can dwell in your own palace apartments. We must appear to be a contented couple in all aspects, until such a time you can be sent to the Sisters without arousing suspicion."

"Then I agree, and say that you will find me a loyal Munte wife, including my willing participation in the public consummation. I shall be an asset at your side." *Until the day when I plunge that Arkith into your heart.* "I have just one small request?"

"Which is?" Mazdek asked impatiently.

"The gladiatorial games I have arranged, might they not be used now, also to celebrate our marriage? It would be most fitting."

Mazdek looked at Renlak, who replied, "It would be a timely distraction for the masses, especially as more news from the provinces filters through about the destruction of Aleskian, and the rampaging of the Bantu horde."

"Very well then," Mazdek said, "enough of all this talk. Seal the document."

*Agreeing to the games, is your first, fatal mistake,* Shaka thought as she picked up the royal seal, melted some wax with the candle, and then pressed the seal firmly in the hot wax, and then down upon the scroll. In this way, she agreed to become the Munte bride, of the High Quaester Mazdek, enabling him to soon become the Emperor of Kappia.

# Chapter Thirty-Three: *Murder at Harwind*

*To encourage privateering against Bruthon commerce in the Great Civil War, the Kappian Senate did not tax privateers who plundered Bruthon ships and ports. Those duly encouraged by the imperial tax relief, included the Burghers of Harwind, who hired two 300-ton frigates owned by the Sea Lords. Captained by Woades and Rogers, eyewitness accounts of the time said that as their ships left Harwind Bay, their bows cut through waters of blood-red algae, the like of which had not been seen before. This was surely an omen of the destruction they would inflict in Bruthon waters, for blood thirstier men, you would be hard to find anywhere. Reader beware, the tale I am about to tell you is not for the faint hearted.*
*Abbie Marson: True Accounts and Great Swashbuckling Tales.*

*A* dawn wind brought the chill of the surrounding hills to the port town of Harwind, which was at the end of the River Erin where it joined the Eastern Tethys Sea. The Erin was ruffled with spray, and square sails slapped against masts while the wind carried away the shouts and drum beats of the oar master as the *Cruel Maid* approached Harwind Bay. Anchored in the bay was a massive sea galleon, bristling with mounted artillery such as catapults, slings and ballista designed to launch projectiles of hefty stones or flaming bolts at an enemy. Huge boarding planks were stowed on the port and starboard sides. Azzadan could tell that these could be raised and lowered like a drawbridge. They had large spikes on the end to imbed into the deck of an enemy ship. As they propelled past the galleon, he noticed the boarding planks were fitted in such a way they could be swung out from the port or starboard sides. Most impressive though, was the gigantic sea harpoon at the bow loaded onto a mighty ballista which sat upon a turntable for manoeuvrability. It was a truly formidable and yet magnificent looking ship.

"The pride of our fleet, the *Red Tide*," Smindy said as she pointed at the massive galleon. Answering Azzadan's questioning look, she then explained, "The *Cruel Maid* is good for rivers and inland coastal waters, but she'll not be able to handle the deep and rough seas we will be venturing into."

Azzadan did not reply, his mind was troubled by other matters. He stood at the bow, his hair and cloak tousled by the wind, feeling the tinge of drizzle on his face. He wore seafaring attire over his ethereal cloak. He put the hood of the seafaring cloak over his head, to protect himself from the bitingly cold wind. His lip curled with anger as he watched the crew manoeuvre the great galley, the *Cruel Maid*, alongside the dock. He never enjoyed coming to the town of his first ever birth so long ago.

When the galley was safely tied alongside and the gangway erected, he was the first to walk down it onto the dock side, where a Fell-blood dock master carrying an armful of wax slates, manifests and cargo logs waited.

"Nobody can land until these forms are all filled in," he declared.

Azzadan lifted the man's chin with his fingers, and stared into his eyes. "Speak to me again, and you will not live to see your bed this night," he threatened coldly. Droplets of rain gathered on the man's bald head. He looked at the cobbled ground, suddenly unable to meet Azzadan's gaze, and mumbled a meek apology Azzadan could not make out.

"Leave him alone," Redboots said cheerily as she joined Azzadan on the dockside. "He works for the Sea Lords, they will take their toll, and harder men then he will extract it if we don't give it with a smile."

"The fearless Redboots is afraid of the Sea Lords?" Azzadan asked mockingly.

"Common sense and a smart business head make me know what battles to fight and those it's best to not even start," she said, and then gave a cheerful a wink.

Looking at the dock master, she smiled and said to him, "Matthow, go and wait in your office, I'll send my man Laro to you. He will sort you out with the toll, but don't stare at his hook or he'll likely gouge out one of your eyes."

The dock master nodded, shuffled his feet, and without a further word or looking at either of them, ran back along the quay from where he had come. In his rush he dropped some wax slates which broke on the ground. He didn't stop to pick them up. He entered a small dockside office and slammed and bolted the door behind him.

"Meek lot these skivvies of the Sea Lords," Azzadan said.

Redboots giggled. "Aye, but he's just a quill scratcher pushing ink around a slate or parchment. Other eyes are watching us though. I pay my dues to the Sea Lords so they let me go about my business unhindered. That's the way it is and that's the way it will continue, so enough of your squawking."

Azzadan shrugged his shoulders indifferently.

"Sometimes the Sea Lords even give me guild business, like blocking the Erin, which yields good coin," Redboots said as she smiled, stretched and yawned, as it started to rain. She sniffed the air. "You smell that? Something's cooking in one of the taverns, probably the fish stew at the Salty Mermaid Inn. I'm going to feast on it whilst the crew gather the supplies needed for the voyage. Do you want to sup and drink with me?"

Azzadan sniffed the air and smelt the food as well, but he had other matters apart from eating and drinking on his mind. "I have some business of my own to attend to first," he grumbled.

Redboots turned her head. "We sail at dawn so use your time well. It is the last time we will step on land for some time, the voyage to Grona is long and hard, we will face seas like you would not dream, and let's hope we don't get found by a monster of the deep." She smiled, clearly relishing the thought of the voyage ahead.

"Smindy!" she shouted.

"Aye captain?" came Smindy's voice from somewhere on the deck of the *Cruel Maid*.

"I want a drinking companion. Laro will see to the ink pushing and the provisions so come and live today with me as though it's our last, for in this trade we never know when it will be."

"Aye captain," Smindy shouted joyfully as she appeared and ran down the gangway to join Redboots.

"Are you joining us? she asked Azzadan, with a hopeful glint in her eye.

"Later. I've a personal matter to deal with first," he replied gruffly.

Azzadan looked around him. Lots of empty crates were sitting on the quayside, the wood slowly rotting. Many of the buildings looked like they were in need of repair, and the cargo ships in the harbour, many of them with the Empire's hammer and snake symbol painted on their hulls, were in poor condition, empty of crews and judging by their waterline their hulls were also empty. It was well known that the Sea Lords, aided by Redboots and pirates of her ilk, were bleeding Harwind dry and blocking any trade from going down the Erin. Once a great trading port where the produce of the Empire was bought and sold, it was now a shadow of its former self.

Azzadan remembered his childhood so long ago during his first lifetime, when he would steal pottery, glass, fabrics, wines, corn and any other produce sold in the markets and along the quays of Harwind. It was several lifetimes ago that the town went into decline, and only three decades or so ago that the Sea Lords took it over. He tried to visit at least once a lifetime, but never had he seen it in such a dire state of repair.

"Keep an eye on things, go pay the toll then visit the governor and tell him to meet me at the Salty Mermaid," Redboots said to Laro as he strolled past her scratching his behind with his hook.

"Aye cap'n," he grunted as acknowledgement.

Redboots and Smindy sauntered off in the direction of the taverns, and Azzadan watched them until they disappeared from sight. For the first time he could recall or remember, he wanted nothing more than to leave the life he was living, and spend the rest of his days with them, being carefree and enjoying every moment in the same way they did. *If only they were Pure-bloods and had more than one life to live, I could spend many lifetimes with them.* Emotions stirred in him he had not felt before. *Why am I so obsessed with them, especially her, Redboots?* He also felt other emotions. If he had fulfilled his mission in returning the Simal and the Seeress Janorra, his debt would be paid, and he would be a Master of the Brew and a member of the Council of Fellows. The humiliation Ishar subjected him to, had made him feel deeply bitter, and the thought that Skidegeat might now get the honours promised to him, was almost too much to bear. *The opportunity to become a master will certainly be denied me, even if I fulfil this mission.* His pride was deeply hurt. *I will forever be a slave to the will of lesser men than I.* He cursed them all, especially Ishar. *You have treated me unjustly!*

Azzadan scratched his arm where he had been injected with the Orange Brew, and sighed again. Ever since he had been denied the chance to find Janorra and reclaim the Simal, gnawing doubts had started to question his loyalty to his Order, for he felt Ishar had betrayed him and made him break his sacred blood-oath. He felt trapped. If he tried to leave the Order, even if it was possible, he would be ruthlessly hunted down. Leaving was not possible because without being given the Orange Brew after each resurrection, he would eventually descend into madness and insanity. It was the one pull that meant every Pure-blood assassin and thief of his Order always returned to the Hall to receive it after each resurrection, as soon as they could. They could go many years without it, but eventually, incurable madness would find them. Only Masters of the Brew, who were specifically selected from the Council of Fellows, were entrusted with the recipe for the Orange Brew, and they were forbidden, under threat of *Final-death*, to share it with anybody else. He would forever be bound to the Order, and therefore trapped, by his need for the toxic brew. There was no way out, and now, it seemed as though he would advance no further in the ranks of his beloved Order. The thought sent him into an even fouler mood.

Leaving the riverside docks behind, Azzadan kicked at loose cobbles on the road. Not even they were being fixed. It was a far cry from the smart pristine town he had left as a New-blood during his first lifetime.

As he moved out of the shadow of the warehouses and onto the square behind the harbour, he crossed the stone bridge that led a across a stream. He leant over the side. The stench of the water, made up of excrement, soapsuds, oil and a few dead rats, rose up. He remembered when, during his youth, he used to fish from that same bridge and catch fresh squiggle backs large enough to eat, from that very stream. *Nothing can live in the foul mire that has become.* His mood became even blacker.

As he made his way across the bridge, Azzadan noticed a company of rough looking men who stood loitering about at the other end. They were drinking from a jug of rum and one or two of them were smoking pipes. Two of the men, noticing him, approached, and were then followed by the others. The first was a tall thin man of uncertain age. Dressed in a large, woollen and none-too-clean cloak pinned in place by a crooked nail with a flattened head, he performed an enthusiastic and over emphasised sweeping bow, whilst the other man, shorter and fatter but similarly attired, circled behind Azzadan.

Azzadan noticed that neither of them had the mark of a Pure-blood beneath their eyes. He guessed their intent, and it made him smile within.

"It looks like you need a new accountant to look after your affairs," the first ruffian said to him as he straightened from his bow. "Hand over your coin, and I will see that it is deposited safely in an appropriate bank for you."

"Come now Hoffer," the man's associate said, "methinks this gentleman would not like his coin in a bank, but would prefer that he donated it to a good cause, such as our drinking and whoring for the day!"

"Move along weaklings," Azzadan said menacingly, as the rest of the men circled around him. He felt the second man, now behind him, try to pick his pocket. In one movement, Azzadan seized the thief's arm, and then broke it in several places, before drawing a small poisoned pin he held between thumb and forefinger. In one darting movement he pricked the man's neck. The work of the poison was instant. Paralysed, the man fell to the ground like a wet sack. The first man, the one who had spoken and tried to distract him, drew a dagger and clumsily thrust it towards Azzadan's throat. Azzadan drew his club, easily parried the dagger and pricked the man in the neck with the same pin. He too collapsed to the ground. The rest of the men, looked at their fallen companions, and then at Azzadan. They hesitated for a moment, before turning and running for their lives.

Azzadan casually sat on the chest of the man who had spoken to him, as the man, still conscious but paralysed, looked up and helplessly stared at him in terror. He searched the man's pockets, and finding a pipe and some tobacco on him, Azzadan filled the pipe, lit it, and began to casually smoke as passers-by rushed past ignoring the scene. He took a few puffs from the pipe, and then threw it aside with a snarl of disgust. He had never liked cheap tobacco.

Azzadan waved down a horse and cart, driven by a poorly dressed one-eyed man. "You know these two?" he asked the man, who leant over from his cart and looked the two paralysed men up and down.

"Nope," the man answered casually. "We get lots of beggars and chancers passing through this place, most are chased out within a day or two. Not seen these two before."

"Good, then load the scum on the back of your cart and take them to the ship called the *Cruel Maid*." He flicked the man a gold coin and said, "Advance payment. Tell the crew Azzadan sent them as food for the cargo, and they are to pay you another gold coin. I'll find you and replace them with you if you don't deliver as instructed."

"They'll arrive," the cart driver said nonchalantly, as he bit into the coin to test if it was real, and smiled with delight when he found it was. He took a cudgel from below his seat. "I'll make sure they don't escape sir," he said eagerly.

"You won't need that," Azzadan said, "they won't be moving for a few days and by then it will be too late." He laughed and walked off as the cart driver got down and began to load the two men onto the back of the cart. He had been wondering how he would find food for the vampire when she was awoken. He had considered kidnapping some beggars from the street during the night, but the two bungling thieves had solved the problem for him. His mood lightened, but only slightly.

Azzadan crossed the square and entered the town proper. The houses inside the town were tall and thin to compensate for the lack of space. Most of the houses hung over the narrow, winding streets, covering the sky so had he not known it was morning, it would have been hard to tell if it was day or night. Nearly all of the buildings were constructed of stone with wooden beams built into them. The air reeked of food, both fresh and rotting. Dirty, unruly children ran about, or some sat in the dark corners of the street, half-starved, hope gone from their eyes.

A woman emptied a slop bucket down a street grating, already partially blocked by faeces. The contents rolled into the streets and Azzadan had to step over them to avoid getting his boots dirty. "Sorry sir," the woman said in alarm when she noticed Azzadan stare angrily at her, before she quickly ran into the house she had emerged from.

Azzadan turned left into a narrow street, walked the length of it and then through a series of alleyways until he came to a street full of old, dilapidated wooden houses, many with red lanterns shining outside. Rickety wooden stairs led up to outside balconies on the upper floors of the buildings, which were mostly populated by women, many of whom were chatting loudly with their neighbours whilst children squatted at their feet. These brightly painted whores called out their services to Azzadan as he passed by below. They made lewd jokes with each other about him as he passed by without giving them a second glance. He came to a house near the middle of the street where a red lantern was brightly glowing. Standing outside, he looked at it for a long time, before trying the door. It opened, so he entered.

Inside the house was a brick floor, slimy with filth. The only furnishing was a dirty flock bedding placed on a box, and two small chairs. The smell of the room and the bad air was unbearable. Sitting in one of the chairs was a rough looking woman of about thirty-nine years of age, unwashed and in tattered clothes. She was poking the embers on a small wood stove with an iron tong. She did not look up when he entered. "A Silver piece for an hour, if you finish early, the price is still the same," she said.

When he did not answer the woman looked up, and after she had gotten over the initial shock, she sneered. "So, the dog returns to its vomit does it?"

"You've recently resurrected mother, you look young," he replied without any trace of emotion. "Why have you returned to this filthy life? What did you do with the coin I sent you, did you receive it?"

"I spent it on gin and drank myself to an early death," she answered deridingly.

"There was enough money for you to leave this all behind," Azzadan responded, fighting the disgust and anger he felt rise within him. He took a purse of coins from his pocket and threw it at her feet where it landed with a jingling sound. "There is enough there to buy a new house away from this disgusting slum. Buy new clothes, get a husband. Start afresh somewhere, buy a barrow and trade vegetables, anything but this," he said.

His mother stood up and strutted towards him. "This disgusting slum was once your home; it was you who left it and me all alone. You visit once a lifetime at most and when you come you expect me to let you dictate how I live?"

"This is not living," he countered.

"And what you do, murdering people is?" she questioned scathingly. "You were nothing more than a common cutthroat and a cheap cutpurse until you met with some high and mighty fellows who now pay you this coin you throw at me. We both sell ourselves, for different services. Why are you here, to taunt me?"

Azzadan paused for a moment, and then said, "If you choose to dwell in this filth and live this life, then at least do what I ask of you."

"Which is?" she asked suspiciously.

"I want you to tout for trade down at the docks, especially with the crew from a galley called the *Cruel Maid*. They transfer to another ship tomorrow, the *Red Tide*, which will set sail. In future, whenever you see either ship alongside, or any from the same fleet, get with the men, find out as much as you can from them, where they have been and where they are going. Don't make it obvious, but when they speak loosely with their head on your pillow, remember what they say."

"You want me to spy for you?" Azzadan's mother turned and walked over to the coin purse he had thrown to the floor, picked it up, guessed its weight in the palm of her hand before opening it and looking inside. "This is generous," she said, "but it will cost you more than this."

"I want to know everything you can find out about the captain, who goes by the name Redboots!"

"Redboots? That is a name known and feared in Harwind. I know little of her business, but I do know she was once first mate to Captain Woades."

"Woades?"

"A blood thirstier man you would have been hard to find. He was a Fell-blood privateer who made his name raiding Bruthon shipping and ports in the Empire's Civil War. It is said Redboots was his lover, until she slit his throat one night for, it was said, the most trivial of reasons." His mother eyed him suspiciously. "What is your interest in this captain?"

"I am to sail with her, on business you need not know. I want you to find out everything you can about her. Find out where her ships anchor when not at Harwind, and what they do when they are not pursuing their trade on the Erin or Tethys Sea." *Redboots has more riches hidden somewhere, if I know where they are, it will help me gain the upper-hand over her should I need it.* "I will pay you very well for such information, if you gain it for me."

His mother laughed cynically. "She has a reputation of being dangerous and cruel, but aye, I'll spy for you, but I want a favour from you in return." She stamped several times on the wooden floor with her foot, making quite a commotion. "Sassy, come here!"

Peering from behind an upstairs door, a young girl of about eight looked shyly around.

"Sassy, come down!"

The girl walked down the rickety wooden stairs, and stood before Azzadan's mother, who looked her up and down.

His mother snorted with disdain. "I have died twice in the last eight years; first time was when I was worse for drink, and fell drunk into the harbour and drowned. The second time, was after giving birth to this brat!"

It was very rare, but not unknown, for a Pure-blood woman to become pregnant after their first lifetime. The news shocked Azzadan.

"Don't look at me like that," his mother said sharply. "I didn't want it, and I don't know why I was cursed with a pregnancy, and don't ask me who the father is, it could be any sea dog from here to Berecoth."

Sassy looked shyly at Azzadan.

"Take her with you," his mother said, "or when she first bleeds, I'll put her to work on the streets."

Azzadan looked at the miserable looking Half-blood child. Her face was bruised and she looked malnourished. "What will I do with her?" he asked his mother.

"Pay some orphanage to look after her or let her serve as a maid in your Order, or give her to Redboots. I don't care, I can't be having another mouth to feed, she costs me coin and as yet earns none in return. Take her, and I'll do what you ask of me. It is not up for negotiation!"

It was not an ideal situation, but Azzadan knew his mother was stubborn enough she would refuse to help him with his request, unless he agreed to this. Besides, Sassy would be better off away from their mother. *I'll find her work on the ships*, he thought to himself.

It took Sassy no time to pack, for the only belongings she owned, were the clothes on her back. When he and Sassy left the house and shut the door behind them, a drunken overweight man was stumbling towards the front door.

"Move out the way, it's my turn with her. I'm one of her regulars," the drunk snarled angrily as he pushed Azzadan out of the way. Azzadan noticed the man was a Pure-blood, not that it would have made any difference had he not been. Taking his knife out, in one swift movement, he slit the man's throat. Sassy let out a short scream and covered her mouth in terror. The man sank to his knees with a look of horror in his eyes as the life gushed out of the slash across his neck.

Some of the prostitutes sitting on their balconies screamed.

Azzadan put his knife away as swiftly as he had drawn it, took Sassy's hand, and muttered to her, "I hate drunkards and gluttons, but worst of all, I hate idiots who have no manners."

*      *      *

The Salty Mermaid tavern was brilliantly lit by numerous bright lamps hanging from the wooden beams in the ceiling. It was gaudily but cheaply decorated. A number of men and women sat around small tables, some were drinking, others smoking pipes, as they laughed and chatted the morning away. There were a considerable number of town guards and soldiers present, employees of the Sea Lords no doubt, but none of them passed more than a passing glance at Azzadan, as he entered the inn accompanied by Sassy.

Throughout the whole tavern there was an air of jollity and a lack of irksome restraint. A plump woman on a stage was singing an upbeat song the words of which were unreservedly vulgar. When the chorus came, more than a few around the tavern not engaged deep in conversation heartily joined in. When that song came to an end, another singer took her place and in contrast to the previous singer, began to sing a song characterized by maudlin sentimentality.

Azzadan noticed Redboots sitting in a corner of the tavern, surrounded by Smindy and several of her men. She was sitting with her feet up, her red boots upon the table. Next to her, was a man dressed in a finely tailored jerkin who was fingering a large velvet hat with a feathered plume that rested on the table in front of him. Azzadan assumed by the man's attire it was the governor, who was talking animatedly with Redboots, who in comparison seemed rather bored. He went and joined them.

"Who is this?" Smindy asked as she looked at Sassy.

Azzadan ignored her question.

"Leave us," Redboots said to her men. They all left so only Smindy, the governor, Azzadan and Sassy remained around the table.

"Ask him," Redboots said to the governor when Azzadan and Sassy were seated and her men had left to join their mates around other tables.

The governor went to speak, hesitated, then spoke in a tone which showed he had not spoken what he had originally intended to say. "Is it true that the Erin will be opened up for trade again?" he asked Azzadan.

"How would I know?" Azzadan answered sullenly, feeling a bit surprised that such a question would be directed at him.

"The enforcer for these Sea Lords is bleeding this town dry. I get my cut and I lead a good life don't get me wrong, but life is not as prosperous as it was when the Empire ruled this port," the governor complained.

"I would disagree," Azzadan replied, "men like you have never invested in the town, and only ever lined your own pockets."

A flicker of annoyance crossed the governor's face, but it was gone as quickly as it had arrived. "Argin, is head of the Skull Guild, and has the ear of the Sea Lords. He is taking more than his share of tariffs the Empire ships and others pay to trade here. He threatened me when I challenged him about it. Meanwhile, Harwind falls apart. We cannot even flush our sewers; this town is a disgrace and it stinks. The Sea Lords ignore the letters I have sent to them complaining about Argin."

"We all have our problems," Azzadan said, disinterested, as a serving maid placed a frothing tankard of beer clumsily on the table before him, spilling some of the contents. He ignored her clumsiness and picked the tankard up, taking a deep swig, leaving froth around his mouth which he wiped away with his sleeve. His thirst quenched; he pushed the tankard away.

"I am in need of your help," the governor said, and then hesitated.

"Just ask him," Redboots urged the governor, in a rather bored manner.

The governor looked around, and then leant in towards Azzadan and whispered. "Argin is a Fell-blood so one death can end him. He is causing me rather a lot of trouble and demanding half the town's income, scanty as it is. He pays the Sea Lords their due, but keeps the rest for himself. I want him dead, and Redboots tells me you might be the man for the job? You could do it tonight, before you sail on the morning tide."

*You couldn't afford to buy the Bethratikus to hire me from my Order,* Azzadan thought angrily. *I have the title Godslayer, that alone means my fee would be worth more than you had earned in all your miserable lifetimes.*

"I'm not interested," Azzadan growled.

"I think you should be, Azzadan of the Order of Ithkall," the governor whispered in a rather threatening tone.

Azzadan shot an accusing look at Redboots. *How does he know who I am?*

She sensed his thought, and shrugged her shoulders. "One of his rats saw you getting off my ship, I suppose," she suggested.

The governor took out a scrunched piece of paper and unwrapped it. On it, was a drawing of Azzadan's face, along with the writing which said:

*WANTED*
*AZZADAN OF THE ORDER OF ITHKALL.*
*REWARD*
*50,000 Gold Kappian Coins.*

"It seems you are badly wanted by the Empire for them to offer this much for you," the governor said. He then asked, "What crime did you commit, apart from belonging to that Order, for them to offer such a reward?"

Redboots took the poster, looked at it, laughed and jested, "I'm almost tempted to hand you in myself."

"Where did you get this?" Azzadan asked the governor. "Are they displayed all over town?"

The governor shook his head. He then glanced over at three men, robed and hooded in black, sitting at a table in the corner of the tavern, deep in whispered conversations among themselves, only pausing to watch who entered or left the tavern. Azzadan followed his stare.

"The Inquisition was here," the governor said in a whispered tone. "They entered the town a few days ago, told me I was not to have this poster copied or distributed across the town, but was to watch out for three men who would come to me. I was paid to give it to them. They are hunting you."

Azzadan shot him a reproachful look, and then looked menacingly at the three men.

The governor continued in whispered tones. "They are Pure-blood bounty hunters. I forged the copy I gave to them. The face those men are looking for is not yours."

Azzadan felt rage rising within him. He snarled to the governor in a whispered tone. "Since when have the Inquisition been welcomed here? The Empire has no hold on Harwind?"

"They did not come openly," the governor said, "but in secret. They threatened me, warned me, but also offered me the reward if I kept an eye out for you. They knew your mother lived here once, and that you were born here. I made false enquiries, and told them she had died the *Final-death* a long time ago, before I was governor, and that during my rule here nobody has ever heard of you, let alone seen you, which is partly true."

"How did you know my mother was born here?" Azzadan asked, and then, "why would you lie on my behalf?" *That is an ample reward they offered.*

The governor smiled slyly. "My little rats scurry here and there and see a lot and hear a lot, and what they see and hear, they squeak to me," he said, "but in this instance, they knew nothing."

Smindy smiled apologetically. "You mentioned her to me, Azzie, on the voyage down the Erin, when we spoke about our childhoods. I secretly sent a raven to the governor." She then added defensively, "You had planned to kill me up until the point when you changed your mind, and then found out who I was."

Azzadan felt the rage rising inside of him and looked murderously at all around the table, and then shot a quick glance at the bounty hunters, before focusing on Smindy. "What is he to you, that you would tell him that?" he asked.

"Let us all relax a little," Redboots said abruptly. "We do business with the governor here all the time, that's how the tide swings here. One of his little rats saw you come off my ship. He came to me with the news about the Inquisition looking for you, now we are telling you. It is in his and my interest, that you get rid of Argin for us, in return for him putting them on a false trail."

"Why should I trust you? The coin offered for me is no small reward."

"Argin has a fortune worth much more," the governor replied, "and then there are the trade tariffs and taxes I will get. My little rats have squeaked in my ears and told me where he keeps his fortune buried. It is simple economics. He is worth more to me dead, than claiming the reward for you."

"Then what's in it for you?" Azzadan asked Redboots.

"I have a good chance of becoming the next leader of the Skull Guild, if Argin is removed," she replied, "but I cannot be associated with his death, for he has more men and ships than I do at this time and they would seek revenge."

"That puts fear into you?" Azzadan asked Redboots.

The look on her face showed she did not like the insinuation. "I fear nothing, but neither am I a fool. I cannot openly raise a hand against a member of my own guild, no more than you could one from your own Order. There would be repercussions. It could fracture my guild, and spill out into a conflict with other guilds. If the guilds fight among themselves, it affects the Sea Lords and their taxes. They do not look kindly upon anybody who inconveniences or angers them. They demand the salt-price for it."

The governor joined in. "Unlike Argin, Redboots mostly keeps her crews under control so they do not harass the locals when her ships are docked here. Nobody objects to a pirate presence if their daily lives are not troubled by them, but when they bother people like Argin's crews do, it's a different matter."

"Do we have a deal?" the governor asked. "My continued silence, for this deed."

"He will do it," Redboots said as she looked around the tavern and smiled as she spotted a salty looking sea captain she knew, raising her tankard of ale in salutation. He returned the gesture.

"We sail for the Tethys Sea and Grona tomorrow," Azzadan growled. "I don't have time to find this Argin and do what you request."

"You don't need to find him, he's over there," Redboots said, pointing with her eyes to the salty sea captain she had greeted. "A few months ago, he burnt down a sacred grove and shrine in a town not far from here. It was a hammer and snake shrine."

The governor smiled sneakily. "I told Argin and his men, that the Inquisition had come here, and their reason was to find whoever was responsible for the destruction of the shrine. He did not care; such is his arrogance."

"It is convenient for us," Redboots said, "as we can blame the Inquisition for his murder. The Sea Lords will not be happy when their man dies, but not even they can touch the Inquisition, who will be held responsible."

"Have you no loyalty to a fellow member of your own guild?" Azzadan asked her.

Redboots waved her hand dismissively. "I get bored of this river and sick of the pungent smells it produces." She frowned. "It is the Skull Guild, with the permission of the Sea Lords, who block the trade. I have to take a turn here patrolling the river with my ships and enforcing the guild's will. If Argin is removed, and I become head of the guild, I will allow trade to flow in return for a tax from each port town, and protection money for their ships." She looked at the governor. "It will be fair and reasonable, not extortionate like Argin demands of you."

"What about good honest pirating?" Azzadan asked.

Smindy laughed and explained the situation to him. "The Tethys Sea does not give us much profit at this time, due to most of the merchants and nations that use the trade routes paying protection to the Sea Lords, so the guilds are rarely allowed to plunder them. The Erin is a foul stretch of water, but it is assigned to our guild, and will be more profitable when trade flows. We can order some of our captains here on the river ships, to enforce the guild's will on our behalf, whilst we take our seagoing ships south into more profitable oceans."

"I will do it then," Azzadan said, as he took the wanted poster of himself and crumpled it up. He looked around. When the governor was not paying him any attention, and he thought nobody else in the tavern was looking at him, he took a tiny metal star out of a hidden pocket in his outfit. With a small flick of the wrist, and only barely glancing in the direction of Argin, he launched the star. It quietly flew across the tavern, unseen and unheard, and slightly grazed his neck before continuing and landing in a wooden beam on the wall of the tavern.

Argin put his hand against his neck as though swatting a mosquito, and then felt it with his fingers. There was only a small nick of blood, so light was the scratch. He looked around quizzically, sniffed his fingers, wiped them on the sleeves of his long coat and dismissed the incident as he continued sipping his ale, laughing and drinking with his men.

"Time, we left," Azzadan said, as he got up and made his way across the tavern. The rest stood and casually followed. On the way out of the tavern he unobtrusively retrieved the metal star imbedded in the wooden beam.

"Well?" the governor asked as he rushed up and joined him when they had left the tavern. "When will you do it?"

"He already has, Argin is as good as dead," Redboots said, laughing loudly.

Azzadan nodded. "I used a slow poison, incurable. It will take about a week for any symptoms to appear. He will be dead within the day when they do." He looked at Redboots who was lustily grinning. "We will be long gone, and beyond suspicion when he dies, for it will look like natural causes."

"If questions are asked, just make sure you fulfil your side of the bargain and get the Inquisition blamed," Azzadan said to the governor. "And keep mine, and the identity of my mother, secret, or I will come for you," he added with a growl.

"I will, I will," the governor said, looking bemused. He then softly said to Redboots, "When Argin dies, I will recommend you to Lord Vansoth, as being worthy to lead your guild and to take his place." He then left, making his way up the street.

As Azzadan walked back towards the docks with Smindy and Redboots, and Sassy following behind, he said, "I found some food for our guest in the cargo hold, for when we wake her up."

"The girl?" Smindy asked, horrified, as she glanced at Sassy.

"No, two men who won't be missed by anybody," Azzadan growled.

Redboots smiled. "I look forward to talking to her, I don't think I've ever met a vampire before," she said.

Azzadan looked quizzically at her, and unconsciously rubbed his neck. "They're not exactly good company. They talk little and you need to tread carefully and warily around them. They are violent with mercurial natures. Even at the best of times they can be unpredictable. Do not offend one for they do not easily forget. They pay back every wrong ever done to them, no matter how long it might take."

Redboots shrugged and said nonchalantly. "There is a long queue of men and women waiting to pay me back for the perceived wrongs, real or no, they think I have inflicted upon them, and those who queued before them and tried to take their revenge are an even greater number - and dead they all be now."

"This is not a man or a woman, but a vampire, and very different. It is no common foe should you make an enemy of it," he warned her.

Changing the subject and looking at Sassy, he said, "This young girl, I would take her on board. Her name is Sassy, she's an eight-year-old Fell-blood."

"You didn't strike me as that type," Smindy said, with an air of mischief mixed with concern.

"It's not like that," he answered her chidingly, and turning to Redboots said. "I want you to take her on as a galley maid or cabin girl or something. She can serve you and be of use."

"We'll see," Redboots said as she looked at Sassy. "You know your way to the docks girl?"

Sassy nodded.

"Then go and find the ship the *Cruel Maid*. Speak to a man named Laro and tell him Captain Redboots has hired you."

"And tell Laro to have the galley serve you up something to eat, you look half-starved girl," Smindy added.

Sassy nodded and ran off towards the direction of the docks.

"Where did you find her?" Smindy asked.

410

"She's my sister," Azzadan growled, as they headed down the street.

A deformed and legless beggar sitting at the side of the street, cried for money as they passed by. "I sailed with you once, before I lost my legs," he said to Redboots who paused a moment and looked at the beggar. Azzadan saw recognition in her eyes. She said nothing, but took a gold coin from her pocket, and flicked it into the man's waiting hands. He screamed with glee and delight at the generous gift.

As they continued down the road, Smindy looked at Azzadan and asked, "What will you do about the bounty hunters?"

"Nothing, for now," he answered. "They think they hunt me in secret, but look for a face different to mine. If they now turn up dead here at Harwind, and resurrect, it will only draw more attention to the place."

"Well, let's not sour the mood," Redboots said, "nor take more chances at the Mermaid. Let us go to the Spikey Perch Tavern, they have ales from the Vargo Goss drinking contest. I wouldn't mind quenching my thirst with a few. Are you up for it now?"

"Of course, he is," Smindy said taking Azzadan by the arm and leading him down the street. "All three of us will make our last night in Harwind one to remember."

Redboots took him by the other arm. "I'll challenge any man there to Harendale, see if any of those old salts want to win a finger of mine. No matter how many lifetimes you live, tonight will be one of those you will remember forever," she said to Azzadan as she threw back her head and began to sing a shanty. Smindy joined in lustily. They both had a good voice, and they sang well.

Azzadan felt his dark and sombre mood finally start to lift. He smiled and said, "I usually don't like drunkards and gluttons, but maybe tonight, I'll make an exception and become one myself."

Smindy and Redboots grinned, and continued their cheerful shanty, that he soon joined in as they strolled towards the Spikey Perch Tavern.

> "*Go loose your topsails,*
> *Your jibs and royals see clear,*
> *Haul home with these sheets, my hearties,*
> *With a light and pleasant gale,*
> *We will crowd aloft our sail,*
> *And far from home we'll go,*
> *Farewell to friends,*
> *Hello to foes,*
> *Vast heaving lads vast heaving,*
> *To the love of battle we goes.*"

# Chapter Thirty-Four: *The Greedy Bena Birds*

*Dear Mr Temmison,*

*Please could you cease and desist with your correspondence on this particular matter, I really am powerless to assist you any further regarding it. You are our most successful author, and as such, as far as we can, we are always committed to accommodating each and every one of your requests and suggestions, as your scholarly work is second to none and highly valued by us. On the matter of the Dwarven language of Sangdalen however, we as your publisher are placed in an impossible situation. The first edition of your work included in full, the entire section you had written on the topic. We were, however, forced by an imperial order to remove this section from any future editions, and were also instructed to recall all of the first editions that had already been released; at some considerable cost to us I must add. I cannot tell you the reasons behind this order, for I do not even know myself. I am your publisher, not a politician. You yourself wrote large sections detailing how sacred and secret the language of Sangdalen is amongst certain factions of the Dwarves. The Empire conducts a huge amount of trade with the Dwarves; perhaps some overly zealous dwarf lord took exception to you for writing about their sacred and secret topics in such an open manner? I do not know. I only know that I cannot disobey an imperial order, and therefore I regret to inform you that no matter how vitriolic your correspondence becomes towards me, future editions of 'Vol VIII, book 1: The Dwarves of the Iron Mountains,' will not contain the same level of details as the first edition. I hope you will understand my position, and that as well as remaining your publisher, I will also remain your true and loyal friend. Phibius.*

*P.S. I have just passed my exams at the academy and have been accepted as an initiate into the Mystery Schools of Kappia. I will remain at this publishing house, and also continue my parish duties, until the 3rd day of the month of Lupoor next year. Please continue to address all correspondence to me until that date. You will be informed as to whom and to where you should address any future correspondence, well in advance of my departure.*

**Magalove: The Lives and Letters of Alberto Temmison.**

*Gilly* wiped her hands on her apron, took it off and folded it neatly before stowing it away in the drawer of a large oak dresser, from which she also fetched a large cake which was cooling on the shelf. She put the cake in a bag and tied it around her waist, slung a rucksack over her back, and took her staff before leaving the room by a far door. "That will do it. Sasna and Farir wait here for my return, you three, let's go me dears," she said cheerily.

Janorra stood, adjusted her sword belt and briefly looked at her companions. She felt comforted by the presence of Scarand, but not with that of Muro. He looked dangerous, and unpredictable. She was also glad that the two Seesnari were not coming with her. Every time she had looked at Farir during breakfast, he was looking at her, and she saw both fear and suspicion in his eyes, which were never a good mix. She did not fully trust the siblings, either. In her opinion, Sasna was motivated by monetary desires, and Farir would do whatever his sister wanted.

Speed was also of the essence. Farir's face was burnt, but not enough to leave any permanent scars, but his shoulder, still heavily bandaged was clearly starting to again cause him some discomfort. He kept rubbing it carefully as though to soothe an itch. *Those injuries might slow him down.* Janorra could tell that Sasna's own wound was also mending slowly, although at times she appeared troubled by it, despite the additional medical care Gilly had given.

Janorra, Muro and Scarand followed Gilly into a passage made of roots, the far end of which was an arch with no door, beyond which was a spiral staircase going upwards, carved into the tree itself. Gilly began to climb the stairs. Looking back, she said, "It is a long climb, me dears, we have places to rest. Old Gilly is afraid of nothing, except falling down these stairs, so make sure one of you catches me if I slip."

When Janorra touched the stairs, which were a living part of the tree, she stretched out both hands and stroked the wooden walls that were each side of the steps. She could feel the texture of its smooth bark, and the very life within which ebbed through the wood. A warm feeling came over her; she felt a delight in the touch of the wood. She sensed that the tree was protecting her, that it empathized with the many sufferings she had endured, and it was giving of its own essence to her. She briefly became aware of the wider Wytchwood, and suddenly was not afraid of it, at least not the part of it that was full of greenery and life. It was as though she sensed the tree speaking to her, making a bargain with her, that if the forest helped her, she must help it.

"Thank you, Martha," she whispered to the tree. Somehow, she felt she had an ally in the forest. For a moment, she forgot her concerns, and her own quest. Gilly had turned around and noticed.

"This is more than a forest, me dear. The Wytchwood is a living force whose spirit senses all of its occupants when they are here. That is due to the last of the elf magic that remains. When those enchantments are depleted, Martha will die, and so will the spirit of the forest."

Janorra felt saddened at the news. "You said there is another Wisdom Tree, here in the same wood?"

"The Elves planted two such trees, each in a place where they sensed great power. The tree on the other side of this wood, who I call Mithilos, is brother to this tree. Poor Mithilos suffers a lot, he has become brittle and enraged. He is dying and is in great pain." She paused for a moment, and as though thinking it might be important, said, "The roots of both trees go deep into the earth and mud of this world, into the very Deadlands themselves, and beyond into other realms."

*Yes, I saw them,* Janorra thought to herself.

Gilly continued. "That is how poor Mithilos uncovered the evil hiding in hidden realms, quite by mistake. That evil corrupted and ruined him. Mithilos' part of the forest has been slowly dying for hundreds of thousands of years, and is only kept from the brink of death by unseen powers. Something terrible lives in that part of the forest, and whatever it is, it used invasive rites and brutal charms upon him. The Elves could do nothing to help Mithilos, and nor could they uncover or find a way to discover what was causing him harm. In fear and distress, they fled, abandoning the Wytchwood, leaving Martha and Mithilos to their fate."

"That seems almost negligent of them," Janorra said.

Gilly sighed. "They were deeply afraid of whatever it was hiding in this place. It was beyond their power to help Mithilos, and they could not bear to watch him suffer so. The maiden we saw in the archive, I don't know for certain, but I think she was a great Elven enchantress, and that she died of a broken heart at not being able to help relieve Mithilos from his suffering. It was that last distress that caused the Elves to flee."

Janorra noticed a wave of grief wash over Gilly, who clearly struggled to stop herself from shedding tears. "I sometimes hear Mithilos' bitterness. He cries out in pain and I grimace at his brittle, outraged voice. He has suffered for longer than anyone knows. I lament that I do not have the power to help him. It is not by chance you are here Janorra, all things are connected."

"Was Yog the cause of this suffering?" Janorra asked.

"No!" Muro barked, but offered no further explanation.

"I don't think so, me dear," Gilly answered. "The evil rumoured to live in that part of the forest, is something else. The Spriggan sometimes talk about the one the text called Yog, although they call her Silverberry. I know little about her really, for they do not tell me much, but the Spriggan blame another power, one hidden, for the misfortune of this forest."

As the spiral stairs became steeper, there was a natural rail, so Janorra held it to aid the climb, and continued to draw comfort from the life of the tree. "I have read about Wisdom Trees in the temple library," she said to Gilly. "The books there say that many were planted by Elves, who were the servants of a goddess named Aeshaldar, an Ashura, who they believe was their first mother. The Wisdom Trees were male and female, brothers and sisters; the first trees that made the great forests. It said these trees are very old and there are now few that are left in the Everglow. I read they were planted in the time when Titans walked the land."

Gilly looked at Janorra inquisitively. "Your knowledge of lore is great. The forest senses great power in you. Your presence here fills it with hope. They both spoke to you, the Wisdom Trees, did they not? Their roots are not only anchored in the physical world, but beyond. When your poor soul left that lifeless body now cocooned by Uilisomor, they would have spoken to you in the realms of the dead."

"They did, in a way, for I saw their roots. I would like to help the one that suffers, if I could. But I do not know how, and my own business is very urgent."

Hope visibly flooded Gilly. "Maybe your own business is connected, me dear, all things are connected."

"Well, the forest did protect me from the Wild Hunt," Janorra said gratefully. "But I lack the knowledge to help the Wisdom Tree. I wouldn't know what to do, but I hope the success of my own quest somehow helps it." *My quest to reclaim the Simal and reach the Baothein cannot be delayed, can it?* She tenderly stroked the wood of the tree. "I don't know how to help your brother," she whispered ever so quietly, and once more felt the life of the forest ebb within her.

Scarand joined in the conversation. "How can you hear the forest?" he asked Gilly.

"By some means, this staff which the Elves left behind, enables me," Gilly replied as she held up the staff. "The Elves nurtured and grew both trees with pleasant charms and songs long ago. Long had the trees been silent until I came upon Martha. The staff was leant against her. I lifted it, and she spoke to me. It gave me quite a fright, I can tell you. She asked me to help her brother. I have done what I can. I have researched and studied many texts, but as yet have found no answer. As a dwarf I lack the natural power and abilities that an elf might have in such matters, and even their kind could not cure the ill or exorcise the evil that torments Mithilos and his part of the forest."

They continued after that, with Gilly chattering idly. It was a long and hard climb up the stairs; it taxed Janorra's strength, despite taking several rests sitting on the chairs on small landings that were seemingly grown into the tree for that singular purpose. During those short rest periods, Gilly regaled them with stories of lore and tales of the forest and of Elves. At one place of rest, she spoke with great sadness, and shared, "I have learnt much from the archive. The Elves once tried to hide themselves away from the calamities that befell the world, and they tried to avoid war at all costs, but it found them. They decided to move from their homes, over defending them, for they feared extinction. The preservation of Aeshaldar's lore is what mattered most to them in the end, they fled to protect such knowledge, lest the world become barren. The archive taught me that when the Elves go to war, they are a formidable force, so the foes they faced must have been terrible indeed to cause them to flee."

414

As they began to climb again, Gilly continued talking. Scarand whispered to Janorra, "She never shuts up, not even for a moment to catch her breath."

Janorra smiled, and whispered back, "I find her knowledge comforting, hope and calmness is upon me in this place, but silence sometimes is just as good."

"She is a wittering fool, even if a Reisic," Muro muttered.

After what must have been an hour, they finally made it to a place very near to the top of the tree. The morning was still young and cold as they finally climbed through an opening onto the floorboards of an upper level, just below the top. There were no windows or walls, simply a series of open arches all the way round supporting the roof, all of which was a natural part of the tree. In each archway a window sill at waist height was broad enough to lean on.

The view from the platform was spectacular, as the Wisdom Tree towered above other trees in the near vicinity. To the north, beyond the forest they could see the Dale of Yarron, and well beyond that they could see distant mountains, the peaks of which were like plumes of white flame, glowing in the morning sun-rise. "The Blue Mountains," Janorra said, "within which are the Crystal Caves, and then beyond them the Tarenmoors. I never thought I would see them with my own eyes." The knowledge of maps she had once studied, had fully returned to her. She drank deeply from the fresh air that was gently blowing onto her face. She looked at the distant mountains; they were indeed a beautiful and glorious sight. For a moment, she had lost herself in the moment, enjoying the view and the soft gentle breeze as well as the soothing sound of the rustling leaves and comfort she had drawn from the forest.

Gilly slid a box to one of the arches and stood upon it so she could see over the sill. "Oh dear, me dears," Gilly said with a troubled tone. "Oh dear," she repeated, "oh dear indeed, me dears."

Janorra's bliss was disturbed, but she was not sure what it was that was troubling Gilly. "What is it?" she asked, as she walked over to her Gilly, and followed her gaze to see what the dwarf was pointing to in the distance beyond the forest.

Scarand joined them. "Bodies, lots of them," he said.

He was right, in the distance, far beyond the wood, Janorra could make out the scene that was clearly the aftermath of a battle. Men, horses, and what looked like some Bantu corpses were littered on the side of the hill where a great gaping hold showed where the moleworm had broken through the surface. There was no sign of anyone living. Fallen banners fluttered in the breeze.

"They are the Baron Daramir's banners, and those of the Hedge Knights," Gilly said. "It looks like they met those Bantu and were killed in a terrible battle."

Scarand scowled at the scene, and scanned the horizon for any signs of life. "It might be that the Bantu on foot, were slain, and that having lost Sasna's trail, the Baron is either himself slain, or has gone to lick his wounds in his castle," he suggested to Gilly. "You would be best making haste, if you wish to make the tunnels to Berecoth, before either return and renew their search."

"You are quite right, me dear," she answered. "And this, is where you must go," she said as she took the box, crossed the room and placing it at the foot of a western facing arch, she stood on it and pointed in the distance. She leant on the sill of the archway. Peeking at the branch, she looked nervously at the edges of it, and gripped the sill more tightly for comfort.

The viewing platform they were on, was cleverly grown from a branch that was thick and wide enough for seven men to stride abreast on. It had been flattened by some Elven magic so it looked like it was easy to walk upon, though on the branch there was no rail, so care would be needed to be taken near the edge. The canopy of foliage above them was green and lush, as was the whole eastern side of the forest. It was only broken by natural gaps through which the sky could be seen. Janorra and the others followed Gilly and gazed in the direction she pointed. To the west, in the far distance, the trees were withered and leafless, as though some dark curse prevented life from growing there.

"That is where Mithilos is, and that is where the Murien showed us we must go," Gilly said, after which she swallowed hard, and looked tentatively at the branch.

Janorra crossed the platform and looked out of an arch to the south-east, where Castle Greytears could be seen in the far distance, over which some dark clouds were gathering though a mist seemed to cover them from full view. She shuddered at the thought of what might have happened had she not been able to escape from there, though she couldn't shake the feeling that the clouds were an ill omen for something far worse than a summer storm. The sight of Greytears and the dying part of the forest, reminded her about the urgency of her quest. She quickly forgot the calmness that had accompanied her during the climb, and the beautiful part of the view, and again remembered the urgency of her mission.

"We must hurry," she reminded Gilly as she re-joined her. "Why have we come up here?"

"To call me Bena birds, me dear," Gilly replied as she took a wooden whistle from her breast pocket. She blew the whistle, which made a sort of crawking sound, and then blew it several more times and waited. They did not have to wait long before a flapping sound could be heard, and two birds, each about the size of the dwarf appeared in the sky, circled and then dived though a gap in the canopy before doing a running landing on the far end of the branch. It was a very clumsy landing for both birds, one of them tumbled over several times before managing to gain its grip. The other seemed to bounce several times, but somehow both managed to remain on the branch and they came to an untidy stop just below the archways where they stood and looked expectantly at Gilly.

"Cake! Crawk! Crawk!" Both birds demanded at the same time.

Janorra looked at the birds in disgust, and curled her nose up at the smell that wafted from them.

"These are Bena birds?" Scarand asked disgustedly.

Another memory returned to Janorra. She recalled reading something about these birds in the temple library when she was studying wildlife lore. She remembered that they would use their wings to fly, but when hunting they favoured using their wings to swim through the deep lakes and underground wells where they hunted large fish, otters and river snakes. They preferred to make their nests in lakes or swampland. They were perpetually hungry, carnivorous birds who also often scavenged in human cities. Well-known as mimics, Bena birds would often imitate the cries of an injured baby animal, as they waited underwater at the edge of a lake, grabbing and drowning any animal curious enough to come close and investigate. They preferred cattle and sheep, but would eat virtually anything. They had even been known to snatch and take small children for a meal. It was said that a mother Bena Bird laid her eggs in water, and there were two different kinds—good and bad. The good eggs floated, and when they hatched, the mother and father raised them, welcoming them into the world and rejoicing in their appearance. The bad eggs sunk to the bottom of the water and hatched there. These bad birds were condemned to live in darkness beneath deep waters in rivers and lakes, and it was said they became terrible and fearsome creatures that never left the deep waters. Bena were powerful birds considered vermin and a pest by many.

416

Gilly laughed at the look of disgust on Janorra's face. "They are not so bad, me dear, once you get used to their smell. They are migratory you know, these two are my friends, siblings, a brother and sister. They come to me every summer and fly off for the winter. I have named them Hogin and Mogin, after two young nephews I had in the Iron Mountains who never used to like washing. It seemed appropriate names, me dear, don't you think?"

"Were these the same two birds watching our journey in the sky?" Scarand asked.

"They were me dear. I had them searching for Sasna and was glad when they told me she travelled here with others. The flying beast often chased them off but Bena are persistent and stubborn creatures when given the right motivation." She looked affectionately at the birds. "Cake is the motivation I give to them." She turned her head and looked at Janorra. "They will help you get your ring, me dear. You see, old Uilisomor is afraid of Bena birds, as they have been known to attack and eat spiders even as big as her you know. They will take you to where she dwells." She then looked at Scarand, Muro and Janorra in turn, and sternly warned. "Remember, you'll not be harming old Uilisomor now, me dears. There will be no need for it, and the forest would not like it."

"Why wouldn't the forest want the spider dead?" Janorra asked, feeling slightly annoyed with Gilly. "That thing killed me."

"I already told you. Uilisomor keeps a lot of nasty old things in the forest at bay, she hunts the things that eat the trees, like the fat wood maggots that hatch from the eggs of the boza flies and stingwings that lay them. Those juicy maggots are bigger than me, me dear. Old Uilisomor can smell them whenever they hatch and she releases a scent that gets them crawling right into her web from wherever they are in the forest, clever old thing she is. So, no, you will not be harming the spider, me dears, as the forest might turn on you."

"So how will I get my ring back?" Janorra asked.

"Oh, my birds will scare her off long enough for you to get your ring back. Old Uilisomor will not come out if my birds are there, she will retreat deep into a cave she lives in, not far from where she trapped you, me dear. You should be able to cut your body from the web, and retrieve the ring. I doubt she has consumed it yet; she likes to give a body a good few weeks of hanging there before the innards are turned to the goo which she drinks. That's why she likes the maggots so much, she doesn't have to wait, she can eat them on the same day."

Janorra turned her nose up in disgust at the thought of the spider treating her discarded body in such a way. In the temple, apart from the times when they were a sacrifice or a meal, the discarded body of a Seer sent to the Deadlands, was treated with great respect and entombed in deep vaults beneath the Argona Temple with much elaborate ceremony and ritual. She looked at the birds and winced. Both birds had long, wide necks and a huge wingspan. They had a long thick beak, short legs and massive partially webbed feet. The excited crawling noise they continued to make as they looked at Gilly was enough to give a headache. Janorra covered her ears with her hands and noticed Scarand do the same.

"They are large enough for a dwarf to fly on," Scarand shouted above the noise.

"Oh, me dear, old Gilly isn't afraid of anything, except flying."

"And spiders and heights," Scarand whispered under his breath to Janorra, who had uncovered her ears. She would have smiled, but the urgency of her task was the only focus of her mind.

The smaller bird had a single white feather on its otherwise bald head. "That's Mogin, the sister, and the larger one is Hogin her brother," Gilly said as she pointed her staff at the birds. A soft blue light emanated from it and rested upon each bird, before sinking into their heads.

"Now tell me, me dears, where are those horrid Bantu. Did you spot them? And what happened to the Baron and his men?"

"Crawk-awk, cake!" Hogin cried flapping his wings whilst looking eagerly at Gilly.

"Ack-ack, cake," Mogin bawled.

Gilly undid the buckle of her bag, took from it the cake she had baked, and broke a couple of pieces off, which she threw to the birds. The birds greedily gulped the pieces down, and Gilly threw some more to them, which were just as quickly eaten. "More cake," Hogin said in between beak fills.

"This is the last piece, Mogin your sister needs fattening up for winter, let her have it me dear," Gilly said as she threw the last piece of cake towards Mogin. Hogin pecked Mogin on her wing. For a moment both birds fought furiously, flapping their ragged feathers and fighting for the piece of cake. Hogin managed to get the cake, greedily gulping it down as he was watched by the envious beady eyes of his sibling.

"That's very greedy, me dear," Gilly said in a reproachful tone.

"Cake," Hogin said in a rusty voice, his golden eyes shining hopefully.

"No more cake for now. Now tell me, the Bantu, did you look for them, me dears?"

"Scary worm sank into the earth, few Bantu that did not follow, dead, ack-ack cake," Hogin cried as he flapped his wings. "Men kill them, ack-ack, but they slew many."

"Five Bantu kill nearly all men, cake, ack-ack," Mogin crawked.

"What about the flying beast?" Gilly asked.

"Follow scary worm into hole, crawk-awk," cake!" Hogin demanded.

Mogin flapped her wings again, "Ack-ack, cake, more cake." She pecked at the branch of the tree, flapping her wings and crawking.

"I'll bake another cake when this business is done, me dears, a really big one. But I need you to help my friend here, to take her to where old Uilisomor lives."

The birds jumped excitedly up and down. "Ack-ack," they both crawked.

"Hogin eat spider?" he asked as he flapped his wings excitedly.

"No, no, me dears," Gilly said sternly as she wagged her finger at the birds. "Old Gilly will not bake you any more cakes if you do. Just take my friends to Bessie, and then on to where Uilisomor lives. Make sure Uilisomor knows you are there so she won't come out until my friends have retrieved something they are looking for."

Hogin looked at Mogin, "No eat spider," it said mournfully.

"Ack-ack," Mogin replied. "More cake if obey?"

"Yes," Gilly said. "A fresh cake if you obey. Mind you, I will need to go to Berecoth soon to buy some more sugar me dears, but I have enough to bake one more big cake. Now, use the forest paths, and take my friends to Bessie, and then to where Uilisomor lives." The dwarf made a shooing sound and signalled to the birds to leave. The two birds spread their wings and jumped off the side of the branch, and effortlessly glided down to the forest floor, weaving in and out of the other trees and branches, and then landing clumsily.

"It seems my way is clear to take Sasna and her brother to the tunnels," Gilly said, sighing with obvious relief.

"Will you join us soon?" Janorra asked her.

"When I have escorted Sasna and her brother safely to the tunnels that lead to Berecoth, I will join you. For now, the forest has agreed to help you, me dear. My birds will take you to meet a friend of mine, Bessie. She wishes to make your introduction; she is the one who knows the way to where we need to go. After that, my birds will take you to find your ring and I will join you as fast as I can."

Janorra looked warily at Gilly. She did trust the dwarf, but setting off into the forest with only Scarand, Muro and the two strange birds to meet whoever knows what and then confront the spider, was not what she had in mind when asking for help.

Gilly must have sensed her uneasiness. "Haste must be the business of the day, me dear. Now off, me dears, follow my birds and trust old Gilly."

"How do we get down?" Janorra asked.

Gilly carefully leant over the side of the sill and pointed. "Oh my, old Gilly never likes this part. Look, over there," she said as she pointed to a rope bridge that led from the branch the viewing platform was on, to the branch of another tree some distance away. In the trunk of that tree you will find a door, you can take the spiral staircase that will lead you to the forest floor where me birds are waiting for you, me dears."

"You're not coming with us even to the forest floor?" Scarand asked.

"Oh no, me dear, I don't like rope bridges. Though you can be sure it is strong, despite its age. The Elves left it behind. It was woven by one of their songs so it is quite safe. Old Gilly will find you. Gaffren is rested and he will gallop with speed to the tunnels with me and the Seesnari on his back. Now, off with you. Old Gilly will find you on my return; I have left instructions for my friend Bessie to meet you at the Spriggans' Glade. Hogin knows the way."

Janorra and the two Davari said their farewell and then climbed carefully over the sills and onto the branch, and made their way to the rope bridge. Scarand tested it before stepping onto the wooden planked flooring, and it appeared strong and robust just as Gilly had said, even though it swayed unnervingly as they crossed it. The door in the trunk of the tree was easy to find and it was unlocked. It took Janorra and the two men little time to reach the bottom of the stairs.

"Couldn't that foolish dwarf have arranged for the birds meet us at the bottom of the tree?" Muro grumbled angrily.

"I think she wanted us to get an overview of the forest," Scarand retorted back, "and I for one am glad I saw the landscape we are in."

The three of them entered the forest floor through an opening that looked like a split in the tree. The opening closed the moment they had all walked through it, and despite briefly trying to find it again out of sheer curiosity and amazement, touching and pushing the trunk where moments before they had just passed through, they could not.

Hogin and Mogin were rummaging for worms and insects, digging up the forest floor. They looked up as Janorra, Scarand and Muro approached. They did not have time to rest as the birds immediately hopped along a forest trail.

"Follow, ack-ack," Hogin squawked.

"If it offers any assurance, I will do all in my power to assist and protect you," Scarand said to Janorra, as they both looked around at the mysterious forest and the trail up ahead that the birds were hopping along. By the noble look in his eye and the bold manner in which he said it, she knew he meant it.

"I thank you, but I do not know the end to which I travel and my task seems all but impossible," she replied.

"As does mine," Scarand said wistfully. "Ever since I entered the Everglow, the hope of ever finding my sisters, constantly tries to leave me." He grew silent for a moment, and then continued. "Every second I tarry or am delayed guilt steals up on me to tell me I am not doing enough…"

Janorra finished his sentence for him, "That you feel you don't understand how important and urgent the task is, and that soon it might be too late."

Scarand nodded grimly. "How do you answer those feelings and thoughts when they come to you?" he asked her.

419

She smiled resolutely. "I have learnt that hope is not a feeling, it is a choice; and even in the midst of despair, I can still choose to carry on. There is no greater hope than that."

"Where there is life, there is hope," Scarand said.

Janorra, herself a scholar and teacher of many a school of wisdom, found comfort in the simple words he spoke. She steeled her resolve. *My only hope is to reach Baothein lands with the Simal. The world will be safe, and I will be protected by their Seers, in this world, and the Deadlands.* For the first time since her escape, she felt a glimmer of genuine hope that she might succeed. The presence of Scarand comforted her.

As Janorra and her companions continued to follow the birds along the westward trail, a strange feeling came upon her, similar to that which she had felt on the stairs when she had stroked the wood. It deepened as she followed the birds deeper into the forest. It seemed to her that she had stepped over a bridge of time, into a corner of the First Age when the Elves still dwelt in the forest.

She knew that Scarand sensed it too, for he looked around at the forest canopy in awe and said to her, "There is the memory of ancient things in this wood. It is as though I have been here before."

"It is indeed alive with memory," Janorra replied, as she had the strange sensation that it was not the first time she had been along these paths, even though in fact it was. It was the memories of others she was sensing and feeling. In her mind's eye she saw the image of two elf lovers in a glade expressing their love for the first time. Then, she saw a maiden feeding a myriad of birds that covered her and sang to her as she sang with delight to them. She smiled with delight at the images, and noticed Scarand do the same.

"I see wonderful visions of things past," he said in awe. "I feel that I am drowning in beauty, even the air I breathe is fresh and pure."

Muro shook his head as though to rid them of images, and muttered under his breath. "Evil images plague my mind in this place. The air is foul."

They marched on, following the Bena birds, until they felt the cool evening come and heard the early night-wind whispering among the leaves of the trees. They rested and slept without fear on the forest floor, in a glade with a small stream running through it with a small pool at the far end.

All night, Janorra had a sense that the forest was protecting them. For the first time for as long as she could remember, she had peaceful dreams. She awoke in the morning feeling refreshed and at peace. Muro was already awake and meditating at the far end of the glade. Scarand was waking from slumber.

"I will bathe," she said to Scarand, as she removed her boots and clothes and climbed down the bank of the pool, and waded into the clear water. Hogin and Mogin, awaking from sleep, watched her drowsily and with curiosity.

The water was cold but its touch was clean. Janorra bathed her face in it, and then waded to the middle until the water was up to her neck. The water was refreshing and rejuvenating. She felt the stain of all travel and weariness wash from her limbs. Scarand joined her, though he kept himself modestly covered, and was careful to avoid staring at her nakedness. Leaving the pool, she quickly dried herself and dressed, before gathering some berries from a nearby bush.

"Wild raspberries," she said, eating with relish and offering some to Scarand who had joined her. She laughed gaily. "This place reminds me of my first life, when I was a child. There was a wood at the end of our garden, it also had a pool and bushes of wild berries," she reminisced.

In that moment, Janorra even toyed with the idea that maybe the Wytchwood was a place she could dwell in. She could abandon her quest; forget all about the world beyond the forest. In here, she need never give thought to such matters again beyond the present moment. Her carefree abandonment did not last long, as it quickly dawned upon her that even if she spent the rest of her life here, one day, she would still die, and, Otan the Obelisk would resurrect her back in Castle Greytears, and by then they would surely know who she was, and remember her previous escape.

It also dawned upon her that she knew little about the abilities of the Wild Hunt, but they were hunting her, and she instinctively knew they would not give up. A shiver of terror briefly swept through her at the thought that the dreadful moleworm and its companions might come crashing through the ground in a shower of earth and mud at any moment. "It is time we left," she said abruptly, gathering her things and adjusting her sword belt.

As they prepared to set out again, Janorra considered that if she died again, she could wander through the Deadlands far from this place, and find another Obelisk, but she would have no idea whether what she might find on resurrection, would be a worse fate than that which she would surely face at the castle. Until she found a safe Obelisk to resurrect at, nowhere was guaranteed to be safe for her. No, she could not dwell in this forest; she must reach Baothein lands, which was her only chance of spending the rest of her lives and days in peace, or an even greater thought, somehow giving herself the *Final-death*. It had dawned upon her just how tired of living she was at times. She looked at Scarand and envied him for only having one lifetime to endure.

"We must have resolves of stone and steel," she said to Scarand, "for tomorrow is unknown, and even in this place, evil might find us at any moment if we are seduced by false securities. We both fail in our quests, if we give up trying to reach the destinations for which we are toiling."

"I understand," he said, "this place is bewitching my senses and priorities as well."

The birds were soon up and about, and Hogin crawked, "Ack-ack, follow," as he hopped down a forest path that led northwards out of the glade. The others followed.

When the path turned westwards, the birds continued northward, going into the shadow of the deeper woods where the trunks of the trees were of mighty girth and their height could only be guessed. They only stopped when they heard a gentle crashing through the forest, as though something of great size was making its way towards them.

"Ack-ack, friendly," Hogin squawked, though he did not need too. Whatever it was that approached them, meant them no harm. Janorra knew it for she could sense it from the forest. Scarand did not seem alarmed either, as out of the shadow of the forest a large tree giant suddenly appeared. The giant was man-like in shape, though its skin was made of bark from which shoots of greenery sprung. It was tall, about twelve feet high and very sturdy. The large feet had twelve toes each, and the hands twelve fingers. The eyes were sad, black, shot through with a milky green light. The giant stared curiously at the small company who stood beneath it.

For a long time Janorra had never totalled how many years she had exactly lived. She was older and wiser by far than any short-lived Fell-blood, but she sensed herself as likened to a child next to this ancient being. How she knew it, she could only guess that the forest was telling her, but she sensed that the creature was the last of its kind, the sole remnant of a very ancient race.

Muro raised his palms defensively, pointing the runes in them at the creature, but the runes did nothing.

The giant smiled at them, a tired, weary, but gentle smile, before carrying on its way into the forest. It soon disappeared into the greenery, and again somehow Janorra knew, that she and her two companions were the last humans who would ever set eyes on such a creature again.

"I have read about them; Tree Gragor, a race that is as old as the earth. I never expected to ever see one," she said with girl-like glee, which soon turned to sadness. "It is the last of its kind. No human will ever see one again."

"Every day that passes in the Everglow, I realise more and more that I know so very little about the true nature of the world," Scarand said in awed reply.

Muro said nothing, but Janorra could tell by the look on his face, that he too was awed by the sight of such a creature, and somewhat alarmed.

Continuing northward, the companions found another stream and followed it to a clear glade where they stopped to rest in the cool air that greeted them. The two birds crawked with delight, as strange music suddenly echoed from the trees: soft joyful horns; the glacial tinkering of harps; a bewildering jumble of melodies that spiralled and rose without the slightest trace of discord all filled the air.

"Friends, ack-ack," Hogin said, which helped to settle Janorra and the two men who had been startled by the suddenness of the music. The sunlight was now directly overhead, and Janorra noticed a group of small figures in the shade of the trees, or seated in the branches, some of whom were playing the music, whilst the others sat there watching them.

"Come," Janorra said to the creatures. She smiled at them, knelt and patted the ground invitingly. Some of the creatures leapt to their feet, and emboldened by her invitation, hurried into the sunlight calling her name.

"Janorra! Janorra! Gilly said you would come," one said as she approached and then tugged curiously at Janorra's leather trousers.

"Gilly told us this morning through the forest, that you were coming," another of the small people said as he looked inside Scarand's boots, before clambering up him and sitting on his shoulder.

Janorra felt no threat from these strange little creatures. "Who are you?" she asked gently.

"We are Spriggan," said one of the small, human like creatures, each of whom were partially clothed with leaves, covering their lichen coloured skin. They looked up at her and smiled. Their wide almond shaped brown eyes were full of wonder.

"Are you going to set the rest of the forest free?" one of them asked her.

"Gilly said the forest finds hope in your appearing," another said, as he walked towards Hogin and Mogin, who both rose to their full height exposing the oily feathers on their chest. Several of the Spriggans ran to the birds, and seemingly oblivious to their smell, began stroking and tickling the birds on the chest. Hogin and Mogin crawked with delight.

"You two are just as stinky as ever," one of the Spriggan said.

"'Ere, bring 'um some of that rotten turnip we found, and that maggot, they'll like that," another suggested.

"Ack-ack, cake," Hogin crawked, followed by Mogin.

"Cake, ack-ack."

"Now we ain't be 'aving no cake you greedy birds," one of the Spriggan playfully said, "but we got some turnip, and a big fat maggot that we caught trying to eat acorns from the Oak of Ages, and that'll 'ave to do you."

More Spriggan emerged from the forest, some carrying a large, wriggling maggot almost as big as themselves, and others some turnips well past their best. The two birds fought over the wriggling maggot, Hogin won, and crawked with delight after swallowing it whole. Both birds then greedily gobbled down the turnips the Spriggan fed to them.

Muro grumpily shooed the Spriggans away when they tried to get near to him, but Janorra and Scarand let them clamber over them, even though they poked and pulled out of curiosity.

"We're not to be delaying you, Miss Gilly told us not too, but she said we could say 'ello," one of the Spriggan said.

"I do 'ope we be seeing you again though, you are so lovely, so beautiful," a young Spriggan female said as she looked up adoringly at Janorra.

"Why, thank you," Janorra replied soothingly.

"So pretty," another Spriggan said. She was different in appearance to the others. Her perfect face – oval in shape, and dominated by her dark almond eyes, canted upward, a smile appearing like a crescent moon through the clouds of a dark night. Her only disfigurement was the ritual scarring that covered her face: deep, circular grooves spiralled down from her forehead and surrounded her eyes, making her look different in appearance to the rest of the Spriggan. "I'm Bessie," she said.

"*Arvivan*," Janorra heard Muro whisper to himself, on noticing the carvings. She wondered what he meant by it.

Bessie ignored him.

Janorra stroked Bessie's twiggy looking hair. Bessie than ran to a nearby white flower, picked it, retuned, and clambering onto Janorra's shoulders, she carefully placed it in Janorra's hair.

"I do declare, you are the most beautiful thing I 'ave ever seen," Bessie stated, and then shot a reproachful glance at Muro who was still shooing other Spriggan away and brushing them off when they tried to climb onto him. "Unlike old grumpy boots over there," she added.

"Old scary eyes webs are not far from 'ere now," a young male Spriggan said to Scarand. "You're not to 'urt 'er, you know that, right?"

"Scary eyes?" Scarand asked.

"Yeah, old, oilo…no, ulesio…oh bother, what is it Gilly calls it?"

"Uilisomor?" Scarand offered.

"Yeah, that's 'er; she used to eat our kind until Gilly spoke to the forest and got 'er to stop. Now she just stares at us if she sees us as she is scuttling about 'er business. If we find them maggot eggs, we take them to the edge of 'er web and she eats 'em when they hatch, and sometimes even before they do."

"Better she eats the eggs than us, and the fat maggots when they 'atch, disease spreaders they are when they turn into flies," Bessie said, and then added, "but I do feel sorry for them."

"Why?" Janorra asked, feeling slightly bemused.

"Because, even maggots are living things, and from their perspective, we must be the monsters." Before Janorra could respond, Bessie shook the thought away, smiled and said cheerfully to Janorra and Scarand. "We must be off now, but I will see you again, soon. Miss Gilly will give us a ticking off if we keep you longer, but we're pleased to meet you ma'am, and you sir." She frowned at Muro. "But not the grumpy one. Look how 'e still shoos us away!"

"I am pleased to meet you as well," Janorra said.

"Bye now," each of the Spriggan said, one after another. The music stopped, and as quickly as they had appeared the Spriggan rushed back into the forest and soon disappeared from sight.

"This place doesn't seem so bad, I wonder why the men of the castle fear it so much," Scarand said as he watched the last of the Spriggan turn, and wave goodbye.

"We have the goodwill of the forest, but I would fear to be here were it not so," Janorra replied, "and a different tale would be told in the west side of the forest, that is a place I would not choose to go, but I fear we must."

Setting out again and heading north from the glade, the forest soon became thick with centuries old thickets and forgotten brooks. It seemed darker in this part of the forest, and the joy Janorra had felt earlier, soon disappeared. The deeper they walked into this part of the forest, the darker it became, and it seemed to her as though dark spectral figures called out to her from under every bower. She became jumpy and held the hilt of her sword.

After an hour of tracking, they saw the first of the gossamer threads, the beginning of Uilisomor's web. The two birds hopped carefully over them. Where the web became thick and unpassable, one of the birds would say, "Ack-ack, chop-chop."

Janorra understood, she got her sword out and cut away at the web, all the time looking out for Uilisomor, but the spider did not appear, although she thought she heard a distant and faint enraged hissing.

"Did you hear that?" she asked, alarmed.

"I did," Scarand replied as he instinctively drew his new bow and notched an arrow for the first time, warily watching the forest around him. Muro raised his hands and the runes in his palms began to glow.

"Put away, put away, ack-ack," Hogin squealed in panic. "Do not harm. No cake for us if she is harmed. Ack-ack."

Scarand reluctantly put the arrow back in the quiver and lowered his bow, and Muro his hands.

Forward they went, slowly and cautiously, stepping over the threads where they could, chopping them where they could not. It was not long before Janorra sensed the spider was watching their progress. She could feel the malice of the creature and knew it was watching their every move, and were it not for the Bena birds she sensed it might pounce at any unexpected moment.

The birds screeched and made a deafening noise.

"Ack- ack, go to your cave, or we eat you," Hogin shrieked.

For the first time, Janorra found comfort and reassurance in the presence of the Bena birds, and was glad for their presence. A part of her had doubted that these birds really could kill the spider, despite the ferocious sharpness at the end of their beaks that looked like they could pierce like a sword. The birds furiously opened and shut their beaks, making a loud cracking noise. It occurred to her that the snap and strength of their closing could easily cut a man cleanly in half, and do considerable damage even to a spider the size of Uilisomor, effortlessly severing off her legs. She had also noticed that from out of their webbed feet, long claws that were like daggers had emerged. These birds were clearly fiercer than she had seen of them so far, and the thought suddenly occurred to her that she would not like one of them to turn on her.

It was quite disturbing when they finally emerged into the glade where Janorra had been killed by Uilisomor just a few days before. Much to her dismay and revulsion, she saw her former body cocooned in the tree; the sight sickened her and made her retch. One foot was slightly sticking out from the cocoon. It was bloated, blackened and covered in dried blood. Tiny maggots crawled in a wound and the skin writhed with larvae and beetles. Janorra could not bring herself to cut down such a disgusting thing.

Scarand must have sensed her uneasiness, and to her relief he took the sword from her, climbed the tree and cut the body down with some difficulty due to the stickiness

424

of the threads sticking to sword and person. Eventually the body dropped to the ground, landing with a sickening thud.

Whilst this was happening, Janorra could sense the displeasure and rage of Uilisomor. The malice of the spider permeated the air and from a distance she heard her hiss with rage.

Scarand cut open the cocoon. Both she and he gasped as they looked upon her own face, pale and corrupt in death. The dried blood on her face was black, the eyes were missing. The stench was sickening. It was a horror she had never hoped to see.

"That is, you!" Scarand declared, horrified as he looked at the corpse.

Muro gloated at the sight with a look of twisted pleasure on his face.

"It was," Janorra replied, as she took the sword from Scarand, and, pulling an involuntary face, cut the ring finger from the corpse. She then pulled the ring off the swollen finger with some difficulty, before removing the Amulet of Ahrimakan from around the corpse's neck. She wiped both items on the grass, though the stench she could not remove. As she touched the amulet, the memories of what it symbolised caused her to shudder.

"I have what I need, let us be gone from this filthy place. The spider has not retreated to a cave, she still watches us, I sense it."

"What about the body, are you just going to leave it for that thing to eat?" Scarand asked.

*What else can I do?* She thought. "It is customary to fulfil a ritual before burning or burying a past body, but we have no time for either ritual or burial, and we have no shovels even if we did."

"We can burn it, I can make fire," Muro said.

Janorra nodded, "Do it, if it can be done in a way the fire will not spread."

"Ack-ack, no fire, the forest hates fire," Hogin warned.

"Ack-ack, only in the stone place is fire allowed," Mogin chimed in.

"We could eat it, ack-ack," Hogin said hopefully, as he stared at Janorra with anticipation glowing in his beady eyes.

Janorra looked at the birds. She had started to grow fond of them, especially after they had posed no threat to the Spriggan which they could easily have swallowed in one gulp. Also, their presence was clearly a deterrent to Uilisomor, for which she was grateful. But, despite this, suddenly she was filled with a new disgust towards them again.

"No," she said. "Definitely no!"

"Then take it to the glade, let the Spriggan brings rocks from the bed of a stream and bury it beneath those. It doesn't seem right to just leave it here," Scarand said as he looked around at the grimness of the place, they were in.

"Ack-ack, Hogin will carry it to the glade," the bird said.

Before Janorra could answer, Hogin picked the half-cocooned corpse up in his large beak and began to hop back in the direction they had come from, with Mogin crawking and hopping excitedly after him.

"Share! Share! Ack-ack," Mogin screeched.

Janorra raced after them.

"Don't you eat it Hogin, or I will make Gilly swear never to make cake for you again. Don't you dare eat my discarded body Hogin! Hogin!"

\*        \*        \*

425

It was past midnight. Sasna could scarcely realize she had been so long underground. She felt a ravenous appetite. Looking up at the dark-black-star-flecked sky, and then back at the stone door that closed and became as one with the large and seemingly innocuous boulder, she shivered.

"I know that look," Farir said to her. "Whatever it is you are thinking, forget it."

"Did you not hear what Gilly said, and see what I saw?" Sasna asked, shaking water from the hood of her cloak which was soggy from the rain that was falling from clouds that were just beginning to hide the moon from sight.

Farir groaned. "Will you never learn?"

"The only reason she told us some of those tunnels were unexplored and dangerous, was to stop us ever going back there. It is said that such ancient dwarf tunnels, could contain treasure untold. Where do you think she got her riches?"

"And who knows what foul things might also lurk in such places?" Farir asked. "She told us there is nothing of worth left in the tunnels she had explored, and she feared to wander into the ones she had not."

"I don't believe her," Sasna said. "When this business with the Sea Lords is over, I intend going back into these tunnels, with or without you."

Farir groaned again and brushed rain from his cloak. "All I know is the filth and dust from that place will take a month to wash off, not even this rain cleans it!"

Sasna ignored his complaint, and looked at a familiar landscape. They were standing on the tallest of a maze of hills, beyond which the land levelled. On the northern bank of the Erin stood a walled town guarded by a moat connected at each end to the river. The last light of the moon, before it was completely hidden by clouds, also showed a port that contained several ships and a variety of boats.

"It will be dangerous," Farir said. "We paid for passage to Harwind, little did we know the one called Captain Redboots planned to take us hostage," he grumbled.

"It was just a miscommunication," Sasna responded. "Whatever the risk, I intend speaking directly with Erik Vansoth. The world is falling to ruins, I will not let the Seesnari fall with it."

"Then we should make haste," Farir said, "and consider ourselves fortunate if we reach the gates of Berecoth before dawn."

Together, they headed down the hill towards the distant town.

# Chapter Thirty-Five: *The Obelisk at Thurog Tor*

*Isabella of Thurog Tor has one of the grimmest reputations as any queen who ever lived. Nobody alive has any memory of her, and there are no contemporary accounts of her reign. I know of her because deep in the ancient tombs below the city, I discovered a crumbling and antique text that told of her rule, during a time now faded from memory. I have no reason to doubt the account is true, although some of the tale is lost due to the past deterioration of the now fragmented transcript. What I did learn from it though, was that she was the last ever Pure-blood queen to rule in the Tarenmoors. She was infamous during her lifetimes as an adulteress, a disloyal mother and a poisoner. She ruled in turbulent times, and under her notorious reign, her kingdom broke away from the Angelivian Empire, and it was that act that led to her Final-death and the end of any Pure-blood reign in the entire Tarenmoors.*
**Temmison Vol VI, Book 1: History of the Kings and Queens of the Tarenmoors.**

*Marki's* dreams were dark and unpleasant. He dreamt that he and Galin were riding up and down the ranks of the Third Legion shouting words of encouragement to the men, but the words seemed bitter and empty.

"Valiant mottos and future aspirations will not lift our gloom," one of the men of the legion had shouted back at them. In his dream, he then walked amongst the camp fires, and listened to the dark mutterings of the men. They spoke of their repetitive torment at the thought of the fate that might have had met their loved ones and their fellow legionnaires left behind at Aleskian. There was much talk in the ranks about the dangers of dying on the march with no safe Obelisk identified. Even in the confusion and chaos of his muddled dream, Marki understood their fear. It was a fear born not of cowardice, but a fear born of those who could find the gift of immortality a curse of never-ending woe if they suffered the misfortune of a physical death far away from a known and safe Obelisk. Marki knew every man of the Third Legion by name. He did not like them all, but by Balagrim's beard he respected each and every one of them, and he had sworn by the Nine Shield-Maidens that he would always do right by them. He made this vow repeatedly to them in his dream, but still some of them murmured, muttered and plotted, before his dreams moved onto Borach.

In the dream about Borach, he saw that a deep darkness and foreboding gloom shrouded his friend. The gloom was not solely due to the mortal and physical wound that would certainly lead to yet another physical death, but the wound he suffered was far, far deeper than that of mere flesh – it pierced the spirit of Borach. It was the haunted scream and despairing wail of Borach, that caused Marki to wake with a start. Cold sweat dripped from his forehead.

"By Balagrim's beard, curse the night-terrors," he muttered.

Sunlight was just appearing through the window of the room he had slept in. Marki jumped out of bed. He had slept fully clothed and armed. Splashing some water onto his face from a bowl that had been left on the table beside the bed, he felt revitalised.

*Despite ill dreams, at least the issue of the Obelisk is resolved for now,* he thought grimly. He did not like the idea of serving someone like Falamore, a man he considered a moral degenerate, but his loyalty to Borach, was foremost. His friend's impending death, and therefore his need of a safe and secure resurrection had made all other issues secondary. *Not all in the legion will agree with the terms I have made for use of the Obelisk, but all other choice was stripped from me.* His particular concern was about Meron, who would not be pleased that he had given the griffin away. *In truth, Meron will be furious and will feel betrayed.*

427

Marki felt it was a bad omen that Falamore had insisted that his two sons, Molamore and Falarain were to accompany the army, and Effgard's son, so they could watch the battle, learn, and gain experience of war. *A war is no place for milklings*, he thought, as he drank some water from the bowl and then tore into a chunk of bread, he had taken to his room with him the night before.

When he left the room, a guard was outside his door. "King Falamore has ordered he is not to be disturbed this day, he wishes to be about drinking and whoring," the guard said abruptly.

*That figures, the degenerate.* Marki yawned, stretched and snapped, "Then take me to Talain. She will be expecting me." The guard nodded and led Marki through the keep. They walked down winding stone staircases, through the Council Chamber, into the Great Hall and then out into the open air by way of the doors he and Effgard had entered by the day before.

Outside, Talain was waiting, and to amuse herself she was pretending to stand stiff to attention next to two guards. The guards looked uneasy in her presence. She grinned and winked as Marki approached.

"I'll show you the Obelisk then," she said, and led him down the steps, across the courtyard to the outer ward that was particularly crowded and noisy that morning, mostly with people who were waiting to catch a glimpse of Marki. "Many have never seen a dwarf before, news of your presence has spread," Talain said, and then winked as she added, "perhaps they have also heard of your giant-sized member."

"Then just as well I am a prime example of the best looking of all dwarves," Marki replied wryly as he scanned the crowd, who were jostling for position to get a better view of him.

"You could earn a small fortune in coin juggling on a street corner here, I would pay to come and see that," Talain said as she pushed her way through the crowd.

Marki followed her and raised his voice to be heard above the din of the crowd. "I can't juggle lass, but I'm nay a bad magician. I can make the contents of a jug of ale disappear right before your very eyes."

Talain pushed past the jostling crowd and made straight for the stables, followed by Marki who was getting annoyed as the crowd pushed and pulled at him, continuously trying to touch him. Some of the people were shouting the name 'Karno,' and hailing Marki as the Servant of Karno. Others were not so polite or respectful. One man barred his way, and patted Marki on the helmet on his head.

"They say its good luck to touch a dwarf," the man said, looking around for approval in an obvious attempt at showing off to the crowd, some of whom cheered him on.

Marki's fist to the man's head was like a hammer blow. He dropped to the ground like a wet sack, unconscious before he even hit it. Those in the crowd, who had cheered, gasped in shock.

"It's not such good luck if a dwarf touches you back," Marki shouted angrily as he stepped over the unconscious man. "Does anyone else want to try and touch this dwarf for luck?" he growled. Nobody else barred their way or tried to touch him after that as the crowd parted so he and Talain could make their way unhindered to the stables.

A groom led Marki's dappled grey pony out the stable door, and another groom led out a fine grey mare for Talain whilst a third groom led out a piebald gelding, upon which was seated Princess Maraya, her hands chained to the saddle. She was skinnier and more hollow-eyed than Marki had remembered from the night before, and several bruises were on her face that had not been there the previous night. Wrapped in a tattered, heavy brown cloak, beneath which was the same raiment she had worn the day before, she shivered in the morning breeze. Her black hair blew wild in the wind. Her face, though bruised, was quite pretty, he thought, though she was clearly malnourished and her eyes devoid of any hope.

"Unchain her," Marki ordered one of the guards holding the reigns of the horse.

The guard hesitated, but Talain said, "Do it. She is now the responsibility of the dwarf, by order of the king."

"My orders are to escort her to the main gate," the guard answered sourly, "and then hand her over to the dwarf."

"She will come with us now. I will answer to the king if needs be," Talain answered just as tartly.

"As you wish," the guard grumbled. He then looked at Marki and said, "I was told to give you the message that your lord and your legion are free to make use of her in whatever way you wish, up until she is handed over to her mother." The guard smirked, and then, unhooking a jangling bunch of keys from his belt and selecting one, unlocked the chains and removed them.

Maraya looked at Marki uncertainly, and then lowered her eyes.

"What does he mean?" Marki asked Talain, puzzled.

The manner in which Talain raised her eyebrows answered his question; she was King Falamore's gift to Borach and the legion, to do with as they wished.

Marki tittered with disapproval once he understood, and addressed Maraya. "Lord Borach would not want an unwilling lassie for that, and I'll not be having any of my men treating you in that way either."

Maraya said nothing, only staring sadly at the ground.

Talain laughed wickedly, flashing her audacious eyes at Marki. "Would you and the men of the legion prefer a boy?"

"Degenerates," Marki uttered under his breath. Looking at Maraya he asked, "Who gave you those bruises? They were not there last I saw you?"

Talain whispered quietly to him so that Maraya could not hear. "Those bruises are the work of Falamore and his men, during their final drunken night with her."

Marki looked at Maraya and of a sudden felt overwhelmed with pity. He tittered and said, "If by trust or kindness I can get you to speak to me, I will. But know lass, you'll not be mistreated whilst in my care and the company of the legion. On that you have my word."

Maraya briefly raised her eyes suspiciously, and looked at Marki as though she was trying to gauge if he was telling the truth, but she stared back at the ground almost immediately.

Marki and Talain mounted up, and dismissing the guards surrounding Maraya, Talain led the way through the winding streets of Thurog Tor. There were many carts on the narrow streets, and to Marki's frustration he and his two companions had to ride slowly, stuck behind a slow trundling cart laden with potatoes and cabbages, not being able to pass until the cart turned down a side-street, the same way they were headed but this street was much wider and they passed with ease. After that they picked up their pace.

Marki didn't react to the excited screams of a woman selling vegetables who shouted, "Look, it's the dwarf, the Servant of Karno is in our neighbourhood." Other people in the crowded street stopped to turn and stare, some shouting similar things themselves.

Talain laughed and tilted her head towards Marki, "They'll soon get used to you. It was the same for me when I first arrived."

Marki grunted nonchalantly and asked, "So, what's your story, how did a Pure-blood, and a Seeress at that, end up in this cesspit of a city?"

Talain curled her nose up. "You ask my story, without first telling me yours, dwarf?"

"Fair point," Marki replied. "Not much to tell really. My people believe the end of the world is coming, Rogrok they call it, a final battle of the gods. They want to make sure they have no part in the cause of it, that, as well as hoping they might escape it, is the reason the Dwarven Clans united after centuries of warring with each other. Each clan burnt their *Book of Grudges* and locked themselves up together in our ancient ancestral home."

"You mean the caves and pot-holes your kind like to dwell in?"

Marki chuckled. He did not take kindly to people insulting him or his ancestral home, but he had summed Talain up and knew she was not being malicious, it was just the way she had about her. "Our kingdom of the Iron Mountains is no cave or pot-hole, though there are those of my kind who prefer more simple dwellings. No lass, it took a thousand years for the greatest masons and builders of our time to carve the dwellings in that mountain and it would take me a week alone to explain their grandeur and beauty, and then there would still be more to tell. It is big enough for all the clans to have their own regions and space in it, deep underground."

Marki lowered his head reflectively as he thought about the ancestral home that he had not seen for more than a hundred years and then said indifferently. "I was roaming the world searching for adventure with my cousin Galin when the call to return was issued. We ignored the call; they shut the Iron Gate, lowered the giant Amroth Bar across it, and sealed it from within. All outside were in effect banished. They'll not open it until this business with Rogrok is done. If the world survives Rogrok, then they will open it."

"But then it could not be Rogrok, if the world does not end?" Talain asked with a sarcastic glint in her eye.

"The world will end as we know it, that is what my kind believe," Marki answered. "What it will be like afterwards, who can tell? It is a vain hope that anything will be left after Rogrok. Surely it must be the end of all things including the Iron Mountains? It is why I chose a life of roaming and adventure rather than being locked away in a mountain, even one I love and call home."

Talain looked visibly surprised by Marki's words. "So, you can never return to your people?

"Sepha and her two hundred Mace-Wardens guard the Iron Gate that leads to the Underways of the Iron Mountains. There is only one thing that would make them open them, to let any of my kind enter, but a dwarf is forbidden to speak of it to any but our own kith and kin. Only the Reisic break this rule."

"Why would you make such a choice to roam this world? Surely you have family who remained behind?"

"My ma is dead, my pa set out when I was just a boy with his brothers to try to find Frabrim, a fabled lost Dwarven stronghold, said to be still full of treasure. He found an old map, showing it to be on an island somewhere to the west in the Panthalassic Ocean. A large expedition was organised at great cost and resource, they set out, and were never heard from or seen again."

"You never desired to find out what happened to them?"

"Oh yes, at first me and Galin wanted to find our papas, but we needed gold to pay for the expedition. Those who had financed the previous one, would not take another risk. So, we left the Iron Mountains to seek our own fortune to pay for it."

"So, what are you doing here?"

"Well, I and Galin were staying at a flea-pit of a town called Berecoth, where we were the bodyguard to the local patrician. Our grandpapa sent us a letter by pigeon telling us the decree the Grand Iron Council had made to shut the gates. But we had no interest in going back home, and sent a letter back stating we were busy."

"Busy, with what?"

"We had entered the Vargo Goss drinking contest, and our pride would not let me or Galin back out of that."

Talain sniggered, opened her mouth then closed it again, before shaking her head with amusement and asking, "You gave up your homeland for a drinking contest?"

"Not just a drinking contest," Marki said, and then added with emphasis, "the world's *greatest* drinking contest, named after the legendary ale drinker Vargo Goss, a dwarf who could even drink a Gragor under the table."

Talain smiled and slowly shook her head in bewilderment as Marki continued.

"It starts in Berecoth, at an inn named the Pike and Perch. Thirty drinkers pay a hefty sum of gold to enter. You all drink equal amounts of the strongest ale there is simultaneously, and whoever quits or passes out first, is eliminated. You are then taken by horse and cart to the next inn on the list, further up the Erin, where you start the next round immediately. Same again, next one to quit or pass out is eliminated. This happens for thirty days, moving from inn to inn until the last man, or dwarf, is left standing."

"And what prize does the winner get?" Talain asked.

Marki beamed with pride. "You get the title, Vargo Goss Legendary Ale Champion!"

"That's it, just a title?"

He looked at Talain, and pompously countered, "No lass, you also get a Golden Jug of Vargo Goss."

"A golden jug, well, if you survived the contest and won, at least you became rich and could fund your expedition, I suppose."

Marki laughed, "Not that sort of golden jug," he said as he lifted his chainmail and unbuttoned the shirt underneath to reveal a chain necklace with a small, elaborate, golden drinking jug pendant attached to the end.

"This is a Golden Jug of Vargo Goss, proof that I am a Vargo Goss Legendary Ale Champion." His face beamed with pride and delight.

"A pendant on a necklace, that's it?"

"And a certificate to display on my wall," Marki said defensively. "Although I lost that a long time ago. Moths ate it I think."

It was not the only necklace that Marki wore. Talain looked at the other strange necklace dangling from his neck. The pendant was a small bone carving of a woman naked except for a tricorn hat and a pair of thigh length boots delicately painted red. It hung from his neck on a rope chain.

"What's that?" she asked curiously.

Marki stroked the figurine tenderly with his fingers. "That is a story for another day when I will tell you about the greatest Fell-blood woman I have ever met, a pirate captain who cut off her own finger, and whilst the stump was still raw, she carved the bone, painted the boots with her blood, and gave it to me after I beat her at Harendale." He grinned with even more pride.

"Anyway, I and Galin, who was second and only passed out shortly before I managed to win the ale contest, were without coin afterwards as the patrician in Berecoth had sacked us for neglect of our duties. So, we wandered up to Kappia, as we heard they were hiring mercenaries. My only possessions were these necklaces, the

431

clothes on my back, the boots on my feet, the armour on my body, and *Old Trusty* here." He patted the hilt of his doubled headed war axe strapped across the back of his shoulders and back.

"Galin and I joined the Kappian Army as mercenaries and were sent to the city of Aleskian where we were attached to the Third Legion, under Lord Borach. We've both been in his service ever since. You know the rest of the story, why we are here in this cess-pit of a city."

Talain looked at Marki, rolled her eyes and pointed to her head, circling her finger in a way that indicated she thought he was crazy.

"I heard Dwarves were…" she paused, and then added, "unique."

They rode in silence for a few minutes, and then she asked, "Do you miss your kin and kind?"

Marki thought for a moment before answering, "Arch, not really. I have an uncontrollable longing for adventure so this is the life for me. I miss my wee sisters, and I'm sure they worry about me. But, as for the rest of them - a company of Dwarves can only be tolerated for so long before they become really annoying, or start bashing each other's heads in."

Marki and Talain looked at each other, and spontaneously burst into loud laughter as they spurred their horses on to a trot. Despite her wild appearance and candid tongue, Marki sensed a roguish honesty in Talain. He felt she was somebody who could be trusted, and he liked her.

"In all seriousness lass, if I had been a member of the Grand Iron Council, I would have voted to have engaged with the world, not lock ourselves away, for that will end badly. A dwarf is bound by the feuds or friendships of kinsman and father. If feuding families in a clan cannot settle a dispute in court, they write it down in a *Grudge Book* and end up fighting between themselves. If a clan feuds with another or among themselves, usually, only bloodied axes or the appearance of a greater threat can solve it. I bet a tankard of ale that in the Iron Mountains each clan has already broken off into several factions, and the clans are even now writing new *Grudge Books* and waging war among themselves over some petty disputes. Border disputes were the causes of most of our wars if truth be told. It's the way of my kind, so I prefer the open sky, and the freedom to choose my own paths. One day, I would like to set out to find out what happened to my father's expedition, but not this day."

The three riders entered an abandoned part of the city reserved for the temples and vaults of the dead. On all sides of them were cracked snowy marble pillars, caked with dirt and overgrown with vines. Golden domes and silver arches some of which had long ago caved in littered the area. Plants and weeds grew through the cracks in the stone path, which was littered with potholes the riders had to take care to avoid. Statues of strange gods that Marki did not recognise, many of which were crumbling or fallen over with age sat in abandoned and uncared for shrines or lay broken on the dusty ground.

"The people believe this part of Thurog Tor is haunted, so nobody comes here, except for me, so it continues to fall into ruin and decay," Talain said.

"I take it Falamore and these people do not pay much attention to these gods then, only this Karno?" Marki asked with a hint of derision.

"Most people keep small wooden carvings of Karno in their houses, and they carry a statue of him into battle, but beyond asking him for victory in battle and the normal blessings people ask a god for, they care little for him and he makes no demands of them."

"Well, advanced warning lass, they might be disappointed when they see the sickly runt, that they think is the incarnation of their god."

Talain paused thoughtfully and then asked: "Do you give time to the gods, dwarf?"

Marki shrugged his shoulders. "Back in Aleskian, when I first arrived there as a mercenary, I would sit for hours listening to the arguments of theologians, philosophers and teachers. More recently, I even attended some of the temple services and got confused by the maze of intricate formulas and complex rituals of the *Aeldar Faith*. I would come away in a haze of bewilderment, sure of only one thing, that they were all touched in the head."

Marki looked around at the relics and ruins of the long-lost civilisation and then added. "The Aeldar religion, like all things of a civilized, long settled people, has lost its pristine essence. It is far too complex for the likes of me," he remarked, almost wistfully. "I remember a quote from Temmison I once read that said, *'no man will be free until the last king is strangled with the entrails of the last priest.'* That made sense to me."

"Temmison?" Talain asked.

"A deceased Kappian author whose works are still widely read," Marki replied. "Come to think of it, I wish I had paid more attention and read what he wrote about these lands, even though it was centuries ago he wrote about them, it might have proved useful now. I never expected to find myself here, so never made the time."

Talain looked around at the ruined shrines and temples. "There are no texts or oral tradition I know of, that has survived the gods once worshipped here. In the Tarenmoors poets and minstrels are the carriers of tradition and faiths, little of it is written down, so when the civilisation that spawns the faith dies, so does their beliefs." She looked again all around her at the ruins, deserted apart from the odd bird flitting between them. "The gods these temples and shrines honour, I call the *Forgotten Gods,* as nobody remembers who they are anymore or why it was the people here once worshipped them. It is sad really, when you think about it."

"That's why I rarely think about it, lass," Marki said. He tapped the shaft of his large axe again. "*Old Trusty* is the only thing I call upon when I'm in trouble. The Dwarven God Balagrim is simple and understandable; he lives deep under the Iron Mountains, in the Middle-World, where it is said he is sitting on a treasure of gold and jewels in the hall of my ancestors. It is useless for us to call on him because he is a miserable self-consumed god who hates weaklings. He gives a dwarf courage and strength at birth, and lets us get on with life, which is all any god should be expected to do. He does not promise us freedom from danger or calamity and we do not demand of him that he should. But even our priestly cast make such a simple belief far more complex than it need be."

Marki looked around more carefully at the eerie abandoned part of the city all around him, then at Maraya. "What about you, lass, do your people give much credence to the gods beyond this dragon skull you worship?"

Maraya looked at him briefly, and then turned her head away, shyly tucking it into her shoulder, ignoring his question.

"She's not spoken hardly a word ever since she came here," Talain said, answering for Maraya. "I think she does understand the Common Tongue very well, but who could blame her for not being in the mood for small talk? Before the dragon skull came, her people worshipped Malagrim, a living Titan, the King of the Giant Halls. They still worship him; they worship many gods, some living, and some mere artefacts like the skull."

Marki raised an eyebrow in surprise, and then burst out laughing. "A living Titan, what jest is this?"

"One you would not find funny, were you ever to cross his path," Talain said with all seriousness. "There are strange things in the Tarenmoors dwarf. You would do well to learn this before you mock."

"So be it," muttered Marki, his eyes burning on Talain's face. "Some Kappians talk of a living Titan that resides under the Kappia palace, and some even stretch the lie that the priests in the Argona Temple have summoned Aeldar Gods from the Void of the Ninth-World."

"You don't believe it?" Talain asked him.

"Why should I? I've never spoken with one who has witnessed it with their own eyes. People tattle about all manner of things. Until a man or woman, I trust, tells me it is so, and that they have seen such a sight with their own peepers, then I will pay little attention to hearsay, the professions of those who reside in temples, or the gossip of tavern drunkards."

"Those words coming from a *Vargo Goss Ale Champion* should be enshrined in the writings of wise men," Talain said with a cheeky smile.

Marki's face and mood softened. He chuckled and then asked her. "So now, you tell me. What are you, a Pure-blood Akkadian woman, doing here in the Tarenmoors?"

A look of sadness swept across Talain's face, and she swallowed hard before speaking. "I was brought here when I was a young girl," she answered, sitting upright in her saddle. "I am the daughter of a Bruthon Baron from the Southern-march, which is south and east of the Bruthon capital, next to the borders of the wild lands of the Horse Lords. I am no common woman, not that you could tell by my markings."

She looked momentarily lost in thought before continuing. "I was abducted by a Half-blood rebel prince during a war with the Horse Lords. His army pillaged and ravaged Bruthon lands. They burnt down my father's castle before pushing west, where they briefly besieged Castle Greytears, but then lifted the siege and pressed west again beyond the Wytchwood, and then northward searching for a land they could make their own. Many of his warriors perished crossing the Abandoned Plain, through thirst or due to the lindworms that rise from the sand there, to consume travellers. The survivors strayed too close to the Giant Halls; many were slain in a fierce battle. The very few who survived, fled east across the plain. Those not eaten by the lindworms, died of thirst, from the heat of the sun or illness. Others were killed by large scorpions which spring up suddenly from lairs in the ground, dragging their screaming victims into the earth, out of sight and hope. Me and a Fell-blood bowman were the last survivors. That is where a strange tale, becomes even stranger."

Marki could tell by the way that Talain took some deep breaths that it was not easy for her to tell her story.

"In your own time lass," he said gently.

"A Gragor, and several Chatti caught up with us. They tortured the bowman, and then flayed him alive for no other reason than their own amusement." Talain choked back a tear.

Marki spoke as tenderly as he was able. "You don't need to describe what they did to you lass; I understand."

Talain shot him a look of rebuke. "No, you do not, for not even I do. Even now I do not understand why they did to me what they did."

Marki again spoke softly, "Aye lass, you can miss out that part, I guess even Chatti have needs. What scoundrel males do with a vulnerable lass needs no explaining. Skip that part and tell me how you came to Thurog Tor."

"Do you want to tell my story for me?" Talain asked reprovingly.

Marki did not answer.

434

"They did not touch me in that way. The only harm they did was..." she paused. "One of them was a Chatti shaman. A Gragor held me down, and the shaman carved these markings into my face, whilst chanting strange words, '*Arvivan,*' is the only one I remember because he kept repeating it. Then they all left, except for the shaman. He placed me on a horse and walked beside it for days until he dropped and died in his tracks, for he ate no food nor drank any water, though he gave me both to keep me alive. He died, the horse wandered on, and I finally passed into delirium from thirst and hunger, and *Awakened* at the Obelisk in this city. The people of Thurog Tor told me I had been seen from the walls, early in the dawn, lying dead beside a deceased horse. They went forth and burnt my body, as is their way, so you can imagine their surprise when I turned up alive and well again the next day. Many of them had never heard of Akkadians or Obelisks; it was my *First-death* and the time I discovered I was a Seer. I taught them the little I knew of the wider world, and the Deadlands, and I have lived here ever since, venerated among them."

Marki whistled. "That's some tale lass," he said. "Did not Falamore, or the men of this place, you know?" He coughed uncomfortably. "Bother you?"

Talain flashed a broad grin, her former gloom gone in an instant. "They were naturally much interested in me, especially the men, but they were also afraid. As I could not speak their language, they learned to speak mine. They are very quick and able of intellect; they learned my language long before I learned theirs. But they were more interested in my stories than in me, even though I am different to their women, and they like the strangeness of that." She laughed cheekily. "But no, they never forced themselves on me. They are afraid of me and treat me with awe and respect, as each time I return from the Deadlands I tell them the stories of what I have seen there."

She continued tranquilly. "Of course, the women are jealous of me, because of the attention I get. The men are handsome enough in their own way, but they have no physical interest as they are afraid of me and think me some sort of goddess, or witch, so they leave me be."

"Those marks, you do them yourself now when you resurrect?"

"No, they appear by themselves. Each time I resurrect, they are there. It must be some Chatti magic. I don't know what they are and used to hate them, but I accept them now, they are a part of who I have become, but I do not know the reason I was given them."

"*Arvivan,*" Maraya said as she pointed at Talain's face, much to Marki's surprise. "*Arvivan,*" she repeated with whispered awe.

Talain smiled. "She said that the first time she laid eyes on me, it's the only word she has ever said to me. I have no idea what it means."

The three riders rode in silence from that point on. They stopped at the entrance of a large stone arch that was worn with age. Carved into the top centre of the arch, was the image of an Obelisk. Their horses became nervous, snorting and whinnying uncomfortably. Due to the nervousness of the horses they dismounted and walked under the arch onto a long stone road, towing their horses by the reins. The road was surrounded both sides by large tombs and vaults of various shapes, sizes and design. Two stray dogs burst out of a pathway between two of the vaults, startling the horses. They were mongrel beasts, big-jawed and ugly. One barked and the other growled, but they ran off down another path when Marki shouted and growled back at them.

Leading the horses by the reins they continued walking along the road in silence, until Talain broke it. "These are ancient tombs. The dead in the Tarenmoors, apart from a few exceptions, are rarely buried now. The people of Thurog Tor burn their dead; they think it is uncouth and unsafe to keep them in vaults as they believe the ghost

435

lingers with a body that is unburnt. What about you dwarf, are you afraid of wraiths and ghosts?"

"I've never seen one, so don't know," Marki said dryly. "I once heard that if an Obelisk dies, or becomes very weak, a fissure can happen between the two worlds and the dead leak into this one. I've never seen it happen, and I'm not sure I want too," he answered. "I think I would prefer an enemy of flesh and blood that *Old Trusty* can manage, over some wisp of a ghost."

Talain snorted. "Most wraiths, except Seers, are harmless enough in the Deadlands, but if they break through into this world, they regain their senses and some of their memories, and that is when they become feral and dangerous. A wild madness and hatred take them over. It is said there are barrows in the Dales of Yarron where the Obelisk Yarath died, and the dead walk there freely, in plain sight for all to see."

Marki shivered. A living foe, he could handle with his axe, the dead in the land of the living, now that was another matter.

"Do you know why or how an Obelisk can die?" Talain asked. "It has never been explained to me," she said, "and I would be interested to know."

"I don't know for sure. Some say that there are rare weapons that can kill them. Also, I remember hearing in Aleskian that if they were not used by Akkadians, after long centuries, they can grow weak and will eventually die."

"I think that may be true," Talain said. "The one we are going to was very weak when I first met it, but it seems a little stronger each time I use it. It never speaks by the way. It just stares at me, and I don't know its name."

"Has Falamore ever been to see this Obelisk?" Marki asked, feeling curious.

"No, nobody ever comes to this part of the city. I told you they believe it is haunted and cursed. They tried to burn it once, but the wind turned on them, and they nearly burnt their own dwellings down, so they just leave it be now."

"It is not unusual for Fell-bloods to be afraid of things that remind them of their short mortality," Marki answered.

"Are you not afraid of death then dwarf?"

He shook his head. "I prefer living, and am in no hurry to die, but I do not fear it. In battle, I always know I could be moments away from it, but that is not the time to dwell upon the matter."

"I have never seen a dwarf in the Deadlands."

"We don't go there when we die. It is said that our god Balagrim lets nine dwarf Shield-Maidens choose which of the dwarf-dead can enter his feasting hall. Only the Reisic are banned; all others have a chance to enter."

"And what sort of qualities do they look for?" she asked.

Marki smiled as he said, "They ask you to tell the best story from your life. Balagrim enjoys the company of those who have lived adventurous lives, and can spend eternity telling him thrilling stories of their deeds whilst drinking with him to lift him from his grim moods."

"So, if you are boring, he won't let you in?"

"Would you want to spend eternity with a bore?" Marki asked and smiled broadly. "I've not annoyed him that I'm aware of and I've lived an adventurous life, so when my time comes there is no reason, I can think of, why the Maidens won't let me in the Drunken Hall to join Balagrim and my dead kin who made it in. I have some great stories to tell, and plan to make some more before I breathe my last."

He stroked the muzzle of his pony as it became restless due to the distant howling of some more dogs. When the beast was calm, he continued.

436

"Our priest used to tell us a story that a company of nine Dwarves died on the same day, I forget exactly how it goes really. But the gist of it was that a door to another world opened, and out of a bright light stepped, the Shield-Maidens. They listened to each of the dead Dwarves' best stories, and only invited two of them in."

"What happened to the others?"

"As the Maidens closed the door on the others, they said to them, *rest brothers,* and their spirits just faded away into nothingness."

"So, you spend an eternity of drunken partying with a bad-tempered god or nothingness? It doesn't sound that great."

"Oh, I don't know, at least nothingness is a kind of peace, and if not that, maybe in Balagrim's halls you also get to tumble around with the Shield-Maidens, so it wouldn't be so bad." He winked at Talain.

"What is the purpose of life if it ends in nothingness?" she asked as she looked him up or down. "There is little point to any life lived that leads to nothingness."

"I myself shall die," he replied, "and if I don't make the grade, there is one thing I know that never dies: the reputation I will leave behind at my death. If I can carve out a name for myself so that those who knew me could sing of my bravery, loyalty and generosity, and that I died a good death, then my name and memory will live on. That is good enough for me."

"What if there's nobody to tell your story, and you die a horrible death?"

"If I know that I made a good end, one worthy of a story that people would want to hear over and over again, even if there was nobody to tell it, I will die with a smile on my face." He waited a moment and then asked, "Should I not be asking you these questions, you have seen death, I have not."

"The Deadlands are still a mystery to me, I know so little, even though I go there often. I have never lived in this world beyond the age of thirty-six."

"Then maybe you should try it," Marki suggested.

"So how long does a dwarf live? I know so little of your kind," Talain asked as she stroked the muzzle of her own horse to calm it as the dogs in the distance howled once again.

"My grandpapa on my mother's side made it to four hundred and thirty-six years, that's considered a decent enough age, though he didn't wear it well. If he laughed too much, he found he would also cough, sneeze, fart and pee all at the same time."

"Quite the party trick," Talain said with a smile as she stopped and ran her finger along the outline of a sarcophagus etched in the stone of a nearby vault. She continued walking. "I don't know why we call them the dead; it is just another form of existence. All humans, even Fell-bloods, have a body in the Deadlands, even if that body dies the spirit within cannot be slain, it still exists. The difference is we Akkadians always get a new body, in this world, no matter how many times we die, but I wonder if that is more of a curse than a blessing."

"What use is a body in the Deadlands if only the Seers are aware of what goes on there?" Marki grunted. "Death is then like a dream one cannot remember when woken from it."

"Somebody in the Deadlands once told me that being a Seer is a gift. He said that I was a guide, that one day all will see, all will know, when the Void is open and the way to paradise is known." She looked at him quizzically, and asked, "You really don't know much about the nature of reality, nor care, do you?"

"I know enough," Marki said defensively. "I know that the basis of life is tragic. Many Pure-bloods see their immortality as a curse, you are right, and they would gladly be gone forever from this world, yet many a Fell-blood still envies them their gift.

Among Fell-bloods only those who suffer too much are willing to leave behind a life as short as theirs. I have no envy for Pure-bloods, as I have lived with them long enough, to know that resurrecting can become a curse when one is tired of suffering. But even you are not immune to a *Final-death*."

Talain looked puzzled, so Marki explained. "You were young when you left your kin. Maybe because of your youth they did not tell you, that even Pure-bloods have only a limited number of lives?"

She looked shock, and was silent for a long while before saying, "No, I was never told that, but in a way, I have always known it."

"There are also weapons that can deal you the *Final-death* in an instant," Marki warned. "You would do well to recognise them, and avoid those who carry such a foul thing. I have a lot to learn about the Tarenmoors, you have a lot to learn about the wider Everglow. In the days ahead, we can be both teacher and student to each other."

They continued along in quiet, until Talain stopped outside of a ruined temple at the end of the road. Inside the middle of the ruin was a large stone vault. "There it is," she said.

Talain handed the reins of her horse to Maraya. "The dogs never come here. You should have no trouble. Wait here for us, we will not be long."

Marki also handed the reins of his pony to Maraya. "Aye, best you wait here lass," he said. "That's if you want to, do what you want lass you're not my slave or prisoner. But I give you my word that at the camp you'll not be touched or harmed by any. I'll hand you safely over to your mother, come what may." He doubted she could escape past the walls of Thurog Tor, and even if she tried, it was no issue for him as he did not consider her his prisoner, she was more of a burden he felt responsible for. If she was not there when he returned, *so be it*, he concluded. He decided he would not bother to look for her, though he hoped that both his and Talain's mounts would still be there when they returned, as it was a long walk back.

Marki and Talain entered the ruin. Crumbled and broken stone crunched beneath their feet. The roof of the ruin was completely gone. Like so many others, it was covered in lichen and overgrown with vines; much of the outer stonework was crumbling. All that remained were half broken columns and a wall here and there. The vault was high and arched at the top, and decorated with stone statues in the image of noble men and women. Marki studied the markings on the door of the vault. Sure enough, there was a symbol of an Obelisk carved into it. He stretched out his finger running it along the markings carved into the stone.

"Now, let's do this shall we?" he said purposefully, ignoring the cold chill that made the hairs on his neck stand. He looked at Talain and gestured with his hand towards the door.

Talain pushed open the stone door of the vault. It opened with a grating sound. A cold wind rushed up from deep below causing a moaning sound that made Marki instinctively grab for his axe.

"You look nervous dwarf," Talain said as she entered ahead of him.

"You talk too much," he replied sourly as he relaxed his grip on *Old Trusty*. He took a deep breath and followed her into the vault.

In the entrance there hung a lantern, already lit, swinging in the draft that came up from below. Talain took it off the hook and held it up.

"That's handy, you keep a caretaker here?" Marki asked suspiciously

Talain looked at the lamp with an expression of wonder. "This lamp was in the Chamber of the Obelisk, the first time I resurrected. It is a perpetual light; it burns continuously without fuel and has done so even since it was lit in ancient times. You

438

cannot blow it out or extinguish it by any means, nor can you mark or destroy the lamp." Her tone inflected a respect, that until then, Marki had not seen in her.

Marki laughed and patted the hilt of his axe. "*Old Trusty* would beg to differ and would wager against the lamp any day." When Talain did not share in the jest, he asked incredulously, "You are telling me that thing has been alight for possibly hundreds or thousands of years and cannot be damaged?"

"Yes, that is what I am telling you," she said reverentially. "The people who once lived here were obviously Pure-bloods. They believed a dead person might need some light on their road to the Valley of the Shadow. Therefore, before the tomb was sealed it was a custom to place an ever-burning lamp inside. The lamp serves as an offering to the god of the dead and keeps evil spirits away. Its light also offers the deceased the required guidance on the journey to paradise in the Underworld and keeps the wisdom of the dead."

"How do you know this, if no record or history of these people still exists?"

"I was told this," Talain said defiantly.

"Told it by whom?"

"A dead bird," she countered with a smile. "Test it, if you wish," she said to him as she put the lantern on the ground.

Marki resisted the urge to take a swing at it. "Let's just be about this business," he said grumpily. Like most Dwarves, he did not like to meddle with things he did not understand. Talain picked the lantern back up. Together they went down into the crypt. The winding stone steps were narrow; Talain led the way with the lantern. Marki could feel the chill coming up the stairs, a cold breath from deep below. They reached the bottom of the stairs, and stepped out into the darkness of the crypt. Talain swept the lantern in a wide semi-circle. Shadows moved and lurched. Marki grabbed the shaft of his axe.

"You scare easily, dwarf," Talain said playfully as she walked ahead.

Although she had said it as a jest, Marki felt embarrassed at the remark, and was glad that the darkness hid the blush he felt on his face. A veteran of many a battle, fearless in the face of the enemy, he did not like how uncomfortable he felt in the vault. Even the crunch of the dirt and loose stone beneath their feet echoed and reverberated all around them. His head quickly turned to and throw at every noise. They made their way deeper into the crypt; flickering light touched the stone floor underfoot, and licked against a long procession of smoothly polished granite pillars that reflected back the light of the lantern. In between the pillars, the dead lay in stone sepulchres. They passed a crowned man and woman laid side by side together, the man holding an iron broadsword, some of which had rusted to nothing long ago leaving nothing but a red stain where once it had been. The shifting shadows seemed to make the stone figures stir as the living walked by. They passed other crowned figures. Talain whispered, respectfully, her words echoing in the domed ceiling overhead.

"These must have been the kings and queens of long ago, no record of their history or deeds survive that I know of, the only proof they once lived is what you see here."

"Are they Pure-bloods?" Marki asked, speaking in the softest whisper he could manage.

"I don't think these ones are, as they do not bear the mark of the Obelisk on their tombs. The Akkadian bodies are entombed much deeper in the crypt; I have only been there once and not again, for the way was confusing, and I died. It is easy to get lost down there, and to not find a way out, for it is endless tunnels lined with sepulchres of men, women and children, and elaborate vaults of what once were greater kings and queens than those we have passed. They must have abandoned this place long ago and we can only guess the reason."

Talain continued to lead the way and Marki followed wordlessly. She pointed at carvings of the Obelisk in the arches over the passageways they went down. Their footsteps echoed off the stones and he began to shiver in the subterranean cold, and hoped Talain would not notice lest she tease him again, mistaking it for fear. They entered a wide, circular chamber.

"There," Talain said, as she held the lantern up high. In the middle of the chamber, surrounded by no more than a dozen empty resurrection cradles, sat an Obelisk. It was small for an Obelisk; its eyes stared into the dim light and did not even turn to face the visitors. Its eyes closed for several seconds at a time as though it was very tired and fighting off sleep. Another lantern, the same as the one she was holding, was hung on a hook high in the vaulted ceiling and shed some light into the chamber.

She pointed to the arch through which they had entered the chamber, where an Obelisk was carved into the stone. "Remember, that marking, leads to and from this place. Look for it at each turning point, and follow. This is where you will meet me and your friend once we have resurrected. Do not wander off the path that leads to here, for the passages run wide and deep and seem never ending. Do not become lost. Make sure you and any delegation come straight here."

"Nay worries of that lass," Marki said. "We will need more than that one lamp you have; we will line the way with lamps, proper ones that need men to put fuel in them. The men detailed to man this place can attend to them and keep them alight." He looked at the Obelisk which closed its eyes for several seconds before half opening them again, and then lazily stared at them both.

"Okay, I'm satisfied that thing is alive, though it looks half asleep or nearly dead. It will do the job. Now let's be gone from this dreadful place."

They made good time on the way back. It was with some relief that Marki emerged from the crypt into the daylight. He took some deep gulps of the fresh morning air. To his pleasant surprise Maraya was still waiting in the distance where they had left her. She watched him as he drank in the air, but said nothing.

Talain put the lantern back on its hook, before leaving the vault and pulling shut the door behind her. She then pointed to a ruined building nearby. "Your men can shelter and put up their tents and belongings in there whilst they wait for the dead to resurrect."

They made their way back through the ruin to Maraya and the horses and all three of them mounted them. Talain led the way back through the abandoned part of the city to the main streets which were busy and thronging with people. It took some time to navigate through the bustling crowds and then on to the main gate of Thurog Tor, where Yizain, the two sons of Falamore, and a small bodyguard were mounted on horses waiting for them. Marki nodded in acknowledgement to them but said no words as they joined them.

"Effgard grew impatient, and has gone on ahead with his son to the camp," Yizain said to Marki. The small party then passed through the gate as it was opened, under the watchful eye of the guards.

"Let's go and meet your Lord Borach then," Talain said once they had passed the gate and hit the open road, spurring her horse to a gallop.

# Chapter Thirty-Six: *A Munte Marriage*

*I was once a maid at the imperial palace. I saw things that still give me nightmares. Once, some Senators complained that the excesses of the Empress Shaka were a drain on the imperial treasury. She invited them to a macabre 'Black Banquet' at the palace. Everything in the banqueting chamber was painted black for the occasion – the walls, the ceiling, the floor, the furniture and everything else. The Senators were told not to bring their womenfolk or any attendants. On arrival they were ushered into the grim and gloomy room. Naked slaves, men and women, painted head to toe in black wore demon masks and danced, I was one of those. Sarcophaguses were carried in, upon which each had the name of a guest inscribed. The Senators sat in terror as Shaka cheerfully discoursed on death and slaughter for an hour. The food, when it came, was served on black dishes, and was that which is usually eaten at ceremonies for the dead, except the meat, which consisted of the severed and boiled hands of women. Each sarcophagus was then opened. The Senators were horrified to see that their naked wives were in them, minus their hands. "Eat up," the Empress said to the Senators, "I will be offended if anything is left over, I want no waste for it would be an excess." In this manner, the Senators were forced to eat the hands of their wives, as the women, their stumps still bloodied and bandaged, stood and watched their husbands consume their grim feast, and all the while, I and the other slaves continued to dance. From what I understand, after that evening none of those Senators ever criticised the excesses of the Empress again.*
**Felicia: The Memoirs of a Former Palace Slave.**

*On* the last night of her imprisonment, Shaka could not sleep. Each time she closed her eyes, her head filled with anger at the thought of the humiliation that awaited her on the morrow. Barefoot, she paced her room, thinking, plotting, regretting that she had been so sure that her position as Empress was unassailable, she had been blind to the plotting of Mazdek that had taken place under her very nose. Her only consolation was that he still needed her, and all the while he did, she was not yet without influence or plan.

The feeling of the fur carpet under Shaka's feet was a warm welcome after the cold hard stone floor of the cell she had previously been kept in. As there were no windows in the room, she was unsure of what time it was but knew that morning could not be that far off. At least by evening, the public marriage ceremony would be over, she would have been sent to the Deadlands and sometime the next day, or in the days soon after, she would resurrect and then *Awaken*. Then, she would play the part of dutiful wife in order to buy time until she could escape the clutches of Mazdek, and plan his overthrow.

Shaka's habitation was quite comfortable after the ordeal of the deeper levels of the dungeons. The room she was in was one of the cells set aside for prisoners who were not to be treated as harshly as those confined in the lower levels. It was a small, plain room furnished with only a bed, a small chair and a desk upon which a beeswax candle gave some light. At her request, she had been provided with all nine volumes of the *Aeldar Books*, but she had not fully read them during her confinement. She had instead concentrated on the several volumes of the *Ancient Gladiatorial Kappian Games and their Customs* that she had also requested. She had read every one of those books, word for word. As she studied them, she had found exactly what she wanted. She knew it was there, but wanted to be able to quote word for word the exact law and custom she required. *Knowledge is power. It will be risky, but Mazdek will be unprepared for what I have planned for him.*

The thoughts plaguing Shaka's mind was that Mazdek knew her too well. She doubted that he would ever really trust her, and it had dawned upon her, that even after the Munte ceremony, he would dispose of her and her children at the earliest opportunity.

The Hammer Knights had proven they were more loyal to their High Quaester, she could not count on them, especially after Mazdek became the Emperor. The nobles, well, for the first time she regretted the numerous times she had humiliated or punished many of them. She had ruled by fear. Fear was only effective when accompanied by power, and she had lost all of that. Her only chance, was to evoke an ancient law at the games to be held in a few days' time. If Mazdek failed to honour the law, he would be publicly shamed. If he did honour it, he would surely be slain, and that would give her time to act whilst he was in the Deadlands. All was not yet lost. *At the games, I have to evoke the law of Maradrith, the law my father enshrined when he took my mother as a Munte bride. It is my only chance.*

Shaka knew most of the nobles had little love for her, and none of that had mattered to her, until now, but she had also favoured some who were members of military families. They had resented the way Mazdek had allowed the Hammer Knights to become more influential in the capital than the legions. She might still find some favour and assistance among them. General Karkson had not allowed the influence of the Hammer Knights to spread in the legions, and Kara Duram was still their stronghold. It was there that they were in the process of disbanding, but that was taking time, so she might yet win them to her cause if she could reach Kara Duram.

Throughout her reign, regret had been a foreign emotion to Shaka. But, during the last week of her imprisonment as arrangements were made for the Munte marriage, it was a frequent visitor in her heart and mind. *I wish General Karkson were still here,* she had often thought to herself. She knew that with one word from her, he would have rallied the legions and been at her side. He would have resisted the schemes and plans of Mazdek. Regret, an emotion that was still strange to her, despite her many long lives, was a feeling she did not like. She had many regrets during that week, but ordering the *Final-death* of her most powerful general who had always been loyal to her, had been the biggest one.

*Karkson had a son and a daughter, born through illicit relations with a woman of noble birth. They had thought it a secret, but I knew of it.* In fact, she had planned to publicly expose and humiliate Karkson and the woman if ever it would amuse her to do so, or if they had caused offence, but now, it was well for her she had not done so. *This knowledge will prove useful to me, if I use it wisely.*

For now, the only people she trusted were her children, and she had not seen them since they had also been imprisoned. *My children will have to accompany me for the ceremony, or it will not be seen as legitimate,* she said to herself. The thought of her children being with her during the procession to the Munte wedding ceremony gave her a small degree of comfort. *We can begin our plans.*

When the gaolers eventually came for her, they were accompanied by four of her maids, all Pure-bloods, and daughters of prominent nobles. Shaka had never really observed them closely before, even Myrene, Karkson's secret daughter. She had certainly never exchanged any pleasantries with them, although she did know all about them and their family backgrounds. Another of the maids, the head maid, named Desira, still bore the burn scar on her face where she, Shaka, had pushed her into a fireplace and held her face against the flame for a reason she could not even at that moment recall. A vague memory also arose, of a time when Regineo had taken offence at another of her maids, Sheena, for some reason. Memories of the maid being pinned to the wall, recoiling from the relentless blows dished out by Regineo who beat her with a golden figurine until her skull was smashed, haunted her of a sudden. Shaka remembered the sound of the crunch of breaking bones, the slap of impacts upon vulnerable flesh. Sheena had died, been resurrected, and returned to her service. The last maid, Mazzie. Shaka wondered: *Have I ever done her wrong? I cannot recall. Regrets, so many regrets.*

Shaka felt strangely comforted to see the maids, it brought her a sense of familiarity, a feeling absent from her during her recent imprisonment. She could instinctively tell that the maids did not share the sentiment. They were clearly nervous as the gaolers slammed the heavy door behind them, turning the key in the lock. Between them, they carried lye soap, a basin of warm water, a towel, a pair of shears, three long straight razors, a simple white wedding gown and a pair of silk slippers.

"Forgive us," our Sarissa, Desira said fearfully, her voice tremoring. "We have been ordered to prepare you for the ceremony."

Shaka had witnessed many Munte weddings, and knew the procedures well. She pulled the chair from under the desk and placed it in the middle of the room. "Just do it," she said softly, as she yanked the shift she wore over her head, and tossed it to the floor. "I will not hold you to account for it, neither this day or in those to come." *I need friends now, wherever I can find them. I must repair the wrongs, and make my maids my allies.*

The hairs beneath her arms were the first to be shaved by the maid named Sheena, who was careful not to touch the Jewellery of Morkroth, the Maidenarz, that was now a permanent and unwelcome part of Shaka's attire even when naked. Shaka noticed that Sheena shuddered in fear whenever she looked at it. The maid called Mazzie shaved her legs. Their hands were trembling with fear as they carried out their work, so much so, that it was a marvel to Shaka they did not accidentally cut her. It was Desira who knelt down, and with great care and gentleness removed the fine black mound of hair between Shaka's legs. Myrene, carefully applied soothing ointment and gently towelled each area, where Shaka had been shaved.

After her body hair had been removed, Shaka sat on the chair, as, without a word, Desira took the shears and began to remove the hair from her head. Shaka sat in stony silence as the shears clicked, and drifts of brunette hair fell carelessly to the floor. She had not been able to tend to it properly whilst imprisoned, and it had become a tangled unwashed mess. As the locks and curls piled up around her feet, she said bleakly and bitterly, "Today I lose two crowns." None of the maids said a word in response, but Shaka could hear their nervous breaths and feel the warmth of it against her skin as they nervously continued with their duties. After she finished with the shears, Desira soaped her head, and then carefully scraped away the stubble with a razor.

When all of her hair was removed, Shaka stood as the maids washed her with the soap and water, and patted her dry with the towel, after which they helped dress her in the splendid white gown, and put the slippers upon her feet. Although they had given no indication that they enjoyed their task, quite the opposite in fact, Shaka could not resist coldly asking the maids, "Do you take pleasure in seeing your Empress humiliated in such a way?"

The maids each looked to the floor, not daring to meet her gaze. "No, my Sarissa," Desira said, after which the others timidly mumbled the same.

*It is time to plant the first seeds*, Shaka said to herself, after which she said, "I am being forced into this Munte marriage, but you are not to speak of it to anyone, for I have agreed to be a loyal wife to Mazdek, when he becomes the Emperor."

Shaka had no doubt, that if her maids were later questioned about any conversations, they had with her, Desira and Sheena would be the ones to tell all, and with little persuasion for they were no doubt glad to see her downfall. Mazzie would probably be of the same ilk, but, Shaka knew they were still terrified of her. *I must gain their confidence; convince them they will fare better with me than with Mazdek. Myrene, is the one who can help turn the maids back to me, if the motivation is right.*

"General Karkson would never have allowed this marriage, he would have opposed it, for he was always loyal to me, and only me. It fills me with woe, that unknown to me, Mazdek had him assassinated with an Arkith. I lost my closest friend, most trusted advisor and my dearest ally." She purposefully did not look at Myrene as she told the lie, but from the corner of her eyes she could tell the girl was startled by the news. Turning to her, she then asked, "Have the people of Kappia not even questioned the absence of the General these past weeks?"

Myrene lowered her eyes to the floor, and Shaka could see tears welling up in them.

"Answer me girl," Shaka said as softly and tenderly as she could fake.

Myrene stammered when she answered. "It was assumed General Karkson had returned to Kara Duram." Unable to hide her emotion, Myrene wiped away a tear.

"I understand your pain, Karkson was loved by many citizens," Shaka said, as she briefly comforted Myrene with an insincere hug. "I also loved him, like a brother, and begged Mazdek to spare him, but he would not heed my petitions." *The seed has been planted. She now thinks Mazdek is responsible for her father's death, and may soon see in me an ally. Now is not the time for me to reveal to her I know she is his daughter.* Still embracing her, she whispered in Myrene's ear, ever so softly, so that the other maids could not hear. "Mazdek has heard a rumour that the general had a secret family - a son and a daughter. He seeks their identity and will imprison them if he discovers who they are. Your secret is safe with me." The slight but momentary widening of Myrene's eyes confirmed to Shaka the words made an impact.

Shaka let go of Myrene, and smiled at her, as warmly as she could. Inside, the humiliation of embracing a maid stung at her pride. *This is the least of the humiliations I must suffer this day.*

Without looking at her, Desira asked, "My Sarissa, are you ready?"

"Yes," Shaka said.

Desira then knocked on the door and shouted loudly, "We are finished."

The gaoler unlocked the door, and the maids, taking the items they had carried in with them rushed out as fast as they were able the moment it was opened.

One of the gaolers shouted up the corridor. Responding, several Hammer Knights came orderly but hastily down it. Their rattling armour was red plate and polished to mirror sheen, but underneath it, Shaka knew they each wore a coarse hair shirt that tormented the skin. One of them entered the cell, took her roughly by the arm and without any courtesy or gentleness pulled her from the room. She felt incensed to be man-handled so roughly yet again, but said nothing. *My time for revenge will come*, she said to herself as she made a mental note of the man's face.

The rough stone steps scraped against the soles of her silk slippers as she was pulled along the corridor, and then up some steep steps where she made her ascent. It was with great relief she finally entered the Courtyard of Tears outside the main door of the Bloody Tower. It was the first time she had tasted fresh air for some weeks, and she breathed it in gratefully. Finally, she was leaving that awful place.

More Hammer Knights were gathered in the courtyard, many of them mounted. They waited silently for several minutes until Aspess and her two brothers were led into the courtyard. Shaka felt relieved they all appeared unharmed, although they shot furtive glances towards her. A large black mare was brought for Aspess. She mounted it side saddle. The two brothers mounted the horses brought for them.

Shaka's four maids returned. They had changed, and were now dressed in gowns of crimson velvet, and between them, they carried the Crown of Maradrith, the crown that had been commissioned for Shaka's mother during her Munte marriage to her father. The maids placed it upon her head. The crown was so decked in precious stones that the weight of it required Shaka to hold it steady with both of her hands.

An open carriage, covered in cloth of gold, was pulled into the courtyard by several large, white stallions, dressed in jewel encrusted bridles, and driven by a naked male slave. The maids helped Shaka into the carriage, and sat behind her, helping her to manage the weight of the crown.

When they were all seated, one of the mounted Hammer Knights blew a trumpet, which was followed by several others in succession outside of the walls of the courtyard. In response to the trumpet blast, bells began to loudly chime and ring out across Kappia city. Shaka swept the faces of the men around her, and the impassive faces of her maids. She laughed bleakly and bitterly. "So, I have bells for my wedding day," she said severely.

Neither the maids or the guards gave any response; they stared impassively ahead as the driver of the carriage flicked the reins and followed the mounted knights outside of the courtyard, through the open gates and onto the *Road of Emperors* where a huge wedding procession awaited her.

The blare of a hundred trumpets split the air from the walls of Kappia, heralding the wedding procession of the Empress Shaka. Her carriage was led to the head of a bodyguard of a thousand Hammer Knights. In the middle of them, in a cage upon a wagon, was chained a wretched looking woman.

"Who is that?" Shaka asked Myrene. The maid gave her a puzzled expression in response, and then said. "Forgive me, my Sarissa, a lot has happened in your absence. That is the Seeress, the one who stole the Simal. She was captured."

*So, Mazdek continues with the plan to deceive and placate the people with a lie until the real Seeress is captured and the true Simal is returned.* The false Seeress was a pitiful sight. Dried blood surrounded her mouth where her tongue had been removed to prevent her from shouting or protesting her innocence. In front of that, upon another wagon, placed upon a velvet cushion on a pedestal was the false Simal. *Mazdek is indeed continuing with his plan to deceive the people.*

The Road of Emperors was an avenue sixty-six feet wide, built of giant limestone paving slabs covering a foundation of brick and asphalt. Shaka sat proudly in her carriage as it was driven towards her capital. It was not pride she felt though; she masked well the deep sense of humiliation and degradation raging inside of her. It was tradition and symbolic that all Munte brides would begin their wedding march having been shaved, washed and dressed at the Bloody Tower. None of her people would even guess or be aware of the horror and humiliation she had endured in that place, they would merely think she was obeying the tradition of thousands of years, as was expected of her. It dawned upon her what a ridiculous tradition it was, and in all her lifetimes she had never wondered about the origins of it or questioned why it was a required part of a Munte ceremony. Perhaps, she wondered, it was because a Munte bride was in effect a prisoner to one man for the rest of their lifetimes.

As the carriage approached the city gate, even before they had reached it, Shaka could hear the sounds of the crowd waiting within the city. Drums pounded and music filled the air, mingling with the sound of voices echoing from the tall buildings and the ringing of the bells. The noise was so great she could barely hear the tramp of the Hammer Knights just a dozen or so paces behind her.

As they approached the main city gate, on either hand, sixty carved griffins, fashioned of red, white and yellow tile on the high walls, towered above the wedding procession. At the Emperor's Gate, the images of bulls and dragons took over from the griffins. The entrance was one of nine massive, bronze-armoured portals in a double-walled, moated fortification system that surrounded the city. Above each entrance, a golden statue of an Aeldar God stood above the symbol of hammer and snake, with Thuranotos above the main middle entrance. In between these statues, banners with the entwined initials of Mazdek and Shaka fluttered in the light breeze.

Plunging into the cool shade offered by the gate, Shaka was surrounded by the sound ringing from the arched tunnel. Just ahead, the light of the sun made a bright arch in the dark. She could already see coloured banners waving, and the soldiers who had linked arms to hold back the huge surging crowd, so that the royal way would remain clear.

Emerging from the cool of the tunnel, into the hot morning sun, the roar of the crowd was deafening. Dancing girls, naked but for small wisps of silk, twirled across the avenue in front of the royal bride, scattering rose petals in her path. The crowd was shouting the name of Shaka and clamouring against each other for her attention, and going wild if they received a glance or a wave. Men pumped the air with their fists whilst chanting madly, as tears rolled down women's cheeks. Shaka knew she was disliked by the majority of the people in Kappia, but it pleased her that she was still so feared, none of them were showing it openly.

Inside the city, the avenue continued and crossed the River Pangarin on a bridge with supports high enough and far enough apart to allow even the largest ships to pass. The ships could be lowered from the Plateau to Lake Pangarin through a series of locks, and was widely considered one of the greatest engineering achievements of the Everglow.

Across the city, in the distance, the large nine-level ziggurat, the Argona Temple, towered over every other building. It bristled with spires and steeples on each level. It was so large it could even be seen across the Argona Plain long before the city ever came into view. Next to the temple the Argona Palace stood, equal in magnificence, only slightly smaller in size so as not to offend the gods. Shaka looked to the north, where the Argona Mountain towered over the city. On its summit stood an Aeldar temple, and not far below that, her Celestial Palace. She longed for this day to be over, and to again find herself in the security of a familiar bedchamber, lined with gold and precious jewels. *Today I endure, soon, I will have my revenge.*

After crossing the bridge, the wedding procession soon left the avenue and entered the smaller streets of Kappia. People had clambered onto every roof and garret. Some held out poles carrying effigies of the Seeress, and jerked stuffed figures hanging in nooses so they danced above the crowds. Shaka waved, and pretended to enjoy the exaltation of her people as she was driven onto the streets of Kappia. Her only chance of ever overthrowing Mazdek, was if she could win back the hearts of her people, and shame him in front of them, but that would take careful planning. Her best chance, was at the upcoming games, when she would publicly evoke a law forgotten by most. First, she had to get the other ingredients of the plan she was hatching into place.

As a Munte bride, Shaka would never be free from Mazdek in the eyes of her people. The moment she became Munte, she would always belong to him, be his property throughout every lifetime they both had. The only chance of release from such a vow would be for him to be shamed into breaking the law, or when he met the *Final-death*, a thought that at that moment she relished.

446

Defying protocol, Aspess and Regineo spurred their horses and rode up next to her carriage.

"He treats you so cruelly, yet you smile, wave and pretend to enjoy the occasion?" Aspess asked her mother bitterly, pitching her voice to be heard above the din of the crowd. She used a secret speech, High Vakkan, known only to those who had trained in the Mystery Schools, and therefore would not be understood by the maids, nor could it be heard above the din of the crowd by the Hammer Knights, some of whom would be familiar with the tongue.

"It is how it must be, for this day, for now," Shaka answered with a grim smile as she and the maids steadied the crown, which rocked upon her head with the movements of the carriage. "Daughter, we must all play our part today, and hope our fortune and fate may change tomorrow."

Aspess turned around, and looked at the fake Seeress, who had been taken from the cage, and was now being led chained, bound and naked further back in the procession just behind the replica Simal. Both were heavily guarded by the Hammer Knights. When the poor wretch being presented as the Seeress passed, the cheers of the crowd turned to ugly boos and jeers, and rotten fruit, vegetables, dung, faeces and even some stones were thrown at her. A few launched themselves from the crowd and kicked or punched her, until soldiers pushed them back.

"I almost pity that poor innocent wretch," Aspess said with an air of indifference.

"Guard your tongue," Shaka reprimanded Aspess harshly, "even when using High Vakkan. None of these fools know what Mazdek has planned for them. When these Fell and Half-bloods are enslaved and shackled, they will beg the gods for my return to the throne of Kappia."

Aspess grimaced. "Mazdek has played a game with us, one we did not know we were a part of. I only signed the marriage contract, when I was taken outside of your cell and told to listen. I heard your screams at the hand of that foul beast Grixen."

Shaka felt her face flush. She hoped Aspess had not heard her in any moment of weakness, especially if at the height of her suffering, she had cried for mercy.

"I told Mazdek, if he stopped hurting you, I would sign and seal the document," Aspess confessed.

Shaka smiled wistfully at her daughter. "He has outwitted us at every turn, but no more. My attention drifted from things that mattered. He saw that and took advantage. His ambition will continue long after he discovers his inability to do the things he promises. We must also play this game now, without a fault, until we are in a position to undo his malice. For today, wave to the crowd and smile."

Regineo then spoke, also using High Vakkan. His voice was full of contempt. "I pity you mother, that already Mazdek has so tamed you, you willingly go along with this charade?" He spat on the ground. "Once I saw your signature and the seal upon the document, I saw no point in resisting what you had agreed to do, but you have thrown away the crown that would one day be mine to inherit!"

Shaka knew her son well, he was no weakling, but he had not had to endure what she had. In her cell, Renlak had told her that it had not been long before Regineo had agreed to willingly sign and seal the document. *You would have broken too, in time, had I refused Mazdek, and you had been subject to the constant persuasions of Grixen!* Guarding her words more than her thoughts, Shaka replied to him, "Nail your will to the task of this day, unpleasant as it is, until such a time as we can speak more freely." She gave a false smile as she took one hand off her crown, steadied it with the other and the help of the maids, and waved to the crowd.

Shaka switched to High Akkadian, so that the maids would understand what she said next. She knew, that both Regineo and Aspess would understand the seed of deceit she was planting in the minds of her maids.

"I will be a loyal Munte wife to Mazdek. I only hope that the legions do not discover it was he who murdered General Karkson. They might not take kindly to such news."

Shaka noticed Myrene stir uncomfortably. *She is again buying the lie.*

Aspess turned her nose up in a snarl. "I look forward to the day we crush that low-born heel-biters head into the sand." She said it in High Vakkan.

Shaka shot a reproachful look towards her daughter and answered her harshly, in the same tongue. "Do not be so open with such words and insults, ears will be leant towards us, many eyes and ears will be upon us at all times ready with whispering tongues to relay our faults to Mazdek. I do not yet trust these maids, but one, I can yet turn to our cause. We must play the part fate has assigned to us. For now, pretend to be loyal, as bitter a taste as that may leave."

Shaka felt it wise to caution her children. In the Empire, to call somebody a heel-biter was one of the worst insults. It conveyed the idea of a friend or adviser who committed treachery, cunning, craft and deceit, like a snake that followed prey for the purpose of biting and poisoning in the heel. The insult applied well to Mazdek, General Karkson had seen it and had mustered the courage to publicly call him out as such, moments before his own *Final-death*.

Once again, Shaka regretted bitterly she had not listened more closely to Karkson. However, if it was reported that she or her children were heard uttering such insults about Mazdek, or giving voice or any hint of rebelling against his schemes, it could invite their immediate demise before they had the chance to form and execute a plan that would undo his schemes.

"Today, you suffer degradation, and we your children are being forced to witness as you become victim to a deep abyss of shame and infamy. Do not expect us to smile as we watch," Regineo said.

"Hold your tongue," Aspess said reproachfully to her brother.

"Let him speak," Shaka said, as she stared at Regineo who was still watching her guardedly.

Regineo's face twisted with anger. "You know the humiliating death I suffered at the hands of the Bantu in Aleskian," he said scathingly to her, "yet you still had one of their foul kind as a guest at a feast. I was butchered by Grixen, in the Bloody Tower. When resurrected I was shown the Munte document that was signed and sealed by you, I did not believe it to be genuine at first."

"I suffered much before agreeing to do so," Shaka confessed, feeling somewhat mortified by the look her son gave her.

"I am ashamed of you mother," he said, "and today that shame will be compounded. You have brought our Empire, my inheritance, to wreck and ruin."

Shaka knew that her son would have given in easily, had he been forced to endure what she had. It occurred to her that Renlak might have told her many lies during his occasional visits to her cell, but concerning Regineo, that was not one of them.

"No injustice will last forever," she answered Regineo. "We might still find loyalty from the legions. There is hope today's events can all be undone."

Regineo's face twisted in confusion and rage. "It is believed Borach *the Betrayer* is now deep in the Tarenmoors, his fate and that of the Third Legion unknown. He knows that I, and therefore you, played a part in what happened at Aleskian. The support of the legions at Kara Duram will erode if ever he or any of his men return and his tale is told."

"Then I trust, you did exactly what I asked of you?"

Regineo looked sullenly at her. "I did. His wife and children were never the ones in the catapults. His family were taken immediately to Kara Duram, but he bought the lie. The plan would have gone smoothly had Borach not slain the one they called Garuk, the Bantu War-leader. The enraged Bantu have proven themselves unpredictable allies. Their rampage at Aleskian was only halted by one of their own masters, a mage of great power named Methruille. When he arrived, he rescued me from the cruelty they intended towards me, and brought the horde under control."

Shaka frowned. "If we gain control of Kara Duram, we can use Borach's family to tame him into subservience, should he ever emerge from where he now skulks." She then asked, "How do the people of Kappia now view the alliance between Mazdek and the Bantu?"

"With suspicion," Regineo answered. "Borach was blamed for opening the gate and destroying the city. But, many Kappians doubt this version of events, and the legions at Kara Duram are refusing to disband as a result. Longshins leads them."

Shaka smiled. "Everything that works against Mazdek, works for us," she said. "We will be able to use this to our advantage." *Longshins, never have I doubted your devotion.*

Regineo's tone was indifferent when he told her, "There are rumours that many Pure-bloods, as well as Fell-bloods, not safe on the plateau, are being slaughtered by the Bantu. Some are being taken beyond the wall, and are being given the *Final-death* in ways entertaining to the Bantu."

"Good, you must do all you can to encourage these rumours. But, if this news is believed in Kappia, why do these fools cheer so loudly?" Shaka asked as she glanced at the cheering crowd.

Aspess answered. "Mazdek has spun the events into a popular narrative that makes him look like the only one who has a solution in these troubled times, and that the blame for events lies far from his door. Plus, these fools look forward to the games, and have been promised much by him if they make this day a joyous one," she said. "He has told them, now the Simal has been returned, the Aeldar will soon be summoned and will rise to fight their enemies. He has convinced them the Bantu will destroy the Baothein and leave Kappia in peace. These commoners believe him, and the nobles dare not voice their concerns openly. The Hammer Knights spy networks are everywhere."

Regineo looked sternly at his mother. "I have already spread the tale among the legions, and secretly sent ravens to Kara Duram, that Mazdek is responsible for the murder of Karkson, and that his failed schemes and alliance with the Bantu are the cause behind this calamity."

"Good," Shaka said.

"No," Regineo replied. "I have heard news from Kara Duram, that I am also being tainted with fault for what happened, for I was seen publicly acting on your behalf at Aleskian."

*This is not good*, Shaka thought.

"The people are saying that I plotted with Mazdek, to discredit and overthrow you, and arrange this Munte marriage."

Shaka thought for a moment before answering: "Then this has become a war of rumour and words. If I regain power, we will write the history that will form the narrative for this time. We will vindicate ourselves, and plant all blame at the feet of Mazdek." She stared coldly at Regineo. "Let those who think it, believe that you are loyal to Mazdek, not to me, and those who do not believe it, let them know that as their truth. Whisper to all a tale that Mazdek plotted Karkson's death, that he deceived me and is responsible for Aleskian's grim fate. Gain the trust and ears of those who might rally to our cause when the time is ripe."

"I am already doing so," Regineo replied. "I have secretly had anonymous pamphlets written and sent to the noble families of the great houses, stating that Mazdek deceived us all with his intentions at Aleskian. Rumours abound that he alone is responsible for Karkson's death. I have also whispered in the ears of the houses still loyal to us, that when the time comes, we will need their bannermen and knights. I am careful who I speak with. Not all families are loyal, some blame you for this catastrophe, and I do not wish Mazdek's spies to catch wind of any plans we make. Through deception I shall also earn their trust and loyalty, by letting them believe I support Mazdek. In that way, we will know who is for us, and who is not."

Shaka looked at her son, studying his cruel features for more than a moment. *This will cause a Third Kappian Civil War, but if that is the price that must be paid to regain my throne, so be it, let it be paid in full!*

"It is a dangerous game you play, tread with care," Shaka warned her son. Then, addressing both Regineo and Aspess, and still conversing in High Vakkan, she said. "This will be a war marked by stealth, murder and betrayal. It will be fought in the council chambers and the forum floor of the Senate, in castle yards and in the barracks. The idle chatter of maids as well as the savagery of the battlefield may determine its outcome. Curb your natures, humble yourselves when you must, win the ear and support of the highborn. Be subtle, be careful. Promise much, make many vows as to the rewards that shall be given to those who will come to our aid when the time to strike is at hand."

Regineo and Aspess acknowledged their mother's words with a nod of their heads, flicked the reins of their horses and fell back in line behind the carriage.

Shaka looked at the cheering and baying crowds. Some of them no doubt were the same people who had written and drawn the derogatory graffiti she could now see on parts of the walls she rode by. No matter, they were fools, and she could yet change their minds in the coming days. She would have to, if she wanted to regain her former power. For now, her thoughts changed to the present. She was not looking forward to what lay ahead. The ritual humiliation of a public Munte marriage was almost more than she could bear, but choice was stripped away from her and somehow, she must endure.

Shaka knew that the news that the Bantu had broken a part of the alliance so quickly and that Mazdek had not been able to fully control them, would either work against her, or for her advantage. It had been his plan, but her decision. If she could successfully lay the blame at Mazdek's door, it would work to weaken his hold on power. An unpredictable Bantu horde rampaging through the Everglow would cause death and destruction, and for those who might survive, a lot of hardship and suffering. Those who suffered and survived, and those who heard of their plight, would want somebody to blame.

Regineo had been present at Aleskian, it would be hard for him to fully distance himself from the calamity, but that would not matter. Once she regained power, she would order history to be rewritten, just as her father had done before her. She could distance herself and all her children from the decisions that had led to the fall of Aleskian, the *Northern Calamity*, as she would name it. Perhaps, for a time, she might even have to distance herself from her son, Regineo, and seek to lay the blame at his door and start rumours that he and Mazdek had planned this betrayal all along. Yes, that might be it; Regineo was despised throughout the Empire. He might make a convenient sacrifice as well as Mazdek to calm the rage that would spread throughout the Empire. When she regained power, Mazdek's punishment would be the *Final-death*, after he had suffered much. Regineo could be exiled until such a time when order was restored, history rewritten and people had forgotten the turbulence of the current times. Then, he could quietly return. *I only hope, that the Simal will again fall into my hands, for only with the backing of the Aeldar Ahrimakan, can I take my rightful place, and he can now only return to the Everglow if Thuranotos summons him from the Arkoom that he is imprisoned within.*

There was no time to consider these matters for now. Shaka could think of no way to prevent or stop the chain of events that were happening. For the time being, she and her children must face whatever indignity and suffering the day had in store for them, and wait for the opportunity to make their move and strike back.

The procession proceeded through the streets of Kappia, until it reached the main square of the city, where the male and female Seers of the Order of the Golden Dawn were dancing around a platform constructed of smooth pine wood, covered with silks, banners, and encrusted with jewels of many kinds. Naked under flowing white robes, the Seers danced in two circles, the men in an inner circle dancing in the direction of the sun, the women in an outer circle moving in the other direction, widdershins. Hundreds of drummers wildly pounded on their drums, cheered on by the huge crowd surrounding the square. Hammer Knights locked arms to keep the crowd back, and to clear a path for the royal bride. Steps led up to a wooden platform elaborately decorated with silks and gold, upon which Mazdek, Marnir and Renlak stood smugly, proudly watching the Empress and her procession ride into the square.

After Shaka's carriage had halted, and with the help of her maids she had disembarked, the drums stopped, and the dancers cleared a way to the platform and threw themselves prostrate to the floor facing it. The crowd fell silent in anticipation. Silk curtains below the platform opened, and a hundred specially chosen Hammer Knights marched proudly from under it and stood behind each of the prostrate dancers, and readied their hammers. At least this time in the Deadlands, Shaka would not have the indignity of not having Seers with her. Each of the dancers would be sacrificed before she was, to await her arrival in the Deadlands so they could escort her immediately to the Obelisk in the temple, where she would await resurrection.

There was something eerie in the stillness with which Mazdek looked at the festive crowd, especially as he stared at the high society of Kappia who sat on the stepped rows of benches behind the platform. An excited babble rose from them as Shaka approached the steps. She recognised many of the faces staring at her. These people were the noble families, merchants rich enough to pay for a seat among the elites, carefree celebrity actors, singers and the leaders of many of Kappia's civic and guild organisations, as well as a myriad of other people chosen to witness, up close, the ritual act of her Munte marriage to Mazdek. There were Senators, members of the Assembly and Magistracy. But, unlike the genuine joy of the common crowd, and some of the more carefree aristocrats, Shaka noticed that some of the people staring at her looked afraid. She could see that behind their smiles, was doubt. Their smiles and joy were clearly for the sake of show only.

The sight of uncertainty on some of the faces in the crowd gave her hope. They knew Mazdek was a low-born, and as such it would be a blow to their pride for them to call him *'their Emperor.'* Perhaps they had heard rumours, or worked out that this Munte marriage was the result of a plot, and was therefore against her will. After all, she had been missing from the imperial court for some weeks and had not addressed the Senate for some time. *Surely the Senate will know I would never willingly agree to a Munte marriage?* The trouble was, even if they did, without the legions, they could not stand against Mazdek and the Hammer Knights who had overtaken the capital city. *Many in the Senate still hate and fear me. It is only the legions who can still win me back my throne.*

451

As the crowd around the platform stared at her, Shaka saw a mixture of reactions on their faces. Some were clearly doubtful, others were afraid, and some were clearly not enjoying the whole spectacle. The only nobles who seemed to be genuinely enjoying her shame, those who showed no pity or compassion, were those she had cruelly mistreated in the past. Several noble women, whom she had ordered into Munte marriages themselves, were clearly smug and happy to be watching her now face the same humiliating situation. They stared at her harshly and the contempt and anger in their faces towards her was clear. She raised her chin with fragile pride, and swallowed the lump she felt in her throat. *Today I endure; soon I will have my revenge.*

The babble of the crowd, which had slowly risen again, died away as one of the Serveri led Shaka slowly up the steps to the stage, followed by her three children. She looked up into Mazdek's cold gaze, and knew even then, her fate was being measured and decided, so she played the part. The Serveri removed the Maradrith Crown, and placed it on a nearby pedestal. Shaka gritted her teeth and smiled as she knelt on her knees before Mazdek, much to his obvious delight.

The ceremony began immediately. It was a formula, a ritual faithfully followed. As Marnir slowly, loudly and authoritatively pronounced every word of the Munte marriage ceremony, each one was like a hammer blow to Shaka. He declared how she, the Empress, by her own free will, surrendered her power, authority, titles and honours, which she freely gave to her husband to be, Mazdek.

She found it hard to breathe, when it came to her turn to repeat the words Marnir spoke, but she did so. "I the Empress Shaka of House Shakawraith, freely agree to the Munte marriage to Mazdek de Lorion of Clarevont." She endured and found strength in the thought that one day she would have her revenge.

Marnir continued, declaring that Shaka willingly forfeited her right to command the legions, which was ironic, seeing as they were supposed to be soon disbanded. It was obvious that he had purposefully not removed the wording from the ceremony, nonetheless. She repeated the words. Marnir then declared that in all things she would obey her husband, the new Emperor, before saying the words she was to repeat.

As serenely as she could, Shaka, kneeling before Mazdek, and gazing up at him, repeated every word accurately. "As a Munte wife, I will obey my husband in all things private and public."

The ceremony was long and arduous, and Shaka dutifully repeated everything she was asked to say. As it drew to a close Mazdek's new titles started to be announced. He was declared Emperor of Kappia, an honoured Osmanian and Simonian, and a whole list of other titles, until it was finally declared that Shaka, by her own free will, was therefore to be forever known as Consort Munte of Emperor Mazdek the First.

The last words of the ceremony were the hardest to say. Shaka felt a tremor in her voice as she announced, "I, Shaka, by my own free will, declare myself Consort Munte to my husband, Emperor Mazdek the First, the de Lorion of Clarevont." That was it; her position, titles, honours and right to rule had been freely surrendered and forever given to Mazdek, until his or her *Final-death.*

In turn, all three of Shaka's children were called forward, and led by Marnir, each publicly announced their support for the marriage. Regineo, the oldest, was first. Dressed in his finest court robes, he played the part well and almost sounded sincere. He signed and sealed with wax the final and legal marriage licence and certificate and stepped aside. Aspess, her second-born, repeated the words Marnir spoke, and though Shaka could tell her daughter was clearly fighting an inner rage at such public humiliation of the royal family, Aspess played her part, signed and sealed both license and certificate, and stepped aside. Caspus did the same.

Renlak shook with fear as he bore witness and with a trembling hand signed and sealed both license and certificate, and with wax, also impressed upon them the seal of his ring of state. Marnir, and then Mazdek signed and sealed them, after which Shaka, rising to her feet, her hand trembling slightly as she did so, also publicly signed and sealed both certificate and license with her imperial stamp.

Shaka swallowed hard as she prepared for the most humiliating part of the ceremony that would now take place. The union would now be sealed, with public consummation. A velvet divan was carried onto the platform. Mazdek held out his hand to his new bride. The leer on his face repulsed her, but there was no dignity in trying to resist him, which would have been an exercise in futility anyway. His face was a grimace of deviant pleasure, eyes wide, mouth snarling, as he approached her. She felt her face redden and blush, as he pulled her white wedding gown up around her waist, and pushed her face down and half-naked onto the divan. He then pulled up his own robe with one hand, whilst he pinned her face down on the divan with the other hand. A tear rolled from her eye as she felt the weight of his body press down upon her. He clumsily and roughly entered her, guiding his manhood with his now free hand. She certainly did not feel pleasure, nor did she feel pain, just an overwhelming sense of humiliation at suffering such grotesque, public attention. But it was the law, the custom. Mazdek had the right under Munte law to prove publicly that he was now her master, and he had chosen to exercise it, making her humiliation complete. Her loathing of him reached a new low, if that were possible. Sweat rolled from his face in streams as he thrusted and grunted, and she felt it drip upon her bare buttocks.

Her only thought as he shunted, was that his arrogance would defeat him soon enough. If she could get everything she planned in place before the games commenced, he would take the bait offered to him on the opening day, of that she was sure, for what other choice would he have but to accept the challenge? During her imprisonment, she had thought long and hard, strained her memory to remember and seize on every detail of Mazdek's weaknesses that might be used against him. She must lull him into a false sense of security, so that he would not get an inclination of what she planned at the games.

It was her own arrogance and sense of invulnerability that he had seized upon, so she had not seen his schemes until they had taken full form, but by then it had been too late. She had learnt the lessons, and they were mistakes she would never repeat again. As his face contorted with perverse lust, she consoled herself with the thought that, *it will be too late for you, when my plans turn against you so soon after this foul marriage is sealed. But for today, I must endure.*

Shaka did not yet know who out of all of the witnesses in the stand would remain loyal to Mazdek, or those who would rally to her when she executed her plan. The humiliation she felt at that moment, was too great for her to turn her head and look at them. Instead, she looked at Aspess, who was vigilant and scanning the faces in the crowd.

Aspess would know which families from the old houses and highborn were enjoying her mother's humiliation, or those who, under her daughter's stare, showed fear and concern. Some of the highborn would themselves harbour ambitions for the throne, of that Shaka had no doubt, and it might be possible there would be more than two sides in the war that was to come. It would require patience for her to learn where each of these people stood, but time was of the essence. *I have to strike at the games, if only I can put all things in place beforehand.* Patience and humility – both were virtues unfamiliar to Shaka, but she must exercise them, no matter how unpleasant a taste it left in her soul. *Today I endure; soon I will have my revenge.*

In the days ahead, Shaka knew she would have to listen to every whisper in court, whilst plotting and planning, working to undo the consequences of this day. When power was back in her hands, she would purge the entire Hammer Knights, banish their Order from the Empire and destroy all history and memory of them. After that, she would have to work out how to deal with the Bantu threat now within the Everglow itself, and find a way to regain the Simal, for without it, her Ahrimakan and her future as an Aeldar Wife and Queen, a goddess, was lost to her. She believed that Mazdek was wrong or lying that the Aeldar would now despise her and easily cast her aside.

It was not lost on Shaka just how perilous a situation she was in. Some nobles were clearly afraid of Mazdek, others despised him, but equally, some were still afraid of her, and some, if not many, despised her for the past treatment she had dished out to them so freely and uncaringly. It seemed impossible at that moment that she would ever get support for her reign again, and for a moment she despaired that all was forever lost. Compliance was her most strategic weapon; make Mazdek believe she had accepted her position. She must play her part; convince him she wanted to be a dutiful Munte wife. His arrogance was such that he might just believe he had truly broken her will and spirit and forced her into obedience to him.

The only merciful part of the public consummation for Shaka was that it was over very quickly. Mazdek pressed his face next to hers, and shielded them from view with the sleeve of his robe, as though he was whispering something private. Then, unseen by the crowd, he contemptuously spat in her face, after which he wiped the spit off with his sleeve, climbed off of her and readjusted his robe.

Shaka got off of the divan, stood to her feet and pulled down her robe. The crowd began to cheer and chant the name of Mazdek.

The final part of the ceremony was about to commence. A heavy golden anvil was carried to the stage by several Hammer Knights. Shaka walked quietly over to it, knelt on her knees, and placed her head on the anvil. A Hammer Knight, dressed in full ceremonial armour, with his face hooded and unseen, stepped up to the anvil, raised his sacred hammer, and brought it down with full force onto her head, smashing her skull, which burst like a ripe melon. The blow killed her instantly.

The one hundred Hammer Knights standing behind the Seers dispatched each and every one of them in the same manner at the same time.

Shaka was no Seer. In the Deadlands she was as blind and unknowing as anyone else. But each time she had died, since she had first mated with an Aeldar, she had become a ghost in the land of the living for just a few minutes before passing into realms beyond. It was the same that day. Her spirit rose from her dead body, and she looked down with disgust at her shattered and ruined skull, as her body slumped onto the white silk cloth that covered the floor of the stage. Skull and brains were splattered on the cloth, and her blood fanned out across it staining it scarlet red. Even worse, the Maidenarz vanished from her physical body, and appeared on her ghostly form. *Even in death I cannot escape this thing,* she cursed.

Shaka knew she had to make the most of this time, and drifted towards the benches where the highborn of Kappia sat. The cheers had died down into excited chatters and murmuring. A trumpet blast sounded the end of the ceremony, and the crowd began to disperse as her corpse and that of the Seers was taken away. Her ghost drifted over to the crowd nearest the stage. She could hear fawning tributes to Mazdek, as people competed with one another to be overheard declaring his praises, as Hammer Knights listened on. But her heightened senses quickly moved on to the more interesting conversations further back, the quiet whispers said between families and close associates, who could not be overheard. She heard one noble boast about some new

454

Fell-blood slaves he had acquired, children, snatched from the outskirts of the Skunfill district.

"They have such fear in their eyes, it's almost like they have feelings," exclaimed the noble. Shaka was not interested in such useless trivia; she needed to find out more important matters so drifted over to where others stood. Another perennial topic caught her ear; the rise of Mazdek was a subject of much quiet debate in one group. These people were clearly talking among those they trusted, in tones where they could not be overhead, their eyes looking around themselves to make sure it remained so.

"It disgusts me that such a low-born is now Emperor," one of the nobles said to which others nodded in agreement. "The Empress is cruel, she has wronged many of us in the past, but at least she has royal blood in her veins."

Another group was outraged that Mazdek had exercised his right of a public consummation. They quietly complained among themselves about his arrogant behaviour, and most of all they were galled by his new titles and position as Emperor, again, for the reason that he was a low-born.

"He is a rough-hewn low-born with no trace of nobility in his blood," one outraged nobleman said to his wife and some close companions in another group.

Shaka also heard some nobles bitterly criticise her, even stating they were glad she had lost her power. These were some of the families she had most wronged in the past, especially among the Senate, many of whom hated her with a passion. However, even among these, her smile grew as she heard the force of the contempt with which they also held Mazdek, who had been systematically stealing their wealth through different schemes and by false accusations. She heard similar statements from most other nobles. She was glad that not all of her support had gone. She did not have much, but the little she had, was still more than that which Mazdek had; she made a mental note of the faces and names of those whose private whispers she heard.

As Shaka's ghost continued to drift through the crowd, she heard talk about the fears some had of possible civil war, others spoke of their fear of the Bantu threat and the way the Bantu had so easily broken the alliance when it suited them at Aleskian. This was all good news to Shaka. Mazdek had the support of the Hammer Knights, a formidable force, but the nobles were far from happy at the recent turn of events.

One refrain that she heard from some groups did not please her. Buried amongst the idle notes of flattery and gossip, there was another, darker theme. Some were talking of her shameful secrets, her forbidden trysts and hidden vices. There was mention that she deserved the humiliation she had just endured. Some Munte brides who themselves had been subjected to such a spectacle, gloated and mocked her for it. But, of most concern, there was talk that Mazdek had chosen the public consummation to dispel the myth that she turned into a snake beast when having intimate relations. She had enjoyed the fear this put into the minds of her people.

"She's just a weak woman after all," said one nobleman to another.

"The she-bitch probably invented the myth herself to make us fear her," his wife replied. The group standing around them laughed scornfully.

Shaka wanted to shout that it was the Maidenarz that prevented her from changing aspect, but in that form, she could not speak in the physical world. She took note of these peoples' faces. *If ever I get this thing off of me, and regain my throne, I will show you what I can become. I will exalt at the terror in your eyes as I stare into them and wrap my coils around you.*

Most disturbing to Shaka, was the next conversation she heard. A conversation between three Senators.

"Her judgement has proved ill," the first one said.

The second replied, "High Quaester Mazdek told me himself that he warned her not to betray Lord Borach and General Karkson, but she dismissed his advice."

"I also blame her for the loss of Aleskian," the first one answered, and then added, "you must refer to him as Emperor Mazdek now!"

The third then said, "Long have I feared she had lost her mind and sanity. Ever since the Black Banquet, when I was forced to eat my own wife's hand, I have waited for an opportunity to get even. That was the reason why I gladly voted and gave support for this Munte marriage, as did others, who were forced to attend that grim event on that fateful evening."

The other two muttered sympathies, one stating he was glad it was an occasion he had not been invited to attend, the other stating he had not been a Senator during that unfortunate time. It dawned upon Shaka that far from being against the will of the Senate, a majority had clearly voted in agreement for the Munte marriage between her and Mazdek. No doubt some had done so due to fear of the Hammer Knights, or were being blackmailed to do so, but others, like these three, because they had lost faith in her, or wanted revenge and clearly despised her. Shaka had been right in what she had said to Aspess and Regineo, support for her reign was deeply divided. Another civil war, was almost inevitable, but preceding that, would come a war of words where truth would be a casualty, and many lies would need to be told to win back support where it was needed. That suited Shaka, lies and deceit had won her the throne from her father, they would win it back for her from Mazdek.

Hope momentarily drained away from Shaka, as the physical world began to ripple, to dissolve and to disappear. A door from the spirit world appeared and opened, and she saw a seemingly endless staircase leading down into the depths of a deep and dark abyss. It was no use trying to resist, as by a force as powerful as gravity, her ghost was sucked into the Deadlands. As she was pulled plummeting down the stairs at an alarming speed, her vision began to fade, and her mind dimmed into nothingness. Shaka's last thought was relief; she felt relieved that a hundred Seers were waiting for her to guide her back to an Obelisk, and back to the land of the living, so that she could plan both her return to power, and plot her revenge.

*Today I endure; soon I will have my revenge.*

# Chapter Thirty-Seven: *Erik Vansoth*

*Almost three-quarters of the world's surface is covered with water and, according to the 9420 Census of Marine Life, our vast oceans probably contain up to two million different species of aquatic life. Many of these creatures are strange and terrifying, such as the Merfolk. Merfolk is the correct term for mermen and mermaids, Temmison is wrong in his use of a different term for this species, and I will not even honour his theory by mentioning it here as it is such poor academic work on his part. Back to topic - I have seen a mermaid. The middle was the shape of a woman. It had a terrible broad face, a pointed forehead, wrinkled cheeks and a wide mouth. It had large eyes and black untrimmed hair. Two great breasts showed her sex. She had two long arms with hands and fingers webbed, like the feet of a goose. Below the middle, she is like a fish, with a tail and fins. It really was a grotesque and somewhat eerie sight. I was just glad it was pickled in a large tank for visitors to view at their leisure.*

*A Mermaid, as described by the Bruthon Missionary Edegal in the Year 9421, after his visit to the Kappian Museum of Monsters and described in his book; Magical, Mystical and Truly Terrifying Creatures.*

*The* timbers of the *Red Tide* groaned and creaked with the pitch and roll of the sea. Azzadan woke stiff and sore from a troubled and uneasy sleep, just as the sky was beginning to take on an orange-red glow from the rising sun, its flickers of light shining through the glazed porthole of the cabin he was in. Smindy was next to him in the cot, half-naked, and gently sleeping. He agilely jumped out of the large cot, and checked for his equipment. To his relief, his clothes and weapons, and his ethereal cloak, were slung carelessly on the deck where he had left them the night before. He cursed himself as he dressed, for his carelessness. Such sloppiness could easily get him killed or robbed of his priceless cloak.

As much as Azzadan admired her, and in a way, felt something akin to a warped love for her, he still knew that Redboots was not to be trusted and might use any opportunity to advance her position even at his detriment. He had been deep in his cups the night before and had clearly lost his wits, letting his guard down so much so that he could only vaguely remember getting into the gig that had rowed the three of them out to her ship, the *Red Tide*. He could not remember how he managed to climb the rope ladders up the ship's side.

*I hate drunkards, yet last night I became one,* he regretfully said to himself as he rubbed his aching head, caught a corked jug of water that was rolling about the deck with his foot, stooped, picked it up, popped the cork and thirstily drank the contents.

Azzadan shook Smindy awake. She awoke startled and took a moment to realise where she was. She got out of the cot, looking around her. She opened a drawer beneath the cot, and took out some fresh clothes and a shawl with which she covered herself. He passed her the jug of water, and she gladly drank from it. She then held her head and groaned, "Never again. It feels like two wrestlers with mallets are fighting inside my head." She opened the door and led him outside. "Well, that was my cabin, I'll show you the rest of the ship."

Smindy then gave him a quick tour of the aft end of the ship. "It's copper-hulled," she said. "Extra-thick copper covers the bow from water-line to keel. Where we will sail, there are giant Teredo worms."

Azzadan stared at her with a puzzled look.

"They are the termites of the sea. As big as a man, they burrow into a ship and eat the timbers, if they are unprotected. A ship will find itself suddenly springing leaks everywhere if the hull is not protected." She seemed to take delight in his concerned expression. "There are far worse creatures than the worms, but this ship is equipped to take care of most of them."

"Only most creatures?" he asked sarcastically.

Smindy grinned. "Why do you think it was so hard for your Order to find a captain to sail there? Only the foolhardy will go to the Grona Sea in a vessel not equipped for it, and only the bravest will do so in one that is. The Sea Lords employ monster hunting ships to keep the numbers of such creatures down. But who knows what might suddenly rise up from the deep?"

She laughed and continued the tour, showing him the Common Space used for music, drinking and socialising during long voyages. Directly above that, was the Assembly Room, where the officers dined and held councils of war. The quarterdeck was above this, with the far end roofed by the 'poop,' and within this space the most senior officers had their cabins, with windows looking out to sea.

"Why do you not have a cabin here?" Azzadan asked her.

"The cabin below is my own space. Whenever I sleep up here, it is in the captain's cabin. Come, I'll show it to you."

Redboots cabin, known as the Great Cabin, was by far the biggest one on board, and was no less elaborate than the one she had on the *Cruel Maid*. The only real difference, apart from the size, was that the transom wall at the back, only had small portholes with toughened glass, only decorated in the centre with a variety of different sea creatures.

Azzadan and Smindy entered the Great Cabin through a side door, passed through it and opened the ornately carved double doors and walked onto the main deck. The crew were scurrying hither and thither, obeying orders bellowed by a bosun's mate. Over their heads the great pyramids of sails were reaching up to the sky, filled with the wind, as the *Red Tide* crashed its way wave by wave across the rough sea. He paused and looked up and briefly watched the mastheads sweeping out great circles across the morning sky. On the starboard quarter the risen sun had just lifted itself out of the sea and hung gloriously over the horizon, sending long glittering trails of golden light towards the ship. It was then he noticed that on the Mizzenmast, the Mainmast, and the Lower Mast, nailed to the top of each and bound with rope to make them secure, was a man, each of them still alive and slowly writhing in pain. Three offerings to Jorgen.

"The Tethys Sea is more demanding and dangerous than the Erin," Smindy said to him as she followed his gaze and looked at the miserable and suffering wretches above. "So, we give more of a sacrifice and a higher one. They were ruffians some of the crew got in a fight with on the streets of Harwind."

Azzadan and Smindy made their way to the poop-deck, where Redboots and Laro were stood side by side, feet apart on the heaving deck, as they steadied themselves and looked through their sextants at the horizon. Her tricorn hat was tucked into her belt, so her red hair was free and tousled as it blew wildly about in the wind. The scarlet jacket she wore was buttoned neatly up to the neck and slightly damp due to the smothered spray that swept across the deck, the droplets covering her in momentary rainbows. Once again Azzadan thought she was the most glorious woman he had ever laid eyes upon. To him, Redboots was a woman of exotic, almost bizarre beauty in an exquisite setting. Both ship and captain were mistress and master of the waves over which they were sailing in solitary grandeur.

*By Skipilos, I think I love this woman,* Azzadan thought. Was it not for his need of the Orange Brew, again, he thought he might decide there and then in that moment to repay the betrayal of his Order, with one of his own, and spend the rest of his days with

458

Redboots sailing where she sailed, until her one life expired? He felt anger rise within him as he remembered the betrayal. He deeply resented the fact he had not been allowed to pursue the Simal and Janorra. Again, bitter thoughts that his Order had failed him tormented his mind. But, were it not for that betrayal, he would not have met Redboots? In a way that caused his emotions to conflict, and it confused him that he also felt glad of it, despite feeling bitter. But, the very sight of Redboots, made his pulse quicken and his breath come sharper. How he lamented in that moment that she was not a Pure-blood and would never see a resurrection when her days were over. *If only she was a Pure-blood, I would gladly spend every lifetime with her was the choice mine alone to make, but she is a Fell-blood. Even so, gladly would I spend just this one with her.*

When they had finished reading and recording the measurements, Redboots and Laro clamped their sextants shut. "Switch to a port tack, then at my order put her head to sea," she bellowed to the helmsman.

"Aye aye cap'n," he bellowed back. The masts creaked and grumbled and the sails flapped as he turned the large wheel to bring the ship to a port tack.

Redboots looked around and noticed Azzadan and Smindy waiting for her. "I'm so glad to get the stench of that filthy Erin washed off of my ship, and most of all, off my skin," she beamed as she joined them, taking in deep gusts of the clean air. "If this wind keeps up, we'll be in range of Grona in four weeks or so, but first we must pay the toll to the Sea Lords. We'll be there before the dogwatches."

Whilst Azzadan stood with Redboots, both quietly enjoying the spray of the sea washing over them and the gusts of wind, Smindy fetched Sassy from below the decks. "It's not good for a young girl to be cooped up below," she shouted up to them as she and Sassy began to play on the upper deck.

Azzadan watched as Smindy and Sassy dressed themselves in ribboned straw bonnets. They were both aglow with youth and high spirits. Dodging sailors about their work, they skipped and ran about the deck, every now and then overwhelmed by gales of laughter. They were soon both pink-cheeked from sun and wind. It struck Azzadan, how innocent they both seemed against the backdrop of the ship they were on. Sassy was indeed innocent, Smindy, not so much, but it seemed in that moment she too had forgotten the cares of a hard life and had become an innocent child again. *By goodness, what is happening to me, do I have feelings for Smindy as well?*

When the sea began to get heavier, Smindy gave Sassy a tonic to help her get over a bout of sea sickness, and took her to the Great Cabin. As Redboots was busy issuing orders, Azzadan soon joined them, and then spent an hour or so playing cards and dice with Sassy, teaching her how to play Harendale, whilst Smindy was plunged deep into accounting books at the table. Sassy rarely initiated any conversation, and when he did, she did not respond that much. He assumed she was of a shy disposition, and soon grew bored of her company. She was not very good and struggled to pick up even the basics of the card game and she was even worse at the dice version. He did feel some sympathy for the poor girl. When the ship jolted rather suddenly and violently as it met with a particularly heavy wave, she looked quite queasy and tucked her head into his arm and said, "I'm scared, Azzie."

"You need to toughen up girl," he responded gruffly, causing tears to form in her eyes. He gently pushed her away, stood, and walked over to Smindy and stood over her shoulder as she poured over the ship's muster book, slop-book, tickets, sick-book, complete-books, bosun's and carpenter's expenses, supplies and returns book, and then studied the general account of provisions purchased and used, together with the quantity of spirits, wine, salted pork and fish, and the log, letter and order books. The victualing of the ship had been recorded in minute detail: 1890 Ib of bread, 120 Ib of

Cocoa, 120 Ib of rum, 240 Ib gallons of beer and so on. He also noticed that in the captain's log, which he flicked open, every detail and event was logged: '3:30. Last of the crew on board. 4.23. Unmoored ship, warped down to buoy. 5.19. Tide was right to set sail.'

Azzadan was surprised that the *Red Tide* was run with such efficiency. "These logs don't show the carefree life that I thought pirating was," he commented with a hint of derision.

Smindy looked at him with all seriousness. "There is a time to be carefree and carless, but running and sailing a ship is not one of them. We are heading towards notoriously turbulent and dangerous waters. One mistake, will kill us all." She then explained to him that, in addition to the dangers, the Sea Lords often boarded guild ships and did surprise inspections, and if they felt that any captain or ship was trying to cheat and hide the percentage of the toll or tariffs, they owed, that captain and ship's career on the Tethys Sea and the inland rivers was over, and they would have to pay the salt-price.

"The salt-price?" Azzadan asked.

"It is not a price anyone with sanity in their brain would want to pay," Smindy answered. "Best to just pay the tolls, and the proper tariffs. The captain takes care of the sailing; I take care of the books. You don't cheat Jorgen from his toll of sacrifices, and you don't cheat the Sea Lords from their toll of coin. They don't accept even honest mistakes without a penalty so I must make sure all is in order."

"Well, I am restless," he retorted. "When you put down your quill, join me in a game of Harendale. The girl is not quick-witted enough to offer a challenge." He walked moodily over to the glazed portholes at the back of the cabin, and stared out of them watching the huge swell of the waves.

When Smindy had finished the books, a short time afterwards, she took a brush and gently brushed Sassy's white hair and wiped the tears from her watery blue eyes. He guessed her tears were due to his refusal to interact with her any longer. He turned and looked at Sassy's pale and delicate skin and doubted she had ever seen much of the sun. This was no life for such a small and tender thing, and he regretted bringing her onto a ship such as the *Red Tide*, but then reflected that, surely, *even this will be a better life than one following in the footsteps of our mother?*

Smindy noticed him watching them, and must have sensed his concern, for she assured him that, "Captain Redboots is never cruel to innocents, we'll look after her well Azzie. I will find a suitable role for her; she will become one of us in time and live a good life full of adventure. She will see much of what this world has to offer. It'll be a dangerous and hard life, but a salt-life can also be a good one."

Smindy's words did assure him, there were worse lives she could live, and despite the harshness and cruelty of life aboard a pirate vessel, it also had much to offer, and it was better than the fate she would have had at Harwind living with his mother.

Azzadan spent the rest of that day, and the two that followed, mostly in idle conversation and activity with Smindy when she was not working on the books. She proved very apt at Harendale and beat him on a number of occasions, much to his annoyance. He suspected she cheated, but could not work out how.

They all slept in the Great Cabin, though Redboots only for a few hours at a time when, exhausted, she slept soundly. It was early evening of the third day at sea, just after the second dogwatch had been called, when Laro could be heard shouting a sighting of land ahead. By then, Sassy was fast asleep in a hammock swinging by the cot bed. Azzadan helped Smindy to pack the books into two satchels, one which she carried whilst he took the other. They then rushed out onto the deck. The ship was just entering the curve of a bay – Henchman Bay.

Azzadan took in the sight. The sun was setting in the west over the port quarter of the ship in a magnificent display of red and gold. The surface of the sea was gilded and glittering. A shoal of flying fish broke the surface and went skimming along, before plunging back beneath, and not far away, was a large mountainous and luscious green island.

"Port Toseucia, the island home of the Sea Lords," Smindy said with a hint of awe as she pointed to a fair-sized town stretching up from an elegant harbour. "And there, high on the hill, is Redboot's manor house." She pointed to a grand house on top of a hill, that stood in acres of land, surrounded by sloping tobacco fields and coffee plantations. "Not that we ever spend much time there, and won't this time for Grona awaits. Slaves tend the house for us when we are away. Oh, Azzie, it is one of the most magnificently furnished houses you will ever see. When we get back from Grona, you must see it."

At first, Azzadan was confused when he shifted his attention away from the house and looked at Toseucia. There seemed to be a forest right down at the water's edge; it was only as they neared the harbour that he realised that the trees were ship's masts. He had never seen so many ships of all shapes and sizes in one place in any of his lifetimes. The *Red Tide*, large as it was, was dwarfed by some of the huge supply ships, the galleons, and the even larger warships. There were small and large galleys, triremes of different sizes, and numerous fat-bellied little merchant ships. By far the largest ship though, was a hulking galleon anchored in the middle of the bay. It had an odd appearance in that it had no masts or sails, and was so large, it looked like a small island itself. Anchored next to it, and attached by thick chains and rope bridges that moved with the motion of the waves, was a fearsome looking war galleon that looked like a terrible sea serpent. The sails bore the same emblem as the flag atop the main mast, a green Kraken in a fight with a silver sky blue Leviathan that had a ship in its jaws, all set against a darker royal blue background.

"The large ship with no masts, is the *Accountant,* one of the toll-ships of the Sea Lords. The one next to it, is named the Kraken; it is the flag ship of Erik Vansoth, First of the Sea Lords," Smindy said to Azzadan.

"Damn it," Redboots hissed as she joined them. "Curse our luck. Erik is here!"

Azzadan raised his eyebrow inquisitively. "Trouble?"

"No," Smindy answered. "When Erik is here, he hosts a Mariners' Ball every evening. Captains like Redboots who are in the Skull Guild, or any seafaring guilds who work with the Sea Lords, are expected to attend if their ships enter the bay. Erik will consider it an insult if we do not go."

"I just wanted to pay the toll and be on our way to Grona," Redboots said with a bored sigh.

The sails of the *Red Tide* were folded away, and she attached to a smaller boat, and was rowed by oar between the numerous ships to as close as she could get to the *Accountant* before laying anchor. She lay there, rocking gently, out in Toseucia harbour, with the *Accountant* on her port beam and beyond it the town of Toseucia, the lights of which were starting to spring to life. The ship's crew fell oddly quiet as they looked at the hulking toll-ship. The only noise came from the creak and groan of the ship as the anchor chain tautened, and a fishing-boat that passed under the stern of the *Red Tide*, laden with tunny and uttering the harsh roar of a conch.

When the fishing-boat had safely passed, and the boat that had rowed them had detached, a supply ship came alongside. A great crane hauled crates of supplies on board. All the crew helped as boxes of leather boots, clothing, candles, food, bedding, medical equipment, and beer and water barrels were carried to the storerooms in the lower-deck. "Harwind did not have enough to supply us with everything we needed," Smindy said, anticipating Azzadan's question.

When this task was complete, the bosun of the *Red Tide* blew his whistle several times and then ordered. "Gig's crew away! Hands to lower the gig!"

"Come with us Azzie," Smindy said to him. They joined Redboots and the other crew and climbed inside the gig, which was lowered away with the shouts and grunts of the crew and the straining of ropes. When the gig was in the water, the ropes were released and the crew rowed the small boat alongside the *Accountant*. Up close, the toll-ship looked more like a massive oblong wooden hulk than an actual ship. At the rear, a flag as large as a sail fluttered in the wind, upon which was the image of a cruel looking mermaid. Scores of other small gigs were rowing towards the toll-ship, were already tied alongside, or were leaving it. The whole scene was a flurry of activity.

The gig of the *Red Tide* was secured by the sailors to one of many small pontoons. All of the crew except one stayed behind in the gig, as Redboots and the others got out and then assailed the long rope ladder, which was about eighty feet in height. Azzadan was not afraid of heights, but it seemed far loftier and more precarious when there was nothing but an insubstantial yielding ladder of moving ropes underfoot. If he fell, he would land on the gig and it would certainly kill him, or worse, just smash and ruin his body. He was not afraid for his skin and not afraid for himself, but he did wonder where the nearest Obelisk might be and hoped there was one on Toseucia. He chided himself for not enquiring.

When they had all successfully assailed the ladder and had safely climbed aboard the toll-ship, they were met by a tubular young man, dressed in old sailcloth trousers and a striped knitted blue and white shirt; he had a marlinspike dangling round his neck. He looked attentively at Redboots and with false deference bowed and said, "Welcome aboard the *Accountant*, your toll-master today will be Bosun Mowett. You are?"

"You know who I am boy, lead the way," Redboots said confidently.

The sailor hesitated, and then said, "Very well ma'am."

The upper deck of the *Accountant* was more like a thriving town than a ship. Every race and nationality were represented: Humans, Gnomes, Dwarves, Halflings and Chatti and virtually every other type of non-human. Azzadan noticed that even a group of Kirani, the mysterious bipedal cat-race from the Sunset Isles wandered about, purring with delight as they sampled the many fish dishes on offer, their tails swishing gracefully as they ate. They stopped by a barrel of jellied eels, and pretending to taste them, they ate their fill, but when they didn't buy anything, the vendor, noticing their ploy angrily chased them off with a stick. Azzadan remembered why he hated the Kirani race so much, especially Skidegeat, the one who had replaced him in recapturing the Seeress Janorra and the Simal.

The young sailor led them among the many taverns, huts, and wooden buildings of various sizes that were built upon the upper deck. Shop vendors and stall-holders were shouting and hollering at Azzadan and his friends as they passed by, offering them a variety of wares and trinkets to buy. The deck was lined with taverns, brothels, and filled with an assortment of traders from booksellers to tailors and a variety of food shops. Ballad singers belted out a mixture of songs, hoping to be thrown a coin by those who passed by. Men, women and children were milling about all chattering excitedly. Dogs ran amok among the throngs of people, picking up or fighting over scraps of food thrown carelessly onto the deck.

They passed a barber's shop, and a red-lipped and pale young woman, with thick-white-blonde plaits chided Azzadan for needing his beard and hair trimmed and his clothes cleaned and mended. She tried pulling him into her shop, offering him a good price but he roughly pushed her away cursing at her, leading to a foul-mouthed tirade from her as a response.

Passing an ironware shop, several Dwarves dressed in sealskin jackets looked up as Azzadan stopped briefly to inspect their wares, fingering the hilt of a cleverly crafted stout looking dagger hanging on a weapon rack.

"Don't touch unless you're going to buy," one of them yelled angrily at him, his mighty waist-length red-beard shaking as he shook his fist.

Azzadan knew better than to get into an argument with a dwarf, for he did not have the time. He didn't like Dwarves; it was always a dangerous matter to tangle with them. He did not fear them, but this short, stocky-race were easily riled, and their axes had a nasty habit of leaping into their master's hands at incredible speed, and when that happened, blood was usually drawn. Azzadan had more important matters to contend with, than getting into a petty fight with a dwarf, so he merely grunted his annoyance and moved on.

The crew of the gig wandered off to a tavern, as Azzadan, Smindy and Redboots entered below decks. They took an open lift, which the sailor operated by a pulley system, taking them as far as it would go. Then, they climbed down ladder after ladder, deck after deck, deeper into the heart of the ship. Each deck was guarded by vicious looking thugs who watched their every move. It would have been pitch dark if it were not for the light of the lanterns that swung with the slow rocking motion of the gargantuan ship. They climbed down more ladders until they were at least level with the ship's waterline. It was a testament to the power of the Tethys Sea that a ship even as large as this, when in a bay, could still be moved by the power of its swell. Through the wooden side of the ship could be heard the slap of the water alongside, and the impact of the waves gently lapping the side. Eventually they reached an iron door guarded by two heavily-armed men, who made them remove every weapon, that they placed on a table before patting them down. Azzadan removed his club and the visible weapons, but kept the concealed ones they did not find when they searched him.

The sailor who had escorted them knocked on the iron door. A hatch opened and a squirrel-faced man looked suspiciously out.

"Who is it?" the man asked.

"Just another captain who thinks I should know who she is," the young tubular sailor said somewhat sarcastically.

Redboots looked at him, and smiled wickedly. "I told you who I was last time we met. I warned you, that if you forgot, I will have to give you cause to remember me," she said, and had a cruel look about her as she winked at him.

"Just let them in Boros," a voice from inside the room commanded. Squirrel-face closed the hatch, and the sound of locks and bolts being released could be heard before the door swung open. Azzadan, Redboots and Smindy entered along with the sailor; the door slammed shut and was locked behind them.

Azzadan looked around; they were in a vast cargo bay, into the middle of which a ship could be floated on the water contained in a purpose-built channel. On the far side of the cargo bay there were a series of massive lifts on ropes, that he figured moved the goods up and down from the storerooms in the upper decks, that in passing conversation Smindy had told him about. The place was huge.

Inside the cargo bay, there were ells of cloths from fine linen to wadmal. There were racks and shelves filled with rolls of fine silks and embroidered fabrics, vats of ale and casks of wine. There were numerous barrels and crates labelled with the produce they held, ranging from olives to fine spices, peppers dark and light, and just about every produce you could imagine. Along the bulkheads there were abundant, huge, iron safes that no doubt contained all manner of gold and jewels. Azzadan's jaw dropped open wide. He had heard about these toll-ships and the wealth they contained, but the seeing of it was greater than anything he had ever been told.

"This cargo bay is one of fifty, and is fed by and services the same number of even larger storerooms on board," Smindy whispered to him.

"Forget any thought of ever returning here to steal. It's impossible," Redboots whispered, when she noticed him gazing in lustful awe.

"Not with an ethereal cloak," he muttered back.

"But there's not one big enough to cover the ship that would be needed to carry all this away, and the dozens of people it would take to load it," she replied in a hushed tone.

"Everything is possible if it is planned well enough," he replied, before squirrel-face interrupted them.

"What are you whispering about? Come, Bosun Mowett is waiting." Squirrel-face led them over to a desk where an extremely obese man dressed in a dirty but finely embroidered tunic, almost bursting at the seams as his body tried to escape it, sat. He was bald, puffy faced, red-cheeked and wore a monocle eye-glass.

"Sit," he said to them as he pointed at the chairs in front of his desk.

"Mowett, you have gotten fatter since we last met," Redboots said.

"And you've still learnt no manners," Mowett snapped back.

Redboots smirked as they sat. Smindy handed Mowett the log books she carried in the leather satchel, and Azzadan followed suite.

As he stared idly around him, Azzadan noticed a Montpellier snake that glided out with a rustling sound from between two barrels, traversing the room in a series of extraordinarily elegant curves, its head held up some eighteen inches from the ground. "A snake!" he cried as he stood up and was about to reach for one of his concealed throwing stars.

Bosun Mowett, whose head was already buried in the log books, looked up and said, "Yes, we have thousands on-board, for the rats. It's a very innocent serpent and only mildly venomous, quite harmless to humans unless you go poking your finger down its throat, now sit-down man."

Azzadan felt his cheeks blush as he sat down. He was not used to being chided by a fat, Fell-blood bookkeeper. He knew every type of snake and knew that kind was not dangerous, but he had not expected to see one in the cargo bay and his reaction had been instinctive.

Mowett looked at Redboots in between flicking through some pages of the log-book. "Well, Miss Red, everything looks in order, as usual. I have sent an inspector on board your ship, as long as his report confirms everything on board is as it should be and matches these records, you will pay the toll and be free to proceed."

"You mean as long as your spies on board confirm we have recorded every sinking and plundering we have done, and set aside the fair share the Sea Lords require of us," Redboots said to him nonchalantly.

"Well, there's never been a problem before so I doubt there will be now, Miss Red," Mowett said. "The inspection will take several hours, as will a more thorough inspection of these books. When you have paid the correct toll, you will be free to proceed. However, first, you must pay your respect to Lord Vansoth at the ball tonight."

"I was hoping to catch the wind heading my way," she sighed.

"Where would that way be?" Mowett asked.

"We have business on Grona Island."

"You go to the Sea of Grona?" Mowett raised his eyebrows in surprise. He opened a drawer in his desk and took out a book, and thumbing through the pages he said, "Hmmm, it's not my business to ask what your business is there, but the toll to enter those waters is not cheap. Only last week one of our hunter-ships slew a great leviathan of the deep that had started troubling the Kappian prison ships. The Empire pays us to guard their milathran and prison ships, so you won't be planning to trouble them, I hope?"

"Of course not, unless they trouble me, although their stubbornness to refuse to pay to protect trade on the Erin is beyond me."

"Well, the political intrigues and wrangling of the imperial court and their motives for imperial policy are often beyond us all, but they don't or can't pay for protection on the Erin so trade is blocked. If they try to break through, they are free to be plundered, for now, but only on the Erin. On the Tethys Sea, including the Sea of Grona, they are to be left alone. Is that clear?"

Mowett looked up from the book, and squinting, stared at her through his monocle. "That reminds me, Captain Argin met an untimely end. He dropped down suddenly in Harwind. Your log says that was your last port of call?" His tone was accusing and suspicious.

It occurred to Azzadan that Argin had died sooner than expected, and that the message of his death had reached the Sea Lords quickly, very quickly indeed.

"I mourn the loss of my guild leader," Redboots said with mock interest. "He was alive and well when I left, and was happily drinking at a tavern. Have your rats look into it, if they suspect any foul play."

Azzadan admired the way in which she casually deflected away even the slightest hint or suspicion of her involvement.

Mowett continued. "Lord Vansoth may wish to speak with you about that, for your guild is now leaderless until somebody else is appointed." He closed one eye and peered at her through his monocle. "If I were a member of your guild, I would not be voting for you to take Argin's place," he said rather pointedly.

"Then it is just as well, that the Skull Guild would not accept the likes of you, even if the Sea Lords allowed you to apply," she answered acidly.

Mowett shook his head with an annoyed fluster, and addressed the tubular sailor. "Mathis, take Miss Red and her companions to accommodation, and show them the shops where they can be outfitted for the ball." He stared at Redboots. "It will not be paid for by the *Accountant*. You will need to buy the appropriate attire yourself, and rent the cabins for the night."

Redboots brushed her hand dismissively. "So be it."

Mowett signalled for squirrel-face to come over, and handed him the log books. "Boros, double check these log books before they are signed off."

He then stared at Smindy. "If Boros confirms that all is well with them, and they match our assessment of your ship's inventory, then they will be signed off and returned to you before you leave."

"I can assure you, all is well," Smindy replied confidently.

*     *     *

For the ball, Azzadan had purchased a shiny leather doublet trimmed with seal fur and belted with an exquisite leather cummerbund. He wore his ethereal cloak about his shoulders, and despite the restriction on weapons, he had concealed some within it that even the most ardent of searches would never reveal, for they were well hidden with charms imbued into the cloak at the time of its crafting.

"I am going to a ball dressed up like a jester without my weapons?" he complained, seeking to hide the fact he had some concealed.

"Nobody, but the Sea Lords carry arms at a Mariners' Ball," Redboots answered. "Apart from guild business, I don't know what else Erik Vansoth might want from me, but stay vigilant."

"He wants from you what he always gets," Smindy said cheekily, and received a hard stare from her captain as a result.

Azzadan stared at Redboots. Her thick red hair was washed and combed, but hanging loose and wild. She wore black trousers, a transparent red white blouse, and nothing underneath. She straightened the lace cuffs and tightened the red scarf she wore, before adjusting the red thigh-length silk boots she had purchased. Tapping the heels on the ground she beamed at Smindy who wore a crimson chemise with fluffy cuffs and an elegantly embroidered white jacket, adorned with a matching scarf. Smindy's hair was tied neatly, with the fringe hanging down beneath the mariner's hat she wore.

A knock on the cabin door alerted them it was time to go to the ball. The same young sailor who had escorted them earlier, Mathis, yawned when Smindy opened the door. He looked at Redboots, and rudely waved with his finger for her to follow as he turned. Azzadan noticed her grimace wildly at the arrogance of the sailor, who clearly felt he was protected in the environment of the Sea Lords.

"You'll remember my name before this night is over boy," Azzadan heard Redboots confidently whisper to herself.

"They don't seem to like her much on here," Azzadan said to Smindy.

Smindy nodded. "The crew of the *Accountant* are arrogant. They bask under the power of the Sea Lords, but most, like Mowett, are men of little true deeds themselves." She hesitated a moment, and then added. "Captain Redboots has risen from humble beginnings, and far exceeded the likes of Mowett. They take umbrage that she has never shown them the deference they think they deserve. Add to that their jealousy, that now Erik Vansoth holds her in the highest esteem, and you have the reasons for their contempt."

They wound their way along the decks until they entered a huge central hall that was shaped like a fish. The hall did not look like it was part of a ship, but more like it belonged in a stone building. The bulkheads on three sides looked like walls and were adorned with tapestries woven with silver seaweed and were most pleasing to the eye. Garlands and pennants hung from ship's masts that reached out from the bulkheads and stretched across the room, revealing images of Jorgen the sea god, and monsters of the deep.

On the fourth side of the hall, there were nine, large, clear portholes built into the starboard side of the ship, all shaped like a starfish, surrounding a similar but much larger central porthole. Azzadan looked outside of one of the nine smaller portholes. The hall was well below the waterline, deep in the bay of the ocean in fact. The sea outside was crystalline and clear with only a greenish tinge, so that all manner of sea-life could be seen swimming above the seaweed which was forty-feet or so below, of which every green strand could be seen swaying in the current in the variegated mosaic of the seabed.

The deck head of the hall, was like the ceiling of a palace, and was so high it was difficult to make out the details of the frescoes decorating it, though they looked like ships, mermaids and other such matters to do with seafaring and the oceans. The central table was huge, long, and, like the hall itself, was also shaped like a fish. It was a smaller version of the shape of the hall. The table was so large around it could easily seat more than two hundred people. Each chair was uniquely shaped and carved out of driftwood. Some guests were already seated at the table, whilst others still stood and were milling about greeting old shipmates whilst others engaged in raucous conversation and jesting.

By far, the most outstanding sight in the entire hall was the massive skull of a kraken that adorned the far deck head behind the main chair, and a large horn the length of three men, that was mounted on golden trestles before it. Azzadan had seen many grand and mysterious sights throughout his lifetimes, but nothing quite like the Hall of the Sea Lords, and he was not a man easily enthralled. "This is incredible," he said to Redboots, as he looked at the impressive skull of the kraken.

Mathis, the young sailor, escorted them over to the top of the table, where Redboots was seated to the left of a large chair at the head of the table. The chair had a high backrest and was carved entirely from mother-of-pearl. Azzadan was told to sit on the right of the chair, and Smindy put next to him.

"My father, Bosun Mowett, wanted you seated at a lesser place on the table," Mathis said, "but Lord Vansoth overruled him."

"Your rudeness knows no bounds," Redboots said to Mathis. "This night, you will learn who it is you speak too. I will insist Erik Vansoth forces you to play me at a hand of Harendale, the victor gets to choose which finger of the losers they get to cut off, and the winners name will be carved onto the chest of the loser as a permanent reminder of this night." She winked as cruelly as before, and, holding up the hand with the missing finger, said, "I have only ever lost once, at Harendale." Mathis didn't say anything, but stared in alarm at the stump where a finger had once been. Trembling, he went and stood to the side of the hall.

"Lords, ladies and gentlemen," a loud voice shouted above the din. "Take your seats." The guests still standing, took a seat at the table as a plethora of nearly naked female slaves carrying crab shaped platters and ornamented jugs made from shells moved towards the table, and were greeted by a joyful murmur from the guests. Carafes of wine and frothing jugs of ale were given to each guest and the platters, full of all manner of foods from the sea, were placed before them on the table: they were filled full of pastry rolls stuffed with delicious looking seaweed, and all manner of skilfully prepared fish both cooked and raw. Freshly cooked lobsters, some the size of a small child, and every type of mussel, whelk and manner of sea-creature you could imagine were there. A bowl of cram, the staple food of many ships due to its longevity and surprisingly delightful taste, was also put before each guest.

Azzadan noticed that the slave who served their food, wore a veil the colour of seaweed that covered her face. She did not flinch as he looked at the most beautiful breasts he had ever seen. They glowed in the yellow-lit hall, and were tipped with seashells to hide the nipples. A small seaweed coloured loincloth preserved her other modesty.

Smindy noticed him watching the woman. "The unveiled ones, are slaves for life and have no will or rights, above that which their masters determine for them," she said. "But the ones who are veiled, like her, are not slaves." She broke the claw off of one of the smaller and more manageable lobsters. "A veiled woman here is sometimes a Bedu noblewoman, maybe the bored wife of a nobleman who runs the merchant fleets and is often overseas. Or, they may be a simple Bedu maid seeking a time of excitement. They come here when their husbands are away, for a month at a time, in the hope that if Erik Vansoth is here, he might choose them one night. If not, they will settle for some other

467

roguish captain, who will have his way for the night and never know their true identity." She cracked the claw with a nutcracker, and pulled out the meat with a small lobster fork. Cutting the flesh in half, she put some on Redboot's plate. "It's the reason the Sea Lord's law states if you lower or remove the veil by force from any of these women, it is at the pain of death. Be warned of that, in case one of them chooses you tonight."

"Chooses me?" Azzadan asked, surprised.

"If, after the festivities, one of the veiled women comes to you and gives you one of the shells covering her modesty, it means she invites you to go with her for the night, but don't remove her veil. It is not allowed. If one of them does not choose you, you may take any of the unveiled ones you desire."

"I have other plans for tonight," Azzadan said as he turned his attention to Redboots who was barely eating; with one hand she was wrapping a lock of hair around her finger, whilst merely plucking at the morsels served her, with a silver fork in her other hand.

"Change them" Smindy said, with a serious smile. "She will be busy in another's company this night."

Azzadan understood the insinuation, and whilst the other guests laid waste to the many other delicacies on offer, he watched Redboots, who looked bored, even as the atmosphere at the table grew livelier and the ample servings of ale, beer and then wine were served and consumed, whilst several fiddlers played lively background music.

The music continued until a tall and curvaceous woman, much appealing to the eye, appeared in the hall. Wearing black trousers and a white-laced blouse, her face was covered by a cavalier styled large black hat with a red feather plume. She blew a conch. The fiddlers grew silent and the crowd fell into a hush as the woman strutted sexily over to the table and nimbly jumped onto it, throwing the conch to a slave, who caught it. The female slaves hastily gathered up the platters, and the guests quickly gathered their jugs of ale, carafes and glasses of wine. With a vigorous kick the woman cleared the ones they were too slow to remove as she strutted along the length of the table.

"Hey shipmates," she shouted as she put her fists on her hips and shook her long black hair. "I see that you need livening up."

The crowd crooned with approval. A number of musicians along with the fiddlers gathered around the table. The woman quickly tapped out a rhythm with the heels of the flamboyant black boots she wore, the silver buckles of which jangled like bells. The drummers repeated the rhythm and the flute and oboe followed. The pipes and fiddles took up the tune, quickly embellishing it, challenging the gaudily dressed woman to quicken her speed and tempo, which she adapted to with ease and began moving rhythmically as the guests cheered and clapped. The piece finished with a final flare accompanied by the woman taking off her hat and throwing it into the crowd, and then the music instantly stopped as the she stood hands on hips, taking deep breaths and proudly enjoying the adulation of the guests.

"Well, if Jorgen answers prayers this is one of them times," Smindy said as she took off her hat and threw it wildly into the air. She shook her hair from her forehead with a sudden jerk of her head, removed her jacket and scarf, and jumped up onto the table. The woman noticed her, and looked on.

"You are good Kira *Buckleboots*," Smindy said, but I am better, and Captain Redboots is better even than me."

"Kira?" Redboots said as she looked up, taking notice of the woman for the first time.

468

The woman, Kira, smiled, flashing several gold teeth. With her heels clicking on the table, she then slowly strutted up the length of the table towards where Smindy stood, looked her up and down, and then stared at Redboots.

"The famous captain looks bored as she waits for the greatest of the Sea Lords to appear. Is she up for the challenge, or are these words of your shipmate as empty as the sails of that old rotten timbered tug of yours on a becalmed day?" Kira narrowed her eyes, a look intensified by her heavy make-up.

The boredom had lifted from Redboots face in an instant as she looked Kira up and down. She put her fork down, stood, and with a single bound she was on the table, kicking away a carafe of wine and jug of ale that was in her way. A hush fell over the guests, who looked on with anticipation.

"I was bored because you move as sluggishly as a fat merchant galleon when it tries to escape the *Red Tide*," Redboots said.

"Words, my old shipmate, mere words," Kira said, as she slowly spun around addressing all around the table. "If anyone else wants to join this next merry dance, then hop up now, and let's dance for Jorgen." Several other women seated around the table, stood up and climbed onto the table, as did one or two men, a bit worse for wear with drink.

"Lead the way," Kira said to Redboots, who put her hands on her hips, and with an upturned head, tapped her feet, cut a caper, and beat out a quick, rhythmic staccato with her heels. Kira, Smindy, and the others on the table copied the steps. One of the men tried to follow suite, but swayed and then drunkenly fell off the table to the jeers and hoots of the other guests.

Redboots laughed, and hopped and changed the tempo. Kira and the other women on the table mirrored her moves perfectly.

"Musicians, play *The Last Voyage of the Island Lass*," Redboots yelled.

The crowd shrieked and applauded.

"With verve!" Kira added.

"And passion!" Smindy shouted.

The drums, fiddles, and other musical instruments began a slow and haunting piece that slowly began to build up in tempo. The dancers on the table stepped in unison with one another.

"Faster," Kira shouted to the musicians, who then sped up the tempo.

"Look lively," Redboots said to them, as the pace picked up even more.

The music began to quickly pick up tempo, until it was at a frenzy, so that none of the other dancers could keep up, each in turn stopping breathlessly and taking their seats, until the only three dancers that remained were Kira, Redboots and Smindy, who beat out the fast rhythm with their heels, so that the table shook and trembled at the pace of the dance. The three women danced and swirled, arms akimbo for parts of the tune and then in the air as the pitch changed.

Toe, heel, toe, heel, toe step forward, step back, arms akimbo. A jump, shoulder's swinging, fist on hips, toe, heel, toe, heel, toe step forward, step back, arms akimbo. The dance reached fever pitch, the table shook and the crowd roared and cheered, everyone clapping and stamping until the very deck of the toll-ship itself seemed to tremble.

Azzadan, a man not in the habit of enjoying much mirth or gaiety, had been in a solemn mood all evening, but even he was lost in the music as he watched the feverish dance. He had no eyes for the other two dancers that remained on the table; he hardly noticed when Smindy could no longer keep the pace and breathlessly stood down from the table collapsing into the chair next to him laughing with sheer joy. He did not even notice the grace and grandeur of the other woman - he only had eyes for Redboots. He could not take his eyes off of the most majestic of women he had ever seen, and in that moment, he knew that he loved her, and that there was nothing he would not do for her. As he watched her there was nothing, nothing in the world but her and the dance… Heel, toe, heel, toe…arms in the air… a jump, arms akimbo, heel toe, heel toe… The wild playing of the musicians was now superfluous to him. It appeared as though time slowed. Redboot's red hair bounced on her shoulders and forehead. Sweat poured off her and blood flowed in her temples. Azzadan felt something he had never felt before. He felt lost, lost to love as he watched her dance. Abandon, oblivion. She was all that mattered to him in that moment and he cursed the gods that such a woman was not a Pure-blood and would only be in the world but a single lifetime. *She may have only one lifetime, but curse the gods if I do not get to spend that with her,* he vowed in that moment.

The musicians finished the melody on a strident, high chord. Kira and Redboots marked the end of the dance with a simultaneous bang of their heels and stood there for a moment, perfectly still, except for their chests which heaved as they caught their breaths. The two women looked at each other. They suddenly hugged, sharing their sweat, their heat, their happiness. They laughed spasmodically, and tears ran down their cheeks. The hall suddenly exploded with one great cheer and the clapping of hands and stamping of feet as the crowd stood and gave them an ovation. To Azzadan's own surprise, he too was standing and clapping as enthusiastically as the most ardent applauder in the hall.

"When you grow tired of pirating, Sharnay, we can go out into the world and earn our living as dancers," Kira said to Redboots.

*Redboots name is Sharnay?* Azzadan asked himself. *It is so beautiful.* He then shook his head. *What bewitchment is this she-pirate putting on me?*

"Never!" Redboots declared, interrupting his thoughts. "You, my sister, take after our mother, and I, our father, may Jorgen guard and rest their roguish souls." She then gracefully exited the table, flopped into her chair and put her hand affectionately onto Azzadan's knee and patted it. The touch shot through him like a heated dagger, filling him with throbbing desire.

"Did you enjoy that my lovely?" Redboots asked him.

*More than you will ever know.*

"He's a mean looking one," Kira said as she looked at Azzadan and smiled, then jumped off of the table and sat on his knee, resting her hand on his other leg. Of a sudden, although their hair was of a different hue, Azzadan suddenly noticed a close resemblance in the way they both smiled, and the words they had just spoken to each other registered with him.

"This is your sister?" he asked.

"My one and only," Redboots replied as she looked affectionately at Kira, and in a manner that belied all of her fierceness, lovingly fondled her sister's hair. "This is my Kira. It has been so many years since we have seen each other. I thought her dead, and perhaps she me, but here we are, Jorgen has reunited us, here in the Hall of the Sea Lords!"

Kira returned the smile, and then tenderly stroked the scar that ran down the left side of Redboot's face, and carefully remarked, "You did not have this the last time I saw you, Sharnay." She then stared at the red boots her sister wore. "You still wear red boots? So, you have not forgotten or forgiven her then?"

"And nor shall I," Redboots said with a grimace.

Kira shrugged, and in an obvious move to change the topic, lifting up Redboot's left hand and noticing the missing finger, she chuckled mildly. "Ha! So, somebody finally beat you at Harendale? That man must have been some cheat!"

"It was not a man, it was a dwarf, and after consuming the amount of ales he was drinking, he was drunker than Vargo Goss himself!" Redboots said with wry amusement. "He swore he didn't cheat, and Dwarves don't usually lie. But by skill or trick, he won the game, and I honoured the bet."

Kira leant over and buried her head in her sister's shoulder, and said, "Sharnay, stay at Toseucia a while. We have so much to catch up on."

"I cannot," Redboots answered. "I am under a salt-oath to my guild and the Sea Lords, to deliver this one to Grona." She looked at Azzadan and smiled.

*Curses to salt-oaths or a Bethratikus, say the word, and I'll linger as long as you wish at your fine house on Toseucia,* Azzadan nearly blurted out, but instead, said it to himself, and then stayed quiet, and listened.

"I did not even recognise your voice, my Kira," Redboots said, pulling Kira onto her lap. "Join me when tomorrow I sail for Grona!"

"I too must say I cannot," Kira answered. "My tale is too long for the telling now. After I left Toseucia when mother and father were killed, like you, I searched far and wide for their killers, and found them."

"You found them?" Redboots asked, her voice uncertain?

"They had found employment with a Pure-blood Sea Lord on the shores of the Northern Ashes, by the rocks called the Kraken's Teeth. I told him my story, and of their deed. He laughed, and said he had forgotten worst crimes he had committed than that which I accused them of, but he agreed to hang them from the nearest ship's mast if I married him. He kept his promise, and they swung from the main mast and kicked their last as we shared our vows."

"Did you bear children with him?"

"No, our marriage bore no fruit, but I did grow to love him, and would even now be there by his side had he not met the *Final-death* at the hands of a usurper. After his sudden and *Final-death* I fled, and came here, to wait for you. I had no money; Erik gave me work. He has paid me one year's advance coin to sing and dance at these feasts."

"I'll double, treble or give ten times back what he has paid you," Redboots said, "unless you were forced to swear a salt-oath to stay until his coin has been satisfied."

"A salt-oath I have sworn, it will be fulfilled within the year, and then, dear sister, I will be free to stand upon your decks, and enjoy the wind and the salt air, and be obligated to none but those whom I choose to sail with, which will be you. Be patient, a year in our short life-spans passes so quickly."

Before Redboots could respond, several loud conches blew and filled the air, as a large and powerful looking figure filled the doorway of the hall.

"It's Erik," Redboots said, as a coy smile reached her lips, as the man took just one step purposefully and arrogantly into the hall.

Erik Vansoth, Lord of the Sea Lords, was a large and physically powerful man. His frame dwarfed the door as he stepped into the hall, accompanied by a dozen unveiled, female slaves, naked apart from a simple loincloth, and a dozen males, all blowing conches. Erik wore leather trousers, no shirt, and a cloak woven of dried seaweed. Rings of gold and jade glistened on his exposed muscled arms. His chest was broad and bare, and upon it was tattooed the emblem of a kraken fighting a leviathan with a ship in its jaws. The large gold rune kraken he wore around his neck, which Azzadan guessed was at least fifty-pounds in weight, hardly weighed on him at all. His boots were cracked leather and had large golden buckles that clanked as he walked. He had a fierce and melancholy visage. His hair and beard were dyed the colour of a green sea, and on top of his head sat a green tricorn hat, adorned with the glistening white teeth from a very large shark. His long beard was forked into many plaits and fastened with silver rings shaped like seashells. He held a scimitar in one hand, a fearsome piece of steel with a black jewel on the pommel, and in the other hand, he held a cruel looking driftwood cudgel. Both were displayed in a manner for all to see.

Azzadan recognised the jewel on the scimitar. *An Arzak - he holds an Arkith!* The way it reflected the light in the hall, and the sheer clarity of it even from that distance, informed him it was a weapon that could deal the *Final-death* to any Pure-blood. *It must be one of those he stole from my Order. This man is extremely dangerous.*

The conches continued blowing as Erik confidently strutted cross the hall and walked up to the Horn of Jorgen and stood before it. A few of the crowd began to shout out. "Erik! Erik! Erik..." They stamped their feet and shook their fists as others added their voice to the swelling chant. The conches stopped, and Erik pointed his scimitar and cudgel at the crowd, moving the one slowly towards the other until silence fell on the room.

"Who here can make a boast that we can raise a glass too?"

One drunk sea captain shouted in jest, "One of my wives is a mermaid the size of a whale, yet even she can confirm I am big everywhere it matters," he boasted, to the amusement of the crowd.

Erik smiled and jested back, "You are a fine man Captain Fress, but she spent last night with me and now you'll find she's stretched so wide, she'll need a bigger mast than that which you can offer her." The crowd roared with laughter, and Fress himself joined in the merriment, even though it was at his expense.

Erik's voice boomed as he roared. "We all have boasts of deeds done, but to sound a note on the Horn of Jorgen, is one that cannot be matched apart from the doing of the deed. A Sea Lord one can become, be he Pure-blood or Fell, man or woman, if he or she can step up to the Horn and sound a note." He raised the scimitar and cudgel in his hands. "But death by my Arkith is the penalty for any that rise to the challenge and fail to sound a note," he warned. "Is there any dare to take the challenge?"

There was not a sound in the hall, until one sea captain shouted, "Sound the horn Erik, sound the horn!" Others soon joined in the chanting, until every voice but Azzadan's was shouting, "Sound the horn Erik, sound the horn!" Erik sheathed the scimitar in its scabbard, and handed the cudgel to a nearby slave, who struggled under its weight until another helped him.

"I will plunge my own Arkith into my own heart, if I fail to blow a note, but never have I failed yet," he boasted as he stepped up to the horn and took a deep breath. The Horn of Jorgen was shiny black and twisted, it took several of the slaves to lift it from the trestle and to hold it in place as Erik put his lips to it and blew. It was bound about with bands of gold and green steel, incised with ancient glyphs that glowed greenly, growing brighter, but no note came. His face went red, then purple, his cheeks were so puffed out they looked about to burst and the muscles and sinews in his neck twitched, thick blue veins pulsing out, but as Erik continued to blow into the horn, no note came, but still, he blew. Then, every line and letter adorned upon the horn began to shimmer with green fire, and finally, it made a noise, Erik sounded a note on it. The sound of the horn was almost deafening, the noise of the horn swelled and intensified, and still Erik blew, until when it seemed the sound would never end, it finally did. Erik's breath failed at last. He staggered and almost fell, but shoved away those who tried to steady him.

"You heard its call, you felt its power," he said breathlessly. Taking some deep breaths, he then roared: "Now hear the words of the greatest of all Sea Lords, Erik Vansoth! I can boast of the far places I have seen. I have sailed to the Sunset Sea and beyond, from land to land I sailed and found the world is round. I have sunk ships aplenty, plundered and sacked towns at will. Kings, lords and nobles have begged me to spare their lives and wives, and some I did at a whim. I have kidnapped some of the most beautiful women in the world and put a baby in their belly. I have killed more men than dinners I have eaten." Murmurs of appreciation rippled through the crowd. "Tonight, those of you who dine here do so as my shipmates, and you will be treated well and fair, I swear it by Jorgen." Even more murmurs of appreciation rose like a crescendo.

"But, one thing I have never done, is break the Sea Lords' code, insulted Jorgen, or gone back on a sacred salt-oath, but some of those who last night supped at my table, have done just that." Less murmurs of gratitude and appreciation.

"I warn you all of this one thing, no godless man may dine at my table and give voice to false words. If such words bubble in your heart, let them not surface on your tongue, for if you hold such thoughts, keep them to yourself, for Jorgen will not be insulted in my hall by your tongue, or you will suffer for it. The sea is never weary, and I am just as tireless in not hearing Jorgen's name spoken ill of in this hall. Are we in agreement shipmates?"

"Aye, aye," was the response and roar of the guests, "we are agreed!"

Azzadan said nothing, nor did he join in with the others. He did not want to join the others for he hated abasing himself by joining in the chorus of approval for Erik's words whether he agreed with them or not, but at the same time he did not want to needlessly offend a host or cause trouble for himself where it need not be found.

Erik noticed Azzadan's silence as he strode towards his pearl encrusted chair, and he stared menacingly at him as he sat in it, whilst the Horn of Jorgen was returned to its place. Azzadan noticed Erik had the mark of a Pure-blood beneath his eye.

"You do not agree to the terms by which you dine in my hall?" Erik barked at him, after he had taken his seat. "I see insolence in your eyes!"

Azzadan looked fearlessly into Erik's eyes, which were the colour of the deep green sea, and he hated him. "Such thoughts do bubble in my heart, but they will not find surface on my tongue, for I am your guest, and shall respect the courtesies required in this hall," he said firmly as he met Erik's fierce gaze. "It would be better for you to not question a man on such matters if his answers can only lead to either a lie coming from his lips, or offence to his host," he added, as he secretly slipped a poisoned pin between his fingers, and calculated that in less than a second Erik would be paralysed long enough for him to remove the Sea Lord's Arkith from the scabbard, and deal him the *Final-death*, if such an action became necessary. Failing that, he could take another pin, or a throwing star, one coated not in a paralysing poison but one that would kill Erik almost instantly. If this all turned sour, Erik would die, and with the cover of his ethereal cloak Azzadan was convinced he could fight his way out of there, and if needs be, invisibly stow away on one of the ships, if Redboots also turned on him, and took the side of Erik.

*Can I yet trust her enough, to side with me, if I slay this wretched Sea Lord?* It was a thought which caused the unusual feeling of dread and despair to briefly sweep over him. Redboots was still a mystery to him, and here, in this hall, where she looked like she belonged and he was still a stranger, he felt that the recent closeness with which he had embraced her and the physical intimacy they had shared, meant very little to her at all.

Erik scowled. "Many of your Order, I know, have little time for the gods; the dedication of many of your own to Skipilos is just mere observance of the rituals, including Ishar, who has caused some to question their own oaths."

Azzadan stared at Erik, feeling puzzled. *How does he know this about Ishar?*

473

"You scurry about in that Rat Warren under Kappia, that you call sacred and secret, but it is neither. Now put away that festering pin you hold between thumb and finger; do you not know I am immune to such petty toxins?"

Azzadan was momentarily caught off-guard. *He knows where my Order dwells and about the concealed pin I hold?*

Erik threateningly leant in towards him. "Make a grab for my Arkith, if you dare, for as fast as you believe you are, I am faster. I can still dive into the deep dark sea and catch a sprint-fish with my own hands, so try me, *Godslayer*, and prick me with that pin, if you dare!" Erik stood, and roared, after he issued the challenge to Azzadan. The other guests, minding their own business, perhaps because they knew better than to interfere or show too much curiosity, discreetly pretended to ignore the commotion at the end of the table.

Azzadan had been trained, relentlessly, over many lifetimes for just such a moment. He had met deadlier foes, but none such as arrogant. Despite Erik's boast, he felt he could best him, and he desperately wanted to put it to the test and deal a death to him, but that was not the purpose for which he was there. Besides, it sounded as though somehow, Erik had access to one of the secret potions that made him immune to the deadly poisons Azzadan's weapons were dipped in. Azzadan put the poisoned pin away.

"Calm yourself, Sea Lord," he said. "I am about other business here, and will not be distracted from it by petty disputes, especially about the gods."

"It is well for you, that it is only Jorgen I honour," Erik said, as he again took his seat. The serving slaves filled the table once again with platters of food, carafes of wine and jugs overflowing with ale. "Those hammer and snake temples that pollute the Everglow are eggshells of faith stuffed with the sour teaching of bad gods. Insult them as you please, but steady your tongue on matters of Jorgen."

Erik looked at Kira, who was still perched on Azzadan's knee. She smiled, patted him on the other knee, and Azzadan felt a soft but sharp prick and in an instant, it was he who was paralysed. Of a sudden, he could not move, nor speak. He was completely paralysed, only able to breathe and move his eyes.

"You are not the only one with poisoned pins at your disposal," Erik said as he grinned unkindly at him, and Kira stared Azzadan in the eyes. He saw the same murderous look that he had seen in her sister's eyes, whenever she wanted to deal out death. Redboots and Smindy, calmly watched the events unfolding, but did not interfere or say anything.

Erik guffawed. "Do you think that in all of my many lifetimes, your Order has not been paid, to send one of your assassins to put me to the *Final-death*? Or, that one of your thieves has not tried to steal my treasures, whilst they skulked about my ships hiding under their ethereal cloaks?" Erik stroked the Arzak in the pommel of his Arkith scimitar. "Some of them, their souls are forever trapped in here and never will they be summoned by an Obelisk back to the land of the living," he said. "And if you think that is just an idle boast, look!" He exulted as he flicked his fingers.

A man appeared from out of nowhere, taking off an ethereal cloak for the briefest of moments, and nimbly jumping onto the table in front of Erik and Azzadan, before concealing himself again. Azzadan recognised the man. *Turis? You were an assassin from my own Order who disappeared, thirty years or so ago.*

"I know the recipe for the Orange Brew that binds you," Erik said with a brazen and challenging grin.

*If that is truly knowledge you have, then many of my Order could be persuaded to serve new masters!* Azzadan thought.

Erik continued. "Turis was not the first sent to kill me, but like the rest, he failed. I spared him the *Final-death*, and offered him the Orange Brew, if he swore loyalty to me. Since then, more of your Order has tried, and each has failed. Their ethereal cloaks I took, and some of them I have bestowed as gifts upon those I saw fit to give them and some I have kept for myself. The Arkiths they carried to give me the *Final-death* are also mine." He laughed triumphantly as he once again stroked the pommel of his scimitar. "This one is my favourite, but I own more Arkiths than any man alive," he added boastfully with no attempt to hide who heard him. "Even your own Order now has only two left."

Azzadan could still not move. He scanned the hall with his eyes. Any other guest who might have noticed the events unfolding at the end of the table, still chose to ignore it, and chatted with their neighbours instead. He looked suspiciously at Redboots, and then at Kira.

"Turis has taught us all about the poisons and potions you use," Erik said. I paid the best alchemists in the world to find antidotes." He grinned. "I can also see your kind when you scurry about hidden under your ethereal cloaks."

"Is this necessary Erik?" Redboots asked, as she looked crossly at him. "You guarantee the safety of all who dine here? It is a sworn salt-oath! Besides you need him Erik!"

"An oath that does not stand if one brings weapons into this hall such as he has done," Erik retorted back, looking malevolently at Azzadan.

Redboots implored Kira. "Kira, he was brought here on my ship, and therefore a part of my crew until my business with him is finished."

"Calm your sails, sister," Kira said as she stood from Azzadan's knee, and looked at a golden ring on her finger from which a tiny pin protruded. "It won't lead to death and will wear off soon."

"It better had, sister," Redboots said scathingly. "I myself have sworn a salt-oath to my guild, and his master has paid me, to get him to Grona. I intend to fulfil this mission or forsake my life in the attempt."

"You serve me well," Erik said to Kira, as he patted her rear. "Now, sing for us soft songs of the sea sweet Kira whilst we eat and talk, I have words to share with our assassin here, and your sister." Kira smiled, got up and joined the musicians, and they began to play soft melodic tunes, whilst she sang loud enough for the guests to hear, but not so loud they also could not hear each other talk.

Erik turned his attention to Redboots. "Mowett tells me you wish to pay a toll to sail to Grona, there is only one reason you would want to voyage there with this Pure-blood and a vampire in your hold," he said, after which he glowered at Azzadan, and then back at her. "My gulls on board your ship, are more loyal to me even than to you. They are all a chatter about it. You wish to raise her husband from the grave in which he sleeps?"

Azzadan knew why Redboots had been open about sailing to Grona; she would not be allowed to do so without paying a toll so had told Mowett about it. The fact that Erik knew about the vampire in the hold, was no surprise to Azzadan, either. It was obvious he had spies on board the *Red Tide,* and the ship had been inspected since anchoring in the bay. It was a cause of concern, however, that Erik seemed to be aware of why they were taking the vampire to Grona. Movement was coming back to him, but he tried not to allow any surprise to show on his face.

"If I pay the toll and do not bother the ships that pay for your protection, you have no business asking my reasons to sail to where I wish," Redboots answered Erik with a flare of defiance. "So many ships now fly your flag of protection on the Tethys, you are putting me and my kind out of business so we plie our trade where we can and for those who will pay us coin."

Erik's moody growl sounded like thunder. "A nasty war is brewing that will drag in all, a bloody fight for life and death, with no mercy shown. Many will fight, only one side will triumph, the others will perish. Your business on Grona affects me, but you can be glad I consider that it will work in my favour."

Redboots took a sip of red wine, and looked at Erik. Azzadan could tell she was considering her next words carefully. "The Sea Lords have mostly stayed neutral in political affairs, you protect those who can afford to pay you, and allow us to plunder those who cannot. Why does that need to change?"

Erik took a deep swig of ale; he wiped the remaining froth from his beard before he answered. "The time is coming when even we might have to choose a side." He looked at Azzadan in the way a cobra might a lion, wary but angry. "I know whose oaths you have sworn and whose coin you take," he said, leaning forward a little towards Azzadan. "There are things I know about the Order of Ithkall, that not even you would be aware of!"

Redboots continued to press her point. "Why are you concerning yourself in this matter?" she asked. "The wars of the Everglow have always been of little interest to you. None can challenge the power of the Sea Lords on the Tethys Sea?"

Erik stared at Azzadan, as though wondering what move to make next. "Salt-feuds I know well enough, but I do not understand the treachery of an Order of thieves and assassins, nor the intrigues of an imperial court and nor do I wish to learn. But the news my chattering gulls bring me from Kappia concerns even me, as this one has a high price on his head."

"The Empire offers a price on his head, what of it?" Redboots asked. "I have a hefty price on my own, after I sank that prize galleon of theirs sent to drive me from the Erin, and the many ships that accompanied it."

Erik poked Azzadan hard in the chest. Although his movement was returning, it was not enough to enable him to snap Erik's finger in half, which he felt the urge to do as the man prodded him. "The coin on the head of this one, puts the reward they offer for you to shame," Erik said to Redboots, "for he stalked his way into the heart of their temple, stabbed one of their gods, and allowed some wretch to get away with the prized Simal."

Azzadan could see Redboots was fuming, her vanity clearly offended. "Then maybe I will raid Kappia itself," she said, "and even loot the very earrings from the Empress' own ears whilst she wears them. Then we will see what reward they think Captain Redboots is worth!"

Erik chortled gustily. "I don't doubt that for one moment my pretty," he said, "but a chain of events is now in motion as a result of what our assassin did. The Empress has been deposed and forced into a Munte marriage to a new Emperor who sits upon the throne, and it is a stroke of fortune for our friend here, that the new Emperor's plans concern me." He began to attack the plate of food put before him like a starving man, and then speaking with his mouth-full added, "the charms and spells on the Great Northern Wall are broken, and the great Gate of Aleskian has been opened. A horde of creatures they call Bantu, pour into the Everglow. It would be easier to count the numbers of every shoal of herring than it would be to put a number to their host."

"That's not possible," Smindy said, and then doubt spread across her face. "We know little of the Empire's affairs beyond their activity on the Erin, but even we have heard the legend that states Aleskian can never be breached."

Erik tapped the side of Azzadan's head in another derogatory manner. "This fool slew one of their Aeldar Gods, lost the Arkoom he used to do it with, and then he lost the Simal he stole from them. He is lucky not to have been given the *Final-death* after such a failure. It is only because Ishar needs him at Grona that he is still alive."

"Why is this your concern?" Redboots impatiently asked Erik.

He stared at her, a glint in his ferocious green eyes. "His Order is desperate; they never intended to give the Simal to the Baothein. They wanted it for themselves." Erik continued to stare at her. "The parasite that sleeps in the hold of your ship is named Velentine, the wife of a long dead bloodsucking lord from times of old, who is buried deep under the Grona prison. Ishar plans to waken them both, in order that the *Fallen* and the Dust Soldiers may be woken in the North, beyond the wall. He wants to use them to wage open war against the Empire; he did not figure that the Bantu hordes would infest the Everglow. Ishar might now ask his new allies to head west, and attack the Bantu strongholds in the North, before focussing on Kappia. I want him to continue with his plans to wage war on Kappia immediately!"

"I know the cargo I carry and the reason for it, but why do the wars of the Everglow now concern you?" Redboots asked Erik.

"The Kappian Empire has withdrawn its forces to where they sit upon that plateau of theirs, the crags of which even the blind and lame could defend. The new Emperor has changed policy. He will sit on his plateau, whist the rest of the world fight to destroy and weaken each other. His army is full of fanatics, who require little pay. He plans to use the coin he saves paying an army, to build up a navy with which he plans to challenge the power of the Sea Lords. It is that which concerns me," Erik said as his face darkened with wrath.

It was not often that Azzadan was impressed, especially when so exposed, but it seemed that whoever the chattering gulls who informed Erik were, they very extremely well informed of events on the land side of the Everglow.

Azzadan stared back impassively as Erik looked at him and spoke. "The poison on that potion is about to wear off. Hold your hand, *Godslayer*, for you would not win any fight you start here. Besides, I have an offer to make to you, one I think you cannot resist."

Azzadan felt movement slowly returning to the rest of his body, starting with his fingers and working its way up his arms. When the poison had fully worn off, which did not take long, he sat and studied Erik. *He is far more dangerous, and better informed, than I would ever have anticipated before meeting him.*

"Do I have your attention?" Erik asked him.

*Oh yes, you have both offended and humiliated me in front of Redboots; you have my attention, my hate, and my sworn vengeance. One day, I will satisfy them.* Azzadan nodded, and stretched his hands, cracking the knuckles. He had never felt so vulnerable before, and felt ashamed that he had been so clearly outwitted and outmanoeuvred by Erik in the presence of Redboots. But, now was not the time to act rashly. Now was the time to listen.

"What is it you propose?" he asked Erik.

"A long time ago, many lifetimes past, my brother, Rorik Vansoth, hunted a leviathan in the seas around Grona. It smashed his ship and he died, resurrecting inside of that prison. It is said you are the only man to ever escape it; is this lie or is this true?"

Azzadan saw no point in lying. "It is true," he said. "I alone know a way in, and a way out."

"And that is the only reason your Order has kept you from the *Final-death* and assigned you this mission is it not?"

"It is," Azzadan reluctantly admitted, and met Erik's eyes for a moment. There was a challenge in them that infuriated Azzadan. He did not like this Sea Lord, and for a brief moment he revelled in the brief thought that where others had failed to slay him with an Arkith, he might be able to grab the one sheathed in Erik's belt and slay him before Turis, his hidden bodyguard could react. He scowled as the thought disappeared as quickly as it came; there was nothing to gain by killing this Sea Lord, for now. *I will wait, for a more opportune and expedient time.*

"You are confident you can awaken this vampire, and get her in and out of Grona?" Erik asked.

"Yes."

"What do you know of her kind?" Erik asked suspiciously.

"I have studied vampires in the past, for once they used to prowl the streets of Kappia long ago, and for a time, I was employed to hunt them. It concerns me that Ishar is now working with such vile creatures. The loss of the Arkoom, and the Simal slipping from our grasp, has led him to making unwise decisions."

"You think that raising those who would be better off staying dead, is folly, yet you still do it?" Erik sneered.

"I am oath-bound by a Bethratikus."

Erik laughed out loud, mockingly. "Ishar cares not for such things. Turis was forced to break an oath he had made on such, and so have others of your Order. Why do you think some have since joined me?"

*I am not the only one Ishar has forced to break a vow?* The news shocked Azzadan, but he did not show it. "Vampires lords are not to be trusted. I am concerned they will make wretched and unreliable allies, but I am bound by a Bethratikus to fulfil my mission."

"The floweriness of your discourse, so liberally littered with un-sophisticated words, is not my concern. I want you to fulfil your oath. Until now the Empire has been of little concern. But if they wish to direct their attention to building a navy to challenge the power of the Sea Lords, that is a different matter. I will make a bargain with Ishar, - to see that he troubles the Empire enough to distract them from building a navy."

"If they are such a concern to you, why do you still protect their milathran and prison ships?" Azzadan asked with veiled loathing.

It was Redboots who answered. "A salt-oath cannot be broken. The Sea Lords have been paid to protect them. The ships that carry milathran back from the Grona mines, are of great value to the Empire."

Erik nodded. "You know our ways well, that is why I always choose to have words with you, my pretty little Redboots," he said, and then to Azzadan. "It is five more years before my contract with the Empire runs out. I cannot, will not, break it until then, for who would then trust a salt-oath I made and wish to pay for my protection? The rest of their fleet is fair game, but not their milathran or prison ships. Alongside their own, they fly my flag of protection."

Redboots interjected. "The Sea Lords will honour the salt-oath, only until it expires which is when the next payment is due. If the payment is rejected, the oath is withdrawn, and the Sea Lords can allow the plunder of milathran from the returning prison ships."

"By which time, they plan to build a navy to contest the rule of the Sea Lords on the Tethys Sea," Erik grumbled. "This war, will work for the Sea Lords, or against us. The sands of time are running out, so little sand remains in the hour-glass until this war spreads, I can almost count the grains," he said to Redboots, and then looked at Azzadan, his tone softening ever so slightly.

478

"I had given up my brother as forever lost. Grona prison is impossible to break into or out of, so we thought, until we heard chattering gulls carry whispers on the wind that the one, they now called the *Godslayer,* had once broken out of it." He leant in towards Azzadan, who could smell the ale on Erik's breath as he added, "The war that is coming is different to all before it. The vampire lord you seek will raise Dust Soldiers in the North, and armies of the *Fallen* will descend upon the Everglow. The Empire, Bantu, the *Fallen,* and every other army there is, will fight each other and few alliances there will be. No blade will go untested in this war, and only one victor will come from it, and they will have to bargain with me to use the rivers or the sea. The land is theirs, but by Jorgen, none shall challenge the rule of the Sea Lords on the waves that are ours!"

"Your concern is unfounded," Redboots said brashly to Erik. "There is not enough coin in the entire Everglow for the Empire to be able to train a navy and build enough ships required to challenge the Sea Lords." She smiled. "It will be a war on land which will affect us very little," she quickly added as she drank more wine.

"A Kraken's egg starts off small, and when it is hatched, the foul Kraken is small enough for a shark to devour it, but left unchecked, it grows into one of the mightiest creatures in the ocean. If you smash its egg before it even hatches, it is no threat, and I will smash whatever navy the Empire tries to build whilst it is still small. I will sail up the Erin myself and smash any eggs the Kappians seek to hatch. I need Rorik to be by my side so together we can face all threats that would challenge the Sea Lords power."

Erik turned his attention again to Azzadan. "You can imagine my delight, when I discovered that Jorgen had carried on his waves the only man known who can break into and out of Grona. Raise the foul parasite queen you are bid to do, and her fouler husband, I care not, it will add to the chaos of the war that will spread on the land. But, rescue my brother at the same time, and I can promise you much. Do we have a deal, *Godslayer?*"

"No," Azzadan said as he grimaced at Erik. "I have sworn a blood-oath on a Bethratikus. I will not accept another blood-contract until I have honoured this one."

Azzadan watched warily as Erik thoughtfully fingered the Arkith in the pommel of his scimitar. *What are you waiting for? Go ahead, try,* Azzadan thought, as he and Erik stared at each other. His senses became very alert, he was sure this time he could move faster than Erik, his hidden bodyguards, or even any who tried to immobilise him again with a pin. The slightest sound out of the ordinary, a faint gush of air revealing hidden movement, and Azzadan would strike. He would not be caught out a second time.

Erik moved his hand away from his scimitar and in an unhurried, non-threatening movement reached inside his seaweed cloak, and pulled out a dagger that he threw onto the table in front of Azzadan. Azzadan recognised it; it was one of the Arkiths his Order had lost. Until that evening, he had not known that assassins from his Order had been sent to kill Erik, and failed, and in so doing, that was how they had lost some of their most powerful artefacts. It seemed a rare opportunity to be able to get at least two of them back.

Azzadan stared at the blade. "It is named *Doombringer,*" he said. *It is a blade in the past I have wielded with my own hand. I could pick it up now and end the reign of this Sea Lord.*

"I do not care for naming weapons," Erik said contemptuously, "only for the death they bring. Those of your Order sent against me, underestimated Erik Vansoth, don't you make the same mistake." The warning looks in his eyes, suggested he was assuming the thoughts racing through Azzadan's mind.

Erik then took out a rolled-up scroll, and waved it in front of Azzadan's eyes. "The recipe for the Orange Brew," he said. "If you want to be free of Ishar, the Arkith and this are both yours, once you free my brother."

Erik laughed when Azzadan hesitated. "Did Ishar not make you break the last oath you swore on a Bethratikus?"

The surprise must have shown on Azzadan's face, for Erik then said, "Turis still has friends inside your Order, and tells me many of your kind are discontent at the repeated breaking of their most sacred traditions and oaths. In the middle of such displeasure, the wealth of the Sea Lords easily finds those who can name a price we can easily meet. The tide is turning, *Godslayer*, and you are better served turning with it." Erik clenched his fist. "It would not surprise me if they gave you the *Final-death* after you raise the bloodsuckers, it might be time for you to find new shipmates, and it might be time for you to earn your own rewards."

Azzadan still felt bitter and betrayed that Ishar had not allowed him to fulfil his previous oath, but he struggled with old loyalties. Although he cared little for Skipilos, or his own Order anymore, he still cared for the honour of the Bethratikus and all that meant to him. He stared at *Doombringer* and then at the rolled-up recipe, and he desired them.

"Fitting rewards for a daring deed. Free my brother and bring him to me, and the Arkith is yours as payment, and so is the recipe," Erik said temptingly. "Then, choose your own destiny; be it to stay bound to Ishar, or to set sail for new seas. The choice will at least be yours."

"You would swear this by one of your salt-oaths?" Azzadan asked him.

"I need make no salt-oath to you on this matter," Erik replied, "and you need not make a blood-one on a Bethratikus to me. Let's call this just an agreement between two men. Take the Arkith, it is yours, an advance payment in return for freeing my brother. When you return with him, the recipe is also yours!"

Azzadan's mind was awhirl. It disturbed him that the secret meeting he had with those of his Order was known about here on the ship of a Sea Lord. The sense of distrust and betrayal he already felt towards his Order and Ishar, spread deeper through him, faster than the poison that had just briefly paralysed him. Everything he had held dear was unravelling before him. The secrecy of his Order had clearly been breached, and he wondered what events and circumstances had led to Turis turning from the Order long ago.

Erik must have sensed his train of thought for he said, "Do not think this new Emperor is not aware your rats scurry around in their warren beneath his own city. The magic that hides your Obelisk from them is fading; they will soon discover your secret halls. They will come for you, and when they do, all of you rats will be exposed and brought to the surface. Ishar knows of this, and already he prepares to relocate, though that is a secret he has guarded well."

Erik grunted. "Take the Arkith. Free Rorik my brother from Grona, and I will give you the recipe when you return him here."

"You trust me?" Azzadan asked, surprised and wary that such a precious and rare item would be handed over to him, before he had fulfilled any obligation.

In answer, Erik said, "Those who follow a code should be held in high esteem, especially by those who employ them, for they know they will keep it. You and I are not so dissimilar. In trades like ours, do we not still see fear and distaste in the eyes of those who pay us to commit their foul deeds for them? Do they not despise us even at the moment when the agreed payment is collected?"

"They do," Azzadan said as he picked up *Doombringer* and studied it. He recognised the touch of it from long ago, and it felt like an old friend. "*Doombringer* is its name," he said for the second time. *I want you to remember, for it will one day bring your doom by my hand, for the indignities you have heaped upon me in this place.* He stared at Erik. "*Doombringer*," he repeated. "I know the tale of this blade, for I helped to create that legend," he said. *I shall increase its fame, and one day soon, all will know it is the final dwelling place of Erik Vansoth.*

"You will see no distaste in my eyes when next we meet if Rorik stands at my side once again," Erik said, "but betray me, know that there will be nowhere you can hide where you will not be found," he added menacingly.

Azzadan smiled. Never, in his wildest dreams, did he ever imagine he would get to be the sole owner of *Doombringer*. He had carried and wielded many an Arkith, but they had belonged to his Order and after the completion of a mission, were always returned to them. Not so long ago, he would have felt duty bound to hand such an artefact over to his Order, who would have made claim to it, as they once owned it. But, since he had been forced to break the sacred oath of the last Bethratikus, things were different now. His Order had betrayed him; he would betray them, at least in this. *Doombringer is mine!*

"For this payment, you will get what you desire," Azzadan said with a grim and gritted smile. "String Rorik's hammock, for when the *Red Tide* brings the vampire lord to his *Fallen*, Rorik will travel the same seas to you," he said.

Redboots banged her fist on the table and scowled at Erik. "What will my payment be for bringing Rorik to you?" she asked pointedly. "I have yet to agree to have his feet step upon my deck; trouble follows him like a stench. He will cause mischief, so I want ample recompense for it!"

"I will forgive you for making this one kill Captain Argin," Erik said, as he switched his gaze between Azzadan and her. "As fond as I am of you my swashbuckling pretty, I would make you pay the salt-price for such a foul deed, if I had the proof and not just an instinct on the matter." He laughed. "Argin was unsettling the friendly ports by not controlling his men or his lusts, so this time, I'll not look for the proof I need to make you pay the salt-price."

Azzadan watched as the colour drained from Redboot's face. She had an uncertain look about her, as she watched Erik warily, like a cat trapped in a corner.

Erik laughed sinisterly. "My dear pretty, return Rorik to me from Grona, and I will support your claim, if you wish to make one, to become leader of the Skull Guild. I will let my support for you be known publicly, and that will secure many votes for you."

"What else would you expect from me, for your support?" she asked.

"Keep the friendly ports welcoming, but make them choose our side. I'll need such as you, to ravage and sack every hamlet, port and town who might side with the Empire along the Erin or the Eastern coast. When my salt-oath to protect them on the Tethys is expired, I'll not renew it and at that time I'll give you a free hand, and all of your ships and crews, to plunder Kappian ships wherever you find them. Do we have a deal?"

Redboots took a sip of wine. If she was surprised that Erik guessed she might have had a hand in ordering Argin's death, apart from the change of colour in her face, beyond that she had not shown it. She smiled coyly. "We have a deal, but, as part of it, you will order that boy, Mathis, and his father Mowett, to play me this night at Harendale for the stakes I demand." She looked over at the young sailor, Mathis, who had pretended not to remember her name, and winked maliciously at him. "If I lose, they can each select a finger of mine to cut off. If I win, then I wish to adorn the necklace around my neck, with a finger bone from the hand of both Mowett and his son. Their sour moods when they talk to me, is an offence I am tired of."

"They will both play you, we are agreed on all things," Erik roared, as he banged his jug of ale onto the table spilling froth over the side. He stood, and raised his hands. The music and singing stopped, and the noise in the hall lowered, as all became silent. "Shipmates, awaiting my return in the hold, were a captain and his crew who tried to cheat the Sea Lords from out of our toll. Tonight, they pay the salt-price."

481

A cheer went up from all in the hall.

"To the portholes," Erik shouted, and a slave began to bang a loud mournful gong, the noise of which rang throughout the ship.

As one, the guests rose to their feet and made their way over to the starfish windows.

"Come, Azzie," Smindy said enthusiastically as she took him by the arm. "I'll wager this is a sight you'll never have seen before."

He stowed *Doombringer* in a sheath inside his cloak, discarding the concealed dagger that was previously sheathed there. Reluctantly, he stood and walked over to the starfish shaped windows with Smindy where the other guests had gathered.

"Watch," Smindy said, and leading him by the hand she pushed her way through the crowd, saying, "Let us through, those who have never seen the salt-price paid get the best view, that is the code, and this man has not seen it."

With some grumbling and muttering, the crowd parted and made way for her and Azzadan.

Azzadan peered out of the large starfish porthole, and watched a large fish swim nonchalantly by. He looked up and thought he could just barely make out the glassy surface of the sea, which was suddenly disturbed by numerous splashes and bubbles. Plummeting to the sea-bed were forty or so stone blocks, and attached above each block by a chain that looped through a ring, fastened onto long shackles on their legs, was a man. The stone blocks hit the seabed causing silt and sand to slightly muddy the waters, which was soon cleared by the current.

Each man attached to a block, floated above it, their hair and clothes swirling slowly with the current, their cheeks puffed as they held onto their breath, in an attempt to cling to life. Azzadan caught the eye of one of them, and saw a look of abject horror and fear, that was exemplified as a hundred or so small mermaids and mermen, each the size of a small child, appeared from out of the seaweed and kelp and swam up to the men. The creatures slowly circled the hapless men, as one, slightly larger than the rest, swam up to the starfish window and looked at Erik through it.

The top half of the mermaid was that of a woman but her face was far from pretty. It was exactly how Azzadan had always imagined a mermaid would look like, pure malevolence. It was for good reason they were considered creatures of ill-omen by most. There were some scales missing from her lower body, and her fishtail was somewhat tattered and torn. Her pendulum-like breasts were deeply scarred. Sharp pointed teeth could be seen between her wide, misshapen lips. At the end of her webbed hands, sharp claws extended from the long fingers.

Noticing the look of disgust on Azzadan's face, Smindy smirked with amusement and said, "There are different types of merfolk, not all are as un-comely as this particular breed."

Erik overhead her comment, and laughed. "My pets are beautiful in my eyes," he said, as he made a feeding gesture with his hands so the creature would understand. He then roared, "Feed, my pretties!"

Rows of razor-sharp teeth were fully exposed as the mermaid attempted what looked like a smile. Her black eyes blinked. With a swish of its scaly fishtail, the creature joined the others, darting through the water with ease. Even through the porthole, the high-pitched screaming could be heard as the creatures circled and with their sharp clawed hands and teeth ripped and stripped the men to mere bones in less than a minute. At first Azzadan could not tell if it was the men who had made the noise in terror, or the creatures themselves, but as it continued even after the men were clearly dead, he concluded it was the grisly creatures. Blood and scraps of leftover flesh rolled with the current, as the skeletons of the men continued to float in the blood-tainted sea. The mermaids and mermen descended back out of sight into the seaweed and kelp from where they had come.

"Such will be the fate of any who do not pay and try to cheat the Sea Lords from our toll," Erik said gleefully as he swivelled around and took Redboots in his arms. "Will you come to my bed wet and willing tonight, my swashbuckling pretty?" he asked her eagerly.

"I will," she replied, with a broad smile. "After my game of Harendale."

"Kira, come join us if you will!" Erik shouted. Kira joined them as arm in arm the three of them walked towards the exit of the hall.

For the first time in many lifetimes, Azzadan felt an insane jealousy. It gnawed at the very root of his soul. The thought of Redboots being in the rough embrace of Erik Vansoth tormented his mind and nearly sent him mad with rage. For a brief moment, he considered making himself invisible with his ethereal cloak, and plunging his newly acquired Arkith into Erik's chest, right there and then.

Smindy must have sensed his mood, as he opened his cloak and stared at *Doombringer,* and then at Erik, for she said, "No man can own her, Azzie, do not let your heart concern itself with the choices she makes."

Smindy took his hand, and accompanied him back over to the table as Redboots, Kira and Erik left the hall to the glaring sound of conches, drowning out their laughing and joking together. On her way out of the hall, Redboots grabbed the young sailor Mathis. "Come, we have a game of Harendale to play," Azzadan heard her say to him.

Azzadan closed his eyes briefly, and in that moment, decided that one day he would make good his oath to kill Erik with the *Final-death,* as with every fibre of his being he fought to control the rage and jealously he felt. When they were seated back at the table, Smindy clasped her narrow white hands together and rested her chin upon them, looking at him with an enigmatic smile etched on her face. The smile quivered on her cheeks along with the crescent shadows of her eyelashes.

"I love Captain Redboots more than life itself," she said, "but it is not that of a romantic kind. Azzie, do not be a fool and love her in that way, for she will never return it. Her feminine façade is treacherous, and many a man have I seen lose himself whilst swept along in the current of it. It is a love that will unman you, make you weak and dependent upon it. Remain your own man, Azzie, and do not drown in the emotions for what you feel for her."

Azzadan abandoned convention, unfastening his doublet he drank a large goblet of wine and then immediately downed it again, after the same woman, who had earlier served their food, re-filled it. Smindy whispered something to the woman, who briefly looked Azzadan up and down as though considering a proposal. She then nodded to Smindy, removed the seashell covering her left breast and handed it to him.

Azzadan took it, as Smindy said, "Come," and, taking him by the hand, they rose to their feet. She took the woman with the other hand and led them from the hall. "We'll take your mind off the matter that troubles it, and give you a night you'll not soon forget," she said to him. "Just remember, we must never know the woman behind the mask, so do not remove it. For, whoever she is, she has chosen to be a bond-slave here for a time, so respect the secret she wishes to keep, for that is the way of things in the Hall of the Sea Lords!"

# Chapter Thirty-Eight: *The Threadweaver*

*And then his voice came faintly and far away, and evil itself looked at me. I trembled with a fear that was darker than the terror of death. I realised this was not their tomb - it was their prison!*
*Confessions of the Priest Named Rual.*

*I'm* so sorry Hogin ate your discarded body, me dear," Gilly meekly said to Janorra as they sat in the Spriggans' glade. "He is a very bad bird and I told him so. No cake for him until I think he is truly sorry for what he did, which may take a while, as them Bena aren't known for having much of a conscience you see, me dear."

Janorra felt that Gilly's empathy was sincere, but she sensed that some of the Spriggan found the situation funny. They tried to hide their mirth behind their hands when she angrily stared at them. Bessie, though, seemed genuinely cross. She looked at Hogin, pointed her finger, wagged it and said crossly, "You are a very greedy old bird. I've a good mind to not give you any more turnips or maggots."

Hogin crawked. "Hogin sorry. Ack-ack." The look of remorse the bird cast at Janorra did not convince her that he was genuinely remorseful.

"Can we get out of this place?" Muro irritably mumbled as several Spriggan clambered over him and climbed on to his shoulders and arms. They tugged his ears and looked at the runes embedded in the palms of his hands. He tensely brushed them off as though they were flies. They landed sprawled on the ground, and then protested and voiced their annoyance at him for treating them so rudely.

Scarand was looking at the Spriggan with curiosity bordering on fascination, and allowing them to clamber over him without protest.

"Well, he did regurgitate it not long after, right before us here in this glade," Gilly said apologetically.

"Only because I forced him to by the power of this ring," Janorra replied crossly. *They should understand how sacred a discarded body is to an Akkadian, especially a Seeress, like me.* The lack of respect offended her deeply.

It slightly eased her mood when she saw that Gilly sensed the level of her annoyance. "Hogin meant no offence, me dear, he really doesn't know any better," she said apologetically and with a sincerity that again convinced Janorra she meant it. "So, me dear, can this be an end to it? At least you now have it buried in this nice glade, covered in nice rocks the Spriggan collected for you."

"I do appreciate that," Janorra said, calming slightly.

"They will keep an eye on it for old Gilly, I made them promise me. They know an old forest-hermit, a spell-caster, who lives in a hovel deep in the forest. They will ask him to put strong charms over it so nothing can disturb it from here on to eternity, me dear. The Spriggan will call it *Janorra's Glade* from now on, you know, in honour of you. So, cheer up, me dear?"

"It was worse for me. I was alive and in the beaks of those disgusting things," Muro complained as he shuddered at the memory. The birds had rescued him and Farir from the Erin on the night the *River Queen* had burnt and sank. The memory of being in the beak of one of them clearly did not evoke pleasant feelings as Janorra could tell by the look of disgust on his face.

Wasn't it the will of Yog?" Scarand remarked, with obvious sarcasm.

Muro shot him a murderous look.

"You owe them your life, me dear," Gilly said in defence of the birds.

"What about a Davari warrior and his wife, did you see anything of them Gilly, might they have survived?" Scarand asked, curiously.

"Oh, I don't know me dear, it may be that one or two others made it out of the Erin, but my birds only had the time to fetch Farir and Muro from the water. I made them a special cake as a reward."

Muro frowned at the mention of Imrand and his wife. He fingered the runes in the palms of his hands, but said nothing.

"Imrand became unpredictable, after he was captured, and that makes him dangerous, should we come across him," Scarand said as a word of caution.

Gaffren snorted impatiently, he was laden with supplies and bags and seemed eager to move. Bessie jumped onto one of his horns and looked up at Gilly, who mounted the goat, sitting in the middle of the saddle. She offered Janorra a helping hand to mount behind her, but Janorra refused, preferring for now to walk.

"Come on Miss Gilly, the Threadweaver will be waiting for us. We sent a message we are coming," Bessie said.

We must go quickly to the palace of ice and rock, where Yog dwells," Muro muttered angrily. "I cannot believe this one you call Silverberry, a Threadweaver, is Yog. We should have no business with Threadweavers. They are deceivers and witches."

"Well, if there is such a place, maybe she knows where it is," Bessie suggested.

"Well, they sound like the same person, me dear," Gilly said to Muro, "only she lives in a cottage."

Bessie was insistent when she spoke. "We need to get permission from 'er to enter the forbidden part of the forest; it's a secret place, and lots of ruins there; she might let us rest at 'er cottage for the night, and we will need some of that refreshing milk."

Gilly looked at Muro. "Who or what we seek is in that part of the forest where we can only enter with the Threadweaver's permission," she said. She then stroked Gaffren's head and looked at Bessie. "You're right Bessie, me dear, we must be setting off. It is a way to go and I would like to make it there before nightfall tomorrow."

The Spriggan, except for Bessie, all remained in the clearing and waved them goodbye as the small company set off from the glade. Janorra looked at the pile of rocks where her former body, regurgitated by Hogin, was now respectfully buried. At least the Bena birds could not get to it. She was pleased that the two birds were not coming with them.

"Time to wash you in the river you smelly old things," she heard one of the Spriggan say to the birds as the company left the glade.

Janorra, walking on foot beside Gaffren, absently brushed away loose strands of her blonde hair. "Why do we need a Spriggan to show us the way?" she asked without looking at Gilly or Bessie. "Do you not know it?"

Gilly answered. "We're going into a part of the forest that is strange even to me, me dear, and I might get lost. Bessie always leads me when I go to parts of the forest I've not been to before. I've never entered that part, I was warned not to, but now I feel I must." She turned and looked at Muro who was walking along behind. "If we have all read our part of the Murien right, the fourth reader is to be found in that part of the forest, and we can't enter there without the Threadweaver's permission and help. It would be too dangerous for us without her blessing."

Scarand exchanged a look with Janorra, but said nothing. Gilly had not noticed and carried on speaking. "The trees in that part of the forest are very mysterious and not always friendly, me dears. They can play mischievous tricks and change the path behind or ahead so an unwelcome traveller gets lost. There are many ways to get lost in the

Wytchwood, which is why I always take Bessie as a guide when I go to unfamiliar parts of the forest."

In her childlike voice Bessie chimed in and spoke loudly so that all in the small company could hear her. "If the trees touch you in that part of the forest, or whisper to you, don't pay them any notice. These ones are disconnected from their Wisdom Tree so have become very naughty. Sometimes they are just curious or even a tad annoyed when they see strangers a wandering, but leave me to speak to them. They will listen to me."

Janorra did not like the sound of that, but she was grateful that fate had led her to finding such travelling companions who knew the forest well. She looked at *Arnazia*, and drew comfort from its presence, before touching the Amulet of Ahrimakan. The amulet bore no use outside of the temple and the summoning chamber, that she knew of, and for the briefest moment she considered tearing it off and casting it aside, but she thought better of it and quickly resisted the urge. *I might yet find another use for this.*

Bessie led them through the forest, often jumping down from Gaffren and racing ahead out of sight, and then occasionally returning to report about the way they should go. Whenever she did, she would have a hand full of berries, nuts, or strange but tasty fruits which she shared among her companions, always making sure Gaffren was served first. The path they followed through the forest was winding, and seemed at times to double back on itself before heading off in new directions. When several forks in the way ahead appeared, Bessie pointed out the direction to take. After a particular turning, the forest soon drew dark and gloomy, and took on a different tone than Janorra had earlier sensed on the way to retrieving her ring. At times it felt like the tip of a branch reached down to touch her shoulder, and she thought she heard a faint unintelligible whisper, but when she turned to look there was nothing there or she thought she saw the branch quickly withdraw with a creak. The others in her party felt the same thing.

"They keep touching and whispering to me," Muro complained angrily as he brushed his shoulder as though something had touched it.

"Be quiet, grumpy," Bessie said bossily. "Best we don't upset the trees. Let them be to satisfy their curiosity."

"I won't be insulted by a twig," Muro said indignantly, "especially not an *Arvivan*." He scowled, and asked aggressively, "Do you remember the ritual?"

Bessie did not answer; instead, she jumped off of Gaffren and ran ahead of the group, lowering her head sulkily and turning back she shouted "*Arvivan!*" Looking petulantly at Muro, she shouted again, this time with more anger, "*Arvivan!*"

"Now, now Mr Muro," Gilly said firmly. "I'll not be having you insult my friends, especially not ones that be helping us, is that clear, me dear?"

"We Ruik, know of the ones called *Arvivan*, the runes showed us," Muro huffed, and then muttered something under his breath about how he objected to being called grumpy.

"How did she get those scars?" Scarand asked.

"It's a long story me dear. She was playing at the edge of the Wytchwood once, when a Chatti shaman captured her and gave her those marks. I know this to be the case as some other Spriggans saw it happen. All Bessie will say about it whenever it comes up, is that word, '*Arvivan*,' and I have no idea what it means. She won't explain any of it to me and I doubt she knows herself what it means." She glanced at Muro, "But you seem to know of it?"

"It is dark and ancient magic," Muro said quietly.

"What sort of magic?" Gilly asked him, clearly surprised, but Muro gave her no answer.

486

The companions walked alongside Gilly who rode Gaffren. They went along dark and winding forest paths that Bessie led them through, and along the way Gilly told them many remarkable stories, sometimes looking at them with her bright blue eyes, at other times as though half speaking to herself. She told them tales of butterflies, bees and flowers, the life and ways of trees and the strange creatures of the forest, both the good and evil ones, those friendly and those not so friendly.

As Janorra listened to the tales of the forest, it momentarily took her mind off of her own troubles and she was glad of the distraction. She began to understand the life of the forest, how ancient and mysterious it was: unlike before, she suddenly felt herself a stranger there.

Gilly spoke of the thoughts of some trees, how they could be dark and strange, resenting those who walked free upon the earth, jealous of those who were not bound by root and time to one spot. She told them that the countless years of some trees had filled them with pride and rooted wisdom, but often they were filled with a deep malice and hatred for things that cut or burnt them. Some of the more sinister trees even resented the squirrels that stole their nuts or the birds that usurped their branches and dared to build their nests. Other trees, she told them, had accepted their lot and were at peace with nature around them, but even they feared the axe and the fire, and would resent those who turned them upon their kin or kind.

Gilly pointed to one tree they passed, a large old oak, gnarled and twisted with age. "That was one of the first young saplings, before the Elves even sang the Wisdom Trees into being; some call it the *Grandfather of the Wytchwood*. The acorn that it grew from was dropped randomly by some bird in the air and it fell into a small crack in the ground, the only fertile place for it to grow. That was in a time when vast herds of wild deer grazed in great flocks upon the wild grasslands, hunted by packs of wargs and other predators. It grew and watched the first men come, Akkadians, before they were blessed with the *Gift of the Obelisks*. They sensed its age so did not cut it down as they knew its ancient life. It stood tall and solitary when they tilled the land as farmers, and in time they built their burial mounds of the kings and queens of old which were placed around it. Look, you can still see the traces of their mounds and some of the ruins of the stone keeps built near it."

Janorra looked at the mounds Gilly pointed at, mounds now covered in trees or undergrowth. Beneath tangled-vines stone doors with strange carvings were barely visible. It fascinated her that an ancient civilisation had once existed here, the only remains of which were the mounds and fragments of a broken ruin here and there littered among the trees and partially hidden by the undergrowth.

Gilly looked at the sight in awe. "It watched as kings of little kingdoms and great ones fought and died, their cities crumbling to nothing. It stood and watched when those burial mounds there were plundered; the gold and precious jewels taken and the bones within left to turn do dust and blow away in the wind.

"It's probably just any old tree," Scarand said innocently.

"Then I dare you to take a sword and try and cut it, and see what the forest does to you, me dear," Gilly said to him sternly. He did not reply, and stared warily at the tree so she continued.

"It bided its time and stood alone for a long time, until the ground around it was fertile enough for it to birth much of this forest. It watched as in time Elves came and sang the Wisdom Trees into shape, and they made the rest of the Wytchwood. The archive said it cried and mourned when the evil came and the Elves left." Janorra noticed that large goblets of sap had hardened long ago on the trunk, each one forming the shape of a tear.

487

They passed the tree and continued on their journey, with Gilly telling them more stories and legends of the forest, before she suddenly fell quiet and would not say another word. They all felt the same gloom descend upon them, but did not know the cause of it, but they felt that over a rise and out of sight there was a dark presence. Before the midday sun rose, they stood on a hill overlooking a valley lush with green trees on one side, and saw the cause of their foreboding. At the far western end of the valley the trees were dead, dying and withered. Before them, was a large and mostly ruined fortress of stone, on an island of rock, surrounded by deep chasms on all sides, with four bridges, one each leading to the north, east, south and west. Two were collapsed, a third, the southern bridge looked on the verge of falling into the abyss, whilst the east facing bridge, was still crossable. It had a large gate house built into the wall of the fortress, the door of which was shut. The fortress rose stark and solitary out of an ocean of trees, its ancient stones, towers and spires blackened by time and weather. Four of the spires were larger than the others, even the one that had partially collapsed. The other three were at various stages of crumbling, with one tilting and leaning so dangerously over the chasm it looked as though it might fall at any moment. The fortress was generally ruined, crumbling, and mostly claimed by creeping vines, roots, trees and brush. The many smaller towers and spires were in a similarly bad condition to the largest ones, having already fallen or looking like they might at any moment. The main citadel at the centre of the fortress, and its dome, could not be seen clearly, as a dark cloud shrouded it from view, ominous as a thunder-cloud; a deep gloom pervaded the air. Around the citadel, behind the walls, was a vast and sprawling stone complex of various buildings.

To the west, beyond the fortress, the last living foliage of the forest had given up the struggle. The trees were dark and bare, twisted and crooked as though in pain. The forest floor was grassless and barren of any foliage. Over the decaying part of the forest hung a vast shadow.

"Is that the dwelling place of Yog?" Muro asked suspiciously. "It cannot be, she lives in a palace of rock and ice, a goddess would not dwell in a place of ruin and decay."

"I've not been here before," Gilly said with a slight tremor in her voice, and then asked Bessie, "Is that where we need to go, me dear?"

Bessie paused a moment and looked at the fortress. "We call it the Old Citadel, for there are no others like it in the Wytchwood. Inside there is where poor old Mithilos suffers," she said sadly, and then tentatively added, "we should speak to Silverberry, unless you wish to turn back?"

"I fear we have little choice but to continue, me dear, and quickly, lest through fear, looking on such sights tempts us to abandon this quest and return to more pleasant realms," Gilly said, after which she looked at Janorra and whispered quietly, "but some of us might no longer have that option."

Bessie sighed. "Down that trail is the Threadweaver's cottage; we must see 'er before we go on into the actual dark part of the forest, 'er cottage is at the edge of it. It will take us the morning and afternoon of tomorrow to reach there. It will soon be nightfall, and I don't know the way in the dark. We should make camp."

"I am eager to find Yog," Muro said impatiently. "If this Threadweaver knows where the palace of ice and rock where Yog dwells is, she must tell me, if not, I'll find it myself. We should press on through the night even if to explore."

Scarand scowled at him. "On the path Bessie might miss something, or even interpret what she sees the wrong way. If she bids us camp, we must camp."

Bessie nodded her head. "There are foul things that live over there in the dark part of the forest, and on the edges of it, that prowl and 'unt at night. The Threadweaver's son also strides there, and none are fouler than 'im. You must never go near the dark forest without 'er permission; none could survive it without 'er 'elp and the delicious milk she will offer. To get both, you must go to 'er cottage, but even the path there is not safe at night." Bessie pointed ahead. "I know a place, very near, where it will be safe to camp. The good Wisdom Tree can still offer us protection there," she chimed.

Janorra did not like the sight of the fortress they looked upon; it made her tremble with fear. She also felt uneasiness at the thought of meeting whoever the Threadweaver was. *Is she the spirit I met in the Deadlands?* However, she just wanted to retrieve the Simal, and if possible, find and rescue Sezareal, and then forever leave the forest before the Wild Hunt re-appeared. She wanted to press on, and reach the cottage, but she had little choice but to trust their guide. Bessie knew the forest, even better than Gilly, so if she advised them to camp for the night, so be it.

They continued along the path and the fortress was soon out of sight; the wood on either side became denser, until suddenly they came out of the shadow of the trees, and before them laid a wide space of grass, littered with old leaves and decaying wood. It sat under a grey dusk, foretelling the impending night which was drawing in fast. On three sides the wood pressed upon it, but on another, thickets and bushes, through which the trail continued. Above them, the first stars twinkled in the sky, but the moon was shrouded by cloud.

Whilst they set up camp, Bessie clambered onto Gaffren and stroked his horns and said, "Look, there are some of those berries you like." She pointed to some wild berry bushes in the midst of the thickets, and led him over to them. "Eat your fill, but don't go a wandering off, it's not safe. You must stay near us, in the clearing." Bessie jumped off as Gaffren began grazing on the lush berries, and she came and sat near Janorra and Scarand, who unrolled the bed rolls Gilly had provided.

"I'll take first watch," Scarand said.

"No need for that," Bessie said. "We are far enough away from the dark forest to be safe here."

"None the less, I'll keep watch anyway," Scarand replied, as he went and stood near Gaffren, stroking the goat's head as it ate.

The companions set up camp, but lit no fire. They had a light meal consisting of apple and cinnamon stuffed pastries that Gilly had previously baked, packed and passed around, and drank from their own water bottles. Gilly and Bessie sat on the grass and spoke together in soft voices. Muro sat in meditation, muttering to himself. Janorra sat alone, wrapped herself in her cloak and blanket to keep out the chill in the air, brushed away the crumbs from the food and enjoyed the tingling sensation in her mouth caused by the seasoning. The wind was sighing in the branches of the trees, and the leaves were whispering. The smells of the forest filled her nostrils; the sharp fresh twang of pine needles and the earthy odour of wet rotting leaves. She stared up at the sky, now beset by night, and watched as the stars grew thicker and brighter, and the moon, now unhidden by the clouds, shone in all of its full lunar glory. Drowsiness stole over her, and she was soon fast asleep.

*      *      *

"Quiet now," Sasna said, "we are near the gatehouse."

489

"I've got my crossbow at the ready here!" One of the guards said, as she and Farir cautiously approached. "Unless you want a bolt in your throat, show your faces, state your names and the business you have in Berecoth."

Sasna blew into her frozen hands, wriggled her fingers and pulled off her hood, exposing her face and hair to the rain which had picked up in its intensity.
Three guards stood in front of the gatehouse, which led into Berecoth.

"Lady Sasna?" one of them asked in surprise.

Farir pulled off his own hood, showing his face.

"Master Farir?" the same guard spurted out.

The guard rushed over to them.

"Good, you know me," Sasna answered.

"We heard that you and you brother had perished on the Erin," another guard said, as he waved a torch in front of her face as if to confirm it was truly her.

"What news in Berecoth?" Sasna asked, "Has the one they call Redboots left?"

"She has," the guard answered, sniffing the air. "But three of her ships remain. The patrician is dead, and the pirate scum have elected one they call Senzas to take his place."

*Senzas, he is the partner of Marlo. I need to speak with him,* Sasna thought, feeling a surge of fresh hope at the prospect of finding passage to Harwind.

"Then take me to him, for I have important business to discuss," she said to the guard.

"As you wish, it's your funeral, Lady Sasna," the first guard said, after which he bellowed an order to open the gate.

*      *      *

Janorra was woken when Bessie burst into loud and jubilant song. She sat up, rubbed her eyes, and stared at the Spriggan, who was jumping up and down in merriment in the glade and singing to the newly risen sun.

*Morning-sun! Morning-sun! 'ow good to see your light.*
*The dark 'as gone, for another day.*
*I watched you chase it away.*
*Morning-sun! Morning-sun! 'ow good to see your light.*

*Yellow-sun! Yellow-sun, 'ow good to feel your warmth.*
*The cold 'as gone, I feel your embrace.*
*I feel your tender rays.*
*Yellow-sun! Yellow-sun, 'ow good to feel your warmth.*

*One more day! One more day! I 'ave lived to see again.*
*I survived the night, and all its frights,*
*To see you rise again.*
*Morning-sun! Morning-sun! 'ow good to see your light.*

"It's how Spriggans always greet the sunrise, me dear," Gilly said. "They have a different song for each day of the week, and the words change according to the seasons."

Janorra listened to the sweet and innocent voice of Bessie, and felt a twinge of envy that such a creature could feel so jubilant to see the dawn of a new day. *Will I ever know the innocence of happiness and freedom from fear?*

They all ate a light breakfast, and following Bessie they set off down the path. Bessie hummed softly and joyfully as she walked, and the gloom of the day before did not seem so bad to Janorra. The shadows of the trees were long and thin on the trail as they headed towards the Threadweaver's cottage. The trail was uneven, and wove its way through ancient oak-trees. They travelled for much of the morning, only stopping for a light lunch before setting off again, and travelling for the best part of the afternoon.

They pressed on for the remainder of the way mostly in silence, only broken by Bessie when she pointed out the direction to take when the trail presented different options. At sunset, the path broke off and led to a clearing wherein sat a cosy but dilapidated looking cottage with a thatched roof. The cottage looked surprisingly pleasant and inviting, despite the poor state of repair it was in. It was surrounded by a white picket fence, and contained a flourishing herb garden, a rich vegetable patch and next to that a beautiful display of coloured flowers of many different varieties, the colours of which were magnified by the few rays of sunset that broke through the forest canopy.

"We are 'ere!" Bessie declared.

"I don't like the look of this," Scarand said suspiciously. "It looks out of place, out of time."

"Like it or not, me dears, Bessie knows the ways of the forest here. I've not met the Threadweaver before, but if we need her permission to pass, then that's what we need." She dismounted Gaffren, held out her hand and Bessie ran up her arm and perched upon her shoulder.

"Take me in, Miss Gilly; Silverberry is waiting for us," Bessie said, and then turning to the others, added, "you best wait 'ere, until I tell you to come. She will be expecting you but best you get an invite as you are new to the forest."

Janorra stood with Muro and Scarand, and watched as Gilly opened the garden gate, walked up the path and knocked on the front door.

"This looks like the dwelling of a witch," Muro growled. "Yog dwells in a palace of ice and rock, not in a hovel."

"We Davari do not consort with witches," Scarand added suspiciously as he stroked the shaft of his bow. "They cannot be trusted, and are best dealt with by an arrow to their heart."

"Don't do anything foolish," Janorra warned them both, and then asked Scarand, "you saw what I did at Castle Greytears, was that not like witchcraft to you?"

He did not reply but held the shaft of his bow firmly.

The door of the cottage opened, seemingly by itself. Bessie and then Gilly exchanged words with the occupant. Gilly then waved at everybody to join her as she entered the cottage. Janorra took a deep breath, and she and the two men entered the garden and cautiously walked up the path to the cottage.

The companions stepped over the wide stone threshold of the cottage. They were in a long low room filled with the light from lamps swinging from the beams of the roof. A round table of dark polished wood was at the centre of the room, and upon it were a number of heavy tomes the leather covers of which were cracked with age. Next to the tomes stood a candle, tall and yellow and burning brightly. In a chair at the table sat a very old and withered looking woman. Her long tangled grey hair rippled down her shoulders; her gown was dirty, dark green and patterned with silver stars. She looked up at the companions.

491

"Come in," she said, with a croaky shrill voice tired from age. "Close the door behind you. Shut out the night before it descends, we do not want to allow the *Untamed Ones* or my son to enter." Scarand, who had been the last one to enter the cottage, looked behind guardedly, and quickly shut the door behind them. He stared suspiciously at the old woman.

Janorra also stared as the old woman slowly stood up. She could hear the sound of bones creaking and joints cracking as the woman moved. When she was stood as far upright as she was able, and mostly still hunched over, she aloofly stared at Janorra, and asked, "Why do you wish to enter the decayed part of the forest and disturb what lies there, my lovely?"

"Something I lost has been stolen from me, and I have reason to believe it is within there," Janorra answered her.

The old-crone cackled with sarcastic laughter. "A thief accuses another thief and wishes to steal back that which she stole." A menacing glare spread across her ancient features. "You cannot enter without my permission, my lovely," the crone said.

"And that is why we are here old witch," Muro said defiantly. "I have come to seek Yog, tell me where her palace of ice and rock dwells that I might seek her."

"We seek your permission, hag," Scarand added. "Give it to us so we may be gone."

Bessie jumped off of Gilly, hid behind her, and peeked out, as with a creaking and snapping sound the crone's head turned, and she fixed her harsh stare on Scarand. He did not flinch.

"So young, so handsome, yet so foolish with his quick tongue. An old lady might be excused for thinking he tired of life already," she said, and then turned her sight on Muro. "Your spirit is a fledgling, compared to the days of this world, even though your body is old, as counted in years by men. Did my sisters not speak to you through the runes, and told you to come visit me here?"

"My business is with Yog, and none of your concern," Muro replied. "Give us what we need to press on, for I long to meet her."

"Yog!" The crone cackled and laughed mockingly. "My sisters and I, never did like the basic names you Davari call us by."

Janorra observed Muro, as uncertainty momentarily crossed his features. When he spoke though, it was with confidence. "It is true that of *The Three Sisters*, Yog has the lesser splendour, but even she has a sinister beauty that terrifies those who behold it. All men are captivated at the sight of her beauty, it is written in the runes. Do not try to pass yourself off as her, hag, for this is no palace of ice and rock." He clenched his fists, and opened them, and the runes in his palms sprang to life. "I will not tolerate such blasphemy!"

The hag flicked her fingers, and both Muro and Scarand fell instantly to the floor as though dead. "Foolish boys," she said.

"What have you done to them?" Janorra asked in alarm.

"They are just sleeping Miss Janorra," Bessie answered.

The hag laughed, showing crooked yellowed teeth. "Ruik like him, worship me and my sisters. Yig and Yag are full of vanity and like to make themselves all pretty for them, for the Davari would not like their true forms, the sight of which would mean death. I used to appear to them in beauty, now I prefer to show myself in this form, although I have many others."

The hag flicked her fingers. Janorra watched in horror as Scarand and Muro stood to their feet, their eyes still closed as if in sleep. Like a puppeteer would pull the strings of a marionette, the hag moved her arms, and Scarand and Muro moved awkwardly with her, as though marionettes manipulated by hidden strings. She made them perform a foolish dance, and then moved them over to the chairs, and sat them heavily in them.

"My sisters have a purpose for him being here," she said, looking at Muro, and then added darkly, "or else I would teach and show him the true form of those he worships, and terror would forever stalk him after the sight of it." Her attention turned to Scarand. "As for the young one, I would keep him here, as a price for his insolence," she said ominously, but then looking at Janorra added, "but fate has bound you together with him, for a time. It is well for him that I will not interfere with the thread my sister has woven for him."

"You are the one they call Yog?" Janorra asked.

"It is one of my many names," the hag answered, "but I do not care for it. You will call me Silverberry."

"We only came for a glass of milk, and permission to enter the dark part of the forest," Bessie said respectfully to Silverberry, peering out nervously from behind Gilly. "These are nice people, except the grumpy one; they just don't know our ways. Those two meant no rudeness by their words." She then quickly added, "I think."

"Well, me dear," Gilly said to Bessie, "we want her to read a text we have brought to her first, as that might tell us exactly where we need to go."

Silverberry slowly turned her creaking head and looked at Gilly.

"I have heard much about you, meddling dwarf," she said to her.

Gilly looked startled, but said nothing, and stared at the ground.

Silverberry's voice was full of derision. "I thought it strange the Wisdom Tree chose a Reisic dwarf to share some of its secrets and spirit with. I have often pondered if it was the right decision. You Reisic show devotion to the thief, the giant Bothgar, my thieving nephew, do you not?" Before waiting for an answer, she added, "I can only think the Wisdom Tree had few choices, so made the best one out of bad options, when it chose you."

Silverberry then turned her attention to Janorra, and a chill ran down her spine. It was as though the hag could see right through her very soul.

"I saw you in the Deadlands," Silverberry said. "On a knife-edge, your destiny rests, and decided it is not. One wrong step will see worlds fall, and a suffering to befall you, that your screams will eternally echo through all domains, if handed to the Aeldar you are." She cackled thoughtfully. "Do not let those who hunt you, catch you," she warned. "When you get what you seek, run!"

Gilly took the Murien out of her backpack, and handed it to Janorra. "It might be best you talk to her about this, me dear," she said.

"With your permission, I would like to travel with my friends to the dark part of the forest," Janorra said, trying to ease the tension, and choosing not to reflect there and then on the ominous warning she had just been given. "You know what it is I have lost?" She handed the Murien to Silverberry. "I think you are the fourth one who is meant to read this."

The old woman took the Murien and cackled again. With great difficulty and slowness of movement, and the sound of creaking bones and cracking joints, she turned, and walked to the kitchen and disappeared from view.

Bessie spoke to both Janorra and Gilly. "Those two silly Davari are lucky they did not get themselves killed, or worse," she said reproachfully. "Now, whatever you do, do not refuse the milk when it is offered to you. She will only offer it once; you will not survive this night nor be able to go deeper into the forest, unless you drink it. It is for your own protection!"

"What is this milk?" Janorra asked.

493

Bessie blushed. "Just drink," was all she answered, as she ran after Silverberry into the kitchen.

Janorra walked over to the table, as did Gilly. She stared at Scarand and Muro. They were both breathing and very much alive, but both in a very deep sleep.

"It seems one does not always recognise their own goddess when such appears before their eyes in a form not pleasing to them, in a place not expected," she observed as she stared thoughtfully at Muro.

"Nobody wants a god to appear in an un-comely form," Gilly added dryly. "Me dear, do you think Silverberry is truly the one the Davari call Yog?"

Janorra did not answer straight away. She began thumbing through the ancient tomes and books on the table, gasping with awe and muttering as she scanned the pages. "This is the language of High Vakkan. This is taught in Kappian Mystery Schools, and few there are that can master such a difficult tongue."

Gilly looked at the strange spidery words written on one of the pages. "It is indeed a strange tongue, and one that I do not know, me dear," she said.

Janorra looked grimly at Gilly, and then towards the kitchen where the shadow of the hag could be seen as she prepared the milk. "Like she said, she has many names, but I do think she is Yog," she said quietly.

"Then, me dear, Muro is a fool to meet the one he seeks, and not to know it was she he sought," Gilly whispered back.

Silverberry returned a few moments later with a tray laden with glasses of watery looking milk. With some difficulty, and hunched over by the apparent weight of the tray, she made her way painfully slowly, with many a crack and creak of bone. She offered a glass of milk to Janorra and Gilly, which they took from the tray. Bessie returned from the kitchen with a small glass she was already greedily drinking from, leaving the stain of milk around her lips and mouth.

Janorra hesitated for a moment, and sniffed the milk. It smelt sour. She curled her nose up in disgust.

"Drink, my lovely," Silverberry said.

Janorra took a hesitant sip of the milk. It was bitter-sweet, but not totally unpleasant, so she emptied the glass in a dozen or so small gulps."

The crone's smile again revealed her yellowed, rotten and broken teeth. She placed the tray on the table, and then using a similar process as before, moved her arms. Two glasses of the milk moved by unseen hands through the air, as Scarand and Muro, still asleep, but moving like puppets, took them and drank the milk.

Janorra, in silence, stood in the light of the swinging lamps that creaked as they swung slowly to and thro of their own accord. She looked out of the window. The sun was setting. Gaffren bleated outside of the door and was let into the cottage by Bessie. Soon, the full moon's soft light spilled down through the trees and filtered in through the cottage windows.

"This milk will help you sleep," Bessie said to Gaffren as she offered him some milk which he lapped up gladly, as Gilly unpacked the supplies from him, took off the saddle, and stroked him affectionately. Gaffren then lay on the floor and went slowly to sleep, bleating softly with content. Gilly and Bessie yawned, stretched their arms, arranged bed rolls on the floor, laid down beside him, and also fell asleep.

"Come now my lovely," Silverberry said, taking Janorra by the hand, before slowly leading her into an adjacent room. "Do not be afraid. I am known by many names, but you may know me as Silverberry. That's what the Elves used to call me. I am not fond of the name the Davari use."

"The Elves?"

"That was in days of old. I left at the same time as they did. I went south into Davari lands, but they went north. I am a Threadweaver, and go where the strands lead me. Fear nothing, for tonight you sleep under my roof, but first, we must talk, and I will show you something."

Janorra did not resist as Silverberry led her to the next room.

The room was sparse, with only two rickety chairs placed around a table, on top of which rested a pedestal and upon that a pair of bronze hands. One hand was empty, the other cradled a dark globe.

"Sit, my lovely," Silverberry said, as she gently guided Janorra to sit on one of the chairs, which creaked and groaned as she sat on it.

Janorra felt a wave of tiredness spread over her as she took the seat, but also a strange calmness. "Are you really the one the Davari call Yog?" she asked calmly.

Silverberry laughed, it was long and high pitched, and unnerved Janorra. When her laughter exhausted itself, the crone took on a more sinister allure. "A long time ago, when I was younger, it used to please me to appear to the Davari in a form of beauty." Her own statement seemed to please her, and a look of self-satisfaction spread across her face. "Oh, how they loved and worshipped me and my sisters. They bowed and scraped the knee and no excesses did they restrict in their devotion." She sighed. "After many centuries of such grovelling, I grew bored of their devotion, and told my sisters I wanted to show myself to them in my true form." A glazed look came over her, as she recounted long distant memories. "My sisters were furious, they wanted to still be seen as objects of loveliness, though long ago had their exquisiteness faded. We argued for a long, long time, and it was this that distracted us, so we did not see Bothgar's plot to carry out his wicked scheme."

When it seemed like she had finished, and there was a long silence, Janorra said, "Muro thinks you dwell in a palace of ice and rock, I think your appearance and your dwelling, are the reasons he cannot now see who you are."

Silverberry seemed pleased. "I did not know that even to this day, the Ruik still worship and seek me, as they do my sisters, but I care little for such tawdry adoration from those who choose a lie." She looked knowingly at Janorra. "In order to know and see the truth, you first have to acknowledge and face the lies that hold you hostage!"

Janorra felt uncomfortable at the scrutinising gaze of Silverberry, who then suddenly said, "I know who you are, and what you have stolen."

Janorra felt a rush of panic, followed by tiredness. *Is she my friend or my foe?*

Silverberry relaxed her gaze. "Few allies you have, but consider me not an enemy, for I have no longer have any desire to see the Aeldar return to this world." She then opened a draw in the table, took out a pipe from inside it, and then a pouch of tobacco with which she began to fill it.

Janorra relaxed a little, but kept her guard up. "The Murien text told us to come here. We hoped you could read it so that we would know where to go. If our journey takes us into the forbidden part of the forest, will you give us your permission to go where we must?"

"Yes, my lovely," Silverberry said, as she produced the Murien and placed it on the table. "I have read the Murien already, so the portal to Garama Aethoros is now open."

"Garama Aethoros?" Janorra asked, "The Fifth World?"

Silverberry nodded. "The Aeldar Wives the Simal seeks are hidden in the deepest and darkest places in that abode, by one called Migdal. The Simal you stole, has woken them up. They are waiting for it to be brought to them."

*Then maybe I should be glad it is no longer in my hands?* Janorra shivered. Her worst fears were confirmed. *The Simal has come here to find the Aeldar Riddles.* "I no longer have it," she confessed, although she sensed Silverberry already knew this. She then asked, "How do you know for sure that they are awake?" She yawned, and despite the seriousness of what she was being told, she desired nothing more than to sleep.

"They used magic at Bothgar's tomb, very recently. I felt them do it. Long ago I slew Bothgar as punishment for theft, but they had taken from him what he himself had stolen. I have waited for them to awaken, and now, finally, they have."

"What did they steal?"

"The last page of *The Prophecy of Rithguar.*"

"Can you tell me, my assistant Sezareal, is she taking the Simal to the Aeldar Wives?"

"I will help you, if you agree to do one thing for me," Silverberry said. "Take the last page of the prophecy and give it to that foolish Ruik. It is part of his thread to return it to my sisters. It is the only reason I let him live." She sighed with anticipated relief. "Then, I might at last go home to my sisters and rest." She cackled, as though sensing Janorra's thoughts. "They will offer you the prophecy, you will see."

Fresh dread filled Janorra, and a new wave of exhaustion hit her. *I have to enter Garama Aethoros? I do not want to go there.*

"They do not yet have the Simal," Silverberry said, as though she was again reading Janorra's very own thoughts. "Sezareal waits at the entrance to Garama Aethoros, you must go and find her and fetch it. You will know what to do, when the time is right." She paused, and added, "Oh, there is one more little favour you can do for me." She pointed at the empty cradle in the pair of bronze hands. "If you find the little bauble that completes this set, have one of your companions, Scarand, yes he will do, have him return it to me, and I will richly reward you."

"What about the Simal?" Janorra asked, "do you also seek that?"

A look of horror spread across Silverberry's face, but she only spoke when she had calmed a little. "No, do not bring it near me, that is the reason when you have it, and you find my lost bauble, have the Davari bring it to me."

"Where is the entrance to Garama Aethoros?" Janorra asked, feeling she already knew the answer.

"The entrance is within a fortress built by the Elves long ago, a fortress then stolen and corrupted by those that now hide there, to mask the gate. The one you call Sezareal, waits outside. You must go to her, take the Simal from her, and then choose the path to take, for many will open up before you."

"How do you know these things?" Janorra asked, as she fought the tiredness and the urge to yawn.

"This thread was written in the Murien, a long time ago. There are many threads, numerous possibilities all based upon the choices you will make. Your fate is not decided, until you choose your path."

"I do not want this responsibility, it was never supposed to be like this," Janorra said, struggling to keep her eyes open as the weariness upon her increased.

"But it is like this," Silverberry said. She then finished packing her pipe, lit it with a match, sucked in the smoke, and blew it back out again making a series of smoke rings, each one of which formed a strange symbol in the air. "Look," she said, as she placed her other hand on the globe. "The Murien shows one thread, *Fabérn,* my little bauble here, shows other possibilities. *Fobéarn,* which is lost inside Garama Aethoros, can show me more. All thinkable destinies are like mere smoke, they might vanish, and new ones appear. The smoke only shows potentials, not certainties, my lovely."

Janorra looked at the symbols in awe, her tiredness briefly leaving her. "High Vakkan," she said respectfully.

Silverberry nodded, and studied the symbol. The black globe, *Fabérn*, hummed and dimly shone, and she stared into it. "Many throughout the Nine Worlds fear the return of the Aeldar, my lovely. Their return must be stopped, or slowed down. Even though you have been chosen by Ashareth, the High Maiden and daughter of En-Sof, some in deeper realms still doubt you are the right one to fulfil this charge."

"I'll happily let another take over this task," Janorra replied. "I saw Ashareth, in a rare place of beauty in the Deadlands. She only gave me the task of taking the Simal and handing it over to a member of the Tarath Guëan to take to the Baothein. It was only out of respect for her, and my desire to escape from that cursed temple, that I accepted. I did not expect to it to all go so wrong. I am not strong enough for the fate of worlds to rest solely on my shoulders."

Silverberry cackled thoughtfully and softly. "This task was given to you by Ashareth, so you can never be alone. When you feel your weakest, that is when you are in fact the strongest." She smiled. "Not all allies are friends, and not all foes are enemies."

"That doesn't make sense to me," Janorra said. The energy coming from *Fabérn* caused the weariness to suddenly leave her and she felt invigorated.

Silverberry cackled as she sucked in more smoke and blew it out in the form of another symbol. "There can be collaboration between opposite powers, for who or what is good or evil is never easily discerned at first. Two powerful sides can work together, for a common goal, which is then the starting point where the real battle between them begins. What is happening, is how it is supposed to be."

"I still don't understand," Janorra said.

"Then listen, very carefully," Silverberry answered, after which she sucked in more smoke and blew it into the air forming another letter, as she stared again into the *Fabérn* which was dimly lit and humming. Janorra again felt fresh energy pulsate through her each time the dim light in the globe shone and it hummed.

Silverberry cackled softly again. "The Baothein want the Simal. They conspired with you to steal it. They sent the Seeress Ashara, named after the goddess, did they not, to find you in the Deadlands?"

"Yes, after my vision of Ashareth, that was when Ashara found me," Janorra admitted softly.

Silverberry stared into the *Fabérn* for a long while before speaking again. "It is wearisome to consider all possible outcomes, but we must. The Baothein are not united on this matter. Some of them want to hide the Simal, and forever deny the Aeldar their return. Others among them want to use it, they wish to seek unknown mysteries and therefore seek the location of the other wives to learn their riddles, and sit at the feet of the Aeldar as students. Most among them, want to find the riddles, but only with the desire to summon each of the Aeldar in turn, so they can slay them with ancient Arkooms. Others, even among the Baothein, wish to summon them to worship them as the Aeldar Cult even has followers there. Some foolish ones, a very few, even believe they can use the Simal to control the Aeldar, to use them for a cause of little importance to others apart from themselves." Silverberry went silent, and stared into the globe for another long period before speaking again. "There are many paths, many choices, each one has the same end; the Aeldar will return to this world." She paused, and then asked, "Do you trust the Baothein to use the Simal wisely? Are you confident you know their true motive? Dark is the human heart, and many secrets and lies there are within it, for a sickness spreads among your race, a sickness of the soul."

"I do not know any other place where it would be safe," Janorra answered honestly. "What they do with it, once I hand it to them, is no longer my concern. Ashareth told me to take it to them."

Silverberry sucked in yet more smoke and blew it into the air forming more letters, merging with the others. The dim light in the *Fabérn* intensified, as did the humming sound. "You and the Baothein were tricked," she murmured, after which she coughed. "They foolishly hired those whose nature is deceit and lies. The one who now boasts he is a *Godslayer*, Azzadan of the Order of Ithkall, never planned to hand over the Simal to the Baothein. You were tricked, and so was he. The Order of Ithkall want to aid the coming of their *Trickster Lord* and his once slain bride, the *Goddess of Chaos*. Master Ishar, also wants to use it to help the Dark Undead, to foment his own power."

"The Dark Undead? I have seen their markings in the Deadlands, but they were old and worn. I had thought such creatures had vanished from the Nine Worlds, or forever slept in tombs deep and unfathomable?"

"Long has she slept, but Queen Velentine, will soon be woken, and she will seek to wake up her husband, Lord Voran. Together, they will awaken the ancient horror that once terrorised Vangalen. Then, many others will be roused from their slumber; the old mysteries are being studied, some will be solved, for new knowledge arises as the old worlds are forced to give up their jealously guarded secrets."

Silverberry wagged her pipe in a telling gesture. "Great events are taking place across the Nine Worlds. You must understand one thing - the Simal has a will of its own. It wanted to come here, to find three more of the Aeldar Wives, to learn *The Riddles*, for it wants to acquire new knowledge, and for a while wishes the Aeldar to be its teacher."

"When I took it, I did not know the Simal would use me, to bring it to Aeldar Wives. I only wanted to escape the place of my suffering, and that is the only reason I agreed to take on such a task."

Silverberry smiled. "You have my permission to enter the forbidden part of the forest. My son will not harm you because you have taken the milk." She looked sternly at Janorra. "You will not be the first to enter that fortress, nor to enter Garama Aethoros."

*I do not plan to enter Garama Aethoros, if the Simal waits outside,* Janorra thought, and even as she did, tried to suppress it lest Silverberry become aware of her intention. Nevertheless, thoughts intruded her mind. *The Baothein can take it there if they wish; I just want to hand the Simal over to them.*

Silverberry cackled. "During the long years many adventurous fools have come to the forest. Those who foolishly wandered into that part of the forest without my permission, my son hunted them and was the source of their demise. Some, I gave permission, to ease my boredom, and though I doubted they would succeed, I hope at least one of them might find my lost *Fobéarn*. They never left, if they did, but I was entertained as I imagined their doom at the hands of Migdal, the one who guards the Aeldar Wives, or his passing from these worlds by theirs. I showed them a way to enter his lair, opened the portal for them, but none of them ever left." She curled her nose up in disgust. "I knew it was beyond their abilities, but I hoped they would slay him so that they could take the prophecy from the Aeldar Wives, and return to me *Fobéarn*. It is Migdal's will and desire that has corrupted this part of the forest, as a deterrent for many who otherwise would come."

Silverberry inhaled and exhaled yet more smoke, forming fresh symbols. "The Ashura chose you to take the Simal to the Baothein, but heed my words. The Simal will seek to do what it wants; you must learn how to stop it. You must control it, not allow it to control you. Even the Baothein do not understand the depth and scope of the Simal's trickery, or its true power. You must learn to thwart its will, even as you do its will, for that is the only way it can be stopped."

"How do I do that, thwart its will?" Janorra asked.

Silverberry laughed. "That, I cannot tell you, for it breaks the rules of the eternal game, and victory, whoever wins, must be won within the rules, or else it all starts over again."

"This is no game!" Janorra said irritably.

"Oh, it is a game, is it not?" Silverberry asked wryly.

"Then whose side are you on?" Janorra asked her suspiciously.

"My own," the crone said, after which she sucked in more smoke and blew it into the air forming more letters, leading to the same response as before from the *Fabérn*.

"When all else is gone, the game been won and lost, me and my sisters will still be here. We will weave mores stories to entertain us through the bleakness of the eternal night. We never take sides anymore; hence the true powers that be neither trust nor doubt us."

Silverberry inhaled more smoke, and blew more smoke symbols. Each time she inhaled and blew out smoke, new letters were formed, as the old ones disappeared. Whenever the light in the *Fabérn* dimmed and the humming sound disappeared, Janorra felt another wave of tiredness hit her, but as the crone inhaled and blew the smoke into the air forming other letters, thus animating the globe again, she felt fresh energy pulsate through her.

"One named Horin will send others to assist you, strange allies you will find, ones you would not expect. One day, into the Labyrinth you must go."

The mention of the Labyrinth stirred new fears within Janorra. She had recently learnt that the Wild Hunt sailed Norvaskun, travelling above the roof of the Labyrinth along the waterways of the Underglow, looking for places where their moleworm, who swam with them, could burrow through to the surface of the earth. *They have already nearly caught me once, why would I go to where they are?* "I do not know the way into the Labyrinth, and the legends says it was sealed by En-Sof. Only his guardians know where the entrances and exits are. Besides, those who hunt me, sail in the canals upon its roof. Why would I wish to go into the Labyrinth, even if it were possible?"

"You may not have a choice," Silverberry said after which she inhaled from her pipe, blew out the smoke, and studied the letter it formed. "You were wise to send the black arrow outside of the forest with the dwarf, where she disposed of it. They are tracking their arrow, and will soon find it, but only then discover they were deceived. You have won time, but into the Labyrinth you must eventually go, for that is a path woven for you, but fraught with danger that route will be. But first, journey to where the ice and snow sits over the land, you will."

The embers in the pipe glowed as Silverberry sucked on it, blowing out smoke as before and reading the signs before looking into the *Fabérn* which was reacting.

"You will soon have few choices," Silverberry said, "but you will not go into the lands of ice and snow, or the Labyrinth alone. Destiny is giving you help, but I see that some of those who journey with you might not survive." A wave of curiosity swept over her face. She looked through the open door towards Gilly who was still lightly snoring and sleeping peacefully in the next room.

Janorra followed Silverberry's gaze, and said, "Do not speak to me of the fate of any I travel with now or in the future. I do not know any of these companions well, but I would not wish the knowledge of their fates to rest with me. I do not wish to know."

Silverberry ignored her and sucked in more smoke from her pipe, and blew out another symbol, read it, and stared into the *Fabérn*.

"The destiny of none is fixed. En-Sof would not allow it to be so for then there is no challenge and neither he nor the others could ever prove their worth, and my kind would grow bored of the threads we weave. I see only shadows of possible futures, not certain ones. You are always free to choose your path but you are not free from the consequences of your choice, and in your choices the fate and destiny of worlds now rest."

"En-Sof abandoned this world long ago, and has left all life at the mercy of malign powers," Janorra said somewhat bitterly. "I have read the books on the *Game of Gods*, but I believed it mere fiction. Yet, you speak as though this is all merely part of some cosmic game to entertain the gods? For what might be a game to them is real to us, we suffer, and the stakes are costly."

Silverberry answered after she drew another mouthful of smoke, and blowing it out formed yet another symbol. "Some call it a game, most call it a war. Conquest is often savage and the consequences for the conquered terrible. En-Sof himself, even the Nameless One, have risked their very existence on the outcome - they will be no more if they lose, or have already lost. War or game, the costs are high and eternal for all participants. But not all powers or players are malign ones. You know much, my lovely, but have much more still to learn about the true nature of existence and reality."

Janorra looked at the fresh letters formed by the smoke from Silverberry's pipe. The smoke disappeared, and an image of a door appeared in the globe. Flashing images of a possible future revealed themselves in the *Fabérn*. She saw a vision of Gilly and another dwarf, a male, running and fleeing for their lives deep in the Labyrinth, pursued by a terrible darkness in the form of a primeval demon. The voices of the two dwarves echoed in the air.

"We're trapped Marki, me dear," Gilly said, her voice trembling with fear, "but Gaffren's death will not be in vain, and neither shall ours. We have bought Janorra time. She still has a chance to get the Simal to the Baothein." She began to weep. "I so hoped to see our people again, me dear, and to take to them the Sangdalen we found."

"I'm not ready to die yet lass, this way!" Marki said as he swung a large axe into a wooden door, smashing and splintering it, and kicking away the parts that remained. "I'll not lose love as soon as I have found it," he thundered, as he took Gilly by the hand and led her through into a cavern from which there was no escape. Like trapped prey, they waited as the demon approached. "This will be a story to tell the Maidens," Marki roared, as he swung his axe and together, with Gilly, charged the demon.

"For me Gaffren!" Gilly cried out.

The vision slowly faded. It was too much for Janorra, she closed her eyes. "Please, do not show me this or any other possible future for myself or any of these people. My heart faints as it is and will need little excuse for withdrawing from my path. I beg you, do not show me the end of any path I must choose for I will not know which is the right one to take when the time comes."

"I see love in her future, and then the terrible pain of loss," Silverberry said with a resigned cackle as she stared at the last vestige of the image. "But nothing is fixed. The Labyrinth might be her doom, and that of the one which she will soon come to love, or it might not be," she said. "There are some destinies that no choices can avoid, but still nothing in the future is fixed until that time of choice arrives. One day soon you will understand this."

"Stop," Janorra pleaded. "Please, stop."

Silverberry grew irate, her features twisting callously. "What you have started cannot be stopped. See further, look deeper beyond the fate of those you travel with," she said coldly and harshly. "You only see what might be, not what will be. The fate of the Simal is what you must focus on, not the mortality and fates of those who will aid you to take it where it must go. Sacrifice them when you must, if a higher purpose you will serve." She paused, and then grew calm as she said, "There are many futures, many outcomes; I cannot weave any certainties into their fates. All I see are possibilities, made true by their choices."

Janorra looked at the new symbol which Silverberry formed with another puff of smoke. "Enough of visions," she said with a quavering voice. "They serve no purpose but to torment me with new fears, and enough of those I have already."

Silverberry put her pipe on the table. The embers glowed brightly, and then went out. The globe, the *Fabérn*, grew silent and dim. "Then I won't show you more my lovely, but I can give you one piece of advice," she said as she smiled and closed her eyes. "The more the three brides lie, the more you should trust them. One tries to hide, one tries to cheat, one plays Harendale and the other two weeps. They seek not what they desire most, but that they shall find, for it comes to them. When you give it to them, have peace of mind."

"I do not understand," Janorra said, as tiredness and exhaustion swept over her once more. "You only speak in puzzles."

"You will understand my lovely, when the time comes, and the destiny of worlds hangs on your choice."

"I am so tired, I wish only to sleep now," Janorra said, yawning.

Silverberry looked at her and said ominously, "Your companions will not wake this night, for he does not come for them, but my son does desire you. It is hard for me to control him at times. He will not bother you in the forest, but he has bargained with me that if you let him in here, he shall take you. Do not, under any circumstance, answer any knock at the door this dark night should you awaken to the sound of it. Ignore any tapping at the window. Your doom is your own, if you open the door, and let him, or one of the *Untamed Ones* into my house." She narrowed her yellowed eyes and began to chant a slow and terrible song.

Janorra, exhausted, depressed and afraid, stood and joined her companions in the adjacent room. She lay down on the bed roll on the floor next to Gilly, and with the haunting song of Silverberry, drifting from the next room into her ears Janorra fell into a very deep sleep which was immediately disturbed by dark dreams and frightful omens.

\*         \*         \*

"We have rogues in the house!" Senzas said with a voice that rang out with accustomed mockery.

"But not fools!" Sasna retorted.

The deceased patrician's manor house was already a shadowy reflection of what it had been the last time Sasna had visited. The heavy silk tapestries that had once adorned the walls of the main hall had been torn down, revealing plaster now covered in crude graffiti formed in words and images. The floor, once covered in rich carpets, was bare boards, littered with cups, plates and uneaten scraps of food. The only remaining visage of its former splendour were the ships' masts, stained and polished, that formed the beams of the lofty vaulted ceiling. A fire in the wide stone fireplace dispelled the dampness of the dawn. Candles in a great silver candelabrum lit the hall, and threw shadows onto the twenty or so pirates who, with cutlasses drawn, surrounded Sasna and Farir.

Senzas sat in a mahogany chair. Beside him sat an unresponsive girl, bruised and beaten. He raised a goblet gallantly to Sasna, and drank unceremoniously. "*Never trust a Seesnari*," he sneered through a curled lip.

"I had an arrangement with your partner Marlo, to arrange passage for me to Harwind. I paid for it in gold. I wish to speak with Lord Vansoth."

"Marlo?" Senzas laughed. "I have not seen him of late. Things have changed since that agreement was made. I now work for Captain Redboots, and she wishes to take you for ransom."

"You will answer to men more powerful than you, if either I or my brother are harmed," Sasna threatened. "My uncle, Saroth Arnton, the High Warden of Ashgiliath, Conqueror of the Seven Towers of Samothrane, Slayer of Barnoth the Wicked, has a message I must speak only to the great Sea Lord, Erik Vansoth!"

Senzas snorted derisively. "Your uncle is a fool to send you into a den of iniquity such as this. I have seen none of the gold you say you paid to Marlo for your intended journey, and he and I were partners in many a crime. What payment do you have for me and my men?"

"Deliver my brother and I safely to Harwind, and help us get safe passage to Lord Vansoth, and I will see you amply rewarded," Sasna said.

Senzas pointed to the twenty or so pirates still circling her and Farir, and said, "It is said you are yet to know a man, Lady Sasna, so, instead, should I not let my men take from you whatever payment they see fit in return for your lives, and only if you please them, then consider your request?"

"Crawl back to the sea you yellow-headed dog," Farir shouted as he started forward.

"Back!" Senzas' voice cracked like a whip, and he threw the goblet he held at Farir. It missed, and clattered harmlessly on the floor. "One more step and I'll gut you like a river fish," he snarled.

From out of the shadows in the hall, previously unseen, a deformed boy crawled out. Sasna immediately recognised him. *Gnarn!*

"With respect Master Senzas," Gnarn said, cowering as though expecting a beating any minute. "Before Gnarn joined the *River Queen*, Gnarn was cabin boy to the *Jolly Raider*. I heard the great Lord Vansoth say to my captain that he wished to negotiate with the Seesnari. Lady Sasna is their envoy, I think Captain Redboots was not aware of this or she would not have issued the orders. Gnarn thinks Lord Vansoth will make you pay dearly if you harm her, for he wills to speak with her."

"You lie, worm," Senzas said threateningly, as he stood to his feet.

Gnarn cowered even further, and whimpering, said, "Gnarn is too afraid of the gallant warrior of the seas named Senzas to tell a lie." He whelped in near panicked hysteria as Senzas approached him. "But Gnarn is more afraid of the great Sea Lord Erik Vansoth. If Gnarn did not speak to the gallant Senzas what he knows, Gnarn fears terrible punishment for his silence."

Senzas kicked Gnarn hard in the ribs, and then stared at him for a full minute as the deformed boy wheezed, cried and whimpered, protesting he was telling the truth. Senzas then looked at Sasna, and stared at her for another full minute before saying. "Erik Vansoth requested this meeting?"

"He did," Sasna lied.

Senzas and some of his men muttered quietly among themselves.

"If you lie, then Redboots will have her salt-price from us all." Reluctantly, he then said, "A ship leaves for Harwind tonight. You will be on it. We will take you to Erik Vansoth." He then pointed a finger at her, "But first, you will visit the rookery, and see to it that a message is sent to your uncle to deliver me payment in gold of a thousand gold coins. On that condition, I will let you go."

"Very well," Sasna said, relief flooding through every fibre of her being.

Senzas looked at Gnarn. "You will accompany her to the rookery, worm, and see to it the message is sent."

"Gnarn will do as you bid, gallant Senzas," he replied.

Sasna and Farir, accompanied by Gnarn, left the manor house and entered the streets of Berecoth. The rain had stopped, and the dawn sun lit up the sky.

"Gnarn is a good liar, mother," he said softly to Sasna. "Gnarn has never seen the one they call Erik Vansoth, but the ungallant Senzas is scared enough of him not to take that chance."

Sasna lowered herself to one knee, and gently kissed Gnarn on the forehead. "You are a good boy Gnarn, mother is glad to see you again."

# Chapter Thirty-Nine: *Strange Visions*

*The Wytches strode through the halls of Hell;*
*Across their paths grim shadows fell*
*Many a victim with their jaws agape -*
*Were to see their fate when it was far too late.*
*Woes betide those who ignore the tales*
*About the Wytches who stalk through the halls of Hell.*
**Old Bruthon Ballad.**

*When* he looked at Sarkisi, naked and laying on the bed, smiling at him, inviting him to join her, all Imrand could think about was Bahri, the leader of the Ikma slavers. He imagined Bahri's face, twisted and leering whenever he had taken Sarkisi by force. The memory revolted him. His member grew flaccid at the thought. Saying nothing, Sarkisi used her hand to work Imrand back to full manhood, but her attempts were in vain. The more Imrand looked at her, felt her grip on his shaft, the more the thought of Bahri lurking in his head sickened him. "I can't," he told her. He pushed her hand away from his groin and held her close. "I am sorry."

She wrapped her arms around him and stroked his hair. "It does not matter," she said, her eyes reddening with tears. "We are together, that is enough."

Imrand tried to keep his rage and frustration in check as he hugged Sarkisi but could not prevent the tears from spilling down his cheeks, onto her shoulder. She drew the sheets over them with a free hand, and he nestled closer, resting his head upon her breast as she stroked his hair. His hands gripped her throat. He began to squeeze. She said nothing as his iron grip choked the life from her.

Imrand awoke startled, sweat beading across his forehead and rolling onto his cheeks. He shot bolt upright, rubbing his eyes. It was not the first time he had been tormented by this dream. It took a few moments before the vagueness of sleep lifted and he became aware of his surroundings. He was in a large cage. Above the cage a lantern swung slightly in a warm breeze. He immediately felt the rage and panic of a caged wolf.

He stood up and noticed a deformed boy rocking to and thro on the ground in a foetal position whilst sucking his thumb. At the far end of the cage he could make out Sarkisi. She was gently speaking to somebody in a soft voice, but he could not see who it was in the dim light, so he took a few steps closer. It was the Seesnari woman, the slaver-trader, the one called Sasna.

"You!" he shrieked menacingly and threateningly as he rushed forward. Both women turned their heads. Sarkisi leapt to her feet and stood before him and the woman, who huddled into the corner of the cage. She grabbed a hold of him to stop him from rushing forward and throttling Sasna. Rage bubbled inside of Imrand. "I'm going to twist her neck off," he said threateningly.

"No, my love, you are not," Sarkisi said gently but firmly as she put her hand on his chest and pushed him away. A red mist descended upon Imrand; he clenched his fists.

"Move out of my way," he said through gritted teeth.

Sarkisi stepped towards him and tenderly stroked his cheek. "Stop and look where we are," she said as gently and firmly as before. "This is a place of illusions."

He looked around him, and the image of Sasna vanished, and was replaced by an image of a leering Bahri who stared at Sarkisi. Imrand lunged towards it, and tried to grab him, but the image vanished as if a mist, and he seized at nothing but air, but then Gerdar appeared, and laughed mockingly at him. The image of Gerdar and the deformed boy sucking his thumb also disappeared.

"They are not real," Sarkisi said to him. "They are not real, my love."

Imrand held Sarkisi by the shoulders, she felt physical.

"Are you real?" he asked her.

"Yes, my love," she answered, and then looked outside of the cage, "but he is just a shadow."

Imrand followed her gaze. Outside of the cage, a hunched figure, dressed from head to toe in a dusty robe with a hood that partially covered his face, was sitting rocking back and forth in a rocking chair, a rusty great-broadsword across his knees, which he was stroking with a taloned finger, making a rasping scraping noise. Two black, fierce and angry eyes stared at Imrand from beneath the hood.

Imrand gasped, taking a short step backwards. His rage towards the imaginary images redirected itself towards the figure. He gathered his wits quickly and ran towards the bars. They were old and rusted, but still strong. He tried to bend them, rattle them, but there was no give at all.

"What are you?" he asked the mysterious figure.

The creature just continued rocking back and forth, saying nothing. Sarkisi joined Imrand and took him by the hand, leading him to the far corner of the cage. She whispered to him, "He only spoke to me once, when you were still unconscious. He said he will take us to them soon, and that we are not to be afraid. He said we could trust him, if we agree to help them."

"Who is he? I'll not let him take you. I won't let him touch you," Imrand said intimidatingly.

"Do you hear that you foul thing?" he shouted at the figure that still just rocked back and forth.

"You won't be able to stop him," Sarkisi said. "There is a powerful magic in this place, I feel it, sense it and see it." She looked around in awe.

"Are we dead? Are we in Hell?" Imrand asked her.

The thought of it made Sarkisi smile compassionately. "We are very much alive my love," she said as she stroked his hair and then too looked at the hunched man. "We will survive this and endure what we must. If we can find out what he wants, we reason with him. I feel in my heart we do not need to be afraid in this place, though my eyes and the sights I see try to convince me otherwise."

Imrand took some deep breaths and studied his surroundings more closely. "Have you seen those Wytches since we have been here? Is it they, he will take us too?"

He watched her narrowly and saw her change colour slightly. "No, I haven't seen them, but yes, I think they are the ones we must meet. Before you woke, he kept talking to himself, saying he was but shadow and was trying to remember." She smiled at Imrand. "Look at us, we have not yet been harmed, that must be a good sign?" He could hear the uncertainty in her voice.

Before he could answer her, the figure spoke. His voice was husky, deep, old. "Who are you? Why have you come to this place?"

"Who are you?" Imrand bluntly countered.

The figure slowly stood up, and when he reached his full height, he was a half-size taller than Imrand. The hood slipped from his head, and the robe opened. His face was utterly without colour, his skin stretched like torn silk over bone, so that every feature of his skull could be seen. He looked very tired. Around the red pupils the sclera of his eyes was as black as night, and they burned with hatred so fierce it took Imrand's breath

505

away. Tufts of withered hair sprang from the creature's scalp. His clothes were withered and torn with age and his body frail, the skin stretched so tight that every bone and inner organ was revealed. The heart pumped slowly and mightily and looked like it would burst from the chest.

Imrand felt a numb heaviness weigh on his limbs, "Who are you, what is your name?" he demanded. A burning wind blew past him. "Who are you?" he asked, as both he and Sarkisi fell to their knees.

"I remember. I am Migdal, the Lord of the Seraphim who stayed in the Nine Worlds," the creature said with a voice booming with pride and pain, as two wings previously hidden unfolded from his back. They were tattered and torn and as ragged as his clothes. "I was guardian of the Simal, hidden deep in the Labyrinth, up until it was stolen from me by a man named Mazdek. My last charge is guardian of the Aeldar Wives, who alone know the Aeldar Riddles that will call and lead their husbands from the Void. I will not fail in this task, as I did in the other. You will assist me."

"Why would we assist you?" Imrand asked.

Migdal laughed, showing a mouth full of sharp fangs.

"Come quickly," he said, "before I fade and forget." He turned and walked away into the shadows.

Sarkisi took hold of Imrand's arm with both her hands. He stood to his feet, and she along with him, as the door to the cage opened by itself.

"Well, you are right, we haven't been harmed so far," Imrand said to Sarkisi as they stepped out of the cage and followed Migdal. "We will at least hear what that thing has to say."

# Chapter Forty: *A Scorched Beard*

*The wyvern is a winged serpentine creature with two eagle-like legs and a barbed tail, the latter of which is usually depicted in art as curled or interwoven. An early example of such art, and perhaps my own personal favourite, is upon the standard of the now disbanded infamous Forty-fourth Legion, depicted in the Kappian Tapestry. Wyverns are pestilent, vicious and envious creatures, and I cannot for the life of me understand why anybody would want to fly on such a foul beast. It also mystifies me that when they are used in a coat of arms, or standard, it symbolises the overthrow of tyranny and evil. Wyverns are visually related to the now extinct Dragon and are often confused with the same.*

*A Wyvern, as described by the Bruthon Missionary Edegal in the Year 9421, after his visit to the Kappian Museum of Monsters as described in his book; Magical, Mystical and Truly Terrifying Creatures.*

*The* horses reared. Marki and Talain kept them under control, although Maraya jumped from her saddle and began to pray and worship as the darkened figure in the sky drew closer. From the brush behind them, came the shouts of the bodyguard protecting Falamore's two sons. The riders had passed through an upland scrub of gorse and heather, growing in a swathe of sandy soil. They were being attacked by something both unexpected and terrifying - an airborne wyvern.

At the first sign of the wyvern, obeying Hozain's barked orders, the princes' bodyguards had scurried them to the shelter and safety of nearby trees. Marki, Maraya and Talain, who had been a few hundred yards ahead of the others, were on their own, caught in the open.

Maraya was on her knees, hands raised towards the wyvern as it descended. She sang and prayed in a tongue unknown to Marki. After its initial swoop, the wyvern landed on the ground in front of Marki with a loud thud.

A near relation to the now extinct dragons, the yellow-scaled beast was far from its usual hunting grounds in the western hills and mountains of the Tarenmoors. It was also donned in armour, with the raven insignia that Marki had learnt showed it belonged to Queen Sharwin. The rider upon it was a skin-clad female barbarian in horned helmet and scale-mail corselet. She seemed momentarily confused as to whom her first target should be, Talain or Marki, or the men seeking cover under the trees. But when she saw Maraya, Marki saw recognition in her eyes. It was a rescue attempt.

The few brief moments it had taken the wyvern rider to observe the situation, was enough for Marki. A seasoned warrior, he had no such hesitation and knew any benefit, however slight, needed to be taken advantage of. With a grunt, he threw his leg over his pony's neck and dropped to the ground, nimbly removing *Old Trusty* as he did so whilst beginning to charge the beast and rider.

The rider on the wyvern, seeing Marki as the most immediate threat, snapped the reins. The angry beast rose up, spread its wings, and beat them to take off. Marki knew that if the beast became airborne again, it would have the advantage. He launched *Old Trusty* through the air with all of his might. The axe flew truly, striking the golden creature squarely at the join of shoulder and wing. Instantly, the wing dropped, and the creature stumbled and failed in its attempt to take to the air. The injured wyvern roared, reared up on its hind legs and inhaled deeply, making a strange clicking sound.

"Move dwarf," Talain shouted from somewhere behind him.

Marki leapt to the left, behind a small sandy clump, as a searing blast of flame cut through the air, scorching the ground where he had been standing moments before. He could feel the heat singeing the hair on his head and beard, and he had to pat himself down to put them out, as he continued rolling, unable to see the wyvern. He could smell the acrid smoke and blackened soil as he heard the wyvern roar wildly.

Marki launched himself upright; the breeze had blown the smoke around him and it sat over the now scattered clump of sand, making him cough violently. The breeze swirled causing the smoke to rise into the air. His cover was gone, the clump alone not enough to hide behind. The wyvern and its rider spotted him. They both fixed their eyes on him. The wyvern began to suck in more air. Marki was about to be targeted with another blast of flames, only this time there was nowhere to dive behind, and he did not have the momentum to run from the path where the flames would surely come any second.

"Come on then, miserable wee beasty," he said under his breath as he stood defiantly staring at the beast and his doom.

Suddenly, a spear sliced through the air, piercing the wyvern in the throat. The creature leapt backwards, staggered and thrashed about as it hit the ground and began to thrash in pain. Its rider was thrown from the saddle. The wyvern screamed in pain and fury, gagged and choked. It shuddered for a long moment and then fell still in death.

Marki looked at Talain who had ridden up behind him. Her shot had been true. He wiped the perspiration from his brow and tried to rein in the look of relief on his face and replace it with a neutral expression.

"That was nay a bad shot lass," he said, as she rode up next to him.

Talain smiled with glee, "That's the first time I have saved a dwarf's arse, and the first time I have slain a wyvern."

Marki exchanged his neutral expression for one of annoyance. "I had the situation under control lass," he said grumpily.

Their conversation was interrupted by the wails and cries of Maraya, who was deeply distressed at the death of the wyvern.

Noise from the side indicated the princes and their bodyguard had left their shelter and were closing in. The two princes and the bodyguard reined in as they regarded Marki and Talain, and the dead wyvern. Hozain had ridden towards the fallen rider, who had not moved since falling from the saddle. He dismounted, drew his sword, decapitated the rider, and picking up the dripping head he led his horse to where they were all standing. He threw the head at the feet of Marki. The rider had a face that was sunburned and weather-beaten.

"Are you sure she was dead? We could have questioned her," Marki asked with some irritation.

Hozain's expression darkened as he looked up at the sky. "She would slow us down. She was just a scout. Probably saw an opportunity to make a name for herself by killing the dwarf who would challenge the *Raven Queen*, and rescuing her daughter. They do not usually scout an area alone. We need to get swiftly to camp before more come."

"Then at least you could have helped us fight it," Talain said somewhat accusingly. "I may have many lives but the dwarf only has one."

Hozain did not look impressed. "My job is to look after the princes, not protect you or the dwarf," he said, as he mounted and spurred his horse on in the direction of the camp. The princes and bodyguard followed.

Marki walked over to the wyvern and retrieved his axe from its broken and ruined body, as well as Talain's spear which he handed to her without comment, only a whistle of respect. His pony, a well-trained mare, had been all too happy to run away from the predator, but returned at his call. He mounted and looked back at the wyvern. "I played a part but it was your kill. That head would make a good trophy on any wall, it's a shame we lack the time to take it to a taxidermist to turn it into one." He jerked the reins of his pony and cantered off.

"Bring the girl," he shouted to Talain.

Talain made sure Maraya was mounted and Marki heard her shrieking and wailing as she passed the dead wyvern. It would be about a half day's ride to where the legion was waiting, on the Plains of Thurogen. It was not an unpleasant ride through the grass of the plains. In fact, so far, except for the wyvern, the Tarenmoors had not proved to be as inhospitable as Marki and the other commanders had feared, but Marki was too experienced in the ways of the world to be naive enough to think that would last. He knew that as well as a place of beauty, it had the potential to be bleak, unforgiving and harsh. The journey to the Kingdom of Thurogen had been mostly without incident for the legion though they had seen signs they were being watched and followed most of the time. However, Marki had a deep-seated feeling that the presence of a scout on a wyvern, meant bad news was not far away.

Marki and Talain rode alone behind the others. She explained to him that there were vast regions of unexplored land in the Tarenmoors and that the civilized kingdoms like Thurogen, whose people were less highly cultured than those of the Empire, though large in extent, occupied a comparatively tiny portion of just one area of the whole region. She told him that the Thurogenite civilization was clearly crumbling; their army was composed largely of untrained farmers and landholders who owed fealty to King Falamore and only took up arms when called, although Effgard's men were fierce warriors who in times of peace often broke into smaller groups and turned to banditry raiding other kingdoms far away. He listened with interest as she told him that beyond the borders of the civilised kingdoms in the central Tarenmoors, there stretched wild and barren expanses of grassland and then deserts. Past the grasslands and deserts, in the jungles, and among the mountains, lived scattered clans and tribes of primitive savages. Talain even suggested that some of these tribes were pre-human in nature.

The remainder of the journey to the camp of the Third Legion was without incident, much to Marki's relief. He had always taken pride in his beard and hair, both of which had been badly burnt in the battle with the wyvern. It caused him embarrassment as one of the legion's scouts excitedly rode up to him and his companions as they reached the outskirts of the camp.

"What happened to you, Commander Marki?" the surprised man asked.

"Does Lord Borach still live?" Marki asked grumpily, ignoring the obvious.

"He does," the man said wearily, "but his suffering is great."

Marki could tell the man had more to say. "Out with-it man, what other news should you speak?"

"A massive army has been spotted encamped a few days' ride to the west.

*That would be Sharwin's army,* Marki thought.

The man continued. "They have airborne wyverns and a multitude of barbarians." The man sounded uncertain as he added, "They also have mercenaries, mounted knights, and worse, they have Chatti and Gragor among them."

Marki scratched his burnt stubble of a beard. He had met one wyvern, and without griffins, a number of them would be a problem to deal with. He reassured himself knowing that they could still be slain. Mounted knights would be a problem, but the legion had met such foes before and bested them. The barbarians were probably an unorganised rabble. But the legion had never met Chatti or Gragor before, and they were reputed to be fierce and difficult foes. "What else?" he barked at the scout.

"They are building siege engines."

Talain interjected. "Sharwin is no fool. She knows it would be foolish for them to fight many battles. How can she defeat a foe that keeps resurrecting and coming at them whilst their numbers weaken? She knows victory depends on winning the first battle, on the Plains of Thurogen. She will then besiege Thurog Tor. She wants control of the Obelisk."

"Are you sure?" Marki asked her. "The walls of Thurog Tor are vast and formidable. Breeching them will be no easy task."

"I'm sure," Talain said. "The siege engines of men would have difficulty breeching such walls, but not those built and operated by Gragor. Sharwin will wait until we are tired from taking out the first two kings, and then she will move to meet us. If she wins, she will throw everything at Thurog Tor, and with Gragor assisting them, it will fall quickly."

*Then blast that fool of a crone's wart Falamore for enraging more foes than we can handle*, Marki thought to himself. They had little choice but to defeat the two other kings Falamore had started war upon, or they might flank them when they met Sharwin's army, and that would be a disaster.

Mark spurred his pony, rode into the camp and quickly instructed some victuallers to make sure Hozain, the princes and the bodyguards were given tents and refreshments. He did not need to check if the legion was preparing for the battle ahead, he knew Galin and Torach well enough to know that every preparation was being made, and the activity around the camp confirmed they were preparing for what lay ahead.

Marki took Talain and Maraya straight to the tent where Borach was resting. He had been relieved to hear Borach was still alive, but very critical and close to death. There was no time to waste. "Can you journey with him from here, to the Deadlands, and get to the Obelisk lass?" he asked Talain as they passed the guards and entered the tent.

"Yes," Talain said, with an air of uncertainty that Marki would have challenged and pressed, had he not been distracted by the sight before his eyes. Borach was lying on the stretcher surrounded by the surgeon and medics. He was soaked in sweat, and mostly lying still, until he twitched and writhed in agony from spasms whilst the medics held him down. In his temple the veins swelled and throbbed. Torach and Galin were also with him. Torach adjusted the patch over his missing eye, and stared at Talain and Maraya with his good one as they walked in.

"We received the raven and the message. It is good news indeed you sent to us cousin," Galin said.

"Which one is the Seeress, her?" Torach asked Marki, who grunted as he pointed to Talain.

"Yes, it is she. How long does Borach have?"

"A few hours at most," the surgeon said.

"Have we heard word from Alwith?" Marki asked.

Galin shook his head.

"Then we have no choice but to trust he delivered the blade to Armun, or it is at least far enough away not to give him the *Final-death*," he said. *By my gran's blisters I hope you succeeded young Alwith.*

Torach tittered as he looked at Talain. "She does not look like a Seeress," he said.

Marki ignored him. "She will do what we have asked of her. Borach will be dead before sunrise, and she will have to take him to the Obelisk, and then return with him to us. We will not enter battle without him."

Torach sighed. "I have discussed tactics with Effgard. He believes Sharwin will wait for us to make the first move, as not all of her army has yet gathered, for many of her warriors are still besieging the city in the south. It is an advantage for her to wait, but not for us. It would be foolish for her to attack when we are this near to Thurog Tor. But, in case we are wrong, we need to be ready for a defensive stance as they already outnumber us at least six to one."

Torach then walked over to a map spread out on a table and prodded it with his finger. "It would be foolish to leave the fortress city of Highguard intact with forces behind us when we meet this *Raven Queen* in battle," he said. "We must move against them swiftly, and then press on to fight her before her forces from the south join her."

Marki nodded. "We will wait for Borach, and then make the first move. I am betting a lizard's tongue Sharwin will want us tired and weakened from battle before she engages us, so will not make a move whilst we attack Highguard. Its walls are crumbled, we should have a swift victory."

Borach regained his senses and briefly opened his eyes. When he spoke, it was laboured and clearly difficult. "Why must you endlessly talk? Send me to the Deadlands. The sooner there, the faster I will be back." He tried to smile, but coughed instead. He took some deep and difficult breaths and looked at Talain. "I thank you, for assisting me," he said.

"It is my honour," she replied, somewhat nervously.

"There's no point waiting until I die from this poison. Now she is here, kill me," Borach said before he groaned, writhed and twitched in another spasm of agony.

"There are certain rituals that must accompany a forced death like this," Torach said.

"To hell with the rituals," Borach barked, regaining his senses once more. "Treat this as a battle death and be away with the rituals until a more convenient time."

Marki and Galin grunted in agreement.

"You ready lass?" Marki asked Talain.

She nodded nervously. "I thought I would have more time to prepare, but I am ready."

"We are out of time lass. We need him back as soon as possible. I'm not happy at asking this of you, but you will have my never-ending gratitude," Marki said respectfully, and then asked, "How would you like to do this? I am not one for raising a blade to a friend, and I already consider you that, as I do him, so it won't be me. One of the legionnaires will give you a swift soldier's death. I promise you it will be quick."

Talain laughed nervously. "I came prepared," she said. She removed a pouch from under her leather corselet, and took two seeds from it. "Blood does not need to be spilt. With these, it takes only a few moments. It is painless, until the last few seconds."

"What the blazes are they lass?" Marki asked.

"They are seeds from the Lacapaziz plant. They are man-eaters, even their seeds are deadly. With your permission, I will give one to him, and then take one myself."

Marki looked at Galin and Torach, and then at the medics. They all nodded.

"Then be done with it," Borach said to Talain.

Talain placed one of the seeds in Borach's mouth. She then gave him some water, and he drank. She clamped his jaw and forced him to swallow.

"I have another set of boiled armour and weapons in the tomb of the Obelisk," Talain said to Marki. "But keep these ones safe for me dwarf, they always seem to fit me more comfortably than the other set."

"I'll do that lass," Marki replied, and then addressed Borach.

"I will bring clothing, your armour, weapons and a horse. I will be ready for you. I will travel at first light with some of our men and take them to the Obelisk at Thurog Tor. I will wait for you both to resurrect."

Talain went and sat down next to Borach, who had suddenly become peaceful. Colour came back to his face, and he sat up. "I feel no pain," he said softly to her.

"You will shortly, but only for a few seconds, and then it will be over," she replied.

Talain took a deep breath. She placed the other seed in her mouth, drank some water, and swallowed. Her breath started to quicken as did Borach's.

"You haven't old us what the Deadlands are like in this region," Marki said.

Talain struggled to speak, but managed to say. "In case you haven't noticed dwarf, I'm dying here. Time enough to tell you that when I return." She winked at Marki and smiled, and then her face contorted in agony as did Borach's.

"Death is but the doorway to new life. We die today, but shall return again. Journey well, the both of you," Torach said, saying the improvised words of a Kappian prayer. Others in the tent also murmured similar words. Talain and Borach writhed in agony for a few seconds and no more, and then with a long exhale of breath, they both lay still and silent.

The surgeon checked for signs of life. "They're dead," he said. "We will tend to their bodies. Effgard told us they could be sent to Thurog Tor for burial in the tombs."

"See to it," Marki said as his eyes filled with tears. Not wanting the others to see, he discreetly left the tent. Although it would hopefully be no less than a day or so before he would see them again, he felt grief and sadness at watching his two friends die. His grief was momentarily put aside when he saw Hozain, a few tents down, attach a message to a raven he took from a saddlebag and then release the bird into the air. The bird flew up high, circled the camp, and headed west. Marki rushed over to him and demanded, "What was in that message? Who are you sending it too?"

Hozain jumped with fright when Marki spoke. "You startled me," he said, grabbing his chest and drawing in breath.

"Answer my questions, what is in that message and who did you send it too?"

"I am informing the queen that the princes have arrived here safely," Hozain replied.

"Thurog Tor is to the south, that bird flew west," Marki angrily countered.

"It will first deliver a message to Effgard, that I will join the main army tomorrow. It will then get where it needs to go," Hozain retorted back before storming off into his tent and angrily closing the flap.

"Skinny little weasel faced lizard head," Marki muttered under his breath. He then pointed to two legionnaires on patrol in the camp, who were passing by and had noticed the exchange. "Stay extra vigilant this night boys," he warned them.

# Chapter Forty-One: *The Voyage to Grona*

*My dear love,*
*I found the missionary Edegal to be the most obnoxious and irritating man I have ever met, and perhaps this is why I so desperately wanted to prove him wrong on his thesis that Titans are extinct, or perhaps even never even existed. Oh, what a delight it would have been to have seen the smugness wiped from off his face. Sadly, it was not to be. I travelled to Grona Island on the Imperial Ship Resolute. For a whole week we anchored off, in the area it is said some sort of grotesque Titan dwells in a cave. I wore a Neblan, as did the captain, but he simply refused to set foot on the island or let me go to it with a launch. He said that if the beast did exist and we were eaten, the necklace might be destroyed and we would then resurrect inside the prison and forever be trapped there. I suppose he had a point. Anyway, sadly, we saw nothing all week, so returned to the mainland whilst the weather still favoured us. I arrived in Kappia city yesterday. Tomorrow I have my interview with the board of the library, and I am thinking that if I were given the position I formerly wrote and told you about, you might change your mind and move to Kappia? I have seen a lovely little cottage in a small village just a few miles outside of the main city, and I think you will fall in love with it if you come and see it. I will write soon.*
*Your loving husband,*
*Alberto.*
**Magalove: The Lives and Letters of Alberto Temmison.**

*To be happy is to be free, to be free you have to be brave.*
**A Pirate Proverb.**

*Redboot's* ship, the *Red Tide*, crashed through the waves. Two companion ships sailed behind her, the *Red Mist* and the *Red Death*, their masts rising and falling like the keys of a giant's harpsichord. Up ahead a pod of whales surfaced, the sunlight glaring off their wet backs as they spumed spray into the morning sky.

Redboots stood on the plunging prow, screaming with pleasure and beaming with delight as the spray of every blast of brine swept over them. "This is what makes me feel alive," she yelled to Smindy, who grinned with equal enjoyment.

"Azzie, don't you just love this?" Smindy shouted to him as another noisy blast of brine splashed over them.

Azzadan's eyes narrowed and his pulse quickened as he looked at Redboots raising her hands to the sky, grinning with delight and sheer ecstasy at nothing more than the enjoyment of the moment. A wave of emotion washed over him as the prow plunged and the brine soaked his skin and clothes afresh: a jumble of joy; laughter; love; pain; treachery; anger, and most of all, jealousy. He wished he could enjoy such simple pleasures with carefree abandon, but he still could not get over the thought of Erik Vansoth touching Redboots on the night of the Mariners' Ball; the very thought repulsed him and set him in a black mood as bitter rage consumed him. *Perhaps I have mistaken her interest in me as affection*, he thought to himself. He noticed that on the necklace she wore around her neck, two more finger bones adorned it. *She beat Mowett and Mathis at Harendale. I think I love this woman, and hate her for not loving me.*

Azzadan said nothing as he turned from the prow of the ship, and walked the length of the surging deck back to the Great Cabin, where he had spent a part of each day playing Harendale with Sassy or talking with Smindy when she was not busy with the ship's books. He was berthed on the Orlop deck, in the dank, fetid bowel of the ship, just above the hold and below the water-line. He had requested the berth, telling

Redboots that from there he could not only keep an eye on the prisoners he had taken in Harwind, but he could also regularly check on the coffin in the hold. He did check on them regularly but he could have done that whilst berthing with her in the Great Cabin, as she had requested him to do, but since she had spent that night with Erik, he had not been able to face going to her cot and embracing her with the passion he truly felt for her. An inner war of love and hate towards Redboots raged within him, and of truth, when the rage rose up within him, he felt afraid he might do something he regretted as he was finding it increasingly difficult to contain the murderous rage he felt. Besides, in such dangerous seas, she often spent the night pacing the deck checking that every man was doing his required duty and the ship had no problems.

The only time during the daytime that Redboots joined them in the Great Cabin, was when she wished to spend time with Armius, a new passenger who had joined the ship before the *Red Tide* had weighed anchor and set off from Henchman Bay off of Port Toseucia. He was a shambolic specimen of a man, whom Azzadan had taken an instant disliking to, so he did not spend much time with him. His ill-fitting clothes were threadbare and old-fashioned. More intriguing was the ugly scar on his cheek, the result of an arrow fired at him some time in the past. The dirk he wore sat uncomfortably in the scabbard; it clearly didn't fit. Armius was a Fell-blood navigator who had been taken on-board to pilot the three ships through the shallow waters of the archipelago where Grona Island was nestled, at the very eastern edge near to where the Everglow ended. The archipelago consisted of a thousand or more islands, though most of them were no bigger than large rocks jutting out of the icy ocean. He had been chosen as he was also a writer and an artist. He had been trebly employed as Redboot's biographer and painter, as well as the navigator.

When not consumed with overseeing the ship, Redboots often retreated to the Great Cabin and posed for Armius him so he could paint her, or she spent hours boasting about her exploits so he could write about them. It was an act of vanity Azzadan found both alluring and infuriating at the same time. He was used to secrecy and stealth, not open displays of boastful vanity of one's deeds, though as Smindy had pointed out to him when he had complained to her of it, that he himself had been vain and had openly boasted about his recently acquired title of *Godslayer*.

"That's different," he had angrily muttered in response.

When Azzadan entered the Great Cabin, Armius was sat at the table eating some leftovers from the meal of the night before, beef and plum pudding which he was washing down with strong ale and punch. Redboots insisted on discipline and order on the ship, and Armius had missed breakfast, so was having to make do with some scraps he had clearly rescued from the ship's galley. It was an act against the hard routine of the ship, but as he was not permanent crew, and his skills were needed, Redboots often overlooked his slovenly lapses, much to Azzadan's annoyance.

"Where's the captain?" Armius asked, inadvertently spitting out food. "Do you know if she will join me today for another session?"

"Can't you eat that in your own cabin, filthy pig?" Azzadan responded dourly, as he went and slumped in a chair.

"I need to be here in case she comes for a sitting," Armius replied, oblivious to the insult. "I won't do the painting until the end of the voyage as my strokes get disrupted with the ship's movement, but I'm doing sketches, making notes for the book and finding out a lot about her." He pushed a nearby parchment across the table towards Azzadan, upon which were some notes accompanied by sketches of Redboots. "Fascinating little filly this one," he said. "I'm going to suggest to her we also do some, erm, natural ones, absent of clothing."

514

Azzadan curled his nose up in disgust, but picked up the parchments and looked at them. Despite the food stains on the parchment, the rough sketches were quite skilful, and showed Redboots in various heroic poses; the writing of Armius was in a gratifyingly apposite style, his large, loose hand scattering the words across the page in lines sometimes so precipitously slanted that it seemed like they would slide off the page altogether. They looked exactly like they were: words written in a rough sea.

"Has she told you anything about her childhood?" Azzadan asked Armius, who just shook his head as he stuffed more beef and plum pudding into his mouth. "She just says she was born from the sea and to it she will return. She mostly talks about her pirating days and how she became a captain when she won a ship at a game of Harendale. She also talks a lot about the time when she was a mere whip of a wench on the *Accountant*."

"You should challenge her to a game one day," Azzadan said, "and offer the fingers of your best hand as the prize. She won't refuse you once your work is done."

"These," Armius said, proudly holding up his fingers which were covered in sticky pie crumbs, "are tools of my trade for the use of sextant, brush and quill, and not for gambling away on a game of Harendale."

Azzadan found the man's company annoying, so he left the cabin and wandered the main deck again. Redboots and her officers were now behind him on the poop deck, the weak morning sun glinting off their telescopes as they scanned the distant horizon. Now and then he dared to glance over the rail, irresistibly drawn at the thought of some of the great sea-creatures that might be lurking below, ready to surface and drag man and ship down to the depths of a watery death. After that, he went and checked on those in the hold, after which he sat sulking in his own cabin, brooding over the thoughts of Redboots in the embrace of Erik Vansoth. He spent the next few days in a similar fashion, and thus the long days at sea went on.

When the seas were calm enough, Captain Blackheart of the *Red Mist* and Captain Whisk of the *Red Death*, accompanied by several of their off-duty officers, would come over to the *Red Tide* and join Redboots in the Great Cabin where they discussed ship matters: how the crews were faring; supplies; ship repairs and the many other responsibilities of a ship's captain. Azzadan always sat in on each meeting, which often took several hours. He mostly just listened and observed, as there was little expertise, he had to offer on such matters.

The official business meetings were always concluded with a meal around the great table, which seated around twelve people. The meal consisted of hams, cheeses and bread washed down by ample amounts of claret as the ship's band played lively music. These were the times he enjoyed most on the voyage, for that was when he saw the Redboots he had first been enamoured by. Throughout these meals she was not the diligent captain of a ship in a rough and dangerous sea, whose sole attention was the ship and its business. During these short periods of respite, she once again relaxed and became Redboots the woman. She was a generous and affable host, and he was fascinated and irritated, both at the same time, as she and her captains tried to outdo each other in the boasting of their deeds and in the singing of song; the meal always ended with cake and a glass of punch before the captains and their officers returned to their own vessels.

*　　　　*　　　　*

The weather had been extremely rough the last four days, so the other captains had not been able to come aboard the *Red Tide*; the three ships communicated through a series

515

of signal flags, either stating that all was well, or if they were facing a particular problem, how they intended to deal with it. The ships made sure they all stayed within sight of each other whenever it was possible, speeding up or slowing down, adjusting their own sail, tack and pace accordingly to keep in sight of the others.

On the eighteenth day of the voyage, the morning after a particularly fierce storm that had raged during the night, and then died out when the sun rose, Azzadan paced the deck. Only the empty rolling sea lay before them and Grona, and his thoughts were increasingly focussing on the destination, and the immense challenge that lay ahead. After breakfast, the officers on duty attended their stations, whilst above and below decks the crew attended to the many tasks required running a ship: the hoisting and lowering of sail, endless cleaning, polishing and sail mending. Others attended to the laundry whilst chefs in the main galley prepared the next meal. The loblolly boys were busily swabbing down decks. Bernsey, the ship's surgeon, arranged his knives, saws, potions and medicines and attended to the ailments some of the crew had come down with. If the deadly perils of the Tethys Sea bothered them, the crew hid their thoughts well; each was absorbed in their own task.

At times during the last few days, Azzadan had even started to enjoy the daily routine he himself had adopted. In between the regular meal times, he checked on the prisoners and the coffin in the hold, spent time with Smindy and Sassy in the Great Cabin playing Harendale, or wandered the ship. He felt reassured by the sight of the orderly calm, ahead of the looming chaos that was surely ahead at Grona, or the many dangers that might appear of a sudden, in the form of adverse weather, or from beneath the surface of the sea in the form of some great monster of the deep. The closer they got to Grona, however, the darker his mood became, and even such a simple pleasure as wandering the ship denied him any satisfaction.

It was later on that eighteenth day out that they spotted the first of the Empire's prison ships. "Ship ahoy!" a voice shouted from the crow's nest in the main mast, and the message relayed throughout the ship.

By then Azzadan had gone to the Great Cabin, and was sitting and playing Harendale with Sassy whilst Smindy worked on the books and Armius sat there sleeping and snoring loudly. All four of them went to the poop deck at the news of a ship's sighting.

Redboots and the officers stood unmoved, their telescopes aimed resolutely at the horizon. At first, Azzadan saw nothing. Then, as his eyes grew accustomed to the pale sky, after the watery light of the shade of the cabin, he noticed a shadow on the horizon, then another and another. Straining his eyes, he counted thirty ships, maybe more, strung out on the seam between sea and sky. Only the empty, rolling sea lay between the *Red Tide* and them.

"They have dropped off their prisoners, and are now stuffed full of a cargo of the rare and expensive milathran," Redboots said regretfully, as she reluctantly ordered the *Red Tide* to stay on its course. "Damn you Erik and your oaths, damn you," Azzadan heard her whisper to herself. He knew it was not easy for her to let such plunder pass by, but he felt pleased she was dedicated and focussed on her current assignment, to get him and the vampire to Grona.

The next sighting, the very same day, was of a gargantuan ctenophore. These creatures were hunters, their bodies consisting of a mass of jelly. When floating, the tendrils could pull a ship and its crew into their city-sized chambers to digest slowly over decades. The one they saw was anchored, after a floating existence of hundreds of years. It had calcified and become a gigantic tower of coral. The umbrella shell like appearance of the top, looked like it offered shelter from the rough seas in the calm waters below it, but any ship foolish enough to be seduced by the false sense of security would become its prey. The *Red Tide*, and its companion ships, steered well clear of it.

*                    *                    *

It was the twenty-first day of the voyage when they first hit disaster. Azzadan was in the Great Cabin, talking to Smindy, trying to find out more about Redboots and her upbringing whilst trying to not sound too interested. Sassy played with a doll as Armius sat there scratching, whilst muttering to himself about fleas and ship's mites, in between idly sketching on a pad. Of a sudden, all four of them realized that the familiar, creaking and thudding sound of the rudder, the heartbeat of their wooden world, was changing. The noise rose to a crescendo as, heaving slowly at first and then with a sudden lurch, the ship slipped steeply to port to go about. Everything from plates, jugs of wine and even the sketch pad crashed off the table, clattering chaotically across the deck. For several long moments, all they could do was to clutch the beams above their heads to stop themselves from being thrown off balance to the side. During this time, the ship held the tilted position, shuddering painfully until slowly it straightened and the lanterns swung vertically again. All the while, a bell clanged furiously, calling the ship's crew to alert.

Azzadan, followed by Smindy, rushed to the upper deck. High above, the wind grabbed the vast sails of the ship and the familiar rolling sensation surged through his body. Redboots had turned them towards the *Red Mist*, which was in the process of being consumed by a beast the like of which Azzadan had never seen before.

The beast's vast gaping mouth had the front keel, hull and a large section of the bow in its jaws; its enormous tongue and several tentacles were slowly wrapping itself sickeningly around the rest of the hull, as its tailed thrashed furiously on the surface of the sea to balance itself. The foremast of the *Red Mist* broke in two. Some of the crew valiantly tried to fend off the beast, but to no avail. No stroke of cutlass or shot of arrow had any effect. Some gave up the fight and jumped overboard and were consumed in moments by shoals of flesh-eating fish that must have followed the monster - the sea frothed and foamed with the blood of those so consumed; the wind carried their screams in the air. The rest, died on the deck, or slid into the monster's mouth, whilst some held onto masts or rails, as the ship was slowly being tilted vertically into the air. As though in slow motion, the jaws of the beast crunched slowly on the ship, the wooden beams and planks cracking loudly, as its small round eyes rolled in almost deviant pleasure.

The *Red Tide* crashed through the waves at full speed, heading towards the creature in a vain attempt to help their stricken sea fellows. The crew adjusted the turntable upon which sat the main, mighty ballista, attuned the height, and aimed the massive sea harpoon at the beast.

"Wait…wait…" Redboots shouted. The crew watched with tense anticipation.

"They will be lost if we don't fire now," the bosun cried.

"Wait!" Redboots yelled. After a few more moments, she bellowed, "Now! Fire!"

The chain attached to the harpoon rattled and sang as the mighty harpoon flew through the air and headed towards the beast. It fell short by a matter of only ten feet or so. The *Red Death*, which had reacted similarly to the *Red Tide*, was still too far away to fire its own huge harpoon.

"Wind it in and fire again!" Redboots shouted. The crew cranked the handle that dragged the chain and harpoon back towards the *Red Tide*, so it could be reloaded and fired again. "Make sure enough barrels are attached, so when we strike it and release the chain, that beast will not go below the surface. We will hunt it to its death," she screamed.

By the time the harpoon was in the process of being dragged out of the sea and onto the *Red Tide* to be reloaded, the stern and the rudder of the *Red Mist* rose fully into the air as the beast swallowed more of the bow, its weight pulling the entire front under. The ship began to break and split in the middle, and the main and mizzen masts toppled. Captain Blackheart, holding a rope with one hand, a cutlass in the other, swung and fought the beast until the last, stabbing and slashing at it even as, in a surge of wave and bubble, the *Red Mist* and the beast disappeared under the vast and blue ocean depths.

The *Red Tide* loaded and armed the vast harpoon at its bow, but it was too late. Redboots watched in horror as the sea stilled, and where her ship the *Red Mist* had been, there was now only an empty frothing and bubbling sea. For the briefest of moments, Azzadan was sure she looked unsure and lost, but if she had, it lasted but an instant. She closed her eyes, wincing as her lips moved rhythmically, the words she was saying confused and indistinct. She then roared and screamed at the sea, and uttered curses at the beast. She quickly regained her composure, her orders rising above the cascade of noise around them. They searched for any survivors, but it was in vain. Not a single one of the crew of the *Red Mist* had survived. There was nothing to be done, the two remaining ships turned back to their course and crashed through the sea, on towards Grona.

A strong gale blew up after the loss of the *Red Mist*, and the two remaining ships were lashed by squalls of freezing rain. Redboots consigned herself to the Great Cabin for most of the day, and would not let anyone join her, posting a guard outside who turned all away, including Azzadan and Smindy. Eventually, in the evening, she summoned them both. Redboots clutched their hands, drawing them so near to her, both Azzadan and Smindy could smell the wine on her breath. She drew them to her cot, and the three of them made love passionately. Once again, Azzadan felt nothing but craving and burning desire for her, all former jealousies and anger gone in an instant. When she slept, he embraced her, and stared at her even as the last candle burnt out and the moon no longer shone its light through the portholes of the Great Cabin, and darkness hid her from his sight. He loved her; of that he was sure. In the darkness, he drew the Arkith, laid the point of it between her breasts and slid it downward, over the curve of her belly. *One thrust, and never again will I have to face the torment of knowing you will be in the arms of another man.* He put the foul weapon away, and softly kissed her on the forehead. *When the spirit of Erik Vansoth dwells within this Arzak, it will not be with yours.*

*      *      *

By dawn of the following day the weather had turned relentlessly cold. A thin blanket of snow and ice covered the *Red Tide*. When the three lovers emerged from the Great Cabin, the crew were busy sweeping off the snow and chipping away at the ice. The sea was flat and calm and frozen at points, but a slight wind stirred among the sails, most of which were folded away. Along with the wind, a strong current moved the ship.

Armius had already taken to the poop deck, and was issuing various instructions as he checked charts, a sextant and a telescope, and ordered which way the rudder should be turned. In the distance, a large group of islands and rocks soon loomed, and the *Red Tide* made its way among them. At one point a mist descended, and they lost most of their visibility, and when it was regained, their sister ship had disappeared, much to the concern of all. It was with relief, joy and much cheering, that the crew of the *Red Tide* greeted her when she re-appeared later that same day.

Redboots did not leave the poop deck all that day, nor during the night, standing with Armius. Smindy and Azzadan also stood with them, as did the other officers on watch, the beaver skin hats they now wore pressed firmly down around their ears. All the crew now wore light furs, gloves and boots, and true to fashion, Azzadan smiled that the furs Redboots wore, were dyed a rich scarlet red. They only left the poop deck to briefly refresh themselves in the Great Cabin below, but never for long. Stewards brought them hot drinks and meals and they ate and drank them where they stood. Early the following morning, the two ships weighed anchor in a bay before a large snow-covered island, surrounded by ice-tipped rocks.

"Grona is the next islands on from here" Armius said, somewhat in awe. "The Kappian ships never come to this bay; we can stay anchored and should not be discovered. The waters are shallow enough that no beast of the deep will disturb us here. We can take a small boat to Grona. That way we will evade the ships guarding it."

"Then it's time to wake our guest in the hold," Redboots said to Azzadan, who nodded grimly.

# Chapter Forty-Two: *The Knock at the Door*

*Fools are they, who open the door, when evil comes knocking.*
*A Bruthon Proverb.*

*Janorra* woke in the middle of the night and sat up startled. A shadow passed by the window opposite her. There was a gentle tapping at the window, followed by a loud knocking at the door, and then eerie silence, only broken by the light snoring of Gilly. None of her companions were stirred from sleep at the noise. Janorra did not react to the knocking - she knew better. The words of Silverberry rang through her mind. *Don't answer any knocking at the door or tapping at the window. You must not let either my son, or the Untamed Ones in.*

Rubbing her eyes, Janorra looked around her. The room was lit only by the faint red glow of flickering embers dying in the hearth. She waited a moment, giving herself time to think. Glancing from window to window, she felt a sudden and curious urge to see who or what was there. Silverberry was nowhere to be seen. Every one of her companions were still fast asleep and blissfully oblivious to the gentle tapping at the window which occurred again, and the loud knocking at the door which followed. When silence resumed, Janorra stood up, and crept silently over to the window. She peered out, but could see nothing, apart from a shadow which passed. The faint visage of a face then appeared in the window. The eyes of it were a fearful red, as though they were lit by the firepits of hell. Janorra gave a wordless cry of terror, but the face disappeared and she was not sure if it had merely been a trick of shadows and light. She moved quickly away from the window, and stepping quietly over to Scarand, who had proven himself so vigilant and alert, even when sleeping, she tried to wake him. No effort of hers could stir him from sleep. It was as though a charm still kept him in a stupor. She returned to her straw mattress. She ignored the tapping at the window and the knocking at the door, which resumed again. Exhaustion soon won over. Wanting to keep her eyes open, she couldn't and was soon fast asleep once more.

*     *     *

Janorra woke early the next morning; she was the first to get up and her body ached everywhere. Moving slowly and stiffly, she washed gently at a basin below a sepia mirror in the corner of the room. She was alarmed to see that her face was a mass of bruises and scratches, and she jumped back with a start. When she looked again in the mirror, what she had previously seen, had been a mere illusion, for the scratches and bruises had disappeared, as did the aches and pains she felt. She walked over to the window where she had heard the tapping the night before and looked out. The night's shadows had receded and the sun brightened up the sky. Gilly soon joined her, as did Bessie.

"Did you hear tapping on the windows and knocking at the door in the night?" Janorra asked them.

"No, me dear," Gilly answered. "I had a peaceful sleep."

"Nor did I Miss Janorra," Bessie said, "but if you did that'll just be Thrarn, the Threadweaver's son. 'E likes to play mischief at night with 'is friends, but you drank 'er milk so you'll be safe in the daytime when we wander where we need to be going. Besides, 'e doesn't like the sun even when it is 'idden by 'eavy foliage. Thrarn only endures the sun if 'e is very angry."

Scarand had joined them, and overhearing the conversation asked Bessie, "What is the milk, and why does it make us safe from him?"

"Oh, it is yum-yum Threadweaver breast-milk," Bessie said innocently. "Thrarn can smell it inside those who drink it and 'e thinks they are family, that's why 'e won't bother them."

Janorra felt like retching, and by the look on her companions faces, she could tell that each of them, except Bessie, felt similar.

Bessie continued. "Even at night in the forest, Thrarn will leave you alone if 'e comes across you once you've drank the milk. It's only when 'e sees people in 'is mother's 'ouse, an insane jealousy comes upon 'im as 'e's not allowed inside; 'e makes such a mess. So, if you let 'im in, who knows what trouble 'e would cause?"

Scarand's face crinkled with disgust and concern. "Breast milk, that is disgusting," he growled, spitting onto the floor and curling his face up.

"It's quite yum-yum," Bessie said, "and very good for you."

"Where is Silverberry this morning?" Janorra asked the Spriggan. She wanted to get the image of the origins of the milk out of her mind.

"She goes to Thrarn's cave at sunrise each day, and feeds 'im. He will suck on 'er teat all day, and that way 'e is satisfied and does less mischief in the forest when night comes." Bessie paused for a moment and scratched her head thoughtfully. "At least that's where I think she goes. I don't know really, it's what we Spriggans tell each other anyway."

Muro had joined them by this time. "What are you talking about?" he asked moodily.

"Nothing of importance," Janorra answered, before Bessie could blurt out the content of their conversation. Janorra understood that Silverberry was a guardian of time, or a Threadweaver as some called them, who were not fully of this world, though their origins were unknown. Muro would understand the true nature of the milk more than the other companions, but even for him, it had not yet dawned upon him that the Threadweaver was indeed Yog, one of the goddesses the Ruik followed, and the one he was searching for. It was best to let the matter drop, she decided, lest the full significance of what they were facing began to dawn upon them, or should Muro feel his part in all of this was now over. Threadweavers guarded areas where the separation between different realms was the thinnest. There were more than three of them, and if Muro began to realise the goddesses he worshipped were no more than Threadweavers, and not in fact real goddesses, it might cause unnecessary complications, that if she could she would avoid, as she felt that despite his bad demeanour, Muro might yet prove to be of use. *For good or ill, I feel his part in this is not yet over.*

"How long does it take to reach the fortress we passed?" Janorra asked Bessie. "For Silverberry confirmed to me that is where we must go."

Bessie put her finger on her chin thoughtfully. "A good few 'ours. We need not rush but nor should we linger for lingering's sake."

"Where is the Murien?" Muro asked.

"I do not know," Janorra replied honestly. "Silverberry last had it, and for all I know she still has it, unless she left it here."

The news did not please either Muro or Gilly, who searched the cottage for the Murien, opening drawers and cupboards, looking under beds and any other place they thought it might be concealed, but they could not find it.

"I wanted to be there when Silverberry read it, me dear," Gilly, who was clearly disappointed, said to Janorra.

"As did I," Muro said, a dark rage bubbling just under his exterior.

521

Janorra tried to placate them both. She said to Muro, "Silverberry told me that our journey will end with you taking *The Prophecy of Rithguar* back to the Ruik, and those you worship." Muro's demeanour changed in an instant, as he studied her, to see if there was any sign of deception, or if she was telling the truth. He acknowledged he believed her with a nod, but said nothing.

Janorra then said to Gilly, "I think your destiny is to come with me, for on that path, in time, you will find the Sangdalen text you seek. Silverberry showed me this as a possible future for you."

Gilly's eyes lit up. "Well, that is good news me dear, that is good news indeed."

Muro, fumbling in his pockets, then declared with an air of surprise, "The Murien. It has been put in my pocket."

\*      \*      \*

Sasna stood with Farir on the prow of the ship taking them to Harwind. Gnarn sat at her feet. She looked up at the sky where the great stars blazed whitely. The deep rumble of thunder sounded in the distance, and far-off lightning flickered across the sky.

"Best get below my lady," the grizzly captain of the ship said as he approached. "A storm is coming, but we'll be in Harwind by morning. A ship awaits you there to take you to Erik Vansoth."

Sasna took Gnarn by the hand, and together with Farir, they made their way below decks to their cabin.

\*      \*      \*

The companions quickly ate a breakfast of fruit and nuts prepared by Gilly from their supplies. Janorra walked to the front door, opened it and stepped outside.

She was soon joined by Scarand who looked at her and said, "You look troubled, did you not sleep well?"

"Look for tracks," she said to him, "for there were strange knocks at the door last night and a tapping at the window."

He looked at her with surprise.

"I tried to rouse you from slumber, but could not," she said as she began walking around the little cottage garden, and looking troubled, Scarand followed at her side. Janorra picked her way towards the window where in the night she had seen the shadow pass. Her tracking skills were poor, but not those of Scarand.

"Foot prints, but none like I have ever seen before," he said as he pointed to the ground. She could see nothing.

"They are faint but fresh, look how the grass is slightly pressed and this blade broken. Something was here not so long ago."

"Something?" she asked.

Scarand followed the tracks a short distance and she tailed him. He followed the prints to the end of the garden, where they disappeared into a glade. "I've never seen tracks like this," he said. "It has three toes and a claw, and is far larger than a man though it leaves such a faint print." There were other prints, but they were even fainter. "These I recognise," he said, "and I would rather not meet those to whom they belong."

"We had better leave this place quickly," Janorra declared, looking back at the cottage. *That innocuous looking place is guarding realms untold.* She then looked up at the sky.

"We have already used up some daylight hours." Warily, she looked at the dark forest beyond the sunny glade. Their companions soon joined them.

Bessie, who was seated upon Gaffren with Gilly, asked cheerfully, "We ready then?"

Janorra, feeling troubled again, nodded silently, and followed as Gilly rode Gaffren out of the garden and into the forest, followed moodily by Muro.

"I can tell that the events of last night have deeply troubled you," Scarand quietly said to Janorra as he walked alongside her. "But we are both alive, so hope yet lives."

It was a full minute before she could answer him. She felt the tremor in her voice when she finally spoke. "I don't know if I can face what is ahead," she said honestly. "I do not know if I am strong enough. I wish I had never taken the Simal. It was supposed to be in the hands of the Baothein by now."

Scarand put a comforting hand on her shoulder. He looked back at the glade and the cottage which were passing out of sight as they continued along the forest trail. The blue smouldering that she had seen at other times returned to his eyes. When he spoke, it was with great solemnity. "Ever since I was brought into this place called the Everglow, I have seen things that I would have scoffed at if others had told me they were real. I don't know what we will face, or where we are going, but I know I must continue going forward or else I know I will never find my sisters. Our paths are joined for now, and if it brings any comfort, know I will do all I can to help you."

Janorra put her hand upon his, and squeezed it appreciatively. *He is brave and kind, but he does not know the horrors that might yet be faced.*

"Until it is time for us to walk a different path, where you go, I will go," he said.

She closed her eyes briefly and bit her lip.

"There are creatures in the Deadlands, called Telamones," she said to him. "I once came across one, by chance I thought at the time, when I was with companions. We slew it, but it was no easy task, and luck as well as skill aided us on that day." She took a breath before continuing. "It is said that when the Aeldar are angered or offended with a person, they release such a creature from the Void, to hunt them down. It is unrelenting, and if it catches them, it returns the victim to the Aeldar, to face unimaginable torments at their hands. It was a Baothein Seeress it hunted on that day, though I did not learn of that fact until later."

"What are the Aeldar like?" he asked her.

"Terrible to behold," she answered. "It is written they once were light, but that faded and turned to a darkness so very deep; darkness born of wrath and fire. They are the primeval night. A ravenous hole is in their essence, annihilating and devouring up any goodness or morality that yields to them. They are the embodiment of discord and chaos. Corruption rules their very nature. Malice forever taints their appearance. They were hurled into the Abyss but seek to escape."

Janorra felt her face go ashen, and paused before she spoke again. "I would rather face the nothingness of *non-being* than be an immortal soul in the hands of the Aeldar." Staring at Scarand, she then added, "Some of the Telamones are wild scavengers, others serve the Aeldar as avenging spirits. These Telamones can still squeeze their form into spirit matter that can inhabit the Deadlands. In appearance their upper bodies are male or female. Their lower body brims with lethal dagger-like hairs, and resembles that of a bloated spider, along with their eight legs. They have many long snakes for hair, each one of which strikes out with razor-sharp teeth that injects a venom that is deadly and poisonous to the soul. Their bodies are as black as coal, on wings like bats they fly. Their eyes are the colour of blood. The favoured weapon they wield is a many-thronged-brass-studded whip, which paralyses a soul once it is lashed. They will hunt me in the Deadlands, I am sure of it. If they catch me, they will consume my soul and

523

vomit me up in front of the Aeldar. I cannot die again until I am in the safety of Baothein lands, or I might suffer the curse of the eternal soul."

"Are you sure that such a horror will be released after you?" Scarand asked her, as he bleakly returned her stare with a look of great concern.

"I have stolen their Simal, and was supposed to hand it over to the Baothein, who would protect me in both the Everglow and the Deadlands. But here I am walking in the Wytchwood. Unless I regain the Simal, the Baothein will not assist me, and only they can protect me from Telamones. I am afraid of this journey, and terrified of what I might face if I die again. But I cannot turn back, for where would I go?"

Scarand reached across with his other hand and clutched her hand in both of his. "In such times as these, the debates and arguments of despair will often visit our minds. All the perils you have faced seem to be drawing together to a point. Your goal is ahead, towards that you must press on." He smiled reassuringly. "I cannot help you in the Deadlands, but I swear by all that I hold dear, I will do what I can to keep you safe in this world." He removed his hands and continued. "We both have been alone and led here by circumstances we have not been the master of." He looked at Muro and said, "I do not trust all of those we walk with." He then glanced at Gilly, Bessie and then again at Janorra. "Gilly and Bessie speak of things that are strange, and their intentions are peculiar and unknown to me. But I trust them, and I trust you, and of recent I have good cause not to trust anyone lightly."

*Especially if they are Seesnari?* Janorra wondered.

His face grew serious. "We both have allies now, of a sort. But powerful forces are at work on both sides of this matter. You must fight when you have no choice, run when you can."

She looked at him, and felt comforted.

"Janorra, I mean it. The Obelisk told you to run, I heard it. Run with all your strength and speed if we face foes we believe cannot be defeated. Do not hesitate to do so when the need arises. I will watch your back." He paused thoughtfully and then added. "I can see that your fate, for good or bad, is tied to this Simal. That is clear even to me. Somehow, you must find the courage to continue this course to whatever end. I give you my word that my will is set to help you until our paths differ, and from my part, that will not be until I know you are safe. No peril or hazard will make me break my word; this I swear by oath to you."

*Death can make you break it unwillingly,* she thought, and then, *if only you could go with me into the Deadlands and face with me the foes I face there, and then return again with me to this life. But you have but one time in this mortal realm and then all trials in it are over for you, and for that, I envy you.*

"Somehow, I will always find my courage again, and set my will to the task," she said, wiping tears from her eye.

"Fear is a good motivator," he replied.

"Fear is my motivation, and yours is love for your sisters," she responded. "Know that when my task is complete, and even during it when I can, I too, will do all in my power to help you find them."

Following the others, they then walked along the forest trail in silence for a long time. The thought of the torment and punishment she would face in the cruel hands of the Aeldar, the Bantu, the Baron, the Empress or any of those who surely pursued her, was more than Janorra could bear. She stopped, and leaning over with one hand on Scarand's shoulder for support, she retched and reeked, losing the contents of that morning's breakfast. When she had finished, she smiled meekly at him.

Scarand must have sensed her thoughts, for he said, "They haven't caught you yet. Do not forsake hope, you may yet reach the place of sanctuary you seek."

*       *       *

"Well done me dear, you led us well," Gilly said to Bessie as she gently stroked her twiggy hair, causing the Spriggan to purr with delight. It was late-afternoon of the day they had left the cottage, for they had travelled at a rapid pace. Gaffren had galloped, and those not seated upon his back, ran at the same pace. The mirth the dwarf expressed hid well the gloom and dread they all felt as the ancient fortress loomed before them. Bessie was the only one it seemed to have no effect on.

A well-worn road descended gently into the valley. Catching their breath, they followed it at a slower pace, until they passed the last vestiges of greenery. They entered into the part of the forest where all was dead bracken and trees, surrounded by impenetrable thickets adorned with savage looking, hooked, red-tipped thorns. A worn and cracked stone path led up to a bridge that crossed the chasm, leading to the fortress within which was the entrance to Garama Aethoros. *I do not plan to enter Garama Aethoros,* Janorra said to herself, *unless choice is taken from me.*

The sight of the ruins of the Old Citadel filled them with horror. The fortress rose into the sky like a grim relic from another, forgotten age. Long lines of crumbling walls and parapets, stationed with crumbling towers that thrust their jagged pinnacles into the sky, surrounded it. Full-sized statues, half-sized effigies, and faces were carved into the stone walls and towers, their horrific features half corroded by long centuries of wind and rain. In the middle of the crumbling walled fortifications, was a citadel, the base of which looked like black marble untouched and untainted by time. The top of the citadel was dominated by a red dome, that had the appearance of uncut crystal. No blemish could be seen upon its round surface. The citadel had been hidden by shadow the day before. Broad marble steps led up to a great golden door near the base of the structure.

The companions trembled as they beheld the ancient fortress, but their attention was soon diverted as Bessie spoke and pointed to something in the sky. "Best we not delay Miss Gilly. I don't like the look of that big old beast flying above us." she said.

Each of the companions looked to the sky. Janorra expected to see the beast that had tracked her from Greytears, but to her surprise but no less horror, a red and golden griffin was circling high in the sky, screeching and descending slowly in wide circles towards them. A rider sat upon it, wielding a powerful looking staff. He was shouting at them, but the distance was too great for them to hear.

*The Empire, have they also found me?* Janorra wondered in fear.

Moments later, with great speed, the Barclugoth appeared. It crashed into the griffin with such a force, it nearly knocked the rider off. The griffin flapped its wings furiously as the Barclugoth snapped at it with its mighty jaws, and slashed at it with its powerful claws.

As the companions watched on, the griffin and Barclugoth fought viciously in a life and death struggle. The Barclugoth struck out with its claws at the griffin's neck, gashing it with a wound that made the creature screech in agony. The griffin managed to turn and bite the Barclugoth's face with its fierce and deadly beak. The Barclugoth suddenly dropped from the sky. As it fell it attempted to right itself. Belching out a garbled scream, it thrashed its great wings in vain, but they had been torn, shredded, and broken by the griffin's claws, and it could not halt its rapid descent. The Barclugoth then fell lifeless through the sky, crashed through the trees some distance away from the companions, and hit the ground with a sickening crunch. But the wounds it had dealt to the griffin, were mortal. The stricken creature managed to stay airborne, but was as torn and broken as the Barclugoth had been. The rider attempted, in vain, to control the beast. He tried to guide it in a tight circle to begin a rapid descent but the griffin's wings failed as it breathed its final breath. It painted the sky with its blood as it plummeted silently and lifelessly to the ground, rider and beast alike crashing through the trees.

"We should not tarry here," Scarand urged.

The travellers ran over the deep and dark abyss by way of the vast stone bridge, adorned with grotesque statues overgrown with thick dead vines and tangled lifeless foliage covering the small wall, upon which were columns that might once have supported a vaulted roof. Gaffren snorted and jerked his head as Gilly tugged at the reins to steady him. The bleached skulls and skeletons of unrecognised creatures, as well as some human ones, frightened them all, even Bessie.

"I've not been upon this bridge before," the Spriggan said nervously, stopping momentarily with the others to catch her breath and check for any signs of pursuit.

"Did the Elves really build this place?" Scarand asked nobody in particular.

Bessie answered him. "They built it before they left Mr Scarand. Forest legend says it was taken from them, and was maybe the reason for their leaving." She looked around warily. "Nobody ever comes to this place, not even us Spriggan, for until now Silverberry has always forbidden us to come 'ere when curiosity got the better of us and we asked for 'er permission. Magic stops this place from crumbling to dust; though by the decay, it must be wearing off."

Scarand looked over the side of the wall and kicked a stone which fell, and after a while the echo of a splash made its way up the abyss. Gilly said gently to him, "Best you don't get to near the edge or lean over too far and fall in there, me dear. If the fall doesn't kill you, there might be hungry things that live in such a place. They are most likely the ones that decorated this bridge." She nervously looked at the skulls and skeletons.

Scarand took a last quick and uneasy look, and moved away from the edge of the bridge, as they set out again at a great pace, wanting to hastily cross the expanse.

Something coursed through Janorra as they left the bridge and passed under the large, rusted, broken and shattered portcullis and approached the closed gate of the outer wall surrounding the fortress. Up close, the walls were exceedingly large and foreboding. They vied in size with those of the Argona Temple in Kappia. As she drew close to them, when under their shadow, the sensation she experienced was one of being drawn, compelled to go even closer, but as she tried, she swayed on her feet and her legs grew numb and heavy under her. Her mind began to cloud, and she might have fallen had Scarand not held her up.

"Come," a whispered voice echoed loudly through the air followed by two other distinct and different voices.

"Come to us," said the second voice.

"We wait," said the third in a cracked whisper.

"Did you hear that?" Janorra asked the others, feeling alarmed by the voices and looking all around her.

"Did we hear what, me dear?" Gilly asked. The puzzled expressions on the faces of the others showed they had not heard the voices.

"Something or someone called to me," Janorra said as she again looked fretfully around her.

"The forest plays tricks on you even here," Gilly replied in a soothing voice intended to give comfort. She dismounted from Gaffren, and walked up to the large iron-bound wooden gates, which were rotten and in bad condition but still intact. Any handle had rusted long ago. She pushed them. They did not budge. The others joined her and tried to help her push, but the doors remained firmly shut.

"They're probably blocked on the other side," Muro said, as he looked up at the walls. "Somebody will need to climb it and have a look."

"I'll do it," Scarand offered, as he pressed himself flat against the side of the outer wall, and searched for hand and footholds. Some of the mortar between the stones was powdery and gone to ash, and he found it easy to get a good grip. Slowly, move by move, he began to climb the wall, pulling himself up stone by stone, fingers and toes digging hard into the crevices between them. Some of the stones looked loose, and as she watched him Janorra could tell he did not like to put his full weight on those ones. He continued climbing, skilfully, until he reached the top, where he grabbed hold of one of the weather-worn gargoyles whose faces stared hideously below. Janorra and the others watched him. He tested it, to see that it was not loose. Confident it would hold his weight, he held onto it with both hands, and managed to swing his legs up onto the top of the gatehouse and disappeared from sight. He was gone for several minutes, and then, from the other side of the gate, they heard a wooden beam being moved and fall heavily on the floor. The gate swung open, and Scarand stood there catching his breath.

"The Vanyr learn to climb when children," was all he said in answer to the questioning looks he was given by some of his fellow travellers.

"You are a thrall, not a true Vanyr," Muro muttered disrespectfully. Scarand ignored the jibe.

They passed through the gates and entered a large courtyard that sat in the shadow of the main structure of the tower. They then walked down a paved passage, long and empty. The only sound was the clatter of Gaffren's hooves on the stone and then cobbled ground. Janorra looked around her with mingled loathing and wonder at the abandoned great houses that stood tall and lonely on either side, over whose doors and their arched gateways many strange letters and images were carved, intermingled with golden hieroglyphics several feet long. No man alive cold read those characters, and Janorra shuddered, the images raised dim conjectures of shapes undreamed of by living mortals. Onward the companions went, warily, weapons at the ready, their restless eyes combing the shadows from side to side. All about them they saw signs of an ancient civilization; marble fountains, voiceless and crumbling, stood in places where the forest-growth and underbrush had invaded the fortress. Broad pavements stretched before them, broken with grass and weeds growing through the wide cracks. They glimpsed walls with ornamental copings, lattices of carven stone that might once have served as the walls of gardens. Ahead of them, through the broken ruins, the dome of the main building gleamed in the sun and the bulk of the structure supporting it became more apparent the further they advanced.

Every street they walked along had houses of different design and wonder, many of which were covered with dead tangled-vines. They entered a great cobbled square, littered with broken stones. It looked like the sort of place where soldiers might once have paraded. Around the square, grotesque statues looked inwards, and against the flow of light and in an abhorrence of nature itself, as though forced by some power unseen, they each cast a shadow that pointed to the main doors of the citadel, which was at the far end of the square.

Muro took the Murien text from his breast pocket and un-wrapped it. The runes and symbols were glowing more brightly than ever they had before. "Yog lives in a palace of ice and rock. I see no such thing here," he grumbled.

The travellers crossed the square and approached the broad marble that led to the entrance to the citadel, which was in a far better state of preservation than the lesser structures they had passed. The thick walls and massive pillars seemed too powerful to crumble before the assault of time and the elements. An enchanted quiet seemed to brood over the building. Cat-like, they reached the top of the steps, and to their surprise, the doors were already open.

"They looked closed from a distance," Scarand said warily, as they all hesitated on the steps.

Far behind them beyond the walls, a hideous, maniacal giggling sound emerged from the forest.

Bessie looked concerned. "That'll be Silverberry's son Thrarn; 'e doesn't like the sun, but all that noise with those two bird things must have drawn him 'ere anyway. Fortunately for us, 'is friends only emerge at night. We best not linger."

"That settles the matter me dears," Gilly said as she spurred Gaffren through the doors and into the tower. The others followed, warily looking behind them.

Janorra shuddered as she entered the citadel, and jumped with a start when, with no rasp of spring or hinge, the doors slammed shut behind them, plunging them momentarily into darkness. No effort of any of them, managed to open the doors again.

"*Mayash*," Gilly said, and the orb at the end of her staff flickered and shone a light around them so they could see each other and their surroundings, but she need not have done so. The red crystal dome on top of the tower, as though awaking from a long undisturbed rest, flickered into life, shedding the entire place with an eerie pulsing crimson light. They were in a great hall, the floor of which was made of clear strengthened glass, the colour of which was tinged by the light from the dome.

"This is a tomb!" Scarand gasped with horror.

Beneath the glass floor, chambers were sunk into the rock and roofed over by the glass floor. Each chamber was filled with several skeletons plus grave goods of gold, silver and jewels. The skeletons were mounted by gold rods onto larges bases and wore elaborate necklaces, earrings and rosettes. They were tall and nimble looking, clothed in armour, bearing weapons and were in various poses for battle. The bones that were revealed, as well as the armour, showed signs of trauma and violence caused by weapons of steel or worse. The skulls were covered by burial masks, made of finely hammered golden glass, that revealed every fine feature of the face that once adorned the skull. The finely sculpted faces, leaving room for small noses and tiny mouths, tapered to pointed delicate looking chins.

"Are they?"

Before Scarand could finish the question, Gilly answered. "Yes, they look like Elves."

"This is not a sightseeing tour," Muro complained as he made his way further into the hall. "I want to find Yog!"

Gaffren's hoof beats clattered and echoed loudly on the glass floored hall, as they took in the sights of the place, they were in. The walls were made of gold, and decorated with repoussé pastoral and hunting scenes of Elves going about their daily business, as well as scenes of them assaulting a fortified city. Liberally placed around the hall, were ornaments of every kind, including stag shaped cups and bowls made of crystal or silver, vases of various shapes and sizes decorated with forest creatures and images, and green figurines of creatures of every type and variety.

"I don't like this place," Bessie said meekly.

They proceeded quickly across the hall, crossing its vast expanse until they came to the centre, where, in the floor was a sunken chamber accessed by a stairway. Going down it into the chamber, they passed a tripartite pillared shrine dedicated to a god none of them recognised. Passing the shrine, they entered a long passage lined with

528

imposing polygonal stone walls. This led to a doorway ornamented with porphyry, and decorated with carved zigzags, spirals, rosettes and leaves. At the end of this were huge oak doors mounted on bronze pivots. The smooth surface of the doors offered no bolts, catches or handles.

Gilly dismounted Gaffren, stood before them, and then searched the sills of the door with nimble fingers; her sensitive tips found projections too small for the eye to see; she pressed these carefully, and in a particular order, until the door crashed open with a loud clang that echoed throughout the passageway.

To answer the astonished look of her companions, she said, "I've not been idle, and have read a lot during my time in the archive. I know how to open an elf door."

Through the doors, was a narrow spiral stairway lined by plain stone walls. "Come then," Muro impatiently growled as he rushed ahead through the doors and down the spiral stairs.

It took the companions a long while to navigate the steps and narrow stair. Gaffren, although nimble of foot, had great difficulty as he was nearly too wide for it, and bleating with complaint and annoyance, there were times when Gilly had to push him to squeeze him through, but eventually they reached the bottom and came instantly to a large natural cave. Crossing the rugged ground with care, they came to the top of a ravine, the result of the ground that once might have been there being eroded. It was now a sharp slope of scree and sliding stones that led into darkness. Being walled in by the cave on either side, and going back to the stairway they had descended being the only other option, they silently pressed on.

Muro was the first to step onto the slope, the rest followed, with Scarand being the last after he peered behind them checking for any pursuer. They slid down it amidst the dust and debris of the scree and stones, but all reached the bottom in one piece.

"At the top of the ravine, did you hear something," Janorra asked nobody in particular.

They heard distant shouting, as though a man were calling after them.

Scarand nodded. "We are being pursued."

A sense of panic filled the entire group, apart from Scarand whose countenance was fierce, and Muro, who had a darkness cross his features. "I will buy you time," Scarand said, as he stood his ground.

"A bow might be no good against whatever he is," Muro snarled mockingly.

"He might be right, we must press on, together," Janorra urged.

They rushed with all speed along the ground until they came to nine paths, separated by walls too large to climb. Janorra picked a path, and ran down it. The rest followed.

"How do we know this is the right way Miss Gilly?" Bessie asked.

"We don't, me dear. This way is as good or as bad as the others, so let's trust Miss Janorra's instinct," was all Gilly gave as an answer.

Down the walled-path they fled, until they entered a doorless room that looked like the workshop of a mage. As they rushed through, Janorra could not stop herself from casting an eye over the workbenches, desks and tables weighed down with numerous items: heavy tomes; scrolls; crucibles; test tubes; phials and jars of assorted items. Book cases around the room were bending under the weight of more heavy tomes of different sizes and colour.

"If only we had time to stay and study," Muro said as he looked gleefully at the dusty books. Picking one up, he gasped with grim surprise. "It is a forbidden, iron-bound book of *Morasos the Cruel*. Do you know how rare this is?"

529

"We do not have time to care, we must press on," Scarand remonstrated, as he looked behind him. "Whoever, or whatever pursues us, is making haste." The sound of shouting, one calling after them, was getting louder.

"You have the heart of a thrall, not a Vanyr," Muro hissed rudely.

"If a bow is useless, then so would be my death if I were to stay and use it," Scarand replied angrily to him. "Stay here old man and read. If you do not die by the violence of our pursuer, perhaps you will be forever trapped in this place and the world will be rid of one more cursed Ruik."

Muro's face twisted with rage. "You, a thrall, dare to speak to me in such a manner?"

"We do not have time for this," Janorra cried with a sense of urgency. "We do not know the nature or purpose of whoever it is that pursues us, and unless choice is stripped from me, I would rather not find out." She turned, and fled down the only other way out of the workshop, a stone-walled corridor.

Muro tucked the book under his arm, and with a last regretful look at the tomes left behind, he followed the others.

The next place they entered was a huge chamber, which blocked them in, except for the way they had come, and a way ahead. The walls and ceiling glistened with runes of every manner and colour. Scarand gasped in awe. Janorra noticed the runes, but her attention was fixed on a large iron-bound door, made of black wood, as well as the many resurrection cradles littered around the floor, some overturned. The door was partially open. Through the opening, they could all see part of the trunk and branches of a giant blackened tree, twisted and gnarled in every grotesque shape imaginable.

"This is a Chamber of Resurrection," Janorra said, "but unlike one I have ever seen before and the Obelisk is not here."

"Mithilos!" Gilly exclaimed, pointing at the tree through the door. "Oh, me poor dear," she added, emphatically.

"The second Wisdom Tree," Janorra whispered, as she tried the door to open it fully. It rasped open with little resistance. The companions entered a large courtyard within a rune-covered cave.

"A rune-cave, like we Ruik have," Muro gasped in awe.

It was not the tree, or the cave, that held their attention however, but the closed portal at the end of the room. The portal was a tall rectangle of white with a shimmering screen of colours playing across the surface like an oily rainbow on water. In front of it, sat a young girl, rocking back and forth whilst holding an orb.

"Sezareal! The Simal!" Janorra exclaimed, but fell into silence as the loud footsteps of their pursuer were heard behind them, entering the chamber. The door slammed shut behind him, blocking off their only visible means of escape. The companions each readied their weapons to face he who stood before them.

# Chapter Forty-Three: *Devious Schemes*

*The daily routine for Hammer Knights when not deployed for war, or not on guard duty:*

❖    **4am.** *Rise for Matins, and attend to horses, then return to bed*

❖    **6am to noon.** *Attend services: Prime (6.15am); Second (9.15am); Third (11.45am). In between services knights will train with weapons, learn battle strategies and groom their horses.*

❖    **Noon.** *Dinner of cooked meats and vegetables will be served. Complete silence throughout the meal will be maintained apart from the priest who will read from Volume V of the Book of Aeldar.*

❖    **3pm.** *Attend afternoon service, followed by weapons training.*

❖    **6pm.** *Attend evening service, followed by supper. After supper silent meditation.*

❖    **9pm.** *Attend Compline, after which knights will receive a glass of wine and water which they will drink as instructions for the following day are given (See note 1 below). After Compline knights will attend to their horses.*

❖    **Midnight.** *To bed in complete silence until 4am.*

*Note 1: The Hammer Knights will perform all of their sacred duties without fail, for this is proof of their devotion and faith towards the Aeldar Gods. If they fail in the most sacred of their duties, especially in regard to specific orders and instructions entrusted to them by a superior, punishment will be in accordance with those prescribed in the holy book.*
**The XXVII Book of Aeldar: The Sacred Duties of the Hammer Knights.**

*After the Battle of Chronicles, Matthias, the High-General of the Hammer Knights and the last to stand at the Kappian Gate when Balian stormed it, was overwhelmed and taken alive. Unknown to himself, he was given water laced with the cruel Maia concoction, a poison if you like, or drug, that alters the mind and heart of even the holiest of men. Thus inflicted, he was then put in a tent with the vilest and most wretched whores that followed Balian's army. Such were the deeds Matthias committed with the whores, even the basest of men in Balian's army blushed at the hearing of them; Matthias was then set free to live with his shame. On returning to the Argona Temple, Matthias requested that he be flayed alive nine times, once for each of the Aeldar he felt his behaviour had insulted. After resurrecting after the ninth flaying, he requested that he be castrated and left to contemplate his shame, and then be driven out of the holy order which he had unworthily joined. Thus, to this day, it is now the standard punishment for any Hammer Knight who defiles himself with a woman, during the Nine Lives of Purity when they guard the sacred temples and palaces of Kappia, to be treated in the same way as Matthias if they break their solemn vows. It is particularly unpleasant for an outsider, to learn that any deviant Hammer Knight must actually request this punishment, lest they be given a harsher sentence if they do not. They genuinely believe that Matthias showed them the way and set the example to be followed, during their time of the Nine Lives of Purity when they are to be solely devoted to guarding the sacred palaces and temples of Kappia city.*
**Temmison Vol II, Book 5: The Wars and Conquests of the Kappian Empire.**

𝒜 bird chirped happily to itself inside a gilded cage, answered from others of its kind from trees in the garden outside the window on the Terrace of the Sun. Shaka stood before a full-length mirror, its edges wound in gold wire like interleaved vines. A stool was put before her and she sat down, allowing one of her maids, Desira, to comb her hair, after which the maid began to plait it, whilst two of the other maids also attended to her.

Shaka felt rage and humiliation build up inside of her, as she remembered that recently Desira had taken shears to her head on the day of the Munte wedding ceremony. *I need my maids as my allies. I shall not punish her, yet.*

"Who is your father?" Shaka asked her. Desira was clearly taken aback, and it amused the Empress, as it was one of the very rare times, she had ever made small talk with a maid, and the discomfort it caused the girl was pleasing to Shaka. Desira was no great beauty, but had a pretty face and a petite slender body.

"Baron Haman, my Sarissa," she answered nervously. "Lord of Castle Blacklake, our ancestral home and a hold always loyal to you."

"And what about you?" Shaka asked the maid named Sheena, who was perfuming Shaka's feet. *She is the most attractive, she will do.*

The maid's hand trembled and she swallowed hard before she answered. "My father was Lord Marion, the Griffin Keeper at Fort Disturbance. He met the *Final-death* a year ago."

"Who took over his position?"

"A man named Cordius, who was highly recommended by General Karkson, my Sarissa," Sheena replied.

"And you?" Shaka asked the third maid, named Mazzie, a plain looking young woman, who was painting Shaka's fingernails.

"My father met the *Final-death* at the hand of an assassin twenty years ago; he was Rodrik, Lord of the Western Marches, and Baron of Kara Duram."

Shaka nodded her head ever so slightly. "I remember your father well. Lord Rodrik was a fierce man with an intense hatred of the Bantu hordes. Didn't he once don a Neblan and go beyond the wall with a Davari army under the command of Lord Borach? Did they not burn a Bantu castle to ashes?"

"It was so, my Sarissa, and both were given the medal of honour by your own hands," Mazzie replied.

Shaka stared at Myrene, who was making the bed and asked. "Who is your father?"

Myrene stopped, turned and faced the Empress and with her head lowered nervously answered, "My father was Lord Myrion of Ormond, a griffin rider from the ancient clans."

*Liar! Your father was General Karkson! I know you have a brother, even if you do not. I also know his true identity, as well as yours.* "I do not recall your father," Shaka said, masking her contempt.

"He was once famed, but the minstrels and bards no longer sing of his deeds," Myrene said meekly.

Shaka pointed to the other three maids who were helping Myrene make the bed. "Look at how my new husband insults me, by replacing some of my Pure-blood maids with Davari. Have they even learnt any High Akkadian yet?"

"No, my Sarissa," Myrene answered. "Their names are Stansia, Marciea and Oliviana. Until recently they were serving Princess Aspess."

Shaka glared menacingly at the maids, who carried on making the beds, averting their eyes to avoid her gaze. She was tempted to drag the Davari maids to the edge of the terrace and throw them off the balcony to the floors below, and under any other circumstances she would not have hesitated to do so. The insult Mazdek had put upon her by replacing some of her Pure-blood maids with Davari slaves, was almost unbearable. But she wanted to avoid any disturbances, and she did not want to scare her

Pure-blood maids. *I must learn to bear this insult for now.* Shaka needed every ally she could find at the moment and wanted to win their trust, as they were vital to her plans.

"I want you to teach these Davari maids High Akkadian, but not in my presence for I will not allow my ears to be polluted with their foul tongue, is that understood?"

Myrene nodded and said, "Your word, my will my Sarissa."

"Then I think, if you serve me faithfully, it is soon time you Pure-bloods will be released from my service, and sent back to your ancestral homes. Would you like that?" The eager looks on each of the Pure-blood maids faces, confirmed to Shaka that was exactly what they wanted, though they were careful not to voice it.

"Our desire is to only serve you, my Sarissa, in whatever manner you wish of us," Myrene said on behalf of each one.

*No, it is not,* Shaka thought sternly. *You fear me and despise me and can't wait to leave my service. I am not sure if you will betray me to Mazdek but I have little choice but to take the risk.* "If you do my bidding, and keep my counsel private and secret, you shall be sent back to your family homes with distinction and honour once I have regained my power. Can I trust you?" *If you betray me, then do not think any suffering you have thus far met here, is even a taste of what is to come."* Each of the Pure-blood maids looked nervously at each other.

Shaka repeated the question. "I have a plan to take us all to the safety of Kara Duram. Once there, you will be released from my service. Can I trust you?"

The Pure-blood maids looked terrified as they met her gaze. "Yes, my Sarissa," each girl said as respectfully as they could before lowering their gaze and returning to their duties.

Her hair now bound in a long plait, her feet perfumed and her nails painted, Shaka stood, allowing the maids to wrap an emerald green dress around her. She tightened the belt, adjusted the fall of the sleeves, cursed at the Maidenarz, the jewellery of Morkroth, and went and sat at her desk. Taking a quill and dipping it in ink, she wrote on three separate parchments. When she finished each letter, she blew on the ink to dry it, rolled it up and then heated some wax which she used to seal it.

Handing the first letter to Desira, she asked. "Do the guards search you when you enter or leave?"

"No, my Sarissa," Desira said.

"Good. Then hide this about your person and give this to no other than Titrius, the Champion of Kappia."

Desira took the letter, and Shaka continued.

"I once gifted him a house by the arena, so he must still reside there. Ask for his whereabouts if you cannot find him, but do not arouse suspicion with your enquiries. Do you understand?"

Desira nodded and slipped the letter between her breasts, so it was out of sight, before disappearing through the curtain over the door.

Shaka handed the second letter to Mazzie. "This is to go to no other than Barazo, the Raven-Keeper at High Perch. He is to send this letter to Kara Duram. It has my seal on it so he is forbidden by law to read it, but if Mazdek has instructed him to check any messages I send, you must tell me." *It is coded so appears of a trivial nature, but Longshins will recognise the code I am using.* "You must tell me if Barazo reads it, do you understand?" Mazzie nodded, hid the parchment about her person and left the room through the same door as Desira.

Shaka handed the third letter to Myrene. "Deliver this to the Princess Aspess."

Myrene nodded, took the letter, hid it and left.

Sheena, who was by far the most shapely and prettiest of the maids, stood there nervously awaiting her orders. Shaka eyed her up and down. "Tell me, the Hammer

Knights who guard my chambers. Do any of them stare at you lustfully when you enter or leave?" Sheena seemed unsure how to answer. "Speak truthfully girl," Shaka snapped.

"Most of them pay us little attention, they take their oaths seriously, but there is one, he makes lewd comments whenever I pass and I feel his stare."

"And how does his companion react to those comments?" Shaka asked.

"He sniggers, and watches me well, with deviance in his eye."

"You are a virgin?" Shaka asked, as she half-smiled and narrowed her eyes.

"Of course, my Sarissa," Sheena said, clearly shocked by the question. "As your handmaidens we are sworn to uphold our purity whilst in your service. No man has ever touched any of us Pure-bloods. I can swear and attest to it by oath, though I cannot vouch for those Davari," she said, casting a look of contempt at the three Davari maids still making the bed."

"The guards adhere to the normal rotation of duties?" Shaka asked calmly.

Sheena thought for a moment. "As far as I know," she answered.

"The one who stares and his companion, when were they last on?"

"They keep the morning watch now, my Sarissa, and are at the door to your chambers as we speak."

Shaka smiled. "Good, then they will be on the first watch this evening." She looked Sheena up and down. "Are you ready to surrender your purity in service to your Empress?" Shaka asked her formally.

Sheena looked terrified, and uncertain.

"I have made oaths…" she began, but was interrupted by Shaka.

"Which I now release you from," Shaka replied brusquely. "These are not normal days, and I require you to do my bidding, whatever that may be."

Sheena nodded. "I am yours to command, you word, my will," she said before looking down at the floor and clutching the sides of her white dress anxiously.

"Then I have a lot to teach you, and very little time to do it," Shaka said as she stood and walked over to the bed, dismissing the Davari maids with a single command and then beckoning for Sheena to follow. "It is not that hard to please a man, and you must quickly learn how." Taking a phial of potion out from the drawer of a table next to her bed, she popped it open, and tipped a couple of drops into a glass of wine. "Drink this," she ordered Sheena, "it is perfectly safe and will make what I am going to ask you to do a lot easier for you." Putting the stopper back in, she handed the phial to Sheena.

"This evening, when the two knights are on duty outside, put two drops of this into two glasses of water, and you drink the rest. You are then to ask them to come into your chambers to investigate a strange noise you thought you heard. Once they investigate and find nothing, offer them the water."

"What is this, and what if they are not thirsty or do not want it, my Sarissa?" Sheena asked nervously.

Shaka smiled. *The water is just back-up. With or without it, the potion you are taking should be enough to have the same effect on them, as it will on you.* "Just do what I command," Shaka said.

*　　　*　　　*

It was later that evening when the Champion of Kappia, Titrius, finally arrived at Shaka's chambers, escorted by the two nervous Hammer Knights, and a blushing Sheena, whose hair and dress were ruffled. Shaka smiled inwardly. Everything, so far, had worked out perfectly. Sheena had done exactly as asked, and lured the knights into her bedchamber. It had not been coincidence that Shaka and the other maids had walked in on them, catching them all in the sexual act, and this whilst the two knights were on sacred guard duty.

"Wait for me inside there," Shaka ordered Titrius, who looked a little bewildered and unsure as he passed through the bead curtain into the room Shaka had pointed towards.

The two guards waited as Shaka cracked open the door to her chambers and peered outside. Servants were moving about the palace lighting the night lamps.

"Remember, if I inform my husband Mazdek of your immoral actions with my maid, and that whilst on a guard duty, he will make you swear before the Jewel of Baramir if there is truth or lie to my accusation. Do you remember what the punishment is for your actions?"

"We could not control ourselves," one of the knights protested.

"What is it you want from us?" the other asked.

*I've got them!* "You will allow into my chambers, any person I wish to be granted access. You will not record these guests in your reports. Your silence and discretion will be the price of my own regarding your act with my maid."

One of the knights nodded, "So be it," he muttered, after which he blushed with shame and embarrassment and looked fearfully away. The other knight also nodded in eager agreement.

"Good, my sons and daughter, have instructions to visit me when you are next on duty. They will enter the palace by a secret passage. You will grant them access to my chambers, and never speak of their visit. Is that understood?"

The knights nodded, and Shaka dismissed them. When they were back on guard duty outside, with the heavy door shut behind them, Shaka smiled at Sheena.

"You did very well," she said.

"I feel soiled and unclean, my Sarissa. The things they made me do." She blushed, and said quietly, "That potion, it is a wicked thing."

Shaka smiled. *You feel shame now, but at the time, the potion made you want to do what you did, as it did them.* "There is so little that is pure in this world, none can walk through it and remain untainted," she said soothingly to the still blushing Sheena.

A tear rolled down the maid's cheek. Shaka gently wiped it away with the tip of her finger, and tasted it, as a touch of Maia would help her in the unpleasant deed, she herself had to do.

The Maia potion she had given to Sheena, who had then put it in the water offered to the knights, was once used by whores in the Kappian brothels, before it was banned, for few men could resist its scent on a woman, and for the woman, it made even the least attractive of men desirable. If a man took it themselves, it made it all but impossible for them to resist the powerful urges the drug made them feel.

Shaka handed Sheena another letter, which she had written earlier. "This is to go to Rachmund, the Master of the Games. Now off with you, and never again speak of this." With more tears welling up in her eyes, Sheena took the letter, and left.

Shaka walked along the corridor and halfway down it, she met Titrius, who had left her room and was now coming the other way. He looked puzzled, and sounded uncertain when he spoke.

"My Sarissa, I should not be here. I am in training for the games; I also have duties to attend too."

Shaka smiled, linked arms with him and turned him back towards her room. "It is your duty to obey your Empress, is it not?"

Titrius nodded. He was a large brute of a man, burly, with a thick bushy beard and thick black locks of hair. His face was scarred and tanned by the sun, and had a weathered appearance. He wore the tunic of a man who had been training hard. It was covered in the dust and grime of the day. The letter had ordered he come immediately without delay. Showing a sealed command from the Empress to attend her, the guards to the entrance of the palace had allowed him in without question. It was only the guards to her chambers that, under orders from Mazdek would have stopped Titrius from entering, even with an imperial order, but now the two currently on guard, were compromised and in her debt in return for her silence.

"I assure you it will not be long before you are back in your ludus, this very night. You shall not be harmed in any way," Shaka said as she drew the heavy curtain across the door when they were both inside her room. Taking two goblets of wine, both laced with Maia, she offered one to Titrius, and sipped the other herself. He accepted the goblet, and took a hesitant sip.

"Drink it all," she said, as she drained her own cup.

Cautiously, Titrius drank the entire contents of the goblet.

Seizing the moment, Shaka pulled free two clasps and her long emerald dress fell to the floor. She walked over to the bed; lay down sideways on it and pulling up one leg, began stroking her hand down her thigh.

Titrius blushed. "Is this what you want me for?" he asked, looking confused, afraid and embarrassed, but his eyes were glazing over. "It is said you change form, and consume those you lay with," he added nervously.

"That is just palace gossip," Shaka purred. *The Maidenarz now prevents me.*

In a few moments, his fear and embarrassment had nearly all gone, and Shaka noticed Titrius looked at her with a raw passion that had been absent before.

"You are married, you are the Emperor's Munte bride," Titrius said, in a last noble effort to resist the urges coursing through his being.

"Yes," Shaka purred. "I am!"

The Champion of Kappia hesitated and looked around at the plush surroundings, then at his Empress who lay there, only wearing the jewelled Maidenarz wrapped around her arm.

"Do you not want to lay with your Empress?"

Titrius looked her up and down, and Shaka could see the blood in his temples pulsing as he tried to resist the urges. The Maia potion was so powerful, that even her just tasting a single tear shed by Sheena, gave enough scent that it would have an effect on Titrius so strong it would be virtually impossible to resist, but she had made sure there was even more in the wine they had both just drank. She needed to be sure he would not give in to any fear or hesitation, as the punishment for sleeping with the Munte bride of an Emperor was severe and terrifying.

"To hell with it," he said as he threw off his robe, and jumped on the bed. "If it's true what they say about you, then so be it, I'll still resurrect a happy man." He lay on the bed beside her and ran his fingers across her breasts and down to her belly. He leaned forward to kiss her on the thigh, moving slowly down her leg towards her ankle. His hands moved beneath her, turning Shaka onto her back as his lips moved on a return course up the inside of her leg. A gentle but insistent tug pulled him alongside her and she held his face in her hands, staring into his eyes, as he played with her nipples with his fingers. They shared a long kiss, tongues meeting tentatively at first. She giggled, running clawed fingers through his chest hair, fingernails slightly scratching the surface. He eased her legs apart and entered her.

The feeling of Titrius touching her revolted Shaka, for so often had she used Maia she was almost immune to it, and it only had a little effect on her own desires, but she hid her grimace for the times when he was not looking at her face. He flopped sideward onto the bed, smiling after the climax of that most intimate and personal of moments.

"You are a great and brave man," she said, barely breathing the words.

"I am?" he asked.

"Of course, you are," she said taciturnly. "Surely you must know the penalty for mating with the Munte bride of your new Emperor?" She ran her finger across his chest, pressing her nail in so sharply and spitefully it drew blood from the long red welt it made.

He jumped off the bed in a panic, the realisation of what he had just done dawning upon him. Putting his robe back on, he said, clearly alarmed. "You tricked me, seduced me. A moment of madness overcame me."

Shaka laughed cruelly and spitefully as she got off the bed, and put her dress back on. "I think I will go now, straight to my husband, and tell him what you have done."

"I'll deny it," Titrius wailed.

"And invite trial in front of the Jewel of Baramir? You wretched fool!" Shaka roared angrily. "Do you think I would by choice lay with a stinking fool like you unless I wanted something from you?"

Titrius shrieked as he went pale, and then dropped to his knees in sheer terror, and began to beg for mercy. Shaka looked at him, and found enjoyment in seeing the great Champion of Kappia begging before her.

"Please, my Sarissa, have mercy on me. I do not know what came over me."

"Go to the public library and read the rules of Munte marriage, it is written in the fifty-ninth chapter, what you must suffer. The seventh verse in particular, describes that which happens to one who has relations with the Munte bride of an Emperor." She shuddered for effect and said, "Quite gruesome and barbaric if you ask me."

"You tricked me, seduced me," Titrius protested.

"That won't change anything, or protect you. The law is the law," she replied stingingly.

"Please, my Sarissa, why would you do this to me? I'll do anything; spare me I beg of you." Titrius was close to tears.

Shaka could not contain the broad smile that spread across her face. It brought her great pleasure to see such a usually bold and fearless man humbled and terrified before her. "Well, there is one little thing I will want you to do at the games for me," she said, "and if you do it, we need never speak of our little romantic tryst this evening, ever again."

"I'll do it, whatever you want," Titrius blurted out eagerly. He looked at her readily awaiting instruction.

"Then listen very, very carefully," she said. "I only have time to tell you this once. On the day of the games, you must do exactly as I now tell you."

# Chapter Forty-Four: *Imrand and the Aeldar Wives*

*His hands had talons; his eyes red like flames burning in the deepest darkness. There was no light, no comfort, and no mercy in them. His stare seared me like fire. And then his voice came faintly and far away, and evil itself looked at me. "Where are the Aeldar Wives?" he asked, after which my soul was drawn from my body across gulfs of echoing time and space. When my soul returned to my body, I trembled with a fear that was darker than the terror of death. I answered him. "We entombed them - three each in prisons from which there is only one means of escape."*
**Confessions of the Priest Named Rual.**

*A bow is a relatively simple device, and an arrow easy enough to make. You pull back the string; energy is stored in it and then released with the arrow, directly at a target. A well-placed arrow can change the course of history.*
**Observations from Phalius the Philosopher.**

*There* was no rasp of spring or hinge, but the door retreated inwards, revealing a room in which lay three sarcophaguses. Imrand and Sarkisi followed Migdal into the room. The carved faces on each coffin were twisted in horror and torment, but Imrand recognised them as the three Wytches that had appeared to them in the wood. Summoned by Migdal, the spirits of the three Wytches rose from out of the sarcophaguses, each of them surrounded by either a red, blue or green eerie light. Imrand cursed, and put his arms protectively around Sarkisi's supple waist. Her eyes were wide with terror, but she did not flinch.

Migdal flicked his fingers, and another door silently opened at the opposite end of the chamber. The three spirits glided up a set of stone stairs, and Migdal followed. "Come," he said to Imrand and Sarkisi, who followed him up the stairs and into a room where there was a long table filled with delights of every kind possible. The table was set in a long chamber filled with a soft light, of red, green and blue hue that seemed to mingle as a mist and become one, before separating again into distinct and separate colours. In the centre of the chamber was the huge trunk of a twisted tree that entered through the floor, and without losing any of its girth, exited from out of the high pinnacle of the space. Imrand felt strangely at ease, unlike in the wood when he had first met these beings. He sensed no threat from them, and glancing at Sarkisi he could tell the terror she had previously felt was easing away.

Neferu, the red Wytch, clad again in red transparent silks, said, "Sit," and flicked her fingers towards the table. Imrand and Sarkisi sat, after which the three Wytches stood at the head of the table. Migdal stood behind them and raised his broken and tattered wings. Neferu landed on her feet, and appeared to take physical form; no sign of age was upon her, except in the depth of her eyes which were wells of deep memory. She spoke in her own tongue, and Imrand understood even though it was not a language he had ever heard before. "It is long since we have seen one of Vanyr's folk in Garama Aethoros," she said, her voice a ghostly whisper.

"A long time, it is," Lefaria echoed as she took form and landed.

"They came with Bothgar. Many long years ago, scores of a thousand centuries and more," Morna said, as she also took form and floated to the ground.

"Many have come to my lair since you have slept," Migdal said to the Wytches, his voice sounding like the thunder, "but they were thieves and were slain by my hand. I brought their corpses and spirits here."

538

Neferu whispered, "Darkness gathers, and the shadows grow longer."

Lefaria whispered, "Very dark. The world falls to ruin."

Morna whispered, "Deep shadows seek to rise and stalk the land again."

"Who are you? Tell us what you want," Sarkisi demanded, a tremor in her voice.

The three Wytches laughed each in turn. The sound filled the chamber and seemed to bounce off of the walls, echoing as it faded.

Neferu spoke. "We have wakened from the long sleep. I am the soul of Neferu, wife of an Aeldar."

Lefaria said, "Look well upon us, princess of the Vanyr. Soon you shall behold us side by side with our husbands in bodily form."

Morna declared, "The race of Men shall love us again."

Why have you brought us here?" Imrand asked.

Neferu answered him: "Our bodies lay in their frames of bones and flesh. New bodies we seek."

Lefaria: "They are now empty shells from which we have awoken. You will help us, for the Simal is here, so very close. Migdal has found it for us."

Morna: "When we return with our husbands to the Everglow, passion will stir the fires of untold numbers of warriors. You will lead them."

Neferu: "We lost hope when we were imprisoned here. Bothgar brought us the *Prophecy of Rithguar*. It said that when the Simal finds Migdal, a prince and princess of the Vanyr would come to help us."

Lefaria: "Hope lives within us again."

Morna: "We have slept, until Migdal woke us to fetch you from Bothgar's tomb."

"Why would I want to help you?" Imrand demanded.

Neferu: "You and your pretty wife will have great rewards."

Lefaria: "Anger is in both your hearts. We can satisfy it."

Morna: "Help us, and we will help you."

"What if we refuse?" Imrand asked.

In an instant the food on the table began to rot and deteriorate. Imrand watched in horror as his hand began to wither and shrivel before him until the skin turned to dust and blew away in an uncanny breeze leaving just the bones on his hand before him. Sarkisi, aged in an instant, until the pile of bones that remained of her skeleton collapsed in the very chair, she sat in. Imrand no longer had flesh himself, he was just a skeleton. He stood to his feet, powered by an unearthly power that still gave him life. The chamber went dark; all he could see was a black emptiness, an abyss of infernal night. In the black abyss there appeared a figure, standing, holding a giant war hammer he swung about his head. The face was expressionless, at the same time beautiful and cruel. Nine horns each shaped differently rose upwards as they sprung from a mass of hair on its head. It looked around him, searching this way and that. It smashed the hammer against the darkness, and it felt to Imrand like the very foundations of creation shook with the impact. He knew that the figure could not see him. Eight other creatures, each more grotesque than the horned figure began to emerge from the darkness. One of them, a foul and giant snake, slithered up to the horned beast and wrapped itself around its leg. The snake noticed Imrand, and with a hiss of pure hatred, it lunged at him. He jumped back instinctively, and the vision faded. He was seated back at the table with Sarkisi; they were no longer a skeleton or pile of bones but back to normal. The food on the table was no longer rotten but fresh and sweet.

The three Wytches looked at them, as though studying their reactions.

"What was that vision?" Sarkisi asked, her voice tremoring with fresh hysteria and fear. "What were those things I saw?"

It occurred to Imrand that his wife had seen the same vision as he had.

"Nine of them. Three of them, our husbands they were," Neferu answered.

"We are Aeldar Wives," Lefaria added.

Morna looked sad when she said, "Nine of them, nine of us. Three of us are within the Simal, saved they are. Three still hide. We three, are now found. The Simal is here, it has woken us, it calls to us. We will join the three that are saved!"

Neferu whispered with longing, "Our reunion with our husbands is so close."

Lefaria: "So close."

Morna: "Help us find our husbands, to call to them with the riddles of their true names, that they might find their own way home to us, from out of the eternal Void!"

"Why do you need our help?" Imrand asked, still feeling deeply unsettled by the disturbing vision.

Neferu and the other two Wytches raised their hands, and suddenly they each seemed tall beyond measurement, and beautiful yet terrible to behold. Each of them slowly faded. Great lights of red, green and blue surrounded where they had been, leaving all else around them in the dark. Then a great white light lit up the room, and the form of Neferu appeared first; it was that of a slender and well-proportioned woman no longer clad in red but naked. Her skin was white as milk and smooth, her voice was gentle and sad when she spoke. "We have slept in the deep dark. The Simal comes to us. Migdal has woken, but he has forgotten who he is, only his shadow which you see before you, sometimes remembers. The Simal comes to us, carried by a thief, but we cannot take it from her; it has to be given to us by one born of the Vanyr."

"You must take it from her when she comes, and give it to us," Lefaria said as she suddenly appeared as if walking from out of a mist; she was also naked.

"You are the children of *Rithguar's Prophesy*. Help us, and great gifts we shall give you, starting with this," Morna said as she also appeared with nothing on and handed Imrand the giant's weapon he had taken from Bothgar's tomb.

Imrand took it, and it shrunk down to the size of a normal sword. He admired the jewelled pommel, the purple-bound hilt, and the long narrow serrated blade. The purple runes on it glimmered and shone with an ethereal light. For the briefest of moments, he considered lunging at the Wytches trying to take them all down in one powerful strike, but he remembered how that had gone for him before, and decided against it. "I will listen to what you have to say," he said.

"*Ormfron*, is the name of the blade," Migdal said. "Arkith it is. Feared by those of Akkadian blood." Migdal flicked his fingers, and of a sudden they were all in a large, tiered circular chamber. In the middle was a firepit, the flames of which leapt up with a roar. Upon the walls hung hundreds of lifeless skeletons, each clad in ancient armour the like of which Imrand had never seen before.

"What is this place?" Imrand asked as he looked around him.

"Some of these were the Elves of the Wytchwood, who, when we arrived, sought to slay us," Neferu answered. "The bodies of some are now entombed, in glass, in their fortress of old. Others are here."

"Some were great kings, queens or heroes from the race of Men, who came to steal from us," Lefaria whispered. "They heard tales of the treasure that lay in Migdal's Lair, and the riches of Garama Aethoros."

"Migdal protected us," Morna said softly. "He took the fortress for himself, and hid the gate to Garama Aethoros, concealed us here, and surrounded it with his lair. They came, he slew them, and brought their bodies and spirits here."

Neferu flicked her fingers, the fire roared and leapt into the air and Imrand was suddenly clothed in Elven glass armour. One of the skeletons on the wall, the one the

540

armour had been removed from, crumbled and fell to the floor with a clatter of the sound of the bones against the bare stone.

Imrand looked at the armour, it was light and fitted him perfectly and of a workmanship made with a skill he could not comprehend, so intricate were the leaf designs upon it. The breastplate, gorget, spaulders and greaves were made of fine green glass and forged in such a way it mimicked the curve of his bulging muscles. The fine rings of a mail tunic were visible between the plates. A thin layer of forest green cloth so expertly tailored separated the pieces of armour so that when he moved, the armour made not a sound. Sabatons protected his feet, and when he walked his footsteps made no sound. His head was encased in a helmet, the likeness of which he could see in a polished metal mirror that momentarily appeared before him. The visor of the helmet was forged into the fine features of a noble elf, but changed and took on the shape of his face and features, and changed to reveal every expression he made. He put *Ormfron* into the sheath that had appeared around his waist. In one hand a finely carved sword appeared, which was shaped like a long and slender leaf, and in the other hand a leaf-shaped shield. On the blade were symbols, and on the face of the shield was shown the whole cosmos: the earth; the waters; the heavens, and all the celestial bodies. Two cities were portrayed in fine and intricate detail. In one city peace reigned; full of hope the people went about their daily business; the other city was beset by foes, and showed scenes of woe and despair, ambush and treachery, death and decay.

Neferu: "The Elvish sword is named *Greendeath*. It was forged with a skill now forgotten, and will melt through any armour like a hot knife through butter."

Lefaria: "The shield is called *Avenger*. We will teach you how to use it, for much magic there is in it."

Morna: "The armour has no name, but *Protector* we call it, for no normal blade can pierce it."

Imrand studied the armour and weapon with savage delight. A strength he had never felt before flushed through him. He turned as he heard a crash and one more skeleton fell from the wall to the floor. When he looked at Sarkisi, she was clothed in similar armour, the visor and helmet taking on the image of her face, and instead of the male muscular physique of his armour, hers was fashioned in the perfection of her own feminine form. In her hand she held a finely crafted bow and a sheath of arrows were slung across her back. The bow glimmered with symbols, and Sarkisi ran her fingers along them.

"That is a Moon Bow," Migdal said. "Its name is *Harnesh*. Any arrow fired when the moon is out, will pierce any armour, your aim will be true, so you will slay any foe."

Imrand and Sarkisi both looked at him as with a long taloned-finger he pointed at them each in turn. "The armour and weapons you now possess, once belonged to a great Elven King and his Queen. They were rulers of Upper and Lower Tangrat, an ancient kingdom now no longer in existence, and forgotten by those who walk in the Outer-World. His name was Tarnash, hers Sarathna. Their legends are written in the symbols of bow and blade. They came to help the Elves of the Wytchwood when we arrived, but they failed in their quest. Only an Arkoom or Arkith, or a weapon made of Elven black glass can pierce the armours you wear, and not many of that kind any longer exist in the world. But an Arkith, we have gifted to you."

Migdal strangely started to fade. "I am forgetting, I do not have long, I am just shadow and must return to my flesh," he said. "Use *Ormfron*, when fighting the Children of the Arnath, and against only those you want to cruelly punish. Use *Greendeath*, for foes that deserve an honoured death." He struggled to breath, and faded even more.

541

"You are given the strength and endurance of a giant, when you wear this armour. It is charmed so that you can carry the weight of a tree for a day and not tire."

Neferu circled Imrand and Sarkisi. "Vengeance you can take on those who have wronged you. Very few will have the strength to resist you with the blades and bow you both now wield. *Ormfron*, Arkith it is, the *Final-death* it gives to any born of Pure-blood. With *Ormfron, Greendeath, Avenger* and *Harnesh*, you can walk the world of men like the heroes of ancient tales, protected by armour none can now forge the like of."

"Invincible you will be, like a goddess," Lefaria said as she circled Sarkisi. "The bow always aims true at night, never a mark will it miss, though when the sun is out your own skill must guide your aim, but even then, foe it will slay."

"With these you can forge your own kingdom," Morna said as she circled them both. "*Ormfron* once slew the Oracle of Ongrath in a time now forgotten by mortals, and *Greendeath* killed the legendary giant Hanrahar, whose blows could not pass *Avenger*. *Harnesh*, when on a hunt once slew Harmingder the Werewolf, a creature so fierce the gods themselves once shuddered at the mention of his name."

"These gifts are yours, if you help the Aeldar Wives," Migdal said.

Images of Bahri and Gerdar appeared. They were in a tent in the desert, with more chained slaves around them, as Bahri and his men ill-treated an unfortunate Davari woman. Imrand felt an almost uncontrollable rage surge within him. He then saw Sasna and her brother, sailing on a ship approaching a storm, and wished nothing more than to pierce their flesh with *Ormfron or Greendeath*. He then saw the twisted hunch-back and the other two black terrors that had captured him and Sarkisi, and again felt an irresistible rage.

"Their names are Regineo, Caspus, and Aspess. They are the children of an Empress. Their lust for hunting Davari has led to your misery," Migdal said. In turn, each image dispersed as a mist. "None will stop you from satisfying your vengeance, with these gifts we bestow, if you fain give us your aid."

Imrand made his decision instantly. "I will," he said fiercely, and then asked, "tell me what I must do?"

The Wytches whispered excitedly among themselves.

Neferu answered: "Take the Simal when it comes!"

Lefaria: "Give it to us you must!"

Morna: "These gifts are yours for your help!"

Of a sudden, gold coins and jewels, like raindrops, fell around them, making loud tinkling sounds as they hit the floor. Imrand and Sarkisi watched in awe, resisting the temptation to fall to their knees and scoop them up.

Neferu: "Help us, and take as much as you can carry."

Lefaria: "Each one is ancient and worth more than a city."

Morna: "Men have sold their souls to lust upon the beauty of these coins. You have the strength now, to carry them far."

Neferu:" What say you?"

"Lefaria: "Speak!

Morna: "Answer us!"

Imrand smiled, and the Elven helmet shifted form to match the joy and exultation that spread across his face. "I will do as you ask," he said.

"As shall I," Sarkisi said melodiously.

"Your will, our will," they said together.

542

# Chapter Forty-Five: *The Dark Paths*

*A special curse is reserved for those who willingly join that Empire of black magicians. The sages of Cragan practice foul necromancy, thaumaturgy of the most odious and evil kind, grisly magic taught them by demons of the old worlds. And of all the sorcerers of that accursed Empire, none was so foul or great as Horin of Cragan. He hides in the Deadlands along Dark Paths I cannot find; but find him I will, and he will pay for his crimes. Any who can offer me information, will be amply rewarded for their trouble.*
*A poster distributed by The Wizard Hunter General of Baothein.*

*At* first, there was nothing but darkness. Talain's senses returned slowly, in small increments. Images flashed, some understandable and some not; places, faces, struggles and then quiet. It was always the same, both when she entered the Deadlands, and then returned to the Everglow. Her memories and knowledge of the other life was always incomplete. Even after the *Awakening*, often she could not immediately recall everything she had been through in the Deadlands. It was the same whenever she died, and entered that place. Talain knew that the reason was she lacked the formal training a Seer should have in one of the Mystery Schools. But she had been self-taught, and she was getting better and faster at remembering. *Why am I in the Deadlands?* she asked herself, feeling confused.

Talain's vision was blurred, and deafening sound filled her ears. It was so loud she blocked it out with her fingers. The darkness slowly ebbed away; her surroundings came into view until she could fully see. A face welled and ebbed in the darkness, a man, tortured and screaming, his eyes rolling back in his skull, his tongue swollen and protruding. The sight triggered something in her memory, she remembered. *He is Borach, I am Talain.* The sight of Borach, tortured, screaming in front of her, filled her with fear. *What is happening?* she inwardly shouted.

Talain and Borach were in a valley, surrounded on two sides by small cliffs littered sparsely with brush and bush. He had the appearance of a grey wraith, as was normal for an Akkadian who was not a Seer. She had remembered reading this somewhere, but his form was changing, and why she did not know. Talain watched with growing fear as a physical transformation overtook the wraith, Borach. The fires of hate smouldering in his eyes grew brighter. His skull-like face grew hard and grey, like a bust carved out of stone, and his eyes shrank to mere slits. He grinned, a deathlike grin that sent chills down Talain's spine. His body shook violently, as if something inside of him fought to get out. Then she saw it, for a mere flash of a second. It was a spirit, as dark as night and dripping with ancient evil. If it did loose itself, she did not know if she could slay it. Her temptation was to run.

Horin had given her weapons and armour that she used whenever she entered the Deadlands, but he had always cautioned, every time she visited him at the Dark Paths, to be careful what creatures she engaged in combat. He had often warned her that she still had so much to learn and that she had less knowledge than a novice at a Mystery School. This became searingly obvious to her at that moment. She did not even know if Borach could be free from the foul spirit that had him in its grip, but it did appear as though the spirit was trying to escape from Borach's essence. Sensing her, the evil spirit within Borach's wraith reached out and grabbed her, wrapping its cold fingers around her throat. Both wraith and spirit cackled like a madman, bloody spittle and froth dripping from their jaws. Borach's face twisted into a mask of hate, and his slitted eyes burned with a baleful fire. A high-pitched scream burst from his lips.

Talain's instincts screamed within her. Her breath came in sharp gasps, her heart hammered in her chest. The wraith that was Borach was feral; the evil spirit more so. She regretted her arrogance thinking she could lead him through the Deadlands. A memory returned. She had promised somebody she could, sworn she would do it. *Ah yes, the dwarf, I promised him I would help his friend.* Another memory returned. *I told King Falamore I could do it.* Both promises had been made in good faith. She had believed it at the time, but had not realised that the wraith she had promised to escort back to the Obelisk at Thurog Tor would be both feral and possessed.

Horin had not taught her how to deal with such a situation. Trying to lure Borach through the Deadlands in this state was an invitation to disaster, for both him and her, but she had given her word to Marki, and to King Falamore. The evil spirit was draining the life essence from her as its finger pressed ever tighter around her throat, she felt weak and sick, and panicked. In one movement she drew her sword, it flashed down, crunching through Borach's head, shoulder and into his chest. Wrenching her blade free, again and again she struck until the wraith that had been Borach grew unrecognisable. The wraith Borach fell to the floor dead. The evil spirit that had possessed it, left the remains of the wraith's corpse, flew into the air like a ball of fire, laughed hideously, and flew into the distance out of sight, its screeching slowly fading.

Talain reeled away from the corpse, her sword falling from her grasp. She stumbled backwards and slid to the ground, cradling her head in her hands. Regaining her composure after a minute or so, she stood to her feet. *This wasn't supposed to happen*, she said to herself. Many times, she had wandered through the Deadlands, but always alone, never had she tried to escort somebody before. She remembered hearing at school when a little girl that the Seers' in Bruthon had many lifetimes of training before they could escort somebody through the Deadlands. It dawned upon her for the first time, that she might not know as much as she thought she did, despite having had many journeys in this place and numerous lessons from Horin. Dealing with a situation like this though, had not be one of those lessons.

Picking up her sword, she sheathed it and walked towards Borach's wraith corpse. It was impossible to pick up, a weight that not even a hundred men could move. She screamed and jumped back when it suddenly hissed, and turned into a mist, and took on a different, lighter wraith like form that floated in the air. It was his essence. She tried to touch it with her hands, but her hand passed through it. The essence wraith that was Borach, of its own accord, with eyes closed, began to drift aimlessly, quietly moaning. The evil spirit returned and watched her from a distance.

Talain regretted her own arrogance, but in her defence, whilst in the Everglow she had not fully remembered everything she had been taught or warned about whilst here in the Deadlands. More memories returned. Horin had warned her not to get into situations she was not ready for, and in this matter, she had received no lessons and did not fully know what was happening, as she had never been with another Akkadian in the Deadlands. Her knowledge was patchy. She herself had died a second-death here a few times, and each time when she resurrected afterwards, she could only remember what she had seen up to the point of death, a death usually inflicted by some foul beast or monstrosity. But, each time, she had resurrected back at Thurog Tor, for to that Obelisk she had always headed. She hoped beyond hope, that somehow, the watery essence that was now Borach, would be summoned and drawn to the Obelisk at Thurog Tor, and would be resurrected there. But his essence was drifting aimlessly, and mostly towards the south, and nothing she attempted could get it to change direction. *Please, don't drift south. The only Obelisk that way is at Foulway, and none would want to resurrect there.* She instinctively knew, that the evil spirit that watched her, would return the moment she left Borach's essence alone. Suddenly, another memory returned, one that struck terror in her heart. It was something Horin had once said to her. *'Savage Telamones, soul-eaters, scavenge at Foulway. Do not stray near to that place lest they pick up your scent. Always stay within range of the Obelisk at Thurg Tor.'*

Talain knew that Borach's very existence was at stake. The evil spirit called to him. His essence picked up speed as if blown by a wind. It aimlessly drifted towards the south, from where the spirit was calling and coaxing it to come. She tried to persuade his essence, his spirit, to follow her, but it just moaned and moved ever towards the south. Her hands passed through it when she tried to grab it and pull it with her. She quickly decided that it was impossible for her to try to guide him in this form to the Obelisk at Thurog Tor. His essence still drifted towards the south, and no tempting, coaxing or effort of hers could get it to do what she wanted. She understood enough to know that in the Deadlands, all the dead had a second body, that if it died, it released the essence of that person, the spirit. The further south the essence of Borach headed, the more the chance that Telamones, the scavengers of the Deadlands, might soon pick up the scent. It was beyond her knowledge to know how to lead a bodiless spirit in that place. She had not expected some foul spirit to have possession of Borach. She regretted that she had ever taken on the task.

Thinking quickly, Talain realised she only had two choices. The first was to follow, and then guard Borach, if he continued to drift towards the south into Telamone territory. In such a case, the Telamones would come when they picked up his scent. She had never seen one, but Horin had warned her that Telamones were fearsome and brutal creatures and well beyond her ability to fight. The second choice was to seek help as fast as she could. *Horin! I must seek the help of Horin,* she told herself. Borach's spirit could not see her, hear her, and she had no way to manipulate or lead it. For now, she had to take a chance and leave him. Speed was essential, if she was to save him.

Talain turned and ran down the valley with all her might. She could see the Black Hills in the far distance beyond the valley, and once she was near them, she knew the trails would be familiar. The Gate of Horin was not that far, she must enter the Dark Paths and urgently seek his help. With all her strength and might, she ran over the loamy soil, leaping over the tiny spears of green that were sprouting through dead, coppery bracken until she reached a barren, red landscape, where the air hung heavy with smoke and the smell of sulphur mixed with the stench of death and decay. It almost overwhelmed her. Plumes of gasses erupted around her, foul, yellowish geysers and red fumaroles. It was torturous ground to travel on, but she kept moving as fast as she could, all of the while berating herself in quiet mutters at her own foolishness for getting into a situation that was clearly beyond her ability to cope with.

It took her over an hour to reach the shadow of the Black Hills, where she entered a lush valley that was in striking contrast to the ground she had just traversed. At the end of the valley, she found the glowing firestones, ones that in the past she had placed, that led to one of the gateways to Horin's Path, or as it was also called, the Dark Paths. He had previously warned her it was a path she should travel less and less, but the reason for the warning eluded her. Something tickled the edge of her consciousness, but she could not grab a hold of it. She reasoned with herself that surely her current predicament was of more importance, so she continued. It was not long before she soon lost track of all time as she ran, and ran, and followed the path of the stones, not stopping or resting until breathing became hard and laboured, and her spirit body ached with exhaustion.

Reaching the end of the path lit by the glowing firestones, Talain slid down an incline and stumbled to a halt, looking at a cluster of bleached stones that she had also placed there long ago to help show her the way. The stones pointed to a tall monument; a slab of arched rock supported by two others. The monument was invisible from any other angle, except when looking on in a straight line from where the stones pointed. Slowly, catching her breath, she walked towards the monument, not taking her eyes off it even for a second, nor deviating from the path even the slightest to her left or right, lest she lose the way.

Slowly, step by step she continued, until she stood before the monument, the Gate of Horin that led to the Dark Paths. A hooded figure clothed in a tattered black robe and cape appeared as she approached, and barred her way. It held a wooden staff, on the end of which was a black stone, the key to the gate. Talain felt a terrible dread welling up in the core of her being. With every movement, it was as though the shadows had become caught in the creature's robes and dragged them along. It planted the staff in the ground and clutched the knotted wood with both hands, its talons wrapping around it with a clicking sound.

"Please, I need to enter the Dark Paths and speak to Horin," she pleaded.

An ashen face stared at her from under the hood. "Go back from whence you came, or pay the price," the figure said with a rasping voice.

"I will pay the price," she said, as she reached for her sword. The blade, which in her hands had always easily left the scabbard the moment she gripped the hilt, would not let itself be drawn. It resisted her, stuck in its scabbard as if glued in tar. She tugged at it, and eventually it was drawn, but in a motion that was unnaturally slow. The ground trembled and shook beneath her. As she peered anxiously at the ground, she noticed it was starting to ripple, as though the patch of soil had become a miniature, windswept ocean beneath her feet. It took her an age and much effort to slowly draw the sword across her palm. Blood began to trickle. She struggled but eventually managed to sheath her sword, and then held out her palm, dripping with blood. The hooded figure reached out with its staff so the blood dripped onto the black stone. It grinned, and made a noise which she could not tell was pleasure or pain. It waved the staff behind it; a circular inscription appeared between the two stone pillars beneath the arch, an ancient hieroglyph of some kind that glimmered in the dark. Strange sensations in the pit of her stomach visited her, rising up into her chest and then throat. For an instant she wondered if she was in danger from the symbols. She felt exposed to a time before time, an era when she had not existed. An ancient gate appeared; she stepped through it, and then fell through it, as though she was endlessly falling until her feet touched solid ground, and all was black and dark. In this way she found herself once more on the Dark Paths.

Several hooded, glowing, cloaked figures riding pale stallions watched her. They signalled for her to follow. It was so dark, she could not see the paths they led her upon, so she followed the glow of the stallions that galloped at full pace. It was not difficult for her to keep up, she ran with all of her strength over a distance she could not calculate, this time without feeling tired or short of breath. Eventually she saw the dark silhouette of Horin's castle upon a hill. The riders silently pointed to a path lit by torches that led up the hill to the castle gates. They did not follow her as she began to run up the path; instead each rider disappeared back into the shadows.

Talain entered the castle by crossing a rickety drawbridge, passing under the open gateway and then pressing on into the main square, where a lone black tree grew through the cracked and broken cobblestones. The door to the main keep was open. She crossed the square and passed through the door with all of her speed, ran up the winding steps of the main tower and entered a large hall, the roof of which was held aloft by mighty pillars with strange carvings etched upon them. Long tapers flickered, sending black shadows along the wall. Velvet tapestries rippled from a wind that blew in from broken windows, causing the aged and tattered silk curtains to dance in its movement. In the centre of the hall was an ebony table that spread virtually the entire length of the hall. Curious statuettes were positioned along its length; they held green candles which burned with a weird green light. At the end of a table, upon a small dais, was a throne-like chair with a high ebony back and wide arms, and feet like bird's claws. A skeletal figured dressed in a decaying ermine robe sat lifeless upon it.

Talain approached the chair cautiously. Underneath the chair was a rock. She bent low, and reaching out she pulled away the rock, and uncovered the small rotting corpse of a bird half-buried beneath it. Maggots and worms slithered between its flesh and bones. She recoiled in disgust, but held out her hand, which of itself started to bleed again. Her blood dripped onto the corpse of the bird, which began to move, before standing to its feet. She instinctively took a few steps back, and the tiny corpse hobbled towards her. As it moved its little bones cracked and popped, shedding goblets of dark, clotted blood. The bird flapped wings with oily feathers stuck to mostly bone. The dead bird tilted its head on one side, and fixed its milky retinas on her. The rotting limbs began to solidify and form healthy flesh, which was soon covered by glowing feathers. The eyes cleared, and stared intelligently at Talain. It was no longer a corpse, but a small, healthy, living bird that stood before her.

"Why have you woken me again?" Horin asked in a time-worn, weary but human voice. Its beak did not move as it spoke. "I have travelled to the voids and gulfs of oblivion. I tire of this realm and do not wish to keep returning."

"Horin, I need your help," Talain answered in desperation.

The bird flapped its wings, and hopped onto the lap of the skeletal figure upon the chair, and merged with the corpse. Sinews and flesh began to grow in an instant, writhing like a vine creeping through the bones until the figure was changed into the form of a youthful man. The ermine robe was renewed, under which clothes appeared. The man stood there dressed in the elegant white robe and clothes from which emanated a bright light, expelling all the darkness around them. Horin sighed with pleasure as broad muscles flexed across his chest and back as he stretched and yawned, shaking off the long sleep.

Talain became aware of sound; from where it came, she could not tell. Hundreds of voices chanted the name of Horin. They were singing glorious ballads and long, rousing epics, describing his past feats in life in extravagant detail. She saw ghostly figures in the hall feasting and dancing. Time stood still. It felt like seconds, like years, and then the sound suddenly stopped, and the ghosts disappeared as quickly as they had come.

Horin took an unsteady step towards her and placed his hand upon her head. "I must read your thread," he whispered. She felt him searching her mind, her memories. He seemed to drink them in and relished the experience. He then frowned, and took his hand from her head as he looked at her disapprovingly. "You were not ready for this, you have taken on much more than you know," he said as a grave look etched his features. "The man, Borach, has been cursed with a foul-blade. Why did you try to escort him through the Deadlands when you lack the required training? His very existence was already in danger without your help. In seeking to assist him you have placed yourself in the same peril he faces."

"I'm sorry, I thought I could help. Can you help me, can you fix it?" she pleaded.
"In fear I slew his spirit body. His essence is drawn to the south and will attract Telamones!"

"Wait here," Horin said. He then flicked his fingers, turned instantly into bird form, and with a flap of his wings flew into the air and out of the castle window. At the same time, a thousand or so darkly clad angels with eyes black as coal appeared, and with a single beat of their delicate wings dropped onto the floor around Talain. They began to dance, and as they danced, they pulled her along with them across a carpet of multi-coloured flower petals, forming a circle around her, holding hands and spinning in the opposite direction. They seemed to flicker with silver fire. As the dance spiralled around her, she closed her eyes and danced with them. The crowns and domes of kingdoms and eternity spread out before her. Talain felt calm and peace, and in an instant it all disappeared, and Horin stood before her again, once more in human form.

The memory of the dance began to fade. Talain struggled to recall the event that she had just seen and heard. It felt like it had happened centuries ago, and at the same time seemed like mere seconds had passed.

Horin had a severe expression on his face. He no longer looked youthful but appeared as old and tired as his voice.

"What is it? What troubles you?" Talain asked.

Horin answered solemnly. "I have seen the threads being woven for this age, and spoken to those who weave them. It has begun; the war of all worlds, a war that will shake the very foundations of all existence. No realm shall escape it, not even this one. The threads of the one you tried to escort are strong and will not be easily broken, but danger surrounds him at every turn. He cannot make many wrongs choices, or his doom and that of others could soon come upon him." He grimaced. "You have acted foolishly, but your folly might be that which saves him. The evil spirit that coaxes his essence still leads him south. Telamones have already picked up his scent. They are coming for him. We must hurry!"

Horin's appearance changed. His skin withered, as a fierce gale began to howl around him. Numerous will-o'-the-wisps covered him, and when they left, his appearance was fearsome to behold. A rusty helmet with buffalo horns swayed above his now skull-like face, its gaping eye sockets burning with a livid flame. His skeletal chest was covered in a rusty cuirass and the rest of his body in rusting armour pieces. He whistled, and out of a mist appeared a skeletal steed cloaked in a ragged caparison. Horin mounted it, and the steed reared up and neighed horrifyingly.

"Come," Horin said as he offered Talain his hand. She took it, and he pulled her up onto the steed behind him. He spurred on the steed, and roared with wild, horrifying laughter. They galloped though the hall, down the winding steps of the tower, across the square and drawbridge and onto the Dark Paths. They rode with speed to the Gate of Horin where the hooded, glowing cloaked figures riding pale stallions fell in behind them. Through the gate they went, through the lush valley and onto the barren red plain and beyond. Talain had no idea how long the journey was, for it seemed like seconds and yet at the same time hours, days, months or years. They came to the place where she had entered the Deadlands, and then raced south until they saw the spirit of Borach drifting ever on towards its doom.

Horin dismounted the skeletal steed, and took Talain from the saddle and stood her on the ground. He then examined the essence, and wailed in despair over Borach. "He is a mighty lord, a noble heart dwells within him, but it has been broken and infected with evil. A foul-blade born of a fouler place and tainted with dark curses has wounded him in the land he lives in. The evil of it shows itself here. You cannot cure him; you cannot protect him. You were foolish to agree to escort one such as him, but your folly has been revised in that you sought my aid."

Deep, terrifying, haunting wailing sounds filled the entire valley. Horin sniffed the air. His eyes burned brightly.

"Telamones are here. They hunt him." A look of surprise spread across Horin's features. "But not all of these Telamones are from Foulway. There are others, far worse. Sent ones. From the Void." He looked around guardedly as in the very far distance, the gigantic outlines of Telamones began to emerge. "The sent ones, hunt another." He listened intently to the fierce, low wailing sounds the creatures made. "They call out a name." He then said a name, very slowly. "Janorra…" As if responding to the name, the terrifying wailing in the distance increased. Horin continued. "They hunt one named Janorra, a woman that is known to me, as are her threads, the possibilities of which I now see before me. They seek her scent for when next she comes to the Deadlands." The dark outlines of the Telamones began to take more distinct shapes. "There are many of them. Such numbers are beyond even me and my warriors. We must act with haste!"

Horin waved his hand. Several angels appeared, each as black as the night. They effortlessly picked up Borach and lifted Talain from the ground, and with a flap of their wings they lifted them high into the air. Horin changed into bird form, and was soon flying at their side.

"Talain," he said looking at her with seriousness and concern. "It is one thing for you to travel here alone, but quite another to travel when such foes have been unleashed from realms deeper than this. You cannot lead a legion of the dead through here, nor can you help Borach again. You are not qualified or ready. It is beyond you, and foolish you were to agree to such a task. Beyond this one time; you must not visit the Dark Paths again."

"Why not?" Talain asked. "I need you, for you are my guide and teacher."

"You have paid the blood price too many times. Each time you come to me, you lessen your chances of going back to the land of the living, ever. I am soon done with these realms. My work is almost finished; I have made amends for my past crimes. I regret that I ever showed you the way to the Dark Paths for your spirit is not yet strong enough to travel there as often as you have desired or needed. I could not see this until now."

"I do not want to go back when I am with you," she said. "I want to stay here with you or go to whatever realms you now dwell in, or shall move onto!" *I love you, Horin, like a daughter loves a father.*

"You cannot. Your thread is not yet woven to its full length. Your destiny will not be forged here, but in the Everglow, in the land of living where reality is dimmed and knowledge so little. You are to be tested and there you must prove yourself."

"I have sworn and given my word to help him, and his legion," Talain said as she looked at Borach's essence being carried through the air by two of the dark, shadowy angels. "I cannot go back on my word!"

Horin frowned. "Greatness and folly abide within you in equal measures. You have agreed to a task that is beyond your ability to carry out."

"Then help me, please. I cannot let them suffer due to the foolishness of a rash promise that I made in ignorance."

Horin's bird like face softened. "Like a daughter you are to me," he said. "I will order my Pale Riders to take the dead of the legion to the Obelisk at Thurog Tor if they die and come here. I have spoken to many Obelisks as well as thread-masters. I will lead the Telamones on false trails away from here. We must aid these men. Great events are afoot, and part of them they are."

"What about him?" she asked Horin as she looked at the spirit of Borach being carried by the angels. The sky grew dark as thunder rumbled, and a few seconds later flared with the sharp, blinding glare of lightning.

"When you wake in the Everglow, you must tell Borach to find the one named Janorra," Horin finally said. "His destiny is tied in with hers. She stole the Simal from the Argona Temple in Kappia city. She is currently to be found in the Wytchwood. Tell him he must not tarry for she is not safe there. He must help her take the Simal to the Baothein, or doom will be his. She can cure him of the evil disease upon his soul. In places my Pale Riders cannot reach, she will guide the dead of his legion through other lands he must go to, for she is destined to travel with them. Beyond this I can tell you no more, for it was knowledge kept from me. Many paths will be open to them and I do not know which they will choose. You will need her help and must seek it out, but she herself is in terrible danger. Here in the Deadlands Telamones hunt her. In the Everglow, the Wild Hunt pursues her, as do the Order of Ithkall. Soon, the Dark Undead will also seek her for they will soon appear again in the world. The Simal must not fall into any of their hands."

"The Wild Hunt? The Order of Ithkall? The Dark Undead? Who or what are they?"

"Borach will know. You must tell him of these things when you return to the land of the living. This war he is engaged in on behalf of the petty rulers in the Tarenmoors will have no influence on the greater threads being woven. Their kingdoms might be crushed and burnt to ashes when the Bantu arrive in their lands. He must find Janorra. Let the foolish kings and rulers of the Tarenmoors unite against the Bantu or destroy themselves. Theirs are trivial threads that have little consequences beyond their petty desires and insignificant fates."

The angels landed gently on the ground, placing Borach and Talain next to the Obelisk at Thurog Tor. Horin landed with a gentle flap of his wings beside them.

"Talain, your training is not sufficient that you might quickly remember these events or my words when you leave the Deadlands and return to the Everglow, but it is imperative you try. Borach must find the one called Janorra, in the Wytchwood, for their threads are woven together. Their fate and doom are terrible, if their paths do not cross. Implore him to seek her! You must try to remember this; the destiny of many requires it."

Horin looked at her fondly. "Farewell Talain. I have but a little work left to do in these realms, before I leave them forever. I have seen it in our fates. We will meet again, but the next time will be our last."

"No!" Talain wailed. "Horin, don't leave me. I need you. I'm afraid without you."

Horin sighed. "My crimes were many in life, dark secrets I sought and obtained. In death, I was imprisoned in the Dark Paths, until angels I had conversed with in life, showed me how to turn it into my domain. I have sought to amend my crimes and worked for the good of many, since death, but still I am cursed and there are those that hunt me still." His head twitched and he scanned the skies and his surroundings. "They will surely find me, for many will now come, and I shall be but a bird in the mouth of a wolf when he that swore to find me discovers my domain. I will not be there when he does. Cragan cannot have peace for long, wherever we flee for sanctuary."

Talain felt her senses growing numb as the Deadlands and Horin began to fade.

She faintly heard his voice, as in the distance. "Do not return to the Dark Paths. I will find you, when we next need to speak."

Her memory began to slip away, as the Obelisk drew her spirit and that of Borach into its cold embrace.

550

# Chapter Forty-Six: *Borach Awakes*

*One of the great mysteries about the Obelisks and Akkadian resurrection is the fact that during their first lifetime, if a Pure-blood Akkadian dies before the age of thirty years, they are sometimes never resurrected. A few cases of this have been recorded, but it is hard to find accurate statistics. It is only after the age of thirty, and nobody really knows the reason why, that resurrection after death is usually guaranteed for at least a few lifetimes, mostly more. If a person makes it past thirty and dies, they are resurrected already physically matured at the age of thirty every single time afterwards. During their first lifetime, an Akkadian does not have the mark of an Obelisk; this appears only after their first resurrection. It disappears when they are on their last, natural, final lifetime, so mercifully, unless they die beyond the Everglow without a Neblan, or by an Arkith, whenever they are resurrected without the mark of the Obelisk, they know that it is for the final time. It is also, surely significant, that Akkadian women can only breed during their first and final lifetimes, although there are exceptions to this rule and sometimes Pure-blood women do become pregnant at other times but it is very rare. Perhaps in the wisdom of the gods this is to stop the world being over populated? Yet again, we really don't know, although theologians and philosophers have endless theories and beliefs for the reasons behind this.*

*I will end this section by saying that as far as records show, the most times a person has ever been resurrected was 192. This was a Kappian noble lady. She died at 42 years of age during her first lifetime, and thereafter (not counting the automatic 30 years of age she was resurrected at) she lived in total for 6570 years, meaning that not including the resurrection age of thirty, she lived roughly on average 34 years after each resurrection, although the records do show that on more than a few occasions she did live for more than 60 years after each resurrection, and on frequent occasions less than 10 years. The lowest number of records for resurrection recorded was just a mere 52. Once again, nobody knows why the amount of times an Obelisk will resurrect somebody, appears to be so random. Milathran, however, is said to increase the number of times a person might be resurrected, as the Obelisks themselves receive some sort of energy when resurrecting a person who takes it, hence the reason it is so valuable and expensive. It all truly is a mystery.*

**Temmison Vol IX, Book 5: The Obelisks.**

*With* a grunt, Borach pushed himself upright. He managed to move to a sitting position in the bed. As sensation returned, it brought with it a dull ache. He swung his legs over the side, and wobbling, stood and lurched across the floor. He recognised the familiar surroundings of his campaign tent. *The Awakening must have happened whilst I slept?*

He looked in a mirror and muttered. *I have the mark of the Obelisk. I still have to endure this life, when a Final-death is now preferred.* He was startled when, in the reflection of the mirror, he noticed a wild looking young woman carefully watching him. "Who are you?" he asked her curtly as he turned abruptly around to face her.

Strangely, the woman sighed with relief. "Go and fetch Commander Marki," she said to a servant who nodded and left the tent promptly. "My name is Talain," she then said to Borach.

Borach recognised the name; it was the Seeress he had heard spoken of during his illness, and who he had briefly met.

"I remember," he said.

She attempted a smile. "Your *Awakening* was traumatic. You passed out and have slept for longer than was expected. I am waiting for you. I have delivered you safely from the Deadlands as I promised."

Borach sensed uncertainty in her voice, as though she was troubled but could not remember why.

"Have all of your memories returned?" he asked her.

"Yes, the important ones in this world. Although, our time in the Deadlands is still vague to me, and I feel troubled. I sense that we met misfortune there although I cannot yet remember exactly what the nature of it was."

"Well, here I am, and for resurrecting at a safe Obelisk, for that, I suppose I owe you my gratitude," Borach declared as he stared at the strange woman. He then noticed another woman standing near a table upon which were refreshments. "I need water, and something to eat," he ordered, as from the corner of the tent the young woman hurried forward and offered a platter filled with bread and cheese, and a crystal goblet filled with water.

Borach shook his head. "I am among strangers. Who is this?" he asked as he looked the woman up and down. The woman turned her head away and stared at the ground.

"Her name is Maraya," Talain answered. "She will tend to your needs. She knows the Common Tongue, although even in her mother tongue she is sparse with her words and speaks little, so do not expect many words from her."

Borach took a piece of bread from the platter, bit a chunk off and ate hungrily. Taking the goblet, he washed it down, spilling water down his chin as Marki burst into the tent and nearly stumbled such was his haste.

"By Balagrim's beard, Bor, you're awake!" he shouted with delight. Borach scowled as Marki lunged across the tent and threw his arms around him, pulling him into a tight hug. Tears rolled down his friend's cheeks. "It's good to see you my old friend, you have no idea the fright you put upon us," the dwarf said.

Borach cautiously patted his friend on the shoulder and looked at him. Marki's usually neatly trimmed hair and beard looked patchy in places.

"A damn wyvern," Marki muttered grumpily under his breath as he noticed Borach's questioning gaze. "Young Talain here killed the oversized chicken!"

Any other time, Borach would not have been able to resist gently mocking his friend for his appearance and obvious discomfort, as Dwarves were often vain about such things, but he felt a deep darkness in his own soul that could not find any humour in the situation. "Best you bring me up to speed with recent events," he said sullenly to Marki.

It took Marki and the commanders, who by then had joined them, a good hour to brief and update Borach on recent events. He was far from pleased at finding himself in the service of a Tarenmoor king named Falamore, but he understood that Marki and the commanders had acted within the confines of a few choices that had to be made fast.

"The griffin, I wanted it named Yianna," he said moodily, "but you have given it away!"

"We had no choice," Marki said defensively. "We had to name it Karno." He cautiously glanced at Meron whose face glowered with displeasure. Ignoring Meron, Marki continued. "The people consider the griffin an incarnation of a god of theirs of the same name; it was part of the deal I had to make."

Borach noticed the anger that burned in Meron's eyes towards Marki, but Meron said nothing.

"It's only a name Bor," Marki said apologetically, "and it was a sickly thing. They will tend it and give it a good life!"

"Then so be it," Borach said as he stared sternly at Meron and then Marki. "If this has been the cause of any dispute between you two, I order an end to it. We have enough issues to deal with!"

Borach's mood was dark; he was in no mood to debate the name of the griffin any further or to mediate between Meron and Marki over the decision to give it to King Falamore. Meron ever so slightly, defiantly, shook his head, but did not openly protest, although Borach noticed he involuntarily clenched his fists as he shot another angry glance at Marki.

*I will have to speak to Meron and Marki another time on this matter to resolve any dispute.* "Now leave me to my thoughts. I had not expected to return to the Everglow and find myself in another war as a mercenary to some Tarenmoor king." *I have not even had the chance to properly mourn Yianna and my children, and now urgent matters demand my time and attention.* "I will study the maps and ledgers and call for you when I wish to discuss our tactics in the battles to come."

Everybody except Marki and Talain left the tent.

"What is it?" Borach snapped.

"Meron is not happy about the griffin," Marki said, stating the obvious. "I had no choice Bor," he protested. "King Falamore is stubborn, and time was not on our side. Meron is a blithering fool if he cannot see reason behind my actions!"

"The three of us will share words on the matter soon," Borach assured his friend.

Borach noticed that Talain was still looking at him warily.

"What is it woman?" he growled at her.

She answered apprehensively. "I have something I need to share with you, I sense it, but I cannot recall what it is but I know it is urgent. Do you remember nothing from our time in the Deadlands?" she asked him, with a look that showed she was hoping he might enlighten the situation.

"Of course, I don't," he barked as his mouth twisted with rage. "I am not a Seer, and what sort are you if you cannot recall what happens in the Deadlands? Be gone!" He clenched his fist to contain the anger he felt welling up within him. He was glad that she had the perceptiveness to sense his mood and not to press the issue, so he watched her walk to the exit of the tent. Before leaving, she turned and said to him.

"I am untrained and lack the education the Mystery Schools give, but if I do recall what happened in the Deadlands, do not delay in hearing me on the matter for I sense great events are unfolding and that I have a message for you. You would be foolish to not hear what I have to say when I remember what it is."

As Talain walked out of the tent for the briefest moment Borach considered calling her back. *Could it be Yianna who has a message for me?* He quickly dismissed the notion. Yianna had met the *Final-death*; she would have been through the burning purge and would now be in the Hall of Ancestors in the Paradise of Moisshar, the patron goddess of Aleskian, whose worship had been banned since the spread of the Aeldar religion throughout the Empire. The irony did not escape him that the Aeldar priests would consider such thoughts blasphemy. His musings were interrupted by Marki.

"Talain is a good girl," Marki said softly. "I trust her; do not be overly harsh with the words you speak to her," he appealed. "It was a stroke of good fortune we found a Seeress at all, albeit her lack of formal training."

"I'm sorry my friend," Borach said. "I would like nothing more than to go into a period of mourning for Yianna and my children, but my thoughts now have to turn to this war we have to fight, and the dire situation we find ourselves mired in."

"I understand," Marki said.

Borach walked over to him, held Marki warmly by the shoulders and said, "So do I, old friend. I understand the decisions that were made, and why. Choice was stripped from you. I am grateful, even if my mood is sour."

Marki nodded. "Thank you, Bor." He took something from out of his pocket and handed it to Borach and said, "We searched everywhere for Yianna and the bairns, just in case it was trickery that faked their capture. I found this, which confirmed they were in the hands of our foes at Aleskian. Do not give in to false hopes, for many of those I have entertained since we left that fateful city, and all have come to nought."

Borach immediately recognised Yianna's locket. He took it and stared silently at it.

"Call for us when you are ready," Marki said softly as he left the tent.

Borach knelt on his knees just looking at the locket, as painful memories returned. Despite Marki's cautious words, again, hoping against hope, he wondered if the message Talain had for him from the Deadlands might somehow be from Yianna. He regretted that the legion's Seers had not been able to come with them into the Tarenmoors for they would recall with clarity any event in the Deadlands. Whatever it was Talain had to say, it would have to wait until she could recall it.

# Chapter Forty-Seven: *The Gallows of Kara Duram*

*Griffin, also griffon, gryphon etc., from old High Akkadian meaning hooked. In heraldry the male griffin is called Alce; the winged variety Opinicus. Griffins are strange in that you do find the male and female genders, but they are gender fluid — meaning they can become male or female depending on the environment they are kept in and the conditions. For instance, the griffin keepers told me that when it comes to griffin eggs, males will hatch in hot conditions, while females will emerge from cooler eggs. Why this happens is a mystery, but the griffin keepers will incubate the eggs so that the male to female ratio is about one male griffin to five females. The males are bred for fighting and used by the legions; the females are mostly sold as pets to rich aristocrats. Griffins can asexually reproduce, meaning they can self-impregnate, but this usually only happens if an available mate is not around. Given the right conditions, griffins prefer an actual mate for sexual reproduction. The male griffins start the mating ritual with some bipedal wrestling. Their bout of wrestling can go on for several days and the females are expected to watch and look interested. If the male wins over a female's favour, after licking her fur for some time he reveals his hemipene — which is basically a sort of double-headed penis. If all goes to plan and eggs are fertilised, the male no longer pays any attention to the female, and plays no part in the raising of the offspring when they are hatched.*
**Griffin mating rituals, as described by the Bruthon Missionary Edegal in the year 9419, after his visit to the city of Aleskian and described in his book; Magical, Mystical and Truly Terrifying Creatures.**

*General* Longshins, Cordius, and thirty or so generals from the legions, stood on the ramparts of the Kara Duram Fortress, and watched the bodies of General Shinther and the other Hammer Knights, hanging from the gallows and swinging in the wind; they listened to the creaking of the ropes. "Such shall be the end of all traitors," Longshins muttered.

"What shall happen to them when they resurrect?" Cordius asked.

"We will interrogate some of them, give the *Final-death* to others," Longshins replied as he unrolled the message that he had received from the Empress Shaka. Scanning the parchment again, he addressed the generals.

"Our Sarissa has been vilely betrayed by Mazdek. She assures us she had nothing to do with Lord Borach's betrayal."

"That does not explain Prince Regineo's part in the events at Aleskian," Yianna said as she stepped from the shadows. "He let my husband believe me and the children were to be sent to the *Final-death*, if he did not comply to imperial orders."

Longshins answered impatiently. "Our Sarissa assures us that Mazdek had given false orders to the prince, and he was only acting on what he believed were her orders. Mazdek has betrayed and tricked us all."

"Do you believe her?" Yianna asked questioningly. "I cannot see how Mazdek could have acted without her compliance. The fact that he also tricked her with subtlety and guile, is the reason she now protests her innocence? It is convenient."

"Be that as it may," Longshins said, "she is coming to Kara Duram. I will never bow the knee to Mazdek. The only hope of restoring stability back to Kappia, is to see him toppled and Shaka back on the throne."

"Then I hope your faith is not misplaced general," Yianna replied.

"We must have the best scholars at Kara Duram work on a charter she will be forced to sign, to bring justice to the Empire and make the imperial family more accountable," one of the other generals said, a grizzly scarred looking veteran.

Longshins scowled at him. "We are men of the Imperial Kappian Legions. We will not break our oaths to her, in the time of her greatest need."

The grizzled veteran nodded: "It is a reason why many of us were slow to disband." He looked at the bodies swinging from the gallows. "I have never trusted those fellows, but until a few days ago, even you were ordering us to obey the commands that came from Kappia."

"That was when I believed the Empress was in charge," Longshins replied moodily. "Mazdek has usurped her." He held the parchment up in the air. "In her own words, she writes how Mazdek forced her into this Munte marriage. If all goes well, she will be with us before the sun sets on this day."

"We have taken a great risk. Mazdek's army will come for us," another general said.

"Then we will fight and defeat them," another replied, receiving the muttered agreement and 'ayes' of others.

Longshins nodded approvingly. "I have word that the Seventeenth Legion defeated the Hammer Knights on the Steps of Narzoum. We control the fortresses there, but our victory was only because we took them by surprise." He pointed to the Steppes of Kara Duram. "Mazdek's Hammer Knights outnumber us by ten to one. We will soon be under siege and it is possible a Bantu army may also lay siege to the Steps of Narzoum. Food supplies are low, and it will be hard to get more. If Shaka manages to escape and arrives here, it will increase the morale of the city to know they fight for the old order, which will be re-established and reformed." He looked at those around him.

A greying general from the Ninth Legion spoke. "I have many questions, but we need the Empress as a figurehead if we are to have any chance of winning this war. If victory does become ours, and we establish stability, the imperial family can be subjected to testing by the Jewel of Baramir, and in that way we can find out the truth of how this whole mess came to be."

Longshins scowled. "So, the Empress will have your support?"

"Aye," or something similar, the thirty or so generals standing on the ramparts muttered, each in turn.

Yianna implored Longshins. "Send word to my husband quickly that I and the children still live. He must know what we plan. It might be possible he could make it here to Kara Duram before the Bantu horde cut him off."

Longshins looked at Cordius and raised an eyebrow questioningly.

"It's saddled," Cordius said, anticipating the question.

"Are you sure you want to attempt to ride it?" Longshins asked him hesitantly.

Yianna noticed a look of uncertainty that briefly swept over Cordius, but he suppressed it. When he spoke, it was with confidence. "The Hammer Knights, just like they did here at Kara Duram, slew all of the griffins at Fort Disturbance except those kept as pets. They butchered Mariekon, my own cherished mount. I escaped on foot. The ones still alive here at Kara Duram are all too small to carry a man, except one. It is not fully trained, but for the good of the Empire, I will take the risk and attempt to fly it."

"For the Empire!" Longshins shouted.

The rest of the generals joined in the chant. Yianna, stayed silent.

*      *      *

Cordius adjusted the leather riding tunic he wore and made sure the laces of the long boots he was wearing were firmly tied. Griffins were not horses. They did not easily accept a saddle or a man on their back and when angered or threatened, they attacked.

It was said in the *Book of Griffin Lore* that the rider did not choose the griffin, but the griffin chose the rider. Cordius remembered his griffin, recently slain by the Hammer Knights. It was the first griffin he had ever tamed and ridden, and named Mariekon the Cannibal, the great grandson of Krikoarn. Mariekon had slain seventeen men, and maimed several others, before he had allowed Cordius to mount him and become his rider. He had been given his name as one night shortly after being tamed he had broken free from his cage, and somehow got into the hatchery at Aleskian and gorged himself on the new-born griffin hatchlings and eggs. A coppered coloured beast streaked with the red colours of sunset, Mariekon had been one of the fiercest griffins Cordius had ever known and would not accept ever being caged or tethered, so he had been allowed to fly free. When he was younger, he had often disappeared for several months at a time, only to be occasionally glimpsed flying low over the Largon Lakes, snatching prey from the waters, or cattle and even men from the fields or roads; eventually he always returned and allowed Cordius to ride him again and finally he had submitted fully to his rider. Cordius did not have the luxury of time to indulge another griffin of similar temperament. Marieke was the son of Mariekon, one of his many offspring, and so far, had proven to be of a similar ilk to his father. Having been rejected for breeding or by use of the legions for being too small, until a few days ago, Marieke had been kept in a cage as the pet of a wealthy merchant at Kara Duram.

"If the griffin will not submit to you, and refuses you as its rider, it will be slain and we will be done with it," Longshins said sullenly to Cordius. "If, or when, we come under siege, we will not be able to spare the meat to feed a griffin that is of no use to us."

"Then let us be about this," Cordius said, as he and Longshins left the ramparts and made their way to where the griffin was caged.

Cordius walked with Longshins. He turned his head. Yianna was following them, walking and conversing with one of the generals, but she was out of earshot. He spoke quietly to Longshins. "I will need a few days to adjust to the griffin, before I try to set out with my passenger. The Lady Yianna will not be happy, when she learns of this."

"It is necessary. She won't know, until after you have left," Longshins muttered.

As they approached the large square on top of the fortress from which griffins took off and landed, they could hear a great commotion. A medium-sized griffin, partially hidden by a blanket covering the iron cage, was raging and smashing against the bars of its prison. Cordius, followed by the others, approached a ring of men standing around a stage constructed of wooden planks, upon which the cage stood.

"We've saddled it, but it's not happy," one of the men said to Cordius, as he used a long pole to pull the carpet from off of the cage. The air filled with the smell of offal mixed with an unpleasant stench of rotting carrion. The legionnaires, who were watching, muttered and stepped back a bit. Inside the cage, which was far too cramped for it, the male griffin thrashed about wildly.

"It is an unpredictable beast," another man said. "The owner mostly kept it in this cage which is far too small for it."

Cordius did not take his eyes off of the griffin, which, enraged by the saddle on its back and the confines of its prison, banged against the bars of the cage, biting them and vainly trying to spread its wings in the cramped confines. The griffin screeched furiously as Cordius approached, the stench of the creature assaulting his nose. He drew even closer, and held out a hand, almost touching the cage.

"Cordius has taken leave of his senses trying to fly that thing," he heard one legionnaire mutter to another, his words only just being heard over the din of the noise. Cordius knew he was taking a huge risk, but he was willing to try. Lord Borach had been one of his father's closest friends, and although Borach was not aware Karkson had a secret son and a daughter, Cordius felt duty bound to at least try and deliver the vital message to Borach that Yianna and their children were still alive. In addition, he was to deliver the message that a growing resistance movement was forming at Kara Duram and on the Steps of Narzoum, in opposition to Mazdek.

The griffin hurled itself at the bars of the cage, raking them with its teeth. Two bars of the cage started parting under the force of the enraged griffin, tearing nails out of the frame.

"Run," a legionnaire shouted at the top of his voice behind him. "The cage is breaking."

The bars of the cage broke, and the top of the cage flew off as the griffin smashed free and struggled out of the wreckage of its prison.

One legionnaire had a blow-pipe in his mouth and was puffing his cheeks ready to fire a dart tipped with pollydust, that would put the creature to sleep.

"Wait!" Cordius shouted, as he stepped in front of the griffin, which screeched, stood on its hind legs and spread its wings as though about to attack. Cordius began to softly sing the *Song of the Griffin Tamer*. The haunting melody seemed to immediately start to pacify the creature. The griffin calmed as Cordius slowly walked towards it with his hand outstretched, softly singing the ancient song. The griffin lowered itself onto all four legs, folded its wings, and reached out its neck to sniff Cordius' still outstretched hand. Cordius felt as though he was acting without his conscious will or participation. The creature cooed, sniffed his hand, and even submitted to him stroking it on its feathered neck. It then, unexpectedly, spread its wings, screeched, and with a spring from its powerful legs and flaps of its wings it launched itself into the air, knocking Cordius onto the ground.

"Missed it!" the legionnaire with the blow-pipe shouted, as he fired the dart, missing the creature which was already soaring high into the air.

Longshins was by Cordius' side in an instant, and helped him to his feet, assisting in brushing the dust and dirt off of his riding tunic.

"You were warned it was not trained or ready to ride," he said reproachfully. "Now who knows what mischief it might reek in the towns and hamlets on the Steppes? If it ever comes back, it is to be slain!"

"He takes after his father," Cordius said pensively. "The same happened the first time I tried to ride him. He will be back, I know it, and he will let me ride him." He stared after Marieke who was now high in the sky and flying off towards distant clouds.

Yianna took a step towards Cordius as she watched the creature disappear from sight. "That griffin was the last hope of reaching my husband with news of recent events," she said as tears filled her eyes.

"He will be back," Cordius assured her, "and I will attempt to ride him again."

"A plague be on all griffins," Longshins growled. "They are more trouble than they are worth. I was not entirely opposed to the culling of such erratic beasts."

Cordius looked at Longshins, and spoke respectfully. "General, do not be hasty in slaying the beast if it returns. Marieke will let me fly him. Wherever Lord Borach is, I will find him, even if I have to search to the ends of the Everglow."

Longshins let out a quiet, unintelligible guttural growl.

# Chapter Forty-Eight: *The Kappian Games*

*I have never been a fan of gladiatorial games, they are a brutal and messy affair and I have neither the taste nor the stomach for them, so have rarely attended. The few times I have observed them, have merely been to pursue scholarly interest on the subject, and I felt it was appropriate to include a discourse here, as such games are usually held after a significant victory in war, or after an imperial coronation or marriage. It is custom that the games always commence with a variety of entertainments, and before any blood is shed, a short address is given by the ruler, be they emperor or empress, and they are expected to stay in attendance throughout the first day. After their opening address, the slaughter commences, and usually consists of some poorly armed captives or slaves being pitted against some poor unfortunate beast, to rouse the crowd so that they might be excited for the more skilful gladiatorial combat that will take place after the ceremonial lunch held by the ruler for dignitaries and special guests.*

*The Kappians have a strange custom, that dates back to the time of Malerian IV, and that is, if a new emperor has recently obtained the crown, the Imperial Champion of Kappia may challenge him (This custom only applies to male rulers). The emperor is bound by tradition to always accept the challenge. The following contest is merely for show, as the Champion, who by law must always be a Pure-blood, after a ceremonial display of combat, willingly surrenders and allows the emperor to slay him. The Champion is well rewarded financially for this, and when resurrected receives the title of 'Emperor's Champion' from the emperor, who has ritually and ceremonially proven himself to be the supreme warrior amongst all Kappians.*

***Temmison Vol II, Book 5: Wars and Conquests of the Kappian Empire.***

*It* was the first day of the Kappian Games, the *Great Games* as it had been named. To celebrate the return of the Simal, the punishment of the Seeress, and the Munte marriage of the Empress to Mazdek, a whole month of chariot racing, wrestling, boxing, athletics, acrobatics and of course gladiatorial combat had been planned at different venues throughout Kappia city. The opening ceremony in the great Kappian Arena was filled to capacity. After the fanfare of music, acrobats, dancing girls, speeches and the official opening of the games was concluded, a crowd of a hundred-thousand screamed and roared with delight as the first of the gladiators walked onto the sand of the arena. Every seat was filled; the galleries were packed with a teeming mass of people, all intent on enjoying the combat and merciless slaughter they were about to witness. In Kappian gladiatorial games, there was no clemency or mercy given to the loser, you killed or were killed, you fought to the death, and you either won, or died. If you were a Pure-blood you might resurrect and fight again; if you were a Fell-blood or a Half-blood, death was permanent, so the stakes were higher.

The gladiators, Fell-bloods, Half-bloods and Pure-bloods, paraded around the curved walls of the amphitheatre. They walked past the Beast Gate, from which, during the games, all manner of ferocious creatures might emerge, which some of them would have to eventually face. They walked past the Gate of Woe, through which for no other purpose other than the sheer entertainment of the crowd, some innocents, perhaps even some unfortunates from the crowd, might be forced to walk through, often naked and unarmed, to be dismembered, butchered and slain or thrown to wild beasts for the amusement of the baying crowd. The gladiators then walked past the Gate of Death, through which many of their corpses would be carried out. Finally, they walked past the Gate of Life, through which, if they won enough bouts or showed enough courage and skill, they would be allowed to walk through as free men and women, having won their liberty, to be showered with riches beyond their wildest dreams. The gladiators, playing to the crowd, passed each gate and finished their spectacular parade and left the arena.

"It's always the same," Regineo said with barely concealed disgust as he looked disapprovingly at the crowd seated above and around the Gate of Death. "Those seated there queued for most of the night to get the prime spots to see the dead corpses carried out. It would be amusing if they were the first to face some beast unarmed."

Shaka was covered in a red robe, that partially hid the unique and Shurien armour she wore, named after the ancient empress who had designed it. She wore it underneath the robe, as custom dictated. Custom also dictated that she should have been wearing the golden ceremonial Empress Armour for such an occasion, but that armour was mostly decorative, unlike the Shurien she wore which was forged for the purpose of providing powerful protection for the wearer, as well as being lavish in cosmetic beauty. She knew many would notice and criticise her for not observing the etiquette of wearing the correct armour for the opening of the games, but the pettiness of ceremonial and social customs was far from being foremost on her mind. She looked venomously at her son and leaning in close so as not to be overheard, said, "At any other games, I would indulge your wish. Remember our purpose today and do your part. Do not get caught in any other distraction!"

"I know what to do, and what I should be wearing," Regineo retorted abruptly. "It will be a few hours before we get our chance to escape. We might as well enjoy the festivities until then. Order some of those arrogant fools gloating over the Gate of Death to be thrown to the beasts!"

Aspess quietly, but sharply rebuked him. "Don't be a fool, brother. There must be no other thought on your mind except that for which we have planned." She took from her pouch a beautiful ring of Juram, slipped it on her finger, next to a strange dark ring whose stone shimmered like a pool of oil, and then put on a pair of red silk gloves to cover her hands, and then the gloves of her black, Shurian glass armour, over the top of the silk ones. Unlike the unique Shurien set of armour Shaka wore, there were three sets of Shurian armour known to be in existence. Each of her three children owned a set, and were wearing it on that day, contrary to tradition. They also wore a red robe over their armour, in line with the customs and traditions of the games.

Aspess turned her head, looking all around, to make sure nobody was overhearing their conversation. Content no prying ears were trying to listen in, she lifted up her hand and quietly declared, "The Juram crystal on this ring is the last one we could find anywhere in the Empire. It cost us dearly, but was worth the price." She lowered her voice even more, and whispered to her mother and Regineo. "It will take us all the way to Kara Duram, where General Longshins awaits our arrival. If we are fortunate, it will not break, and we might then use it if at some other time, if we are again in great need."

"It will not break, the Aeldar will favour me," Shaka replied.

Aspess looked hauntingly at her mother, "Your messages all met with success?" She glanced suspiciously towards Shaka's maids, all standing a short distance behind them. "We should hope none of these messages were intercepted and we are not betrayed."

Shaka smiled slightly, and turned her head to glance at her seven maids. She watched each of them intently for a moment. The Pure-bloods Desira, Mazzie, Myrene, Sheena and the three Fell-bloods Stansia, Marciea and Oliviana all lowered their gaze. As far as Shaka knew, they had not betrayed her confidence. It would have been impossible to have made the plan to escape without their assistance; she had promised the Pure-blood maid's freedom for their help once they reached Kara Duram.

"Mazdek ordered them to spy on me, but their fear of me is greater than that of him. They have not betrayed me, or I would have seen it in their eyes." *Mazzie informed*

560

*me that Barazo opened and read my letter to Kara Duram, but he was too dim-witted to see anything of significance in it to bother to report it to Mazdek, and even if he had, it would have been dismissed as of little importance, appearing only as a mundane matter and one letter among many I send out each week.*

Recent experiences had taught all of the imperial family and their servants to be cautious, and Shaka was glad Aspess and the maids all understood the nature of the risk they were taking. If Mazdek had discovered their plan, it would entertain him to let them think they were undetected, and then to foil them at the last moment. He could only have discovered their plan if one of the maids, or those they had contacted, had not been true and loyal to Shaka, or if a message had been intercepted which was unlikely as she had received an answer to each message.

Caspus joined them at that moment. He was eating pastries and offered one to his mother. She curled her nose up, refused it and resisted the temptation to chide her son for his lack of dignity. Crumbs dropped onto his red robe and some on the black Shurian armour he wore, as he munched at the friable snack he held with his fingers.

"Is all in place?" she quietly asked when he had taken a seat in front of her.

He answered with a single nod of his head.

Before Shaka could say anything more, the crowd suddenly began to shout in a seemingly unending chorus. *'Mazdek! Mazdek! Mazdek!'*

Being driven on a golden, ivory-decorated chariot, pulled by two magnificent stallions, Mazdek entered the arena surrounded by Hammer Knights running alongside, each of them dressed in their finest ceremonial armour. In the chariot, sitting alongside him, was Grixen, the Bantu Ambassador, and Renlak, who had retained his office and was now the Emperor's Hand. Shaka looked calculatingly at Mazdek as he waved at the crowd. He was dressed in the finest ceremonial Emperor armour, the male version of the set she should have been wearing. A grand and exquisite sword was elegantly sheathed at his side. "Enjoy your moment, whilst it lasts," she hissed under her breath.

The chariot came to a halt in the centre of the arena. With an extravagant sweep of his hand, Mazdek motioned for silence and the roar of the crowd hushed. "People of Kappia," he roared. He raised a hand and extended a finger. "Firstly, I have returned the Simal to our great city and today, you will witness the punishment of the renegade Seeress. All who see her fate will weep in terror and know that the will of the Aeldar is not to be contested." The people roared and cheered until he motioned again for silence. He raised a second finger alongside the first. "I have quelled the rebellion started by Lord Borach, which led to the fall of Aleskian."

"*Final-death* to all traitors," some shouted amidst the cheers from the crowd, in support of Mazdek.

Two fingers became three. "We have made an alliance with the Bantu army. Once they have purified the Everglow of the lesser races and destroyed the Baothein, they will withdraw from the Everglow, and Aleskian will be given over to us once more, that we may rebuild our Empire stronger and larger than ever before." The crowd did not cheer so enthusiastically and some stirred uneasily, especially those who were not Pure-bloods. "The Nine Aeldar will return to the Everglow, and they will lead our Empire into a greatness the like of which the world has never seen before." The crowd cheered, this time with more enthusiasm. He raised a fourth finger. "But the true reason for the celebration of these games is that our Sarissa, the Empress Shaka, had seen it is the will of the Aeldar for her to submit to my wise rule, when she became my Munte bride, and I your new Emperor!" The crowd cheered and roared again.

Shaka clenched her fists and ground her teeth in quiet fury.

When the crowd again became silent, Mazdek said. "Enough words from me, my precious people. The arena will now be prepared for a special first event, the like of which you have not seen before on these glorious sands!"

As the crowd cheered, the chariot driver manoeuvred the chariot to the steps that led to the imperial box. The golden barred gate that protected the stairway was opened, and Mazdek, Grixen and Renlak stepped down from the chariot and made their way to where Shaka and her children were seated, in the imperial box, which was surrounded by an assortment of other nobles, who were just far enough away that any conversations the imperial family had could not easily be overheard.

Grixen pursed his lips in cruel amusement as he took a seat behind Shaka. "I trust you are well?" he asked sarcastically as he leaned over towards her. His lips curled over his fangs in an unintended gesture. "I have so missed our appointments together."

"I have not missed the foul stench of your breath, ambassador," Shaka replied dryly.

Renlak sat next to Grixen but said nothing about the discourtesy Grixen and Shaka openly showed towards one another.

Shaka continued to taunt Grixen. "Perhaps the day may soon come, when our roles might be reversed, and we can commence our meetings again, ambassador," she said tersely. She looked briefly at the arm on which the Maidenarz, covered by her armour, was on, and then back at Grixen. "If this thing ever comes off, I can show you the true meaning of fear and pain."

Grixen looked at her with a puzzled expression on his face that she assumed was the result of the unexpected defiance she had just shown toward him and the threat she had issued. He was about to say something when Mazdek took his seat next to Shaka.

"The people of this city adore me," Mazdek declared triumphantly, as the crowd cheered and chanted his name.

"Such praise may be short-lived, if they discover the length of your deception, or the shortness of your courage," Shaka said as charmingly and inoffensively as she could. Before Mazdek could answer she turned, looked at Grixen and asked.

"Did you not assure us the real Simal would be returned to us by now? If those you call the Wild Hunt are as skilled and efficient as you say they are, why is the Simal not already sitting in the heart of the Argona Temple once again?"

There was a long pause, and before Grixen answered, Mazdek filled the silence. He took out of a sheath on his belt the Arkith that had once belonged to Aspess, the one with which she had given the *Final-death* to General Karkson. He pressed the tip of it against Shaka's side, making sure those around him could not see what he was doing.

"You would be well reminded, my dear bride," he whispered venomously as he falsely beamed beatifically at Shaka, "that there are many souls within here, in perpetual torment, who would find some small solace if you and your filthy brood were to join them within its eternal confines. The tip of this can easily pierce that fine armour you wear underneath your robe."

The chilling warning served as a sharp reminder to Shaka to play her game very carefully indeed. *His days are numbered. I must guard my tongue, for now.*

Mazdek then noticed she was not properly attired. "Why are you not wearing the correct ceremonial armour?" he asked her suspiciously.

Shaka's facial expression did not change as the lie left her lips. "A Munte bride is not entitled to wear the same armour as her husband on such a grand occasion. Lesser attire must be worn, by her and her children, as a sign of subservience to their new master."

Shaka cast a disapproving look at Renlak. "Surely you have refreshed your memory and read the seven volumes of the *Ancient Gladiatorial Kappian Games and their Customs*, to be able to advise Emperor Mazdek on all of the traditions to be observed today?"

Renlak shifted uneasily in his seat. "Of course," he replied to Shaka, his eyes momentarily shifting from side to side.

Her outward expression did not change, but inwardly Shaka smiled. Renlak would not dare to admit he was not sure of every exact custom for the games. The books she had mentioned were a laborious and tiresome read, and with all of the recent massive constitutional changes her marriage to Mazdek had set in motion, Renlak and his advisors would simply not have had the time to go over every single detail in regard to every practice and tradition to be adhered to at the games.

Mazdek eyed her suspiciously, and warned, "Do not embarrass me this day, in front of this crowd. It is our first major public appearance together since our wedding. You have agreed to play your part."

Shaka glanced at the Arkith and then said, as sweetly as she could, attempting to mask both her disgust and anger, "Please, husband, put that away, it is unnecessary. I was just advising caution. The mood of the crowd is like a game of Harendale, the fortunes of any player can reverse quickly at the turn of a card or the roll of a dice. Today, you must show them you are now the true emperor!" The words left a vile taste in her mouth, but the hidden significance of her words and what they would entail, made her smile warmly inside. She smiled as amiably as she could at him.

Mazdek sheathed the Arkith and the crowd suddenly roared and distracted the conversation. The very structure of the arena seemed to shake with the reverberations. From out of a trapdoor, a huge cage had been raised by pulleys into the arena. It was covered in an animal skin and was then hidden from view by a hastily installed grove of potted trees and bushes that surrounded the cage so that none could see what was inside. Hundreds of Davari slaves, men, women and children, were led into the arena through the Gate of Woe. The women and children were unarmed, whilst the men were armed with axes, clubs, spears or bows with only one arrow. Those armed were dressed in fur-skin armour and led to one side of the arena, those unarmed to the other. One of the Davari was armed with a sword and protected by a rectangular shield; he was dressed differently than the others, being donned in scant plated armour, and was made to stand in the middle near the grove of trees.

"That is their chief," Mazdek said with delight as he looked at the man with the sword and shield. "He is supposed to be a famous and brave warrior. Today, his mettle will be tested for all to see!"

*As will yours my dear,* Shaka thought smugly to herself.

When Rachmund, the Master of the Games, stood on the podium, the crowd went silent with anticipation; only excited murmurs and whispers could be heard as he began setting the scene.

"Imagine, people of Kappia, a scene before you. You have heard, that in the thickest parts of the primordial forests, giant black wargs roam, and on the vast and icy-plains to the south of the Everglow, white and grey ones live. These fierce beasts, prey on the Davari, who make arrogant boasts that they hunt them in turn."

The crowd became almost delirious with delight and expectation. Rachmund continued. "How many of us have not heard the arrogant and boastful songs the Davari sing of how their great warriors have felled such beasts and adorned their huts with their skins? What if, people, we had captured one of these giant wargs, from one of the great forests, for these games?" The crowd murmured with excitement.

"What if, people of Kappia, we could now see for ourselves if the Davari boasts are true? Can their chief, armed only with a sword and shield, protect the women and children, and lead his warriors to victory, as their arrogant songs boast?"

A hushed anticipation fell upon the crowd.

563

Rachmund lifted his hands and held them there as the atmosphere in the crowd intensified. He brought them down in one swift movement, shouting, "Release the warg!"

Complete silence fell over the crowd, as, hidden from sight behind the trees and bushes, the grating sound of the cage door being opened was heard. Except for that, no other sound could be heard in the arena, until a large sniff, followed by a deep throaty growl, was heard coming from within the grove of trees.

The Davari chief shouted something to the armed men. Realising their only chance of survival was to kill the creature lurking in the grove of trees, cautiously, they advanced towards the grove. Some of the trees were knocked over as a giant black warg, far bigger than the norm, sprang out onto the sands. The chief roared and shouted out a challenge to the creature, but it was distracted by the shouts and screams of the women and children. The beast snarled in anger as some of the women and children began to run, trying to flee to the very edges of the arena; it launched itself at them, and was upon them in moments. There was no escape for the Davari women and children who attempted to climb into the safety of the crowd, for the throng was protected by iron-bars and a wall that could not be climbed, and any that leaped high enough to grab hold of the ledges, had their fingers prized off by the crowd, so the poor hapless victim fell or was pushed back into the arena and the waiting jaws and claws of the warg. The warg reaped devastation as with gnashing teeth and sweeping, raking claws it tore the terrified women and children to pieces in moments. Driven to fresh delirium by the scene of slaughter, the crowd stood on their collective feet and roared with excitement.

The Davari warriors were now rapidly advancing upon the beast as it mangled and maimed and tore limb from limb off of those who had panicked. The women and children, who had not fled, ran to the warriors and joined their ranks. Born amid the harshest environments imaginable, reared where life was unimaginably brutal and only the strongest and most ruthless survived, it was not the first time some of them had faced such a foe. Many a village had been raided by such beasts, it had hunted them on the icy-plains or in the snow-capped mountains, but some Davari had themselves actively hunted such a creature. Their chief had taken charge and was still giving instructions to those who followed him. They steadily advanced towards the beast which was distracted by its short reign of terror and carnage amongst the weakest of its foes.

At the command of the chief, the Davari with spears hurled them at the beast, and those with bows, but only one arrow, fired them. Spear and arrow hit the left side of the beast piercing the flank as well as the front and hind quarters. With an enraged coughing-growl, audible over the crowd's own bloodthirsty roars, the beast spun and faced its attackers. The chief roared as he charged towards it, his warriors followed without heed for safety, all cohesion lost in the rush to kill the incandescent beast, which in turn began to hurtle towards them with great lunging strides. The chief held out his shield before him, and was the first to reach the warg, attempting to plunge his sword in its neck, but he was knocked aside by the impact and a sweep of its paw, the claws of which tore his armour apart.

The other Davari attacked the swirling mass of tooth and talon that was the black warg, which tore into them, its ebon claws ripping their armour as easily as if it was silk and tearing asunder the flesh beneath it. Axes and clubs bludgeoned the beast, and though mortally wounded, still it ferociously fought back slaying and butchering until only it and the chief remained alive.

The mortally wounded warg eyed its prey warily as the chief, the last survivor, got to his feet and shook off the daze that had temporarily incapacitated him. Both man and beast bore grievous wounds, and they circled each other, as alone, they faced their foe across the sand. The valiant chief held his sword and shield up, and charged; at the same time, with lightning speed the warg took several large strides and then sprang at him. The warg came at him with all the fury of a thing that knows only the source of its pain standing before it; it hooked its claws over the rim of the shield, and cut through it like a knife through butter, using its weight to wrench the tattered remains of the shield from the stricken chief's hand. The force of the impact knocked the Davari backwards, his sword spilling uselessly onto the sand as he fell and hit the hard surface. As he struggled to rise and regain his sword, the warg lunged forward and knocked him over with a swipe of his paws, shredding the skin of his back to the bone, but the chief was fast, he rose again, lunged for the sword, grabbed it, turned and plunged it into the warg's neck as the beast renewed its attack. The sword must have missed the immediate vital organs and hit mostly skin and fur, for even though blood poured from the wound, it did not deter the warg who seized the torso of the man in its mouth, its jaws snapping as it threw back its head, attempting to bury its incisors through the remains of the tattered armour, which, after a few bites, it finally managed. The Davari chief still fought valiantly but could not get a hold of the hilt of his sword still buried in the creature's neck, so instead, with powerful hands, he grabbed the jaws of the beast, and tried to prize them apart in a last attempt to free himself from their iron grip. The sinews on his muscular arms and powerful chest swelled and went taut as a cable as he tried to wrench open the warg's mouth, but it was in vain, as the last of his life and strength left him, and with a final throw of its head back, the warg tossed him into the air, and with another snap of the jaws, the beast ended the life of the valiant chief. The warg shook its head furiously, and tossed him aside, throwing him into the air to land crumpled, broken and dead on the sand. One of the Davari maids whimpered at the death of the Davari chief, but Shaka did not turn to look at which one it was.

"Now that is the smell I associate with an arena - blood," Grixen said as his eyes narrowed deliriously. "I almost wanted the Davari chief to win, despite the fact I would have lost my wager." He looked at the sight with sheer delight as two dozen or so animal handlers emerged from doors set in the arena's walls, hurrying across the sand with their restraining nets and poles to coax the warg back to its cage.

"Perhaps he did win, in a way, and you will still lose," Shaka said, as the creatures back arched convulsively and it struggled to breathe, making great wheezing and snorting noises as blood sprayed from its nose and mouth. It managed to issue its last ever furious howl, before it fell to the sand, its paws twitching as the last of its life left it. Some of the crowd cheered and roared with delight, others booed and hissed.

Shaka laughed mockingly at Grixen. "You won't win any coin for a draw."

Grixen pulled a surly face, and Shaka realised how close she was to offending him again – it pleased her. She smirked. Despite the threat Mazdek had given her, he would not dare to do anything in public, and soon, if all went well, she and her children would have escaped his clutches, and be safe at Kara Duram. If her plan failed, then her fate was sealed anyway, so meanwhile she would enjoy taunting the foul ambassador every chance she got. After all of the suffering he had inflicted upon her, she could not resist provoking him further.

"Perhaps, husband, we should let the ambassador have the warg's cock. I'm sure he would think of something to use it for."

Grixen raised his hand as though to strike her and snarled. Shaka felt a dark fury flow through her veins, and with her eyes, dared him to do it. If he did, it would not go unnoticed in a crowd of this size. They would surely turn against him.

"You would strike the Empress in front of all these people, ambassador?" she asked him, darkly enjoying the moment.

Mazdek's mood had soured. "I will have the fur made into a rug for my quarters, if it is not too damaged," he said to Grixen. "You can have the claws, fangs and heart, the sale of them will more than replace whatever coin you lost on the bet."

"Indeed," Renlak joined in. "Charm dealers and apothecaries will pay a lot; some warg body parts are worth more than a wagon load of gold, they'll be bidding high for the claws and fangs, and even more for the heart."

"Come now, husband, let us eat, before we enjoy the spectacles this afternoon will offer," Shaka suggested to Mazdek.

Ignoring her, Mazdek moodily stood and began to make his way to the extravagant dining room behind the box, where lunch was being served.

"It is not the loss of coin that so offends and angers me," Grixen said to Renlak, his face fixed in an angry scowl and his voice dangerously controlled. He looked coldly at Shaka and hissed, "She does!"

Shaka raised an eyebrow, clearly enjoying the Bantu's discomfiture. She leant over and put a finger on his chest and prodded him rudely. "I fear you have very little time left, ambassador. If I were you, I would leave now," she whispered. "I think you will find that what is planned for this afternoon will not be attuned to your specific tastes."

"You dare to threaten me, powerless as you are?" Grixen asked with an exasperated growl.

Shaka's face twisted with hate and fury, as with lowered voice full of intent she said, "The beast within me is sleeping, not dead. Look into my eyes and know that one day, it will come for you!"

"How dare you," Grixen growled.

"Your first mistake was thinking that I am your weakened prey," she responded.

"You cannot withstand the storm," Grixen hissed.

"I am the storm," Shaka declared.

"Mother!" Aspess said, interrupting the exchange. She gave Shaka a look that reminded her of the words of caution she herself had earlier issued. *My daughter is right, I must not get distracted.*

Aspess continued. "Emperor Mazdek will lose face if he leaves, so honour requires him to be at the games during this afternoon's festivities. But I am sure Ambassador Grixen will not want to be humiliated by the petty rituals that must take place this afternoon? He must play a part if he stays but surely, he has been properly briefed?"

Aspess fixed her glare on Renlak whose eyes widened with concern. "You have briefed Grixen what is required of him, as our guest," she asked Renlak.

"What are you talking about?" Grixen asked, a perplexed look crossing his face.

Shaka enjoyed his concern. "This afternoon the entertainment is mostly full of ritual and ceremony followed by executions. You should rest, and then return refreshed for when the Seeress and the Simal are to be paraded, this evening. Her death will be most entertaining. You cannot accept the challenge if you are not present."

Grixen frowned and stared at her with a bemused look, and asked Renlak, "What is she talking about?"

Shaka fixed her gaze on Renlak and raised her eyebrows in feigned surprise. "You have played a role in organising these games, have you not spoken with Rachmund the Master of Games to enquire what Grixen's role will be?"

Renlak shot her a worried glance.

Shaka said, casually, "Titrius, our Champion, intends to challenge Grixen, to a fight to the death. He wishes to test his mettle against the first Bantu to ever set foot in

Kappia. It is his right to challenge anybody he wishes." She glanced at Grixen. "I am sure the ambassador will not want to decline the offer and humiliate his people?"

Renlak and Grixen gave each other a concerned look.

Shaka pressed the matter. "Having proved he is still Champion, Titrius will then be rewarded with gold and titles by Emperor Mazdek." She smiled politely. "He must then challenge the Emperor himself, in a showcase fight Mazdek will be allowed to win, but Mazdek must say the exact words after he kills the Champion to legitimise his warrior status over the armies of Kappia. I forget exactly, what those words are."

The colour drained from Renlak's face.

Shaka looked at him with feign disapproval. "Really, have you not read the ancient laws and customs, and informed yourself about the specific role a new male emperor must play in the games, if he has just ascended to the throne through marriage to a Munte bride? If Mazdek does not fulfil the laws and etiquette required of him, he will be humiliated in front of this huge crowd. He will look to you as to where to place the blame. His rule will not be seen as legitimate if he does not fulfil his role."

As Shaka expected, Renlak's look of shock and horror showed he was not aware of the ancient laws and customs to which she referred, for he had never presided over games put on to honour a new emperor and his Munte bride. She had reigned for so long, and he had watched her preside over so many games, she had gambled that he assumed he knew the protocols, and therefore had not checked how they applied to a newly crowned male emperor.

"The nobles will be judging you and the Emperor this afternoon, for some of them will still remember what is supposed to happen."

Renlak's look was one of utter dismay, so Shaka again took advantage of the moment. "Mazdek hates public embarrassment and surprises, as his Hand, I suggest you go to the great library and do some fast research and then brief him. You still have time. Read the fifth chapter of volume five of *Ancient Gladiatorial Kappian Games and their Customs*. It shouldn't take you more than an hour or more of reading. Or is it chapter one hundred and fifty-five? I forget, for those books are so long and tedious."

Renlak paused for a moment, undecided what to do. "Can you not just tell me, what is expected of Mazdek?" he asked meekly. "Or maybe Rachmund can?"

Shaka feigned indignation. "No, it is not my duty. If a mistake is made, I do not wish to be blamed for it. The responsibility to advise Emperor Mazdek on this matter is yours alone. Rachmund is only an announcer. He will run the games according to the instructions given to him by the Hand. I suggest you make the most of the time you have before Titrius enters the sands later this day."

"Off you go," Aspess said to Renlak as she made a shooing gesture with her hand. "It will be you he will blame if he suffers any public embarrassment today."

Without further hesitation, and in a great hurry, Renlak left.

Grixen still sat there looking puzzled. "It is called the Champion's Challenge," Aspess said, taking him by the arm in mock affection and helping him to stand. As she led him towards the dining room she said, "The Champion can challenge anyone in the crowd, and coward they will be called, if they do not rise to it."

Regineo sneered as he joined them. "Titrius is not in agreement with your presence here and wishes to demonstrate how a Kappian warrior can so easily slay your kind."

"He plans to kill you slowly, slicing one body part off at a time," Aspess said.

"He cannot challenge me. I am a guest and an ambassador here." Grixen protested.

"Oh, he can do it, and he plans to do so, for it is our law and custom. He will issue the challenge in front of the whole arena, and you must either fight him to the death, or decline the challenge," Aspess said. "After you have declined or he has killed you, he has a ceremonial fight with the new emperor, which the Champion as a courtesy must lose."

"I am not a warrior!" Grixen complained.

"Then you will be mocked as craven by the entire crowd if you refuse to fight him," Aspess said gleefully, "and your own kind will hear of it with shame."

"This is an outrage," Grixen griped. "I am an ambassador. Nobody would dare to challenge me!"

"The Champion of Kappia dares to do so, and will, after lunch," Aspess added with a smirk. "It is his right to do so, and the rumour is he intends to do just that."

"But like I said, you don't have to be here, ambassador," Shaka suggested, enjoying the look of shock on Grixen's face, but presenting no mirth or warmness in her voice. "We are trying to save you this humiliation. If you leave now, the Champion will have to challenge somebody else to fight."

Mazdek was already lying on a divan when Shaka and her children, followed by the maids entered the dining room; other nobles and invited guests were filing in. A slave girl had already given him a glass of wine and two others were vying over each other to feed him grapes. Shaka narrowed her eyes and watched as Grixen entered the dining room, paused, and then left in a hurry.

"Where's he going?" Mazdek asked Shaka when she joined him at the sumptuous table laid out with all manner of culinary delights.

"Oh, he is suddenly not feeling that well. I think he will decide to stay away from the games this afternoon," she said smugly.

\*　　　　\*　　　　\*

A blast of horns blew to alert the crowd that the festivities of the afternoon were about to begin. Shaka was pleased that Renlak had not yet returned. Her plan was working perfectly. Caspus had been to the great library that morning and made sure that every tome Temmison had ever written about the rules and customs of Kappian games, were removed from their usual place and hidden on obscure shelves where it would take weeks to find them among the many hundreds of thousands of books the library housed. Grixen, fearing a challenge to fight to the death, would not be back.

"Renlak probably has some important matter of state or a matter about the games to deal with; I am sure he will inform you if it is of any importance, whereas the ambassador seems to have lost interest," Shaka said to Mazdek when he again inquired as to their whereabouts.

"They left without even having lunch with the invited guests," Mazdek complained, his voice harsh with suspicion and anger. "You had better not be up to any of your tricks!" he warned, his voice trailing off as Rachmund took to the podium.

"Relax, husband; I made a promise to you and I intend to keep it," Shaka lied as reassuringly as she could. Her plan had worked perfectly so far. All it needed now was for Rachmund the Master of the Games, and Titrius the Champion of Kappia, to take the next step, and not lose their courage.

"Lords, ladies and gentlemen," Rachmund roared. Shaka cringed inwardly as she looked at the hairy, sweaty man addressing the crowd. Even with a drop of Maia potion, laying with Rachmund to get him to do what she required, had been even more repulsive to her than the act with Titrius had been. The result was the same, however. Rachmund was terrified of the consequences of being punished for laying with the Munte bride of the Emperor, so had agreed to do what she required of him.

"It has long been our custom and law, to allow the Champion of Kappia, to issue a challenge to any in the arena. A challenge, they cannot refuse, lest they be called craven," Rachmund yelled as Titrius, armed with a net and trident, stepped forward into the arena, accompanied by the noise and adulation that arose from the crowd.

Rachmund continued. "Titrius wished to challenge the Bantu Ambassador, but it seems he must have got wind of the news, for he has left the games and gone to bed like a milkling." The crowd roared with laughter and mockery.

"What is the meaning of this?" Mazdek hissed under his breath as he stared angrily at Rachmund and then at Shaka. "I will not allow the ambassador to be treated so shamefully!"

Shaka smiled falsely at him. "Relax husband, it is tradition to taunt foreign ambassadors. No harm would have come to Grixen so let the crowd have their sport."

Rachmund continued. "It would usually be our custom and tradition at normal games that our champion then offers a challenge to the Champion of Asheroth who is here with us today." The crowd booed as the champion of Asheroth, armed with spear and shield, stepped into the arena. He played along and gestured rudely to the crowd.

Rachmund continued. "The champions would fight to the death for the first fight; the loser would then resurrect so that they may also contend again at the last fight of the games; but these are not normal games; these games are to celebrate the crowning of our new Emperor and to honour him and his Munte bride!" He paused for a moment and turned to look up at the imperial box. "In line with our ancient laws and customs, our champion is required to issue a challenge to our new Emperor, Mazdek I. They will fight to the death."

"Fight me, Mazdek the First!" Titrius roared.

A deathly silence fell over the entire crowd, as they turned and looked towards the imperial box, where Mazdek sat next to Shaka.

It took Mazdek a moment to realise what Rachmund and Titrius had said. He scowled and fidgeted uncomfortably as the crowd watched him, waiting for a response. "They cannot do this," Mazdek protested to Shaka under his breath.

"Be at ease husband," Shaka whispered to him, feigning surprise and concern. "Surely Renlak briefed you on the ancient laws and customs, and the duties and ceremonies required of you this day?"

Mazdek returned a blank stare to her.

"Kappian games etiquette and law requires that the Champion of Kappia must challenge any new male emperor to a fight to the death."

"It is now ceremonial only," Aspess said, sounding sincere. "In the times of old, it was always customary for a new male emperor to show off his prowess on the sands and prove himself against the champion. Malerian II was the last to do it for real; he lost and was slain and was therefore humiliated in front of all of Kappia."

Shaka joined in. "So, Malerian changed the rules. Now, a fight between any new emperor and the champion is just for show. Titrius will allow you to slay him, and you will be declared *Supreme Warrior of the Kappian Empire*!"

"I am surprised Renlak has not briefed you about this," Regineo added.

Mazdek eyed them each in turn, his face twisted with suspicion. Some in the crowd were beginning to shout and chant, "Fight him! Fight Titrius! Prove yourself!"

Shaka smiled reassuringly and said, "It is only an old law and custom. I think we should do away with it really. It is not a true contest and is now only an opportunity for a new emperor to show off and demonstrate his total rule." She could tell by the changing glint in his eye, Mazdek was torn between suspicion as well as imagining the cheer and flattery of the crowd after he performed such a duty, and also, he was clearly considering the reaction he might get if he refused.

"Refuse the challenge if you wish," Shaka said mockingly. She then added scathingly, "But you will show yourself to be craven in front of the entire crowd if you do not wish to accept."

"It is law and custom," Aspess declared reproachfully to Mazdek. "It would not look good if you refused. You must accept the challenge. You will be perfectly safe."

"Accept the challenge, unless you are craven," somebody in the crowd shouted, and not by mere chance. Shaka had planned this down to the last detail possible. The evening before her maids had visited the taverns in disguise and reminded many people in Kappia of the old law and custom and what would be expected of a new emperor at the games. It was a chant that was soon taken up by others, and then more, until the entire crowd in the arena were calling for Mazdek to accept the challenge.

Mazdek's features were a mixture of emotions. Shaka could tell he was trying to weigh up all options. "If you refuse to even step upon the sands and face him, you will be shamed in front of all Kappia, and forever be called gutless," she whispered derisively to him.

"It is just a ceremony. If you refuse, law and custom states that another can take up the challenge and make a claim to be emperor and take his bride," Regineo declared.

My brother is right," Aspess said. "If you do not fight Titrius, another can accept the challenge on our behalf; but know that, in the minds of the crowd, that person will then have a claim to the crown as well as a right to take my mother as wife!"

The roar of the crowd and the chant for Mazdek to accept the challenge grew to fever pitch.

Mazdek's face contorted with fury. "If this is the result of your guile and trickery, you will pay!" he warned Shaka menacingly.

Shaka stood and motioned for silence with her hands. When the crowd was quiet, she said. "My husband, Emperor Mazdek the First, gladly accepts the challenge made by the Champion of Kappia." The crowd roared their approval.

Mazdek stood and went as pale as the colour of milk. His reign and rule would be forever damaged, unless he accepted the challenge, and Shaka could tell by the look on his face that he knew it.

"You planned this," he hissed with rage from the corner of his mouth to her. He looked towards the Hammer Knights who were guarding the imperial box. Shaka felt alarm rise within her, she knew he was about to order them to seize her and her children.

"Be at peace husband, please," she said as reassuringly as she could as she took him by the arm. She felt him tense as she began to lead him from the box. "It is custom that myself and our children, for you are now their father, accompany you to the sands. Look, Regineo, Caspus and Aspess have donned their finest armour for the occasion to honour you, as have I." Shaka's maids helped the siblings take their cloaks and silk gowns off. Once the clothing was removed, their fine glass armours the colour of the darkest night, made with exceptional legendary skills by smiths of a bygone age, glinted gloriously in the sunlight. The maids then helped Shaka unclasp her own robe to reveal her own splendid armour. It was white, lined with gold and jewels, and emblazoned with the emblem of the now disbanded imperial guard, the green upper torso of a naked women with a snake head with the fangs bared, emblazoned on a background of red. Two sparkling rubies formed the eyes of the snake.

Rachmund quietened the excited cheers of the crowd as the imperial family, followed by the maids, made their way down the steps towards the sands of the arena.

570

Shaka could feel the tenseness in Mazdek's arm, so she tried to reassure him. "Today, I will prove my loyalty to you, my Serissia, so that all may see who the true ruler of Kappia is." It stung Shaka's pride like a nest of angry hornets, to address Mazdek with the masculine version of the title she so adored for herself. It stung her even more, as she gracefully bowed her head, but it worked, she felt his tenseness lessen slightly.

Every eye in the arena was upon them as they made their way towards the sands, and Shaka knew that her fate depended on Mazdek believing the next words that came from her mouth. "Titrius will not dare to strike and harm you. You are now the Emperor, and this is but the first small test of your rule. It is but a trifling ceremony that will please the crowd and for you to gain the title you will need, to have influence over men you will have to call to fight the Empire's wars in times of need."

"Very well. But if I discover any mischief of yours behind this, I will hand you over to Grixen, and no plea or cry of mercy you ever utter will be listened too. You will suffer unimaginably until all of your lives have expired," he warned through gritted teeth.

"I know that full well, husband," Shaka said as charmingly as she could. "I have accepted my fate. You are my husband; I am your loyal and faithful Munte bride. This is just an ancient custom that will prove your worth, ceremonially, to the people of Kappia." Arm in arm with Mazdek and followed by her children and maids, they made their way down the last of the stairs. A dozen or more Hammer Knights followed them. The golden gate was opened for them, and they all stepped onto the sands. One of Shaka's maids carried her plumed helm, and helped her put it on as the other maids helped her children don their Shurian helms.

Rachmund and Titrius both bowed low as Mazdek approached them.

"I was not aware of this law or custom," he said menacingly to Rachmund. "Why was I not informed about this?"

"Apologies, my Emperor," Rachmund said grovelingly. "Your Hand, Renlak, was supposed to inform you? I did remind him to do so."

"I will be honoured for you to send me to the Deadlands this day, my Serissia," Titrius said as he bowed even lower.

Shaka took grim delight that both Rachmund and Titrius had told their lies with skill. She had checked up on them, and as planned, their families had already left Kappia and were well on their way to the safety of Kara Duram, safe from the revenge Mazdek would surely have on all those and their families who played any part in the events about to happen.

"I am merely the announcer and assumed he had informed you of this custom," Rachmund said reverentially as he prostrated himself before Mazdek.

"We will merely clash swords a couple of times, my Serissia," Titrius said, "just for show. I will then drop my sword, kneel before you as my Emperor and you will give me a warrior's death. Put your sword between my shoulder blades and plunge it in as far as you can. I will return to the games in a few days' time after I have resurrected, and the ancient law and custom dictates, in this same arena I must swear allegiance to you, the Supreme Warrior of the Kappian Empire. In front of this crowd I will willingly kneel and swear sacred oaths never to raise sword against you again. You will win the respect of all warriors in the Empire, my Serissia."

"It is all part of the custom and show, and earns you the title Supreme Warrior, sire," Rachmund said. "Forgive me if this was not explained to you before this day."

Rachmund, his nose still pressed to the sand then said, "When you fight Titrius, to prove your prowess and courage, your men are not allowed to be on the sands. Only you and your kin."

To Shaka's surprise and concern, a puffing and panting Renlak ran towards the centre of the arena. When he reached it, he bowed briefly to Mazdek and tried to catch his breath as fast as he could. "Forgive me, my Serissia. I was not aware of this custom. I have been to the library and checked, and by chance and with the assistance of one of the librarians found the tomes that state the rules and customs for games such as these. The fight with the Champion is just a ceremony, not a real battle," he said as he wheezed and gasped for more breath.

Mazdek and Renlak spoke in muttered whispers for some time. Shaka pursed her lips in sweet amusement. She had not expected Renlak to return so soon, but he had, and was informing Mazdek that all was as it was supposed to be. *All except one thing.* She smiled inwardly. Renlak had just assured Mazdek, that all was being conducted according to custom and law.

When they had finished talking, Mazdek ordered his men to leave the sands and said to Rachmund, "I am content that all is according to custom; proceed."

Rachmund stood. Shaka was delighted that both he and Titrius were playing their part perfectly and were very convincing. Their families safely ushered out of Kappia, their crimes of lying with her secret, she knew their loyalty was now only to her. She also knew that loyalty was born out of fear for the consequences of their own actions, not out of any love or respect they had for her. She remembered words her father had once spoken to her. *'Fear is a good motivator.'*

Mazdek looked relieved as he drew his sword. He walked over to Renlak, handed the Arkith to him, and ordered him to leave the sands. That was the only part of Shaka's plan that did not go perfectly, but she had planned for every eventuality. She had instructed Titrius that if Mazdek had the Arkith about his person, then he was to wound him with the normal sword, and give him the *Final-death* with the Arkith, but if he did not carry the Arkith or handed it to somebody else, he was to just wound him and allow her to give the killing blow. In any eventuality, she would win. If Mazdek was given the *Final-death*, she knew the Hammer Knights would not support her yet, so she still planned to escape, leaving the Empire and Kappia in turmoil until she could return with the legions to take back control. If Mazdek was not given the *Final-death*, he would still be humiliated in the eyes of all of Kappia, and she would still escape and plot her return to power from behind the walls of Kara Duram. Escaping was not her only goal that day. Mazdek had to be humiliated, and she wanted the crowd to see her kill him and then escape publicly. That way, they would know that the whole marriage had been a sham and she did not support his claim to be the Emperor.

Aspess smiled dispassionately as she and her brothers stood next to their mother, and Titrius and Mazdek drew their swords and took a fighting stance. Shaka thumbed the hilt of her own sword, and wished it was an Arkith. Titrius bowed to Mazdek. Shaka pulled down the visor of her plumed helm, protecting the entirety of her head.

"Let the Champion's Challenge begin," Rachmund declared.

The packed stands around them boomed with a raucous cacophony, as the crowd yelled, bellowed and hooted, all cheering their preference for the Emperor, who's Hammer Knights were strategically placed around the stadium watching for any signs of dissent. The massive structure seemed to shake with the reverberations. Mazdek and Titrius advanced with blades ready to strike. The elderly Mazdek shuffled on his feet, whilst Titrius glided with the seasoned footwork of a professional gladiator. Their blades met, but it was playful and light, and thus they danced around each other, striking blade against blade with little effort. Once or twice, Mazdek did seek to take advantage of the situation, and try to catch Titrius by surprise with a more serious lunge or blow, but due to his age, he was slow, and Titrius easily dodged or defended the blow.

"I tire," Mazdek said to Titrius in between wheezed breaths. "Let us end this."

"As you wish," Titrius said, using no title to address Mazdek.

As planned, Titrius wheeled around until Mazdek was in the position Shaka wanted him. He then lunged, and in one strike, severed Mazdek's sword arm. Mazdek, his face contorted in crumpled agony, fell to his knees shrieking in agony as he tried to stem the flow of blood pouring onto the sand from the ruined stump of what was left of his arm. The din of the crowd quietened in an instant.

Shaka wasted no time. Drawing her sword, she moved swiftly towards Mazdek. She wrenched his helmet off, took his chin in one hand and pulled his contorted face around to look at her. She coldly stared him in the eyes and said, "I won't be able to attend your funeral and resurrection husband, but I will be there on the day you are given the *Final-death* for your treachery." She pushed his face away and grasping the hilt of her sword with both hands, swung the blade and took his head off in one swipe. It flew into the air as the crowd grew silent, and landed with a clatter as it bounced several times on the sand before coming to a still at her feet.

The crowd were in mixed confusion. They stood there looking bewildered and confused, not knowing what they were seeing being played out on the sands below them. The Hammer Knights in the stand were already rushing towards the openings into the arena. Aspess had already taken off her glass glove and the silk one beneath it, and holding them in her other hand; she held forth the hand upon which she wore the Ring of Juram. She chanted the incantation and then muttered the final words, "Baforme, entrendren."

A shimmering blue portal appeared. Titrius, Rachmund, her two sons and maids, as instructed, quickly stepped through the Juram portal and instantly disappeared. Shaka held her sword up high with one hand and picking up the head of Mazdek with the other, she also held it up high for all to see.

"Mother, we do not have long," Aspess urged her.

The crowd was still in stunned silence. The only noise in the arena was the Hammer Knights barking orders and trying to get to the sands. One or two arrows hit her armour but they bounced off harmlessly.

Shaka took her own helmet off and shouted to the crowd. "I Shaka, of House Shakawraith, am the true Empress and ruler of Kappia. I declare this Munte marriage null and void!" She hurtled the head of Mazdek across the sands. It made a sickening crunching noise as it landed and bounced along the ground.

"Mother, we must go," Aspess said with pressing urgency.

Shaka and Aspess stepped into the portal. The rising din of the crowd disappeared in an instant. It had been a long time since Shaka had travelled through any sort of portal, but she laughed with hysterical delight as she felt the familiar sensation of spinning through time in slow motion. After a few moments, she and Aspess stepped out of the other side of the portal. Her sons, her maids, Titrius and Rachmund, and a delegation of Kappian generals were waiting for her.

Aspess immediately muttered an incantation that closed the portal behind them.

"Welcome to Kara Duram, my Sarissa," General Longshins said as he and the other reception party in the room cheered and bowed their heads low.

Shaka continued laughing with feverish pleasure. Her plan had worked perfectly. She had finally escaped the clutches of Mazdek, and for now, was safe at Kara Duram.

573

# Chapter Forty-Nine: *A Guilty Soul*

*The sword that slays the king wins the war, but the wielder never becomes king.*
*A Kappian Proverb.*

*Apprentice:* "Master, why do you not feel fear?"
*Gothberg:* "Everything I was afraid of has already happened to me. In life I have feared nothing, except my god and my wife."
*Apprentice:* "But look at your terrible foe, and see how the armour of the knights that guard him shine and sparkle in the sun, yet yours is so dented and worn."
*Gothberg:* "Knights in shining armour, may never have had their mettle tested in battle."
*Apprentice:* "But master, I have always seen you as a peaceful man."
*Gothberg:* "You were a fool to think the reason I was peaceful, was because I didn't know how to be violent."
*Apprentice:* "Don't do this master; I beg of you; you are a good man."
*Gothberg:* "Beware the darkness that lies in good men, if ever it is roused. For those I love, I will do great and terrible things."
*Apprentice:* "But master, you look so worn and weary as though life has hung a heavy weight around your neck."
*Gothberg:* "In life, I have not been broken by my trials and testing, I have been forged, for this very moment."
*A passage found on a torn and faded parchment in the Lower Archives of the Great Kappian Library. It is widely reputed to be a factual account of the last words of Gothberg the Great Before he slew the Cyclops of Cyracrose and his minions. Sustaining mortal wounds himself, the only other piece of the parchment that has survived the tides of time, states that Gothberg did not survive the encounter.*


*Borach* sat back on his haunches and stared at the golden crown that lay in a pool of blood. The gold glimmered in the last rays of dusk streaming through the windows of the palace of Highguard. In the stillness he could hear the noises of the city beyond the palace, the sound of doors being broken, women screaming and defiant citizens shouting their protest before being put to death. He noticed the smears of blood on the crown, left by his fingers. It was the blood of King Marsin the Pureheart. Effgard had told great tales about this king, including those of his wisdom, justice and mercy.

Guilt flooded Borach's soul as he stood. One day he hoped to meet Yianna in the Fair Havens beyond the Outer World; he feared the shame he would feel when he looked her in the eyes knowing what he had just done. He backed away from the blood smeared crown that lay on the stone floor, staring at it as though it were a snake about to strike at him. Trailing bloody footprints, he crossed back to the throne where the body of the king lay slumped.

The old decrepit king had been unable to fight, and had instead chosen to die with dignity and defiant courage. His last words had been: "I am a descendant of Gothberg the Great, last of my line. I will not grovel under King Falamore's table." Marsin had then fallen on his own sword which pierced him through the heart. He died almost instantly.

That he had killed himself, made it worse for Borach. He looked with disgust at the king's sword he had pulled from the body. The blood of the king trickled across the runes on the blade and dripped onto the floor.

"I would have given you horses, a carriage and freedom, for you and your family," Borach said regretfully to the corpse.

Torach entered the hall and strode to Borach's side, but he said nothing.

Borach did not turn his head, as with self-disgust he said, "This king did not deserve to die like this; nor did the rebel barons we have slain in this petty war."

Torach sighed deeply. "It is regretful, but better he and his family are dead, or they would now live like beggars under Falamore's table."

It had taken the legion and a few thousand of Effgard's men less than a month to destroy the rebel barons. Effgard remained with the main army, but Hozain and Falamore's two sons had accompanied the legion.

The stone cities and keeps of the rebel barons had been flattened and burnt to the ground. Some barons had been lords of little more than settlements or hamlets with wooden keeps and had hardly been worthy of the title baron. Most of their land consisted of settlements with a few hundred or so stone huts with straw roofs, and some farms. The main towns had not been much grander. In each one, the houses had surrounded a large hall in the centre backed by a keep. Wooden palisades or shoddily built stone walls had surrounded the hamlets, and some had several stone towers and ramparts from which the walls had been defended. They had been no defence against the legion, whose forces were swelled by the men Effgard had been able to spare.

At each settlement, several hundred apish looking warriors had drawn up outside the palisades gathering in one large unruly group. They had worn patterned woollen trousers and jerkins, carried axes and spears and bore swords with animal faces, lightning bolts, crossed axes and many other designs. Their unruliness in battle meant they were no match for the well-organized legion, and each battle had been more of a slaughter than any sort of contest. The warriors of each settlement had been brave but rash and had fought as individuals rather than as one unit. They had wasted their numerical advantage, and their lives, needlessly charging the ranks of the legion, whose disciplined fighting style made short work of them with no losses. Once the legion had killed the settlement defenders, Effgard's men, accompanied by Hozain and Falamore's two sons, entered to plunder, pillage and kill whoever remained.

On the hillside meadows around the main settlements cattle and sheep had wandered untended, oblivious to the several hundred legionnaires and the mob of Effgard's men that had poised at the top of the hills observing the scenes.

"It's a pitiful dump. Not worth fighting over. I say we pass by and head straight for the capital of King Marsin and then for battle with Sharwin," Marki had said on one occasion, but to no avail, as it was one of the settlements they had agreed to take.

Each ensuing battle had lasted for little more than half a day. At the largest of the towns, the baron, rather than allowing himself and his family to be captured, had paraded his wife and children on the palisade when the last of his warriors fell. In full view of the legion, and much to their dismay and distress, he had defiantly decapitated his wife, daughters and sons, and threw their bodies off of the walls, before jumping off himself and falling to his death. The remainder of the women and children that survived had soon been rounded up as spoils of war and loaded into wagons that some of Effgard's men rode slowly back to Thurog Tor.

Borach remembered that, at that town, Marki and Talain had ridden up beside him. Marki had looked grim, the distaste obvious in his voice when he had spoken to Borach. "Falamore's sons are ripping grisly and bloody trophies from their victims. I say we send the monstrous little hobgoblins back to their stench of a father. The work we do here is foul enough but their deeds leave a far worse taste in the mouth. Their guardian, Hozain, sent another raven just this morning, to whom, I do not know."

Talain had agreed with him. "They display a cruelty I had not noticed in them before," she had said.

Borach had considered sending the boys back to their father along with the spoils of war, but he had allowed them to remain. In fact, he had considered it an advantage having them there, for, if Falamore changed his mind or altered their agreement, the princes would be a bargaining tool he could use to persuade him to see sense.

The cattle and sheep that wandered the hills had been butchered and salted, as provisions for the legion. There had been no joy or mirth as each settlement was burnt to the ground. After battle, Borach, surrounded by Marki, Galin, Meron and Torach had sat in the saddle of his horse and watched the smoke billow into the air.

Borach had been blinded by rage and duty when they had destroyed the settlements, but Highguard, the fortress of King Marsin, had affected him deeply. It was not a minor settlement, but a major city surrounded by numerous villages and hamlets. When the legion had surrounded it, Borach knew it would be a long siege and a waste of time they did not have, but King Marsin had been betrayed. The gates of his fortress had been opened during the night, and the legion and Effgard's men had entered and fought ferociously all night, and then for the next two days.

The King's Hall had been the last bastion to hold out. Borach had fought his way into the keep with a small contingent of Effgard's men and when they were killed, alone he had fought a path to the King's Hall, but when he arrived there, he had found it unguarded. King Marsin had been seated proudly on his throne. The old king had looked at Borach and declared, almost prophetically, "When you arrive in the halls of your ancestors and meet your fathers and grandfathers, and join your wife and heirs at the table to feast; will you boast of and be proud of the deeds you have done this day, or will you hang your head in shame?" The old king had then stood, turned to face his throne, and had fallen on his sword.

The final words the king had said to Borach had pierced his very soul. Borach rushed over to him, but as he got there, the great king had breathed his final breath, and the light from his bright eyes dimmed and were extinguished. As Borach drew the sword from the king's body, the crown that had fallen from the old man's head rolled to his feet. Borach had picked it up, but then dropped it in horror as his thoughts had immediately turned to Yianna and his own children. The king's words had pierced him more than any sword could. He had waited there in silent shock until Torach had joined him. "This is not what Yianna would have wanted," he whispered to himself quietly under his breath. He then turned towards Torach and asked, "What have we become?"

Borach threw the king's sword, and the crown, to the stone floor. They landed with a loud clatter. He turned, and followed by Torach, walked outside of the throne room and along the corpse strewn corridors as though in a drunken daze. When they reached the outside, the stench of thousands of funeral pyres filled the air along with a black oily smoke that rose over the city. It had taken two days to completely take the city and would take another five to collect and dispose of all of the bodies and sort out the captured prisoners. It was a grim task made all the more laborious due to Falamore's instructions to check every corpse, and each prisoner, in order that King Marsin's family might be identified. The inner keep around the palace had held out until that day, but finally the legion had managed to bring the gatehouse down with the battering ram they had made, and elsewhere the final carnage was still taking place. Marki had been assigned to take the towers carved into the mountain the city sat below, but Torach and a bodyguard had been with Borach. They had become separated in the confusion of battle, and Borach had found himself fighting only with Effgard's men to aid him.

With tormenting thoughts of shame and Yianna in his mind, Borach walked out of the inner ward, through the gatehouse and into the city. *What would Yianna think?* The very question dominated his thoughts. Yianna knew she had married a soldier, a warrior, but Borach had always fought for the security and interests of the Kappian Empire, with the blessing of the Empress Shaka, and with a sanctioned *War Scroll* from the Senate legalising and legitimising any cause or war he had previously fought in. Now, he found himself fighting for a despot king for no other reason than they had needed to use his Obelisk. *I feel shame and guilt for my actions.*

The realisation of his new reality, made Borach feel soiled and dirty. In that moment, he envied Fell-bloods that they did not have to live so many lives and could so easily end their existence in the physical world. He felt, not for the first time, that his Akkadian blood was a curse, and he wished he had the means there and then to end his existence in the Everglow. All he could think of was Yianna and how she would disapprove of the actions he was engaged in.

Two horses were brought to Borach and Torach which they mounted and then began the journey to the camp. They observed that the soldiers of the legion not detailed on corpse burning were at work with the engineers, levelling every building, destroying stone by stone the thick curtain wall of the city, and then shattering each brick and stone with sledgehammers so that they could not be used to rebuild the city or wall again.

A woman clutching a child to her chest ran out of a side-street and almost into Borach's horse. She stopped and looked at him in alarm, and then fearful of whatever she was running from, she chanced a quick glance behind her as several of Effgard's men ran out into the street after her. "Please, my child, help me," she pleaded to Borach.

Borach put his horse between the woman and the men and snarled at them. "Leave this one alone."

The men gripped their weapons and looked at each other, and Borach could tell they were considering attacking him, but one of them muttered something to the others, and whatever it was convinced them, for they turned and headed down the street no doubt to look for more unprotected prey.

"Come," Borach said to the woman as he offered her a hand which she took. He pulled her, still clutching the child, behind him onto the saddle.

Near the gate, Falamore's two sons were busy cutting trophies off of corpses; ears, noses and fingers. They were being guarded by their bodyguards and watched by Hozain, who noticed Borach and rode up to him.

"Did you find the king?" he asked. "I have heard a rumour that his family threw themselves from the tower? Is this true?"

"If you had entered the battle yourself, you might have seen with your own cowardly eyes what took place here," Torach barked.

Hozain protested something about they were supposed to bring royal captives back to Falamore. Borach did not answer but spurred his horse and brushed past him.

"King Falamore gave explicit instructions to keep the king alive if possible and bring him and the crown to Thurog Tor," he shouted petulantly as Borach rode off. "Alive or dead he is to have his testicles removed and hung around his nose. That is King Falamore's wish."

Hozain's protest grew distant as Borach reached the scene where the battle of the gate had been fought earlier that day. Most of the corpses had been cleared, but some remained, and the wounded from both sides had been brought here and were being tended by medics. He particularly noticed two of Effgard's men, one who had lost a leg, and another who was trying to stop his innards from spilling out of a slash across his stomach. Both men were wailing, howling, and shouting oaths and execrations. The noise these men made was in stark contrast to the dead who lay silent where they had fallen. They looked like sheaves cut down by the hand of a reaper.

Borach rode past the carnage without stopping, left the city through the main gate which was now guarded by his own men, and rode out to the encampment. Torach left him near the camp to intervene between a group of legionnaires who were arguing with some of Effgard's men, in a situation that looked like it might come to blows. They were pushing a man about, a town guard, who was pleading for his life. The legionnaires were wanting to spare him, Effgard's men to have cruel sport with him.

Borach entered the camp and soon arrived at his pavilion. He dismounted before helping down the woman, who was still clutching her child, from the horse. She attempted to run, and he made no effort to stop her, but the guards at the tent caught her. He then entered the pavilion without acknowledging the guards and glanced briefly at the maps laid out on a table, before taking a feathered quill, which he dipped in a pot of ink and then scrawled a crude skull over the city of Highguard. He slumped into a chair and breathed deeply.

Borach had intended summoning his commanders once he had eaten and bathed, but without pomp or any ceremony, Marki stormed past the guards and into the tent. Usually Borach would stand to direct his friend to a chair, but he was in no mood to do so and stayed seated. Marki was clearly in no mood for any courtesies either.

"Should we be happy now that Highguard is destroyed and a famed king of legend and his kin are killed or captured, to be treated like dogs at the feet of Falamore?"

"Marsin is dead," Borach said, as Maraya approached and offered him a large goblet of wine. He snatched it unceremoniously from her and drank it down in one go, placing the empty goblet clumsily onto a nearby table. He then looked at the woman holding her child, who with some commotion had pushed past the guards and nervously followed him into the tent. He said to Maraya, "Look after her; she and the child are to be protected and treated well."

Maraya nodded and took the woman by the hand and led her from the tent.

"Have you found his wife and children?" Borach mournfully asked Marki, "I heard a rumour they are dead?" The last words of the king were still etched upon his mind. *If I can save Marsin's family, I will protect them from Falamore.*

Marki grimaced. "It is true. They were barricaded in a tower, high on the mountain and like the last lot, threw themselves from it when we tried to force entry," he said with revulsion. "They all prefer death to the fate Falamore will give them."

Borach cupped his face in his hands. The field outside the encampment was filled with guttural shouts and screams, and the sound of iron cutting through flesh. The pitiful cries and shrieks of terror drifted through the air into the pavilion where Borach sat, as Effgard's men put to the sword the men of fighting age they had captured. They were killing what remained of the population of Highguard.

Marki was clearly agitated. "This is not battle Bor, it is slaughter. I and the men are sick of it, and we don't even have a *War Scroll* to justify it," he said as he spat in disgust.

"Sit, Marki," Borach ordered as he gestured to his friend.

Marki sagged down into the cushioned couch opposite with a long breath of exhalation.

"King Marsin is dead, his city all but destroyed. We now only have the *Raven Queen's* army to defeat, and our obligations to Falamore are complete," Borach offered as encouragement.

578

Marki frowned at him. "You did not answer my question," he asked roughly as he looked at Borach with recrimination. "Are you happy at what we are doing here?"

Borach felt a surge of rage he could not control. He threw the empty goblet at Marki, who managed to punch it away with his gloved fist as he stood and faced Borach who shouted, "This was a deal you made. You sold us like common mercenaries to this foul king to do this wretched work."

Marki, his fist tightly clenched, looked angrily at Borach, and then his features softened as his rage subsided. "I did what I had to do Bor, what other choice did I have?" His armour clanked noisily as he sat down heavily on the couch, his head slumping into his chest. "You're right, this is my doing."

Borach's rage also disappeared, and he felt a sudden surge of love and compassion for his old friend. He stood up, walked around the table, went over to him and sat down on the couch next to him. Putting his hand on Marki's shoulder he said, "Am I happy with this wretched work? You know me better than that old friend."

Marki let out a wail. He removed an iron glove from his right hand, threw it to the floor, and wiped away the tears that formed in his eyes. "I am battle sworn and think nothing of it when it is just. But I do not enjoy this senseless slaughter. I made a deal with that potbellied whey-face Falamore and we are in his service until this work is done but I do not see what different choices I could have made." He again spat on the floor in disgust and said bitterly, "To hell with Falamore. It is not right, a whole city butchered to satisfy the revenge of one man. If my heart would let me, I would turn on Falamore rather than continue with this, but I have sworn oaths and given my word. The honour of the legion is at stake whichever way we turn."

Talain entered the tent and sensing the mood she walked over to Maraya who had returned and stood at a table, and with her help poured wine into fresh goblets which she then handed to Borach and Marki. "That's the last of the wine, until any we get from Highguard turns up here." They drained the contents in one.

"Twenty-seven men of the legion are dead in total," Talain said as she looked at *Old Trusty* sheathed across Marki's back. "I'll go to the Deadlands and get them, but I have no more seeds left. Make my death quick and painless, I want you to do it, not one of your men."

"I cannot do it lass, not to a friend," Marki answered.

Borach stood to his feet and walked over to the campaign table where several scrolls were flattened out with iron paper weights on top of the map. He scanned the scrolls and then picked one up and still looking at it said, "The battle report says the dead are twenty-six, what has happened?"

"A few minutes ago, one of the men slipped and fell from the wall when taking down the stones," she answered as she walked over to the table and picked up the ale jug, which was empty. "There might be more that die taking the few houses in the inner ward." She put the jug back down on the table and sighed. Maraya took the jug and filled it from a barrel of ale inside the tent. She filled three cups with ale and passed them around.

"Thank you, lass, and I'll need more," Marki said as he gently took it from her and drained it in one go. He curled his nose up in disgust. "Is this the brew we recently took from those we vanquished? I hope that we take from Highguard tastes better than this pig swill."

"Have your memories from your last visit to the Deadlands returned to you yet?" Borach asked Talain impatiently, as he threw the report back onto the table. He tried to mask the contempt he felt. *If she were a proper Seer, trained at the Mystery Schools, she would have full recollection by now.*

"My memories are still vague, but yes. I remember some of what took place and before I return to the Deadlands to escort your men, I would speak to you of it." She looked at Maraya, and then Borach. "In private."

"Leave," Borach ordered Maraya, who promptly left.

"Spit it out then lass," Marki said as he consumed more ale, curling his nose up at the taste.

Talain swallowed hard, and it was obvious to Borach that whatever it was she was about to say, would not come easy.

"Have your own Seers ever spoke of one they called Horin?" she asked him.

"No," he answered, "but all Akkadians are taught the *Legend of Horin*. It is a famous tale, is this the one you speak of?"

"I cannot tell if they are the same, for I know nothing of the legend, only the person."

Borach thought for a moment, trying to recollect the details of the story. "Horin was a Cragan, a foul magician in the Craganite Empire. He was entombed in an eternal coffin for betraying their secrets. He escaped by taking on the form of a bird, and now seeks to rectify his past wrongs with good deeds. It is said he gifted the Masters of the White Order with powerful staffs of gold and ivory, and the Masters of the Black Order with staffs of silver and ebony. But, when he gifted it to them, he gave a warning, that if a Master of the White Order used the power of his staff, an equal amount of power is made available to a Master of the Black Order, and vice-versa."

"Ah, I am no Akkadian but I have heard that tale," Marki said. "Horin intended to bring balance into the world, but not knowing the true nature of the sentient races, he only introduced chaos, and now neither side knows who has more power than the other for they have both indiscriminately used their staffs."

"The legend states that is how the Grey Council, the Tarath Guëan was formed. An ancient order that attempts to bring balance to the Everglow, lest the end of days come," Borach said. He then asked Talain, "Why do you speak of him?"

Talain took a while before she responded, and when she did, her words were cautious and measured. "My memory is vague, but I think they are one and the same, as I recall that the Horin I know can take the form of a bird or a man. He told me you were to seek one named Janorra. She is a Seeress of great power and one who can cure the disease upon your soul."

"What disease?" Borach asked.

"The blade that wounded you, *Ungweethon*, has injured your very spirit."

*Not nearly as much as Yianna and my children's death has*, he nearly replied, but instead, feeling curious, asked menacingly, "What sort of disease is upon my soul?"

"There is a foul spirit attached to you in the Deadlands. I sought the aid of Horin; he helped me get you back to Thurog Tor. Creatures called Telamones were hunting your soul."

"Soul-eaters?" Marki asked. "If only I were a Seer and a Pure-blood, I would guard Lord Borach myself in the Deadlands."

"Do not wish such a curse upon yourself," Borach said darkly. The news troubled him more deeply than he was willing to show openly. "Continue your tale woman; I do not have time to waste unless what you say is important."

"Janorra, a Seer, is in terrible danger. Horin told me the Wild Hunt seek her."

Borach and Marki exchanged a concerned look.

"Go on lass," Marki encouraged.

"The Order of Ithkall seeks her, and soon so will the Dark Undead."

"Ithkall's thugs? That den of assassins has passed from the world," Marki said, and then looked questioningly at Borach. "Haven't they?"

"Vangalen, isn't that a cult that once lived in a city in the north, beyond the wall?" Borach asked.

Marki shrugged his shoulders. "Never heard of them."

"Why would these fiends be after her?" Borach inquired.

"She stole the Simal from Kappia city. Your destiny is tied to hers. Horin told me you must help her get it to the Baothein," Talain urged.

Marki laughed, but it was born more of concern than mockery. "Lass, I think you are getting your memories confused after your *Awakening*. We hate the Baothein with a passion, as they do us. What you say cannot be right."

"The Simal?" Borach asked. "I have heard mention of such an artefact, one it is said they use to summon the Aeldar at the Argona Temple."

"If you believe such nonsense," Marki jibed.

Borach grimaced. "We are done with Kappia. It is Hammer Knight business to get back trinkets they have lost. If we see them, we will kill them on sight. Neither will we assist the Baothein in obtaining a bauble they could use for whatever foul purpose is in their deceitful hearts."

Talain sounded desperate. "Horin urged me, to insist, that you must find the one named Janorra. She is in a place called the Wytchwood, and is in great peril. Your destiny is tied in with hers. If you do not help her, your doom will find you."

"Now lass," Marki said affectionately. "I'm fond of you and friend I consider you. But you must be wrong on this. I suggest you focus on helping our dead legionnaires get back to Thurog Tor for resurrection, and not trouble yourself with other confusions that might play tricks on your mind."

Talain was insistent. "I am not confused. The memories, vague as they are, came to me this morning. Horin said that his Pale Riders will help the legion resurrect, wherever you might die, if you find the Seeress Janorra. She will lead you where to go. Your destinies are entwined. You must find her!"

"Is that all?" Borach asked her impatiently.

Talain nodded.

"Then dispatch yourself to the Deadlands, without haste, and bring my men to Thurog Tor."

"I will, for I desire to see Horin before he leaves," she said, "but I urge you to reflect on my words."

"I will, now leave, and do not expect Marki to do a deed he is not willing to do," Borach said coldly. "One of my men has been ordered to give you a swift death. See Commander Torach, he will take you to him."

Talain paused for a moment, clearly wanting to say more, but thought better of it, and turned and left the tent. When she was gone, Borach asked Marki, "What do you make of that then?"

"I trust the lass to not do wrong by us," he answered, "but her reliability I question. Her skills as a Seer are raw, and she is untrained. I'd prefer to have a trained and more experienced Seer give you a message from the Deadlands."

"She is all we've got," Borach replied. "Until now, Horin was nothing but a myth in a book, but I have heard many Seers speak of what they have seen and heard in the Deadlands, and I know better than to presumptuously disregard any tale about that place on the first hearing of it."

"I sense there is a but coming," Marki said.

"But her memories are vague, and not clear. It disturbs me she claims to consult with one called Horin, and that his riders are supposedly helping our men, and make claims of what they want in return. I agree with your counsel, I cannot act and make decisions based on a vague tale told by a Seer I do not fully know, and whose skills are undeveloped." Borach walked over to the maps on the table and slowly moved his finger across one of them until he found what he was looking for. Marki joined him.

"The Wytchwood she mentioned is far to the south from here," Borach said, pointing to a location on the map. "Even if we wanted too, there is no way we could get there surrounded by the foes we have made by engaging in this war. We must finish the task at hand and meet the *Raven Queen* in battle."

"Very well," Marki answered as he stretched his arms and yawned. "We can leave some of Effgard's men here to finish up. I suggest we move the legion to the Plains of Thurogen tomorrow and join with the main army. If Effgard has seen success in his endeavours, we can make a move on the *Raven Queen* before her forces are all gathered and maybe we can choose the ground where we must fight."

"Agreed," Borach said, as Torach entered, leading by the point of a sword the man Borach had seen was the source of contention between his and Falamore's men. "Who is this?" he asked.

"He says his name is Balash, he was the Hand of King Marsin," Torach replied.

Balash looked nervous, and it reflected in his voice when he spoke. "We had heard rumours a legion from Kappia fought for King Falamore. When I saw your banners fluttering in the winds, I knew my city was doomed. It was I who secretly opened the gate of Highguard for you. Surely that was an act worthy of some reward?"

Borach's eyes smouldered with a fire that rarely lit the eyes of less principled men. He said to Torach. "Take him to the King's Hall and smear his face in the blood of his king, and then take him to the same tower Marsin's family threw themselves from. He can choose to die quickly by throwing himself off, or I will have him taken into the wild, where his head will be smothered in honey, and have him buried to his neck, so that whatever foul creatures or insects prowl such places, can feast on him whilst he still lives."

A look of terror spread across the man's face. Whimpering, he threw himself on his knees before Borach and begged for mercy. "Spare my life. I gave you the city. It would still be under siege had I not opened the gate. I thought you would reward me."

"Your reward will be a quick death when you throw yourself from the tower," Borach said with lowered voice. "Your king did not deserve such a betrayal."

# Chapter Fifty: *Yianna and Shaka*

*The merchant Yangil sent his servant to the market of Riversweep to buy some fresh prawns. Before very long the servant came back without the prawns. White and trembling, and in great agitation he said to his master, "Down in the market place by the harbour I was jostled by a woman in the crowd, and when I turned around, I saw that it was death who jostled me. She looked at me and made a threatening gesture. Master, please lend me your griffin that I might hasten away and fly to Kara Duram to avoid her. I will hide there so death will not find me this day."*

*The merchant loved his servant, so lent him his griffin and the servant flew away in great haste. Later the merchant went down to the harbour to buy the prawns himself. He saw death standing in the crowd and went over to her and asked, "This morning, why did you frighten my servant whom I love? Why did you make a threatening gesture to him?"*

*"That was not a threatening gesture," Death said. "It was only a start of surprise. I was astonished to see him in Riversweep, for I have an appointment with him tonight in Kara Duram."*

*The Fireside Ramblings of Rambold the Philosopher.*


*Yianna* crumpled the piece of paper in her hand and stared out from the upper window of the house that she had been born in many lifetimes ago. The sun shone through the open window along with a fresh breeze. It was a welcome relief after the damp and dark dungeon the Hammer Knights had imprisoned her in. From her vantage point she could see the thick stone parapet of the inner-city wall. It had crenellations cut into it every five feet for archers and ballista. The heads of the Hammer Knights, and those of any who had fought alongside them, were mounted in between the crenels, impaled on iron spikes so they looked over the fortress city of Kara Duram. General Longshins had dispatched them with the regimental Arkith. They had met the *Final-death*.

Not surprisingly, Kara Duram was in a state of confusion. It had been believed that the fall of Aleskian and the disbanding of the legions was an imperial act sanctioned by the Empress Shaka herself. Her secret letters to General Longshins had protested her innocence and blamed it all on the vile usurper Mazdek. She had admitted wishing to join in an alliance with the Bantu to destroy the Baothein but had insisted that Mazdek had secretly engineered the destruction of Aleskian and the disbanding of the legions. Since her escape from Kappia to Kara Duram, she had publicly vowed in the name of Ahrimakan that Mazdek was entirely to blame for the calamities now befalling the Kappian Empire. Yianna doubted her story, after all, Shaka and truth had never been easy bedfellows, and Yianna remembered the role Prince Regineo had played in the fall of Aleskian when he had openly sided with the Hammer Knights.

Yianna's words to General Longshins and the other generals about doubting Shaka's version of events had fallen on deaf ears, perhaps in part because since her arrival at Kara Duram Shaka had restored the Praetorian Guard, her personal imperial bodyguard, of which Longshins had once been a captain of. It was only in the last day or two that Yianna had hear rumours that during his service in the guard, he and Shaka had been lovers. In whispered gossip, some had even dared to suggest that he was the real father of Aspess and Caspus. Whatever the truth of it, Yianna knew that Longshins and Shaka's acquaintance went back to her first lifetime, when she just a young princess, and lasted throughout the early centuries of her tumultuous rule after she had ascended to the throne.

Learning of the relationship that had once existed, Yianna now regretted she had confided in Longshins about her questions regarding Shaka's role behind the events that had occurred at Aleskian. A few days later, her son Biran had been forced to join the city-watch and she had not seen him since, or her daughter who had been sent to help at the griffin stables. Yianna had been refused access when she tried to see either of them, but she had seen both of them from a distance at work and they looked safe and well. She knew she had to tread carefully; uncrumpling the piece of paper she held she read again the summons to have lunch with the Empress. No doubt Shaka would be aware that Yianna had tried to sow doubt in some minds about her role in recent events, a slight that would not sit easy with the vindictive ruler. As a result, Yianna's days had been anxious, her nights restless; she feared for her children and longed for news of her husband, Borach. There was nothing she could do for any of them. Feelings of helpless despair had visited her often, as they did again as she looked at the note.

The clank of armour-shod feet on the pavement outside alerted Yianna to the arrival of the Praetorian Guard. She went slowly down the stairs, crossed the entrance hall and waited until the loud knocking stopped, and only then opened the door. A young captain, dressed in the imperial armour of the Praetorian Guard, minus the helmet, which he carried under one arm, saluted her.

"We are to escort you into the presence of her Imperial Majesty Shaka of House Shakawraith."

Yianna nodded and stepped out of the house, closing and locking the door behind her. She noticed the cloaked and hooded man across the street who made no attempt to conceal himself; obviously a spy reporting on the comings and goings at the house.

Yianna wore the latest fashion of Kara Duram that many noble women wore. It was clothing that had been donated to her by an unknown benefactor after she had been released from the dungeon. The fabric was coloured with a purple dye made from murex shellfish, upon which was a faded pattern. The dress itself was a long skirt, belted at the waist, with a red underskirt that was a tiered wraparound tied with a cord belt also at the waist, and could be seen through the slits in the tunic. The top was a tight short-sleeved indigo bodice made of several pieces of material, decorated with intricately woven braid, and fastened under the bosom. It was drawn back to expose the shape of the breasts and sewn together to give a bit of uplift. The clothing was faded and was well past its best. Necklaces, bracelets, earrings, hairpins and ankle bracelets completed the assemble. It was not very practical, and restricted movement a fair bit, but it was plain for all to see that she, Yianna, was a member of the nobility. Sumptuary laws had always been in place in the city, and were designed to distinguish different classes from each other. According to these laws, those not born of nobility could imitate the clothing worn by the upper classes. Cloths of gold and purple silk, according to these laws, were reserved for the nobility and could not be used by the common people.

It had been many lifetimes since she had been to the city of her birth, so she wanted all in Kara Duram to be reminded she descended from the ancient ruling class. She had been the only Pure-blood child, and apart from her children, she was not aware of any other living relatives she had in the city, although she had known her father had sired a number of Half-blood children whose now Fell-blood descendants might still be alive somewhere in the city. The Half or Fell-blood children would not have been allowed to use the family name, so it would be difficult for her to trace any descendants of her father's line, and they might not even be aware of the distant connection. Her family name was well remembered in the city, especially among the other nobles. In such troubled times, such connections might help her, should the Empress Shaka choose to be vindictive, for the Empress needed the support of the nobility in the city, which she would soon lose should she attempt to harm any of them, or kill them off.

584

As they made their way through the streets towards Shaka's abode, the throngs of people parted to make way for the small party. Yianna glanced furtively around her and looked at the many-coloured stream of the Kara Duram streets, which were exotic, hybrid, flamboyant and clamorous. She heard many different tongues being spoken and saw a variety of people. Memories walked with her. It was a far different place from the city she had known in the youth of her first lifetime. As they crossed the Square of Triumph, she noticed that the statue of Merokash, a Kuranian hero of ancient times who had served the gods of the *Old Faith*, which had stood proudly there during her first lifetime, had recently been toppled. Some debris and rubble remained, but the main statue itself had been broken up and removed; all that remained were the feet, around which several children climbed over and played upon. A memory, until then forgotten, resurfaced, and she wondered if the graffiti she and her friends had once scratched on those feet during her childhood when she also had played around them, was still there. It probably was, and as much as she desired to do so, now was not the time to stop and look, so she passed by with only a glance.

As they passed the square and entered Red-Lantern Street, she inadvertently met the gaze of a bold-eyed, red-lipped harlot whose short skirt bared her lily-white thighs at each insolent step. Behind the brashness of the harlot's stare, Yianna also sensed uncertainty, and with good reason. Since the conversion of the Empire from the *Old Faith* to that of the Aeldar religion the High Quaester Mazdek and the Empress Shaka had, until recently, always shown a united front in their devotion. Even when it caused a civil war and the Empire broke into three factions, Kappia had been united, insisting the Aeldar would soon permanently return to the Everglow.

In Aleskian, the news that some of the Aeldar had been summoned from the Void and had taken human form for short periods of time had been met with scepticism and even a degree of ridicule. Whatever the truth of it, the Empire was once again divided and was again at war with itself. The issue now, was not only about who should rule, but who had the true claim to be the guardian of the new faith? Both Shaka and Mazdek declared themselves the rightful ruler of the Empire and the leader of the *Aeldar Faith*. There was also the Baothein threat, only checked because a Bantu horde was within the Everglow itself, and if the rumours were true, was heading towards Baothein lands. The most immediate danger, for Kara Duram, was the fact that Mazdek made claim to the throne in Kappia, and Shaka was now at Kara Duram defying that claim even though she had become his Munte bride. Lawyers, even in Kara Duram, were arguing over whether or not she had an actual claim to the throne anymore because she was, in effect, still legally his Munte bride. Few in the city doubted that it would not be long before the city was under attack by a vast army of Hammer Knights. Even though the city was carrying on as normal, the tension in the air was palpable and the city was preparing for a siege.

As well as the threat of a siege, the Aeldar religion was splintering and fracturing into many different sections, even in Kara Duram. Theologians and scholars were hotly debating who had the rightful claim to the throne, and to be leader of the faith, Mazdek or Shaka, and which of them the Aeldar Gods would side with? Some said that as Mazdek alone now had access to the Simal, meaning that only he could summon the three whose riddles were known, the Aeldar would side with him. Plus, many of them also said, by complying with the Munte marriage, Shaka had legally given the Kappian throne to Mazdek so she no longer had any legitimate claim to it. Others insisted that because she was forced into the Munte marriage and had been promised by Ahrimakan that one day she would rise to become an Aeldar Wife, that the Aeldar would rain down their wrath on Mazdek for his deeds and side with her. They said, that was the reason why, since the Simal had been recaptured, Mazdek had not dared to summon any of the three Aeldar whose riddles were known. It was whispered in the taverns that the reason he did not summon them, was that he feared their displeasure. It was small wonder many of the people no longer knew who, or what, to think and believe in.

Despite the controversy, General Longshins and the other generals, supported Shaka, and had publicly executed every Hammer Knight within the city. With the support of the legions, none would dare to openly challenge Shaka's power. Some priests in Kara Duram, who had sided with Mazdek and preached against Shaka from their temple pulpits, had mysteriously disappeared, and this, had started to silence Shaka's more vocal opponents, and was the cause that whatever her critics thought, they were now mostly taking their grievances to the private sphere. Even so, it was well known in the city, and Yianna had heard it said, that many of the priests and Seers at Kara Duram, who, though publicly swearing loyalty to Shaka, still believed in private that she was responsible for the calamities they faced and that the Aeldar had abandoned her. Those who preached from the temple pulpits in the city now, whatever they thought in private, hailed Shaka as the true ruler of the Empire and head of the *Aeldar Faith*.

As they weaved their way through the streets, Yianna's apprehensions grew. She masked her fears behind a face kept composed and stern. It did not go unnoticed by her that some off-duty legionnaires glowered darkly at her. These tall supple warriors had forged the Empire with their blood and steel over many lifetimes; she did not know any of them, as they were from the legions forty to forty-eight who had only guarded Kara Duram for a few centuries or more, and before that had fought invasive wars in the place the Empire now called the Borderlands, far to the west, lands lost to barbarian invaders during the civil war when none of the factions could spare the resources or men to guard them.

The soldiers clearly recognised her. It was clear they were aware she was the wife of Borach, who until recently had been declared as Borach *the Betrayer*. She wondered if their dark stares were the result of their questioning how he could have let such a great city as Aleskian fall into the hands of the Bantu horde; it was being said that rather than defend the city, he had fled like a craven to hide in the Tarenmoors. Rumours, questions and doubts were rife in the city on many matters, and Yianna no longer knew who she could trust. Since her release, she had seen nobody from the legions that had once guarded Aleskian, nor any of their families or any of the citizens. General Longshins had assured her that those from the legions sent from Aleskian prior to its fall, and the survivors who had managed to flee after it, along with their families and other citizens had been sent to the Fortress of Margazul to reinforce those who now sought to guard the iron, tin, gold and silver mines, which would soon be targeted by Mazdek and the Hammer Knights. Yianna longed for his words to be proved to be true, to allay her doubts and fears. She felt alone and friendless in the city of her birth.

As they turned the final corner, Shaka's abode came into view. It was the last occupied house on top of a large hill on a street which ran south. Yianna knew it from her youth. The herringbone masonry was a familiar sight. It had once been the home of Rambold the Philosopher, who had met the *Final-death* during her first lifetime, in mysterious circumstances. She and many of the other children of Kara Duram's nobility had often sat with him by his fireside as he told them many tales of the world, and short fables with a thoughtful meaning. His former house was a grand old mansion, but not the sort of palace Shaka would be used to, Yianna observed, for the Hammer Knights had burnt the actual palace of Kara Duram down when the legions turned on them. The old palace was nothing now but rubble and ruin, as was most of the northern part of the fortress city where the fiercest fighting had recently taken place. It was this final act of vandalism that had helped turn many Kuranians against the Hammer Knights, giving their support to the legions. Recently, the citizens of the great fortress city had stood by as they were forced to endure and suffer the wilful destruction of some of their most ancient and prestigious architectural heritage. The Hammer Knights, during the short time they had been in charge of Kara Duram, had systematically removed and destroyed anything they felt dishonoured the *Aeldar Faith*. Fortunately, the great walls that surrounded the city had not been damaged in the fighting.

A wide garden, enclosed by a wall, where date palms grew thick, separated Rambold's former house from the other houses on the street. As Yianna advanced down the road, she noticed that beggars, so plentiful in Kara Duram, were nowhere to be seen near here. In fact, the entire road was empty of any people. *No doubt the indiscriminate violence the imperial family are known for, keeps people from venturing too near to their new abode,* Yianna thought to herself.

The gate to the house did not open upon the road, but upon the alley which ran between an abandoned house and the garden of the date palms. The young captain jerked rapidly at a rope which rang a bell somewhere inside the garden. He augmented the clamour by hammering on the iron-bound teak gate with the hilt of his sword. A wicket opened in the gate and the sullen face of a Fell-blood slave peered through.

"Open," the captain ordered. The slave craned his neck to stare at who was with him; he opened the gate without comment and then closed it again behind them and bolted it. The guards stayed by the gate but Yianna followed the captain through a garden where great pale blossoms loomed over them. They passed the guards at the entrance to the house and entered. Inside the large reception hall, several guards halted a game of cards to stare at Yianna with cryptic speculation in their eyes. They said nothing, and when she had passed, lowered their eyes and continued with their game.

Yianna followed the captain down a windowless corridor lit by golden lamps. "What is your name?" she asked him, trying to ease the increasing tension she felt by engaging in small talk. It was the only conversation on the entire journey so the captain was a bit taken aback.

"I am Captain Fellblower," he answered.

"You are recently resurrected? You look so young and fresh."

"I was slain in the battle for Kara Duram. One of those blasted hammers cracked my skull open like an egg. I resurrected about a week ago."

"You are not a Kuranian, are you?"

"No, I was born in the port city of Karadesh on the eastern coast," the captain replied respectfully, as he halted at a guarded door across which a heavy iron bar rested in powerful metal brackets. The guards lifted the bar, and he led Yianna into a well-appointed lounge, the windows of which, she instantly noted, were small and strongly set with twisted bars of iron, tastefully gilded with gold. *There have been some modifications since Rambold lived here. This now looks more like a prison than a home. Are the bars to keep people out, or Shaka within?*

Yianna shuddered slightly as the heavy door closed behind them and she heard the bar slide back in place. She carefully studied her surroundings. There were lavish ornamental rugs on the floor, a luxurious couch and ornately carved stools in the room. A large stairway led to the upper levels of the house. The captain led her up them to the fourth floor, then along a corridor and into a room with an outside balcony upon which some guards stood. Even in her youth, Yianna had not been to this part of the house. The stupendous view from the balcony overlooked the southern part of the city below

587

it, down the other side of the hill. It showed much of the city and the plain beyond it; black, acrid looking smoke filled the skies above the plain.

"Wait here," the captain said quietly. He then walked across the room and out onto the balcony, and Yianna heard him speaking to some people out of her line of sight.

The captain returned, and said, "The Empress Shaka awaits you."

Yianna tentatively walked with the captain across the room and out onto the balcony. The Empress Shaka and her daughter, Princess Aspess, were seated on comfortable divans. Seven maids stood ready to attend them. Yianna had never met Shaka or Aspess before, but recognised them through the numerous paintings and statues she had seen of them, as well as the images of Shaka that adorned imperial coins. She felt the skin crawl between her shoulders as she looked at the two women. All the tales she had heard about them came back to bead her flesh with clammy sweat.

The two women paid her no attention. Yianna felt curious at the sight before her; the old locksmith from the Iron-gate Market, who had served her not a week ago when she had purchased some items, was also present, and was nervously fiddling with something on Shaka's arm and neck.

"I am sorry, my Sarissa," the grey-haired old man said with a trembling voice. "I have never seen locks like these. If you say it exists in two-worlds, then it is beyond my skill to unlock it. You will need a Seer with a vast knowledge of locks and charms, as it might need to be unlocked on the other side of life before it can be unlocked here."

"Have your cutters even made a mark on the chain that links the arm and the neck? Look how slender it is, you must be able to cut it?" Shaka asked impatiently.

The old man moaned in fear. "My cutters are the sharpest and strongest there are in Kara Duram, and never has a chain of this slenderness resisted them. They do not even leave a tiny scratch. I am at a loss what to do."

"Then gather your tools and be gone, fool," Aspess said sharply to him as she stood to her feet.

The old man quickly gathered his tools and threw them without ceremony into a leather bag, and without even closing it he hurriedly left the balcony. He almost bumped into Yianna and the captain such was his haste.

"Have me escorted me from this place," he begged the captain, who instructed one of the guards to lead the old man from the house.

Aspess noticed Yianna standing there. "Welcome, do join us *Feya* Yianna of Aleskian," she said, using the courteous title Yianna had been given when she had married Borach.

"My Sarissa, your highness," Yianna replied, as she entered the balcony, bowed her head and curtsied first towards Shaka, and then Aspess. Shaka was dressed in an elegant gold, sleeveless silk gown, over which she wore a luxurious white tunic embroidered with lace and gems and trimmed with fur. She wore a circlet shaped as a snake with the head rearing out as if to strike, and on her left arm, a small, live corn snake wrapped itself around her forearm. It flicked the air with its tongue. However, it was the elaborate arm and neck bracelet that caught Yianna's eye. She had never seen anything so magnificent in appearance.

"Your adornment is so beautiful," she said to Shaka, who for a brief moment almost snarled, before regaining her composure.

Shaka stared at Yianna and coldly smiled, in the manner of a fiend sizing up prey. She had the coldest eyes Yianna had ever seen. She was beautiful, but in a cruel way, as though the deeds of her lives were marked upon her otherwise flawless features. Yianna apprehensively returned the smile with a polite nod of her head.

Bitterness tainted Shaka's voice when she spoke. "It is a curse. A thing that exists in two worlds and follows me from one to the other. I would remove it, but to do so I would also have to order somebody to remove both my head and my arm, and still it would be upon me when I resurrect."

*I am sure there are many in the Empire who would gladly oblige,* Yianna thought.

"My mother jests," Aspess interjected. "She has made a vow to wear it until the usurper Mazdek has paid for his treachery and crimes."

Yianna did not even need to sense the lie; she had heard the locksmith's words. Also, there had been no trace of amusement in Shaka's tone. Whatever the jewellery piece was, it was clear she detested it and wanted it removed.

Aspess, dressed in an emerald coloured Kappian tunic, folded and wrapped around her, and fastened with ruby buttons, silver clips and pins, pointed to the horizon beyond the balcony, in a clear attempt to change the topic.

Yianna focussed on the prominent view the balcony offered over the inner and outer city. Now her view was unrestricted, she could see that the high curtain walls of the furthermost battlements bristled with spears, swords and ballista. There was an archer at every crenel and arrow slit. Pots of bubbling boiling oil were at the ready over the murder holes. Catapults with flaming fire pots next to them sat upon the roofs of stout inner keeps. The great drawbridges that spanned the moats were up. The heavy oak and iron-gates were shut and barred and every portcullis was down. In the distance, far beyond the walls, black smoke still rose in the air. Villages on the plains were ablaze.

"It has begun," Yianna involuntarily whispered under her breath as a cold hand clutched at her heart.

Aspess followed her gaze. "Mazdek's army is at the Red Fork. My mother has kindly allowed all Pure-bloods into Kara Duram. The Fell-bloods outside have been ordered to defend the fields and holdfasts. It seems they are not doing that well."

"Kara Duram will never fall," Shaka said cockily. "It is mostly a Pure-blood army of veteran legionnaires from Karadesh that we now have defending it. I have every confidence in General Longshins."

*It will fall if starvation and then disease visits the fortress,* Yianna thought.

"Please, sit," Aspess said curtly as she pointed to the divan she had just been sitting on. Yianna complied and sat, whilst Aspess stood behind her. From the instant she sat, Yianna felt that somebody else was watching her; she turned her head first to the right, and then to the left. On her right was a vase the size of a man; depicted on it, among other signs of motherhood was a servant handing a Kuranian mother her baby. To her left, was a similar vase, but it depicted men drinking. A huge leather wine bag was being poured into the mouth of a man, who in the next image then turned into a half-beast. Again, the image was familiar, as it was a common image warning the men of the city that too much self-indulgence with wine could turn them into beasts. Her eyes however, were drawn to the curtain at the far end of the balcony. There was somebody standing behind it. She could not see who it was, but she could feel their eyes watching her. She ignored the sensation.

Shaka clapped her hands and the maids left. When they had gone, she said, "I have mourned deeply for the fate of Aleskian, and that of your husband. I hope Lord Borach will return to us soon." Her voice was laced with false sincerity.

Yianna stayed silent, but her curiosity must have shown itself on her face for Shaka smiled and added. "There is a young man named Cordius. A griffin he was trying to tame has returned, and it has since allowed him to fly it. He is to take to the skies again, and search far and wide to seek your husband. He will bring message to him to join us in our fight against Mazdek, the one who alone is responsible for the calamity that befell the great city of Aleskian that I cherished so much."

Yianna again sensed the lie; she wanted to get to the truth of the matter, and despite her fears, wanted to test the Empress, but not push her too far, so she chose her words bravely but tactfully. "The orders my husband obeyed, had all of the necessary imperial seals upon them, my Sarissa, including your own. It is most troubling Mazdek could achieve such a plan unnoticed." *I know it was you. Lies drip from your tongue.*

"The depth and scope of his trickery and treachery have no end," Aspess barked angrily.

"Indeed, he was deceitful and aided by traitors," Shaka said, eyeing Yianna warily, looking more perplexed than angry at the verbal probing.

*If you did not know about it, then you are incompetent. If you allowed it, but it turned out differently to your expectations, then you are still responsible.* Yianna chose not to air her thoughts but instead said, "A wise man once said that an empire that is defeated by external enemies, can rebuild, but one that crumbles from within, is ultimately doomed. I fear for the future, my Sarissa."

Aspess laughed acidly and said heatedly. "Do you think we do not know whose house this once was which we now dwell in? The treacherous Rambold also wrote that the Kappian Empire was like some stricken beast too stupid to know its doom was near, that it floundered ingloriously trying to get back on its feet. He was publicly whipped for the statement!"

"I am impressed with your knowledge, Princess Aspess," Yianna replied respectfully. "I assume you have studied his biography and some of his works during your stay here?"

"I have," Aspess said menacingly. "Until recently the house was full of statues and tributes to him along with quotes from his supposed wisdom; but I found his loyalty lacking so you would be prudent to consider with care who and what you quote in front of her Imperial Majesty."

Yianna bowed her head with false reverence, her tone grave when she spoke to Shaka. "I only quoted Rambold, because I am one of those who wish to serve you and see the sickness that now dwells within the heart of our Empire, removed." *You two women are part of the sickness that has brought the great Kappian Empire to its knees.* "Whatever service I can be to the Empire in seeing all treachery punished and corrected, then I shall seek to serve the realm well." *Your foul reign is coming to an end; you two are like the stricken beast that cannot see its own doom approaching.*

"Some in my mother's Empire take their oath more seriously than others," Aspess said reproachfully, and then pressed her lips together.

Yianna gave a polite nod; her previous apprehensions had been replaced by anger and revulsion at having to converse with the architects of Aleskian's doom, but she did not want it to show. When she spoke, she tried to sound as meek and respectful as she could. "My family are at your service. I hope Cordius is successful in his mission to find my husband."

"That news is pleasing," Aspess said with a smirk.

The maids returned with jugs of honeyed wine and a tray of sweetcakes. One of the maids poured a bit of the wine into a glass, tasted it, and then filled three glasses and handed one to each of the women, along with a sweetcake on a plate.

Aspess took a sip of the wine and took a bite from a sweetcake. Yianna had not thirst or hunger, but out of politeness did the same. The wine was so strong it stung her eyes.

"Did you like the clothing I had sent to you as a gift?" Shaka asked her.

Yianna felt both uncomfortable and resentful, now that she knew who the unknown benefactor was, especially that the clothing was worn.

"I have arranged for a trunk load of more clothing to be sent, all of it will be new, and some jewellery as well." Shaka added.

"You are most generous, my Sarissa, thank you." *When the city is under siege, and the city in a state of starvation, those so lavishly dressed will only cause resentment from the impoverished. You know this.*

"I have another gift for you," Shaka said. "I understand that you have no servants or slaves? What must the other Kuranian nobility in this city think of you living in such an impoverished state since your release from confinement?"

Yianna did not reply.

"Myrene has been teaching these Davari maids High Akkadian. They have made good progress. They will serve you well. Myrene will accompany them and oversee their education; it is the last act of service I require from her before she is realised from my service."

Yianna knew it was a cruel move for Shaka to burden her with mouths to feed, at a time when, if the siege was long, food would soon enough be in short supply. *I have no wealth or income; where will I get the coin to feed them?* "Thank you, my Sarissa."

"I will also give you him as a temporary bodyguard." She pointed to the captain who had escorted Yianna. "You, what is your name?"

"I am Captain Fellblower, my Sarissa."

"See to it the paperwork is completed for *Feya* Yianna to take ownership of these Davari slaves; after that, neither you nor they are to leave her side, she must always be attended too."

"Yes, my Sarissa."

Yianna had no doubt that the Davari maids would have been instructed to spy on her, as would the captain and Myrene. She had no need of maids, nor a bodyguard that she was aware of. The captain would no doubt look after himself using the legion's victuals, but without any income, having three slaves and a maid, was mouths for her to feed, during a time when due to the coming siege, food would soon be rationed and in short supply. Already, the price of bread in the city had escalated rapidly. However, she knew better than to refuse the gift. *I now have spies inside my house as well as outside of it.*

"Thank you, my Sarissa. You are most generous."

"There is one small favour I ask in return," Shaka said.

*Of course, there is.* "Anything you ask, my Sarissa."

"It is your daughter who will complete the act of service. I just ask for her mother's blessing upon the endeavour."

Yianna felt her heart freeze inside of her. *Yana? What peril are you putting my daughter in?* It took all of her discipline not to allow her emotion to show on her face, although she could not stop the side of her mouth twitching anxiously. She waited a moment, as Shaka watched her like a hawk, and then she asked as composedly as she could, "What act of service is it you have asked of my daughter?"

"Your daughter Yana is to deliver a message to your husband."

Panic struck Yianna. It took all of her effort to remain composed. "The city will soon be under siege, how is she to find him and deliver this message?"

The answer to the question dawned upon Yianna almost as soon as she had asked it. On the skyline, a griffin rose into the sky. Seated upon it were two people; the rider in the front saddle gripped the reins as the griffin rose high into the sky; the passenger seated on the saddle behind him, gripped on tightly. Although it was impossible to tell from that distance, Yianna instinctively knew the passenger was her daughter Yana!

"It is rumoured that already the flying beasts of the Bantu swarm in the skies, but Cordius will make it through and find him," Shaka said gleefully as she leant in towards Yianna. The corn snake on her wrist flicked the air with its tongue.

"It is believed your husband is in the Tarenmoors," Aspess said brashly.

Yianna had been raised in all the ways of courtesy. Despite the fear and anguish that struck her heart to see her daughter riding into the perils of the Tarenmoors to seek her father, she did not react verbally, but try as she might she could not stop the emotions from reaching her face nor the quiver of her lips. She felt a sick feeling in her gut, a sense of dread closed around her heart.

"So, do we have your blessing upon this small act of service that is required from your daughter?" Aspess asked. "You did say your family was at our service?"

Yianna tried to speak, but no words came out, and neither could she meet the gaze of the Empress or Aspess; instead she just stared at the corn snake still writing around Shaka's arm and flicking its tongue into the air.

"You are a sour woman," Aspess griped sharply. "We generously bestow gifts upon you, yet you are not pleased to see your daughter ride off in the service of her Empress? It is believed your husband scurried into the Tarenmoors; she has gone with Cordius to implore him to return and swear new oaths to my mother."

Yianna felt her face flush, and in an instant the last of her fear turned to wrath. She was so angry that even had her manners allowed, for a moment she still could not speak. *IS THERE NO END TO YOUR MADNESS?* She wanted to shout, but, composing herself and turning her head away to hide an unbidden tear, she calmly replied, "It has my blessing, my Sarissa. I will pray that my daughter's quest meets with success, and that the day will come when she and my husband will enter Kara Duram. I am sure he has already sworn new oaths in his heart and intends to keep every one of them." *My husband is no fool. He knows, all of these calamities are your doing! He will have his revenge!*

*  *  *

When Yianna had left, General Longshins stepped from behind the shadow of a curtain, where he had listened to the entire conversation. He walked past the vase and without prompting sat on the divan next to Shaka. "Borach was a good man, I had no quarrel with him," he said to her.

Shaka's face curled with distaste. "He and his men are the last ones who can tell a version different to ours, about what happened at Aleskian. It is essential they are lured here, and persuaded by our version of events, or are silenced."

"They will never make it through the Bantu hordes, which fan out over our former provinces like blood spilt in water," Longshins retorted.

"The Bantu seek revenge upon Borach, it is good for us if they end him; if not, and by some small chance he makes it here, he will swear loyalty to me, or he will be put to the *Final-death*, the same as the others were," Shaka snarled, glaring at him.

Longshins frowned. "He will never risk his family. If he is found, and does by some small chance make it here, I will speak with him. Even if he swears loyalty to you, he will always know you had a hand with what happened at Aleskian."

"You do not waiver general, do you?" Aspess asked.

Longshins took Shaka's hand in his own. He spoke tenderly, but with a certain roughness. "I served your father, and was by his side as we reforged this mighty Empire from the dust and ruins of defeat; I served you when we expanded it until you ruled half of the Everglow. Now, it is again in dust and ashes and you rule but a few fortresses,

592

but I will be by your side as we rebuild it again. I will slay who I must, even Borach, if it comes to that." He smiled affectionately and kissed Shaka on the forehead. "The Aeldar will all be raised, and you shall become as they. My solemn oath is to serve you alone."

He then stood and roughly embraced Aspess before letting her go. "You, daughter, have no less a place on my heart than your mother. On the day you were born, the Spirit of Sharnath that dwells deep within the Argona Temple called to your mother and I. We took you to her. Sharnath immersed you in the Pool of Lythisius, filled with the sacrificial blood of that Seraph. Sharnath was the only ever female of the *Firstborn* Titans. She held you under that bubbling froth until you gave out your last breath, and your lungs and body were filled with the blood of Lythisius. Then, the first prophecy was fulfilled. When she lifted your lifeless corpse from the pool, the essence of Lythisius entered you. You coughed, and came alive again."

Aspess smiled. "It is the first time I have ever heard you call me daughter, father," she said.

"And the first time you have called me father," Longshins replied with an equally warm smile, "but you know what the prophecy requires, and the rewards for fulfilling it."

Aspess nodded. "I am to breed with Thuranotos when he is summoned. The child of that union, a Titan of great splendour, shall be sacrificed. Those who drink his blood will control the Simal. Whoever commands the Simal, will even have power over En-Sof should he return?" She smiled at her mother. "The blood of my child from that union, will be my gift to you, mother."

Shaka beamed and triumphantly declared. "Thank you, daughter, it is no less than I deserve." Her voice then became serious and grave. "But heed the warning of the prophecy. Until then, no man may copulate with you, as it is written in the *Book of Sharnath*."

"I find my amusements, elsewhere," Aspess said. "Do you not think Yianna was…desirable?"

Shaka stood, took her daughter's hand and kissed it. "Find your pleasures where you wish, as long as you do not dishonour the prophecy. If you do, the spirit of Lythisius will leave you, and Sharnath will find another." It was then she noticed, for the second time, the strange ring upon her daughter's finger. She stared at the stone which rippled like a pool of oil and for a moment she seemed to be hypnotized by its beauty.

"Where did you get this?" Shaka asked her. "I first noticed it at the games, but until now, have given it no heed. It is such a strange ring."

Aspess looked at the ring, and suddenly the colour drained from her face. "That is strange. Until now, I had forgotten I wore such a trinket."

Longshins grabbed her hand and looked at the ring. "Perhaps it is through some charm you had not noticed or remembered you wore such a thing? Who gave it to you?"

"Yes, who gave it to you?" Shaka asked suspiciously.

Aspess' face went as pale as white powder. "I had forgotten, but now I remember. It was a gift from the Lord of Morkroth!"

# Chapter Fifty-One: *The Horror in the Hold*

*What can I say about vampires? Not a lot, for one distant look at the spires and towers of Old Vangalen made me sick with such a dread and fear, it was enough for me to realise it was a place I had no desire to visit. I turned around and fled from that land as hastily as I could.*
*Temmison Vol XV, Book 3: Cities of the Northern Badlands.*

*The Red Tide* anchored in the bay of a small and desolate uninhabited island, that mostly consisted of snow-covered bitter tundra littered with the odd vacant hill. The wind blew down the icy slopes to such a degree that the ship groaned and creaked with the pitch and roll of the sea, upon which ice floes drifted.

It was pitch dark in the decks down below the level of the sea's surface, the only light being that which the small group carried. Through the wooden hull of the ship could be heard the slap of the water alongside, and the impact of the waves hitting the planking a deck or so above. Azzadan and his companions crouched low so as not to bang their heads on the low bulkheads as they walked over to a steep ladder that led deeper into the ship. A rat squeaked and scurried past them, but it was not a surprise to see one this far down in the belly of the ship. Gaining a hand and foothold, and carefully carrying the candles and lanterns, the group began the descent into the deepest hold of the ship.

When they reached the bottom of the ladder, Azzadan fumbled in his pocket for a match, as an uncanny wind had blown out the candles and lanterns that the small party held, so they had descended the final ladder in eerie darkness. After the candles and lamps were lit again, the small party also consisting of Redboots, Smindy, Armius and two crewmen, made their way into the deepest part of the ship, where they stood outside of the compartment within which the sarcophagus was stored, having been previously lowered through several hatches that, when opened, led straight to the upper deck.

The door creaked and complained loudly as it was unlocked and opened. On entering the compartment, the stench of sweat and faeces hit them. Their eyes fell immediately on the strange looking sarcophagus on one side, and then to the two men Azzadan had taken prisoner at Harwind, who were chained in the corner on the other side. They looked at him with sheer horror in their eyes. Every feature of their faces was terror-stricken, and they whimpered. He had fed and watered them himself throughout the voyage and cleaned much of their mess. During his first visit, they had threatened him with all manner of violence if he did not release them, and he had stayed silent. Their threats soon stopped, and after just a few visits, had changed to pleas for mercy, until eventually they had begged and cried for their lives and freedom. He had ignored them, just tending to their needs, even resetting and mending the arm he had broken on one of them. At no point had he engaged with them in any substantial conversation, and eventually, they had given up trying to reason with him, because he had always stayed silent, beyond what he needed to say to attend to their needs. He felt no mercy or compassion for the two men as they were scum in his eyes; but, neither did he have any particular desire to taunt or torment them. He considered their suffering and predicament as more than enough for them to endure, as they waited in the dark for a fate that, unknown to them, was now about to be unleashed.

The small party gathered around the sarcophagus, grim-faced and silent, their shadows leaping about the compartment in the swaying light of the candles and lanterns. Without ceremony, the lid was prized open and the two crewmen carefully lifted out the corpse within, which was wrapped in dry bandages, and chained with heavy iron links coated in milathran, a powdered metal said to be despised by the vampire kind. They paused to allow the dust to settle, as the compartment filled with the smell of rancour and decay. The mummified corpse looked very small. It was placed on a table, and Azzadan stepped forward and unlocked the padlock on the chain, which he carefully, but unavoidably noisily, unwrapped from around the body. He then started to gently remove the bandages, careful to avoid lifting off the mottled skin along with them.

When the corpse was naked, Smindy unfolded the clothing she had brought along for the vampire. She dressed the corpse in the gown and then took out of the sarcophagus a thick golden chain, on which hung a red pendant the size of a baby's fist and handed it to Azzadan.

"Are you sure we are safe, Azzie," she said somewhat uncertainly as she looked fretfully at the corpse. It was the first time he had ever seen any fear in Smindy.

He smiled and nodded reassuringly to her. *By Skipilos I hope so*, he thought to himself as he picked up the milathran chain and bound the hands and feet of the corpse with it. "You can sweep up this dust afterwards and make a tidy sum selling it to an apothecary," he said, trying to lighten the mood.

"Damn the dust, the milathran on that chain must be worth more in gold than all of the wealth in the fabled city of Alesandrin," Redboots said with a greedy glint in her eye.

Azzadan took the pendant and walked over to one of the men chained in the corner; he took out a knife from under his own cloak and cut the man on the arm, causing the poor wretch to moan in panic even though it was in fact only a small nick. He rubbed the pendant in the blood, and returned to the table, before gently putting the chain and pendant around the neck of the corpse, so that the blood trickled onto the neck.

None of them had been sure exactly what to expect, but the long, still silence had not been it. They waited a full minute or so, before Redboots asked impatiently, "Maybe it needs more blood?"

*These are the exact instructions we were given.* "Wait," Azzadan answered tensely as he put his hand on her forearm.

Redboots was about to say something, but whatever it was, she did not have the opportunity. The infernal scream that came from the corpse of the vampire took them all by surprise; they held their ears as the noise deafeningly reverberated around the timbers. Armius and the two crewmen shivered and cowed in fright and would have run from the compartment had not Redboots, with a harsh stare, ordered them to contain themselves. Smindy went pale, but stood alongside Azzadan and Redboots, who both remained unflinching. The scream soon ceased, and the dried flesh on the corpse began to change, filling with colour and new life as traceries of blue veins mapped the inside of the creatures now pale white skin. There was the uncomfortable sound of bones clicking together and a loud noise like rustling leaves and a rushing wind, as the corpse renewed itself and slowly transformed into the vibrant and fresh body of a young woman.

"Noisy little bitch isn't she," Redboots whispered.

The vampire sat up, opened her eyes, and swung her legs over the side of the table. With a flick of her hands and feet, the heavy chain that bound them snapped and the links scattered like rain in all directions, clattering against the wood of the ship. She howled horribly with fury as she stood to her feet, swaying unsteadily at first, until she found her balance, and then a calm and serene expression spread across her features and she became deathly quiet. She did not move or make a sound for a full minute or so but just stood there staring blankly ahead. She was exquisitely beautiful, for a vampire, with long hair the precise colour of black ink. Her eyes were as black as the darkest of nights apart from the deeply crimson pupils. Her floor-length white gown with the lace sleeves belled out around her slim arms, swayed as though moved by a secret wind. She took a first unsteady step, and then another, and then walked bare foot around the compartment, looking down at the broken chain links coated in the milathran her kind despised.

"Only the purest milathran can hold a Queen of the Night," she sneered. "What fools bound me with tainted alloys upon my death?" For the first time she seemed to notice the other occupants in the compartment, looking at them as though awaking from a dream. "You did this to me?" she asked accusingly.

The vampire paced slowly around Azzadan and the others in the manner a wolf might size up its prey before pouncing. Vital energy pulsed from her like blood from an open wound. Azzadan knew that she could sense the vitality pouring off everybody in the compartment, possibly even the whole ship, and that to her it would be like a wave of energy that would fill her with a drunken dizziness. He only hoped she could control her hunger until she was fed. She looked at them and then hissed, revealing the razor-sharp fangs that were death under her red lips.

"Welcome, my Lady Velentine," Azzadan said deferentially as he bowed his head.

She looked uncertain for a moment, and tilted her head as though trying to remember. "Velentine…yes…yes…that was my name. Velentine. I am the Queen of the Vangalen."

"Was," Redboots retorted brusquely.

Velentine turned her head in an instant and looked quizzically at Redboots, and bared her fangs in a threatening gesture.

Azzadan pointed towards the two men chained in the corner, who were speechless with horror. "Dinner is served, my lady," he said.

Velentine turned her head in another instant and eyed the men savagely. She then walked unsteadily over to the first man and knelt beside him, sniffing him. The man began to scream the high, wordless scream of a man terrified of facing death. Velentine took his wrist, almost gently, but the man's struggles were in vain as with superior strength she turned it so the flesh of his inner arm lay bare. He pulled and twisted at his chains, cried like a child and whimpered like a dog. Her finger nails grew into long talons, piercing his flesh, causing him to scream in agony and terror. She then looked him in the eyes and stood to her feet, holding him in the air with the strength of one arm, her hand around his throat. As her gaze met his, the man seemed to slowly relax, and he became suddenly quiet, still and passive, as though a powerful charm had overcome him. Of a sudden he no longer seemed afraid but stared at her as though he was in a trance, in love almost, as he willingly offered his neck to her.

"My kind call this the *Stinging Kiss*," she whispered to him, as seductively, she lowered her mouth to his neck. At first, he did not even struggle as the life was drained from him. The only noise in the compartment was the sucking and slurping sound she made as she greedily drank his blood, and the whimpering terror of her second victim. Then, as the last of life was drained from him, his feet involuntarily hammered a frantic beat on the deck, slowed and then stopped. She dropped his lifeless body and turned to look at the other man who was gasping in horror, unable to catch his breath due to the panic that had seized him. She tormented him for a moment, taking his arm, which was in a sling that Azzadan had put it in, and twisted it, causing him to finally catch his breath and scream out in pain. She then finished him in the same manner as his companion. He died willingly, and silently. Velentine knelt and studied the corpses, as though fascinated by them.

Azzadan instinctively rubbed his own neck as he remembered when, not so long ago, he had died to the *Stinging Kiss* of a vampire. He recalled how he had been frozen by bonds and powers he could not see, dark forces that he thought had been wielded by the mind of Ishar, but now understood was the power of a vampire. A vague memory that he also had offered his neck willingly arose in him. He had been powerless to do anything as the woman had sprung from the couch and taken his life in a similar manner, and he wondered if, despite the anger he had felt, the same vacant trance like look had also been upon his own face as the life was drained from him.

"Foul things," he muttered involuntarily under his breath.

When Velentine had finished revelling in the ecstasy and energy her feeding had given her, she stood and slowly approached Azzadan, baring her bloodied fangs. He and the others instinctively took a step backwards. Blood dripped and dribbled repulsively down her face and fanned out on the front of her white gown. She wiped away the blood from her face with the sleeve of her gown and then sniffed the air, and said, "I smell sweeter blood, untainted blood, for which I thirst."

"You won't be having any of my crew now," Redboots said brashly, as she planted her feet firmly and put her hand on the hilt of her cutlass. "You'll have to stay thirsty if that's what you're thinking."

"A child," Velentine whispered as she circled the small party of people. Her voice rose in ecstasy and fervour. "I smell the sweet blood of a Half-blood child on this ship. Give her to me. I command it."

"Not Sassy," Smindy pleaded as she looked at Redboots and then Azzadan, saying, "Azzie, not Sassy, she's your kin."

Azzadan felt a hard knot at the centre of his stomach, and the short hairs on his neck bristled. He felt repulsed by the creature that stood in front of him, but he needed to gain her trust. "You have slumbered for many centuries, my lady, much has happened in the world whilst you have slept. You have fed, that must be enough for now. I wish to tell you our reason for waking you, for our business is urgent and to your benefit."

"Fed?" Velentine asked indignantly. "You give me the blood of two common wretches and call that being fed? Give me the sweet blood of the child I smell, for it is that, I crave."

Azzadan swallowed hard to supress the revulsion and anger he felt rising within. He was as cold and ruthless as any man alive, or so he had supposed, but the thought of Sassy being given over to this creature was a step not even he was willing to consider.

"Dismiss that thought," he barked. "We are here to aid you and your clan. Vangalen is nothing more than a ruin, and your kind are homeless and scattered across the world. We have woken you for a reason."

"Vangalen is destroyed?" Velentine cried out, her voice soft and wretched. Such was the power of the emotion she expressed, for a brief moment, Azzadan almost felt compassion for her, as grief washed over her face, and she stood glowering and sad, and spoke in a voice full of absolute misery and despair. "Fair but dark were the many pillared-halls of Vangalen. Tall and pointed were its spires. Cold and fresh were the springs that flowed into Lake Varez-âlium, upon whose blissful shores the Lord of Night won my heart as he sang to me the *Song of Valgarazzan*."

"My Master Ishar, of the Order of Ithkall, bid me to bring you here to Grona and waken you that you might come with me and rouse your husband, Lord Voran, from his slumber."

The grief vanished from Velentine in a moment, and it seemed to Azzadan that a shadow and flame, strong and terrible, clouded her as though a rending in the world of sight had appeared. She clenched her talons in rage, the noise of which was like the sound of stone grating glass. "Voran sleeps?" she hissed. "The Lord of Night was vanquished?" She looked at Azzadan strangely, and he could see an anger born of absolute hate that replaced the despair of but a moment ago. It showed in her eyes, as a dark and savage ire.

"Of course, why else would my love let me sleep the long, dark sleep?" she hissed.

In that moment she seemed to Azzadan as tall as a giant, darkness and cruelty was etched on her every feature. He felt a desire to bow his knee as he realised, he was in the presence of a fiend from the ancient world, so beautiful and dreadful did she appear to him. He felt his stomach clench, and for a moment he almost looked away, but steeled himself to keep his gaze fixed on hers.

"We can waken him, my lady," he said, composing himself to make sure his voice was steady and firm. "That is our purpose, and we shall see it done."

Velentine's rage slowly faded, and she appeared as normal size again, her features calm and serene once more as she walked to the far end of the hold, her back to them. Only her extended talons showed she was no mere woman.

"What does it feel like to have lived so many lives, yet remember so little of them," she said, somewhat mournfully as she turned her head towards Azzadan. "I remember everything, each moment of every day I have ever lived. Nothing is forgotten, especially not those I owe a debt of vengeance towards. I feel the pain of that even now."

In an instant, Velentine had crossed the length of the room and stood before him. His skin prickled with her nearness, the smell and taint of blood was still fresh upon her hot breath. She stroked his cheek with the long talons of her hand, but left no mark, even though he felt his cheek begin to burn. She sniffed him and curled her nose up in disgust. "A Pure-blood," she said, "protected by vampire powder."

She sniffed the air again, and smirked, as she looked at Smindy and Redboots in turn. "You two Fell-bloods, have also protected yourselves?"

"I would not have the likes of you aboard, without protecting myself and she who is closest to me," Redboots said defiantly.

"But not your crew," Velentine sneered, "nor the little one. She who I desire most is not tainted with the powder you three have polluted yourselves with."

Azzadan regretted not bringing more vampire powder with him. It was expensive, and he had not expected to find companions whose fate he would actually care about. Sassy was not protected, and Velentine desired her. It dawned upon him Redboots and Smindy had taken precautions the same as he had, but, perhaps due to the rarity of vampire powder and the cost, the rest of the crew was not.

Velentine walked around to the back of him. He felt her breath prickle on the back of his neck. "Give me the child," she said in an almost innocent manner.

"Azzie no!" Smindy cried.

Azzadan turned and looked at Smindy. Behind her, Armius and the two crewmen were cringing in terror.

Velentine, in an instant, was before Smindy. She struck her hard on the face, and Smindy fell to the floor. "That foul powder only means I will not give you the *Stinging Kiss*, it does not mean I cannot kill you," Velentine said with utter contempt etching her voice.

Smindy stood; she took her hands away from her face and though shaking, stood tall. She looked at Redboots, who was staring as though mesmerized by Velentine.

"Cap'n, not Sassy, we don't harm innocents."

Redboots closed her eyes, opened them, and shifted uncomfortably on her feet, as though waking from a deep sleep. "You can't have the child," she said to Velentine somewhat angrily as she tightened her grip on the hilt of her cutlass, and drew it.

"Enough! Velentine screamed.

In a moment, Azzadan could no longer move. He felt the same paralysis, as he had the last time, he had met a vampire, and Velentine was clearly much more powerful than Lagrinda.

In an instant Velentine stood before Redboots and sniffed. "I can smell your mortality, the sweet rot of corruption in your soul. The power of authority you think you have is based on fear, and where there is fear, loathing is never far away." She laughed at Redboots; it was shrill and condescending. "Darkness has you," she said. "Your small acts of kindness cannot redeem a soul as drenched in filth as yours."

"I don't care who or what you are, this is my ship, you'll not have the child," Redboots snarled defiantly through gritted teeth. Azzadan could tell Redboots was trying to strike Velentine with her cutlass, but she was moving slowly as one through water, and Velentine danced mockingly around her.

Velentine then closed her eyes and lifted her hands; misty smoke swirled and rose from them and disappeared into the wood of the ship. "Though eight thousand years have rolled their cycles, since the daughter of Veros revelled in red feasts amid the black halls of my ancient home, still they sing of me in song and legend, or how else would the Sons of Ithkall have known where to find the tomb within which my husband laid me?"

Azzadan, paralysed, was still unable to move or speak. He could see from the corners of his eyes that the others were also as helpless as he, and Redboots was still trying to swing her cutlass, but in such slow motion, it was as if she was in a different dimension of time.

With her eyes closed, Velentine danced again around Redboots and said to her. "To win immortality you must entertain death. If you woo the king of darkness like a lover, his gift will be life. Not life as you, a mere Fell-blood mortal woman understands it; not a life where you will grow old and shrivelled, worn-out like a hag, before death consumes you, but life where we fade into the shadows to cheat age and death itself." She then stopped in front of Redboots and stared her in the eyes. Redboots became motionless.

"My lord and master, my husband, Voran, would desire you as a sister of the night, I know it," she said, "but you have cheated him through some vile powder, and stolen your own destiny, so, know this! I see that death hunts you; it comes for you sooner than you think. In that moment before your eyes close forever in your demise, you will see the true nature of reality; you will know fear like you have never known, as you see the empty, black eternity that awaits you. In that moment you will beg Lord Voran for the gift of life, and one of us you would have become, for he would have gifted a soul as black as yours with it. I shall end your days. With your own eyes you will watch as I pull your heart from your chest with my own hand; I foresee it. This is the prophecy of Velentine for you, oh rotten soul!"

Again, Velentine was in front of Azzadan, in an instant, moving with a speed faster than the eye. "I sense your love for her," she said, turning her head towards Redboots. "Disappointment and rage are the only reward you will receive for your misplaced affections. You are a Pure-blood; she is nothing but a Fell-blood. You should value her life no more than you do that of the barnacles that cling to the hull of this ship!"

Through the corner of his eyes Azzadan could tell Redboots was still straining against the power that held her, trying to speak and defy the creature that so threatened

599

them all, but she could hardly move a muscle. The door of the compartment creaked as it opened, and as though in a trance or sleep-walking, Sassy walked in, surrounded by wisps of the whirly smoke that had earlier left Velentine's hands.

"You heard my call, sweet child," Velentine said softly and seductively to Sassy. "Come to me!"

Sassy walked over towards Velentine. Azzadan strained with every fibre of his being attempting to break the invisible bonds that bound him, but he could not move or speak. Velentine sensed it, for she looked at him and smiled, as one amused.

"I know the name of she whose blood, teeth, dust and bones were used to make that which you consumed, for I smell her dark essence. That powder you have taken makes your blood taste vile to me, for we do not drink the essence of our own, but it does not diminish my power over you." She laughed mockingly and said, "Foolish mortals!"

Velentine's eyes shone in the dim light like that of a predatory animal. She stood motionless, only steadying herself against the rocking of the ship, her gaze fixed firmly on Sassy. "Sweet child, so pretty. You remind me of a daughter I once had; I have changed my mind, you will not die, but live!"

Fury rose within Azzadan as he helplessly watched Sassy offer her neck to Velentine, who said, "I will taste but a little of your blood and grant you some of mine. It is a great gift I give you; a gift of the Sisterhood of the Night. If I am to rebuild Vangalen, I will need to raise a new brood to call my own."

Sassy did not resist as Velentine bit into her neck, but the vampire did not drain the life from the child. The change over Sassy was gradual, as her eyes became as black pits and her pupils crimson whilst her hair turned white. She seemed to float in the air as Velentine waved a hand.

"Let me show you what happened to our people!" Velentine said. Her hair stood on end and fluttered as though she were standing against a fierce wind as she raised her hands and screamed, "I am coming, my beloved."

Azzadan watched as Velentine waved her hand, and like a curtain being opened to a past reality he watched the fall of Vangalen. He saw a great field of battle where countless corpses littered the ground for miles around. Crows were stripping the flesh from dead men's faces, feral wargs and netherhounds were burrowing into the entrails of horses. Snakes slithered through empty eye sockets. Torn and frayed banners fluttered in the wind, on the ground where they had been planted, abandoned by their owners. Great war machines, broken and smouldering lay strewn about like some god's abandoned toys. Behind the scene, the towers and spires of Vangalen were burning and toppling to the ground.

"My husband was once one of the Seraphim. In a deep dark place, I found him, and taught him to remember who he was." Velentine hissed in fury. "My husband and I will take our revenge on those who betrayed us, and then we will seek out any who show allegiance to the Aeldar, and flay and slay them we will. I am sworn to destroy those wretched pretenders to the ancient thrones of the Nine Worlds." She smiled wickedly at Azzadan. "It is said Skipilos too, was once one of the Seraphim, this is why your master Ishar, seeks an alliance between our Orders." Her smile twisted into a furious grimace. "Morkroth betrayed us. He wanted to ally with the Aeldar. We would trust a fish with a maggot more than our destinies with those abominations!" She pointed at the scene of devastation and howled with fury. "Look at how Morkroth, he who we once called ally, treated our people. But see my husband, do you see him?"

"I see him," Sassy said with a voice that sounded other-worldly. "He has six wings, and eyes all over his body. He wraps his prey in his wings and feeds on their blood. He is beautiful to behold."

Whatever it was Sassy could see, it was in addition to the scene Azzadan was witnessing.

"I see him!" Sassy said, wonderment and awe upon her face which glowed with a strange light. "I see him! I see him! He is more beautiful than the night!"

The scene slowly faded and disappeared.

Azzadan noticed that both Redboots and Smindy had the same vacant, trance like look on their faces, as did Armius and the two crewmen. In an instant, Velentine was then stood in front of one of the crewmen and stroked his cheek. Several overlapping circles appeared on his skin where she had stroked it.

"What is your name?" she asked.

"Vardy," he answered vacantly.

She sniffed him. "You have the blood of nobility in you, yet here you are, living a wretched life on a ship as foul as this. Where are you from, and who are your kin?"

"I am Seesnari. I am the nephew of Saroth Arnton, the High Warden of Ashgiliath, Conqueror of the Seven Towers of Samothrane, Slayer of Barnoth the Wicked."

Velentine gave an amused, yet mocking smile. "Are you now? I set you free, you are now one of my marked ones," she said to him.

Azzadan knew exactly what this meant. He had read that the *Marked* would go insane with a pain that would drive them out of their minds, unless they obeyed and did the bidding of the vampire that had marked them. He knew that they didn't rest or sleep and would become fierce, mindless killers, unless their vampire overlord controlled them.

Velentine took Sassy by the hand, and walked over to the sarcophagus, she climbed in, as, still holding her hand, so did Sassy. "Now leave me and my daughter to rest," Velentine commanded. "Death will come to any who disturb me before I have gained my full strength. When I am ready, we will go to Lord Voran." She closed the lid of the coffin, and suddenly the others in the room could move again.

Smindy, quickly followed by Redboots, ran over to the coffin and tried to wrench it open. No effort could budge the lid.

"Sassy!" Smindy cried.

Redboots was enraged, her face a knot of anger and hate. "I'll kill the bitch!" she threatened as she struck the lid of the coffin several times with her cutlass. The sound of the steel upon the lid made a loud ringing clang, but only silence came from within the sarcophagus. Redboots flew into even more of a rage. She continued to furiously try and open the lid to the sarcophagus, but her enraged efforts were in vain, so she kicked against it and then banged on it with the hilt of her cutlass, all the time uttering vile curses, threats and blasphemies. When she finally gave up, she leant on it, catching her breath.

Vardy opened the door to the compartment, and, with a voice of one speaking from another world, said, "You must leave. Velentine will send for you when she is ready."

Redboots hissed with fury and ran over to him, her cutlass raised in the air to strike him.

"Don't, captain," Smindy shouted as she grabbed Redboot's forearm before the killing blow could be dealt. "He's one of us, despite the foul magic that has now taken hold of him."

601

Redboots momentarily closed her eyes, and bit her lip as though trying to suppress her fury. Taking a lantern, she stormed out of the hold. Azzadan, Smindy, Armius and the other crewman left. The door shut behind them.

Once outside, it was as though Azzadan and the others had woken from a strange dream. Redboots shot a hateful glance at Azzadan. "I did not know the depths of the foulness of the creature you dared bring upon my ship," she growled. "She has turned Sassy into the same darkness that she is, and who knows what she has done to Vardy!"

Azzadan knew that it was rumoured that a vampire lord could control vast numbers of people with runes such as she had placed upon Vardy's cheek. He also knew that it was said a vampire was at their weakest after they woken from a long sleep, so he doubted that Velentine could control more than one crewman with a rune, in her present state. Human weapons could not slay a vampire lord, of which Velentine was, but the Arkith he had about him could. He regretted not using it, but the feeling quickly passed. He knew they hated milathran, it burnt and hurt them, but whoever had bound Velentine with the chain around her, had clearly not used one with enough purity to disempower her upon waking. It had all gone so badly wrong.

"I curse the day you stepped onto my ship with that thing!" Redboots shouted at him.

"That may be," Azzadan answered moodily. "Velentine will gain in power after she has rested, and more so each day after that. It might not be long before she can control the minds of all upon this ship."

"Then we must kill her," Redboots snarled. "I have a silver dagger in my cabin with which I can pierce her heart."

"Silver is not as potent against her kind as some believe it to be," Azzadan replied.

"But you have an Arkith, when she next awakes, she can be slain with that?" Smindy asked.

Azzadan again considered it for a moment, and then decided against it – the moment of his regret had gone. "Yes, she can, but it will not be done by my hand, not yet. Like it or not, we have accepted this mission. We have no choice in this matter but to continue as planned. Sassy is lost to us; we have to accept that fact."

Smindy looked accusingly at him. "Are you saying we should still go ahead with this plan after what we have just witnessed in there? That thing is out of control. There is no way we can trust that fiend!"

"I agree," Armius said. He was visibly shaking. "We should abandon this folly now!"

The other crewman began to whimper. "I'll fight foes of flesh and blood for you, cap'n, and so will the men, but you can't expect us to have that thing in our midst? I saw what it did to Vardy!" He turned and tripped as he tried to scramble in a panic along the passageway towards the ladder.

Redboots was upon him in a moment, kicking him in the back so that he stumbled and fell. She drew her cutlass, and with a violent stab, tried to pierce him through the heart but he rolled and dodged just in time to avoid the thrust.

"Please, no cap'n," he begged.

Her second thrust did not miss; it pierced him cleanly through the heart. He died in an instant. Redboots wiped the blood from her cutlass on the man's clothing and sheathed it. She sheathed handed the lantern to Smindy, and ran her hands through her hair, as though trying to buy time to think.

Smindy looked at Redboots with horror. "Captain, what are you doing? What madness has befallen you now? He was a good and loyal pirate."

"He was one of Erik's spies," Redboots said, "but that was not my reason. The last thing we need is panic spreading among the rest of the crew." She breathed deeply,

602

straightened her tunic and did her best to smooth down her hair. "Azzadan is right. There is no turning back now. We have to see this through to the end, come what may."

"You heard what she said would become of you," Smindy responded incredulously. "This will end in your death!"

"I have cheated death before, and will do so again," Redboots roared. "I accept or believe in no destiny other than that which I carve with my own cutlass."

"What about Sassy?" Smindy protested as she panted anxiously, "that thing turned her into a monster, we all saw it with our own eyes, and what about Vardy, what has he become?"

"She only has the power to control him for now," Azzadan said uncertainly.

"I'll scuttle this ship if I have to, and leave her drowned at the bottom of this ocean," Redboots seethed, her anger overcoming her reason again.

Azzadan tried to calm her. "I have a Bethratikus to fulfil, and you, your salt-oath. Once done, we can all be away from this business. We must collaborate with Velentine, for now. We have no other choice but to finish what we have begun, come what may."

Redboots took a couple more, deeper breaths. "Then it's decided, come what may, we proceed."

Azzadan doubted the sincerity of her words, for he had seen that look before, not on her, but on others who were hiding their real intentions. Whatever words were coming out of her mouth, he could see by the look in Redboot's eyes that she wanted revenge on Velentine. He just hoped that she wouldn't do anything reckless and would see the sense behind fluffing their sworn obligations, whatever the cost.

"Red, don't do anything stupid," he said as he put his hand on hers reassuringly. "We will fulfil our oaths and then be done with her."

Redboots laughed, but there was no mirth in it. She pulled her hand away. "I don't fear death and I am not afraid of that fanged-bitch," she said contemptuously. "I'll do what I must for our oaths to be fulfilled, but I will not die by her hand in the attempt. If she tries something like what just happened in there again," she pointed her cutlass at the door. "Then I swear a higher oath, that by Jorgen I will find a way to kill her." She pointed her cutlass at Azzadan, and declared, "And if you try to stop me, you as well!"

Not only had the words stung him, but the hateful way at which Redboots looked at him, wounded his soul.

"I will think of something," he said. "Velentine still needs us to get into Grona, I will speak to her when she awakes. She will see reason." *I hope she will. Velentine is more savage and erratic that I had dreaded. I don't know if she can be reasoned with.*

Redboots laughed cynically and made her way to the ladder. She turned, looked at them all, but especially Armius who was still shaking with fear.

"We will not mention to the crew what has taken place here. I do not want a mutiny." She looked at the corpse. "Azzadan, you will cut him up. We will dispose of him overboard, secretly, during the night. I will explain his and Vardy's absence somehow, and wait to see what the fanged-bitch does next." She turned and began to climb the ladder.

Disturbing thoughts crossed Azzadan's mind. *When Velentine and Voran are reunited we will face a greater danger, for we now know her kind are unpredictable and cannot be trusted. I must come up with my own plan on how to deal with that.*

# Chapter Fifty-Two: *The Raven Queen*

*Some of the rulers in the Tarenmoors are so vain it takes more than an hour just to announce all of their titles. Strangely, some end their titles with a variation on the season of the year. Let me explain. We Akkadians have developed a calendar, but calendars are tricky things. We have twelve months to a lunar year. Each month should start at a new moon, but at the end of a year of twelve lunar months, there are nearly eleven days left over. Neither a month nor a year lasts an exact number of days, so we Akkadians have calculated a calendar that allows us to start each month at the start of a new moon. This lunar calendar allows us to start each month without our festivals losing their exact place in the seasons. In contrast, the people of the Tarenmoors have a basic sonar calendar and divide their year into two seasons – summer and winter. This makes it difficult to provide an exact a date for anything that happens there, when trying to write their history, and also creates some confusion as to what ruler I might be referring to. For instance, the last in a long list of titles for Queen Alstiace is 'Of the Summer Sun.' In winter this will change to 'Of the Winter Moon.' They are particularly offended if the correct title is not used, which might be confusing to you the reader, so I felt the need to clarify that Queen Alstiace of the Summer Sun is the same person as Queen Alstiace of the Winter Moon, and the appropriate title must be used when I refer to her deeds and the time of year when she did them. Time and time again I tried to convert them to our superior twelve-month calendar, or at least memorise it, but they just laugh. I even tried to come up with a rhyme but have failed to do so. I therefore teach their children to recite that: Jagrian, Fengrian, Hengrian, Magrian, Karian, Rhian; these six months form the summer season. Mupoor; Nuppoor, Lupoor, Luppoor, Terrapoor and Derrapoor, are the winter months. I must do better, but I am old. Maybe at my next resurrection I will again have the fresh faculties to solve such a simple matter but for now it alludes me.*
**Temmison Vol IV, Book 2: History of the Kings and Queens of the Tarenmoors.**

*The* host of Queen Sharwin, the *Raven Queen of the Summer Sun*, gathered for battle on the seventh day of the seventh month of Mupoor. She had assembled her forces on the slope of a valley at Rua-Sacoth, an ancient shrine in a valley of the same name, situated on the western edge of the Plains of Thurogen. A second army, consisting of savage barbarians, had come up from the south, moved onto the plains and flanked Borach's army. They had made retreat to Thurog Tor impossible. The battle, would indeed be decisive.

On the opposite slope, Borach and his army formed up in battle array against Sharwin's forces. Only the fertile valley with its lush meadows lay between them. Their camp and supplies were in the Gorge of Elamah. To protect this from the flanking force, Borach had little choice but to leave a significant number of defenders looking after the supplies and camp. They had force-marched all night to reach the valley and the men were visibly tired.

Marki scratched his still charred beard anxiously. "We walked right into this one Bor," he said scathingly. "It could be a disaster."

Borach made no comment. His eyes carefully scanned the opposite hill, upon which Sharwin's raven banners could be seen fluttering in the wind, along with those of her allies. The entire army must have consisted of fifty thousand or more.

Effgard, seated on his horse, also scanned the lines of the enemy army. "Bossian Knights, mercenaries from the Westmarch. I have longed to meet them in battle," he said eagerly, as he pointed at over a thousand well armoured horsemen clad in gleaming steel.

Alongside the knights were lines of pikemen, archers and men-at arms; their armour and weapons were crude and assorted in comparison to those of the knights. Mostly though, Sharwin's army was made up by the horde of half-naked tribesmen who stood on the mountain waving crude weapons and shrieking savage war cries that reached down into the valley and echoed up onto the slope where Borach sat upon his mount.

A raucous noise of horns, drums and iron beating against shields erupted as several Gragor appeared on the ridge behind Sharwin's army.

"Giants," Marki said, pointing to the Gragor. The races of Gragor and Dwarves had been enemies as long as anybody could remember. "I'd like to take one of them cloud huggers down with *Old Trusty*," he growled.

"That would be a fight worth watching," Effgard remarked.

Marki snorted derisively. "It is said by my kind, that Balagrim only lets folk keep growing in height until they're perfect, so it didn't take us Dwarves that long."

Effgard laughed, long and loud.

Talain remarked spiritedly, "Then you will get a lot taller before your days are over, dwarf."

Marki chortled.

Borach was in no mood to engage in the repartee of those around him. "Go fetch Maraya," he barked to Talain, who, after a short insolent stare at his manner, spurred her horse and rode off.

Borach again studied his enemies. The Gragor looked like they would be fierce foes. Not only were they tall and well armoured, they were holding lethal looking spiked clubs that were slung over their shoulders. *Those clubs could take several men down at once*, he observed. Even from that distance he could make out that one of the giants was female. He had been told about her. Reputed to be a terrible beauty, she was dressed as an ancient dragon priestess. As he watched her, a band of well armoured and heavily armed Chatti also appeared. They were seated in chariots pulled along by vicious looking wargs that growled and snapped at each other. In their midst, within an open top golden cart, also pulled by wargs, appeared the dragon skull that the tribes worshipped, and over that flew a yellow banner with a red dragon upon it.

"That'll make a good trophy if we can capture that," Marki said dryly.

"They will protect that skull at all costs," Effgard replied pragmatically, as with a grim demeanour he scanned the enemy ranks. He then turned his head behind him and looked at the hill filled with the men of his own army, and those who would be led by Borach and Hozain. "My scouts have reported the army flanking us has not moved," he said. "It will take them half a day or so to get here if they do."

"Then we need to win this battle before they decide to join in," Marki said, "and I am concerned there have been no reports as to the location of the wyvern riders and the host that travels with them."

Borach turned his head and looked at his own legion, planting their shields in the ground, the back lines readying their javelins to throw, and the front line readying their spears to make their stand or charge, depending on the orders given. In their middle, the golden griffin standard was proudly planted, gripped by Popparus and next to him, stood the man holding the legion's banner, which flapped in the light wind. Whether defending or attacking, as long as the legion maintained its discipline and line, which Borach knew they would, then they stood a chance, even against such overwhelming numbers as they faced. If the army behind them moved, however, or the mysteriously unlocated wyverns and the army with them turned up, it would change everything. Marki had spoken the obvious, Borach concluded. This battle had to be won swiftly.

The legion was the centre and by far the strongest unit and the most disciplined and experienced of all of the United Army, although not the largest. The Gragor, even though fierce, were not great in number, so he considered the main threat for the legion as being the armoured knights. He wished that he himself had a disciplined cavalry, as the many horse riders Effgard had brought who were positioned on the left wing of the centre, were already dismounting from their shaggy garrons, as they preferred to fight on foot. Borach had not been able to persuade Effgard that fighting on horseback would give them more manoeuvrability and options. Effgard had insisted that was not how his men fought.

Seranim archers stood at the front of the legion. Hired by Falamore, Borach had been informed they were the most skilled archers of any race. They were demoralised though, as they had not yet received any pay for the month and no spoils of war. *I should have allowed them to join us at Highguard*, Borach thought regretfully. As much as he had despised the looting and pillaging, he disliked even more having demoralised men with him. Shemite slingers and skirmishers from the Reach were in front of the archers. Lightly armoured, clad mainly in decorative tunics and boiled leather, they could move fast and attack the enemy with devastating effect using their slings to hurl stones that could crush the skull of even a helmeted soldier. *I would prefer a defensive stance and for Sharwin to make the first move*, he thought, but he knew that would be risky in case she waited for the army behind them to begin to move, or for the wyverns to turn up. Time was on her side, not his. He had hoped to catch her unprepared and whilst her forces were still split. Not knowing the location of the third army, however, was a concern to him. *What happened to my scouts? They should have returned by now.*

To the right of the legion were several thousand-foot soldiers, Falamore's men, led by Hozain. They were all as crudely armed and fitted as most of the army opposite. Most of them were not even trained soldiers, but farmers or tradesmen drafted in for the battle. Some were armed only with a pitchfork or a shovel. Karno the griffin was safely caged at the back of the army and protected by a carefully selected group of legionnaires, chosen by Meron, who had insisted they would be the ones to guard it. Karno would not fight in the battle, the creature was still too sickly and weak, but its presence inspired the men of Effgard and Falamore. It now belonged to Falamore, and he had insisted Karno was present at the battle even if not fighting in it. Meron had become very disgruntled as a result.

On foot, Galin approached Borach.

"Have the other scouts yet returned?" Borach asked him.

Galin, his helmet under his arm, his axe across his back, shook his head. "Not all of them, some are long overdue. Those who have returned cannot see any other armies sneaking up on us, but we have no eyes on where the wyvern riders are. The scouts sent out to look for them have not returned." He sighed with frustration.

Marki spoke. "What I don't understand is why those flanking us have not moved. They have no siege engines so cannot take Thurog Tor, and they cannot get here in time for the battle. They are just waiting, but for what?"

"My guess is, if this goes badly for us, they are there to prevent us retreating back to Thurog Tor, or elsewhere," Effgard remarked. "The fate of Thurogen, will be decided here in this valley, today, and I am sure the wyverns will make an appearance."

Marki slammed his mailed fist on his leg in frustration. "That's not good. I don't like this Bor, something foul is afoot here. There are no wyvern riders I can see in the enemy camp. It could be they were sent to hunt down our scouts, and they might have got some of them. We know those men; they would have returned unless dead or prevented from doing so."

606

Borach grimaced, his spirits sank; the odds were against them as it was. If another third army was approaching from the rear, without constantly updated reports he had no way of knowing it. The fact that some of the scouts had not returned, was sign enough that they were captured or dead, as no other reasonable explanation could explain why they had not returned. They had been under strict orders to report back before the sun had risen.

Dread spread through Borach's innermost being, as it started to dawn upon him that force marching overnight to catch Sharwin unawares, might have been a fateful tactical error. They had marched into a valley in which they might easily become trapped.

"We will fight, and face whatever foes we must, wherever they come from," he declared, and then looking up at the sky, added, "even if from the air." He wished he had griffins that could fight with him, and riders that could scout for him.

"Give us the signal when we are to join the fray," Galin said as he saluted and set out to return to his depleted cohort.

Borach had divided the undermanned legion into three reduced cohorts, all consisting of roughly two hundred plus men. Marki, Galin and Torach had command of a cohort each, and Borach overall command of them.

Borach had faith in the discipline of the legion. He also knew the mercenaries would listen to orders, as long as the battle was not being lost, but he could not trust Falamore's men, who were under the orders of Hozain who had other ideas how to fight this battle, as did Effgard and his men. Borach knew that maintaining discipline was the key to victory against such uneven numbers, but the warrior mentality of Hozain and Effgard was that battle consisted of each man fighting for himself, his honour and that of his family, and how he chose to do that was of his own free will, so they did not easily take orders from another. It was a mentality that differed greatly from that of the well-disciplined legion, and try as he might, Borach had not been able to persuade Hozain or Effgard that obeying orders was the key to winning such a battle as they faced.

Although it had been named the United Army, in truth it was three armies, who would each do their own thing. Borach looked up at the grey sky and cursed the fates that he had ended up in such a precarious and chaotic war. *At least me and my men will resurrect at Thurog Tor if we die*, he thought, *all except my dear friends Marki and Galin. I could not bear to lose them this day*. As he was pondering on gloomy thoughts, whilst trying to plan for every surprise event that might happen during the battle, there was a commotion in the ranks of Falamore's men and they started to part and cheer. Borach heard the unmistakable sound of music. Slaves carried Blondel and her two sons on sequined palanquins, surrounded by a large bodyguard. Accompanying them on foot was Effgard's son, Davino, who played a small lyre and sang soothing songs. They had come from the Gorge of Elemah to watch the battle.

"Are they mad? Wyverns could have got them on their way here," Marki said.

*Would that have been such a bad thing?* Borach thought. He did not voice it as he knew Effgard had a fondness for the queen, not to mention a love for his own son.

With great effort, the slaves put the cumbersome palanquin on the ground. Davino stopped playing the music and stood there looking in awe at the army across the valley.

Hozain rode up to his queen. Without a greeting, Blondel insisted discourteously, "I want Sharwin captured alive. She will live out her days under my husband's table!"

Hozain nodded.

Marki whispered a bit too loudly to Borach, "That weasel Hozain will be helping her milklings collect grisly trophies from those we will slaughter for her today."

Blondel shot him a furious look, but said nothing.

Marki scoffed, but before he could say anything further, Talain returned, accompanied by Maraya who was also on horseback.

"Shagor! Shagor!" Maraya shouted excitedly as she pointed to the opposite mountain at the female Gragor, who was using her spear to point to one of the male Gragor. Even from that distance, Borach could tell the male she pointed at was a massive, savage and lethal looking creature with muscled arms that rippled with brutish strength. His body was smeared in blood and covered with human scalps and animal hides. A fearsome spiked club was sloped over his shoulder. The Gragor lumbered down the mountain and into the valley with long, gaping strides.

"Barathi comes!" Maraya said, somewhat ominously.

Shagor, and then her brother, roared something, that none amongst the ranks of Borach understood except Maraya and Blondel.

"What are they saying, lass?" Marki asked Maraya.

Maraya smiled. "Shagor wants you to look at her brother, Barathi; he is a famous Gragor warrior. He is challenging a champion from this army to meet him in battle. If your champion wins, the Gragor and Chatti will not join the battle today. If you lose, they will see every last man in this army killed and fed to their wargs and wyverns. This is the way of the Gragor, they will be true to their word, as honour in battle is their highest virtue."

Marki snarled and drew *Old Trusty*, "I'll meet the oversized offal bag in battle and will soon cut him down to size. A beast is a beast no matter the size!"

"The honour will be mine," Effgard said with an equally ferocious snarl as he drew his own axe.

Hozain gasped nervously, "That's the largest Gragor I have ever seen, and I would not want to fight him."

"That's why nobody will remember your name," Marki growled to him, as he unstrapped *Old Trusty* and swung it around with a battle cry.

Borach drew his blade, and with a dark and menacing look towards the Gragor, said, "I will be the one to face him. This is my order and command, and it shall be obeyed."

Marki began to laugh. "Then you'd better be quick about it, look, Effgard's boy has already accepted the challenge!"

Borach looked into the valley. Unnoticed, Davino had slipped away and sprinted down into the valley and was already running across the open space to face the giant.

"No! No! Foolish boy!" Effgard shouted. "Come back! Do not steal the honour that belongs to me!" Effgard reared his horse, and it was clear to all that he intended charging down the hill to intervene.

Hozain shouted at him. "Your boy has accepted the challenge, if you intervene, you will dishonour yourself, your family name, and the Gragor."

"To the netherworld with it," Effgard snarled.

"Hozain is right," Blondel urged. "You cannot intervene and bring this dishonour upon us. We will mourn for Davino, even as we curse his folly, yet praise his courage."

Effgard stilled his horse, paused a moment, and let out a long and anguished wail, as one who was about to lose a son, or an honour belonging to him. Borach was not sure which.

Marki waited until Effgard grew silent, and then sighed and said dryly, "Shame. He was a nice lad; very polite. One day I'll honour his bravery with a mug of ale, and his death with another, as minstrels sing his ballad. But his foolishness means we will be fighting Gragor and Chatti today after all."

They all watched as Barathi stopped and stared at the young Davino with contempt and roared something towards where Borach sat upon his horse, once again unintelligible to all except Maraya, who looked at Borach and said, "Barathi asks why you insult him and send a boy to fight him? He calls you craven, and your men cowards, for not daring to face him in single combat."

"I'll fight him," Borach snarled as he spurred his horse to make his way down the valley.

"Stop," Maraya said. "Davino has accepted the challenge. You must now let them fight, or you will be seen as a man with no honour and the Gragor and Chatti will never trust any words you speak."

Borach halted his horse and looked down into the valley where Effgard's son Davino stood, defiantly facing the Gragor. He knew he had to allow events to unfold as they would. "The stupidity of youth," he roared, as he turned his horse back and rejoined the others. "He deserves a pointless death. I have no pity for him; the rest of us face a greater task for his foolishness."

Effgard looked at him with a venomous stare.

They all watched and could hear as Davino began to sing; the breeze caught his words which floated musically across the valley and up the sides of both hills.

"He sings of the deeds of our ancestors, and of my valour, his father," Effgard said, suddenly finding fresh pride in his son.

After the song had finished, Davino cried out to Barathi. "I am Davino, a servant of En-Sof, you come with club and spike, but I will smite you and cut off your head with your own dagger and feed it to the birds of the air. Fight me or run back to your ranks in fear."

"So be it!" Barathi roared in the Common Tongue, his head jolting with the force of his words, spraying drool everywhere. "I will gnaw your flesh, crunch your bones and use what is left of them as a toothpick!"

"Is he trying to drown the boy?" Marki asked mockingly.

Without further hesitation Barathi lumbered over to Davino and lurched after him.

Likewise, Davino ran quickly towards him to meet him in battle. He undid a sling from his belt, put his hand into his bag, took out a stone and began to swirl the sling. Faster and faster it whirled around his head, until he released the stone, which flew through the air at a great speed, before sinking into the forehead of Barathi, who briefly stopped in his stride and rocked back on his heels, disorientated. Davino continued running towards him.

Barathi regained his senses and swung his massive club at the boy, who ducked beneath it and skidded to his feet a few feet away. The giant's club imbedded itself in the earth showering the boy with dirt and dust. The force of the blow caused the ground to tremble and shake with such force Davino momentarily lost his footing but regained it just as quickly. Barathi's first effort to release his club from the ground was not successful so he let it go and struck at Davino with both of his massive fists. The boy was too quick and dodged them, flipping over in several summersaults until he was a short distance away from the mighty blows of the giant.

The second attempt of Barathi to release his club was successful. Holding it with both hands high above his head he ran towards the young Davino, who put another stone in the sling, and running towards Barathi he swirled it through the air, faster and faster, and then slung it with all of his young might. The stone hurtled through the air and hit the giant in his left eye and sunk deep into it. Barathi roared in fury, but his roar died out as he came to a stop. He staggered unsteadily on his feet before his head slunk to his chest. Drool and blood came out of his mouth and he fell to his knees, and then onto his face hitting the earth with a mighty crash.

Both armies stood in stunned silence, as Davino ran up to the giant and true to his word, removed the dagger from the giant's belt and with great effort, cut off his head. He was not strong enough to lift it, so instead, put one foot upon Barathi's decapitated head, as the sweet and melodious roar of his triumph filled the valley.

For a moment, there was more stunned silence, and then Effgard let out the mightiest roar and cheer that a man could possibly give.

Marki was the first to speak. "Have you ever seen the like of it?" he shouted in bewildered awe and disbelief. "A giant slain by a boy! Davino *the Giantslayer* he will be called!" He laughed, cheered, roared and shouted as did all of the men in the United Army. "If he were a dwarf that would be a story worthy to tell the Maidens and Old Balagrim himself!" Marki declared to Effgard.

Borach was the only one not cheering. "We still have a battle to fight," he said sullenly, and pointed to the valley, "your jubilation might be short-lived."

The United Army gradually became silent occasioned by the fact that the female Gragor, Shagor, had descended quickly into the valley and with great speed had approached Davino. She and he exchanged words but none except they could hear what was said. She picked him up and taking a vial from a pouch she uncorked it and covered him with oil. She then turned to both armies and roared something in her own tongue.

"What's she doing?" Marki asked in alarm, "I thought you said they had honour?" he asked as he turned to Maraya.

"She has anointed him, and is honouring Davino for his victory, and declaring the Gragor and Chatti will honour their word and not fight today," Effgard said. "According to their custom, Davino must not fight anymore this day so she is taking him to her tent to sit with her."

"Will the boy be hurt?" Marki asked.

Effgard grimaced. "No, the Gragor will bestow great honours upon him for his bravery and victory, honours that should have been mine. My own son has robbed me of these, but he will be safe."

"You are strange folk with stranger ways," Marki muttered as he shook his head in disbelief.

The United Army let out another cheer as Shagor held Davino up, to honour him, before she gently put him on the ground, and held his hand. Then, she roared something in Borach's direction.

"Quiet!" Marki bellowed to the army as he spurred his pony and rode up and down the ranks. "Quiet! Let us hear what she says to us!" He returned to Borach's side as the army quietened and Shagor roared more words. Blondel's face curled with rage as the words boomed and echoed through the valley.

"What did she say?" Borach asked Maraya.

Maraya had a look of sheer delight on her face. "She says that Falamore has already been slain by Yizain. She has his head."

"Lies! Treason!" Blondel shrilled.

"She lies! This is a trick!" Hozain said.

Shagor took something from out of a bag slung over her shoulder. She hurtled the object with mighty force. It hurtled through the air near to the ranks of Borach's army. It landed several feet away from him, and all could see it was the severed head of King Falamore.

Maraya still looked ecstatic as Shagor continued to shout. "She says Yizain flew to them by wyvern to deliver Falamore's head; he has made a claim for the throne; he ordered us to lay down our arms so he could speak terms of peace with Sharwin."

Shagor then took something else out of her bag and with a terrible cry hurtled it up the hill. It landed near a similar place, and they could see it was the head of Yizain.

Hozain stared in disbelief at the head of his brother.

"Sharwin rejected his claim," Maraya said with equal thrill.

"Women always have a way of complicating things," Marki sniped.

Blondel was so furious she struggled to get the words out as she spoke to Hozain and Effgard and said, "Attack them. Attack them now! Kill! Kill the Gragor. Kill them all! Kill any who will not fight for my revenge!"

"Stop this folly!" Borach roared before Hozain or Effgard could act. "They would have us act rashly."

Again, Shagor shouted something out.

Maraya translated it. "My mother wishes to speak with you, Lord Borach, and Lord Effgard." She turned and looked contemptuously at Hozain. "You as well," she spat out. Hozain appeared rattled and nervous, and unsure what to do.

As Shagor turned and led Davino up the hill towards her own ranks, a wild looking figure left a pavilion, mounted a horse and began to ride towards the valley. A cloud of birds began spiralling and swooping around the figure, thrashing wildly and tumbling after her like a screaming storm.

"My sister, Sharwin, the *Raven Queen of the Summer Sun*," Effgard said with grudging respect. A roar went up from the host around her. Sharwin, surrounded by several mounted warriors and the swirling storm of ravens, rode her horse into the valley.

"Come with me," Borach said to Maraya. He spurred his horse and followed by Marki and Effgard they rode into the valley to meet Sharwin, accompanied by the fading screams and curses of Blondel as they made their way silently down the hill past their army. Hozain remained behind.

When the two parties met, the appearance of Sharwin was not what Borach had expected. Even seated upon her mount, he could tell that in stature she was quite tall. In appearance, she was most terrifying and the glance of her eyes fierce. A great mass of tangled black hair fell to her hips. Her voice was harsh when she spoke a command to her ravens to settle. The birds landed and rested upon the ground, squawking quietly as they waited for further instructions from their mistress.

"Imagine a king who fights in his own battles, now that would be a sight!" Sharwin scornfully said to Effgard. "Why did you choose to fight for that fat oaf of a brother of ours, who lived in ease whilst others took up their swords for him?" She laughed derisively. "Effgard the *Wargheart*? Once your name was a legend, now it is nothing more than a minstrel's memory and today you will be forgotten by history, or remembered by it as Falamore's ninnyhammer."

"Be careful who you insult, sister," Effgard countered with a snarl. "This battle will never be forgotten, nor those who make a name for themselves in it. Today, if we fight, I will seek your head as surely as the wolf hunts the lamb."

Borach looked at the vast numbers behind Sharwin that he and his army were up against, and in an attempt to avoid battle, he chose to attempt diplomacy. He turned his head and said to Maraya, "Go to your mother. You are free."

Far from being pleased to see her, or at hearing the words, Sharwin looked at Maraya with disgust, and then at Borach. "She comes from the loins of a coward who snivelled under my brother's table," she said furiously. "She is no longer welcome at my hearth. After my victory, she will be given to any of my men who choose to pleasure themselves with her."

The response was not what Borach had expected.

Maraya lowered her head in shame.

Sharwin did not seem to care. "After my victory today, I will accept fresh seed in me and a new line of succession shall be bred. I shall birth true and honourable heirs."

"Motherly love," Marki retorted sarcastically.

Sharwin fixed her gaze on him, and then again at Borach before addressing Effgard again. "You choose interesting allies, brother. A dwarf, an Akkadian, and brothers who are traitors to their own king?"

"What do you mean, brothers?" Effgard asked her.

"Why do you think Hozain has not ridden down here to face me?" She smiled knowingly. "Look, already he turns and runs."

Borach looked behind. Led by Hozain, Falamore's men were retreating from the field of battle. Blondel and her sons were following them.

"What is going on?" Borach demanded of Sharwin.

"Blondel feels she has a claim to the throne of Thurogen," she said answered with cruel mirth. "Yizain was to become her puppet husband, king in all but power. She planned for Hozain and his men to turn on you in battle, and fight with us, if we agreed to the demands, she sent by Yizain."

"This can't be true," Effgard said, looking bewildered. "She betrayed Falamore?"

"It is very true, my foolish brother," Sharwin replied, with ridicule. "Even in the ranks of my own army it was whispered she despised our fat brother. Any tears she sheds, and anger she displays, is for the death of Yizain, not for fat Falamore."

"Then it is good for this plot to be revealed, before we cross swords, sister," Effgard said. "You have acted with honour."

Sharwin scowled. "The throne of Thurogen is mine by birth right, but I will not seize it by any other way but honest battle, or my claim will be challenged. Brittle my reign would be, if I ascended it by such a disgraceful deed committed on the field of battle."

Effgard spoke gravely. "Blondel has acted treacherously, but her folly has been exposed. I long to shed blood, and lust for a fight, for my axe is thirsty, but the truth of it is we no longer have a need for the battle this day, for I do not want the throne of Thurogen. I see reason and would have peace now our brother is dead."

Sharwin cocked an eyebrow in scathing surprise, but said nothing.

Effgard continued. "As long as I have maids to warm my bed and ales to fill my cup, I will fight your wars for you, as I swore to do so for Falamore. Sister, my allies here report of an enemy that comes from the North, from far beyond the Everglow. They come our way. I would speak with you on this."

Sharwin sneered. "This day I only care for the enemies I see before me and shall see their destruction; if new foes come from the North, I shall slay them in the same manner."

Effgard beseeched her. "Sister, the spirit of the raven possesses you and robs you of your reason. We can fight new foes together. I have no desire to make a claim for the throne, our brother is dead, and you can have it."

"But you have conditions, do you not?" she asked knowingly.

"Only two. Do not burn Thurog Tor to the ground, nor kill everyone who dwells within the city; revoke that oath. Then, break your alliance with the Chatti and Gragor, and have no more dealings with them. There is no need for this battle if you agree to these terms."

"There will be no peace until all my enemies are vanquished," Sharwin replied. She laughed, though her eyes did not reveal merriment, but were burning with hatred. "I was told how the people jeered, mocked and laughed at the humiliation of my husband and daughter when they were paraded through the streets of Thurog Tor. For that, they

612

will pay! I swore oaths on the skull of the dragon that every last man, woman and child of that city would be slain, or I would die in the attempt."

"I will not let you do that," Effgard said. "Revoke your oaths, break your alliance, and we shall have peace, for I too have sworn an oath to protect Thurog Tor, and one to never ally with the foul Chatti and Gragor."

Sharwin's face twisted with indignant rage. "If I revoke my oaths, then none I make in the future will have any worth!"

"Oaths made by a woman, are of less worth to the gods than those of a man," Effgard countered, somewhat conceitedly. "They will understand you uttered the words and performed such ceremonies under great burdens of emotion. Revoke your oaths, or we shall do battle."

Sharwin's face contorted even further with primal fury. "Then today will be your ruin, brother. This is the day you die. I will have your head for a footstool!" She looked Marki and then Borach up and down. "I will turn your skull into a drinking bowl, Akkadian, and yours for a pot to pee in, dwarf," she said.

Marki tittered sarcastically and countered, "Then if you win, you will have plenty of drinking bowls but only one pot to pee in, for Pure-bloods will come back and fight you again and again. You will have to kill them each time they resurrect!"

Sharwin raised an eyebrow in surprise, and her demeanour relaxed a little. "So, it is true what I have heard about Akkadians? I had heard tale of Talain, but doubted the truth of it."

"It is true mother," Maraya said, somewhat sheepishly. "I have seen Talain die, and then the Obelisk returns her to the world of the living. The Pure-blood myth is true."

Sharwin laughed derisively. "By the time they resurrect, Thurog Tor will be but ash and ruin, and they will be bound with chains the minute they appear at the Obelisk," she said grimly as she looked at Borach with curiosity. "You are the pets my brother sent to try to have me chained and fed with scraps under his table, like a miserable dog?" She scoffed with more mockery and laughter. "Why should I fear my enemy who flees from his enemy to seek sanctuary in the Tarenmoors? In fleeing your imagined foe in the North, have you not neglected your warrior's duty in bolting from one field of conflict, and even now are letting Effgard talk you out of another battle before you?"

Borach replied, "Treachery vanquished me, where the sword could not. My foe is not imagined. Like you, I have muttered oaths. One day I will return to my homeland and avenge myself on those who have wronged me."

Sharwin looked at Borach brazenly. "Ever since I heard the myth of Pure-bloods, I have longed to know if it were true, and if it was, to bear a son with such blood coursing through his veins." She caressed her breast seductively, as she spoke with sardonic and beguiling sweetness. "All men must pay the cost of an eye to see my glory, some will pay with both. If you prove yourself this day in battle, when you resurrect, I might consider you as a potential mate. I will breed a Pure-blood child with you, who will be my heir. In this, you will have no choice. If you resist, it is not your arms and legs I will need."

"Degenerate heathens," Marki muttered.

"It is an honour for him," Sharwin replied scathingly, and turning her fierce gaze again upon him, said to Borach, "You will be the first since my husband to see my naked beauty. In time, I might even let you keep one eye, or both, and you will know a love the like of which only the gods have seen before now. We will have many children born to us, all Pure-bloods. They will mate and breed more Pure-bloods."

"That's not how it works," Marki said with exasperation. "Any child you have with him will be Half-bloods, and will never resurrect."

"Enough!" Borach shouted boldly at Sharwin. "You speak as one who has already won the battle. We swore oaths to Falamore, but he is dead, and we are now free from them. You will not spare Thurog Tor, and we are allied with Effgard as much as we were with the fat king, so a battle it is."

Sharwin again turned her ferocious gaze upon him, "I shall consider today a mere practice for a contest with a worthier foe that will come," she said. "If today I die, I will not beg for more time nor will I cry. I have lived and loved and earned glory for my name. I will leave this life with a smile on my face singing my own death song."

Effgard sighed with regret and said, respectfully, "I pledge to you, sister, I will give you the proper funeral rites and build a pyre so high it will touch the heavens; naked you shall be when I light it and both my eyes I will keep as I feast upon the scene of your defeat."

"I will bestow upon you the same honour, brother, but your skull I will keep," she answered, "and I will see that the corpses of your men are treated with respect."

Sharwin then snarled, turned her horse, spurred it and rode away surrounded by her warriors. "*Mechen!*" she shouted to the ravens, who all took to the air, flew high, circled and then swooped and attacked Borach and his companions. The hundred or so ravens filled the air with their scornful din. Borach raised his hands as they slammed into him. Most died, hitting him with such force their necks broke, but others remained alive, pecking at his face, clawing at his arms and beating their wings furiously against his armour. He was nearly tipped from his mount as it reared in a sudden panic. Trying to free himself from the thrashing wings, he punched at the birds and then drew his sword; the runes on the blade glistened. He and his companions slew many of them; any birds left alive and able to do so, turned and flew after Sharwin, whose hideous mirth could be heard as she continued to ride towards her army to rejoin it.

Sharwin raised her arm and shouted something. The birds that had rejoined her hung motionless in the air for a moment. Then they burst into flames and dropped to the ground dead.

"Cursed woman," Borach said furiously as he looked at the dead birds on the floor around him.

"I like her, if I'm honest," Marki said, sincerely. "I like her a lot."

"What's with those birds?" Borach asked.

"The birds are for show," Effgard answered with a grim smile. He turned to Maraya, "Ride to the Chatti. They will give you sanctuary, even if your mother will not."

Without a word, Maraya spurred her horse and headed towards where the Chatti watched upon the hill.

The three of them turned their horses and galloped away to return to their own army. "Apart from the obvious, I'm not sure I understand what else your sister was saying to Bor?" Marki asked Effgard.

"Some folk in the Tarenmoors believe Pure-bloods and resurrection at an Obelisk to be a myth," he answered. "Sharwin believed our brother Falamore had made up a lie about the one we call Talain. My sister has always wanted to breed with a male Pure-blood, if it was ever proved true to her, they exist."

"I got that bit," Marki said, "but what about the eyes?"

"It is said my sister has never let any man since her husband see her nakedness. She lets her birds peck out both eyes of any she now orders to her bed. I think she just promised that one day, if love grows between them, after a resurrection she might let Borach keep one, and maybe after time, both of his eyes."

"Why does she blind the men?" Marki asked.

614

Effgard chuckled. "She feels humiliated that her husband has grovelled under the table of Falamore begging for scraps; she disowned such a husband as unworthy of her for accepting such disgrace over death, and said all men were unworthy to look upon her naked beauty, until they prove otherwise. But by then they are already blinded, so she desires a Pure-blood now she has discovered there is truth to the myth."

"And I thought some of our dwarf lasses were coarse and wild," Marki said as he spat at first with disgust, and then, considering the matter, burst into laughter. "Despite her toxic tongue and insults, I really do like your sister," he said. As his laughter dissipated, he grimly added, "I wish she had seen sense and avoided this battle though."

"So, do I," Effgard replied. "I would have had peace with her, but it is not to be."

Borach said nothing, but even he felt a grudging respect towards the fierce Sharwin, although also feeling grievously insulted. By the time he and his two companions arrived back at their front ranks, Hozain's men had fully left the army and were already marching out of sight.

"Let the treacherous cowards go," he said to Marki and Effgard, as they watched them disappear. It was some relief to him that the mercenaries, who looked perplexed at the situation, had remained.

Effgard laughed grimly. "Now we know why my sister kept that other army behind, she is clever, and knew Hozain would turn tail and flee to Thurog Tor once his treachery was revealed. He will die today!"

*So, might we*, Borach thought to himself, as he again wondered where the unlocated wyverns were.

The host on the opposite side of the valley was already in motion, trotting down the long and gentle slope. The measured tramp of the armoured horse made the ground tremble. Banners flung out long silken folds in the light breeze; lances that swayed like a bristling forest, dipped and sank as their pennons fluttered about them.

"Hold your position," Borach ordered, as Effgard's men fidgeted with tension and excitement, as they began to issue their battle cries. Borach had tried to encourage them to fight as one, but the instinct that battle, even a big one, was a contest of many individuals, was so ingrained in them that he had little faith Effgard's men would obey any of the orders they were given, even by their own commander. The legion and mercenaries, were far more disciplined.

*"Neither you nor I need to control my men in battle,"* Effgard had said in the days before the battle, *"they just need to be unleashed."* Borach had known then, as he knew now, the words were brave but foolish.

The centre of Sharwin's host, the tribesmen, reached the centre of the valley, and began to charge uphill. Behind them, the pikemen and archers halted halfway down the hill. The mounted knights manoeuvred down the hill at a measured pace and formed a wedge formation in the valley.

Borach knew their tactic. He issued an order. "Do not charge," he shouted to what was left of the United Army. "Their main centre will attack us and feign retreat, do not follow!"

"That's not the way we fight," Effgard said with a forbidding smile. "I have told you, me and my men will win victory our way, or face our deaths as we see fit."

"Then be prepared to greet your ancestors in their halls," Borach replied fiercely, "for many more of you will die than is necessary, if again you fail to take heed and see sense in my tactic."

Rage spread across Effgard's face, twisting his features. "My own son, proud of his deed as I am, has already robbed me of slaying a Gragor this day! You will not steal any remaining honour from me! You fight as you wish; I and my warriors will conduct ourselves on the field of battle as we see fit. The blood rage is upon us; do not judge us harshly for following the way of our ancestors." His features softened slightly. "If we see victory this day, I would still like to call you, and the dwarf, friend."

Borach grimaced and snarled as the sky grew thick, darkened by the arrows that filled the air, fired by the enemy host. The legion, as one, took their shields from the ground. He and the legion instinctively raised shields to protect themselves from the arrow storm. The Seranim archers and the Shemites, also shielded themselves, as did Effgard's men, as the storm of arrows rained down.

Several arrows thudded against Borach's shield, piercing it and protruding from the other side, the barbs just a few inches from his face. He cut the shafts off with one stroke of his sword. "Fire at will," he ordered the Seranim archers and Shemite slingers, who, after obeying and firing a return volley, withdrew to a distance behind the legion where they could use their ranged advantage on the advancing army. Many men on both sides fell at the first exchange of arrows which found every unprotected crevice in their armour.

The enemy tribesmen started to ascend the hill to the front ranks and were rapidly approaching the United Army with surprising speed and agility. The legion again planted their shields in the ground, and released their javelins and spears with deadly effect, as the archers and slingers picked out enemy tribesmen. The whistling of arrow shafts and stones in the air, the clanging of steel and shrieks, combined with shouts of fury and pain, filled the air as the front ranks of the two hosts met. Shields splintered, men on both sides fell dead or wounded. After a furious first encounter, lasting an hour or more, the enemy tribesmen suffered many losses, but had made little impact on the ranks of the United Army, so they began to retreat at full pace down the side of the valley.

"Hold your ground, do not follow," Borach urged Effgard and his men, to no avail, as Effgard roared and, followed by his own men, began to charge after the retreating host. Blood rage had entered their hearts; they did not listen and charged down the slope of the valley after the retreating enemy.

Marki rode along the ranks of the legion, shouting and barking the order to hold ground. He then rode along the lines of mercenaries, some of whom were already adopting a melee stance, and were following Effgard, or, were preparing to charge. Such was his authority, that most of them stopped the charge and reformed their line.

Borach cursed with anguish of spirit, as Effgard and his men, screaming strange heathen oaths, caught up with Sharwin's fleeing host, and fought the retreating host up the hill.

"It will be death to follow," Marki said to Borach.

Marki shook his fist in rage when the mounted knights turned and charged along the vale, flanking Effgard in the middle of the valley. So hot and focused were Effgard and his men in pursuit of their enemy, cutting down those they had caught up with, the first they became aware of the flanking counter-charge was when the knights crashed into them, cutting them down like they were sheaths of wheat at the mercy of a sickle.

Sharwin's retreating tribesmen turned, and fought, trapping Effgard and his men between them and the knights. The pikemen and men-at-arms began to march with rapid speed towards Effgard and his men, circling them on their unprotected right and left flanks, so that they were surrounded on all sides.

Some of Effgard's men panicked and began to run in different directions, but there was nowhere to run. Some, in their confusion, even turned on each other, hacking their own comrades down in their muddle. Most, fought bravely, but in vain, and fell quickly in large numbers, especially when more arrow storms rained down upon them.

"Blistering fools with boils for brains!" Marki shouted in frustration.

The mounted knights fought their way through the entire undisciplined ranks of Effgard's men. Once the knights were clear, Sharwin's archers rained down more showers of arrows upon the confused and hapless men who were in complete disarray. Her host feigned another retreat, and then turned and engaged, as the knights reformed as a wedge, and then recharged, all but finishing what remained of those who had charged against Borach's orders. Her tribesmen charged in and killed the remainder of Effgard's men, hewing and slaying, until the last of those who had charged were dead, about three thousand in all.

The last one standing was King Effgard. His mighty chest heaving and glistening with sweat, and with the red axe gripped in his blood smeared hand, the bodies of the men and horses he slew mounted up around him. He threw back his head and laughed as a dozen arrows pierced him. "This valley shall be my pyre!" he roared as a Bossian Knight slashed down with his great sword, severing shoulder-bone and breast. Effgard sank to the earth, laughing mightily through a gurgle of gushing blood before the light went from his eyes. One of the knights cut off his head and stuck it on the end of a lance which he raised high, causing a cheer to erupt from Sharwin's ranks.

Sharwin's army roared in triumph as they watched the death of Effgard. Those who had not yet joined the battle, on command, began a measured march down into the valley, and then towards the legion, whilst the rest reformed.

The legion and mercenaries, all that was left of the United Army, maintained their position, despite the chaos and carnage that had unfolded before their eyes.

Borach bellowed at them all to hold their courage, as a few of the Seranim turned, dropped their weapons, and began to flee. The remainder took heart, and though fidgeting with fear, stayed their ground.

Borach signalled to a trumpeter, who sounded out several long blasts from a horn. He looked at Popparus and the bannerman, and said to them, "Hold the standard and banner well this day, my loyal friends."

The Third Legion, all three cohorts, began to advance towards the oncoming host, accompanied by the mercenaries, whose supply of stone and arrows being nearly exhausted, had taken a melee stance and were following Marki.

The United Army marched down the hill and into the valley of death. Moments later, some of the mercenaries stopped in their tracks as they pointed to the air. A large number of wyverns had appeared in the sky. Swooping down attacking as one, they dived and confronted what was now Borach's army. Some of the mercenaries fled in fear at the ferocity of the wyverns and their riders, as the knights who were reforming to the east of the valley, swung around, preparing for a second charge.

"Square formation!" Borach ordered, at which the legion complied immediately, forming into several squares.

The mounted knights gathered around the standard of their commander, a black horse upon scarlet, and waited for the wyverns to do their damage before they charged.

Marki shouted in wrath as the wyverns tore through the United Army. Some of the mercenaries were now in full flight, terrified by the savagery of the beasts. A few wyverns attacked the square formations of the legion.

Borach, filled with a red wrath, felt bitterness and regret that he had no griffins, which would easily tear the lesser wyverns apart. Instead, he watched as the foul beasts tore men apart with their ferocious claws and teeth, and the rest spewed out burning fire.

The remaining Seranim archers and Shemite slingers, as they had been ordered in such a scenario, used their remaining arrows and stones, or picked them from the ground or a corpse, and aimed at the wyvern riders. Their aim was deadly and true, and brought many of them down. Some of the corpses of the riders fell from the saddles, others got caught up in the stirrups, or became tangled in the reigns, sending their mounts into either confusion or a mad frenzy.

"Brace!" Borach shouted as the mounted knights charged. The legion bore the full impact of the charge, but the wyverns, now mostly riderless, enraged and out of control, turned on the mounted knights.

"Finally, a stroke of luck," Marki shouted, "lest this day be a complete disaster."

*More a stroke of folly by the knights, to charge when the wyverns were still inflicting damage upon us,* Borach thought.

The knights retreated with heavy losses, as the out of control wyverns tore into horse and rider alike. Borach felt grudging respect for their commander who stood his ground, and fought a riderless wyvern that had felled his horse. The commander died with a sweep of the beast's claws, moments before the Seranim archers brought it down with the last of their arrows.

"Advance!" Borach shouted above the din of noise, seeing the opportune moment to press the attack. The legion took up their shields and formed a line as they began an ordered march towards the pikemen and men-at-arms who had by now, again reached the valley and were seeking to flank them, as a large rabble of shrieking tribesmen charged from the centre. What was left of the wyverns turned upon the pikemen and men-at-arms, or pursued the mounted knights who had survived the failed charge. The knights fled the field of battle in complete disarray on their panicked mounts.

*Another stroke of good fortune,* Borach thought to himself, as he watched the riderless wyverns, out of control, rampaging into the ranks of their own army.

Sharwin's pikemen fixed their pikes into the ground, and several of the wyverns impaled themselves on them. Other wyverns were hacked to death by the swarming tribesmen who had joined the fray, but the beasts made them pay a heavy price in death as they spewed forth their fire, before their life ebbed from them, and the fierce beasts let out a mournful and heart-rending death moan. Borach felt no pity for them.

More wyverns fell, wounded, screeching in fury and pain at a deadly arrow storm from their own side. The remainder took to the air and with a few flaps of their wings they landed in the midst of the enemy archers and into another hail of arrows. Several wyverns fell but they did not falter. They tore into the archers in a fury of tooth and claw, and many of the foes fell in swift succession before their wild onslaught.

Borach only had time for the briefest of thoughts, and again, it was of relief that the wyverns had turned on their own allies, for it had turned the tide of battle and but for that small stroke of chance, it may have had a different outcome. In the midst of the chaos, he heard Marki and Galin laughing with delirious delight.

"To me! To me!" Borach cried to his cohort, as the legion increased the speed of its advance to a full charge, maintaining formation. Singing an ancient battle song of Aleskian, Borach charged ahead of his army into the fray.

*Men of Aleskian, my wrath boils like the surging river*
*Like a god enraged, my foes engaged, I shall fight for thee*
*I will see our enemy smote, on this, the field of his ruin*
*Fight, fight for me, fight with me, for glory waits for thee*

As one, his cohort, began to murmur and chant a haunting and intimidating barritus, and their crescendo rose as one and filled the valley as with a mighty roar they charged into the fray.

Over the din, Borach heard his ever faithful fellow Marki sing his own ballad of war.

"A story for Balagrim and the Maidens!" Marki shouted as he roared a battle cry that would weaken the knees of the stoutest enemy. His cohort followed, crying a battle chant as they plunged into the heart of chaos itself.

Right into the press rode Borach. His spear shivered as he threw it at the enemy commander of the men-at-arms, skewering him, leading to instant death. Out swept his sword and he spurred towards the enemy standard and hewed down staff and bearer. The rest of the legion crashed into the tribesmen and cut them down swiftly in massive numbers.

About forty or so of the legion, including Torach, fell to the innumerable rain of arrows that came down upon them, as he and his cohort, charging the archers, became their main focus. The arrows killed friend and foe alike, but the Seranim archers and Shemite slingers extracted a heavy price as with precision, and on the move, they picked up stray arrows and stones, and took down one after another of Sharwin's archers, or joined in the melee.

The ferocity of the legion was such that what remained of the *Raven Queen's* army in the valley turned and fled, only this time it was not a ruse; panic had spread among them. They fled in all directions, being pursued by the United Army. The mercenaries followed Marki and his cohort; the fierce dwarf leered wildly as the blood rage consumed him. Many fell before his dreadful axe strokes.

Borach's cohort reformed and hunted new foes. A sizeable portion of Sharwin's army, a few thousand in number, the pick of men, stood around her, still unfought, though the stones and arrows of the advancing ranged mercenary units were beginning to hail down upon them. What remained of Torach's cohort, having dispatched the enemy archers, joined Borach's cohort.

Sharwin could be heard screaming orders over the noise of the battle. "Fight to the death!" she screamed at those around her.

"Protect the Queen!" a general roared, before a Seranim arrow pierced his throat and ended his life.

Led by Borach, the men of the legion kept advancing and had soon engaged the first ranks of those seeking to protect Sharwin. Marki and his cohort joined them. It was gory and bloody work, and the longest and hardest fought battle of the day. Legionnaires, swordsmen, tribesmen and mercenaries mingled in one torrent of chaos and destruction. Try as they might, Sharwin's men could not hold back the disciplined line of the legion as they steadily fought their way towards her, inch by bloody inch, and foot by gory foot. About a hundred or so, more legionnaires, fell in the encounter, only to be replaced by those behind them. Several hundred mercenaries fell, but not nearly as many casualties as fell from the army of Sharwin. She stood in the midst of the battle, surrounded by ravens that attacked her foes. Deadly was every stroke of the sword she wielded.

After several hours of hard-fought battle, the last of the foes fell trying to protect their queen. The tent of Sharwin was surrounded and unprotected, and, when the last of her ravens were slain, she fled into it. Borach and Marki approached the entrance to the pavilion and tearing the flap open, they entered. Sharwin stood there, and formidable was her appearance. Her armour was rent and covered in blood, her clothes torn so that she was all but naked. The notches on her sword and the wounds to her body confirmed she had not been idle or inactive in the fierce battle. Her eyes blazed under her tussled mane of hair. She knelt on the floor, put the pommel of her sword on the ground, the tip of it against her breast, and leant on it ready to fall upon it.

"Stop!" Borach shouted.

She hesitated a moment and looked up. "I will not give you the satisfaction of having me enslaved!" she said with fury and determination.

"I vow to the gods I will not allow that fate to become yours," Borach promised, and he meant it. "Before today I have met foes with a courage that equals your own, but few they have been, and the world is a lesser place without them. You are needed in the days ahead, Queen Sharwin. Stay your hand. Both of your brothers are dead. You have my word you will not be harmed or handed over to any that would enslave you."

"I have learnt that in this world, the words of few men can be trusted," Sharwin said. She then grinned and uttered a short death song as she let the full weight of her body fall against her sword, piercing through her chest and out of her back.

Marki ran to her, knelt, wailed, held her head in his hands, and lamented. "Silly lass. What was said, was meant, for we are not men without honour."

Borach listened as Marki made her a promise. "I shall pay the most skilled of minstrels to write songs about you, and I shall drink in your honour and sing them, whenever I raise a jug of ale and tell of your tale, for few women like you have walked this world."

Sharwin smiled, and blood gurgled from her mouth, but no word could she speak.

Borach inwardly screamed with anguish and fury of spirit as the light of life left her eyes. He then sunk to his knees and bemoaned the death of one so brave and fierce, as Sharwin the *Raven Queen of the Summer Sun*.

A dark raven, black as the night, in the form of a spirit, left her body through her mouth, and in a rush of air flew outside of the pavilion.

"I tire of war," Borach muttered mournfully to himself. "I tire of life itself in a world such as this."

# Chapter Fifty-Three: *The Chatti*

*The wars of the Tarenmoors have been so many and numerous, many of the races to the south of it have been hurled back into a state of savagery. They are loosely knit clans, entirely ignorant of the rise and fall of the great civilisations. Some, in the remotest regions of the Everglow, believe the existence of a Pure-blood race of humans who resurrect at the ancient Obelisks, is merely a myth. I proved them wrong on more than one occasion, with some unfortunate mishap or other...Only those who dwell in some of the ancient cities that still remain, have any semblance of what you could call culture. It is therefore no small surprise that from the hard environment of the distant west, some of the Chatti, whose own numbers have been depleted by numerous tribal wars and their harsh volcanic environment, have migrated east. Such a migration required crossing the Great Cohga Lake, and the Great Isola Range, which consists of a series of hazardous plateaus and dangerous, gigantic mountain ranges that separate the far-west of the Everglow, from the east. At some point in their history, on their journey heading east, the Chatti made peace with the fierce Gragor, a race of giants said to have descended directly from the Titans themselves. I sat in an encampment with some Chatti and Gragor one evening, not far from the Giant Halls; they spoke of their plans and ambitions of becoming the undisputed power in the Tarenmoors, controlling the warlike clans and tribes of barbarians that now mostly live there.*
**Temmison Vol I, Book 2: History of War in the Tarenmoors.**

*The* roar of the battle had died away; the shout of victory had faded and all that could be heard were the cries of the wounded and dying. Like decaying leaves on a forest floor, the fallen littered the valley; the sinking sun shimmered on the burnished helmets, armour and broken swords of the dead or dying. In silence great warhorses lay amongst the heavy regal folds of silken standards, along with their riders, overthrown in pools of curdling crimson. About them and among them, were strewn slashed and trampled bodies; legionnaires, archers, pikemen and tribesmen, their armours, whether skilfully or crudely wrought, all rent and shattered alike and covered in the gore of a violent death. Borach and Marki, having left the tent of Sharwin, walked among the broken bodies and watched riderless horses racing down the valley, or in a state of distress and confusion walking among the dead.

Marki shook his head and sighed, and then called over a nearby legionnaire. "Gather the bodies of Effgard and Sharwin; when time allows, we will build a funeral pyre worthy of the legends they forged in their lifetimes. We will let it climb as high as time and man can build it." The legionnaire nodded and marched off to obey the order. He then turned towards Borach. When he spoke, his voice was etched with sadness and regret. "Effgard was a fool to lose his life so rashly; war has changed, the men he fought today fight differently than those he encountered in his youth."

"He was a fool not to take note of our counsel and caution," Borach agreed. He felt no pity that Effgard had died due to his own folly.

"Aye, a fool, but I liked and admired him," Marki said glumly.

Borach's murderous eyes blazed from beneath his dented helmet as he gazed at the grizzly scene of devastation. The aftermath of a battle was never a pleasant sight to look upon. His own armour was tattered and splashed with blood, his blade red to the hilt. From the corner of his eye he noticed movement on both sides of the top of the valley. What he saw, filled him with dismay. "It looks like our work here is not yet done," he said as he pointed with the tip of his sword. All around them, on every side, more tribesmen had appeared. Throughout the battle, the Chatti and Gragor had stood on the hill watching. At no point had they joined in the fighting, and neither did they appear like they were about to engage in any fighting then, but these news foes looked ready to charge. There was a commotion in the camp, but from that distance Borach could not make out what the cause or source of it was, nor did he have the time to reach it to find out. He instinctively knew that the legionnaires guarding Karno at the camp would make a valiant stand, but would soon be overcome by the sheer swarm of numbers. To add to his woes, the skies above suddenly became dark, as a thousand or more enemy wyverns and their riders flew over the valley in disordered array. The screeching of the beasts filled the valley with ominous notes of death.

"By Balagrim," Marki murmured quietly under his breath.

Borach turned to look at his own army. Most of his men bore the wounds of battle. About four hundred legionnaires, half of the Shemite and Seranim archers and only a hundred or so of Effgard's men had survived. Some of them sank to their knees and wailed in despair when they saw more of the enemy forces surrounding them. The battle had been costly indeed, the survivors already exhausted. Borach knew that it would be beyond any of them to fight a new and fresh foe and win such a fight. He and his men would try and would die and then resurrect, but there would be no escape for his old friend Marki, or any of the others not born with pure Akkadian blood. Behind him, the survivors of his army began to form defensive positions as the officers barked orders.

Marki sighed wearily. "I was so looking forward to a mug of ale and a warm fire to cook some meat upon." He then smiled savagely and boldly. "I guess a dwarf who has chosen this life will have to more than earn even such scant rewards."

"You have more than earned them today, my friend," Borach said, as he looked at his old comrade. "But life does not always give us what we are due."

Marki looked up at the sky, dark with wyverns and black clouds. "When you resurrect, have the bards and minstrels write songs and poems of my deeds, and make sure they say I died a noble and brave death, for that I will do." He smiled as he touched the painted finger bone hanging on the necklace around his neck. "I am not afraid to die, I have a story ready to tell the Maidens, and many more to tell Balagrim," he said. "My only regret is that I still have some wrongs in my *Book of Grudges* I have not yet redressed. I keep it tucked away in my trunk with my other few belongings. Top of the list is a dwarf called Old Grundy, who stole a maiden from me I was once due to wed."

"That is a tale you have never told me," Borach said.

"Aye, after all of these years it still pains my heart to tell it. If you ever meet a dwarf with such a name, and he has a crooked nose, a blind right eye and a left ear missing, it will likely be him. Will you kindly remove his head from his shoulders for me, and then strike him from my list?"

"I will," Borach promised.

Marki then smiled and said, "Then if this is my time, it is as good a day as any to die, but I will extract a heavy price from those who wish to take my life from me." He then swung his axe around his head and roared defiantly at the surrounding enemy, before shouting at them. "As my grandfather used to say. In a morning, if a dwarf draws his axe for battle, and by sunset he still fights, then those who have not yet killed him, should run!"

"Wait, look!" Borach said as he pointed at a rider setting off from the Chatti camp on the hill. It was Talain; her horse galloping at full speed towards him and Marki, leaping over the mounds of corpses or trampling them underfoot. Borach wiped the blood of battle from his blade, as Talain rode up to him.

622

Talain dismounted, caught her breath and said, "They want to talk, up there on the hilltop, in their camp. A Chatti shaman, Chasotha, wishes to discuss the terms of our surrender."

"That's a bad idea. We'll not be surrendering to any boneheaded Gragor or hairy faced Chatti!" Marki said defiantly.

"You should hear them out, should you not?" Talain said, ignoring him and making her plea directly to Borach. "All in our camp are dead. They have captured Karno. I slew several foes with my spear. A Chatti appeared. He would not fight me, only fending off my blows. He said he would not kill me because I was '*Arvivan*.' I was taken to Chasotha. He wishes to talk, to make some sort of treaty with you. I am bringing you that message."

"Tell him to come and talk to *Old Trusty*," Marki growled defiantly as he shook his heavy axe.

"Has there not already been enough death this day? Would it not be wiser to at least hear what Chasotha has to say?" she asked him.

Marki growled like an angry wolf.

Borach looked around him; his men looked completely exhausted, and they were completely surrounded. He made an instant decision, walked over to his horse, mounted, and said to Marki, "Prepare the men to defend this position if the talks do not go well."

"I'll be damned if I will," he replied rebelliously. "Galin can fulfil that role. My place is by your side, this could be a trap."

"If it is a trap and they slay me, I will resurrect at Thurog Tor. It is better for you to stay; the legion needs you."

"A dwarf is judged by the manner in which he lived as well as died. I'll die at some point, if it's today or tomorrow or a hundred years from now; my story for the Maidens is ready to tell. You are my friend and commanding officer Bor, but I shall be my own master in this matter. I'm coming with you, orders or not."

Borach knew it was useless arguing with his friend, and he had neither the patience nor the desire to do so. "Very well, as you wish it."

Marki mounted his pony, and he and Borach followed Talain. The three of them rode over to Galin, who was wounded and bloodied from battle, but still issuing orders to his men. Borach issued defensive instructions to him, and then set off for the place up on the hill where the Chatti were camped beneath their dragon banners. The surviving tribesmen from Sharwin's army cursed, yelled and hurled vile taunts as the three of them made their way past their lines, but none attacked. They continued up the hillside, riding past the hulking Gragor and into the Chatti camp. The giants looked down at them with menacing stares and held their large weapons at the ready. Borach shifted uncomfortably in his saddle and stroked the muzzle of his horse to calm it down, as it was juddering and threatening to rear, as a pack of wargs snarled hungrily.

"I told you this wasn't a good idea," Marki muttered under his breath.

The three riders approached a massive fur covered pavilion and dismounted. Outside of it, stood a Chatti, who held a large staff and had an air of superiority and authority about him. He was clad in beaten plates of iron, wolf and bear pelts, and stood in front of the cart upon which was the large dragon skull.

"Well by Balagrim, that skull looks real enough," Marki said with a gasp of awe.

"He is Chasotha, the Chatti shaman," Talain said sullenly as they approached the Chatti.

Chasotha grinned bleakly. His teeth were yellow and filed. He said nothing as he slowly observed Talain, Borach and Marki in turn.

623

Borach had heard about the Chatti race, but until then, he had never seen or met one up close. He knew they had a reputation for primal ferocity that could not be underestimated. Living mostly in the harsh tundra and volcanic mountains far to the west, only the strongest and most ruthless and cunning survived. They were bred tough, perhaps because more than once in history, their race had been on the verge of extinction, but they had survived, and forged a crude civilisation, and since those times migrating and raiding bands of the Chatti had spread across the Everglow, as their presence in the Tarenmoors was more than proof of. The Chatti were taller and more powerfully built than all but the mightiest of men. No two were identical, but they were all similar in appearance and cladding so it was hard for any except a trained eye to tell them apart. They each had the same thick red hair that covered the entirety of their faces, excepting the eyes, mouth and nose.

"Come," Chasotha said, and then turned and headed towards his pavilion, entering without ceremony through the flap at the entrance. As the three of them warily followed, the Chatti warriors surrounding them howled a guttural refrain, a deafening ear-splitting chant that was discordant, melodious and hideous at the same time. It spoke of delirium, loss of restraint and control, and a pleasure for battle and bloodlust. Borach felt uncomfortable that the sound touched some deep part of his own soul. It stirred a dim memory from the past when he too had longed for nothing more than the sounds and chaos of battle, and of a sudden even the blood he had shed that day did not satisfy the urges within him. He fingered the pommel of his sword and resisted the urge to draw it and attack them.

Once they were all inside the pavilion, which was internally decorated with animal pelts and leathers, and filled with more raucous Chatti and sullen looking Gragor, Chasotha raised his hands, and the din of the Chatti was silenced. He took a seat on a crudely carved knobbly wooden chair. Smoke from lamps and a fire pit created a thin haze inside the tent. A warg, just a young pup, chewing a human leg bone, got up and strutted over and sat in front of Chasotha, head beneath his feet. Chasotha ruffled its ear affectionately, as the pup continued chewing and licking the bone. He waited for the din to quieten down before he spoke. "I am Chasotha," he said with a gruff and hard voice. His face and head were covered in the same red hair, only his nose, lips and black eyes with their dilated green pupils, as bright as spring grass, could be seen through it.

"Speak then," Borach said boldly, "and let us see if you are indeed a race with honour, or if you lure us here under false pretences."

Chasotha cocked an eyebrow. "Is this insolence or courage?" he asked with a throaty growl, as some of the Chatti reached for their weapons.

Borach gripped the hilt of his sword, still in its scabbard, and Marki reached for his axe, but did not draw it.

"Call it what you will you red-faced baboon," Marki said defiantly, which caused a roar of protest from some of the offended Chatti. "If your warriors draw their weapons, your head will be leaving your shoulders the very second after they do."

The young warg stopped chewing its bone and began to growl boldly at the dwarf.

"Stop it!" Talain shouted, glancing nervously between Marki, Borach and the Chatti. The tension lifted when she spoke, and several of the Chatti muttered something in awe. "*Arvivan*," they muttered to each other.

"It is small wonder, there are few who like your race, dwarf," Chasotha said bad-temperedly.

"And I've not met your kind before, but the minstrels hardly sing of your sweetness, so don't think we'll be surrendering our weapons as we talk," Marki replied stubbornly.

"Keep your weapons," Chasotha responded brusquely. "If it was your death I sought, I would not use subtlety or deceit. You are surrounded by my warriors and would already be dead if that was my design."

Borach looked around him. It was true, the fierce looking Chatti had them surrounded along with the quiet but menacing looking Gragor, one of whom he observed was Shagor, who towered over them.

Marki grumbled and appeared ready for a fight as Shagor walked over to him, the ground pounding under her footsteps. She stared down at him, but said nothing. Marki stood his ground fearlessly. "I heard tale you were a terrible beauty, it's the second time I've seen you this day and to my eyes, you're an ugly brute," he said as he stared back at her.

The Chatti began to argue, shout, and gesticulate at each other and towards Marki. Some called for his death. "She understands the Common Tongue," Chasotha said gruffly. "Gragor insult each other before they mate for life, she might take such words as a proposal. Take a care you are not wed to her before the day is out, dwarf."

Marki's eyes widened with alarm. "No offence was meant lass," he said as he looked up almost apologetically at Shagor, "and no compliment either. By Balagrim are all the females in these lands insane?"

The grin disappeared from Shagor's face. "I not like dwarves," she said with a deep and hoarse voice. She growled, turned around and stomped off moodily to stand beside Chasotha.

"Women," Marki tittered as he shrugged his shoulders.

'Stay your tongue Marki,' Borach wanted to say sternly to his friend, but he respected him and his ways too much to seek to shame him in front of an enemy, even if he was not being helpful. Dwarves were not known for their diplomatic skills and Marki was not making matters any better.

"I have not summoned you here to discuss the ascetics of female Gragor," Chasotha barked impatiently, "and nor will I be riled by the rudeness of Dwarves." He gestured to the other Chatti to calm themselves. The storm of debate quickly blew itself out. "You should count it good fortune, dwarf, that you proved yourself this day on the field of battle, for it is Chatti custom that a warrior can speak his mind freely, without consequence, when our council is assembled." He looked at the other Chatti who were still staring furiously at Marki. "It is also our custom, however, that one warrior can challenge another if they so wish, but I have brought you here under a promise of peace, and no fight shall take place unless you start it, dwarf."

Marki nodded. "It is also a dwarf custom that each warrior who has proven himself in battle can speak his mind freely at any gathering," he said. "The blood-rage is still upon me, and I will not have my tongue stilled if there are words I wish to speak in this gathering, be the consequences what they may. I will speak my mind!"

Chasotha stared at him a moment, and them guffawed. "Then I might not like you, dwarf, but you have my respect and may speak as you wish, as shall I." He paused and looked around at the assembled Chatti and Gragor. "Many here are, or were, chieftains, and all present have proven themselves many times in past battles. Not all of the chieftains are in agreement with the decision that has been reached today, and clearly that difference continues, but the majority are, so we will all unite behind it as my word on this matter is final. None have challenged me to battle over it, for I speak with the authority of Malagrim, Lord of the Giant Halls."

Some of the Chatti grumbled among themselves despondently.

"What decision would that be?" Borach asked cautiously.

"That you are allowed to live, and walk away from this field of battle," Chasotha said curtly. "If you agree to our terms."

Borach said nothing. It was better to allow Chasotha to continue, for it was obvious he would soon state what those terms would be.

"The arrival of your legion has caused quite a stir," Chasotha said, a look of displeasure and distaste evident upon his face. "You have disrupted our plans. We had not expected the outcome of this day to lead to the humiliating death of Barathi at the hands of a mere boy, and then the death of Queen Sharwin."

"It has been a dark day's work that has brought us no pleasure," Borach said sternly, "and my own hand would have fought Barathi, had the boy not acted in haste and without my consent." Chasotha looked at him in a manner that Borach could sense he was being studied, like some sort of oddity or curiosity.

"I liked Sharwin," Marki interjected, "and we would have spared her, but her distrust of men moved her own hand against her well-being. She was not harmed by our hand."

Chasotha nodded. "The Raven Spirit that left her body, returned to us, and told us you offered her life, before it found a new host. That is the only reason why you still live."

Marki chortled acerbically. "The men who fell by my axe today fell because it was swung by my arm. That is why we still live. I have yet to test you Chatti in battle, as I remember you being more spectators than participants. Do not kill us with your words when you have yet to draw your swords."

Chasotha snarled. "Look into my eyes and see how badly at this moment I want your death, dwarf," he said with bared teeth, "but in peace I brought you here, and that I will honour."

"My friend is rash with his words," Borach said, "but it is his right to speak as he wishes, even if they are not the words I would choose to be spoken at this moment. What is it you want with us?"

Chasotha closed his eyes momentarily, and when he opened them, continued. "One of the most difficult problems which confront any leader in a time of war, is to alter plans in the light of changing circumstances. The nature of war is ceaseless change. For this reason, plans require continuous review and readjustment."

Despite his fierce and savage countenance, it was becoming obvious to Borach that Chasotha was no fool, and that he had a sharp and astute, instinctive intellect. He was also coming across as a creature with a code of honour. Marki's impulsive and reckless manner with words would have offended impetuous men possibly leading to thoughtless action, but Chasotha was clearly guided by his own principles, and in control of his decisions. "Sharwin would not listen to reason, when Effgard attempted to persuade her to make peace with him," Borach said.

Again, Chasotha nodded. "She had sworn to raze Thurog Tor, and Effgard had sworn to defend it. They had been fighting since they were children. When you look deep into their eyes, you know neither would ever back down."

"Well, Thurog Tor has an empty throne as a result, so what is this new plan you have?" Marki asked.

"I wanted Sharwin to win this day, but I did not want her to destroy Thurog Tor," Chasotha answered. "I could not have stopped her by any persuasiveness of words, only by force, but she was an ally, so that I would not do. I would have stood by her side and allowed the city to burn."

"You don't intend to destroy it then?" Borach asked.

"No," Chasotha answered. "We have seen the storm that comes from the North. Lord Malagrim wishes it to be halted at the walls of Thurog Tor. I lament Sharwin's death, but the fates have worked it for our favour. She was…impetuous with her actions, like your dwarf is with his words." He stroked the head of the warg who had returned to licking its bone, and ignored Marki's surly stare.

Chasotha continued. "There is a lot we can learn from a warg. They are often there, watching, waiting, keeping to the shadows. When they hunt, they are the most patient and relentless foe there is. Their prey often senses them, but cannot see or hear them. But, when they pounce from out of the shadows, death is in their jaws. Quietly they will endure pain, silently they will suffer, and patiently they will wait. They are loyal to their own pack. When they howl at the moon, it is said among my kind that they do so because they are mourning for those that death has taken outside of their reach."

"I bet like any dog, they still lick their own balls though," Marki said dryly, somewhat ruining the atmosphere.

Chasotha eyed him angrily, but continued regardless. "These rulers of the Tarenmoors are impatient and warlike, the women as much as the men. Peace can never reign among them, until their enemies are slain or captured, even if those enemies are siblings, sons or daughter, mothers or fathers. We aligned with Sharwin to make her supreme ruler under our supervision." He shook his head, clearly regretting her death. "We counselled her not to separate her army, but she was stubborn and did not listen, and it has cost her more than victory this day. If all of the wyverns had been here, a different tale would be told of the Battle of Rua-Sacoth."

Borach knew full well that Marki was about to unleash another string of insults, for the battle rage within his friend had not yet fully subsided. Borach caught his eye, and though he would not forbid him to speak, Marki understood. Whatever words he had been about to utter, the dwarf reluctantly held them in, if only out of respect for Borach whose ways were different.

Chasotha clapped his hands, and from behind the chieftains, Maraya stepped forward holding a crimson stained sack dripping droplet of blood. She tipped the contents onto the hard ground. The heads of Blondel's two sons clattered and rolled upon it before resting at the feet of Borach, their cold eyes fixed in death and eerily looking up at him. Marki sighed, and said regretfully, "Blondel was a mean spirited and angry lass, and they were strange boys, but it almost brings me pity to know her heart would break at seeing their fate."

"They both died like the curs they were," Maraya said angrily to nobody in particular, "and the curse upon my mother has now come upon Blondel, and fool enough she is to welcome it."

"Curse?" Borach asked.

Chasotha lent forward, his eyes glittered. "When Sharwin died, the Spirit of the Raven entered Blondel. Madness has taken a hold of her for a time. We allowed her to wander off, babbling to herself, into the wilderness, for we shall not kill the one who the spirit now dwells within."

"You intend for her to rule Thurogen?" Borach asked bluntly, "or will you take the throne?"

Chasotha looked and sounded sincere when he answered. "No, she and her husband will," he replied as he pointed to Maraya. "When he is of age, the boy who slew Barathi shall wed her. We have spoken with him, and though he mourns the death of his father, he has agreed to it. Davino has proven himself worthy to be a future king not just by his acts today, but of those past, for long have we watched him, watched you all."

"As puppet rulers?" Borach asked, already knowing the answer.

A sinister look spread across Chasotha's face. "Maraya and Davino will lead Karno into Thurog Tor; the people of the city are like sheep without a shepherd. We will offer them peace, and a new king and queen. They will accept this plan, or together, they will all die." He huffed in derision, and added, "In the name of King Malagrim of the Giant Halls, I offer you peace, so that together we can face the coming threat. Will you accept, or do you wish to fight on?"

"What do you know of the coming threat?" Borach inquired.

"Everything that you know, and more," Chasotha answered. "Malagrim has had the perfect spy in Falamore's halls and very little has gone unnoticed by him, or by me," he said with a sly grin. "None of your plans or conversations had in the presence of Talain have gone unobserved."

"She is a spy?" Borach blurted out in surprise, instinctively gripping the hilt of his sword.

"She is *Arvivan*, the perfect spy," Chasotha replied.

Talain drew her spear and swung it in around in a curt arc, bringing the tip to rest against Chasotha's throat. The warg startled, growled at her, but did not attack.

To Borach's surprise, the Chatti warriors did not react to try to protect Chasotha, who sat their grinning as she pressed the tip of the spear against his throat.

A look of misery spread across Marki's face, that affected his speech. "Tell me it's not true lass?" he asked Talain in desperation.

Talain was gasping in shock, nervously taking deep breaths. Her eyes rested on Marki, pleading with him to believe her. "I am no spy," she said, and then turning her gaze upon Chasotha, she protested indignantly. "I am no spy, and even if by the threat of death, you will tell them that!" Her eyes darted back and forth between Marki and Chasotha. She choked up, close to tears. "Falamore was far from perfect, and many of his ways disgusted me, but he gave me a home and never did wrong by me. I would never have repaid him with betrayal. I have not known you long dwarf, but friend I now call you, so I swear to you, I would not act falsely towards you, or your Lord Borach."

Talain looked at Borach, and he saw sincerity in her eyes, and believed her.

"You did not even know you were a spy," Chasotha said as he reached towards the spear and pushed the tip aside. "Away your spear and it will be explained to you."

Talain hesitated a moment, and then reluctantly withdrew her spear and slung it across her back.

Chasotha clapped his hands. The flaps of the tent opened wide, and two dozen or so tribesmen carried the huge dragon skull into the tent and placed it in the centre. Borach gaped in wonder, having had more pressing matters on his mind, he had paid only the barest attention to it when they had ridden up to the camp. The skull was large enough that you could ride a horse through the open jaws. It was as black as onyx, and smooth as polished stone. The white teeth were as long as sabres and looked just as sharp.

Chasotha took a torch from a sconce at the end of a pole in the ground, stood, and walked into the mouth of the skull. "Come, all three of you," he said, beckoning for his guests to follow. When Chasotha held the torch up to the white teeth, the flames had no effect for they had once felt much hotter fires.

Cautiously, Borach, Marki and Talain followed Chasotha into the mouth of the dragon skull and continued until they were standing within the skull itself. At the roof of the skull, the flame revealed a small blue stone.

"An Omphalos Stone," Chasotha said. "This skull is more than ten thousand years old, and this dragon was the last of its kind. Nobody can any longer remember what his name was in life. His deeds and record, his tale, good or bad, is forgotten by time. This stone, once the beast's brain, was shrunk by ancient and powerful magic now forgotten; but those who know the ritual still have the power to see through the eyes of an *Arvivan*." He looked at Talain, "A word in the ancient dragon tongue that means dragon-eye. For this purpose, you were chosen and marked as an *Arvivan*, when just a child."

Talain instinctively put her hands to her face and touched the ritual scarring. "You disfigured me for your schemes?"

"Watch," Chasotha said, and then mumbled an incantation that none could understand but he, and then he said, "*Arvivan*, Bessie."

Of a sudden, Borach, Marki, Talain and Chasotha were in a forest, watching a party of travellers whose image filled the skull. One was a Spriggan, who had the same markings as Talain on her face; another was a female dwarf riding a horned, aged goat. The others were an Akkadian woman and two Davari men.

"By Balagrim's beard what mischief is this?" Marki said as he gripped his axe.

"Listen," Chasotha said impatiently, "for they cannot see or hear us."

"There it is again Miss Gilly," the Spriggan said to the dwarf, "that sense that I am not alone but being watched. It has become more and more frequent of late."

"It's the forest me dear, I have the same sense at times, it's these trees," the female dwarf said.

"It's not the trees Miss Gilly, I tell you, and I don't like it. I don't like it at all," the Spriggan protested.

The woman, a blonde with a beauty the like of which Borach had never seen before, walked over to the Spriggan and let the creature clamber onto her shoulders.

"I sense it too, Bessie," she said as she looked around her. "There is ancient magic at work, it's not the forest. There is something or someone else watching us."

"There is power that lies hidden within this place. It is not possible to pass through unnoticed, me dears," the female dwarf said.

The woman looked around her again. "I sense it is something else, older magic than even the forest remembers; but what, I do not yet know."

"It's not the Wytchwood or anything in it, Miss Janorra," the Spriggan said. "It happens at random times ever since I was given these marks on my face all of them years ago. It happened the other day when I was minding my own business and taking a poop of all things. Now who wants to watch a Spriggan poop?"

Chasotha muttered an incantation and the vision disappeared. "Sometimes we may see things we didn't intend too," he said gruffly, contritely and with embarrassment. "We are not interested in the pooping of a Spriggan I can assure you of that."

"Who was the dwarf, the female one?" Marki asked. "I have seen her face before, but when, I have forgotten by time. She is magnificent."

"She is one who dabbles in Elven lore, most unusual of your kind she is," Chasotha replied to Marki.

Talain was still tracing the ritual scarring on her face. "You have been able to watch me whenever you chose because of these?"

"In both the land of the living, and the Deadlands," Chasotha said, regaining his composure. "It is how we know the threat you speak of is true," he added, looking at Borach. "For we have many *Arvivan* throughout the Everglow and see what they see and hear what they hear. We know many things. The Bantu horde is burning and pillaging without restraint as they head towards Baothein lands." He mumbled another incantation, and then said, "*Arvivan*, Michelgoa." There appeared the image of a wounded man, his face scarred with the ritual markings of *Arvivan*. He was kneeling before the thane of some unknown great hall. "The main Bantu host passed us by and heads west, my lord," the man said, gasping for breaths which came painfully to him. "Bands of their marauders, large in number, burn our villages and desecrate our land. They head this way and were fast on our heels until we used the secret ways to come here quickly. By this time tomorrow, this hall will be overwhelmed by them."

The old thane stood, with some difficulty. His voice was tired but firm. "Then fetch my armour and my sword. This foe is like a hungry and rabid wolf. A shepherd does not waste time or emotion just hating such a foe who stalks his flock. He kills it or is killed by it."

Chasotha muttered another incantation and the image disappeared. His tone of voice was foreboding when he spoke. "Doom approaches us all. Only in the strength of many bonded by unity, can any hope be found. It will not be long before they come south into the Tarenmoors, and that is why they must find an allied and united force to face them and halt their advance. If they are not stopped in the Tarenmoors, sooner or later, they will find a way to the Giant Halls. Malagrim has bidden us to find a way to stop them. It is the reason we needed to end this pointless war, now the throne of Thurogen is vacant."

"The second vision I understand, but why did you show us the first?" Borach asked Chasotha, but before allowing him to answer, he turned to Talain and asked. "Is Janorra not the name of the one you said I was to seek out?"

"Yes, it is, but I am furious that I have been used as some seeing device for a Chatti shaman," Talain answered, shaking with rage and barely able to contain her emotion as she looked angrily at Chasotha. "One of you forced these marks upon me when I was a small girl and not even death removes them. You had no right!"

"It is an honour to be *Arvivan*," Chasotha calmly replied.

His answer only agitated Talain more. "It brings me no honour. I should be able to choose what causes I serve, to whom I give my allegiance, and not be forced to serve powers and masters I know not of."

Chasotha stood tall and looked at Talain ominously, and spoke brusquely. "You have served a higher purpose than your own miserable existence. It is a gift you have been given. You may not see that now, one day you will, it is an honour to be *Arvivan*." The other Chatti in the pavilion murmured in agreement.

"Enough of this," Borach said commandingly. "You can figure out the morality and workings of this another time, Talain." He then looked at Chasotha and demanded, "Why did you show me that woman, Janorra, what do you know of her?"

"I know she is the one who has stolen the Simal," Chasotha answered.

Borach snarled. "I will not call you a liar in your own pavilion, but this news you have is surely errant. You could have spied upon me in my own tent when Talain tried to recall vague memories. She is wrong on this matter, and therefore, so are you. If there truly is such an artefact called the Simal, it is hidden and guarded deep in the Argona Temple in Kappia where no thief could steal it."

"It is your knowledge that is lacking," Chasotha replied sternly. "The woman you saw, is named Janorra. She stole the Simal and then lost it. She now seeks it." He stroked his beard thoughtfully. "Your Empire has lost a great treasure, and been greatly affected by this theft. They now tell the lie that it has been returned to them, and the woman we have just seen is dead. The Kappian Empire is now at war with itself over this matter."

Borach grimaced. "I no longer care; I have nothing but hatred for the Kappian Empire, although loyal servant I once was. My only concern is to survive and live enough lives to have revenge upon those who have wronged me, even if that is the royal family itself. But…" A thought occurred to him, which he gave voice to. "Perhaps the theft of the Simal set off the chain of events that led to all of my trouble and grief? If so, the woman named Janorra, is responsible for the *Final-death* of my family." He clenched his fist and gritted his teeth. "If there is truth to my thought, then I shall also have my revenge upon her," he added threateningly.

"Lay that charge at her feet, if you must," Chasotha said. "But a far greater cause than your need for retaliation is at stake. The future and fate of us all may rest upon the outcome of her quest."

"What quest?" Marki asked, momentarily placing a reassuring hand on Borach's arm.

"To find the Simal," Chasotha answered. "She seeks that which she has lost. On this quest, she now has companions, but great is her peril. Your Empire has allied itself with the Bantu. Their Wild Hunt pursues her, and they know her whereabouts. They have set a trap so that when she regains the Simal, they will take it from her, and return it, and her, to the new Emperor in Kappia."

"New Emperor?" Borach asked, failing to hide his surprise. It also dawned upon him that the Empire truly was in league with the Bantu. *That explains why Aleskian fell*, he mused.

"A man by the name of Mazdek has usurped the throne, the Empress Shaka has fled to Kara Duram where the legions have come to her cause," Chasotha answered, looking studious whilst he waited for a response.

"Mazdek? That vile son of a rotting maggot," Marki growled angrily. "He will stop at nothing to fulfil his ambition. He is riddled with superstition and seeks the return of his gods to this world. That much we have heard."

"We have many *Arvivan* in the Kappian Empire, we see many things," Chasotha said as he continued to thoughtfully stroke the fur on his face whilst still staring at Borach. "The Tarenmoors must unite, for that Bantu horde will come here, and if they conquer these lands, there will be nothing to stop them using their foul moleworms to cross the Abandoned Plain. In their arrogance they will march up to the gates of the Giant Halls themselves. Though we Chatti and Gragor are mighty, we are still few in number and cannot face such a host alone. If you accept the peace we offer, the war between the kingdoms of the Tarenmoors will end. We must be ready to face new foes."

"Peace between us would make sense," Borach growled. "You wanted Sharwin to defeat Falamore and build up the defences of the Tarenmoors," he then said, as a statement not a question.

Chasotha nodded. "She was never the perfect choice; she would have started more wars and finished the blood-feuds she had with others even whilst the Bantu host marched towards her, for strong-willed and impulsive she was, but she was the best choice we had. We had not expected the arrival of a Kappian Legion at Thurog Tor, so our plans were adapted." He smiled. "Today, the boy Davino proved himself a hero in the eyes of all, so our plans were adapted again. What man amongst the tribes will not follow a giant slayer, if they know he is to rule with the blessing of Karno?" He looked at Maraya. "You and he, under my guidance, will unite all the kingdoms, clans and tribes, and with our support and the god Karno by your side, we can build up a defence in the Tarenmoors to stand against the coming storm."

"So, you expect me and my men to guard Thurog Tor?" Borach asked.

Chasotha shook his head. "No, for when the war starts, the Bruthon will strike the Seesnari, and from there they can make their way up the River Erin to make war with the Chatti and Gragor. I want you to assist the Seesnari in capturing one of the main Bruthon strongholds, Castle Greytears. From there, you can stop the advance of the Bruthon, even attack their lands and seize their territories. You can give yourself

631

whatever title you wish, but you will be lord of both the castle and the Obelisk there. Eventually, as your power grows, you can begin to open up trade along the river."

Borach and Marki exchanged a look. "I do not have enough men to take such a castle, and although I am not familiar with the politics of the Nine Kingdoms, I do recall that the Seesnari are not a military force of any might."

"They are not," Chasotha answered. "But the Bruthon King is also weak. Every lord and baron of his has their own private army. He cannot unite them, except for one cause."

"Which is?" Borach inquired.

"War, with us and the Seesnari! Since pirate scum have blocked trade along the eastern route of the Erin, much of the Davari trade slave has gone north up the Erin, to our Giant Halls and from there we sell to the Baothein or the western kingdoms. The Bruthon King makes secret alliances among the Nine Kingdoms, and plans to strike the Seesnari as soon as he can get his lords and barons to stop squabbling and unite. If he succeeds, we will lose much trade and income, at a time when we need to make preparations for a defensive war against the Bantu horde."

"How do you know the plans of the Bruthon King?" Borach asked. The answer dawned upon him even before Chasotha offered it.

Chasotha gave Borach a knowing look. "We have *Arvivan* in his halls; we know his plans, and so we have made our own. We have allied with the Seesnari, and with slave gold, we have paid for many mercenaries to assist us in taking Greytears. The mercenaries will stay as long as the gold fills their purses, but they have no interest in defending a castle for the rest of their days, and nor do we want to pay them for a task that others are better suited for. We need a longer-term plan than that."

"So, because it has an Obelisk, you figure who better than a Kappian Legion full of Pure-blood Akkadians to defend Greytears, once it is taken?" Marki asked as he cocked an eyebrow.

"The timing of your arrival is fortuitous to say the least," Chasotha replied. "But before you take Greytears, you must assist us in frustrating the plans of Kappia and the Bantu, by taking the Simal and giving it to us."

"Why do you need our help with that?" Marki asked.

"Indeed," Borach added. "You could negotiate with me, and still pursue the Simal, but you speak as though it is a wish yet to be acted upon. Why do you want it?"

"My Lord Malagrim desires the Simal; he wishes to gaze into it; it will be safe in the Giant Halls."

"Then go get it for him," Marki said.

"They can't," Talain answered.

"We offer you help," Chasotha interrupted. "We will give you an army of barbarians, and what Chatti and Gragor we can spare. If you take Castle Greytears, we will have free movement along the Erin from there to the Giant Halls, and together we will resist the encroaches of the Bruthon. Taking Greytears will be of mutual benefit to you, as well as to ourselves. But we require a sign of your goodwill. Helping us capture the Simal, will build trust between us both."

"I understand your tactical strategy against the Bruthon, but why do you need our help with the Simal?" Borach enquired. "If there is to be trust between us, then truth must be spoken."

Chasotha answered glumly. "Neither Chatti or Gragor can enter the Wytchwood, for the forest itself will rise up against us; ancient charms and spells prevent us from stepping foot there. Those of us who have disobeyed wisdom and entered, have never returned. Old resentments still linger in that place."

632

"So, you just want us to march south from here and go get the Simal for you, and then take a castle?" Marki asked.

"No, the lands to the south of here are wilder and more savage than even these ones. There are tribes we cannot reason with, beasts of sky and land to contend with, and that is even before you get to the treacherous Blue Mountains. Beyond them, are the ancient barrows in the Dale of Yarron, where the dead walk in the land of the living. You must come to the Giant Halls with us, and from there we will provide you with the means to safely get to the Wytchwood."

"If the Wild Hunt gets the Simal before we do, they will take it onto the canals of the Underglow," Borach said. "We cannot follow them there, for we do not know how to enter such a place."

"The Gragor and Chatti have a way to enter the Underglow," Chasotha said with a toothy grin, "and we would hunt them there. That was our plan all along, but it is a vast place, and the chances of us finding them are slim. It is better to get to the Simal, before they do. In that, you can assist us. Then, together we take Castle Greytears."

"So, it is a race against time then," Marki stated. "But, tell me, if you desire the Simal so much why did you not send some of these barbarians to get it?"

Chasotha nodded in acknowledgement. "They are undisciplined. Seeing a beautiful Akkadian woman with something rumoured to be as wondrous and alluring as the Simal, I fear their lower natures would win over some of them. They would look at it and take it for themselves; on this matter, we can take no chances."

"Your plan is still fraught with risk and uncertainty," Borach said.

Chasotha grinned widely. "Are not ventures of such boldness always so?" he asked. "When your legion's dead have resurrected at Thurog Tor, you must march with my warriors across the Abandoned Plain to the Giant Halls. From there great river ships will take our army to Castle Greytears. Those so assigned, can fly by wyverns and go into the Wytchwood, to find the Simal before the Wild Hunt succeeds in the task."

Marki cleared his throat again and looked at Borach. "We've trouble enough, though owning an Obelisk outright would cheer the hearts of the men no end, and whatever path we choose, is going to involve more clashing of swords sooner or later."

Chasotha nodded. "The Bruthon army has never recovered from your civil war. Their lords remain weak and divided, now is the time to strike, before they can unite together with the allies, they are seeking to make among the Nine Kingdoms."

"It would be a smart move strategically Bor," Marki said thoughtfully. "To own a castle of our own, with its own Obelisk."

Borach growled. "I know the value Kappia places upon the legendary Simal. Though many speak of it, none I knew had seen it, so it was hard to separate truth from saga. If it does exist, and is now lost to them, to deny them its return, would enable me to strike a blow at their heart." He looked firmly at Chasotha. "One condition I have. The woman named Janorra, is not without blame in setting forth the events that led to my family's suffering. She will be mine, to do with as I wish, if I agree to this." It was a statement, not a question.

"She is of no consequence to us," Chasotha said dismissively. "There is one thing, though."

"Speak," Borach demanded.

"We have discovered that a wizard, now among the *Banished* from the Tarath Guëan, also seeks the Simal, although he has yet to appear. It must be that he searches for it, without success as yet."

"By Balagrim's honour," Marki shouted. "I knew there would be more to this." He then spat on the ground with disgust. "Your mummy let you bash your potty on your head too often when you were a bairn laddie, if you think we will be fighting a wizard from the Tarath Guëan."

Some of the Chatti muttered discontentedly, but Chasotha seemed unruffled by Marki's response.

"This wizard, what is his name?" Borach asked.

"He is known as Armun," Chasotha answered.

"Armun? He is known to us, from a time long ago."

"Aye, and only recently we had sought his help, although we did not know he was now *Banished*, a title of shame given to those expelled from the Tarath Guëan," Marki added.

Borach spoke grimly. "Powerful he still is. If he seeks the Simal and wishes to take it by force, we might not be able to stop him, with only the blades of men."

"That is why we need to move fast," Chasotha said. "We will monitor Janorra through our *Arvivan*. We may yet still have time, but with more delay, the chances of success might slip from us. We must act swiftly. Once the Simal is safely inside the Giant Halls, not even the whole might of the Tarath Guëan could get it, let alone just one of them. Armun, exiled and alone, will give up his quest."

"What if I refuse this offer?" Borach asked.

Chasotha shrugged, but the determination in his voice was convincing. "You return to your men in the field, and the battle continues. You will face defeat this day and die. We will have taken Thurog Tor and will be waiting for you, when you resurrect, or, at the least, we would have surrounded the walls of Thurog Tor, and our war continues. If our siege is not quick or successful, and the Bantu horde arrives, we will retreat to the Giant Halls and face them when they come, whilst you face them alone, at Thurog Tor." He paused, and made a friendly gesture with his hand, and his smile was both bitter and sweet. "I would rather you stood with us, then against us."

Borach fingered the hilt of his blade. He looked at Marki, who sighed and said, "I'll support whatever you decide Bor, that goes without saying, even if it means dealing with a wizard. This is not without risk, but an Obelisk and a castle of our own for the lads? That's not bad, and if we can stop those Bantu and Mazdek getting his hands on the Simal again, it would be a good day's work."

Borach then looked at Talain, who still looked in shock at all she had learnt and the meaning of what it meant to be *Arvivan*.

"I don't like what he has done to Falamore," she said as she looked scathingly at Chasotha, her brow furrowing with disgust as she then looked at the heads of Falamore's sons lying on the floor outside of the dragon skull. "But it seems that today, you have little choice." She looked at Chasotha and regarded him in silence for a moment, before saying to Borach, "I will follow you, but know that in doing so, these Chatti get to see and hear all we say and do, whenever they wish to spy upon us."

Borach's features tightened with resolve. "Then it's decided," he said, looking decisively at Chasotha. "We are with you."

"Good," Chasotha said, clapping his hands. "We will march before the week is out. The sooner we get to the Giant Halls, the faster we can make plans for war." He then looked at Talain and said, "If you also serve us well in this, there is a way for us to remove the marks of *Arvivan*. It is difficult and comes at a price; serve us well and at a time of my selecting, I will give you this choice."

# Chapter Fifty-Four: *The Banished*

*The First Age was The Golden Age of Creation, when the Nameless One, he who made En-Sof released his power into En-Sof, not knowing it would weaken his very being. The Second Age was The Age of the Aeldar, who seeing the chance to take the Nine Worlds for themselves, struck at the Nameless One and his servant En-Sof with relish. The Third Age was The Age of the Titans, a time when the hybrid children of gods and men walked the earth. The Fourth Age came after the Aeldar were banished and many of the Titans slain, these are the Forgotten Times and such is the age named. The Fifth Age was an Age of Darkness when those who lived cursed the very breaths that sustained them. The Sixth Age is now, The Age of Men. It is our privilege to usher in a Seventh Age, a new Age of The Aeldar. This is why we say in the tongue of The Ancients, 'Aquilon el twant braetho ey ilyiados,' which means, 'Awake, come and give free life my sacred ones.'*
**Extract from a sermon preached by High Quaester Mazdek in the Argona Temple.**

"*Move* out of my way!" Janorra said to her companions as she drew her sword and faced the man.

Scarand readied his bow and aimed an arrow as Muro dropped the book he carried, and raised the palms of his hands; the runestones began to glow.

"Put away your weapons fools," the man huffed as he planted his staff on the ground, leaned on it for support, and fought to catch his breath.

Janorra stayed alert, her sword still drawn, as she studied the stranger. Signs of exhaustion strained his every feature. He had one white milky eye, the left one, the other was black, and his stare was intense and harsh. His grey-white hair flowed across his shoulders and down his back and was equal in length to his long flowing beard, once neatly knotted and styled, but now a tangled mess, speckled with gold, gems, leaves and twigs. He wore a long grey robe, torn and etched with the grime and dirt of much travel. Along with the rimmed pointed hat he wore, the robe was an obvious sign to Janorra he was a sage, as was the ebony staff he leant upon. He gripped the staff with both hands, his long fingers impatiently strumming the shaft. On the end of the staff was a white orb streaked with black lightning that shifted and move across the surface. The clasps that held the orb in place were fashioned in the shape of griffin talons.

"Who are you, state your purpose and the reason you pursue us?" Janorra demanded.

The man stood upright, as far as his age allowed him to do so. "Far and wide, for many weary months have I searched for you, troublesome Seer," he said. "I did not expect to find you here in this place, but the sight of a Barclugoth made me realise the Wild Hunt are on your trail."

*Months? I have not been gone from the temple that long, have I?*

Gilly must have understood the puzzled look on her face. "The Wytchwood has a way of distorting time, me dear, especially when we spend time in or near a Wisdom Tree. You might have been here a bit longer than you realised."

*How long has it been?* Janorra had more pressing matters to deal with though, than to seek an answer to that particular question right at that very moment. "I am no troublesome Seer," she said defensively. "Tell me who you are and why do you pursue me?" She continued to slowly move towards Sezareal but continued facing the sage with her sword pointed towards him.

"I am not your enemy. I am Armun, formerly a grand Master of the Grey Council, also known as the Tarath Guëan," the man declared wearily.

*Formerly? None can leave the Grey-Council – you were expelled from it.* It then dawned upon Janorra. "Azzadan mentioned you. I was supposed to bring the Simal to you."

"A task in which you failed," Armun said, with regret.

"You have the title *Banished* and are exiled from the Tarath Guëan?" Janorra asked suspiciously. With the tip of her sword still pointed towards him, she continued to back cautiously away from him, still slowly making her way towards Sezareal, who still sat on the ground rocking back and forth as she stared blankly at the closed portal.

"I was expelled because of you," Armun said wearily. "You were supposed to return the Simal to me, and then I was to take it to the Baothein to guard it, and you were promised a place of sanctuary. It was I who, for that purpose, recruited Azzadan of the Order of The Clawed Hand, that treacherous Brotherhood of Ithkall!" He banged his staff on the ground in a momentary flash of anger. The black lightning inside the orb arced wildly as if trying to strike somebody.

"Steady old man," Scarand warned, still aiming an arrow at Armun who dismissed the threat with a wave of his hand.

"Don't point twigs at me," Armun barked.

"Explain yourself," Janorra said as she reached Sezareal, and in one movement sheathed her sword and snatched the Simal from her. She quickly put it inside the backpack slung over her shoulders and then breathed a momentary sigh of relief. *I have it*, she said to herself as she put her hand on the pommel of her sword, ready to draw it again should she need to do so. "I knew it was the Tarath Guëan, with the support of the Baothein, who recruited Azzadan to help me in the task, but only once did he tell me your name, and I did not know you were now exiled and one of the *Banished*. Surely, he reported back to you the reason for the trouble that has befallen my quest?"

Armun banged his staff on the ground in another flash of temper, causing Scarand to draw his bow taught again, and Muro to ready himself.

"It's okay," Janorra said to Scarand and Muro. They relaxed, but only slightly. If Armun was once a member of the Tarath Guëan, a bow and even Muro's runes would pose little threat to him all the time he held his staff.

Armun drew up to his full impressive height, even though he was hunched with age. Fury twisted and contorted his face. "Azzadan proved treacherous!" he spat out. "I sent him to assist you in your task, and I have regretted it ever since. It was discovered he planned to steal it from you once it was outside of the Argona Temple. It seems the Brotherhood have a plan of their own for the Simal, and dark it is, for it involves ancient enemies of all that is good in the Everglow, little that may now be." He sighed deeply. "The Council blame me for not foreseeing this, heaping upon me more shame." He furrowed his eyebrows in displeasure, but his look soon turned to sadness. "It was an error for which I have paid a heavy price. I am now not only *Banished*, *Bane* they now call me, and bear those cursed titles must I, but even so, I must correct my failures. The fate of many rests in my hands."

The news both shocked and surprised Janorra. *Azzadan wanted to steal the Simal from me? Armun was deceived and sent false allies to assist me in such a task?*

Armun interrupted her thoughts. "The Simal should be safe now in Baothein lands. It is not, but at least it is now back in your hands and not that of the Brotherhood." He pointed his staff towards the outside. "Marcioaka, my griffin, my oldest and most trusted friend, in the last of his many great deeds, slew the Barclugoth that tracked you from the skies above." A tear ran down his dirt-stained face, cleaning it along its path. He pulled a twig and leaf from his beard and threw them to the floor. "His last great noble act, was taking the brunt of our fall, to spare me so I could continue my most urgent of tasks." He wiped his face with his sleeve. "My heart breaks at his death, but beneath you, the Wild Hunt row Norvaskun along the canals of the Underglow on the roof of the Labyrinth; they seek an exit but their absence here shows they have not yet found one; but…" he held up his staff for emphasis. "They might burst forth at any moment, for they will find a way to break through the power of the forest sooner or later. They have with them moleworms that can tunnel through the earth. Thank whatever gods you will that those dark waterways are not easy to navigate and are fraught with danger even for them, as that is surely another reason for their delay."

"We have already seen them," Scarand said, "and barely managed to escape after we did. The forest somehow helped us."

Armun looked at him gravely. "Many dark sorcerers there are, in those sombre and wild lands beyond the Great Northern Wall, and none as powerful as he who travels with them. The power of this forest is keeping them at bay, and even Methruille has not yet found a way, but not for long. He will be seeking help from darker powers he would have sent for. Time is of the essence. We must head immediately to Baothein lands. With Aleskian fallen, and the Aleskian Gate open, there is none to hold back the tide of evil now entering the Everglow."

Armun's words momentarily stunned Janorra. "Then my worst fears are confirmed, as my vision showed me," she said. "Only the fall of Aleskian could explain the presence of such foul creatures as the Wild Hunt in the Everglow."

Armun's face briefly softened, and then transfigured with a fiercer intensity as he noticed Gilly, who stood there holding Gaffren by the reins as she rubbed and stroked his ears, calming him. Armun strode over to her, sniffed her, and then stared as he clenched his fist, and several times banged the side of his head with it in frustration. "It has brought me no displeasure, that your kind have locked themselves away in their Iron Mountains," he said with no attempt to hide his annoyance. "You always dabble in matters beyond your comprehension and then marvel that the world thinks you witless, whilst you consider yourselves wise… Harrumph!"

Gilly looked questioningly at him.

Armun unclenched his fist and momentarily cupped his face in his hand before raising it and his staff in exasperation. "The Wytchwood used its power to hide the scent of the Seeress from the Barclugoth, but it could not hide the scent of the arrow you brought into it, a scent you still carry. Do you have it upon you, or has just the scent of it lingered?"

"Erm, I disposed of it, me dear," Gilly answered meekly.

Armun's mood grew worse as his features twisted with anger. "You should not have picked it up in the first place, or should have discarded of it sooner. The forest did not know that, but a dwarf who claims to know lore should have known better!"

"Oh dear," Gilly said remorsefully and then stuttered, "oh dearly dear, me dear."

"By scent alone you know about the arrow?" she asked him.

"It has a scent of evil, from other worlds, so yes, I can smell it upon you," he growled. "I am of two minds to make you leave, and to take with you those that touched the arrow. Of what use are you to me?"

"Where would we go?" Gilly asked.

"I don't know and wouldn't care," Armun barked. "I should make you take that twig with you and ask it to lead you somewhere far from here where you can do no more mischief."

"'Ere, I ain't no twig," Bessie protested, but cowered when Armun turned his stare upon her.

Gilly frowned at Armun, but spoke courteously. "There's no need to be so rude, me dear. I have resisted the wisdom of my own kind, and sought to defend nature against the covetous powers whose aim is to possess, exploit and despoil it. I'll not pretend I don't make a mistake here and there, but since the Elves left, this forest and those who dwell within it have not seen a better friend than me!"

"That's right, you...you...old bossy boots," Bessie shouted crossly at Armun, but hid behind Gilly when he furrowed his brow at her.

Armun stared firmly but thoughtfully at Gilly and then Bessie, and then after a short silence, said, "I am not fond of Dwarves, and I don't even know of what race the twig is, but you might both be of use yet. Can you lead us through this forest?"

"Yes, me dear," Gilly answered docilely.

Bessie said nothing, but looked sulkily at Armun.

"Then that is what must be done," he said. "You will lead us from this forest, but no meddling in any other affair unless I instruct otherwise, is that clear?"

Gilly and Bessie nodded compliantly.

Looking at Janorra, Armun's face softened slightly with resignation. "Come, we have a long road ahead of us, one fraught with danger. We must make haste to the lands of the Baothein. Once we leave this cursed forest, we will leave these fools to their own fate. If they choose another path it might be, they can do you a favour and mislead the Wild Hunt, take them far away from you whilst we find a safer path to travel. The death of their Barclugoth will be a setback to them, but they will soon enough replace it."

Armun relaxed a little. "Come now, I cannot touch the Simal – you will carry it still. We must be quick; the Bantu pour into the Everglow like hot lava flowing from a volcano and all roads north will soon be blocked."

Armun turned away, and appeared about to say something else, but before he could, a faint humming vibration began to fill the place they were in.

Armun turned to face the source of the noise. It was emanating from the portal just behind Janorra. Puzzlement spread across his face, then alarm. "Step away from it, now!" he instantly urged her, his voice panic-stricken.

Janorra did not need to be asked twice, but as she went to move away, Sezareal stood to her feet and grabbed her by the hand; she tried to pull away, but the young girl had her in a grip with a strength that belied her size. The shimmering screen of colours that danced across the surface of the rectangular portal grew brighter, and the humming vibration that emanated from it grew louder.

"The portal is opening. Step away!" Armun shouted as he ran towards Janorra, trying to grab her. The shimmering screen of colours danced wildly across the surface of the portal and grew ever brighter, and the humming vibration that emanated from it grew to an almost unbearable pitch, and then stopped suddenly, as a door opened in the portal.

Janorra could not break free from Sezareal's grip.

Sezareal opened her eyes; they were black and formless. "They are waiting for you," she said with a ghostly monotone voice, and then with a mighty pull, swung Janorra around and pushed her through the open portal.

# Chapter Fifty-Five: *Fort Guardian*

*Kuthma, a grey-eyed tawny-haired chief, once emerged from out of the Tarenmoors with a horde of barbarians dressed in wolfskins and scale-mail. He had ridden into the North to invade the rich uplands the Kappian Empire had failed to adequately guard. Eventually he was driven back, but not without great cost in loss of life and wealth to the Kappians. It was after this event, that they built a line of defensive forts to prevent such an invasion ever occurring again. Decadence, neglect or just sheer forgetfulness, have allowed these forts to fall into ruin and disrepair.*
**Temmison Vol II, Book 2: History of the Kappian Empire.**

*Fort* Guardian stood on the western bank of the Black River, guarding the bridge that crossed it, before the southern flow of the river diverted towards the east. It had taken Cordius and Yana more than a day to reach it by foot. The stillness of the fort was so primeval, that even Yana and Cordius' breath seemed like a disturbance. The only sign of the previous inhabitants, was the rotting corpse of the Fort Commander, Captain Armachief that they found on a stairwell leading to a watchtower. His thin, gaunt face was set in a frozen horror; his throat had been slashed from ear to ear as if by a razor-sharp blade. Cordius shook his head and straightened to scowl down at the dead Fell-blood man. "I met him once," he said to Yana. "He would not have abandoned his post. We must assume his men did not share the same commitment" Only human footprints were in the blood that surrounded the corpse, evidence the man had died at the hands of his former comrades.

Treading carefully, climbing the tower to survey the horizon, did little to ease the fears Cordius and Yana felt.

"Look," Cordius said to Yana. She followed where his finger pointed. To the east, beyond the river, a swarm of flying creatures, as thick as a colony of bats filled the air. "Garâtons. They spy out the land for the Bantu. We should consider turning back to Kara Duram."

"No," Yana declared. "You return if you wish, I will press on south. I must find my father."

Cordius shook his head uneasily, and a look of despair overwhelmed him. Gloom filled his voice. "The way back to Kara Duram on foot, will be fraught with danger now, but it is still the better option. If we make it in range of a safe Obelisk, we stand a better chance of survival than continuing with this foolish errand. Without Marieke…"

Yana interrupted him. "There are many Bantu patrols and scouting parties we would need to avoid, if we attempt to return. If we continue, we do not know the dangers ahead, but we stand more of a chance. Only the finding of my father will make the risk we have taken worthwhile."

Cordius did not argue, but Yana could tell by the look on his face, he was struggling with frantic terror and self-doubt. From the skies, they had seen many Bantu patrols, and even glimpsed the tail end of a vast army. Now, the sight of garâtons in the sky, showed the extent of the danger they were in.

"Do you think Marieke will come back?" Yana asked hopefully.

The look Cordius gave her, followed by a grunt, was answer enough. Although tethered when they had rested for the night before, the griffin Marieke had chewed through the rope and had flown off. Avoiding the question, Cordius said, "We will rest here tonight; decide what to do in the morning. This fort was abandoned in haste, there might still be some supplies we can use."

Cautiously, they made their way to the courtyard. It was there, that they saw the monstrous three-toed prints of a garâton in the dust of the courtyard. It made their scalps prickle.

"The Bantu have been here," Cordius said in alarm, "but it was after the fort was abandoned as there was no battle here." He pointed to some large footprints mingled with those of the garâton. "Bantu riders."

"Will they return?" Yana asked, as the sweat of fear dripped down her face.

"Perhaps," Cordius replied. "They did not find the corpse so did not thoroughly search the place."

They made their way across a courtyard, and into the gardens, where the small orchard, vineyards and vegetable patches which supplied fruit, vegetables and herbs for the fort, were overgrown. The garden's fish pond was undisturbed and unkempt. The whole scene, set against the glow of the setting sun, was peaceful and quiet.

"The Bantu did not come here for supplies," Cordius remarked. "They are probably just mapping the area, finding places that they can use to garrison, if they intend occupying these lands."

Quietly making their way to the kitchen they found some dried fruit and fish, and quickly ate, washing it down with some weak ale; after their meal, they refilled their knapsacks with as much supplies as they could carry. Moving deeper into the keep, they found a room at the bottom of some stairs that led to a parapet on the walls of the fort. It had a window that faced the courtyard. The room was secure, and also offered the means of a quick escape from the fort should one be needed. "I'll stand watch. You had better sleep," Cordius said. "You will need your strength. The journey back to Kara Duram by foot, will not be an easy one."

Yana met Cordius' gaze squarely. "I have told you; I am not returning to Kara Duram. I am heading south, to find my father."

# Chapter Fifty-Six: *Garama Aethoros*

*His hands had talons; his eyes were red like flames burning in the deepest darkness.*
*There was no light, no comfort, and no mercy in them. His stare seared me like fire. "Do not come*
*to Garama Aethoros to harm the Aeldar Wives," he warned menacingly, after which my vision faded*
*and my soul was drawn again across gulfs of echoing time and space.*
**Confessions of the Priest named Rual.**

*It* took a few moments before Janorra realised what had happened, and the moment it
dawned upon her that she had been pushed through the portal, a shockwave of terror
swamped through her being. Her first, dizzy and disconnected thought was that she had
been captured. She moaned inwardly in despair and instinctively shut her eyes, waiting
for something or somebody to seize her. When, after a few moments nothing had
happened, she cautiously opened her eyes.

*When will all of this horror end?* She rubbed her forehead, took some deep breaths, and
tried to push back the terrifying thoughts that flooded to the surface. She regretted that
her first instinct had been to wait meekly for her fate. *Focus! I have been in dark places before
and faced many dangers.* She took more calming, deep breaths. *Now, where am I? What is this
place?* She raised her hand softly spoke an incantation. *"Rayfro musila mephor."* A white
light shone from the jewel in *Arnazia*, dispelling the darkness. Warily, she looked around
at her surroundings. The milky veil of an ethereal mist filled the air, and she could dimly
see the portal behind her. She stepped towards it, and gently pressed one hand upon it.
The colours on the surface shimmered and rippled as she touched it. Her hands met
hard resistance. The portal was closed. Taking out the Simal, she held it up to the portal,
in the hope that it might open. It did not.

"Ashareth help me," Janorra whispered, and then said *"Myrash; Benthos; Heiorthian!"*
The portal did not react or open. Turning away from it in frustration, she noticed that
she was at one end of a long shadowy tunnel that seemed to be cut through solid red
stone. It led downwards on a gentle slope. She took some more deep breaths and tried
to summon her inner calmness as she again prayed to the goddess for help. "Ashareth,
once again, I am afraid. Help me, please." *I must remain calm and alert*, she then told
herself. Swallowing hard, she drew her sword and then took the first steps forward
along the downward path, continuing cautiously. For what seemed like an hour, she
walked, until she finally came out upon a crossroads. Here, the milky mist evaporated,
and she could see that the floor, ceiling and walls were highly polished and gleamed
dully. From the fretted arched ceiling swung ebony censers filling the corridors ahead,
and to the right and the left, with dreamy perfumed clouds that filled them with a
strange mix of red, blue and green shifting light.

The tunnel to the left was not silent. From somewhere below, very deep, echoed up
sounds that did not belong in the sane world. From the tunnel to the right, came a
screeching squeal of demonic mirth, followed by long shuddering howls accompanied
by screams of terror. The screams stopped, and only the greedy sucking of slavering lips
followed by the crunch of bone could be heard. Then silence; deadly, eerie silence.

Panic almost consumed Janorra, but she took some more deep breaths. *Whatever I see
or hear, I must not panic*, she told herself, *and besides, if the desire to run overtakes me, which way
do I go?* Steeling herself, she continued on, deciding to go through the tunnel ahead, as
she had heard no noise coming from it. As she walked, she looked at the walls of the
tunnel, which were carved with figures of Titans, half-forgotten Gods and Heroes from

an ancient age. The floor was adorned with esoteric symbols so ancient and ghastly that her skin crawled when she looked at them.

After walking for a tense hour or so, she eventually came to another crossroads, and heard the pad of stealthy feet in the mouth of the tunnel to the right, and then briefly caught the glimpse of a shadowy form that was grotesque in outline, in the tunnel to her left. She felt whatever the creatures were, they were watching her from beyond the mist, and in terror she held up *Arnazia* and her sword protectively, but neither creature came into the tunnel. *I might feel like a mouse in a trap, but this mouse is not without power,* she told herself, and then the thought occurred to her that in some strange way she might be being guided as in which direction to go, so she again chose the passage ahead. As she continued, it appeared that was indeed the case, for each time she came to a crossroads in the tunnels where there was more than one direction to choose, she always chose the tunnel from which no noise emerged from which was mostly ahead, but sometimes to the left or the right. Eventually, she found herself in another tunnel that led down, down and down without any other choice, and for more than what felt like a half a day she walked it in a silence which was only broken by her own heavy breathing and the soft padding of her footsteps echoing on the walls of the tunnel. Hunger, thirst and exhaustion, soon took its toll and she sat to rest. In her knapsack she had a little water and some food, and she ate and drank gladly.

After a short rest, Janorra continued. Eventually she came to a large circular chamber, lit only by nine large runes each glowing on the walls, and some words in an ancient tongue that she somehow recognised. Looking up at each of the runes in turn, she held up *Arnazia* and slowly and softly read out the words that appeared next to them; "*Vispin; Makarto; Vanor; Farginashy; Muntin; Kildoso; Judgir; Kojko; Vargin.*"

When Janorra had said the last word, a sphere appeared which was translucent, scintillating and had sheets of energy arcing the light blue surface. The sphere flattened out, separated, and with a crack, split, and beneath each of the nine runes a doorway of ebony coloured wood appeared. Three of the doors were broken, the ones with the words *Vispin, Makarto* and *Vanor* above them, and the entrance of each of these doors were blocked with debris. Three other doors were closed and barred, the ones with the runes *Farginashy, Muntin* and *Kildoso* above them, and three were open, the ones with the runes *Judgir, Kojko* and *Vargin* overhead.

Janorra walked cautiously towards the three open doors, and still holding up *Arnazia,* looked into each of them in turn. It dawned upon her where she was: *I am at the entrance, the gate of Garama Aethoros, the abode of the Aeldar Wives, or Aeldar Riddles, as some call them.* Long forgotten knowledge resurfaced; the words were names. The three doors that were closed, held an abode of three Aeldar Wives yet to be discovered. The three broken doors once held three who were now within the Simal. The three open doors, were no doubt the place where three more now dwelt. *What have I done? Cursed am I to find myself in such a situation and place.* She swallowed hard, panic won over, and she turned and began to run back to the tunnel she had come down, but a solid wall now blocked her path. She screamed in despair and horror; her scream echoed down the passageway of the three doors that were open. When the only sound that remained was her own sobbing, she once again took some deep breaths, and calmed herself.

*I have no other choice,* she told herself, as with *Arnazia* raised above her head and her sword pointing forwards, she stepped towards the door with the name *Vagarin* above it. She felt a faint jerking movement as she passed the door, a sense of dislocation as though reality itself was moving, and she felt unease. Once she had passed, the door shut behind her with a loud slam that made her spin around with a start. *See the place of terror where your schemes have brought you!* She reproached herself as she nervously looked

642

around and tried the door. It would not open. There was only one way to go, ahead, so with panted breath she made her way along a corridor which was covered in terrifying runes that covered the ceiling, floors and walls. Her ring as well runes in the walls and ceiling lit the way ahead. There was no other visible source of light, except that coming from *Arnazia* and the runes. She could read some of the runes, but other were a mystery to her. *There is so much knowledge here*, she told herself, in an effort to swamp the thoughts and feelings of fear still pounding her mind and heart. Looking at one of the runes, she knew it, it read, *'Flesh and blood cannot dwell long in a place such as this. You must hurry.'* It was incentive enough. She picked up the pace as she continued down the corridor, again sensing the faint jerking movements of shifting reality.

Janorra moved swiftly towards another door at the other end of the corridor and tried the handle. To her relief it opened, so she passed through to find herself in yet another corridor, exactly like the one she had just been in, except there was a thick layer of dust on the floor. The door shut by itself behind her, and on studying it, she was disturbed to observe that it was damaged by many sword strokes. Looking ahead, she saw on the ground, partially buried by the dust, the bones of a man, still clad in skilfully wrought mail. The iron belt was imbedded with gold and rubies, the hauberk gilded and covered with diamonds. The now fleshless skull, still with its hair, was covered in a plumed helm rich with gold and jewels. The finger-bones still clutched a notched and broken sword, as though he had hewn at the closed door in his last despair as life gave way to death. She gazed at the remains of the once great knight, and then passed by without touching or disturbing them.

Janorra then walked the length of the corridor into the next one, and so on, corridor after corridor, all similar in appearance and design, and each time a door closing behind her. Each time she left a corridor and entered another, she felt the same faint jerking movement, and a growing sense of dislocation and sense that reality itself was moving. She continued until fatigue won over her, and she slumped to the floor in exhaustion and despair. She had already consumed the last of her food and water, but once she had regained enough strength through a brief rest, she stood and walked ahead, at times half-running, passing through about a dozen or so similar corridors, each one plain and undecorated except for the many and varied runes. She tried to read and interpret as many of the runes as she could as she sped along, all the time the doors behind her closing so there was only the way ahead to go.

Janorra moved through baffling and intricate passages, from room to room, from court to court, from courtyards into rooms, from rooms into galleries, from galleries into more rooms, and thence into yet more courtyards. Each courtyard was made from different coloured marble and surrounded by colonnades: red; green; orange; yellow; purple; blue; black, white and various other shades in between, all adorned with runes, symbols, or painted and carved art of numerous styles and depictions.

Eventually, she came to a pyramid, roughly three hundred and forty feet in height, with carved animals, beasts and gods covering it. An underground passage was built through it. Janorra did not have time to stare in wonder at the magnificence of the structure, so she quickly traversed the underground tunnel, and coming out at the other end, entered a vast oval shaped hall. Another door closed behind her, blocking her way back. The floor of the hall was littered with statues, some intact, others ruined whilst still on their bases, and some toppled onto the floor. The walls of the hall sported trophies - the skeletal remains of hundreds of warriors: dwarf; elf; human, and some of which were strange races unknown to her. Most skeletons were still wearing the full armour they once wore in life, and were clutching swords, axes, spears or bows. Some wore robes and held staffs. Janorra hoped that the skeletons were lifeless, their spirits long departed, and that the evil in that place kept them as trophies, nothing more. She was sure the skeletons were no guardians of that hall, just ornaments, the bodies of trespassers and adventurers throughout the long eons and ages who had stumbled by chance or design during some distant age upon the place, their remains collected by the evil that dwelt there. She stood there silently, observing the bizarre scene, and looking as to where she might go. She momentarily froze with terror when one of the skeletons crashed to the floor with a loud noise before crumbling to dust leaving behind only the cladding and armour that had adorned it, and a sword.

Janorra again reproved herself that her reactions were slow. Cautiously she walked closer and noticed that the armour and sword were of a type she had never seen before. A scathing, high pitched mocking laughter echoed through the hall. It was a harsh, chilling sound, and filled her with the desire to flee as in her mind's eye she witnessed scenes of madness that were beyond her sane experience. A ghostly figure, carrying some sort of orb, appeared at one end of the hall, and ran towards her, accompanied by two others. Janorra let out a small involuntary whimper of terror but held her sword towards the apparitions and readied *Arnazia*. The ghosts did not notice her, and passed by in a rush, and of a sudden she realised it was a woman wearing the armour and carrying the sword that now lay on the floor before her, and two companions accompanying her. She watched as the woman and her companions repeatedly tried to find a way out of the hall, without success. The speed of the image grew faster as she watched the women live out their last moments, die and fade in that very hall, after which a power unseen moved their corpses and pinned them to the wall.

"So, this is my fate?" Janorra screamed. It felt as though her voice was magnified a thousand times as it echoed throughout the hall. "If I die here, where will I resurrect?"

"Do not fear; they are deceivers," a soft voice behind her said.

Janorra spun around, and this time reacted with instinct, swiftly swinging her sword at the spectral female form behind her. The sword passed harmlessly through the air, and the ghost looked dispassionately at her. "All fears here are an illusion," the ghost said. "Take my armour and sword. They have an ancient power for which I have no use for anymore."

"Who are you?" Janorra demanded, as she recognised that the spectre was the woman she had just seen in her mind's eye.

"I am from a time long-forgotten in the world, a queen of lands and people, now diminished in time. I was Yimsha, once Queen of the Golden Lands. My tale was one of greatness, but foolishness and greed led me to this place. Here, in Garama Aethoros, my tale became one of woe. Do not die here, or you will roam Garama Aethoros eternally; remember, all fear here is just an illusion.'

After those words, the spectre pointed to her armour and sword and again said, "Take them." She then pointed to the base of a ruined statuette. "Take what you find there." She then slowly disappeared.

Janorra found herself alone again in the hall. She knelt down and brushed away the thick layer of dust covering the armour and sword. Despite its age, underneath the dust, the armour was in good condition. It was golden in colour; on the chest-piece was emblazoned the emblem of a chariot with a warrior queen inside of it hunting a Titan. The tasset had rune-shaped jewels encrusted within it, as did the bracers, greaves and the circlet for the head. The leotard was made from the skin of a creature she did not know, finally interwoven over the top with fine metal mesh, gold in colour, that looked extremely delicate, but on testing it, Janorra could tell it was incredibly strong. She cleaned the armour as best as she could and, not really knowing why, she quickly undressed, put the leotard on and donned the armour over the top of it. It left her neck,

644

upper arms and upper legs bare and unprotected, but it felt right to wear such magnificent armour. It was flexible, robust and incredibly light. Throwing her own sword to the floor, she picked up the new sword and felt a power pulse through her. She decided to keep it to discover what the power within it was capable of. Curiosity sent her over to the base of the ruined statue to which the spectre had pointed. Next to it, under some rubble and dust, was a strange looking orb, the one she had seen the woman carry in the vision. She brushed off the rubble and the dust; the orb was smaller than the Simal, white in appearance. "It looks similar to the orb *Fabérn* that Silverberry used," she whispered to herself.

"It is, but the name of this one is *Fobéarn*," she heard Yimsha say in a ghostly whisper.

Janorra swung around, but nobody was there. Not knowing why, she slipped the orb inside her backpack, in a pocket that separated it from the Simal.

Swinging the sword once to get its measure, panther-like Janorra walked around the hall, poised to strike left or right. *Perhaps even a charmed sword is as a straw against the power of this darkness,* she thought to herself, but holding the sword invigorated her and brought some comfort. She noticed three doors, tried two of them but they were locked; the third opened and she found herself in a curved corridor. The door slammed shut behind her as she stepped into the passage, and try as she might, it would not open again, so once again the only way to go was ahead. Following the curve of the passage, she came to an ivory arch that led into a broad, square chamber. The walls were of red marble, the floor of jade and the ceiling of fretted gold. She saw divans of rich satin, gold-worked footstools that looked like they had been carved from single rubies, a disk-shaped table carved from a single untainted diamond. On one of the divans was a woman reclining, and behind her stood a man; both were watching her. The man scowled as he met Janorra's startled glare.

"Who are you?" Janorra asked.

The man and woman were both clothed in armour so fine, it covered yet showed their every feature, and at first, Janorra wondered if they were even human. In girth and breadth, the man was tall; the muscles on his limbs swelled and rippled with every movement. The woman, whose feminine subtleties were accentuated, stood.

"Come," she said to Janorra. "They are waiting for you."

"Who is waiting for me?" Janorra demanded, as she trod warily into the chamber and pointed the tip of her sword towards the man and woman. "Tell me who you are?"

"I am Sarkisi," the woman answered, "and this is my husband, Imrand." Sarkisi held out her hand in a gesture of invitation. "Come, follow us. Migdal and the Aeldar Wives wish to speak with you."

Sarkisi and Imrand turned and left the chamber through a gold-gilded arch. Grasping her sword firmly, having no other choice, Janorra fretfully followed them.

# Chapter Fifty-Seven: *The Giant Halls*

*Volcanoes burst from the earth and terrific earthquakes shook down the shining cities of the ancient empires. Whole races were blotted out. The Gragor fared only a little better than other races. A small colony survived and settled among the Mountains of Varascua, where they built great halls and cities. It was there, that King Malagrim, a Titan, first strode onto the pages of history!*
***Temmison Vol I, Book 1: History of the Gragor.***

*The* bodies of the barbarian chieftains were burning on orderly rows of pyres that had been set up on the battlefield. The grandest and greatest pyres were those of Effgard and Sharwin and were of such magnificence, they would burn long after all of the others were already reduced to ash and ruin. The pyres of Falamore and his sons were sizeable, as befitted their rank, but apart from size they were shown little more respect than the many tribal warriors who had fallen. The rest of the bodies of the barbarians, as was their custom, were left on the field of battle. The wyverns were allowed to feed on them, and other carrion eaters were gathering around. The vultures and crows circled over the battlefield, before landing to compete with jackals and the odd young warg, ripping at the already rotting human flesh, tearing off lumps and tatters of it and swallowing them whole.

Marki hawked and spat on the ground in disgust and shuddered. "It makes my flesh crawl to see how they treat their common dead," he said, almost apologetically. "Bury me under stone, as is the dwarf way when I meet the Maidens." He looked up from his pony at Borach. Borach knew as well as Marki, that it was not always possible to retrieve the corpses from a battle, let alone bury them, if the battle was lost, but he replied tactfully to his dear friend.

"I will," he said grimly.

The bodies of those fallen in the legion, had been carried to Thurog Tor, to be mummified and entombed in the abandoned part of the city near to the Obelisk. Karno, in a cage on top of carts being pulled by adoring tribesmen, had been taken by Davino, Maraya and a delegation of Chatti to Thurog Tor. Meron, Stamis and a handful of legionnaires had insisted on going with Karno. Borach could have ordered them to stay, but tensions were running high, and it was better for all they left with at least a semblance the legion was still unified.

"I don't think we will see Meron again," Marki said dryly, "and though I have no fondness for him, he had his uses."

"We will see him again," Borach replied, and then said to himself, *though whether he will then be friend or foe, only time will tell.*

The last of the legion's newly resurrected dead, those who had been killed in the battle, had now returned and were back in the camp on the slopes of the Valley of Elamah, away from where the wind blew the smoke from the pyres. Torach was among them. He rode up to where Borach and Marki were watching the pyres. Talain accompanied him.

After polite greetings, Torach said to Borach, "Meron and Stamis refused to share words with me, or sup with me, after I had resurrected."

Borach acknowledged the words with a nod, but did not reply.

"Horin kept his word, he returned your dead to the Obelisk at Thurog Tor," Talain said to Borach. "All are accounted for and back in the camp."

"You did well lass, to find us such an ally in the Deadlands," Marki replied. "But where we are going, those who die, will soon be out of the reach of it. Your own skills will be needed."

Borach noticed that Talain smiled uneasily, and looked anxious as she briefly glimpsed at him and then averted her eyes. He wanted to question her, but a Chatti in a chariot appeared on the horizon and sped towards them, stopping when he was close enough to be heard without having to shout.

"The week is out; preparations have been made. Chasotha wishes us to march before the noon of this day."

"Tell Chasotha we are ready," Marki said.

The Chatti chariot rider rode off.

Borach spurred his horse, and followed by the others, headed towards the camp.

"I'm sure going to miss that stubborn-headed Effgard," Marki said glumly, as he turned and took a last look at the burning pyres.

*      *      *

When the legion was prepared, they had set out on their march. It took about four days to march to the edge of the Abandoned Plain. The legion, the Chatti, Gragor and a sizable force of barbarian tribesmen had marched in loose formations. The dragon skull had been carried on a cart pulled along with ropes by tribesman who took turns with the heavy burden. It had often got stuck in the terrain and it took some time and effort to free it even with the help of the Gragor.

When the army had reached the plains, it was as far removed from anything resembling civilisation, or any terrain Borach or any of the legionnaires had seen before. Stretching before them, was miles of empty desert. They had all heard stories of the Abandoned Plains, Borach had read many tales himself. It was a place he had never intended to see, let alone attempt to cross. The tales he had read told that, beneath the sands of that place, large savage insects lurked, that would suddenly spring from their burrows to drag the unwary traveller down below the surface. Even worse, the stories told of giant lindworms, unseen and burrowed, that followed below the surface and hunted those who tried to cross the plain.

Chasotha had assured Borach he knew the trails where the sand and ground were too hard for the lindworms to burrow or hunt, and where the burrows of the insects could be spotted by scouts, and therefore avoided. The first few days of traversing the plain, proved that Chasotha's skill as a guide was indeed remarkable. As they marched across the plains, at times sandstorms blew up from out of nowhere, huge windswept freaks that engulfed them all in dust and grit and forced them to close their eyes and hunker through by tying a short rope to the person in front of them. He led them along hard and barren trails for three days, where the only sign of life apart from them, was a giant lindworm that broke through the surface of the sand a mile or so away, only to burrow again out of sight. The size of the creature had amazed them all, except Chasotha and the Chatti, who boasted they had seen bigger.

On the fifth day since they had entered the plains, they had come to an oasis, where they stopped and took much needed rest as they ate and replenished their water supplies. They set out again the next day and marched for a further six days. On the fifteenth day since they had left the camp at Elamah, in the far distance they spied the outline of mountains, and as they continued marching towards them, columns of spiralling rock formations that spiked skyward, like a forest of stone spears, for more than a hundred feet or so into the air, came into view.

"The Fangs of Ard-Rhaeus," Chasotha declared with an air of awe to Borach on first seeing them. "We need to pass through them, it is the only safe way to get to the Mountains of Varascua, where King Malagrim dwells within the Giant Halls. Any other route attempted, you have to deal with the lindworms and other creatures that inhabit the deep sands of the Abandoned Plain."

As is often the case with desert landscapes the rocky columns were further away than they appeared, and it was several hours later before they arrived at the base of them. They then slowly made their way through the rock formations until they came to a solid wall, only broken by a fissure that led into a large cave. The crack in the rock face was large enough for a Gragor to pass, and for men to enter three-abreast. Inside, the cave was dark and cool, a welcome relief to all from the burning sun and desert heat. The Chatti had brought with them a supply of torches made from dried reeds and resinous sticks of wood. They lit some, and passed them along the line at various intervals, so all could see where they were going as they entered the cave. It was a slow and tedious process. The sunlight from the entrance soon disappeared, the further from it they trudged.

In the darkness, only seen by the light of the torches, they came to a deep chasm, over which spanned a narrow stone bridge, only just wide enough for the cart with the dragon skull on it to pass. A large stone sentinel, taller than a Gragor, and shaped in an image that was neither beast nor man, stood at the entrance to the bridge, blocking the entrance with an iron shield and holding a curved steel sword above its head in a threatening manner. The dust-covered shield and sword were intricately decorated, and the bottom of the shield was planted in a layer of dust.

Chasotha looked at the sentinel with awe, and said to Borach, "The Ard-Rhaeus."

The statue and the bridge were the first things they had seen since they had entered the plains that were not a natural formation. The sentinel, although not alive, seemed to stare at them in hostile fashion, its ruby eyes cold and without empathy.

Chasotha spoke something in an old tongue that Borach had never heard before, and causing a spiral of dust, the shield raised to allow them to pass, as did the sword, showering them in a scattering of dust and sand. When in position, and free from the debris that had covered it, both the sword and shield appeared as shiny and pristine as if they had just that minute come off the blacksmith's anvil.

Marki cursed as he brushed the dust from him, and more than a few legionnaires gave the sentinel worried glances as they walked under its shadow and between its legs to cross the bridge.

Peering over the side of the bridge, Borach could see no bottom to the dark chasm below them. Even the slightest whisper, echoed hauntingly on the walls of the chasm, and sounded so alarming they crossed the bridge mostly in silence with the only noise the reverberating of their footsteps, the noise of the wheels of the cart and the grunting and heavy breathing of the tribesmen carefully guiding it across the narrow confines of the bridge. It was with relief they crossed the bridge safely. The other side was guarded by another sentinel, different to the one before, but they passed under it in the same manner. They then entered another cave which, with the onset of night approaching, they camped within and slept. When the first rays of the new morning shone into the cave, they left it, and entered daylight. They marched for the remainder of the day through the Fangs of Ard-Rhaeus. The trail was well worn and snaked through large rocky pillars to their left and right, which partially shaded them from the fierce sun. Each night they camped near pools of fresh water supplied by great waterfalls whose flow disappeared deep into the earth below. In their own way, the Fangs of Ard-Rhaeus had their own lonely beauty.

They marched during the day time, and camped at night, and so on for another four days. At dawn on the fifth day, Marki stood next to Borach and said, "The Bantu will have a hard job crossing these plains if they don't know the way." He wiped the sweat from his brow and took in deep breaths of the fresh air. Borach, however, was looking ahead, and Marki's gaze soon followed his and the dwarf whistled in wonder at the sight they were observing, that had been hidden by the dusk the evening before. Lined against an orange and purple sunrise, they saw the mighty towers and walls of a great city the like of which none of the men of the legion had seen before; it was quite literally carved out of a mountain. Its colossal minarets, towers and spires lifted towards the heavens and stood as tall as the other surrounding mountains. Along the parapets they could make out the distinct outline of fierce looking Gragor patrolling the city walls.

"The Giant Halls, the realm of King Malagrim," Chasotha said with a grin as he beamed at the breath-catching sight before them.

The city was of such splendour, it did draw the eye. The legionnaires, who had seen many a grand sight, spoke among themselves in wonder.

Marki drew breath and whistled. "I've seen dwarf architecture that is a sight to behold, but even I must admit, this is some feat of craftmanship."

Borach studied the scene before him. Gigantic stairs chipped from the stone face of the walls zigzagged from ledge to ledge. Some of the ledges looked natural; others were regular and neat, evidently chiselled out over years or decades. Ranks of rough, square holes pierced the wall – windows into interior chambers. It was such a staggering accomplishment it was hard to gauge the scale or how many decades or centuries it would have taken to hack out such a magnificent structure from the rock of a mountain.

Borach also observed that it could be easily defended. The only approach was through a valley also carved into the mountain. A handful of Gragor could hold the canyon mouth against an army with little need to do anything more than roll boulders down the scree or throw them into the middle of the valley, upon any advancing host. Just a few hundred archers with enough arrows, could pick off an entire army and where the valley bottlenecked towards the far end, a small number of infantry soldiers, could fend off invaders who might have made it past any consistent volley of rocks or arrows.

Shagor bellowed with joy at the sight of the city, and blew a large horn, the bellowing sound of which echoed across the sands and was met with return blasts of greeting from the walls. She looked down at Marki, smiled, prodded her chest and said, "Mountains of Varascua. Shagor's home."

Marki whispered under his breath, "I'd kind of figured that out for myself lass."

The army slogged its collective way towards the city for more than two hours, confronted by rolling terrain of sharp rocks and twisted thorn that was riven by deep gullies that looked to have once been riverbeds. The deep gullies, surrounded by vertical walls of rock, were the only way the terrain could be crossed. Borach noted that such terrain would provide many opportunities to set ambushes on any advancing army, even before they reached the mountains and the valley.

Borach noted Marki must have had a similar thought, for his friend said, "The Giant Halls are surely unconquerable. Even if a traitor led them on the right trails across the Abandoned Plains and through the Fangs of Ard-Rhaeus, this terrain and then their defences, would be all but impossible to conquer."

"Such a place can only be taken by treachery within," Borach said, "so let us hope our new allies do not have a viper in their nest."

The terrain, even in the gullies, soon became so challenging, that no one spoke in more than a whisper, and even then, it was short and only as necessary. The trek was physically demanding and they were feeling numbed by the strain of the long and strenuous journey since they had left the camp at Elemah. They had traversed dry and hostile terrain, but due to the skill of Chasotha as a guide, they had crossed unharmed with no deaths. As they walked through the gullies, being careful on the uneven ground, Borach also noted something else and he pointed them out to Marki. Near the top of the gullies, cleverly hidden from all but the sharpest eye, were water spouts carved in the shape of all manner of beasts.

"By Balagrim," Marki said with a look of awe, "they can even flood these gullies if they wished."

They continued for the next hour in complete silence. A harsh wind blew sand and dirt through the gullies they traversed. Borach pondered that even Marki, normally comfortable and free at sharing his thoughts and making wry comments, remained silent. Leading his pony on foot, Marki was concentrating on putting one foot in front of the other, as they edged ever nearer towards the Giant Halls. The dwarf rubbed his eyes, bloodshot from the sandstorms they had endured. Borach stretched in his saddle, his own limbs were stiff and ached, and he was glad the journey was almost over. He rubbed his own bloodshot eyes with the back of his thick wrist.

By the time they reached the valley that led to the Giant Halls, they had been marching for the better part of the day, and the onset of dusk was beginning. They negotiated the valley watched by patrolling Gragor and Chatti, passed the bottleneck, and approached the enormous gates to the Giant Halls. The gates grated and whined as they were opened. The air changed, it felt foul and the wafting smell of strange foods greeted them. As they passed under the massive gates of the Giant Halls, torches gleamed and smouldered luridly. They revealed that cemented into the structure of the gates, were the skulls and bones of many races and creatures. Borach and Marki exchanged an uneasy glance that was not unnoticed by Chasotha.

"The Gragor are an ancient and inscrutable race, powerful and merciless to their enemies, but they also have honour. You enter here as an ally, and need fear no betrayal," he said.

Borach snarled in uneasy exasperation. He had once heard that strangers were not often welcome in the Giant Halls. It was said outsiders were only tolerated when they came as ambassadors or legitimate traders, yet here he was, even if an invited guest, leading a depleted legion of Pure-bloods into the place. He had no choice but to continue, so with wary eyes and a hand ready to draw his sword should it be needed, he spurred his horse and followed Chasotha up a huge ramp that passed under a gated arch and eventually entered into a large shadowy street. The legion, accompanied by the Chatti, Gragor and tribesmen they had travelled with, marched down the street which was empty of people, until they entered a larger, main street.

"The Gragor live in another part of the city, and only an invited guest can go there, under pain of death," Chasotha said. "In this part of the city, we Chatti and Fell-bloods live."

Borach looked around him. The street was not like any Kappian city at dusk, where brightly-clad people laughing and strolling along the pavements would be going in and out of the shops and stalls, which would be wide open and displaying their variety of wares, brought from across the Kappian Empire and beyond to be sold in the cities and towns. There was no bright blaze of lamps and cressets, under which street entertainers would perform: jugglers; minstrels; actors and about every form of entertainer you could imagine. Here, the stalls, shops and houses were closed at dusk. The only lights along the street were large torches at regular intervals. The Chatti and Fell-bloods walking the streets were fairly few; they stopped and stared as the strange procession

650

marched by them. A strange restlessness ran through the place, a stirring of ancient ambitions long frustrated, and a whispering none could define except those who whispered.

Borach found the scene gloomy and unreal; the whispering of the people; the angry stares, the great black walls that rose on each side of the streets in which the shops and houses were built into. Even though this part of the city had been built for human habitation, there was a grim massiveness about it that he found overpowering and oppressive.

The Gragor that had accompanied them across the Abandoned Plains left them, as did most of the Chatti, and the barbarians who had accompanied them took the cart carrying the dragon skull to a different part of the city. Chasotha and a few of his warriors led Borach and the legion through the city for a good part of an hour, until they were led out onto a large plateau that jutted out from the city, beneath which was a large lake. On the plateau, tents and pavilions had already been set up and wagons full of provisions were being emptied by Fell-blood Davari slaves, men and women, who were storing them and beginning to cook food.

"You will camp here tonight," Chasotha said. "These slaves will serve you food and ale. Tomorrow we begin preparations. You will speak to Malagrim. When we are ready, we make haste to the Wytchwood; war beckons."

Borach nodded.

"Oh, there is one more thing," Chasotha said. "At night time, there is a curfew in the city. It is wise that nobody walks the streets so order your men to remain in their camp when the moon rises, the slaves will also sleep here. Those who guard the halls are released at night; you don't want them hunting your men through the streets. Rest well, for tomorrow you meet Lord Malagrim, King of the Gragor."

# Chapter Fifty-Eight: *The Aeldar Wives*

*I am Yimsha, Queen of the Golden Lands.*
*I have heard of a place named Garama Aetheros.*
*With my enchanted sword and armour, enter I shall and none will I fear;*
*Reavers and reapers, men who are bold, come, come with your Queen.*
*I carry Fobéarn's Orb. Fear not.*

*Who will come with me to riches untold?*
*Only the brave, will risk the grave, to prove themselves bold.*
*It is far away, far away, but I am Yimsha the brave.*
*For gold and treasure come, come and risk the long dark grave.*
*I carry Fobéarn's Orb. Fear not.*

*Dear Garnelle,*
*This is the fragment of the Song of Yimsha I found in the Kappian Library that I told you about. I believe it refers to an imagined queen who dared enter the fictitious realm of Garama Aethoros. Further research cannot be carried out as no historical records mention this queen, hence our conclusions here are that it is a work of fiction. The corners of the page are seared with burn marks, as you can see, and sadly this is all that has survived; how or when this fragment came into the possession of the Kappian Library nobody knows. Myself and some of my team of scholars think it was probably during the period of the Aethian Conquests, for it is known they set fire to their libraries rather than have us Kappians capture their literary works, but it is on a different type of papyrus than can be made from the reeds which currently grow in that region, so this casts doubt as to its origin. As you are the foremost scholar on what little is known of the Aethian Conquests, please have a look and let me know your thoughts?*
*Your dear friend,*
*Alberto Temmison.*
**A letter found in the Kappian Library written by Temmison to the noted scholar Garnelle.**

*Janorra* followed Imrand and Sarkisi through a maze of torch-lit passageways, until they came to a long straight corridor. It had a muraled wall on one side and on the other there were occasional arched doorways, behind which stairs led either upwards, or some downwards, into some murky depth. She stopped at one mural and gasped with horror. It was a picture of her, holding the Simal. She did not pause for long; there would be time enough to ponder such a mystery another time. She quickly caught up with her two guides and they walked until they came to a large bronze double-door. A cluster of rusty chains hung from three great iron rings set in the bronze and were attached to three iron gibbets, within each of which a skeleton dangled.

Janorra glared at the skeletons warily, and noticed the bones were splintered and broken as if by some savage blows. It caused a surge of dread to shoot through her. She fought down the unreasoning panic of a trapped animal. *I have Arnazia, my sword, and can even use the power of the Simal if I must, though sparingly.* She gave in to the dread. "Enough. Take me back!" she shouted as Imrand and Sarkisi stopped at the door and Imrand was about to knock. They turned to her. Imrand growled gutturally.

Sarkisi smiled compassionately, and said, "I understand your fear. They just want to speak to you."

"I do not wish to speak with them, I want to be gone from this place," Janorra wailed, anguish forcing her to her knees.

Sarkisi spoke reassuringly. "It feels like my husband and I have been a long time in this place. It is still strange to us, but we have not been harmed and, I think, neither shall you be. Migdal and the Wives just want to talk with you."

Imrand shook his head derisively as he stared at Janorra, who Sarkisi helped up from her kneeling position. Janorra sheathed her sword.

Imrand knocked loudly on the door, and it opened seemingly by itself, to reveal a downward winding stair which they traversed. With each step downwards, Janorra felt she was descending into some hell. She involuntarily shivered; she sensed something extremely ancient and evil was waiting for them at the bottom of the stair. Every step downward sounded startlingly loud in the dim light and stillness, and it was only her instinct, born of many lifetimes, in both the world of the living and the dead, that prevented her from collapsing in complete and hopeless despair. These instincts had enabled her to lie hidden and silent in the Deadlands when wild beasts of the dead had prowled covertly around her, hunting her, sniffing the air for her scent which she had masked by arcane tricks. As well as instinct, logical reasoning assured her that if the power in this place had wanted to take her by force, it might have been a battle already faced. So, as she went downward following her two guides, she did not scream, weep or rave as a lesser woman might have, even though her limbs quivered with the intensity of her emotions, which burnt fiercely with raging turmoil within her bosom. She took deep breaths, steadied herself as best she could, and prayed silently to her goddess that even in such a place as this she might find strength and assistance when needed. At the foot of a stair, to her surprise, they came into a serene looking wooded glade.

"Where have you brought me?" she asked Sarkisi as they made their way to the centre of the clearing. Her question was still unanswered, when three spectral figures appeared. The first, a perfectly shaped woman clad in red transparent silks, floated in the air. Her beauty shone as the sun. Golden hair floated slowly around her as though she was drifting in water, and she smiled a radiant smile. The second wore green silks and had white hair with streaks of black and she also smiled, her beauty and skin were like the moon. The third, wore silks of blue and her hair was dark, with flecks of white; her beauty was like the stars. Each was a beauty of sinister allure; although their faces were different, they each shone with a radiance and exquisiteness that Janorra had not seen the like of before, except when in the presence of a Goddess of the Ashura, such as Ashareth of whom she had seen with her own eyes in the Deadlands.

"You are Wytches, Aeldar Wives?" Janorra asked tentatively, as she instinctively took out the Simal, and held it in one hand, as though she was partially controlled by its power.

"Give us the Simal," the one in red silks softly said.

"That is what we seek," green silks said with a charming voice and beguiling smile.

"Why else would you be here?" blue silks whispered elegantly.

*Ashareth, strengthen me,* Janorra silently prayed. Somehow, deep within, she found an inner strength. "It does not belong to you," she said defiantly as she held up her ring. At that moment, it dawned upon her, that the skeletons at the entrance, were the remains of the bodies of these three women. "You have no power over me, strong you are in spirit but long ago your bodies grew weak and your power has all but vanished. I have knowledge of lore as ancient as you."

As one, the Wytches laughed, serenely yet mockingly. "She thinks she knows as much as us," they laughingly whispered among themselves.

"I know the chant of the *Aeldar Incantation of Theodrisa*. If I speak it, pain and torment will be yours!"

The three ghosts froze in shock, all laughter suddenly gone, and then after a moment they screamed in a manner that tore at the nerves of Janorra, and by the look of Sarkisi and Imrand, at them as well, as they covered their ears as though in great pain.

Janorra's lips curled in contempt at the Wytches, and she held *Arnazia* up to them. It was as though they suddenly sensed the terror of being prey, for they stopped screaming, and stared at her in horror.

"A Ring of Theodrisa? Wait," red silks shrieked in panic, as her image rippled, briefly faded and re-appeared. Though her body was still that of the fairest of maids her face became a loathsome melange of youth and ancient malice, and then returned to beauty.

"Stop, listen to us," green silks said in fear. Her hair momentarily billowed around a thorn-crowned head, and barbed thorn vines wound their way along her legs and arms and across her torso, before she returned to her former image.

"Please, mercy," blue silks whispered in horror. For a brief moment, dark tattoos garlanded her body, and she appeared as a witch-hag of old from the terror stories Janorra had been told to frighten her as a child, so long ago.

Something in the way the spirits spoke, touched Janorra deep within. *They are truly afraid.*

"I am Neferu," the wraith in red silks said to Janorra.

"I am Lefaria," green silks said.

"I am Morna," blue silks whispered.

"If you sing *The Song of Theodrisa* in this place, in the presence of that ring, it will torment us, but you also will be forever trapped here, and will awake to nothing but pain," Neferu pleaded ardently.

"Blood demands blood in a place such as this; pain demands pain," Lefaria warned.

"*The Song of Theodrisa* cannot be sung in Garama Aethoros when such a ring is also here. Do not let that be the path of your choosing in this moment," Morna added with a malevolent look on her face, as she grew tall beyond measurement and her face terrible yet beautiful.

"Forever trapped," Lefaria said as she also grew and changed appearance into something dreadful and foul.

"Our pain will be terrible if you sing *The Song of Theodrisa* and we are not inside the Simal," Morna groaned.

"She confuses us," Neferu screamed, undergoing the same transformation as the other two. "See how we speak out of turn and lose all of our beauty? Our husbands will not be pleased to learn we do not respect the sacred order of their earliest rank."

"Forgive us sister," Lefaria sobbed. "We are so close to what we desire but cannot see clearly. Where is Migdal?"

"We are sorry," Morna whimpered, "so long we have waited. Migdal will help us?"

"If she will not give it to us, take it from her," Neferu screamed at Imrand.

"Take it for us!" Lefaria shrieked.

"Take it now!" Morna screeched.

With the speed of a seasoned warrior, Imrand tried to snatch the Simal out of Janorra's hand. She had no chance to react. The moment he tried to touch it, he withdrew his hand before he could, and screamed out in pain, and dropped to the floor.

The three Wytches shrunk and transformed back into apparitions of feminine beauty. "He cannot take it," they said in frightened surprise.

To Janorra, the Wytches suddenly seemed so small and powerless. She hesitated, not knowing what to do. "We wish to be free from this our prison, and enter the Simal," Neferu warily said. "Please, come and speak to Migdal with us," she begged.

"We cannot enter unless you give it to us," Lefaria said. "Migdal will explain."

"Trust us, we can help each other," Morna pleaded with a desperate whisper.

A parting in the glade appeared, and the three Aeldar Wives went through it. "Come," they said, their words sounding like a single whisper from other worlds. "You must speak to Migdal!"

Imrand, clutching his hand and grimacing in pain, stood. He glared at Janorra and said, "There is no going back. The only way is forward."

"Follow," Sarkisi said, her voice dripping with uncertainty. Imrand and I are trapped here, as are you, until you give them what they desire." She and Imrand followed the Wytches through the door.

Full of doubt, but seeing no other option, Janorra followed and went through the parting in the glade; she found herself on a twisted woodland path, and followed the others until they came into another glade in which was a large iron-strapped door. The three wraiths gathered around it. The door opened, and the wraiths went through it. "You must speak to Migdal," they said as one. "Come! Follow!" Imrand and Sarkisi followed, as did Janorra, after a moment of hesitation. She took a deep breath, and still holding the Simal in her hand, she stepped through the door into a corridor.

The corridor they were in was different than the ones Janorra had traversed before. The floors were carpeted in red with a black pattern, and there were framed paintings on the walls, in between which, were ghastly murals that surrounded the paintings. The art showed scenes of murder, torture, execution and slaughter in the name of some dark god Janorra had never seen any images of until then. If there was a narrative aspect to the murals, she could not discern it fully, but she guessed they had something to do with some great conquests of a past primordial age. Nowhere, not even in the Deadlands, had she ever seen suffering and pain celebrated as it was here. The art was a twisted view of life and death, and whoever had painted it, thought pain was amusing and suffering comical.

The further she walked down that corridor, the less convinced Janorra became that she was stronger than the three Wytches. She sensed that something profoundly evil, more so than they, dwelt at the end of it; it was gnawing away at every trace of confidence she had. At the end of this final corridor, stood a black door, twisted in the frame in such a manner it looked as though the wood itself was in pain. The symbol on the door sent a shiver of terror through her; the thought in her mind pushed itself out of her mouth as she spoke involuntarily. "This symbol should not exist in this realm or in any world," she whispered in horror, "I have seen it's like before, in the Deadlands, but there it was lesser."

Imrand and Sarkisi covered their eyes so as not to look at the symbol. Sarkisi trembled and whimpered, until comforted by her husband.

Janorra had only ever seen such a symbol before in the Deadlands and knew what it meant. *I need to get out of here fast,"* she thought, as she looked at the symbol of a black, winged-heart gripped by clawed talons, carved into the door. *This is the heart of darkness, they have led me into a trap,"* she thought as the twisted door opened and the Wytches passed through, followed by Imrand and Sarkisi.

*All fear here is just an illusion*, Janorra told herself, trying to dispel the fresh terror she felt. *I must go on; I have no other choice.* With great trepidation, she passed through the twisted door and entered a great chamber. She let out a short cry of dismay as the door slammed shut behind her and disappeared. Central to the huge cavern was an island of stone in a subterranean lake, only reached by a single bridge of stone. On the island was an Obelisk that was dirty, damaged and broken. It was in the middle of an elaborate ceremonial construction surrounded by stone columns linked by arches. Stone gargoyles sat upon each arch, looking menacingly outwards. The style and craftsmanship of it all was distinct in terms of design and the skill with which it was fashioned.

"No human hands made this," Imrand said as he furrowed his brow and studied the scene before him, sniffing the air which smelt of mildew and rotting flesh.

Sarkisi gripped his arm, "I am afraid," she whispered.

It occurred to Janorra that neither Imrand nor Sarkisi had seen this sight before. The whole scene, including the architecture, was obscene. Her eyes, however, were soon drawn towards a figure chained to the Obelisk. It was a withered figure, a head taller than a man. It had the body of a man, but tattered wings spread out from behind its back. It looked lifeless. Janorra knew what, and who, it was. She had only heard about the *Fallen* before and had hoped never to come across one.

"This is Migdal," she stated to herself. "I had hoped it not true I would meet him."

The three Wytches drifted over the bridge to the centre of the island. Janorra and her two guides cautiously followed.

*Arnazia*, began to shine, and she drew strength from its presence. The Simal, began to vibrate violently and she had to use both hands to hold it, lest she dropped it. *All fear here is just an illusion*, she repeated to herself again and again, attempting to find her courage, take the next step, and remember the nature of the place she was in.

When the three Wytches had reached the centre of the island, they turned and watched, and waited for the others to join them. Janorra, Imrand and Sarkisi walked cautiously across the bridge, and then stood in a semi-circle around them and the Obelisk.

Neferu spoke in a loud, shrill voice, and sounded very angry. Her voice echoed through the chamber. "Give it to us!" she demanded. "Give us the Simal!"

"Now!" Lefaria demanded.

"Give it to us," Morna hissed.

The three Wytches gave a shrill of laughter, and then each spoke something unintelligible in turn. Janorra of a sudden became frozen to the spot; she could not move or speak.

"Migdal empowers us now," Neferu said confidently.

"She cannot stop us now," Lefaria laughed arrogantly.

"She is not so strong now," Morna scorned.

"If the man cannot touch it, the Davari woman must take it from her. Kill her, and take it from her. Do it now!" the three Wytches said as one to Imrand and Sarkisi.

Imrand drew his sword as he slowly and guardedly approached Janorra, whilst Sarkisi notched an arrow in her bow and pointed it at Janorra.

"Get it for us!" Neferu shouted at Imrand and Sarkisi.

"Now!" Lefaria demanded.

"Don't wait any longer!" Morna hissed.

From deep within, Janorra summoned her deepest strength and inwardly prayed to Ashareth and the Ashura. Somehow, she managed to blurt out the words, "*Rayfro os ey braetho iliyray osn em*," which means, *light of my life, shine on me*. She felt the power of the Ashura fill her, and *Arnazia*, her ring, began to pulse with power. Movement and speech fully returned to her. "Stay back," she warned Imrand who was almost upon her. He hesitated and looked at the Wytches for instruction.

656

"I am the only one here who can touch the Simal and not go insane," she warned him, "you might kill me, but if your wife touches it, her mind will be forever lost to you." She held tightly onto the Simal as it vibrated even more violently.

"She thinks she is stronger than us," Neferu said indignantly.

"The arrogance of the wretch," Lefaria said.

"We will show her," Morna hissed angrily.

"You will show me nothing," Janorra shouted defiantly, remembering that all of the fear was just an illusion. "Those Davari can threaten me, they can kill this body, but they cannot take the Simal and they cannot give it to you." She looked at the Wytches. "You can neither touch it nor take it, unless it is given to you by a Pure-blood."

"The prophecy said it shall be a Davari who offers it to us," Neferu said.

"It was told long ago," Lefario added.

"Fulfilled, it will be," Morna then said.

"A prophecy is only as accurate as the one who utters it," Janorra retorted, "and I warn you the prophecy was wrong and false."

Imrand dropped his sword and pounced on Janorra with panther-like speed. He was a daunting image of strength and moved with a swiftness that prevented her from uttering any incantation to stop him. His great hands closed on her throat. She made no attempt to dodge or fend them away. Her own hands instinctively darted to his thick neck as she dropped the Simal, which fell to the floor with a heavy thud. Her eyes widened as she felt the thick cord of muscles that protected his throat. She was no match for his brute strength. His lips drew back from his teeth in a grinning snarl, made worse by the grotesqueness of the helmeted mask he wore. She felt the veins beginning to stand out on her temples. The wind whistled from between her parted teeth as his iron fingers ground deeper into her yielding throat muscles. She grasped his wrists trying to tear away those inexorable fingers which were crushing her jugular and windpipe. She tried to speak an incantation, so that the power of *Arnazia* might restrain him, but she could not utter a word, so tight was his grip.

"I want to leave this place. If neither I nor my wife can touch that thing, you will give it to them," he snarled. Of a sudden, Janorra felt him loosen his grip. He stared, mesmerized, at Yimsha's circlet which she wore around her forehead. He then looked into her eyes, and for no reason Janorra could think of, he let go of her neck.

"Forgive me, Queen Yimsha," he wheezed, "forgive me."

Janorra sat up. Blood trickled down her breast from the wounds Imrand's fingers had drawn in the skin of her neck, which was unprotected by Yimsha's armour that she wore. Her blonde hair was damp, sweat ran down her face, and her chest heaved as she coughed and fought to catch her breath. She felt exhausted, brutalised and full of despair.

"I will serve you Yimsha," Imrand said, a glazed look coming over his eyes.

At the same time, Sarkisi lowered her bow and reached for the Simal. She took it, and stood tall, but would not stare into it.

"We have it," Neferu shrilled gleefully.

"It is ours!" Lefaria shrieked.

"Give it!" Morna wailed mournfully.

As one entranced, Sarkisi, still refusing to look at it, took the Simal over to the Wytches and held it out for them to take. Each of them in turn tried to take it, but some power unseen stopped them when they touched it. Their hands were forced away, and they screamed in pain as though their spectral flesh had been scorched with a burning fire.

"I told you," Janorra gasped, "only a Pure-blood can give it to you." She looked at Sarkisi, who, although resisting, had her head turned by an unseen power, and she stared into the Simal. A Look of both awe and horror spread across her face.

Janorra remembered that the power of the Simal could reach into the furthest recesses of the heart and make anything real that it desired. It was a thing that had been formed in the heart of creation, shaped in the fires of a primordial existence when gods and giants roamed the foundations of the universe. It was not an item to be handled by those without the lore and knowledge to do so.

Sarkisi moaned in despair, "Against such power, what can mere mortals hope to achieve in one lifetime? I am assailed by visions of things only a god should know."

"What dream or nightmare binds her?" Imrand shouted as he broke free from whatever trance he was in, and ran to Sarkisi. She had a haunted look on her face that spoke of some reality that ought never to be dragged into the mind of somebody in this world. He tried to take the Simal from her, but a bolt of light shot from it and threw him back several feet. He landed dazed, next to Janorra, but was soon back on his feet. Picking up his sword, he raised it, and pointed it at Janorra. "What devilry is this?" he demanded.

"Her mind will be forever lost, unless you let me take it from her," Janorra urged him, as she stood to her feet. He pressed the point of his sword against her neck, drawing fresh blood.

"She lies!" Neferu shouted furiously.

"It is ours!" Lefaria squealed, as again she tried to take the Simal to no avail, the wraithy flesh of her hands searing with a sizzling and burning sound causing her to howl with pain.

"It is ours!" Morna howled.

A deranged look of insanity spread across Sarkisi's face. "I no longer wish to be of this world," she cried hysterically, her voice tainted with ecstasy and dismay of equal measure. "Reality is immense, so very, very vast."

Imrand looked desperately at Sarkisi, and then at Janorra. "Take it, take it from her," he pleaded, as Sarkisi howled with utter madness. He lowered his sword. "Help her, please," he begged, desperation etched on his every feature.

Janorra rushed over to Sarkisi and snatched the Simal from her. The light from it went out in an instant. She briefly examined Sarkisi who had a blank look on her face.

Imrand rushed over to his wife and held her in his arms. "Will she recover?" he asked, his voice panic stricken.

Before Janorra could answer, a moaning issued from the withered figure chained to the Obelisk. He began to wake, and stepped away from it as far as he could, being still bound by the chains. He folded his wings and looked around as one waking from a slumber.

Janorra stared at him with dismay. His face was utterly without colour, his skin stretched like torn silk over bone, so that every feature of his skull could be seen. He looked very tired. Around the red pupils the sclera of his eyes was as black as night. Tufts of withered hair sprang from his scalp. His clothes were withered and torn with age and his body frail, the skin stretched so tight that every bone and inner organ was revealed. The heart pumped slowly and mightily and looked like it would burst from the chest.

Janorra felt a numb heaviness weigh on her limbs when he stepped towards her, and it was not just due to exhaustion. She fell to her knees. "You are Migdal, one of the *Fallen*," she said, detecting this was the greater evil she had earlier sensed. His eyes burned with hatred so fierce it took her breath away. A burning wind blew past her when he roared in fury. The strength in her legs gave out and she again collapsed on the floor.

"Give the Simal to him, or he will give you the *Final-death*," Neferu shrieked in a voice so frenzied it echoed and clattered around the stones.

"He will kill you unless you give it to him," Lefaria threatened.

"Do it!" Morna hissed furiously.

Migdal moved towards Janorra, and reached out for the Simal, but he could not take it; his hand was instantly pushed back by a powerful unseen force as he frantically tried to grab it. The Simal again burned with a fierce bright light that caused him to shield his eyes and made the three Wytches recoil in horror.

"Give it to me," Migdal roared, growling in anguish as he tried to take the Simal, again only to be repulsed as before by its unseen power. He braced himself, as winds from unseen realms pushed him back, away from the Simal.

"Give it to us," Neferu said fiercely.

"Now, or our power will make you tremble," Lefaria warned.

"This is your last chance, give it or face our wrath," screamed Morna.

Janorra slowly stood to her feet. Somehow, as though the Simal was unwillingly telling her, she knew instinctively that none of them, except Imrand, could harm her and he was too busy seeking to comfort and wake his wife from whatever dream or nightmare held her.

"Kill her, give it to us and you will be free," Migdal growled at Imrand.

Imrand snarled at him, and shouted with disdain, "I tried that, it didn't work. This armour, powerful as it is, does not protect me from that thing you call the Simal."

Picking up Imrand's discarded sword, Migdal, his chains rattling, struggling against the wind, stepped forward and swung the sword overhead. It came crashing down towards Janorra's head, but a bubble of protective light appeared around her and the sword bounced harmlessly off. The hate and anger in Migdal's eyes glowed with fresh intensity.

Deep in her mind, Janorra felt a voice whisper to her. *'Command them; they cannot harm you. They are in your power whilst I am near to you and you hold Fabérn.'* The voice took her by surprise. It was that of Yimsha, and came from the jewel in the circlet that Janorra wore.

"Enough!" Janorra screamed at the top of her voice. The wind stopped, and everything became deathly quiet. "Kneel," she said, with little confidence, to the Wytches. Mist like hands emerged from the circlet around her head and forced them one by one, against their will, slowly to their knees. The three Wytches grudgingly knelt, screaming, protesting noisily and violently, struggling fiercely but in vain against the power forcing them against their will.

"Kneel," she said to Migdal, who eyed her warily. "That will not work on me," he said angrily, as the wind around him stopped.

"Then I shall sing *The Song of Theodrisa* and we will see the outcome," she threatened.

"To sing that here will mean your *Final-death*," Migdal threatened in return, but Janorra saw a flash of vulnerability in his previously fierce features.

"There are things worse than the *Final-death*. I have no desire to live or exist any longer," she answered honestly to him. "All existence is suffering, and of that I have had my fill. I have lived long enough to know that the living can envy the dead, and the gift of being a Pure-blood is in truth a curse."

"The *Final-death* and then torment will be yours, if you utter Theodrisa's verses here," Migdal shrieked, "in the presence of one of her rings of power." His words made Janorra hesitate, for she could not tell if they were a threat or a warning.

'*Tell him to remember who he is. Tell him he is Migdal, greatest of all Seraphim,*' Yimsha whispered in Janorra's mind.

"You are Migdal, the greatest Seraphim," Janorra shouted.

Migdal paused, and stared at her quizzically. His features softened and for the briefest moment, he appeared less evil, and as though memory was returning to him. "Are you Mazdek's ally? Did he send you to Garama Aethoros?" he asked.

Janorra had not expected those two questions. *Is this the cause of his hostility if he believes this to be true?* She decided to answer honestly. "I stole the Simal from Mazdek, who claimed one of his ancestors found it. He is no ally of mine."

"Then why are you here in Garama Aethoros?"

"It is against my will," she replied. "I was to take the Simal to the Baothein, but chance or powers unseen have led me here. I believed it was you or the Aeldar Wives who brought me here against my will."

Migdal studied her for a long moment. His eyes rolled back and his body shuddered. "I remember. Yes, I remember now. A thief stole the Simal from me. It has grown in power since that time. It will not let me touch it. Why?" He looked momentarily confused, and then asked. "Tell me, have any of the Aeldar been summoned?"

Instinctively, Janorra felt she should answer the question. "Yes. Three of them, at different times but they cannot maintain a physical form for long." She decided not to tell him that Ahrimakan had been slain the last time he had taken physical form, and that his spirit was trapped in the Arzak of an Arkoom. She would need to know Migdal's motives and agenda before she volunteered any more information, and why there was a sudden change about him. He seemed calm, unlike before. '*You can trust him, for now,*' she heard Yimsha whisper. '*All the time he remembers who he is, you can trust him.*'

*But can I trust you?* Janorra wondered, but did not give voice to the thought.

Migdal stared blankly at the Simal.

The Aeldar Wives wept as the invisible hands still gripped them.

"Help us, Migdal," Neferu pleaded.

"We want to enter the Simal; that we might soon summon our husbands," Lefario wailed.

"Make her give it to us," Morna pitifully begged.

"You must come with me, before I forget," Migdal said to Janorra. He waved his hand, and of a sudden, the two of them were alone on a small hill, overlooking a compound. The compound was about seventy-five to a hundred feet in length, and was enclosed by a fence of linen curtains attached to poles and fastened to the ground with ropes and stakes. Towards the rear of the compound was a tent, a structure of about fifteen by forty-five feet in size. It was a structure made of wood, and covered with the skin of various sorts of animals, which had been dyed red. It was not particularly attractive to look at. The gates were made of purple and scarlet yarn woven into twined linen. "Follow," Migdal said, as, now free from chains, he walked towards the gate. "I will soon forget, and then we must leave here." Janorra cautiously followed. It was then that she noticed, in all, Migdal had once had six wings. Where the other four had been, there were now just scarred stumps. Passing through the curtains, and into the courtyard, Janorra continued to follow Migdal, and they passed a bronze altar that was still smoking with some sort of burnt offering. Fresh blood had formed in a small tray at the base of the altar. Migdal dipped his finger in it, and marked himself, and then Janorra with the blood. He did the same to the Simal. It shimmered in Janorra's hands as the blood touched it.

Janorra felt a river of purity wash through when the blood touched her. Not far from that was a bronze basin, where Migdal performed a ceremonial purification, washing his hands and feet. Of a sudden, for the briefest of moments, a glory and light shone around him, and Janorra saw that his body was covered in eyes, that opened and looked in all directions. Such was his beauty and magnificence, she almost fell to her knees to worship him, and had to resist the temptation. The eyes closed, and the glory disappeared, but in form, he was not as tragic as before. Migdal stood there looking at her. "Wash, in the same manner that you saw me do," he ordered.

Janorra obeyed. The touch of the water was cool, invigorating, and seemed to cleanse her very soul. "I feel clean," she said meekly.

"Wash the Simal," Migdal said, and again Janorra obeyed, submerging it into the water and rubbing her hands over the surface of it. When she took it out, it was a clear colour of crystal blue.

"Good. We can now safely enter," Migdal said as he walked towards the tent.

Janorra followed. They entered the tent through a screen made of blue, purple, and scarlet yarn woven into fine twined linen. She didn't know how she knew, but she sensed the door faced to the east.

"The east, is from where En-Sof shall return from, and the direction from which the Nameless One, shall arrive," Migdal said, as though anticipating her enquiry. Janorra nodded, and did not give voice to the question already answered.

Once inside the tent, Janorra saw that it was divided into two chambers. She and Migdal were inside a front chamber, about fifteen by thirty feet in size, the walls of which were made of dark wood overlaid with gold, and draped with pure-white linen. The wood rested in silver sockets sunk into the ground. The chamber contained a table with bread upon it. Across from it was a lampstand fashioned after an apple tree. It had nine arms, branches, which were hammered from a solid piece of gold. At the end of that room was an altar where sweet smelling incense was burning.

"This is a holy place," Migdal said. "Here, I remember who I am."

"What is beyond there," Janorra asked, looking at the entrance to the other compartment, where a veil separated the two chambers. The veil was made with blue, purple and scarlet yarns and fine linen. Embroidered on that curtain were images of Seraphim, Cherubim, and other angels.

"Your death. You cannot enter there," Migdal said ominously.

"I would welcome death, if it meant non-existence, or to dwell forever in the Fair Havens," Janorra replied softly.

"If the Aeldar return to Pangaea, not even the Fair Havens will be a safe abode," Migdal remarked. "Nowhere in the Nine Worlds will be safe."

The statement troubled Janorra, so she changed the topic. "What is this place?" she asked, feeling overwhelmed by the beauty and sanctity of her surroundings.

"This is just the shadow of a greater reality, of once what was, but still is. It is an image of the place we were ordered to build. The second chamber is the place where the Nameless One, was supposed to meet with the Seraphim and Aeldar, when he finally came to Pangaea – but he never came." A sadness spread across the face of Migdal. "This chamber we are in, is the image of the place where I did meet and converse with En-Sof, and if he returns, it is in the true reality this image represents, where I will meet with him again, but only when he finds me and releases me from my self-imposed prison, for I am now but a shadow and memory in the world, even to myself." A deeper sorrow spread across his face. He stood there staring at Janorra and the Simal, as one deep in thought and undecided what to do. "Do you wish to be gone from Garama Aethoros?" he asked.

"Yes, I do," Janorra replied wearily.

Again, Migdal paused, studying her for a long time before speaking. "Then you will see things you do not know, if you answer my next question truthfully," he finally said.

Janorra nodded agreement, but was wary, expecting anything. "I will answer you openly," she replied honestly.

"Good, in this place no lie can be told, it is more powerful than any truth stone." Again, Migdal studied her, sternly, for a long while. "Do you serve the Aeldar? Do you wish to see them return from the Void to rule in the Everglow?"

Janorra felt fresh invigoration, feeling strength from *Fobéarn's* orb enter her. *'Speak the truth, or he will never let you leave Garama Aethoros,'* Yimsha whispered to her innermost mind. *'I was never brought to this place, but my mistake was to lie about my motive,'* she added. *'No Obelisk can reach you here. Tell him the truth.'*

"I was forced to serve them, but I despise the Aeldar," Janorra answered, "and would see an end to them. It is the reason I stole the Simal, so that the Baothein could guard it and stop them from being summoned again. You owe me the truth as well, are you an ally of the Aeldar? Why do you want the Simal?" Janorra feared what the answer might be.

Migdal continued staring at her, before answering, "No, I am not their ally. The Simal has grown in power and will no longer let me touch it. It seeks the Aeldar Wives; it has found three of them, and they have already entered it. Three more it has now found, by your hand, against your will, and they now seek to enter. The other three, I have lost. I know not if they have hidden themselves in secret parts of Garama Aethoros, or have returned to the Outer World. You must search for them here, or there, but to return here you must use a different entrance hidden in the physical world."

"I have no desire to ever return here," Janorra said. "I know what you are, but why do you guard the Aeldar Wives if you are not a servant of the Aeldar?"

Migdal laughed mockingly, but his mirth did not last for long and melancholy sadness again quickly etched upon his features. "I do not serve them," he uttered with sincerity. "*The Book of Aeldar* tells lies about us Seraphim."

"Then tell me what it is you desire, and why did you try to kill me, and take the Simal from me?" Janorra asked animatedly.

"I did not remember who I was," he answered.

"You do now?" she asked.

"I am Migdal, the last of the Seraphim who stayed true to the charge En-Sof gave us," Migdal answered with a rasping voice booming with pride and pain, as the two frayed wings unfolded from his back to their full length. They were tattered and torn and as ragged as his clothes. "Nine of us there were. Look into the Simal, order it to show you the truth, to reveal to you what it desires most. Not even the Simal can lie in a place like this, for though this place is but a shadow of a true reality, it is not without power. The Simal has been cleansed, and for a time, whilst here, it will remember its true purpose before corruption tainted it."

Janorra's expression matched her mood - puzzled and hardened. Not that long before, Migdal had tried to kill her and take the Simal. For all she knew, this could be an act and he was trying to trick her. "Show me the truth, and reveal your desire," she reluctantly said to the Simal, as she took a deep breath and warily looked into it. She felt as though she fell into it, into a dark chasm; the world began to spin. Her mind plummeted into blackness and whirled away on the currents of time. She pictured shapes moving through the Nine Worlds and saw a torrent of places and people, a bewildering collection of scenes that left her feeling bewildered. There were scenes from her childhood, so many lifetimes ago. Flashes of memories from each of her lifetimes appeared before her and disappeared in an instant. She did not need to be told that dark powers were involved in the things that had happened to her: she could feel them, they made her skin crawl, and there was the illusion of a foul stench in the air as she watched evil hunt and circle her during past lives.

In the Simal, Janorra then saw Silverberry, and heard her whispered words. '*The more the three brides lie, the more you should trust them. One tries to hide, one tries to cheat, one plays Harendale and the other two weeps. They seek not what they desire most, but that they shall find, so when you give it to them, have peace of mind.*'

Janorra then saw a vision of En-Sof, being sent by the Nameless One, to complete and perfect the Nine Worlds that had been forged at the beginning of time. En-Sof, accompanied by nine powerful and majestic angelic beings, the Aeldar, descended to the Nine Worlds, as did the Seraphim, also nine in number, the most splendid of whom was Migdal. They came to the tent she was standing in. It was in the physical world of Pangaea, on top of a large mountain, part of a range of smaller mountains. *The Forbidden Mountain?* She asked herself. Though she had never seen it with her own eyes until then, she had seen sketches and drawings of it in books and knew of its existence.

Migdal appeared next to her, and looked so lovely. He pointed at the vision and the assembled beings. "Look at how beautiful we were," he said. "Now, watch and listen. When the Simal has shown you what it now must, it will bring you back to me." He then faded away from next to her, but not from the vision.

Janorra then saw a myriad of moving images. She saw that En-Sof, the Seraphim and the Aeldar were accompanied by an uncountable army of angels, commanded by Cherubim. She listened as the Seraphim were given charge of four of the Nine Worlds, and the Aeldar that of another four; their charge was to beautify and furnish them with all things that were good, so that the Nameless One, when not away on business in other realms, could one day come and rest in them.

En-Sof was given the title the *Primary Draftsman*, and upon the Aeldar and Seraphim, was bestowed the title *The Architects*, and to one Aeldar, Thuranotos, and one Seraphim, Migdal, the title *Grand Architect* was granted. Much power was entrusted to them. The world of Pangaea, the first of the Nine Worlds, was chosen as the place where the Nameless One would meet with En-Sof and the two *Grand Architects*, during his planned temporary visits and sojourns. Thuranotos and Migdal were charged to visit the other worlds which they were responsible for, and return to En-Sof to report on progress, that together the three of them would work together to beautify, govern and maintain the unity of the Nine Worlds, all for the Nameless One.

The vision changed: Janorra was then shown that the Everglow was created as a special place within Pangaea, where the Nameless One could hold a conclave with the two *Grand Architects* and the *Master Draftsman*, En-Sof, whenever he visited. The Nameless One intended to descend at the *Tent of Conference* on the Forbidden Mountain.

The vision then showed Janorra the Nameless One, who was forging the Simal in a place that she had not the words to describe. He himself, was but a shape and faint outline, but she saw that he invested great power and intellect into the Simal, that it might replenish En-Sof, whenever he touched it, for much energy he released into his work. She then watched as the Nameless One gave the Simal to En-Sof, and forbade any but he to touch it, and he wrote many laws concerning the Simal. En-Sof held the Simal and brought it with him to Pangaea, and declared he could see things past and present in the realms beyond the Nine Worlds, but the future was clouded. En-Sof declared himself the Watcher Guardian of the Simal, vowing to keep it safe until the Nameless One appeared. She watched as mountains rose and fell, streams carved huge chasms in the earth and became mighty rivers, and desert wastelands and ice ages came and went, and all the time En-Sof stared into the Simal.

The Seraphim respected the Simal and the laws that were written by the Nameless One, but Janorra saw that the Aeldar Thuranotos, secretly desired its power and knowledge, and begrudged that only En-Sof was allowed to touch it, and gaze into it. He secretly whispered his malcontent into the ears of the other Aeldar. Janorra was horrified as over the eons of time, when a day was like a thousand years, she saw a very faint, but dark shadow, begin to corrupt the essence of the Aeldar as they watched En-Sof stare into it. They desired the Simal, and grew in their malcontent.

One day, En-Sof looked up, and declared, "Now, we can begin!" Through the power of the Nameless One imbued in the Simal, En-Sof, the *Master Draftsman*, populated the Everglow with the races of Men, Dwarves, and Elves, who were, along with the children they would breed, created to assist *The Architects* in the building of Pangaea, which was the first of the Nine Worlds. Many other races and species were made to populate Pangaea and the Everglow, for the enjoyment of the Nameless One that he might walk and talk with them, and learn from them, when he finally visited. All manner of creature did En-Sof create, that he might please the Nameless One when he came.

Janorra watched as En-Sof stood at the entrance to the *Tent of Conference*, looking into the Simal and then towards the east, calling out day and night to the Nameless One, asking him to come and see the progress of the work, but silence was his only reply, and his countenance grew sad. Then, one day, a Cherub of fearsome magnificence descended from the east. His sword was bloodied, his clothes rent, his exhaustion clear for Janorra to see. The Cherub whispered in En-Sof's ears, and though she could not hear the content of the words that were spoken, it was obvious En-Sof received disturbing news from this messenger who had appeared from dimensions and realms beyond the Nine Worlds. The messenger left, to return from whence it had come, and En-Sof sat and wept, and looking again into the Simal, a look of horror spread across his one peaceful face. He became greatly distracted and troubled, and then, exerting great power, he created the ancient Obelisks, for a purpose Janorra was not shown, and then from the Simal he created two smaller Orbs of Power, that he gifted one each to Thuranotos and Migdal, to enable them to finish the making of the Nine Worlds. Janorra recognised the orbs, for their names were *Fabérn* and *Fobéarn*.

Janorra watched, and such was the distraction of En-Sof, he rushed the work, and in so doing, made a fateful error, and he wounded and weakened himself with the effort. The blood of En-Sof fell to the ground, and he attempted to use the power of the Simal to heal himself, but in creating *Fabérn* and *Fobéarn* from it, he had damaged and corrupted the Simal itself. Un-beknown to En-Sof, Thuranotos had secretly watched him, and when En-Sof went to inspect the Obelisks, Thuranotos secretly wiped up the blood that had dripped from the wound of En-Sof. He kept it in a phial that he hid well in deep and dark places. Janorra continued to watch. In the vision, another Cherub from other realms brought further bad news to En-Sof. He stood at the entrance to the *Tent of Conference*, and held the Simal up high, but he could not see beyond the Nine Worlds, and even within them his vision was blurred when he looked into it. En-Sof gathered the Aeldar and Seraphim, and told them that he must leave the Nine Worlds to discover what was taking place, for great and malicious events were unfolding. He entrusted the completion of the Nine Worlds to the Seraphim and Aeldar. Great power he gave to them, not knowing this further weakened his own self. Before leaving, he charged the Cherubim and lesser angels with painting the skies, shaping the mountains, rivers and landscapes, according to his design, and he charged the Seraphim to build the

Great Wall that surrounds the Everglow, that only those creatures and races chosen to do so, those with the most beauty, might dwell within it, and be companions of the Nameless One should he come. Those not chosen for this purpose, were to live in peace and harmony, outside of the Great Wall.

Janorra observed that with great speed and efficiency, the Seraphim built the Great Wall, helped by the race of Elves who worked tirelessly with grace, skill and agility, so that the wall was finished even before En-Sof had completed all of his preparations to leave. Their work done, eight of the Seraphim, with half of the Cherubim and angels, returned to their four worlds, for much work had they to do in them, lest the Nameless One visit, for they considered their task in Pangaea complete, and wished to not disappoint the Nameless One should he come. Only Migdal remained behind in Pangaea. Janorra watched as the angels that remained in Pangaea, continued to beautify the surface of the world, according to the designs of En-Sof. En-Sof had charged the Aeldar with building the Labyrinth, where gardens, mazes, lakes, towns and cities and a palace for the Nameless One were to be built. The magnificence of the palace, stunned Janorra, and no description she could think of would do it justice. The Labyrinth was built deep underground in the belly of the earth, and ran the entire length and breadth of the Everglow. On its roof, was built the Underglow, an elaborate system of below the surface canals, waterworks, rivers and seas, so that the Nameless one might sail and cruise upon them for his leisure, and enjoy the beauty of the many jewels that were imbedded in the cavernous roofs, providing a stunning light with which to see all that had been made. The races of Dwarves and Men were charged with assisting the Aeldar in the build, but they argued among themselves, and so the work was slowed.

Janorra watched as En-Sof made final preparations to leave the Nine Worlds, before the Labyrinth was completed, but he wrote laws, that were to be obeyed throughout all of the Nine Worlds, that peace and harmony might always remain, and in the deepest parts of the Labyrinth that had been completed, he destroyed the maps, and skilfully hid the Simal in a Forbidden Citadel, so that only he might know of its location, and he forbade any but he to enter, and many great and powerful *Protectors* he set at the gates. This infuriated the Aeldar, for tired they were from their labours, and they desired the power to be gained from the Simal. When En-Sof left the Nine Worlds, he vowed to one day return. After his departure, in secret the Aeldar sought the Simal, thinking to reason with or slay the *Protectors*, but they could not find the Forbidden Citadel where it was hidden.

Migdal discovered the plans of the Aeldar, and rebuked them for it, a thing which angered them and grew their resentment towards him. Whilst he was sleeping, the Aeldar came upon him, bound him with great chains, and threw him into the deep places of the earth, from which he could find no escape. They did this that they might seek the Simal without hindrance to their desire. Janorra was horrified as she watched these events happen.

Janorra saw that the remaining Cherubim and angels heard of Migdal's treatment at the hand of the Aeldar. In fear, they tried to flee Pangaea and warn the Seraphim who had left, as to what was taking place in the First World of Pangaea, but they were stopped by the Aeldar, who began to hunt them down and imprison them. Death entered Pangaea at this time.

In fear, the other angels hid themselves in the rivers, lakes, ponds, trees, mountains and inanimate objects of the world, and any other place where the Aeldar could not find them. The Elves had busied themselves, and had already sung into being the plants and the great forests, and the wisdom they had already learned, they bestowed upon certain trees. When the angels hid in the trees and forests, the Elves communed with them, and many secrets they were taught. The angels taught the Elves to fear the Aeldar and their devious plans.

Within the great forests they had sung into being, Janorra observed that the Elves built great fortresses to protect themselves, and among them civilisations grew which the Aeldar grew jealous of, for the palaces the Elves made for themselves, became more splendid than those that the Aeldar would inhabit, on their return to their own, uncompleted worlds. The Aeldar whispered against the Elves, in the ears of the races of Men and Dwarves, who grew discontent that they still laboured on the Labyrinth and the Underglow, whist the Elves enjoyed rest and pleasure from their main labour of building the Great Wall. "It was the lesser task they were given," the Aeldar declared in their speeches to the races of Men and Dwarves, and thus their bitterness grew, and turned to open hostility towards the Elves, who confined themselves to the safety of their forest homes, a place they named the Elven Abodes.

The images and sounds of the vision seemed so real to Janorra, it felt like she was actually there, as they moved before her eyes. She watched as the Aeldar looked at the daughters of men and became discontent at the restrictions to their lusts and the pleasure denied them by the written laws of En-Sof; they secretly plotted war against him, should he ever return. Janorra heard their dark mutterings, and watched in horror as the light of their essence further dimmed, and the shadow within them grew ever darker.

It was as though Janorra was among them when, she witnessed that, weary of their own labour, which was now unwatched by the Aeldar, some Dwarves and Men travelled to the great forests to see if it was true that the Elves lived lives of leisure. The timing could not have been worse, for taking rest from building their fortresses and palaces, the Elves held a week-long festival, where music played and they danced, sang, feasted and made merry. The Men and Dwarves arrived the day the festival began, and in secret they watched, until they could stomach no more. Returning to their own kind, they spread their discontent and tales of laziness, and the angry mutterings among their own people intensified and turned into outright hatred for the Elves.

Some angels that had hidden in nature or inanimate objects, again tried finding a way to other worlds to warn the Seraphim of the clouds of conflict growing within Pangaea, but those that tried were caught before they could leave, and cruel was their suffering at the hands of the Aeldar. Janorra wept in pity for them even as the vision showed her their travail. Disfigured they became in body and soul, and it amused the Aeldar to release such tormented creatures back into the world, where they began to inflict much trouble and woe on all living things, and the very creation itself. Once creatures of great beauty, these abominable creatures hunted and consumed other species, and any not of their own kind.

Janorra saw that served by the races of Men and Dwarves, the Aeldar continued to grow bored with working on the Labyrinth and the Underglow. They longed to work on their own worlds, and they resented En-Sof that the task the Seraphim had been given, was the lesser of the two. They became lazy and insolent, and none of their achievements satisfied them any longer, so with purpose and intent, they changed part of the layout of the Labyrinth. Again, they sought the Simal, and searched for the gate that led to the Forbidden City within the Labyrinth. This time, they had no desire to attempt to reason with the *Protectors*, but intended to slay them through guile and deceit, but they could not find the gate that led to the city, and they howled with rage. It was then, frustrated, and tired with the monotony of their task in overseeing the completion of the Labyrinth and the Underglow, they wandered and walked the entire expanse of the Everglow, looking for fulfilment, distraction and other things that might amuse them. Thus, the Second Age, the Aeldar Age, began, as they left their appointed tasks unfinished, and settled within the Everglow. Intending to also go beyond the Great Wall to explore the rest of Pangaea, and finding they could not, their anger towards En-Sof turned to hatred, for he had made it so that they were limited to the Everglow, and this discovery made them hate him the more. It was then, that they openly rebelled against all that En-Sof had written. It was with intent, that they set out to defile the Everglow, and those that lived there, and they sought for themselves wives from among the most beautiful women among the race of Men. Nine maidens they chose, daughters of one named Belroth, a foreman whose life was devoted to the completion of the Labyrinth and the Underglow for his Aeldar masters. Twelves daughters in all Belroth had, but three were rejected, and nine chosen. The three rejected, Janorra saw with horror, were those the Davari now named as Yag, Yig and Yog.

Janorra wanted to shout and warn the daughters of Belroth, maidens of great beauty and innocence, as the Aeldar changed into the form of men, and sought to win their hearts, but she knew it was futile, for the events she was witnessing had already taken place, long ago in ancient history. Each of the nine chosen daughters of Belroth, he who guided the race of men in their part of the building of the Labyrinth, were seduced in turn by a different Aeldar who appeared in the form of a man. Janorra witnessed the seduction of the first six maidens, and dread filled her heart.

Janorra watched as the last three maidens were seduced. She saw Neferu as a sweet and innocent young woman, sitting in a forest glade. Her head, crowned by her golden hair, was draped in a garland of spring flowers. One of the Aeldar, in the appearance of a man, came and sat with her and gave her gifts of great magnificence and wooed her with smooth words, and she gave herself to him. Lefaria sat in her father's garden, wearing a dress woven with an intricate weave of leaves and spun gold. Another of the Aeldar came to her, and in similar manner she was seduced. Morna, wearing a blue cloak that shimmered in the moonlight swung on a swing as an Aeldar danced and sang for her and won her heart. No resistance she offered him, when reaching out to touch her, he did.

Still within the Simal, Janorra watched as an ancient corruption infested the innocence of the nine maidens, each in their turn, the last being the three she was with. Neferu, hid behind a veil as her beauty turned grotesque. Lefaria cried and covered her face behind a mask, in order to cheat her father of the truth when he found her and asked of her day. Morna played with Harendale cards as she heard the weeping of her sisters, and she dared not face her own truth and the twisting of her beauty. Janorra felt compassion, for indeed, they had not sought nor known what they would desire most, but they had found it when the Aeldar had come as gods among men. Each of the nine maidens lied to their father about the truth of what had happened, for great was their shame and intense was their fear. When Belroth discovered their secret, he took a knife to slay each of them, but they wept and begged for mercy, and through love and pity for them, he tamed his wrath.

Fearing their father's wrath would soon consume his pity and love, when the maidens realised that they were with child, Janorra saw how each of them fled and were secretly wedded, without their father's knowledge and against his will, to the Aeldar who had seduced them. They gave birth to babies that were not human, the First Titans - the *Firstborn*. The *Firstborn* grew majestic and great in size, and in turn bred with other women and made more of their kind to populate Pangaea. Much mischief did these Titans do.

Janorra discovered, through the vision, that it was during the Aeldar Age that the Labyrinth and the Underglow were finally completed, under the direction of Belroth, who in anger and disillusionment with the Aeldar, tore up the final plans and maps and hid the pieces from them. Belroth gave these fragments to the most trusted of his workforce, Men and Dwarves alike, and charged them with guarding or hiding the fragments, as they were made of a substance which he could not destroy. He spread much rumour amongst them, so that in time, Men and Dwarves began to resent and distrust the Aeldar. Some of these Dwarves fled the Everglow, and found a new home in the Iron Mountains, where they built a glorious kingdom, that was soon split into many factions through disputes and rivalry. Some Men, fled far to the icy south, and became known as the *Resenters*, which is the meaning of the word Davari. They soon descended into savagery, and like the Dwarves, made war among themselves.

The jealousy of the Aeldar towards the Elves grew. With the help of some Titans, and the Men and Dwarves who had remained in the Everglow, the Aeldar by force, conquered and stole the Elven fortresses and palaces. Many Elves were slain. The survivors fled to the north, beyond the Great Wall, and left the Everglow. In time they became Light, Dark or High Elves, and much animosity grew between them.

The Aeldar broke their promise to share the spoils of war with the Titans, Men and Dwarves who had fought with them. They made the former Elven Abodes their own homes where they dwelt with their wives and bred more foul offspring, and during their feasts they mocked those who had helped them. Janorra watched, transfigured by what she was seeing. During these days, the Aeldar Wives gave birth to more Titans, who themselves bred among each other, and became more numerous than all the other races, and thus began the Third Age, the Age of the Titans.

The Dwarves, who had remained in the Everglow, began to build their own great fortresses and citadels, with the help of Titans, born from women who were not Aeldar Wives. A great Realm they soon became. Those of the race of Men who had also remained in the Everglow, also built great civilisations, and their numbers grew rapidly. Janorra watched as the Aeldar grew concerned at the growing might and power of their former workforce. Belroth, whispered words to the Dwarves, Men and Titans, any who would listen, about the mockery the Aeldar directed at them, and in addition to the truth, he also spread many rumours and lies.

It troubled the Aeldar when they heard the whispers of war, and the rumours Belroth had spread. Belroth then hid himself, in places where he would not have to face the Aeldar wrath. The Aeldar once again sought the Simal, and when they heard that Belroth had torn up the maps and plans for the Labyrinth and Underglow and distributed the fragments among Men and Dwarves, they demanded that any who had them, hand them over. Some Dwarves and men made forged copies and passed them over, and the deception was not noticed by the Aeldar, for great had been their laziness and complacency in overseeing the completion of the build.

The nine Aeldar Wives saw the great architectural wonders that Dwarves, Titans and Men had made for their own habitation. As Aeldar Wives, the once pure maidens had become arrogant and cruel after losing their innocence. The *Firstborn*, watched in horror, as the masqueraded loveliness of their mothers faded over time, and soon their foulness could not be hidden. Their fathers, the Aeldar, were blinded to it, and they could not see the corruption of their wives' beauty, and all manner of deceit and treachery did their wives whisper in their ears. They resented the illegitimate children of their husbands, and their descendants, as well as the children the other Titans had spawned. They named them the *Impure*.

In jealous spite, the Aeldar Wives desired the cities that Dwarves, Men and Titans had built, and they desired them for their own offspring, the *Firstborn*. They persuaded their husbands to make more war, and take what they desired. This became known as the *War of Devastation*. Some Dwarves, Men and Titans who survived, also fled to the south or to the west, and escaped the Everglow, beyond the Great Wall, where the Aeldar could not pursue them. Some, stayed loyal to the Aeldar, despite the great betrayal they themselves had endured. The descendants of these Dwarves came to be known as Euarian Dwarves. The descendants of the race of Men who fought for the Aeldar, were given the blood of En-Sof, and thus the race of Pure-bloods was born. The reason as to why En-Sof created the Obelisks was then revealed to Janorra. En-Sof had created them, after news of the trouble the Nameless One faced in other realms, so that if ever he was slain, they would restore his spirit and essence to a new body. The Obelisks were created by him, and for himself. His spirit would rest in the Fifth World, now known as the Deadlands, until the Obelisks brought him back to the Outer World, also known as Pangaea. With the blood of En-Sof running through their veins, the race of Men so gifted, became known as Akkadians, and in a twist of nature, the Obelisks brought them back to life whenever they died within the Everglow. Their spirits waited, in the world Janorra knew as the Deadlands, one of the worlds the Aeldar had once been given to create as a place of beauty. Never, had En-Sof intended it, to be a place where the dead would inhabit, whilst waiting for the Obelisks to bring them back. The Obelisks groaned under this heavy burden, and some of them began to go insane, for great was their confusion.

The vision moved on. Janorra saw a group of the angels who had stayed hidden. They revealed themselves at this time, and were slain by the Aeldar. Finding themselves in the Deadlands, they created the Fair Havens, but hid it well, so the way could not be found, only shown to those they trusted to go there. These angels, became the Ashura. It was they who gave sight to the first Seers in the Deadlands.

There was no time for Janorra to reflect, the images she was seeing changed again. Those who had not been gifted with the blood of En-Sof, resented the Aeldar, as did the Titans, including the *Firstborn*. They believed the blood of En-Sof should have been given to them, and they hated their fathers, the Aeldar, for not bestowing it upon them. In return, the Aeldar feared the growing number of Titans, who, in time made war against the Aeldar and the Akkadians. To their dismay, and at great cost to themselves, they discovered that no weapons could harm the Aeldar. For fear of the war being lost, it was during this time, that some Titans went north and sought help from the Elvish race, who had sent message that they had discovered how to make weapons they called Arkooms, which could slay the Aeldars' bodies. These weapons had forged into them, Arzaks, powerful soul-gems, wherein the Aeldar spirits could be trapped inside after their bodies were slain. Inside these Arzaks they would be imprisoned until the day when En-Sof or the Nameless one might come to summon and judge them for their foul deeds, and face a day of wrath. They also made lesser weapons called Arkiths, also forged with Arzaks upon them, by which the spirits of Pure-bloods might also be trapped, to wait for a day of judgement. Few of these weapons were made, as a long time did it take to fashion even one, and rare and unusual were the resources that were needed to make them.

It was not a unanimous decision among the Elves, when some of them shared the secret methods of forging Arkooms, Arkiths and Arzaks with the Titans. Those that did so, made the choice out of fear the Aeldar would one day find a way where they might leave the Everglow. These became the Dark Elves. Such was the division among the Elves over the decision, in disgust, many of them left Pangaea, and sailed to an archipelago of islands, far in the north of the Tethys Sea, near the edge of the known world, wherein they disappeared from known history. These became the High Elves. Janorra remembered legend said they built the Solar City, a place of fame and fable. She watched as the Elves that remained, those who had not given away their knowledge, became the Light Elves. Some hid in the Great Northern Forest of Pangaea, and thus became known as Wood or Forest Elves. Some hid in mountains, caves or along the great rivers, their environmental location now giving their name: Mountain Elves; Cave Elves; River Elves and even Marsh Elves, and many such more connotations.

Janorra watched with dismay as the Elves that remained, lost their purity, and grew dark in soul as they shared their knowledge with the Titans. Day and night for years, together with the Titans, the Elven smiths hammered in their forest forges, and shared their deepest secrets with them. Nine Arkooms did they form in this time, one for each of the Aeldar. On their return to the Everglow, the Titans carried these rare and powerful weapons. Janorra watched them teach the Dwarves and Men how to forge such weapons. Nine were made by the Dwarves, in their deep forges heated by the lava of the earth. Nine were made by the race of Men, who forged them at their sky forges.

Janorra then saw the Aeldar meet in a Council of War, and great fear was among them when they heard about the weapons that had been fashioned against them. It was news of these weapons, that made the Aeldar sue for peace, and a false truce did they offer to the Titans, and to the *Firstborn* who led them. Tricked by this false truce, many of the *Impure*, as well as each of the *Firstborn*, were invited to the Argona Temple, a place the Akkadians had built where they honoured, served and worshiped the Aeldar. It was during this, the *Feast of Stone,* that the Titans who had attended, had their eternal spirits trapped inside their own physical bodies, which were fossilised, by arcane knowledge that the Aeldar used. It was a cruel and harsh judgement, but one the Aeldar believed was just punishment for the Titans desiring to wield such terrible weapons as the Arkooms against them. Many times, Janorra had passed by those dreadful stone prisons deep in the heart of the Argona Temple, and now she knew that indeed, there was truth behind the legend and stories she had heard. She trembled at the cruelty of the Aeldar. So cruel was this punishment, it struck fear into the hearts of all who heard of the fate of the *Firstborn* and the *Impure*. It was this fear that led to the *Resenters* and the remaining *Impure*, choosing to make peace with the Aeldar, after which they fled into the far reaches of the Everglow, or beyond, still fearing retribution when the Aeldar considered it an opportune time.

As some had feared, the peace did not last long, for the Aeldar still desired revenge. To protect themselves, they desired to own the Arkooms for themselves. It caused Janorra great emotional pain, as she watched those *Resenters* who had remained in the Everglow, be driven to near extinction, such was the retribution they faced with none to defend them against the Aeldar wrath. Such was the size of the Akkadian army sent against them, that Janorra covered her ears, so great was the stamping sound of their marching feet, and so loud were the screams of those slaughtered. The Pure-bloods learnt a costly lesson though, when they pursued the survivors beyond the Great Wall of the Everglow, for they discovered that any Pure-blood who died beyond the wall, was never returned to the land of the living by the Obelisks. However, the Aeldar recovered the Arkooms the race of Men had made. Finding they could not destroy these weapons, they hid them in separate and far flung places, where they might not ever be found.

Janorra then learnt, through the vision, that it was at this time, the Aeldar committed perhaps their greatest act of evil, when they sacrificed some of the Obelisks, and turned them into numerous Neblans, in order that the Akkadians might safely go beyond the Great Wall to slay their foes, and have their spirits kept safe within a Neblan should they die there. The sacrificing of some Obelisks, was such an act of evil, that she heard the world itself weeping and mourning, and she saw in the vision that it was then that so much of the beauty of the world became lesser or even corrupted. The Aeldar themselves could not bear the suffering of the Obelisks, their screams, and the fading of the world, so it was for their own sake, not out of mercy, that they stayed their hand and slew no more Obelisks.

The *Impure*, in order to have continuing peace with the Aeldar, were instructed to hand over their Arkooms, and then betray and make war with the few Euarian Dwarves who had remained. This they did, handing over their Arkooms, after which short and brutal was the campaign against the Dwarves, for it was with surprise that the *Impure* fell upon their former allies. The Arkooms of the Dwarves were given to the Aeldar, and well-hidden all of these weapons were.

The *Impure* were given the abodes that they and the Euarians had made, so the last Eurorian Dwarven habitations within the Everglow were taken from them, and they were virtually wiped out as a civilisation, though a few survivors fled to the furthest parts of the world.

Janorra then watched as two of the Ashura, found a way to travel to the worlds where the eight other Seraphim dwelt. They were oblivious to what had happened in Pangaea. Such was their outcry when they heard the news, the Seraphim wept and rent their clothes. When they returned to Pangaea, and saw the destruction the Aeldar had wrought upon the First World, Pangaea, they howled with despair. But the Seraphim were wise, and did not immediately reveal themselves to the Aeldar. With the help of the Ashura, they searched in the deep places for Migdal. Many long centuries passed until they found him, and were able to free him from his chains, but only by cutting off four of his wings. When, together with Migdal, they returned to the world of Pangaea, many empires had already risen and fallen, for it had pleased the Aeldar to play at games of war among themselves, pitting the races of Pangaea against each other.

Janorra then watched as, led by Migdal, the Seraphim and Ashura searched in the deep subterranean places of the world for the Forbidden City where the Simal was hidden. By chance, more than skill, they found it. But, no reason would the *Protectors* listen to as to why Migdal needed the Simal, and they would not let him nor any of his companions enter the city. The Seraphim and Ashura disagreed as what to do next. The Ashura would have no part in fighting the *Protectors*, so they left, hoping that En-Sof would soon return and restore order to the chaos in the world. The Seraphim, chose otherwise. In a mighty battle, they slew the *Protectors* of the Forbidden City. This was their undoing, for corrupted they then became, their nature grew twisted and callous.

Janorra continued to watch as, now armed with the power of the Simal, Migdal and the Seraphim, turned one of their own worlds, the Void, into a prison for the Aeldar. It was after this that, still fuelled by his anger, Migdal waged war upon the Aeldar with stealth and deceit, and one by one, using the power of the Simal, he defeated them, sending them to the Void where they were bound and chained in prisons dark and deep, waiting for the day when En-Sof would return, or the Nameless One would come, to judge them for their deeds. Before withdrawing from the world, Migdal searched for the Aeldar Wives, but their father, Belroth, feared Migdal's wrath, and in mercy, hid them and gave them new names, each a riddle in its own right. Thus, began the Fourth Age, the Forgotten Age, a time of barrenness in the world.

In time, Migdal and the Seraphim found Belroth. Janorra watched as they tortured him, until such was his torment, he finally gave up the three locations of his daughters. They had been hidden in three locations - three daughters in each one, deep within the world of Garama Aethoros, a world that the Aeldar had failed to complete.

Because of the corruption that had spread throughout Pangaea, as well as the result of their deeds, Migdal and the other Seraphim, turned foul. Janorra saw their light fade.

All apart from Migdal hid, for ashamed they were, of what they had become. The Seraphim, including Migdal, lost the grace En-Sof had bestowed upon them. Once creatures of light and beauty, they became dark and cold. Migdal retained his sanity, but the other eight became wild and uncontrollable, and in torment disappeared into the deep and dark places of the world, and Janorra saw, what woe would come upon any unfortunate creature that might now stumble upon such wild and hopeless beings the Seraphim had become. It was learning of the fate of the Seraphim that caused the lesser angels to lose hope. They turned onto dark paths, and sought out the great sages of the new emerging power, the Cragan Empire, led by one called Horin, a Pure-blood man who had discovered many secrets of the Nine Worlds, and had been the first of the Pure-bloods to be given the gift of sight in the Deadlands, by the Ashura. The lesser angels allied themselves with Horin, who taught his descendants and followers how to see in the Deadlands. Cruel was the reign of Horin, and suffer the world did, under the weight of his rule.

Janorra saw that Migdal searched far and wide in Garama Aethoros for the Aeldar Wives, and eventually he found them. Because of the foul deeds the Simal had been used for, it had become corrupted itself, and it tried to trick Migdal, into allowing the Aeldar Wives to enter it. But Migdal learnt that if they did, the Simal could be used to summon the Aeldar from the Void, back to the world of Pangaea. He imprisoned and hid the Aeldar Wives in three locations, three in each one, in prisons deeper than even Belroth had known, where they also would wait to be judged for the malevolence they had inflicted upon the world, and for their evil deeds.

Janorra sensed that Migdal grew to dread the Simal, for it had become sentient and alive, and he feared the extent of the intelligence that dwelt and grew within it. Janorra watched him return it to the Forbidden City, where he hid the Simal within it, burying it as deep as he could dig, and guarding it only with his own shadow as he surrounded it with riddle, mystery, magic and charm. He lamented as he left the city, for he regretted that the *Protectors* had been slain by his hand, for he wished they were there to guard the Forbidden Gate. Great was his wailing that there was now nobody to guard the Simal. He trusted that so difficult was it to find, that none would.

Before Migdal returned to Garama Aethoros, where the Wives were imprisoned, Janorra watched Migdal seek out the Dwarves and Davari, who now dwelt and thrived to the south of the Everglow, beyond the Great Wall. He chose the wisest among them, the Ruik and Reisic, who had hidden the plans and designs of the Labyrinth in secret texts. Other clandestine languages he taught to them, and hid great secrets, including where he and the Aeldar Wives would be hidden, in texts that were called Murien. The Ruik and Reisic were entrusted with the charge that when En-Sof returned to Pangaea, they would come together, and would surrender the texts to him, so that En-Sof could find Migdal, who would tell him how such chaos had spread throughout the Nine Worlds. The three rejected daughters of Belroth were left to watch over the Ruik, but Janorra was not shown how darkness overtook them and they became, Yag, Yig and Yog. Janorra did not hear in the vision the former names of Yag or Yig, but she heard that Yog's original name was Silverberry. It amazed and terrified her that, one born of such beauty, could become what Silverberry now was. '*In pride, we let the Ruik worship us, and vain we became,*' she heard Silverberry's voice drift over time and space.

Janorra then watched as Migdal chained himself in Garama Aethoros, in chains he himself could not break, lest he be tempted to wander the world before the return of En-Sof, and thus cause more chaos, for he could no longer trust himself. But En-Sof never returned, and so The Fifth Age began, The Dark Age. During this time, history became legend, and legend became myth, until the origin of the world was forgotten by many and kept only by a few who held onto what was called the *Old Faith*.

The Dark Age was a time cursed with violence, oppression, war and crime, more than the world had yet seen. It was a time when the races of Pangaea were constantly at war, even among themselves. It was during this time that some of the Dwarves from the Iron Mountains left Pangaea for fairer places beyond the sea, as their mountainous lands had become surrounded by all manner of ghouls and foul creatures, but Janorra was not shown where they went. At this time many Light Elves left the North, as constant war was making them darker and bitterer. Some went to the West, sailing on great ships to forgotten islands where it was said their light returned and fair their countenance became.

Janorra then watched as the great libraries of past ages fell into ruin and dust, forgotten by time and memory, but some texts survived, or had been copied, and scholars studied them. During the Dark Age, she saw a young scholar, an ancestor of Mazdek, Galaeroth, a Seer of exceptional ability, find a secret text in the Deadlands that was supposed to remain hidden but had become uncovered by the sands of time. It was a text called *The Song of the Simal*. During centuries of research and exploration lasting many lifetimes, searching in the Everglow and the Deadlands, he discovered many more such texts and finally learnt how to read them, and that was how he discovered knowledge about the Simal and the secret of the Aeldar and their Wives. He sought the Forbidden City, and found it. The shadow of Migdal that guarded the city did not see him enter, for long had it slept. Galaeroth found the Simal, took it, and used its power to wake and then trick the shadow of Migdal into returning to Garama Aethoros. Galaeroth, followed in secret, and that is how he found the first three Aeldar Wives, sleeping, as was Migdal, due to the long age they had been hidden and locked away in their forlorn prison.

On waking, Migdal was powerless against the Simal, and the Aeldar Wives told Galaeroth secrets about it, and willingly gave him their names and entered, but not before teaching him how to find their husbands, and how they might be summoned. Migdal was powerless to stop Galaeroth, but even when commanded with the power of the Simal, he did not give up the other two entrances to Garama Aethoros. Their locations, and that of the other six Aeldar Wives, remained hidden from Galaeroth.

Janorra watched all of this in horror. Galaeroth left Garama Aethoros with the Simal, vowing to find the other entrances in the physical world so he could return and discover the other wives. At that point, the visions slowly diminished, and Janorra found herself back in the present. She staggered and shook her head at all she had seen and heard.

"I know what the Simal showed you, for it was in my mind's eye as well, as I gazed into it," Migdal said to her. "It was with trickery, guile and discovered knowledge, that Galaeroth stole the Simal from my shadow in the Labyrinth. Again, I have failed En-Sof. I see that the Simal can no longer be controlled by me for it now has a will of its own. It knows I wait and seek the judgement of those it would one day be forced to summon, so it pursues a goal to summon them now so that the Aeldar might grow in power before the return of En-Sof. Six Aeldar Wives the Simal has now found. It is only a matter of time before it comes for the last three."

"It appears I can still master the Simal," Janorra replied.

"Not outside of this place," Migdal said sombrely. "It will let you think you control it, but the truth is, it is seeking to use you. Do not trust it." He looked at her sombrely. "I was wrong to try and slay you, and take it from you. I did not remember who I was, and even now, I am starting to forget. Here, in this tent, I am just shadow. I see that my part in the fate of the Simal is over. It will not allow me to even touch it, as it has no more use for me, but it does for you. Through guile it brought you here against your will."

"It showed me so much," Janorra said. "All of the history I thought I knew, about the origins of the Nine Worlds, I knew so little, and even what I did know, and now think I know, is fragmented knowledge. What I know is...incomplete."

"Put right the mischief Galaeroth and now Mazdek have caused," Migdal said. "Long ages I waited for the Nameless One, and he never came. En-Sof promised to return, but still we wait." Slowly, Migdal began to very slowly fade. "I am forgetting again. Soon, we will return to Garama Aethoros. Tell the Simal that when it returns, it is to return the minds of the one you call Sezareal, and the one named Sarkisi. They are to gaze into it, and it will release their minds."

"The one called Sezareal is an innocent, but the one named Sarkisi, her husband tried to kill me and take it from me. Why should I grant her this mercy?" Janorra asked.

"They have suffered much," Migdal said sombrely, even as he faded, as have you. He looked at her with a momentary pity in his eyes. It might be you have met an elf at some point, and forgotten," he said. "I saw in the Simal that you once wrote and performed plays about them? Those plays might have been stories told to you by one of their kind, that their tales might not be entirely forgotten."

The thought had never occurred to Janorra. Before she could respond, Migdal coughed and said, "I am quickly forgetting, my shadow will return to my body, where I will sleep until woken again, so listen to my words carefully. Here, I am my shadow, and again I have remembered who I am, or was. When we return to Garama Aethoros, I will quickly forget again." Misery etched his every feature. "When the minds of Sezareal and Sarkisi are returned, they will also be able to carry the Simal, but when they look into it, they will no longer see anything. You might find in them, new allies, if you tell them the peril the Nine Worlds face." Migdal started to breathe heavily, as though he was struggling for breath, as he continued to fade. "Do not let Mazdek possess the Simal again. You cannot let him, or another, get a hold of it. Take it to those you believe to be true, who will prevent the return of the Aeldar." He stared intensely at Janorra, the fierceness and hatred that had previously shone in his eyes in Garama Aethoros, was now replaced with intense sadness and regret. "When En-Sof returns, my only hope of grace is mercy; I face a miserable eternal immortality, if I fail further. Are the motives of those you plan to give the Simal to pure and true?"

"I do not truly know," Janorra answered, "but I do not know what else to do with it. Regret plagues my every moment, that I ever stole such a thing as this."

"Folly has plagued all our steps. I could not find the other Seraphim, those you call the *Fallen*. They did not answer when I called for them, now, seeing again into the Simal, I remember why."

Janorra considered the situation briefly.

"Why has En-Sof never returned?" she asked him.

Migdal lowered his head. "It could be that En-Sof has forgotten the Nine Worlds, he only assisted in creating them, but by leaving he allowed the causes of chaos to surface and those powers have corrupted the Simal itself. En-Sof serves the one who made all other things; I can only surmise that they now struggle for their own survival in the realms beyond the Nine Worlds, if they survive at all, so they no longer consider this a place of importance."

"How can they lose such power, if they once possessed the gift of life and the making of matter itself?"

"A foolish question, but one I will answer." Migdal sighed, as he faded even more. "We Seraphim once believed, that in creating all things, the Nameless One, He Who Is, gave of his own essence and weakened himself too much when he created life. The most powerful of those he formed tried to overthrow him, in realms unguessed." He paused, and then said, "The Aeldar desire to rule the Nine Worlds. If they return from the Void, they will gain power and knowledge of such a magnitude, were En-Sof to return, or the Nameless One was to appear, they might be able to defeat even them in battle. The Aeldar must be stopped. They cannot be allowed to return, for they will learn the secret of all things if they gain possession of the Simal."

Janorra finally sighed with relief. "On that matter, we have the same goal and purpose," she said softly. "I would desire to leave the Simal in Garama Aethoros, that you might guard it?"

"I cannot touch it now, and if I could, there is no place I can hide it where it won't be found. I know that now." He looked around him, and then at her. "The race of Men must guard it and now decide its fate. I will guard the three remaining Aeldar Wives for they also have woken and shall call to the Simal. It will find them, but by whose hands? I think our paths may cross again, soon, Janorra," Migdal said.

"I do not want to carry the Simal," Janorra pleaded. "I was supposed to hand it over to others, long before now."

Migdal struggled for breath, and breathed deeply before speaking again. "He reached out and touched Janorra on the head, even as he was still slowly fading away. "You see it, where you must go, where you can find me again and the last three. Where Grimmer dwells, is where I can be found."

Janorra almost froze with horror at the vision that entered her mind. "I cannot go there; I must take the Simal to the Baothein."

"You have not understood," Migdal said sternly. "Mazdek will find the final entrance to Garama Aethoros, sooner or later. He will find the last three Aeldar Wives, and if the Simal is there, they will enter, and he would take it. You must take it out of Garama Aethoros, find the last Three Wives, and only then take it to a place where he cannot find it. You must soon leave Garama Aethoros."

"I do not know how to leave Garama Aethoros," Janorra said. "If I did, I would."

"You must give the Simal what it wants," Migdal replied. "It will then let you leave."

"Let the Aeldar Wives enter it?" she asked.

"Yes, for that is why the Simal brought you to Garama Aethoros. The Simal now uses the desires of men and women, as it has used you, for its own purposes. It forbids me to even touch it for it knows my desire is to stop it, and it fears me the most."

"My desire to steal it and be free from my suffering at the temple, was useful to it. I see that now," Janorra remarked, "but if what you say is true, then it knows I too seek to frustrate its goals and stop the Aeldar from returning?"

"It knows that, but for now, it still believes it can use you to fulfil its purpose. You have some power it, but do not for one moment, ever believe you have total control. Use it rarely and even then, sparingly. Only if there is no other choice, should you tap into its power. Mazdek believed he controlled it, and he has lost it, if but for a time. You must keep it from him, for he believes he can control the very Aeldar themselves through the Simal, and who knows what knowledge he has obtained; it might be that he will find a way to subdue even them, if he has not already, for he has surrendered his humanity to powers very dark." Migdal's face grew taut with the strain he clearly felt, as he continued to very gradually fade. "Through the Simal, the secrets of all things, can be discovered in time, for the Nameless One imbued it with his own power and intelligence. Everything, is in danger, if it falls again into the wrong hands, and the Aeldar are summoned."

"You are fading. Will you take me with you when you leave this place?" Janorra asked.

"Yes," Migdal said, as he looked at her. She drew back as he reached out a hand towards her, but then, she allowed him to take a hold of the chain that held the Talisman of Ahrimakan she wore around her neck. He looked at it, and said, "The Simal showed me your hand had a part in imprisoning Ahrimakan in an Arkoom." He let the chain go, leaving it around Janorra's neck. "Only Thuranotos himself has the power to free him from such an abode. If Thuranotos' wife is found, and the Simal discovers the Riddle of his name, he will return, when summoned. This is the purpose the Simal seeks, the desire it pursues above all others – the return of Thuranotos."

Janorra shuddered. "I saw that in the vision, and was also warned of this, a long time ago, by the one called Horin, whose image we saw," she said.

Migdal's face contorted with anger and hatred. "That was a name I had not heard in a long time, until your vision. That Cragan Sorcerer thinks his good deeds in the after-life, might negate the evil he committed during his lifetimes in Pangaea. En-Sof will judge him harshly, no matter what amends he seeks to make."

Janorra understood, and when she spoke, her words were solemn. "He has been an invaluable ally to me in the Deadlands. It was he who gifted me my sword, Fury, and the armour that bedecks me when I wander in that place. It is said, that those he touches during their first visit to the Deadlands, or those who touch him, are gifted as Seers, though I consider sight in that place not a gift, but a curse."

"Many of mine own angels were beguiled by the sweetness of his words and the cruel deceptions his tongue uttered," Migdal said, "but enough of him. I sense the essence of Ashareth around you, it is she whom you follow? Did she not gift you with sight?"

Janorra nodded. "She did, she also showed me the true nature of the Aeldar, and the nature of the war they will bring, if they return to this world."

"The old world will be against the new," Migdal said. "Tell me what Ashareth showed you!"

A wave of sadness swept over Janorra; she shuddered, as memories and visions of things she would rather forget, flashed through her mind. "Ashareth took me to the Void. She showed me what this world would be like, under the rule of the Aeldar. Outside the fortresses they will build, the world will become a wilderness of toppled trunks and blackened stumps. Sudden violent ruin will come upon the world, which will be filled with hideous corpses. Many will be bereaved, millions maimed, and many more dead, but still, the Aeldar followers will hunt the survivors who remain alive. Horror and mourning will be everywhere. The rivers will dry up, the civilisations we know, will fall into ruinous shambles. Those who survive the next *War of the Aeldar*, will become impoverished. Terror and sorrow will be their meat and drink." She stared at Migdal, who was watching her intently, as he very slowly, continued to fade. She continued. "I saw the Aeldar laugh as the world was plunged into peril. Their eyes feasted on the morbid desolation they beheld. *'It is the birth pangs of a new world,'* they said to one another, *'one that will be forged to our liking.'* They then unleashed new terrors on the world, which brought more flame and death. Out of the greatness of the metals they had forged in the void, weapons were made, which were the work of long-dead smiths and sorcerers, who imbibed them with irresistible might. A magic controlled these weapons, as though they lived. No conscience did they have, as they set the world ablaze..." she paused, momentarily feeling too traumatised to continue.

676

Migdal finished the sentence for her. "Metal shaped like the dragons and beasts of old, hearts filled with flame and hate, with a desire for nothing more than the destruction of what is, to make way for what the Aeldar wish there to be."

Janorra looked at him, "You have seen this as well?"

Migdal scowled. "I have read the last page of *Rithguar's Prophecy*, and seen the things you have seen," he said. "This future you see, is but the past relived, in another time." He handed her a worn page of text. "Give this to a Ruik," he said.

Janorra took the page and tucked it beneath her armour.

Migdal had almost completely faded, and was flickering in between realities. Janorra had many questions and was not sure which to ask first. All she said, was a verse she remembered from *The Book of the Old Faith*. "En-Sof is merciful, and with mercy follows hope." She then added, "Can we hope these things will not come into this world, Migdal?"

"I do not know if En-Sof will return, or can," he answered, "and if he does, will he be in time? The Simal is ever learning, and works diligently towards the return of Thuranotos, for it delights in the chaos he has brought, and longs to be used by him to learn more knowledge of evil." He closed his eyes for a long moment, and when he opened them, Janorra saw a gentleness in them that had not been there before. "The Simal is not evil in itself, it just seeks knowledge, both that which is good, as well as that which is evil. Perhaps, not all light has gone out. We must make our own hope. The evil of the Aeldar Wives was born from pain. They fear ceasing to exist more than they fear suffering, as that has been their companion throughout these long and dark years, and used to it they are." He looked hopefully at Janorra. "I now look on them, and take pity. But it is not out of that, that I ask you to give them the Simal. It is the only choice before you, and for now, we must let the Simal make the next move."

Before Janorra could protest, or ask any further questions, Migdal again flickered in and out of reality. He tried to say something, but it was unintelligible as his voice was broken. He folded his wings, waved his hand, and his form completely disappeared as a morning mist evaporates.

*      *      *

Janorra was instantly back with the Aeldar Wives, who appeared to not have noticed she had even been gone. "All life is suffering that leads to death," Neferu croaked.

"Are you the one to suffer?" Lefaria asked.

"Or are you the one to cause suffering?" Morna asked.

"We are innocent, give us the Simal and we will spare you," Neferu shouted.

"Give us the Simal, and we will let you go," Lefaria whispered.

"We will destroy you if you do not," Morna screeched.

Janorra finally understood the words of Silverberry. She realised the Wytches were lying about their ability to destroy her. The words of Silverberry rang through her mind. *'The more the three brides lie, the more you should trust them. One tries to hide, one tries to cheat, one plays Harendale and the other two weeps. They seek not what they desire most, but that they shall find, so when you give it to them, have peace of mind.'*

Whatever Migdal had been in the Tent of Meeting, he was no longer. He roared and shrieked in fury at Janorra. The chains once again bound him to the Obelisk, and against his will, they drew him to it. *He has forgotten again, who he is*, she wailed to herself. Soon, Migdal had fallen back asleep.

*This is a dice I must cast, even if the future of the Nine Worlds and perhaps beyond will be determined by the outcome.* Janorra understood what she had to do. *They cannot take it, only a*

*Pure-blood can give the Simal to them.* Slowly and with apprehension, she stepped towards Neferu, and handed the Simal to her.

Neferu, snatched it and stood to her feet looking into it with glee and ecstasy. She reached out to Lefaria and Morna, who also seized it with their hands. They all stood, staring with lust and wicked joy, into the Simal. The Simal turned to a fiery red and flames within it danced wildly and lit their faces. Neferu uttered a word in a language that Janorra could not even comprehend, and with a shimmer of air, she was slowly sucked into the Simal and disappeared, her final look joy and relief. Lefaria also uttered a word, as did Morna, and the same thing happened to them. All three wives were gone in an instant. The Simal fell to the floor, landing with a thud, and did not move.

Janorra walked over and picked up the Simal. When she touched it, the light went out and it turned a jet-black colour. "Three more Aeldar can now be summoned, six in total, though Ahrimakan is now trapped in an Arkoom. Six Riddles can now be spoken," she whispered to herself, to strengthen her resolve. *I must not let Mazdek get it.*

Imrand stood there watching her as he held Sarkisi tightly. He had removed the Elven helmets from their heads, and for the first time Janorra saw their own faces. She walked over to them. "Give her back her mind," she said to the Simal, as she held it before Sarkisi's blank face. Sanity was slowly restored to her. Her eyes were restored from the black colour, back to their own.

"What happened?" Sarkisi asked Imrand, looking confused.

Imrand roared with joy and kissed Sarkisi all over her face.

"Thank you," he said to Janorra. "Thank you."

Janorra wrapped the Simal in a cloth and returned it to her rucksack. "Are you still my foes?" she asked them.

"Not if you are not ours," Imrand responded.

"Good, then we should quickly leave this place, if we can," Janorra said.

Imrand and Sarkisi agreed, donned their helmets, and the three of them set out immediately. Imrand and Sarkisi led the way for the first part. They had retrieved large bags of gold and jewels kept in the room they had stayed in. Janorra saw no point in arguing with them to leave it behind. They carried the bags with ease.

"The armour, it gives you strength?" she asked them.

"It was a gift from the Wytches, in return for us helping them," Sarkisi answered, "and yes, when wearing it we are strengthened, and not subject to normal fatigue."

Imrand took a small bag of jewels, and handed them to Janorra. "There might be a time you need them," was all he said.

Janorra took them, and placed them in her rucksack. He was right. *I do not know what further perils are ahead, or what I might need to fulfil my quest*, she said to herself.

Together, the three of them worked out the way back to the Skeletal Hall, as they named it. All the doors that had closed, opened as they approached them, and with great difficulty and after many turns and mistakes, for the way looked different, the three of them traversed the network of corridors and passages, and eventually they found their way back to the vast oval shaped hall, where the skeletal remains still hung silently. "If only we had means to take more of these armours and weapons," Imrand said regretfully as he looked around the hall. "What powers and secrets do they have?"

"We have gifts enough, husband," Sarkisi said. "I do not ever wish to return here. Avert your eyes and do not desire what you cannot take."

Imrand nodded reluctantly. "I do not know the way beyond here," he said to Janorra, "for we have not been past here before."

"Then follow me," Janorra said, "for I *have* been this way before." They left the place quickly and ascended the corridors, tunnels and stairways. All other exits were blocked, and only one way available to them, so they quickly found the portal, which shimmered and turned red in colour, through which, they could now see the outside world. Janorra saw her other traveling companions. She, Imrand and Sarkisi stepped through the portal and were back in the world of Pangaea, in the same rune-cave, from where she had been taken against her will into Garama Aethoros.

*        *        *

A chaotic scene met Janorra and her companions as they rushed into the Chamber of Resurrection. Sezareal, her eyes and face still a blank, was seated behind Gilly on Gaffren, who was bleating hysterically, and trying to buck them. It took every effort of Gilly's to calm him. Bessie had clambered onto the neck of the goat and was holding on as tightly as an infant would its mother. She looked terrified, and clenched her eyes shut. Scarand readied his bow, Muro raised his palms and the runes in them began to glow.

Armun stared at Janorra with bemusement, and pointed his staff at her, clearly not recognising her in her new attire of Yimsha's armour.

"It's me, Janorra," she shouted, "and these are Imrand and Sarkisi, who assisted me."

Armun hesitated, and furrowed his brow trying to study her face. Finally, he recognised her and sighed as a momentary look of relief spread across his face.

Imrand and Sarkisi had dropped their sacks of treasure, spilling some of the contents on the ground, and squared up to Muro and Scarand, who were staring curiously at them after Janorra announced them. Finally, they recognised their features beneath the armour that moulded to them so perfectly.

"What ails between us, will wait," Muro said to Imrand as he lowered his palms, and Scarand his bow. "There is a more immediate foe to fight."

Imrand snarled indignantly and gave a dismissive snort, but he and Sarkisi also lowered their weapons.

Janorra watched, in stunned silence along with the others, as the broken Obelisk that Migdal had been chained too slowly appeared. When it had fully materialised, it opened its eyes. It looked lost and bewildered. It said nothing, but let out a long painful moan, and then became briefly alert, and asked in a tired voice, "What is my name? I cannot recall it." It then drifted back to a sleeplike state.

Looking through the open door to the rune-cave, they then noticed the Wisdom Tree, formerly withered, had already began to come back to life and blossom and bloom, but there was no time for Janorra to take in the sight and marvel, for a reddish smoke filled the air.

Armun stared in amazement at Imrand and Sarkisi, who were now trying to gather up the spilled treasure back into their sacks. "My eyes have not seen armour such as that, in many an age," he said suspiciously, and then rebuked them, "leave that, we fight for our lives."

Imrand ignored him, and continued as before, aided by his wife.

"Fools," Armun muttered.

Of a sudden, the whole fortress shook, and the runes turned a blackish-purple, and then all manner of colours, as the door to the chamber glowed red.

"The Wild Hunt is outside," Armun said to Janorra, sweat beading on his forehead, as he pointed his staff at the door and the runes, muttered something and repeated the process pointing his staff at the runes. Both times white energy shot from it, and turned them back to their original colour. He lent on his staff and looked ever so weary. "They appeared shortly after the portal turned red. This place was built to keep foes out. We

679

locked all the doors that lead to this chamber and the cave, and I bound them with powerful charms months ago, so that only we could enter and leave for food and water, but I do not know how much longer I can contain them. There is one with them, whose power matches or even surpasses my own."

*Months? It seems like mere hours to me since I entered Garama Aethoros.* There was no time for Janorra to ponder. She took a moment to absorb more details of the surroundings. The workbenches from the mage's workshop, the desks, tables, heavy tomes, numerous scrolls and other items had all been brought into the cave.

"Did you learn anything from them?" she asked looking at Armun and then Muro.

"We found another way out of here, by the knowledge we gained," Muro growled. "But we had to lock it, using arcane arts. It will take time to unlock."

The fortress shook again, with the same result to the iron-bound door and runes as before, only this time the door momentarily bent inwards, and appeared as though it would splinter apart. Armun waved his staff which cracked and arced with power, shooting fresh bolts of lightning into the rules which glistened with the energy sent into them, and the iron-bound door corrected itself.

Armun trembled slightly. "Do you have it? Do you have the Simal?"

"Yes," she replied, as she walked up to Gaffren, pointed her ring and muttered something to him. Of a sudden, he became calm.

"Thank you, me dear," Gilly said, trying to catch her breath. Bessie opened one eye, a look of terror in it.

Taking it from her knapsack, Janorra held the Simal before Sezareal's blank face. "Give her back her mind," she said to it. A faint light issued from it, and sanity was slowly restored to her. Her eyes returned to their original colour.

"I have seen things, that will forever haunt me," Sezareal said.

"You will soon see them through the eyes of this lesser reality," Janorra replied, "and as a dream, the memories will fade, for higher knowledge does not last long here."

Sezareal looked at Janorra as though suddenly recognising her, and absolute hatred formed in her eyes. "You were going to give me to that…that thing. My sister, Jezareal, she is still in that wicked temple." Her face contorted with hate. "A curse on you Janorra the Seeress, a curse!" she screamed.

The Obelisk opened its eyes and squinted as one looking at the light after a long time in the darkness. It stared at Janorra, blinked its eyes, and then spoke in a voice so loud, it drowned out any response she was going to give to Sezareal. "I have been returned to the Everglow, I am Morothrarn, an Arnath." A joyous realisation dawned upon it as it remembered who it was. The Obelisk then asked, "Does King Tharmacay still rule in…erm…where was his throne now? Hmmm…such an empire the world had never seen. It will last until the last day of the Final Age such is its power and stretch."

Janorra fought back the surge of regret and the emotions that Sezareal's words created in her. "I have never heard of him," she answered respectfully to Morothrarn. *It would not be good to offend him, lest I need his assistance.*

"Who are you?" the Obelisk asked her.

"I am Janorra," she replied, "I am a Child of the Arnath, an Akkadian."

"Hmm, Janorra…Janorra…Child of the Arnath…why are these words familiar to me?" the Obelisk asked itself. Of a sudden, a deranged look of insanity slowly crossed the Obelisk's face and it said, "Oh yes, before I forget, I have a message for you." It paused but a moment and then shouted, "Run Janorra! Run!"

# Chapter Fifty-Nine: *Borach and Malagrim*

*Temmison wrote a history on the Giant Halls, but as with most of his work it is probably more legend than accurate history, and not as reliable as more critical works by those with far greater academic qualifications than he. Can I request it is removed from this renowned library, whose famous and well won reputation is sorely sullied by having such a gross work of fiction pretending to be history among its shelves?*

**A fragment of text found in the Kappian Library - Source believed to be Edegal.**

*Borach* and his two dwarf commanders stared at the sight before them, as the first of men might have stared in some primordial dawn. He shook his head. His chest heaved and glistened with sweat. The morning sunrise, partially dimmed by mist, revealed that Lake Gargos, above which they had camped, was filled with hundreds of ships and barges, the size of which he had never seen the like before. The barges were not built for war, but merely for transportation, but they were guarded by equally large war galleys, bristling with oars powered by Davari slaves who rowed to the steady beat of a drum, as the galleys practiced manoeuvres across the lake.

Lake Gargos stretched far southwards, where it eventually became a part of the River Erin. To the east of the lake, was the desert the legion had recently crossed. To the west, was a great forest that stretched as far as the eye could see.

"I never thought I would set eyes on the Everdark Forest," Marki remarked, after which he plunged his head in a trough of water, spreading drops everywhere as he re-emerged and shook it. "My folk used to talk in lowered tones about that place. They say you can walk from one end to the other, and never see a glint of daylight, so dense is the foliage. I'm just glad our business won't be taking us there."

Borach turned his head and nodded behind him. Marki whistled as he followed his gaze and took in the sight. Beyond the human part of the city, whose buildings were large enough, the great constructions of the Giant Halls reared their hulking structures against the morning sky. The Halls were on an island of rock surrounded by a large chasm only crossed by a singular bridge. They rose high into the sky, so high that they ascended into cloud and mist. The night before had hidden their full scale, but now, in the light of the new dawn, they looked indescribably menacing.

"I once thought this place was only legend," Galin said. "Until of late, I'd never met any who had actually laid eyes on it, and neither did I expect to do so myself."

Borach gritted his teeth; he was in no mood for idle chatter. "Any word from Meron and those who went to Thurog Tor?"

"None," Galin said. "Perhaps he will know?" Chasotha joined them near the edge of the plateau. He grinned widely. "A wyvern rider arrived this morning. The people of Thurog Tor surrendered and accepted the plan proposed. Davino will be king and Maraya will be wife to him when he is old enough. The city is now preparing for the Bantu threat." He then pointed towards some of the barges that were being rowed by Gragor towards the harbour walls that stretched out beneath the plateau. "The barbarian army is embarking, and your legion will also embark today, we cannot waste time before we go south and lay siege to Castle Greytears; but you must first select twenty of your men to accompany you on the quest to the Wytchwood."

"Only twenty?" Borach asked, looking at him questioningly. "If we come across the Wild Hunt, it will be a tough battle."

The wild looking Chatti stroked his red facial hair thoughtfully and said, "Last night I spoke with the Lord of the Giant Halls. King Malagrim will speak to you now."

Galin went to attend to his duties, and Borach and Marki followed Chasotha through the city. Unlike the quiet and lifelessness of the evening before, it was now full of life, with people from dozens of nations about the streets, but still there was something sinister and dark about it. A group of large Cinoan Reavers stood outside of a tavern from which the stale smell of wine and rank sweaty bodies drifted on the breeze, and the snatches of obscene songs could be heard coming from within. The reavers silently watched Borach and Marki, with dark angry eyes, as they passed. They looked dangerous. Each had great broadswords strapped to their bulky frames.

Marki watched the men carefully from the corner of his eye. "You let those untrustworthy Cinoan gutter rats openly wear steel on these streets whilst they drink?" he asked Chasotha. "We once waged war with Cinoa, the men are without honour or principle."

Chasotha grunted. "Many Mercenaries have gathered here; they will travel with us to war. We have a curfew at night. As long as they cause no trouble in the day, we let them carouse and see no reason to disarm them. It may be the last time they ever get to have such a day."

Borach noticed Marki scowl at the Cinoans as they walked by. They scowled back with equal dislike. One of them, looked directly at Chasotha and growled, "I don't savour the prospect of fighting alongside untrustworthy Dwarves and their Kappian masters. Their honour and word are worth nothing."

"By Balagrim's beard," Marki hissed, exasperated and annoyed. "I'll silence that arrogant mouth." He reached for *Old Trusty*, but Chasotha held up a hand to stop him.

The Cinoan threw down his tankard of ale and approached. "I am Malchus, a captain from the Reaver Halls of Cinoa, a warrior who fought alongside Aram Bakash," he said, puffing his chest proudly out. "Do not think those from the Halls have completely forgotten the crimes of the legions." He scowled with barely suppressed rage.

"Aram Bakash is allied with us the war against the Bruthon," Chasotha replied aggressively to Malchus. "If you accept his coin, you will accept our allies as your own, as does he."

Malchus did not reply. With a final contemptuous look at Marki and Borach, he spat on the floor, and turned back to his companions, making some remark only they could hear, which they raucously laughed at.

Borach and Marki followed Chasotha, the dwarf still muttering threateningly about Cinoans as they continued on their way. The crooked, paved streets of the city were covered with heaps of refuse and puddles. A variety of different people were strolling along the pavements going in and out of the shops and stalls, which were wide open and displaying their variety of wares. A strange restlessness still ran through the place. The people, those who were clearly the everyday citizens, were clearly wary and cautious of the many armed men moving about the city and walking their streets in large groups.

Once again, Borach felt the place overpowering and oppressive. A band of rascals, mostly children, followed them, dressed only in every stage of rags and tatters. Some drunken soldiers, men, swaggered along the road, arm in arm with strident women clad in tawdry finery who bawled with shrill laughter. On the pavement, a Seesnari wench sat laughing on the knee of a fat and gross tawny-haired Zenobian, who thrust his face into a huge tankard of frothing ale in between his bawdy jests and boasts.

Borach was glad when they left that quarter of the city, but his pleasure was short-lived and disappeared when they entered onto a broad path that was empty of people and shaded by massive sinister walls on both sides. He had the feeling they were being watched, but he could not tell from where. They followed the path and soon came to a spectacular bridge that spanned a large chasm in the ground. The bridge was carved in the shape of a six-winged Seraph that stretched its arms over the chasm, with its body descending into it. The head was turned to one of the arms so as you approached the centre, you passed through the mouth which was a gateway to the other side of the bridge, and large enough for a Gragor to pass through. The facial features on the head were corroded by thousands of years of wind and dust storm and were half erased. The eyes were large jewels that were chipped and covered in dirt, but in places still sparkled in the sunlight.

Marki's eyes widened at the sight of such a marvellous structure. "Despite its age and weathering, I can tell that whoever made this, were incredible masons," he said as he admired the workmanship. "I thought only Dwarves could build a bridge such as this."

"It was built long ago," Chasotha said, "during the time of the Titans."

Marki chuckled, but said nothing.

The words evoked a vague memory in Borach. It stirred somewhere in his brain – a memory of when over a dying fire in his hall, whilst deep in his cups of wine, Yianna had once read to him Temmison's account of his visit to the Giant Halls. He had told a tale of a terrifying Titan who dwelt in the place. His work had since been discredited by many historians, following suit of Temmison's contemporary Edegal, but in that moment, the thought grew inside of Borach – could it be true? Until then, he had assumed Malagrim was just another Gragor. *Could he in truth be an actual Titan?*

Before he could question Chasotha, they reached the centre of the bridge, and saw horrific creatures sitting in the shadows of the mouth of the statue's head. They had flaming yellow eyes that sat beneath low protruding brows. Their heads were peaked and their mouths were filled with long and sharp yellow fangs that dripped saliva as they snarled with primitive fury at the approaching trio. The creatures stank with a bestial reek. They were covered from head to toe in dense dirty hair, their bodies heavy with iron muscles that showed sheer brute strength.

"By Balagrim's beard," Marki said as he instinctively reached for his axe.

Chasotha stopped him. "These are the reason there is a curfew. Their kind has been in this city as long as memory recalls. They are allowed to hunt any who travel the streets at night. He then pointed to some battered Cinoan armour pieces lying nearby. "Despite our warnings, there are still those who break the curfew. It seems they found a feast last night."

Before Borach could say anything, a young woman stepped out of the shadows. She was wildly beautiful and dressed in a doeskin loin clout and jewelled moccasins. Her shimmering black hair was as dark as night and bound back by a jewel encrusted gold band, curiously wrought in a design that resembled the muscular frame of the beasts that surrounded her.

"These are Moravey," she said, her voice sweet and innocent, but laced with a heavy accent. "They dwell deep in the Everdark Forest, as do my people. Long ago, we learnt to tame them, and since Lord Malagrim allowed my kind to come here, their kind has served as guardians of the Giant Halls protecting its treasures from those who would steal them."

"I trust you know what you're doing lass," Marki said, "but if I were you, I'd still watch my back around beasties that look as ferocious as that, or you might not live a long life."

683

The woman giggled merrily. "I am older than you, dwarf," she replied, "and more knowledgeable about Moravey than you clearly are."

Borach studied the young woman's face and could not see the mark of an Akkadian. "You are Pure-blood?" he asked her.

The woman again laughed merrily. "I am not, I am Ascenti. Pure-bloods are not the only ones gifted with long years within the Everglow, but I only have one death and one life, so I must make sure I only devote it to a worthy cause."

She looked Borach and Marki up and down, and then asked Chasotha, "You bring an Akkadian and a dwarf to the halls of King Malagrim?

Chasotha bowed his head respectfully to the woman. "I sent message ahead, they are expected."

"Indeed, they are. Chasotha you will return to make preparations with the army; you two will follow me."

The girl turned and headed through the Seraphim's mouth, as Chasotha headed back the way he had come. A chill went down Borach's spine as he and Marki walked past the beasts and followed the girl, and both gripped the hilt of their weapons. Although the Moravey snarled, bared their fangs and stared wildly as they passed them, to Borach's relief, the beasts did not follow.

"By all the Maidens, what other babbling reeling-ripe varlets will we meet in here?" Marki mumbled to himself as they reached the end of the bridge and passed under a high vaulted arch to a broad marble stairway that led into an enormous domed citadel. "Will you not tell us your name lass," he asked the woman.

She briefly turned her head, smiled, and carried on through the citadel without answering him, and silently led the way up another set of marble stairs, and through two massive bronze doors which were opened and closed by unseen hands as they passed.

They walked up countless flights of stairs, and along numerous corridors, all big enough for Gragor to walk through. The size of the place was intimidating, and Borach had never felt so small. Neither the stone walls nor the marble floors they traversed had any decorations whatsoever. The monotony of the arduous walk, ever heading upwards, was only broken by high windows in the walls which gave fantastic views of the city and the Everdark Forest, both of which were soon hidden from view by the mist of the clouds. They ascended higher and then eventually even the clouds were beneath them when they looked out of the windows. Finally, they came to an enormous passageway, at the end of which were two gigantic golden doors, eloquently carved.

"Sit here," the girl said as they approached the doors, pointing to a long stone bench seated with a velvet cushion. When Borach and Marki were sat, she took a gong and banged a large symbol. The noise echoed throughout the passageway and was so loud, both Borach and Marki covered their ears.

With the noise still ringing in their ears, the girl joined them on the seat and said, "My name is Bonnie. I have never met an Akkadian or a dwarf before." She looked in turn at Borach and Marki, studying them both with an innocent curiosity. "You look like a sensible man," she said to Borach, and then to Marki, "Malagrim does not like Dwarves, even less will he like an opinionated one. I do not know the reason for his dislike, but you should wait to be spoken too, and then cautious in your response if he does choose to address you."

Marki growled fiercely, "I have not yet decided if I like Malagrim, so the same caution should apply to him when he addresses me. I'll not be starting any trouble, so your Malagrim would be wise not to be the cause of any either." Marki tapped *Old Trusty*. "After your words, I'll not be leaving my friend outside if that is the price of entry. I have chosen the iron life and that is my battle call. I'll not stand before this oversized Gragor unarmed if he is looking to pick a fight with me."

Bonnie did not appear to take offence. She smiled merrily and replied, "Silly dwarf, Malagrim cannot be killed by mere mortal weapons, forged without runes of power, and no Titan can. Your axe would only tickle or scratch him."

If the situation had not been so serious, even Borach might have smiled at the befuddled look on Marki's face. He admired the raw courage and tenacity of his dear friend, but by the sounds of it, who they were about to meet, was no ordinary Gragor. *Can it really be true, that Malagrim is a Titan?*

The three of them waited outside for more than an hour. During this time Bonnie explained to them that it was rare to have so many strangers in the city. Usually, outsiders were not welcome, but war was coming. Malagrim had opened the city up, and many mercenaries had come. They would be setting out the following day to wage war with Bruthon. Eventually, with hardly a sound, the golden doors glided open. A man dressed from head to toe in coloured exotic bird plumes, set on a harness of leather and copper, emerged. He danced with fantastic bounds and prancing and whirled around.

"Great Balagrim, now we have a foolish savage dancing around meaninglessly," Marki whispered to Borach under his breath.

The man stopped in front of them as suddenly as he emerged and stood there frozen with statuesque stillness. The plumes rippled once and settled about him. From amidst the plumes, a scarred and weathered face, very old, peered out. "King Malagrim awaits you," he said with a lisp, and turning, he leaped and cavorted back into the hall.

Bonnie stood from the seat and led them through the doors into a hall so long, it was the length of several bow shots. Neither Borach nor Marki had seen the like before. They both let out an involuntary gasp of awe at the sight before them. Sparsely hung lanterns that hung from the rafters gave a moody, smoky light but revealed a magnificent setting. The hall was filled with golden statutory, each figure several times the size of a large Gragor and reaching up into a domed ceiling. Fierce expressions were on their faces, and their sightless eyes gazed down the hall towards a red coloured throne at the far end of the hall, upon which sat a giant figure that looked like a statue.

The floor was made of highly polished black marble interlaced with white marble and traceries of gold. As they passed the statues, Borach noticed names chiselled in runes and letters unknown to him beneath each set of feet. Loneliness suddenly flowered within him. The surroundings were so foreign - it struck him just how far from home he was. A destroyed home, but still a place his heart ached for.

The ceiling of the hall was so high, neither Borach nor Marki could see the designs upon it, but they did notice the jewel hanging from the middle of the vaulted dome. Held by great golden chains, was a gigantic diamond as big as a man-sized house. It was not the only marvel. Around the hall, heaped in staggering excess, piles of jewels of every kind sat upon beds of golden coins. There were piles of diamonds, rubies, emeralds, sapphires, opals and every other type of jewel. Chests overflowing with necklaces, bracelets, and jewellery of every kind sparkled. The wealth was staggering.

Above them, mounted upon the walls, were gigantic gem-crusted harnesses and armour pieces that could very well have once been worn by ancient Titans of the old world. Silver-scaled corselets, golden helms with rich plumes, massive jewel-hilted swords in cloth-of-gold sheaths and virtually every other type of richly embellished weapon, were fixed alongside them. On tables made of silver, goblets, plates and jugs carved from single jewels glittered in the light of the few lanterns around the hall.

Despite the dimness of the hall, the light sparkling off of the many treasures was so dazzling, Borach and Marki had to initially shield their eyes, and when they uncovered them, they did not know where to look first, as they followed Bonnie and the dancing savage through the hall. Borach and Marki strode solemnly and cautiously between more than sixty statues. As they drew nearer, their eye was drawn completely to the figure on the throne, and the throne itself. The figure seated on the throne, was three times the size of a normal Gragor, and sat as still as a statue. The throne itself was carved from a single ruby. It was blocky, unadorned and cut with unyielding precision and skill.

The figure on the ruby throne remained motionless, staring at the diamond in the ceiling, as though mesmerized by it. He paid no heed as Bonnie, and the plumed man who was still leaping and dancing, led Borach and Marki down the hall towards him.

"Is that a statue?" Marki asked Borach in a hushed whisper.

Borach amicably shrugged his shoulders, he himself was not sure.

Bonnie and the plumed savage prostrated themselves on the floor before the figure, and then respectfully stood up.

"My lord," Bonnie said. "I present to you Lord Borach, and Commander Marki of the Third Kappian Legion."

Malagrim did not move at all. He sat still and motionless, staring at the massive diamond hanging from the ceiling. Then he blinked, and his face darkened as he slowly moved his head to look at the two visitors. Strong features shadowed his chiselled, clean-shaven face. He had a grim, ancient and intelligent look in his eyes. A nine-pointed crown lined with nine rubies rested on his head, the hair of which was grey and fell to his shoulders. Over his powerful chest, flowing from his shoulders to his elbows and from his thighs down to his knees, he wore a white shirt of mail. Pure, raw strength emanated from him.

Malagrim silently stared at Borach and Marki for a long while. Out of respect, they stood with their heads slightly bowed, and did not return their initial stare at him, any longer than was polite. When Malagrim finally spoke, his voice was calm, but strong and booming, and deadly serious. "I don't like Dwarves," he said.

Borach glanced at Marki; he could tell the remark made his friend boil over with fury and annoyance. His chest swelled, and, making sure he was stretched to his full height, Marki fixed his gaze on Malagrim and replied, "Then I am not too keen on Titans, if they cannot show basic courtesy to a guest who has been invited into their halls."

Malagrim stared impassionedly at Marki for a long while. Borach took the opportunity to study Malagrim more closely. He was bare-footed, had the body of a man, but the tail of a lizard, and was ferocious to behold. Even so, Borach noticed that Marki still returned the stare. The Titan and the dwarf examined each other silently, neither of them blinking. Malagrim's face did not change when, eventually he said, "But I do admire their courage."

Borach sighed with silent relief as the tension lessened. But then to the left, he heard a plea for help. Turning his head, he saw a dark-skinned man, a Zinoban, who was bound and being led by ten females, all similar in appearance to Bonnie, apart from they were naked from the waist up.

"Help me, please," the man begged faintly, looking at Borach and Marki with a pleading look. He was hardly able to get the words out due to his terror, evident on his every feature and in his wide eyes. The women stripped him naked and used silk ropes to peg him out on the floor between four golden posts.

Bonnie looked at the man, and said to Borach, "When they enter the city, the mercenaries are warned not to try and steal the treasures of King Malagrim. Most of them do not get very far, but he and three of his companions, scaled the outer wall to a height even above the clouds. Quite an impressive feat really."

Borach noticed that the man's body was covered in bite marks and the slashes of claws, evidently the work of the Moravey.

"The Moravey do not initially kill or eat those who try to break into the halls themselves," Bonnie said, clearly anticipating the unspoken questions Borach had. "A special punishment is reserved for them. His comrades have already been punished."

From out of a dark shadow, Shagor appeared. She carried a bag that was filled with large golden rocks.

"Balagrim be praised, at least she is not naked to the waist," Marki whispered to Borach. Borach nudged his friend, urging silence.

The man began to whimper, then to shriek and scream. One of the women gagged him with a silk cloth. The women then began to circle him. The man writhed and strained against his bonds but could not break them. The plumed shaman leaped over towards the man, and taking out a knife from his belt, he raised it to the heavens, and began shouting prayers and ululations, before carving a rune, into his chest.

Shagor took out the first rock of gold, and hefted it down onto the man's left leg, smashing and mangling it. She then took another, and crushed his right leg, and then with further rocks of gold, his arms, and then finally, his ribcage. Four Moravey then emerged from the shadows and tearing off the man's bonds and lifting off the rocks of gold, they dragged him off, still alive, into the shadows.

"Now, they can eat," Bonnie said. "The rune will keep him alive, until the heart is eaten, and that is saved for last. It is a particularly nasty death, but a deserved one for those who try to steal from King Malagrim's halls."

Marki whistled in shock and amazement. "Well, we are honest men lass," he said.

Borach turned his attention back to Malagrim, who had not watched the grim spectacle; his gaze was again fixed on the diamond hanging from the ceiling.

"My Lord Malagrim is tired," Bonnie said. "I am instructed to tell you, that you are to find the Simal. A sage by the name of Armun, one of the Tarath Guëan, has been sent to aid a Seeress named Janorra. She stole the Simal, and is seeking to take it to the Baothein. Armun plans to assist her in her quest. They wish to take the Simal to the Baothein, but, my Lord Malagrim desires it. You are to capture her, and bring her along with the Simal to Lord Malagrim."

"The Baothein?" Marki growled. "The Tarath Guëan usually remain neutral in the affairs of this world. Why would Armun involve himself in a matter such as this?"

Bonnie seemed indifferent to the question. "It is not our concern. The Simal must be brought here."

"What news do you have of the woman named Janorra," Borach asked.

"She has the Simal and is inside Garama Aethoros. We see through the eyes of the *Arvivan*, Bessie. They wait outside for her to emerge, but were losing hope, for she has been inside that place for longer than expected, but the colour of the portal has changed. This means she will be emerging soon. This is good for us. The timing is well and we are ready with our plans.

"We do not wish to make an enemy of the Tarath Guëan," Borach said.

"I will deal with Armun," Bonnie replied. "For I know that such a task is beyond your abilities."

"What will Malagrim do with the Simal?" Borach asked.

"He will keep it as a treasure, and spend his days looking into it to gain knowledge." Bonnie shrugged her shoulders. "What will you do to the woman named Janorra?" she

687

asked innocently, tilting her head with curiosity. "Chasotha said you feel she has wronged you?"

"I do not know," he answered. "If she had not stolen the Simal, it would not have set up a chain of events that led to the death of my family. She is partly responsible for their fate."

"It seems a lot of people want to find this woman, Janorra," Marki observed.

Borach gave a further explanation. "A Seeress who travels with us, told me that one named Horin, who dwells in the Deadlands, sent me a message through her, that I was to help her take the Simal to the Baothein. But if you want it here, it makes no difference to me, as long as Kappia is denied getting a hold of it."

Bonnie looked nervously at Malagrim, and then back at Borach. "Do not mention the name Horin in front of Lord Malagrim again," she urged him quietly.

Borach noticed a slow angry frown starting to spread across the features of Malagrim. He began to clench his fists, grit his teeth, as he slowly turned his head to look at them. The frown started to transform into a look of sheer rage, as his features contorted, expressing a primal fury that gave him a savage and terrifying look.

"Come, perhaps we should continue this conversation elsewhere," Bonnie suggested, as she looked with concern at Malagrim. She quickly turned and made for the exit to the hall, urgently signalling for Borach and Marki to follow, which they did without protest.

The three of them exited the hall the same way they had entered, and Bonnie led them through some different passageways, down numerous stairways, until they came upon an outside balcony that overlooked the city and the Everdark Forest. She invited them to sit on one of the benches around a table, and then wasted no time in addressing the matter of the Simal.

"The Baothein wish to possess the Simal, so that they can summon the Aeldar back to this world to slay them with an Arkoom," she said. "It is a good motive, but the Simal will not be safe with them. There is no guarantee they will survive the war that is even now gathering at their borders."

"We are no friends of the Baothein," Marki said. "We have no desire to get involved in some dispute over a religious relic. Especially not a dispute with the Tarath Guëan."

"Armun is alone; he has been banished from the Tarath Guëan for his part in this matter," Bonnie replied. "I am Ascenti. My kin and I can deal with him, but we cannot contend with the Wild Hunt who pursue the Seeress, as there are only twenty of us Ascenti left in this world – we cannot fight a Wild Hunt."

"There are only twenty of you left?" Borach asked, somewhat sympathetically.

Bonnie glanced briefly at the forest. "There are many strange creatures in a place such as that," she said somewhat skittishly. "It is why the last of us left our ancestral home and sought sanctuary here in the Giant Halls."

"Surely the Gragor and Chatti can deal with the Wild Hunt?" Marki enquired.

"They cannot enter the Wytchwood, it will be death for them," Bonnie responded. "There are ancient curses on that place, and there is an ancient enmity between the Wytchwood and the races of Gragor and Chatti."

"What makes you think those curses won't affect us?" Borach asked.

"Because it has allowed the woman Janorra to walk there, and it seems to help her. If we go there with you to assist her, we will remain unharmed by the Wytchwood itself. I sent one of my people, a forest-whisperer, to speak to it and ask permission to enter."

Marki chortled. "Talking forests? Has the world gone mad?" He stopped laughing when Bonnie looked at him gravely.

"Do not presume you understand the true nature of all life in this world," she said.

"Have you yet heard back from this forest-whisperer?" Borach asked.

"Yes," Bonnie replied immediately. "We may enter, but only a few of us."

"How many?" Borach asked.

"Twenty of us Ascenti, and twenty from your legion. The forest will not allow any more than that to enter."

"Twenty skinny young lasses and twenty of our men to fight a Wild Hunt?" Marki shook his head. "We are no cowards lass, but neither are we fools."

"Marki is right," Borach remarked. "The more men we can take, the better."

"We Ascenti only have twenty royal-wyverns, enough to carry us and one of your men each as a passenger. Besides, we had to gain permission from a Threadweaver. There is a special liquid she gave us that we must drink, and even with a small sip each, there is only enough for around forty or so."

"What liquid?" Borach asked suspiciously, and then added, "And what is a Threadweaver?".

"Do not concern yourself with what the liquid is," Bonnie said somewhat evasively. "It is not poisonous, but it will protect us from a creature that lurks there. The Threadweaver is merely an inhabitant that dwells and protects that part of the forest."

"But she cannot protect this Seeress from the Wild Hunt though," Marki remarked somewhat sarcastically.

"No, she chooses not to involve herself in this matter, any more than she has done so already," Bonnie replied.

Borach stroked his chin thoughtfully, and then said, "This is fraught with risk. The Wild Hunt are ferocious warriors."

"It is a rescue mission, and need not be a full-scale battle," Bonnie suggested. "But we need to move fast. The Threadweaver told us the Wild Hunt is very close to finding a way out of the Underglow. They will find the Seeress, capture her and the Simal, and return it to Mazdek who is now the Kappian Emperor. It is the agreement he made with the Bantu."

Although they had heard this news before, her words still shocked both Borach and Marki in equal measure. "The Empire I once served and love, has allied itself with our bitterest enemy," Borach said. "I cannot find the words to express the betrayal I feel. Maybe you had better tell us everything you know. If our taking the Simal strikes a blow at Mazdek and frustrates his plans, we will willingly be involved."

For the next hour, Bonnie told them all the news that had been learnt through *Arvivan* spies. Borach and Marki sat and silently listened, only interrupting to ask for more details or information regarding a specific event. They looked at each other with dismay when Bonnie had finished.

A thought flashed through Borach's mind. *If Shaka and her brood have escaped to Kara Duram, and the legions have remained loyal to her, they clearly do not know that she was the one who betrayed me and handed Aleskian over to the Bantu.* He looked at Marki, and by his friend's knowing look, the same thought had also occurred to him.

"One day, we will make sure everyone at Kara Duram knows what Shaka ordered to be done there," Marki growled.

"I cannot say I feel any pity for the Empress Shaka," Borach said with barely concealed anger, "for the deeds of her lawless family ended up at my door." He briefly buried his hands in his face, and then looked up. "Until recently, the talk of the Aeldar and this Simal, was only the topic of rumours, and the people of Aleskian paid little heed to them, even when the Aeldar priests preached their long sermons." He sighed. "If the Simal is as truly powerful as you say, why is it wisdom to allow Malagrim to possess it. A foul mood crossed his soul when we even said a name that angered him."

"He knew Horin from ancient times," Bonnie said, "a tale not immediately relevant to our current concern."

"But who should own the Simal is relevant," Borach remarked.

"Bonnie paused briefly, before speaking. "The Tarath Guëan, once dwelt in the White Towers of Baothein. It might be they wish to dwell there again instead of in a wilderness hovel. The Simal would make them very powerful. I fear that they have sent Armun on a secret task, and their banishment of him is only a pretence so they do not alienate political powers that otherwise leaves them alone. We cannot take the chance of the Simal falling into the hands of an allied Baothein and Tarath Guëan."

"We are no friends of the Baothein," Marki said, "and I would not desire to help them in any matter. But, surely bringing the Simal to a place of safety must override any other concerns or squabbles at this time? And to do that, would be best served by actually getting hold of the blasted thing before starting fights with the likes of Armun and possibly the Tarath Guëan, would it not?"

Borach shared Marki's disquiet. "Long have I known Armun. He is a sage of no small consequence, and I have considered him acquaintance in the past. Do you expect us to make an enemy of him, just because it is demanded, and without us even being consulted on the matter?"

"Those with power do not have to include you in their deliberations," Bonnie answered.

"Then they will have to start doing so," Borach said indignantly.

Bonnie nodded gravely. "You cannot escape the politics of your situation. The Everglow will soon become a crucible of war. An age of reckoning is upon us. Refusing any union or alliance will weaken us all, but recalling the Aeldar even if to slay them, is an act of folly. Who knows what powers they have obtained in the Void? Lord Malagrim knew them of old, and if he states it is wiser to leave them where they are, then the Simal is safer in his hands."

Borach felt troubled, and looked at her seriously, whilst Marki snorted with derision and said, "I no longer care for the fate of the Simal. The Empire betrayed us and lost it; I don't care who gets it now, as long as they don't. Let Armun or Malagrim have it, let's just find it!"

Bonnie studied them, and then said, "You need us, and in this, we need you. You retain your freedom and can walk away any time you wish to do so, even right now; but first consider this - your actions will have impact far beyond what you intend."

"I do not trust the Baothein," Borach said grimly, "but never have I been keen on this *Aeldar Faith*. If Armun wants them to have it and they want it to slay them, I would hear his thoughts before deciding."

Bonnie spoke softly. "There is little time left to deliberate. The Seeress will soon leave Garama Aethoros. The Wild Hunt seeks her and will take it unless we are swift, or, Armun will have it and take it to the Baothein. If you do not assist us, we will offer you no further help. You have to decide your course, and you have to choose now, who you will side with. Malagrim or Armun?"

*It may be that I may have to reconsider many a great thing in the days ahead.* Borach thought as he remembered the words Talain had relayed to him from Horin, and the vision he had seen of Janorra in the Wytchwood. If she was responsible for setting into motion the events that led to the *Final-death* of his wife and the fall of Aleskian, then he wanted justice.

"It seems events are shaping our destiny, my old friend," he said to Marki, and then to Bonnie. "I will help you get the Simal, but, as already agreed, the Seeress Janorra is mine to deal with as I see fit. Those are my only terms."

"What?" Marki protested indignantly. "Bor, we cannot make an enemy of Armun over this, especially before hearing him on the matter. He will not take it lightly."

"Your honour is noble," Borach said to him, "but our current path is clear. We must help Bonnie get the Simal, and in so doing, see what paths then open up. We will deal with the challenges faced when we walk them."

"I don't remember us signing up for this Bor," Marki said under his breath.

"I'll not order any of my men to come with me to the Wytchwood, including you. Any who wish to follow me on this course of action, will need to be volunteers."

Marki sighed. "I could have easily spent my days without any regret that I had never entered a talking forest," he said, "but despite my reservations, count me in Bor. I'll go with you."

Borach smiled, and put a friendly hand on Marki's shoulder. "I never doubted that for one moment," he said warmly.

Bonnie clapped her hands and looked genuinely happy for the first time. "Good," she said. "Lord Malagrim will be pleased."

"Will he now? When we left him, a look of malicious wrath was upon his face," Marki said glumly.

"Lord Malagrim is often in a dark mood, but this decision will be pleasing to him," Bonnie said reassuringly to Marki, and then turning to Borach. "Your legion will soon head south with the main army to Greytears; when you return to your camp, gather up twenty of your fiercest warriors and wait for me. I will make swift preparations and send for you when I am ready for us to leave."

Bonnie took a small bell from the table, and rang it. One of the women who had earlier brought in the Zinoban thief arrived. She was more modestly attired, having a robe cloaked around her. "Balaria," Bonnie said to her, "escort these two back to their camp."

Borach resisted allowing his mind to turn to morbid matters as he and Marki followed Balaria back to their camp. He had an intense hatred for the Baothein and had no qualms about helping prevent them from acquiring the Simal. But, Armun had helped him on a number of occasions throughout the long years of his lives. He did not desire making an enemy of him, but if he helped Bonnie take the Simal, then that is surely what would happen. The question as to why Armun had been removed from the Tarath Guën and had become one of the *Banished* bothered him. It also troubled him, that who or what Bonnie and the surviving Ascenti were, if she was confident that she could contend with a sage as powerful as Armun, she had powers Borach had not yet witnessed, and that might yet prove to be a valid cause for concern.

# Chapter Sixty: *Velentine*

*Any Titan that survived the great purge, was levelled to a bestial plane such was the brutishness of their treatment. The few survivors that still walk the world, are now little more than savage beasts stalking among the ruins of a world now strange to them. A heavy price that race has paid, for rising to destroy their Aeldar masters. We will set out to capture one and bring it in chains to be paraded throughout Kappia; perhaps we could build an enclosure for it in the zoo or even teach it to do tricks in my circus. Yes, we will head to Grona where it is said one still lurks in deep caves beneath the mountains. Minstrels will sing ballads of my deeds in the taverns across the world, bards will tell my stories everywhere, when a living Titan I bring to Kappia. Already my legends and deeds will never be forgotten, so great am I. Just think how much more I will be celebrated when I capture the living Titan of Grona and bring it to you, here at Kappia? Yes, I will bring it back alive, or my name is not Zosoara the Great!*

*This is the only known fragment of text about the life of Zosoara the Great. It was found in the Kappian Library. A note accompanying it says thus: 'Zosoara spoke these words before he boarded a ship to set sail for Grona. Neither he, or any that set sail with him, were ever heard from again.' - Source Believed to be Edegal.*

*For* two days, strange voices and ghostly tones were heard, even on the upper deck of the *Red Tide*. Their source was the hold in which Velentine and her new companions were resting. The entire ship at times seemed to be covered with a flickering, powerful red light. Some of the terrified crew complained that they had seen misshapen silhouettes suddenly appear in parts of the ship, and skulking shapes of horror that took them to the fringe of lunacy. Azzadan knew these were not just rumours issued by frightened men; the day before he himself had seen the faint image of a man with black wings that spread out from his back like that of a crow. It looked at him, and took off into the sky, leaving behind some black feathers on the deck that Azzadan had picked up, proving it had been no mere hallucination.

"Look," he had said to Redboots, "these black feathers are no figment of a zealous imagination." She had said nothing in reply, but merely sharpened the edge of her cutlass as she murderously stared at it, rhythmically honing the blade with a whetstone.

Not for the first time, the mutterings of mutiny were being whispered among the crew. Some of them drew their weapons and slashed and thrust ferociously at sounds or movements they heard or imagined. One crew member even had the audacity to give the order to 'heave up the anchor' whilst another tried to stab Redboots in the back with a cutlass. She had heard him draw the blade from its sheath, and just in time had drawn her own weapon, turned and disarmed hm. Whether or not the man had been thrusting at an imaginary foe or attempting to kill her, she was not sure, but she had him crucified to the main mast, and the man who had given the order to heave anchor was thrown overboard, where he died in the freezing waters of the sea in a matter of seconds. Azzadan knew she would soon lose control of her crew if she did not maintain strict order enforced by brutal discipline.

Only Azzadan and Redboots had dared venture down into the hold, despite the warning of Velentine not to disturb her rest. Outside the compartment in the hold, the door seemed to flicker with a powerful red light coming from within, and shifting and changing hieroglyphics shone in the wood before vanishing. On seeing the strange happenings, Azzadan had felt it was wiser to heed the warning of Velentine, and had to stop Redboots from trying the door. She had felt incensed that there was a part of her own ship she could not go into, but fortunately for Azzadan, she had finally listened to reasoning, and had not disturbed whatever was going on behind the door.

On the third day, the ship became strangely silent, until the now dead man crucified to the mast, pulled his flesh against the nails, and ripped himself off of the mast and descended into the hold. Azzadan and Redboots tried to follow him, but the hatch into the lower decks where the hold was, were slammed shut behind the man by unseen hands, and no amount of effort by any of the crew could open it. It was obvious to them the crucified crewman was going to become one of the marked.

Azzadan paced back and forth along the deck of the *Red Tide*, as if some inner fire would not let him stand motionless. He had not weighed the consequences of tampering with matters as dark as this, and he had not considered the ambitions Velentine herself might have. He had been too caught up in his own thoughts and ambitions, from which he still could not break free.

It occurred to him that thousands of years of diabolism, and a tradition of ancient evil beyond his conception had shaped and formed Velentine. The ambition of Ishar to aid the restoration of the ancient, black, grisly kingdom of Vangalen suddenly seemed to him like a big mistake, and he was not sure he wanted any more part to play in it. He had seen it, a possible glimpse of the future in a dream. Smindy and some of the crew also reported the same dream, and when questioned whether or not she had experienced it, Redboots had given no reply.

Those who had the dream all reported that they had seen visions of Velentine waking Lord Voran, after which they made plans to enslave the world, and with a deluge of blood worked to wash away the present order to restore the past. The brutishness with which they enslaved all other races and lifeforms, was of the like that Azzadan, himself no stranger to death and cruelty, had woken with the cold sweat of foreboding. His brain had reeled when he tried to understand what he had seen in his dream. He had seen the black towers and spires of Vangalen rise, and how the bodies and blood of the peoples of the Everglow, had been used to furnish the mortar and the stones for the rebuilding of it.

"Azzadan, what have we done?" Smindy asked him, as he continued his pacing. She looked very vulnerable, standing there, dismay written all over her face. Redboots stood behind her; her face was sullen with a dark rage. She stared at him, waiting for an answer to Smindy's question.

Redboots summed up what she was thinking, what they were all thinking, when she said, "Give me an enemy whose skull I can cleave to the teeth and I'll be happy, but no matter how sharp the sword wielded by flesh and blood, it cannot kill creatures from worlds beyond."

"But this can," Azzadan remarked, as he tapped the Arkith that had been given to him by Erik Vansoth.

"Then give it to me, that I can go down and slay that foul horror in the hold," Redboots said as she reached out for the Arkith.

Azzadan stepped aside, and put his hand on the hilt, to protect the weapon from being taken, not to threaten Redboots. "No," he said, "I have sworn on a Bethratikus, and will not forsake my oath." Redboots snarled and stormed out of the cabin, followed by a more sympathetic Smindy who shrugged doubtfully before she followed.

Cold sweat gathered thick on his flesh. Icy doubts assailed Azzadan. His wild, chaotic years of serving the Order, as an assassin and a thief, had bred in him bitterness beyond common conception. He had never before been concerned if he was the cause of ruin to anybody who associated with him. That was until he had met Smindy and Redboots. Gone was the carefree smile on their faces and the adventurous bravado that had so drawn him to them. The loathing of his present position increased his bitterness to a type of madness, as Redboots slammed the cabin door shut behind her.

Azzadan knew Redboots had good reason to be in such a dire mood. Earlier that day, she had tried to contact the companion ship, the *Red Death*, but inexplicably, there was no reply to the flags, and then after a thick mist had immediately descended, the ringing of ships bells that were used to attempt to communicate from ship to ship, alerted them there was clearly a problem. She and Azzadan had taken a gig and rowed over to it, and to their horror the ship had been abandoned. Not a single member of the crew was left on board. Meals were unfinished, jugs of ale and wine only sipped or half-drunk. The gigs and launches were still on board; the crew would die if they had tried to swim in the freezing waters. They had clearly left in a rush, but they had not used the boats to do so, so how had they left? It did not make any sense, and where could they go? The only place they could go would be the barren island, but Redboots had scanned it with her telescope and she could see no signs of life on there. She and Azzadan had both agreed it was better not to tell the crew of the *Red Tide*, the mystery of whatever it was that had happened on the *Red Death*.

*      *      *

It was the first hour of the fourth day that Velentine appeared on the upper deck with Sassy and the two marked crewmen. Sassy and the crewmen wore expressionless black masks partially covered by the frayed hooded cloaks they wore, attire that had not been provided for them by any in the world of the living. The men stank of mould and decay. The man who had been crucified, move awkwardly, as though his flesh still struggled with his injuries, yet no moan or complaint came from him. Sassy ignored the desperate calls of Smindy to come to her, and when she tried, Smindy was unable to approach her. It was as though an invisible hand pushed her back when she attempted to do so.

"She is mine. You cannot approach unless I allow it," Velentine hissed at Smindy. She herself wore a hooded cloak, but no mask. She stood with her three companions; their outlines etched against the stars. No man could approach her without some apprehension, and Azzadan felt every nerve tingling as he walked up to Velentine. He briefly considered breaking his oath, donning the ethereal coat, drawing the Arkith and plunging it into her heart. He was convinced that with the advantage of invisibility and his speed and skill honed over many lifetimes, he could commit the deed before she could react, but the closer he got to her, the more his mind filled with monstrous doubts and a sense of his own peril mixed with wild suspicions. When he stood before her, a wave of futility washed over him. His flesh crawled with revulsion and he cursed himself for a fool that he had already talked himself out of it. *She is using some trickery against my mind.*

"I am ready to leave, to awaken Lord Voran," Velentine said to him. "You do not need to come with me."

The two marked crewmen, now Velentine's assistants, walked over to the launch, and unassisted by anyone else, they lowered it into the water.

"I have to come with you," Azzadan said, "for I have my own business within Grona, and I doubt that even you could enter it without me showing you the way."

"I'm coming too," Redboots said, her eyes hard, angry and wary as she approached Azzadan, and whispered ominously. "I want to find out what this fanged bitch has done to the crew of the *Red Death*." She spoke in a tone soft enough so the crew of the *Red Tide* still above deck would not hear.

"I'll come too, captain," Armius said, "for it is a perilous journey to Grona even from here and you might need all my skill to navigate the waters." Redboots nodded in appreciation.

"I'll come," Smindy said.

Redboots shook her head. "No! I need you here, you are to take command until I return, make sure these cringing curs do not leave without us. That is an order."

Smindy offered no dispute, but merely said, "Whatever that thing has done to Sassy, if you can, try to reverse it. Bring her back and save her."

Redboots nodded. The seven of them climbed down the ladder into the gig.

Armius steered the gig as the two marked crewmen rowed it through the icy darkness. The *Red Tide* was soon out of sight. The air seemed so cold to Azzadan; it was like breathing another element. The only noise was the gentle lapping of the water against the hull of the boat, the rhythmical clack of the oars, and the creak of the oar-locks.

Thick clouds in the sky soon obscured the stars. Azzadan strained his eyes across the black restless water, but he could not penetrate the darkness. Armius navigated using a small compass that gave a feint light on the face so the points and needle could be seen. When the clouds cleared, he used the stars to find their way.

Velentine and her companions sat in silence, hardly moving. Azzadan was concerned to notice that Redboots, who was sitting behind her, hardly took her eyes of the vampire. She fingered the hilt of her cutlass; an uneasy feeling rose in Azzadan, as it was not hard for him to guess what might be going through her mind. She set a wild and ferocious figure sitting there, her glorious hair blowing softly in the breeze, her mouth twitching involuntarily, no doubt as she imagined ways of killing Velentine. He had no doubt this bloodthirsty maiden of the seas, whose gory legends were sung in taverns wherever there was a port, would seek at some point to take her revenge for whatever it was Velentine had done to the crew of the *Red Death*.

All of those in the boat were soon chilled to the bone, their cloaks covered in snow and ice, but none of them complained. To give Armius rest and to warm his hands, Redboots and Azzadan took turns at the tiller, and then when the wind was sufficient, they raised the small sail of the gig. The two oarsmen, without being given orders, stopped rowing and brought the oars inboard.

When the morning arose, the bright sunlight did not affect Velentine in the slightest. *Another vampire myth dispelled*, Azzadan thought; he had half suspected and hoped that she might sizzle up in the sun as a twig thrown onto a fire, but she did not. By the disappointed look on Redboot's face, it was clear to him she had imagined a similar desire.

The morning sun also revealed that several triangular fins were cutting the water as they followed the boat. The one thing that pleased him about the sight was that it distracted Redboots from staring at Velentine. She briefly leaned over the side of the boat, and then stood. The sail bellied as the wind swept over the waves, and the white crests danced along the sweep of the wind. Redboots stood in the aft of the boat, planting her feet to the heave of the deck. She breathed deeply and folded her arms impatiently, as though daring the sharks to attack. Queen of the blue ocean, she was still. As though sensing her challenge, the fins disappeared beneath the water, and were not seen again.

They sailed on, throughout the rest of the day, until night fell. Such was the cold, Azzadan felt that death would soon visit him, Redboots or Armius if they continued throughout the night. Redboots made no complaint when he suggested stopping at an island they passed. They made a small fire around which the three of them huddled, whilst Velentine and her companions stood by themselves, as shadows in the darkness. After a meal of dried fish, and melted snow for drink, the humans caught some scattered sleep. Velentine and her companions disappeared into the night, only to return early the next morning. Frozen blood was smeared around Velentine's mouth.

For the next day and night, they sailed past several bleak islands. On the third day, the rising sun revealed that the character of the coastline had changed. No longer did they sail past flat and barren icy shores. Now the shore was full of cliffs, with blue hills of ice marching behind them. The cliffs soon gave way to mountains, from which streams and rivers poured into the sea. So, at last they passed the mouth of a broad river that mingled its flow with the ocean. They passed under a long and windy natural tunnel in the mountain. They rowed through the tunnel until they entered a vast stretch of sea. In the distance to the north, they saw the great black walls built into the side of the island mountain of Grona.

"Grona prison," Azzadan said in awe, as an involuntary shudder twitched his broad shoulders. It was only then, that Velentine stirred. She stood, and lowered her hood. Her piercing eyes regarded the island mountain sharply. "Where does the guardian of this prison have its lair?" she asked, as she licked her lips as though enjoying a primitive appetite for bloodlust.

"To the north side of the mountain, it is through there, that there is a secret entrance and exit to the prison. I know a way we can get in and out, without disturbing the creature." The moan of the icy wind mingled with the gentle laugh of Velentine.

Azzadan was unsure why she had laughed. "We are upwind of the island, we must make sure we stay that way, lest it get our scent."

Armius adjusted the sail, and commented, "You make it sound like it will be easy to sneak past the guardian?"

Azzadan nodded. "It is not easy, but we must try; I doubt such a beast can be slain in battle, by any means we possess."

Velentine sneered, "What a servile philosophy, to crawl on your belly and hope you are not noticed. I will not sneak past it. This creature will bow the knee to me."

"I doubt that will happen," Azzadan said meaningfully. "It is as tall as a tower; it has three eyes around its head so can see in all directions. It looks slow and cumbersome, but its appearance is not true to the fact that it is fast. The spiked-club it wields, when swung with its strength, could shatter a castle into tiny fragments of stone. We will avoid a confrontation; it is possible, I have done it before!"

Velentine stretched her jawbones in a grin that made her look grotesque. "What a puny race you are. You will see my power, and know why your kind fears the night, the darkness in which you shivered as I and my kin stalked and hunted your ancestors in times of old." She looked at the island of Grona. "All beasts and races will bow. The world will again quake in fear, at the name of Voran, and his Queen, Velentine."

Azzadan felt a fierce impatience. Doubts rarely assailed him, but as he looked at Velentine staring menacingly at Grona, and behind her, Redboots staring just as menacingly at her, an uneasy feeling washed over him once again.

*You be the fool if you must. I and my companions will use stealth.* "Then enough talk, let's be about this business," he said moodily, as he took the helm of the boat, whilst Armius adjusted the sail again, and they caught the wind that thrust them towards Grona prison.

# Chapter Sixty-One: *Bonnie*

*I tried to trade with the Children of the Molach, but was lucky to escape with my life. Deep below the Everdark Forest, they have built their dens, interconnected by a vast subterranean network. In the abandoned halls of the once proud Ascenti, I had agreed to meet a Molach Chief. As we approached the hall, I saw the Ascenti nobles, now naught but gnawed bones, in clothes reduced to rags by the winds of time. We were ambushed. Up from the ground the Molach burst. We fought for our lives, but against such numbers and implacable ferocity, we were helpless against a verminous horde. The tide of monstrous rat men flowed over us one by one, dragging my men down, into the earth, to be eaten alive. My men screamed as the yellow chiselled-teeth sunk into their soft-flesh, and the chittering, that hideous chittering the Molach made as they feasted! I fled for my life. It is my enduring shame, that one of those I left to die, was my own son, blood of my blood, and flesh of my flesh. Oh, the shame! Oh Beruz, my son, how I miss you. It was terror that controlled me that day. Forgive me!*
*A merchant's account of an attempt to trade with The Children of the Molach.*

*Dawn* was creeping into the eastern horizon, bringing a welcome respite from the coldness of the night. The peak of the cliff on which Bonnie stood upon, jutted out over the ancient city of the Giant Halls, and overlooked Lake Gargos. The waters shimmered and reflected the sky. The ships and barges that had moved upon it in a flurry of activity the day before had all but gone.

"Your men have set sail down the river with Chasotha to Castle Greytears," Bonnie said to Borach as he, Marki and Galin approached. "They will meet up with the Seesnari, and mercenaries from many nations. The Obelisk there, will soon be yours. It was a good day, for you, Lord Borach, when you made the choice to ally with King Malagrim and join your cause to ours."

Borach studied Bonnie carefully. She was dressed in a scale-mail corselet and carried a horned helmet under her arm. Her hair was shaved off except for a single lock at the back and wisps over her forehead. A large arcane staff with a blue orb was strapped across her back. Unlike the day before, when she had seemed like a simple maid, Borach thought the attire made her look like one of the ancient heroines of song and tale.

"Allies?" Marki asked. "The wyvern rider who tried to kill me near Thurog Tor, was dressed just like you lass," he said, rather indignantly. "And by Balagrim what have you done with your hair?"

"Have you Dwarves not invented wigs yet?" she asked playfully. "Is that why your own hair and beard still lack substance, since your encounter?"

Marki grunted something unintelligible and Galin chortled.

"Wig or not, I liked your hair the way it was yesterday," Marki grumbled. "That wyvern who attacked me, was it one of yours?"

Bonnie eyed him with a glint of seriousness. "That was a common-wyvern, ridden by a Chorkortos, not a royal one. You would not have survived had it been a royal one, ridden by one of my people, the Ascenti."

Marki murmured with disapproval. "Don't be so sure of that, lass," he said, and then grumpily added, "I'd rather be with the legion, than on this fool's errand," to which Galin shook his head in agreement, "but me and Galin agreed to come, so let us be about it."

"We will join the army in time to watch the Gragor crush the walls of Greytears," Bonnie said, as she smiled triumphantly. "The attack will not commence until we arrive."

Bonnie unstrapped the staff from her back, held it up to the sky, and began to sing. It was an eerie call, to the royal-wyverns she was attempting to summon from the Everdark Forest. After a few moments, she stopped.

Borach grew impatient. "Are you sure it will work?" he asked her, as he eyed the skies for any sign of the beasts emerging from the clouds in the bright blue sky.

Bonnie did not immediately reply to him. Instead, she drank in deep gulps of air, let out another eerie call, and then only after a while said, "No song is older than the *Dragonsong*." The orb on the end of the staff began to glow. "Our royal-wyverns cannot resist the *Dragonsong*, nor the call of an Omphalos stone. They are coming."

A serious expression grew on Bonnie's face. "In the Everdark Forest, there is a mountain range we call the Wyvernspine. In red-lit caves beneath it, the walls once echoed with the chants of our minstrels, who sang the songs of ancient days, when dragons and royal-wyverns were as common in the skies above the Everglow, as sparrows and doves." She smiled, and Borach could see the look on her face was pained. "*The Dragons of Maezador* once flew into those caves for sanctuary, when the Titans and Aeldar hunted them for sport in days long ago. Hidden by the acrid smoke, those glorious creatures of wing, scale and claw, coiled around the hottest vents. There they fell into slumber and deep dreams. As the mountains cooled, so too did the fire of their hearts go out, and thus, they died, and dragons were no more." Bonnie closed her eyes a moment and a tear rolled down her cheek.

Borach could tell Marki was about to say something, but he caught his eye, and shook his head to dissuade him against it, for he knew that Dwarven songs and memories were not so keen on the dragon kind, of whom it was sung that they once burned cities and ate many, and thus Dwarves did not consider them a noble race, and had bid good riddance to their kind from the world.

Bonnie wiped away the tear with the back of her hand. "Common-wyverns will hatch on any ledge or perch, but royal ones require the hot steam and magna that now flows again beneath those mountains. That is where we take their eggs to hatch. In great braziers, we burn aromatic oils, and sing the *Dragonsong* to the eggs of the royal-wyverns. It is pleasing to the fledglings within, and teaches them courage and nobility. The adults also rest there, when we are not flying them."

"How do your people know the *Dragonsong*?" Borach asked.

"An old Ascenti dream-weaver stumbled upon the caves, just days before the last dragon died. She entered the creature's dreams, and there she heard the *Dragonsong*, and the old songs of valour. She sang them for days, but could not raise the beast from its slumber. She sang with all of her might, as with despair, she watched its mighty chest rising and falling with the rhythm of its ancient and slowing heart, and then it beat one more time, and the last dragon was gone from this world."

Borach was pleased that Marki said nothing. He could sense that any hurtful words he traded with Bonnie, might be short lived and quickly forgotten, but potent while the effect of them lasted. It was an area where he and his friend differed most. Borach preferred silence over rash words, whereas his friend often spoke exactly what was on his mind.

"The women of my family have flown with the flocks for thousands of years, and none know the way of the royal-wyvern like we do," Bonnie said, "but since the Children of the Molach burrowed under the forest, and built their diabolical dens, their numbers have decreased. It is fortunate the heat of the Wyvernspine keeps them away from the sacred nesting grounds."

Borach had heard of a diabolical race of large humanoid rat-creatures that now inhabited some parts of the earth beneath the Everglow. Until then, he had not realised they were responsible for the demise of the Ascenti. He knew little of them, but had heard tales from explorers and traders who came from the west to Aleskian. They said that the Molach rarely appeared above ground, unless to spring on unsuspecting prey, but contact had been made with some of their chiefs. It was rumoured in the west, that if a colony of Molach set up beneath a city, they were harbingers of disease, and entire cities had been wiped out by the resulting plague. The one good thing, was that the various colonies were irreconcilably divided, and mostly fought among themselves, thus reducing their own numbers through genocidal campaigns that left no survivors among the defeated side. Borach shuddered and tactfully decided to change the topic.

"A griffin will rarely allow any but its rider to fly upon it, unless it takes a liking to the companion of the rider," he politely informed Bonnie, "but if you say these royal-wyverns will allow us on as passengers, regardless, I will trust you."

"The *Dragonsong* tames them to do our will," Bonnie said, as somewhere below them, they heard the moaning screech of a common-wyvern being wheeled up the rampart.

"He is a magnificent beast," said Bonnie admiringly, as the wyvern was wheeled into sight, and led from his cage, "but his splendour pales into insignificance when you see those which we shall fly today." The beast thrashed and flailed about furiously. His wings were pinioned to his side by chains, his legs shackled, but still he writhed. He roared in the direction where Borach and Bonnie stood.

Another screech, several, could be heard from the skies above. Borach felt a rush of wind above him, and turned to see three royal-wyverns descending from the clouds, to land on the ledge several metres away. They were far bigger than the common-wyvern, and much more colourful. Each of them was armoured and saddled, and behind the twin saddles was a large pack of what appeared to be travel supplies. Two of the royal-wyverns had a rider in the saddles, one was rider less. The two female riders were dressed in similar fashion to Bonnie. They made ululating trilling sounds as the beasts drew to a still.

"Do you know how royal-wyverns mate?" Bonnie asked Borach, who shrugged his shoulders. "It is far more glorious than the way griffins do so. A female, takes off on a nuptial flight and flies to the highest possible altitude, and the males pursue her. Only the strongest male can survive at such a height, and that is the one that gets to breed with her, up there, beyond the clouds!"

The three royal-wyverns circled the common one. "Your sacrifice, is honoured," Bonnie said, as she held the staff and pointed the Omphalos stone towards the common-wyvern, and to the royal ones, she said, "Feed!"

As she sang the *Dragonsong*, in a tongue with words the like of which Borach had never heard, the royal-wyverns lunged at the hapless common-wyvern and ripped it to shreds, screeching hysterically as they greedily tore off lumps and then gulped down its flesh.

The scrunched-up scowl on Marki's face revealed his displeasure at the grisly sight. It was not something Borach enjoyed watching either, but it was not long before the royal-wyverns had consumed the entirety of the creature, bones and all, so that all which was left on the ground were the last remnants of limbs still clasped by the chains, that fell to the ground with a loud clank. The royal-wyverns licked up the entrails and blood.

Once the feeding frenzy had finished, one of the women dismounted from the smallest of the wyvern.

"We are ready," she said to Bonnie. "The other riders have gone ahead with their passengers."

Bonnie ended her song and looked at Borach. "Those of your men you selected to ride with my Ascenti riders, and the woman you call Talain, left this morning. They will prepare camp for us. You will ride behind me. Your talkative dwarf, if he still wishes to come, will ride behind Sernea, and the other one behind Saisha."

"I am nobody's dwarf," Marki said huffily.

Another rider dismounted and smiled at Marki. "I am Sernea," she said. The woman's face was hideously scarred, as though some creature had once gnawed at it.

"I get the ugly one then," Marki tactlessly whispered to Galin, a bit too loudly, causing Sernea to give him a reproachful look, but she said nothing.

Galin looked at the wyverns the women had dismounted from. "They're also not sweet to the eye, much uglier than griffins," he remarked.

*Dwarves and their diplomacy*, Borach thought to himself as he observed the creatures more closely. The head and wings were green and yellow in colour, shot through with multi-coloured stripes, as was the reptilian body. They only had two legs, and a tail ending in a diamond-shaped tip. He had heard that there was a sea-dwelling variant dubbed the sea-wyvern, which had a fish tail in place of a barbed one.

Borach still could not understand the words that Bonnie again began to sing. As she continued singing, the largest of the royal-wyverns came over and lowered its long neck, which rippled with peristaltic motion, and watched Bonnie as she sang. The beast made a gentle cooing noise, intermittent with clicking from the back of its throat. It then moved closer to Borach, so that its face was just a few feet from his. Its moist breath, unsurprisingly, smelled like raw meat. Its eyes were cold and filled with primordial savagery.

Bonnie stopped singing, and stroked the creature on the forehead and then whispered in his ear. The beast cooed and clicked, and then lowered its body to the ground. Bonnie mounted and offered Borach her hand. He took it and with a strength that surprised him, she pulled him into the saddle behind her. "His name is Drasi," Bonnie said, patting the beast on the head.

Marki and Galin moaned and grumbled as Saisha and Sernea helped them into the saddles of their mounts, the two dwarves moaning and complaining all the while that if dwarves were meant to fly Balagrim would have given them wings. The sight made Borach briefly smile; his friends had never enjoyed flight. The two riders then mounted, when the dwarves had settled.

Bonnie secured the staff over her shoulder and took the reins of the beast. "It is time," she said, loud enough for all to hear. "The Omphalos Stone has shown us, the thief who has the Simal, will soon emerge with it. Armun, once of the Tarath Guëan, now one of the *Banished*, waits to take it and her to the Baothein. The Wild-Hunt has set a trap for them, where they wait in the shadows. We too, will be waiting, unseen until the last moment. The Wild Hunt will learn the fear of becoming prey." A ferocity spread across her feminine features. "Lord Malagrim desires the Simal, and we shall bring it to him." The female riders made louder ululating trilling sounds and shrieked their delight.

*I hope this all works out*, Borach thought. The offer of a castle and a safe Obelisk, as well as an ally army to help him take it, had been an offer he just could not refuse. The Chatti, Gragor, Seesnari and an army of mercenaries were going to lay siege to Greytears, along with what was left of the Third Legion. Strategically it all made sense.

With the Bantu soon to descend from the north, and the opportune Bruthon to the east, and for the Seesnari the eight kingdoms to the west of them, the allied armies needed each other. They had decided to strike first, and plant Borach and his men in Greytears as a buffer against the Bruthon threat. The only thing he did not like about the plan, was the fact he had to go with Bonnie to capture the Simal. He had wanted to travel with his men down the river, but it seemed as though fate was leading him to the cursed Wytchwood. He curled his nose with disgust, as he remembered the foul-tasting milk like liquid that they had to drink, for some strange reason.

"I long for open skies and soaring cliffs, and the thrill of hunting like a hawk," Bonnie said as she urged her wyvern towards the edge of the cliff. She shouted to Borach, "Hold on tight," as the wyvern claws gripped the edge of the plateau and it folded its wings back with regal poise. Borach carefully made sure his feet were firmly in the silver stirrups, and that he was well-positioned in the gilt-worked red leather saddle, holding the grips tight. Bonnie flicked the reins of the gold-tasselled, red-leather bridle.

"Fly Drasi," she ordered. The royal-wyvern bent his legs, and with a mighty thrust, pushed himself off the cliff and with a jump, a beat, a thrash of its wings it launched into the air. Instead of ascending, it drew back its wings and dived. Down and down the wyvern and its riders plummeted, twisting and spiralling so that it felt out of control. Borach's breath was snatched away, but he gripped with his knees, and clutched his hands on the saddle grips even tighter, as he held on with all of his strength and might. If he lost focus for a second, he thought he might lose his grip and fall, so he held on tighter, and readjusted his position in the saddle.

Bonnie shrieked with sheer delight, her joy escalating as the water of the lake came ever closer. At the last moment, just when it seemed they would crash into the water, Drasi adjusted his tail and spread his wings so they went into a glide that took them level with the lake. He flapped his wings with a mighty whoosh, and continued to slowly flap them as with great speed he soared over the surface of the lake, much to Borach's relief.

It was not long before they, and the other wyvern riders, had crossed the lake and caught up with the fleet of ships and barges sailing down the River Erin. The men of the legion cheered, as did the Chatti and Gragor, as the party flew by at an amazing speed. Shagor, in particular, waved joyfully, jumping up and down, causing complaints from those on the barge as it rocked and creaked with the force, especially from Popparus who vociferously tried to calm her excitement, along with the bannerman who was knocked over and nearly stomped on by her.

When they had past the fleet, the three wyverns ascended into the sky, beyond the clouds to perhaps to gain their bearings, and then back into them again to stay out of sight. In this way they continually ascended and descended.

It had been many lifetimes since Borach had flown a griffin, and this was the first time he had been on the back of a royal-wyvern, which was much faster. Never had he flown so fast as then. His hair whipped his face and his eyes watered in the wind as he leaned and looked over Bonnie's shoulder. She whooped and yelled with excitement, and he could not help but do the same as clouds floated around them. For a few moments, he felt carefree, and forgot all of his troubles. Even more so, when Sernea and her wyvern drew alongside them. Borach noticed Marki's eyes were clenched shut, and despite coaxing by Sernea for him to open them, much to Borach's amusement he merely angrily grumbled something and refused to do so.

They flew for most of that day, southwards, following the course of the river. Despite the thrill and joy of it all, Borach was glad when they came to a place near a large forest where other royal-wyverns and their riders were waiting for them. Drasi was

701

blowing hard by then, a sign of imminent exhaustion. *They are faster than a griffin, but don't have as much endurance as one,* Borach noted to himself.

Bonnie turned Drasi in a sharp bank and roll manoeuvre, and they glided to the clearing. The creature landed on the dusty ground with a short run, a loud click of his claws and a thrash of his wings to slow him down. Saisha and Sernea's wyvern landed in the same way.

"Well done Drasi," Bonnie said to the beast as she dismounted her weary mount and stroked the creature's head.

Borach dismounted. Both man and beast felt grateful for the chance to rest.

"Blustering spitspewers," Marki shouted as he angrily fell off his wyvern into the dirt. "Call me an excrement-wallowing boil-brained dribbling profligate wind-breaker if after this day I ever get on one of these beasts again."

"I will, Sernea," said, "for we will not be here long and you will either have to stay here or get back on."

Marki just growled as he stood up, brushing the dirt from himself. Galin did not fare much better, and was also bitterly complaining that dwarves were born to keep their feet firmly on the ground.

The wyverns were heaving for breath, their dry tongues lulling from their mouths. Ascenti warriors came and took the travel packs off, and led the exhausted creatures to some large pools of fresh water, which were fed by a stream. The royal-wyverns drank greedily, and did not protest when the women filled buckets of water and began to wash them down as others fed them with strips of already prepared meat. Next to the pool, other royal-wyverns rested, and near them, eating, or resting on travel mattresses, sat their Ascenti riders, and the legionnaires who had ridden with them.

Marki joined Borach and Bonnie, as did Talain and Galin. "This day has served to remind me, why no dwarf I know likes flying," Marki grumbled, much to their amusement, as he rubbed his rump to remove the saddle weariness. Talain laughed wearily, and slapped him on the shoulders in a friendly fashion. She then grew serious and addressed Borach. "There is a brooding atmosphere to this place," she said.

Hand on her hips, Bonnie turned about to survey her surroundings and Borach followed her gaze. They were on a plain consisting of both dust and grass. Large rocks surrounded it, and were positioned in such a way that somebody had put them there both as a means of defence as well as concealment, and judging by their size, it must have been Gragor, Borach assumed. To the far north, beyond the rocks, were mountains whose tops were hidden by clouds. Bonnie's gaze turned towards the south, and Borach's followed hers. He stiffened and caught his breath when, through the only opening in the rocks, he noticed afresh the primitive and sombre looking forest a half-mile or so to the south, made more sinister looking by the dim twilight and onset of night that made the giant trees appear forbidding and unwelcome.

"Is that it, the Wytchwood?" he asked Bonnie.

"Yes," she answered sombrely, as she shivered with a twitch of her delicate shoulders. "We Ascenti once sought sanctuary there, when we first left our homes. It is how we got to know the Threadweaver that dwells within."

"I have heard terrible stories about that place," Talain said.

Bonnie took her staff and removed the Omphalos stone, and as though anticipating his question, she said to Borach, "No, it is not the same one in the dragon skull, and not as powerful. But with it, we can see the *Arvivan* named Bessie, and those with her." She held it in the palm of her hand. Unlike before, the images did not appear around them, but she said, "Look into it." When he did, Borach could see the strange creature called Bessie, who was sitting sulkily on the floor. Around her, her companions were resting.

"That is Armun," Borach said as the image of a weathered mage appeared. He sat resting his eyes, and next to him were the female dwarf, a goat, and two Davari.

Bonnie spoke as she pointed to the image of a red-coloured portal. "When it is red like that, it means Janorra is about to re-enter this world, we hope, with the Simal. We do not know how they have the same means to know it, but the Wild Hunt will also be likely to appear when she does. We will take them all by surprise, and take the Simal from her whilst Armun and his companions are fighting them."

"What if he turns and fights us?" Marki asked. "Even a *Banished* was once one of the Tarath Guëan. They usually stay neutral in political affairs, as they did during the civil war, but even if we attack Armun, there might be a reckoning with them one day."

"Recently, we asked for their help regarding a rather foul blade that came into our possession," Galin said.

"Did they help?" Bonnie asked.

"We don't know," Marki answered blankly. "The man we sent to them, never returned to us. But back to this matter, it is distasteful for me to now make an enemy of Armun in seeking to frustrate his plans, as much as I disagree with him taking that blasted Simal to the Baothein, whom I hate with a passion."

"I agree," Borach said. "If we can avoid making an enemy of Armun that would be a preferred course to take. We can help them deal with the Wild Hunt, and then speak to him, to see if he can be reasoned with."

"It is hard to reason with the Tarath Guëan," Bonnie replied curtly, "especially one now a *Banished*. But we can try. I do not want to slay Armun unless I have too."

Borach suddenly looked at Bonnie in a different way. *If she can slay one of the Tarath Guëan, she must be more formidable than she appears.* "On occasion, during the course of my long years of lives, I have met Armun," he said to Bonnie. "He is bad-tempered, but a reasonable man, and also a dangerous one; if you can slay him, then you can restrain him? It might be that we can reason with him to help us bring the Simal to Malagrim, rather than the Baothein."

"That is a better move than trying to just take it from him," Marki said, "only a tickled-brained mewling would not consider that as a best option."

Bonnie stood there, clearly deep in thought. She turned her glare towards the Wytchwood. Any previous sweetness about her appearance had gone, and Borach noticed again fierceness in her. It lasted but a moment, and then her sweet smile returned. "We are agreed then," she finally said. "We will fight the Wild Hunt with Armun, and then, attempt to reason with him." She looked at her companions. "If reasoning does not work, I will take the Simal, Armun and his companions would be foolish to try to stop me."

"Do not act rashly," Borach warned her.

"Rest whilst you can," Bonnie said. "I will watch our quarry through the Omphalos. When Janorra emerges, we must quickly make our move."

*     *     *

The Fortress City of Kara Duram occupied a hillside that was roughly circular in shape, and was surrounded by a vast moat. The huge walls were designed in a convex curve, some twelve miles in length. Six gates opened through them, leading to bridges that crossed the moat and led to the Steppes of Kara Duram, a mighty grassland criss-crossed with many farms, villages and settlements. Shaka stood on a battlement and looked out upon the vast host of Hammer Knights camped on the grasslands around

703

the fortress. The number of their banners could not easily be counted, and nor could the number of great siege engines they were constructing.

"They will try to secure the Obelisk at any cost," Aspess said to her mother, "so we can expect an attack quickly."

"We should use the Juram and abandon this place, even these great defences cannot endure indefinitely against such a host, if they do delay," Regineo urged.

"And go where?" Shaka asked, almost serenely.

"Your sister still rules as the White Queen of the Baothein, surely she would show mercy and offer us sanctuary?"

Shaka snorted derisively. "The Bantu will soon ravish her lands, and she will be no more than a footnote in history."

"What if you fall into the hands of Mazdek? You know the depths of cruelty he will expose you too," Regineo persisted.

"We will not lose this battle, and even if we did, I will not fall again into the hands of Mazdek," Shaka said as she fingered the Arzak on the pommel of the Arkith that she held. She gazed reflectively into its deep and dark depths. "Maybe an eternity inside one of these things, is not as bad as some people think. Maybe even inside there, they need an empress to rule them. But no, we will not lose this battle."

"Then I wish I could share your confidence," Regineo said with a tone of disgust.

Shaka waved her hand dismissively. "You soon will," she said.

"What have you got planned, mother?" Aspess asked suspiciously.

A sadistic grin spread across Shaka's face. "In days as dark as these, empires are forged or lost, and new allies we must seek. Dear daughter, here we will take a stand, but not alone. Now, cover your noses." She clapped her hands. "Bring him in," she shouted.

Caspus appeared with Longshins and another, and suddenly a horrid stench filled the air that nearly made her retch. "I present to you, Chief Ratgorn, of Clan Fanghaw," Caspus stuttered.

Shaka covered her nose as a hideous creature suddenly appeared. It stood as a man, but had the appearance of a mutated rat. Yellow chiselled teeth hung over the side of lips that were black. It's beady and malicious eyes blinked, as its whiskers and nose twitched, and it made a low involuntary chittering noise. It wore armour that was covered in dirt and grime, although it appeared as though some attempt had been made at cleaning it.

"What is it?" Regineo shrieked, as he took a step back in terror.

Aspess laughed sarcastically at his response. "One of the Children of the Molach," she slowly said as she stared at the creature with wonder and recognition, and then looking at her mother, she smiled knowingly. "You never cease to amaze me, mother. I would never have thought of that."

"Have your tunnels, reached my son?" Shaka asked Ratgorn.

Ratgorn nodded enthusiastically. When he spoke, his voice was high and shrill, grinding to the ears to listen too. "We cannot burrow through rock, but we burrowed through clay and found a way into the sewers under Kappia, and where they were broken, we entered. From there, we found our way to Erespatagor and freed him from his prison. He slowly slithers his way here as we speak, hiding during the day, and moving at night."

"Slowly?" Shaka asked.

"Great were the torments Mazdek had inflicted upon him," Ratgorn replied, "for your son refused to join their cause."

"And what of Kappia?" Shaka asked.

"Our Plague Priests sneak from the sewers at night into the Skunfill district; disease and illness spreads throughout the city." Ratgorn laughed hysterically. "We post the pamphlets you gave us; the people blame Mazdek for this calamity." Ratgorn sniffed the air. "The eyesight of my kind is poor above ground, but I can smell that the enemy is at your gates."

"They are here," Aspess answered, and looking at her mother observed, "if Kappia rebels whilst Mazdek is here, he will have to retreat."

"Indeed, he will," Shaka said, and then looking at Ratgorn, whilst trying to hide her disgust, asked, "are your traps set under the battleground?"

Ratgorn nodded, and his face twisted with hatred. "My colony is small, after the attempted genocide at Molarash, but there are enough of us to turn the tide of battle in your favour. If we sneak, attack where not expected, disappear and reappear, we will cause terror in their ranks and slay many. When they retreat, we will follow. In the darkness of night, our Plague Priests will appear and spread disease in their camp."

Shaka's grin spread widely. "Then, when my son gets here, we will not wait for them to attack us. When the Horns of Kara Duram sound, we begin the attack."

"When victory is yours, I get my reward?" Ratgorn asked suspiciously.

"You will be given suitable land to build your dens and replenish your colony, as we agreed," Shaka said, "but then you must leave when you are at strength."

"Oh, we will," Ratgorn said. "The Everdark Forest is our home now. The vile Clan Fornesh slaughtered us, drowned our elders, and ate our young." His face grew incandescent with rage. "They took my closest kin, tied them to stakes near the Wyvernspine, and laughed as the wyverns ate them alive."

Shaka cast her eyes back across the Steppes of Kara Duram and the army encamping there. "Then we both have those on whom we wish to exact our revenge," she said, as her own rage boiled inside of her.

\*　　　　\*　　　　\*

"I'm sorry lass," Marki said to Sernea as he used a stick to stoke the embers of the fire to revive it. In the distance wolves howled at the full moon.

"What for?" she asked nonchalantly.

"For, you know, being rude earlier – about your looks." He felt sheepish, and was genuinely sorry. "I was agitated about the flight here, and sometimes, this foolish old gibber mouth of mine opens and speaks before my brain can stop it." He threw some logs onto the fire, and continued to stoke it until it flared into life. "If brains were grain, I wouldn't have enough to feed a baby chick."

"As I was about to mention," Talain said drolly, and smiled wryly.

"Well, I'm sorry lass," he said to Sernea. "Will you forgive an insensitive old dwarf?"

"Of course," Sernea replied, as she blew, and took a mouthful of the hot soup that she drank from a wooden cup.

"I'll tell you how I got these," Talain said to Sernea, as she pointed to her own face, "if you'll tell me how you got those scars."

Sernea smiled wearily. "The Chatti are hopelessly divided, perhaps more so than any other race. It is why they could not fight the Children of the Molach when they first appeared under their lands." She took another sip of soup. "The Chatti fled east, to avoid the disease and corruption that nearly wiped them out. That is how we first came into contact with some of them, when they entered the Everdark Forest." She stared hauntingly into the now revived fire. "We allowed them to pass, and they went to the Giant Halls and found sanctuary."

705

"The Gragor were dying out, still are, so they made an alliance with the Chatti," Talain added, looking at Marki.

Sernea nodded. "The Chatti warned us the Children of Molach would come, but we waited for nearly a century, and they never did, after which we grew lapse, and soon forgot the warnings." She stared up at the night sky, with eyes full of regret. "When they emerged from the ground, we did not even know what or who was attacking us." Her eyes closed and she sighed deeply. "The battle was over before it even started really." She stared over at Bonnie who was at the other side of the camp, still staring into the Omphalos, and then at the other Ascenti, most of who were sleeping or seated around similar campfires quietly talking to others gathered there. "All of my sisterhood, were out on a hunt that day with some of the men, but I was sick." The memories were clearly causing her immense pain and she swallowed hard before she could speak again. Looking over at one of the royal-wyverns, she pointed at it and said, "Freylash, is her name. I have raised her since she was an egg. Our bond is strong."

Marki looked over at the wyvern she had pointed at, and considered it no better looking than his first observation, but this time, he said nothing.

"The bond between Freylash and I, is a very strong one; she sensed my distress that day. She and other wyverns came, and drove the Molach back underground. Freylash bit the head off the one that was attacking me, after which I drifted into a haunted sleep." She looked at the other Ascenti. "When they returned, I was the only survivor, for Freylash guarded me." She bowed her head. "We begged the men who returned from the hunt, not to go down into the burrows to search for more survivors, but they would not listen to reason. None of them ever returned." She put the cup down, and covered her face with her hands. "We Ascenti, cannot produce children with any of the other races of men, that we know, and we have tried, so we are the last of our kind." She uncovered her face, smiled bravely and looked at the other Ascenti around the camp. "Once we few here pass, the Ascenti will be no more."

Marki sobbed out loud, and put a comforting hand on Sernea's shoulder.

# Chapter Sixty-Two: *The Battle of the Wytchwood*

*Every empire which has enjoyed prosperity and power for a considerable time, is eventually destroyed when an attitude of discontent towards the existing order is allowed to take root and flourish. When that occurs, the end is inevitable. However, it is often one small thing that tips the scales and decides the future fate of kingdoms and empires.*
*Observations from Phalius the Philosopher.*

*It* had been more than an hour since Janorra had left Garama Aethoros, and still they were trapped in the rune-covered cave and Chamber of Resurrection. The Wisdom Tree was revitalising and beginning to flourish with new life. The Obelisk that had appeared in the Chamber of Resurrection had stayed quiet, its eyes mostly closed, though occasionally it momentarily opened them and suddenly shouted the words, "I have a message, but I cannot remember what it is, nor can I remember my name." After each time it spoke, it again fell silent, and eventually went back to sleep.

For the last hour, Muro had stood at the side of the cave, muttering and chanting at the wall.

"We could not chance opening the secret exit, until you had returned," Armun had said to her in way of explanation. "We had to put charmed locks on all entrances and exits, to keep the Wild Hunt out. It takes time to undo the locks we put on it." He had then briefly explained that the exit they were going to attempt to open, only led to the fortress itself. "If the Wild Hunt are already inside the fortress, they might be waiting for us, or prowling for another way into this cave."

Janorra shuddered at the thought. "Is he more suited to this task than you?" she asked, staring over at Muro who continued chanting to the wall.

"He is surprisingly knowledgeable, for a Fell-blood," Armun replied, and looking at the door added, "The Wild Hunt has a powerful mage with them, and I fear I know who it might be. I must counter his attempt to enter, whenever he assails the door, or it will soon break." He looked over at the Obelisk, who was again sleeping. "He is still too weak for me to draw power from him."

*Janorra felt like a trapped animal.* "How did the Wild Hunt know I had left Garama Aethoros?" she asked Armun.

"No doubt through some dark art," he replied glumly. He looked around at the others. Gilly was stroking Gaffren, keeping him calm. Bessie was sleeping, whilst Scarand paced up and down, bow in hand, a moody countenance upon his face.

"I have learnt much about these companions, whilst you were in Garama Aethoros," Armun said. "The Spriggan persuaded her kind to bring us supplies. She is terrified, but loyal to the dwarf, who..." he paused. "Gilly is remarkable, in her own way." He then looked at Scarand. "Much misery has beset his soul since he has been here. He desires nothing more than to find his sisters, but he is wise for one so young. He knows his best chance is to have the mark of a slave removed, and to learn of the world he now inhabits." Armun smiled compassionately. "I have taught him the essentials of the art of the sword, during the time we waited for you. He is a fast learner and is already becoming quite skilled. I have also taught him much about the Everglow. When the Simal is safe in Baothein lands, I will assist him in his own quest, that much I have promised him."

"Then he gains powerful allies that he will need," Janorra said, and then she looked across at Muro. "What about him?"

A look of distaste spread across Armun's face. "His soul is black, he speaks little. All I know of him is what Scarand told me. I knew of the Ruik before, but not the extent of their foulness." He then glanced at Imrand and Sarkisi, who were sitting there with their helmets off. Sarkisi slept with her head in her husband's lap, as Imrand affectionately stroked her hair. "What do you know of them?"

"That their love is strong, and in a time of danger, he will secure her life, even if it means sacrificing ours," Janorra answered. "Beyond that observation, I know little, for we had no time for pleasantries inside Garama Aethoros. If the opportunity allows, when we have found a way out of this, I will question Scarand for more knowledge about them." *When I find a way to escape the Wild Hunt, or if?* She quickly dismissed the sickening thought.

The very foundations of the fortress shook once more, runes came alive, the door turned red, and Armun waved his staff, and countered whatever magical force was trying to break the door down. Janorra thought he looked so weary. She resisted every temptation to attempt to use the Simal to aid them. Armun had warned passionately against daring such an attempt. "Already, it has been in your possession too long," he said, "but I dare not touch it, or look into it, for it might drain what little of my power is left, if it considers those outside of this cave, ally to itself."

Janorra looked over at Muro. *Hurry, find a way to open the secret exit. Being trapped in here is torment to my soul.*

The fortress shook again, the runes on the cave ceiling danced with a myriad of fresh colours, the door turned red, and Armun waved his staff again, to counter the force, as Gaffren bleated with fresh terror.

\*　　　　\*　　　　\*

"The Seeress has returned to this world," Bonnie shouted at the top of her voice, as she ran around the camp and roused all those who were sleeping. "Mount your pets, we must ride with the wind, lest our prize is stolen from us."

"Are you sure she has the Simal?" Borach asked her.

"I am sure," Bonnie said, but he observed that she looked troubled.

"What is it?" he asked.

"I cannot see through the eyes of an *Arvivan*, when it sleeps, so it was hard to know when to time our move. Too soon, or too late, both increase the risk. The Spriggan is now awake. They have opened an exit to the cave, and are fleeing the Wild Hunt. Urgency is a must."

Borach understood, but the camp was ready. On waking, they were quickly mounted, and all the royal-wyverns took to the air with their riders and passengers. This time, Borach felt no exhilaration as they soared through the skies towards the Wytchwood. He was also pleased to observe that unlike before, Marki muttered no complaints as he mounted Freylash, sitting in the saddle behind Sernea. Grimness smouldered on Marki's face, and Borach knew his friend was ready for battle.

\*　　　　\*　　　　\*

Methruille stared at the iron-bound door. "They have found another way out," he roared angrily at Gaishak.

A fury burned in Gaishak's eyes. "Dotherekin, you and your scum rats guard this door. The rest, with me." With great swiftness, followed by other Bantu, Gaishak made his way through various passages and caves, until he stood outside of the fortress. It was dusk. In the sky above, two dozen or so garâtons patrolled. Marigoof, Barikoff and about two score or so of Bantu were in heated debate.

"What 'ave ya peepers goggled?" Gaishak unceremoniously asked Barikoff.

"Some boys are 'unting in the fortress, some on the wall. The bridge is guarded." He looked at Marigoof. "The *Mad One* is convinced 'e and 'is boys peeped something moving through the forest, and 'e came 'ere to gas-pipe about it."

Marigoof looked at the shrunken head of his brother on his shoulder, nodded as though he was in agreement with it, and said to Gaishak. "We're not bloba-blabbing. Something big and nasty is moving through the trees. I'll load me dice to wager its waiting for dark before it comes out to play."

Gaishak growled, baring his fangs and said to Barikoff, "Be ready with ya dabbers then. Kill whatever tries to cross the bridge, from 'ere or the forest. Don't kill the Seeress if she tries to cross. We want 'er alive."

Barikoff nodded, and followed by some Bantu, headed back towards the bridge.

Methruille emerged from within the fortress. "Follow!" he ordered Gaishak and Marigoof. Some of the Bantu began to blow their loud horns, signalling orders.

*  *  *

"The power in my staff and soul are almost drained," Armun said wearily to Janorra. He looked exhausted as he led them towards another great spiral stair. Gilly was seated on Gaffren and Sezareal behind her, whilst Bessie clung to Gaffren's neck. Scarand and Muro followed, as did Imrand and Sarkisi at a slightly slower place because of the sack of gold and treasure each of them still carried. They had hastily been running through the fortress for more than thirty minutes. Armun peered out of one of the windows, it was nearly dark, with a full moon already rising. The Bantu horns and loud cries could be distinctly heard. "We explored this place thoroughly whilst we waited for you," he said to Janorra, struggling to catch his breath in between words. "The bridge to the east will be guarded, but there is a bridge to the south, it is in a perilous condition, so much so they might not bother watching it. If we remain unseen, we might make it across under the cover of darkness."

Janorra remembered seeing the bridge on the way to Silverberry's cottage, and again when they had later approached the fortress. It had looked very perilous as though it might collapse if anyone attempted to cross it.

Armun noticed her concerned look. "If it is unpassable, then we will have no choice but to fight and cross by the eastern bridge!" He then noticed that Imrand and Sarkisi, weighed down with their sacks, finally caught up with them all. "Drop what you are carrying, fools, we are in a flight for our lives," he urged them.

Imrand and Sarkisi, who now both had their helms donned, looked at each other, and then at Armun. "I do not follow your lead," Imrand snarled, as he dropped the sack and drew his sword. "With this I will buy an army to wipe out all who have wronged me. I will not leave it behind."

"Work together, or we will not survive this place," Armun shouted, his voice booming angrily, "what good will your gold do you from your graves?"

"I do not follow your lead!" Imrand angrily repeated.

"Then go your own way!" Armun barked. "We do not have the time for this, and will lock the doors behind us." Leaving Imrand and Sarkisi behind, he impatiently signalled for the others to follow, as some force hit the fortress and made it shake, causing dust and debris to fall from the vaulted ceiling. Halfway up the stairway he paused to catch his breath, and to see if Imrand and Sarkisi were following. They were

709

not. "The spells I have placed around this place are failing. The mage the Bantu have with them is very powerful. We will run if we can, but will fight if we must!"

The fellows fled up the stairwell. The cries and horns outside grew fainter as they reached the top of the long stair and stepped out into a large corridor formed of stone blocks and plank flooring. Scarand, was the last to reach the landing. The walls of the keep shook and momentarily glowed, as something hit them again, causing dust to fall from the vaulted ceiling above them. A loud crashing sound, as though a wall had collapsed, was heard. The fierce yells of the Bantu and the horn-calls suddenly stopped.

"They are inside," Armun said, as he slammed shut the wooden door at the top of the stair and slid the large iron bolts across. "This will be but a piece of parchment to them. My Staff must be used sparingly, I will not use the power it has left to collapse the stone and block the stair." He looked around him, despair briefly crossing his face. "They will soon be upon us, and I am so weary."

From beyond the door, they heard the fierce yells of the Bantu, and an equally fierce war cry from Imrand. "It is regrettable," Armun said, "but whoever those fools are, we must leave them to the fate they have chosen."

*       *       *

Imrand and Sarkisi made their way back down the stairs and onto a large landing. The wall at the far end had collapsed, and through the dust and debris, a score or more Bantu emerged into the fortress. At the top of the stair, they heard the sound of the door being shut and bolts slid across.

Imrand again dropped his sack of treasure and stood next to Sarkisi. He looked at the dagger in her belt. "Do not let them take you alive," he said. She nodded, drew her bow, and aimed at the Bantu who were yelling and screaming ferociously as they charged down the corridor. Sarkisi fired shot after shot and several of the Bantu fell.

Imrand, his sword raised above his head, gave out an equally ferocious war cry, as he charged the Bantu.

*       *       *

Janorra's instincts were telling her that Armun was right, but it did not sit well with her that Imrand and Sarkisi had stayed behind. However, any delay would be perilous to them, so she followed Armun and the others to the end of the corridor, which branched off right and left. "This way," Armun said, as he took the left turning, and from there went through a doorway that led to a narrow set of stone steps leading upwards. At the top they ran through a low archway that led out onto a parapet.

Janorra sensed something, a presence, lurking unseen and close on the parapet. Armun must have sensed it as well, for he spun around. There was no time for him to utter a word, as a powerful blast of heat and fire shot towards him. It was only his instinct and staff that saved him, and them, as he swung it in an arc muttering some words. It threw a distinctive, transparent, lucid white shield in the shape of a half-bubble around the companions.

To Janorra's horror, a figure emerged, as from an unseen realm. Intangible at first it started to take form and flung back its hood revealing itself in all of its ghastly horror. It was a man with a withered grey face, and eyes as black as night. Three Bantu appeared with him. One of them was extremely large, with bits of bone decorating his hair, another with half of his face missing, replaced by metal iron-spiked teeth, and the third with a shrunken Bantu head on his shoulder. Behind them, scores of yelling Bantu, using ropes attached to grappling hooks, were clambering onto the parapet.

"Methruille!" Armun said, horror spreading on his face and tinting his voice. "I was right when I thought I sensed your foul reek."

Other-worldly whispers could be heard as Methruille spoke, his words trickling out with slow and deliberate malice. "You are tired, your power weakens; the Tarath Guëan have forsaken you in your moment of greatest need, *Banished*!"

"You too are *Banished*, but I shall not enter the depths of darkness that I now see you are a bed-fellow with," Armun retorted, his voice full of alarm.

Methruille sneered. "The Tarath Guëan grew weak, and turned their back on the Outer World, though not all of us. Give the woman and the Simal to me, and you and the others can live." He slapped his hands together in an imperious gesture, and then spread his palms slowly. The air between them caught fire and formed into a fiery ball spinning slowly between his hands, which grew in intensity with every moment that passed.

"Never," Armun growled through gritted teeth. "I shall not yield to the likes of you, treacherous one."

"So be it," Methruille said scornfully. The protective shield around Armun and the others rippled and shimmered as he hurled the fire-bolt at it, but it held, just.

The air inside the bubble became very hot, and the faces of them all were lit by a red glow. The companions stood rooted with horror staring at the enemy they faced. Gaffren was hysterical with fear, and jumped and kicked, knocking Muro and Scarand to the ground, and nearly bashing Janorra senseless.

Armun thrust his hand forward, and the bubble burst, but sent a wave of energy back towards Methruille and the Bantu who were knocked back, falling to the ground.

Scarand stood to his feet, slightly dazed, and fired his bow at one of the Bantu fallen to the ground, but missed. He remembered that Armun had formerly instructed him that arrows needed to be tipped with specially forged steel to pierce Bantu skin or their armour, but their eyes were good targets if exposed. His second shot was true to the mark, and pierced the Bantu through the eye, killing it instantly. His third shot, bounced off the metal of the spike-mouthed Bantu, who was shaking his head as it roared in anger and got back on its feet. The feral looking Bantu briefly looked at the brutish band gathering behind him, and then at Janorra and her companions.

"Get 'em boys!" he roared.

\*       \*       \*

Imrand was a lethal storm of flashing blades. The Bantu weapons, which would inflict lethal wounds on the flesh beneath any normal armour, had no effect on that which he wore. The last Bantu lowered his blade in mute surprise, just before Imrand performed a swift pirouette and sliced his sword, *Ormfron*, through the brute's neck, sending its head spinning along the passageway. His blood splattered face and furious snarl made a fearsome sight, as he approached Sarkisi, who was retrieving her arrows from the bodies of the fallen Bantu. "This bow and these arrows, slay them with ease," she said.

"The world will learn to fear us, my love," Imrand replied.

Sarkisi retrieved the last arrow, wiped the blood from it and returned it to her quiver. She gently caressed her husbands helmed face, her voice was quiet and dangerous, "Those who have shamefully slighted us and driven us to despair, will weep at the ruin and desolation we will wreak upon them and their kin. Nothing shall come between us ever again."

711

Sarkisi felt her veins throbbing with a strange vitality, and from the look on Imrand's face, she knew he had the same sensation. The armour gave them the sense of a powerfulness they had never experienced before. It was intoxicating and wonderful, an unnatural vigour. She and Imrand threw back their heads, and issued a war cry the like of which the world had not heard for many a long age.

*      *      *

The Bantu were fast. The metal-mouthed one was upon Scarand before he could release another arrow. He fought him with a sword. Neither he nor his foe gave way, so relentless was their determination to slay the one that stood before them.

Janorra found herself in her own life and death battle with a grotesque looking Bantu, who thrust at her with his spear, which she parried aside, whilst dodging an axe and spear that had been hurled by other Bantu charging along the parapet.

Gilly aimed her staff, and hollering, shot a bolt of power that hit Methruille but had little effect. Gaffren bolted, and with Sezareal on the back, Bessie clinging to his neck, and Gilly desperately trying to control him, he bolted along the parapet, down some stairs to a lower battlement, and leapt over the side, landing clumsily onto the courtyard below spilling his riders onto the ground. Janorra had no time to see how they fared as she parried yet another powerful thrust from the Bantu's spear.

Muro stepped into the fray, and from the runes in his palms came fire and ice, which he fired, one at the foe facing Janorra, the other at the one fighting Scarand, causing the Bantu to protect themselves with defensive manoeuvres. Metal-mouth snarled, but he lost his footing on some spilled blood and fell to the ground.

When he had fired the shots, Muro grabbed Janorra by the arm. "Give it to me, I know you have it," he said.

Janorra remembered the instruction Migdal had given to her, and without thinking it through, she took the last page of the *Prophecy of Rithguar*, and handed it to Muro. He smiled maniacally, and shoved it beneath his tunic. "Run," he said to Janorra, and then turning to Armun said, "I will stand with you. The runes have told me I will not die here this day. I shall return home!"

Armun turned towards Janorra, and with dismay and fear in his voice said, "We will hold them here as long as we can, you must reach the eastern bridge. Run, Janorra, run!" He looked at Scarand. "Do what you can to protect her," he said.

Janorra wasted no time, and followed by Scarand, she turned and fled at full flight along the parapet towards one of the large spires. Passing through a low archway, and reaching the entrance to the tower, the door of which had long since perished, she turned and took a last look at Armun, who said, "I am Keeper of the Staff of Ashtar, Warrior of Idrisa, servant of the Tarath Guëan of the Grey Council. Evil shall not prevail this day!" He banged the staff on the ground, and a white transparent shield spread before him and Muro.

Methruille drew himself up to his full height, fire and darkness surrounded him, as he hurled another fire-bolt, causing Armun's protective shield to shatter like broken glass. Armun fell to one knee as a large number of Bantu appeared. Within seconds, scores of Bantu black-feathered arrows pierced him. Muro used his runes of ice and fire to deflect the ones headed towards himself. Armun, mortally wounded, fell to his knees, and whispered something in Muro's ear.

Muro protected them by a wall of ice he formed. He then fired a bolt of fire towards the Wytchwood. It arced high and long, and hit the dead bracken, which caught light instantly, the fire quickly beginning to spread.

"Run, Janorra, run!" Armun shouted, with his last breath. They did. He pointed his staff and shot a bolt from it, causing the stone around an arched doorway to collapse behind them, to protect her and Scarand, buying them a small amount of time.

Janorra stood momentarily before the pile of rubble, coughing and brushing away the dust that covered her. She could see through a small hole, and she watched Muro take Armun's staff, before fleeing down the same stairs from which they had entered the parapet.

Janorra stared with wide-eyes at the sight of Armun falling, and Muro fleeing. The wall of ice began to melt, and Janorra saw the enraged face of Methruille, who was using his own staff to clear a path to her.

"Come," Scarand urged, as he pulled her through an open doorway that led to the spire. The stairs were collapsed, and they had no choice but to make it through the ancient rubble to another doorway. To her dismay, the parapet was filled with Bantu who were charging towards her, from both directions. Scarand fired the last of his arrows. Janorra heard the blaring of horns and the guttural grunting of the closing Bantu. "We've got 'er trapped," she heard one of them gloatingly roar.

*      *      *

Gaffren charged maniacally around the courtyard, bucking and kicking at anything in sight. He was as much a danger to his dismounted riders, as he was to the Bantu now pouring into the courtyard.

A score of arrows and spears came towards Gilly, Bessie and Sezareal. One arrow hit Bessie in the throat. She reeled around for a moment, clutching at the arrow and gurgling brown blood; "Oh, not like this miss Gilly," Bessie said, before she dropped to the ground, lifeless.

Gilly wailed in despair. "Oh, me poor dear, me poor Bessie," she cried.

A spear hit Sezareal full in the chest; the impact of it slammed her against the parapet wall with such force that her breath exploded from her lungs. She slumped lifeless to the floor. Gilly continued to wail in despair. Gaffren bleated in terror at the sound of the horns and the sight of the Bantu as he continued to wildly charge around the courtyard kicking his hind legs at anything in range. When he came near to her, Gilly managed to grab the reins and leap into saddle, but he was still bucking furiously. She yanked the reins and roared with such might, her actions momentarily brought the terrified goat under control.

"Take the stumpy alive if you can," one of the Bantu ordered the others.

"Oh, me poor foolish Gaffren," Gilly said as she tried to comfort the goat as the Bantu surrounded them in a circle. She whispered in his ear. "It looks like this is where Gilly and Gaffren take their last stand, me dear. Now, for Balagrim's sake, help me make it a good one so I can tell a good story to the Maidens." In an instant the grief and despair on Gilly's face turned to fury, as, more in panic than courage, Gaffren lowered its head and charged the Bantu. "For me Gaffren!" she roared. Above her, from the corner of her eye, a shadow descended.

*      *      *

A spear narrowly missed Imrand's head and thudded into the door of the house which he and Sarkisi were passing. He dropped the sack of treasure, gripped the shaft and wrenched it free, and then hurled it back at the Bantu who had launched it, skewering

713

him. He turned as he heard footsteps behind them, and saw Muro, who had left the fortress and was running down the street towards them.

"What are you doing old man?" Imrand angrily asked him.

"Getting out of here," Muro replied. He looked at the treasure. "Looks like you've got your hands full. Carry it, and follow me."

"Why would I follow you?" Imrand asked impatiently.

"Because you're going the wrong way," Muro answered, as he beckoned for them to follow him.

*         *         *

Freylash furiously beat her wings as she descended from the sky. From what Marki could see, a garâton had latched onto the wyvern's underbelly and was biting and tearing into it with its teeth and claws. Some of the other wyvern riders were in a similar battle. One rider and its wyvern, plummeted towards the ground. He was aggrieved to see Talain was the passenger. In a blur, Marki saw three black shapes clinging to the stricken creature's tattered gut as it hurtled past them, taking itself, its rider and passenger, and the beasts attacking it to their deaths as together they crashed into the ruined fortress, hitting the side of a tower, toppling it, and then falling lifeless to the ground.

Sernea frantically tried to get her own wyvern under control. Cursing under his breath, with one arm Marki grabbed hold of one of the straps of the saddle, and closing his eyes, swung to the underside of the wyvern. With the other arm, he swung *Old Trusty*, and slew the garâton which let go and plummeted to the fast approaching stone of the courtyard below. With the thrashing of its great wings, Freylash managed to slow the descent enough so that when Marki lost his grip, the drop into the courtyard, was not lethal. He hit the ground rolling and tumbling for several feet, with all the wind and half the life battered out of him. He found himself in the middle of a furious fight. Remembering her from the vision of *Arvivan*, he did not have time to make any introductions, but he knew that the female dwarf fighting from the back of a goat was not his immediate enemy. Surrounded, and convinced that his death was upon him, the dwarf acted according to his instinct. How he regained his feet, he could not even have told the Maidens, but he stood, and even before he had caught his breath, still winded, he hurled himself towards the nearest Bantu. He felt *Old Trusty* pierce the brute's armour and the creature was dead in an instant. Marki fought like a wild beast, and no foe was able to stand before the ferocity of he and *Old Trusty*.

Freylash and Sernea crashed to the ground heavily, and no movement did they make. The female dwarf upon the goat took her own share of foes, until the goat stumbled and she fell to the ground. In an instant Marki stood protectively over her, with his axe in his hand, and slew the last of the Bantu.

The female dwarf lay where the goat had thrown her, but she was struggling to a sitting posture. Marki, checking no enemies were advancing upon them, then held out his hand to the dwarf. "I'm Marki, lass," he said, "I'm pleased to make your acquaintance."

The female dwarf stared at him in astonishment. Her mouth moved, but initially no words came out. "My arrival here is a long story, lass," Marki said, "and one I'll tell you when we have more time."

Gilly, then took his hand, and allowed him to help her to her feet. "I'm Gilly, me dear, and I'm pleased, and very surprised, to make your acquaintance."

The enemies now dead, the goat scrambled unsteadily to his feet. "And this, is me Gaffren," Gilly said, as she took his reins.

714

Marki wasted no more time on conversation. He ran over to Sernea, who lay on the ground dead, her neck broken. Marki let out a loud wail. Freylash, her underbelly shredded and her intestines spilling onto the ground, snorted. Her mouth opened wide, and she snapped on empty air as though trying to defend herself from any foes. The wyvern tried to get to its feet, but lurched and fell back to the ground almost instantly. The creature gratingly roared and harshly bellowed in distress.

Gilly joined Marki. "There's pain in her voice," she said sympathetically. "It would be kinder to end her, for this death will be prolonged and one full of agony."

Marki knew she was right. Tears filled his eyes as he raised *Old Trusty*. He struck downward with all the strength of both arms, driving the axe deep into Freylash's skull. The body of the creature twitched and flickered momentarily. The scales along her back and flanks turned from a hue of vibrant colours, to a dull lurid red, and then the light went out of her eyes.

Marki wiped away the tears from his eyes, and looking at the body of Sernea he said, "If I survive this day, I'll come back and retrieve your body. You'll get a decent funeral according to the rites of your kind. On this you have my word."

"I must find my friend me dear, her name is Janorra," Gilly said to Marki as she mounted Gaffren. She held out a hand. He took it, but said no words as he climbed into the saddle behind her, for despite the short time he had known them, his grief for Sernea and Freylash, was still too raw. Talain, he knew, would return from death, but they would not.

*   *   *

Bonnie and Borach landed on the parapet, and were not unscathed. The aerial battle with the garâton had been brutal. Several riders and their wyverns were dead, the others were all injured to a lesser or greater degree. The surviving wyverns spewed out fire towards the Bantu, who began to make a disorderly retreat back over the parapets.

"Methruille!" Bonnie shouted at the mage who blocked their way.

The mage stared back at her in disbelief and alarm. "Ascenti?" he asked. "Long had I hoped the stories were true that your kind were in this world no more."

Borach watched Bonnie smile ferociously. The mage, muttered some words, and much to Borach's surprise, took his hat off, pulled the hood of his cloak over his head, and disappeared from sight.

It was then that Borach noticed, at the base of a large spire, the battle was still intense. A man and a woman were locked in a ferocious fight with a number of Bantu who had them trapped. He recognised the woman from the vision of *Arvivan. The Seeress Janorra!*

Without thinking, he lunged towards the fray and was joined by Bonnie, whilst her wyvern, still spewing fire, pursued the Bantu who were retreating. Other Ascenti were landing on the parapet and they and their mounts joined the battle.

A Bantu, who had a severed shrunken head attached to his shoulder, stood in Borach's way. Borach swung his sword. The Bantu dodged sideways, but was not fast enough. Borach's sword missed the Bantu's head, but swiped the shrunken head toppling it clean over the parapet.

The Bantu stopped and stared at his shoulder in horror, where the head had been. "My brother!" he shouted furiously.

"Then join him," Borach said, as he put the heel of his boot in the Bantu's stomach, and shoving with all of his might, propelled him over the side of the wall. He did not have time to look over the side, as another Bantu, a large one, rushed towards him. The Bantu stopped as it recognised him.

"The former Lord of Aleskian," the Bantu sneered through bared fangs. "I am Gaishak the Corpse-eater, and today, I will feast on your flesh."

Borach said nothing in reply. Their swords met in a mighty clash, sending sparks up into the air. The strength of Gaishak was self-evident, by the power with which he swung his sword. But battle rage had consumed Borach. All he could think of was gaining revenge for Yianna and his children. On and on he and the Bantu fought, until he started to see doubt in the Bantu's eyes. With one mighty stroke from Borach, the Bantu's strength faltered, and he failed to completely parry it. Borach drove the point of his sword into Gaishak's body. The blade went into flesh, sinew and bone, right up to the hilt. Gaishak dropped his sword and fell to his knees. He shook his head from side to side and his mouth opened to its widest extent. Borach, still grasping the hilt, put his boot on Gaishak's chest and managed to tear the blade out. Most horribly, the Bantu's silence was broken. Though he knew the tongue, the words that issued from Gaishak's blood-streaming jaws did not make any sense to Borach, nor did they sound like anything that could have been produced by any civilised voice. This exhibition of primordial fury would have chilled the blood of a lesser man, but in that moment Borach felt akin to it, and saw in Gaishak's wrath a counterpart to that which had recently taken a hold of him in his darkest moments. The incomprehensible raging and ferocity of the roar of the creature fleetingly held Borach with a comprehending fascination. Borach quickly regained his senses, and with one stroke, removed Gaishak's head from his shoulders.

*       *       *

Scarand and Janorra slew the last of the Bantu that stood before them. Surprised by the arrival of wyverns and their mysterious riders, the other Bantu began to retreat. However, it was the new sight that emerged that brought Janorra fresh horror. Their armour was distinct and recognisable; her heart sank. "Kappian legionnaires," she said to Scarand. "The Empire has found me." She watched as the man took the head off of the large Bantu he had been fighting. He glanced very briefly at her, but more Bantu descended upon him, and his focus turned towards fighting them.

Janorra did not hesitate, but turned and ran with all haste until she thought her lungs would burst. She ran along the parapet, until she came to some stairs which she instinctively ran down, and then she fled at random through the fortress. Scarand caught up with her, and they did not stop until they came to a door, which was ajar.

"Come, quickly," he said, pulling her through the door and then shutting and bolting it behind them. The sound of the horns and battle disappeared.

They found themselves in some sort of library, although most of the books had longed turned to dust and ruin. They made their way down the cavernous hall, pressing through the weight of the silence, and catching their breath, watching for movement and listening for sounds that would signal danger or pursuit. They reached the end, but their way was barred by an ancient bronze door, the frame of which was set into the wall with pins and metal plates. Its surface was dull and overgrown with mould. Scarand brushed off the handle, seized it with both hands, and twisted hard. Nothing.

"There are locks and plates above and below the handle," Janorra said, peering closely at the door. "We will never open it unless we learn the sequence, and that would take more time than we have."

To their left, a long, circular iron stairway, its interlocking sections connected by catwalks and platforms, wound in serpentine fashion about the shelved walls leading to a door at the top.

"We need to go up then," Scarand said.

They began to climb, wearily ascending the steps at a slow but steady pace, the only sound their footfalls on the stairs and their panting for breath in the otherwise silent library.

By the time they reached the door, the furious sound of somebody trying to burst through the library door they had entered by, could be heard.

Janorra hoped beyond hope the door before her would open. If it did not, they were trapped. She tried the handle. The latch clicked, and the door opened. She and Scarand sighed with relief and stepped into a long corridor that branched off to the left and right. Choosing the right, they fled down it and then through a doorway that led to a narrow set of stone steps leading downward into an inner courtyard clouded with smoke.

From beyond the walls, raging red flames from the Wytchwood licked into the air. In the distance, they once again heard the blowing of horns and the distinctive sound of sword clashing against sword and shield, they heard the roar of the Bantu mixed with the roar of men, women and the screeching of wyverns.

Janorra and Scarand looked at each other, but said nothing. They heard the sounds of pursuit behind them. Picking up the pace the two of them headed down the stairs and through the courtyard to a place where the outer wall was crumbled and cracked. They managed to squeeze through the hole, and found themselves by the southern bridge. If it had earlier been guarded, it was not now.

Like the eastern bridge the southern one was monstrously massive, but what remained of it was on the verge of collapse. Just one small section was intact, but it looked so fragile, that it might break under the weight of Scarand and Janorra were they to attempt to cross it. Janorra and Scarand looked at each other indecisively.

"Stop!" a voice behind them roared. Janorra spun around to see the man who had slain the large Bantu clambering through the hole in the wall, followed by a woman. A large wyvern descended from the air landing on the ground with a heavy thud. The brute reared up on its mighty hind legs and elongated its neck and body, as though ready to breathe fire, or to charge and lash out with its spiked tail. The woman said something to it; the creature roared and bellowed, and settled to watch her would be prey with the patience of its reptilian kind.

Scarand raised his sword and had already turned to face the new foes. He glanced at Janorra and said, "Go, I'll delay them long enough for you to get across."

"No," Janorra said, "do not waste your life vainly. If we hurry, and what little of the bridge remains, holds, we can make it to the shelter of the trees, where that beast will not be able to land. We might find a way through the smoke and flames." The fire in the Wytchwood was spreading fast, but she would rather face that peril, and the uncertainty of the ruined bridge, than the certainty of being caught by her pursuers.

Scarand nodded, and turning to the bridge, he and Janorra stepped onto it. Bricks and mortar broke loose beneath them, plummeting into the abyss below, but enough still remained for them to continue on. So rapid was their flight, and such was her haste and panic, that halfway across, Janorra fell, and the Simal came out of her rucksack and rolled across the thin remnant of the bridge. It teetered on the edge, where it glimmered and glowed with ghastly light.

"Do not look into it," Janorra shouted to Scarand in alarm as he rushed to pick up the Simal. "Do not even touch it." She got up, and walking carefully to the edge, as more bricks and mortar crumbled and broke loose, she picked the Simal up and placed it in her rucksack.

Behind them, a large section of the bridge noisily gave way and collapsed, falling into the depths. Scarand took Janorra's hand. "We can still make it," he said, as they again began to run. More bricks and mortar crumbled behind them as they made haste to the other side. They made it by mere seconds, as the last of the bridge tumbled into the abyss. Exhausted, Janorra sat down and leant with her back against a tree and closed her eyes wearily. She opened them when she heard a screech, and she and Scarand watched as, on the other side, the woman and man mounted the wyvern, which took to the skies in pursuit of them.

Pulling her to her feet, Scarand urged, "We need to get under the cover of the trees." She did not resist, stood to her feet, and again, they ran.

*  *  *

From under the shadows of a ruined colonnade, Imrand watched, along with Muro and Sarkisi, the battle on the eastern bridge. The moon was now fully in the sky, and shed an eerie light upon the scene. The Bantu guarding it were in a ferocious fight with some creatures that had emerged from the forest, and had literally smashed down the gate, splintering the rotten wood and rusted iron.

"What is it?" Sarkisi asked, looking at the foul form of the monstrous creature which, along with some companions, was attacking the Bantu. Three times the height of a man, naked except for a cloth over its loins, its body was covered with boils and knotted with lumps and warts. Blood-streaked thighbones were dangling from a belt. They clattered together as the creature moved, making an unsettling noise. It had a spiked tail with which it impaled Bantu, lifting them into the air and then crashing them into the ground. It roared as it also swung a large spiked club at the Bantu, knocking them over or crushing them with its feet.

"That must be Tharn, the son of one named Silverberry," Muro answered. "He is angry intruders have entered here."

Sarkisi readied *Harnesh*, her Moon Bow, "Should we intervene?" she asked.

Muro shook his head. "Let them fight it out. We will kill the victors, cross the bridge, and make good our escape."

All three of the Davari knew the creatures that were with Tharn - Moravey. "They call them *Untamed Ones* here," Muro said. The Moravey had the same peaked heads and yellow fangs as the ones that dwelled in the mountains of their own lands, but whereas those in the Davari lands were covered in white hair to help them blend in with the snow, these ones had black hair, but beneath it, the brutish strength of their kind was evident. They carried clubs and attacked the Bantu with a ferocity that the Bantu matched in kind.

The battle on the bridge was brutal and prolonged, but eventually the Bantu prevailed. The Moravey were slain, and Tharn was mortally wounded. Two dozen or so flaming arrows were imbedded in his flesh, and several spears, but still he fought on, savagely swinging his club and crushing any Bantu that got within its range. The Bantu continued to fire more arrows into him, and Tharn's strength ebbed away, until with a final groan, he crashed to the ground dead. The Bantu were not without their losses, and many those were. Only seven out of fifty, survived the deadly encounter.

"Now," Muro said to Sarkisi, who unleashed a deadly volley of arrows. Each one found its mark. The Bantu armour was pierced as a knife through melting butter. Death was instant for the last Bantu on the bridge.

"This truly is a weapon of legend," Sarkisi said as she looked at the moon, and then with awe at the bow which was glowing with a faint whitish light. "I will build new legends and tales with it, and all shall fear to face *Harnesh* when the moon shines," she said.

Wasting no more time, with Imrand and Sarkisi picking up and carrying their treasure, the three Davari crossed the bridge and disappeared into the forest.

*      *      *

With Marki and Gilly on his back, Gaffren galloped at full pace through the street. Jumping over cracks in the broad pavements, dodging vines and ruined walls. "The bridge is most likely guarded, we will have to fight our way across it," Gilly said.

"Good!" Marki roared. "I have some scores to settle this day!" After witnessing the deaths of Sernea and Freylash, he was in a dark mood, and the battle rage was consuming him. As they approached the bridge, there was no sign of life, only dead bodies. Gaffren slowed as they crossed. Carnage was all around them.

"Poor Thrarn," Gilly remarked as she passed his corpse. "Bessie described him to me once, it is him. I am sure."

Marki made no comment as he looked at Thrarn and then at the dead Moravey. Fearsome in appearance though they were, he regretted that he had not been given the opportunity to test himself against one. Looking at the Wytchwood, where a fire was now raging and smoke billowing into the air, the sounds of battle could be heard in the air. "The Bantu in the fortress are dead," he said. "My friends need my axe." He pointed to where the sounds of battle were, where the fire was raging. "Will you and your sweet goat take me there or need I go on foot lass?" he asked Gilly.

"I too have friends that might need my assistance, me dear," Gilly said, as she spurred Gaffren into action and headed towards the sounds of battle.

*      *      *

As Janorra and Scarand headed deeper into the Wytchwood, they saw a scene just as worse as the nightmares they had just experienced. The Wytchwood, even here, was ablaze. Bantu arrows had set the trees alight, as well as the fire Muro initially began.

"How can this be?" gasped Janorra, "I thought Gilly said the forest would protect itself from such a danger."

"Clearly not this foe," Scarand replied as he looked at the fires with a shocked expression, shaking his head in bewilderment. Through the trees and smoke, they saw Bantu moving swiftly, but had not spotted them.

"Curse these creatures of chaos," Janorra cried. "Should we head to the dark part of the forest where the trees are dead?"

"No," Scarand said, "when the fire reaches there, it will spread faster than we can run."

There was a waist high blanket of smoke, drifting beneath the boughs. The two companions made their way through it, gasping for air whenever the smoke cleared. Ahead of them, they heard the blaring of a horn, and the growl of Bantu. They began to run away from the sound, but with the fire, heat and smoke, everything was confusion. A squall of embers followed them as they hurried through the trees and an ominous heat washed over their faces. The crackling of burning wood filled the air. They limped through the thickening smoke, the fumes filled their lungs and when they coughed their chests were wracked with dreadful pains.

719

Behind them, a dozen or so Bantu appeared. A wave of flaming black-feathered arrows whistled through the trees, thudding into branches and trunks all around them. Janorra and Scarand covered their mouths with the ends of their cloaks, handkerchiefs and their hands, and soon found themselves driven by the fire towards a large open glade. More black-feathered arrows whistled past them, wrapped in pitch-soaked rags and spitting flames. Branches around them exploded as the arrows hit home. The scraps of flame spread out like a net and soon spread to other trees. The Wytchwood groaned as if in pain; they were trapped by fire either side of them.

"They are missing on purpose. They're trying to herd us," Scarand shouted above the roar and cackle of flames. Janorra looked, he was right. Through the flames she could see Bantu with bows. They were clearly aiming at the trees, not them. The marksmanship of the Bantu was incredible, they were vaulting over flaming stumps as they fired and not a shot missed its mark, hitting the trees around the two companions, herding them no doubt towards a trap.

"This way," Janorra shouted, as she ran, weaving drunkenly through the trees no longer knowing which way she was heading. Their choices were few. The fires were spreading faster and faster, leaping from tree to tree. Above all the clamour, the constant din of the Wild Hunt's horns rang out. Bantu, shrouded in smoke moved among the chaos, untouched by the flames, using their flaming arrows to herd the companions towards a direction they left clear. They had no choice but to head towards it, and soon entered a very large glade. Scarand took a quiver of arrows from a dead Bantu, but only three were in it.

The companions were not the only ones who had been herded towards the glade. As they approached the glade the scene was far more disturbing than they thought. Within it, Janorra noticed some Spriggan. *What are they doing here?* A masked Bantu was spreading fire around the edges of the glade, to trap them, and others were hacking down any Spriggan who darted across their path trying to escape the flames. Noticing her, one of the Spriggan ran towards Janorra, but an arrow through the neck felled the poor thing before it could reach her.

Through the trees, Janorra saw some Kappian legionnaires in a life and death struggle with the Bantu; in her mind, they were both were trying to capture her, and she did not know into whose hands it would be worse to fall. The soldiers, about a dozen in number, were soon trapped by flames. Many of them stumbled and dropped to their knees, as fiery arrows embedded in their necks.

Janorra ran to the edge of the glade, but it burst into flame. A Bantu exploded from a hedge to their right. She lashed wildly, her blade opened the beast's throat and it fell, reeling back into the smoke. The flames immediately consumed it.

The heat near the edge was too intense, so Janorra and Scarand moved nearer the centre of the glade. There was nowhere else for them to run. They were trapped and clearly exposed. They huddled together, back to back, in an attempt to protect their flanks. Dozens of Bantu began loping out of the shifting smoke-filled gloom and flames, leering, snorting and brandishing brutal weapons as they encircled them both.

Scarand fired the last of his arrows. The first arrow, a Bantu one he had picked up, buried deep within a Bantu's broad shoulder blades. He watched in horror as the creature wrenched the arrow free without a murmur of pain. The second arrow, fired more clumsily, bounded off of the chest armour of another. The mocking howling of the Bantu filled the air. His third arrow, hit the same Bantu in the eye and it fell silently into death. Several larger Bantu rushed through the only entrance and exit.

"We got the soft-'ole and an orf-chump," one of the Bantu said gleefully as another roared, "take 'em alive boys."

The Bantu approached them. Janorra felled the first that came within her reach, swinging and stabbing furiously at the sword wielding creature as it charged. Her blade embedded deep between his ribs and his armour quickly turned crimson, but she could not remove the blade, so she let go of it, took the Simal from the rucksack and held it in front of her, hoping with all hope that some power from it might save them.

The Bantu were upon them in seconds. Scarand fought like a blood-mad barbarian, his strength and ferocity like that of a wild beast, and he slew two, but he was no match against the numbers he faced and several Bantu soon overpowered him and trussed him up in rope bonds.

Janorra fought wildly as a one-eyed Bantu, snatched the Simal from out of her hand, but his hand made a sizzling sound as though flesh was touching a hot surface. He dropped it immediately, and in retaliation struck a blow to her head with his fist. She fell helplessly to her knees, and was soon immobilised and trussed up.

Scarand continued to struggle in his bonds. One of the Bantu laughed. It was the one he had fought earlier, with a half-metal face and iron spikes for teeth. He licked his lips and ground his teeth and then said, "Look boys, he's madder than a Gragor's flea."

"Bite the orf-chump's nose of Frogin," the one-eyed Bantu said to him. He held his hand limply as it still sizzled from being burnt by the Simal. He snarled at Scarand and then looked at Janorra.

"We can make the orf-chump die painfully later," Froglin replied. "We're not to 'urt the soft-'ole. Not yet, anyway."

"Oh, go on," the Bantu said. "Let me 'ave a maffick with the soft-'ole, and then I'll gis u a turn at the snog."

"No, Scopold, no!" Froglin shouted.

Another of the Bantu looked at Janorra, and then at the shrunken, decapitated head on his shoulder, which he stroked tenderly. "Marigoof lost 'is brother for a while. I wanna find the one that lopped 'im off," he said.

Scopold gingerly attempted to pick the Simal up again. Again, it burnt him and he screamed in pain as he dropped it. He cupped Janorra's face in his large, blood-stained hand, held up his injured one and rasped. "We'll give the Empire scum Shrimakan and you, but you will be ours to 'ave some fun with before we do." He snarled, baring his fangs and a mouth full of filed and sharpened teeth. "Me and the boys will maffick, strip the skin from your gigglemug, flay the flesh from your bones, and when you resurrect, we will start again."

His breath stank. Janorra felt bile rise in the back of her throat, opened her mouth to scream, but vomited instead. The Bantu laughed as she knelt there trembling.

"Where's Gaishak?" another Bantu asked Froglin.

"He's maggot food," Froglin replied.

A mage ran into the smoke-filled glade followed by several other Bantu. He smiled wickedly when he saw Janorra, and even more so at the sight of the Simal laying on the ground. He approached and picked it up. The grin on his face widened. "We have the Shrimakan," he said triumphantly. The Simal glowed wildly as he muttered dark incantations. It was clear to Janorra, he was trying to use magic to take the Simal into another realm, away from the present danger, but she knew that no spell or invocation known to any being living or dead, no matter how powerful, could transport the Simal through such means. It was clear to her he had no Jula to use. Wherever he wanted to take the Simal, he would have to carry it. This truth soon dawned upon him. Without taking his eyes off of the Simal, he said to the Bantu, "Pick the prisoners up. We need to get back to Norvaskun. Our entrance to the Underglow is not far."

721

"Do what Methruille says boys, it's 'ome time," Froglin roared after which he snapped his teeth together several times in glee.

Instantly a horrible roar shook the woods. The aimless snapping and crackling of the burning trees changed to a sustained crashing as a wyvern came like a hurricane straight into the clearing, followed by several others. Blood smeared the scaly, flabby lips and dripped from the huge mouth of the first wyvern. The sporadic flames of the forest did not seem to bother it in the least, but the two riders, covered in smoke and grime, jumped off the creature's back and were soon followed by those on the other wyverns.

"The *Betrayer* has joined with the Ascenti," Methruille sneered.

\*　　　　\*　　　　\*

Borach was in no mood for small talk. With his blade drawn he ran towards the nearest Bantu. "For Aleskian!" he roared.

"For me Gaffren!" Borach heard a female voice roar as a goat with two riders burst through the smoke. To Borach's great surprise, one of the riders was Marki.

Marki grinned a toothy smile as he jumped off the goat and matched Borach's stride. "By Balagrim Bor, you look like you could use a hand. This is Gilly, by the way, and the goat is Gaffren."

Borach grinned morosely, but did not reply. He lunged towards the first Bantu he reached; the long straight blade impaled the beast and stood out a foot and a half between his shoulders.

Marki attacked the nearest Bantu, swinging *Old Trusty*. A choking cry escaped the Bantu as the head fell back limply, disclosing a throat that had been severed from ear to ear.

Freeing his sword, Borach saw the Bantu he had fought earlier. This time, it was not the severed shrunken head he hit, but he swung his sword with all of his might and the actual head of the Bantu and the shrunken one, flew from the shoulders, the neck spurting black blood and goo. The wyverns themselves joined in the battle, tearing into the Bantu forces.

The steel of *Old Trusty* flashed as Marki dipped and rolled, slicing throats and severing limbs, performing a lethal dance; a whirling storm of limbs and steel. The Bantu tried to fight back, tried to parry the blows, but the fury of Marki, backed by that of Gilly who swung her staff with amazing skill, meant that the fight was lost almost as soon as the Bantu realised it had begun, but all too quickly they rallied.

Borach unleashed the full might of his fury, and none there was that faced him, who could stand before him.

Another wyvern circled overhead and then landed with a run and skidded to a halt. Turning, it was upon the Bantu with a ferocity that matched their own. It was a carpet of claws and snapping beak as it ripped many of them to shreds. Through the work of the riders and the wyverns, Borach, Marki and Gilly, the glade was soon carpeted with a pile of scattered and bleeding Bantu corpses, but those that remained alive were relentless and did not give up. Others dashed through the banks of smoke, glimpsing the fight, and joining in with unyielding fury.

Several wyverns were killed, along with their riders, Ascenti and Kappian alike. The fierce fray had casualties on both sides.

Bonnie faced Methruille. Sparks and bolts of lightning came from their staffs, but neither could outmanoeuvre the other, and in the ferocity of the fight, Methruille dropped the Simal and was unable to retrieve it. The surviving Bantu, along with Methruille, were pushed back, and when it was clear the battle was lost to them, one of their horns blasted, and the last few survivors, along with Methruille, quickly disappeared into the flame and smoke enveloping the forest.

Before he disappeared from sight, Methruille pointed at Janorra. "We will find you again. The Wild Hunt will never give up," he scowled.

Borach stopped to catch his breath as he surveyed the scene. There was no jubilation among the victors, the cost in lives had been too high, and only eight of the royal-wyverns had survived the encounter, but one was mortally wounded. Bonnie and Saisha, bloodied from the battle, approached the wounded one, and mercifully put the stricken beast out of its suffering. Marki wiped the blood off of *Old Trusty*, cleaning it on the bodies of the Bantu. The terrified goat, Gaffren, ran up to Gilly. She caught its reigns, and sang softly to it as she calmed it. When the goat was under control, Borach watched as she cut the cords binding the Davari man and the Seeress Janorra.

Borach felt a fury rise up within him, when he saw Janorra retrieve the Simal. He ran towards her and raised his sword, fully intending to slay her where she stood. Gilly was between them in an instant, and a swipe from her staff aimed at his feet, knocked him to the ground.

"Don't you touch her, me dear," Gilly warned.

Marki was there in an instant. "Bor, don't," he pleaded. "Enough blood has been shed this day.

"Her actions led to the fall of Aleskian, and the *Final-death* of Yianna and my children," Borach sputtered, the pain in his voice evident to all. He got to his feet and stared venomously at Janorra.

"I am only responsible for my choices, not those of others," Janorra retorted back, and then, her voice and face panic-stricken, she asked. "Do you intend to return me to Kappia?"

"We are no longer soldiers or friends of Kappia lass," Marki said. "We are exiles." He reached out a hand towards Borach, but the fury within Borach was still too strong. He snarled, turned away, and stormed off into the smoke and haze in the same direction Methruille and the Bantu had retreated.

"We'll protect you lass," Marki said encouragingly to Janorra, before he turned, and followed Borach.

# Chapter Sixty-Three: *New Friendships*

*He is a good friend that speaks well of us behind our backs.*
**A Dwarven Proverb.**

*Marki* looked at Gilly more closely and felt himself blush; *she is so pretty*. He then bowed politely in the manner of Dwarves and said, "I've not really introduced myself properly. I am Commander Marki, *Vargo Goss Legendary Ale Champion*, and Son of Maladrith the Blacksmith of Clan Margor of the Iron Mountains."

"A *Vargo Goss Ale Champion*? My, that is a feat to be proud of, me dear," Gilly replied as she curtsied and then added, "I am Gildaora, daughter of Garalayith, *Knitting Champion* of Clan Gomar, also of the Iron Mountains, but most call me Gilly." She pointed to her goat, "And this, as you know, is me Gaffren."

"Well, you can hold your own in a scrap lass," Marki said, followed by a whistle of admiration.

"As can you," Gilly replied, after which she blushed and looked at the ground.

"Did you have a hand in that handy drop of rain?" Marki asked her.

"No, me dear," Gilly answered. "But there might have been other friends of the Wytchwood, elementals, who had a hand in that downpour. It completely put out the fire, so I do not think it mere coincidence."

Borach, Bonnie and Talain approached. "That's all of them resurrected and *Awakened*," Talain said to Marki as he looked at the sleeping Obelisk and those gathered around it. "Apart from Armun. He has not fully *Awakened* yet."

Marki raised his eyebrows in surprise. "It's been only a few hours since some of them resurrected," he said.

Talain eyed Janorra curiously. "She is very skilled. Using her ring, she was able to *Awaken* each of the resurrected incredibly quickly."

"Except Armun?" Marki inquired.

Talain frowned. "According to her, he will take more time to regain his memories. She thinks it is a miracle that the Obelisk was able to resurrect anyone at all. It has been trapped in the place called Garama Aethoros for longer than anybody knows, and is very weak."

Borach looked suspiciously at Janorra. "I have ordered her every move to be watched."

Marki looked over at the Pure-blood men who had died in the battle, now resurrected. They had clothed themselves in their former armour and clothes, which, damaged as they were, had been retrieved from the field of battle. Some of them were guarding Janorra and the Simal, whilst others were preparing their equipment for the upcoming trip. Galin sat there sullenly, as Janorra attended to a grievous wound inflicted upon his arm during the battle. Another woman was watching her, anger written all over her face. "Who is that?" Marki asked, as he lit his pipe, sucked on it, and when it came alive, he sucked some more and then blew out the smoke.

"Her name is Sezareal," Borach answered. "She is somehow connected to the Seeress, but there seems to be no love lost between them."

"Armun looks glum," Marki observed, as he pointed with his pipe towards him. Armun was sitting on a cradle, near to the Obelisk, his back slumped.

"Very few of his memories have returned," Talain said, "but of those few that have, he seems most concerned to have lost his staff."

"It helps me he does not have his memories," Bonnie stated. "I must take the Simal to Malagrim as soon as I am able. When Armun finally remembers his own task, I will have to kill him, if he resists my purpose, and leave whilst he is still in the Deadlands."

"You do not have it?" Borach asked.

Bonnie frowned. "No. I tried to take the Simal from the Seeress, she stopped me. It is some trickery of hers. I have blackened her eye for her defiance, but beyond that, did her no harm. I will try again soon. We may have to slay her."

"Janorra is my friend, me dear," Gilly snapped at Bonnie, clearly annoyed. "You'll not harm her, or take the Simal against her will, or mine, nor that of the Wytchwood, for I will tell the forest to resist you. You are not the only one with a few tricks up your sleeve! Or a staff with power."

Bonnie snorted derisively. "This matter is not your concern!"

"I am making it my concern, me dear," Gilly irately retorted. "This forest is my friend, not yours. I will not have you harm Janorra again, or you will have me and the Wytchwood to reckon with!"

Bonnie stared at Gilly with a look of utter contempt.

"Enough!" Borach snapped impatiently. "Take the Simal, but do not harm the woman until I have spoken with her. I will soon find out, one way or another, what her involvement is in the matters that have led to my woe."

Bonnie paused before addressing Borach. "The Simal felt as heavy as a mountain to me when I tried to take it. I dropped it, and when I tried to pick it up again, it became scorching to the touch." She seemed concerned. "I could not take it. It…it resisted me!" She laughed dismissively. "I am sure it is just some trick the woman used. I will figure out a way to take it and overcome her mischief."

"I have no love for magic items, let me tell you," Marki added to the conversation. "More trouble than they were worth. My kind wisely steer well clear of them." He then looked apologetically at Gilly and smiled sheepishly. "Well, mostly."

"Then if you cannot yet take it, you will leave the Simal with the Seeress for now, for it must come with us away from this place," Borach ordered Bonnie, and then said to all, "the Wild Hunt suffered a heavy defeat, but they will not give up looking for the Simal and the Seeress and will return. We must leave this place."

"The Simal will be returned to Malagrim, that was our agreement," Bonnie reminded Borach.

"It was," he acknowledged, "but it will be a dangerous journey to return to the Giant Halls, and one that must be prepared for and planned properly."

"Then the sooner we set out the better," Bonnie said. "The Simal has to be taken on foot; we would do well to set out before the Wild Hunt recover from this defeat. If I cannot carry it to Malagrim, I will make the woman Janorra to do it for me!"

"Do not test me on this, me dear," Gilly warned Bonnie. "I will not allow Janorra to be forced to do anything she is not willing to do." She looked directly at Borach. "Me dear, it would be wise to hear Armun on this matter, when his memories have returned."

Borach looked at both Bonnie and Gilly. Both had a determined look on their faces and stared at each other defiantly. He sighed deeply. "Whether by means of Janorra's trickery, or the Simal itself, it seems you cannot carry it," he said to Bonnie. "We cannot tarry here. We have seen what the Wild Hunt can do, and we have lost all but seven of the royal-wyverns, and all but three of their riders. They all fought well in the battle. If the Bantu return with reinforcements, we might not win the next encounter."

"Then what do you suggest?" Marki asked.

"The Simal stays with us, for now," Borach stated. "Rash moves, unplanned, would not be wise." He looked around at the chamber. "We will leave here and join with the rest of our forces gathering for the siege at Greytears. The Simal will be secure there, in the middle of a host. We can form a plan what to do with it, whilst beginning the conquest of Greytears." He looked at Bonnie. "It seems that, after all, we might have no choice but to hear Armun on this matter when his memories have returned. He would be a better ally than an enemy."

Bonnie snorted. She was clearly not pleased.

"In the matter of the Simal, I am determined we not act in haste," Borach stated. "My decision is made."

"I agree," Marki said cautiously. "Gilly here, has agreed to lead us through the Wytchwood to the Erin, where we can signal our boats to collect us."

"I will bury my friend Bessie first, me dear," Gilly said to Borach. "That is not up for negotiation."

Borach nodded. "Very well then," he said. "The Ascenti wish to deal with their dead as well, and some of my men have their own bodies to respectfully bury as they see fit. We will leave after these matters have been promptly dealt with."

"Will you join me, me dear?" Gilly asked Marki.

"Yes, I will lass," he gently answered.

"I will ask Miss Janorra as well," Gilly said, "she and Bessie had become friends in the short time they knew each other."

"No!" Borach said firmly. "She will be held under guard and watched at all times."

Gilly looked at Marki, looking for support.

Marki raised his eyebrows sympathetically. "It is best she stays here lass," he said.

*        *        *

Gilly wailed with misery, as some Spriggans took the corpse of Bessie from her arms. "Oh, my poor dear Bessie," she wailed. Marki, who stood behind her, put a comforting hand on her shoulder, but said nothing.

"Don't you worry Miss Gilly," one of the Spriggan said. "It's only Bessie's body that's dead, 'er spirit is now a part of the forest. We are sure we 'eard 'er singing from the other side last night; perhaps she sang a lament with old Silverberry for Thrarn."

"You did?" Gilly asked hopefully, wiping away a tear.

"We think we did, Miss Gilly," another Spriggan answered, "though it could 'ave been the wind rustling through the leaves."

The Spriggans laid Bessie's body in a hole in the ground, that had already been prepared.

"Janorra's glade is the right place to lay her," a Spriggan said. "Bessie always liked it 'ere, and she was really fond of Miss Janorra, so she won't mind a tad being buried next to 'er. We'll plant some golden flowers on their mounds, as a forever memory to them."

The Spriggan filled in the hole with their little shovels, and then planted seeds on the two burial mounds. Of a sudden, strange music suddenly echoed from the trees, soft joyful horns and the glacial tinkering of harps, a bewildering jumble of melodies that spiralled and rose without the slightest trace of discord. A hundred or so Spriggans appeared, as did the two Bena birds Hogin and Mogin, who joined in the music with out of tune squawking.

"We 'ave a party at Spriggan town, will you join us Miss Gilly?" one of the Spriggan asked.

Gilly looked at Marki who patted her warmly on the shoulder and said, "It is your choice, but my advice is we need to be getting back to the Obelisk and then on our way. We want to reach the main army at Greytears, as soon as we can."

"My friend Mr Marki is right, me dear," Gilly said to the Spriggan. "We have a perilous journey to make, that delaying any further, only increases the risk." She smiled warmly at the Spriggan. "That reminds me, can we assure our friends for certain the forest will allow them safe passage out? Have you heard from Silverberry?"

"It will," a peculiar looking Spriggan answered. "The forest is thankful that the visitors saved it from those nasty old Bantu. It will let them leave unmolested. Silverberry will be mourning for Thrarn, so we 'ave not disturbed 'er."

"Well give Bessie and old Thrarn a right good send off," a Spriggan said as the funeral procession slowly proceeded into the greenery of the forest. Soon the music faded, as did the sound of the Bena birds, and they were soon all out of sight.

"Well by Balagrim, I never thought I would see such a sight," Marki said as he slapped his thigh." He then looked conscious of his joviality, coughed, and said, more sympathetically, "When you are ready, my dear Gilly."

She turned to him and smiled warmly. "I am ready, Mr Marki, me dear." She took his hand, and they made their way through the forest back towards the Old Citadel.

*   *   *

Marki and Gilly arrived at the Old Citadel just as the funeral procession for the Ascenti was about to begin. They joined Talain and Galin who greeted them. Bonnie, Saisha and a third Ascenti whose name Marki did not know, silently led the procession on foot. The bodies of the dead were carried by the legionnaires. The Ascenti women showed no signs of effeminate mourning as they marched ahead. They were dry-eyed, their faces grim-set. The bodies of the deceased were put on prepared pyres, made up of dead wood that had been collected, as no living tree would they dare cut down in such a place as the Wytchwood. The fires were lit, and the procession watched the flames and smoke soar into the sky. After a short time, Bonnie and the other two Ascenti, turned and left. The funeral party dispersed.

Marki, followed by Gilly and Galin approached Bonnie, who stood by a ruined fountain. His eyes were filled with tears. "I mourn for all your dead, but the most for Sernea," he said. "Though I knew her but for a short time only, my respect for her was immense." He then added. "No words were spoken, no mention of their names."

Bonnie nodded. "The obsequies we have observed, are appropriate for Ascenti heroes. We believe it is not only in war that discipline needs to be maintained, but in mourning as well. We do not like wild displays of emotional incontinence."

"Then you would not like a dwarf funeral," Marki said. "There is weeping and mournful wails everywhere, and the songs of lament often pass well into the night."

"You are right, I would not like that," Bonnie responded tetchily.

Saisha and the other Ascenti woman joined them.

"What about the dead wyverns, what happens to them?" Talain asked.

A look of sadness swept over Bonnie's face. "We leave them where they have fallen. They will rot until the bones are left to bleach in the sun, or nature reclaims them. Others wyverns often eat them, if food is scarce. The survivors have eaten their fill."

Saisha then added, "It is not unusual for us to turn some of their bones, teeth, skin or scales into jewellery or some implement with a more practical use, such as a drinking horn, for the sake of remembering them. We have collected enough of their remains for this. They will be honoured."

The third Ascenti woman spoke, addressing Bonnie. "Five of the wyverns, including Drasi bear significant wounds. We have released them to go to the Wyvernspine to recover, but Drasi flew off in a different direction. The wounds on the other two mounts are minor. They can carry the weight of a rider, but not a passenger as well."

Bonnie nodded. "Drasi will return to the Wyvernspine when he is ready. You and Saisha take the other two and meet with the army gathered at Greytears. I am going on foot. Make sure the boats are there to meet us at the agreed spot."

Saisha and the other woman nodded, turned and left.

Bonnie looked sternly at Marki. "My people have been ravaged by disaster. This battle cost us more dearly than any others. Only three Ascenti now remain in this world."

"You have paid a very heavy price lass," Marki agreed.

"Then you will know that I will not consider it a crime or a betrayal, to do what I must, if Borach forbids my efforts to return by any means, the Simal to Malagrim. I consider it my solemn duty."

"He has not denied you this, lass," Marki said. "He only wishes to hear Armun on the matter and to plan any journey to take it there properly. Perhaps Armun might even agree to your demands and ally with you to make it so?"

Bonnie inhaled and then exhaled impatiently. "I will go to Greytears with you, but know this. The Simal is better off in the hands of Malagrim, and from there, I will form a band to journey with me. If I still cannot carry the Simal myself, then I will drag Janorra there, in chains if I must." She glanced at Borach. "You must convince Borach of the folly of attempting to stop me." She turned and left abruptly.

"There's going to be trouble ahead," Galin warned, as he rubbed the stitches on his arm.

"Don't I know it," Marki grumbled, as he turned and stared at Gilly who was glaring at Bonnie as she strode off.

*       *       *

Much to Janorra's relief, the journey through the Wytchwood was without event or incident, although a slow dreadful wailing, the type of somebody in deepest grief, had filled the air. It eerily echoed throughout the Wytchwood. "It is Silverberry mourning for Thrarn, before she leaves this place," Gilly had informed the others.

As they walked Marki had questioned Janorra and Scarand intensively about the escape from Greytears, and both had told them how they managed it. She had only offered a partial account for the reason she had left the Argona Temple, and had only provided vague answers to his questions. Talain had been a welcome distraction, as she had also walked by her side for much of the journey, asking many questions about the Deadlands, and trying to discover any knowledge Janorra was willing to share about being a Seer. Janorra did not tell her much, for she was still learning who she could trust, but she used the time to avoid Marki's further intense questioning of her.

They made it to the banks of the Erin on the morning of the third day after they had set out. Saisha and her wyvern greeted them, as did several boats who ferried them across the river. On the other side, Chatti, Seesnari, a few legionnaires and some heavily armoured mercenaries met them. Gilly led Gaffren by the reins, and they all made their way by foot, through the forest trails, and then to a main road where horses waited for them. No horse would allow Janorra to mount it when she tried. Each one she attempted to mount reared up and went into a state of panic, confirming what she already knew, about animal-kind dreading such immediate nearness to the presence of the Simal. She could, however, without incident sit in the back of one of the wagons

728

being pulled by a team of horses. Scarand joined her, as did Marki, after he had been updated by a legionnaire. He continued his line of questioning about anything they might remember about Castle Greytears that might be of help for the siege and battle that lay ahead.

A fire flashed in Scarand's eyes, and he in turn questioned Marki about Kappia, and sought information on what might be the fate of such as his sisters, Marciea and Oliviana. Janorra felt compassion for Scarand, as a look of wild despair and anguish replaced the anger in him, when Marki confessed he had only visited the city once, a long time ago, and that there was little he could offer in way of helpful information. Janorra told him all that she could remember about the city, though mostly, she had been confined to the Argona Temple, so could not offer him much more beyond that which she had already shared with him previously.

As they journeyed along the road, they passed scorched fields and poisoned wells, and then entire villages that were burned to the ground. The air was thick with smoke and warped by the heat of the some of the buildings which were still burning. The crackling of the flames mixed among the sobs of terrified villagers, who looked half-starved. They sat or stood by the roadside wearing only tattered rags, most of them with shoeless feet, whilst children ran alongside the horses and wagons begging for food.

Marki did not appear to be indifferent to the suffering all around him, but neither did he seem particularly disturbed by it, as though it was a sight familiar to him.

"Did your forces do this?" Janorra asked with disgust.

"No, lass," Marki answered. "The Baron of Greytears did not want to leave anything outside the castle that we might find use of." He looked at a child who ran alongside the wagon with hands out, imploring them for some food. Marki picked up a ration bag and threw it to the child, who grabbed it and ran off. He threw several other ration bags onto the road, where other children and villagers rushed and then fought with each other over the contents. "It seems the Baron does not want too many mouths to feed within the castle," he said, "but my hope is it won't be a long siege."

The moon was rising in the sky by the time they reached the large army camp. The night was cold. The guards let them enter with no trouble. Two guards led the party swiftly through the site. Inside the camp, horses, tied to hitching-posts, stamped and snorted, and steam belched from their nostrils. The camp was swarming with soldiers, many of them mercenaries. Some wore padded jackets and round helmets and walked around carrying out whatever errand they were upon. Others were heavily armoured, and wore cavalry helmets with feathered plumes; they led horses by the reins, horses whose saddles were hung with lances, crossbows and shields. Janorra noticed the emblems on the shields of the knights, most of which she did not recognise except for those that bore a golden stripe between two lion heads, the Zarnan family coat of arms showing these men were Knights of Zinabar, a small but proud kingdom to the west she had once visited during her first lifetime when she was a carefree actress. Many of the soldiers and some of the legionnaires were sitting around campfires cooking their evening meal, or having already eaten, were lying down, in keeping with the practice that in a time of war, you sleep where and when you can, and get up when you are woken. Some plucked on lyres or stringed instruments, and sang quiet baleful songs about battles past, and the one they would soon face, as well as the families they had left behind, as they wandered in strange lands to fight for Lord Borach. Others were doing exercises, running around flagpoles, carrying wooden swords and wicker shields. They struck at wooden posts as they ran around the poles.

Those who knew where they were going dispersed, the others were led to some tents. Borach and Marki were led to the largest pavilion in the camp. Armun was taken away, under heavy guard, and Bonnie was led by the two Ascenti women to a remote part of the camp, where the wyverns were as far away from the horses as it was possible to be, so they would not spook them. Sezareal was led away elsewhere.

"You two are in there," a guard said to Janorra and Gilly, pointing to a large pavilion. "You will have guards outside."

Janorra saw little reason to protest, and in truth, the presence of guards was actually quite welcome, for they would be looking out to protect her. Scarand was taken to the tent next to theirs.

A maid waited inside the tent where there was a bowl off fresh water, soap, towels, food, a change of clothes, and everything Janorra and Gilly might need. After eating a meal in relative silence, Gilly and Janorra washed and changed their garments. "I will have these cleaned for you, and returned in the morning," the maid said.

Janorra was reluctant to allow Yimsha's armour to be taken from her, but the maid persuaded her it would all be returned in the morning, polished and clean. Janorra relented, and after she had tucked the knapsack with the Simal safely away, she and Gilly went immediately to bed. Janorra fell into a deep and peaceful sleep, and although she knew many dangers still lay ahead, for that night at least, with the guards outside, and being inside the camp of a large army, she felt secure and safe, a feeling she had not experienced for a long while.

*   *   *

Janorra woke promptly at dawn. Gilly had already left the tent. To her relief, the Simal was still secure under the bed, and Yimsha's armour was placed neatly on a rack. Janorra washed, ate a light breakfast consisting of a piece of fruit she took from a bowl, and then donned the armour and the knapsack with the Simal. The armour had been cleaned and looked pristine. The familiar odour of linseed oil and rosin varnish, brought no feelings of nostalgia, for it only reminded her of the Hammer Knights who guarded the Argona Temple. Putting the ringlet on, she whispered, "Yimsha?" wondering if the spectre might appear if summoned. Nothing happened. Janorra concluded that perhaps Yimsha had only been able to appear inside of Garama Aethoros.

Janorra stepped outside of the tent. The air was fresh and cool. "Did you see where Gilly went?" she asked one of the several guards around the tent.

"Follow me," the guard answered.

Janorra followed the guard. They moved speedily past the many soldiers who were already busy with various chores and duties. She ignored the wolf whistles and crude comments made by some of the mercenaries as she passed their tents. They arrived at a pavilion outside of which sat Gilly, sucking on her pipe and blowing out smoke rings. Her eyes were shut contentedly as though she were asleep. Marki sat next to her, his head in his chest, snoring loudly as he rested on a small wooden crate.

"Good morning," Janorra said.

Gilly opened her eyes, and beaming with a wide smile, said, "Good morning me dear." She looked warmly at Marki. "He was woken in the night to attend a briefing. A scout has returned and brought news from the north." She nudged Marki, who woke with a start.

"What? Wait? Where?" he asked, rubbing his eyes.

"We only shared breakfast together," Gilly said in way of explanation to Janorra, "and old sleepy head here fell back asleep."

"A soldier needs to grab sleep every chance he gets in times like these," Marki protested unapologetically. Addressing Janorra, he then said, "Sit woman, sit!"

Janorra sat on one of the crates outside of the tent, and soon, Scarand joined them.

Marki stared strangely at Janorra, who grew uneasy at the way he looked at her. "Do you have something to say?" she asked him.

"Aye, I do lass," he replied. "Last night, before we let her sleep, Lord Borach and I spoke extensively to Sezareal, and it was quite a tale she told us." He paused and then asked, somewhat dubiously, "Is it true, that an Aeldar God was actually summoned and slain?"

"It is true," Janorra answered. "Or, at least, I hope the Arkoom that was plunged into its foul chest, did what it was supposed to do."

Marki shook his head. "By Balagrim, I had often thought the Aeldar were merely the figments of over excited imaginations. Now, tell me the account of it, and your life in the temple, in your own words."

Janorra then recounted to the three of them, what led to her imprisonment at the Argona Temple, her life and experiences whilst there, and how she escaped, including how Azzadan had hopefully slain Ahrimakan.

Her audience of three, listened, mostly in stunned silence, only asking for clarification on a point here or there. When she had finished recounting the tale, Marki said, "That is some story less. Some story."

"Do you believe me?" Janorra asked him.

He hesitated before answering. "After all I've seen since the fall of Aleskian, I have no reason to doubt you, and I sense no lie upon your lips or a look of such in your eye." He slapped his leg. "Yes, by Balagrim, I do believe you," he said, "and it certainly explains why the young Sezareal, carries such a hatred for you. Her tale of how you both escaped is similar in many details."

"I did not do what I did to those sisters out of malice," Janorra said, feeling somewhat ashamed.

"I do not doubt it," Marki answered, "and after hearing your account, I find I cannot judge you harshly for your actions. Give Sezareal time. Grief and anguish are still heavy on her heart, due to not knowing the current circumstance of her sister." He looked at Scarand, and remarked, "as you would well understand, young fellow."

Scarand nodded, but Janorra could tell a deep melancholy was upon him, and he gave no other reply.

Janorra watched in awe as two Gragor passed by. Their slow lumbering gate and heavy steps, made the ground tremor slightly as they passed. The Chatti with them, looked fierce and unrelenting. They stared at Janorra with curiosity as they passed by, but they said nothing. In the distance, a trumpet blared.

"Come," Marki said. The war council is about to start, and we are all summoned." He then looked apologetically at Scarand. "Except for you. I'm afraid you will have to find other things to occupy your time."

Scarand looked grim. "Then have me taken to the one named Sezareal; I would speak some more with her, and learn from her what I might about the city of Kappia."

Marki looked at Janorra, and as though anticipating the reason behind the look, Scarand said to her, "She will not taint my heart towards you. I just want to speak with her and learn what I can about the city of Kappia, for her mind had not returned to her when we waited for your reappearance from Garama Aethoros."

"Then do so," Janorra said calmly, "if it puts your mind at rest. Perhaps you might discover that which might aid you in your own quest."

# Chapter Sixty-Four: *The Council of War*

*The Kirani are cat-like creatures that can walk upright. They believe that if they die in their homeland, an island called Kranitark somewhere on the western sea, their spirit goes to the paradise of Kirano. If they die outside of their homeland, they believe their spirit is doomed to walk the world until the day the world ends, when they will be reunited with their clans in Kirano. This does not, however, prevent the more courageous of them from travelling far and wide. In fact, it is considered a badge of honour and courage for any Kirani to travel widely and those that do so are honoured with the title Courageous Traveller and are much sought after as mates if they return home. Their favourite food is chicken. They have an absolute obsession for it. They also like their home comforts, a nice warm bed and a soft companion to cuddle up with, but don't let these nicer qualities deceive you. They are extremely ferocious and deadly in a fight.*

*Temmison Vol 1, Book 6: Peoples and Races of Pangaea.*

*It is tempting to say that there were never a people as unfortunate as the Cinoans. Their almost utter destruction was the product of Kappian rapacity at its worst; the country had immense wealth and was reputed to be quite staggeringly rich in diamonds and rare jewels. It was this fact that first brought it to the attention of Emperor Maopold III, who conquered and colonised it, turning it into a virtual labour camp, and hence from that time on Cinoan history is one of brutal servitude. The most iconic tapestry I have seen of this time depicts a weeping father, at a quarry, crouched over the severed hand and foot of his daughter, punished because she had failed to meet her quota of bricks for the day. The wicked do not always get their just deserts. Maopold III died his Final-death peacefully in his bed, on the third day of the month of Hengrian in the 102nd Year of the Golden Lion. Perhaps due to his wickedness, the Obelisks simply refused to return him to the land of the living again.*

*Temmison Vol II, Book 5: The Wars and Conquests of the Kappian Empire.*

*Janorra* followed Gilly and Marki as they made their way down a freshly-trodden path towards the large pavilion in the centre of the camp. Seesnari pennants fluttered in the wind, outside of the tent, as well as those of the Seranim, the Third Legion, the Chatti and several others that she did not recognise. She felt a lump in her throat as they entered the tent, as perilous thoughts were going through her mind. *I am still free. Whatever this council decides for me, what if I just decided...not to do it?* Inside, the tent was dimly lit by oil lanterns. Disturbingly for Janorra, the cacophony of conversation fell to an immediate and portentous silence as she entered, and every eye became fixed upon her. The gathering consisted of people either standing or seated around a large oval table that ran most of the entire length of the tent. It was adorned with various refreshments of wine, water, fruit and nuts. Among the gathering, there were several Seesnari nobles; fierce looking Chatti warriors; even a small delegation of three Kirani, the cat people from Kranitark in the Sunset Islands. One of the Kirani briefly stood, and turned full circle as is the Kirani way when introducing themselves. He had the striped face of a tiger, but stood upright like a man and wore black leather armour, shiny knee-length buckled boots, and a strange looking cloak ornamented with eccentric looking glyphs. It reminded her of the cloak Azzadan wore, and for a moment, she froze in terror, lest this strange looking Kirani might also be from the Order of Ithkall, but there was no clawed hand on his clothing that she could see. If he was an ally of Azzadan, there was nothing she could do about it at that moment, but she took her knapsack off and held it tightly, feeling the shape of the Simal inside of it. The Kirani then took his seat after performing an elaborate bow towards Janorra which included his striped bushy tail swishing across the front of his booted legs. Janorra had never seen a Kirani before. Their prowess was as proverbial as it was exotic, and they had a reputation for being crooks, cheats, and incessant thieves. It was said of them their charm was fused with ruthlessness, their dash with determination, to potent effect. She wondered why such a creature would be present at the council. Also, present, were a score or so of mercenary captains and several men of the Third Legion, including Borach, who stared sullenly at her as Marki ushered her to a seat in between Talain and Bonnie. Janorra looked around to see if she could see Armun, but he was not in attendance. *I wish I could consult with him concerning the Kirani, among other matters.* She took her seat, placed the knapsack on the table, and held onto it tightly, refusing the goblet of water offered to her by Talain.

"We're right behind you, me dear," Gilly whispered reassuringly to Janorra, as the two dwarves took a standing position behind her.

"We are all here," Borach declared without any opening courtesies, "apart from Master Armun. He still has not fully *Awakened*, so his presence will be of little use to us at this time. We have two matters to discuss at this council," he said. "The siege of Greytears will be our first." His face then involuntary curled up with distaste, "And then we must sort out the mess this Seeress has caused."

Gilly promptly interrupted Borach. "This Seeress has a name, and, if I may, I would like to make her introduction to this council."

Borach paused, opened his mouth to speak, but then, as one who had reconsidered, impatiently waved his hand in a gesture permitting Gilly to speak. "This is the Seeress Janorra, me dears," she said. "Her journey has been perilous and long, and I have sojourned with her for much of a part of her trials. She will be treated with courtesy by this council, for I consider her a friend, and if she is made an enemy of by you, then consider me such as well." A murmur of protest arose from many of those present.

"Somebody, silence that noisy self-indulgent dwarf with a fly swatter," one of the mercenary captains muttered.

Janorra heard Marki give an angry threating growl behind her. "Any Cinoan scum that tries it, will have his head quickly parted from his shoulders," he snarled.

The mercenary captain laughed dismissively and then whispered something to a scantily clad female slave standing next to him. The slave nodded, and left the tent.

"Malchus, remember your place and hold your tongue," one of the Seesnari nobles objected.

Janorra briefly studied Malchus' appearance, and caught his eye. His hair was spiked in the middle, shaved at the sides, with his head dyed blue, the same colour of his painted lips. He bared his filed teeth in an attempt at a smile, and then turned a furious gaze upon the noble who had rebuked him, but before he could say anything Borach banged his heavy fist on the table, causing the jugs and goblets near him to jump slightly and land again with a clatter. "Enough," he shouted.

"Indeed, gentlemen and ladies," a Fell-blood man said. "We all have a common cause, let us not squabble among ourselves." The man looked at Borach. "May I be the first to address this esteemed gathering?" he asked, somewhat insincerely.

"Say your piece," Borach moodily responded.

The man stood as he spoke. He had a short, broad back and well-developed muscles that were not hidden by the velvet doublet he wore. His hair was spectacular and curly, like a lion's mane, and he stood with a dignified posture. His voice was strong and commanding, confident and charming. He bowed gracefully to those gathered. "I am Maruk, the envoy for the Lord of the Mardoni. I am ambassador at the court of the Seesnari. Like our Seesnari allies, we consider the Bruthon an imminent threat. Our army is small, so mostly consigned to defending our own borders, but we have provided a significant amount of gold to pay for the mercenary forces that are gathered." He coughed, as though slightly embarrassed. "That gold is limited in supply, and might be exhausted if this turns into a long siege. If Greytears is to be taken, it will need to be done quickly, or the Giant Halls will have to contribute much more."

"Here! Here!" Some Seesnari nobles voiced in agreement. One of them stood and addressed the council. "A long siege is out of the question." Janorra studied the Seesnari delegation. Consisting of men and women, they were proud and stern of glance, all cloaked and booted as if just arrived from a journey on horseback. Their garments were rich, but stained with the dirt from recent travel. It was then that Janorra noticed Marlo seated among them, the pirate who had escaped with her from Greytears. He acknowledged Janorra with a nod.

A fierce looking Chatti was the next to speak. "I am Chasotha," the Chatti said. "We have Gragor and Chatti that right now are building mighty siege machines to break down the walls, but it takes time to build them. If we are to take Castle Greytears, haste might not be an option for us."

"We do not have the luxury of time," the Seesnari noble who had rebuked Malchus said. He was a tall man with a fair and noble face, blond-haired with locks shorn about his shoulders and blue-eyed. Barely out of his youth, he wore a richly embroidered black leather tunic and a green waistcoat. He had a necklace of gold upon which a stone of emerald green was set. Across his back, a long and elegant ebony bow rested and a quiver full of arrows with silver feathers. He then introduced himself. "I am Lord Starlen, son of Saroth Arnton, the High Warden of Ashgiliath, Conqueror of the Seven Towers of Samothrane, Slayer of Barnoth the Wicked." He stared arrogantly and proudly at the gathering, and then at Bonnie and a female warrior, the latter of whom was dressed in scanty armour that showed a lot of flesh covered in old scars, fresh minor wounds and dirt. She had taken off her horned helmet. Her scale-mail corselet had a raven insignia upon it and Janorra gathered she was a wyvern rider who no doubt had brought the fresh news from the north. "Perhaps, Chasotha, your scout will tell the whole council what she informed us about on her return."

Chasotha nodded at the woman, "Seressi is of the Crenwall tribe, and considered one of our finest scouts. Speak of what you have seen."

Seressi rubbed her eyes as though to take the tiredness from them. "I flew north, with a dozen other scouts. A wyvern can fly higher than most beasts, so we were able to fly undiscovered whilst seeing the Bantu's flying beasts below us. I have seen that there are two main Bantu forces. One army is marching south into the Tarenmoors, the other west towards Baothein lands. Numerous raiding parties of some considerable size are fanning out and causing terror, burning and pillaging, destroying all in their wake. They are slaughtering the great herds of aurochs that are on their migration route from the west to the grazing lands of the Tarenmoors, herds my people hunt to provide us with stores for the winter months. The meat the Bantu do not take or eat, they leave to rot. Entire herds have been slaughtered and are rotting in the wild places. My people will starve unless we find other sources of supplies." Her voice seethed with anger.

Marki interrupted. "I was in the briefing you gave earlier. You left out the part that many Cinoans from the Reaver Halls now join the Bantu in this pillaging," he said as he stared accusingly at Malchus.

"We are mercenaries, loyal to none but those who pay us gold to do their slaughter for them," Malchus responded defiantly. He looked scornfully at Marki, and then at Chasotha. "Those hired by the Bantu will be loyal to them. Malagrim pays me and my men, our blades are his, even if they are called upon to slay Cinoan flesh."

734

Janorra noticed that Marki was about to say something else, but he was stopped by a glare from Borach. "You would not be here if your loyalty to our coin was doubted," Chasotha said to Malchus. He then said to Seressi. "Inform the council of the numbers of the Bantu army?"

"The two armies are hordes I could not number. Their lines stretch further than the eye can see, even from a height," she replied.

"Tell them about Aleskian!" Chasotha said glumly. "You saw with your own eyes that it has been razed to the ground?"

"It is nothing more than a ruin of ash and rubble, the smoke of which even now still rises to the sky," she replied.

Marki and the other legionnaires groaned loudly. Borach stayed silent, grimly looking at the floor.

Malchus, the Cinoan laughed merrily as though he had just heard good news.

"You think such news is amusing?" Marki challenged him, drawing *Old Trusty* in a threatening manner.

"Silence your tongue you womanish pygmy," Malchus retorted with a dismissive wave of his hand. "Dwarves are known for their profligate dandyism, as well as they are known for their illegality and self-aggrandisement during their episodes of drunken brawling. I'll not lower myself to crack your skull and dirty my hammer with dwarf blood, even if just to cease your incessant prattling."

Janorra turned her head and noticed that Marki's face twisted with rage. He coiled his legs, as though ready to jump onto the table and charge at Malchus. Gilly firmly grabbed his arm. Marki looked at her and grimaced. She said something to him that nobody else could hear. Marki frowned. "Ha!" he snorted with rage, as he stood down, sheathing his axe, scowling and muttering and still glowering angrily at Malchus who continued to sneer with derision.

Janorra knew well the reason behind Malchus' anger. The very lands they were now on had once been Cinoan ancestral lands, in a time long before the existence of the Kappian Empire. History recorded that at that time, the Dwarves and Davari drove them from their lands, and they had never been able to return, as new settlers and kingdoms had soon risen. The Cinoans had travelled to the north and west and settled new lands bordering the Baothein, but they had never forgotten their ancestral hatred of both Dwarves and Davari, nor the land they had been driven from. In more recent times, before the Empire's civil war, the legions, led by Lord Borach, had entered Cinoan lands to put down a growing military threat as well as to quash the bands of raiders that constantly came from the scores of Reaver Halls. It was said it was a decade of blood and smoke, and the Cinoans had learnt first-hand about the wolf-like savagery of which the legions were capable. Cinoa had been soaked in blood. The minstrels still sang songs that the battle-hardened legions seemed as though forged of iron, and had been impossible to withstand. Many of the Reaver Halls had been destroyed and were now the habitation of wild animals and lonely spirits. The legions' Seers took their dead to the nearest safe Obelisks to resurrect, and so they kept coming until the Cinoan royalty and nobles were captured, and were taken to grovel before the Kappian Senate in Kappia, before being imprisoned or executed. The legions had brought back to Kappia Cinoan slaves by the tens of thousands, and uncounted plunder in groaning wagon trains. The Cinoan kingdom had been destroyed, and those that survived had become wanderers or bands of traveling raiders and mercenaries, with no place to call their home. *Another example of Kappian cruelty*, Janorra thought, and though she considered Malchus a far from pleasant man just by the look of him, she empathised with his rage.

"We have enemies enough, this council is called to discuss matters at hand, not resolve grudges and disputes, be they ancient or recent," Chasotha said fiercely, looking at Malchus and then Marki as a furrow of displeasure creased his forehead. "Continue with your tale, Seressi."

"After spying on the Bantu from on high, I flew east over the Kappia Plateau. Kappia is now at war with itself." She looked at Borach. "The city your people call Kara Duram, is besieged by those whose emblem is that of hammers and snakes."

The news shocked Janorra, and by the look on Borach's face, and that of the other legionnaires, it was clear they felt a similar surprise. Borach said nothing.

"The other more minor details, will be in my full report," Seressi said to Chasotha who replied, "you have done well. Go, rest, for we will be in more need of your scouting expertise in the days ahead." Seressi excused herself from the meeting and left.

Starlen spoke up. "The scouts have made us aware that the Bantu presence inside the Everglow is now split into two forces. One moves west towards Baothein lands, the other south towards the Tarenmoors. They pose a threat to us all, but my immediate concern is with the threats we the Seesnari face." He stabbed a finger towards the west. "To the west, three of the Nine Kingdoms share a border with us, and two of them we have fought before. They might again become snakes who bite the heel to make war and invade us if they thought it an opportune moment." He glanced at Marlo. "The Bruthon share this border with us, but we have learnt, by the treatment at their hands of my cousin Lady Sasna, that they mean war. Long have we traded with Kappia and sold them slaves which we traded along the Erin, past Bruthon ports, for which we paid high tariffs. They were so weakened by the Empire's civil war they can no longer protect the river from pirate scum, so our trade now trickles north to the Giant Halls and from there west or north into the lands beyond. If we open up the Erin again, we Seesnari have agreed to supply food and other goods to Malagrim, as payment for his assistance in this war."

Chasotha chimed in. "The Giant Halls can defend themselves, but the Bantu threat will stop the flow of trade through it, and our supply chains. Auroch meat is provided to us as tributes by the Tarenmoor tribes, their slaughter is a strategic move by the Bantu to limit our resources. The routes among the Erin must be opened up. It will be a lifeline for the Giant Halls, and the Tarenmoors, if we are to hold them back in the war that is now approaching our door."

"Indeed," Starlen said. "We Seesnari have sent an envoy to Erik Vansoth, one of the Sea Lords with a proposal. Part of that, involves destroying the Bruthon threat." He then glanced at Chasotha. "Some Chatti will head north to bolster the defence of the Tarenmoors. It has been agreed that Castle Greytears be given to Lord Borach, and from there, other Chatti will raid and weaken Bruthon lands. We must, once and for all, end the Bruthon threat as a first priority." He paused momentarily before continuing, and glanced around the room at those present. "The Hedge Knights of the Bruthon have long been engaged at their south-eastern border, protecting Bruthon lands from the raiding parties sent by the Horse Lords of Rhonbea and the Southern Marches." He pointed his finger in the air, and wagged it in a manner of warning. "But…it has come to our attention, news from our spies that the Bruthon king is on the verge of forging a peace treaty with the Horse Lords. This means, many Hedge Knights might soon be freed up to come and join the defence of Greytears. If we do not take the castle soon, it will be reinforced by many more well-trained armoured knights. The castle must be taken quickly, before that happens. Do you not agree, Lord Borach?"

Borach sighed heavily. "My men are the only Akkadians fighting on our side, in this battle. Death for them, near the walls of Greytears, will mean a resurrection inside of an enemy castle, if our Seer fails." He looked at Talain briefly, and then addressed Starlen. "I concur the sooner it is taken, the better it is for all, but Chasotha makes a valid point that a siege cannot be undertaken quickly."

Malchus spoke: "My men have already started to dig tunnels to undermine the walls. I counsel we put every spare man to work on them, including making the lazy Kappians dig a tunnel for themselves."

Janorra heard the groan of rage Marki issued, but before he could interject, Starlen firmly rebuked Malchus. "There is no love lost between you and the Kappians, but the incessant insults will stop now."

"Silence your tongue Seesnari, I take no orders from you," Malchus said as he used his sleeve to wipe away red wine that had spilled from the goblet he drank from and onto his beard.

Starlen looked at him in the manner of one who was surprised at not being treated with respect. "You are present at this conclave, that you might be better prepared to understand the situation we face, for which you accept gold," he said.

Malchus' response was to crudely burp, and then he said, "We have been paid Chatti gold, for our tunnelling expertise, not Seesnari. Speak to those in your employ as you wish, but I will not be silenced from speaking freely in this council of war. I do not trust Kappians. If we Cinoans dig a tunnel, Kappians will not use it."

When Borach stood, Janorra noticed he narrowed his eyes, and held the Cinoan in those slitted orbs. She read no friendliness; she saw only a fire as alien and hostile as that which burns in the eyes of a wolf about to pounce upon a sheep. He appeared menacing in every aspect, and when he spoke, nobody doubted the determination in his words.

"This Cinoan, will leave this conclave now, or I will cleave his skull to his teeth."

Malchus rose to his feet, and there was no fear in his mind or heart, as was evident for all to see. He stood with the demeanour of a man who had proven his worth on many a field of battle. "Those are the words of a typical Kappian dog, *or Borach the Butcher* as he is known among the women and children that survived the scourging of Cinoa." Malchus drew his war hammer as Borach drew his blade.

Marki jumped onto the table, *Old Trusty* already in his hands.

"Such a dog as he, would threaten me at a council where it was said all could speak their mind?" Malchus' voice rose to a loud and deep roar, and was filled with bitterness, deep and sharp. "I would bend him over a table and take him like a whore if it had not been for the fact that dwarf cock has been there first."

Chasotha also stood, and placed himself between Malchus and Borach. Such was the roar of his voice, all in the council, many of whom were also drawing their weapons, ceased and turned their eyes upon him.

"All will be given a voice here, and no blood will be shed, or it will be the undoing of us all." He stared at Marki, "Stand down dwarf!" Looking at Malchus and Borach, he ordered them, "Sheath your weapons, for if either of you shed blood here, I will expel you and all your men from this camp to fight it out wherever and however you will."

It was with obvious reluctance, that both Borach and Malchus sheathed their weapons, and took to their seats. Marki had raised *Old Trusty*, the veins on his head bubbled as though he was resisting the urge to launch it at Malchus.

"Marki me dear," Gilly said softly and soothingly, "don't do it, I beg of you."

Chasotha glowered at Marki, "Restrain yourself," he warned, with less anger than before, "for the sake of us all, you will not shed blood at this council, master dwarf."

Marki lowered his axe, and with many mutterings and curses, stood down from the table and went to storm out of the pavilion cursing Cinoans. Gilly restrained him, and whispering in his ear, managed to encourage him not to leave.

"Have you finished with your inflammatory insults? Chasotha asked Malchus.

The female slave who had earlier left, returned, and handed Malchus a small fur bag, which he took.

Malchus then defiantly replied to Chasotha, "No, I have earnt the battle right to have my say and will not hold my tongue for fear or favour of any, especially not amongst this band of craven thugs. I will have my say!"

"Then have it," Chasotha said fiercely to him, and then to Borach, "and you will listen, and then have yours."

Malchus was barely restraining his anger as he opened the small bag, and took from it a withered hand adorned with a jewelled ring. "I no longer call any man lord, or king. No man or woman should be given an eminence so great it prevents them from being brought to account for their deeds." Using the withered hand, he pointed accusingly at Borach. "This is the hand of my wife, all that I could find of her in the aftermath of the Kappian invasion of my homeland. He and his legions slaughtered my people in our own backyard, and not content to subject us to just the most abject terms, they ruined us and flushed us from our land. They trampled women and children under their horse's hooves, and their legions' booted feet. Many of our sacred Reaver Halls went up in flames, as they transported my people to their glutted slave markets, where our women and children were sold for a pittance of coin."

"Whilst you were pillaging and doing the same elsewhere," Marki objected.

"Let him speak!" Chasotha roared.

"We raided the villages and hamlets of our enemies, not systematically destroyed entire peoples," Malchus shouted back to Marki. He looked at Chasotha, and again pointed accusingly at Borach. "In their cities, was heaped the plunder of many lands. Their fleets of purple-sailed war galleys plundered the Tethys Sea, until the Sea Lords rose against them. The peoples of the Everglow, in many lands and provinces, bowed to their rule as far west as Shuna. Their armies ravaged the borders of Makigia in the east until it was swallowed by their rule." Malchus looked at Starlen. "Their royalty even wears Obelisk necklaces that they may cause suffering in the snowy lands of the Davari, using portals of Juran, where they appear as cowards and disappear again, using the Ikma to bring slaves for you to buy and sell."

"We know this," Maruk, said, "and where has it got them? The Kappian Empire is now on its knees, the rot within has caused it to all but collapse, and even their own cities are razed to the ground and a legion flees to the Tarenmoors for sanctuary. But, the situation in the Everglow has changed, a greater threat now faces us all. We all, must forget past grievances, Malchus, for the greater good."

"I see a threat before me, and it reeks of both Akkadian and Dwarven blood," Malchus replied as he looked ferociously at Borach and then at Starlen. "They say *never trust a Seesnari*, I say never trust a Kappian! Do not trust them to be a buffer, for they will only do so as long as it suits them. Give Greytears to us Cinoans, for this is our ancient homeland, and when we regain it, we will not easily forsake it like these dogs that are worse than any sell swords."

Janorra looked at Borach. His head was hung, so he was staring at the floor.

"I am not a man of politics," Malchus said, "but I know that business with Kappia has always been conducted by the fashioning of alliances and the doing down of rivals. Borach, was, until recently, a loyal servant of the vile Kappian Empire that all of us here revile." He turned to Starlen. "We will defend your borders with the Bruthon, if you grant Castle Greytears to us. We will swear an eternal allegiance to you, never to break faith from our part, and every Cinoan warrior spread throughout the ends of the Everglow would return to reclaim all land of ours claimed now by Bruthon. The Seesnari do not own a foot of land we claim to be ours, so ask this; would you not rather have a Cinoan sit on the seat of rule in Greytears and be your eastern neighbours?" He looked with contempt at Borach and the legionnaires. "Or would you prefer this untrustworthy cur, who until recently was loyal to the empire that has brought so much ruin to us all?" The conclave broke out in uproar again, and even Chasotha could not quieten them. Different delegates began to argue, one with another. Janorra noticed the only ones who did not seem affected were the Kirani, who sat there purring as though they were enjoying the spectacle. The one who had earlier spoken, noticed her looking at him, winked, and smiled, baring his fangs in a friendly gesture.

Borach rose again, and stood still. He said nothing, but stared at Malchus, who also stood and fixed his gaze upon Borach. Eventually, one by one, the delegates became quiet, as they stared at the two men, staring at each other, neither backing down.

Borach spoke softly, but vehemently. "I was born seventy-four lifetimes ago, during the reign of *Maopold the Proud*, under whom my father served as Lord of Aleskian."

"It is not possible for a man who has lived so long, to have any honour left," Malchus sneered.

"And less so for a man who has Cinoan blood running in his veins," Marki bellowed.

Borach raised his hands. Such was the aura of his demeanour that all went quiet. "Once, the Kappian Empire was a republic; we were called citizens, not subjects. We walked tall, and displayed our abilities to our full advantage and displayed *Vir*, our word for honour and courage, virtues we considered our greatest strengths. Every man was obliged to shoulder his duties as a citizen and by work and diligence, could prove himself, and advance in the empire, where justice and peace reigned." He shook his head regretfully and grimaced. "Maopold proved himself to be a vicious tyrant, more than deserving of his nickname. He changed the empire so that it came under the sole rule of one man, himself." He scowled. "A terrifying poison afflicted the heart of Kappia. We heard about it in Aleskian, but seldom bore witness to it. It seems to be in the nature of rulers that they hold good men in more suspicion than the bad, and dread the talents of others, and that is often the reason for their undoing. Maopold met the *Final-death*, sleeping peacefully in his bed, and his daughter Shaka became ruler. My father met the *Final-death*, by an assassin wielding an Arkith. I then became the Lord of Aleskian, and fought the wars I was ordered to fight, as I did under Maopold's reign."

Borach looked at Marki and asked, "What is the primary role of a legionnaire?"

"A soldier is loyal to his lord, and does what he is told," Marki mumbled as he shot an irritated glance at those in the conclave who turned and stared at him.

"And at what point does he stop doing what he is told?" Borach then asked.

"When he's dead," Marki replied.

Borach smiled wryly. "That is the answer I knew my most loyal and trusted friend would give." The smile soon faded from his face when Malchus shouted, "And a man who fights for coin is loyal only to his purse, but one who fights for his ancient homeland, will be deterred from no other cause, if he is true to his people."

Borach looked at Malchus, and Janorra noticed his previous anger towards the Cinoan had passed. "There is also another answer, I know it now. A soldier can also stop doing what he is told, when he realises that the age he lives in, is a rotten one: when he can see that the empire he once loved and served is in truth, diseased, debased and degraded. When his eyes are open, and he sees that even the so-called peace the empire once brought to the world was founded upon nothing nobler than the exhaustion of cruelty, and the subjugation of those not able to resist."

Janorra noticed that Borach's eyes smouldered more vividly.

"The Empress Shaka sent my own wife and children to their *Final-death*. My city, was razed to the ground." The look Borach gave Malchus, was so ferocious, that although the Cinoan did not avert his gaze or show any weakness, Janorra could tell neither did he wish at that moment to interrupt. "That is when I swore, like you Cinoan, that I will serve no man but myself, no cause but that which will bring me but a moments reprieve from my torment." He then said to Malchus, "I will offer you no apology, for I obeyed my orders, as you do yours. Before you were born, my father invaded your lands, and I accompanied him. In more recent times, in your own life time, when your people rose up and rebelled against Kappian rule, I obeyed my orders and did what I did to your lands." He sighed deeply. "Now, we all face a grave and merciless threat from the Bantu. I will hold my peace in the matter of our own past disputes, if you will yours. When this matter is done, and Greytears is taken, then, if you wish to take up past disputes with me, I will allow you to wield the Arkith my legion owns, so that the winner in a man to man combat, will see his foe no more in this world. Are we agreed?"

"You would give me the chance to give you the *Final-death* in single combat?"

Borach solemnly nodded, "I will."

"Then we are agreed," Malchus seethed, "and after I have removed you from this world, I will whip your pup of a dwarf in combat and silence his own profane tongue."

Marki shouted a response. "If you still steal the air from this world after combat with Borach, then I will gladly face you as well!"

"Then it is done," Chasotha declared, "but Greytears will be in the hands of the legion if we succeed to take it." Looking at Malchus he added, "We pay you the agreed gold to do our bidding, not for you to make claims on what you think should be yours. You may take that to Malagrim when this matter is done."

"He would not grant me an audience on the matter before," Malchus replied," but if you say to me my case will be heard before him when, after the battle of Greytears, I have slain *Borach the Butcher* and his pup of a dwarf, then I will hold my peace for now and fight the battle that is ahead of us."

"It is agreed," Chasotha said. "The matter now is, how can we take this castle quickly?" He looked at the Kirani. "Skidegeat, and his two companions, are masters of stealth."

Janorra looked at Skidegeat's two companions, and noticed they were female Kirani.

Chasotha continued. "They tried to enter Castle Greytears, unseen, but could not. We do know though, that it takes more than twenty men to work each of the three winches it takes to operate the main gate. We would need sixty men at least."

When Skidegeat spoke, he purred the words out, his accent exotic and strange, his manner polite. "I am Skidegeat, at your service. My companions are Zasorra and Zosasha. Together, we own a rare Arkith…" The admission sent a chill down Janorra's spine, and again, she wished Armun was present to give counsel.

Skidegeat continued, "Baron Daramir has an Inquisitor of no small power, who has placed wards along the walls, and possibly the main keep, so I, Skidegeat, and my companions could not pass undetected. He clearly fears an assassination attempt whilst under siege. We would set off many alarms and alert the castle to our presence."

Marki offered a suggestion. "There are already Aeldar tunnels under the castle. It is how Janorra escaped from the castle, along with Sasna, your cousin, Starlen, and that man with no nose. We might quietly gain entry with a sizeable force at night, take control of the towers to the approach and open the gate from within."

Borach spoke. "I was informed the exit into the castle would be guarded, as are the tunnels, by some beast. The entrance also, cannot be easily found." He stared harshly at Janorra. "Can it?"

Janorra felt uncomfortable at the way Borach looked at and spoke to her. It was clear, that for the tragedy that had befallen his family, and the destruction of the city of Aleskian, he partly blamed her for, if not fully. She sensed he believed that her taking the Simal had set into motion a sequence of events that had led to the current circumstances. It was not, however, a time for her to be obstinate or uncooperative.

"Aeldar doors were not made to be seen when shut. We left the tunnels in haste, under the cover of darkness. I am not sure I could find the door again," she confessed.

"I possibly could," Marlo offered, "for it was near to where I hid my boat." He looked apologetically at Starlen, who gazed at him reproachfully. "I had no idea Janorra was here until she entered this tent," Marlo said, "and I could not open such a tunnel, I lack the skill, that's why I did not offer it previously as a solution."

"It would serve us no good," Janorra said, seeking to end the conversation, for she wished no delay in heading to Baothein once Armun was *Awakened*, and had no desire to get involved in the matter of capturing Greytears. "The tunnels are guarded by a fearsome beast, a Minotaur; even if you got past it, there are traps set for the unwary. If you get past all of these, there is no way to open the Aeldar door to enter the sanctuary. Only the incumbent priest and the local Inquisitor know how to do that."

"Or a Seeress of the Aeldar Faith, from the Argona Temple," Borach growled at Janorra. "You opened the exit door. I do not believe you if you say you cannot open the one to the sanctuary within the castle."

Marki looked at Janorra, and asked sincerely, "Lass, we need your help as much as you will be needing ours. If we can get you in the tunnels, is it possible you might be able to get us in the temple sanctuary?"

Janorra bit her lip in frustration. She needed the goodwill of others, if she was ever to reach Baothein lands. "It is possible," she finally blurted out after an intense pause, "but I cannot guarantee it, and they are sure to have put guards in the sanctuary, and possibly wards guarding it as well. Before that, there is the creature. The *Theos Murphor incantation* rarely works twice on the same beast, and although the priest told me that not all the traps were set, some have been. It was good fortune we did not fall foul of any last time. The risks are very great."

"I'll slay the wee beastie and make a steak out of it," Marki said. "*Old Trusty* will make short work of that bovine monstrosity. I say we give it a shot, and try to get into the castle that way to open the gates."

"I know the priest well, me dear," Gilly said to Marki, raising her voice to overcome the disordered chatter that had broken out in the tent. The council grew quiet. "He does not always wake in time for early morning prayers, is often late and in an agitated rush. If all seems quiet, I wouldn't mind betting any guards in the sanctuary might take the opportunity to sleep. The priest is easily scared, if you do catch him there, it would not take much effort to get him to cooperate. His courage would evaporate with the right persuasion."

Skidegeat gave a wide grin and looked at each of his female companions. "Once any wards have been disarmed, Skidegeat and his companions can dispatch any patrols on the streets," he said, "do you not think?"

"Zasorra thinks we could do it," the Kirani to his left, who had grey fur and black stripes purred.

"Zosasha concurs," the other companion said. "We can clear a way to the gates."

Chasotha banged his fist on the table, and smiled at the three Kirani. "I knew hiring you as sell swords was a good idea," he beamed. Janorra was not so sure.

"Then it is agreed," Borach said wearily. "We will continue to build siege equipment, tunnel towards the walls, whilst seeking to open the gates by stealth. Now, for our second item. What to do with the Simal?"

Janorra had said as little as possible during the previous debate, only contributing when pressed. Now, she was determined to make her stand and speak her mind. "This matter cannot be decided, until Master Armun has *Awakened*. I can only think that whatever magic was used on him in the battle with the mage known as Methruille, still works its mischief for a time, and the loss of his staff of power, has weakened his ability to *Awaken* speedily. *Ashareth, help Armun to Awaken, I need his help to get to Baothein lands.*"

For the first time in the council meeting, Bonnie spoke. "Malagrim desires the Simal. I have vowed to bring it to him." She stared at Janorra with ferocity. "Your will in this matter, or that of Armun, is irrelevant."

Janorra felt a courage born of desperation rise up within her. She unfastened the clasps of the knapsack, took out the Simal, and placed it on the table in full view of everybody. Even though wrapped in a cloth, it glimmered and glowed with a ghastly light and began to make a humming noise. "Then take it to him," she challenged Bonnie. She slowly turned her head, so her gaze swept over those in the conclave in her line of sight. "Take it, any of you, if you dare," she challenged. "But first hear my words and heed them well. It took me three lifetimes to master the cerebral and mystical techniques required to carry such a powerful artefact. Insanity, and eventually death, takes those who try to hold such an object casually."

Janorra knew it was a risk, but one she was willing to take. "Skidegeat, would you and your companions like to attempt to pick up the Simal, and look into its depths?"

For the briefest of moments, Janorra noticed that the Kirani lost his cool demeanour. It was just a flash, a mere moment before he regained it, but it was telling.

"Skidegeat has no interest in such a bauble," he purred.

"Then Bonnie, you failed last time you tried to pick it up. If you succeed this time, do you believe you can carry such an item and not be tainted by its allure and power? You wish to take it to Malagrim, but no beast of sky or land will carry it, such a journey would be made on foot, even whilst the Wild Hunt searches for it. If any of you has a Jula, it takes a special art that only Armun has, to prepare for the Simal to be taken by such means, and even that has proven unreliable. He must be heard on this matter."

Bonnie leant over the table, and reached out a hand towards the Simal. The humming of the Simal grew in intensity, so that some began to cover their ears, and a powerful light began to emanate from it, so that all in the tent except Bonnie and Janorra shielded their eyes. "My eyes, my eyes!" Bonnie shrieked as eventually she withdrew her hand before she touched it, and covered her own eyes.

"Put it away," Borach shouted.

Janorra did not hesitate. She took the Simal, put it back in the knapsack and fastened the straps and clasps. The humming died down and the light faded.

"By Balagrim, I would never have believed such a thing," Marki declared.

"I will not have this matter decided, until Master Armun has *Awakened*," Janorra repeated. "He will be heard on this, and meanwhile, I request more guards, day and night, to protect me and the Simal, lest folly overtakes any and they seek to seize it from me, or do me harm." She looked at Chasotha and Borach. Chasotha nodded assent.

"So be it," Borach said, as he turned his eyes sourly upon Janorra. "Marki will choose guards you can trust." Borach stood, and declared, "This council is over. Our decisions have been made. See to them, each to their own task!"

# Chapter Sixty-Five: The Prophecy of Rithguar

*A bird does not sing because it has an answer. It sings because it has a song. A prophet does not speak because he desires to talk. He speaks because he has a prophecy.*
**A Davari Proverb.**

*The Nine Seraphim will remember what they once were, before the Nameless One returns. He will bring the renewal of all things, and Judgement shall come.*
**A segment from the Prophecy of Rithguar.**

When they reached the banks of the Erin, Imrand and Sarkisi stopped to listen. Muro drew deep breaths. They heard no noise of pursuit behind them. Imrand dropped the sack of treasure and drew *Ormfron*, as Sarkisi dropped her sack and notched an arrow in *Harnesh*. "It is time for you to go your own way, old man," Imrand said to Muro as he pointed *Ormfron* at him. "No foe can stand against me now! Leave, or die!"

Muro held up the palms of his hands, the runes in them began to glow. "Do not be too hasty trusting your new toys; even they have their limitations and such armour is not a defence against the runes of the Ruik!"

"We shall see," Imrand threatened as he took a step towards Muro and Sarkisi drew the bow and aimed it at Muro.

"How do you intend crossing the river? Muro asked.

Imrand quickly glanced at the Erin. They were at a bend in the river where the water flowed slowly.

Muro laughed maliciously. "It might look calm here, but the currents under that smooth surface, are still deadly, as are the creatures that might lurk beneath the surface, ready to eat you and your pretty wife. You need me."

"We will find a way to cross it, somewhere," Sarkisi answered, glancing both directions of the river.

"You have nothing I need, old man," Imrand said as he took another cautious step towards Muro.

"We are more powerful together. The runes have gifted us, all three, more than we could have foreseen," Muro said. Watched by Imrand and Sarkisi, he walked towards the river and muttered an incantation. Holding up the hand with the ice rune, ice shot from it and hit the surface of the river, freezing a thin path across the water almost immediately. Muro stepped onto the roughly surfaced ice, and began to cross the Erin. Turning back to the two watching him, he said, "I will melt it when I get to the other side, so I would not delay, if I were you."

Imrand sheathed *Ormfron*, picked up the sack of gold and jewels, and adjusted them to a comfortable position over his shoulder. Sarkisi put away *Harnesh*, and picked up her sack of treasure. They quickly followed Muro in crossing the Erin. Once they were all on the other side of the river, Muro melted the ice with his fire rune, and the river began to flow again as if nothing had happened.

"We are now joined together," Muro said to them both, "and are more powerful together." He took out of his pocket a text and held it up. "I have this, the *Prophecy of Rithguar.*"

"Of what use to me is a piece of scrap parchment?" Imrand asked.

Muro laughed sinisterly. "Knowledge of the possible fates. We Ruik, through this, can learn the location of the last three Aeldar Wives, and the last entrance to Garama Aethoros which will lead to them."

"I am done with Wytches. Of what use is such knowledge to me?" Imrand asked.

"The entrance is hidden far to the south, in Davari lands," Muro said wolfishly. "The Simal will be brought there, in time, and you can have an army waiting for whoever comes to enter that foul place. If you possessed the Simal, and whoever can carry it, you can bring every empire and kingdom in this foul place of the Everglow to its knees." Muro pointed across the Erin to the north, and grinned demonically. "It is time we Davari, rose up, and forever rid the world of those born of Akkadian blood."

Realisation dawned upon Imrand. "Then that makes that piece of parchment very valuable indeed, and extremely dangerous," Imrand said cautiously.

"Why should you fear any danger, if your boast be true that no foe can now stand against you?" Muro asked sarcastically.

"What do you want, old man?" Imrand demanded impatiently.

Muro giggled with insane excitement. "Power, but of a different type to which you seek." He unstrapped Armun's staff which was secured across his back. "I now possess the staff of a Tarath Güean. In the desperate moment of an impending death, Armun asked me protect it, to wait for him to resurrect, and hand it back. But it is now mine!" Almost lovingly, he caressed the staff, and ran his eyes up and down the length of it. "I will take this to the Ruik caves, and together with my brothers, we will unlock its secrets and master its use." He looked at Imrand. "You must raise an army. When the time is right, the Ruik will come to your aid, and together, we will rid the world of all that is impure."

Imrand and Sarkisi exchanged a glance, and then Imrand asked Muro. "The Ruik would march north with me, to wage war upon my enemies within the Everglow?"

Muro smiled. "The *Prophecy of Rithguar* commands that the Davari burn the Everglow until it is nothing but ash and ruin."

Imrand grinned ferociously. "Then I am willing to let our past differences be cast aside. Together, we will journey back to our people, and there we will prepare for our destiny." The grin quickly disappeared from Imrand's face. "But first, before I return to the Vanyr, I will pay a visit to Bahri and Gerdar of the Ikma. I will not be distracted from this revenge, old man."

"That is acceptable to me," Muro said with a sneer. "There must be farmsteads ahead, where we can find horses and take what supplies we need for our journey. Then, we must find a way to leave the Everglow, and that, might be a quest in itself for we cannot just go walking into Ashgiliath and demand they open the gates."

"We will find a way to return home," Imrand said. "I heard much talk in the slave-pens. Ashgiliath does not hold the only exit from this accursed place." He looked around him. "We will leave, and when we return to these lands, it will be at the head of a vast army, and merciless shall my vengeance be upon all living things that oppose us."

Sarkisi took one look behind her before she followed her husband and Muro as they headed along a natural trail in the forest. "Home," she whispered to herself.

*  *  *

Cordius and Yana had waited for as long as they could, but Marieke had not returned, so they had agreed to continue on foot in the hope that the griffin would find them. Through dark woods, up and down masking slopes of sombre hills they had travelled, hoping to find some sign of the Third Legion's trail and the direction they might have travelled in. They drank from dusky streams that flowed without little sound, and hunted rabbits and squirrels for meat, or ate berries from bushes for sustenance. Their main companions were the lone winds that whispered down the passes. At night, they huddled together to protect themselves from the cold night air of the Tarenmoors.

"Do you think we will ever find my father?" Yana asked Cordius, as she trembled like a leaf from the cold, and huddled even more closer to him.

Cordius stroked her hair reassuringly. "Marieke will return, and we will take to the skies again, and find our bearings."

Yana looked cautiously up at the sky. "But what about those garâtons? We have seen many of them in the skies above in recent days, only good fortune provided us with places to seek refuge out of their sight. Surely it is human foes they hunt?"

Cordius kissed her softly on the head. "Marieke is more than a match for a garâton and its rider. He will find us, just wait and see."

Yana smiled, but she did not feel reassured. *I never thought I would be lost in the Tarenmoors. Oh, what a fate,* she bemoaned to herself. A deep moroseness fell upon her, as she looked out of the entrance of the cave they sheltered in, and saw a hostile and bleak wilderness below. *Father, where are you?*

∗      ∗      ∗

The Fortress City of Kara Duram occupied a hillside that was roughly circular in shape, and was surrounded by a vast moat. The huge walls were designed in a convex curve, some twelve miles in length. Six gates opened through them, leading to bridges that crossed the moat and led to the Steppes of Kara Duram, a mighty grassland criss-crossed with many farms, villages and settlements. Shaka stood and looked out upon the vast host of Hammer Knights camped on the grasslands around the fortress. Their number could not be counted, and nor could the number of great siege engines they were constructing. Like the sound of an ominous and angry thunder, the great boom of countless drums beating in uniformity filled the air.

"My grandmother remembered the time when the Hammer Knights were formed," Shaka said wistfully. "They started as a small monastic order. Little was it known they would become a military order of such size and influence."

"We should use the Juram and abandon this place, even these great defences cannot endure indefinitely against such a host," Aspess urged her.

"And go where?" Shaka asked, almost serenely.

"Your sister still rules as the White Queen of the Baothein, surely she would offer us sanctuary?" Aspess replied.

Shaka waved her hand dismissively. "We would become nothing more than bargaining chips. In days as dark as these, empires are forged or lost. No, dear daughter, here we must make a stand. Do not let the noise they make disturb you, for that is the purpose of the drums, to make a noise to unnerve even the stoutest of hearts."

"What if you fall into the hands of Mazdek? You know the depths of cruelty he will expose you too," Aspess asked.

"If we lose this battle, I will not fall again into the hands of Mazdek," Shaka said as she fingered the Arzak on the pommel of the Arkith that she held. She gazed into its deep and dark depths. "Maybe an eternity inside one of these things, is not as bad as some people think. Maybe even inside there, they need an empress to rule them?"

∗      ∗      ∗

The creature climbed grotesquely to the summit of the cliff. A hundred or so serpentine bodies, without the heads, served as the monster's legs and arms. Its torso was neither man nor beast, but a hideous deformity of nature. Upon the head were many eyes and mouths, and the creature whined as an enraged-beast in pain whenever it moved.

"You see the slime that drips from the beast's body?" Azzadan said to Redboots and Velentine. "If we cover ourselves in that, it will not detect our presence. We should be able to move, by stealth, to the cave wherein we can gain entrance, by a secret way, to Grona Prison."

Velentine grinned strangely. "You have not seen the power that can be wielded by a Queen of the Dark! I shall not sneak past such a dim-witted creature. I shall tame it, make it my servant, my pet." She stepped out from behind the rocks where they had taken shelter.

"What are you doing?" Azzadan asked in alarm.

"She's insane," Redboots said as they reached to pull Velentine back, but she moved with a speed they could not match, and glided over the ground swiftly until she stood in full view of the beast.

"Come!" she said in a voice so loud that it filled the air and bounced off of the face of the cliff; she raised her arms. "Come to your queen!"

The creature noticed her at once, and fixed its many eyes upon her, as with great speed it half-climbed, half-slid down the mountain gripping it with its serpentine limbs. It rushed over to Velentine and stretched to its full height, which was seven times that of a man. It paused and studied her, with an almost naive curiosity.

Velentine spoke in a tongue that the world had not heard for ten-thousand years or more.

"She's mad," Redboots said.

"Maybe not," Azzadan replied, as the creature used its limbs to lower itself docilely to her height, as Velentine continued to utter the words of ancient Vangalen. She reached out and stroked the creature. Turning back to Azzadan and Redboots, she calmly said about the creature, "It is now in my service." Her voice then became more animated, when she commanded Azzadan, "Now, take me to Voran. Take me to the tomb of my husband. Long has he slept. My desire is to awaken him without delay."

*     *     *

"Then is it agreed, Erik Vansoth, Lord of the Sea Lords?" Sasna asked.

Erik banged his mighty fist on the table, causing the platters to jump and bounce upon it, and the glasses of wine and mugs of ale to spill. "Your uncle offers generous terms, so it is agreed," he roared, meat, spit and wine flying from his mouth. "By Jorgen, my fleets will pillage and burn every Bruthon town and village along the Erin. We will even sail up to the Giant Halls where it is said the Titan Malagrim, sits upon a throne. I will unseat him myself, for his kind have no place in the world I will forge!"

His face turned grim and foreboding. "If your uncle swears this salt-oath with me, woe betides him if he proves the saying true, *never trust a Seesnari!*"

Sasna smiled reassuringly, and stroked the head of Gnarn who sat contentedly at her feet. "My uncle will honour his word, and any oath he makes, for we long for the slave trade to flow along the Erin again, so riches and prosperity can rain upon us all." She paused, and then added, "The Seesnari will not make war with Malagrim, but neither shall we aid him if you choose to do so. For the right price, my uncle will let you use our ports, even that of Ashgiliath. He has given me his word on this, to pass on to you."

"We will use your ports, but no price we will pay, only swear a salt-oath not to sack and raid Seesnari towns and cities," Erik said, as he watched for Sasna's response.

"I am sure he will agree that a salt-oath will be sufficient, as long as it protects our trade routes along the Erin," Sasna replied politely.

Erik's grim look, slowly morphed into a smile. He turned to Kira. "Now, Kira, sing and dance for Sasna and her brother, Fergo."

"Farir," Farir corrected him.

Erik roared back, "This is my hall, if I say you are called Fergo, then by Jorgen tonight you are called Fergo!"

Farir did not reply but sulkily downed his wine, as Kira stood to her feet and winked at Sasna. "I know a shanty of old, said to be from the time when the Seesnari once sailed the Tethys Sea, a time when their women folk sailed great ships with their men. It is called, *The Maiden's Gale.*"

Kira began to sing. Sasna was more than pleased that she had finally fulfilled her mission, and although she smiled outwardly, she could not help but feel a sense of trepidation as she looked at the fearsome Erik Vansoth, who closed his eyes as he listened to the haunting melody and words of the song that Kira sang. Sasna's thoughts were consumed elsewhere. *These are perilous times; if my uncle makes one wrong move, or breaks this oath, the gleaming spires of Ashgiliath will surely be toppled into the dust, and in time will fade from living memory.*

*  *  *

Skidegeat purred contentedly as Zasorra and Zosasha groomed him, platting his hair and combing his facial fur. "Lord Borach has ordered the Seeress to accompany us into the Aeldar tunnels," Zasorra said, "is that when you plan to take it?"

Skidegeat laughed gently. "Maybe, my dear Zasorra," he replied. "If she is foolish enough to carry it with her into such a place. But I have already observed she mistrusts us, so we might need to earn her trust." He took Zasorra's hand as she combed his fur and kissed it. "We need her to carry the Simal for us, willingly. This mission requires we earn her trust, and compliance. Our patience will win this from her. Azzadan lacked the appeal and personality such a task involved, so it is of no small surprise he bumbled the mission."

Zasorra and Zosasha laughed. "Ishar should have trusted you with this mission from the start," Zasorra said. "If he had, the Simal and the Seeress would already be safe in the Halls of Ithkall."

"Indeed, they would, my lovers," Skidegeat purred, as he bared his fangs, and closed his eyes whilst the two female Kirani continued to groom him. "Indeed, it would."

*  *  *

Borach, Torach and Marki were assembled alone around the large table in the main pavilion. "If it were not for Armun, I would either kill her with the Arkith and throw the wretched Simal into the Erin, or let Bonnie take them both to the Giant Halls, as she desires," Borach said dourly, as he looked at looked at his two commanders with furious eyes. "I blame her for the death my family."

"You know my loyalty to you could never be doubted, Bor," Marki said, equally as dourly, "but the former would not sit right with me. I have heard her tale; she is as much a victim of Kappia as are Yianna and the bairns. Let this go, I implore you by

747

Balagrim, as I could not live with my conscience if harm came to her by your hand and I did or said nothing."

"It is pointless debating this again," Torach remonstrated. "We must wait until Armun is *Awakened*, as has been already agreed."

"Any news on that?" Marki asked.

Torach shook his head. "I know little of the ways of the Tarath Guëan, nobody does, but Bonnie thinks his *Awakening* is hampered by the loss of his staff. It is as though a part of him is missing, she says." He clenched and unclenched his fists in frustration. "Bonnie said the Simal seemed as heavy as a mountain when she even considered trying to pick it up, and no muttering, song, spell or incantation she knows can rid her of that impression."

"Then we press ahead with the plan," Borach said. "Marki, you take a company of men along with the Seeress and the Kirani, to the place that Marlo fellow shows you. Enter the Aeldar tunnels, gain entry to the castle and open the main gates at night. We will be ready to assault the city on your signal."

"So be it," Marki said. He waited behind when Torach left the pavilion. Taking Borach affectionately by the shoulders, he said to him, "In times of war, our own blades have made widows of wives, and husbands' widowers. Our own actions have led to an abundance of fatherless children and motherless babes in the world. Be not so quick to condemn the actions of Janorra that inconsequently led to your own misery. That was never her goal or intention, as it was not ours to leave a trail of misery, in the wars we fought for Kappia."

Borach looked morosely at the table as he leant upon it.

"Bor, come on," Marki pleaded. "Janorra is not responsible for what happened to Yianna and the bairns. When we have captured Greytears, listen to her tale yourself, by Balagrim. I know you will find pity in your heart for her, and release the anger you feel towards the lass!"

Borach smiled at his old friend. "I will hear her tale," he said, "but if Armun has not *Awakened* by the time we have Greytears, then I feel we must let Bonnie take the Simal to Malagrim. It will be safe in the Giant Halls, and it will be one less burden I must concern myself with."

"Agreed," Marki said, "after Greytears, if Armun is not himself again, then Bonnie must take Janorra and the Simal to Malagrim, and we must help her do it, but Gilly won't be happy."

*      *      *

Janorra felt a rare spark of anger ignite something inside of her. "I see Lord Borach murdering me with his eyes every time he looks at me," she said to Scarand. "If he is going to do it, then he should be the man and put action to his thoughts!"

"Do not be so rash," Scarand cautioned, "you have a powerful ally in Gilly, and that other dwarf, Marki, seems quite taken with her. He clearly has influence over the one named Borach."

Her anger softened. "He blames me for the *Final-death* of his family, and maybe he is right," she moaned, "and on top of that I have the hatred of Sezareal to contend with. You have spoken with her; how did she seem?"

Scarand was blunt in his answer. "She does blame you." He took a breath. "But I do not. I see how you had few choices, apart from the ones you took."

His word gave her but a little comfort. "I pray to Ashareth that Armun will fully *Awaken* soon. He will take me to the safety of Baothein lands. Here, I am surrounded by those who hate me and wish to force me to take the Simal to the Giant Halls."

"May I come in me dears?" Gilly shouted from outside the entrance to the tent.

"Enter," Janorra replied.

Gilly entered, smiling broadly. "They are waiting for you," she said to Janorra.

Janorra knew who she meant. Marki, Marlo, the Kirani and two score or more of legionnaires were going to attempt to enter Greytears by way of the Aeldar Tunnels, and she was being forced to go with them. Picking up her backpack from the floor, she looked at Gilly. "I have buried the Simal, in the ground under my bed. Please, guard it for me."

"Me dear, I do not want to be near that thing," Gilly said cautiously.

"Please Gilly. I do not trust the Kirani. There is something about them that…scares me. I cannot take it with me but nor can it remain unguarded. Move into this tent until I return, please?"

Gilly sighed reluctantly. "Okay, me dear, I will do as you say. Me and young Scarand here, will guard it with our lives until you return. We will tell no one it is here, me dear, and one of us will always stay awake and keep an eye on the place it is hidden."

She looked at Scarand. "Isn't that right, me dear?"

"I cannot assist you with this until I return," he answered.

"Why is that, me dear?" Gilly asked.

"I showed the letter Sasna gave me, to one of the Seesnari delegation. He was not happy, but after showing it to Starlen, the Seesnari have agreed to honour Sasna's oath. Some of them travel back to Ashgiliath tomorrow, and I am to go with them. I will be given papers proving my freedom. When I return, I will bear the brand of a free man."

"Do you trust the Seesnari?" Janorra asked him.

"I see no reason not to," he replied. He looked at Janorra intensely. "I wish nothing more than to begin the search for my sisters, but the best chance of success I have is for me to ally with you for this time, until Armun is *Awakened* at least. I have sworn to assist you until you and the Simal are safe, but I must seize this chance to go to Ashgiliath. I will return in a week or two, as a free man, when my business there is concluded."

"Well then, me dears," Gilly said, "I will guard the Simal, by myself, until both of you return." She must have anticipated the question behind Janorra's concerned gaze for she said, "No, me dear, I will not be tempted to dig it up and take a look at it."

Janorra thanked them both. Adjusting her armour and sword, she put on her knapsack minus the Simal, and left the tent.

*         *         *

In the Chamber of Summoning within the ruined fortress of the Wytchwood, the Obelisk opened its eyes. It was alone. The only sign of life was the Wisdom Tree flourishing in the cave next door. A dim memory woke from deep within it. "I remember my name," it boomed to itself. "I am Milotron. My name is Milotron." It laughed, and speaking to the empty chamber it then said. "I have a message to deliver." It then roared, "Run Janorra, Run!"

*To be continued…*

# *Appendix*

Each of the characters that appear in *the Simal - To Slay a God*, have an extensive back story. To discover more of their history and exploits prior to their appearing on the pages of this epic saga, you can visit our website at www.TheSimal.com

You can also visit The Simal Youtube channel.
https://www.youtube.com/channel/UCfMU1xd_-Vlr5t9vlLv8cJA

On both the website and channel you will also find a glossary, maps, artwork and a lot of information both about the author and the epic world of the Simal that he has created. News and publishing dates for the next book continuing this story will appear on both the Website and Youtube channel.
The next book, *The Simal – Into the Labyrinth*, will continue the tale of Janorra and the Simal.

On the Youtube channel you can leave comments. Sean would love to hear from you, and will be interactive with fans of the Simal series of books.

More information on the world of the Simal is just a click away.

urce UK Ltd.
UK
31219
1B/264/P